HELLI

BRIAN ALDISS was bor
service in Burma and the Far East, he turned to writing,
his *Horatio Stubbs* trilogy reflects those wartime days.
His most famous sf novels include *Hothouse* and the
Helliconia trilogy.

He has won all the major sf awards. He has also
published contemporary novels, and his Hugo Award-
winning history of science fiction, *Trillion Year Spree*
(with David Wingrove), and a memoir of his writing
life, *Bury My Heart at W. H. Smith's*. He is a past
chairman of the Society of Authors, and a Fellow of the
Royal Society of Literature. His most recent work is a
collection of short stories, *The Secret of This Book*.

By Brian Aldiss

The Brightfount Diaries	Galaxies Like Grains of Sand
The Hand-Reared Boy	Hothouse
A Soldier Erect	The Dark Light Years
A Rude Awakening	Greybeard
The Malacia Tapestry	Earthworks
Life in the West	The Saliva Tree
Report on Probability A	Cryptozoic
Frankenstein Unbound	Barefoot in the Head
Dracula Unbound	The Eighty-Minute Hour
Brothers of the Head	Enemies of the System
Trillian Year Spree	Moreau's Other Island
(with David Wingrove)	A Tupolev Too Far
Somewhere East of Life	The Secret of This Book
Non-Stop	

Voyager

BRIAN ALDISS

HELLICONIA

Book One: Helliconia Spring
Book Two: Helliconia Summer
Book Three: Helliconia Winter

HarperCollins*Publishers*

Voyager
An Imprint of HarperCollins*Publishers*
77–85 Fulham Palace Road,
Hammersmith, London W6 8JB

This one-volume paperback edition 1996
1 3 5 7 9 8 6 4 2

First published in Great Britain in three volumes:
Helliconia Spring published by Jonathan Cape 1982
and in paperback by Grafton 1983
Copyright © Brian Aldiss 1982
Helliconia Summer published by Jonathan Cape 1983
and in paperback by Grafton in 1985
Copyright © Brian Aldiss 1983
Helliconia Winter published by Jonathan Cape 1985
and in paperback by Grafton in 1986
Copyright © Brian Aldiss 1985

The Author asserts the moral right to
be identified as the author of this work

ISBN 0 00 648223 6

Set in Electra

Printed in Great Britain by
Caledonian International
Book Manufacturing Ltd, Glasgow

INTRODUCTION

A publisher friend was trying to persuade me to produce a book I did not greatly wish to write. Trying to get out of it, I wrote him a letter suggesting something slightly different. What I had in mind was a planet much like Earth, but with a longer year. I wanted no truck with our puny 365 days.

"Let's say this planet is called Helliconia," I wrote, on the spur of the moment.

The word was out. *Helliconia!* And from that word grew this book.

*

Science of recent years has become full of amazing concepts. Rivalling SF! We are now conversant with furious processes very distant from our solar system in both time and space. Cosmologists, talking of some new development, will often say, "It sounds like science fiction". A perfectly just remark, reflecting as it does the relationship that exists between science fiction and science.

This relationship is not capable of precise definition, since science permeates our lives, and both scientists and writers are wayward people. It is a shifting relationship. What is clear is that science fiction functions in predictive or descriptive mode. It can attempt either to stay ahead of science, to foresee future developments or discontinuities; or it can dramatise newly achieved developments, making the bare (and, to some, arid) facts of science accessible to a wide readership.

An example of the former method (the "Wait and See" method) is Gregory Benford's novel, *Timescape,* in which he talks of the intricacies of time in a way which has only recently entered discussion by the scientific community.

An example of the latter method (the "Digestive Tract" method) is H. G. Wells' *The Time Machine,* in which he demonstrates, as it were, the possibility of solar death – a startlingly new idea when Wells wrote.

In *Helliconia,* the Digestive Tract method is employed. In 1979, while this book was a mere building site, its foundations open to the alien sky, James Lovelock published a small book entitled, *Gaia: A New*

Look at Life on Earth. The name Gaia was suggested by Lovelock's friend (I might even claim him as a friend of mine) William Golding, the novelist. The classical Gaia was the goddess of the Earth in Greek mythology; Lovelock was outlining an impersonal updated version of that gubernatory personage. Lovelock pointed out that the continued survival of a living Earth is miraculous. Life survives despite an amazingly narrow range of chemical and physical parameters – parameters subject to fluctuation.

How is it that the Earth's temperature has not long ago increased, as has happened on "our sister planet" Venus; that the salinity of the oceans has not become more toxic than the Dead Sea; that atmospheric oxygen has not become tied down in oxides, or that hydrogen has not escaped from the upper atmosphere? Lovelock's answer, known as the Gaia Hypothesis, is that everything on the earth, the biomass, constitutes a single self-regulatory entity – living, of course, but of course without conscious intention. Gaia has no particular centre, no prime minister or parliament, no *Fuhrer*; not even a Greek goddess; it functions through its unfocused complexity, built up over millions of years. The implication is that the work of bacterial and other forces have built, and maintain, the living world we know, best to suit themselves – a process in which humanity has played small part.

I gave myself up to James Lovelock's arguments in his first book and succeeding ones in the way that, in an earlier phase of existence, I had surrendered myself to Thomas Hardy's novels.

Interestingly, Lovelock is an independent biologist of a rather old-fashioned kind, unsupported by universities or other institutions. And his hypothesis relies on the mode of close observation and enquiry which is such a marked feature of Charles Darwin's work. Darwin perceived where we merely see. Lovelock points out that what he calls "city wisdom" has become almost entirely centred on problems of human relationships; whereas, in a natural tribal group, wisdom means giving due weight to relationships with the rest of the animate and inanimate world.

He says, "I speak from personal experience when I say that those of us who go forth in ships to travel to remote places . . . are few in number compared with those who chose to work in city-based institutions and universities."

From travel, investigation, and perception, Lovelock built up his integrative hypothesis. I was wildly excited by it. Whether it was *true* or not, I felt that it was just and should be proved by research, and that here was a thesis which delivered new understanding. Lovelock wrote during the period of the Cold War, when we lived in the shadow of nuclear war, and the threat of nuclear destruction, followed by nuclear winter. Had nuclear winter come about, it would have been the ultimate profaning of nature, the rape and slaughter of Gaia.

These intellectual and emotional ideas were in my mind when I sat down to the seven year task of writing *Helliconia*. I hoped in it to dramatise on a wide scale the workings out of Lovelock's hypothesis.

*

The story between these covers is just a scientific romance. It talks about pretty ordinary fallible people living within fallible systems, just like us – together with the alien who also has a share in us. Although it may not look like it, I did not intend to place a great scientific emphasis on this introduction. SF, that spectral entity, is not science but fiction, bound to obey many of fiction's ordinary rules, possibly with an extra imaginative dimension – there is no proof whatsoever that life exists elsewhere in the galaxy.

Deeply interested in the workings of the world of affairs, of economics and ideology and religion, I had written a novel (*Life in the West*) concerning such matters, of which I was merely a bystander. The novel met with enough success for me to hope to do something similar on a larger scale.

So at first I thought of an allegory, with the three major power blocs represented by three Helliconian continents. Happily, this scheme soon faded away – although three continents were left behind by the tide, Campannlat, Hespagorat, and Sibornal.

For by then creative instincts flooded in, washing away more didactic ones. All the conflicting impulses with which our minds are filled seemed to rise up and organise themselves in a remarkable way. Whole populations seemed to assemble, with a great rustle of garments, from the dark. This astonishing creative process, with its seeming autonomy, is one of the major pleasures of writing.

Naturally, I had to find a story. Three stories, in fact.

There I already had general ideas, once I realised that I desired to assemble a large cast of characters.

What I could not grasp to begin with was *what the Helliconian vegetation would look like*.

I was stuck. My three most able advisers, Tom Shippey, Iain Nicholson, and Peter Cattermole, had done their best to drum philological and cosmological facts into my head. Still I could not think what a tree on Helliconia would look like. If I could not imagine a tree, I told myself, I was incapable of painting the whole new binary system I – *we* – had devised.

One evening in 1980, I was travelling from Oxford to London by train, to attend some function or other at the British Council. The time was towards sunset as the train passed Didcot power station. My wife and I had often talked about the station's cooling towers; were they not, from a distance at least, beautiful? Wasn't the industrial landscape beautiful? Would John Keats have found such sights "a joy forever"?

The towers on this occasion stood with the sun low behind them. They breathed forth immense clouds of steam into the still-bright sky. Towers and steam were a unity, black against the light background.

Yes! *They were Helliconian trees!*

The cooling towers, those cylinders with their corsetted Victorian waists, were the trunks. The billowing ragged forms of steam were the foliage. The foliage would emerge from the trunk only at certain times of year.

That moment of revelation was what I needed. I started to write my scientific romance. Among the many characters with whom I became involved, I felt most affection for Shay Tal, who stands her ground at Fish Lake; the lovely summer queen, MyrdemInggala; young Luterin; and especially Ice Captain Muntras, who plies a trade once fashionable on Earth in the days before refrigerators, selling what is sometimes prized, sometimes cursed.

As the whole matter had seemed to unfold from that one word, Helliconia, so we believe the whole universe has unfolded from the primal atom. The principle is similar. It is also contained emblematically in the second book of this novel. A defeated general walks through a Randonan forest, a great rain forest swarming with life, a seemingly permanent thing. Yet, only a few generations earlier, it all burst out of a handful of nuts.

When the third and final volume was published, my enthusiastic publisher, Tom Maschler, asked me over a drink, "What would you say Helliconia's really all about?"

I shrugged. "A change in the weather . . . ," I said.

*

Most so-called contemporary novels are freighted with nostalgia. Perhaps one reason for either loving or shunning science fiction is that it is relatively free of the poisons of forever looking back. It looks to the future, even when it looks with foreboding.

Science fiction has a remarkable and expanding history this century.

It has diversified from cheap paperbacks and magazines to all forms of culture, whether acknowledged or otherwise, from pop to grand opera. It is a curious fact that a large proportion of SF takes place off-Earth, sometimes very far off. One day, a cunning critic will explicate these mysteries.

Meanwhile, here is another story, taking place a thousand light years from Earth. But less far from its concerns.

For this first one-volume edition, I have added appendices. They contain some of the stage directions, as it were, of the drama. The drama can be read and, we hope, enjoyed without them; the appendices form something of a separate entertainment.

BRIAN W. ALDISS

1996

ACKNOWLEDGEMENTS

Thanks for invaluable preliminary discussions go to Professor Tom Shippey (philology), Dr. J. M. Roberts (history) and Mr. Desmond Morris (anthropology). I also wish to thank Dr. B. E. Juel-Jensen (pathology) and Dr. Jack Cohen (biology) for factual suggestions. Anything sound philologically is owed to Professor Tom Shippey; his lively enthusiasm has been of great help all along.

The globe of Helliconia itself was designed and built by Dr. Peter Cattermole, from its geology to its weather. For the cosmology and astronomy, I am indebted to Dr. Iain Nicolson, whose patience over the years is a cause for particular gratitude.

Dr. Mick Kelly and Dr. Norman Myers both gave up-to-date advice on winters other than natural ones. The structure of the Great Wheel owes much to Dr. Joern Bambeck. James Lovelock kindly allowed me to employ his concept of Gaia in this fictional form. Herr Wolfgang Jeschke's interest in this project from its early days has been vital.

My debt to the writings and friendship of Dr. J. T. Fraser and to David Wingrove (for being protean) is apparent.

To my wife, Margaret, loving thanks for letting Helliconia take over for so long, and for working on it with me.

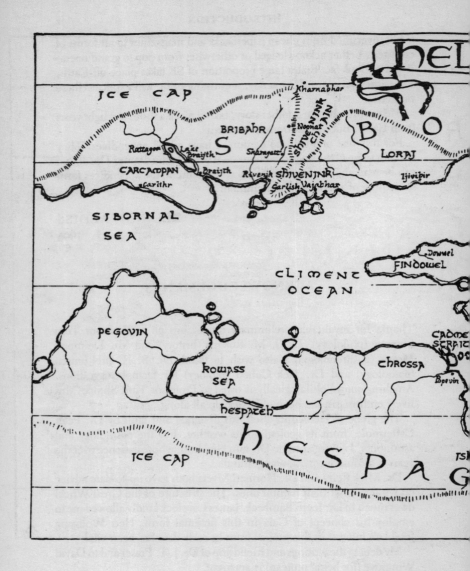

LICONIA

Polar Circle 55°

ICE CAP

R N A L

Old Askitosh · USKUTOSHK · Askitosh · North Tropic · 35° · KUJ-JUVEC · Futhir

Persecution Bay

PANNOVAL SEA · Koriantura · UPPER HAZZIZ · CHALCE · Bandriat

· Rungobandryaskosh · GULF OF CHALCE

BRASTERL · Nnydwesh · Norrdal · PANNOVAL · Isturiacha · HAZZIZ · MORSTRUAL · ARDENT SEA

CAMPANNLAT · Pannoval City · R.Vakk · QUZINE MTS. · MADURA DESERT · MORDRIAT · · Haccuth · Equator

WESTERN BARRIERS · ROONSMOOR · R.AVER

Powachet · OLDORANDO · Ousna

ONIPOT · QUAIN · · Yicch · R.Takissa · R.Mar

RADADO · Purporian · RACE · R.Hacal · Akace · Matrassyl · THRIBRIAT · Vallos

· Ordelay · OSOILIMA · VALLGOS

LEEAT IS. · RANDONAN · BORLIEN · Ottassol

· Gravabagalinien

· Poorich · Keevasien · SCIMITAR SEA

SEA OF EAGLES · South Tropic 35°

Hande · NARMOSSET SEA · Oiishst · Loidryardry · DIMARIAM

ICE CAP

ORAT · Polar Circle 55°

MK

My dear Clive,

In my previous novel LIFE IN THE WEST, I sought to depict something of the malaise sweeping the world, painting as wide a canvas as I felt I could confidently tackle.

My partial success left me ambitious and dissatisfied. I resolved to start again. All art is a metaphor, but some art forms are more metaphorical than others; perhaps, I thought, I would do better with a more oblique approach. So I developed Helliconia: a place much like our world, with only one factor changed—the length of the year. It was to be a stage for the kind of drama in which we are embroiled in our century.

In order to achieve some verisimilitude, I consulted experts, who convinced me that my little Helliconia was mere fantasy; I needed something much more solid.

Invention took over from allegory. A good thing, too. With the prompting of scientific fact, whole related series of new images crowded into my conscious mind. I have deployed them as best I could. When I was farthest away from my original conception—at the apastron of my earliest intentions—I discovered that I was expressing dualities that were as relevant to our century as to Helliconia's.

It could hardly be otherwise. For the people of Helliconia, and the non-people, the beasts, and other personages, interest us only if they mirror our concerns. No one wants a passport to a nation of talking slugs.

So I offer you this volume for your enjoyment, hoping you will find more to agree with than you did in LIFE IN THE WEST—and maybe even more to amuse you.

Your affectionate
Father

Begbroke
Oxford

HELLICONIA
SPRING

CONTENTS

PRELUDE

Yuli   1

Embruddock   75

I · Death of a Grandfather   79
II · The Past That Was Like a Dream   88
III · A Leap from the Tower   104
IV · Favourable Temperature Gradients   114
V · Double Sunset   125
VI · "When I Were All Befuddock . . ."   144
VII · A Cold Welcome for Phagors   162
VIII · In Obsidian   178
IX · In and Out of a Hoxney Skin   212
X · Laintal Ay's Achievement   244
XI · When Shay Tal Went   253
XII · Lord of the Island   274
XIII · View from a Half Roon   289
XIV · Through the Eye of a Needle   313
XV · The Stench of Burning   337

Why have so many heroic deeds recurrently dropped out of mind and found no shrine in lasting monuments of fame? The answer, I believe, is that *this world is newly made*; its origin is a recent event, not one of remote antiquity.

That is why even now some arts are still being perfected: the process of development is still going on. Yes, and it is not long since the truth about nature was first discovered, and I myself am even now the first who has been found to render this revelation into my native speech. . . .

Lucretius: *De Rerum Natura*
55 BC

PRELUDE

Yuli

T his is how Yuli, son of Alehaw, came to a place called Oldorando, where his descendants flourished in the better days that were to come.

Yuli was seven years old, virtually a grown man, when he crouched under a skin bivouac with his father and gazed down the the wilderness of a land known even at that time as Campannlat. He had roused from a light doze with his father's elbow in his rib and his harsh voice saying, "Storm's dying."

The storm had been blowing from the west for three days, bringing with it snow and particles of ice off the Barriers. It filled the world with howling energy, transforming it to a grey-white darkness, like a great voice that no man could withstand. The ledge on which the bivouac was pitched afforded little protection from the worst of the blast; father and son could do nothing but lie where they were under the skin, dozing, once in a while chewing on a piece of smoked fish, while the weather battered away above their heads.

As the wind expired, the snow arrived in spurts, twitching in feather-like flurries across the drab landscape. Although Freyr was high in the sky—for the hunters were within the tropics—it seemed to hang there frozen. The lights rippled overhead in shawl after golden shawl, the fringes of which seemed to touch the ground, while the folds rose up and up until they vanished in the leaden zenith of heaven. The lights gave little illumination, no warmth.

Both father and son rose by instinct, stretching, stamping their feet, throwing their arms violently about the massive barrels of their bodies. Neither spoke. There was nothing to say. The storm was over. Still they had to wait. Soon, they knew, the yelk would be here. Not for much longer would they have to maintain their vigil.

Although the ground was broken, it was without feature, being covered with ice and snow. Behind the two men was higher ground, also covered with the mat of whiteness. Only to the north was there a dark grim greyness, where the sky came down like a bruised arm to meet the sea. The eyes of the men, however, were fixed continually on the east. After a period of stamping and slapping, when the air about them filled with the foggy vapour of their breath, they settled down again under the skins to wait.

Alehaw arranged himself with one befurred elbow on the rock, so that he could tuck his thumb deep into the hollow of his left cheek, propping the weight of his skull on his zygomatic bone and shielding his eyes with four curled gloved fingers.

His son waited with less patience. He squirmed inside his stitched skins. Neither he nor his father was born to this kind of hunting. Hunting bear in the Barriers was their way of life, and their fathers' before them. But intense cold, exhaled from the high hard hurricane mouths of the Barriers had driven them, together with the sick Onesa, down to the gentler weather of the plains. So Yuli was uneasy and excited.

His ailing mother and his sister, together with his mother's family, were some miles distant, the uncles venturing hopefully towards the frozen sea, with the sledge and their ivory spears. Yuli wondered how they had fared in the days-long storm, if they were feasting even now, cooking fish or hunks of seal meat in his mother's bronze pot. He dreamed of the scent of meat in his mouth, the rough feel of it meshed in saliva as it was gulped down, the flavour. . . . Something in his hollow belly went *whang* at the thought.

"There, see!" His father's elbow jabbed his biceps.

A high iron-coloured front of cloud rose rapidly in the sky, dimming Freyr, spilling shade across the landscape. Everything was a blur of white, without definition. Below the bluff on which they lay stretched a great frozen river—the Vark, Yuli had heard it called. So thickly covered in snow was it that nobody could tell it was a river, except by walking across it. Up to their knees in powdery drift, they had heard a faint ringing beneath their heels; Alehaw had paused, putting the sharp

end of his spear to the ice and the blunt end to his ear, and listened to
the dark flow of water somewhere beneath their feet. The far bank of the
Vark was vaguely marked by mounds, broken here and there by patches
of black, where fallen trees lay half-concealed by snow. Beyond that,
only the weary plain, on and on, until a line of brown could be made
out under the sullen shawls of the far eastern sky.

Blinking his eyes, Yuli stared at the line and stared again. Of course
his father was right. His father knew everything. His heart swelled with
pride to think that he was Yuli, son of Alehaw. The yelk were coming.

In a few minutes, the leading animals could be discerned, travelling
solidly on a wide front, advancing with a bow wave preceding them,
where their elegant hoofs kicked up snow. They progressed with their
heads down, and behind them came more of their kind, and more,
without end. It appeared to Yuli that they had seen him and his
father and were advancing directly upon them. He glanced anxiously
at Alehaw, who gestured caution with one finger.

"Wait."

Yuli shivered inside his bearskins. Food was approaching, enough
food to feed every single person of every tribe upon whom Freyr and
Batalix ever shone, or Wutra smiled.

As the animals drew nearer, approaching steadily at something like
a man's fast walking pace, he tried to comprehend what an enormous
herd it was. By now, half of the landscape was filled with moving animals, with the white-and-tan texture of their hides, while more beasts
were appearing over from the eastern horizon. Who knew what lay
that way, what mysteries, what terrors? Yet nothing could be worse
than the Barriers, with its searing cold, and that great red mouth Yuli
had once glimpsed through the scudding wrack of cloud, belching out
lava down the smoking hillside. . . .

Now it was possible to see that the living mass of animals did not
consist solely of yelk, although they made up the greater part. In the
midst of the herd were knots of a larger animal, standing out like
clumps of boulders on a moving plain. This larger animal resembled a
yelk, with the same long skull about which elegant horns curled protectively on either side, the same shaggy mane overlying a thick matted
coat, the same hump on its back, situated towards its rump. But these
animals stood half as tall again as the yelk which hemmed them in. They
were the giant biyelk, formidable animals capable of carrying two men
on their backs at the same time—so one of Yuli's uncles had told him.

And a third animal associated itself with the herd. It was a gunnadu,
and Yuli saw its neck raised everywhere along the sides of the herd. As
the mass of yelk moved indifferently forward, the gunnadu ran excitedly to either flank, their small heads bobbing on the end of their
long necks. Their most remarkable feature, a pair of gigantic ears,
turned hither and thither, listening for unexpected alarms. This was the

first two-legged animal Yuli had seen; below its long-haired body, two immense pistonlike legs propelled it. The gunnadu moved at twice the speed of the yelk and biyelk, covering twice as much ground, yet each animal remained where it was in relation to the herd.

A heavy dull continuous thunder marked the approach of the herd. From where Yuli lay against his father, the three species of animal could be distinguished only because he knew what to look for. They all merged with one another in the heavy mottled light. The black cloud-front had advanced more rapidly than the herd, and now covered Batalix entirely: that brave sentinel would not be seen again for days. A rumpled carpet of animals rolled across the land, its individual movements no more distinguishable than currents in a turbulent river.

Mist hung over the animals, further shrouding them. It comprised sweat, heat, and small winged biting insects able to procreate only in the heat from the burly-hoofed flock.

Breathing faster, Yuli looked again and—behold!—the creatures in the forefront were already confronting the banks of the snowbound Vark. They were near, they were coming nearer—the world was one inescapable teeming animal. He flicked his head to look in appeal at his father. Although he saw his son's gesture, Alehaw remained rigidly staring ahead, teeth gritted, eyes clenched against the cold under his heavy eye ridges.

"Still," he commanded.

The tide of life surged along the riverbanks, flowed over, cascaded over the hidden ice. Some creatures, lumbering adults, skipping fauns, fell against concealed tree trunks, dainty legs kicking furiously before they were trampled under the pressure of the march.

Individual animals could now be picked out. They carried their heads low. Their eyes were staring, white-rimmed. Thick green trails of saliva hung from many a mouth. The cold froze the steam from their upthrust nostrils, streaking ice across the fur of their skulls. Most beasts laboured, in poor condition, their coats covered with mud, excrement, and blood, or hanging loose in strips, where a neighbour's horns had stabbed and torn them.

The biyelks in particular, striding surrounded by their lesser brethren, their shoulders enormous with grey-bunched fur, walked with a kind of controlled unease, their eyes rolling as they heard the squeals of those who fell, and understood that some kind of danger, towards which they were inevitably to progress, threatened ahead.

The mass of animals was crossing the frozen river, churning snow. Their noise came plain to the two watchers, not solely the sound of their hoofs but the rasp of their breath, and a continued chorus of grunts, snorts, and coughs, a click of horn against horn, the sharp rattle of ears being shaken to dislodge ever persistent flies.

Three biyelks stepped forth together on the frozen river. With sharp resounding cracks, the ice broke. Shards of it almost a metre thick reared up into view as the heavy animals fell forward. Panic seized the yelk. Those on the ice attempted to scatter in all directions. Many stumbled and were lost under more animals. The cracking spread. Water, grey and fierce, jetted into the air—fast and cold, the river was still flowing. It rushed and broke and foamed, as if glad to be free, and the animals went down into it with their mouths open, bellowing.

Nothing deterred the oncoming animals. They were as much a natural force as the river. They flowed ever on, obliterating their companions who stumbled, obliterating too the sharp wounds opened in the Vark, bridging it with tumbled bodies, until they surged up the near bank.

Now Yuli raised himself on to his knees and lifted his ivory spear, his eyes blazing. His father seized his arm and dragged him down.

"See, phagors, you fool," he said, giving his son a furious, contemptuous glare, and stabbing ahead with his spear to indicate danger.

Shaken, Yuli sank down again, as much frightened of his father's wrath as by the thought of phagors.

The yelk herd pressed about their outcrop of rock, lurching by on either side of its crumbling base. The cloud of flies and stinging things that sang about their twitching backs now enveloped Yuli and Alehaw, and it was through this veil that Yuli stared, trying to get a sight of phagors. At first he discerned none.

Nothing was to be seen ahead but the avalanche of shaggy life, driven by compulsions no man understood. It covered the frozen river, it covered the banks, it covered the grey world back to the far horizon, where it tucked itself under the dun clouds like a rug under a pillow. Hundreds of thousands of animals were involved, and the midges hung above them in a continuous black exhalation.

Alehaw dragged his son down and indicated a spot to their left with one shaggy eyebrow. Half-hidden beneath the skin that served as their bivouac, Yuli stared at the advance. Two giant biyelks were lumbering towards their coign of vantage. Their massive white-furred shoulders were almost on a level with the ledge. As Yuli blew the midges away from before his eyes, the white fur resolved itself into phagors. Four of them, two riding on each biyelk, clung tight to the hair of their mounts.

He wondered how he had missed sighting them before. Though they merged with their giant steeds, they exhibited the presence of all who ride while others travel on foot. They clustered on top of the biyelks' shoulders, directing their moody bull faces ahead towards the higher ground where the herd would stop and graze. Their eyes glared out under upward-curving horns. Every now and again, one would shoot out his white milt, curving it up the slot of his powerful nostrils, to remove plaguing midges.

Their clumsy heads pivoted above the bulk of their bodies, which were completely covered with long white hair. The creatures were all white, except for their pink-scarlet eyes. They rode the striding biyelks as if they were part of them. Behind them, a crude leather carrier holding clubs and weapons swung to and fro.

Now that Yuli was alert to the nature of the danger, he discerned other phagors. Only the privileged rode. The rank and file of their nation went on foot, proceeding at a walking pace matching that of the animals. As he watched, so tense he dared not even brush the flies from his eyelids, Yuli saw a group of four phagors pass within a few metres of where he and his father lay. He would have had no difficulty in spearing the leader between the shoulder blades, had Alehaw given the command.

Yuli looked with particular interest at the horns that passed him, two by two. Smooth though they appeared in the dull light, the inner and outer edges of each horn were sharp from base to tip.

He coveted one of those horns. Horns of dead phagors were used as weapons in the savage recesses of the Barriers. It was for their horns that learned men in distant towns—couched in dens remote from storm—referred to phagors as the ancipital race: the species with two sharp edges.

The leading ancipital strode along dauntlessly. Lack of an ordinary knee joint made his an unnatural-looking stride. He marched mechanically as he must have done for miles. Distance was no obstacle.

His long skull was thrust forward in typical phagor fashion, low between his shoulders. On either arm he wore hide straps, to which were attached outward-pointing horns, their extremities tipped with metal. With these, the creature could prod away any animal that walked too close to him. Otherwise, he was unarmed; but to a nearby yelk, a bundle of possessions had been tied, a bundle including spears and a hunting harpoon. Adjacent animals also involuntarily carried baggage belonging to the other phagors in the group.

Behind the leader were two more males—so Yuli assumed—followed by a female phagor. She was of slighter build, and carried some kind of bag tied round her middle. Under her long white hair, pinkish dugs swung. On her shoulders rode an infant phagor, clutching uncomfortably at its mother's neck fur, its head clamped down on her head. Its eyes were closed. The female walked automatically, as though in a daze. It was a matter for conjecture for how many days she and the others had been walking, or how far.

And there were other phagors, spread thinly round the outskirts of the moving concourse. The animals took no notice of them, accepting them as they accepted the flies, because there was no alternative to acceptance.

The noise of the drumming hoofs was punctuated by laboured breathing and coughing and breaking wind. Another sound rose. The phagor who led the small group was emitting a kind of hum or growl, a rough noise delivered over a vibrating tongue which varied in pitch; perhaps it was intended to cheer the three who followed. The sound terrified Yuli. Then it was gone, and the phagors too. More animals streamed by and eventually more phagors, continuing stanchlessly. Yuli and his father lay where they were, occasionally spitting flies from their mouths, waiting for the time to strike and win the meat they desperately needed.

Before sunset, the wind got up again, blowing as before off the ice-caps of the Barriers, into the faces of the migratory army. The attendant phagors marched with their heads down, eyes slitted, and long trails of saliva fanned from the corners of their mouths and froze across their chests, as fat freezes when thrown out on the ice.

The atmosphere was iron. Wutra, god of the skies, had withdrawn his shawls of light and shrouded his domain with overcast. Perhaps another battle had been lost to him.

From under this dark curtain, Freyr became visible only when it reached the horizon. Blankets of cloud rumpled back to reveal the sentinel smouldering in a perspective of golden ashes. It shone out with spirit over the wastes—small but bright, its disc no more than a third as large as that of its companion star, Batalix, yet Freyr's light was greater, fiercer.

It sank into the eddre of the ground and was gone.

Now was the time of dimday, which prevailed in summer and autumn, and which almost alone distinguished those seasons from even less merciful times. Dimday suffused a dazed half-light across the night sky. Only at times of New Year would Batalix and Freyr rise and set together. At present their lives were solitary, hidden frequently behind cloud which was the billowing smoke from Wutra's war.

In the manner of day's turning to dimday, Yuli read the weather omens. Driving winds would soon be conjured up with snow on their breath. He recalled the rhyme they chanted in Old Olonets, the tongue of magic, of past things, of red ruin, the tongue of catastrophe, fair women, giants, and rich food, the tongue of an inaccessible yesterday. The rhyme had been recalled in the croupy caves of the Barriers:

> Wutra in sorrow
> Will put Freyr to barrow
> And us to the billow

As if responding to the changing light, a general shudder passed across the mass of yelk, and they stopped. Groaning, they settled where they were upon the trampled ground, tucking their legs beneath their bodies. For the enormous biyelk, this manoeuvre was not possible. They stood where they were and slept, ears across eyes. Some of the phagor groups gathered themselves together for companionship; most simply flung themselves down indifferently and slept where they fell, jamming their backs against the flanks of supine yelk.

Everything slept. The two figures sprawled on the rock ledge dragged their sheltering skin over their heads and dreamed, empty-bellied, with their faces buried in their folded arms. Everything slept, except for the mist of biting and sucking insects.

Things that were capable of dreams struggled through the uneasy mirages that dimday brought with it.

In general, the view, with its lack of shadow and constant level of suffering, might have appeared to anyone scrutinising it for the first time to represent not so much a world as a place awaiting formal creation.

At this stage of quiescence, there was a motion in the sky hardly more energetic than the unfolding of the aurora which had hung above the scene earlier. From the direction of the sea came a solitary childrim, sailing through the air some metres above the prostrate mass of living things. It looked to be no more than a great wing, glowing red like the embers of a dying fire, beating with a steady lethargy. As it passed over the deer, the animals twitched and heaved. It skimmed over the rock where the two humans lay, and Yuli and his father twitched and heaved, like the yelk seeing strange visions in their sleep. Then the apparition was gone, heading on lonely for the mountains in the south, leaving behind it a trail of red sparks to die in the atmosphere like an echo of itself.

After a while, the animals woke and rose to their feet. They shook their ears, which bled from the attentions of the gnats, and again started forward. With them went the biyelks and gunnadus, scuttling here and there. With them too went the phagors. The two humans roused, and watched them go.

Throughout another day the great progress continued, and blizzards raged, plastering the animals with snow. Towards evening, when wind was blowing tattered cloud across the sky and the cold held a whistling edge, Alehaw sighted the rear of the herd.

The rear was not as tight as the vanguard had been. Stragglers from the herd trailed back several miles, some limping, some coughing pitifully. Behind and beside them scurried long furry things with bellies near the ground, waiting the chance to nip a fetlock and bring a victim crashing down.

The last of the phagors marched past the ledge. They did not walk at the rear, either from respect for the low-bellied carnivores or because the going was difficult over such trampled ground, piled with scumble.

And now Alehaw rose, motioning his son to do likewise. They stood, clutching their weapons, and then slithered down to level ground.

"Good!" said Alehaw.

The snow was strewn with dead animals, in particular round the banks of the Vark. The break in the ice was plugged with drowned bodies. Many of those creatures who had been forced to lie down where they stood had frozen to death as they rested, and were now turned to ice. The lumps of which they composed the red core were unrecognisable in shape after the blizzard.

Delighted to be able to move, young Yuli ran and jumped and cried aloud. Dashing to the frozen river, he skipped dangerously from one unidentifiable lump to another, waving his hands and laughing. His father called him sharply to heel.

Alehaw pointed down through the ice. Black shapes moved, obscurely seen, partly defined by trails of bubbles. They streaked the turbid medium in which they swam with crimson, boring up beneath the frozen layers to attack the banquet provided for their benefit.

Other predators were arriving by air, large white fowl coming in from the east and the sullen north, fluttering heavily down, brandishing ornate beaks with which they bored through the ice to the flesh underneath. As they devoured, they fixed on the hunter and his son eyes heavy with avian calculation.

But Alehaw wasted no time on them. Directing Yuli to follow, he moved to where the herd had stumbled across fallen trees, calling and waving his spear as he went, to frighten off predators. Here dead animals were readily accessible. Although badly trampled, they still preserved one part of their anatomies intact, their skulls. It was to these that Alehaw addressed his attention. He prized open the dead jaws with the blade of a knife, and adroitly cut out their thick tongues. Blood spilled over his wrists onto the snow.

Meanwhile, Yuli climbed among the tree trunks, collecting broken wood. He kicked the snow away from one fallen trunk, contriving a sheltered place in which he could make a small fire. Wrapping his bowstring round a pointed stick, he rubbed it to and fro. The crumbled wood smouldered. He blew gently. A tiny flame sprang up, as he had seen it do often under the magical breath of Onesa. When the fire was burning well, he set his bronze pot on it, and piled snow in to melt, adding salt from a leather pocket he carried in his furs. He was ready when his father brought seven slimy tongues in his arms, and slipped them into the pot.

Four of the tongues were for Alehaw, three for Yuli. They ate with grunts of satisfaction; Yuli trying to catch his father's eye and smile, to show satisfaction; but Alehaw kept his brows knit as he chewed, and his gaze down at the trampled ground.

There was work still to be done. Even before they had finished eating, Alehaw got to his feet and kicked the smouldering embers aside. The scavenger birds nearby rose momentarily, and then settled again to their feast. Yuli emptied the bronze pot and secured it to his belt.

They were almost at the place where the great herd of animals reached the western limit of its migration. Here, on higher ground, they would seek out lichen under the snow, and graze on the strands of shaggy green moss that wrapped the larch forests about. Here, too, on a low plateau, some of the animals would reach their due term and bring forth their young. It was to this plateau, no more than a mile off, that Alehaw and his son made their way through the grey daylight. In the distance, they saw groups of other hunters, heading in the same direction; each group deliberately ignored the others. No other group consisted of two people only, Yuli noted; that was the penalty his family paid for being not of the plain, but of the Barrier. For them, everything was more arduous.

They walked bent double, up the incline. The way was strewn with boulders, where an ancient sea had once withdrawn in the face of encroaching cold—but of that aspect of affairs they knew and cared nothing; only the present was of importance to Alehaw and his son.

On the lip of the plateau they stood, shielding their eyes against biting cold in order to peer forward. Most of the herd had disappeared. All that remained of its still active numbers were occasional swarms of flying insects and the pungent smell. It had left behind on the plateau those of its members who were propagating.

Among these fated individuals were not only yelk but the flimsier gunnadu and the bulky bodies of giant biyelk. They lay inert, covering a wide area, dead or almost dead, sometimes with sides heaving. Another party of hunters was moving closer among the dying animals. Grunting, Alehaw gestured to one side, and he and Yuli moved over in the direction of a broken cluster of pines, near which a few yelk lay. Yuli stood over one to watch his father kill the helpless beast, already labouring its way into the grey world of eternity.

Like its monstrous cousin, the biyelk, and the gunnadu, the yelk was a necrogene, giving birth only through its death. The animals were hermaphrodite, sometimes male, sometimes female. They were too crudely designed to have within them the apparatus of mammals such as ovaries and wombs. After mating, the spurted sperm developed within the warm interior into small maggotlike forms, which grew as they devoured the stomach of their maternal host.

A time came when the maggot-yelk reached a main artery. It could then spread in its numbers like seed in the wind throughout the host animal, causing death within a short while. This event occurred unfailingly when the great herds reached the plateau at the western limit of their range. So it had done throughout ages that no one could count.

Even while Alehaw and Yuli stood over the beast, its stomach collapsed like an old bag. It threw up its head and died. Alehaw plunged in his spear, in ceremonial fashion. Both men dropped to their knees in the snow, and with their daggers ripped up the belly of the animal.

The maggot-yelk were within, no bigger than a fingernail—almost too small to see but collectively delicious to taste, and highly nourishing. They would help Onesa in her illness. They died on exposure to the freezing air.

Left to themselves, the maggot-yelk would live in safety inside the skins of their hosts. Within their little dark universe, they would not hesitate to devour each other, and many were the bloody battles fought in aorta and mesenteric arteries. The survivors grew through successive metamorphoses, increasing in size as they decreased in numbers. At length, two or possibly three small rapid-moving yelks would emerge from throat or anus, to face the starveling world outside. And this emergence would be achieved just in time to avoid death by trampling, as the herds moved slowly into position on the plateau for their return migration northeastwards towards far Chalce.

Dotted over the plateau, among the animals simultaneously procreating and dying, stood thick stone pillars. The pillars had been set there by an earlier race of men. On each pillar was carved a simple device: a circle or a wheel with a smaller circle at its centre. From the centre circle, two opposed curved spokes radiated to the outer one. Nobody present on the sea-sculpted plateau, animal or hunter, attended to these decorated pillars in the least degree.

Yuli was engrossed with their catch. He tore off strips of hide, weaving them crudely into a bag, into which he scraped the dying maggot-yelk. Meanwhile his father was dissecting the carcass. Every bit of the dead body could be utilised. From the longest bones, a sledge would be built, lashed together with strips of hide. Horns would serve as runners, to ease their having to pull the sledge all the way home. For by then the little carriage would be loaded high with good solid joints of shoulder and rib and rump, covered over with the rest of the skin.

Both worked together, grunting with effort, their hands red, breath in a cloud above their heads where midges gathered unnoticed.

Suddenly, Alehaw gave a terrible cry, fell backwards, tried to run.

Yuli looked round in dismay. Three great white phagors had crept from a place of concealment among the pines, and stood over them. Two sprang on Alehaw as he got up, and clubbed him to the snow. The other struck out at Yuli. He rolled aside, yelling.

They had completely forgotten about the dangers of phagors, and had neglected to keep any watch. As he rolled and sprang and avoided the swinging club, Yuli saw the other hunters nearby, working calmly on the dying yelk just as he and his father had been doing. So determined were they to get on with the work, to build their sledges and be off—so near was starvation—that they continued about their business, glancing up at the fight only now and again. The story would have been different had they been kin of Alehaw and Yuli. But these were plainsmen, squat unfriendly men. Yuli yelled to them for help, without avail. One man nearby hurled a bloody bone at the phagors. That was all.

Dodging the swinging cudgel, Yuli started to run, slipped, and fell. Up thundered the phagor. Yuli fell into an instinctive defensive pose, resting on one knee. As the phagor dived at him, he brought up his dagger in an underarm movement and sank it into the broad gut of his attacker. He watched with shocked amazement his arm disappear into stringy stiff pelage and that coat immediately belch into thick gold gore gushing everywhere. Then the body smote him, and he went rolling —rolling then by volition, rolling out of harm's way, rolling into what shelter offered itself, rolling panting behind an upthrust shoulder of dead yelk, from where he looked out on a world suddenly turned enemy.

His assailant had fallen. Now he picked himself up, nursing that golden patch in his gut with enormous horned paws, and staggering mindlessly, crying "Aoh, aoh, aohhh, aohhhh. . . ." He fell head first and did not move again.

Behind the fallen body, Alehaw had been beaten to the ground. He lay crumpled, but the two phagors immediately seized him and one of them arranged him over his shoulders. The pair looked about, stared back at their fallen comrade, glanced at each other, grunted, turned their backs on Yuli, and began to march away.

Yuli stood up. He found his legs, bound inside his fur trousers, were shaking. He had no idea what to do. Distractedly, he skirted the body of the phagor he had killed—how he would boast of that to his mother and uncles—and ran back to the scene of the scuffle. He picked up his spear and then, after some hesitation, took his father's spear as well. Then he set off to follow the phagors.

They were trudging ahead, making heavy weather of getting uphill with their burden. They soon sensed the boy following them, and turned now and again, halfheartedly trying to drive him off with threats and gestures. Evidently they did not think him worth expending a spear on.

When Alehaw recovered consciousness, the two phagors stopped, set him on his feet, and made him walk between them, encouraging him with blows. Uttering a series of whistles, Yuli let his father know that he was nearby; but whenever the older man ventured to look over his shoulder, he received a clout from one of the phagors that sent him reeling.

The phagors slowly caught up with another party of their own kind, consisting of a female and two males; one of the latter was old and walked with a stick as tall as himself, on which he leaned heavily in his progress uphill. Every now and again, he stumbled in the piles of yelk droppings.

Eventually, the scatters of scumble appeared no more, and the smell died from their nostrils. They were moving along an upward path the migratory herd had not taken. The winds had dropped, and spruce trees grew on the slope. There were now several knots of phagors climbing up the hillside, many of them bowed beneath carcasses of yelk. And behind them trailed a nine-year-old human being, fear in his heart, trying to keep his father in sight.

The air grew thick and heavy, as if under enchantment. The pace was slower, the larches closer, and the phagors were forced to bunch more closely. Their rough song, scraped across their horny tongues, sounded loudly, a hum that on occasions rose to a scalding crescendo and then died again. Yuli was terrified, and fell further behind, darting from tree to tree.

He could not understand why Alehaw did not break from his captors and run back downhill; then he could grasp his spear again, and together the two of them would stand side by side and kill all the shaggy phagors. Instead, his father remained captive, and now his slighter figure was lost among the crowding figures in the twilight under the trees.

The humming song rose harshly and died. A smokey greenish light glowed ahead, promising a new crisis. Yuli sneaked forward, running doubled up to the next tree. Some kind of building stood ahead, fronted by a double gate, which opened slightly. Within, the faint fire showed. The phagors were shouting, and the gate opened more. They began to crowd in. The light was revealed as a brand, which one of their kind held aloft.

"Father, Father!" screamed Yuli. "Run, Father! I'm here."

There was no answer. In the murk, which the torch further confused, it was impossible to see whether or not Alehaw had already been pushed inside the gate. One or two phagors turned indifferently at the shouts, and shooed Yuli away without animosity.

"Go and zzhout at the wind!" one cried in Olonets. They wanted only full-grown human slaves.

The last burly figure entered the building. Amid more shouting, the gates closed. Yuli ran to them crying, banging against their rough wood as he heard a bolt being shot home on the other side. He stood there for a long while with his forehead against the grain, unable to accept what had happened.

The gates were set in a stone fortification, the blocks of which were crudely fitted into each other and patched with long-tailed mosses. The edifice was no more than an entrance to one of the underground caves in which the phagors, as Yuli knew, had their existence. They were indolent creatures, and preferred to have humans working for them.

For a while, he ranged round about the gate, climbing up the steep hillside, until he found what he expected to find. It was a chimney, three times his height and of impressive circumference. He could climb it with ease, because it tapered towards the top and because the blocks of stone of which it was made were crudely set together, allowing plenty of foothold. The stones were not as freezingly cold as might have been expected, and free of frost.

At the top, he incautiously stuck his face over the lip, and was immediately jerked backwards, so that he lost his hold and fell, landing on his right shoulder and rolling in the snow.

A blast of hot, foetid air, mixed with wood smoke and stale exhalation, had erupted at him. The chimney was a ventilator for the phagor warrens below ground. He knew he could not climb in that way. He was shut out, and his father was lost to him forever.

He sat miserably in the snow. His feet were covered by skins, laced in place up the legs. He wore a pair of trousers and a tunic of bear fur, stitched in place by his mother with the fur next to his skin. For additional warmth, he had on a parka with a fur hood. Onesa, during a period when she was feeling well enough, had decorated the parka with white scuts of an ice rabbit round the shoulders, three scuts to each shoulder, and had embroidered the neck with red and blue beads. Despite which, Yuli presented a forlorn sight, for the parka was stained with the remains of food and fat drippings, while dirt caked the fur of his garments; they smelt strongly of Yuli. His face, a light yellow or beige when clean, was wrinkled brown and black with dirt, and his hair straggled greasily about his temples and collar. He had a flat-nostrilled nose, which he began to rub, and a broad, sensuous mouth, which began to pucker, revealing a broken front tooth among its white neighbours, as he started to cry and punch the snow.

After a while, he rose and walked about among the forlorn larches, trailing his father's spear behind him. He had no alternative but to retrace his steps and try to return to his sick mother, if he could find his way back through the snowy wastes.

He realised also that he was hungry.

Desperately forsaken, he started a hullabaloo at the closed gates. There was no kind of response. Snow began to fall, slowly but without cease. He stood with fists raised above his head. He spat, the gob landing on the panels. That for his father. He hated the man for being a weakling. He recalled all the beatings he had received from his father's hand—why had his father not beaten the phagors?

At last, he turned away through the falling snow in disgust, and began to walk downhill.

He flung his father's spear away into a bush.

Hunger battled with fatigue and got him back as far as the Vark. His hopes were immediately dashed. None of the dead yelk remained undevoured. Predators had arrived from every corner and torn away their meat. Only carcasses and piles of bare bones by the river awaited him.

He howled in wrath and dismay.

The river had frozen over and snow lay on the solid ice. He scraped the snow away with his foot and stared down. The bodies of some of the drowned animals still remained in the ice; he saw one where the head of the yelk hung down into the dark current below. Large fish ate at its eyes.

Working strenuously with his spear and a sharp horn, Yuli bored a hole in the ice, enlarged it, and waited, standing above it with spear poised. Fins flashed in the water. He struck. A blue-flecked fish, its mouth open in amazement, shone at the spearpoint as he pulled it forth dripping. It was as long as his two hands outstretched and placed thumb to thumb. He roasted it over a small fire and it tasted delicious. He belched, and slept for an hour, propped between logs. Then he started to trek southwards, along a trail the migration had all but obliterated.

Freyr and Batalix changed sentry duty in the sky, and still he walked, the only figure moving in the wilderness.

"Mother," cried old Hasele to his wife, before he even got back to his hut, "Mother, see what I found by the Three Harlequins."

And his ancient crone of a wife, Lorel, lame since childhood, hobbled to the door, stuck her nose out in the biting cold air, and said, "Never mind what you found. There's gentlemen from Pannoval waiting to do business with thee."

"Pannoval, eh? Wait till they see what I found by the Three Harlequins. I need help here, mother. Come, it's not cold. You waste your life stuck in that house."

The house was rude in every extreme. It consisted of piles of boulders, several of them taller than a man, interspersed with planks and timbers, and roofed over with hides on top of which turfs grew. The interstices of the boulders were stuffed with lichen and mud, to make the interior windproof, while spars and whole tree trunks propped the edifice at many points, so that the whole affair most resembled a defunct porcupine. To the main structure, additional rooms had been added in the same spirit of improvisation which had prompted the original. Bronze chimneys thrust up into the sour sky, smoking gently; in some rooms, pelts and hides were dried, in others sold. Hasele was a trader and trapper, and had made enough of a living so that now, towards the end of his life, he could afford a wife and a sledge pulled by three dogs.

Hasele's house perched on a low escarpment which curved away eastwards for several miles. This escarpment was strewn with boulders, in some places split, in others piled one on top of the other. These boulders provided shelter for small animals, and so made good hunting grounds for the old trapper, who was no longer inclined to wander as far afield as he had done in the days of his youth. On some of the more monumental piles of stone, he had bestowed names, the Three Harlequins being one. At the Three Harlequins, he dug in salt deposits for the mineral he needed to cure his hides.

Smaller stones littered the escarpment, each subtending from its eastern side a raked cone of snow, its size varying according to the nature of the stone, pointing precisely away from the point from which the west wind whistled off the distant Barriers. This had once been a beach, belonging to a long-vanished sea coast, the north coast of the continent of Campannlat, when times had been more favourable.

To the eastern side of the Three Harlequins grew a little thicket of thorn bushes, taking advantage of the shelter of the granite to thrust forth an occasional green leaf. Old Hasele valued these green leaves in his pot, and set snares all round the bushes in order to keep off animals. Unconscious and entangled in the sharp twigs lay the youth he had discovered, whom he now dragged with Lorel's aid into the smokey sanctuary of his hut.

"He's no savage," said Lorel admiringly. "See here how his parka is decorated with beads, red and blue. Pretty, ain't they?"

"Never mind that. Give him a mouthful of soup, mother."

She did so, stroking the lad's throat until the soup went down, when her patient stirred, coughed, sat up, and whispered for more. As Lorel fed him she looked down, pursing her lips, at the swollen cheeks and eyes and ears, where countless insect bites had caused blood to flow and mat beneath his collar. He took more soup, then groaned and slumped back again into a coma. She held him to her, putting an arm round him, under his armpit, rocking him, remembering ancient happinesses to which she could no longer give a name.

Guiltily looking round for Hasele, she found he had padded off already, eager to do business with the gentlemen from Pannoval.

She laid the youth's dark head down, sighing, and followed her husband. He was sipping spirits with the two large-built traders. Their parkas steamed in the warmth. Lorel tugged at Hasele's sleeve.

"Maybe these two gentlemen will take this sick youth you've found back with them to Pannoval. We can't feed him here. We're starving as it is. Pannoval is fat and rich."

"Leave us, mother. We're negotiating," Hasele said, in a lordly way.

She hobbled out the back of the building, and watched as their captive phagor, shuffling under his chains, secured their dogs in the snow kennel. She looked beyond that bowed back to the gritty grey landscape to the miles of desolation that faded into a desolate sky. From somewhere out in that wilderness, the youth had come. Perhaps once or twice a year, people, alone or in pairs, straggled dying from the ice deserts. Lorel could never gain any clear impression of where they came from, only that beyond the desert were mountains colder still. One fugitive had babbled of a frozen sea that could be crossed. She made the holy circle over her dry breasts.

In her younger days, it had teased to have no clearer picture. Then she had gone wrapped to stand on the escarpment and stare northwards. And childrims flew overhead, waving their solitary wings, and she had fallen to her knees with a dazed impression of men—massed and holy, rowing the great flat wheel of the world to some place where the snow did not always fall or the wind always blow. She went indoors crying, hating the hope the childrims brought her.

Though old Hasele had dismissed his wife in a lordly way, he took note of what she said, as he always did. When his deal with the two gentlemen from Pannoval was concluded, and a small pile of precious herbs and spices and wool fibres and flour balanced against the skins the men would load on their sledge, Hasele raised the question of their taking the sick youth with them back to civilization. He mentioned that the youth wore a good decorated parka, and therefore—just possibly, gentlemen—might be someone of importance, or at least the son of someone important.

Rather to his surprise, the two gentlemen agreed that they would be very happy to take the youth with them. They would have to make a small charge of an extra yelk skin, to cover the youth and defray the extra expense. Hasele muttered a bit, and then gave in with a good grace; he could not afford to feed the boy if he lived and, if he died— it never pleased him to feed human remains to his dogs, and the native habit of mummification and aerial burial was not his way.

"Done," he said, and went to fetch the least good skin he could quickly lay his hands on.

The youth was awake now. He had accepted more soup from Lorel, and a warmed leg of snow rabbit. When he heard the men coming, he lay back and closed his eyes, one hand tucked inside his parka.

They surveyed him only casually, then turned away. Their plan was to load the sledge with their acquisitions, spend some hours here being entertained by Hasele and his wife, getting drunk, sleeping it off, and then set out on the challenging journey south to Pannoval.

All this was done, and a fine noise was made as Hasele's spirits were consumed. Even when the gentlemen slept on a pile of skins, their snores were loud. And Lorel secretively tended Yuli, feeding him, bathing his face, smoothing his thick hair, hugging him.

In early dimday, when Batalix was low, he was gone from her, still feigning unconsciousness as the gentlemen lifted him on to their sledge, cracked their whips, scowled to achieve some fortification between their hangovers and the brow-clamping cold, and were off.

The two gentlemen, whose lives were hard, robbed Hasele and any other trapper they visited to the maximum extent that the trappers allowed themselves to be robbed, knowing as they did so that they would themselves be robbed and cheated when, in their turn, they had to trade in the skins. Cheating was one of their methods of survival, like wrapping up well. Their simple plan was, as soon as they were out of sight of Hasele's ramshackle edifice, to slit the windpipe of their newly acquired invalid, to pitch his body into the nearest snowdrift, and to see to it that only the good decorated parka—together possibly with the under tunic and trousers—reached the safety of the market in Pannoval.

They halted the dogs and braked the sledge. One of them drew a gleaming metal dagger and turned back towards the prostrate figure.

At which moment the prostrate figure rose up with a yell, hurling the skin that had covered him over the gentleman's head, kicking him ferociously in the stomach, and running furiously into the distance, taking a zigzag course to avoid any speeding spears.

When he considered himself far enough away, he turned, crouching behind a grey stone, to see if he was followed. In the dull light, the sledge had already disappeared from view. There was no sign of the two gentlemen. Save for the whistle of the west wind, all was still. He was alone in the frozen waste, some hours before Freyr-rise.

A great horror came upon Yuli. After the phagors had taken his father to their underground lair, he had wandered for more days than he could count through the wilderness, dazed by cold and lack of sleep, crazed by insects. He had completely lost his way, and was close to death when he collapsed into the thorn bush.

A little rest and nourishment had quickly restored his health. He had allowed himself to be loaded onto the sledge, not because he at all trusted the two gentlemen from Pannoval, who smelt all wrong to him, but because he could not bear the old crone who insisted on touching him in a way he disliked.

Now, after that brief interlude, here he was, in the wilds again, with a sub-zero wind plucking at his ears. He thought once more of his mother, Onesa, and of her illness. The last time he had seen her, she had coughed, and blood bubbled out of her mouth. She had looked upon him in such a ghastly way as he left with Alehaw. Only now did Yuli realise what that ghastly look meant: she had never expected to see him again. It was useless seeking to get back to his mother if she were a corpse by now.

Then what?

If he was to survive, there was only one possibility.

He rose, and at a steady jog trot followed in the wake of the sledge.

Seven large horned dogs of the kind known as asokins pulled the sledge. The leader was a bitch called Gripsy. They were known collectively as Gripsy's team. They rested for ten minutes in every hour; at every other rest period, they were fed foul-smelling dried fish from a sack. The two gentlemen took it in turn to trudge beside the sledge and to lie on it.

This was a routine Yuli soon understood. He kept well back down the trail. Even when the sledge was out of sight, as long as the air was still his keen nose could detect the stink of men and dogs running ahead. Sometimes he drew near to watch how things were done. He wanted to see how to handle a dog team for himself.

After three days' continuous travelling, when the asokins were having to take longer rests, they reached another trapper's post. Here the trapper had built himself a small wooden fort, decorated with horns and antlers of wild animals. Lines of skins flapped stiffly in the breeze. The gentlemen stayed here while Freyr sank from the sky, pale Batalix also died, and the brighter sentinel rose again. The two gentlemen screamed with the trapper in their drunkenness, or slept. Yuli stole some hardtack from the sledge and slept fitfully, rolled in a skin, in the sledge's lee side.

On they went.

Two more stops were made, interspersed with several days' journeying. Always Gripsy's team drove roughly southward. The winds became less chill.

At last, it became apparent that they were getting close to Pannoval. The mists towards which the team pulled proved solid stone.

Mountains rose from the plain ahead, their flanks deeply covered with snow. The plain itself rose, and they were working through foothills, where both gentlemen had to walk beside the sledge, or even push it. And there were stone towers, some with sentries who challenged them. The sentries challenged Yuli too.

"I'm following my father and my uncle," he called.

"You're lagging behind. The childrims will get you."

"I know, I know. Father is anxious to get home to Mother. So am I."

They waved him on, smiling at his youth.

At last, the gentlemen called a halt. Dried fish was thrown to Gripsy and her team, and the dogs were staked out. The two gentlemen picked a snug little corrie on the hillside, covered themselves with furs, applied alcohol to their insides, and fell asleep.

As soon as he heard their snores, Yuli crept near.

Both men had to be disposed of almost at the same time. He would be no match for either in a fight, so they must have no warning. He contemplated stabbing them with his dagger or bashing their brains in with a rock; either alternative had its dangers.

He looked about to see that he was not watched. Removing a strap from the sledge, he crept close to the gentlemen, and managed to tie a strap round the right ankle of one and the left ankle of the other, so that whoever jumped up first would be impeded by his companion. The gentlemen snored on.

While undoing the strap from the sledge, he noticed a number of spears. Perhaps they had been for trade and had not sold. He did not wonder at it. Removing one from its confining strap, he balanced it and judged that it would throw badly. For all that, the head was commendably sharp.

Returning to the corrie, he nudged one of the gentlemen with his foot until the gentleman rolled with a groan onto his back. Bringing the spear up as if he were about to transfix a fish, Yuli transfixed the gentleman through his parka, his rib cage, and his heart. The gentleman gave a terrible convulsive movement. Expression horrible, eyes wide, he sat up, grasped at the shaft of the spear, sagged over it, and then slowly rolled back with a long sigh that ended in a cough. Vomit and blood seeped from his lips. His companion did no more than stir and mutter.

Yuli found that he had sunk the spear so fiercely it had driven through the gentleman and into the ground. He returned to the sledge for a second spear and dealt with the second gentleman as he had with the first—with equal success. The sledge was his. And the team.

A vein throbbed at his temple. He regretted the gentlemen were not phagors.

He harnessed up the snarling and yelping asokins and drove them away from the spot.

Dim shawls of light rippled in the skies overhead, to be eclipsed by a tall shoulder of mountain. There was now a distinct path, a track that broadened mile by mile. It wound upwards until it negotiated a towering outcrop of rock. Round the base of the rock, a sheltered high valley was revealed, guarded by a formidable castle.

The castle was partly built of stone and partly hacked out of the rock. Its eaves were wide, to allow snow to avalanche from its roofs to the road below. Before the castle stood an armed guard of four men, drawn up before a wooden barrier which barred the road.

Yuli halted as a guard, his furs decorated with shining brasses, marched up.

"Who're you, lad?"

"I'm with my two friends. We've been out trading, as you see. They're away behind with a second sledge."

"I don't see them." His accent was strange: not the Olonets to which Yuli was accustomed in the Barriers region.

"They'll be along. Don't you recognise Gripsy's team?" He flicked the whip at the animals.

"So I do. Of course. Know them well. That bitch is not called Gripsy for nothing." He stepped to one side, raising his sturdy right arm.

"Let her up, there," he shouted. The barrier rose, the whip bit, Yuli hollered, and they were through.

He breathed deep as he got his first sight of Pannoval.

Ahead was a great cliff, so steep that no snow clung to it. In the cliff face was carved an enormous representation of Akha the Great One. Akha squatted in a traditional attitude, knees near his shoulders, arms wrapped round his knees, hands locked palms upward, with the sacred flame of life in his palms. His head was large, topped with a knot of hair. His half-human face struck terror into a beholder. There was awe even in his cheeks. Yet his great almond eyes were bland, and there was serenity as well as ferocity to be read in that upturned mouth and those majestic eyebrows.

Beside his left foot, and dwarfed by it, was an opening in the rock. As the sledge drew near, Yuli saw that this mouth was itself gigantic, possibly three times taller than a man. Within, lights could be seen, and guards with strange habits and accents, and strange thoughts in their heads.

He squared his young shoulders and strode forward boldly.

That was how Yuli came to Pannoval.

Never would he forget his entry into Pannoval, and his passing from the world under the sky. In a daze, he steered the sledge past guards, past a grove of beggarly trees, and stopped to take in the roofed expanse before him under which so many people lived out their days. Mist compounded with darkness, as he left the gate behind, to create a sketchy world with forms but no outlines. It was night; the few people moving about were wrapped in thick clothes which in their turn were wreathed by nimbi of fog, encircling them, floating about their heads, moving after them in slow swirls like threadbare-cloak trails. Everywhere was stone, stone carved into walls and divisions, stalls, houses, pens, and flights of steps—for this great mysterious cave tipped away up towards the interior of the mountain, and had been hewn over the centuries into small level squares, each separated from the next by steps and flanking walls.

With forced economy single torches fluttered at the head of each flight of steps, their flames oblique in a slight draught, illumining not the concourse but the misty air, to which their smoke contributed further opacity.

Ceaseless action of water through long eons had carved out a number of linked caves in the rock, in various sizes and on various levels. Some of these caves were inhabited, and had become regularised by human endeavour. They were named, and furnished with the necessities of rudimentary human life.

The savage halted, and could proceed no farther into this great station of dark until he found someone to accompany him. Those few outsiders who, like Yuli, visited Pannoval, found themselves in one of the larger caves, which the inhabitants knew as Market. Here much of the necessary work of the community was carried out, for little or no artificial light was required, once one's eyes had become accustomed to the dimness. By day the place rang with voices, and with the irregular knock of hammers. In Market, Yuli was able to trade the asokins and the goods on the sledge for things necessary to his new life. Here he must stay. There was nowhere else to go. Gradually he became accustomed to the gloom, to smoke, to smarting eyes, and to the coughing of the inhabitants; he accepted them all, along with the security.

It was his fortune to fall in with a decent fatherly trader called Kyale, who, with his wife, ran a stall in one of the small squares of Market. Kyale was a sorrowful man with a downward-turning mouth partly concealed by blackish moustaches. He befriended Yuli for reasons Yuli could not understand, and protected him from swindlers. He also went to some trouble to introduce Yuli to this new world.

Some of the echoing noises of Market were attributable to a stream, the Vakk, which ran through the rear end of Market, deep in its own chasm. This was the first free-flowing stream Yuli had ever seen, and it remained for him one of the wonders of the settlement. The splashing waters filled him with pleasure and, with his animistic faith, he regarded the Vakk as almost a living thing.

The Vakk had been bridged, so that access was gained to the end area of Market, where increasing steepness of the ground necessitated many steps, which culminated in a wide balcony housing a huge statue of Akha, carved from the rock. This figure could be seen, its shoulders rising from shadows, even from the far side of Market. Akha held in his outstretched hands a real flame, which a priest replenished at regular intervals, appearing from a door in Akha's stomach to do so. The people of Akha presented themselves to the feet of their god regularly; there they offered up all manner of gifts to him, which were accepted by the priests, unobtrusive in black-and-white-striped robes. The supplicants prostrated themselves, and a novice swept the ground with a feathery brush, before they dared gaze hopefully up at the black stone eyes high above them in the web of shadow, and retreat to less holy ground.

Such ceremonials were a mystery to Yuli. He asked Kyale about them, and received a lecture that left him more confused than before. No man can explain his religion to a stranger. Nevertheless, Yuli received a strong impression that this ancient being, represented in stone, fought off the powers raging in the outer world, particularly Wutra, who ruled the skies and all the ills associated with the skies. Akha was not greatly interested in humans; they were too puny for his concern. What he wanted was their regular offerings, to keep him strong in the struggle with Wutra, and a powerful Akhan ecclesiastical body existed to see that Akha's desires in this respect were carried out, in order that disaster did not descend on the community.

The priesthood, in alliance with the militia, had the governance of Pannoval; there was no one overall ruler, unless one counted Akha himself, who was generally supposed to be out prowling the mountains with a celestial club, looking for Wutra and such of his dreadful accomplices as the worm.

This was surprising to Yuli. He knew Wutra. Wutra was the great spirit before whom his parents, Alehaw and Onesa, offered prayers in time of danger. They had represented Wutra as benevolent, the bringer of light. And, as far as he recalled, they never mentioned Akha.

Various passages, as labyrinthine as the laws issued by the priesthood, led to various chambers adjoining Market. Some of these chambers were accessible, some forbidden of entry to common folk. About the forbidden regions, people were reluctant to talk. But he soon observed wrongdoers being dragged off there, hands tied behind their backs, winding up dark stairways into the aularian shadows, some to the Holies, some to a punishment farm behind Market called Twink.

In due course of time, Yuli traversed a narrow passage choked with steps which led to a large regularised cave called Reck. Reck also contained its enormous statue of Akha, here seen with an animal hanging on a chain about his neck, and dedicated to sport; Reck was the site at which mock battles, displays, athletic contests, and gladiatorial combats were held. Its walls were painted crimson and sang-de-boeuf, with swirling decorations. Much of the time Reck was almost empty, and voices boomed through its hollow spaces; then citizens with an especial bent for holiness came and wailed up into the high-vaulted dark. But on the glowing occasions of the games—then music sounded, and the cavern was crowded to overflowing.

Other important caverns opened from Market. At its eastern side, a nest of small squares or large mezzanines led up between flights of steps impeded by heavy balustrades to an extensive residential cavern called Vakk, after the stream that surfaced here, sunk deep in its gurgling ravine. Over Vakk's great entrance arch was much elaborate carving, with globular bodies entwined between flowing waves and stars, but much of it had been destroyed in some forgotten roof-fall.

Vakk was the oldest cavern after Market, and was filled with "livings," as they were called, dating back many centuries. To one arriving on its threshold from the outer world, viewing—or rather, guessing at—its mounting and confused terraces that climbed back into obscurity, Vakk in the uncertain light was a daunting dream where substance could not be distinguished from shadow, and the child of the Barrier felt his heart quail in his chest. A force like Akha was needed to save anyone who trod in such a thronged necropolis!

But he adapted with the flexibility of youth. He came to look on Vakk as a prodigal town. Falling in with guild apprentices of his own age, he roamed its muddle of livings which were clustered on many floors, often leading one from another. Cubicle was stacked on cubicle in profusion, the furniture in each fixed because carved from the same rock as floors and walls, all in one flowing line. The story of rights of ways and privacies in these organic warrens was complex, but always related to the guild system of Vakk, and always, in case of dispute, to be settled by the judgement of a priest.

In one of these livings, Tusca, Kyale's kindly wife, found Yuli a chamber of his own, only three doors from where she and Kyale lived. It was roofless and its walls curved; he felt as if he had been set down within a stone flower.

Vakk sloped steeply, and was dimly lit by natural light—more dimly than Market. The air was sooty with the exhalations of fat lamps, but clerics collected tax on every lamp, which had numbers stamped on their clay bases, so that they were used sparingly. The mysterious fogs which afflicted Market had less power in Vakk.

From Vakk, a gallery led direct to Reck. There were also, on lower ground, ragged arches leading to a high-roofed cavern called Groyne, which had good clean air, although the inhabitants of Vakk thought the inhabitants of Groyne rather barbarous, chiefly because they were members of more lowly guilds, slaughterers, tanners, diggers of chert and clay and fossil wood.

In the honeycombed rock adjoining both Groyne and Reck was another large cavern full of habitations and cattle. This was Prayn, which many avoided. It was being energetically extended by the sappers' guild when Yuli arrived. Prayn collected all the night soil from the other suburbs and fed it to swine and noctiferous crops, which thrived on heat. Some of the farmers in Prayn bred as a sideline a strain of bird called a preet, which had luminous eyes and luminescent patches on its wings. Preets were popular as cage birds; they added a little brightness to the livings of Vakk and Groyne—though they also were the subject of taxes collected by priests for Akha.

"In Groyne they are gruff, in Prayn pretty tough," went a local saying. But Yuli found the people lifeless, except when roused by the games, rare exceptions being those few traders and trappers living in Market in terraces of their own guild, who regularly had occasion to be blessed by Akha and sent on business in the outside world, as had been the case with the two gentlemen of his acquaintance.

From all the major caverns, and from smaller ones, paths and tunnels led into the blind rock, some ascending, some descending. Pannoval was full of legends of magical beasts that came in from the primordial dark of the rock, or of people who were spirited away from their livings into the mountain. Best to stay put in Pannoval, where Akha looked after his own with his blind eyes. Better Pannoval, too, and taxes, than the cold glare of outside.

These legends were kept alive by the sayers' guild, members of which stood on every stairway, or waited on terraces, and spun fantastic tales.

In this world of nebulous gloom, words were like lights.

To one other section of Pannoval, which figured largely in people's whispered discourse, Yuli was not allowed to make his way. That was the Holies. The Holies could be reached by gallery and stair from Market, but it was guarded by the militia, and set apart by repute. No one went voluntarily through its winding approaches. In the Holies lived the militia, forever guarding the law of Pannoval, and the priesthood, forever guarding its soul.

All these arrangements were so magnificent to Yuli that he could not see their meanness.

It took Yuli little time to find how closely the people were governed. They expressed no surprise in a system to which they had been born; but Yuli, accustomed to open spaces and the easily comprehended law of survival, was astonished at the way in which their every movement was circumscribed. Yet they thought themselves uniquely privileged.

With his legitimately acquired stock of skins, Yuli planned to purchase a stall next to Kyale, and set up shop. He discovered that there were many regulations that forbade anything so simple. Nor could he trade without a stall—unless he had a special licence—and for that he would have to have been born a member of a hawkers' guild. He needed a guild, an apprenticeship, and certain qualifications—a kind of exam—that only the priesthood could confer. He also needed a two-part certificate from the militia, together with insurance and references. Nor would he be able to trade until he owned a living. Yet he could not possess the room Tusca had rented for him until he was fully accredited with the militia. He was unable to meet even the most elementary qualification: a belief in Akha and a proof of regular sacrifices to the god.

"It's simple. First you, as a savage, must attend a priest." That was the dictum of a sharp-faced militia captain before whom Yuli had to appear. He confronted Yuli in a little stone room, the balcony of which was a metre or so above one of Market's terraces, and from which one might survey the whole animated scene.

The captain wore a floor-length cloak of black and white over the customary skins. On his head he wore a bronze helmet displaying the holy symbol of Akha, a kind of two-spoked wheel. His hide boots came halfway up his calf. Behind him stood a phagor, a black and white woven band tied round its hairy white brow.

"Pay attention to me," growled the captain. But Yuli found his eyes ever drifting towards the silent phagor, wondering at its presence.

The ancipital stood with an air of taciturn repose, ungainly head thrust forward. Its horns were blunt; they had been sawn short, and their cutting edges dulled with a file. Yuli saw that it had a leather collar and thong about its throat, half-concealed under white hair, a sign of its submission to man's rule. Yet it was a threat to the citizens of

Pannoval. Many officers appeared everywhere with a submissive phagor beside them; the phagors were valued for their superior ability to see in the dark. Ordinary people went in fear of the shambling animals that spoke basic Olonets. How was it possible, Yuli wondered, for men to form liaisons with the same beasts who had imprisoned his father—beasts that everyone in the wilds hated from birth?

The interview with the captain was dispiriting, and worse was to come. He could not live unless he obeyed the rules, and they appeared interminable; there was nothing for it—as Kyale impressed upon him—but to conform. To be a citizen of Pannoval, you had to think and feel like a Pannovalian.

So he was consigned to attend the priest in the alley of livings where he had his room. This entailed numerous sessions at which he was taught a ritualised history of Pannoval ("born from Great Akha's shadow on the eternal snows . . .") and forced to learn many of the scriptures by heart. He also had to do whatever Sataal, the priest, told him to do, including the running of many tedious errands, for Sataal was lazy. It was no great consolation to Yuli to find that the children of Pannoval went through similar courses of instruction at an early age.

Sataal was a solidly built man, pale of face, small of ear, heavy of hand. His head was shaven, his beard plaited, in the manner of many priests of his order. There were twists of white in the plaits. He wore a knee-length smock of black and white. His face was deeply pocked. It took Yuli some while to realise that, despite the white hairs, Sataal was not past middle age, being only in his late teens. Yet he walked in a round-shouldered way suggesting both age and piety.

When he addressed Yuli, Sataal spoke always kindly but remotely, keeping a gulf between them. Yuli was reassured by the man's attitude, which seemed to say, This is your job and mine, but I shall not complicate it by probing into what your inner feelings are. So Yuli kept quiet, applying himself to the task of learning all the necessary fustian verses.

"But what do they mean?" he asked at one point, in bewilderment.

Sataal rose slowly in the small room, and turned about, so that his shoulders loomed black in a distant source of light, and all the rest of him flowed into encompassing shadow. A dull highlight gleamed on his pate as he inclined his head towards Yuli, saying, admonishingly, "Learning first, young fellow, then interpretation. After learning, then less difficulty in interpretation. Get everything by heart, you hardly need it by head. Akha never enforces understanding from his people, only obedience."

"You said that Akha cares nothing for anyone in Pannoval."

"The important point, Yuli, is that Pannoval cares for Akha. Now then, once again:

"Whoso laps Freyr's bane
Like a fish swallows ill bait:
When it groweth late
Our feeble frames he will burn."

"But what does it mean?" Yuli asked again. "How can I learn it if I don't understand it?"

"Repeat it, son," said Sataal sternly. " 'Whoso laps . . .' "

Yuli was submerged in the dark city. Its networks of shadows snatched at his spirit, as he had seen men in the outer world catch fish with nets under the ice. In dreams, his mother came to him, blood flying from her mouth. Then he would wake, to lie in his narrow cot staring up, far up, far beyond the confines of his flower-shaped room, to the roof of Vakk. Sometimes, when the atmosphere was fairly clear, he could see distant detail, with bats hanging up there, and stalactites, and the rock gleaming with liquid that had ceased to be liquid; and he wished he could fly away from the traps he found himself in. But there was nowhere else to go.

Once, in midnight desperation, he crawled through to Kyale's home for comfort. Kyale was annoyed at being woken, and told him to go away, but Tusca spoke to him gently, as if he were her son. She patted his arm and clutched his hand.

After a while, she wept softly, and told him that indeed she had a son, a good kind lad of about Yuli's age, Usilk by name. But Usilk had been taken from her by the police for a crime she knew he had never committed. Every night, she lay awake and thought of him, concealed in one of those terrifying places in the Holies, guarded by phagors, and wondered if she would ever see him again.

"The militia and the priests are so unjust here," Yuli whispered to her. "My people have little to live on in the wilds, but all are equal, one with another, in the face of the cold."

After a pause, Tusca said, "There are people in Pannoval, women as well as men, who do not learn the scriptures and think to overthrow those who rule. Yet without our rulers, we should be destroyed by Akha."

Yuli peered at the outline of her face through the dark. "And do you think that Usilk was taken . . . because he wanted to overthrow the rulers?"

In a low voice she replied, holding tightly to his hand, "You must not ask such questions or you'll meet trouble. Usilk was always rebellious—yes, perhaps he got among the wrong people. . . ."

"Stop your chatter," Kyale called. "Get back to your bed, woman—and you to yours, Yuli."

These things Yuli nursed in himself all the while he went through his sessions with Sataal. Outwardly, he was obedient to the priest.

"You are not a fool, even if you are a savage—and that we can change,"

said Sataal. "Soon you shall progress to the next step. For Akha is the
god of earth and underground, and you shall understand something of
how the earth lives, and we in its veins. These veins are called land-
octaves, and no man can be happy or healthy unless he lives along his
own land-octaves. Slowly, you can acquire revelation, Yuli. Maybe, if
you are good enough, you could yourself become a priest, and serve Akha
in a greater way."

Yuli kept his mouth shut. It was beyond his ability to tell the priest
that he needed no particular attentions from Akha: his whole new way
of life in Pannoval was a revelation.

The days followed one another peacefully. Yuli became impressed
with the never varying patience of Sataal, and began disliking his instruction periods less. Even away from the priest, he thought about his
teaching. All was fresh and curiously exciting. Sataal had told him that
certain priests, who undertook to fast, were able to communicate with
the dead, or even with personages in history; Yuli had never heard of
such things, but hesitated to call them nonsense.

He took to roving alone through the suburbs of the city, until its thick
shadows took on for him colours of familiarity. He listened to people,
who often talked of religion, or to the sayers who spoke at street corners,
who often laced their stories with religion.

Religion was the romance of the darkness, as terror had been of the
Barriers, where tribal drums warded off devils. Slowly, Yuli began to
perceive in religious talk not a vacuum but a core of truth: the way in
which people lived and died had to be explained. Only savages needed
no explanation. The perception was like finding an animal's trail in the
snow.

Once he was in a malodorous part of Prayn, where human scumble
was poured into long trenches on which the noctiferous crops grew.
Here, the people were pretty tough, as the saying had it. A man with
short-cropped free-flowing hair, and therefore neither a priest nor a
sayer, ran up and jumped onto a scumble barrow.

"Friends," he said, standing before them. "Listen to me for a moment,
will you? Just stop your labours and hear what I have to say. I speak
not for myself but for the great Akha, whose spirit moves inside me. I
have to speak for him although I put my life in danger, for the priests
distort Akha's words for their own purposes."

People stopped to listen. Two tried to make a joke at the young man's
expense, but the others stood in submissive interest, Yuli included.

"Friends, the priests say that we have to sacrifice to Akha and nothing
more, and he will then keep us safe in the great heart of his mountain.
I say that is a lie. The priests are content and do not care how we the
ordinary people suffer. Akha tells you through my lips that we should
do more. We should be better in ourselves. Our lives are too easy—once
we have made sacrifices and paid taxes, we care nothing. We merely

enjoy, or go to the games. You hear so often that Akha cares nothing for us and everything for his battle with Wutra. We must make him care— we must become worthy of his care. We must reform ourselves! Yes, reform! And the easy-living priests must reform themselves also. . . ."

Someone called to say that the militia were coming.

The young man paused. "My name is Naab. Remember what I say. We too have a role in the great war between Sky and Earth. I will be back to speak if I can—speak my message to all Pannoval. Reform, re- form!—Before it is too late . . ." As he jumped down, there was a surge among the crowd that had gathered. A great tethered phagor rushed forward, with a soldier at the other end of his leash. It reached forward and grabbed Naab's arm with its powerful horned hands. He gave a cry of pain, but a hairy white arm went round his throat and he was led away in the direction of Market and the Holies.

"He shouldn't have said such things," a grey man muttered, as the crowd dispersed.

Yuli followed the man on impulse, and grasped his sleeve.

"The man Naab said nothing against Akha—why should the militia take him away?"

The man looked furtively about. "I recognise you. You're a savage, or you wouldn't ask such stupid things."

For answer, Yuli raised his fist. "I'm not stupid or I would not ask my question."

"If you weren't stupid, you'd keep quiet. Who do you think has power here? The priesthood, of course. If you speak out against them—"

"But that's Akha's power—"

The grey man had slipped away into the dark. And there in that dark, that ever watchful dark, could be felt the presence of something mon- strous. Akha?

One day, a great sporting event was to be held in Reck. It was then that Yuli, acclimatised to Pannoval, underwent a remarkable crystalisa- tion of emotion. He hurried along to the sports with Kyale and Tusca. Fat lamps burned in niches, leading the way from Vakk to Reck, and crowds of people climbed through the narrowing rock passages, struggled up the worn steps, calling to one another, as they filed into the sports arena.

Carried along by the surge of humanity, Yuli caught a sudden view ahead of the chamber of Reck, its curved walls flickering with light. He saw but a slice of the chamber to begin with, trapped between the veined walls of the passage along which the rabble had to pass. As he moved, so into that framed distant view moved Akha himself, high above the heads of the crowd.

He ceased to listen to what Kyale was saying. Akha's gaze was on him; the monstrous presence of the dark was surely made visible.

Music played in Reck, shrill and stimulating. It played for Akha.

There Akha stood, broad and horrible of brow, its large stone eyes unseeing yet all-seeing, lit from below by flares. Its lips dripped disdain.

The wilderness held nothing like this. Yuli's knees were weak. A powerful voice inside him, one he scarcely recognised as his own, exclaimed, "Oh, Akha, at last I believe in you. Yours is the power. Forgive me, let me be your servant."

Yet alongside the voice of one longing to enslave himself was another, speaking simultaneously in a more calculating manner. It said, "The people of Pannoval must understand a great truth which it would be useful to get to comprehend by following Akha."

He was astonished at the confusion within himself, a war that did not lessen as they entered the chamber and more of the stone god was revealed. Naab had said, "Humans have a role in the war between Sky and Earth." Now he could feel that war alive within him.

The games were intensely exciting. Running races and spear throwing were followed by wrestling between humans and phagors, the latter with their horns amputated. Then came the bat shoot, and Yuli emerged from his pietistic confusions to watch the excitement. He feared bats. High above the crowd, the roof of Reck was lined with the furry creatures, dangling with their leather wings about their heads. Archers came forward and shot in turn at the bats with arrows to which were attached silken threads. The bats, when hit, fell fluttering down, and were claimed for the pot.

The winner was a girl. She wore a bright red garment tight at the neck and long to the ground, and she pulled back her bow and shot more accurately than any man. And her hair was long and dark. Her name was Iskador, and the crowd applauded her wildly, none more so than Yuli.

Then there were the gladiatorial combats, men against men, men against phagors, and blood and death filled the arena. Yet all the time, even when Iskador was tensing her bow and her lovely torso—even then, Yuli thought in terms of great joy that he had found an amazing faith. The confusions within would be banished by greater knowledge, he assumed.

He recalled the legends he had listened to round his father's fire. The elders had spoken of the two sentinels in the sky, and of how the men on earth had once offended the God of the Skies, whose name was Wutra. So that Wutra had banished the earth from his warmth. Now the sentinels watched for the hour when Wutra returned, to look again with affection on the earth, and see if the people behaved better. If he found they did, then would he remove the frosts.

Well, Yuli had to acknowledge that his people were savages, just as Sataal claimed; how else would his father have allowed himself to be dragged away by phagors? Yet there must be a germ of truth in the tales. For here in Pannoval was a more reasoned version of the story. Wutra was now merely a minor deity, but he was vengeful, and he was loose

in the skies. It was from the skies that peril came. Akha was the great
earth god, ruling underground, where it was safe. The Two Sentinels
were not benign; being in the sky, they belonged to Wutra, and they
could turn against mankind.

Now the memorised verses began to make sense. Illumination shone
from them, so that Yuli muttered with pleasure what had previously
given him pain, gazing upon Akha's face as he did so:

> *"Skies give false prospects,*
> *Skies shower extremes:*
> *Against all such schemes*
> *Akha's earth overhead protects."*

Next day, he went humbly to Sataal and told the man that he had
been converted.

The pale heavy face of his priest regarded him, and Sataal drummed
his fingers on his knees.

"How were you converted? Lies fly about the livings these days."

"I looked at Akha's face. For the first time I saw it clear. Now my
heart is open."

"Another false prophet was arrested the other day."

Yuli smote his chest. "What I feel inside me is not false, Father."

"It's not so easy," said the priest.

"Oh, it is easy, it is easy—now everything will be easy!" He fell at the
priest's feet, crying his delight.

"Nothing's so easy."

"Master, I owe you everything. Help me. I want to be a priest, to
become as you."

During the next few days, he went about the lanes and livings noticing
new things. No longer did he feel himself encased in gloom, buried underground. He was in a favoured region, protected from all the cruel
elements that had made him a savage. He saw how welcome the dim
light was.

He saw too how beautiful Pannoval was, in all its chambers. In the
course of their long habitation, the caves had been decorated by artists.
Whole walls were covered with painting and carving, many of them
illustrating the life of Akha and the great battles he had fought, as well
as the battles he would fight when again enough humans had faith in his
strength. Where the pictures had grown old and faint, new ones had
been painted on top of them. Artists were still at work, often perched
dangerously on top of scaffolding that reached towards the roof like the
skeleton of some mythical long-necked animal.

"What's the matter with you, Yuli? You attend to nothing," Kyale
said.

"I'm going to be a priest. I've made up my mind."

"They'll never let you—you from outside."

"My priest is speaking to the authorities."

Kyale pulled at his melancholy nose, slowly lowering his hand until the tugging operations were taking place at one end of his moustache, as he contemplated Yuli. By now, Yuli's eyesight had so adjusted to the dimness that every nuance of expression on his friend's face was clear. When Kyale moved without a word to the back of his stall, Yuli followed.

Again grabbing his moustache for security, Kyale placed his other hand on Yuli's shoulder. "You're a good lad. You remind me of Usilk, but we won't go into that. . . . Listen to me: Pannoval isn't like it was when I was a child, running barefoot through the bazaars. I don't know what's happened, but there's no peace any more. All this talk of change— nonsense, to my mind. Even the priests are at it, with wild men ranting about reform. I say, let well enough alone. Know what I mean?"

"I know what you mean, yes."

"Well, then. You may think that it would be soft, being a priest. So it might. But I wouldn't recommend it at present. It's not as—as secure as it used to be, if you follow me. They've become restive. I hear they often execute heretical priests in the Holies. You'd do better here indentured to me, making yourself useful. Understand? I'm speaking to you for your own good."

Yuli looked down at the worn ground.

"I can't explain how I feel, Kyale. Sort of hopeful . . . I think things ought to change. I want to change myself, I don't know how."

Sighing, Kyale removed his hand from Yuli's shoulder. "Well, lad, if you take that attitude, don't say I didn't warn you. . . ."

Despite Kyale's grumpiness, Yuli was touched that the man cared about him. And Kyale passed on the news of Yuli's intentions to his wife. When Yuli went to his little curved room that evening, Tusca appeared in his doorway.

"Priests can go anywhere. If you become an initiate, you'll have the run of the place. You'll come and go in the Holies."

"I suppose so."

"Then you may find what has happened to Usilk. Try to, for my sake. Tell him I still think of him. And come and tell me if you can find any news of him."

She put a hand on his arm. He smiled at her. "You are kind, Tusca. Don't your rebels who want to bring down the rulers of Pannoval have any news of your son?"

She was frightened. "Yuli, you will change in all ways when you're a priest. So I'll say no more, for fear of injury to the rest of my family."

He lowered his gaze. "Akha strike me if I ever harm you."

On the next occasion when he appeared before the priest, a soldier was also present, standing behind Sataal in the shadows with a phagor on a leash. The priest asked Yuli if he would give up everything he possessed to walk in the path of Akha. Yuli said that he would.

"Then it shall be done." The priest clapped his hands, and off marched the soldier. Yuli understood then that he had now lost his few possessions; everything but the clothes he wore and his knife which his mother had carved would be taken by the military. Speaking no further word, Sataal turned, beckoning with one finger, and began to walk towards the rear of Market. Yuli could do nothing but follow, pulse beating fast.

As they came to the wooden bridge spanning the chasm where the Vakk leaped and tumbled, Yuli looked back, beyond the busy scene of trade and barter, out through the far archway of the entrance, catching a glimpse of snow.

For some reason, he thought of Iskador, the girl with the dark hair flowing. Then he hurried after his priest.

They climbed the terraces of the worship area, where people jostled to leave their sacrifices at the feet of the image of Akha. At the back were screens, intricately painted. Sataal whisked past them, and led into a narrowing passage, up shallow steps. The light became rapidly dimmer as they turned a corner. A bell tinkled. In his anxiety, Yuli stumbled. He had reached the Holies sooner than he had bargained for.

Just for once in crowded Pannoval, nobody else was about. Their footsteps echoed. Yuli could see nothing; the priest ahead of him was an impression, nothing, blackness within blackness. He dared not stop or reach out or call—blind following was what was now demanded of him and he must treat all that came as a test of his intentions. If Akha loved chthonic darkness, so must he. All the same, the *lack* of everything, the void that registered itself on his senses only as a whispered noise, assaulted him.

They walked forever into the earth. So it seemed.

Softly, suddenly, light came—a column of it appearing to strike down through a stagnant lake of darkness, creating on its bed a circle of brightness towards which two submerged creatures advanced. It silhouetted the heavy figure of the priest, black and white garb swirling about him. It allowed Yuli some sense of where he was.

There were no walls.

It was more frightening than total darkness. He had already grown so accustomed to the confines of the settlement, to having a cliff, a partition, a fellow's back, a woman's shoulder, always within jostling distance, that agoraphobia seized him. He went sprawling, uttering a gasp as he fell to the paving.

The priest did not turn. He reached the place where the illumination fell and marched steadily on, shoes clack-clacking, so that his figure was lost almost immediately behind the misty shaft of light.

Desperate at being left, the youth picked himself up and ran forward. As the shaft of light impaled him, he stared up. High above him was a hole through which ordinary daylight shone. Up there were the things he had known all his life, the things he was renouncing for a god of darkness.

He saw ragged rock. Now he could comprehend that he was in a chamber larger than the rest of Pannoval, and higher. At a signal—perhaps the tinkling bell he had heard—someone somewhere had opened a high door onto the outside world. As warning? As temptation? Or merely as a dramatic trick?

Maybe all three, he thought, since they were so much more clever than he, and he hurried on after the priest's disappearing figure. In a moment, he sensed rather than saw that the light behind him faded; the high door had closed. He was again in unbroken darkness.

They at last reached the far side of the gigantic chamber. Yuli heard the priest's steps slow. Without faltering, Sataal had reached a door, on the panel of which he rapped. After some delay, the door opened. A fat lamp floated in the air, borne above the head of an ageing woman who sniffed continuously. She allowed them to pass into a stone corridor before fastening the door behind them.

Matting covered the floor. Several doors confronted them. Along both walls, hip high, ran a narrow band of carving, which Yuli wanted to look at more closely but did not dare to; otherwise the walls were undecorated. The sniffing woman knocked at one of the doors. When response came, Sataal pushed it open and motioned Yuli in. Bowing, Yuli passed his mentor's outstretched arm and marched into the room. The door closed behind him. That was the last he saw of Sataal.

The room was furnished with detachable furniture of stone, covered with coloured rugs. It was lit by a double lamp standing on an iron holder. Two men sat at a stone table, and looked up without smiling from some documents. One was a militia captain, his helmet with its wheel insignia resting on the tabletop by his elbow. The other was a thin grey priest with a not unfriendly face, who blinked as if the mere sight of Yuli's face dazzled him.

"Yuli of the Outside? Since you have come this far, you have taken one step on the way to becoming a priest of Great Akha," the priest said in a reedy voice. "I am Father Sifans, and first of all I must ask you if you have any sins that destroy your peace of mind, to which you wish to confess."

Yuli was disconcerted that Sataal had left him so abruptly, without even a whispered farewell, though he understood that he must now give up such worldly things as love and friendship.

"Nothing to confess," he said sulkily, not looking the thin priest in the eye.

The priest cleared his throat. The captain spoke.

"Youth, look at me. I am Captain Ebron of the North Guard. You entered Pannoval on a sledge teamed by asokins called Gripsy's team. It was stolen from two renowned traders of this city named Atrimb and Prast, both of Vakk. Their bodies were found not many miles from here, with spears through them, as if they had been done to death in their sleep. What say you about this crime?"

Yuli stared at the floor.

"I know nothing of it."

"We think you know everything. . . . Had the crime been committed within the territory of Pannoval, it would carry the penalty of death. What do you say?"

He felt himself shaking. This was not what he had expected.

"I have nothing to say."

"Very well. You cannot become a priest while this guilt lies on you. You must confess the crime. You will be shut up until you speak."

Captain Ebron clapped his hands. Two soldiers entered and grasped Yuli. He struggled for a moment, to test their strength, had his arms sharply wrenched, and allowed himself to be led away.

Yes, he thought, the Holies—full of priests and soldiers. They've got me properly. What a fool I am, a victim. Oh, Father, you abandoned me. . . .

It was not even as if he had been able to forget about the two gentlemen. The double murder still lay heavy inside him, although he always tried to rationalise it by reminding himself that they had attempted to kill him. Many a night, as he lay on his cot in Vakk, staring up at the distant vault, he saw again the gentleman's eyes as he sat up and tried to pull the spear from his entrails.

The cell was small and damp and dark.

When he recovered from the shock of being alone, he felt cautiously about him. His prison was featureless except for an ill-smelling gutter and a low shelf on which to sleep. Yuli sat on it and buried his face in his hands.

He was given plenty of time to think. His thoughts, in the impenetrable darkness, took on a life of their own, as if they were the figments of delirium. People he knew, people he had never seen, came and went about him, engaged in mysterious activities.

"Mother!" he exclaimed. Onesa was there, as she had been before her illness, slender and active, with her long serious face that readily broke into a smile for her son—though it was a guarded smile with lips scarcely parted. She bore a great bundle of twigs on her shoulder. A litter of little horned black piglets walked before her. The sky was a brilliant

blue; both Batalix and Freyr shone there. Onesa and Yuli stepped along
a path out of a dark larch forest and were dazzled by the brightness.
Never had there been a blue like that; it seemed to tint the piled snow
and fill the world.

Ahead was a ruined building. Although it had been solidly built in
the long past, weather had broken it open like an old tree fungus. Before it stood a flight of shallow steps, now ruined. Onesa flung down
her twigs and sprang so eagerly up the steps that she almost skipped.
She raised her gloved hands as she went, and even offered a snatch of
song to the crisp air.

Rarely had Yuli seen his mother in such spirits. Why did she feel
like that? Why not more often? Not daring to put these questions
direct, yet longing to have some personal word from her, he asked,
"Who built this place, Mother?"

"Oh, it's always been here. It's as old as the hills. . . ."

"But who built it, Mother?"

"I don't know—my father's family, probably, long ago. They were
great people, with stores of grain."

This legend of his mother's family's greatness was well-known to him,
and the detail of the store of grain. He marched up the ruined steps,
and pushed open a reluctant door. Snow scattered in a cloud as he
shouldered his way inside. There was the grain, golden, piles of it,
enough for them all for ever more. It started running towards him in
a river, great piles of it cascading down, over the steps. And from under
the grain, two dead bodies heaved to view, struggling blindly towards
the light.

He sat up with a great cry, sprang to his feet, stood up, paced to the
cell door. He could not understand where these alarming visions came
from; they seemed not to be a part of him.

He thought to himself, *Dreams are not for you, dodger. You're too
tough. You think of your mother now, yet you never showed her affection. You were too afraid of your father's fist. You know, I really
believe I hated my father. I believe I was glad when the phagors carried
him off—weren't you?*

*No, no. . . . It's just that my experiences have made me hard. You're
hard, dodger, hard and cruel. You killed those two gentlemen. What
are you going to be? Better to confess to the murders and see what
happens. Try and love me, try and love me. . . .*

*I know so little. That's it. The whole world—you want to find out.
Akha must know. Those eyes see everything. But me—you're so small,
dodger—life's no more than one of those funny feelings when the
childrim flies overhead.*

He marvelled at his own thoughts. Finally he cried for the guards to
open his door, and found that he had been incarcerated for three days.

For a year and a day, Yuli served in the Holies as a novice. He was not allowed to leave the halls, but dwelt in a monastic nocturne, not knowing whether Freyr and Batalix swam separately or together in the sky. A wish to run through the white wilderness gradually left him, erased by the penumbral majesty of the Holies.

He had confessed to the murder of the two gentlemen. No punishment followed.

The thin grey priest with the blinking eyes, Father Sifans, was the charge-father over Yuli and other novices. He clasped his hands and said to Yuli, "That unhappy incident of the murders is now sealed behind the wall of the past. Yet you must never allow yourself to forget it, lest, in forgetting, you come to believe that it never happened. Like the many suburbs of Pannoval, all things in life are interwoven. Your sin and your longing to serve Akha are of a piece. Did you imagine that it was holiness that led a man to serve Akha? Not so. Sin is a more powerful mover. Embrace the dark—through sin you come to terms with your own inadequacy."

"Sin" was a word often on Father Sifans' lips at one period. Yuli watched it there with interest, with the absorption pupils devote to their masters. The way the lips moved was something he imitated to himself later, alone, using the movements to repeat all that he had to learn by heart.

While the father had his own private apartment to which he withdrew after instruction, Yuli slept in a dormitory with others of his kind, in a nest of dark within the dark. Unlike the fathers, they were allowed no pleasures; song, drink, wenches, recreation were forbidden, and their food was of the most spartan kind, selected from the offerings made by supplicants of Akha daily.

"I can't concentrate. I'm hungry," he complained once to his charge-father.

"Hunger is universal. We cannot expect Akha to fatten us. He defends us against hostile outside forces, generation by generation."

"Which is more important, survival or the individual?"

"An individual has importance in his own eyes, but generations have priority."

He was learning to argue the priest's way, step by step. "But generations are made up of individuals."

"Generations are not only the sum of individuals. They contain also aspirations, plans, histories, laws—above all, continuities. They contain the past as well as the future. Akha refuses to work with individuals alone, so individuals must be subdued—quenched, if necessary."

Slyly, the father taught Yuli to argue. On the one hand, he must have blind faith; on the other, he needed reason. For its long journey through the years, the entombed community needed all defences, needed both prayer and rationality. The sacred verses claimed that at some time in the future, Akha, in his lonely battle, might suffer defeat and the world undergo a period of intense fire descending from the skies. The individual must be quenched, to avoid the burning.

Through the entombing halls went Yuli, with all these ideas declaiming themselves in his head. They stood his understanding of the world upside down—but therein lay much of their attraction, since every revolutionary new insight only emphasised his previous ignorant state.

Among all the deprivations, one sensory delight stole upon his bewilderment to soothe him. The priests found their way through the dark labyrinth by wall-reading, an arcane mystery in which Yuli was soon to be initiated. There was also another directional clue, intended to delight. Music. At first, Yuli in his innocence imagined that he heard the sound of spirits overhead. He could make nothing of the tickling line of melody played on a one-stringed vrach. He had never seen a vrach. If not a spirit, could it be the wail of wind through a crevice somewhere in the rock?

His delight was so secret that he asked no one about the sounds, not even his fellow novices, until walking one day unexpectedly with Sifans into a religious service. Choirs were important, and monody even more so, with a single voice launched into the hollows of the dark; but what Yuli came to love most were the interventions by inhuman voices, those of the instruments of Pannoval.

Nothing similar was ever heard in the Barriers. The only music the besieged tribes there knew was a prolonged drumming, on a drum made of hide; clacking, of animal bones struck together; and clapping, of human hands, accompanied by a monotonous chant. It was the luxurious complication of the new music that convinced Yuli of the reality of his still awakening spiritual life. One great tune in particular took him by storm, "Oldorando," which had a part for an instrument that soared about all others, then dived into their midst, finally to retreat into a secure melodic refuge of its own.

Music became almost an alternative to light for Yuli. When he talked to his fellow novices, he found that they felt little of his exhilaration. But they—he came to realise—all carried a much greater central commitment to Akha himself than he. Most of the novices had loved or hated Akha from birth; Akha was nature to them as he was not to Yuli.

When he wrestled with such matters during the sparse hours allotted to sleep, Yuli felt guilt that he was not as the other novices. He loved the music of Akha. It was a new language. But was not music the creation of men, rather than of . . .

Even when he choked off the doubt, another doubt sprang up. How about the language of religion? Wasn't that also the invention of men —perhaps pleasant, ineffectual men like Father Sifans?

"Belief is not peace but torment; only the great War is peace." That part of the creed at least was true.

Meanwhile, Yuli kept his own council, and fraternised only superficially with his fellows.

They met for instruction in a low, damp, foggy hall named Cleft. Sometimes they went in utter darkness, sometimes in the glow of wicks carried by the fathers. Each session ended with the priest pressing his hand to the novice's forehead, gesturing at his brain, an action at which the novices laughed later in their dormitory. Priests' fingers were rough, from the wall-reading by which they navigated briskly about the labyrinths of the Holies even in the most pitchy blackness.

Each novice sat in a curiously shaped dock, built of clay bricks, facing his instructor. Each dock was decorated in individual low-reliefs, to make their identification in the dark easier. Their instructor sat opposite and above them, astride a clay saddle.

When only a few weeks of the novitiate had lapsed, Father Sifans announced the subject of heresy. He spoke in a low voice, coughing as he did so. Worse than nonbelief was to believe wrongly. Yuli leaned forward. He and Sifans had no light, but the charge-father in the next box did, a fluttering flame which served to throw a foggy orange nimbus about Sifans' head and shade his face. The old man's white-and-black gown further disintegrated his outlines, so that he merged with the dark of the chamber. Mist rolled about them, trailing anyone who walked slowly by, practising wall-reading. Coughs and muttering filled the low cavern; water dripped ceaselessly, like small bells.

"A human sacrifice, Father, did you say a human sacrifice?"

"The body is precious, the spirit expendable. One who has spoken against the priesthood, saying they should be more frugal to aid Akha . . . You are far enough on with your studies to attend his execution. . . . Ritual from barbarous times . . ."

The nervous eyes, two tiny points of orange, flickered in the dark like a signal from a remote distance.

When the time came, Yuli walked through the lugubrious galleries, nervously trying to wall-read with his fingers. They entered the largest cavern in the Holies, called State. No light was allowed. Whispering filled the air as the priesthood assembled. Yuli surreptitiously took hold of the hem of Father Sifans' gown in order not to lose him. Then a voice of a priest, declaiming the history of the long war between Akha and Wutra. Night was Akha's, and the priests were set to protect their flock through the long night's battle. Those who opposed the guardians must die.

"Bring forth the prisoner."

There was much talk of prisoners in the Holies, but this one was special. The tramp of the militia's heavy sandals could be heard, a shuffling. Then brightness.

A shaft of light blazed down. The novices gasped. Yuli recognised that they stood in the vast chamber through which Sataal had led him, a long while ago. The light source was as before, high above the multitude of heads; it appeared blinding.

At its base stood a human figure, tied to a wooden framework, legs and arms spread. It was in the upright position, and naked.

Even as the prisoner gave a cry, Yuli recognised the dense impassioned face, square, and framed by short-cropped hair. It was the young man he had once heard speak in Prayn—Naab.

His voice and message were also recognisable. "Priests, I am not your enemy, though you treat me like one, but your friend. Generation by generation, you sink into inaction, your numbers grow less, Pannoval dies. We are not just passive votaries of Great Akha. No! We must fight with him. We must also suffer. In the great war between Sky and Earth, we must play our part. We must reform and purify ourselves."

Behind the bound figure were militiamen in gleaming helmets, guarding him. Others arrived, bearing smoking brands. With them marched their phagors, checked by leather leads. They halted. They turned inward. They hoisted their brands high above their heads, and the smoke rose in leisurely braids upwards. Forward creaked a stiff cardinal, bowed under black-and-white garb and an elaborate mitre. He struck a golden staff against the ground three times, crying shrilly in the Priestly Olonets, "Have done, have done, have done. . . . O Great Akha, our Warrior God, appear to us!" A bell tinkled.

A second pillar of the brilliant white light, solidifying rather than banishing the surrounding night. Behind the prisoner, behind the phagors and the soldiers, Akha appeared, reaching upwards. A murmur of expectation came from the crowd. It was a skeletal scene, the militia and the massive white beasts all but transparent, Akha chalky in the column of light, the whole embedded in obsidian. In this representation, the semihuman head of the god thrust forward, and his mouth was open. The eyes were as sightless as ever.

"Take this unsatisfactory life, O Great Akha, and use it for Thy satisfaction."

Functionaries moved smartly forward. One began to crank at a handle set in the side of the frame holding the prisoner. The frame began to creak and shift. The prisoner cried softly once, as his body was forced to bend backwards. As the hinges on the framework opened, his body arched back, exposing his helplessness.

Two captains marched forward with a phagor between them. The great beast's blunted horns had been capped with silver and reached almost to the height of the soldiers' eyebrows. It stood in the ungainly customary stance of a phagor, head and prow of chest thrust forward, its long white hair stirring slightly in the draught that blew through State.

Music sounded again, drum, gongs, vrachs, drowning out Naab's voice, and the sustained warble of a fluggel rising high above them. Then everything stopped.

The body was bent double now, legs and feet twisted somewhere out of sight, head right back, exposing throat and thorax, gleaming pale in the column of light.

"Take, O Great Akha! Take what is already Thine! Eradicate him."

At the priest's scream, the phagor stepped a pace forward and bent down. It opened its shovel mouth and applied rows of blunt teeth to either side of the proffered throat. It bit. It raised its head, and a great morsel of flesh came up with it. It moved back into place between the two soldiers, swallowing noncommittally. A trickle of red ran down its white front. The rear column of light was cut off. Akha disappeared back into his nourishing darkness. Many of the novices fainted.

As they jostled out of State, Yuli asked, "But why use those devilish phagors? They're man's enemy. They should all be killed."

"They are the creatures of Wutra, as their colour shows. We keep them to remind us of the enemy," said Sifans.

"And what will happen to the—to Naab's body?"

"It will not be wasted. Every item is of some application. The whole carcass may go for fuel—perhaps to the potters, who always need to fire their kilns. I really don't know. I prefer to keep myself aloof from administrative details."

He dared say no more to Father Sifans, hearing the distaste in the old priest's voice. To himself, he said over and over again, "Those evil brutes. Those evil brutes. Akha should have no part of them." But the phagors were all over the Holies, padding patiently along with the militia, their noctilucent eyes peering here and there under their craggy brows.

One day Yuli tried to explain to his charge-father how his father had been caught and killed by phagors in the wild.

"You do not know for sure they killed him. Phagors are not always entirely evil. Sometimes Akha subdues their spirit."

"I'm sure he's dead by now. There's no way of being certain, though?"

He heard the father lick his lips as he hesitated, and then leaned towards Yuli in the blackness.

"There is a way of being sure, my son."

"Oh, yes, if you mounted a great expedition from Pannoval north—"

"No, no . . . other ways, more subtle. You will one day understand the complexities of Pannoval more fully. Or perhaps you won't. For there are entirely other orders of the priesthood, warrior mystics, of which you do not know. Perhaps I had better say no more. . . ."

Yuli urged him on. The priest's voice sank still lower, until it was almost lost under the splash of a water drip near at hand.

"Yes, warrior mystics, who forswear the pleasures of the flesh and in return gain mysterious powers . . ."

"That's what Naab advocated, and was murdered for it."

"Executed after trial. The superior orders prefer us, the administrative orders, to remain as we are. . . . But they . . . they communicate with the dead. If you were one of them, you could speak with your father after death."

Into the dark, Yuli stammered his amazement.

"There are many human and divine capacities which can be trained, my son. I myself, when my father died, fell into a fast through sorrow, and after the passage of many days saw him clear, suspended in the earth which is Akha's as if in another element, with his hands over his ears, as if he heard some sound he disliked. Death is not an end, but our extension in Akha—you recall the teaching, my son."

"I'm still angry with my father. Perhaps I have difficulty because of that. He was weak at the end. I wish to be strong. Where are these—these warrior mystics of whom you speak, Father?"

"If you do not believe my words, as I sense, it is pointless my telling you anything further." The voice held a nicely calculated shade of petulance.

"I'm sorry, Father. I'm a savage, just as you say. . . . You think the priesthood should reform itself, as Naab claimed, don't you?"

"I take a middle way." He sat leaning forward tensely for a while, blinking as if there was more to be said, and Yuli heard his dry eyelids flutter. "Many schisms divide the Holies, Yuli, as you will come to see if you take your orders. Things are less easy than they were when I was a boy. Sometimes it seems to me . . ."

The water drops went splash-splash-splash and someone coughed distantly.

"What, Father?"

"Oh . . . you have heretical thoughts enough, without my planting more. I can't imagine why I talk to you. That's the end of instruction for today, boy."

Talking not to Sifans, who liked to proceed by equivocation, but to his fellows, Yuli gradually learnt something of the power structures that held the community of Pannoval together. The administration was in the hands of the priests, and they worked with the militia, one reinforcing the other. There was no final arbitrator, no great chief, like the chiefs in the tribes of the wilderness. Behind each order of the priesthood lay another. They faded off into the metaphysical darkness, in obscure hierarchies, none finally with the power to command all the others.

Some orders, went the rumour, lived in more distant caverns in the mountain chain. In the Holies, habits were lax. Priests might serve as soldiers and vice versa. Women came and went among them. Under all the prayer and learning was confusion. Akha was elsewhere. Somewhere —somewhere there was greater faith.

Somewhere along the receding chain of command, thought Yuli, must be Sifans' order of warrior-mystics, who could commune with the dead and perform other amazing acts. The rumours, really no more to be listened to than the drip of water down a wall, whispered of an order elsewhere, set above the inhabitants of the Holies, who were referred to, when they were referred to at all, as the Keepers.

The Keepers, according to the whisper, were a sect to which admission was by election. They combined the dual role of soldiering and priesthood. What they kept was knowledge. They knew things unknown even in the Holies, and that knowledge gave them power. By keeping the past, they laid claim to the future.

"Who are these Keepers? Do we see them?" Yuli asked. The mystery excited him, and as soon as he heard of them he longed to be part of the mysterious sect.

He was speaking again to Father Sifans, almost at the end of his term. The passage of time had matured him; he no longer mourned his parents, and the Holies kept him busy. He had discovered recently in his charge-father an intense relish of gossip. The eyes blinked faster, the lips trembled, and the morsels slipped out. Every day, as the two men worked together in the prayer hall of their order, Father Sifans allowed himself a small ration of revelation.

"The Keepers can mix among us. We do not know who they are. Outwardly, they look no different from us. I might also be a Keeper, for all you know. . . ."

Next day, after prayer, Father Sifans beckoned Yuli with a mittened hand and said, "Come, since your novice term is nearly up, I'll show you something. You recollect what we were talking about yesterday?"

"Of course."

Father Sifans pursed his lips, squeezed his eyes together, raised his little sharp nose like a shrew's towards the ceiling, and nodded his head sharply a dozen times. Then he set off at a stiff mincing pace, leaving Yuli to follow.

Lights were rare in this section of the Holies and, in some places, forbidden entirely. The two men moved now with assurance through total darkness. Yuli kept the fingers of his right hand extended, lightly touching a carved skein unwinding on the wall of the corridor. They were passing through War-borw, and Yuli was now wall-reading.

Steps were indicated ahead. Two of the luminous-eyed preets fluttered in a wicker cage, punctuating the junction between the main passage, a side one, and the steps. Yuli and his old charge-father progressed steadily upwards, *clack-clack-clack*, up stairs, along passages punctuated by more stairs, avoiding by habit others who walked in the limestoned dark.

Now they were in Tangwild. The wall-scroll on the rock under Yuli's fingers told him so. In a never repeating design of intertwined branches sported small animals which Yuli considered must have been figments of some long dead artist's imagination—animals that hopped and swam and climbed and rolled. For some reason, Yuli imagined them all in vivid colours. The band of wall-scroll carving ran for miles in all directions, never more than a hand-span wide. This was one of the secrets of the Holies; nobody could get lost in the labyrinthine dark once he had memorised the various patterns that identified the sectors and the coded signs signalling turns or steps or corridor divisions, all woven into the design.

They turned into a low gallery which the resonance of sound told them was otherwise unoccupied. Here, the wall-scroll was of quaint men squatting with out-turned hands among wooden huts. They must be outside somewhere, Yuli thought, enjoying the scenery beneath his palm.

Sifans halted, and Yuli bumped into him. As he apologised, the old man rested against the wall.

"Be silent and let me enjoy a good pant," he said.

In a moment, as if regretting the severity of his tone, he said, "I'm getting old. On my next birthday, I shall be twenty-five. But the death of an individual is nothing to our Lord Akha."

Yuli feared for him.

The father fumbled about the wall. Moisture ran down the rock and soaked everything.

"Hah, yes, here . . ."

The charge-father opened a small shutter, permitting light to blaze in upon them. Yuli had to shield his eyes for a moment. Then he stood by Father Sifans and looked out.

A grunt of astonishment escaped him.

Below them lay a small town, built on a hill. Crooked lanes ran up and down, sometimes fronted by quite grand houses. They were intersected by alleys, where riotous building concocted a maze of dwellings. To one side, a river ran in a chasm, and livings perched dangerously on its very edge. People, tiny as ants, moved among the lanes and jostled inside roofless rooms. The noise of their traffic rose faintly to where the men stood peering down.

"Where are we?"

Sifans gestured. "That's Vakk. You've forgotten it, haven't you?"

He watched with some amusement, his nose screwed up, as Yuli stared down, open-mouthed.

How simple he was, he thought. He should have recognised it was

Vakk without having to ask, like a savage. He could see the far archway leading to Reck, faint as ice in the distance. Nearer, squinting, he made out familiar livings and the alley where his room had been, and the home of Kyale and Tusca. He recalled them—and the beautiful black-haired Iskador—with longing, but his feelings were muted, because there was no point in yearning for a bygone world. Kyale and Tusca would have forgotten him, as he had them. What chiefly struck him was how bright Vakk appeared, for he remembered it as a place of deep shadow, lacking all colour. The difference marked how greatly his sight had improved during his stay in the Holies.

"You recollect that you asked me who the Keepers were," said Father Sifans. "You asked if we saw them. Here is my response." He indicated the world below them. "The people down there do not see us. Even if they look upward, they are still unable to spot us. We are superior to them. So are the Keepers superior to mere members of the priesthood. Within our fortress there is a secret fortress."

"Father Sifans, help me. Is that secret fortress . . . is it friendly towards us? Secrecy is not always friendly."

The father blinked his eyes. "The question should be rather, Is the secret fortress necessary to our survival? And the answer to that is, Yes, whatever it costs. You may find that a strange answer, coming from me. I am for the middle way in everything but this. Against the extremities of our life, against which Akha seeks to defend us, extremes are called for.

"The Keepers keep Truth. According to the scriptures, our world has been withdrawn from Wutra's fire. Many generations ago, the people of Pannoval dared to defy Great Akha and went to live outside our sheltering holy mountain. Towns like Vakk which we see before us were built under the naked skies. Then we were punished by fire, which Wutra and his cohorts sent down. A few survivors lived to return to our natural home, here.

"This is not merely scripture, Yuli. Forgive the blasphemy of that 'merely.' This is scripture, I should say. It is also a history that our people have lived. The Keepers in their secret fortress keep that history, and many things that still survive from the period of naked skies. I believe they see uncloudedly what we see clouded."

"Why are we in the Holies not considered fit to know these things?"

"Enough to know them as scripture, a parable. Myself, I believe that the naked knowledge is kept from us, first, because those in power always prefer to hoard knowledge, which is power, and second, because they believe that armed with such knowledge we might again attempt to return to the outside world of naked skies at such time as Great Akha banishes the snows."

Yuli thought with racing thoughts. Father Sifans' frankness astonished him. If knowledge was power, where stood faith? It occurred to him that he was possibly being tested, and was aware of the priest awaiting his answer with alert interest. Playing safe, he brought in the name of Akha again.

"Surely, if Akha banishes the snows, that is his invitation to return to the world of skies? It is not natural for men and women to be born and die in darkness."

Father Sifans sighed. "So you say—but you were born under the skies."

"I hope to die there, too," Yuli said, with a fervour that surprised himself. He feared that his unpremeditated response would provoke his charge-father's anger; instead, the old man placed a mittened hand on his shoulder.

"We all desire conflicting desires. . . ." He struggled with himself— either to speak or to stay silent—then said calmly, "Come, we will return, and you shall lead the way. Your reading of the wall-scrolls is becoming excellent."

He closed the shutter on Vakk. They regarded each other as the night rushed back. Then they returned through the dark sleeve of the gallery.

Yuli's initiation as a priest was a great event. He fasted for four whole days, and came light-headed before his cardinal in Lathorn. With him went three other young men of Yuli's own age, also due to take all the vows of a priest, also to sing for two hours, standing in stiff clothes and unaccompanied by music, the liturgies memorised for the occasion.

Their voices rose thinly in the great dark church, hollow as a cistern.

> *Darkness be our guise*
> *Ever, and sting the sinner within*
> *To sing. Bremely we begin*
> *Priests, priests, of great rate,*
> *Golden in ancient Akha's gaze,*
> *Armoured in ancient right.*

A solitary candle stood between them and the figure of the seated cardinal. The old man remained motionless throughout the ceremony; perhaps he slept. A breeze blew the candle flame fluttering in his direction. In the background stood the three charge-fathers who had sponsored the young men to priesthood. Yuli could see Sifans dimly, his nose wrinkled upwards like a shrew's in pleasure, nodding to the chant. No militia were present, or phagors.

At the end of the initiation, the stiff old figure decked out in its black and whites and chains of gold rose to its feet, raised its hands above its head, and intoned a prayer for the initiates:

". . . and grant finally, O Ancient Akha, that we may move ever more deeply into the caverns of thy thought until we discover within ourselves the secrets of that illimitable ocean, without bound or dimension, which the world calls life, but which we privileged few know to be Everything that is beyond Death and Life. . . ."

Fluggels began to play, swelling music filled Lathorn and Yuli's heart.

Next day, he was given his first task, to go among the prisoners of Pannoval and listen to their troubles.

For newly ordained priests there was an established procedure. They served first in the Punishment area, and then were transferred to Security before being allowed out to work among the ordinary people. In this process of hardening off, they were fortified in the distancing between them and the people implied in their ordination.

Punishment was full of noise and burning brands. It also had its quota of warders, drawn from the militia, and their phagors. It was situated in a particularly wet cavern. A light rain fell most of the time. Anyone who looked up could see the beads of moisture swinging downwards on a crooked path, teased by wind from stalactites far overhead.

Warders wore heavy soles to their boots, which sounded on the pavements. The white-coated phagors which accompanied them wore nothing, able to rely on their natural protection.

Brother Yuli's job was to work duty spells with one of the three guard lieutenants, a coarse thick man called Dravog, who walked as if he were crushing beetles and spoke as if he were chewing them. He constantly beat his leggings with his stave, making an irritating drumming noise. Everything that concerned the prisoners—including the prisoners themselves—was meant to be banged. All movements were executed to gongs, any delay was punished by application of a stave. Noise was the order of the day. The prisoners were a sullen lot. Yuli had to legitimise any violence and frequently patch its victims.

He soon found himself opposed to Dravog's mindless brutality, while the unremitting hostility of the prisoners eroded his nerves. The days spent under Father Sifans had been happy even if he had not always appreciated that at the time. In these harsh new surroundings, he missed the dense dark, the silences, the piety, and even Sifans himself, with his cautious friendliness. Friendship was not a quality Dravog recognised.

One of the sectors of Punishment was a cavern called Twink. In Twink, squads of prisoners worked at demolishing the rear wall to enlarge the work space. The toil was endless. "They're slaves, and you've got to beat them to keep them going," Dravog said. The remark gave Yuli an uncomfortable glimpse into history—probably much of Pannoval had been opened up in this way.

The rubble from the excavation was carried away in clumsy wooden

carts, which needed the efforts of two men to shift. The carts trundled
to a place somewhere in the warrens of the Holies where the Vakk ran
far below ground level and a deep pit waited to receive the rubble.

Twink contained a farm worked by the prisoners. Noctiferous barley
was grown for bread, fish were farmed in a pool fed by a stream which
poured from the rock. A quota of larger fish was culled every day.
Diseased fish were dug into long banks where enormous edible fungi
grew. Their pungent odour cut across the senses of anyone entering
Twink.

Nearby, in other caverns, were more farms, and chert mines. But
Yuli's movements were almost as circumscribed as those of the pris-
oners; Twink formed the limit of his beat. He was surprised when
Dravog, in conversation with another warder, mentioned that one of
the side passages leading from Twink would take him into Market.
Market! The name conjured up a jostling world he had left behind in a
different life, and he thought nostalgically of Kyale and his wife.
"You'll never be a proper priest," he told himself.

The gongs were struck, the wardens shouted, the prisoners strained
their grudging bodies. The phagors shambled back and forth, sticking
their milts up their slotted nostrils, and occasionally exchanging a
grunted word with each other. Yuli hated their presence. He was
watching four prisoners under the eye of one of Dravog's warders
trawl in the fish pool. To do this, the men were forced to get into the
freezing water up to their stomachs. When their net was full, they
were allowed to climb out and drag the catch onto the bank.

The fish were gout. They were a pale strawy white, with blind blue
eyes. They struggled hopelessly as they were dragged from their natural
element.

A rubble cart was passing, pushed by two prisoners. One of its
wheels struck a stone. The prisoner shouldering the nearside shaft
staggered and fell. As he went, he struck one of the fishers, a youth
stooping to get a hold on the end of the net, who plunged head first
into the water.

The warder began to shout and struck about him with his stave. His
phagor hopped forward and grasped the prisoner who had slipped,
lifting him off his feet. Dravog and another warder came running up
in time to beat the young prisoner about his head as he dragged himself from the pool.

Yuli grasped Dravog's arm.

"Leave him alone. It was an accident. Help him out."

"He's not allowed in the pool on his own," Dravog said savagely,
elbowing Yuli out of the way and striking again.

The prisoner climbed out with blood and water pouring from his
head. Another warder rushed up, his brand hissing in the rain, his

phagor behind him, eyes pink in the shadows. He shouted, sorry to have missed the excitement. He joined with Dravog and the other warders in booting the half-drowned prisoner back to his cell in the next cavern.

When the commotion had died and the mob disappeared, Yuli cautiously approached the cell, in time to hear a prisoner in the adjoining cell call, "Are you all right, Usilk?"

Yuli went to Dravog's office and collected the master key. He unlocked the cell door, took a fat lamp from a niche in the passage, and entered.

The prisoner sprawled on the floor in a pool of water. He was supporting his torso with his arms, so that the outline of his shoulder blades stuck painfully through his shirt. Head and cheek were bleeding.

He turned a sullen look at Yuli, then, without change of expression, let his head droop again.

Yuli looked down at the soaked and battered skull. Tormented, he squatted by the man, setting the lamp down on the filthy floor.

"Scumb off, monk," the man growled.

"I'll help you if I can."

"You can't help. Scumb it!"

They remained in the same positions, without moving or speaking, and water and blood mingled in the puddle.

"Your name's Usilk, I believe?"

No response. The thin countenance remained pointing down at the floor.

"Is your father's name Kyale? Living in Vakk?"

"Leave me alone."

"I know—I knew him well. And your mother. She looked after me."

"You heard what I said. . . ." With a sudden burst of energy, the prisoner flung himself on Yuli, beating at him rather feebly. Yuli rolled over and disengaged himself, jumping up like an asokin. He was about to fling himself into the attack when he paused. With an effort of will, he controlled himself and pulled back. Without a word more, he collected the lamp and left the cell.

"A dangerous one, that," Dravog said to him, permitting himself a sly grin at the priest's expense, seeing his flustered appearance. Yuli retreated to the brothers' chapel, and prayed in the dark to an unresponsive Akha.

There was a story Yuli had heard in Market, a story not unknown to the ecclesiastics in the Holies, about a certain worm.

The worm was sent by Wutra, wicked god of the skies. Wutra put the worm into the labyrinth of passages in Akha's holy mountain. The worm is large and long, its girth being about equal to that of a passageway. It is slimy, and it slides along noiselessly in the dark. Only its breathing can be heard, issuing from its flabby lips. It eats people. They are safe one moment; the next, they hear the evil breathing, the rustle of long whiskers, and then they are swallowed.

A spiritual equivalent of Wutra's worm was now at large in the labyrinths of Yuli's thought. He could not prevent himself seeing, in the thin shoulders and blood of the prisoner, the gulf that lay between preachments and practice in Akha. It was not that the preachments were so pious, for mainly they were practical, stressing service; nor was it that life was so bad; what troubled him was that they were at odds.

There returned to his memory something that Father Sifans had said to him. "It is not goodness and holiness that lead a man to serve Akha. More often it is sin such as yours." Which implied that many among the priesthood were murderers and criminals—little better than the prisoners. Yet they were set over the prisoners. They had power.

He went about his duties grimly. He smiled less than he had. He never felt happy working as a priest. The nights he spent in prayer, the days in thought—and in trying, when possible, to forge some sort of contact between himself and Usilk.

Usilk shunned him.

Finally, Yuli's time in Punishment was completed. He entered a period of meditation before going to work with the Security Police. This branch of the militia had come under his notice while working in the cells, and he found within himself the ghost of a dangerous idea.

After only a few days in Security, Wutra's worm became ever more active in his mind. His task was to see men beaten and interrogated and to administer a final blessing to them when they died. Grimmer and grimmer he became, until his superiors commended him and gave him cases of his own to handle.

The interrogations were simple, for there were few categories of crime. People cheated or stole or spoke heresy. Or they went to places that were forbidden or plotted revolution—the crime that had been Usilk's. Some even tried to escape to Wutra's realm, under the skies. It was now that Yuli realised that a kind of illness gripped the dark world; everyone in authority suspected revolution. The illness bred in the darkness, and accounted for the numerous petty laws that governed life in Pannoval. Including the priesthood, the settlement numbered almost six and three quarter thousand people, every one of whom was forced into a guild or order. Every living, guild, order, dormitory, was infiltrated by spies, who themselves were not trusted, and also had an infiltrated guild of their own. The dark bred distrust, and some of its victims paraded, hangdog, before Brother Yuli.

Although he loathed himself for it, Yuli found he was good at the work. He felt enough sympathy to lower his victim's guard, enough destructive rage to tear the truth out. Despite himself, he developed a professional's taste for the job. Only when he felt secure did he have Usilk brought before him.

At the end of each day's duty, a service was held in the cavern called Lathorn. Attendance was compulsory for the priesthood, optional for any of the militia who wished to attend. The acoustics of Lathorn were excellent: choir and musicians filled the dark air with swelling veins of music. Yuli had recently taken up a musical instrument. He was becoming expert on the fluggel, a bronze instrument no bigger than his hand, which he at first despised, seeing other musicians play enormous peetes, vrachs, baranboims, and double-clows. But the tiny fluggel could turn his breath into a note that flew as high as a childrim, soaring up to the clouded roof of Lathorn above all conspiring melody. With it, Yuli's spirit also flew, to the traditional strains of "Caparisoned," "In His Penumbra," and, his favourite, the richly counterpointed "Oldorando."

One evening, after service, Yuli left Lathorn with an acquaintance, a shriven fellow priest by the name of Bervin, and they walked together through the tomblike avenues of the Holies, to run their fingers over new carvings even then being created by the three Brothers Kilandar. It chanced that they encountered Father Sifans, also strolling, reciting a litany to himself in a nervous undertone. They greeted each other cordially. Bervin politely excused himself, so that Yuli and Father Sifans could parade and talk together.

"I don't enjoy my feelings about my day's work, Father. I was glad of the service."

As was his fashion, Sifans responded to this only obliquely.

"I hear marvellous reports of your work, Brother Yuli. You will have to seek further advancement. When you do, I will help you."

"You are kind, Father. I recall what you told me"—he lowered his voice—"about the Keepers. An organisation for which one can volunteer, you said?"

"No, I said one could only be elected to the Keepers."

"How could I put my name forward?"

"Akha will aid you when it is necessary." He sniffed with laughter. "Now you are one of us, I wonder . . . have you heard a whisper of an order above even the Keepers?"

"No, Father. You know I don't listen to whispers."

"Hah, you should. Whispers are a blind man's sight. But if you are so virtuous, then I will say nothing of the Takers."

"The Takers? Who are they?"

"No, no, don't worry, I will say not a word. Why should you bother your head with secret organisations or tales of hidden lakes, free of ice? Such things may be lies, after all. Legends, like Wutra's worm."

Yuli laughed. "Very well, Father, you have worked me up to sufficient interest. You can tell me everything."

Sifans made tsking noises with his thin lips. He slowed his step, and sidled into an alcove.

"Since you force me. Very regrettable . . . You may remember how the rabble lives in Vakk, its rooms all a huddle, one on top the next, without order. Suppose this mountain range in which Pannoval lives is like Vakk—better, like a body with various interconnected parts, spleen, lungs, vitals, heart. Suppose there are caverns just as large as ours above us and below us. It's not possible is it?"

"No."

"I'm saying it is possible. It's a hypothesis. Let us say that somewhere beyond Twink there exists a waterfall, falling from a cavern above ours. And that waterfall falls to a level below ours, some way below. Water plays where it will. Let us say that it falls into a lake, the waters of which are pure and too warm for ice to form on them. . . . Let us imagine that in that desirable and secure place live the most favoured, the most powerful, the Takers. They take everything of the best, the knowledge and the power, and treasure it for us there, until the day of Akha's victory."

"And keep those things from *us* . . ."

"What's that? Fillips, I missed what you said, Brother. Well, it's just an amusing story I tell you."

"And does one have to be elected to the Takers?"

The father made little clicking noises with his tongue. "Who could penetrate such privilege, supposing it existed? No, my boy, one would have to be born to it—a number of powerful families, with beautiful women to keep them warm, and perhaps secret ways to come and go, even beyond Akha's domains. . . . No, it would need—why, it would need a revolution to get near such a hypothetical place."

He stuck his nose in the air and giggled.

"Father, you tease the poor simple priests below you."

The old priest's head went to one side, judicially. "Poor you are, my young friend, and will most like remain so. Simple you are not—and that is why you will always make a flawed priest, as long as you continue. That is why I love you."

They parted. The priest's declaration troubled Yuli. Yes, he was a flawed priest, as Sifans said. A music lover, nothing more.

He washed his face in icy water as his thoughts burned. All these hierarchies of priesthoods—if they existed—led only to power. They did not lead to Akha. Faith never explained precisely, with a verbal precision to rival the precision of music, how devotion could move a stone effigy; the words of faith led only to a foggy obscurity called holiness. The realisation was as rough as the towel on which he dried his cheeks.

Lying in the dormitory far from sleep, he saw how old Sifans' life had been stripped from the old man, real love had been starved from him, until he was left only with teasing ghosts of affection. He did not really care—had perhaps ceased to care a while ago—whether those beneath him had faith or not. His hints and riddles expressed a deep-rooted dissatisfaction with his own life.

In sudden fear, Yuli told himself that it would be better to die a man in the wilderness than a dry mouth here in the shadowy safeties of Pannoval. Even if it meant leaving behind his fluggel and the strains of "Oldorando."

The fear made him sit up, casting off his blanket. Dark winds, the restless inhabitants of the dormitory, blew about his head. He shivered.

With a kind of exultation matching the exultation he had experienced on entering Reck long ago, he whispered aloud, "I don't believe, I believe nothing."

Power over others he believed. He saw it in action every day. But that was purely human. Perhaps he had actually ceased to believe in other than human oppression during that ritual in State, when men had allowed a hated phagor to bite the words from young Naab's throat. Perhaps Naab's words might still triumph, and the priests reform themselves until their lives held meaning. Words, priests—they were actual. It was Akha that was nothing.

Into the moving dark he whispered the words, "Akha, you are nothing!"

He did not die, and the winds still rustled in his hair.

He jumped up and ran. Fingers unwinding the wall-scroll, he ran and ran until he was exhausted, and his fingertips raw. He turned back, panting. Power he wanted, not subjection.

The war in his mind was stilled. He returned to his blanket. Tomorrow, he would act. No more priests.

Dozing, he started up once again. He was back on a frozen hillside. His father had left him, taken by the phagors, and he flung his father's spear contemptuously into a bush. He recalled it, recalled the movement of his arm, the hiss of the spear as it embedded itself among the tattered branches, the knife-sharp air in his lungs.

Why did he suddenly recollect that insignificant detail?

Since he had no powers of self-analysis, the question remained unanswered as he drifted into sleep.

The morrow was the last day of his interrogation of Usilk; interrogations were permitted for only six days consecutively, then the victim was allowed to rest. Rules in this respect were strict, and the militia kept a suspicious eye on the priesthood in all these matters.

Usilk had said nothing useful, and was unresponsive alike to beating and cajolery.

He stood before Yuli, who was seated on an inquisitorial chair carved elaborately from a solid chunk of timber; it served to emphasise the difference between the state of the two men, Yuli outwardly at ease, Usilk half-starved, ragged, shoulders bowed, face wan and without expression.

"We know that you were approached by men who threaten the security of Pannoval. All we wish is their names and then you can go free, back to Vakk."

"I did not know them. It was a word in the crowd."

Both question and answer had become conventional.

Yuli rose from his chair and walked round the prisoner, giving no sign of his emotions.

"Usilk, listen. I feel no enmity for you. I respect your parents, as I told you. This is our last session together. We shall not meet again, and you will certainly die in this miserable place, for no reason."

"I have my reasons, monk."

Yuli was surprised. He had expected no response. He lowered his voice.

"We all have reasons. . . . I will put my life in your hands. I am unfit to be a priest, Usilk. I was born in the white wilderness under the skies far to the north of Pannoval, and to the wilderness I wish to return. I will take you with me, I will help you to escape. That's true speaking."

Usilk raised his gaze to Yuli's. "Scumb off, monk. That trickery won't work on me."

"It's true speaking. How can I prove it? You wish me to blaspheme against the god to whom I made my vows? You think I can say these things lightly? Pannoval has shaped me, yet something in my inner nature makes me rebel against it and its institutions. They bring shelter and content to the multitude, but not to me, not even in the favoured role of priest. Why not, I cannot say, except that it is how I am made. . . ."

He choked back his flow of words.

"I'll be practical. I can get a spare monk's cassock for you. When we go from this cell later, I will help you slip into the Holies and we will escape together."

"Scumble on your tricks."

Yuli fell into a rage. It was all he could do to stop himself attacking and beating the man. He flew in fury to the instruments hanging on the wall, and lashed at his chair with a whip. He seized the fat lamp that stood on the table and thrust it under Usilk's eyes. . . . He hit himself on the chest.

"Why should I lie to you, why betray myself? What do you know, after all? Nothing, nothing worth having. You're just a thing, snatched up from Vakk, your life without meaning or importance. You have to be tortured and killed, because that is your destiny. Fine, go ahead with it, enjoy feeling your strength die day by day—it's the price you pay for pride, and for being a cretin. Do what you will, die a thousand times. I've had enough. I can't bear the torment. I'm off. Think of me as you lie in your own scumble—I'll be out, free, free, under the sky where Akha's power can't reach."

He shouted these words, careless who heard him, blazing before the beaten pallor of Usilk's face.

"Scumb off, monk." Just the same sullen phrase he had used all week.

Jumping back a pace, he brought up the whip and struck Usilk with the stock across his broken cheek. All his force and rage went behind the blow. His glaring gaze saw by the lamp's uncertain light exactly where on the cheek under the eye and across the bridge of Usilk's nose the stock struck. He stood with whip half-raised, watching as Usilk's hands came up towards the injury, how his knees buckled. He swayed and fell to the floor, resting on knees and elbows.

Still clutching the whip, Yuli stepped over the body and quitted the cell.

In his own confusion, he was scarcely aware of the confusion round him. Warders and militia were running here and there in an unexpected manner—the normal progress through the dark veins of the Holies was a funereal walking pace.

A captain came along briskly, holding a flaring torch in one hand and shouting orders.

"You're one of the priest-interrogators?" he demanded of Yuli.

"What of it?"

"I want all these rooms cleared of prisoners. Get them back to their cells. The injured are going to be put in here. Look sharp."

"Injured? What injured?"

The captain roared his annoyance. "Are you deaf, Brother? What do you think all the shouting's been about this last hour? The new borings in Twink have collapsed, and many good men are buried. It's like a battlefield down there. Now, get moving and get your prisoner back in his cell, fast. I want this corridor cleared in two minutes."

He moved on, shouting and cursing. He was enjoying the excitement.

Yuli turned back. Usilk still lay crumpled on the floor of the interrogation room. Stooping, he seized him under the shoulders and dragged him into an upright position. Usilk moaned and appeared semiconscious. By levering one of the prisoner's arms over his shoulder Yuli could persuade him to walk after a fashion. In the corridor, where the captain still roared, other interrogators were removing their victims, hustling excitedly, nobody exactly looking displeased at this interruption to routine.

They headed into the dark like shadows. Now was his chance to disappear, while the excitement was on. And Usilk?

His rage was dying, his guilt returning. He was aware of wishing to show Usilk that he was sincere in his earlier offer of help.

The decision was made. Instead of heading towards the prison cells, he turned towards his own quarters. A plan grew in his mind. First, he had to revive Usilk, to prepare him for escape. It was useless to think of taking him to the brothers' dormitory, where they would be discovered; there was a safer place.

Wall-reading, he turned off before the dormitories, propelling Usilk up a winding stair, off which, in a warrenlike arrangement, the chambers of some of the fathers led. The band of carving under his hand kept him informed of where he was, even when the darkness grew so intense that phantasmal crimsons drifted through it like submerged weeds. At Father Sifans' door, he tapped and entered.

As he had calculated, there was no response. At this time of day, Sifans should be engaged elsewhere. He pulled Usilk in.

He had stood outside this door many times, but had never entered it. He was at a loss. He helped Usilk to sit, leaning with his back against a wall, and groped about for the lamp bracket.

After some blundering against furniture, he found it, and spun the chert wheel attached to the bracket. A spark flew, a tongue of light grew, and he lifted the lamp from its socket and looked about him. Here were all Father Sifans' worldly goods, few in number. In one corner stood a small altar with a statue of Akha, greasy with handling. There was a place for ablutions. There was a shelf supporting one or two objects, including a musical instrument, and a mat on the floor. Nothing more. No table or chairs. Lost in shadow was an alcove which Yuli knew without looking would contain a cot where the old father slept.

He moved into action. With water from the basin, piped from the rock, he washed Usilk's face and tried to revive him. The man drank a little water, puking as he did so. On the shelf in a tin was some doughy barley bread; Yuli fed some to Usilk and ate a chunk himself.

He shook Usilk's shoulder gently. "You'll have to forgive my temper. You provoked it. I'm only a savage at heart, not fit to be a priest. Now you see that I spoke truth—we are going to escape from here. With a rockfall in Twink, it should be easy to get away."

Usilk merely moaned.

"What do you say? You're not that bad. You'll have to move for yourself."

"You will never trick me, monk." He looked at Yuli through slitted eyes.

Yuli squatted down beside him. The movement made Usilk flinch away. "Look, we have already committed ourselves. I have committed myself. Try and understand. I'm asking nothing from you, Usilk—I'm just going to help you get out of here. There must be some way to escape through the north gate dressed as monks. I know an old trapper

woman called Lorel, not many days journeying north from here, who
will allow us shelter while we grow used to the cold."

"I'm not moving, man."

Smiting his forehead, Yuli said, "You'll have to move. We are hiding
in a father's room. We can't stay here. He's not a bad old boy, but he'd
surely report us if he discovered us."

"Not so, Brother Yuli. Your not-so-bad old boy is a grave of secrets."

Jumping up, Yuli turned and stood face to face with Father Sifans,
who had emerged quietly from the alcove. He put forward a papery
hand in a protective gesture, fearing attack.

"Father . . ."

The gesture became one of reassurance as Father Sifans blinked at
him in the wan light.

"I was resting. I was in Twink when the roof fell in—what a mess!
Fortunately, I was not in great danger, but a piece of rock flew and hit
my leg. I can advise you that there will be no escape through the north
gate; the guard have closed it and declared a state of emergency, just
in case the worthy citizens do something unwise."

"You're going to report us, Father?" From the olden days, the days
of his adolescence, he had kept one possession, the bone knife which
his mother had carved in her well days. His hand crept beneath his
cassock and grasped the knife as he asked his question.

Sifans sniffed. "Like you, I shall do something unwise. I am going
to advise you on the best route to take to leave our country. I am also
going to advise you not to take this man with you. Leave him here, I'll
see to him. He's close to death."

"No, he's tough, Father. He'll recover quickly when the idea of freedom really sinks in. He's been through much, haven't you, Usilk?"

The prisoner stared up at them, across a blackened cheek which had
already swollen enough to close one eye.

"Also, he is your enemy, Yuli, and will remain so. Beware of him.
Leave him to me."

"It's my fault he is my enemy. I will make amends and he will forgive
me when we are safe."

The father said, "Some men do not forgive."

As they stood regarding each other, Usilk made clumsy movements to
rise to his feet, and stood gasping, resting his forehead against the wall.

"Father, I hardly can ask you this," Yuli said. "For all I know, you
are a Keeper. Will you come with us to the outer world?"

The eyes blinked rapidly. "Before my initiation, I felt I could not
serve Akha, and I attempted once to leave Pannoval. But I was caught,
because I was always one of the docile kind, and not savage like you."

"You never forget my origins."

"Oh, I envied savagery. I still do. But I was defeated; my wish was
subverted by my nature. I was caught and treated—well, as to how I

was treated, let me merely say that I also am a man who cannot forgive. That was long ago. Since then I have gained promotion."

"Come with us."

"I will remain here and nurse my injured leg. I always have my excuses, Yuli."

Taking a stone from the floor, the father drew a sketch on the wall for Yuli, explaining an escape route to him. "It is a long journey. You must travel beneath the Quzint Mountains. You will find yourself at last not in the north but the more clement south. Stay well, and prosper." Spitting on his hand, he erased the marks on his wall and tossed the stone into a corner.

Finding nothing to say, Yuli put his arms round the old man, so that his frail arms were pinned to his side, and hugged him. "We'll go at once. Farewell."

Usilk said, speaking with difficulty, "You must kill this fellow, kill him now. Or, as soon as we leave, he will give the alarm."

"I know him and I trust him."

"It's a trick."

"You and your damned tricks, Usilk. I won't let you touch Father Sifans." This was said in some agitation, as Usilk came forward and Yuli put out a detaining arm to keep him from the old priest. Usilk struck at his arm, and for a moment the two wrestled together, until Yuli pushed him off as gently as possible.

"Come on, Usilk, if you're fit enough to struggle. Let's go."

"Wait. I see I'll have to trust you, monk. Prove yourself true by freeing a comrade of mine. His name's Scoraw and he worked with me at the fish pool. He'll be in Cell 65. Also fetch a friend of mine from Vakk."

Stroking his chin, Yuli said, "You're in no position to dictate anything." Every delay meant danger. Yet he saw that it was necessary to make some gesture to placate Usilk, if they were to agree at all. Sifans' plan made it clear that they had a dangerous journey ahead.

"All right, Scoraw. I remember the man. He was your revolutionary contact?"

"Are you still trying to interrogate me?"

"Very well. Father, may Usilk stay here with you while I collect this Scoraw? Good. And who is the man in Vakk?"

A kind of smile moved briefly over Usilk's broken face. "Not a man, a woman. My woman, monk. Name of Iskador, queen of archery. Lives at the Bow, Bottom Alley."

"Iskador . . . yes, yes, I know her—I knew her once by sight."

"Get her. She and Scoraw are tough. We'll see how tough you are later, monk. . . ."

The father tweaked at Yuli's sleeve, and said softly to him almost inserting his nose into Yuli's ear. "My apologies, I have changed my mind. I do not dare to be left alone with this surly and stupid person. Please take him with you—you have my assurances I shall not leave my room." He clutched fiercely at Yuli's arm.

Yuli clapped his hands together. "Very well. Usilk, we go together. I'll show you where you can steal a habit. Put it on, go and collect Scoraw. I will go down into Vakk and collect your girl, Iskador. We will meet at the inner corner of Twink, where there are two passages leading off, so that we can escape if necessary. If you and Scoraw do not come, I shall have to leave without you, knowing you have been captured. Is that clear?"

Usilk grunted.

"Is that clear?"

"Yes, let's move."

They moved. They left the shelter of Sifans' small room and launched themselves into the thick night of the corridor. Fingers to wall-scroll, Yuli led on, forgetting in his excitement even to bid farewell to his old mentor.

The people of Pannoval at this time were hardheaded. They had no great thoughts, except to keep their stomachs fed. Yet they had a kind of small change in stories, which were bartered about by storytellers from time to time.

At the great entrance, by the guardhouses, before a visitor to Pannoval came among the terraces of Market, trees grew—small in number and stunted, but definitely green trees.

They were properly prized for their rarity, and for their habit of yielding an occasional harvest of wrinkled nuts called roofers. No tree managed to crop every year, but every year one tree or other had a few lime-coloured roofers dangling from its outer twigs. Most of the roofers had maggots in them; but the dames and children of Vakk and Groyne and Prayn ate the maggots along with the flesh of the nut.

Sometimes the maggots died when the nut was cracked. The poor little story had it that the maggots died of shock. They believed that the interior of their nut was their whole world, and the wrinkled case that contained it the sky. Then, one day, their world was cracked open. They saw with horror that there was a gigantic world beyond their world, more important and brighter in every way. It was too much for the maggots and they expired at the revelation.

Yuli thought of the maggots in the roofer nuts as he left the gaunt shadows of the Holies for the first time in more than a year, and returned, dazzled, to the busy world of ordinary life. At first, the noise and the light and the bustle of so many people reduced him to a state of shock.

All the challenge and temptation of that world was epitomised by

Iskador, Iskador the beautiful. The image of her face was fresh in his mind, as if he had seen her only yesterday. Confronting her, he found her even more beautiful, and could only stutter before her.

Her father's living had several compartments and was part of a small factory for making bows; he was the grand bowmaster of his guild.

Rather haughtily, she allowed the priest in. He sat on the floor and drank a cup of water, and slowly managed to tell her his tale.

Iskador was a sturdy girl of no-nonsense appearance. Her flesh was milky white, contrasting with her flowing black curly hair and her hazel eyes. Her face was broad, with high cheekbones, and her mouth wide and pale. All her movements were energetic, and she folded her arms over her bosom in a businesslike way as she listened to what Yuli had to say.

"Why doesn't Usilk come here and tell me all this rigmarole?" she asked.

"He is collecting another friend for the journey. He could not come into Vakk—his face is a bit bruised at present, and would excite unwelcome attention."

The dark hair hung down on either side of the face, framing it with two wings. Now the wings were flicked impatiently aside with a toss of the head, as Iskador said, "Anyhow, I have an archery contest in six days, which I want to win. I don't want to leave Pannoval—I'm happy enough here. It was Usilk who was always complaining. Besides, I haven't seen him for *ages*. I've got another boyfriend now."

Yuli stood up, flushing slightly.

"Fine, if that's how you feel. Just keep quiet about what I've told you. I'll be off and take your message to Usilk." His nervousness before her made him more brusque than he intended.

"Wait," she said, coming forward with extended arm, a well-shaped hand reaching out towards him. "I didn't say you could go, monk. What you tell me is pretty exciting. You're meant to plead on Usilk's behalf, begging me to come along with you."

"Just two things, Miss Iskador. My name is Yuli, not 'monk.' And why should I plead on Usilk's behalf? He's no friend of mine, and besides . . ."

His voice tailed off. He glared angrily at her, cheeks colouring.

"Besides what?" There was a hint of laughter in her question.

"Oh, Iskador, you're beautiful, that's what besides, and I admire you myself, that's what besides."

Her manner changed. She put her hand up so as to half-hide her pale lips. "Two 'that's what besides' . . . both rather important. Well, Yuli, that does make a bit of difference. You're not unpresentable yourself, now I come to look at you. How did you get to be a priest?"

Sensing the turn of the tide, he hesitated, then said boldly, "I killed two men."

She seemed to spend a long while regarding him from under her thick eyelashes.

"Wait there while I pack a bag and a strong bow," she said at last.

The collapse of the roof had sent an anxious excitement through Pannoval. The event most dreaded in popular fancy had occurred. Feelings were somewhat mixed; with dread went a relief that only prisoners and warders and a few phagors had been buried. They probably deserved everything that Great Akha sent them.

At the rear of Market, barriers were drawn up, and the militia were out in force to keep order. Rescue teams, men and women of the physician's guild, and workers, were moving back and forth at the scene of the disaster. Throngs of onlookers pressed forward, some quiet and tense, others merry, where an acrobat and a group of musicians encouraged them to be cheerful. Yuli pushed through the melée with the girl behind him, and people gave way to a priest out of long custom.

Twink, where the disaster had occurred, had an unfamiliar look. No onlookers were allowed, and a line of brilliant emergency flares was set up to assist the rescuers. Prisoners fed powder into the flares to maintain their brightness.

The scene was one of grim action, with prisoners digging and other ranks behind waiting to take over when they rested. Phagors had been set to hauling away the rubble carts. Every so often, a shout went up; then digging became more feverish, and a body would emerge from the earth, to be passed to waiting physicians.

The scale of the disaster was impressive. With the collapse of a new boring, part of the roof of the main cave had fallen in. There had been more than one subsidence. Most of the floor was piled high with rock, and the fish and fungus farm had largely been obliterated. The source of the original weakness that led to the disaster was a subterranean stream, which now gushed from its course, adding a flood to the other difficulties.

The rock fall had almost buried the rear passages. Yuli and Iskador had to scramble over a pile of debris to get there. Fortunately, this action was concealed from enquiring eyes by a still larger pile of debris. They climbed through without being stopped. Usilk and his comrade Scoraw were waiting in the shadows.

"The black and white suits you, Usilk," Yuli commented sarcastically, referring to the priestly disguise both prisoners wore. For Usilk had come eagerly forward to clutch Iskador. Perhaps displeased by his battered face, she kept her distance, appeasing him by holding his hands.

Even in his disguise, Scoraw still looked the prisoner. He was tall and thin, with the droop to his shoulders of a man who has spent too long in a cell too small. His hands were large and scarred. His glance—

at least during this encounter—was indirect; flinching from meeting Yuli's eyes, he took little sips of sight when Yuli's attention was elsewhere. When Yuli asked him if he was prepared for a difficult journey, he merely nodded, grunted, and shrugged a bag of possessions further on to his shoulder.

It was an inauspicious start to their adventure, and for a moment Yuli regretted his impulse. He was throwing away too much to consort with two characters like Usilk and Scoraw. First, he perceived, he must assert his authority, or they would meet nothing but trouble.

Usilk evidently had the same thought in mind.

He pushed forward, adjusting his pack. "You're late, monk. We thought you'd backed out. We thought it was another of your tricks."

"Are you and your mate up to a hard journey? You look ill."

"Best to get going and not stand about talking," Usilk said, squaring his shoulders and pushing forward between Iskador and Yuli.

"I lead, you cooperate," Yuli said. "Let's get that clear, then we'll all agree together."

"What makes you think you're going to lead, monk?" Usilk said jeeringly, nodding to his two friends for support. With his half-closed eye, he looked both sly and threatening. He was feeling pugnacious again, now that the prospect of escape was offered.

"Here's the answer to that," Yuli said, bringing his bunched right fist round in a hard curve and sinking it into Usilk's stomach.

Usilk doubled up, grunting and cursing.

"Scumb you, you eddre . . ."

"Straighten up, Usilk, and let's march before we're missed."

There was no more argument. They moved after him obediently. The faint lights of Twink died behind them. But at Yuli's fingertips went a wall-scroll, serving as his sight, teasingly formed of beads and chains of tiny shells, spinning out like a melody played on a fluggel, leading them down into the enormous silences of the mountain.

The others did not share his priestly secret, and still relied on light to get about. They began to beg him to go more slowly, or to let them light a lamp, neither of which he would do. He seized on the opportunity to take Iskador's hand, which she gave gladly, and he walked in a steady delight to feel her flesh against his. The other two contented themselves with clinging to her garment.

After some while, the passages branched, the walls became rougher, and the repeating pattern gave out. They had reached the limits of Pannoval, and were truly alone. They rested. While the others talked, Yuli kept clear in his mind the plan that Father Sifans had sketched for him. Already, he regretted that he had not embraced the old man and bidden him farewell.

Father, you understood much about me, I believe, for all your odd ways. You know what a lump of clay I am. You know that I aspire to good but cannot rise above my own dull nature. Yet you did not betray me. Well, I did not knife you either, did I? You must keep trying to improve yourself, Yuli—you're still a priest, after all. Or am I? Well, when we get out, if we get out . . . And there's this wonderful girl . . . No, no, I'm not a priest, old father, bless you, never could be, but I did try and you helped. Fare you well, ever. . . .

"Get up," he called, jumping to his feet and assisting the girl to hers. Iskador rested a hand lightly on his shoulder in the dark before they set off again. She did not complain about being tired when Usilk and Scoraw began to do so.

They slept eventually, huddled together at the foot of a gravelly slope, with the girl between Usilk and Yuli. Night fears got to them; in the dark, they imagined that they heard Wutra's worm slithering towards them, its jaws open and its slimy whiskers trailing.

"We'll sleep with a light burning," Yuli said. It was chill, and he held the girl tight, falling asleep with one cheek against her leather tunic.

When they woke, they nibbled frugally on the food they had brought. The way became much more difficult. There had been a cliff fall, and they crawled for hours on their bellies, nose to toe, each calling to the other unashamedly, in order to keep in touch in the overmastering night of the earth. A freezing wind whistled through the slot they had to work their way through, icing their hair to their heads.

"Let's go back," Scoraw begged, when at last they could stand, bent-backed, and draw in breath. "I prefer imprisonment to this." Nobody answered him, and he did not repeat the suggestion. They could not go back now. But the great presence of the mountain silenced them as they proceeded.

Yuli was hopelessly lost. The rock collapse had thrown him out of his reckoning. He could no longer remember the old priest's map and was almost as helpless without the repeating pattern at his fingers as the others. A whispering noise grew and he strove to follow it. Bars of evil and unidentifiable colour drifted before his staring eyes; he felt that he was pressing through solid rock. His breath broke from his open mouth in sharp gasps. By mutual consent, they rested.

The way had been leading downhill for hours. They staggered on, Yuli with one hand to the side, one arm raised above his face, so that he did not strike his head against rock, as he had already done on several occasions. He felt Iskador clutching his habit; in his present state of fatigue, the touch was merely an annoyance.

With his mind rambling, he began to believe that the way he breathed controlled the diseased colours he saw. Yet that could not be entirely correct, for a kind of luminosity was creeping into view. He plunged on, ever down, squeezing his swollen lids tight together and then releasing them. Blindness was descending upon him—he was seeing a faint milky light. Looking round, he seemed to see Iskador's face as in a dream—or a nightmare, rather, for her eyes were staring, her mouth gaping, in the ghostly disc of her face.

At his gaze, her awareness returned. She stopped, clutching at him for support, and Usilk and Scoraw barged into them.

"There's light ahead," Yuli said.

"Light! I can see again. . . ." Usilk grasped Yuli's shoulders. "You scumbing villain, you have brought us through. We're safe, we're free!"

He laughed greatly, and rushed ahead, arms outstretched as if to embrace the source of the light. In joy, the others followed, stumbling down the rough ground through a light that never was before, unless over some unknown northern sea where icebergs swam and clashed.

The way levelled out, the roof withdrew. Pools of water lay at their feet. They splashed through, and the path led up again steeply, until they were reduced to a walk, and the light grew no stronger, though there were now fierce noises all round.

Suddenly, they were at the end of the way, and stood daunted on the lip of a fissure. Light and noise surrounded them.

"Akha's eyes," gasped Scoraw, and stuck a fist between his teeth.

The fissure was like a throat, leading down into the belly of the earth. They could look up at the gullet, some way above. From the brink of the gullet, a river burst, and plunged down into the fissure. Just below where they stood, the force of the falling water struck rock for the first time. Its energy created the intense drumming they had heard. It then cascaded into depths where it was lost to view. The water was white even where it did not foam, and shot through with livid greens and blues. Although it radiated the dim light in which they rejoiced, the rocks behind it seemed no less bright: they were coated in thick whirls of white and red and yellow.

Long before they had finished gazing upon this spectacle, and looking at the white ghosts of each other, they were drenched by spray.

"This isn't the way out," Iskador said. "This is a dead end. Where now, Yuli?"

He pointed calmly to the far end of the ledge on which they stood. "We go by that bridge," he said.

They made their way carefully towards the bridge. The ground was slimy with ropey green algae. The bridge looked grey and ancient. It had been built of chunks of stone carved from the rock nearby. Its arch curved up, then stopped. They saw that the structure had collapsed, and was no more than a stub of a bridge. Through the milky light, another stub could be seen dimly on the far side of the chasm. There had once been a way across, but no more.

For a while, they stood staring across the gulf, not looking at one another. Iskador was the first to move. Bending, she set her bag down and pulled her bow from it. She tied a thread to an arrow of a kind she had used when Yuli saw her prize-winning performance, a long time ago. Without a word, she placed herself at the edge of the chasm, a foot firm on the edge, and raised the bow. She drew back her arm as she did so, squinting along it almost casually, and let fly.

The arrow seemed to curl through the spray-laden light. It reached its zenith over an outcrop of rock, glanced against the rocky wall above the waterfall, and fell back, its power spent, until it clattered at Iskador's feet.

Usilk clapped her shoulder. "Brilliant. Now what do we do?"

For answer, she tied stout cord to the end of the thread, and then picked up the arrow and drew in the thread. Soon the leading end of the cord ran over the projecting ledge, and travelled back down to nestle in her hand. She then produced a rope on which she made a noose, drew that over the projection too, slipped the other end of the rope through the noose, and pulled the whole thing tight.

"Do you wish to go first?" she asked Yuli, passing him the rope end. "Since you are our leader?"

He looked in her deepset eyes, wondering at her cunning, and the economy of her cunning. Not only was she telling Usilk that he was not the leader, she was telling him, Yuli, to prove that he was. He chewed this over, finding it profound, then grasped the rope and squared up to the challenge.

It was alarming but not too dangerous, he estimated. He could swing across the chasm and then, walking against vertical rock, climb to the level of the lip over which the waterfall poured. As far as they could see, there was space to climb in and avoid being swept away by the water. The possibilities that followed could be assessed only when he was up there. He certainly was not going to show fear in front of the two prisoners—or Iskador.

He launched himself rather too hurriedly across the abyss, his mind in part on the girl. Striking the opposite cliff rather clumsily, his left foot slipped on green slime, he jarred against the wall with his shoulder, swung into spray, and lost his grip on the rope. Next second, he was falling down the chasm.

Amid the roar of water came their united cry—the first time they had genuinely done something in unison.

Yuli struck rock, and clung there with every fibre of his being. He squeezed his knees up under his body, fought with his toes, and gripped the rock.

His fall had been no more than two metres, though it jarred every bone in his body, and had been broken by a boulder protruding from the cliff. It afforded him little more than a foothold, but that was enough.

Gasping, he crouched in his awkward position, scarcely daring to move, his chin almost on a level with his boots.

His anguished gaze fell on a blue stone lying below his eyes. He focused on it, wondering if he was going to die. The stone would not come sharp. He felt that he might have reached out over the ledge where he crouched and picked it up. Suddenly his senses told him the truth of the matter—he was not looking at a nearby stone but a blue object far below. Vertigo seized him, paralysing him; accustomed to the plains, he had no immunity against such an experience.

He closed his eyes and clung. Only Usilk's shouts, coming from a long way off, forced him to look again.

Distantly below lay another world, to which the fissure in which he crouched served as a kind of telescope. Yuli had a view no bigger than his hand into an enormous cavern. It was illuminated in some way. What he had taken for a blue stone was a lake, or possibly a sea, since he had a glimpse only of a fragment of a whole whose size he could not attempt to guess. On the shore of the lake were a few grains of sand, now interpretable as buildings of some kind. He lay in a cataplexy, staring senselessly down.

Something touched him. He could not move. Someone was speaking to him, clutching his arms. Without will, he allowed himself to cooperate in sitting up with his back against the rock, and locking his arms about his rescuer's shoulders. A bruised face, with damaged nose, slashed cheek, and one closed black and green eye swam before his vision.

"Hang on tight, man. We're going up."

He managed then to hold himself against Usilk, as the latter worked his way slowly upwards and eventually hauled them, with enormous labour, over the rock lip from which the waterfall poured. Usilk then collapsed, flat out, panting and groaning. Yuli looked down for Iskador and Scoraw, just visible on the other side of the fissure, faces upturned. He also looked more sharply down, into the fault; but his vision of another world had disappeared, eclipsed by spray. His limbs trembled, but he could control them sufficiently to help the others to join him and Usilk.

In silence, they clutched each other thankfully.

In silence, they picked their way amid the boulders on the side of the rushing stream of the waterfall.

In silence, they went on. And Yuli kept silence over the vision of the other world he had glimpsed. But he thought again of old Father Sifans; could it have been a secret fortress of the Takers, momentarily revealed to him amid the wilderness of rock? Whatever it was, he took it inside himself and was mute.

The warrens in the mountain seemed endless. Without light, the party of four went in fear of crevasses. When they judged it to be night, they found a suitable nook to sleep, and huddled together for warmth and company.

Once, after climbing for hours along a natural passage strewn with boulders from a long-vanished stream, they found a niche at shoulder height, into which all four could scramble, to tuck themselves away from the chill wind that had been blowing in their faces all day.

Yuli went to sleep immediately. He was roused by Iskador shaking him. The other men were sitting up, whispering apprehensively.

"Can you hear?" she asked.

"Can you hear?" Usilk and Scoraw asked.

He listened to the wind sighing down the passage, to a distant trickle of water. Then he heard what had disturbed them—a continuous rasping noise, as of something moving fast against the walls.

"Wutra's worm!" Iskador said.

He clutched her firmly. "That's just a story they tell," he said. But his flesh went cold, and he grasped his dagger.

"We're safe in this niche," Scoraw said. "If we keep quiet."

They could only hope he might be right. Unmistakably, something was approaching. They crouched where they were, peering nervously into the tunnel. Scoraw and Usilk were armed with staves, stolen from the warders of Punishment, Iskador had her bow.

The noise grew louder. Acoustics were deceptive, but they thought it came from the same direction as the wind. There was a rasping element to the noise now, and a rumble as of boulders being thrust heedlessly aside. The wind died, blocked perhaps. A smell assailed their nostrils.

It was a ripe aroma of festering fish, of scumble, of rotten cheese. A greenish fog permeated the passage. Legend said Wutra's worm was silent, but now it approached with a roar, whatever it might be.

Moved more by terror than courage, Yuli peered from their lair.

There it was, coming fast. Its features could hardly be discerned behind the bank of green luminescence it pushed along in front of it. Four eyes, banked two and two, whiskers and fangs gigantic. Yuli pulled his head back in horror, choking. It was approaching irresistibly.

Next moment, they all four had a sight of its face in profile. It plunged by, eyes glaring insanely. Stiffish whiskers brushed their furs. Then their vision was blocked by scaley ribs, rippling by, blue-lit, scouring dust in upon them, choking them with filth and stink.

There were miles of it, then it was past. Clutching each other, they peered out of their hiding place to see the end of it. Somewhere at the beginning of the boulder-strewn passage was a wider cave through which they had come. A convulsion was taking place down there; the green luminescence, still visible, rippled.

The worm had sensed them. It was turning round and coming back. For them. Iskador stifled a cry as she realised what was happening.

"Rocks, fast," Yuli said. There was loose rock they could throw. He reached towards the sloping back of the niche. His hand struck something unsuspected and furry. He drew back. He struck his chert wheel. A spark flew and died—living long enough for him to see that they were keeping company with the mouldering remains of a man, of which only bones and his enveloping furs remained. And there was a weapon of sorts.

He struck a second spark.

"It's a dead shaggy!" Usilk exclaimed, using the prisoner's slang for phagor.

Usilk was right. There was no mistaking the long skull, from which the flesh had dried, or the horns. Beside the body was a staff capped by a spike and a curved blade. Akha had come to the aid of those threatened by Wutra. Both Usilk and Yuli reached out and grabbed the shaft of the weapon.

"For me. I've used these things," Yuli said, wrenching at it. Suddenly, his old life was back, he recalled facing a charging yelk in the wilderness.

Wutra's worm was returning. Again the scraping noise. More light, livid and green. Yuli and Usilk ventured a quick look out of the niche. But the monster was unmoving. They could see the blur of its face. It had turned and was facing back in their direction, but did not advance.

It was waiting.

They chanced a look in the other direction.

A second worm was bearing down on them from the direction the first had come. Two worms . . . suddenly, in Yuli's imagination the cave system was crawling with worms.

In terror, they clung to each other, as the light grew brighter and the noise nearer. But the monstrous creatures would be concerned only with each other.

Following a wave of foetid air, the head of the monster plunged by, four eyes glaring as it stared to its front. Bracing the lower half of his newly acquired spear against the side of the niche, Yuli thrust the point out beyond the rock, hanging on with both hands.

It pierced the churning side of the worm as it charged forward. From the long opening tear in its body, a thick jamlike substance gushed, and flowed down the full extent of its body. The monster was slowing before its whiskered tail had passed the shelf where the four humans sprawled.

Whether the two worms had been intending to fight or mate would never be determined. The second worm never reached its target. Its forward motion petered out. Waves of crudely telegraphed pain caused the body to ripple, the tail to lash. Then it was still.

Slowly, its luminescence died. All was quiet, save for the sough of the wind.

They dared not move. They scarcely dared change their position. The first worm was still waiting somewhere in the darkness, its presence indicated by a faint green glow, scarcely discernible over the body of the dead monster. Afterwards, they agreed that this was the worst part of their ordeal. Each supposed in his or her private thoughts that the first worm knew where they were, that the dead worm was its mate, and that it was only waiting for them to stir to plunge forward and be revenged.

Eventually the first worm did move. They heard the slither of its whiskers against the rock. It slid cautiously forward as if expecting a trap, until its head loomed over the body of its dead adversary. Then it began to feed.

The four humans could no longer stay where they were. The sounds were too terrifyingly suggestive. Jumping clear of the spilt ichor, they regained the passage, and scampered away into the dark.

Their journey through the mountain was resumed. But now they stopped frequently and listened to the sounds of the dark. And when they had need to speak, they spoke in low tremulous voices.

Occasionally, they found water to drink. But their food gave out. Iskador shot down some bats, but they could not bring themselves to eat the creatures. They wandered in the labyrinth of stone, growing weaker. Time passed, the security of Pannoval was forgotten: all that remained of life was an endless darkness to be traversed.

They began to come upon bones of animals. Once, they struck a chert and discovered two human skeletons sprawling in an alcove, one with an arm about the other; time had robbed the gesture of any gentleness it might once have possessed: now there was only bone to scrape against bone, and terrifying grin to respond to the skull's grin.

Then, in a place with a colder airflow, they heard movements, and found two red-furred animals, which they killed. Close by was a cub, mewling and poking up its blunt nose at them. Tearing the cub apart, they devoured it while the flesh was still warm and then, in a sort of raging paroxysm of awakened hunger, devoured the two parents as well.

Luminescent organisms grew on the walls. They found signs of human habitation. The remains of a shack and something that might have been a boat sprouted a crop of fungi. Nearby, a chimney in the cavern roof had encouraged a small flock of preets. With her unfailing bow, Iskador downed six of the birds, and they cooked them in a pot over a fire with fungi and a pinch of salt for flavour. That night, as they slept together, unpleasantly vivid dreams visited them, which they attributed to the fungi. But when they set off next morning, they came after only two hours of walking to a low wide cavern into which green light filtered.

In one corner of the cave, a fire smouldered. There was a crude pen, inside which were three goats, their eyes bright in the twilight. Three women sat nearby on a pile of skins, an ancient crone with white hair, and two younger women. The latter ran off squealing when Yuli, Usilk, Iskador, and Scoraw appeared.

Scoraw ran forward and jumped in with the goats. Using an old utensil lying nearby as a pail, he milked the goats into it, despite the unintelligible cries of the crone. There was little milk to be had from the animals. What there was, they shared before moving on, casting the utensil down behind them as they left before the men of the tribe returned.

They entered a passage that turned sharply and had been barricaded. Beyond lay the mouth of the cave and, beyond that, open country, mountainside and valley, and the brilliant light of the realm ruled by Wutra, god of the skies.

They stood close together, for now they felt the bonds of unity and friendship, regarding the beautiful prospect. When they regarded each other, their faces were full of merriment and hope, and they could not keep from shouting and laughing. They skipped about and hugged one another. When their eyes were accustomed sufficiently to the brightness they could shield their brows and gaze up to where Batalix flitted among thin cloud, his disc a pale orange.

The time of year must be near the spring equinox, and the time of day noon, for two reasons: Batalix was vertically overhead, and Freyr was sailing below her to the east. Freyr was several times the brighter, spilling its light over snow-covered hills. Fainter Batalix was always the faster sentinel, and would soon be setting while Freyr lingered still at zenith.

How beautiful the sight of the sentinels was! The seasonal pattern of their dance in the heavens returned fresh to Yuli's mind, making him open heart and nostrils. He leaned on the carefully wrought spear with which he had killed the worm and let his body fill with daylight.

But Usilk laid a detaining hand on Scoraw, and lingered in the mouth of the cave, looking out apprehensively. He called to Yuli, "Wouldn't we do better to stay in these caves? How are we supposed to live out there, under that sky?"

Without removing his eyes from the landscape ahead, Yuli sensed that Iskador stood halfway between him and the men at the cave mouth. Without looking back, he answered Usilk.

"Do you remember that story they told in Vakk, about the maggots in the roofer nuts? The maggots thought their rotten nut was the whole world, so that when the nut cracked open, they died of shock. Are you going to be a maggot, Usilk?"

To that Usilk had no answer. But Iskador had. She came up behind Yuli and slipped her hand into the crook of his arm. He smiled and his heart sang, but he never ceased staring hungrily ahead.

He could see that the mountains through which they had come would provide shelter southward. Stunted trees no higher than a man grew sparsely, and grew upright, which indicated that the chill west wind of the Barriers no longer had power here. He still retained his old skills, learnt from Alehaw long ago. There would be game in the hills and they could live sensibly under the sky, as the gods intended.

His spirit rose, swelling until he had to fling his arms out wide.

"We will live in this sheltered place," Yuli said. "The four of us will stay united, whatever else happens." From a snowy fold of hillside, distantly, merging into the evening sky, smoke rose. He pointed ahead. "People live there. We'll force them to accept us. This shall be our place. We'll rule them, and teach them our ways. From now on, we live under our own laws, not other people's."

Squaring his shoulders, he set off down the slope, among a shallow stand of trees, and the others followed, Iskador first, walking proudly, then the others.

Some of Yuli's intentions worked out, and some did not.

After numerous challenges, they were accepted in a small settlement sheltering under a protective fold of mountain. The people lived on a squalidly primitive level; because of their superior knowledge and their boldness, Yuli and his friends were able to impose their will on the community, to rule it, and to enforce their own laws.

Yet they never became truly integrated, because their faces looked different, and the Olonets they spoke went with a different lilt from the local variety. And they discovered that this settlement, because of its advantages, always lived in fear of raids from a larger settlement some way off on the banks of a frozen lake. Indeed, these raids were made more than once during the years that followed, with great suffering caused, and loss of life.

Yet Yuli and Usilk became cunning, and maintained their cunning because they were outsiders, and built ferocious defences against the invaders from Dorzin, as the larger settlement was called. And Iskador taught all the young women how to make bows and use them. They came to perform with great skill. The next time the invaders arrived from the south, many died with arrows in their chests, and then there were no more attacks from that direction.

Yet inclement weather beat upon them, and avalanches rolled down from the mountains. There was no end to storms. Only in cave mouths could they grow a few maggoty crops or sustain a few mangey animals to give them milk and meat, so that their numbers never grew, and they were always hungry, or seized by illnesses that could be ascribed only to the malignant gods (of Akha, Yuli allowed no mention).

Yet Yuli took the beautiful Iskador for his woman, and loved her, and looked every day on her broad strong face with comfort. They had a child, a boy they called Si, in memory of Yuli's old priest in Pannoval, who survived all the pains and dangers of childhood, and grew up wild. Usilk and Scoraw also married, Usilk to a small brown woman named Isik, curiously like his own name; Isik, despite her stature, could run like a deer and was intelligent and kind. Scoraw took a girl named Fitty, a capricious lady who sang beautifully and led him a hell of a life, and produced a baby girl who died after one year.

Yet Yuli and Usilk could never agree. Although they united in the face of common danger, Usilk at other times displayed hostility to Yuli and his plans, and tricked him when he could. As the old priest had said, some men never forgive.

Yet a deputation came from the larger settlement of Dorzin, which had suffered losses following an outbreak of disease. Having heard of Yuli's reputation, they begged him to rule them in place of their dead leader. Which Yuli did, to be away from the vexation of Usilk, and he and Iskador and their child lived by the frozen lake, where game was plentiful, and administered the laws firmly.

Yet even in Dorzin there were almost no arts to relieve the monotony of their hard life. Though the people danced on feast days, they had no musical instruments beyond clappers and bells. Nor was there any religion, except for a constant fear of evil spirits and a stoic acceptance of the enemy cold, and sickness, and death. So that Yuli became at last a real priest, and tried to instill in the people a feeling for their own spiritual vitality. Most men rejected his words because, although they had welcomed him, he was an outsider, and they were too sullen to learn new things. But he taught them to love the sky in all its moods.

Yet life was strong in him and Iskador, and in Si, and they never let die the hope that better times were emerging. He kept the vision he had been granted in the mountains, that there was possibly a way of life more enjoyable than the one immediately granted, more secure, less subject to the chances and the elements.

Yet he and his beautiful Iskador grew older for all that, and felt the cold more with the passing years.

Yet they loved the lakeside place where they lived and, in memory of another life and another set of expectations, called it by the name of Oldorando.

This is as far as the story of Yuli, son of Alehaw and Onesa can go. The story of their descendants, and what befell them, is a far greater tale. All unknown to them, Freyr drew nearer to the chilly world: for there was truth buried in the obscure scriptures Yuli rejected, and the sky of ice would in due process of time become a sky of fire. Only fifty Helliconian years after the birth of their son, true spring would visit the inclement world that Yuli and his beautiful Iskador knew.

A new world was already poised to be born.

Embruddock

And *Shay Tal said*:

You think we live at the centre of the universe. I say we live in the centre of a farmyard. Our position is so obscure that you cannot realise how obscure.

This I tell you all. Some disaster happened in the past, the long past. So complete was it that no one now can tell you what it was or how it came about. We know only that it brought darkness and cold of long duration.

You try to live as best you can. Good, good, live well, love one another, be kind. But don't pretend that the disaster is nothing to do with you. It may have happened long ago, yet it infects every day of our lives. It ages us, it wears us out, it devours us, it tears our children from us. It makes us not only ignorant but in love with ignorance. We're infested with ignorance.

I'm going to propose a treasure hunt—a quest, if you like. A quest in which every one of us can join. I want you to be aware of our fallen state, and to maintain constant alertness for evidence as to its nature. We have to piece together what has happened to reduce us to this chilly

77

farmyard; then we can improve our lot, and see to it that the disaster does not befall us and our children again.

That's the treasure I offer you. Knowledge. Truth. You fear it, yes. But you must seek it. You must grow to love it.

I

DEATH OF A GRANDFATHER

The sky was black, and men bearing torches came from the south gate. They were thickly wrapped in skins, and trod with a high step to get through the snow lying in the lanes. The holy man was coming! The holy man was coming!

Young Laintal Ay hid in the porch of the ruined temple, his face shining with excitement. He watched the procession trudge by between the old stone towers, each one encrusted on its east face with the snow that had arrived earlier in the day. He noticed how colour existed only at the spluttering ends of the torches, on the end of the holy father's nose, and in the tongues of the six-dog team that pulled him. In each case, the colour was red. The heavy-laden sky—in which the sentinel Batalix was buried—had leached all other colours away.

Father Bondorlonganon from distant Borlien was fat, and made fatter by the enormous furs he wore, furs of a kind not used in Oldorando. He had come alone to Oldorando—the men who accompanied him were local hunters, each one already known to Laintal Ay. It was on the father's face that the boy focussed all his attention, for strangers came seldom; he had been smaller, less tough, on the occasion of the father's last visit.

The holy man's face was oval, and massively creased by horizontal lines, into which such features as his eyes fitted as best they could. The lines seemed to compress his mouth into a long cruel shape. He sat his sledge and stared about him suspiciously. Nothing in his attitude suggested he liked being back in Oldorando. His gaze took in the ruined temple; this visit was necessary because Oldorando had killed its priesthood some generations ago, as he knew. His uncomfortable stare rested a moment on the boy standing between two square pillars.

Laintal Ay stared back. It seemed to him that the priest's look was cruel and calculating; but he could hardly expect to think well of a man who was coming to perform last rites over his dying grandfather.

He smelt the dogs as they went by, and the tarry scent of burning torches. The procession turned and was heading up the main street, away from the temple. Laintal Ay was in two minds about following. He stood on the steps and hugged himself, watching as the sledge's arrival attracted people from their towers, despite the cold.

In the murk at the far end of the lane, under the big tower where Laintal Ay and his family lived, the procession halted. Slaves appeared to deal with the dogs—they would be housed in the stable under the tower—while the holy father climbed stiffly from his perch and bundled into shelter.

At the same time a hunter approached the temple from the south gate. It was a black bearded man called Aoz Roon, whom the boy greatly admired for his swaggering air. Behind him, shackles clamped round horny ankles, trudged an ancient phagor slave, Myk.

"Well, Laintal, I see the father has arrived from Borlien. Aren't you going to welcome him?"

"No."

"Why not? You remember him, don't you?"

"If he didn't come, my grandfather wouldn't be dying."

Aoz Roon clapped him on the shoulder.

"You're a good lad, you'll survive. One day, you will rule Embruddock yourself." He used the old name for Oldorando, the name in fashion before Yuli's people came, two generations before the present Yuli, who now lay awaiting the priest's rites.

"I'd rather have Grandfather alive than be a ruler."

Aoz Roon shook his head. "Don't say that. Anyone would rule, given the opportunity. I would."

"You'd make a good ruler, Aoz Roon. When I grow up, I'm going to be like you, and know everything and kill everything."

Aoz Roon laughed. Laintal Ay thought what a fine figure he cut, as his teeth flashed between bearded lips. He saw ferocity, but not the priest's slyness. Aoz Roon was in many ways heroic. He had a natural daughter called Oyre, almost Laintal Ay's age. And he wore a suit of black skins unlike anyone else's, cut from a giant mountain bear he had slain single-handed.

Carelessly, Aoz Roon said, "Come on, your mother will want you at this time. Climb on Myk and he'll give you a ride."

The great white phagor put out his horned hands and allowed the boy to scramble up his arms onto his bowed shoulders. Myk had been in servitude in Embruddock a long while; his kind lived longer than humans. He said, in his thick, choking voice, "Come on, boy."

Laintal Ay reached up and clasped the horns of the ancipital for security. As a sign of his enslavement the sharp double edges of Myk's horns had been filed smooth.

The three figures trudged up the time-worn street, heading towards warmth as the dark closed in on another of the countless nights of winter —a winter that had ruled over this tropical continent for centuries. Wind shifted powdery snow from ledges; it drifted down on them.

As soon as holy father and dogs had entered the big tower, the onlookers disappeared, scurrying back to their billets. Myk set down Laintal Ay in the trampled snow. The boy gave Aoz Roon a cheery wave as he dashed himself against the double doors set in the base of the building.

A stench of fish greeted him in the murk. The dog team had been fed on gout hooked from the frozen Voral. They jumped up as the boy entered, barking savagely on their leashes, showing their sharp teeth. A human slave who had accompanied the father shouted ineffectually to them to keep quiet. Laintal Ay growled back, keeping his fingers wrapped under his arms, and climbed the wooden stairs.

Light filtered from above. Six floors were piled above the stable. He slept in a corner on the next floor. His mother and grandparents were on the top floor. Between lived various hunters in his grandfather's service; as the boy passed by, they turned their broad backs to him, being already busy packing. Laintal Ay saw, as he climbed to his floor, that Father Bondorlonganon's few belongings had been deposited here. The man had installed himself, and would sleep nearby. No doubt he would snore; grown-ups generally did. He stood looking down at the priest's blanket, marvelling at the strangeness of its texture, before going upstairs to where his grandfather lay.

Laintal Ay paused with his head through the hatch, staring into the room, viewing everything from the perspective of the floor. This was really his grandmother's room, the room of Loil Bry since girlhood, since the time of her father, Wall Ein Den, who had been lord of the Den tribe, Lord of Embruddock. It was filled now with Loil Bry's shadow. She stood with her back to a fire burning in an iron brazier close by the opening through which her grandson peered. The shadow loomed upon walls and low-beamed ceiling, threateningly. Of the elaborate tapestried gown that his grandmother always wore, nothing transferred to the walls but an uncertain outline, with sleeves converted to wings.

Three other people in the room appeared dominated by Loil Bry and her shadow. On a couch in one corner lay Little Yuli, his chin jutting above the furs that covered him. He was twenty-nine years old, and worn out. The old man was muttering. Loilanun, Laintal Ay's mother, sat next to him, clutching her elbows with her hands, a woebegone look on her sallow face. She had not yet noticed her son. The man from Borlien, Father Bondorlonganon, sat nearest Laintal Ay, his eyes closed, praying aloud.

It was the prayer as much as anything which halted Laintal Ay. Normally he loved to be in this room, full of his grandmother's mysteries. Loil Bry knew so many fascinating things, and to some extent took the place of Laintal Ay's father, who had been killed while on a stungebag hunt.

Stungebags contributed to the foetid honey smell in the room. One of the monsters had been caught recently, and brought home bit by bit. Broken shards of plating, chopped from its back, helped fuel the fire and keep the cold at bay. The pseudo-wood burned with a yellow flame, sizzling as it burned.

Laintal Ay looked at the west wall. There was his grandmother's porcelain window. Faint light from outside transfused it with a sullen orange glow, scarcely competition for the firelight.

"It looks funny in here," he said at last.

He came up one more step, and the bright eyes of the brazier gleamed at him.

The father unhurriedly finished his prayer to Wutra and opened his eyes. Netted among the compressed horizontal lines of his face, they were unable to open far, but he fixed them gently on the boy and said, without preliminary greeting, "You'd better come here, my lad. I've brought something from Borlien for you."

"What's that?" He held his hands behind his back.

"Come and see."

"Is it a dagger?"

"Come and see." He sat perfectly still. Loil Bry sobbed, the dying man groaned, the fire spat.

Laintal Ay approached the father warily. He could not grasp how people could live in places other than Oldorando: it was the centre of the universe—elsewhere there was only wilderness, the wilderness of ice that stretched for ever and occasionally erupted in phagor invasions.

Father Bondorlonganon produced a little hound and placed it in the boy's palm. It was scarcely longer than the palm. It was carved, as he recognised, out of kaidaw horn, with a wealth of detail which delighted him. Thick coat curled over the hound's back, and the minute paws had pads. He examined it for a while before discovering that the tail moved. When it was wagged up and down, the dog's lower jaw opened and closed.

There had never been a toy like it. Laintal Ay ran round the room in excitement, barking, and his mother jumped up to shush him, catching him in her arms.

"One day, this lad will be Lord of Oldorando," Loilanun said to the father, as if by way of explanation. "He will inherit."

"Better he should love knowledge and study to know more," said Loil Bry, almost as an aside. "Such was my Yuli's preference." She wept afresh into her hands.

Father Bondorlonganon squeezed his eyes a little more and enquired Laintal Ay's age.

"Six and a quarter years." Only foreigners had to ask such questions.

"Well, you're almost at manhood. In another year, you'll become a hunter, so you'd better soon decide. Which do you want more, power or knowledge?"

He stared at the floor.

"Both, sir . . . or whichever comes easier."

The priest laughed, and dismissed the boy with a gesture, waddling over to see his charge. He had ingratiated himself: now, business. His ear, attuned by experience to the visitation of death, had caught the sound of a change in the rate of Little Yuli's breathing. The old man was about to leave this world for a perilous journey down along his land-octave to the obsidian world of the gossies. Getting the women to aid him, Bondorlonganon stretched the leader out with his head to the west, lying on his side.

Pleased to be released from inquisition, the boy rolled on the floor, fighting with his horn dog, barking softly back at it as it furiously exercised its jaw. His grandfather passed away while one of the most savage dogfights in the history of the world was taking place.

Next day, Laintal Ay wished to stay close to the priest from Borlien, in case he had more toys hidden in his garments. But the priest was busy visiting the sick, and in any case Loilanun kept firm hold of her son.

Laintal Ay's natural rebelliousness was curbed by the quarrels that broke out between his mother and his grandmother. He was the more surprised because the women had been loving to each other when his grandfather lived. The body of Yuli, he who was named after the man who came with Iskador from the mountains, was carted off, stiff as a frozen pelt, as if his last act of will was to hold himself rigidly away from his woman's caresses. His absence left a black corner in the room, where Loil Bry squatted, turning only to snap at her daughter.

All the tribe were built solid, buttressed with subcutaneous fat. Loil Bry's once renowned stature still lingered, though her hair was grey and her head lost between her shoulder bones as she stooped over the cold bed of that man of hers—that man loved with intense passion for half a lifetime, since she first beheld him, an invader, wounded.

Loilanun was of poorer stuff. The energy, the power to love, the broad face with seeking eyes like dark sails, had missed Loilanun, passing direct from grandmother to young Laintal Ay. Loilanun was strawy, her skin sallow; since her husband died so young, there was a falter in her walk—and a falter too, perhaps, in her attempt to emulate her mother's regal command of knowledge. She was irritable now, as Loil Bry wept almost continuously in the corner.

"Mother, give over—your din gets on my nerves."

"*You* were too feeble to mourn your man properly! I'll weep, I'll weep till I'm taken, I'll bleed tears."

"Much good it will do you." She offered her mother bread, but it was refused with a contemptuous gesture. "Shay Tal made it."

"I won't eat."

"I'll have it, Mumma," Laintal Ay said.

Aoz Roon arrived outside the tower and called up, holding his natural daughter Oyre by the hand. Oyre was a year younger than Laintal Ay, and waved enthusiastically to him, as he and Loilanun stuck their heads out of the window.

"Come up and see my toy dog, Oyre. It's a real fighter, like your father."

But his mother bundled him back into the room and said sharply to Loil Bry, "It's Aoz Roon, wishing to escort us to the burial. Can I tell him yes?"

Rocking herself slightly, not turning, the old woman said, "Don't trust anyone. Don't trust Aoz Roon—he has too much effrontery. He and his friends hope to gain the succession."

"We've got to trust someone. You'll have to rule now, Mother."

When Loil Bry laughed bitterly, Loilanun looked down at her son, who stood smiling and clutching the horn dog. "Then I shall, till Laintal Ay becomes a man. Then he'll be Lord of Embruddock."

"You're a fool if you think his uncle Nahkri will permit that," the old woman responded.

Loilanun said no more, drawing her mouth up in a bitter line, letting her regard sink down from her son's expectant face to the skins which covered the floor. She knew that women did not rule. Already, even before her father was put under, her mother's power over the tribe was going, flowing away as the river Voral flowed, none knew where. Turning on her heel, she shouted out of the window, without more ado, "Come up."

So abashed was Laintal Ay by this look of his mother's, as if she perceived he would never be a match for his grandfather—never mind the more ancient bearer of the name of Yuli—that he hung back, too wounded to greet Oyre when she marched into the chamber with her father.

Aoz Roon was fourteen years of age, a handsome, swaggering, young hunter who, after a sympathetic smile at Loilanun and a rumple of Laintal Ay's hair, went over to pay his respects to the widow. This was Year 19 After Union, and already Laintal Ay had a sense of history. It lurked in the dull-smelling corners of this old room, with its damps and lichens and cobwebs. The very word *history* reminded him of wolves howling between the towers, the snow at their rumps, while some old boney hero breathed his last.

Not only was Grandfather Yuli dead. Dresyl also had died. Dresyl, Yuli's cousin-brother, Laintal Ay's great-uncle, the father of Nahkri and Klils. The priest had been summoned and Dresyl had gone down rigid into the dirt, the dirt of history.

The boy remembered Dresyl with affection, but he feared his quarrelsome uncles, those sons of Dresyl, Nahkri and the boastful Klils. As far as he understood these things, he expected that—no matter what his mother said—old traditions would guarantee it was Nahkri and Klils who would rule. At least they were young. He would make himself a good hunter, and then they would respect him, instead of ignoring him as at present. Aoz Roon would help.

The hunters did not leave the hamlet this day. Instead, they all attended the funeral of their old lord. The holy father had calculated exactly where the grave should be, close by a curiously carved stone, where the ground was softened enough by hot springs for burial to be possible.

Aoz Roon escorted the two ladies, wife and daughter of Little Yuli, to the place. Laintal Ay and Oyre followed, whispering to each other, with their slaves and Myk, the phagor, following them. Laintal Ay worked his barking dog to make Oyre giggle.

Cold and water created a curious stage for grief. Fumaroles, springs, geysers, burst from the ground to the north of the hamlet, pouring across naked rock and stone. Driven by the wind, the water from several geysers fanned out westwards in a curtain, to freeze before it struck the ground, building up into elaborate fanciful shapes, intertwining like rope. Hotter springs, lashing this superstructure with warm water, kept it in a perilous state of plasticity, so that chunks would break off from time to time, to fall clacking to the rock and gradually be washed away.

A hole had been dug to accommodate the old hero, once conqueror of Embruddock. Two men with leather buckets laboured to bale water out of it. Wrapped in a coarse cloth without decoration, Little Yuli was lowered in. Nothing went with him. The people of Campannlat— or those who bothered to learn the art—knew only too well what it was like down below, in the world of the gossies: there was nothing anyone could take with them to help.

Huddled about the grave was the population of Oldorando, some one hundred and seventy men, women, and children.

Dogs and geese also joined the crowd, looking on in a nervous animal way, whereas the humans stood passively, changing their weight from foot to foot. It was cold. Batalix was high, but lost in cloud; Freyr was still in the east, an hour after its rise.

The people were dark and of substantial build, with the great barrel bodies and limbs which were the heritage of everyone on the planet at this period. The weight of adults at present was close to twelve staynes in the local measure, whether male or female, with little variation; drastic changes would occur later. They huddled in two groups of roughly equal numbers, their breath cloudy about them, one group of hunters and their women, one of corpsmen and their women. The hunters wore suits of reindeer skin, the bristly pelage of which was so thickly matted that even strong blizzards could not blow the hairs apart. The corpsmen wore lighter garb, generally of ruddy deer pelts, suited to a more sheltered life. One or two hunters wore phagor pelts, boastfully; but those hides were generally reckoned too greasy and heavy for comfort.

Steam rose from both groups, to be snatched away by the breeze. Their coats gleamed with moisture. They stood unmoving, watching. Some of the women, remembering strands of the old religion, threw down a large brassimip leaf each, as being about the only green stuff freely available. The leaves blew about uncertainly, wumping as they turned over. Some trundled into the soggy hole.

Ignoring everything, Bondorlonganon proceeded with the business in hand. Squeezing his eyes shut as if he would crack them like nuts, he recited the prescribed prayer to the heathens gathered about him. Mud was shovelled into the hole.

These things were kept short, out of respect for the weather and its effect on the living. As the hole filled, Loil Bry gave a terrible cry. She ran forward, and threw herself on her husband's grave. Aoz Roon was quick to catch her up and hold her, while Nahkri and his brother looked on, arms folded, half in amusement.

Loil Bry broke away from Aoz Roon's hold. Stooping, she grasped two handfuls of mud and smeared it over her face and hair, crying as she did so. Laintal Ay and Oyre laughed with delight. It was fun to see adults doing silly things.

Although the holy man continued with the service as if nothing had happened, his face wrinkled with disgust. This miserable place, Embruddock, was known for its lack of religion. Well, their gossies would suffer, sinking through the earth to the original boulder.

Tall and old, the widow of Little Yuli ran among the crackling ice structures, through the mist, down to the frozen Voral. Geese took off in dismay before her as she went crying along the bank, a crazed hag of twenty-eight hard winters. Some of the other children laughed, until their mothers silenced them in shame.

The stricken old lady capered on the ice, with stiff, rickety movements like a puppet. Her figure was dark grey against the greys, blues, whites of the wilderness before which all their dramas were played out. Like Loil Bry, all present there were balanced on the edge of an entropy gradient. The children's laughter, the sorrow, the madness, even the disgust, were human expressions of a war against perpetual cold. None knew it, but that war was already tipping in their favour. Little Yuli, like his great ancestor, Yuli the Priest, founder of the tribe, had emerged from eternal dark and ice. Young Laintal Ay was a precursor of the light to come.

Loil Bry's scandalous behaviour lent spice to the feasting that was held after the funeral. All celebrated. Little Yuli was fortunate, or accounted so, for he had a father to welcome him to the world of gossies. His former subjects celebrated not only his departure but a more worldly journey—the holy man's return to Borlien. For that, the priest had to be well filled with rathel and barley wine, to keep out the cold on his trip home.

Slaves—they too Borlienians, but Father Bondorlonganon overlooked that—were despatched to load the sledge and harness up the yelping dogs. Laintal Ay and Oyre went along to the south gate with a merry crowd to see him off.

The priest's face squeezed itself into something like a smile at the sight of the boy. He bent suddenly and kissed Laintal Ay on the lips.

"Power and knowledge to you, son!" he said.

Too overcome to reply, Laintal Ay lifted the toy dog in salute.

In the towers that night, over a last bottle, tales were told again of Little Yuli, and of how he and his tribe had arrived in Embruddock. And of how unwelcome they were.

As Father Bondorlonganon was drawn back, pickled, across the plain to Borlien, the clouds parted. Above him, beading the night sky, were the prodigal stars.

Among the constellations and the fixed stars was a light that crawled. Not a comet but Earth Observation Station Avernus.

From the ground below, the station appeared as no more than a point of light, casually watched by travellers and trappers as it passed overhead. Close to, it revealed itself as an irregular and complex series of units with a number of specialised functions.

The Avernus housed some five thousand men, women, children, and androids, all of the adults specialising in some aspect of the planet below. Helliconia. An Earth-like planet with particular interest for the people of Earth.

11

THE PAST THAT WAS LIKE
A DREAM

Laintal Ay, overcome by warmth and fatigue, fell asleep long before
the celebrations were over. The stories went on over his head, much
as the winds blew about the planet, in a cold fury of possession.

The stories were of the activities of men, above all of his heroism, of
the way he killed such-and-such a devil animal, of the way enemies were
defeated, and in particular—on this evening after the burial—of how
the first Yuli had come down out of darkness to found a new way
of life.

Yuli captured their imaginations because he had been a holy man, yet
had rejected faith in favour of his people. He had battled with and
defeated gods who now had no name.

An elemental quality in Yuli's character, something between ruthlessness and fair-mindedness, awoke a response in the tribe. His legend
grew in their minds. So that even his great-grandson, another Yuli,
"Little" Yuli, could ask himself in times of stress, "What would Yuli
have done?"

That first place he named Oldorando, to which he went with
Iskador from the mountain, did not prosper. It could do no more than
survive. It existed precariously on the edge of a frozen lake, Lake Dorzin,

88

and could merely bow beneath the elemental furies of winter, unaware that those furies were about to exhaust themselves. Of that, there was no hint in Yuli's lifetime. Perhaps that was another reason why the present generation in the stone towers of Embruddock liked to speak of him: he was their ancestor who lived in deep winter. He represented their survival. Their legends were the first part of their awareness to admit of the possibility of a change in climate.

Together with the towns hived in the great mountain ranges of the Quzint, that first wooden Oldorando lay close to the equator, in the middle of the extensive tropical continent of Campannlat. Of the concept of that continent, nobody in Yuli's time had knowledge; their world was limited by the hunting territory and the encampment. Only Yuli had experience of the tundras and zastrugi which stretched away to the north of the Quzint. Only Yuli had experience of the foothills of that enormous natural feature which formed the western end of the continent, known as the Barriers. There, among fast-moving frosts, volcanoes situated over four thousand metres above sea level added their own kind of intransigence to the weather, spreading a lava plateau over the ancient impact rocks of Helliconia.

He was spared knowledge of the awesome territories of Nktryhk.

To the east of Campannlat looms the Eastern Range. Hidden from the eyes of Yuli and all other men behind cloud and storm, the earth here gathers itself up into range after enormous mountain range, culminating in a volcanic shield across which glaciers grind their way down from peaks over fourteen thousand metres high. Here the elements of fire and earth and air existed almost in their pure form, held in a cold fury too great to permit a mellowing into alloys less opposed. Yet even here, at a slightly later date—by the time of the death of Little Yuli—even on ice sheets penetrating almost to the stratosphere, ancipital life might be observed, clinging to existence, rejoicing in the storm.

The howling white wilderness of the Eastern Shield was known to the phagors. They called it Nktryhk, and believed it to be the throne of a white wizard who would cast the Sons of Freyr, the hated man-things, out of the world.

Stretching north and south for almost three and a half thousand miles, Nktryhk separated the inner part of the continent from the chill eastern seas. Those seas lashed against the cliffs of Nktryhk, which reared precipitously eighteen hundred metres above the waters. The waves turned to ice as they burst upwards, bearding the cliffs with icicles or falling back to the swell as hail. Of this the scattered human tribes knew nothing.

Those generations lived by the hunt. The hunt formed the subject matter of most of the stories to be told. Although hunters hunted together and helped each other, ultimately the hunt concerned one man's

courage as he faced alone the savage beast who turned to confront him.
Either he lived or he died. And if he lived, then others might live, the
women and children back in safety. If he died, the tribe died, very likely.

So Yuli's people, that small band by the frozen lake, lived as they
had to, as committed as animals to their mode of existence. The listeners
to the story enjoyed accounts of the lake settlement. There, fish were
trapped in ways still so minutely described that the methods had been
imitated in the Voral. Heads of deer were thrown into melt holes by
the river's edge to collect much-relished eels, just as Yuli had once done.

Yuli's people also fought giant stungebags, killed deer and savage
boar, and defended themselves against phagor raids. Depending on season, quick crops of barley and rye were grown. The blood of enemies
was drunk.

Men and women produced few children. In Oldorando, they matured
by the age of seven years and were ageing by the time they were
twenty. Even when they laughed and rejoiced, frost stood by their
elbows.

The first Yuli, the frozen lake, the phagors, the intense cold, the past
that was like a dream: these vivid elements of legend were known to
everyone, and often retold. For the little herd of people who sheltered
out their lives in Embruddock were confined in ways to which that confinement blinded them. At puberty, they were each stitched into the
skins of animals; the animals enfolded them. But dreams, and the past
that was like a dream, gave them extra dimensions in which they could
all live.

Huddled close in Nahkri's and Klils' tower, after Little Yuli's funeral,
everyone took pleasure once more in sharing in the past that was like a
dream. To make the past more vivid, or perhaps to dim the present,
everyone drank rathel, dispensed by Nahkri's slaves. Rathel was the
most highly valued liquid in Embruddock, after red blood.

Little Yuli's funeral gave them the chance to break the unvarying
routine of life, and to live imaginatively. So the great tale of the past,
of two tribes uniting, even as man and woman unite, was again retold.
The tale was passed from mouth to mouth, much like the rathel mug,
one narrator taking over from the next with hardly a pause.

The children of the tribe were present, eyes gleaming in the smouldering light, as they sipped rathel from their parents' wooden mugs. The
tale they heard was called familiarly the Great Tale. At any festival, not
merely at a burial or a coming of age, or at the festival of the Double
Sunset, someone would be sure to cry, as darkness came slanting in,
"Let's have the Great Tale!"

It was a history of their past, and much more than that. It was all
the art the tribe had. Music they lacked, and painting, and literature,

and almost anything fine. What had existed, the cold had devoured. But there remained the past that was a dream; that survived to be told.

No one was more responsive to this tale than Laintal Ay, when he could manage to stay awake for it. One of its themes was the union of two conflicting sides; that he understood, for the division concealed by that union, in which the tribe had to believe as an article of faith, was— had been—a part of his family life. Only later, as he grew up, did he discover how there was never union in anything, only stifled dissent. But the narrators in the fuggy hall, in this Year Nineteen After Union, gleefully conspired to tell the Great Tale as one of unity and success. That was their art.

The narrators jumped up one by one, declaiming their piece with varied assurance. The first narrators spoke of Great Yuli, and of how he came from the white wildernesses north of Pannoval to the frozen lake called Dorzin. But one generation gives place to another, even in legend, and soon another narrator rose, to speak of those, scarcely less mighty, who followed Yuli. This narrator was Rol Sakil, the midwife, who had her man and her pretty daughter, Dol, by her side; she gave a certain emphasis to the spicier aspects of her share of the tale, which was much relished by her audience.

While Laintal Ay dozed in the warmth, Rol Sakil told of Si, son of Yuli and Iskador. Si became the chief hunter of the tribe, and all feared him, because his eyes looked in different directions. He took a locally born woman called Cretha or, according to the style of her tribe, Cre Tha Den, who bore Si a son named Orfik and a daughter named Iyfilka. Both Orfik and Iyfilka were valiant and strong, in days when it was unusual for two children to survive in one family. Iyfilka went with Sargotth, or Sar Gotth Den, who excelled in catching myllk, the two-armed fish beneath the ice of Lake Dorzin. Iyfilka could crack the ice with her singing. Iyfilka bore a son to Sar Gotth whom they called Dresyl Den—a famous name in the legend. Dresyl fathered the famous brothers, Nahkri and Klils. (Laughter.) Dresyl was Laintal Ay's great-uncle.

"Oh, I adore you, my baby!" Iyfilka cried to her child, fondling him and smiling. But this was at a time when tribes of phagors were travelling in kaidaw-drawn sleighs over the ice, striking at human habitation. Both the pleasant Iyfilka and Sar Gotth were killed in a raid, running away by the bleak lake's shore. Some afterwards blamed Sar Gotth for being a coward, or for not being vigilant enough.

The young orphan, Dresyl, was taken to live with his uncle, Orfik, who by now had a son of his own called Yuli, or Little Yuli, after his great-grandfather. Although he grew enormous, he was known as Little in memory of his ancestor's greatness. Dresyl and Little Yuli became inseparable friends, and so remained through life, despite the trials that were to come. Both in their youth were great fighters, and lusty men who seduced the Den women, causing much trouble by their enjoyments. Some tales could be told on that score, were not certain folk present. (Laughter.)

One and all said that Dresyl and Yuli, the cousin-brothers, looked alike, with their powerful dark faces, hawk noses, small curling beards, and bright eyes. Both stood alertly and were of good build. Both wore similar furs with trimmed hoods. Their enemies prophesied they would meet with the same fate, but it was to prove otherwise, as the legend will relate.

Certainly, the old men and women whose daughters were in jeopardy prophesied that this pestilential pair would come to a bad end—and the sooner the better. Only those daughters themselves, lying with their legs open in the dark, and their lovers mounted on them, knew how beneficial the cousin-brothers were, and how different, one from the other; they knew that in their inward natures Dresyl was fierce and Yuli gentle, gentle as a feather and as ticklish.

At this point in the story, Laintal Ay roused. He wondered sleepily how it could ever have been that his ancient grandfather, so bent, so slow, had ever managed to tickle girls.

One of the corpsmen continued the story.

The elders and the old shaman of the lakeside tribe met together to decide how Dresyl and Yuli should be punished for their lechery. Some spat anger when they spoke, because in their hearts they were jealous. Others spoke piously since, being old, they could follow no course but virtue. (The storyteller laid this simple wisdom on thick, and assumed a piping voice, to make his audience laugh.)

Condemnation was unanimous. Although their numbers were depleted by disease and the phagor raids, and every hunter was needed, the elders decided that Little Yuli and Dresyl should be expelled from the settlement. Of course, no woman was allowed to speak in the friends' favour.

The message was conveyed. Yuli and Dresyl saw nothing for it but to leave. As they were gathering up their weapons and kit, a trapper arrived at the camp, half dead, from another tribe on the eastern fringes of the lake. He brought word that phagors were again approaching, this time in some force across the lake. They were killing any humans they came across. This was at the time of a double sunset.

Terrified, the men of the settlement promptly gathered up their women and possessions and set fire to their homes. They began at once to move southwards, Little Yuli and Dresyl among them. At their retreating backs, fire flew in robes of red and black into the sky, until eventually the lake was lost from view. They followed the Voral River, travelling day and night, for Freyr shone at night during this period. The ablest hunters travelled ahead and to either side of the main body, seeking food and safety. In the emergency, Yuli and Dresyl were provisionally forgiven their sins.

The party consisted of thirty men, including the five elders, twenty-six women, and ten children under seven, the age of puberty. They had with them their sleighs, pulled by asokins and dogs. Following were numerous birds and a variety of hounds, some little more than wolves or jackals, or crosses between the two; these last were often the playthings of the children, given to them as puppies.

Several days of travel followed. The weather was clement, although game was scarce. One Freyr-dawn, two of the hunters, Baruin and Skelit, who had been acting as scouts, returned to the main body and reported a strange town ahead.

"Where the river meets a frozen stream, water bursts into the air with great noise. And mighty towers built of stone stand up into the sky." Such was Baruin's report, and the first description of Embruddock.

He described how our stone towers stand in rows, and are decorated with brightly painted skulls, to ward off intruders.

They stood in a shallow valley full of gravel, discussing what should be done. Two more hunters arrived, dragging a trapper they had caught returning to Embruddock. They threw him to the ground and kicked him. He said that the Den tribe lived in Embruddock, and were peaceful.

Hearing there were more Dens about, the five elders immediately said that they should make a detour round the hamlet. They were shouted down. The younger men said that they should attack immediately; they could then be accepted on a basis of equality by this distantly related tribe. The women vociferously agreed, thinking it would be pleasant to live in stone buildings.

Excitement rose. The trapper was clubbed to death. All—men, women, and children—dipped their fingers in his blood and drank, that they might prevail before the day was done.

The body was thrown to the dogs and birds.

"Dresyl and I will go forward and take in the lie of the land," Little Yuli said. He stared challengingly at the men about him; they dropped their gaze and said nothing. "We will win the day for you. If we do so, then we shall be in command, and will tolerate no more nonsense from these old men. If we lose the day, then you can throw our bodies to the animals."

"And," said the next speaker to take up the story, "at Little Yuli's brave speech, the canine company looked up from their feast and yelped their agreement." The audience smiled seriously, recalling that detail from the past that was like a dream.

Now the story of that past became more tense. The audience drank less rathel as it listened to how Dresyl and Little Yuli, the cousin-brothers, planned to take the silent town. With them went five chosen heroes, their names well-remembered: Baruin, Skelit, Maldik, Curwayn, and Big Afardl, who was killed that day, and by a woman's hand.

The rest of the party remained where they were, so that the noise of their hounds did not give the game away.

Beyond the icy river was no snow. Grass grew. Hot water gushed into the air, sending curtains of steam across the area.

"It's true," murmured the audience. "It still occurs as you say."

A woman drove black hairy pigs up a path. Two children played naked among the waters. The invaders watched.

They saw our stone towers, the strong ones, the ruinous ones, all laid out in streets. And the old city wall reduced to rubble. They marvelled.

Dresyl and Yuli skirted Embruddock alone. They saw how square our towers are, with walls sloping inwards all the way up, so that the room on the top floor is always smaller than those below. How we keep our animals in the bottom floor for warmth—up the ramp to save them in case the Voral floods. They saw all the animal skulls, brightly painted and facing out, to scare intruders. We always had a sorceress, didn't we, friends? At this period, it was Loil Bry.

Well, the cousin-brothers also saw two aged sentries up on top of the big tower—this very tower, friends—and in no time they had nipped in and despatched the greybeards. Blood flowed, I have to tell.

"The flower," someone called.

Oh, yes. The flower was important. Remember how the lake people said that the cousin-brothers would meet with the same destiny? Yet when Dresyl grinned and said, "We will do well ruling this town, brother," Yuli was looking at the little flowers at his feet, flowers with pale petals—probably scantiom.

"A good climate," he said, in surprise, and plucked the flower and ate it.

They were scared when they first heard the Hour-Whistler blow, for that famous geyser, known to all, was not known to them. They recovered, and then disposed their forces so as to be prepared for the time when both sentinels were set and the hunters of Embruddock returned home, bearing with them the spoils of the chase, all unsuspecting.

Laintal Ay roused at this point. There were battles in the past that was like a dream, and one was about to be described. But the new story-teller said, "Friends, we all had ancestors in the battle that followed, and all have gone since to the world of gossies, even if they were not despatched prematurely on that occasion. Suffice it to say that all present acquitted themselves valiantly."

But he, being youthful, could not dismiss the exciting part so lightly and continued despite himself, eyes glowing.

Those innocent and heroic hunters were surprised by Yuli's stratagem. Fire suddenly bloomed from the top of the herb tower, and tall flowers of flame rose into the evening air. The hunters naturally shouted out with alarm, dropped their weapons, and ran forward to see what could be done.

Spears and stones rained down on them from the top of the neighbouring tower. Armed invaders appeared from concealment, shouting and thrusting their spears at unguarded bodies. Our hunters slipped and fell in their own blood, but some invaders they managed to slay.

Our town contained more armed men than the cousin-brothers calculated for. Those were the brave corpsmen. They appeared from everywhere. But the invaders were desperate and hid in houses they had taken over. Young boys also were forced to fight, including some of you here, now past your prime.

The fire spread. Sparks streamed overhead like husks at a winnowing, as if they would light the sky. Carnage grew in the streets and ditches. Our women took up swords from the dead to fight off the living.

All acquitted themselves valiantly. But boldness and desperation won the day—not to mention the leadership of him who this day went down to the world of the gossies to be with his ancestors. Eventually, the defenders threw down their weapons and rushed away in the gathering dark, screaming.

Dresyl's blood was up. An avenging fury rose on his brow. He had seen Big Afardl slain beside him—and from behind—and by a woman at that.

"That was my good old grandmother!" cried Aoz Roon, and laughter and cheers rose on all sides. "There was always courage in our family. We are of Embruddock stock, and not of Oldorando."

Dresyl could scarcely be recognized for his fury. His face turned black. He ordered his company to hunt down and kill every surviving man of Embruddock. The women were to be gathered into the stable of this very tower, friends. What a terrible day that was in our annals. . . .

But the victorious men, led by Yuli, took Dresyl forcibly and said to him that there must be no more killing. Killing brought bitterness. From the morrow, all must live in peace, to make a strong tribe, or there were not enough souls to survive.

These wise words meant nothing to Dresyl. He struggled until Baruin brought a bucket of cold water and flung it over him. Then he fell down as if in a swoon, and slept that dreamless sleep which comes only after battle.

Baruin said to Yuli, "You sleep too, with Dresyl and the others. I will keep watch, in case we are surprised by a counterattack."

But Little Yuli was unable to sleep. He said nothing to Baruin, but he had been wounded, and his head was light. He felt himself near to death, and staggered outside to die under Wutra's sky, into which Freyr was already preparing to ascend, for it was the third quarter. He walked down the main street here, where grass grew coarse among streams of mud. Freyr-dawn was the colour of mud, and he saw a scavenging hound slink away, full-bellied, from the corpse of one of his fellow hunters. He leaned against a crumbling wall, breathing deep.

Opposite him was the temple—ruined then as now. He stared without understanding at the decorations engraved in the stone. Remember, in those days, before Loil Bry civilized him, Yuli was by way of being a barbarian. Rats snicked in at the doorway. He moved to the temple hearing only a rushing in his ears. In his hand he held a sword taken from a fallen adversary—a better weapon than any he possessed, made of good dark metal here in our forges. This he held before him as he kicked in the door.

Inside, tethered milch sows and goats scuffled. Field implements used to be stored there in those days. Looking about, Yuli saw a trap-door in the floor, and heard voices whispering.

Taking hold of the iron ring, he heaved up the door. Down in the pool of darkness under his feet, a smoking lamp burned.

"Who's there?" someone called. A man's voice, and I expect you know whose it was.

It was Wall Ein Den, then Lord of Embruddock, and well-remembered by us all. You can picture him, tall and upright, though his youth had fled, with a long black moustache and no beard. All remarked on his eyes, which could outstare the boldest, and his haggardly handsome face, which in its time moved women to tears. This was the historic meeting between him, the old lord, and Little Yuli.

Little Yuli went slowly down the steps to him, almost as if recognising him. Some of the masters of corps were there with Lord Wall Ein, but they did not dare speak as Yuli came down, very pale, clasping his sword.

Lord Wall Ein said, "If you are a savage, then murder is your business, and you had best get it over with. I command you to kill me first."

"What else do you deserve, hiding in a cellar?"

"We are old, and powerless in battle. Once it was otherwise."

They confronted each other. Nobody moved.

With a great effort, Yuli spoke, and his voice seemed to him to come from far away. "Old man, why do you leave this great town so poorly guarded?"

Lord Wall Ein replied with his usual authority. "It was not always thus, or you and your men would have met a different reception, you with your poor weapons. Many centuries ago, the Land of Embruddock was great, stretching north to the Quzints and south almost as far as the sea. Then Great King Denniss ruled, but the cold came and destroyed what he had wrought. Now we are fewer than ever we were, for only last year, in the first quarter, we were raided by the white phagors riding like the wind on their giant mounts. Many of our best warriors, including my son, were killed defending Embruddock, and now sink towards the original boulder."

He sighed, and added, "Perhaps you read the legend carved on this building, if you can read. It says, 'First phagors, then men.' It was for that legend and other matters that our priesthood was slain, two generations ago. Men must be first, always. Yet some days I wonder if the prophecy will not come true."

Little Yuli heard the lord's words as if in a trance. When he attempted to reply, no words rose to his bloodless lips, and he felt the power drain from his inner eddre.

One of the old men, between pitying and sniggering, said, "The youth has a wound."

As Yuli staggered forward, they backed away. Behind them was a low archway with a passage beyond, dimly lit from an overhead grating. Unable to stop now that he had started, he marched down the passage, dragging his feet. You know that feeling, friends, whenever you are drunk—as now.

It was damp in the passage, and warm. He felt the heat on his cheek. To one side was a stone stairway. He could not understand where he was, and his senses were failing.

And a young woman appeared on the stair, holding a taper before her. She was fairer than the skies. Her face swam before his vision.

"It was my grandmother!" cried Laintal Ay, shrill with pride. He had been listening excitedly, and was confused when everyone laughed.

At that time, the lady had no thought of bestowing any little Laintal Ays upon the world. She stared at Little Yuli with wild eyes, and said something to him which he could not understand.

He attempted a reply. The words would not come to his throat. His knees buckled. He sank down to the floor. Then he collapsed entirely, and all there believed him to be dead.

At this thrilling juncture, the storyteller made way for an older speaker, a hunter, who took matters less dramatically.

Wutra saw fit to spare Yuli's life on that occasion. Dresyl took command of the situation while his cousin-brother lay recovering from his wound. I believe that Dresyl was ashamed of his bloodlust and now took care to behave in a more civilized way, finding himself among civilized people like us. He may also have remembered the kindness of his father, Sar Gotth, and the sweetness of his mother, Iyfilka, killed by the hated phagor herd. He took over Prast's Tower, where we used to store salt, living at the top of it and issuing orders like a true commander, while Yuli lay in bed in a low room beneath.

Many at the time, myself included, disliked Dresyl, and treated him as a mere invader. We hated being ordered about. Yet when we understood what he intended, we cooperated, and appreciated his undoubted good points. We of Embruddock were demoralised at that time. Dresyl gave us our fighting spirit back, and built up the defences.

"He was a great man, my father, and I'll fight anyone who criticises him," shouted Nahkri, jumping up and shaking his fist. He shook it so energetically that he almost fell over backwards, and his brother had to prop him up.

None speaks against Dresyl. From the top of his tower, he could survey our surrounding country, the higher ground to the north, where he had come from, the lower to the south, and the geysers and hot springs, then strange to him. In particular, he was struck by the Hour-

Whistler, our magnificent regular geyser, bursting up and whistling like a devil wind.

I recall he asked me about the giant cylinders, as he called them, spread all over the landscape. He had never seen rajabarals before. To him they looked like the towers of a magician, flat on top, made of strange wood. Though not a fool, he did not know them for trees.

He was mainly for doing, not looking. He ordered where all his tribe from the frozen lake would be quartered, distributed in different towers. There he showed a wisdom we might all follow, Nahkri. Although many grumbled at the time, Dresyl saw to it that his people lived in with ours. No fighting was allowed, and everything fairly shared. That rule as much as anything has caused us to intermingle happily.

While he was billetting families, he had everyone counted. He could not write, but our corpsmen kept a tally for him. The old tribe here numbered forty-one men, forty-five women, and eleven children under the age of seven. That made ninety-seven folk in all. Sixty-one folk from the frozen lake had survived the battle, which made one hundred and fifty-eight people all told. A goodly number. As a boy, I was glad to have some life round the place again. After the deaths, I mean.

I said to Dresyl, "You'll enjoy being in Embruddock."

"It's called Oldorando now, boy," he said. I can still remember how he looked at me.

"Let's hear more about Yuli," someone called out, risking the wrath of Nahkri and Klils. The hunter sat down, puffing, and a younger man took his place.

Little Yuli made a slow recovery from his wound. He became able to walk out a short way with his cousin-brother and survey the territory in which they found themselves, to see how it could best be hunted and defended.

In the evenings, they talked with the old lord. He tried to teach them both the history of our land, but they were not always interested. He talked of centuries of history, before the cold descended. He told how the towers had once on a time been built of baked clay and wood, which the primitive peoples had developed in a time of heat. Then stone had been substituted for clay, but the same trusted pattern observed. And the stone withstood many centuries. There were some passages underground, and had been many more, in better times.

He told them the sorrow of Embruddock, that we are now merely a hamlet. Once a noble city stood here, and its inhabitants ruled for thousands of miles. There were no phagors to be feared in those days, men say.

And Yuli and his cousin-brother Dresyl would stride about the old lord's room, listening, frowning, arguing, yet generally respectful. They asked about the geysers, whose hot springs supply warmth to us. Our old lord told them all about the Hour-Whistler, our unfailing symbol of hope.

He told how the Hour-Whistler has blown punctually every hour ever since time began. It's our clock, isn't it? We don't need sentinels in the sky.

The Hour-Whistler helps the authorities keep written records, as the masters of corps are duty-bound to do. The cousin-brothers were astonished to find how we divide the hour into forty minutes and the minute into one hundred seconds, just as the day contains twenty-five hours and the year four hundred and eighty days. We learn such things on our mothers' laps. They also had to learn that it was Year 18 by the Lordly calendar; eighteen years had our old lord ruled. No such civilized arrangements existed by the frozen lake.

Mind, I say no word against the cousin-brothers. Barbarians though they were, they both soon mastered our system of makers corps, with the seven corps, each with different arts—the metal makers being the best, to which I'm proud to say, without boasting, I belong. The masters of each corps sat on the lord's council then, as they do now. Though, in my opinion, there should be two representatives from the metal-makers corps, because we are the most important, make no mistake.

Following a lot of jeering and laughter, the rathel was passed round again, and a woman in late middle age continued the legend.

Now I'll spin you a tale a lot more interesting than writing or time-keeping. You'll be asking what befell Little Yuli when he got better of his wound. Well, I'll tell you in a dozen words. He fell in love—and that proved worse than his wound, because the poor fellow never recovered from it.

Our old Lord Wall Ein wisely kept his daughter—poor pampered Loil Bry Den, who was in such a pother today—out of harm's way. He waited until he was sure that the invaders weren't a bad lot. Loil Bry was then very lovely, and with a well-developed figure, enough for a man to get hold of, and she had a queenly way of walking, which you will all remember. So our old lord introduced her to Little Yuli one day, up in his room.

Yuli had already seen her once. On that terrible night of the battle when, as we've heard, he nearly died of his wound. Yes, this was the black-eyed beauty with the ivory cheekbones and lips like a bird's wing, whom our friend mentioned. She was the beauty of her day, for the women from Lake Dorzin were a plain lot, to my mind. All her features were precisely drawn on the velvet of her skin, and those lips, so trimly curving, were painted in delicate cinnamon. To speak truth, I looked a bit like that myself when I was a young girl.

Such was Loil Bry when Yuli first saw her. She was the greatest wonder of the town. A difficult, solitary girl—people didn't care for her, but I liked her manner. Yuli was overwhelmed. He forever sought occasions when he could be alone with her—either outside or, better still, cloistered up close with her in her room in Big Tower where she still lives to this day, with that porcelain window. It was as if she gave him a fever. He could not control himself in her presence. He used to swagger about and boast and swear in front of her and make a real fool of himself. Many men get like that, but of course it doesn't last.

As for Loil Bry, she sat there like a little puppy, watching, smiling behind her high cheekbones, her hands folded in her lap. Of course, she encouraged him, needless to say. She wore a long heavy gown, decorated with beads, not furs like the rest of us. I heard that she wore furs underneath. But that gown was extraordinary, and reached almost to the ground. I'd like a gown like that. . . .

The way she speaks, it still is a bit of a mixture of poetry and riddles. Yuli'd never heard anything like it up on Lake Dorzin. It flummoxed him. He boasted all the more. He was bragging about what a hunter he was when she said—you know her musical voice—"We live out our lives in all kinds of darkness. Should we ignore them or explore them?"

He just goggled at her, sitting there looking lovely in her cloth garment. It had beads stitched on it, as I said, lovely beads. He asked if it was dark in her room. She laughed at him.

"Where do you think is the darkest place in the universe, Yuli?"

Poor fool, he said, "I've heard that far Pannoval is dark. Our great ancestor, whose name I bear, came from Pannoval, and he said it was dark there. He said it was under a mountain, but I don't believe that. It was just a way of speaking in those times."

Loil Bry regarded her fingertips, resting like little pink beads on the lap of that lovely garment.

"I think the darkest place in the universe is inside human skulls."

He was lost. She made a proper fool of him. Still, I must watch my tongue about the dead, mustn't I? He was a bit soft, though. . . .

She used to bemuse him with romantic talk. You know what she used to say? "Have you ever thought how we know so much more than we can ever tell?" It's true, isn't it? "I long to have someone," she'd say, "someone to whom I could tell everything, someone for whom talk is like a sea on which to float. Then I'd hoist my dark sail. . . ." I don't know what she said to him.

And Yuli would lie awake, clutching his wound and who knows what else, thinking of this magical woman, thinking of her beauty, and her troubling words. ". . . Someone for whom talk is a sea on which to float . . ." Even the way she turned her sentence seemed to him to be Loil Bry's way and no one else's. He'd long to be on that sea, sailing with her, wherever it was.

"That's enough of your womanly nonsense," cried Klils, struggling to his feet. "She put a spell about him, Father said so. Father also told us of the good things Uncle Yuli did at first, before she made him stupid." He went on to tell them.

Little Yuli got to know every inch of Oldorando while he was recovering. He saw how it is laid out, with the big tower at one end of the main street and the old temple at the other. In between, the women's house, the hunter's homes on one side, the towers of the makers corps on the other. The ruins farther out. How all our towers have the heating system of stone pipes carrying hot water from springs through them. We couldn't build anything half so marvellous today.

When he saw how the place was, he saw how it should be. With the aid of my father, Yuli planned proper fortifications, so that there would be no more attacks—especially no more phagor attacks. You've heard how everyone was set to digging a mound with a ditch on its outer side and a stout palisade on top. It was a good idea, though it cost a few blisters. Regular lookouts were drilled and posted at the four corners, as they still are. That was Yuli's and my father's doing. The lookouts were given horns to blow in case of a raid—the self-same horns we use today.

There were proper hunts as well as proper lookouts. People were almost starved before the merging of the tribes. Once the entire town was enclosed, Dresyl, my father, got the hunters breeding a proper hunting dog. Other scavengers could be kept out. Packs of hunting dogs could bring down game and run faster than we could. That was not much of a success, but we might try again some time.

What else? The guilds were able to make up their numbers. The colour-makers corps enlisted some children among the newcomers. New mugs and platters were made for everyone from a vein of clay they know about. More swords were hammered out. Everyone had to work for the common good. No one went hungry. My father nearly worked himself to death. You drunken lot ought to remember Dresyl while you're remembering his brother. He was a lot better than that one. He was, he was.

Poor Klils broke into tears. Others also began to cry, or laugh, or fight. Aoz Roon, himself staggering slightly under the weight of rathel he had drunk, grabbed up Laintal Ay and Oyre, and hustled them off to bed and safety.

He looked blurrily down at their passive faces, trying to think. Somewhere in the course of the telling of the legend of the past that was like a dream, the future of the lordship of Oldorando had been decided.

III

A LEAP FROM THE TOWER

On the day after Little Yuli's burial and the celebrations marking that occasion, everyone had to go back to work as usual. Past glories and discomforts were forgotten for the time being, except perhaps by Laintal Ay and Loilanun; they were continually reminded of the past by Loil Bry, who, when she was not weeping, liked to recall the happier days of her youth.

Her chamber was still hung with tapestries of ancient lineage, now as then. Ducts of hot water still gurgled under the floors. The porcelain window still gleamed. This was still a place of oils, powders, and perfumes. But there was no Yuli now, and Loil Bry herself had decayed into old age. Moths had got the tapestries. Her grandson was growing up.

But before Laintal Ay's time—in the days when the mutual love of his grandparents flowered—a trivial-seeming incident occurred which in its repercussions was to set a disastrous mark on Laintal Ay and on Embruddock itself: a phagor died.

When he had recovered from his wound, Little Yuli took Loil Bry as his woman. A ceremonial was held to mark the great change that had come to Embruddock, for in this union the two tribes were symbolically united. It was agreed that the old lord, Wall Ein, and Yuli and Dresyl should rule Oldorando as a triumvirate. And the arrangement worked well, because everyone had to strive hard together to survive.

Dresyl worked without cease. He took for his woman a thin girl whose father was a sword maker; she had a singing voice and a lazy glance. Her name was Dly Hoin Den. The storytellers never said that Dresyl soon grew disappointed with her; nor did they say that part of her initial attraction for Dresyl was that she represented a pretty but anonymous member of the new tribe into which he wished to integrate. For, unlike his cousin-brother, Yuli, he saw team spirit as the clue to survival. His work was never for himself; nor, in a sense, was Dly Hoin.

Dly Hoin bore Dresyl two boys, Nahkri and, a year later, Klils. Although he could spare little time apart with them, Dresyl doted on his sons, lavishing on them a sentimental love denied him by the deaths of his parents, Iyfilka and Sar Gotth. He instilled in the boys and their friends many legends concerning their great-great-grandfather, Yuli, the priest from Pannoval who had defeated gods whose names were now forgotten. Dly Hoin taught them the rudiments of annotation but nothing more. Under their father's care, both boys became adequate hunters. Their house was always full of noise and alarms. Fortunately, a clownish element in their characters—in Nahkri's, in particular—was never perceived by their fond father.

As if to defeat the predictions of those who had claimed that the cousin-brothers would meet one and the same fate, Little Yuli became self-absorbed to almost the extent that Dresyl absorbed himself in the community.

Under the influence of Loil Bry, Yuli grew soft, and hunted less and less. He sensed the hostility of the community towards Loil Bry, with her exotic ideas, and withdrew himself from it. He sat in the big tower and let the storm winds blow outside. His woman and her ancient father taught him much that was mysterious, both about the world that was past and the world below.

So it came about that Little Yuli embarked upon that sea of talk on which Loil Bry's dark sail flew free, and lost all sight of land.

Speaking of the world below, one day in the second quarter of the year, Loil Bry said to Little Yuli, gazing at him with her lustrous eyes, "My splendid one, you commune in your head with the memory of your parents. You see them sometimes as if they still walked the earth. Your imagination has the power to conjure up the forgotten sunlight in which they walked. Yet here in this empire of ours we have a method of communing direct with those who have gone before. They still live, sinking down in the world below towards the original boulder, and we can reach them, as a fish dives to feed on the riverbed."

He murmured in exchange, "I would like to talk to my father, Orfik, now that I am old enough to have sense. I would tell him of you."

"We also set store by our wonderful parents, and their parents, who had the strength of giants. You observe the stone towers in which we live. We cannot build them, yet our parents did. You see how scalding earthwater has been trapped in pipes to heat our towers. We cannot manage that art, yet our parents did. They are gone from our sight, yet they still exist as gossies and fessups."

"Teach me these things, Loil Bry."

"Because you are my lover, and my pulses rise up when I behold your flesh, I will teach you to speak direct to your father and, through him, to all your tribe who ever lived."

"Is it possible that I could speak even to my great-grandfather, Yuli of Pannoval?"

"In our children our two tribes will merge, my lover, as they do in those infants of Dresyl's. You shall learn to speak with Yuli, and mingle his wisdom with ours. You are a great person, my lover, and not a mere tribesman, like the poor fools outside; you shall be greater by speaking direct with the first Yuli."

Much though Loil Bry cared for Little Yuli, because she needed someone on whom to build a great love, she foresaw that he would fall further into her power if she taught him esoteric arts; with his protection she could remain in sumptuous idleness, as she had done before the invasion.

Much though Little Yuli loved this indolent, intelligent woman, he perceived that she might bind him to her by such devices, and resolved to learn from her all he could and not be deceived. Something in their temperaments or their situation rendered him deceived nonetheless.

Loil Bry gathered to her an old learned woman and an old learned man. With their aid, she taught Yuli the discipline of father-communing. Yuli gave up the hunt entirely in order to contemplate; Baruin and others provided their food. He began to practice pauk; in that trance state, he hoped to meet with the gossie of his father, Orfik, and commune through the gossie with fessups, the ancestral gossies sinking down through the lower world towards the original boulder, from which the world began.

At this time, Yuli rarely went out. Such unmanly behaviour was a mystery in Oldorando.

Loil Bry had roved greatly in the countryside about Embruddock when a girl, as her grandson, Laintal Ay, would come to do. She wished Yuli to see for himself how stones marking land-octaves trailed all round the continent.

Accordingly, she engaged a grey, hawkish man, by name Asurr Tal

Den. Asurr Tal was the grandfather of Shay Tal, later to play a great part in affairs. Loil Bry commanded Asurr Tal to take Yuli into the lands to the northeast of Oldorando. There she had once stood, watching day turn to dimday and dimday to brief night, and felt the pulse of the world flow through her.

So Asurr Tal took Yuli on foot in a clement season. It was early winter, when Batalix rose well to the south of east, shining there alone for less than an hour—the interval diminishing day by day—before the second sentinel also rose. A wind blew, but the sky was as clear as brass. Although Asurr Tal was withdrawn and rather bent, he managed the distance better than Yuli, who was out of training. He made Yuli ignore the distant wolves and study all he saw in terms of esoteric art. Asurr Tal showed him stone posts, such as there had been by Lake Dorzin. The posts were set solitary in wild places, each marked with a symbol of a wheel with a ring at its centre, and two lines connecting ring with wheel. He expounded their meaning in a singsong voice.

He said that the posts bore a symbol in which power radiated from a centre towards a circumference, as power radiated from ancestors to descendants, or from fessups via gossies to the living. The pillars marked land-octaves. Every man or woman born was born on one octave or another. The power in land-octaves varied with the season, determining whether infants were born male or female. The land-octaves flowed everywhere until they reached the distant seas. People lived most happily when they conformed to their own land-octaves.

Only when they were buried on their correct land-octaves could they, as gossies, hope to communicate with their living children. And their children, when their time came to make the journey to the world below, should also lie along the correct land-octave.

With his hand held like a chopper, old Asurr Tal chopped at the hills and valleys about them.

"Remember that simple regulation, and father-communing can be established. The word grows fainter, like an echo along mountain valleys, from one vanished generation to the next, throughout the kingdoms of the dead, who outnumber the living as lice outnumber men."

As Little Yuli regarded the barren mountainside, a strong revulsion rose in him against this teaching. Not long since, his interest had been only with the living, and he had felt himself free.

"This business of talking to the dead," he said heavily. "The living should have no traffic with the dead. Our place is here, travelling on this earth."

The old man snickered, caught Yuli's furred sleeve in a familiar way, and pointed downwards.

"You may think so, you may think so. Unfortunately, it is the rule of existence that our place is both here and down below, down in the grit. We must learn to use the gossies as we use animals for our benefit."

"The dead should keep in their place."

"Oh, well . . . as for that, you'll be dead one day, yourself. Besides, Mistress Loil Bry wishes you to learn these things, does she not?"

Yuli desired to shout, "I hate the dead and want nothing of them." But he bit off the words and stood silent. And so he was lost.

Although he learned how to perform the rituals of father-communicating, Little Yuli was never able to communicate with his father, much less with the first Yuli. The dead yielded no response. Loil Bry explained this by saying that his parents had been buried in an incorrect land-octave. Nobody fully understood the mysteries of the world below. In trying to understand more, he sank further under his woman's power.

All this time, Dresyl worked for the community, consulting with the old lord. He never lost his love for Yuli, even making his two sons study some of the lore that their strange aunt readily poured forth. But he never permitted them to stay long, lest they become bewitched.

Two years after Nahkri was born to Dresyl, Loil Bry presented Little Yuli with a daughter. They named her Loilanun. With the midwife's help, Loilanun was born in the tower under the porcelain window.

Loil Bry, assisted by Yuli, gave their daughter a special present. They gave her, and through her all Oldorando, a calendar.

Owing to the disruptions of the centuries, Embruddock had had more than one calendar. Of the three old calendars, the most generally known was the so-called Lordly. The Lordly simply counted years from the accession of the last lord. The other two were antiquated, and one, the Ancipital, regarded as sinister; it had been abandoned for that reason, and for that reason had never entirely died. The Denniss went in for large numbers, and was not perfectly understood since the priests had been expelled from the town.

Under these old calendars, the birth of Loilanun fell, respectively, in the years 21, 343, and 423. Now her birth date was declared to be the Year Three After Union. Henceforth, dates would be kept with reference to the number of years since Oldorando and Embruddock came together.

The population received this gift with the same stoicism they received the news that there was a band of ancipital marauders in the vicinity.

One Batalix-dawn, when the clouds were thick as phlegm and hoarfrost speckled the ancient breastworks of the hamlet, the horns of the lookout sounded from an eastern tower. Immediately, there was stir and shouting. Dresyl ordered all women to be locked in the women's tower, where many of them were already at work. He assembled his men, armed, at the barricades. His little sons came forth trembling to join him and stare towards the rising sun.

In the grey dawn distance, horns showed.

The phagors attacked in strength. Among their number were two who rode on kaidaws, their own particular animals—animals horned and mailed in fibrous red fur thick enough to withstand any cold.

As they were assailing the barricades, Dresyl had one of his men break down a small earth dam previously built to pen in the hot waters of a geyser. Phagors notoriously hate water. A scalding flood now burst upon them, swirling about their knees, causing awful confusion in their ranks. Some hunters leaped forward to press home their advantage.

One of the kaidaws went down in yellow mud, hoofs thrashing, and was killed by a well-flung spear to the heart. In panic, another of the great beasts made a standing jump, clearing the barricade. It was the legendary spring jump of the horned horse, which few humans ever witnessed. The animal came down among the warriors of Oldorando.

They clubbed the kaidaw to death and captured its rider. Many other brutes were maimed by stones. The attackers retreated at last, while only one defender had been killed. All were exhausted. Some flung themselves into hot springs to restore their energies.

This was a great victory for united action, declared Dresyl. He strode about in a kind of fury, brow dark with triumph, shouting to all that they were now one tribe, and had been blooded. Henceforth, all must work for all, and all would prosper. The women gathered round to listen, whispering while the men lay flat, recovering. It was the Year Six.

Kaidaw meat was good. Dresyl ordered a feast of celebration, to start when both sentinels had set. The kaidaw carcass was parboiled in the earthwaters, and then roasted over fires lit in the square. Barley wine and rathel were provided to celebrate the victory.

Dresyl made a speech, as did the old lord, Wall Ein. Songs were sung. The man who had charge of slaves brought forward the captured phagor.

Nobody present that evening in the Year Six had any reason for misgivings. Humans had again fought off their legendary foes and everyone intended to celebrate the occasion. The celebrations would include the putting to death of their captive.

The inhabitants of Oldorando had no way of knowing how special a personage their captive was among the ancipital race, or that his death would drift down the backwaters of the years until terrible retribution would be visited on them and their offspring.

Everyone fell silent as the monster stood among them, glaring at them with his large scarlet eyes. His arms were lashed behind his back with leather rope. His horned feet pawed restlessly at the ground. In the gathering dark, he seemed immense, the bogeyman of all their nocturnal dreams, a creature from uneasy dimday sleeps. He was clad in shaggy white fur, stained by mud and battle. He stood challengingly before his human captors, giving off a resonant smell, his boney head with its two long horns thrust forward between his shoulders. His thick white milt appeared foraging up the slits of his nostrils, first one, then the other.

This brute wore strange accoutrements. A broad stomacher fashioned from hide was strapped round his girth; spurs at ankle and wrist supported protruding spikes. The elegant razored horns were capped with metal. It fitted his gigantic skull like a harness, coming to a two-pronged point in the centre of the forehead between the eyes, curving behind the ears, and fastening elaborately under the jaw so as to encompass the long boney chops.

Baruin stepped forward and said, "See what our concerted action has achieved. We have captured a chief. By his headgear, this beast leads a component. Look at him well, you young men who have never before seen a fuggie close, for they are our traditional enemy, in darkness and light."

Many young hunters stepped forward and tugged the creature's matted hair. He stood unmoving and let forth a fart like a small thunderclap. They fell back, alarmed.

"Fuggies organise their herds into components," Dresyl explained. "Most can speak Olonets. They take humans as slaves, and are beastly enough to eat their captives. As a chief, this brute understands all we say. Don't you?" He clouted its rough shoulder. The monster stared coldly at him.

The old lord, standing beside Dresyl, spoke.

"The male phagors are called stalluns and the females gillots or fillocks, that I know. Males and females alike go on raids and fight together. They are creatures of ice and darkness. Your great ancestor Yuli warned against them. They are bringers of illness and death."

Then the phagor spoke, using the Olonets in a hoarse churring voice.

"You worthless Sons of Freyr will all blow away before the final storm! This world, this town, belong to us, the ancipitals."

The women in the crowd were frightened. They threw stones at the evil thing that spoke in their midst, and shouted, "Kill him, kill him!"

Dresyl raised an arm, pointing.

"Drag him up to the top of the herb tower, friends! Drag him to the top and throw him off."

"Yes, yes," they roared, and at once the bolder hunters ran forward, seized the great stubborn bulk and, by sheer force, thrust it towards the nearby building. Great cheering and commotion reigned, children ran screaming round their elders.

Among those urchins were the two sons of Dresyl, Nahkri and Klils, both scarcely out of toddling stage. Because they were so small, they were able to stagger through the legs of the milling adults, and so came up against the right leg of the phagor, rising like a shaggy column before their eyes.

"You touch it."

"No, you."

"You daren't, coward!"

"You're a coward too!"

Putting forth chubby fingers, they touched the leg together.

Heavy musculature moved below a rug of hair. The limb lifted, the three-toed foot stamped down in the mud.

Though these monstrous creatures could master the Olonets tongue, they were far from human. The thoughts in the harneys of their heads ran aslant. Old hunters knew that inside their barrel bodies they carried their intestines above their lungs. From their machinelike walk, it could be seen how their limbs were jointed in a different way from a man's; at what should have been elbow and knee, phagors could bend lower arms and legs in impossible attitudes. That distinction alone was enough to strike terror into small boys' hearts.

For a moment they were in contact with the unknown. Pulling back their hands as if they had been burnt—in truth, the ancipital body temperature was cooler than man's—the two urchins looked at each other with wild eyes.

Then they burst into howls of fear. Dly Hoin swept the boys into her arms. By then, Dresyl and others had shifted the monster on.

Although the great animal struggled in its bonds, it was hammered through the entrance and into the tower. The crowd, restless in the square, listened to the noise within, which worked its way up the building. A cheer rose in the thick air as the first hunter emerged on the roof. Behind everybody, the kaidaw carcass roasted, untended; its flavours mingled with wood smoke to fill the bowl of the square, full of upturned faces. A second cheer, louder than the first, arose when the phagor chief was dragged into view, black against the sky.

"Throw it down!" screamed the crowd, united in hate.

The monstrous chief fought with his jostling captors. He roared as they prodded him with daggers. Then, as if realising that the game was up, he jumped up onto the parapet and stood there, glaring down at the jostling mob below.

With a last burst of rage, he snapped his bonds. He jumped forward, arms outstretched, with a massive spring that carried him away from the tower. The crowd tried too late to scatter. The great body hurtled down, crushing three people beneath it, a man, a woman, a child. The child was killed outright. A groan of terror and dismay rose from the rest there assembled.

Even then, the great animal was not killed. He raised himself up on his shattered legs to confront the avenging blades of the hunters. Everyone pierced him through, through the thick coat, through the dense flesh. He struggled on until his curdled yellow blood streamed across the trampled ground.

While these terrible events took place, Little Yuli remained in his chamber with Loil Bry and their infant daughter. When he made to dress and join the fight, Loil Bry cried that she felt unwell and needed his company. She clung to him, kissing his lips with her pale mouth, and would not let him go.

After this, Dresyl felt contempt for his cousin-brother. But he did not go and kill him, as he had a mind to, although these were savage times. For he remembered a lesson and recognised that killing divided tribes. When his sons ruled, this was forgotten.

This forbearance of Dresyl's—based on a friendship begun in his boyhood, before Dresyl had a beard or grey in it—stood the community in good stead, and earned him new respect. And the things Little Yuli learned at the expense of his fighting spirit were fruitful in the days to come.

Immediately after the shock caused by the appearance of the phagor chief in its midst, the community underwent another ordeal. A mysterious illness, accompanied by fever, cramps, and body rash, seized half the population of Oldorando. The first to go down were the hunters who had pushed the phagor to the top of the herb tower. For some days, little hunting was done. The domesticated pigs and geese had to be eaten instead. A woman with child died of fever, and the whole hamlet sorrowed to lose two precious lives to the world below. Yuli and Loil Bry, together with their daughter, escaped the illness.

Soon the communal bloodstream was purged of its malady, and life went on as usual. But the news of the slaying of the phagor spread forth from the community.

And for a while the climate continued harsh towards mankind. The cold winds picked out the seams of any badly stitched garment.

The two sentinels of light, Freyr and Batalix, went about their duties as appointed, and the Hour-Whistler continued to blow.

For half of the year, the sentinels shone together in the skies. Then the hours of their setting slipped further apart, until gradually Freyr ruled the sky by day and Batalix the sky by night; then night scarcely seemed night, day scarcely light enough to be called day. Then the sentinels again became reconciled: days became bright with both lights, nights became pitch.

One quarter, when there were only shrill stars looking down on Oldorando, when cold and dark were intense, the old lord, Wall Ein

Den, died; he descended to the world below, to become himself a gossie and sink down to the original boulder.

Another year was finished, and another. A generation grew up, another grew old. Slowly numbers increased under Dresyl's peaceful rule, while the suns performed their sentry duties overhead.

Although Batalix showed the larger disc, Freyr always gave out more light and more warmth. Batalix was an old sentinel, Freyr young and lusty. From one generation to the next, no man could positively swear that Freyr grew towards manhood, but so said the legends. Humanity endured—suffering or rejoicing—from generation to generation, and lived in the hope that Wutra would be victorious in the world above, and ever sustain Freyr.

These legends carried reality within them, as a flower bulb carries the flower within its flesh. So humans knew without knowing they knew.

As for the animals and birds, still many in numbers though few in species, their senses were more closely bound by the magnetic fluctuations of the globe than were mankind's. They also knew without knowing they knew. Their comprehensions told them that ineluctable change was already at hand—was indeed rising under the earth, in the blood-stream, in the air, in the stratosphere, and in all that was in the biosphere.

Above the stratosphere rode a small self-contained world built from the elements of metals gathered in the rich fields among the stars. From the surface of Helliconia, this world appeared in the night sky as a star itself, travelling swiftly overhead.

It was the Earth Observation Station Avernus.

The binary system of Freyr and its companion, Batalix, was closely watched by the Avernus. In particular, the families on the station studied Helliconia, and had done so for more than one of its slow Great Years about Freyr—or Star A, as it was known on the station.

Helliconia was of unique interest of the people of Earth, and never more so than at this period. Helliconia revolved about Batalix—Star B, as it was known on the station. Both sun and planet were beginning to accelerate in their orbit. They were still almost six hundred times as distant from Freyr as Earth is from its primary. But the distance was diminishing, week by week.

The planet was now several centuries past apastron, the coldest part of its orbit. There was new purpose in the corridors of the Observation Station; everyone could read the message in the increasingly favourable temperature gradients.

IV

FAVOURABLE TEMPERATURE
GRADIENTS

Children follow their parents or they do not. Laintal Ay grew up knowing his mother as a quiet woman, given to the same kind of studious seclusion as her mother and father. But Loilanun had not always behaved like that, before life defeated her.

In adolescence, she rejected the gentle tutelage of Loil Bry and Little Yuli. She screamed at them that she hated the cloistered atmosphere of their room—which, as they grew older, they were increasingly reluctant to leave. After a violent quarrel, she left them, went to live in another tower with relations.

There was plenty of work. Loilanun became useful at grinding and tanning. While making a pair of hunting boots, she met their future wearer and fell in love with him. She was scarcely at the age of puberty. She ran out with the hunter on bright nights, when no one could sleep. There was the world in all its appalling beauty about her for the first time. She became his woman. She would have died for him.

Manners were changing in Oldorando. He took Loilanun out with him on a deer hunt. Once Dresyl would never have permitted women running with them; but his command had become less certain as he grew older. The deer hunters met with a stungebag in a narrow defile.

Before Loilanun's eyes, her man was run down and pierced through by one of the creature's horns. He died before he could be carried home.

Brokenhearted, Loilanun returned to her parents. They received her back, placidly absorbing her, comforting her. As she lay in the scented shadows, life stirred in her womb. She had conceived. She remembered the joy of that occasion when her time came and she gave birth to a son. She called him Laintal Ay, and him too her parents placidly accepted. It was spring of the Year After Union 13, or 31 by the old calendar of Lordly Years.

"He will grow into a better world," said Loil Bry to her daughter, regarding the baby with her lustrous eyes. "Histories tell that a time will come when the rajabarals will be thrown open, and the air will be heated with the heat of the earth. Food will be plentiful, snow will disappear, people will be naked to each other. How I longed for that time when I was young. Laintal Ay may see it. How I wish he had been a girl—girls feel and see more than boys."

The child liked to watch his grandmother's porcelain window. It was unique in Oldorando, though Little Yuli maintained that there had once been many more, all now broken. Year after year, Laintal Ay's grandparents had lifted their eyes from their ancient documents to watch the window turn pink, orange, and crimson with sunset, as Freyr or Batalix descended into a bath of fire. The colours would die. Night would stain the porcelain black.

In the old days, childrims had come, fluttering about the towers of Oldorando, those selfsame apparitions the first Yuli had seen when struggling across the white wilderness with his father.

Childrims came only at night. Sparks like feathers would flare behind the porcelain window, and the childrims would be there, slowly circling, a single wing flapping. Or was it a wing? When the people ran out to look at them, their outlines were confusing, never clear.

The childrims caused strange thoughts in human minds. Yuli and Loil Bry would lie upon their rugs and skins and feel that all the thoughts in their heads were coming alive at the same time. They saw scenes they had forgotten, and scenes they had never known. Loil Bry often cried and covered her eyes. She said it was like communing with a dozen fessups at once. Afterwards, she longed to experience some of the unexpected scenes once more, but once they had gone they could never more be recalled; their confusing beauty vanished like a fragrance.

The childrims sailed on. No man could fathom their going or their coming.

Their rightful habitat was the upper troposphere. Occasionally, electric pressures forced them to descend close to the surface of the planet. Neural currents in the brains of men and animals held a brief attraction for them, causing them to pause and circle as if they too were creatures of intelligence. Then they rose again and were gone. Depending on local whims of the great magnetic storm sweeping across the Helliconian system, the childrims might sail in any direction, onwards, upwards, swept along with the magnetic tides, circulating without perception or need of rest.

Yet not circulating for ever. Because the electric entities that human beings called childrims could not change. So nothing was more vulnerable to change than they.

Temperatures across the tropical continent of Campannlat varied greatly at any one time. On a mild day in the summer, while Loilanun sat playing listlessly with her young son, the ground temperature in Oldorando climbed several degrees above zero. Only a comparatively few miles north, by Lake Dorzin, there might be ten degrees of frost. In summer, when the sentinels worked day and night, there was no frost at all in sheltered parts, and cereal crops grew.

Three thousand miles from Oldorando, in the Nktryhk, daily temperatures showed wide variation, from minus twelve degrees centigrade to minus one hundred and fifty degrees, about the temperature at which krypton turns to liquid.

Change accumulated, at first as what may be termed latent change. Then its effects were rapid, as temperature gradients in the upper atmosphere responded to increased radiations from Freyr. The process was steady but quantal. On one occasion, Earth Observation Station Avernus recorded a twelve-degree rise in temperature at a 16.6-mile equatorial altitude within the course of an hour.

With this warming up, stratospheric circulation increased strongly, and the planet was swept by storms. Jet streams were observed over Nktryhk travelling at speeds in excess of two hundred seventy-five miles per hour.

Suddenly, the childrims were no more.

The beginnings of what was to spell a renascence for mankind and animals brought disaster for the childrims. The conditions that created them dispersed between one year and the next. Their vortices of piezoelectric dusts and charged particles were too fragile to survive a more dynamic system. They were gone, leaving behind them evanescent trails of sparks in the rarefied upper air. The sparks soon died.

Yuli and Loil Bry looked in vain for the childrims. Laintal Ay soon forgot he had ever seen them.

Groups of phagors were emerging under the greenish sky common at that altitude, where the sentinels—when not buried in cloud—directed their rays through multitudinous ice crystals. The phagors, stalluns and gillots alike, moved into position with their inhuman gait. Many had birds perched on their shoulders or flying just above them. The birds and the phagors were white, the terrain white or brown and exsiccated black, the sky beyond livid green. The living things were outlined against the Hhryggt Glacier.

The course of the glacier was divided at one point by a massif of plutonic rock which, like an infernal castle, had withstood centuries of siege. The ice had scoured its walls, yet it survived, rearing its bunched towers towards the sky. Where the ice river fell away was a firn-covered plateau. Here stood the ancipital leader, immobile, while the cohorts of his crusade assembled.

It was the components belonging to the kzahhns of Hrastyprt who first decided to bring destruction upon the Sons of Freyr who lived in the remote plains. The young kzahhn was Hrr-Brahl Yprt. He would lead the crusade. It was his grandstallun, the great Kzahhn Hrr-Tryhk Hrast, who had been destroyed by those distant Sons. Under Hrr-Brahl Yprt would the legions ride forth in revenge.

For under Hrr-Brahl Yprt the component had prospered, regaining strength lost since Freyr last burned the world. Force of numbers as much as conscious decision urged it from its altitudinous fastnesses to begin this migration of irresistible scale.

Vengeance moved in their harneys, but action was triggered by favourable temperature gradients in the stratosphere. A heat message thrilled along the five-hundred-mile length of the glacier, as it spilled down from the airless plateau of High Nktryhk to the excoriated valleys east of the Oldorandan plain, drawing out ancipitals from its eaves and crevices.

Hrr-Brahl Yprt waited, motionless. He too heard the heat message across his air-octave.

The precursor of major climatic change activated other forms of life in the region, forms on which the phagors were in part dependent for protein. Protognostic tribes called Madis also occupied the boulder-strewn land of the glaciers. Gaunt, perpetually undernourished, they too began to resume a nomadic habit. They drove before them goat and arang, the quadruped that lived on lichens or rocklice. The Madis sought lower pastures. But they would not travel before the phagor crusade left the way clear.

The young Hrr-Brahl Yprt growled an order to mount. Only the highest among his officers had kaidaws to ride. These rusty red steeds were mounted as soon as the order came, the officers seating themselves behind their animals' humps.

That order came late in the Year 13, according to Loil Bry's modest calendar. According to the ancipital calendar, it was the Air-Turn or Year 353 After Small Apotheosis of Great Year 5,634,000 Since Catastrophe. By a more modern reckoning, it was late in the year 433.

Laintal Ay was then an infant, dandled on the knee of his widowed mother.

The time would come when he would have to confront the whole might of Hrr-Brahl Yprt's crusade.

Beside the kzahhn's kaidaw stood a creaght, or young male phagor, bearing a towering standard.

Hrr-Brahl Yprt was as tall as a well-built man and weighed almost half as much again. His keratinous three-toed feet formed a base for thick flanks, massive thews, and a chest broader than any man's.

His head, wedged between sturdy shoulders, was remarkable. It was long, narrow, boney, with prominent ridges above the eyes, giving those eyes, sheltered by long sweeping lashes on which frost glittered, a marked stare. His horns, set back behind his ears, curved forward before turning upwards, in the manner of his line. They were veined grey, as if made of marble, and their edges were deadly sharp. These weapons were used only in combat with other phagors, never against other species; their tips could never be sullied by the red blood of a Son of Freyr.

Hrr-Brahl Yprt's prominent muzzle was black behind the arches of his nostrils, just as his grandstallun's had been. It accentuated the command of his gaze. An air of ferocious authority was reinforced by his every movement.

An elaborate face crown had been wrought by his weapon makers for this crusade. The crown formed almost a fleur-de-lys pattern down the young kzahhn's long nose. It curved about the base of his horns and sprouted two sharp iron horns of its own, which protruded laterally.

When threatening a subordinate, the kzahhn wrinkled up his lip to show two lines of blunt longitudinally ridged teeth, flanked by long incisors.

His body was accoutred with armour: chiefly, a sleeveless jacket of stiff kaidaw skin with three capes and a belt, which latter broadened over his girth into a sort of sporran serving to conceal his genitals swinging under the coarse matted hair of his pelvis.

The name of his kaidaw was Rukk-Ggrl. After mounting Rukk-Ggrl, the young kzahhn raised his hand. An immense curled musical instrument, reamed from a stungebag horn, was sounded by a human slave. Its diaphony echoed across the grey wastes.

Following this mournful call, other slaves appeared from a cave in the plutonian massif, carrying between them the figures of Hrr-Brahl Yprt's father and great-grandstallun.

These illustrious forebears were in a state of tether, slowly sinking towards the final vortices of nonbeing. This marked diminution of the life process had caused them to shrink in size. The great-grandstallun was now almost entirely transformed into keratin.

At the appearance of the totem objects, a stir went through the hosts of the component assembled, male and female. They stretched over the frozen ground, many standing out against the sky on nearby ridges or banks of shattered stone, where their outlines were confused by the brilliant cloud piling up. Some leaned on spears, their huge birds above them. All, when stationary, assumed the daunting immobility of their kind. Only an occasional flicking ear indicated that they were alive. They shifted their positions so as to direct their regard on their young leader and the leaders of the past.

The totem figures were presented to the kzahhn. The human slaves knelt in abasement before him.

Hrr-Brahl Yprt dismounted, to stand between his ancestors and his kaidaw. After making a bow, he humbly buried his face in the rufous hair of the flank of Rukk-Ggrl. His comprehension left his harneys. In a kind of trance, he summoned the spirits of his father and great-grandstallun back to the living present.

The spirits came before him. They were little whiskery figures, no higher than snow rabbits. They uttered squeaks of greeting. As they had never done in real life, they ran on all fours.

"O my sacred forebears, now integrating with earth," cried the young kzahhn, in the thick tongue of his kind, "at last I go to avenge him who should be standing now between you, my valorous grand-stallun, Great Kzahhn Hrr-Tryhk Hrast, who was killed by the peltless Sons of Freyr. Years of trial lie ahead. Strengthen my arm, warn us of danger, hold horns high."

His great-grandstallun appeared to be standing deep inside Rukk-Ggrl. The keratinous image said, "Go, hold horns high, remember enmities. Beware friendship with the Sons of Freyr."

This remark was useless to Hrr-Brahl Yprt. He scarcely thought himself likely to feel other than hatred for the traditional enemy. Those in tether were not always wiser than those in air.

The keratinous image of his father was larger than that of the great-grandstallun since he had entered tether more recently. The image bowed to his son and spoke, sketching a series of pictures in his son's harneys.

Hrr-Anggl Hhrot showed his son an image which the young kzahhn understood only in part. To a human, it would have been incomprehensible. Yet it was a view of the known universe, as pictured by the ancipital race, a view that largely conditioned their approach to life.

A busy organ pumped lustily, expanding and contracting. It consisted of three parts, each somewhat resembling a human fist clenched tight. The parts were interdependent, and of different colours. The grey third was the known world, the dazzling white third Batalix, the mottled black third Freyr. When Freyr puffed itself large, the other parts shrank; when Batalix grew, so did the known world.

This busy organ was surrounded by steam. Through the steam ran yellow threads, the air-octaves. The air-octaves wavered as if in flight from Freyr, yet nevertheless curled about it in some instances. The Freyr-third put forth black exopodites which tugged at the air-octaves, drawing it closer to the known world. It frothed. It grew.

These images were familiar to the young kzahhn and intended to reassure him before he set forth. He understood also the warning that the pictures conveyed: that the air-octaves the crusade would have to follow were becoming more chaotic, and that the perfect sense of direction he and all his kind possessed would be disturbed. The crusade would make slow progress, taking many air-turns, or years.

He thanked the keratinous image with deep churring in his throat.

Hrr-Anggl Hhrot revealed more pictures. These had the scent of ancient things. They were drawn from a well of remembered wisdom, from the heroic ages when Freyr was negligible. An angellike army of keratinous predecessors could be seen, confirming the images.

Hrr-Anggl Hhrot showed what would happen when air-turns to near a stallun's number of toes and fingers had lapsed across the triple organ. Slowly, mottled black Freyr would drag itself into concealment behind Batalix. Twenty times in successive air-turns would it behave so. This was the terrifying paradox: that though the Freyr-part grew larger, it would hide itself behind the shrinking Batalix-part.

The twenty concealments marked the beginning of Freyr's period of cruel dominance. From the twentieth concealment onwards, the ancipital component nations would fall under the power of the Sons of Freyr.

Such was the warning—but it contained hope.

The poor ignorant Sons would become terrified by the concealments of Freyr, who whelped them. The *third* concealment would demoralise them most. *That* was the time to strike against them, that was the time to arrive outside the town where the great kzahhn, Hrr-Tryhk Hrast, had been destroyed. That was the time of revenge. The time to burn and kill.

Remember. Be valiant. Hold horns high. War has begun!

Hrr-Brahl Yprt behaved as if he had received the flow of wisdom for the first time. He had received it many times. It was unalterable. It served him for thought. All of his component with ancestors in tether had received the same images many times over previous quarters. The images came from the known world, from the air, from the long dead. They were incontrovertible.

All component decisions were the result of such flows of wisdom from keratinous ancestors. Those who made the past outnumbered the living. The old heroes lived in an heroic age when Freyr waxed puny.

The young kzahhn emerged from his moment of tether. The host about him stirred, flicked ears. The birds above them were stationary. Again the discordant horn was blown, and the doll-like images were carried away to their cave in the natural fortress.

It was time to move forward.

Hrr-Brahl Yprt swung himself up into Rukk-Ggrl's high saddle. The movement dislodged Zzhrrk, his white cowbird. It wheeled up into the air, and then settled again on Hrr-Brahl Yprt's shoulder. Many of the host had their own cowbirds. The harsh croak of the cowbird was sweet to a phagor ear. The birds played a useful role in ridding the phagors of the ticks that infested their bodies.

This tick, an unconsidered creature, formed a vital link in the complex ecological structure of the world—and an undisclosed bond between deadly enemies.

While the young kzahhn was in tetherlike communication with his ancestors, livid clouds had drawn over the snowscape. Light was reflected back and forth between overcast and ground. In the diffused, nonpolarized illumination, where no shadows were cast and living things became spectres, human beings would have been lost. There was no horizon. Everything was pearly grey.

Whiteout meant little to the ancipital army, with its air-octaves to follow. Now that the communication ceremony was finished, foot servants led four kaidaw ponies forward through the whiteout. The single humps of the animals were scarcely fleshed out; their rough coats were still dapple. Astride each pony was one of the kzahhn's four fillocks. Each fillock wore eagle feathers or pallid papilionaceous rock flowers woven into her head-hair. This quartet of young beauties had been selected by the component to keep the Kzahhn Hrr-Brahl Yprt company during the years of the crusade.

A cool breeze, forty degrees below zero, blew from the glacial heights to the east, to ruffle the delicate filaments of the coats of the ancipital damsels. Beneath those filaments lay the thickly matted phagor coat, almost impenetrable to cold except when soaked with water.

The breeze stirred the cloud cover. As though a shutter had been opened at a window, the shapes of the known world returned. The host of creatures was revealed, and the sheer walls of Hhryggt behind them, and the four fillocks, ghostly pale at first. The whiteout thinned. Ahead, bleak defiles became visible which would lead to a place of destiny twelve thousand metres nearer sea level.

The Hrastyprt standard was raised.

The young kzahhn raised a hand as signal, pointed forward.

He dug his horned toes into Rukk-Ggrl's flank. The beast lifted its horned head and moved forward over the brittle firn. The host got slowly under way with its unnatural shambling movements. Slate grated, ice rang. Cowbirds floated high on updraughts. The crusade had begun.

Its consummation would come as the ancestral images predicted, when Freyr concealed itself behind Batalix for the third time. Then the kzahhn's army would strike the Sons of Freyr who lived in that accursed town where Hrr-Brahl Yprt's noble grandstallun had been killed. That great old kzahhn had been forced to jump from the top of a tower to his death below. Vengeance was on its way: the town would be obliterated.

Perhaps it was no wonder that the infant Laintal Ay cried at his mother's knee.

Year by year, the crusade progressed. The inhabitants of Oldorando remained in ignorance of that distant nemesis. They laboured in the toils of their own history.

Dresyl was no longer as energetic a leader as he had been. He stayed more and more in town, fussing with details of organisations which had gone smoothly before he interfered. His sons hunted in his stead.

The scent of change made everyone restless. Young men in the makers corps wanted to leave and take up hunting and trapping. The young hunters themselves would not behave. Dresyl already had a hunter under his command who had a natural daughter by an older man's wife. Such behaviour was becoming common, and fights with it.

"We behaved better than that when I was a lad," Dresyl complained to Aoz Roon, forgetting the pranks of his own youth. "We'll be murdering each other next, like the savages of the Quzint."

Dresyl could not decide whether to try and crush Aoz Roon or make the man conform by praising him. He inclined to the latter, for Aoz Roon was becoming famed as a cunning hunter, but such moves angered Dresyl's son Nahkri, who felt enmity for Aoz Roon, for the sort of reasons known only to the young.

Dly Hoin, Dresyl's unsatisfactory wife, fell ill and died, even as the Year 17 After Union died away. Father Bondorlonganon came and buried her on her side in her land-octave. When she had gone, a gap opened in Dresyl's life, and he felt he loved her for the first time. Sorrow ruled his heart thereafter.

Despite his years, he learned the arts of father-communing and achieved pauk in order to speak again with his departed Dly Hoin. He met her gossie drifting in the world below. She upbraided him for lack of love, for wasting their life, for being cold of temperament, and many other things that made his heart grieve. He fled from her vituperation, her snapping jaws, and ever after was a more silent man.

Sometimes he spoke to Laintal Ay. The boy was brighter of mind than Nahkri or Klils. But Dresyl stayed away from his old cousin-brother, Little Yuli; whereas before he had felt contempt for Yuli, now he felt envy. Yuli had a living woman to love and make happy.

Yuli and Loil Bry continued in their tower, and tried not to take note of their grey hairs. Loilanun kept an eye on Laintal Ay, and watched as he entered more fully into the rude pleasures of a new generation.

Remote under the Quzints lived a religious sect called the Takers. The first Yuli had once had a glimpse of them. Secure in a gigantic cavern heated by interior warmth, the sect was virtually impervious to temperature gradients in the upper atmosphere. But they maintained a clandestine liaison with Pannoval; from that warren came a perception that, in its way, induced as important a change as any temperature gradient.

Although the perception was wrongheaded, it held beauty for the rigid minds of the Takers, and seemed to possess the truth that goes with beauty.

Takers, male and female, wore an elaborate garment which enveloped them from the chin to the ground. In profile they presented the look of a half-open flower turned upside down. Only this external garment, the charfral, was worn.

The charfral could be seen as emblematic of Taker thinking. Their understandings had become codified through many generations, the ramifications of their theology manifold. They were at once lascivious and puritanical. Even the repressive stratification of their religion contained its paradoxes, and had led to a neurotic form of hedonism.

Belief in the Great Akha was not incompatible with organised lechery, for one basic reason: Great Akha paid no attention to mankind. He fought against the destructive light of Wutra, and this served mankind's interest; but it was not for mankind but himself that Akha fought. It did not matter what mankind did. The ethics of eudemonism sprang from man's powerlessness.

Long after his death, the prophet Naba changed all that. Naba's words eventually filtered down from Pannoval to the cavern. The prophet promised that if men and women forswore concupiscence, and lying so indiscriminately one with another that no one knew his own father, then the Great Father, Akha himself, would have regard for them. He would allow them to participate as warriors in the war against Wutra. The war would be brought to an early close. Mankind—this was the essence of Naba's message—was not powerless unless it chose to be so.

Mankind was not powerless. For the buried Takers, the message was persuasive. It could never be so persuasive in the Holies of Pannoval; there, people had always taken it for granted that mankind could act. But down in the cavern, the charfrals began to burn. Chastity set in.

Within a year, the Takers changed their temperament. The old rigid codification was directed to a restrictive virtue, in the name of the stone god. Those who could not conform to the new morality were executed by the sword, or fled before the sword fell.

In the heat and dialectic of the revolution, it was not enough for the Takers to convert themselves. It never is. Revolutionaries must go forth and convert others. The Faith-Trip of Akha's Naba was undertaken. Through a hundred miles of underground passages, the Faith-Trip went to spread the message. And the first stop on the way was Pannoval.

Pannoval was indifferent to the returning word of its own prophet, who had been executed and forgotten long ago. It was actively against an invasion of fanatics.

The militia turned out in strength, and battle was joined. The fanatics were prepared to fight. They wanted nothing better than to die for the cause. If others died too, so much the better. Their gossies, howling down the land-octaves, urged them to conquer. They flung themselves forward. The militia did its best throughout a long, bloody day. Then it turned and ran.

So Pannoval bowed to the message of potency and to the new regime. Charfrals were hastily made up especially to be burnt. Those who did not conform fled or were killed.

Those who fled made their way to the open world of Wutra, to the everlasting plains of the north. They went at a time when the snow was in retreat. Grasses grew. The two sentinels kept better watch over the skies, and Wutra himself seemed less savage. They survived.

Year by year, they spread northwards in search of food and a sheltered corner of land. They spread along the Lasvalt River to the east of the great plains. They raided the migratory herds of yelk and gunnadu. And they moved towards the isthmus of Chalce.

At the same time, those ameliorating temperatures were causing a stir among the peoples of the frigid continent of Sibornal. Wave after wave of rugged colonisers moved southwards, down the isthmus of Chalce into Campannlat.

One day, when Freyr ruled alone in the sky, the northernmost tribe from Pannoval met the southernmost part of the exodus from Sibornal. What happened then had happened many times before—and was fated to happen again.

Wutra and Akha would see to that.

Such was the state of the world when Little Yuli left it. Salt traders from the Quzints arrived in Oldorando with news of avalanches and freak happenings. Yuli—now quite ancient—hastened down to see them when they arrived, slipped on some steps, broke his leg. Within a week, the holy man from Borlien was calling, and Laintal Ay was delighting in his carved dog with the moveable jaw.

An epoch was over. The reign of Nahkri and Klils was about to begin.

V

DOUBLE SUNSET

Nahkri and Klils were in one of the rooms of the herb tower supposedly sorting deer skins. Instead they were looking out of the window and shaking their heads at what they saw.

"I don't believe it," Nahkri said.

"I don't believe it, either," Klils said. "I just don't believe it at all." He laughed until his brother slapped him on the back.

They watched a tall aged figure running crazily along the banks of the Voral. Nearby towers obscured the figure, then they saw it again, skinny arms and legs flying. It stopped once, scooping up mud to plaster over its head and face, then ran on with its tottering gait.

"She's gone mad," Nahkri said, smoothing his whiskers pleasureably.

"Worse than that, if you ask me. Crazy, high in the harneys."

Behind the running figure went a more sober one, a boy on the verge of manhood. Laintal Ay was following his grandmother to see that no harm came to her. She ran ahead of him, crying aloud. He followed, glum, silent, dutiful.

After shaking their heads, Nahkri and Klils put them together. "I can't see why Loil Bry's behaving like that," Klils said. "You remember what Father told us?"

"No."

"He told us that Loil Bry only pretended to love Uncle Yuli. He said she didn't love him at all."

"Ah, I remember. So why's she keeping up the pretence now that he's dead? It doesn't make sense."

"She's got some clever scheme, with all that learning, you see. It's a trick."

Nahkri went over to the open trap. Women were working below. He kicked the door shut and turned to face his younger brother.

"Whatever Loil Bry does, that's not important. Nobody understands what women do. The important thing is that Uncle Yuli's dead and now you and I are going to rule Embruddock."

Klils looked frightened. "Loilanun? Laintal Ay—what about him?"

"He's still a kid."

"Not for long. He'll be seven, and a full hunter, in two more quarters."

"For long enough. It's our chance. We're powerful—at least, I am. People will accept us. They don't want a kid ruling them, and they had a secret contempt for his grandfather, lying about all the while with that madwoman. We must think of something to tell everyone, to promise them. Times are changing."

"That's it, Nahkri. Tell them times are changing."

"We need the support of the masters. I'll go and speak to them now —you'd better keep away, because I happen to know that the council think you're a trouble-making fool. Then we win round a few leading hunters like Aoz Roon and the others, and everything will work out."

"What about Laintal Ay?"

Nahkri hit his brother. "Don't keep saying that. We'll get rid of him, if he's any trouble."

Nahkri summoned a meeting that evening, when the first sentinel had left the sky and Freyr was moving towards a monochromatic dusk. The hunting party was home, most of the trappers were back. He ordered the gates closed.

As the crowd assembled in the square, Nahkri appeared on the base of the big tower. Over his deerskins he had thrown a stammel, a coarse woollen garment of red and yellow, without sleeves, to lend himself dignity. He was of medium height, with thick legs. His face was plain, his ears large. Characteristically, he jutted his lower jaw forward, giving his features an ominous, top-heavy quality.

He addressed the crowd in a serious way, reminding them of the great qualities of the old triumvirate, of Wall Ein, of his father, Dresyl, and of his uncle, Yuli. They had combined bravery and wisdom. Now the tribe was united; bravery and wisdom were common qualities. He would carry on the tradition, but with new emphasis for a new age. He and his brother would rule with the council, and would always give ear to what any man had to say.

He reminded them all that phagor raids were a continual threat, and that the salt traders from the Quzint had spoken of religious wars in Pannoval. Oldorando must stay united and continue to grow in strength. Fresh efforts were needed. Everyone must work harder. The women must work harder.

A woman's voice interrupted him.

"Get down off that platform and do some work yourself!"

Nahkri lost his presence of mind. He gaped at the crowd below him, unable to think of a reply.

Loilanun spoke from the crowd. Laintal Ay stood beside her, looking down at the ground. Fear and anger shook her frame.

"You've no right to be up there, you and your drunken brother!" she called. "I am Yuli's issue, I am his daughter. Here stands my son, Laintal Ay, whom you all know, who will be a man in two quarters. I have as much wisdom and knowledge as a man—gleaned from my parents. Maintain the triumvirate, as you were intended to do by your father, Dresyl, whom all respected. I demand to rule with you—women should have a voice—I love our family. Speak up for me, everyone, see that I get my rights. Then when Laintal Ay is of age, he will rule in my stead. I'll train him properly."

Feeling his cheeks burn, Laintal Ay looked about under his lowered brow. Oyre was gazing at him sympathetically and made a sign.

Several women and a few men started to shout, but Nahkri had recovered his poise. He outshouted them.

"No one is going to be ruled by a woman while I have anything to do with it. Who ever heard of such a thing? Loilanun, you must be as soft in your head as your mother to think of it. We all know you had bad luck with your man being killed, and everyone's sorry, but what you say is all nonsense."

The people all turned and looked at Loilanun's flushed worn face. She returned the gaze unflinchingly and said, "Times are changing, Nahkri. Brains are needed as well as brawn. To be honest, a lot of us don't trust you and your blockhead brother."

Many murmured in Loilanun's favour, but one of the hunters, Faralin Ferd, said roughly, "She's not going to rule me—she's only a woman. I'd rather put up with those two rogues."

At this there was much good-hearted laughter, and Nahkri carried the day. As the crowd cheered, Loilanun pushed her way through it and went somewhere to weep. Laintal Ay followed her reluctantly. He felt sorry for his mother, he admired her; he also thought in his harneys that it was absurd for a woman to expect to rule over Oldorando. Nobody had ever heard of such a thing, as Uncle Nahkri said.

As he paused on the edge of the crowd, a woman called Shay Tal came to him and touched his sleeve. She was a young friend of his mother's, with a fine complexion and a keen, hawklike look. He knew her as strange and sympathetic, for she occasionally visited his grandmother, bringing bread.

"I'll come with you to comfort your mother, if you don't mind," Shay Tal said. "She embarrassed you, I know—but when people speak from the heart it often embarrasses us. I admire your mother as I admired your wise grandparents."

"Yes, she's brave. But still people laughed."

Shay Tal looked scrutinisingly at him. "Still people laughed, yes. But many of those who laughed admire her nevertheless. They are scared. Most people are always scared. Remember that. We must try to change their minds."

Laintal Ay went along with her, suddenly elated, smiling into her severe face.

Fortune favoured Nahkri and Klils. That night, a furious wind blew from the south, shrieking continuously among the towers like the Hour-Whistler itself. Next day, the fish trappers reported a glut of fish in the river. The women went down with baskets and scooped up the gleaming bodies. This unexpected plenty was taken as a sign. Much of the fish was salted, but enough was left over to provide a feast that night, a feast at which barley wine was drunk to celebrate the new rule of Nahkri and Klils.

But Klils had no sense and Nahkri no wisdom. Worse, neither had much feeling for their fellow men. In the hunt, they performed no better than average. They often quarrelled with each other over what was to be done. And because they were aware in a shadowy fashion of these defects, they drank too much, and so quarrelled the more.

Yet luck remained with them. The weather continued to improve, deer were sometimes more plentiful, and no diseases struck. Phagor raids ceased, though the monsters were sighted occasionally a few miles away.

Fruitful monotony attended the lives in Oldorando.

The rule of the brothers did not please everyone. It did not please some of the hunters; it did not please some of the women; and it did not please Laintal Ay.

Among the hunters was a party of young bloods who formed a company together, and resisted Nahkri's attempts to break them up. Of these, the leader was Aoz Roon Den, now in the full flower of manhood. He was large of frame, with a frank expression on his face, and could run on his two legs as fast as a hog on four. His figure was distinctive;

he wore the skin of a black bear, and the fur enabled him to be picked out at a distance.

That bear was one he had wrestled with and killed. In pride at the feat, he carried the animal back from the hills unaided, and threw it down before his admiring friends in the tower where they lived. After a rathel party, he had summoned in Master Datnil Skar to skin the animal.

And there had been a touch of distinction in the way Aoz Roon had arrived in this tower. He was descended from an uncle of Wall Ein's who had been Lord of the Brassimips. The brassimips were an area and a vegetable vital to the local economy; from the brassimips came the feed for the sows that yielded milk for rathel. But Aoz Roon found his family tyrannical, revolted against it early in life, and established his niche in a distant tower, along with bright sparks of his own age, the mirthful Eline Tal, the lecherous Faralin Ferd, the steady Tanth Ein. They drank to the stupidity of Nahkri and his brother. Their drinking parties were widely regarded as distinguished.

In other ways also, Aoz Roon was distinguished. He was a man noted for courage in a society where courage was common coin. During the tribal dances, he could turn a cartwheel in the air without touching the ground. And he believed strongly in the unity of the tribe.

Nor did the presence of his natural daughter, Oyre, stop women admiring him. He had caught the eye of Loilanun's friend, Shay Tal, and responded warmly to her unique beauty; but he gave his heart to no one. He saw that one day Nahkri and Klils would meet with trouble and fall before it. Since he understood—or thought he did—what was good for the tribe, he wished himself to rule, and could not allow any woman to rule his heart.

To this end, Aoz Roon cultivated his comrades with good fellowship and also paid attention to Laintal Ay, encouraging the boy to come by his side on the chase when he officially reached the years of a hunter.

Out on a deer hunt to the southwest of Oldorando, he and Laintal Ay became separated by flooded ground from the rest of the company. They had to detour through difficult country studded with the great cylinders of rajabarals. There they came on a party of ten traders lying round a grass campfire, torpid after drink. Aoz Roon despatched two of the number as they slept, without any of the others rousing. He and Laintal Ay then rushed from cover holding animal skulls before their faces and screaming. The remaining eight traders surrendered in superstitious fear. This story was told in Oldorando as a great joke for many years.

The eight had traded in weapons, grain, furs, and anything else that came to hand. They came from Borlien, where the people were traditionally regarded as cowards, and travelled from the seas of the south

to the Quzints in the north. Most of them were known in Oldorando—
and known as cheats and swindlers. Aoz Roon and Laintal Ay brought
them back to serve as slaves, and shared their goods among the people.
For his personal slave, Aoz Roon kept a young man called Calary,
scarcely older than Laintal Ay.

This episode brought Aoz Roon more prestige. He was soon in a position to challenge Nahkri and Klils. Yet he held back, as was his way,
and consorted with his fellow bloods.

Unrest was growing among the makers corps. In particular, a young
man by the name of Dathka was attempting to break away from the
metal-makers corps, refusing to service his long term as apprentice. He
was taken before the brothers. They could get no submission from him.
Dathka disappeared from everyone's ken for two days. One of the
women reported that he was lying bound in an infrequently used cell,
with bruises on his face.

At this, Aoz Roon went before Nahkri and asked that Dathka might
be allowed to join the hunters. He said, "Hunting is no easy life. There
is still plenty of game, but the grazing grounds have altered with this
freak weather the last few years have sent us. We're hard pressed, as
you know. So let Dathka join us if he wishes. Why not? If he's no good,
then we'll kick him out and think again. He's about Laintal Ay's age,
and can team up with him."

The light was dim where Nahkri stood, supervising slaves who were
milking the rathel sows. Dust filled the air. The ceiling was low, so that
Nahkri stooped slightly. He appeared to cringe before the challenge of
Aoz Roon.

"Dathka should obey the laws," said Nahkri, offended by Aoz Roon's
unnecessary reference to Laintal Ay.

"Permit him to hunt and he'll obey the laws. We'll have him earning
his keep before those welts you set on his face can heal."

Nahkri spat. "He's not trained as a hunter. He's a maker. You have
to be trained to these things." Nahkri feared that various secrets belonging to the metal makers might be given away; the crafts of the
corps were closely guarded and reinforced the rulers' power to rule.

"If he won't work, then let's subject him to our hard life and see how
he survives," Aoz Roon argued.

"He's a silent, surly fellow."

"Silence is an aid on the open plains."

Finally Nahkri released Dathka. Dathka teamed up with Laintal Ay
as Aoz Roon said. He developed into a good hunter, delighting in the
chase.

Silent though he was, Dathka was accepted by Laintal Ay as a brother.
There was not an inch to choose between them in height, and less than
a year in age. Whereas Laintal Ay's face was broad and humorous,

Dathka's was long, and his glance perpetually cast downward. Their expertise as a team became legendary during the chase.

Because they were so much together, old women said of them that they would one day meet the same fate, as had been predicted in an earlier age of Dresyl and Little Yuli. As then, so now: their fates were to differ greatly. In these young days, they merely seemed alike, and Dathka excelled to such an extent that the vain Nahkri grew proud of him, patronising him, and sometimes making reference to his own far-sightedness in releasing the youth from his bondage with the corps. Dathka kept silent and stared at the ground when Nahkri went by, never forgetting who had beaten him. Some men never forgive.

Loil Bry was not the same after the death of her man. Whereas she had formerly clung to her scented chamber, now, old and vulnerable, she chose to wander in the wilderness of green springing up about Oldorando, talking or singing to herself. Many feared for her, but none dared approach, except Laintal Ay and Shay Tal.

One day, she was attacked by a bear driven down from the hills by fresh avalanches. Dragging herself along, wounded, she was set on by wild dogs, who killed and half ate her. When her mangled body was found, women gathered it up and carried it home weeping.

Then was the extravagant Loil Bry buried in traditional fashion. Many women wailed their grief: they had respected the remoteness of this person, born in the time of snows, who had managed to remain in the midst of them and yet live a life completely apart. There was a kind of inspiration in such remoteness: it was as if they could not sustain it for themselves, and so lived it through her.

Everyone recognised the learning of Loil Bry. Nahkri and Klils came to pay their respects to their ancient auntie, though they did not bother to order Father Bondorlonganon over to supervise her burial. They stood about on the edge of the mourning crowd, whispering together. Shay Tal went with Laintal Ay to support Loilanun, who neither wept nor spoke as her mother was lowered into the sodden ground.

As they left the place afterwards, Shay Tal heard Klils snigger and say to his brother, "Still, brother, she was only another woman . . ."

Shay Tal flushed, stumbled, and would have fallen if Laintal Ay had not grasped her round the waist. She went straight to the draughty room where she lived with her aged mother, and stood with her forehead to the wall.

She was of good build, though she had not what was termed a child-bearing figure. Her outward merits lay in her rich black hair, her fine features, and the way she carried herself. That proud carriage attracted some men, but repelled many more. Shay Tal had rejected an advance by her genial kinsman, Eline Tal. That had been long enough ago for her to notice that no other suitors approached—except Aoz Roon. Even with him, she could not subdue her spirit.

Now, as she stood against the moist wall, where grey lichens scrawled their skeletal flowers, she resolved that Loil Bry's independence should serve as an example to her. She would not be *only another woman*, whatever else they said of her over her grave.

Every morning at dawn, the women gathered in what was known as the women's house. It was a kind of factory. By first light, figures would steal forth from ruinous towers, huddled in their furs and often with additional swathings against the cold, and make their way to this place of work.

A saturating mist filled these mornings, divided into blocks by the shadowing towers. Heavy white birds passed through it like clouds. The stones ran moisture, and mud oozed underfoot. The women's house stood at one end of the main street, near to the big tower. Some way behind it, down a slope, flowed the Voral, with its worn stone embankment. As the women straggled to work, geese—the fowl of Embruddock—came up to be fed, honking and clattering. Every woman had a titbit to throw them.

Inside the house, when its heavy creaking door was closed, the eternal women's tasks were performed: the grinding of grain for flour, boiling and baking, the stitching of garments and boots, and the tanning of hides. The work of tanning was particularly difficult, and was overseen by a man—Datnil Skar, master of the tawyers and tanners corps. Salt was involved in the tanning process, and the tanners traditionally had charge of it. Also involved was the soaking of the hides in goose scumble, work too degrading for men to undertake. The toil was enlivened by gossip, as mothers and daughters discussed the shortcomings of men and neighbours.

Loilanun was forced to work here with the other women. She had become very thin and her face held a yellowy hue. Her bitterness against Nahkri and Klils ate at her vitals so much that she scarcely spoke even to Laintal Ay, who was now allowed to go his own way. She befriended no one but Shay Tal. Shay Tal had a certain fey quality, and a way of thought far removed from the dumb endurance that was a marked characteristic of the women of Embruddock.

One chill dawn, Shay Tal had just climbed from her bed, when a knocking sounded on the door below. The mists had penetrated the tower, beading everything in the room where she slept with her mother. She was sitting in the pearly darkness pulling on her boots when the knock came a second time. Loilanun pushed open the downstairs door and ascended through the stable and the room above it to Shay Tal's room. The family pigs shuffled and snorted warmly in the dark as Loilanun felt her way up the creaking steps. Shay Tal met her as she climbed into the room, and clutched her cold hand. She made a gesture of silence towards the darkest corner of the room, where her mother lay sleeping. Her father was away with the other hunters.

In the dung-scented confinement of the room, they were little more than grey outlines, but Shay Tal detected something amiss in Loilanun's hunched appearance. Her unexpected arrival suggested trouble.

"Loilanun, are you ill?" She whispered the words.

"Weary, just weary. Shay Tal, throughout this night, I spoke with my mother's gossie."

"You spoke with Loil Bry! She's there already. . . . What did she say?"

"They're all there, even now, thousands of them, below our feet, waiting for us. . . . It's frightening to think of them." Loilanun was shivering. Shay Tal put an arm round the older woman and led her over to the bed on the floor, where they sat huddled together. Outside, geese honked. The two women turned their faces to each other, seeking signs of comfort.

"It's not the first time I've been in pauk since she died," Loilanun said. "I never found her before—just a blank down there where she should be—scratched emptiness. . . . My grandmother's fessup was wailing for attention. It's so lonely down there. . . ."

"Where's Laintal Ay?"

"Oh, he's out on the hunt," she said dismissively, immediately returning to her theme. "So many of them, drifting, and I don't believe they talk to each other. Why should the dead hate each other, Shay Tal? We don't hate each other—do we?"

"You're upset. Come on, we'll go to work and get something to eat."

In the grey light filtering in, Loilanun looked quite like her mother. "Maybe they have nothing to say to each other. They're always so desperate to talk to the living. So was my poor mother."

She began to weep. Shay Tal hugged her, while looking round to see if the sleeper stirred.

"We ought to go, Loilanun. We'll be late."

"Mother was so different when she appeared . . . so different, poor shade. All that lovely dignity she had in life was gone. She has started to . . . curl up. Oh, Shay Tal, I dread to think what it will be like to be down there permanently. . . ."

This last remark was forced from her in a loud voice. Shay Tal's mother rolled over and grunted. The pigs below grunted.

The Hour-Whistler blew. It was time to be at work. Arm in arm, they shuffled downstairs. Shay Tal called the pigs softly by name to quiet them. The air was frosty as they leaned on the door to close it, feeling the rime on its panels powder under their fingers. In the greys and sludges of early morning, other figures made for the women's house, armless as they clutched blankets about their shoulders.

As they moved among the anonymous shapes, Loilanun said to her companion, "Loil Bry's gossie told me of her long love for my father. She said many things about men and women and their relationships I don't understand. She said cruel things about my man, now dead."

"You never spoke to him?"

Loilanun evaded the question. "Mother would scarcely let me get in a word. How can the dead be so emotional? Isn't it terrible? She hates me. Everything gone but emotion, like a disease. She said a man and a woman together made one whole person—I don't understand. I told her I didn't understand. I had to stop her talking."

"You told your mother's gossie to stop talking?"

"Don't look so shocked. My man used to beat me. I was scared of him. . . ."

She was panting and lost her voice. They crowded thankfully into the warmth of the house. The soak pit of the tannery steamed. In niches, thick candles made from goose fat burned with a sound like hair being ripped from hide. Twenty-odd women were gathered there, yawning and scratching themselves.

Shay Tal and Loilanun ate lumps of bread together, and took their ration of rathel, or pig's counsel, before moving over to one of the pestles. The older woman, now her face could be seen more clearly, looked ghastly, with hollows under her eyes and her hair matted.

"Did the gossie tell you anything useful? Anything to help? Did she say anything about Laintal Ay?"

"She said we must collect knowledge. Respect knowledge. She scorned me." Talking through her face full of bread, she added, "She said knowledge was more important than food. Well, she said it was food. Probably she was confused—not being used to it down there. It's hard to understand all they say. . . ."

As the supervisor appeared, they moved over to the grain.

Shay Tal looked sideways at her friend, the hollows of whose face were now filled with an ashen light from the eastern window. "Knowledge can't be food. However much we knew, we'd still have to grind the corn for the village."

"When Mother was alive, she showed me a drawing of a machine powered by the wind. It ground the grain and women didn't lift a finger, she said. The wind did the women's work."

"The men wouldn't care for that," Shay Tal said, with a laugh.

Despite her caution, Shay Tal's resolution hardened; she became the most extreme of the women in defying what was unthinkingly accepted.

Her special work was in the boilery. Here, the flour was kneaded with animal fat and salt, and steamed over troughs of rapid-flowing water from the hot underground springs. When the dark brown loaves were ready, they were cooled, and a lean girl named Vry distributed them to everyone in Oldorando. Shay Tal was the expert of this process; her loa /es had the reputation of tasting better than those of any other cook.

Now she saw mysterious perspectives beyond the loaves of bread. Routine no longer contented her, and her manner became more remote. When Loilanun fell ill of a wasting disease, Shay Tal took her and Laintal Ay into her house, despite her father's protests, and patiently tended the older woman. They talked together for hours. Sometimes Laintal Ay listened; more often, he grew bored and went off on his own.

Shay Tal began to pass ideas to the other women in the boilery. She talked in particular to Vry, who was at a malleable age. She talked about the human preference for truth over lies as resembling the need for light above dark. The women listened, muttering uneasily.

And not only the women. In her dark furs, Shay Tal had a majesty felt by the men, too—Laintal Ay, among others. With her proud bearing went proud talk. Both the looks and the talk attracted Aoz Roon. He would listen and argue. He released a vein of flirtatiousness in Shay Tal, who responded to his air of authority. She approved of his support of Dathka against Nahkri; but she allowed him no liberties. Her own liberty depended on allowing him none.

The weeks passed, and great storms roared over the towers of Embruddock. Loilanun's voice grew weaker, and one afternoon she passed away. In her illness, she had transmitted some of Loil Bry's knowledge to Shay Tal and to other women who came to see her. She made the past real to them, and all that she said was filtered through Shay Tal's dark imagination.

Loilanun, as she faded, helped Shay Tal to found what they called the academy. The academy was intended for women; there they would seek together to be something other than drudges. Many of the drudges stood wailing by her deathbed until Shay Tal, in a fit of impatience, threw them out.

"We can observe the stars," Vry said, raising her waiflike face. "Have you ever studied how they move on regular paths? I would like to understand the stars better."

"Everything valuable is buried in the past," Shay Tal said, looking down at the countenance of her dead friend. "This place cheated Loilanun, and cheats us. The gossies wait for us. Our lives are so circumscribed! We need to make better people just as we need to bake better loaves."

She jumped up and flung open the worn window shutter.

Her shrewd intellect saw immediately that the academy would be mistrusted by the men of Embruddock, and by Nahkri and Klils above all. Only the callow Laintal Ay would support her, though she hoped to win over Aoz Roon and Eline Tal. She saw that whatever opposition the academy met with, she would have to fight—and that fight was necessary to give new spirit to all. She would defy the general lethargy; time had come for progress.

Inspiration moved Shay Tal. As her poor friend was buried and she stood with a hand on Laintal Ay's shoulder, she caught the eye of Aoz Roon. She burst into speech. Her words carried wild and loud among the geysers.

"This woman was forced to be independent. What she knew helped her. Some of us are not to be owned like slaves. We have a vision of better things. Hear what I say. Things will be different." They gaped at her, pleased at the novelty of her outburst.

"You think we live at the centre of the universe. I say we live in the centre of a farmyard. Our position is so obscure that you cannot realise how obscure.

"This I tell you all. Some disaster happened in the past, in the long past. So complete was it that no one now can explain to you what it was or how it came about. We know only that it brought darkness and cold.

"You try to live the best you can. Good, good, live well, love one another, be kind. But don't pretend that the disaster has nothing to do with you. It may have happened long ago, yet it infects every day of our lives. It ages us, it wears us out, it devours us, it tears our children from us, as it has torn Loilanun. It makes us not only ignorant but in love with ignorance. We're infested with ignorance.

"I'm going to propose a treasure hunt—a quest, if you like. A quest in which every one of us can join. I want you to be aware of our fallen state, and to maintain constant vigilance for evidence as to its nature. We have to piece together what has happened to reduce us to this chilly farmyard; then we can improve our lot, and see to it that the disaster does not befall us and our children again.

"That's the treasure I offer you. Knowledge. Truth. You fear it, yes. But you must seek it. You must grow to love it.

"Seek the light!"

As children, Oyre and Laintal Ay had often explored beyond the barricades. Dotted about the wilderness were stone pillars, the insignia of old tracks, which served as perches for the large birds doing sentry duty over their domain. Together, they scrambled across forlorn ruins, skull-like remains of habitations, backbones of ancient walls, where rime scoured gate towers and age under-ate everything. Little the kids had cared. Their laughter echoed against these stranded anatomies.

Now the laughter was subdued, the expeditions more strained. Laintal Ay had reached puberty; he underwent the blood-drinking ceremony, and was initiated into the chase. Oyre had developed a mischievous will, and walked with a more springy tread. Their play became tentative; old charades were abandoned as carelessly as the structures they haunted, never to be reenacted.

The truce of innocence between them was ended finally when Oyre insisted that her father's slave, Calary, come on one of their excursions. This development marked their last expedition together, though neither realised it at the time; they pretended to hunt for treasure as before.

They came on a pile of masonry from which all trace of timber had been filched. Leaves of brassimips thrust up among the remains of a monument where old skilled work sank to loam crust. Once, as children, they made this their castle: here they had been a host defying charge on charge of phagors, and had imitated the cheerful imaginary sounds of battle.

Laintal Ay was preoccupied with a more troubling panorama which unfolded in his mind. In that panorama—slightly resembling a cloud, but also seeming to be a declaration by Shay Tal, or perhaps some ancient proclamation carved on rock—he and Oyre and their reluctant slave, and Oldorando, and even the phagors and unknown creatures inhabiting the wilderness, were whirled about in a great process . . . but there the light of his intellect went out, to leave him wondering on the edge of a precipice at once dangerous and glamorous. He knew not what he did not know.

He stood on an eminence of the ruin, looking down at Oyre below him. She was doubled up, investigating something far removed from his concern.

"Is it possible there was once a great city here? Could anyone rebuild it in times to come? People like us, with wealth?"

Getting no answer, he squatted on the wall, staring down at her back, and added more questions. "What did all the people eat? Do you think Shay Tal knows about such things? Is her treasure here?"

She, sewn into her furs, stooping, looked from above more like an animal than a girl. She was prying into an alcove among the stones, not really attending to him.

"The priest who comes from Borlien says that Borlien was once a huge country that ruled all Oldorando farther than hawk can fly."

He set his keen gaze across the countryside, which a thick cloud layer made tenebrous. "That's nonsense."

He knew as perhaps Oyre did not that the territory of hawks was circumscribed even more severely than that of men. Shay Tal's address had brought to his notice other circumscriptions in life, which he now chewed over fruitlessly while scowling down at the figure below. He was vexed with Oyre, he could not say why, longing to probe her in some way, to find tongue for what lay beyond silence.

"Come and see what I've found, Laintal Ay!" Her bright dark face looked up at him. Her features had recently fined towards womanhood. He forgot his vexation and slithered down the declivitous wall to land beside her.

She had fetched from the alcove a small naked living thing, its pink rat face distorted with alarm as it wriggled in her grasp.

His hair brushed hers as he looked down at this new arrival in the world. He cupped his rougher hands round hers till their fingers were interlocked round the struggling centre.

She raised her gaze to regard him direct, her lips apart, smiling slightly. He smelt her scent. He grasped her about her waist.

But beside them stood the slave, his face showing sullen comprehension of the flame of new intuition which flew between them. Oyre moved a pace away, then pushed the baby mammal carelessly back into its nook. She scowled down at the ground.

"Your precious Shay Tal doesn't know everything. Father told me in confidence that *he* thinks she is definitely strange. Let's go home now."

Laintal Ay lived with Shay Tal for a while. With his parents and grandparents dead, he was severed from his childhood; but he and Dathka were now fully fledged hunters. Disinherited by his uncles, he determined to prove himself their equal. He thrived and matured early, growing up with a genial expression on his countenance. His jaw was firm, his features clear-cut. His strength and speed soon became generally noticed. Many girls cast a smiling glance on him, but he had eyes only for Aoz Roon's daughter.

Although he was popular, something about him made people keep their distance. He had taken to heart Shay Tal's brave words. Some said he was too conscious of his descent from the Great Yuli. He remained apart, even in company. His one close friend was Dathka Den, corpsman turned hunter, and Dathka rarely spoke, even to Laintal Ay. As someone said, Dathka was the next best thing to no-one.

Laintal Ay eventually took up residence with some of the other hunters in the big tower, above Nahkri's and Klils' chamber. There he heard the old tales re-told, and learned to sing ancient hunters' songs. But what he preferred was to take supplies and snow shoes, and rove the countryside newly emerging into green. He no longer sought Oyre's company on such expeditions.

At this period, nobody else ventured out alone. The hunters hunted together, the swineherds and gozzards had their fixed paths near the settlement, those who tended the brassimips worked in groups. Danger

and death so often accompanied solitude. Laintal Ay acquired a reputation for eccentricity, although his good-standing was not damaged,
because he added considerably to the number of animal skulls which
adorned the stockades of Oldorando.

The storm winds howled. He travelled far, untroubled by the in-
hospitality of nature. He found his way to unfrequented valleys, and
to broken old remains of towns from which the inhabitants had long
since fled, leaving their homes to wolves and weather.

At the time of the festival of Double Sunset, Laintal Ay made his
name in the tribe with a feat that rivalled his and Aoz Roon's achievement of capturing the Borlienian traders. He was travelling alone in
high country to the northeast of Oldorando, over deep snow, when a
hole opened under his feet, and he fell in. At the bottom of the drift
sat a stungebag, waiting for its next meal.

Stungebags resemble nothing so much as collapsed wooden huts,
covered by makeshift thatch. They grew to great lengths, having few
enemies but man, feeding rarely, being inordinately slow. All that
Laintal Ay saw of this one, curled at the bottom of its trap, was its
asymmetrical horned head and gaping mouth, in which the teeth appeared to be made of wooden pegs. As the jaws closed on his leg, he
kicked out and rolled to one side.

Fighting against the encompassing snow, he brought up his spear
and wedged it far back in the hinges of the stungebag's mouth. The
animal's rhythmic struggles were slow but powerful. It knocked Laintal
Ay down again, but was unable to close its mouth. Jumping away from
the probing horns, he flung himself on the back of the beast, clinging
to stiff tufts of hair which burst from between octagonal armour
plates. He pulled his knife from his belt. Clutching the hair with one
hand, he hacked away at the fibrous tendons that held one of the plates
in place.

The stungebag screamed with rage. It too was impeded by the snow
and could not roll over sufficiently to crush Laintal Ay. He managed
to sever the plate from its back. The plate was splintery, and in texture
woodlike. He jammed it down the beast's throat, and then commenced
to cut the clumsy head off.

It fell. No blood ran, only a slight whitish ichor. This stungebag
had four eyes—there was a lesser breed with two. One pair stared forward in the skull; the other looked backward and was set in hornlike
protrusions at the back of the skull. Both pairs rolled over into the
snow, still blinking in disbelief.

The decapitated body began to burrow backwards through the snow
at its fastest rate. Laintal Ay followed, struggling through chunks of
falling snow until it and he emerged into daylight.

Stungebags were proverbially difficult to kill. This one would keep
travelling for a long while before falling to pieces.

Laintal Ay let out a whoop of exhilaration. Bringing out his flints, he jumped up on the neck of the creature and set light to the coarse fur, which burnt with a furious sizzling noise. Evil-smelling smoke billowed into the sky. By burning one side or the other, he was able to do a rough job of steering. The creature shunted backwards towards Oldorando.

Horns sounded from high towers. He saw the spray of geysers. The stockade loomed, decorated with skulls painted in bright colours. Women and hunters ran out to greet him.

He waved his fur cap in return. Seated at the hot end of a blazing wooden caterpillar, he rode it backwards in triumph through the lanes of Embruddock.

Everyone laughed. But it was several days before the stink died from rooms along his triumphal route.

The unburnt remains of Laintal Ay's stungebag were used up during the festival of Double Sunset. Even slaves were involved with this event—one of them was offered as a sacrifice to Wutra.

Double Sunset coincided in Oldorando with New Year's Day. It was to be Year 21 by the new calendar, and celebrations were in order. Despite everything that nature could do, life was good and had to be secured by sacrifice.

For weeks, Batalix had been overtaking its slower fellow sentry in the sky. In midwinter, they came close, and days and nights were of equal length, with no dimday intervening.

"Why should they move as they do?" Vry asked Shay Tal.

"That's how they have always moved," Shay Tal said.

"You don't answer my question, ma'am," said Vry.

The prospect of a sacrifice first, with a feast succeeding, lent excitement to the ceremony of the sunsets. Before the ceremonies began, there was dancing round a mighty fire in the square; the music was of tabor and pipe and fluggel—which latter instrument some claimed was invented by Great Yuli himself. Rathel was provided for the dancers, after which all, in a glow of sweat beneath their hides, moved beyond the stockades.

A sacrificial stone lay to the east of the old pyramid. The citizens gathered about it, standing at a respectful distance, as one of the masters commanded.

Lots had been drawn among the slaves. The honour of being victim fell to Calary, the young Borlienian slave belonging to Aoz Roon. He was led forth, hands lashed behind his back, and the crowd followed expectantly. A cold stillness filled the air. Overhead was barred grey cloud. To the west, the two sentinels sank towards the horizon.

Everyone carried torches fashioned from stungebag hide. Laintal Ay led his silent friend Dathka to walk along with Aoz Roon, because Aoz Roon's beautiful daughter was there.

"You must feel sorry to lose Calary, Aoz Roon," Laintal Ay said to the older man, making eyes at Oyre.

Aoz Roon clapped him over the shoulder. "My principle in life is never to feel regret. Regret's death to a hunter, as it was to Dresyl. Next year, we will capture plenty more slaves. Never mind Calary." There were times when Laintal Ay mistrusted his friend's heartiness. Aoz Roon looked at Eline Tal, and both laughed together, emitting rathel fumes.

Everyone was jostling along and laughing, except for Calary. Taking advantage of the crowd, Laintal Ay seized Oyre's hand and squeezed it. She gave him an answering pressure and smiled, not daring to look at him directly. He swelled with exhilaration. Life was truly wonderful.

He could not stop grinning as the ceremony proceeded more seriously. Batalix and Freyr would disappear simultaneously from Wutra's realm and sink into the earth like gossies. Tomorrow, if the sacrifice proved acceptable, they would rise together, and for a while their parades across the sky would coincide. Both would shine by day, and night be left to darkness. By spring, they would be out of step again, and Batalix commencing dimday.

Everyone said the weather was milder. Signs of improvement abounded. Geese were fatter. Nevertheless, a solemn silence fell over the crowd as they faced towards the west and their shadows lengthened. Both sentinels were leaving the realm of light. Illness and ill things were presaged. A life must be offered lest the sentinels depart forever.

As the double shadows extended, the crowd grew still, though it shuffled its feet like a great beast. Its cheerful mood evaporated. It became faceless in the smoke from the raised torches. The shadows spread. A greyness which was not to be dispersed by the torches blanketed the scene. People were submerged in evening and the massed psyche of the crowd.

Elders of the council, all grey and bent, came forth in line, and called out a prayer in shaky singsong. Four slaves brought Calary forward. He staggered between them with his head hanging, saliva flecking his jaw. A flight of birds wheeled overhead, the sound of its wings like rainfall, and was gone towards the western gold.

Upon a sacrificial stone, lozenge-shaped, the sacrificial victim was laid, his head set in a depression carved in its leprous upper surface, directed to the west. His feet were secured in a wooden brace, pointing to the direction—now slatey with oncoming night—where the sentinels would next appear if they completed their perilous journey. Thus, in his body, with its vents and passages, the victim represented the mystic union between the two immense mysteries of human and cosmic life: as above, so, with an effort of massed will, below.

The victim had already shed its individuality. Although its eyes rolled, it made no sound, stilled as if awed by the presence of Wutra.

As the four slaves stepped back, Nahkri and Klils appeared. Over their furs they had assumed cloaks of stammel, dyed red. Their women accompanied them to the edge of the crowd, then left them to proceed alone. Their straggling rat beards for once lent solemnity to their visages; indeed their pallor matched that of the victim on whom Nahkri bent his regard as he picked up the axe. He hefted this formidable instrument. A gong was struck.

Nahkri stood there, balancing the axe in both hands, the slighter figure of his brother just behind him. As the pause lengthened, a murmur came from the crowd. There was a time for the sundering stroke: miss that time, and who knew what might befall the sentinels. The murmur expressed an almost unspoken mistrust of the two ruling brothers.

"Strike!" cried a voice from the massed ranks. The Hour-Whistler sounded.

"I can't do it," Nahkri said, lowering the axe. "I won't do it. A fuggie, yes. Not a human, not even a Borlienian. I can't."

His younger brother lurched forward and grasped the instrument. "You coward—making us look fools before everyone. I'll do it myself and shame you. I'll show you who's the better man, you queme!"

With teeth bared, he swung the axe up on his shoulder. He glared down into the stark face of the victim, which stared up from its depression as from a grave.

Klils' muscles twitched, appearing to disobey him. The blade of the instrument signalled back the rays of sunset. Then it was lowered, and rested against the stone, while Klils leaned over the shaft, groaning.

"I should have drunk more rathel. . . ."

An answering groan came from the crowd. The sentinels now had their discs entangled with the unkempt horizon.

Individual voices made themselves heard.

"They're a couple of clowns. . . ."

"They listened too much to Loil Bry, I say."

"It was their father stuffing them full of head learning—the muscles are weakened."

"Have you been on the nest too much, Klils?" That coarse shouted question drew laughter, and the sullen mood was broken. The mob closed in as Klils let the axe slip into the trampled mud.

Aoz Roon ran forward, breaking away from his fellows, and seized up the instrument. He growled like a hound, and the two brothers fell away from him, protesting feebly. They stumbled back farther, arms raised protectively, as Aoz Roon swung the axe above his head.

The suns were going down, half sunk with glory in a sea of dark. Their light was spilled like yolk from two goose eggs, drab gold, as if phagor and human blood were mingled over the stagnant waste. Bats flittered. The hunters raised their fists and cheered Aoz Roon.

Sun rays converged on the pyramid, and were split into bars of shadow by its peak. The divided lights ran precisely along the flanks of the worn stone on which the victim lay, defining its shape. The victim himself was in shadow.

The blade of the instrument of execution swung in sunlight, bit in shade.

After the clean clop of the stroke came a united sound from the crowd, a kind of echoing stroke from lungs exhaling in unison, as though all present also gave up the ghost.

The victim's head fell severed to one side, as if kissing the confining stone. It began to drown in blood, which gushed up from the wound and spread, trickling down into the earth. It was running still as the last segment of the sentinels drowned below the horizon.

Ceremonial blood was the thing, the magic fluid that fought non-life, precious human blood. It would continue to drip throughout the night, lighting the two sentinels among the vents and passages of the original boulder, seeing them safe to another morning.

The crowd was satisfied. Bearing their torches aloft, they made their way back through the stockade to the ancient towers, which were now smoulderingly black against the cloudscape, or mottled with phantom light as the torches grew nearer.

Dathka walked by Aoz Roon, who was given respectful clearance by the crowd. "How could you bear to lop your own slave?" he asked.

The older man shot him a contemptuous look. "There are moments of decision."

"But Calary . . ." Oyre protested. "It was so frightening."

Aoz Roon brushed his daughter's objection aside. "Girls can't understand. I filled Calary full of rungebel and rathel before the ceremony. He felt nothing. He probably still thinks he's in the arms of some Borlienian maid." He laughed.

The solemnities were over. Few doubted now that Freyr and Batalix would arise on the morrow. They moved in to celebrate, to drink with extra cheer, for they had a scandal to whisper about, the scandal of the feebleheartedness of their rulers. There was no more delightful subject over mugs of pig's counsel, before the Great Tale was retold.

But Laintal Ay was whispering to Oyre as he clutched her in the dark. "Did you fall in love with me when you saw me ride in on my captured stungebag?"

She put out a tongue at him. "Conceited! I thought you looked silly."

He saw that the celebrations were going to have their more serious side.

VI

"WHEN I WERE ALL BEFUDDOCK..."

All he could see before him was the land rearing up, making a clear bow of horizon close at hand. The tiny springy plants underfoot stretched to that horizon and, away below him, to the valley. Laintal Ay stopped, resting with his hands on one knee, breathing heavily, and looked back. Oldorando was six days' walk away.

The other side of the valley was bathed in a clear blue light which picked out every detail with lucidity. The sky above was slatey purple with future snowstorms. Where he stood, all was in shadow.

He resumed his upward trudge. More land emerged over the curved near horizon, black, black, unassailable. He had never been there. Farther, the top of a tower rose as the near horizon sank beneath his progress. Stone, ruined, built long ago to an Oldorando mould, with the same inward-sloping walls, and windows placed at each of the four corners on each of the floors. Only four floors stood.

At last Laintal Ay surmounted the slope. Large grey birds cropped outside the tower, which was surrounded by its own debris. Behind, the unassailable hill, enormous, its blackness lit by the slate sky. A line of rajabarals interposed themselves between him and infinity. Chill wind rattled against his teeth, so that he drew his lips together.

What was the tower doing, so far from Oldorando?

Not so far if you were a bird, not so far at all. Not so far if you were a phagor mounted on a kaidaw. No distance if you were a god.

As if to emphasize the point, the birds took off, wings clattering, flying low over the moor. He watched them until they were out of sight and he alone in the great landscape.

Oh, Shay Tal must be right. The world had once been different. When he had talked about her speech to Aoz Roon, Aoz Roon had said that such matters were not important; they could not be changed; what was important was the survival of the tribe, its unity; if Shay Tal had her way, the unity would be lost. Shay Tal said that unity was unimportant beside the truth.

His head occupied by thoughts that moved across his consciousness like cloud shadows over the landscape, he went into the tower and looked up. It was a hollow ruin. The wooden flooring had been pulled out for fuel. He set his pack and spear down in a corner and climbed up the rough stonework, taking advantage of every foothold, until he stood perched on the top of one of the walls. He looked about him. First he looked for phagors—this was phagor country—but only barren and inanimate shapes met his survey.

Shay Tal never left the village. Perhaps she had to invent mysteries. Yet there was a mystery. Looking over the gigantic landforms, he asked himself in awe, *Who made them? What for?*

High on the great round hill behind him—not even a foothill to the foothills of the Nktryhk—he saw bushes moving. They were small, a sickly green under the dense light. Watching intently, he recognised them as protognostics, clad in shaggy coats, bent double as they climbed. They drove before them a herd of goat or arang.

He deliberately let the time go by, experienced the drag of it across the world, to watch the distant beings, as if they held the answer to his questions, or to Shay Tal's. The people were probably Nondads, itinerant tribesmen speaking a language unrelated to Olonets. As long as he watched, they toiled through their allotted landscape and seemed to make no progress.

Closer to Oldorando were the herds of deer that supplied the villages with much of their food. There were several ways of killing deer. This was the method preferred by Nahkri and Klils.

Five tame hinds were kept as decoys. The hunters led these beasts on leather reins to where the herd grazed. By walking in a crouched position behind the deer, the men could manoeuvre their mobile cover close to the herd. Then the hunters would rush forth and hurl their spears with the aid of spear throwers, killing as many animals as possible.

Later, they dragged the carcasses home, and the decoys had to carry their dead fellows on their backs.

On this hunt, snow was falling. A slight thaw about midday made the going heavy. Deer were scarcer than usual. The hunters walked eastwards steadily for three days over difficult ground, leading their decoy deer, before they caught sight of a small herd.

The hunters were twenty in number. Nahkri and his brother had restored themselves to favour after the night of the Double Sunset by a liberal distribution of rathel. Laintal Ay and Dathka travelled beside Aoz Roon. They spoke little during the hunt, but words were scarcely necessary when trust had been established. Aoz Roon, in his black furs, stood out as a figure of courage against the surrounding desolation, and the two younger men kept to his side as faithfully as his huge dog, Curd.

The herd was cropping on the crest of a slight rise some way ahead, and to windward of the men. It was necessary to work round to the right, where there was higher ground and their scent would not carry.

Two men were left behind holding the dogs. The rest of the party moved up the slope, over two inches of slushy snow. The crest of the rise was marked by a broken line of tree stumps, and a heap or two of shattered masonry, well-rounded by the force of centuries of weather. They were in dead ground, and the herd was visible only when—on hands and knees now, trailing their spears and spear throwers—they came to the top of the rise and surveyed the field.

The herd comprised twenty-two hinds and three stags. The latter had divided the hinds between them, and occasionally roared defiance at each other. They were shaggy and ill-conditioned beasts, their ribs showing, their reddish manes trailing. The hinds foraged complacently, heads down most of the time, nuzzling the snow aside. They grazed into the wind, which blew into the faces of the hunters as they crouched. Large black birds strutted under their hoofs.

Nahkri gave the sign.

He and his brother led out two of the tame deer, walking them round to the left flank of the herd, keeping the animals between them and the grazing hinds, who ceased foraging to see what was going on. Aoz Roon, Dathka, and Laintal Ay led out the other three decoys, working round to the right flank.

Aoz Roon walked his hind, keeping its head steady. Conditions were not absolutely as he liked them. When the herd fled, they would run away from the line of hunters, instead of towards them; the hunters would be deprived of excitement and practice. Had he been in charge, he would have spent more time on preliminaries—but Nahkri was too unsure of himself to wait. The grazing was to his left; a straggling grove of denniss trees separated the grazing from broken and rocky ground on the right. In the distance stood harsh cliffs, backed by hills, on and on, with mountains in the far distance, thunderous under plumes of purple cloud.

The denniss trees provided some cover for the hunters' approach. Their silvered, shattered trunks were denuded of bark. Their upper branches had been stripped away in earlier storms. Most of them sprawled horizontally, pointing their tusks away from the wind. Some lay entangled, as if locked in eon-long battle; all, so abraded were they by age and elements, resembled cordilleras in miniature, riven by chthonic upheaval.

Every detail of the scene was checked by Aoz Roon as he advanced under cover of his deer. He had been here often before, when the going was easier and the snow reliable; the place was sheltered and afforded the wide visibility the herds preferred. He noted now that the dennisses, for all their appearance of death, even of fossilization, were putting out green shoots, which curled from their boles to hug the ground on their leeward side.

Movement ahead. A renegade stag came into view, emerging suddenly from among the trees. Aoz Roon caught a whiff of the beast—with a sourer smell he did not immediately identify.

The new stag thrust itself rather awkwardly on the herd, and was challenged by the nearest of the three resident stags. The resident advanced, pawing the ground, roaring, tossing its head to make the most of its antler display. The newcomer stood its ground without adopting the usual defensive posture.

The resident stag charged and locked antlers with the intruder. As the points came together, Aoz Roon observed a leather strap stretched across the antlers of the newcomer. He immediately passed his hind back to Laintal Ay and faded behind the nearest tree stump. Leaving the cordage of its grounded trunk, he ran to the next tree in line.

This denniss was blackened and dead. Through its broken ribs, Aoz Roon sighted a yellowish lump of hair, protruding between farther trees. Grasping his spear in his right hand, drawing back his arm for a blow, he began to run as only he could run. He felt the sharp stones under the snow beneath his boots, heard the bellowing entangled animals, watched as the great dead wood bole loomed—and all the while he sped as silently as he could. Some noise was inevitable.

The hair moved, became the shoulder of a phagor. The monster turned. Its great eyes flashed red. It lowered its long horns and spread wide its arms to meet the attack. Aoz Roon plunged his spear in under its ribs.

With a churring cry, the great ancipital fell backwards, borne over by Aoz Roon's charge. Aoz Roon was carried down too. The phagor wrapped its arms about Aoz Roon, digging its horned hands into his back. They rolled in the slush.

The black and the white creatures became one animal, an animal that fought with itself in the midst of an elemental landscape, struggling to tear itself apart. It struck against a silvered root and again became two component parts, black half below.

The phagor pulled back its head, opening its jaws ready for a strike. Rows of yellow teeth, spadelike, set in grey-white gums, confronted Aoz Roon. He managed to drag an arm free, grasp a stone, and thrust it between the heavy lips, the teeth, as they closed upon his head. Aoz Roon stood, found the shaft of the spear still in the monster's body, and bore his weight upon it. With a harsh exhalation of breath, the phagor gave up the ghost. Yellow blood spurted up from the wound. Its arms fell open, and Aoz Roon climbed panting to his feet. A cowbird rose from the ground nearby and flapped heavily towards the east.

He was in time to see Laintal Ay despatch another phagor. Two more ran from the shelter of a horizontal denniss. Both galloped away on one kaidaw, heading for the cliff. White birds followed with sweeping wings, screeching towards the echoes that returned to them from the wilderness.

Dathka came over and clutched Aoz Roon's shoulder without speaking. They regarded each other and then smiled. Aoz Roon revealed his white teeth, despite his pain. Dathka kept his lips together.

Laintal Ay came up, exulting. "I killed it. It died!" he said. "Their bowels are in their chest, their lungs in their bellies. . . ."

Kicking the phagor body aside, Aoz Roon went to lean against a tree stump. He breathed out strongly through mouth and nostrils to rid himself of the sick milky stench of the enemy. His hands trembled.

"Call Eline Tal," he said.

"I killed it, Aoz Roon!" Laintal Ay repeated, pointing back at the body lying in the snow.

"Fetch Eline Tal," Aoz Roon ordered.

Dathka went over to where the two stags still struggled, heads down, antlers locked, scuffling the snow to mud with their hoofs. He took out his knife and cut their throats like an old hand. The animals stood and bled yellow blood until they could stand no longer, whereupon they collapsed and died, still locked together.

"The strap between the antlers—that's an old fuggie trick to catch game," Aoz Roon said. "When I saw it, I knew they were about. . . ."

Eline Tal ran up with Faralin Ferd and Tanth Ein. They pushed the younger men away and supported Aoz Roon. "You're meant to kill these vermin, not cuddle them," Eline Tal said.

The rest of the herd had long since fled. The brothers had killed three hinds between them and were triumphant. The other hunters arrived to see what had gone wrong. Five carcasses was not a bad kill; Oldorando could eat when they got home. The phagor carcasses would be left where they were to rot. Nobody wanted their skins.

Laintal Ay and Dathka held the decoy hinds while Eline Tal and the others examined Aoz Roon. The latter threw off their detaining hands with a curse.

"Let's scumb off," he said, clutching his side with a look of pain. "Where there were four of the vermin there may be others."

Lumping the dead hinds onto the backs of the decoys, dragging the stags, they commenced the trek home.

But Nahkri was angry with Aoz Roon.

"Those rotten stags are starved. Their meat will taste like leather."

Aoz Roon said nothing.

"Only vultures eat stag in preference to hind," Klils said.

"Keep quiet, Klils," Laintal Ay shouted. "Can't you see that Aoz Roon is hurt? Go and practise swinging an axe."

Aoz Roon kept his gaze down at the ground, saying nothing—which angered the elder brother still more. The eternal landscape stood silent about them.

When at last they got within sight of Oldorando and its sheltering hot springs, the tower lookouts blew their horns. The lookouts were men too old or sick to hunt. Nahkri had given them an easier task—but if their horns did not sound the moment the hunting party appeared in the distance, he stopped their ration of rathel. The horns were a signal for the young women to stop work and come out beyond the barricades to meet their men. Many were fearful lest there had been a death—widowhood would entail menial jobs, bare subsistence, early death. This time, they counted heads and rejoiced. All the hunters were returning. This night, there would be celebrations. Some of them might conceive.

Eline Tal, Tanth Ein, and Faralin Ferd called out to their own women, employing endearments and abuse in equal measure. Aoz Roon limped on alone, saying no word, though he looked up under his dark brows to see if Shay Tal was there. She was not.

No women greeted Dathka either. He made his youthful face long and hard as he pressed through the welcoming gaggle, for he had hoped Shay Tal's unobtrusive friend Vry might have shown herself. Aoz Roon secretly despised Dathka because no women ran up to clasp his arm, although he was himself in the same situation.

Under those dark brows, he watched a hunter catch the hand of Dol Sakil, the midwife's daughter. He watched his own daughter, Oyre, run to grasp the hand of Laintal Ay; he reckoned to himself that they would suit each other well enough, and that there might be advantage from the match.

Of course the girl was headstrong, whereas Laintal Ay was rather soft. She would lead him a dance before consenting to be his woman. Oyre was like the precious Shay Tal in that respect—difficult, pretty, and with a mind of her own.

He limped through the wide gates, head down, still nursing his side. Nahkri and Klils were walking nearby, fending off their screeching women. They both threw him a threatening look. "Keep your place, Aoz Roon," Nahkri said.

He looked away, hunching a shoulder against them.

"I wielded the axe once and, by Wutra, I'll wield it again," he growled.

The world trembled before his sight. He gulped down a mug of rathel and water, but still sickness rose in him. He climbed to the lair he shared with his companions, indifferent for once how the game he had helped kill was stripped. Once in his room, he collapsed. But he would not suffer the slave woman to cut open his clothes or examine his wounds. He rested and hugged his ribs. After an hour, he went out alone and sought Shay Tal.

Since it was near a sunset, she was taking crusts of bread down to the Voral to feed the geese. The river was wide. It had unfrozen during the day, revealing black water fringed by shelves of white ice across which geese came honking. When they were both young, it was always frozen from bank to bank.

She said, "You hunters go so far away, yet I saw game on the other side of the river this morning. Hoxneys and wild horses, I believe."

Dark and moody, Aoz Roon looked down upon her and grasped her arm. "You've always a contrary idea, Shay Tal. Do you think you know better than the hunters? Why didn't you come out at the sound of the horn?"

"I was busy." She took her arm away and started to crumble the barley crusts as the geese surrounded her. Aoz Roon kicked out at them and grasped her arm again.

"I killed a fuggy today. I'm strong. It hurt me but I killed the dirty thing. All hunters look up to me, and all maidens. But it's you I want, Shay Tal. Why don't you want me?"

She turned a face with stabbing eyes up to his, not angry, but containedly angry. "I do want you, but you would break my arm if I went against you—and we should always be arguing. You never speak softly to me. You can laugh and you can scowl, but you can't coo. There!"

"I'm not the sort to coo. Nor would I break your lovely arm. I would give you real things to think about."

She answered nothing, but fed the birds. Batalix buried itself in snow, casting gold into strands of her hair which were loose. In the crisp dead scene, all that moved was the black rift of water.

After standing awkwardly regarding her, shifting his weight from one foot to another, he said, "What were you so busy at earlier?"

Not returning his gaze, she said intensely, "You heard my words on the doleful day when we buried Loilanun. I was speaking mainly to you. Here we live in this farmyard. I want to know what goes on in the world

beyond it. I want to learn things. I need your assistance, but you are
not quite the man to give it. So I teach the other women when there's
time, because that's a way of teaching myself."

"What good's that going to do? You're only stirring up trouble."

She said nothing, staring across at the river, on which was cast the
last of the day's beggarly gold.

"I ought to put you over my knee and spank you." He was standing
below her on the bank, gazing up at her.

She looked angrily at him. Almost immediately, a change came over
her face. She laughed, revealing her teeth and the ribbed pink roof of
her mouth, before covering them with her hand. "You really don't
understand!"

Using the moment, he took her strongly into his arms. "I'd try to coo
for you, and more besides, Shay Tal. Because of your lovely spirit, and
your eyes as bright as those waters. Forget this learning which all can
do without, and become my woman."

He whirled her around, her feet off the ground, and the geese scattered indignantly, stretching their necks towards the horizon.

When she was standing again, she said, "Speak in an ordinary way to
me, Aoz Roon, I beg. My life is twice precious, and I can give myself
away once only. Knowledge is important to me—to everyone. Don't
make me choose between you and learning."

"I've loved you a long while, Shay Tal. I know you're vexed about
Oyre, but you should not say no to me. Be my woman at once, or I'll
find another, I warn you. I'm a hot-blooded man. Live with me, and
you'll forget all about this academy."

"Oh, you just repeat yourself. If you love me, try to hear what I'm
saying." She turned and started to walk up the slope towards her tower.
But Aoz Roon ran forward and caught up with her.

"Are you going to leave me with no satisfaction, Shay Tal, after
making me say all those silly things?" His manner was meek again,
almost sly, as he added, "And what would you do if I were ruler here,
Lord of Embruddock? It's not impossible. You'd have to be my woman
then."

In the way she looked at him, he saw why he pursued her; just momentarily, he felt to the essence of her as she said softly, "So that's how
you dream, Aoz Roon? Well, knowledge and wisdom are another kind
of dream, and we are fated each to pursue his own dream separately. I
love you too, but no more than you do I want anyone to have power
over me."

He was silent. She knew he found her remark hard to accept—or
thought he did; but he was pursuing another line of reasoning, and said,
with a hard glance, "But you hate Nahkri, don't you?"

"He doesn't interfere with me."

"Ah, but he does with me."

As usual when the hunt returned, a feast was held, with drinking and eating into the night. In addition to the customary rathel, newly fermented by the brewers corps, there was dark barley wine. Songs were sung, jigs danced, as the liquors took hold. When the intoxication was at its height, most men were drinking in the big tower, which commanded a view down the main street. The ground floor had been cleared, and a fire burned there, sending its smoke curling against the metal-lined rafters. Aoz Roon remained moody, and broke away from the singing. Laintal Ay watched him go, but was too busy pursuing Oyre to pursue her father. Aoz Roon climbed the stairs, through the various levels, to emerge on the roof and gulp the cool of the air.

Dathka, who had no talent for music, followed him into the darkness. As usual, Dathka did not speak. He stood with his hands in his armpits, staring out at the vague looming shapes of night. A curtain of dull green fire hung in the sky overhead, its folds shading into the stratosphere.

Aoz Roon fell back with a great roar. Dathka grasped him and steadied him, but the older man fought him away.

"What ails you? Drunk, are you?"

"There!" Aoz Roon pointed into the vacant dark. "She's gone now, damn her. A woman with the head of a pig. Eddre, the look in her eyes!"

"Ah, you're seeing things. You're drunk."

Aoz Roon turned angrily. "Don't you call me drunk, you shrimp! I saw her, I tell you. Naked, tall, thin-shanked, hair from slit to chin, fourteen dugs—coming towards me." He ran about the roof, waving his arms.

Klils appeared through the trapdoor, staggering slightly, holding a femur of deer on which he was gnawing. "You two have no business up here. This is the Big Tower. Those who rule Oldorando come here."

"You scumble," Aoz Roon said approaching. "You dropped the axe."

Klils coshed him savagely on the side of the neck with the deer bone. With a roar, Aoz Roon grasped Klils by the throat and tried to throttle him. But Klils kicked his ankle, pummelled him under the heart, and drove him back against the parapet surrounding the roof, part of which crumbled and fell away. Aoz Roon sprawled with his head hanging over into space.

"Dathka!" he called. "Help me!"

Silently, Dathka came up behind Klils, took him with a firm grasp about the knees, and lifted his legs. He swung the man's body, angling it across the wall, and over the seven-floor drop.

"No, no!" cried Klils, fighting furiously, locking his arms about Aoz

Roon's neck. The three men struggled in the green dark, accompanied by the sound of singing from below, two of them—both befuddled by rathel—against the willowy Klils. Eventually they had him, prizing away his grip on life. With a last cry, he fell free. They heard his body strike the ground below.

Aoz Roon and Dathka sat gasping on the parapet. "We got rid of him," Aoz Roon said finally. He hugged his ribs in pain. "I'm grateful, Dathka."

Dathka answered nothing.

At last, Aoz Roon said, "They'll kill us for this, the scumble. Nahkri will see to it they kill us. People hate me already." After another wait, he burst out angrily, "It was all that fool Klils' fault. He attacked me. It was his fault."

Unable to endure the silence, Aoz Roon jumped up and paced about the roof, muttering to himself. He snatched up the gnawed femur and flung it far out into the gloom.

Turning on the impassive Dathka, he said, "Look, go down and speak to Oyre. She'll do what I say. Get her to lead Nahkri up here. He'd wear a pig's nose if she suggested it—I've been watching the way that scumb's eyes go to her."

Shrugging his shoulders, saying nothing, Dathka left. Oyre was currently working in Nahkri's household, much to Laintal Ay's disgust; being well-favoured, she had an easier time of it than other women.

After Aoz Roon had hugged himself and shivered and paced the roof and projected oaths into the darkness, Dathka returned.

"She's bringing him," he said shortly. "But it's ill-advised, whatever you have in mind. I'll have no part in it."

"Keep quiet." It was the first time anyone had ever given Dathka that order. He slouched back in deepest shadow when figures started climbing through the trapdoor—three figures, the first of them being Oyre. After her came Nahkri, mug of drink in hand, then Laintal Ay, who had decided to stay close to Oyre. He looked angry, and his expression did not soften when he looked at Aoz Roon. The latter scowled back.

"You stay downstairs, Laintal Ay. You need not be involved in this," said Aoz Roon harshly.

"Oyre's here," replied Laintal Ay, as if that was sufficient, not budging.

"He's looking after me, Father," said Oyre. Aoz Roon brushed her aside and confronted Nahkri, saying, "Now, you and I have always had a quarrel, Nahkri. Prepare to fight it out with me directly, man to man."

"Get off my roof," ordered Nahkri. "I will not have you here. Below's where you belong."

"Prepare to fight."

"You were ever insolent, Aoz Roon, and you dare to speak up again after your failure in the hunt. You've drunk too much pig's counsel." Nahkri's voice was thick from wine and rathel.

"I dare and I dare and I do," cried Aoz Roon, and he flung himself at Nahkri.

Nahkri threw the mug in his face. Both Oyre and Laintal Ay took Aoz Roon by the arms, but he shook himself free, and hit Nahkri across the face.

Nahkri fell, rolled over, and brought a dagger from his belt. The only light to be had was a glow coming up from a fat wick burning on the floor below. It glinted on the blade. The green folds in the sky lent nothing more than a tincture to human affairs. Aoz Roon kicked at the knife, missed, and fell heavily on Nahkri, winding him. Groaning, Nahkri began to vomit, making Aoz Roon roll away from him. Both men picked themselves up, panting.

"Give it up, both of you!" cried Oyre, clinging to her father again.

"What's the quarrel?" Laintal Ay asked. "You provoked him over nothing, Aoz Roon. The right's on his side, fool though he is."

"You keep quiet if you want my daughter," roared Aoz Roon, and charged. Nahkri, still gasping for breath, had no defence. He had lost the dagger. Under a rain of blows, he was carried to the edge of the parapet. Oyre screamed. He tottered there for a moment, then his knees buckled. Then he was gone.

They all heard him strike the ground at the foot of the tower. They stood frozen, guiltily regarding one another. Drunken singing came up to them from inside the building.

> "When I were all befuddock
> A-going to Embruddock,
> I saw a pig a-doing a jig,
> And fell down on me buddock . . ."

Aoz Roon hung over the edge of the parapet. "That's done for you, I imagine, Lord Nahkri," he said in a sober voice. He clutched his ribs and panted. He turned to survey them, marking each with his wild eye.

Laintal Ay and Oyre clung silently together. Oyre sobbed.

Dathka came forward and said to them in a hollow voice, "You'll keep silent about this, Laintal Ay, and you, Oyre, if you care for your lives—you've seen how easily life's lost. I shall give out that I witnessed Nahkri and Klils arguing. They fought, and went over the edge together. We could not stop them. Remember my words, see the scene. Keep silent. Aoz Roon will be Lord of Embruddock and Oldorando."

"I will, and I'll rule better than those fools did," said Aoz Roon, staggering.

"You see you do," said Dathka quietly, "for we three here know the truth about this double murder. Remember we had no part in it: this was your doing, all of it. Treat us accordingly."

The years in Oldorando under the lordship of Aoz Roon were to pass much as they had under previous leaders; life has a quality rulers cannot touch. Only the weather became more freakish. But that, like many other things, was beyond the control of any lord.

The temperature gradients in the stratosphere altered, the troposphere warmed, ground temperatures began to climb. Lashing rains fell for weeks at a time. Snow disappeared from lowlands in tropical zones. Glaciers withdrew to higher ground. The earth turned green. Tall plants sprang up. Birds and animals never seen before came bounding over or past the stockades of the ancient hamlet. All patterns of life were reforming themselves. Nothing was as it had been.

To many older people, these changes were unwelcome. They recalled untrammelled vistas of snow from their youth. The middle-aged welcomed the changes, but shook their heads and said that it was too good to last. The young had never known anything different. Life burned in them as in the air. They had a greater variety of things to eat; they produced more children; and fewer of those children died.

As for the two sentinels, Batalix appeared the same as ever. But every week, every day, every hour, Freyr was growing brighter, hotter.

Set amid this drama of climate was the human drama, which every living soul must play out, to his own satisfaction or disappointment. To most people, this weaving of minute circumstance was of the utmost importance, each seeing himself the centre of the stage. All over the great globe Helliconia, wherever small groups of men and women struggled to live, this was so.

And the Earth Observation Station recorded everything.

When he became Lord of Oldorando, Aoz Roon lost his lighthearted manner. He grew morose, for a while shunning even the witnesses and accomplices to his crime. Even those who maintained some access to him did not perceive how much his self-imposed isolation owed to ceaseless fermentation of guilt; people do not trouble to understand one another. Tabus against murder were strong; in a small community where all were related, even if distantly, and where the loss of even one able-bodied person was felt, consciousness was so precious that the dead themselves were not allowed to depart utterly from their fellows.

It happened that neither Klils nor Nahkri had children by their women, so that only their women were left to communicate with their men's gossies. Both reported from the spirit world only raging anger. The anger of gossies is painful to endure, for it can never be relieved. The anger was attributed to a fury the brothers would naturally feel at an outburst of drunken fratricidal madness; the women were excused further communication. The brothers and their hideous end ceased to be a common topic of conversation. The secret of the murder was kept for the present.

But Aoz Roon never forgot. On the dawn of the day after the killing, he had risen wearily and rinsed his face in icy water. The chill merely reinforced a fever he had been suppressing. His whole body raged with a pain that seemed to lumber from organ to organ.

Shivering with an anguish he dared not communicate to his companions, he hurried from his tower, his hound Curd by his side. He got himself into the lane where, in the phantasmal mists of first light, only swathed bodies of women were to be seen, moving slowly to work. Avoiding them, Aoz Roon stumbled towards the north gate. He had to pass by the big tower. Before he knew it, he was confronting the broken body of Nahkri, sprawled at his feet, its eyes still open in terror. He found the ugly corpse of Klils, lying on the opposite side of the tower base. The bodies had not yet been discovered or the alarm given. Curd whimpered and jumped back and forth over Klils' sodden body.

A thought pierced his daze. Nobody would believe that the brothers had killed each other if they were found lying on different sides of the tower. He grasped Klils' arm and tried to move the body. The corpse was stiff, and immobile as if it had rooted itself in the ground. He was forced to bend down, thrusting his face almost in the wet rotted hair, to pick up the body under its arms. He heaved again. Something had happened to his great careless strength. Klils would not move. Gasping, whimpering, he went to the other end and tugged at the legs. Geese honked distantly, mocking his efforts.

At last he shifted the corpse. Klils had fallen face downwards, and his hands and one side of his face had frozen to the mud. Now they broke away, and the body bumped over the dead ground. He dumped it by its brother, an unmoving, meaningless thing which he tried to wipe from his mental vision. Then he ran for the north gate.

A number of ruinous towers stood beyond the barricades, often surrounded by—or indeed ruined by—the rajabarals that loomed above their remains. In one of these monuments to time, overlooking an icy stretch of the Voral, he found refuge. A littered room on the second floor was intact. Although the wooden stairs had disappeared long ago, he was able to scramble up a pile of rubble and pull himself through into the stone chamber. He stood panting, resting one hand against the wall for support. Then he took his dagger and commenced frantically to cut himself free from his skins.

A bear had died in the mountains to clothe Aoz Roon. No one else wore a similar black fur. He ripped it off heedlessly.

At last he stood naked. Even to himself, the sight was shaming.

Nudity had no part in the culture. The hound sat and panted, and watched, and whimpered.

His body, with its hollow belly and marked muscle, was consumed with the flamelike pattern of a rash. The tongues lapped him all over. From his knees to his throat, he burned.

Clutching his penis in misery, he ran about the room, crying in many kinds of pain.

To Aoz Roon, the fire on his body was an imprimatur of guilt. Murder! Here was the effect; his dark mind leaped to the cause. Never for one moment did he cast his memory back to the incidents of the hunt, when he had been in close contact with the great white phagor. Never could he reflect that the lice which afflicted that shaggy species had transferred themselves to his body. He was without the knowledge to make such connections.

The Earth Observation Station rode overhead, observing.

Aboard it were instruments that enabled the observers to learn things about the planet beneath them that the inhabitants did not know. They comprehended the life cycle of the tick that had adapted itself to parasitism on both phagor and humanity. They had analysed the composition of the andesitic crust of Helliconia. From the smallest to the greatest, all facts were there to be collected, analysed, and signalled back to earth. It was as if Helliconia could be dismantled, atom by atom, and despatched to an alien destination across the galaxy. Certainly, it was in a sense being recreated on Earth, in encyclopaedias and Eductainment media.

When, from the Avernus, the two suns were seen to rise in the east above the shoulders of the Nktryhk Range, some of whose peaks towered into the stratosphere, and glory and shadow burst from them, penetrating the depths of the atmosphere with mystery, there were romantics aboard the station who forgot their facts and longed to be part of the rude activities taking place down on the bed of the ocean of air.

Grumbling and cursing, wrapped figures made their way through the murk to the big tower. A chill wind raged from the east, whistling between the ancient towers, slamming into their faces and conjuring rime on their bearded lips. Seven o'clock of a spring evening, and blackest night.

Once they got inside the tower, they jammed the rickety wooden door behind them, straightened up, and exclaimed. Then they mounted the stone steps that led to Aoz Roon's room. This room was warmed by the hot water flowing through the stone pipes in the basement. Upper rooms towards the top of the tower, where Aoz Roon's slaves and some of his hunters slept, were farther from the heat source, and consequently colder. But tonight the wind, squirrelling in through a thousand cracks, made everything icy.

Aoz Roon was holding his first council as Lord of Oldorando.

Last to arrive was old Master Datnil Skar, head of the tawyers and tanners corps. He was also the oldest person present. He came slowly up into the light, looking cautiously, half wary of a trap. The old are always suspicious of changes in government. Two candles burned in pots in the centre of a floor luxuriously covered with skins. Their ragged flames slanted towards the west, in which direction two pennants of smoke trailed.

By the uncertain light of the candles, Master Datnil saw Aoz Roon, seated on a wooden chair, and nine other people, squatting on the skins. Six of them were the masters of the other six makers corps, and to them he bowed individually after a courtesy towards Aoz Roon. The other two men were the hunters Dathka and Laintal Ay, sitting together rather defensively. Datnil Skar disliked Dathka for the simple reason that the lad had quit his corps for the feckless life of a hunter; such was Datnil Skar's opinion; and he also disliked Dathka's habit of silence.

The only female present was Oyre, who kept her dark gaze fixed uneasily on the floor. She sat partly behind her father's chair, so as to remain in the shadows that danced against the wall.

All these faces were familiar to the old master, as were the more spectral ones ranged on the walls below the beams—the skulls of phagors and other enemies of the hamlet.

Master Datnil seated himself on a rug on the floor next to his fellow corpsmen. Aoz Roon clapped his hands, and a slave woman came down from the floor above, carrying a tray on which were a jug and eleven carved wooden cups; Master Datnil realised when a measure of rathel was handed to him that the cups had once belonged to Wall Ein.

"You are welcome," Aoz Roon said loudly, lifting his cup. All drank the sweet cloudy liquid.

Aoz Roon spoke. He said that he intended to rule with more firmness than his predecessors. He would tolerate no lawlessness. He would consult the council as before, the council to consist as before of the masters of the seven makers corps. He would defend Oldorando against all enemies. He would not let women or slaves interfere with decent life. He would guarantee that nobody would starve. He would permit people to consult their gossies when they wished. He thought the academy a waste of time when the women had work to do.

Most of what he said was meaningless, or meant only that he intended to rule. He spoke, it could not but be noted, in a peculiar way, as if he wrestled with demons. His eyes often stared, he clutched the arms of his chair as if he was struggling with an inward torment. So that although his remarks were themselves inconsequential, the manner of delivery was horrifyingly original. The wind whistled and his voice rose and fell.

"Laintal Ay and Dathka will be my chief officers, and see my orders are carried out. They're young and sensible. All right, damn it, that's enough talk."

But the master of the brewers' corps interrupted in a firm voice, saying, "My Lord, you move too fast for those of us with slow wits. Some of us might like to ponder on why you appoint as your lieutenants two saplings, when we have men of oak about us who would serve better."

"I've made my choice," said Aoz Roon, rubbing his trunk to and fro against the back of his chair.

"But perhaps you have made it too fast, sire. Consider how many good men we have . . . what of your own generation, such as Eline Tal and Tanth Ein?"

Aoz Roon brought his fist down on the chair arm. "We need youth, action. That's my choice. Now you may go, all of you."

Datnil Skar rose slowly, and said, "My Lord, forgive me, but such hasty dismissal damages your merit, not ours. Are you ill, are you in pain?"

"Eddre, man, go, can't you, when asked? Oyre—"

"The custom is for your council of masters to drink to you, to toast your reign, sire."

The gaze of the Lord of Embruddock rolled up to the beams and down again.

"Master Datnil, I know you old men are short of breath and long on words. Spare me. Go, will you, before I have you replaced too. Away, all of you, my thanks, but go, away into this beastly weather."

"But—"

"Go!" He groaned and clutched himself.

A surly dismissal, and the old men of the council departed muttering, blowing out their toothless cheeks in indignation. Not a good omen. . . . Laintal Ay and Dathka left, shaking their heads.

As soon as he was alone with his daughter, Aoz Roon fell on the floor and rolled about, groaning, kicking, and scratching himself.

"Did you bring that medicated goose fat from Mistress Datnil, girl?" he asked his daughter.

"Yes, Father." Oyre produced a leather box containing a soft hunk of grease.

"You're going to have to rub it on my body."

"I can't do that, Father."

"Of course you can, and you will."

Her eyes flashed. "I will not do it. You heard what I said. Get your slave woman to do it. That's what she's for, isn't it? Or else I'll get Rol Sakil."

He jumped up, snarling, and took hold of her. "You'll do it. I can't afford to let anyone else see my state, or word will spread. *They'll find out, don't you see?* You'll do it, damn you, or I'll break your eddring neck. You're as difficult as Shay Tal."

When she whimpered, he said, with fresh anger, "Close your eyes if you're so squeamish, do it with your eyes shut. You don't have to look. But do it fast, before I go out of my harneys."

As he began to strip himself of his skins, still with madness in his look, he said, "And you will be spliced to Laintal Ay, to keep you both quiet. I want no argument. I've seen the looks he gives you. It'll be your turn one day to rule Oldorando."

Off came his trousers, and he stood there naked in front of her. She closed her eyes tightly, turning away her face, sick with disgust at this humiliation. Yet she could not shut out the sight of that hard, spare hairless body, which seemed to writhe under its skin. Her father was covered to his throat with scarlet flames.

"Get on with it, you great silly fillock! I'm in agony, damn you, I'm dying."

She reached out a hand and began to plaster the sticky lard across his chest and stomach.

Afterwards, Oyre fled from him, spitting curses, and ran from the building, to stand with her face turned to the chill wind, retching with disgust.

Such were the early days of her father's reign.

A group of Madis lay in their shapeless clothes, sleeping uneasily. They rested in a broken valley trackless miles from Oldorando. Their sentry dozed.

Walls of schist surrounded them. Under the onslaughts of frost, the rock broke into thin layers which crunched underfoot. There was no vegetation, except for an occasional stunted holly bush, the leaves of which were too bitter even for the omnivorous arang to eat.

The Madis had been caught in a thick mist which frequently descended on these uplands. Night had come and they had remained dispiritedly where they were. Batalix-rise had already visited the world, but dark and mist still reigned in the cold cleft of the canyon, and the protognostics still slumbered uneasily.

The young kzahhn's crusade commander, Yohl-Gharr Wyrrijk, stood on an eminence some feet above them, watching as a mixed party of warrior gillots and creaghts under his orders crept up on the defenceless group.

Ten adult Madis made up the company crouched in the obscurity.

They had with them a baby and three children. Beside them were seventeen arangs, sturdy goatlike animals with thick coats which provided most of the humble needs of the nomads.

This family of Madis was institutionally promiscuous. The exigencies of their existence were such that mating took place indiscriminately; nor were there any tabus against incest. Their bodies lay pressed together to conserve heat, while their horned animals crawled in close against them, forming a kind of outer ring of defence against the bone-numbing cold. Only the sentry was outside this circle, and he lay innocently with his head resting on the pelage of one of the arangs. The protognostics had no weapons. Their one defence was flight.

They had relied on the mist for protection. But the sharp eyes of the phagors had found them out. The extreme difficulty of the terrain had cut Yohl-Gharr Wyrrijk off temporarily from the main body of Hrr-Brahl Yprt's command. His warriors were almost as starved as the prehumans upon whom they were descending.

They bore clubs or spears. The crunch of their approach over the beds of schist was covered by the snores and snuffles of the Madis. A few more steps. The sentry woke from a dream and sat up, full of terror. Through the dank mist, ugly figures emerged like ghosts. He gave a cry. His companions stirred. Too late. With savage cries, the phagors attacked, striking without mercy.

In almost no time, all the protognostics were dead, and their little flock with them. They had become protein for the crusade of the young kzahhn. Yohl-Gharr Wyrrijk climbed down from his rock to give orders for its distribution.

Through the mist, Batalix arose, a dull red ball, and peered into the desolate canyon.

It was the Year 361 After Small Apotheosis of Great Year 5,634,000 Since Catastrophe. The crusade had now been eight years on its way. In five more years, it would arrive at the city of the Sons of Freyr which was its destination. But as yet no human eye could see the connection between the fate of Oldorando and what happened in a remote and leafless canyon.

VII

A COLD WELCOME
FOR PHAGORS

L ord or not, *he'll* have to come to *me*," Shay Tal said to Vry proudly, when in a still dimday they could not sleep.

But the new Lord of Embruddock also had his pride, and did not come.

His rule proved neither better nor worse than the previous one. He remained at odds with his council for one reason and with his young lieutenants for another.

Council and lord agreed where they could for the sake of a peaceful life; and one matter on which they could agree without inconvenience to themselves was on the subject of the troublesome academy. Discontent must not be allowed to breed. Needing the women to work communally, they could not forbid them to gather together, and so the prohibition was useless. Yet they did not revoke it—and that vexed the women.

Shay Tal and Vry met privately with Laintal Ay and Dathka.

"You understand what we're trying to do," Shay Tal said. "*You* persuade that stubborn man to change his mind. You are closer to him than I can manage."

All that came of this meeting was that Dathka started making eyes at the reticent Vry. And Shay Tal became slightly more haughty.

Laintal Ay returned later from one of his solitary expeditions and sought Shay Tal out. Covered with mud, he squatted outside the women's house until she emerged from the boilery.

When she appeared, she had with her two slaves bearing trays of fresh loaves. Vry walked in a docile way behind the slaves. Once more, Oldorando's bread was ready, and Vry set off to supervise its distribution —though not before Shay Tal had snatched a spare loaf for Laintal Ay. She gave it to him, smiling and throwing back her unruly hair.

He munched gratefully, stamping his feet to warm them.

Milder weather, like the new lord, had proved more a convulsion than an actual progression. Now it was cold again, and the moisture beading Shay Tal's dark eyelashes froze. All about, white stillness prevailed. The river still flowed, broad and dark, but its banks were fanged by icicles.

"How's my young lieutenant? I see less of you these days."

He swallowed down the last of the loaf, his first food in three days.

"Hunting has been difficult. We've had to travel far afield. Now that it's colder again, the deer may move nearer home."

He stood alertly, surveying her as she stood before him in her ill-fitting furs. In her coiled quietness was the quality that made people admire and stand back from her. He perceived before she spoke that she saw through his excuse.

"I think much of you, Laintal Ay, as I did of your mother. Remember your mother's wisdom. Remember her example, and don't turn against the academy, like some of your friends."

"You know how Aoz Roon admires you," he blurted out.

"I know the way he has of showing it."

Seeing that he was disconcerted, she was more kind, and took his arm, walking with him, asking him where he had been. He glanced now and again at her sharp profile as he told her of a ruined village he had visited in the wilds. It lay half buried among boulders, its deserted streets like dried streambeds, fringed with roofless houses. All its wooden parts had been taken or had rotted away. Stone staircases ascended to floors that had long since disappeared, windows opened on prospects of tumbled rock. Toadstools grew in the doorsteps, driven snow accumulated in the fireplaces, birds made their nests in flaking alcoves.

"It's part of the disaster," said Shay Tal.

"It's what happens," he said innocently, and went on to tell of a small party of phagors he had stumbled across—not military ones, but humble fungusmongers, who had been as scared of him as he of them.

"You risk your life so needlessly."

"I need to . . . I need to get away."

"I have never left Oldorando. I must, I must—I want to get away as you do. I'm imprisoned. But I tell myself we are all prisoners."

"I don't see that, Shay Tal."

"You will see. First, fate moulds our character; then character moulds our fate. Enough of that—you're too young."

"I'm not too young to help you. You know why the academy is feared. It may upset the smooth running of life. But you tell us that knowledge will contribute to a general good, isn't that right?"

He regarded her half-smilingly, half-mockingly, and she thought, gazing back into his eyes, Yes, I understand how Oyre feels about you. She assented with an inclination of her head, smiling in return.

"Then you need to prove your case."

She raised a fine eyebrow and said nothing. He lifted his hand and uncurled his dirty fingers before her eyes. In his palm lay the ears of two grasses, one with seeds arranged in delicate bells, the other shaped like a miniature teazle.

"Well, ma'am, can the academy pronounce upon these, and name them?"

After a moment's hesitation, she said, "They are oats and rye, aren't they?" She searched in her mental store of folk wisdom. "They were once a part of—farming."

"I picked them beside the broken village, growing wild. There may have been fields of them once—before your catastrophe. . . . There are other strange plants, too, climbing against the ruins in sheltered spots. You can make good bread with these grains. Deer like them—when the grazing's good, the does will choose the oats and leave the rye."

As he transferred the green things to her hands, she felt the rasp of the rye's beard against her skin. "So why did you bring them to me?"

"Make us better bread. You have a way with loaves. Improve the bread. Prove to everyone that knowledge contributes to the general good. Then the ban on the academy will be lifted."

"You are very thoughtful," she said. "A special person."

The praise embarrassed him. "Oh, many plants are springing up in the wilderness which can be used to benefit us."

As he made to go, she said, "Oyre is very moody nowadays. What is troubling her?"

"You are wise—I thought you would know."

Clutching the green seeds, she hitched her skins about her body and said warmly, "Come and talk to me more often. Don't disregard my love for you."

He smiled awkwardly and turned away. He was unable to express to Shay Tal or anyone else how witnessing the murder of Nahkri had clouded his life. Fools though they were, Nahkri and Klils were his uncles and had enjoyed life. The horror would not go away, though two years had passed. He also guessed that the difficulties he experienced with Oyre were part of the same involvement. Towards Aoz Roon, his feelings were now intensely ambivalent. The murder estranged his powerful protector even from his own daughter.

His silence since the deaths implicated him in Aoz Roon's guilt. He had become almost as speechless as Dathka. Once he had fared forth on his solitary expeditions out of high spirits and a sense of adventure; now sorrow and unease drove him forth.

"Laintal Ay!" He turned at Shay Tal's call.

"Come along and sit with me until Vry returns."

The summons pleased and shamed him. He went quickly with her into her old rough refuge above the pigs, hoping none of his hunter friends saw him go. After the cold outside, its fug made him sleepy. Shay Tal's furfuraceous old mother sat in a corner against the garderobe, droppings from which fell immediately to the animals below. The Hour-Whistler sounded the hour; darkness was already gathering in the room.

Laintal Ay greeted the old woman and sat himself down on skins beside Shay Tal.

"We'll collect more seed and plant little fields of rye and oats," she said. He knew by her tone she was pleased.

After a while, Vry returned with another woman, Amin Lim, a plump, motherly young woman who had appointed herself Shay Tal's chief follower. Amin Lim went straight to the rear wall of the room, sitting cross-legged with her back to the stonework; she wished only to listen, and to be within sight of Shay Tal.

Vry was also self-effacing. She was of comparatively slight build. Her breasts scarcely made more show under her silver-grey furs than two onions would have done. Her face was narrow, but not without its good looks, because her eyes were deep-set and brilliant against the pale skin. Not for the first time, Laintal Ay thought that Vry bore a resemblance to Dathka; perhaps that accounted for Dathka's attraction to her.

The one feature that marked Vry out was her hair. It was rich and dark. When seen in sunshine, it disclosed itself as dark brown, rather than the bluey black of Oldorandan hair. Her hair was the only indication that Vry was of mixed extraction; her mother had been a slave woman from the south of Borlien, light of hair and complexion, who had died when she entered into captivity.

Too young to feel resentment against her captors, Vry had been fascinated by everything in Oldorando. The stone towers and the hot water pipes had particularly excited her childish admiration. She poured out questions and gave her heart to Shay Tal, who answered them. Shay Tal appreciated the child's lively mind, and took care of her as she grew up.

Under Shay Tal's tuition, Vry learned to read and write. She was one of the most ardent members of the academy. Of recent years, more children were born; in her turn, Vry was now teaching some of them the letters of the Olonets alphabet.

Vry and Shay Tal began to give Laintal Ay an account of how they had discovered a system of passageways under the town. With a grid of passages running north–south and east–west, the system connected all the towers, or had once done so; earthquakes, floods, and other natural disasters had blocked some passages. Shay Tal had hoped to reach the pyramid that stood half-buried by the sacrifice grounds, since she believed that structure to contain treasures of all kinds, but sludge had buried the necessary passages up to the roof.

"Many things connect of which we have no understanding, Laintal Ay," she said. "We live on the surface of the earth, yet I have heard that in Pannoval people live comfortably beneath it, and in Ottassol to the south, according to some traders. Perhaps the passages connect with the world below, where live the gossies and fessups. If we could find a way to them, in the flesh and not just in the spirit, then we should possess much buried knowledge. That would please Aoz Roon."

Overcome by the warmth, Laintal Ay merely nodded in drowsy fashion.

"Knowledge is not just a buried thing like a brassimip," Vry said. "Knowledge can be generated by observation. I believe there are passages through the air similar to the passages beneath us. When it is night, I watch the stars as they rise and set in progression across the sky. Some go by different passages—"

"They're too far away to influence us," said Shay Tal.

"Not so. All are Wutra's. What he does there will influence us."

"You were afraid underground," said Shay Tal.

"And I believe the stars scare you, ma'am," retorted Vry promptly.

Laintal Ay was amazed to hear this shy young woman, no older than he, drop her usual deferential manner and speak out to Shay Tal in this way; she had changed as much as the weather of late. Shay Tal appeared not to mind.

"Of what use are the underground passages?" he asked. "What do they signify?"

"They're just a relic of some old forgotten past," Vry said. "The future lies in the heavens."

But Shay Tal said firmly, "They demonstrate what Aoz Roon denies, that this farmyard in which we live was once a grand place, filled with arts and sciences, and people that were better than we. There were more people, there must have been—all now transformed to fessups—dressed grandly, as Loil Bry used to dress. And they had many thoughts like brilliant birds in their heads. We are all that remains, us, with mud in our heads."

Throughout the conversation, Shay Tal referred ever and again to Aoz Roon, gazing intensely into the dark corner of the room as she spoke.

The cold went, and rains came, then cold again, as if the weather at this period was specially designed to plague the people of Embruddock. The women did their work and dreamed of other places.

The plain was striped by folds which ran roughly in an east–west direction. Remains of snowdrifts still lay cupped in the synclines on northern sides of crests—tattered reminders of the snow desert that had once swathed the whole land. Now green stalks poked through the stippled snow, each stalk creating its own miniature rounded valley over which it was sole ruler.

Against the snow lay gigantic puddles, the most remarkable feature of the new landscape. They barred the entire landscape with parallel fish-shaped lakes, each reflecting fragments of the cloudy sky overhead.

This area had once formed rich hunting grounds. The game had gone with the snows, heading for drier grazing in the hills. In their place were flocks of black birds, wading phlegmatically on the margin of the transient lakes.

Dathka and Laintal Ay sprawled on a ridge, watching some moving figures. Both young hunters were soaked to the skin and in a bad humour. Dathka's long hard face was creased into a scowl which hid his eyes. Where their fingers pressed into the mud, half-moons of water appeared. All about them were the sipping sounds of hydropic earth. Some way behind, six disappointed hunters squatted on their haunches, concealed behind a ridge; as they waited indifferently for a command from their leaders, their eyes followed birds winging overhead, and they blew softly on their damp thumbs.

The figures being observed were walking eastwards in single file along the top of a ridge, heads low before a fine drizzle. Behind the file lay a broad curve of the Voral. Moored against the Voral's banks were three boats which had brought the hunters to invade traditional Oldorandan hunting grounds.

The invaders wore heavy leather boots and scoop-shaped hats which betrayed their origins.

"They're from Borlien," Laintal Ay said. "They've driven off what game there was. We'll have to drive them off."

"How? They're too many." Dathka spoke without taking his gaze from the moving figures in the distance. "This is our land, not theirs. But there are more than four handsful of them. . . ."

"There's one thing we can do: burn their boats. The fools have left only two men behind to guard them. We can deal with them."

With no game to hunt, they might as well hunt Borlienians.

From one of the southerners they had recently captured, they knew the state of unrest that prevailed in Borlien. The people there lived in mud buildings, generally two stories high, with the animals below and their owners above. Recent unprecedented rains had washed the huts out of existence; whole populations were homeless.

As Laintal Ay's party made its way towards the Voral, keeping from view of the boats, the rain increased. It came from the south. This was the beginning of the winter period. The rain fell capriciously in gusts, sprinkling the moving figures, then settling in more sullenly, until it beat a tattoo on their backs and moisture ran down their faces. They blew it from the ends of their blunt noses. Rain was something none of them had experienced until a few years ago; not a man in the party but wished for the crisp days of his childhood, with snow underfoot and deer stretching to the horizon. Now the horizon was hidden by dirty grey curtains, and the ground leaked.

The murk worked in their favour when they reached the riverbank. Here thick succulent grasses had sprung up as high as a man's knee, despite recent frosts, grasses that bowed and shimmered under the pressure of the downpour. There was nothing to be seen as they ran forward except wavering grass, the overburdened clouds, and muddy water the colour of cloud. A fish plopped heavily in the river, sensing an extension of its universe.

The two Borlienian guards, crouching for shelter in their boats, were killed without a struggle; perhaps they thought it better to die than get any wetter. Their bodies were cast into the water. They floated against the boats, and blood spread from their corpses, while the firemaker of the party tried vainly to make fire; the river was shallow at this point, and the bodies would not go away even when struck at by oars. With air trapped under their skins, they drifted just below the rain-pocked surface of the water.

"All right, all right," Dathka said impatiently. "Leave the firemaking. Break up the boats instead, men."

"We can use the boats ourselves," Laintal Ay suggested. "Let's row them to Oldorando."

The others stood and watched impassively as the two youths argued.

"What will Aoz Roon say when we return home without meat?"

"We'll have the boats to show him."

"Even Aoz Roon doesn't eat boats." Laughter greeted the remark.

They climbed into the boats and juggled with the oars. The dead men were left behind. They managed to row themselves slowly back to Oldorando, the rain beating continually in their faces.

Aoz Roon's reception of his subjects was morose. He glared at Laintal

Ay and the other hunters with a silence they found more daunting than words, since he offered them nothing to refute. At last, he turned from them and stood staring out of his open window at the rain.

"We can go hungry. We have gone hungry before. But we have other troubles. Faralin Ferd's party have returned from foraging in the north. They sighted a party of fuggies in the distance, riding kaidaws and heading this way. They say it looks like a war party."

The hunters looked at each other.

"How many fuggies?" one asked.

Aoz Roon shrugged his shoulders.

"Were they coming from Dorzin Lake?" Laintal Ay asked.

Aoz Roon merely shrugged his shoulders again, as if he found the question irrelevant.

He swung round on his audience, fixing them with his heavy gaze. "What do you think is the best strategy in the circumstances?"

When there was no reply, he answered his own question. "We're not cowards. We go out and attack them before they arrive here and try to burn Oldorando down, or whatever is in their thick harneys to do."

"They won't attack in this weather," an older hunter said. "The fuggies hate water. Only extreme madness can drive them into water. It ruins their coats."

"The times are extreme," Aoz Roon said, striding restlessly about. "The world will drown under this rain. When's the eddring snow coming back?"

He dismissed them, and paddled through the mud to see Shay Tal. Vry and her other close friend, Amin Lim, were sitting with her, copying out a design. He sent them packing.

He and Shay Tal looked warily at each other, she at his wet face and his air of having more to say that he could express, he at the wrinkles under her eyes, the first white hairs glinting in her dark locks.

"When will this rain stop?"

"The weather's getting worse again. I want to plant rye and oats."

"You're suppose to be so wise, you and your women—you tell me what will happen."

"I don't know. Winter's setting in. Perhaps it will get colder."

"Snow? How I'd love the damned snow back, and the rain gone." He made an angry gesture, raising his fists, then dropping them again.

"If it gets colder, the rain will turn into snow."

"Wutra's scumble, what a female answer! Have you no certainty for me, Shay Tal? No certainty in this damned uncertain world?"

"No more than you have for me."

He turned on his heel, to pause at her door. "If your women don't work, they won't eat. We can't have people idle—you understand that."

He left her without a word more. She followed him to the door and stood there, frowning. She was vexed that he had not given her a chance to say no to him again; it would have renewed her sense of purpose. But his mind, she realised, had not really been on her at all, but on more important questions.

She hunched her rough garments about her and went to sit on her bed. When Vry returned, she was still in that attitude, but jumped up guiltily at the sight of her young friend.

"We must always be positive," she said. "If I were a sorceress, I would bring back the snows, for Aoz Roon's sake."

"You are a sorceress," Vry said loyally.

News of the approaching phagors travelled fast. Those who remembered the last raid on the town spoke of nothing else. They talked of it at night as they tumbled, rathel-rich, into their beds; they talked of it at dawn, grinding grain by goose light.

"We can contribute more than talk," Shay Tal told them. "You have brave hearts, women, as well as quick tongues. We'll show Aoz Roon what we can do. I want you to listen to my idea."

They decided that the academy, which must always justify its existence in the eyes of the men, should propose a plan of attack that would spare Oldorando. Choosing suitable ground, the women would reveal themselves at a safe place where the phagors would see them. When the phagors approached, they would be ambushed by the hunters, waiting concealed on either flank to cut them down. The women screamed and cried for blood as they discussed the idea.

When the plan had been discussed to their satisfaction, they chose one of their prettiest girls to act as emissary to Aoz Roon. The girl was almost of an age with Vry; she was Dol Sakil, daughter of the old midwife, Rol Sakil. Oyre escorted Dol to her father's tower, where the girl was to present Shay Tal's compliments and to request him to come to the women's house: there a defensive proposal would be presented to him.

"He won't take much notice of me, will he?" Dol said. Oyre smiled and pushed her ahead.

The women waited while the rain poured down outside.

It was midmorning when Oyre returned. She was alone, and looking furious. Finally she burst out with the truth. Her father had rejected the invitation—and kept Dol Sakil. He regarded her as a present from the academy. Dol would live with him from now on.

At this news, a high anger overcame Shay Tal. She fell to the floor. She danced with rage. She screamed and tore her hair. She gestured and swore vengeance on all imbecile men. She prophesied that they would all be eaten alive by phagors, while their supposed leader lay in bed copulating with an imbecile child. Many other terrible things she said. Her companions could not calm her and went in fear of her. Vry and Oyre were driven away.

"It is a vexation," said Rol Sakil, "but it will be nice for Dol."

Then Shay Tal gathered her clothes about her body and stormed down into the lane, to stand before the big tower where Aoz Roon lived. The rain poured on her face as she cried aloud the scandal of his conduct, daring him to show himself.

Her noise was so great that men of the makers corps and some hunters ran out to listen. They stood against the ruinous buildings for shelter, grinning, with folded arms, while the downpour beat the steam from the geysers close to the ground, and mud bubbled between their boots.

Aoz Roon came to the window of his tower. He looked down and shouted to Shay Tal to go away. She shook her fist at him. She screamed that he was abominable, and his behaviour such that all Embruddock would meet with disaster.

At this juncture, Laintal Ay arrived and took Shay Tal by the arm. He spoke lovingly. She stopped screaming a moment to listen. He said that she must not despair. The hunters knew how to handle phagors. Aoz Roon knew. They would go out and fight when the weather improved.

"When! If! Who are you to make conditions, Laintal Ay? You men are so weak!" She raised her fists to the clouds. "You will follow my plan or else disaster will strike you down—and you, Aoz Roon, you hear? I see it all clearly with an inner eye."

"Yes, yes." Laintal Ay tried to hush her.

"Don't touch me! Just follow the plan. The plan or death! And if that fool leader, so called, hopes to remain leader, he must give up Dol Sakil from his couch. Raper of children! Doom! Doom!"

These prophecies were uttered with wild assurance. Shay Tal continued her harangue with variations, damning all ignorant and brutal men. Everyone was impressed. The downpour increased. The towers dripped. The hunters grinned mirthlessly at each other. More onlookers arrived in the lane, eager for drama.

Laintal Ay called up to Aoz Roon that he was convinced of the truth of what Shay Tal said. He advised Aoz Roon to fall in with the prophecies. The women's plan sounded a good one.

Again Aoz Roon appeared at his window. His face was as black as his furs. Despite his anger, he was subdued. He agreed to follow the women's plan when the weather improved. Not before. Certanly not before. Also, he was going to keep Dol Sakil. She was in love with him and needed his protection.

"Barbarian! Ignorant barbarian! You're all barbarians, fit only for this stinking farmyard. Wickedness and ignorance have brought us low!"

Shay Tal marched up and down the lane in the mud, screaming. The prize barbarian was the uncouth rapist whose name she refused to speak. They lived only in a farmyard, a pool of mud, and they had forgotten the grandeur that once was Embruddock. All the ruins lying outside their miserable barricades had once been fine towers, clad in gold, all

that was now mud and filth had once been paved with fine marble. The
town had been four times its present size, and everything had been
beautiful—clean and beautiful. The sanctity of women had been respected. She clutched her wet furs to herself and sobbed.

She would no longer live in such a filthy place. She was going to live
at a distance, beyond the barricades. If the phagors came by night, or
the wily Borlienians, and caught her, why should she care? What had
she to live for? They were disaster's children, all of them.

"Peace, peace, woman," said Laintal Ay, splashing along beside her.

She rejected him contemptuously. She was only an ageing woman
whom nobody loved. She alone saw truth. They would regret it when
she was gone.

Thereupon, Shay Tal suited deeds to words, and commenced moving
her few goods to one of the ruinous towers standing among the rajabarals, outside the fortifications to the northeast. Vry and others assisted
her, splashing back and forth through the rain with her poor possessions.

The rain stopped next day. Two remarkable events occurred. A flock
of small birds of a kind unknown flew over Oldorando and wheeled
about its towers. The air was full of their twittering. The flock would
not settle in the village proper. It alighted on the isolated towers
beyond, especially on the ruin to which Shay Tal had exiled herself.
Here the birds set up a remarkable noise. They had small beaks and
red heads, with feathers of red and white on their wings, and a darting
flight. Some hunters ran forth with nets and tried to catch the birds,
without success.

The event was considered an omen.

The second event was even more alarming.

The Voral flooded.

Rain had caused the river to rise. As the Hour-Whistler sounded
noon, a great swell approached from upstream and the direction of
distant Dorzin Lake. An old woman, Molas Ferd, was down by the
riverbank collecting geese scumble when she sighted the swell. She
straightened as much as she was able and stared in amazement as a
wall of water bore down on her. Geese and ducks took fright, clattering
up to perch on the barricades. But old Molas Ferd stood where she was,
shovel in hand, staring openmouthed at the waters. They rushed upon
her and hurled her against the side of the women's house.

The flood filled the village before subsiding, washing away grain, invading people's homes,—drowning sows. Molas Ferd was battered to
death.

The hamlet was turned into a swamp. Only the tower where Shay Tal
had taken up residence was spared the onslaught of muddy waters.

This period marked the true beginning of Shay Tal's reputation as a
sorceress. All who had heard her cry out against Aoz Roon sat inside
and muttered.

That evening, as first Batalix, then Freyr set in the west, turning the flood waters to blood, the temperature dropped dramatically. The village was filled with thin crackling ice.

Next Freyr-dawn, the town was aroused by Aoz Roon's angry shouting. The women, scuffling into their boots to go to work, listened in dismay, and woke their menfolk. Aoz Roon was taking a leaf from Shay Tal's book.

"Out you come, damn you all! You're going to fight the phagors today, every one of you! I set my resolve against your idleness. Rise, rise, all of you, get up and fight. If phagors are to be found, then phagors you will fight. I fought them single-handed, you scum can fight them together. This will be a great day in history, you hear me, a great day, even if you all die!"

As the dawn clouds scudded bleakly overhead, his great figure in its black furs stood on top of the tower, fist waving. With his other hand, Aoz Roon clutched a struggling Dol Sakil, who fought and yelled to get out of the cold. Eline Tal loomed behind them, grinning feebly.

"Yes, we'll slay the milk-struck phagors according to the women's plan—you hear that, you idle quemes of the academy?—we'll fight according to the women's plan, for good or ill—carry it out to the letter. By the original boulder, we'll see what happens today, we'll see whether or not Shay Tal talks sense, we'll see what her prophecies are worth!"

A few figures were emerging in the lane, clattering through the thin ice, staring up at their lord. Many clutched each other timidly, but old Rol Sakil, mother of Dol, cackled and said, "He must be well developed, yelling like that—that's what our Dol said he was. Bawls like a bull!"

He came to the edge of the parapet and glared down at them, dragging Dol with him, still shouting.

"Yes, we'll see what her words are worth, we'll test her. We'll test Shay Tal in battle, since you all seem to think so much of her. Do you hear me, Shay Tal? We'll make or break today, and blood shall flow, red or yellow."

He spat down at them, then withdrew. The trapdoor slammed after him as he climbed back into his tower.

When they had eaten some black bread, everyone set forth, urged on by the hunters. All were subdued, even Aoz Roon. His storm of words had blown itself out. They proceeded in a southeasterly direction. The weather remained below freezing. The day was still, the suns were lost in cloud. The ground was hard and ice crackled underfoot.

Shay Tal went with them, keeping in with the women, her mouth pursed, her skins swinging about her thin body.

Progress was slow, for the women were unaccustomed to walking distances that meant nothing to the men. They came at length to the

broken plain from which Laintal Ay's hunting party had sighted the
Borlienians only two days before the Voral flooded. Here lay the series
of ridges with shallow flood lakes between, glinting like stranded fish.
Here the ambush could be set up. The cold would bring out phagors,
if there were any. Batalix had set, unseen.

They went down into the plain, men first, the women following, in
confused groups. All were apprehensive under the hard sky.

By the edge of the first flood lake, the women halted, looking at Shay
Tal in none too friendly a fashion. They realised the danger of their
position, should any phagors arrive—particularly if they came mounted.
No amount of anxious glancing about could reassure them on that
score, for the ridges restricted their view.

They were exposed to danger and the elements. The temperature
remained two or three degrees below freezing. Quiet reigned; the air
was hard. The shallow lake lay silent before them. It was some forty
metres wide by one hundred metres long, occupying the hollow between
two ridges with its unwelcoming expanse. Its waters were motionless
but still unfrozen, reflecting the sky without a ripple. Its sullen appearance increased a certain supernatural fear which fell upon the women
as they watched the hunters disappear over the ridge. Even the grass
at their feet, crisped by frost, seemed under a curse, and no birds cried.

The men were unhappy about having their womenfolk nearby. They
stood in a neighbouring depression, by another lake, and complained
about their leader.

"We've seen no sign of phagors," Tanth Ein said, blowing on his
nails. "Let's turn back. Supposing they destroyed Oldorando while we
were away? A fine thing that would be."

The cloud of breath about their heads united them as they leaned
on their spears and looked accusingly at Aoz Roon. The latter paced
about, keeping himself separate from them, his expression black.

"Turn back? You talk like women. We came to fight, and fight we
will, even if we throw our lives to Wutra while we do so. If there are
phagors near, I'll summon them. Stand where you are."

He went at a run to the top of the ridge behind him, so that the
women were again within his view, intending to shout at the top of his
voice and awaken all the echoes in the wilderness.

But the enemy was already in view. Now, too late, he understood why
they had seen no more wandering Borlienians; they had been driven off.
Like old Molas Ferd before the flood, he stood paralysed before the
sight of humanity's ancient enemy.

The women straggled at one end of the fish-shaped lake, the ancipitals
grouped at the other. The women made frightened and uncertain movements; the ancipitals were motionless. Even in their surprise, the women
responded individually; the phagors could be seen only as a group.

It was impossible to make out the number of the enemy. They merged together with the late afternoon mists filling the hollow, and with the scarred greys and blues of the scene. One of them gave a thick protracted cough; otherwise they might have been lifeless.

Their white birds had settled on a ridge behind them, at first with some jostling, now spaced out regularly, with heads submissively on one side, like the souls of those departed.

From their frosty outline, it could be determined that three of the phagors—presumably the leaders—were mounted on kaidaws. They sat, as was their habit, leaning forward with their heads close to their mounts' heads, as if communion was in progress. The foot phagors clustered against the flanks of the kaidaws, shoulders hunched. Nearby boulders were not more still.

The cougher coughed again. Aoz Roon threw off his spell and called to his men.

They climbed along the crest of the ridge, to stare at the enemy in dismay.

In response, the phagors made a sudden move. Their strangely jointed limbs geared themselves from immobility to action with no intermediate stage. The shallow lake had checked their advance. They had a well-known aversion to water, but times were changing; their harneys said "Forward." The sight of thirty human gillots at their mercy decided them. They charged.

One of the three mounted brutes swung a sword above his head. With a churring cry, he kicked his kaidaw, and mount and rider burst forward. The other brutes followed as one, whether mounted or running. Forward they dashed—into the waters of the shallow lake.

Panic scattered the women. Now that their adversary was almost on them, they ran hither and thither between the ridges. Some climbed one side, some the other, making small sharp noises of despair, like birds in distress.

Only Shay Tal remained where she was, facing the charge, and Vry and Amin Lim clung to her in terror, hiding their faces.

"Run, you fool woman!" bellowed Aoz Roon, coming down the ridge at a run.

Shay Tal did not hear his voice above the shrieks and the furious splashing. She stood firm at the end of the fish lake and flung out her arms, as if gesturing to the phagor horde to halt.

Then the transformation. Then the moment that ever after in the annals of Oldorando would be referred to as the miracle of Fish Lake.

Some claimed later that a shrilling note rang through the frosty air, some said a high voice spoke, some vowed Wutra struck.

The whole group of marauders, sixteen in number, had entered the lake, led by the three mounted stalluns. Their rage drove them into the alien element, they were thigh deep in it, churning it up with the fury of their charge, when the entire lake froze.

One moment, it was an absolutely still liquid, lying, because undisturbed, unfrozen at three degrees below freezing point. The next moment, disturbed, it became solid. Kaidaws and phagors all were locked in its embrace. One kaidaw fell, never to rise again. The others froze where they were, and their riders froze with them, hemmed in ice. The stalluns behind, brandishing their arms—all were trapped, held in the grip of the element they had invaded. None took as much as one further step. None could fight free to gain the safety of the shore. Soon, their veins froze within their bodies, despite the ancient biochemistries that coloured their bloodstream and protected it from the cold. Their coarse white coats became further sheathed in rime, their glaring eyes frosted over.

What was organic became one with the great inorganic world that ruled.

The tableau of furious death was absolute, carved from ice.

Above it, white birds wheeled and dipped, crying with gaping beaks, finally making off to the east in desolate flight.

Next morning, three people rose up early from a skin bivouac. Powdery snow had fallen during the night, giving the wilderness a peppery appearance. Freyr ascended from the horizon, casting watery purple shadows over the plain. Several minutes later, the second faithful sentinel also struggled free into Wutra's realm.

By then, Aoz Roon, Laintal Ay, and Oyre were on their feet, beating and stamping circulation into their limbs. They coughed, but were otherwise silent. After looking at each other without speaking, they moved forward. Aoz Roon stepped out onto the lake of ice, which rang beneath his tread.

The three of them walked across to the frozen tableau.

They stared at it almost in disbelief. Before them was a monumental piece of statuary, fine in detail, wild in imagining. One kaidaw lay almost under the hoofs of the other two, the greater part of its bulk submerged by brittle waves, its head rearing up in fear, its nostrils distended. Its rider struggled for control, half fallen from its back, terrible in immobility.

All the figures were caught in mid-action, many with weapons raised, eyes staring ahead to the shore they would never reach. All were encased in rime. They formed a monument to brutality.

Finally, Aoz Roon nodded and spoke. His voice was subdued.

"It did happen. Now I believe. Let's get back."

The miracle of Year 24 was confirmed.

He had sent the rest of the party back to Oldorando the previous evening, under Dathka's leadership. Only after he had slept could he believe he did not dream the incident.

Nobody else said anything. They had been saved by a miracle; the thought dazed their minds, silenced their tongues. They trudged away from the alarming sculpture without another word.

Once they were back in Oldorando, Aoz Roon ordered one of his slaves to be taken by two hunters to Fish Lake, to the site of the miracle. When the slave had seen the tableau with his own eyes, his hands were lashed behind his back, he was faced towards the south, and booted on his way. Back in Borlien, he would tell his fellows that a powerful sorceress watched over Oldorando.

VIII

IN OBSIDIAN

The room in which Shay Tal stood erect was ancient beyond her computation. She had furnished it with what she could: an old tapestry, once Loil Bry's, once Loilanun's—that illustrious line of dead women; her humble bed in the corner, built of woven bracken imported from Borlien (bracken kept out rats); her writing materials set on a small stone table; some skins on the floor, on which thirteen women sat or squatted. The academy was in session.

The walls of the room were leprous with yellow and white lichen which, starting from the single narrow window, had, over uncounted years, colonised all the adjacent stonework. In the corners were spiders' webs; most of their incumbents had starved to death long ago.

Behind the thirteen women sat Laintal Ay, legs folded under him, resting his chin on his fist and his elbow on his knee. He looked down at the floor. Most of the women gazed vacantly at Shay Tal. Vry, Amin Lim, were listening; of the others, she could not be sure.

"The effects in our world are complex. We can pretend they are all a product of the mind of Wutra in that eternal war in Heaven, but that is too easy. We would do better to work things out for ourselves.

We need some other key to understanding. Does Wutra care? Perhaps we have sole charge of our own actions. . . ."

She ceased to listen to what she was saying. She had posed the eternal question. Surely every human being who had ever lived had had to face up to that question, and answer it in her own way: have we sole charge of our own actions? She could not tell the answer in her own case. In consequence, she felt herself totally unfit to teach.

Yet they listened. She knew why they listened, even if they listened without understanding. They listened because she was accepted as a great sorceress. Since the miracle at Fish Lake, she was isolated by their reverence. Aoz Roon himself was more distant than before.

She looked out through the ruinous window at the ecrhythmous world, now freeing itself from the recent cold, its slimes and snows spatchcocked with green, its river streaked with muds from remote places she would never visit. There were miracles. The miraculous lay beyond her window. Yet—had she performed a miracle, as everyone assumed?

Shay Tal broke off her talk in mid-sentence. She perceived that there way a way of testing her own holiness.

The phagors charging at Fish Lake had turned to ice. Because of something in her—or something in them? She recalled tales about phagors dreading water; perhaps the reason was that they turned to ice in it. That could be tested: there were one or two old phagor slaves in Oldorando. She would try one out in the Voral and see what happened. One way or the other, she would know.

The thirteen were staring at her, waiting for her to go on. Laintal Ay looked puzzled. She had no idea what she had been saying. She perceived that she had to conduct an experiment for her own peace of mind.

"We have to do what we're told . . ." one of the women said from the floor, in a slow puzzled voice, as if repeating a lesson.

Shay Tal stood listening to someone tramping up the steps from the floor below. There was no way in which she could answer politely a statement she had been contradicting since the Hour-Whistler last blew; any interruption was welcome at this point. Some of the women were irredeemably stupid.

The hatch was flung open. Aoz Roon appeared, looking rather like a great black bear, followed by his dog. Behind him came Dathka, to stand poker-faced in the rear, not even casting a glance at Laintal Ay. The latter stood rather awkwardly, and waited with his back to the cold wall. The women gaped at the intruders, some giggling nervously.

Aoz Roon's stature seemed to fill the low room. Though the women craned their necks at him uneasily, he ignored them and addressed Shay Tal. She had moved back to the window, but stood facing him, framed against a background of muddy village, fumaroles, and the parti-coloured landscape stretching to the horizon.

"What do you want here?" she asked. Her heart beat as she beheld him. For this above all she cursed her new reputation, that he no longer bullied her, or held her arms, or even pursued her. His whole manner suggested this was a formal and unfriendly visit.

"I wish you to come back into the protection of the barricades, ma'am," he said. "You are not safe, living in this ruin. I cannot protect you here in the event of a raid."

"Vry and I prefer living here."

"You're under my control, for all your reputation, you and Vry, and I must do my best to protect you. All you other women—you should not be here. It is too dangerous outside the barricades. If there was a sudden attack—well, you can guess what would happen to you. Shay Tal, as our powerful sorceress, must please herself. The rest of you must please me. I forbid you to come here. It's too dangerous. You understand?"

All evaded his gaze except the old midwife, Rol Sakil. "That's all nonsense, Aoz Roon. This tower is safe enough. Shay Tal's scared off the fuggies, we all know that. Besides, even you have been here on occasions, haven't you now?"

This last was said with a leer. Aoz Roon dismissed it.

"I'm talking about the present. Nothing's safe now the weather's changing. None of you enter here again or there will be trouble."

He turned, raising a beckoning finger to Laintal Ay.

"You come with me." He marched down the steps without a farewell, and Laintal Ay and Dathka followed.

Outside, he paused, pulling at his beard. He looked up at her window. "I'm still Lord of Embruddock, and you had better not forget it."

She heard his shout from within, but would not go to the window. Instead, she stood where she was—alone despite the company—and said in a voice loud enough for him to hear, "Lord of a rotten little farmyard."

Only when she heard the squelch of three pairs of boots retreating did she deign to glance out the window. She watched his broad back as he trudged with his young lieutenants towards the north gate, Curd trotting at his heel. She understood his loneliness. None better.

As his woman, she would surely not have lost stature, or whatever it was she valued so highly. Too late to think of that now. The rift was between them, and an empty-headed doll kept his bed warm.

"You'd better all go home," she said, afraid to look directly at the women.

When they got back to the muddy main square, Aoz Roon ordered Laintal Ay to stay away from the academy.

Laintal Ay flushed. "Isn't it time that you and the council gave up your prejudice against the academy? I hoped you'd think better of it since the miracle of Fish Lake. Why upset the women? They'll hate you for it. The worst the academy can do is keep the women content."

"It makes the women idle. It causes division."

Laintal Ay looked at Dathka for support, but Dathka was gazing at his boots. "It's more likely to be your attitude that causes division, Aoz Roon. Knowledge never hurt anyone; we need knowledge."

"Knowledge is slow poison—you're too young to understand. We need discipline. That's how we survive and how we always have survived. You stay away from Shay Tal—she exerts an unnatural power over people. Those who don't work in Oldorando get no food. That's always been the rule. Shay Tal and Vry have ceased working the boilery, so in future they will have nothing to eat. We'll see how they like that."

"They'll starve."

Aoz Roon drew his brows together and glared at Laintal Ay, "We will all starve if we do not cooperate. Those women have to be brought to heel, and I will not tolerate you siding with them. Argue with me any more and I'll knock you down."

When Aoz Roon had gone, Laintal Ay gripped Dathka's shoulder. "He is getting worse. It's his personal battle with Shay Tal. What do you think?"

Dathka shook his head. "I don't think. I do what I'm told."

Laintal Ay regarded his friend sarcastically. "And what are you told to do now?"

"I'm going up by the brassimips patch. We've killed a stungebag." He exhibited a bleeding hand.

"I'll be there in a while."

He walked by the Voral, idly watching the geese swimming and parading, before following his friend. He thought to himself that he understood both Aoz Roon's and Shay Tal's points of view. To live, all had to cooperate, yet was it worth living if they merely cooperated? The conflict oppressed him and made him long to leave the hamlet—as he would do if only Oyre were to agree to come with him. He felt that he was too young to understand how the argument, the growing division, would resolve itself. Slyly, seeing nobody was looking, he brought out from his pocket a carved dog given him long ago by the old priest from Borlien. He held it forward and worked its tail. The dog began to bark furiously at nearby geese.

Someone else was wending her way towards the brassimips and heard the imitation dog bark. Vry saw Laintal Ay's back between two towers. She did not intrude on him, for that was not her way.

She skirted the hot springs and the Hour-Whistler. An easterly breeze took the steam from the waters as it emerged from the ground, to blow it hissing across wet rock. Vry's furs were pearled with a bead of moisture at every hair end.

The waters ran gargling, yellow and chalky in their crevices, full of an infectious fury to be somewhere. She squatted down on a rock and absentmindedly dipped her hand in a spring. Hot water ran up her fingers and explored her palm.

Vry licked the liquid off her fingers. She knew the sulphurous flavour from childhood. Children were playing here now, calling to each other, running across slippery rock without falling, agile as arangs.

The more adventurous children ran naked, despite the stiff breeze, inserting their androgynous bodies into clefts between rocks. Spuming waters cascaded up their stomachs and over their shoulders.

"Here comes the Whistler," they called to Vry. "Look out, missus, or you'll get a soaking." They laughed heartily at the thought.

Taking the warning, Vry moved away. She thought that a stranger here would credit the children with a sixth sense, able to predict exactly when the Hour-Whistler blew.

Up it went, a solid column of water, muddy for a moment then brilliant pure. Ascending, it whistled on an ascending note—its unvarying note, sustained for an unvarying duration. The water sailed upwards to about three times the height of a man before falling back. The wind curved the jet towards the west, hammering the rocks where Vry had squatted a moment earlier.

The whistle stopped. The column died back into the black lips of earth from which it had sprung.

Vry waved to the children and continued up the brassimip track. She knew how they knew when the geyser was about to blow. She still remembered the thrill of wriggling naked between ochre rocks, plugging one's body into the streaming earth, toes among hot slimes, flesh tickled by bursting bubbles. When the hour was near, a tremor shook the ground. One wedged oneself into the rock and felt in every fibre the strength of the earth gods as they tensed themselves to deliver their triumphant ejaculation of hot liquids.

The path she followed was trodden mainly by women and pigs. It wandered hither and thither, unlike straighter paths created by hunters, since its course had been dictated largely by that wayward creature, the hairy black sow of Embruddock. To follow the direction in which the track tended was to arrive eventually at Lake Dorzin; but the path ceased long before that, at the brassimip patch. The rest of the way was still a wilderness of marsh and frost.

As she moved up the path, Vry wondered if all things aspired to a highest level, and if there was a competing force trying to drag them to the lowest. One looked up to the stars, one ended as a gossie, a fessup. The Hour-Whistler was an embodiment of the two opposed forces. Its spouting waters always fell back to earth. In her unobtrusive way, she willed her spirit to soar to the sky, the region she studied without Shay

Tal's aid, the place of sublime movement, the riddling place of stars and suns, of as many secret passages as the body.

Two men came towards her. She could see little of them but legs, elbows, and the tops of their heads, as they staggered downhill under heavy loads. She could identify Sparat Lim by his spindly legs. The men were carrying slabs of stungebag. After them came Dathka, carrying only a spear.

Dathka gave her a grin of welcome and stood to one side of the path, surveying her with his dark eyes. His right hand was bloody, and a thin trail of blood ran down the spear shaft.

"We killed a stunge," he said, and that was all. As usual, Vry was both embarrassed and comforted by his lack of words. It was pleasant that he never boasted, unlike many of the young hunters, less pleasant that he never revealed his thoughts. She tried to feel something for him.

She halted. "It must have been a big one."

"I'll show you." He added, "If you'll let me."

He turned back along the track and she followed, unsure whether she ought to speak or not. But that was silly, she told herself; she understood perfectly that Dathka desired to communicate with her.

She blurted out the first thing that came into her head.

"How do you account for human beings in the world, Dathka?"

Without a backward glance, he said, "We came up from the original boulder." He spoke without the consideration she would have wished him to give to such an important matter, and there the conversation languished.

She regretted that there were no priests in Oldorando; she could have talked to them. Legends and songs related that Embruddock had once had its fair share of priests, administering an elaborate religion which united Wutra with the living of this world and the fessups of the world below. One dark season before Wall Ein Den ruled, when breath froze on people's lips as it issued forth, the population rose and slew the priesthood. Sacrifices had ceased from then on, except on festival days. The old god, Akha, was no longer worshipped. No doubt a body of learning had also been lost. The temple had been stripped. Now pigs were housed in it. Perhaps other enemies of knowledge had been about, when pigs were preferred to priests.

She risked another question of the ascending back.

"Do you wish you understood the world?"

"I do," it said.

She was left wrestling with the brevity of the reply; did he understand or did he wish he understood, she asked herself.

The forces that had thrown up the Quzint Mountains had folded the earth in all directions, causing attendant deformations like buttresses, like the roots of trees, to extend outwards for many miles from

the mountains themselves. Between two such rocky extrusions grew a
line of brassimips which had long been essential to the local economy.
Today, the plot was a scene of mild excitement, and several women
were clustered round the open tops of the brassimips, warming themselves and herding their pigs while watching the work in progress.

Dathka indicated that this was where the stungebag was killed.

His gesture was scarcely necessary. The carcass lay about in piles,
sprawling up the desolate hillside. Towards its tail, Aoz Roon himself was investigating it, his yellow hound about his heels. The stubby
legs of the immense corpse pointed into the air, fringed by stiff black
hairs and spines.

A group of men waited about the body, laughing and talking. Goija
Hin supervised the slaves, human and phagorian, who wielded axes.
They were splitting the fibrous carcass into slabs that could be carried
down to the hamlet. They stood up to their knees in coir and woody
sections of the stungebag's flesh. Great splinters flew as they dismembered the remains.

Two older women dodged about with buckets, gathering up spongey
white entrails. They would boil the mess down later to distill a coarse
sugar from it. The coir would be used for ropes and mats, the flesh for
fuel for the various corps.

From the paddlelike digging paws of the stungebag, oils would be
extracted to form a narcotic called rungebel.

The older women were exchanging impolite remarks with the men,
who grinned and stood in nonchalant poses about the hillside. It was
unusual for stungebags to venture near human habitation. The beasts
were easy to kill, and every part of them was useful to the fragile economy. The present kill was thirty metres long, and would benefit the
community for days to come.

Pigs ran squealing round Vry's feet as they rooted among the fibrous
debris. Their swineherds were working below in the brassimips. Nothing
of the giant trees was visible above ground except heavy fungoid
leaves, cossetting the earth with their twisted growth pattern. The
leaves stirred like elephant ears, not from the prevailing breeze but from
draughts of warm air blowing out of the crowns of the trees.

A dozen brassimips formed the patch. The tree rarely grew singly.
The soil about each tree bulged upwards and was starred with cracks,
suggesting the considerable bulk of vegetation below. The heat that the
trees syphoned up to their leaf system enabled the plants to thaw
frozen ground, so that they continued to grow even in permafrost
conditions.

Jassiklas lived under the leathery leaves. They took advantage of the
sheltering warmth to put forth timid brown-blue flowers. As Vry
stooped to pick one, Dathka returned to her side and spoke.

"I'm going into the tree."

She construed this as an invitation to join him, and followed. A slave was pulling up leather buckets full of chips from the interior and throwing them to the pigs. Pulped brassimip chips had fed Embruddock's pigs through the dark centuries.

"That's what attracted the stungebag," Vry said. The monstrous animals were as fond of brassimip as the pigs.

A wood ladder led into the tree. As she followed Dathka down, her eyes came for a moment level with the ground. As if drowning in earth, she saw the leather leaves waving about her. Beyond the backs of the pigs were the men, fur-clad, standing among the wreckage of the giant stungebag. There was snowy high ground and a sky of slate over all. She climbed down into the tree.

Warm air assailed her cheeks, making her blink, carrying with it a perfumed rotting smell that both repelled and attracted her. The air had come from a long way down; brassimip roots bored far into the crust. With age, the core of the tree commenced a fermenting process which released a hardening substance resembling keratin. A tube formed through the centre of the tree. A heat pump was established, warming leaves and underground branches with heat trapped at lower levels.

This favourable environment created a refuge for several sorts of animal, some decidedly nasty.

Dathka reached out a hand to steady Vry. She climbed off the ladder beside him and stood in a bulb-shaped natural chamber. Three dirty-looking women were working there. They greeted Vry, then went on scraping chips of brassimip flesh from the walls of the trees, loading them into the bucket.

Brassimip had a flavour rather like parsnip or turnip, but was bitter. Humans ate it only in times of starvation. Normally, it made pig feed—in particular, feed for the sows whose milk went to the making of rathel, Oldorando's staple winter drink.

A narrow gallery opened to one side. It led into the topmost branch of the tree, the leaves of which would surface in a bunch some distance away. Mature brassimips had six branches. The topmost branches were generally left to grow without interference; being nearest to the surface, they harboured a variety of sheltering nasties.

Dathka indicated the central tube going down into the darkness. He climbed down. After a moment's hesitation, Vry followed, and the women paused in their labours to watch her go, smiling part in sympathy, part in mockery. Directly she got into the tube, it was completely dark. Below was only the eternal night of earth. She thought that she, like Shay Tal, was having to descend into the world of fessups to gather knowledge, despite her protests.

The tube was marked by growth rings which formed ridges. The ridges were used as steps. The tube was narrow enough for anyone ascending or descending to plant her back securely against the opposite side of the tube.

Rising air whispered in their ears. A cobwebby thing, a living ghost, brushed Vry's cheek. She resisted an impulse to scream.

They climbed down to a point where the second branches left the main trunk. Here the bulb-shaped chamber was even smaller than the one above; they stood close, heads together. Vry could smell Dathka and feel his body against hers. Something stirred in her.

"See the lights?" Dathka said.

There was tension in his voice. She fought with herself, terrified by the lust that flooded her. Should he lay a finger on her, this silent man, she would fall into his arms, would rip away her furs, strip herself naked, fall copulating with him in the dark subterranean bed. Obscenely delightful images filled her.

"I want to go up again," she said, forcing the words from her throat.

"Don't be scared. Look at the lights."

In a daze, she looked about, still catching his scent. She was staring into the second branch down from the surface. There spots of light, starlike—galaxies of red stars, imprisoned in the tree.

He shuffled in front of her, eclipsing constellations with his shoulder. He thrust something pillowlike into her arms. It was light, covered with what she took for coir, as stiff as the hairs of a stungebag. Its star eyes looked unwinkingly up at her. In her confused state she did not identify it.

"What is it?"

For answer—perhaps he felt her desire after all; but could he make no stronger response, if so?—Dathka stroked her face with a clumsy tenderness.

"Oh, Dathka," she sighed. Trembling took her, beginning from the viscera and spreading through her eddre. She could not control herself.

"We'll take it up. Don't be scared."

The black-haired pigs were scuttling among the brassimip leaves as they emerged into daylight. The world seemed blindingly bright, the ring of axes intolerably loud, the scent of jassiklas unduly strong.

Vry sank down and listlessly regarded the small crystalline animal she held. It was in a state like the phagor's tether, curled into a ball with its nose tucked into its tail, its four legs folded neatly into its stomach. It was immobile, and felt as if made of glass. She could not uncurl it. Its eyes fixed her with a remote gaze, unwinking between immobile lids. Through its dusty grey coat, striations of faded colour showed.

In some way, she hated it, as she hated him—so insensitive to a woman's feelings that he had mistaken her trembling for the vibrations of fear. Yet she was grateful that his stupidity had prevented her from certain disgrace, grateful and resentful.

"It's a glossy," Dathka said, squatting by her, looking aslant into her face as if puzzled.

"A gossie?" For a moment she wondered if he was trying to be uncharacteristically funny.

"A *glossy*. They hibernate in the brassimips, where it's warm. Take it home."

"Shay Tal and I have seen them west of the river. Hoxneys. That's what they're called when they emerge from hibernation." And what would Shay Tal have thought if . . .

"Take it," he repeated. "A present from me."

"Thank you," she said, with contempt. She rose, emotions in place again.

She found she had blood on her cheek, where he had stroked her with his cut hand.

The slaves were still hacking away at the monstrous carcass. Laintal Ay had arrived, and was talking to Tanth Ein and Aoz Roon. The latter summoned Dathka vigorously, waving his hand over his head in command. With a resigned look of farewell to Vry, Dathka made off towards the Lord of Embruddock.

The busy things men did were nothing to her. She tucked the glossy between her arm and her shallow bosom and turned downhill towards the distant towers.

When she heard the sound of someone running to catch her up, she said to herself, Well, he's too late now, but it was Laintal Ay.

"I'll walk down with you, Vry," he said. As she remarked, he seemed in a carefree mood.

"I thought you were having trouble with Aoz Roon."

"Oh, he's always a bit touchy after a brush with Shay Tal. He's a great man, really. I'm pleased about the stungebag, too. Now that the weather is warming up, they're harder to find."

The children were still romping by the geysers. Laintal Ay admired her glossy, and burst into a snatch of hunter's song:

> *"The glossies that sleep*
> *When the snowdrifts are deep*
> *Will wake up to eddre-filling rain,*
> *And then hoxneys will spread*
> *With their high-stepping tread*
> *Across the plain, across the flower-thrilling plain."*

"You are in a good humour! Is Oyre being nice to you?"

"Oyre's always nice."

They went their different ways, Vry heading for her ruined tower, where she showed her present to Shay Tal. Shay Tal examined the little crystalline animal.

"It's not good to eat at this stage of its life. The flesh may be poisonous."

"I don't plan to eat it. I want to guard it till it wakes."

"Life is serious, my dear. We may have to go hungry if Aoz Roon sets himself firmly against us." She contemplated Vry for a while without speaking, as was increasingly her habit. "I shall fast and defy him. I need no material things. I can be as ruthless with myself as he can be with me."

"But really he . . ." Words failed Vry. She could utter no reassurance to the older woman, who continued determinedly.

"As I told you, I have two immediate intentions. First, I shall conduct a scientific experiment to determine my powers. Then I shall descend into the world of the gossies, to hold concourse with Loilanun. She must now know much that I don't. Depending on what I learn from these things, I may decide to leave Oldorando entirely."

"Oh, don't leave, please, ma'am. Are you sure that's the right thing to do? I'll go with you if you go, I swear!"

"We'll see about that. Leave me now, please."

Feeling deflated, Vry climbed the ladder to her ruinous room. She flung herself down on her couch.

"I want a lover, that's what I want. A lover . . . Life's so empty. . . ."

But after a while, she roused herself and looked out of the window at the sky, where clouds and birds sailed. At least it was better to be here than in the world below, where Shay Tal planned to go.

She recalled Laintal Ay's song. The woman who had written the song—if it was a woman—had known that the snow would eventually disappear and that flowers and animals would emerge. Perhaps it would happen.

From her nighttime observations, she knew that there were changes in the sky. The stars were not fessups but fires, fires burning not in rock but air. Imagine a great fire burning in outer darkness. As it came nearer, its warmth would be felt. Perhaps the two sentinels would draw nearer, and warm the world.

Then the glossies would come back to life, turning into hoxneys with high-stepping tread, just as the song had it.

She determined to concentrate on her astronomy. The stars knew more than the gossies, for all that Shay Tal said, though it was shocking to find that one disagreed with such a majestic person.

She tucked the glossy into a warm corner by her couch, wrapping the pathetic little thing in fur so that only its face showed. Day by day, she willed it to come alive. She whispered to it and encouraged it. She longed to see it grow and skip about her room. But after a few days, the gleam in the glossy's eyes dimmed and went out; the creature had expired with never a blink.

Despairingly, Vry took it to the crumbling top of the tower and flung the bundle away. It was still wrapped in furs, as if it were a dead baby.

A passion of restlessness seized Shay Tal. More and more, her statements became preachments. Though the other women brought her food, she preferred to starve herself, preparing to go into deep pauk to confer with the illustrious dead. If wisdom was not found there, then she would look farther afield, beyond the farmyard.

First, she determined to test out her own powers of sorcery. A few miles away to the east lay Fish Lake, scene of her "miracle." While she teased herself as to the true nature of what had happened there, the citizens of Oldorando were in no doubt. Throughout that cold spring, they made pilgrimages to gaze upon the spectacle in the ice, and to tremble with fear not unmixed with pride. The pilgrims encountered numbers of Borlienians who also came to marvel. Once, two phagors were seen, cowbirds perched with folded wings upon their shoulders, standing mute upon the far shore, regarding their crystalline dead.

As warmth returned to the world, the tableau began to slip. What was awesome turned grotesque. One morning, the ice was gone, the statuary became a heap of decomposing flesh. Visitors encountered nothing more impressive than a floating eyeball or a mop of hide. Fish Lake itself drained and disappeared almost as rapidly as it had formed. All that remained to mark the miracle was a pile of bones and curving kaidaw horns. But the memory remained, enlarging through the lenses of reminiscence. And Shay Tal's doubts remained.

She went down into the square in the afternoon, at an hour when milder weather tempted people to walk out and talk in a way once foreign to them. Women and daughters, men and sons, hunters and corpsmen, young and old, strolled forth to pass the time of day. Almost anyone would put himself or herself at Shay Tal's beck and call; almost no one wanted to talk to her.

Laintal Ay and Dathka were standing with their friends, laughing. Laintal Ay caught Shay Tal's glance, and came over to her reluctantly when she beckoned.

"I'm about to conduct an experiment, Laintal Ay. I want you with me as a reliable witness. I won't get you into further trouble with Aoz Roon."

"I'm on good terms with him."

She explained that the experiment was taking place by the Voral; first, she had a mind to explore the old temple. They walked together through the crowd, Laintal Ay saying nothing.

"Are you embarrassed to be with me?"

"I always take pleasure in your company, Shay Tal."

"You need not be polite. Do you think I am a sorceress?"

"You are an unusual woman. I revere you for that."

"Do you love me?"

At that, he was embarrassed. Instead of answering directly, he cast his gaze down to the mud, muttering, "You are like a mother to me, since my mother died. Why ask such questions?"

"I wish I were your mother. Then I could be proud. Laintal Ay, you also have an inwardness to your nature. I feel it. That inwardness will distress you, yet it gives you life, it is life. Don't ignore it, cultivate it. Most of these people jostling us have no inwardness."

"Is inwardness the same as conflict?"

She gave a sharp laugh, gripping her body with her forearms.

"Listen, we are trapped in this wretched hamlet among meagre personalities. A whole series of greater realities can be happening elsewhere. So much must be done. I may leave Oldorando."

"Where will you go?"

She shook her head. "Sometimes I feel that the mere crush of dull people will cause us to explode, and we'll all scatter from here across the world. You note how many babies have been born of recent years."

He looked round at all the friendly familiar faces in the lane, and suspected that she was talking for effect, though there were more children.

He put his shoulder to the door of the old temple and heaved it open. They entered and stood silent. A bird was trapped inside. It flew round and round, darting close to them as if scrutinizing them, then soared upward and escaped through a hole in the roof.

Light filtered down through the gaps, creating shafts through the twilight in which particles of dust whirled. The pigs had recently been moved to outside sties, but their smell still lingered. Shay Tal walked restlessly about, while Laintal Ay stood by the door, looking out into the street, remembering how he used to play here as a child.

The walls had been decorated with paintings executed in a stiff manner. Many had been spoiled. She looked up at the tall alcove above where the sacrificial altar stood, its stone dark still with something that could have been blood. Too high for vandals easily to deface hung a representation of Wutra. Shay Tal stood staring up at it, fists on hips.

Wutra was depicted, head and shoulders, in a furry cloak. His eyes glared down from a long animallike face with an expression which could be interpreted as compassion. His face was blue, representing an ideal colour of sky, where he dwelt. Rough white hair, almost manelike, surmounted the head; but the most startling departure from the human norm was a pair of horns thrusting upwards from his skull and terminating in silver bells.

Behind Wutra crowded other figures of a forgotten mythology, mainly horrendous, teeming through the sky. On his left and right shoulder perched his two sentinels. Batalix was depicted as oxlike, bearded, grey and old, with rays of light streaming from his spear. Freyr was larger, a virile green monkey with an hourglass suspended round his neck. His spear was bigger than that of Batalix, and also radiated rays of light.

She turned away, saying briskly, "Now my experiment, if Goija Hin is ready."

"Did you see what you wanted?" He was puzzled by her abruptness.

"I don't know. Later, I may know. I plan to go into pauk. I would have liked to ask one of the old priests whether Wutra was supposed to preside over the world below as he does over the earth and sky. . . . So many discontinuities."

Meanwhile, Goija Hin was bringing Myk out of the stable under the big tower. Goija Hin was the slave master, a man who exhibited all the stigmata of his calling. He was short but immensely solid, with bulging arms and legs. His features fitted clumsily on his low-browed face, which was adorned with wisps of whisker, randomly sited. His garments were leather and, waking or sleeping, he was accompanied by a leather knout. Everyone knew Goija Hin, a man impervious to blows or thought.

"Come on, Myk, you brute, time to make yourself useful," he said, speaking in his customary low snarl.

Myk ambled forth promptly, having grown up in slavery. He was the phagor longest in servitude in Oldorando, and could remember Goija Hin's predecessor, a man of far more terrible aspect. Black hairs grew in his patchy coat. His face was wrinkled, and the sacks under his eyes were messy with rheum.

He was always docile. On this occasion, Oyre was nearby to soothe him. While Oyre patted his bent shoulders, Goija Hin prodded him with a stick.

Oyre had acted as intermediary for Shay Tal and asked her father for permission to use a phagor in Shay Tal's experiment. Aoz Roon had carelessly told her to take Myk, since he was old.

The two humans led Myk to a curve of the Voral where the river flowed deep. Shay Tal's ruined tower stood not far away. Shay Tal and Laintal Ay were already waiting when the trio arrived. Shay Tal stood peering into the depths of the stream as if trying to decipher its secrets, her cheeks hollow, her expression bleak.

"Well, then, Myk," she said challengingly, as the beast approached. She regarded him calculatingly. Scrawny sacks of flesh hung down from his chest and stomach. Goija Hin had already strapped his hands behind his back. His head rolled apprehensively between his hunched shoulders. When he saw the Voral, he ran his milt anxiously up his nostril slits several times in quick succession, uttering a low cry of fear. Could it be that water would turn him into a statue?

Goija Hin gave Shay Tal a rough salute.

"Tie his legs together," Shay Tal ordered.

"Don't hurt him too much," Oyre said. "I've known Myk since I was a small girl and he's entirely docile. He used to give us rides, didn't he, Laintal Ay?"

Thus appealed to, Laintal Ay came forward. "Shay Tal won't hurt him," he said, smiling at Oyre. She regarded him questioningly.

Attracted by possible excitement, several women and boys came up to see what was going on, and stood in knots on the bank.

The river ran deep in the curve, cutting into the near bank only a few inches below the ground on which they stood. On the opposite side of the river, where it was shallower, a thin shelf of ice remained, preserved from direct sun by an overhang. This wafer jutted out towards deeper water, elaborately marked in glassy whorls, as if the water itself had taken a knife to carve it.

When Goija Hin had bound the legs of the unfortunate Myk, he pushed him to the edge of the river. Myk stuck his long head in the air, curled back his lower lips onto his stubbly chin, and let out a trumpet of fear.

Oyre clutched at his coat, begging Shay Tal not to harm him.

"Stand back," Shay Tal said. She gave the signal to Goija Hin to push the phagor in.

Goija Hin set his thick shoulders to Myk's ribs. The phagor tottered then plunged into the river with a splash. Shay Tal raised her arms in imperious gesture.

The watching women gave a shout and rushed forward. Rol Sakil was among them. Shay Tal motioned them back.

She stared down into the water and could see Myk struggling below the surface. Swathes of his coat came roiling upward with the disturbed water, brushing the surface like yellow weed.

The water remained water. The phagor remained alive.

"Pull him up," she ordered.

Goija Hin had Myk by two straps. He tugged and Laintal Ay helped. The old phagor's head and shoulders broke the surface and Myk gave a pathetic cry.

"Don't killydrown poor me!"

They dragged him ashore and he lay panting at Shay Tal's feet. She chewed her underlip, frowning at the Voral. The magic was not working.

"Throw him in again," one of the onlookers called.

"No more water or I finish," Myk said, thickly.

"Push him in again," Shay Tal ordered.

Myk went in a second time, and a third. But the water remained water. No miracle happened, and Shay Tal had to conceal her disappointment.

"That's enough," she said. "Goija Hin, take Myk away and feed him extra."

Oyre knelt compassionately by Myk's throat, crying and patting him. Dark water flowed from the phagor's lips and he began coughing. Laintal Ay knelt and put his arm round Oyre's shoulder.

Disdainfully, Shay Tal turned away. The experiment showed that phagors plus water did not make ice. The process was not inevitable. So what had happened at Fish Lake? Equally, she had not managed to turn the Voral to ice, as she had wished to do. So the experiment did not prove she was a sorceress. It did not prove she was not a sorceress; it seemed to prove that she had turned the phagors at Fish Lake to ice—unless there were other factors involved she had not considered.

She paused with her hand on the rough stone of the doorway to her tower, feeling the rasp of lichen against her palm. Until she found another explanation, she would have to treat herself as others treated her, as a sorceress. The more she starved, the more she respected herself. Of course, as a sorceress, she was destined to remain a virgin; sexual intercourse would destroy her magical powers. She gathered her furs against her lanky form and climbed the worn stairs.

The women on the bank looked from Myk's half-drowned body, surrounded by a growing puddle, to Shay Tal's retreating figure.

"Now what did she want to go and do that for?" old Rol Sakil asked the company. "How come she didn't drown the stupid thing properly while she was about it?"

The next time the council met, Laintal Ay rose and addressed them. He said that he had heard Shay Tal lecture. All knew of her miracle at Fish Lake, which had saved many lives. Nothing she did was directed to the ill of the community. He proposed that her academy should be recognised and supported.

Aoz Roon looked furious while Laintal Ay spoke. Dathka sat rigid in silence. The old men of the council peered at each other under their eyebrows and muttered uneasily. Eline Tal laughed.

"What do you wish us to do to aid this academy?" Aoz Roon asked.

"The temple is empty. Give it to Shay Tal. Let her hold meetings there every afternoon at promenade time. Use it as a forum, where anyone can speak. The cold has gone, people are freer. Open the temple as an academy for all, for men, women, and children."

His resounding words died into silence. Then Aoz Roon spoke.

"She cannot use the temple. We don't want a new lot of priests. We keep pigs in the temple."

"The temple is empty."

"From now on, pigs are kept in the temple."

"It's a bad day when we put pigs above the community."

The meeting eventually broke up in some disorder, as Aoz Roon marched out. Laintal Ay turned to Dathka, his cheeks flushed.

"Why didn't you support me?"

Dathka grinned sheepishly, tugged his narrow beard, stared down at the table. "You could not win if all Oldorando supported you. He has already banned the academy. You waste your breath, my friend."

As Laintal Ay was leaving the building, feeling disgusted with the world, Datnil Skar, master of the tawyers and tanners corps, called to him and grasped his sleeve.

"You spoke well, young Laintal Ay, yet Aoz Roon was right in what he said. Or, if not right, not unreasonable. If Shay Tal spoke in the temple, she would become a priestess and be worshipped. We don't want that—our ancestors got rid of the priests some generations ago."

Laintal Ay knew Master Datnil for a kindly and modest man. Restraining his anger, he looked down at the worn face and asked, "Why tell me this?"

Master Datnil looked about to see that no one was listening.

"Worship arises from ignorance. Believing in one fixed thing is a mark of ignorance. I respect attempts to drum facts into people's heads. I wanted to say that I am sorry you were defeated, though I don't agree with your proposition. I would be willing to address Shay Tal's academy if she will have me."

He removed his fur hat and set it on the lichenous sill. He smoothed his sparse grey hair and cleared his dry throat. He looked about him and smiled nervously. Although he had known everyone in the room since he was born, he was unaccustomed to the role of speaker. His stiff clothes creaked as he shifted from one foot to another.

"Don't be afraid of us, Master Datnil," Shay Tal said.

He caught the note of impatience in her voice. "It's only of your intolerance I'm afraid, ma'am," he replied, and some of the women squatting on the floor hid smiles behind their hands.

"You know what we do in our corps, because some of you work for me," Datnil Skar said. "Membership in the corps is for men only, of course, for the secrets of our profession are handed down from generation to generation. In particular, a master teaches all he knows to his personal novice or chief boy. When a master dies or retires, then the chief boy becomes master in his turn, as Raynil Layan will soon take over my position. . . ."

"A woman could do that just as well as any man," said one of the women, Cheme Phar. "I've worked for you long enough, Datnil Skar.

I know all the secrets of the brine pits. I could pickle myself, if need arose."

"Ah, but we have to have order and continuity, Cheme Phar," said the Master mildly.

"I could give the orders all right," said Cheme Phar, and everyone laughed, then looked at Shay Tal.

"Tell us about the continuity," the latter said. "We know, as Loila-nun taught us, that some of us are descended from Yuli the Priest, who came from the north, from Pannoval and Lake Dorzin. That's one continuity. What about continuity within the corps, Master Datnil?"

"All members of our corps were born and bred in Embruddock, even before it was Oldorando. To many generations."

"How many generations?"

"Ah, a good many . . ."

"Tell us how you know this."

He wiped his hands on his trousers.

"We have a record. Each master keeps a record."

"In writing?"

"That's correct. Writing in a book. The art is passed on. But the records are not to be disclosed to others."

"Why do you think that is?"

"They don't want the women taking over their jobs and doing it better," someone called, and again there was laughter. Datnil Skar smiled with embarrassment, and said no more.

"I believe that secrecy served a protective purpose at one time," Shay Tal said. "Certain arts, like metal forging and tannery, had to be kept alive in bad times, despite starvation or phagor raids. Probably there were very bad times in the past, and some arts were lost. We cannot make paper any longer. Perhaps there was once a paper-makers corps. Glass. We cannot make glass. Yet there are pieces of glass about —you all know what glass is. How is it that we are more stupid than our ancestors? Are we living, working, under some disadvantage we don't fully understand? That's one of the big questions we must keep in mind."

She paused. No one said anything, which always vexed her. She longed for any comment that would push the argument forward.

Datnil Skar said, "Mother Shay, you speak true, to the best of my belief. You understand that as master I am under oath to disclose secrets of my art to nobody; it's an oath I take to Wutra and to Embruddock. But I know that there were once bad times, of which I am not supposed to speak. . . ."

When he fell silent, she helped him with a smile. "Do you believe that Oldorando was once bigger than it is now?"

He looked at her with his head on one side. "I know you call this town a farmyard. But it survives. . . . It's the centre of the cosmos.

Well, that's not answering your question. My friends, you found rye and oats growing north of here, so let's speak of them. To the best of my belief, that place was once carefully tended fields, enclosed against wild beasts. The fields belonged to Embruddock. Many other cereals grew there and were cultivated. Now you cultivate them again, which is wise.

"You know we need bark for our tanning. We have a job to get hold of it. I do believe—well, I know . . ." He fell silent, then he said quietly, "Great forests of tall trees, which yield bark and wood, grew to the west and north. The region was called Kace. It was hot then, and there was no cold."

Someone said, "The time of heat—that's a legend left over from the priesthood. The sort of tale we're supposed to get out of our minds in the academy. We do know that it was once *colder* than it is now. Ask my grandma."

"What I'm saying is that, to the best of my belief, it was hot before it was cold," Datnil Skar said, slowly scratching the back of his grey head. "You should try to understand these things. Many lives go by, many years. There's a lot of history vanished. I know you women think that men are against you learning, and it may be so; but I speak sincerely when I say that you should support Shay Tal, despite various difficulties. As a master, I know how precious knowledge is. It seems to run out of the bottom of a community like water out of a sock."

They stood and clapped him politely when he left.

At Freyr-set, two days later, Shay Tal was pacing restlessly in her room in the isolated tower. A shout came from below. Immediately she thought of Aoz Roon, though the voice was not his.

She wondered who would venture beyond the barricades when light was growing dim. Putting her head out of the window, she saw Datnil Skar, his figure insubstantial in the dusk.

"Oh, come up, my friend," she cried. She went down to meet him. He appeared clutching a box, smiling nervously. They sat down facing each other on her stone floor, and she poured him a measure of rathel.

After some idle conversation, he said, "I think you know that I am due to retire soon as master of the tawyers and tanners corps? My chief boy will take my place. I'm getting old and he long ago knew all I have to teach."

"You come here because of that?"

He smiled and shook his head. "I come here, Mother Shay, because I—I experience an old man's admiration for you, for your person and your worth. . . . No, let me say it. I have always served and loved this community, and I believe you do the same, though you have the opposition of many men. So I wanted to do you a good turn while I was able to."

"You're a good man, Datnil Skar. Oldorando knows it. The community needs good people."

Sighing, he nodded. "I have served Embruddock—or Oldorando as we should call it—every day of my life, and have never left it. Yet scarcely a day's gone by . . ." He broke off in his shy way, smiled, and said, "I believe I am speaking to a kindred spirit when I say that scarcely a day has gone by since I was a lad when I haven't wondered . . . wondered what was happening in other places, far away from here."

He paused, cleared his throat, then said more briskly, "I'll tell you a tale. It's only brief. I remember one terrible winter when I was a lad when the phagors attacked, and disease and famine followed. Many people died. And the phagors were dying too, although we didn't know it at the time. It was so dark, I swear days are brighter now. . . . Anyhow, the phagors left behind a human boy during the slaughter. His name was—I'm ashamed to say I've forgotten it, but to the best of my belief it was something like Krindlesheddy. A long name. Once I knew it clearly. The years have made me forget.

"Krindlesheddy had come from a country a long way to the north, Sibornal. He said that Sibornal was a land of perpetual glaciers. I was selected to be chief boy in my corps, and in Sibornal he was to be a priest, so we were both dedicated to our calling. He—Krindlesheddy or whatever his name was—thought our life was easy. The geysers kept Oldorando warm.

"As a young member of the priesthood, my friend had belonged with some colonists who moved south to escape the cold. They came to a better land by a river. There they had to fight with the local inhabitants of a realm called—well, the name has gone after these many years. A great battle raged, in which Krindlesheddy—if that was his name—was injured. The survivors fled, only to be caught by raiding phagors. It was mere fortune that he escaped them here. Or perhaps they left him because he was wounded.

"We did what we could to help the lad, but he died after a month. I cried for him. I was only young. Yet even then I envied him because he'd seen something of the world. He told me that in Sibornal the ice came in many colours and was beautiful."

As Master Datnil finished his story, sitting meekly beside Shay Tal, Vry entered the room, on her way to the floor above.

He smiled kindly at her, saying to Shay Tal, "Don't send Vry away. I know she's your chief boy and you trust her, as I wish I could trust my chief boy. Let her hear what I have to say." He laid his wooden box on the floor in front of him. "I have brought the Master Book of our corps for you to see."

Shay Tal looked as if she would faint. She knew that if this borrowing was discovered, the makers corps would kill the master without hesitation. . . . She could guess at the inner struggle the old man had gone through before bringing it. She wrapped her thin arms about him and kissed him on his wrinkled forehead.

Vry came and knelt down by him, excitement on her face.

"Let's have a look!" she exclaimed, reaching out a hand, forgetting her diffidence.

He put his hand over hers, detainingly.

"Notice first the wood of which the box is made. It's not from a rajabaral; the grain is too beautiful. Notice how it's carved. Notice the delicate metal chasing that binds the corners. Could our metal-makers corps do such fine work today?"

When they had examined the details, he opened the box. He brought out a large tome bound in heavy leather, tooled with an elaborate design.

"This I did myself, Mother. I rebound the book. It's the inside that's old."

The pages inside were carefully, often elaborately, written by a number of different hands. Datnil Skar turned the pages rapidly, even now reluctant to reveal too much. But the women clearly saw dates, names, lists, and various entries and figures.

He looked up into their faces, smiling a grave smile. "In its way, this volume gives a history of Embruddock over the years. And each surviving corps has a similar volume, of that I am certain."

"The past is gone. We're trying now to look outward to the future," said Vry. "We don't want to be stuck in the past. We want to go out . . ."

Indecisively, she let the sentence die, regretting that in her excitement she had brought herself to their attention. Looking at the faces of the other two, she saw they were older and would never agree with her. Although their aims were in general agreement, a difference existed that could never be bridged.

"The clue to the future lies in the past," Shay Tal said, comfortingly but dismissively, for she had made such remarks to Vry before. Turning to the old man, she said, "Master Datnil, we greatly appreciate your brave gesture in letting us look at the secret book. Perhaps some day we may examine it more thoroughly. Would you tell us how many masters there have been in your corps since records commenced?"

He closed the book and began packing it in its box. Saliva trickled from his old mouth, and his hands shook badly.

"The rats know the secrets of Oldorando . . . I'm in danger, bringing this book here. Just an old fool . . . Listen, my dears, there was a great king who ruled over all Campannlat in the old days, called King Denniss. He foresaw that the world—this world which the ancipitals

call Hrrm-Bhhrd Ydohk—would lose its warmth, as a bucket slops
water when you carry it down a lane. So he set about founding our
corps, with iron rules to be enforced. All the makers corps were to preserve wisdom through dark times, until warmth returned."

He spoke chantingly, as from memory.

"Our corps has survived since the good king's time, though in some
periods it had no wherewithal to tan leather. According to the record
here, its numbers once sank to a master and an apprentice, who lived
below ground a distance away. . . . Dreadful times. But we survived."

As he was wiping his mouth, Shay Tal asked what period of time they
were discussing.

Datnil Skar gazed at the darkening rectangle of window as if contemplating flight from the question.

"I don't understand all the notations in our book. You know our
confusions with the calendar. As we can understand from our own
day, new calendars represent considerable dislocations. . . . Embruddock—forgive me, I fear telling you too much—it didn't always belong
to . . . our sort of people."

He shook his head, darting his gaze nervously round the room. The
women waited, motionless as phagors in the old dull room. He spoke
again.

"Many people have died. There was a great plague, the Fat Death.
Invasions . . . the Seven Blindnesses . . . tales of woe. We hope our
present Lord—" again a glance round the room—"will prove as wise
as King Denniss. The good king founded our corps in a year called 249
Before Nadir. We do not know who Nadir was. What we do know is
that I—allowing for a break in the record—am the sixty-eighth master
of the tanners and tawyers corps. The sixty-eighth . . ." He peered
shortsightedly at Shay Tal.

"Sixty-eight . . ." Trying to hide her dismayed astonishment, she
gathered her furs about her with a characteristic gesture. "That's many
generations, stretching back to antiquity."

"Yes, yes, stretching right back." Master Datnil nodded complacently, as if personally acquainted with vast stretches of time. "It's
nearly seven centuries since our corps was founded. Seven centuries,
and still it freezes of nights."

Embruddock in its surrounding wilderness was a beached ship. It still
gave the crew shelter, though it would never sail again.

So greatly had time dismantled a once proud city that its inhabitants
did not realise that what they regarded as a town was nothing more
than the remains of a palace, which had stood in the middle of a
civilisation obliterated by climate, madness, and the ages.

As the weather improved, the hunters were forced to go in increasingly long expeditions in search of game. The slaves planted fields and dreamed of impossible liberty. The women stayed at home and grew neurotic.

While Shay Tal fasted and became more solitary, Vry became full of a repressed energy and developed her friendship with Oyre. With Oyre, she talked over all that Master Datnil had said, and found a sympathetic listener. They agreed that there were puzzling riddles in history, yet Oyre was lightly sceptical.

"Datnil Skar is old and a bit gaga—Father always says so," she said, and limped found the room in parody of the Master's gait, exclaiming in a piping voice, " 'Our corps is so exclusive we didn't even let King Denniss join. . . .' "

When Vry laughed, Oyre said, more seriously, "Master Datnil could be executed for showing his corps Master Book about—that's proof he's gaga."

"And even then he wouldn't let us look at it properly." Vry was silent, and then burst out, "If only we could put all the facts together. Shay Tal just collects them, writes them down. There must be a way of making a—a structure from them. So much has been lost—Master Datnil is right there. The cold was so bitter, once on a time, that almost everything inflammable was burnt—wood, paper, all records. You realise *we don't even know what year it is?*—Though the stars might tell us. Loil Bry's calendar is stupid, calendars should be based on years, not people. People are so fallible . . . and so am I. Oh, I'll go mad, I swear!"

Oyre burst out laughing and hugged Vry.

"You're the sanest person I know, you idiot." They fell to discussing the stars again, sitting on the bare floor close together. Oyre had been with Laintal Ay to look at the fresco in the old temple. "The sentinels are clearly depicted, with Batalix above Freyr as usual, but almost touching, above Wutra's head."

"Every year, the two suns get closer," Vry said, decisively. "Last month, they virtually touched as Batalix overtook Freyr, and no one paid any notice. Next year, they will collide. What then? . . . Or maybe one passes behind the other."

"Perhaps that's what Master Datnil meant by a Blindness? It would suddenly be dimday, wouldn't it, if one sentinel disappeared? Perhaps there will be Seven Blindnesses, as once before." She looked frightened, and moved nearer her friend. "It will be the end of the world. Wutra will appear, looking furious, of course."

Vry laughed and jumped to her feet. "The world didn't end last time and won't do so this time. No, perhaps it will mark a new beginning." Her face became radiant. "That's why the seasons are growing warmer. Once Shay Tal has done her ghastly pauk, we will tackle the question anew. I shall work at my mathematics. Let the Blindnesses come—I embrace them!"

They danced round the room, laughing wildly.

"How I long for some great experience!" Vry cried.

Shay Tal, meanwhile, showed more clearly than before the little bird bones below her flesh, and her dark skins hung more loosely about her body. Food was brought her by the women, but she would not eat.

"Fasting suits my ravenous soul," she said, pacing about her chilly room, when Vry and Oyre remonstrated with her, and Amin Lim stood meekly by. "Tomorrow I will go into pauk. You three and Rol Sakil can be with me. I will dredge up ancient knowledge from the well of the past. Through the fessups I will reach to that generation which built our towers and corridors. I will descend centuries if necessary, and confront King Denniss himself."

"How wonderful!" Amin Lim exclaimed.

Birds came to perch on her crumbling window sill and be fed the bread Shay Tal would not touch.

"Don't sink into the past, ma'am," Vry counselled her. "That's the way of old men. Look ahead, look outward. There's no profit in interrogating the dead."

So unused to argument had Shay Tal grown that she had difficulty in refraining from scolding her chief disciple. She looked and saw, almost with startlement, that the diffident young thing was now a woman. Her face was pallid, with shadows under her eyes, and Oyre's the same.

"Why are you two so pale? Are you ill?"

Vry shook her head.

"Tonight there's an hour of darkness before dimday. I'll show you then what Oyre and I are doing. While the rest of the world was sleeping, we have been working."

The evening was clear at Freyr-set. Warmth departed from the world as the younger women escorted Shay Tal up to the roof of the ruinous tower. A lens of ghost light stretched upwards from the horizon where Freyr had set, reaching halfway to zenith. There was little cloud to conceal the heavens; as their eyes became accustomed to the darkness, the stars overhead flashed out in brilliance. In some quarters of the sky, the stars were relatively sparse, in others they hung in clusters. Overhead, trailing from one horizon to the other, was a broad, irregular band of light, where the stars were as thick as mist, and there occasional brilliances burned.

"It's the most magnificent sight in the world," Oyre said. "Don't you think so, ma'am?"

Shay Tal said, "In the world below hang fessups like stars. They are the souls of the dead. Here you see the souls of the unborn. As above, so below."

"I think we have to look to an entirely different principle to explain the sky," Vry said firmly. "All motions here are regular. The stars advance about that bright star there, which we call the polar star." She pointed to a star high above their heads. "In the twenty-five hours of the day, the stars rotate once, rising in the east and setting in the west like the two sentinels. Doesn't that prove they are similar to the two sentinels, only much farther from us?"

The young women showed Shay Tal the star map they were making, with the relative positions of stars marked on a vellum sheet. She evinced little interest, and said, "The stars cannot affect us as the gossies do. How does this hobby of yours advance knowledge? You'd do better to sleep at night."

Vry sighed. "The sky is alive. It's not a tomb, like the world below. Oyre and I have stood here and seen comets flaring, landing on the earth. And there are four bright stars that move differently from all the others, the wanderers, of which the old songs sing. Those wanderers sometimes double back in their passage across the sky. And one comes over very fast. We'll see it presently. We think it's close to us, and we call it Kaidaw, because of its speed."

Shay Tal rubbed her hands together, looking apprehensively about. "Well, it's cold up here."

"It's colder still down below, where the gossies lie," Oyre retorted.

"You keep a watch on your tongue, young woman. You're no friend of the academy if you distract Vry from her proper work."

Her face became cold and hawklike; she turned away quickly, as if to shield Oyre and Vry from its sight, and climbed back downstairs without further words.

"Oh, I shall pay for this," Vry said. "I shall have to be extra humble to make up for this."

"You're too humble, Vry, and she's too haughty. Scumb her academy. She's scared of the sky, like most people. That's her trouble, sorceress or no sorceress. She puts up with stupid people like Amin Lim because they pander to her haughtiness."

She clutched Vry with a sort of angry passion and began to list the stupidities of everyone she knew.

"What upsets me is that we did not get the chance to make her look through our telescope," Vry said.

It was the telescope that had made the greatest difference to Vry's astronomical interest. When Aoz Roon had become lord, and had gone to live in the big tower, Oyre had been free to grub through all kinds of decaying possessions stored there in trunks. The telescope had come to light tucked among moth-riddled clothes which fell to pieces at the touch. It was simply made—perhaps by the long-defunct glass-makers corps—being no more than a leather tube which held two lenses in place; but when turned upon the wandering stars, the telescope had the power to change Vry's perceptions. For the wanderers showed distinct discs. In that, they resembled the sentinels, though they did not emit light.

From this discovery, Vry and Oyre had concluded that the wanderers were near to the earth, and the stars far away—some very far. From trappers who worked by starlight they had the names of the wanderers: Ipocrene, Aganip, and Copaise. And there was the fast one they had named themselves, Kaidaw. Now they sought to prove that these were worlds like their own, possibly even with people in them.

Gazing at her friend, Vry saw only the general outlines of that beautiful face and powerful head, and recognised how much Oyre resembled Aoz Roon. Both Oyre and her father seemed so full of spirit—and Oyre had been born outside agreements. Vry wondered if by chance—by any remote chance—Oyre had been with a man, in the dark of a brassimip or elsewhere. Then she shut the naughty thought away and turned her gaze to the sky.

They stayed rather soberly on the top of their tower until Hour-Whistler sounded again. A few minutes later Kaidaw rose and sailed up to the zenith.

Earth Observation Station Avernus—Vry's Kaidaw—hung high over Helliconia, while the continent of Campannlat turned beneath it. The station's crew devoted most of their attention to the world below; but the other three planets of the binary system were also under constant surveillance by automatic instrumentation.

On all four planets, temperatures were rising. Improvement overall was steady; only on the ground did anomalies register on tender flesh.

Helliconia's drama of generations in travail was set upon a stage sparsely structured by a few overriding circumstances. The planet's year about Batalix—Star B to the scholars of the Avernus—took 480 days (the "small" year). But Helliconia also had a Great Year, of which the people of Embruddock knew nothing in their present state. The Great Year was the time Star B, and its planets with it, took to make an orbit round Freyr, the Star A of the scholars.

That Great Year took 1825 Helliconian "small" years. Since one Helliconian small year was the equivalent of 1.42 terrestrial years, this meant a Great Year of 2592 terrestrial years—a period during which many generations flourished and departed from the scene.

The Great Year represented an enormous elliptical journey. Helliconia was slightly larger than Earth, with a mass 1.28 times Earth's; in many respects, it was Earth's sister planet. Yet on that elliptical journey across thousands of years, it became almost two planets—a frozen one at apastron, when farthest from Freyr, an overheated one at periastron, when nearest Freyr.

Every small year, Helliconia drew nearer to Freyr. Spring was about to signify its arrival in spectacular fashion.

Midway between the high stars in their courses and the fessups sinking slowly towards the original boulder, two women squatted one on either side of a bracken bed. The light in the shuttered room was dim enough to render them anonymous, giving them the aspect of two mourning figures set on either side of the prostrate figure on the couch. It could be determined only that one was plump and no longer youthful, and the other gripped by the desiccating processes of age.

Rol Sakil Den shook her grizzled head and looked down with lugubrious compassion on the figure before her.

"Poor dear thing, she used to be so nice as a girl, she's no right to torture herself as she does."

"She should have kept to her loaves, I say," said the other woman, to make herself agreeable.

"Feel how thin she is. Feel her loins. No wonder she's gone weird."

Rol Sakil was herself as thin as a mummy, her frame eroded by arthritis. She had been midwife to the community before growing too old for such exertions. She still tended those in pauk. Now that Dol was off her hands, she hung on the fringes of the academy, always ready to criticise, rarely prepared to think.

"She's got so narrow she couldn't bring forth a stick from that womb of hers, never mind a baby. Wombs have to be tended—they are the central part of a woman."

"She has much to look to beside babies," said Amin Lim.

"Oh, I've as much respect for knowledge as the next person, but when knowledge gets in the way of the natural facilities of copulation, then knowledge should move over."

"As for that," Amin Lim said with some asperity, from the other side of the bed, "her natural facilities were set aback when your Dol settled herself in Aoz Roon's bed. She feels deeply for him, as who doesn't? A presentable man, Aoz Roon, besides being Lord of Embruddock."

Rol Sakil sniffed. "That's no reason why she should go off intercourse entirely. She could always fill in time elsewhere, to keep herself in training. Besides, *he* won't come round knocking at *her* door again, you mark my words. He's got his hands full with our Dol."

The old woman beckoned Amin Lim nearer to bestow a confidence and they put their heads together over the supine body of Shay Tal. "Dol always keeps him at it—both by inclination and policy. A course I'd recommend to any woman, you included, Amin Lim. I hazard you enjoy a length now and again—it ain't human not to, at your age. You ask your man."

"Oh, I daresay there isn't a woman as hasn't fancied Aoz Roon, for all his tempers."

Shay Tal sighed in her pauk. Rol Sakil took her hand in her own withered one and said, still using a confidential mode, "My Dol tells me as he mutters terribly in his sleep. I tell her that's the sign of a guilty conscience."

"What's he got to be guilty about, then?" Amin Lim asked.

"Now, then—there I could tell you a tale. . . . That morning, after all the drinking and carrying on, I was about early, as of old. And as I went out, well wrapped against the cold of morning, I come on a body in the dark and I says to myself, 'Why here's some fool drunk out of his wits, lying asleep on the ground.' There he was, at the base of the big tower."

She paused to observe the effect of her story on Amin Lim, who, having nothing else to do, was listening intently. Rol Sakil's little eyes became almost hidden in wrinkles as she continued.

"I'd never have thought a mite more of it—I likes a drop of pig's counsel myself. But round the other side of the tower, what do I find but another body lying there. 'That's two fools drunk out of their wits, lying asleep on the ground,' says I to myself. And I'd never have thought a mite more of it, but when it's given out that young Klils and his brother Nahkri were found dead together, lying at the bottom of their tower, why, that's another matter. . . ." She sniffed.

"Everyone said that's where they were found."

"Ah, but I found them first, and they weren't together. So they didn't fight together, did they? That's fishy, Amin Lim, isn't it? So I says to myself, 'Someone went and pushed them two brothers off the top of the tower.' Who might it be, who stood most to gain by their deaths? Well, girl, that's something I leave to others to judge. All I says is, I says to our Dol, 'You cultivate your fear of heights, Dol. Don't you go near no edges of towers while you're with Aoz Roon,' I says. 'Don't you go near no edges of towers and you'll be all right. . . .' That's what I says."

Amin Lim shook her head. "Shay Tal wouldn't love Aoz Roon if he did that kind of thing. And she'd know. She's wise, she'd know for sure."

Rol Sakil rose and hobbled nervously about the stone room, shaking her head in doubt. "Where men's concerned, Shay Tal is the same as the rest of us. She doesn't always think with her harneys—sometimes she uses the thing between her legs instead."

"Oh, hush with you." Amin Lim looked sorrowfully down at her friend and mentor. Privately, she wished that Shay Tal's life were ruled more in the way Rol Sakil indicated: she might then be happier.

Shay Tal lay stretched out stiffly on her left side, in the pauk attitude. Her eyes seemed barely closed. Her breathing was scarcely audible, punctuated by long-drawn-out sighs. Looking at the austere contours of that loved face, Amin Lim thought she was watching someone facing death with composure. Only the mouth, growing tighter occasionally, indicated the terror it was impossible to suppress in the presence of the denizens of the world below.

Although Amin Lim had once gone into pauk herself, under guidance, the fright of seeing her father again had been enough for her. The extra dimension was now closed; she would never again visit that world until her final call came.

"Poor thing, poor little thing," she said as she stroked her friend's head, lovingly regarding its grey hairs, hoping to ease her passage through the black realm lying below life.

Though the soul had no eyes, yet it could see in a medium where terror replaced vision.

It looked down, as it began to fall, into a space more enormous than the night sky. Into that space, Wutra could never come. This was a region of which Wutra the Undying had no cognisance. With his blue face, his undaunted gaze, his slender horns, he belonged to the great frosty battle taking place elsewhere. This region was hell because he was not. Every star that gleamed was a death.

There was no smell except terror. Every death had its immutable position. No comets flared down here; this was the realm of entropy absolute, without change, the event death of the universe, to which life could respond only with terror.

As the soul did now.

The land-octaves wound over real territory. They could be likened to paths, except that they more resembled winding walls, endlessly dividing the world, only their tops showing above the surfaces. Their real substance went down deep into the seamless ground, penetrating to the original boulder on which the disc of the world rested.

In the original boulder, at the bottom of their appropriate land-octaves, the gossies and fessups were stacked, like thousands of ill-preserved flies.

The gaunt soul of Shay Tal sank down on its predestined land-octave, negotiating a course between the fessups. They resembled mummies; their stomachs and eye sockets were hollow, their boney feet dangled; their skins were coarse as old sacking, yet transparent, allowing a glimpse of luminescent organs beneath. Their mouths were open like fish, as if they still recalled the days when they breathed air. Less ancient gossies had their mouths stuffed with things like fireflies which issued forth in smokey dust. All these old put-away things were without motion, yet the wandering soul could sense their fury—a fury more intense than any of them could have experienced before obsidian claimed them.

As the soul settled between their ranks, it saw them suspended in irregular rows which stretched to places she could not travel, to Borlien, to the seas, to Pannoval, to far Sibornal, and even to the icy wildernesses of the east. All were relegated here to being units of one great collection, filed under their appropriate land-octaves.

To living senses, there were no directions. Yet there was a direction. The soul had its own sail. It had to be alert. A fessup had little more volition than dust, yet fury pent in its eddre gave it strength. A fessup could swallow any soul sailing too close, thus freeing itself to walk upon the earth again, causing terror and disease wherever it went.

Well aware of danger, the soul sank through the obsidian world, through what Loilanun had called scratched emptiness. It arrived finally before the gossie of Shay Tal's mother. The drab thing appeared made of wires and twigs, which formed patterns like dried halters of breasts and thrusting hipbones. It glared at its daughter-soul. It showed its old brown teeth in its slack lower jaw. It was itself a brown stain. Yet all its details could be viewed, as a pattern of lichen on a wall can perfectly depict a man or a necropolis.

The gossie emitted a noise of unceasing complaint. Gossies are negatives of human lives and believe nothing good of life in consequence. No gossie considers that its life on earth was long enough, or that its tenure there achieved the happiness it deserved. Nor can it believe that it has earned such oblivion. It craves living souls. Only living souls can give ear to its endless grievances.

"Mother, I come dutifully before you again and will listen to your complaints."

"You faithless child, when did you last come, how long, and reluctant, oh, always reluctant, evermore reluctant, as in those thankless days—I should have known, I should have known—when I bore you not wishing another offspring squeezed from my poor sore loins—"

"I will listen to your complaints—"

"Pah, yes, reluctantly, just as your father cared nothing, nothing for my pain, knew nothing, did nothing, just like all men but who's to say children are any better sucking your life from you—oh, I should have known—I tell you I despised that clod of a man always demanding, demanding everything, more than I had to give, never never satisfied, the nights of grief, the days, caught in that trap, that's what it was, and you come here, a trap designed to swindle me out of my youth, pretty, yes, yes, I was pretty, that damned disease—I see you laughing at me now, little you care—"

"I care, I care, Mother, it's agony to behold you!"

"Yes, but you and he you cheated me out of it, out of all I had and all I hoped for, he with his lust, the filthy pig, if men only knew the hatreds they stir when they overpower us, override us in the dim unendurable dark, and you with that piddling feebleness, that ever sucking mouth forever with that mouth like his prod demanding too much, too much by far in patience and your scumble ever needing wiping, witless, wailing, wanting something all the while, the days, the years, those years, draining my strength, ah my strength, my sweet strength and I once so lovely, all stolen, no pleasure left for life, I should have known, no life my mother promised me at her breast and then she too no better than the rest dying damn her dying curse the stinking milkless bitch that bore me dying when I needed her. . . ."

The little thing's voice scratched against the pane of obsidian, trying to get at the soul.

"I do sorrow for you, Mother. I am now going to ask you a question to help take your mind off your sorrows. I will ask you to pass that question on to your mother, and to her mother and her mother's mother, and so down to remote depths. You must find me an answer to the question, and then I shall be so proud of you. I wish to discover if Wutra really exists. Does Wutra exist, and who or what is he? You must send the question back and back until some far fessup returns an answer. The answer must be full. I wish to understand how the world works. The answer must come back to me. Do you understand?"

A reply was screamed at her before she had finished speaking.

"Why should I do anything for you after the way you spoilt my life and why and why and why and what care I down here for any of your stupid problems you mean little piddling fool, it lasts for ever being down here, you hear, for ever and my sorrow too—"

The soul broke into the monologue.

"You have heard my demand, Mother. If you do not carry it out to the letter, I shall never visit you again in the world below. No one will address you ever again."

The gossie made a quick gulp at the soul. The soul remained just out of harm's reach, watching dusty sparks issue from the unbreathing mouth.

Without another word, the gossie began to pass on Shay Tal's question, and the fessups below snapped in fury at it.

All hung suspended in obsidian.

The soul was aware of other fessups nearby, hanging like shabby jackets on pegs in a midnight hall. Loilanun was there, and Loil Bry, and Little Yuli. Even Great Yuli was hanging here somewhere, reduced to a furious shade. The soul's father's gossie was nearby, more feared even than its mother's gossie, its wrath surging at her like a tide.

And the voice of the father's gossie was like the scratching of the nails of a hand on a windowpane.

". . . and another thing, ungrateful girl, why weren't you a boy, you wretched failure you knew I needed a boy wanted a boy a good son to carry on the miserable suffering of our line, so I'm regarded as a laughingstock by all my friends not that I thought aught of that gang of miserable cowards, ran from danger they did, ran when the wolves howled and I ran with them not knowing if I could have my time again —my time again oh yes my damned time again—and the wind blowing fresh in the lungs and every joint on the move down the trail where the deer flickered free with their white scuts bobbing—oh, the time again— and no involvements with that sexless breastless hag you call your mother here in the clutches of this unbreathing stone I hate her hate her hate you too you prattling scumble you'll be here one day soon yourself yes here for ever in the tomb you'll see. . . ."

And there were other messages from other dried mouths, tail ends of grunts, sticking into her fabric like old animal bones protruding from soil, verdigrised over with earth, age, eddre, envy, and poisonous to the touch.

The soul of Shay Tal waited amid the venoms, sail aquiver, waited for her answer. And eventually a message travelled up from dry insensate mouth to dry insensate mouth through the obsidian, passing something like a response to the question through the crystallized centuries.

". . . all our festering secrets why should you share them you prying slut with slime for harneys why should you presume to share that little that we have here in our destitution far from sun? What once was knowledge is lost, leaked from the bottom of the bucket despite all that was promised, and what remains you would not understand you would not understand whore nothing you'll ever understand except the final throes of heart giving in for all your pretensions and Wutra what of him he did not aid our distant fessups when they lived. In the days of the old iron cold came the white phagors out of the murk and took the town by storm making the humans their slaves who worshipped their new masters by the name Wutra because the gods of ice winds ruled. . . ."

"Stop, stop, I wish to hear no more—" cried the soul, overwhelmed.

But the malicious gale blew over her. "You asked you asked you could not stand the truth you mortal soul, you'll see when you get here. To find your wish of useless wisdom you should journey far to far Sibornal there to seek the great wheel where all is done and known and all things understood as pertains to existence on your side of the bitter bitter grave, yet good none good will it do you you prying dry-quemed failure of the dead's daughter for what is real or true or tested or a testament to time even Wutra himself except this prison where we find ourselves all undeserving . . ."

The soul, quailing, hoisted sail and floated upwards through the bleak mansions, through rank after rank of screaming mouths.

The word, the poisonous word, had come from the far fessups. Sibornal had to be her goal, and a great wheel. Fessups were deceivers, their endless rages led them to limitless malice, but their powers in that

respect were limited. It seemed true that Wutra had deserted not merely
the living but the dead as well.

The soul fled upward in anguish, scenting far above it a bed on which
lay a pallid body without movement.

Above ground, processes of change, endless periods of upheaval, expressed themselves through such biological beings as animals, men, and
phagors.

From the northern continent, Sibornalans still moved southwards
across the treacherous isthmus of Chalce, propelled by a sporadically
improving climate to seek more hospitable lands. The inhabitants of Pannoval expanded northwards across the great plains. Elsewhere, too, from
a thousand favoured habitats, people began to emerge. On the south of
the continent of Campannlat, in such coastal fortresses as Ottassol,
numbers multiplied, growing fat on the abundance of the seas.

In that haven of life, the sea, many things moved. Faceless beings
shaped like men climbed to the shore, or were washed by storms far
inland.

And the phagors, too. Lovers of cold, they also were propelled by
change, seeking new habitats along benign air-octaves. Over all the three
measureless continents of Helliconia, their components stirred and reproduced and fought the war against the Sons of Freyr.

The crusade of the young kzahhn of Hrastyprt, Hrr-Brahl Yprt, came
slowly down from the high shoulders of Nktryhk, proceeding through
the mountains, always obeying the air-octaves. The kzahhn and his
advisers knew that Freyr was slowly gaining the ascendancy over Batalix,
and so moving against them; but that knowledge could not speed the
pace of their advance. Often they stopped to make raids, on the protognostic peoples humbly traversing the snowfields barefoot, or on components of their own kind towards whom they smelled hostility. No sense
of urgency burned in their pale harneys, only a sense of destination.

Hrr-Brahl Yprt rode Rukk-Ggrl, and his cowbird rode mainly on his
shoulder. Sometimes it took off with a clatter of wings, climbing to soar
above the company, whence it could watch with its beady eyes the long
procession of stalluns and gillots, most of them on foot, tailing all the
way back to the defiles of higher ground. Zzhrrk would ride the updraught so that he maintained a position directly above his master for
hours at a time, wings outstretched, only his head moving from side to
side, alert for other cowbirds gliding nearby.

There were little knots of the protognostic peoples, generally Madis
trying to lead their goats to the next thorn or ice bush, who sighted the
white birds from afar. They would cry to each other and point. All knew
what the distant cowbirds signified. And they would escape while they
had the chance, from death or captivity. Thus the insignificant louse

that lived on phagors, burrowing in their coats, a titbit for cowbirds, became an unknowing instrument in saving the lives of many a protognostic.

The Madis themselves were infested with parasites. They feared water, and the yearly application of goat dripping to their lean carcasses increased rather than hampered infestations, but their insects played no accountable role in history.

Proud Hrr-Brahl Yprt, his long skull adorned with face crown, looked up at his mascot soaring high above, before glaring ahead again, alert for possible danger. He saw the three fists of the world in the harneys of his head, and the place at which they would eventually arrive, where lived the Sons of Freyr who had killed his grandfather, Great Kzahhn Hrr-Tryhk Hrast, who had dedicated his life to despatching the enemy in uncounted numbers. The Great Kzahhn had been killed by the Sons in Embruddock, and so had lost his chance of sinking into tether; thus was he destroyed for ever. The young kzahhn admitted to himself that his nations had been less active in killing Sons than they should have been, indulgently seeking instead the majestic ice storms of High Nktryhk, for which their yellow blood was brewed.

Now amends were being made. Before Freyr grew too strong, the Sons of Freyr in Embruddock would be eliminated. Then he would himself fade into the eternal peace of tether with no stain on his conscience.

As soon as she was strong enough, Shay Tal leaned on Vry's shoulder and took herself down the lane to the old temple.

The doors of the temple had been removed and a fence substituted. In the dim interior, pigs squealed and rooted. Aoz Roon had been true to his word.

The women picked their way among the animals and stood in the middle of the muddied space, while Shay Tal stared up at the great ikon of Wutra, with his white hair, animal face, and long horns.

"Then it's true," she said in a low voice. "The fessups spoke true, Vry. Wutra is a phagor. Humanity has been worshipping a phagor. Our darkness is much greater than we guessed."

But Vry was looking up hopefully at the painted stars.

IX

IN AND OUT OF A
HOXNEY SKIN

T he enchanted wildernesses began to chart their riverbanks with succulent-stemmed trees. Mists and fogs were syphoned from reviving bournes.

The great continent of Campannlat was some fourteen thousand miles long by five thousand miles wide. It occupied most of the tropical zone in one entire hemisphere of the planet of Helliconia. It contained staggering extremes of temperature, of height and depth, of calm and storm. And now it was reawakening to life.

A process of ages was bringing the continent, grain by grain, mountain by mountain, down into the turbid seas that fringed its coastline. A similar trend, as remorseless, as far-reaching, was increasing its energy levels. Climatic change triggered an acceleration in metabolism, and the ferment of the two suns brought forth eructations from the veins of the world: tremors, volcanic eruptions, subsidences, fumaroles, immense suppurations of lava. The bed of the giant creaked.

These hypogean stresses had their parallels on the planetary surface, where carpets of colour sprang from the old icefields, green spears thrusting up before the last dregs of snow rotted into the soil, so urgently did Freyr call them forth. But the seeds had packaged themselves against precisely that advantageous moment. The flower responded to the star.

After the flower, again the seed. And those seeds provided the energy requirements for new animals that streamed across the new veldts. The animals too were packaged to the moment. Where few species had been, proliferation was. Crystalline states of cataplexy were exercised away under cantering hoofs. Moulting, they left haystacks of discarded winter hair behind them, which was seized upon immediately for nesting material by birds, while their dung provided foodstuffs for insects.

The long fogs were alive with darting birds.

Multitudinous winged life flashed like jewels across what had been sterile icefields only a moment before. In a torment of life, the mammals stretched their legs in full gallop towards summer.

All the manifold terrestrial changes following the one inexorable astronomical change were so complex that no man or woman could comprehend them. But the human spirit responded to them. Eyes opened and saw afresh. All across Campannlat, the human embrace had new passion in its sap.

People were healthier, yet disease spread. Things were better, yet things were worse. More people died, yet more people lived. There was more to eat, yet more people went hungry. For all these contradictions, the prompting was ever outward. Freyer called, and even the deaf responded.

The eclipse that Vry and Oyre had anticipated occurred. The fact that they alone in Embruddock had expected it was a source of satisfaction, although otherwise the effects of the eclipse were alarming. They perceived how terrifying the event was to the uninitiated. Even Shay Tal dropped on her bed and hid her eyes. Bold hunters stayed indoors. Old men had heart attacks.

Yet the eclipse was not total.

The slow erosion of Freyr's disc began early in the afternoon. Perhaps it was the sloth of the whole thing which was so disturbing, and its duration. Hour by hour, the erosion of Freyr increased. When the suns set, they were still locked together. There was no guarantee that they would appear again, or appear again whole. Most of the population ran out into the open to watch this unprecedented sunset. In ashen silence, the maimed sentinels slid from view.

"It's the death of the world!" cried a trader. "Tomorrow the ice will be back!"

As darkness descended, rioting broke out. People ran madly with torches. A new wooden building was set on fire.

Only the immediate intervention of Aoz Roon, Eline Tal, and some of their strong-armed friends saved a more general madness. A man died in the fire and the building was lost, but the rest of the night remained quiet. Next morning, Batalix rose as usual, then Freyr, entire. All was well—except that the geese of Embruddock stopped laying for a week.

"What happens next year?" Oyre and Vry asked each other. Independently of Shay Tal, they began serious work on the problem.

On the Earth Observation Station, the eclipses were merely a part of a pattern predicated by the two intersecting ecliptics of Star A and Star B, which were inclined to each other at an angle of ten degrees. The ecliptics intersected 644 and 1428 terrestrial years after apastron or, in Helliconian terms, 453 and 1005 years after apastron. On either side of the intersections were ranged annual eclipses; in the case of Year 453, an imposing array of twenty eclipses.

The partial eclipse of 632, heralding the series of twenty, was viewed by the scholars on the Observation Station with correct scientific detachment. The ragged fellows barging through the lanes of Embruddock were treated to compassionate smiles by the gods who rode high overhead.

After the mists, after the eclipse, floods. What was cause, what effect? Nobody wading through the residual mud could tell. The land to the east of Oldorando, as far as Fish Lake and beyond, lost its herds of deer, and food became scarce. The swollen Voral acted as a barrier to the west, where abundant animal life was frequently sighted.

Aoz Roon showed his gift for leadership. He made his peace with Laintal Ay and Dathka and, with their aid, drove the citizens to build a bridge across the river.

Such a project had never been attempted in living memory. Timber was scarce, and a rajabaral had to be cut into suitable lengths. The metal-makers corps produced two long saws with which an appropriate tree was sawn up. A temporary workshop was established between the women's house and the river. The two boats stolen from Borlienian marauders were carefully broken up and reassembled to form parts of the superstructure. The rajabaral was turned into a thicket of chocks, wedges, planks, bars, struts, and posts. For weeks, the whole place was a timberyard; curls of shavings floated away downstream among the geese; Oldorando was full of sawdust and the fingers of its labourers of splinters. Thick piles were hauled and driven with difficulty into the bed of the river. Slaves stood up to their necks in the flood, tied to one another for safety; amazingly, no lives were lost.

Slowly, the bridge grew, and Aoz Roon stood there, calling them on. The first row of piers was washed away in a storm. Work began again. Wood was driven against wood. The thuggish heads of sledgehammers took their arcs from the air to land with a thwack on great wooden wedges, the tops of which turned to fur under repeated blows. A narrow platform crept out across the waters and proved secure. Dominating the

operation stood the bear-wrapped figure of Aoz Roon, swinging his
arms, wielding a mallet or a whip, encouraging or cursing, ever active.
They remembered him long afterwards over their rathel, saying, with
admiration, "What a devil he was!"

The work prospered. The workers cheered. A bridge four planks wide
with a handrail along one side spanned the dark Voral. Many of the
women refused to cross it, disliking the glimpse of fast water through
the gaps between the planks, and the everlasting *splap-flub* of current
again the piles. But access to the western plains had been won. Game
was plentiful there, and starvation was averted. Aoz Roon had reason
to be pleased.

With the arrival of summer, Freyr and Batalix parted company, rising
and setting at different times. Day was rarely so bright, night rarely
entire. In the increased hours of daylight, everything grew.

For a while, the academy also grew. During the heroic period of the
bridge building, everyone worked together. The shortage of meat meant
for the first time an increased awareness of the importance of grain.
The handful of seeds that Laintal Ay had pressed on Shay Tal became
a clutch of fields, where barley, oats, and rye grew in profusion and
were guarded from marauders as being among the precious possessions
of the Den tribe.

Now that several women could reckon and write, the grain that was
harvested was weighed and stored and fairly rationed; any carcasses
brought in were tallied; fish yields were noted. Every pig and goose in
the town was entered on a balance sheet. Agriculture and accountancy
brought their own rewards. Everyone was busy.

Vry and Oyre had charge of the cereal fields, and of the slaves working
there. From the nearer acres, they could see the big tower in the distance,
over the waving ears of grain, with a sentry standing there on watch.
They still studied the constellations; their star chart was as complete
as they could make it. Stars were in their conversation often as they
prowled among the grasses.

"The stars are always on the move, like fish in a clear lake," Vry said.
"All the fish turn together at the same moment. But the stars aren't
fish. I wonder what they are, and what they swim in."

Oyre held a grass stalk up to the nose that Laintal Ay admired so
much and closed first one eye and then the other.

"The stalk seems to move back and forth across my vision, yet I know
it's still all the while. Perhaps the stars are still and it's we who
move. . . ."

Vry received this and was silent. Then she said in a small voice,
"Oyre, my beauty, perhaps it's so. Perhaps it's the earth that moves all
the while. But then . . ."

"What about the sentinels?"

"Why, they don't move either. . . . That's right, we move, we go round and round like an eddy in the river. And they're far away, like the stars. . . ."

". . . But coming nearer, Vry, because it's getting warmer. . . ."

They gazed at each other, mouths open, eyebrows slightly raised, breathing lightly. Beauty and intelligence flowed in them.

The hunters, released by the bridge into the west, gave little thought to the revolving sky. The plains were open for their despoliation. Green rose up everywhere, crushed under their running feet, their sprawling bodies. Flowers burst. Insects that flew no more than a man's height above the ground blundered among pale petals. Game in plenty was near at hand, to be brought down and dragged back to the town, spotting the new bridge with its dull blood.

With the growth of Aoz Roon's reputation, Shay Tal's went into eclipse. The diversion of women into labour connected either with the bridge or with agriculture weakened her hold on the intellectual life of the community. It hardly appeared to bother Shay Tal; since her return from the world below, she increasingly shunned companionship. She avoided Aoz Roon, and her gaunt figure was seen less often about the lanes. Only her friendship with old Master Datnil prospered.

Although Master Datnil had never again allowed her as much as a glimpse of the secret book of his corps, his mind wandered frequently to the past. She was content to listen to him unwinding the skein of his reminiscence, peopled with bygone names; it was not unlike, she thought, a visit to the fessups. What seemed dark to her held luminance for him.

"To the best of my belief, Embruddock was once more complicated that it is now. Then it suffered a catastrophe, as you know. . . . There was a mason-makers corps but it was destroyed some centuries ago. The master of the corps was particularly well thought of."

Shay Tal had observed before his endearing habit of speaking as if he were present during the events he described. She guessed he was recalling something he had read in his secret book.

"How was so much building achieved in stone?" she asked him. "We know the labour of working in wood."

They were sitting in the master's dim room. Shay Tal squatted before him on the floor. Because of his age, Master Datnil sat on a stone set against the wall, so that he could rise easily. Both his old woman and Raynil Layan, his chief boy—a mature man with a forked beard and unctuous manners—came and went in the room; the master kept his talk guarded in consequence.

He answered Shay Tal's question by saying, "Let us go down and walk in the sun for a few paces, Mother Shay. The warmth is good for my bones, I find."

Outside, he put his arm through hers and they walked down the lane where curly-haired pigs foraged. Nobody was about, for the hunters were away in the west veldt and many of the women were in the fields, keeping company with the slaves. Mangy dogs slept in the light of Freyr.

"The hunters are now away so much," Master Datnil said, "that the women misbehave in their absence. Our male Borlienian slaves harvest the women as well as the crops. I don't know what the world's coming to."

"People copulate like animals. The cold for intellect, the warmth for sensuality." She looked above their heads, where little wanton birds swooped into holes in the stonework of the towers, bearing insects for their young.

He patted her arm and looked into her pinched face. "Don't you fret. Your dream of going to Sibornal is your kind of satisfaction. We all must have something."

"Something? What?" She frowned at him.

"Something to hang on to. A vision, a hope, a dream. We don't live only by bread, even the basest of us. There's always some kind of inner life—that's what survives when we become gossies."

"Oh, the inner life . . . It can be starved to death, can't it?"

He stopped by the herb tower and she paused with him. They regarded the blocks of stone forming the tower. Despite the ages, the tower stood well. The blocks fitting neatly one into the other raised unanswered questions. How was stone quarried and cut? How was it built up so that it formed a tower which could stand for nine centuries?

Bees droned round their feet. A flight of large birds moved across the sky and disappeared behind one of the towers. She felt the day going by in her ears, and longed to be seized up in something great and all-embracing.

"Perhaps we could make a small tower out of mud. Mud dries good and solid. A small mud tower first. Stone later. Aoz Roon should build mud walls round Oldorando. At present the village is virtually unguarded. Everyone's away. Who will blow the warning horn? We are open to raiders, human and inhuman."

"I read once that a learned man of my corps made a model of this world in the form of a globe which could be rotated to show the lands on it—where was once Embruddock, where Sibornal, and so on. It was stored in the pyramid with much else."

"King Denniss feared more than the cold. He feared invaders. Master Datnil, I have kept silent for a while with respect to many of my secret thoughts. But they torment me and I must speak. . . . I have learnt

from my fessups that Embruddock . . ." She paused, aware of the
burden of what she was going to say, before completing her sentence.
". . . Embruddock was once ruled by phagors."

After a moment, the old man said, in a light conversational tone,
"That's enough sunlight. We can go in again."

On the way up to his room, he stopped on the third floor of the tower.
This was the assembly room of his corps, smelling strongly of leather.
He stood listening. All was silent.

"I wanted to make sure that my chief boy was out. Come in here."

Off the landing was a small room. Master Datnil pulled a key from
his pocket and unlocked the door, looking round once more, anxiously.
Catching Shay Tal's eye, he said, "I don't want anyone butting in.
What I'm about to do in sharing the secrets of our corps carries the
death penalty, as you understand. Ancient though I may be, I want the
last few years of my life out."

She looked round as she stepped into the small cubbyhole off the
assembly room with him. For all their caution, neither of them saw
Raynil Layan—as chief boy of the corps, due to inherit Master Datnil's
mantle when the old man retired. He stood in the shadows, behind a
post supporting the wooden stair. Raynil Layan was a cautious, precise
man, whose manner was always circumspect; he stood at this moment
absolutely rigid, without breathing, showing no more movement than
the post that partly protected him from view.

When the master and Shay Tal had entered the cubbyhole and
closed the door behind them, Raynil Layan moved with some alacrity,
his step light for so large a man. He applied his eye to a crack between
two boards which he had engineered himself some while ago, the better
to observe the movements of the man he would supplant.

Distorting his face by tugging considerably on his forked beard—a
nervous habit imitated by his enemies—he watched Datnil Skar remove
from its box the secret record of the tawyers and tanner corps. The
ancient spread it open before the gaze of the woman. When that information was laid before Aoz Roon, it would mark the end of the old
master—and the beginning of the rule of the new. Raynil Layan descended the stairs one step at a time, moving with quiet deliberation.

With trembling finger, Master Datnil pointed to a blank in the pages
of his musty tome. "This is a secret which has weighed heavy on me for
many years, Mother, and I trust your shoulders are not too frail for it.
At the darkest, coldest time of an earlier epoch, Embruddock was over-
run by the accursed phagors. Its very name is a corruption of an ancipital
name: Hrrm-Bhhrd Ydohk. . . . Our corps was then driven out into
caves in the wild. But both men and women were kept here. Our kind
was then in servitude, and the phagors ruled. . . . Isn't that a disgrace?"

She thought of the phagor god Wutra, worshipped in the temple.

"A disgrace not yet past. They ruled us," she said, "and are worshipped still. Doesn't that make us a race of slaves to this day?"

A fly with viridian plates on its body, of a kind only recently seen in the settlement, buzzed from a dusty corner and alighted on the book.

Master Datnil looked up at Shay Tal in sudden fear. "I should have resisted the temptation to show you this. It's nothing you should know." His face was haggard. "Wutra will punish me for this."

"You believe in Wutra despite the evidence?"

The old man was trembling, as if he heard a step outside that spelt his doom. "He's all about us. . . . We are his slaves. . . ."

He struck out at the fly, but it eluded him as it set off in a spiral for a distant target of its own.

The hunters watched the hoxneys in professional amazement. Of all the life that invaded the western plains, it was the hoxney that, in its sportiveness, most embodied the new spirit. Beyond the settlement was the bridge, and beyond the bridge the hoxneys.

Freyr had called forth the glossies from their long hibernation. The signal had gone from sun to gland; life filled their eddres, they unrolled and lived again, crawling out of their dark comfortable places to stretch, to abound in movement—to rejoice and be hoxneys. To be herds and herds of hoxneys, to be careless as a breeze, to be striped and hornless, to resemble asses or small kaidaws, to gallop and gambol and graze and plunge hock-deep into delicious grasses. To be able to outstrip almost anything else that ran.

Every hoxney bore stripes of two colours, running horizontally from nose to tail. The stripes might be vermilion and black, or vermilion and yellow, or black and yellow, or green and yellow, or green and sky blue, or sky blue and white, or white and cerise, or cerise and vermilion. When the herds threw themselves down to rest, sprawling like cats, their legs carelessly stretched, they faded into the landscape, which also had put on new shows for the new seasons. Just as the hoxneys had broken from the glossy state, so "the flower-thrilling plain" transformed itself back from song into reality.

At first, the hoxneys had no fear of the hunters.

They galloped among the men, snorting with glee, tossing their manes, throwing up their heads, showing wide teeth made crimson by chomping veronika, raige, and the scarlet dogthrush. The hunters stood perplexed, caught between delight and the lust of the hunt, laughing back at the sportive beasts, whose rumps zithered with fire where the light of the sentinels touched them. These were the beasts that drew the dawn across the plains. In the first enchantments of meeting, they seemed impossible to kill.

Then they'd fart and be off like volted zephyrs, thundering between the pointless brown steeples that ants were raising everywhere, wheeling about, gazing mischievously back, shaking manes, whinneying, often charging back again to prolong the game. Or, when they tired of that, and of grazing with their soft muzzles to the floor, the stallions would set upon their fillies, rolling them in delight among the tall white orling flowers. Calling with shrill dove notes like laughter, they plunged their striped prods into the willing quemes of the mares, then pranced off, dripping still, to the applause of the hunters.

The mood of ease had its effect on the men. No longer were they so keen to return to their stone rooms. After they had brought down a capering animal, they delighted in lying by the fire that roasted it, talk-ing of women, bragging, singing, sniffing the sage, dogthrush, and scantiom that blossomed about them and, crushed by their bodies, gave out pleasing aromas.

Generally speaking, they were harmonious. When Raynil Layan ap-peared—it was unusual to see a man of the corps in the hunting grounds—the mood was broken for a while. Aoz Roon went apart from the others and talked to Raynil Layan with his face to the far horizon. When he returned, his expression was grim, and he would not tell Laintal Ay and Dathka what had been said.

When false evening came to Oldorando, and one or other of the two sentinels scattered its ashes over the western sky, the hoxney herds scented a familiar challenge. Lifting their nostrils to the flushed air, they watched for sabre-tongues.

Their enemies also sported bright colours. Sabre-tongues were striped like their prey, always black and one other colour, a blood colour, gen-erally scarlet or a rich maroon. Sabre-tongues bore a close resemblance to hoxneys, although their legs were shorter and thicker, and their heads rounder, the rotundity emphasised by lack of visible ears. The head, set on a sturdy neck, housed the sabre-tongue's chief weapon: fast in pursuit over short distances, the sabre-tongue could project a sword-sharp tongue from its throat and sever the leg of a hoxney as it fled.

Having once seen this predator in action, the hunters held it in re-spect. The sabre-tongue, for its part, showed the men neither fear nor aggression; mankind had never appeared on its menu nor, as far as it knew, was it on mankind's.

Fire seemed to attract the animal. Sabre-tongues developed a habit of slouching up to the campfire in twos, male and female, to sit or sprawl there. They licked each other with their white sword tongues and would devour pieces of meat the men threw them. Yet they would never allow themselves to be touched, drawing away snarling from a cautiously proffered hand. The snarl was sufficient warning for the hunters; they had seen what damage that terrible tongue could do, used in anger.

Brakes of thorn tree and dogthrush were in blossom about the landscape. Beneath their heavy boughs the men slept. They dwelt among blossom and its cloying scents, with flowers never seen or smelt before, except by long-gone fessups. In the dogthrush thickets they found the hives of wild bees, some brimming with honey. The honey fermented easily to make beethel. On the glutinous beethel the men got drunk and pursued one another through the grasses, laughing, shouting, wrestling, until the curious hoxneys came to see what all the fun was about. The hoxneys too would not permit a man to touch them, although many a man tried when caught up by the beethel, running across the veldt after the frolicking animals until he fell over and slept where he lay.

In the old days, the return home had been the crowning pleasure of the hunt. The challenge of the chill snowfields had been exchanged for warmth and sleep. That was altered. The hunt had become play. Their muscles were no longer stretched, and there was warmth on the flowering veldt.

Also, Oldorando held less attraction for the hunters. The hamlet was growing crowded as more children survived the hazards of their first year on earth. The men preferred convivial beethel binges on the plain to the complaints that often attended their return.

So they no longer came back boastfully in the old tight-knit bunch, straggling home instead in ones and twos, in a less obtrusive way.

These new-style returns held one excitement previously absent, at least as far as the women were concerned; for if the men had their irresponsibility, the women had their vanity.

"Let's see what you've brought me!"

That, with variations, was the popular cry, as women dragged their brats out to meet their men. They went as far as the new bridge and waited there, standing on the east bank of the Voral while the kids threw stones at the ducks and geese, waiting impatiently for the men to arrive with meat—and skins.

The meat was their due, their necessity, and it was no good a hunter coming back without meat.

But what aroused frenzies of delight in the hearts of the women were the skins, the brilliant hoxney skins. Never before in their impoverished lives had they visualised a change of garb. Never before had the tanners been in such demand. Never before had the men been driven out to kill for the sake of killing. Every woman wished to possess a hoxney skin—preferably more than one—and to dress her offspring in one.

They competed with each other for brighter skins. Blue, magenta, aquamarine, cherry. They blackmailed the men in ways men enjoyed. They preened themselves, they stained their lips. They paraded. They dressed their hair. They even took to washing themselves.

Correctly worn, with those electric stripes running vertically up the body, hoxney skins could make even a dumpy woman look elegant. The skins had to be properly cut. A new trade prospered in Oldorando: tailor. As flowers put forth bells and spikes and faces along the lanes between the ancient worn towers, and flowering ivies climbed the towers themselves, so the women began more to resemble flowers. They decked themselves in bright colours their mothers had never set eyes on.

It was not long before the men, in self-defence, also cut off their old heavy furs and took to hoxney skins.

The weather became still and threatening, and the rajabarals steamed from their flat lids.

Oldorando was silent under towering cumulus. The hunters were away. Shay Tal sat alone in her room writing. She no longer cared about her appearance, and still went round in her old ill-fitting skins. In her head she still heard the creaking voices of fessups and her parents' gossies. She still tried to dream of perfection and travel.

When Vry and Amin Lim came down from the room above, Shay Tal looked up sharply and said, "Vry, what would you think of a globe as a model of the world?"

Vry said, "It would make sense. A globe rotates most smoothly of all figures, and the other wanderers are round. So we must be too."

"A disc, a wheel? We've been brought up to believe that the original boulder rests on a disc."

"Much we were brought up to believe is incorrect. You taught us that, Mother," Vry said. "I believe our world revolves round the sentinels."

Shay Tal sat where she was, contemplating them, and they fidgeted under her inspection. Both of the younger women had shed their old skins and wore bright hoxney suits. Stripes of cerise and grey ran up Vry's body. The ears of the dead animal adorned her shoulders. Despite all Aoz Roon's threatened restrictions on the academy, the skins had been presented to her by Dathka. She walked more confidently. She had acquired glamour.

Suddenly, Shay Tal's temper flared up. "You stupid wenches, you silly gillies, you are defying me. Don't pretend you aren't. I know what goes on under that air of meekness. Look at the way you dress nowadays! We get nowhere with our understanding, nowhere. Everything seems to lead us to fresh complexities. I shall have to go to Sibornal, to find this great wheel the gossies speak of. Perhaps real freedom, clear truth, lives there. Here is only the curse of ignorance. . . . Where are you two going, in any case?"

Amin Lim spread her hands to demonstrate their innocence. "Nowhere, ma'am, only to the fields, to see if we've cured the mildew on the oats."

She was a big girl, even bigger at this time with the seed her man had planted within her. She stood there pleadingly, released by a slight flicker of assent in Shay Tal's eye, whereon she and Vry almost scuttled from the oppressive room.

As they retreated down the dirty stone steps, Vry said resignedly, "There she goes again, blowing up, as regular as the Hour-Whistler. Poor thing, something is really worrying her."

"Where's this pool you mentioned? I don't feel like walking far in my condition."

"You'll love it, Amin Lim. It's only a little way beyond the northern fields, and we can walk slowly. I expect Oyre's there."

The air had thickened to an extent where it no longer carried the scent of flowers, but emanated a metallic trace of its own. Colour appeared dazzling in the actinic light; the geese looked supernaturally white.

They passed between the columns of great rajabarals. The stark cylinders with their concave curve were better suited to the geometries of a winter landscape; with the growing lushness they formed a forbidding contrast.

"Even the rajabarals are changing," Amin Lim said. "How long has steam been coming out of their tops?"

Vry did not know and was not particularly interested. She and Oyre had discovered a warm pool, knowledge of which they had so far kept to themselves. In a narrow valley, the mouth of which pointed away from Oldorando, fresh springs had burst forth from the ground, some at a temperature near boiling, some rushing down to meet the Voral in a cloud of vapour. One spring, damned by rock, flowed a different way and formed a secluded pool, fringed by verdure but open to the sky. It was to this pool that Vry led Amin Lim.

As they parted the bushes and saw the figure standing by the pool, Amin Lim shrieked and threw her hand to her mouth.

Oyre stood on the bank. She was naked. Her skin shone with moisture and water dripped from her ample breasts. With no sign of shyness, she turned and waved excitedly to her friends. Behind her lay her discarded hoxney skins.

"Come on, where you have been? The water's glorious today."

Amin Lim stood where she was, blushing, still covering her mouth. She had never seen anyone naked before.

"It's all right," Vry said, laughing at her friend's expression. "It's lovely in the water. I'm going to strip off and go in. Watch me—if you dare."

She ran forward to where Oyre stood and began unlacing the cerise and grey suit. Hoxneys were tailored to be climbed in and out of. In another minute, the suit was thrown aside and Vry stood there naked, her more slender lines contrasting with Oyre's sturdy beauty. She laughed in delight.

"Come on, Amin Lim, don't be stuffy. A swim will be good for your baby."

She and Oyre jumped into the water together. As it swallowed up their limbs, they squealed with delight.

Amin Lim stood where she was and squealed with horror.

They had gorged down an enormous feast, with bitter fruits to follow the slabs of meat. Their faces still shone with fat.

The hunters were heavier than they had been last season. Food was all too plentiful. The hoxneys could be slaughtered without anyone's having to run. The animals continued to come close, capering among the hunters and rolling their parti-coloured bodies against the hides of their dead fellows.

Still wearing his old black furs, Aoz Roon had been talking apart to Goija Hin, the slave master, whose broad back was still visible as he trudged towards the distant towers of Oldorando. Aoz Roon returned to the company. He grabbed up a chunk of rib still sizzling on a stone and rolled over in the grass with it. Curd, his great hound, frisked playfully with him, growling, until Aoz Roon brought a branch of fragrant dogthrush down to keep the brute from his meat.

He kicked out at Dathka in a friendly way.

"This is the life, friend. Take it easy, eat as much as you can before the ice returns. By the original boulder, I'll never forget this season as long as I live."

"Splendid." That was all Dathka said. He had finished eating, and sat with his arms wrapped round his knees, watching the hoxneys, a herd of which was wheeling fast through the grass not a quarter of a mile away.

"Damn you, you never say anything," Aoz Roon exclaimed good-humouredly, pulling at his meat with his strong teeth. "Talk to me."

Dathka turned his head so that his cheek rested on his knee and gave Aoz Roon a knowing look. "What's going on between you and Goija Hin then?"

Aoz Roon's mouth went hard. "That's private between the pair of us."

"So you won't talk either." Dathka turned away and regarded the cantering hoxneys once more, where they wheeled below the high cumulus piling up on the western horizon. The air was full of green light, robbing the hoxneys of their brilliant colour.

Finally, as if he could feel the black regard of Aoz Roon through his shoulder blades, he said, without shifting his gaze, "I was thinking."

Aoz Roon flung his chewed bone to Curd and lay flat under the blossoming bough. "All right, then, out with it. What have you been saving up all your lifetime to think?"

"How to catch a live hoxney."

"Ha! What good would that do you?"

"I wasn't thinking of good, any more than you were when you called Nahkri to the top of the tower."

A heavy silence followed, in which Aoz Roon said no word. Eventually, as distant thunder sounded, Eline Tal brought round some beethel. Aoz Roon demanded angrily of the company in general, "Where's Laintal Ay? Wandering again, I suppose. Why is he not with us? You men are getting too lazy and disobedient. Some of you are in for a surprise."

He got up and walked heavily away, followed at a respectful distance by his hound.

Laintal Ay was not studying hoxneys like his silent friend. He was after other game.

Since that night, four long years ago, when he was witness to the murder of his uncle Nahkri, the incident had haunted him. He had ceased to blame Aoz Roon for the murder, for he now understood better that the Lord of Embruddock was a tormented man.

"I'm sure he thinks himself under a curse," Oyre had once told Laintal Ay.

"He can be forgiven a lot for the western bridge," Laintal Ay replied, in a practical way. But he felt himself spoiled by his involvement in the murder, and increasingly kept his own counsel.

The bond between him and the beautiful Oyre had been both strengthened and distorted by that night when too much rathel had been drunk. He had even become wary with her.

He had spelt out the difficulty to himself. "If I am to rule in Oldorando, as my lineage decrees, then I must kill the father of the girl I wish to make mine. It's impossible."

No doubt Oyre also understood his dilemma. Yet she was marked out as his and no one else's. He would have fought to the death any other man who went near her.

His wild instincts, his sense for the cunning trap, for the unregarding moment that spells disaster, made him see as clearly as did Shay Tal that Oldorando was now left regularly vulnerable to attack. In the present warm spell, nobody was alert. Sentries droused at their posts.

He raised the question of defence with Aoz Roon, who had a reasonable answer.

Aoz Roon said dismissively that nobody, friend or foe, travelled far any more. A mantle of snow had made it easy for men to go wherever they pleased; now everywhere was choked with green things, with thickets growing denser every day. The time for raids was past.

Besides, he added, they had had no phagor raids since the day Mother

Shay Tal performed her miracle at Fish Lake. They were safer than they had ever been. And he passed Laintal Ay a tankard of beethel.

Laintal Ay was not satisfied with the answer. Uncle Nahkri had considered himself perfectly safe that night he had climbed the stairs of the big tower. Within a couple of minutes, he was lying in the lane below with his neck broken.

When the hunters went out today, Laintal Ay had got no further than the bridge. There he turned silently back, determined to make a survey of the village and see how it would fare under an unexpected attack.

As he commenced circling the outskirts, the first thing he observed was a light plume of steam on the Voral. It rode along on a certain line in midstream, never deviating, seeming to advance above the dark rapid glide of the water, yet ever remaining in the identical place. Feathers of vapour shredded back from it along the breast of the river. What it signified he could not determine. He proceeded with a sense of unease.

The atmosphere grew heavier. Saplings were springing up over mounds that had once been buildings. He viewed the remaining towers through their slender bars. Aoz Roon was right in one respect: it had become difficult to get round Oldorando.

Yet warning images formed in his mind. He saw phagors riding kaidaws, leaping obstacles and charging into the heart of the settlement. He saw the hunters straggling home, loaded with bright skins, their heads heavy from too much beethel. They had time to witness their homes burnt, their women and children dead, before they too were trampled under savage hoof.

He forced his way through prickly bushes.

How the phagors rode! What could be more wonderful than to mount a kaidaw and ride it, master it, share its power, be one with its action? Those ferocious beasts submitted to no mount but a phagor: or so the legends said, and he had never heard of the man who had ridden a kaidaw. The very notion made one dizzy. Men went on foot. . . . But a man on a kaidaw would be more than the equal of a phagor on a kaidaw.

Half concealed by bushes, he could see across to the north gate, which stood open and unguarded. Two birds perched on top of the gate, twittering. He wondered if a sentry had been posted that morning, or if the man had deserted his post. The silence, through the heavy air, took on a booming quality.

A shambling figure came into his line of vision. It was immediately recognisable as the slave master, Goija Hin. Behind him went Myk, led by a rope.

"There now, you'll enjoy this afternoon's work," Laintal Ay heard the slave master say. He stopped beyond the gate and tied the phagor to a small tree. The creature's legs were already chained. He patted Myk almost affectionately.

Myk looked at Goija Hin with apprehension. "Myk can sit here in the sunshine some time."

"Not sit, stand. You stand, Myk, you do as you're told, or you know what you'll get. We're going to do exactly as Aoz Roon says, or we'll both be in trouble."

The old phagor made a growling sound. "Trouble is always all round us in the air-octaves. What are you Sons of Freyr but trouble?"

"Any more of that I rip your stinking hide off," Goija Hin said, without malice. "You stay there and do what we were told and you'll have your chance on one of us Sons of Freyr in a minute."

He left the monster where he was concealed from gaze and marched off with his flat-footed walk, back towards the towers. Myk promptly lay down on the ground and was lost to Laintal Ay's view.

Like the trail of vapour riding on the Voral, this incident made Laintal Ay uneasy. He stood waiting, listening, wondering. The twittering stillness was one he would have regarded as unnatural only a few years ago. He shrugged his shoulders and walked on.

Oldorando was unguarded. An undertaking must be made to rouse the hunters to a sense of peril. He observed that steam seeped from the caps of the bare rajabarals. There was another portent he could not interpret. Thunder rumbled, far to the north, yet with intimate menace.

He crossed a brook which bubbled and let forth steam, the vapour snarling itself among teeth of fern growing from the bank. When he bent to dip his hand, he found the water tolerably warm. A dead fish floated past, tail uppermost, just under the surface. He squatted there, looking across it at the tangle of new green through which the tops of the towers showed. No hot spring had existed here before.

The ground trembled. Reed trailed in the water, for ever uncurling; newts flashed in it then were gone. Birds rose crying over the towers, then sank again.

As he waited for the tremor to be repeated, the Hour-Whistler blew nearby, the sound of Oldorando he remembered since the cradle. It lasted a fraction longer than usual. He knew exactly how long it lasted; this time, the note was sustained for an instant more than it should have been.

He rose and continued his perimeter prowl. When moving with difficulty through raige bushes which reached to his thigh, he heard voices. With the prompt response of a hunter, Laintal Ay froze, then moved forward cautiously, bent double. Ahead was a sharp rise in the ground, patched by thyme bushes. He sank down on his hands among the fragrant leaves, to peer forward cautiously. He felt his stomach swing under him—his lean arc of belly had become convex with recent good living.

Voices—female—again. He raised his head and looked over the mound.

Whatever he had expected to see, the reality was far more de..ghtful. He found himself gazing into a hollow, in the centre of which lay a deep pool surrounded by verdure. Wisps of steam rose from the water and drifted into the bushes round about, which dripped moisture back into the pool. On the far side of this pool were two women dressing themselves in their hoxney skins; one was heavy with child; he quickly identified her as Amin Lim and her companion as Vry. Standing near him on the edge of the pool, her beautiful back turned to him, was his adored and self-willed Oyre, naked.

When he realised who it was, he gasped with pleasure, and lay where he was, regarding those shoulders, that sweep of back, those glowing buttocks and legs, with a delight that caught his breath.

Batalix had broken free from one of the giant purple castles of cloud, to flood the land below with gold. The sentinel's rays scattered obliquely over Oyre's cinnamon skin, which was pearled about her shoulders and breasts with water drops. Runnels of water chased themselves down the mazes of her flesh, finally spreading to the stone on which she stood, as if to unite her, naiadlike, to the nearby element they shared. Her pose was relaxed, her feet were slightly apart. One hand was raised, to wipe away water from her eyelashes as she watched her friends preparing to leave. Oyre's was the carelessness of an animal—unconscious at this moment of the hunter's predatory regard, yet poised for escape if need be.

Her dark hair clung wetly to her skull, damp tails of it curling about her shoulders and throat, lending her an otterlike quality.

Laintal Ay could catch only glimpses of her face from where he crouched. He had never seen any naked body before, male or female; custom, reinforcing cold, had banished nudity from Oldorando. Overcome by what he saw, he allowed his face to sink into the fragrant thyme. Pulses beat heavily in his temples.

When he could raise his head and look upon the sight again, the movement of her buttocks as she waved her friends good-bye and turned away worked a strong enchantment in him. He breathed a different air. Oyre now regarded the pool almost drowsily, gazing into its pure depths, her lashes gleaming against her cheeks. At her next movement, he could consider her pudendum, covered with tiny wet pigtails, her superb belly, and the cunning whorl of her navel. All was momentarily revealed as she flung up her arms and jumped into the pool.

He was alone with the heavy sunlight and the steam rolling into the bushes until she surfaced again, laughing.

She climbed out quite near him, her breasts swinging clear of her body, jellying lightly against each other.

"Oyre, golden Oyre!" he called in ecstasy.

He rose.

She stood in a crouch before him, a pulse throbbing by a little hollow on her neck. Her regard was heavy upon him, her dark eyes lustrous, yet with a kind of sensuous dullness induced by the general ripe warmth. He saw anew the beauty of the short oval of her face, framed in otter hair, and the sweetness about her eyebrows and the folds of her eyelids. Those eyebrows were arched at present, but after her first surprise she showed no fear, simply looking at him with parted lips, awaiting his next move as if puzzled as to what it might be. Then, belatedly, she curled one hand down and covered her queme. The gesture was more provocative than protective. Well aware of her beauty, she possessed a natural composure.

Four little lascivious birds fluttered down between them, overcome by the heaviness of the afternoon.

Laintal Ay strode across the grass and clutched her, looking fiercely into her eyes, feeling her body against his furs. He reached forward and grasped her, kissing her passionately on the lips.

Oyre stepped back and licked those lips, smiling slightly, her eyes narrowed.

"Strip yourself. Let Batalix see how you are made," she said.

The words were part invitation, part taunt. He unlaced his neckties, then grasped the opening of his tunic and tugged, so that the stitches tore. With loud ripping sounds, the tunic came away and he flung it down. Then he treated his trousers similarly, and kicked them off. He was aware of how his prod stood out stiff from his body, as he crossed to her.

Oyre grasped his outstretched arm, pulled, kicked at his shin, and stepped back swiftly, propelling him full length into the water.

The moist lips of the pool closed over Laintal Ay. It felt astonishingly hot. He surfaced, yelling for breath.

She leaned down laughing with her hands on her handsome knees.

"You wash yourself before you are fit for me, you flea-bitten warrior!"

He splashed her, smacking the surface of the water between laughter and anger.

When she helped him out, she was considerably softer. She felt slippery in his grasp. As they knelt down in the grass, he slid a hand between her legs, feeling her fine details. Immediately, his seed burst from him across the grass.

"Oh, you fool, you fool!" she cried, and caught him a slap across the chest, her face distorted by disappointment.

"No, no, Oyre, it's all right. Give me a minute, please. I love you, Oyre, with all my eddre. I want you always, always. Come to me, rouse me again."

But Oyre stood up, full of annoyance and inexperience. Despite his coaxing words, he felt enraged with her, with himself. He jumped up beside her.

"Scumb you, you shouldn't be so pretty, you minx!"

He grabbed hold of her arm, swung her brutally round, and thrust her towards the steaming pool. She grabbed his hair, snarling and screeching. Together they tumbled into the water.

He got an arm about her back, caught her underwater, kissed her as they surfaced, grabbing a breast with his left hand. Laughing, they climbed to the muddy bank, rolling over together. He hooked a leg round hers and climbed on top. She kissed him passionately on the lips, thrusting her tongue into his mouth even as he entered her queme.

There they lay in the secret place, serene, ecstatic, making love. The mud beneath them, plastering their sides, emitted comfortable noises, as if full of microbes all copulating to express their joy in life.

She was climbing languorously into her hoxney skins. The soft pelts were distinctively marked with dark blue and light blue stripes, each stripe varying in width as it chased its way down Oyre's body. The afternoon had become stifling, and thunder rumbled near at hand, occasionally breaking into claps like sharp cries of protest.

Laintal Ay sprawled close, watching Oyre's movements, eyes half-closed.

"I've always wanted you," he said. "For years. Your flesh is a hot spring. You'll be my woman. We'll come here every afternoon."

She said nothing. She started singing under her breath.

> "The stream on its way
> Glides like our day . . ."

"I want you badly, every day, Oyre. You want me too, don't you?"

She looked at him and said, "Yes, yes, Laintal Ay, I wanted you. But I cannot be your woman."

He felt the ground tremble under him.

"What do you mean?"

She seemed to hesitate, then she leaned towards him. When he automatically reached for her, she pulled herself away, tucked her breasts into her tunic, and said, "I love you, Laintal Ay, but I am not going to become your woman.

"I always suspected that the academy was just a diversion—a consolation for silly women like Amin Lim. Now the weather's fine, it has fallen apart. To be honest, only Vry and Shay Tal care about it—and possibly old Master Datnil. Yet I value Shay Tal's example of independence, and imitate it. Shay Tal will not submit to my father—though I expect she desires him madly, as everyone does—and I follow her example: if I become your possession, I become nothing."

He scrambled up on his knees, looking wretched. "Not so, not so. You'll be—everything, Oyre, everything. We're nothing without each other."

"For a few weeks, yes."

"What do you expect?"

"What do I expect. . . ." Her eyes rolled upwards, and she sighed. She smoothed back her still damp hair and looked away, at the young bushes, at the sky, at the birds. "It's not that I have such a high regard for myself. I can do so little. By remaining independent like Shay Tal, perhaps I can achieve something."

"Don't talk that way. You need someone to protect you. Shay Tal, Vry—they're not happy. Shay Tal never laughs, does she? Besides, she's old. I'd look after you and make you happy. I want nothing better."

She was buttoning up her tunic, looking down at the toggles which she herself had designed (to the tailor's amazement), so that the skins could be put on and off without trouble.

"Oh, Laintal Ay, I'm so difficult. I have difficulty with myself. I don't really know what I want. I long to dissolve and flow like this wonderful water. Who knows where it comes from, where it goes to?— from the very eddre of earth, maybe. . . . I do love you, though, in my horrid way. Listen, we'll have an arrangement."

She stopped fiddling with her tunic and came to stand looking down at him, hands on her hips.

"Do something great and astonishing, one thing, one deed, and I'll be your woman for ever. You understand that? A great deed, Laintal Ay —a great deed and I'm yours. I'll do whatever you wish."

He got up and stood away from her, surveying her. "A great deed? What sort of great deed do you mean? By the original boulder, Oyre, you are a strange girl."

She tossed her damp hair. "If I told you, then it would no longer be great. Do you understand that? Besides, I don't know what I mean. Strive, strive . . . You're getting fat already, as if you were pregnant. . . ."

He stood without moving, his face hard. "How is it that when I tell you I love you you insult me in return?"

"You tell me truth—I hope; I tell you truth. But I don't mean to hurt you. Really I'm gentle. You just released things in me, things I've said to no one else. I long for . . . no, I can't say what the longings are for . . . glory. Do something great, Laintal Ay, I beg you, something great, before we grow too old."

"Like killing phagors?"

Suddenly she laughed on rather a harsh note, narrowing her eyes. For a moment, her resemblance to Aoz Roon was marked. "If that's all you can think of. Provided you kill a million of them."

He looked baffled.

"So you imagine you're worth a million phagors?"

Oyre pretended to smite herself hard on the forehead, as if her harneys had come loose. "It's not for *me*, don't you see? It's for yourself. Achieve one great thing for your own sake. Here we're stuck in what Shay Tal says is a farmyard—at least make it a legendary farmyard."

The ground trembled again. "Scumble," he said. "The earth really is moving."

They stood up, shaken out of their argument, ignoring each other. A bronze overcast spread from the aerial castles, which now took on purple hearts and yellow edges. The heat became intense, and they stood in the midst of an oppressive silence, backs to each other, looking about.

A repeated smacking sound made them turn towards the pool. Its surface was marred by yellow bubbles which rose and grew until they burst, to spread filth through the hitherto clear water. The bubbles sailed up from the depths, releasing a stink of rotten eggs, coming faster and blacker. Thick mist filled the hollow.

A jet of mud burst from the pool and sprayed into the air. Gobbets of scalding filth flew, pocking the foliage all about. The humans ran in terror, she in her garb the colour of summer skies.

Within a minute of their leaving, the pool was a mass of black seething liquid.

Before they could get back to Oldorando, the skies opened, and down came the rain, grey, and chilling to the flesh.

As they climbed into the big tower, voices could be heard overhead, Aoz Roon's prominent among them. He had just arrived back with allies of his own generation, Tanth Ein, Faralin Ferd, and Eline Tal, all sturdy warriors and good hunters; with them were their women, exclaiming over new hoxney skins, and Dol Sakil, who sat sulkily apart on the window sill, regardless of the rain beating down. Also in the room was Raynil Layan, his skins perfectly dry; he fingered his forked beard and looked anxiously back and forth, without either speaking or being spoken to.

Aoz Roon spared his natural daughter no more than a look before saying challengingly to Laintal Ay, "You've been missing again."

"For a while, yes. I'm sorry. I was inspecting the defences. I—"

Aoz Roon laughed curtly and looked at his companions as he said, "When you enter in that state, with Oyre with her fancy garb unlaced, I know you have been inspecting something other than the defences. Don't lie to me, you young fighting cock!"

The other men laughed. Laintal Ay went crimson.

"I'm no liar. I went to inspect our defences—but we have no defences. There are no sentries, no guards, while you were lying drinking in the wilderness. Oldorando could fall to one single armed Borlienian. We're taking life too easy, and you set a poor example."

He felt Oyre's steadying hand on his arm.

"He spends little time here now," Dol called, in a teasing voice, but was ignored, for Aoz Roon had turned to his other companions and said, "You see what I have to endure from my lieutenants, so-called. Always impudence. Oldorando is now concealed and protected by green, growing higher every week. When the warlike weather returns, as return it will, that will be time enough for war. You're trying to make trouble, Laintal Ay."

"Not so. I'm trying to prevent it."

Aoz Roon walked forward and confronted him, his immense black figure towering over the youth.

"Then keep quiet. And don't lecture me."

Above the noise of the downpour, cries could be heard outside. Dol turned to stare out of the window and called that someone was in trouble. Oyre ran to join her.

"Stand back," Aoz Roon shouted, but the three older women also jostled to get close to the window. The room became even darker.

"We'll go and see what's happening," Tanth Ein said. He started down the stairs, his great shoulders almost blocking the trap as he descended, with Faralin Ferd and Eline Tal after him. Raynil Layan remained in the shadows, watching them go. Aoz Roon made as if to stop them, then stood indecisively in the middle of the dull room, regarded only by Laintal Ay.

The latter came forward and said, "My temper ran away with me; you shouldn't have called me a liar. Don't let that mean that my warning goes unheeded. Our responsibility is to keep the place guarded as we used to."

Aoz Roon bit his lip and did not listen.

"You get your ideas from that damned woman Shay Tal." He spoke absently, one ear cocked to the noises outside. Masculine shouts were now added to the earlier cries. The women at the window also set up a great noise, running about and clinging to Dol and to each other.

"Come away!" cried Aoz Roon, grabbing Dol angrily. Curd, the great yellow hound, started to howl.

The world danced to drumming rain. The figures below the tower were grey in the downpour. Two of the three burly hunters were lifting a body from the mud, while the third, Faralin Ferd, was endeavouring to put his arms about two old women in rain-soaked furs and direct them towards shelter. The old women, uninterested in comfort, raised their faces in grief, rain pouring into their open mouths. They were recognisable as Datnil Skar's woman and an ancient widow, the aunt of Faralin Ferd.

The women had dragged the body in from the north gate between them, covering it and themselves with mud in the process. As the hunters straightened up with their burden, the body was revealed. Its visage was distorted and masked by blood so caked that the rain did not wash it away. Its head fell back as the hunters heaved it high. Blood still gouted across its face and garments. Its throat had been bitten out, as cleanly as a man bites a great mouthful from an apple.

Dol began to shriek. Aoz Roon pushed past her, thrust his burly shoulders into the window space, and called down at those below, "Don't bring that thing in here."

The men chose to disregard him. They were making for the nearest shelter. Jets of rainwater were spewing down from the parapets above them. They floundered in the muck with their muddy burden.

Aoz Roon cursed and ran from the room, charging downstairs, Curd following. Caught by the drama of the moment, Laintal Ay followed, with Oyre, Dol, and the other women behind him, jostling on the narrow steps. Raynil Layan came more slowly in the rear.

The hunters and the old women dragged or escorted the dead body into the low-ceilinged stable to drop it on scattered straw. The men stood away, wiping their faces with their hands, as a puddle of water in which blood spiralled leaked from the body, to set afloat wisps of straw, which turned uncertainly on the flood like boats seeking an estuary. The old women, grotesque bundles, cried on each other's shoulders monumentally. Although the face of the dead man was plastered with blood and hair there was no doubt of his identity. Master Datnil Skar, with Curd sniffing at his cold ear, lay dead before them.

Tanth Ein's woman was a personable creature, by name Farayl Musk. She broke into a series of long wailing cries, which she was unable to stifle.

Nobody could mistake the deadly neck wound for anything but a phagor bite. The mode of execution common in Pannoval had been passed on, for when need arose, as it rarely did, by Yuli the Priest. Somewhere outside in the pouring rain was Wutra, waiting. Wutra, for ever at war. Laintal Ay thought of Shay Tal's alarming claim that Wutra was a phagor. Perhaps there really was a god, perhaps he really was a phagor. His mind went back to the time earlier in the day, before he had found Oyre naked, when he had seen Goija Hin leading Myk to the north gate. There was no doubt who was responsible for this death; he thought how Shay Tal would have fresh cause for sorrow.

He looked at the stricken faces about him—and Raynil Layan's gloating one—and took courage. In a loud voice, he said, "Aoz Roon, I name you the killer of this good old man." He pointed at Aoz Roon as if imagining that some present did not know whom he designated.

All eyes turned to the Lord of Embruddock, who stood with his head against the rafters, his face pale. He said harshly, "Don't dare speak against me. One word more from you, Laintal Ay, and I will strike you down."

But Laintal Ay could not be stopped. Full of anger, he cried mockingly, "Is this another of your cruel blows against knowledge—against Shay Tal?"

The others murmured, restless in the confined space. Aoz Roon said, "This is justice. I have information that Datnil Skar allowed outsiders to read the secret book of his corps. It's a forbidden act. Its just penalty is now, as it always was, death."

"Justice! Does this look like justice? This blow has all the stealth of murder. You've all seen—it's carried out like the murder of—"

Aoz Roon's attack was hardly unexpected, but its ferocity knocked his guard away. He struck back at Aoz Roon's face, dancing black with rage before him. He heard Oyre shriek. Then a fist caught him squarely on the side of the jaw.

Detachedly, he saw himself stagger backwards, trip over the sodden corpse, and sprawl powerless on the stable floor.

He was aware of screams, shouting, boots trampling round him. He felt the kicks in his ribs. There was confusion as they took him up like the body they had dropped—he attempting to protect his skull from knocking against a wall—and carried him outside into the downpour. He heard thunder like a giant pulse.

From the steps, they flung him bodily into the mud. The rain came flying down into his face. As he sprawled there, he realised that he was no longer Aoz Roon's lieutenant. From now on, their enmity was out in the open, apparent to all.

Rain continued to fall. Belts of dense cloud rolled across the central continent. An atmosphere of stalemate prevailed over the affairs of Oldorando.

The distant army of the young kzahhn, Hrr-Brahl Yprt, was forced to halt its advance, to shelter among the shattered hills of the east. Its components went into a sort of tether rather than face the downpour.

The phagors also experienced earth tremors, which originated from the same source as those afflicting Oldorando. Far to the north, old rift zones in the Chalce region were undergoing violent seismic upheaval. As the burden of ice disappeared, the earth shook and rose up.

By this period, the ocean that girdled Helliconia became free of ice even beyond the wide tropical zones, which stretched from the equator to latitudes thirty-five degrees north and south. The westward circulation of oceanic waters built up in a series of tsunami, which devastated coastal regions all round the globe. The floodings often combined with vulcanism to alter the land area.

All such geological events were monitored by the instruments of the Earth Observation Station, which Vry called Kaidaw. The readings were signalled back to distant Earth. No planet in the galaxy was watched more intensely than Helliconia.

Account was taken of the dwindling herds of yelk and biyelk which inhabited the northern Campannlat plain; their pasturage was threatened. Kaidaws, on the other hand, were multiplying as marginal lands, hitherto barren, provided grazing.

There were two sorts of ancipital community on the tropical continent: static components without kaidaws, which lived close to the land, and mobile or nomadic groups with kaidaws. Not only was the kaidaw a highly mobile animal in its own right; its fodder consumption forced those who domesticated it to move continuously in search of new foraging grounds. The army of the young kzahhn, for example, consisted of numerous small components committed to a nomadic and often warlike existence. Their crusade was only one aspect of a migration, which would take decades to complete, from east to west of the entire continent.

A tremor which brought down avalanches about the kzahhn's army marked the tail end of an upheaval in the planet's crust which deflected a river of meltwater flowing from the Hhryggt Glacier. A new valley opened. The new river coursed through it, and henceforth flowed westwards instead of north, as previously.

This river burst its way down to become a tributary of the river Takissa, streaming southwards to empty into the Sea of Eagles. Its waters ran black for many years; they carried with them dozens of metric tons of demolished mountain every day.

Flooding caused by the new river through its new valley forced one insignificant group of phagors of the nomadic type to disperse in the direction of Oldorando instead of heading east. Their destiny was to encounter Aoz Roon at a later date. Though their deflection at the time was of little seeming importance even to the ancipitals themselves, it was to alter the social history of the sector.

There were, on the Avernus, those who studied the social history of Helliconian cultures; but it was the heliographers who regarded their science as the most valuable. Before all else came the light.

Star B, which the natives below called Batalix, was a modest spectral class G4 sun. In real terms slightly smaller than Sol, its radius being 0.94 Sol's, its apparent size as seen from Helliconia was 76 percent that of Sol seen from Earth. With a photosphere temperature of 5600 Kelvin, its luminosity was only 0.8 that of Sol. It was about five billion years old.

The more distant star, known locally as Freyr, about which Star B revolved, was a much more impressive object as viewed from the Avernus. Star A was a brilliant white spectral class A-type supergiant, with a radius sixty-five times that of Sol's, and a luminosity sixty thousand

times as great. Its mass was 14.8 times Sol's, and its surface tempera-
ture 11,000K, as opposed to Sol's 5780K.

Although Star B had its constant students, Star A was a greater mag-
net for attention, especially now that the Avernus was moving, along
with the rest of Star B's system, nearer to the supergiant.

Freyr was between ten and eleven million years old. It had evolved
away from the main sequence of stars and was already entering its old
age.

Such was the intensity of the energy it poured out that the disc of
Star A was always more intense as viewed from Helliconia than that of
Star B, though it never appeared so large, owing to its much greater
distance. It was a worthy object for ancipital fear—and for Vry's
admiration.

Vry stood alone on the top of her tower, her telescope by her side.
She waited. She watched. She felt the history of private relationships
flowing towards the morrow like a silt-laden river; what had been fresh
was clogged with sediment. Beneath her passivity was an unformulated
longing to be seized up by some larger thing which would provide
wider, purer perspectives than faulty human nature could command.

When darkness fell, she would look again at the stars—provided the
cloud cover parted sufficiently.

Oldorando was now surrounded by palisades of green. Day by day,
new leaves unfurled and mounted higher, as if nature had a plan to bury
the town in forest. Some of the more distant towers had already been
overwhelmed by vegetation.

She saw a large white bird hover above one such mound without paying it particular attention. She watched and admired its effortless hovering above the earth.

Distantly came the sound of men singing. The hunters were back in
Oldorando from a hoxney hunt, and Aoz Roon was holding a feast. The
feast was in honour of his three new lieutenants, Tanth Ein, Faralin
Ferd, and Eline Tal. These friends of his childhood supplanted Dathka
and Laintal Ay, who were now relegated to the chase.

Vry tried to keep her thoughts abstract, but they drifted back continually to the more emotional subject of defeated hope—hers, Dathka's, whose desires she could not find it in herself to encourage, Laintal
Ay's. Her mood was in tune with the long-protracted evening. Batalix
was down, the other sentinel would follow in an hour. This was a time
when men and beasts made preparations against the reign of night. This
was a time to bring out a stub of candle against some undreamed-of
emergency, or to resolve to sleep until the light of dawn.

From her eyrie, Vry saw the common people of Oldorando—whether or not further on with their hopes—coming home. Among them was the thin crooked shape of Shay Tal.

Shay Tal returned to the tower with Amin Lim, looking grimy and tired. Since the murder of Master Datnil, she had become increasingly remote. The curse of silence had fallen on her too. She was currently trying to follow a suggestion made by the dead master, to dig her way into King Denniss's pyramid, out by the sacrificial ground. Despite the aid of slaves, she had no success. People who went to look at the earthwork being thrown up laughed, openly or secretly, for the stepped walls of the pyramid went on down into the earth without feature. For every foot dug, Shay Tal's mouth grew grimmer.

Moved by both pity and her own loneliness, Vry went down to speak to Shay Tal. The sorceress seemed to have precious little that was magical about her; almost alone among the women of Oldorando, she still wore the old clumsy furs, hanging ungracefully about her body, giving her an outdated air. Everyone else was in hoxneys.

Afflicted by the older woman's woebegone air, Vry could not resist giving some advice.

"You make yourself so unhappy, ma'am. The ground is full of the dark and the past—do stop scratching there."

With a flash of humour, Shay Tal said, "We neither of us see happiness as our prime duty."

"Your attention's so downcast." She pointed out of the window. "Look at that white bird, circling gracefully in the air. Doesn't the sight lift your spirits? I'd like to be that bird, and fly up to the stars."

Somewhat to Vry's surprise, Shay Tal went to the window and looked in the direction Vry pointed. Then she turned, brushing her hair from her brow, and said calmly, "You observe it's a cowbird you pointed out?"

"I suppose so. What of it?" Shadows were already gathering in the room.

"Do you not recall Fish Lake and other encounters? Those birds are the familiars of phagors."

She spoke placidly, in her detached academy manner. Vry was frightened, thinking how self-absorbed she had been to neglect an elementary fact. She put her hand to her mouth, looking from Shay Tal to Amin Lim and back.

"Another attack? What should we do?"

"It appears that I have ceased to communicate with the Lord of Embruddock, or he with me. Vry, you must go and inform him that the enemy may be at his gates while he feasts with his cronies. He will know that I can't be relied on to forestall the brutes, as once I did. Go right away."

As Vry hastened down the path, rain started to drip again. She followed the singing. Aoz Roon and his cronies sat in the lowest room in the tower of the metal-makers corps. Their faces were ripe with the food and beethel set before them. A trencher piled with geese stuffed with raige and scantiom formed the chief dish; its aroma made the starved Vry's mouth water. Those present included the three new lieutenants and their women, the newest master of the council, Raynil Layan, and Dol and Oyre. The last two alone looked pleased at Vry's entry. As Vry knew—as Rol Sakil had proudly announced—Dol now carried Aoz Roon's child inside her.

Candles burned already on the tables; dogs milled in the shadows under the tables. Flavours of cooked goose and raw dogs' piss intermingled.

Although the men were red and shining, despite the piped heating the room felt cold. Rain gusted in, causing streamlets to run between the flags. It was a small dirty room, with cobwebs festooning every corner. Vry took it all in as she broke her news nervously to Aoz Roon.

She had once been familiar with every adze mark on the beams overhead. Her mother had served as a slave to the metal makers, and she had lived in this room, or in a corner of it, and witnessed the degradation of her mother every night.

Although he had looked far gone in drink a moment earlier, Aoz Roon jumped up immediately. Curd started to bark furiously, and Dol kicked him into silence. The other feasters stared at each other rather stupidly, reluctant to digest Vry's news.

Aoz Roon marched round the table, clouting their shoulders as he issued an order to each.

"Tanth Ein, alert everyone and turn out the hunters. God's eddre, why aren't we properly guarded? Mount sentries on all towers, report when all's done. Faralin Ferd, fetch in all women and children. Lock them in the women's house for safety. Dol, Oyre, you two remain here, and you other women. Eline Tal, you have the loudest voice—you stay on top of this tower and relay any messages needed. . . . Raynil Layan, you're in charge of all corps men. Have them paraded at once, go."

After this rapid fire of orders, he shouted them into action, himself pacing about furiously. Then he turned to Vry, "All right, woman, I want to see the lie of the land for myself. Yours is the northernmost tower—I'll look from there. Move, everyone, and let's hope this is a false alarm."

He set off rapidly down to the door, his great hound bursting past him. With a last glance at the stuffed geese, Vry followed. Soon, shouts resounded among the leprous old buildings. The rain was tapering off. Yellow flowers, abloom in the lanes, unbent their heads and stood erect again.

Oyre ran after Aoz Roon and fell in by his side, smiling despite his growled dismissal. She sprang along in her dark blue and light blue hoxney with something like glee.

"It's not often I see you unprepared, Father."

He shot her one of his black looks. She thought merely, He has grown older of late.

At Vry's tower, he gestured to his daughter to stay, and entered the pile at a run. As he climbed the crumbling steps, Shay Tal emerged on her landing. He spared her only a nod and continued upwards. She followed him to the top, catching his scent.

He stood by the parapet, scrutinising the darkening land. He set his hands in a platform across his eyebrows, elbows out, legs apart. Freyr was low, its light spilling through rifts of western cloud. The cowbird was still circling, and not far distant. No movement could be observed in the bushes beneath its wings.

Shay Tal said from behind his broad back, "There's only the one bird."

He gave no answer.

"And so perhaps no phagors."

Without turning or changing his attitude, he said, "How the place is altered since we were children."

"Yes. Sometimes I miss all the whiteness."

When he did turn, it was with an expression of bitterness on his face, which he seemed to remove with an effort.

"Well, there's evidently little danger. Come and see, if you wish."

He then went down without hesitation, as if regretting his invitation. Curd stayed close as ever. She followed to where the others waited.

Laintal Ay came up, spear in hand, summoned by the shouting.

He and Aoz Roon glared at each other. Neither spoke. Then Aoz Roon drew out his sword and marched down the path in the direction of the cowbird.

The vegetation was thick. It scattered water over them. The women got the worst of it as the men pressed back boughs which showered in the faces of those who followed.

They turned a bend where young damson trees were growing, trunks thinner than a man's arm. There was a ruined tower, reduced to two floors and swamped by vegetation. Beside it, under the leprous stone, in a tunnel of sullen green gloom, a phagor sat astride a kaidaw.

The cowbird could be seen through branches overhead, croaking a warning.

The humans halted, the women instinctively drawing together. Curd crouched, snarling.

Horny hands resting together on the pommel of its saddle, the phagor sat its tall mount. Its spears trailed behind it in an unprepared way. It widened its cerise eyes and twitched an ear. Otherwise, it made no move.

The rain had soaked the phagor's fur, which clung about it in heavy grey clumps. A bead of water hung and twinkled at the tip of one forward-curving horn. The kaidaw was also immobile, its head outstretched, its furled horns twisting below its jaws and then up. Its ribs showed, and it was spattered with mud and gashes on which its yellow blood had caked.

The unreal tableau was broken, unexpectedly, by Shay Tal. She pushed past Aoz Roon and Laintal Ay, to stand alone on the path in front of them. She raised her right hand above her head in a commanding gesture. No response came from the phagor; it certainly did not turn to ice.

"Come back, ma'am," called Vry, knowing the magic would not work.

As if under compulsion, Shay Tal moved forward, bringing all her attention to bear on the hostile figure of mount and rider. Twilight was encroaching, light dying: that would be to the advantage of the adversary, whose eyes saw in the dark.

Taking pace after pace forward, she had to raise her eyes to watch the phagor for any unexpected movement. The stillness of the creature was uncanny. Drawing nearer, she saw that this was a female. Heavy brownish dugs showed beneath the soaked fur.

"Shay Tal, get back!" As he spoke, Aoz Roon ran forward, passing her, his sword ready.

The gillot moved at last. She raised a weapon with a curved blade and spurred her mount.

The kaidaw came on with extraordinary speed. At one moment it was still, at the next charging towards the humans down the narrow path, horns first. Screaming, the women dived into the dripping undergrowth. Curd, without being told, raced in, dodging under the kaidaw's prognathous jaw to nip it in the fetlock.

Baring her gums and incisors, the gillot leaned from her saddle and struck at Aoz Roon. Ducking backwards, he felt the crescent slice by his nose. Farther back down the path, Laintal Ay stuck the butt of his spear in the ground, fell on one knee, and pointed the weapon at the chest of the kaidaw. He crouched before its charge.

But Aoz Roon reached out for the leather girth that was strapped around the animal's body, clasping it as the brute thundered by. Before the phagor could get in a second swipe, he worked with the momentum of the charge and swung himself up on the kaidaw's back, behind its mount.

For a second it seemed that he would fall over on the far side. But he hooked his left arm about the gillot's throat and stayed in place, head well out of reach of the deadly sharp horns.

She swung her head about. Her skull was as heavy as a club. One blow would have knocked the man senseless, but he ducked under her shoulder and tightened his stranglehold on her neck.

The kaidaw halted as suddenly as it had started into action, missing Laintal Ay's point by inches. Beset by Curd, it sheered about, furiously trying to toss the great hound with its horns. As it plunged, Aoz Roon brought up his sword with all the force he could muster, and thrust it between the ribs of the gillot, into her knotted intestines.

She stood up in her leather stirrups and screamed, a harsh, rending noise. She threw up her arms and her curved sword went flying into the nearest branches. Terrified, the kaidaw pranced on its hind legs. The phagor fell free, and Aoz Roon with her. He twisted as they fell, so that she bore the brunt of the tumble. Her left shoulder struck the ground jarringly.

From the dusky sky, the cowbird came swooping in, screeching, to defend its mistress. It dived at Aoz Roon's face. Curd leapt high and caught it by a leg. It slashed at him with curved beak, it battered his head with furious wings, but he tightened his grip and dragged it to the ground. A quick change of grip and he had its throat. In no time, the great white bird was dead, its pinions sprawled without motion across the muddy path.

The gillot also was dead. Aoz Roon stood over it, panting.

"By the boulder, I'm too fat for this kind of activity," he gasped. Shay Tal stood apart and wept. Vry and Oyre inspected the dead brute, regarding its open mouth, from which a yellow ichor seeped.

They heard Tanth Ein shouting in the distance, and answering shouts coming nearer. Aoz Roon kicked the gillot's corpse so that it rolled on to its back, causing a heavy white milt to flop from the jaws. The face was severely wrinkled, the grey skin wormlike where it stretched over bone. The body hair was moulting; patches of bare skin showed.

"It has some filthy disease perhaps," Oyre said. "That's why it was so feeble. Let's get away from it, Laintal Ay. Slaves will bury its corpse."

But Laintal Ay had dropped to his knees and was uncoiling a rope from the corpse's waist. He looked up to say grimly, "You wanted me to perform some great deed. Perhaps I can."

The rope was fine and silken, finer than any rope woven from stunge-bag fibre in Oldorando. He coiled it about his arm.

Curd was holding the kaidaw at bay. The mount, taller at the shoulder than an average man, stood a-tremble, head high, eyes rolling, making no attempt to escape. Laintal Ay tied a noose in the rope and flung it over the animal's neck. He drew it tight and approached the trembling creature step by step, until he could pat its flank.

Aoz Roon had recovered his composure. He wiped his sword on his leg and sheathed it as Tanth Ein arrived on the scene.

"We'll keep watch, but this was a solitary brute—a renegade near death. We have reason for continuing our celebrations, Tanth Ein."

As they clapped each other's shoulders, Aoz Roon looked about him. Ignoring Laintal Ay, he concentrated his regard on Shay Tal and Vry.

"We have no quarrel, whatever you imagine to the contrary," he told the women. "You did well to sound the alarm. Come with Oyre and me and join the festivities—my lieutenants will welcome you."

Shay Tal shook her head. "Vry and I have other things to do."

But Vry remembered the stuffed geese. She could still smell them. It would be worth enduring even that hated room for a taste of that superb flesh. She looked in torment at Shay Tal, but her stomach won. She yielded to temptation.

"I'll come," she told Aoz Roon, flushing.

Laintal Ay had his hand on the kaidaw's trembling flank. Oyre stood with him. She turned to her father and said coldly, "I shall not come. I'm happier with Laintal Ay."

"You please yourself—as usual," he said, and marched off along the dripping lane with Tanth Ein, leaving the humiliated Vry to follow behind as best she could.

The kaidaw stood tossing its great bracketted head up and down, looking sideways at Laintal Ay.

"I'm going to make a pet of you," he said. "We shall ride you, Oyre and I, ride you over the plains and mountains."

They made their way through a gathering crowd, all pressing to see the body of the vanquished enemy. Together, they went back to Embruddock, whose towers stood like decaying teeth against the last rays of Freyr. They walked hand in hand, differences submerged in this decisive moment, pulling the quivering animal after them.

X

LAINTAL AY'S
ACHIEVEMENT

The veldt was banded with upstart flowers as far as eye could see, and farther, farther than any man on two legs could investigate. White, yellow, orange, blue, viridian, cerise, a storm of petals blew across the unmapped miles to wash against the walls of Oldorando and incorporate the hamlet into its blast of colour.

The rain had brought the flowers and the rain had gone. The flowers remained, stretching to the horizon where they shimmered in hot bands, as if distance itself were stained for spring.

A section of this panorama had been fenced off.

Laintal Ay and Dathka had finished work. They and their friends were inspecting what they had achieved.

With saplings and thorn trees, they had built a fence. They had chopped down new growth till the sap ran from their blades over their wrists. The saplings had been trimmed and secured horizontally to serve as the bars of the fence. The uprights and horizontals were packed branches and whole thorn trees. The result was almost impenetrable, and as high as a man. It enclosed about a hectare of ground.

In the middle of this new enclosure stood the kaidaw, defying all attempts to ride it.

The kaidaw's mistress, the gillot, had been left to rot where she fell, as the custom was. Only after three days were Myk and two other slaves sent to bury the body, which had begun to stink.

Blossom hung neglected like spittle from the kaidaw's lips. It had taken a mouthful of pink flowers. Eaten in captivity, they seemed not to its taste, for the great gaunt animal stood with its head high, staring out over the top of the stockade, forgetting to munch. Occasionally, it moved a few yards, with its high step, and then came back to its original vantage point, eyes showing white.

When one of its downward-sweeping horns became entangled in the thorns, it freed itself with an impatient shake of the head. It was strong enough to break through the fence and gallop to freedom, but the will was lacking. It merely gazed towards freedom, blowing out sighs from distended nostrils.

"If the phagors can ride it, so can we. I rode a stungebag," Laintal Ay said. He brought up a bucket of beethel and set it by the animal. The kaidaw took a sniff and backed away, bridling.

"I'm going to sleep," Dathka said. It was his only comment after many hours. He crawled through the fence, sprawled on the ground, stuck his knees in the air, clasped his hands behind his head, and closed his eyes. Insects buzzed about him. Far from taming the animal, he and Laintal Ay had earned themselves only bruises and scratches.

Laintal Ay wiped his forehead and made another approach to the captive.

It brought its long head down so as to look him levelly in the eye. It was blowing softly. He was aware of the horns pointing at him, and made coaxing noises, poised to jump aside. The great beast shook its ears against the base of its horns and turned away.

Laintal Ay controlled his breathing and moved forward again. Ever since he and Oyre had made love by the pool, her beauty had sung in his eddre. The promise of more loving hung above him like an unreachable bough. He must prove himself by that imaginary great deed she required. He woke every morning to feel himself smothered in dreams of her flesh, as if buried under dogthrush blossom. If he could ride and tame the kaidaw, she would be his.

But the kaidaw continued to resist all human advances. It stood waiting as he approached. Its hamstrings twitched. At the last possible moment, it bucked away from his outstretched hand, to prance off, showing him its horns over one shoulder.

He had slept in the stockade with it on the previous night—or dozed fitfully, afraid of being trampled under its hoofs. Still the beast would not accept food or drink from him, and shied away from every approach. The performance had been repeated a hundred times.

Finally, Laintal Ay gave up. Leaving Dathka to slumber, he returned to Oldorando to try a new approach.

Three hours later, as the Hour-Whistler sounded, a curiously deformed phagor approached the enclosure. It dragged itself through the fence with awkward movements, so that gouts of wet yellow fur were torn out by the thorns, to remain hanging among the twigs like dead birds.

With a dragging gait, the oddity approached the kaidaw.

It was hot inside the skin, and it stank. Laintal Ay had a cloth tied round his face, with a sprig of raige against his nostrils. He had made two Barlienian slaves dig up the three-day-old corpse and skin it. Raynil Layan had soaked the skin in brine to remove some of its unpleasant associations. Oyre accompanied him back to the enclosure and stood with Dathka, waiting to see what happened next.

The kaidaw put its head low and breathed a soft question. Its dead mistress's saddle, complete with flamboyant stirrups, was still strapped about its girth. As soon as Laintal Ay reached the puzzled beast, he set one foot high in the near stirrup and swung himself up into the saddle. He was mounted at last, positioned in front of the animal's single low hump.

Phagors rode without reins, crouching over the necks of their mounts or holding the harsh frizzled hair growing along the ridge of their necks. Laintal Ay clutched the hair tightly, awaiting the next move. From the corner of his eye, he could see other villagers, strolling across the Voral bridge, coming to join Oyre and Dathka and watch the proceedings.

The kaidaw stood in silence, head still low, as if weighing its new burden. Then, slowly, it began an absurd movement, arching its neck inward, bringing its head round until its eyes, from an upside-down position, could look up and regard the rider. Its gaze met Laintal Ay's.

The animal remained in its extraordinary position but began to tremble.

The trembling was an intense vibration, seemingly originating at its heart and working outwards, much like an earthquake on a small planet. Yet still its eyeballs glared fixedly at the being on its back, and it was bereft of voluntary movement. Laintal Ay also stayed motionless, vibrating with the kaidaw. He remained looking down into its twisted face, on which—so he afterwards reflected—he read a look of intense pain.

When it did finally move, the kaidaw shot upwards like a released spring. In one continuous movement, it came erect and jumped high in the air, arching its spine like a cat's and curling its clumsy legs beneath its belly. This was the legendary spring jump of the kaidaw, experienced at first hand. The jump took it clear over the stockade fence. It did not even brush the uppermost sprigs of thorn.

As it fell, it snapped its skull down between its forelegs and thrust its horns upwards, so that it struck the ground neck first. One of the horns

was immediately driven through its heart. It fell heavily on its side and
kicked twice. Laintal Ay flung himself free and sprawled among the
clover.

Even before he climbed shakily to his feet, he knew that the kaidaw
was dead.

He pulled the stinking phagor skin from his body. He whirled it
round his head and flung it away. It fell into a sapling's branches and
dangled there. He cursed in frustration, feeling a terrible heat inside his
head. Never had the enmity between man and phagor been more clearly
demonstrated than in the self-destruction of this kaidaw.

He took a pace towards Oyre, who was running to him. He saw the
villagers behind, and bands of colour. The colours rose, took wing, became the sky. He floated towards them.

For six days, Laintal Ay lay in a fever. His body was lapped in a
flamelike rash. Old Rol Sakil came and applied goosegrease to his skin.
Oyre sat by him. Aoz Roon came and looked down at him without
speaking. Aoz Roon had Dol with him, made heavy with child, and
would not let her stay. He departed stroking his beard, as if remembering something.

On the seventh day, Laintal Ay put on his hoxneys again and returned
to the veldt, full of new plans.

The fence they had built already looked more natural, dappled all
over with green shoots. Beyond the enclosure, herds of hoxneys grazed
among the bright-coloured pastures.

"I am not going to be beaten," Laintal Ay said to Dathka. "If we
can't ride kaidaws, we can ride hoxneys. They are not adversaries, like
kaidaws—their blood is as red as ours. See if we can't capture one
between us."

Both of them were wearing hoxney skins. They picked out a white-
and-brown-striped animal and approached it on hands and knees. It
was resting. At the last moment, it got up and walked away disgustedly.

They tried approaching it from different sides, while the rest of the
herd watched the game. Once, Dathka got near enough to touch the
animal's coat. It showed its teeth and fled.

They brought up the rope taken from the gillot and tried to lasso the
animals. They ran about the plain for several hours, chasing hoxneys.

They climbed young trees, lying in wait in the branches with the lasso
ready. The hoxneys came sportingly near, pushing each other and whinneying, but none ventured under the bough.

By dusk, both men were exhausted and short-tempered. The nearby
carcass of the kaidaw was being stripped by several scholarly-looking
vultures, whose clerical garb contrasted with the gobbets of golden meat
they were swallowing. Now sabre-tongues arrived, driving the birds away

and quarrelling over the feast among themselves. Soon it would be dark.

The two retired to the comparative safety of their enclosure, ate pancakes and goose eggs with salt, and went to sleep.

Dathka was the first to waken in the morning. He gasped and propped himself on one elbow, hardly able to believe his eyes.

In the cool dawn light, colour had scarcely returned to the world. Grey mist lay in strata, completely screening the old hamlet from their sight. The world lay in a succulent grey-green mist, characteristic of a Batalixian sunrise in these days. Even the four hoxneys now grazing contentedly in the stockade appeared as little more than pewter imitations of hoxneys.

He woke Laintal Ay with a prodding boot. Together, they crawled on their bellies over the wet grass and through the protecting barrier of thorns. When they were beyond the barricade, they stood up quietly, beaming at each other, clasping each other's shoulders in an attempt to keep from laughing.

No doubt the hoxneys had sought shelter from the sabre-tongues. Now they were in deeper trouble.

Drawing their knives, the men cut fresh armfuls of spikey thorn bush, ignoring the tears they gave their own flesh. These sinewy shrubs had grown even in the snows, keeping each cluster of leaf buds protectively rolled into spikes. Now the spikes unfurled into coppery green, revealing the silver curve of true thorns.

The hoxneys had broken a gap in the fence where they had entered. It was not difficult to intertwine the thorns and repair the hole. They soon had the four animals secure.

At which point, Laintal Ay and Dathka fell into an argument. Dathka claimed that the animals should be left without water until they were weakened and would submit to domination. Laintal Ay said that extra feeding and buckets of water would win the day. Eventually his method, being more positive, prevailed.

But they were still a long way from making mounts of the beasts. For ten days they worked concertedly, bedding down in the enclosure every night as the night grew shorter. The capture was a sensation; the whole population flocked across the Voral bridge to watch the fun. Aoz Roon and his lieutenants came every day. Oyre watched at first, but lost interest as the hoxneys spiritedly defied their would-be riders. Vry came frequently, often in the company of Amin Lim, who was carrying her newborn infant in her arms.

The battle for domestication was won only when the young hunters hit on the idea of dividing the enclosure into four with more fences. Once the animals were separated from each other, they became dejected, standing about with their heads low, refusing to eat.

Laintal Ay had been feeding the animals on barley bread. To this diet, he added rathel. Stocks of rathel had been accumulating steadily in Prast's Tower. Even the men now preferred the sweeter beethel or barley wine, and Embruddock's traditional drink was going out of fashion. One result of this was that women were released from the brassimip patch to work in the new fields. There was rathel to spare for four hoxneys.

A small measure mixed with the bread was enough to make the captive animals skip merrily, fall about, and later become slow and heavy-lidded. During their heavy-lidded phase, Laintal Ay slipped a strap round the neck of the hoxney they had named Gold. He mounted. Gold reared up and bucked. Laintal Ay stayed on for about a minute. On a second attempt, he stayed longer. Victory was his.

Dathka was soon astride Dazzler.

"God's eddre, this is better than sitting on burning stungebags," Laintal Ay shouted, as they rode round the enclosure. "We can ride anywhere—to Pannoval, to the end of the lands, to the edge of the seas!"

At last they dismounted and thumped each other, laughing with achievement.

"Wait until Oyre sees me riding into Oldorando. She won't resist me any longer."

"It's surprising what women can resist," Dathka said.

When they were sure enough of their mounts, they rode side by side across the bridge and into town. The inhabitants turned out and cheered, as if aware of the great social change upon them. From this day forth, nothing would be the same.

Aoz Roon appeared with Eline Tal and Faralin Ferd, and claimed one of the other two hoxneys, which was christened Grey. His lieutenants started to quarrel over the remaining animal.

"Sorry, friends, the last one is for Oyre," Laintal Ay said.

"Oyre's not riding a hoxney," Aoz Roon said. "Forget that idea, Laintal Ay. Hoxneys are for men. . . . They present us with immense possibilities. Riding hoxneys, we are on equal terms with phagors, Chalceans, Pannovalians, or any breed you may name."

He sat astride Grey, gazing at the ground. He foresaw a time when he would lead not simply a few hunters but an army—a hundred men, even two hundred, all mounted, striking fear into the enemy. Every conquest made Oldorando richer, more secure. Oldorandan banners flew across the unmapped plains.

He looked down at Laintal Ay and Dathka, who stood in the middle of the lane, reins in their hands. His dark face wrinkled into a grin.

"You've done well. We'll let yesterday rest with yesterday's snows. As Lord of Embruddock, I appoint you both Lords of the Western Veldt."

He leaned forward to clasp Laintal Ay's hand.

"Accept your new title. You and your silent friend are in charge of all hoxneys from now on. They are yours—my gift. I'll see you have help.

You'll have duties and privileges. I'm a just man, you know that. I want all the hunters mounted on broken hoxneys as soon as possible."

"I want your daughter as my woman, Aoz Roon."

Aox Roon scratched his beard. "You get to work on the hoxneys. I'll get to work on my daughter." Something veiled in his look suggested that he had no intention of encouraging the match; if he had a rival to power, it was not his three complaisant lieutenants but young Laintal Ay. To bind him to Oyre was to reinforce that potential threat. Yet he was too cunning actively to discourage his wayward daughter from her interest in Laintal Ay. What he wanted was a contented Laintal Ay, and a stream of armed, mounted warriors.

Although his vision was impossibly grand, yet the epoch would come when all he dreamed of doing was achieved by others a hundred times over. That epoch had its beginnings when he and Dathka and Laintal Ay first sat astride the woolly backs of their hoxney mares.

Powered by the dream, Aoz Roon threw off a state of indolence which had overcome him with better weather, and reverted to the man of action. He had inspired his people to build a bridge: now it was stables and corrals and a shop where harness and saddles were made. The dead gillot's saddle with adjustable stirrups was used as a model for all Oldorandan saddles.

The tamed hoxneys were used as decoys in the manner of captive deer, and more of the wild animals were caught. Despite their protests, all hunters had to learn to ride; soon, each had a hoxney of his own. The age of hunting on foot was dead.

Fodder became an overwhelming problem. The women were driven to plant more fields of oats. Even the old were sent out to do what they could. Fences were built round the fields to exclude hoxneys and other despoilers. Expeditions went out to discover fresh brassimip plants, once it was discovered that hoxneys would eat ground brassimip—the food from the plant where their glossies had sheltered in darker days.

For all these new developments, power was needed. The greatest innovation was the building of a mill; a hoxney, plodding round and round in a circle, ground all the grain required, and the women were released from their immemorial morning chore.

Within a few weeks, days even, the hoxney revolution was well under way. Oldorando became a different kind of town.

Its population had doubled: for every human, there was a hoxney. In the base of every tower, hoxneys were quartered beside pigs and goats. In every lane, hoxneys were tethered, champing down grasses. Along the banks of the Voral, hoxneys were watered and traded. Beyond the town gates, primitive rodeos and circuses were held, with hoxneys in starring roles. Hoxneys were everywhere, in towers, in talk, in dreams.

While auxiliary trades grew up to cater for the new obsession, Aoz Roon furthered his plans for turning his hunters into light cavalry. They drilled incessantly. Old objectives were forgotten. Meat became scarce, promises of more meat more plentiful. In order to stave off complaints, Aoz Roon planned his first mounted foray.

He and his lieutenants chose as their target a small town to the southeast, by name Vanlian, within the province of Borlien. Vanlian was situated on the Voral, where that river broadened into a valley. It was protected on its east side by tall crumbling cliffs honeycombed by caves. The inhabitants had dammed the river to create a series of shallow lakes in which they bred fish, the chief item of their diet. Sometimes traders brought the fish, dried, to Oldorando. Vanlian, with over two hundred inhabitants, was larger than Oldorando, but had no strongholds equivalent to the stone towers. It could be destroyed by surprise attack.

The marauding cavalry numbered thirty-one. They attacked at Batalix-dawn when the inhabitants of Vanlian were out of their caves and attending to their fish harvest. Although their town was surrounded by ditches backed by steep embankments, the hoxneys climbed this fortification with ease, and bore down on the helpless people, their riders uttering wild cries and striking out with their spears.

Within two hours, Vanlian was destroyed. The men were killed, the women raped. Huts were burned down, fires were started in the caves, the dykes regulating the artificial lakes despoiled. A celebratory feast was held among the ruins, with much of the local small ale consumed. Aoz Roon made a speech praising his men and their mounts. None of the cavalry had died, although one hoxney had been mortally wounded by a Vanlianian sword thrust.

The victory against tall numerical odds was achieved so easily because the local people were aghast at seeing brightly clad men riding in on bright steeds. They stood with mouths open to receive their death blow. Only youths and children of both sexes were spared. These were forced to round up their livestock and move off in the direction of Oldorando, driving pigs, goats, and cattle before them. Under the eyes of six cavalry selected as guards, they took a day to make a journey that Aoz Roon and his triumphant lieutenants achieved in an hour.

Vanlian was hailed as a great victory. More conquests were called for. Aoz Roon tightened his grip, and the population learned that conquests call for sacrifices. The Lord addressed his subjects on this question when he and his cavalry had returned from another successful raid.

"We shall never want again," he announced. He stood with his arms akimbo and his legs apart. A slave stood behind him, holding Grey's rein. "Oldorando will be a great place, as legends say that Embruddock was in bygone days. We are like phagors now. Everyone will fear us, and we shall grow rich. We will take in more land, and have more slaves to tend it. Soon, we shall raid Borlien itself. We need more people, there are not enough of us. You women must bear your men more children. Babies will soon be born in the saddle as we spread far and wide."

He pointed to a wretched huddle of prisoners, guarded by Goija Hin, Myk, and others. "These people will work for us, just as the hoxneys work for us. But for a while we must all work doubly hard, and eat less, so that these things come about. Don't let me hear you complaining. Only heroes deserve the greatness that will soon be ours."

Dathka scratched his thigh and looked at Laintal Ay with one eyebrow up and one eyebrow down. "See what we've started."

But Laintal Ay was carried away by excitement. Whatever his feelings for Aoz Roon, he believed many of the things the older man said to be true. Certainly, there was no excitement like that of riding on hoxney-back, being at one with the lively creature, and feeling the wind on one's cheek and the ground thundering by below. Nothing so wonderful had ever been invented—with one exception.

He said to Oyre, gathering her to him, "You heard what your father said. I have done a great thing—one of the greatest things in history. I have tamed the hoxneys. That's what you wished, isn't it? Now you must be my woman."

But she pushed him away. "You smell of hoxneys, just as my father does. Ever since you were ill, you have talked of nothing but those stupid creatures, good only for their skins. Father talks only of Grey, you talk only of Gold. Do something that makes life better, not worse. If I was your woman, I'd never see you, because you're out riding all day and night. You men have gone mad over the hoxneys."

The women in the main felt as Oyre did. They experienced the bad effects of hoxney-mania without its excitements. Forced to work in the fields, they no longer enjoyed a sleepy afternoon's visit to the academy.

Only Shay Tal took a close interest in the animals. The wild hoxney herds were no longer as plentiful as they had been. Taking alarm at last, they moved to new grazing grounds to the west and south, in order to avoid captivity or slaughter. It was Shay Tal who had the initiative to breed from a mare and a stallion. She set up a stud by King Denniss's pyramid in which foals were soon being born. The result was a strain of domesticated and mild-mannered animals, easy to train for whatever job was required.

One of the best mares she christened Loyalty. Over all the foals she exercised great care, but her special attention was directed towards Loyalty. She knew that she now held by a halter her means of leaving Oldorando and getting to far Sibornal.

XI

WHEN SHAY TAL WENT

In sun and rain, Oldorando expanded. Before its industrious inhabitants realised what had happened, it had crossed the river Voral, had leaped the marshy tributaries to the north, had stretched out to the corrals on the veldt and the brassimip patches in the low hills.

More bridges were built. None was heroic like the first one. The corps had relearnt the art of sawing planks, carpenters came forth—among both the free and the slaves—for whom arches and joints and abutments presented few problems.

Beyond the bridges, fields were planted and fenced, sties were built for pigs and pens for geese. Food production had to be dramatically increased, to feed the increasing numbers of domesticated hoxneys, and to feed the slaves needed to tend the extra fields. Beyond or between the fields, new towers were built along the old Embruddock lines, to house the slaves and their keepers. The towers were built according to a demonstration given by the academy, using mud blocks instead of stone, and rising only to two stories instead of five. The rains, heavy on occasion, washed away the walls. The Oldorandans cared little for that, since only slaves lived in the new blocks. But the slaves themselves cared —and demonstrated how straw harvested from the cereal fields could

253

be used as overhanging thatch, to preserve the mud buildings and keep them intact even in heavy rainstorms.

Beyond the fields and new towers were bridle paths, patrolled by Aoz Roon's cavalry. Oldorando was not merely a town but an armed camp as well. Nobody left or entered without permission, except in the traders' quarters—nicknamed the Pauk—developing to the south side.

For every proud warrior mounted on a steed, six backs must bend in the field. But the harvest was good. The ground gave forth abundantly, following its long rest. Prast's Tower had been used in cold times to store first salt, than rathel; now it stored grain. Outside, where the ground had been beaten flat, women and slaves worked to winnow an immense pile of grain. The men turned over the grain with wooden paddles, the women flapped skins tied to square frames, fanning away the chaff. It was hot work. Modesty went by the board. The women, at least the young ones, threw off their smart jackets and worked with naked breasts.

Fine particles of dust rose. The dust stuck to the moist skins of the women, powdering their faces, lending their flesh a furry appearance. It rose in the air, creating a pyramid above the scene, gold in the sunlight, before dispersing to fall elsewhere, deadening footfalls on stairs, staining vegetation.

Tanth Ein and Faralin Ferd rode up, closely followed by Aoz Roon and Eline Tal, with Dathka and younger hunters riding behind. They had returned from a hunt and had brought in several deer.

For a minute, they were content to sit in their saddles, watching the women at work. Among the women were the wives of the three lieutenants; they paid no attention to the jocular remarks of their lords. The frames fanned the grain, the men leaned indulgently forward in their saddles, the chaff and dust flew high, flecking the sunshine.

Dol appeared, walking slowly, heavy with child, and Myk the aged phagor walked by her, driving her geese. With her came Shay Tal, her skinniness emphasised by the plumpness of Dol. When they saw the Lord of Embruddock and his men, both women paused, glancing at each other.

"Say nothing to Aoz Roon," Shay Tal cautioned.

"He's amenable just now," Dol said. "He hopes for a boy."

She strode forward and stood by the side of Grey. Aoz Roon looked at her but said nothing.

She slapped his knee. "Once there were priests to bless the harvest in Wutra's name. Priests used to bless newborn babes. Priests cared for all, men and women, high and low. We need them. Can't you capture some priests for us?"

"Wutra!" Aoz Roon exclaimed. He spat into the dust.

"That's no answer."

His dark eyebrows and eyelashes were dusted with the golden pepper in the air as he switched his heavy glance beyond Dol to where Shay Tal stood, her dark narrow face as blank as an alleyway.

"She's been talking to you, Dol, hasn't she? What do you know or care about Wutra? Great Yuli threw him out, and our forefathers threw out the priests. They're only lazy mouths to feed. Why are we strong while Borlien is weak? Because we have no priests. Forget this nonsense, don't bother me with it."

Dol said, pouting, "Shay Tal says the gossies are angry because we have no priests. Isn't that right, Shay Tal?" She looked appealingly over her shoulder at the older woman, who still made no move.

"Gossies are always angry," Aoz Roon said, turning away.

"They're twitching down there like a bed of fleas," Eline Tal agreed, pointing at the earth and laughing. He was a big, red-cheeked man, and his cheeks wobbled when he laughed. More and more, he had become Aoz Roon's closest companion, with the other two lieutenants playing rather subsidiary roles.

Stepping one pace forward, Shay Tal said, "Aoz Roon, despite our prosperity, we Oldorandans remain divided. Great Yuli would not have wished that. Priests might help us become a more united community."

He looked down at her, and then climbed slowly from his hoxney, to stand confronting her. Dol was pushed to one side.

"If I silence you, I silence Dol. No one wants the priests back. You only want them back because they'll help fortify your craving for learning. Learning's a luxury. It creates idle mouths. You know that, but you're so damned stubborn you won't give up. Starve yourself if you will, but the rest of Oldorando is growing fat—see for yourself. We grow fat without priests, without your learning."

Shay Tal's face crumpled. She said in a small voice, "I do not wish to fight you, Aoz Roon. I'm sick of it. But what you say is not true. We prosper in part because of applied knowledge. The bridges, the houses— those were ideas the academy contributed to the community."

"Don't anger me, woman."

Looking down at the ground, she said, "I know you hate me. I know that's why Master Datnil was killed."

"What I hate is division, constant division," Aoz Roon roared. "We survive by collective effort, and always have done."

"But we can only grow through individuality," Shay Tal said. Her face grew paler as the blood mounted in his cheeks.

He made a violent gesture. "Look about you, for Yuli's sake! Remember what this place was like when you were a child. Try to understand how we have built it to what it is now by united effort. Don't stand in front of me and try to argue differently. Look at my lieutenants' women —tits swinging, working in with everyone else. Why are you never with them? Always on the fringe, mouthing discontent, whining."

"No tit to swing, I'd say," Eline Tal said, chuckling.

His remark had been intended for the delectation of his friends, Tanth Ein and Faralin Ferd. But it also reached the alert ears of the young hunters, who burst into jeering laughter—all except Dathka, who sat silent, hunched in his saddle, alertly surveying the participants in the momentary drama.

Shay Tal also caught Eline Tal's comment. Since he was distant kin to her, the remark stung the more. Her eyes glittered with tears and wrath.

"Enough, then! I'll stand no more abuse from you and your cronies. I'll worry you no more, Aoz Roon, I'll argue never again. You've seen the last of me, you thickheaded, disappointing, treacherous bully—you and your little pregnant cow of a bedmate! At Freyr-dawn tomorrow, I leave Oldorando for good. I shall depart alone, on my mare, Loyalty, and no one will ever see me more."

Aoz Roon flung out his arm. "No one leaves Oldorando without my permission. You're not going from here until you grovel at my feet, begging to leave."

"We'll see about that in the morning," Shay Tal snapped. She turned on her heel, clutched her loose dark furs about her body, and made off towards the north gate.

Dol was red in the face. "Let her go, Aoz Roon, drive her out. Good riddance. Pregnant cow, indeed, the juiceless creature!"

"You keep out of this. I'll settle this my way."

"I suppose you're going to have her killed, like the others."

He struck her across the face, lightly and with contempt, still looking after the retreating figure of Shay Tal.

It was the night period when everyone slept, though Batalix still burned low in the sky. Although slaves twitched in the dreams of dim-day-sleep, some of the free were still about on this occasion. In the room at the top of the big tower, full council was met, consisting of the masters of the seven old corps, plus two new masters, younger men from newly constituted corps, the harness and lorimers, and the outfitters. Also present were Aoz Roon's three lieutenants and one of his Lords of the Western Veldt, Dathka. The Lord of Embruddock presided over the meeting, and serving wenches kept their wooden cups filled with beethel or small beer.

After much argument, Aoz Roon said, "Ingsan Atray, give us your voice on this question."

He was addressing the senior master, a greybeard who ruled over the metal-makers corps, and who had as yet said nothing. The years had curved Ingsan Atray's spine and turned his scanty hair white, so that the great width of his skull was emphasized; for this reason, he was regarded as wise. He had a mannerism of smiling a great deal, though his eyes, barricaded behind wrinkled lids, always looked wary. He smiled now, squatting on the skins piled on the floor for his comfort, and said, "My Lord, Embruddock's corps have traditionally protected the women. Women, after all, are our source of labour when the hunters are in the field, and so on. Of course, times are changing, I grant you that. It was different in the times of Lord Wall Ein. But women also serve as channels of much learning. We have no books, but women memorise and pass on the legends of the tribe, as is seen whenever we tell the Great Tale on feast days—"

"Your point, please, Ingsan Atray . . ."

"Ah, I was coming to it, I was coming to it. Shay Tal may be difficult and so on, but she is a sorceress and learned woman, widely known. She does no harm. If she leaves, she will take other women with her, and so on, and that will be a loss. We masters would venture to say that you were correct in forbidding her to leave."

"Oldorando's not a prison," Faralin Ferd shouted.

Aoz Roon nodded curtly, and looked about. "The meeting was called because my lieutenants disagreed with me. Who agrees with my lieutenants?"

He caught the eye of Raynil Layan, nervously stroking his forked beard.

"Master of the tanners corps, you always like to air your voice—what have you to say?"

"As to that—" Raynil Layan gestured dismissively. "There is always the *difficulty* of preventing Shay Tal leaving. She can easily slip away, if so disposed. And there is the general principle . . . Other women will think . . . Well, we don't want discontented women. But there's Vry, for instance, another thinking woman, yet attractive, and *she* gives no trouble. If you could rethink your order, many would be grateful to you. . . ."

"Speak out and don't mince your words so," Aoz Roon said. "You're a master now, as you wished, and don't have to cringe."

Nobody else spoke. Aoz Roon glared at them. All avoided his gaze, burying their faces in their cups.

Eline Tal said, "Why are we worrying? What's the odds? Let her go."

"Dathka!" the lord snapped. "Are you going to grant us a single word tonight, since your friend Laintal Ay has not put in an appearance?"

Dathka set down his beaker and looked directly at Aoz Roon.

"All this debate, this talk of principle . . . it's rubbish. We all know you and Shay Tal long wage great personal war. So *you* decide what to do, not us. Kick her out now you have your chance. Why bring us into it?"

"Because it concerns you all, that's why!" Aoz Roon pounded his fist on the floor. "By the boulder, why does that woman always have such a grudge against me, against everyone? I don't understand. What rotten maggot chews at her harneys? She keeps on the academy, doesn't she? She sees herself in a long line of female troublemakers— Loilanun, Loil Bry, who became Little Yuli's woman. . . . But where would she go? What would happen to her?"

His sentences seemed wild and disconnected.

No one answered. Dathka had spoken for all of them; all were secretly aghast when he said what he did. Aoz Roon himself had nothing more to say. The meeting broke up.

As Dathka was slipping away, Raynil Layan grasped Dathka's arm and said softly, "A cunning speech you made. With Shay Tal out of the way, the one you fancy will head the academy, won't she? Then she'll need your support. . . ."

"I leave the cunning to you, Raynil Layan," Dathka said, pulling away. "Just keep out of my path."

He had no trouble in finding Laintal Ay. Despite the lateness of the hour, Dathka knew where to go. In Shay Tal's ruined tower, Shay Tal was packing, and many friends had come to bid her farewell. Amin Lim was there with her child, and Vry, and Laintal Ay with Oyre, and several other women beside.

"What was the verdict?" Laintal Ay asked Dathka immediately, coming to his side.

"Open."

"He won't stop her leaving if she's bent on it?"

"Depends how much he drinks during the night, he and Eline Tal and that crew—and that wretched hanger-on, Raynil Layan."

"She's getting old, Dathka; should we allow her to go?"

He shrugged, using one of his favourite gestures, and looked at Vry and Oyre, who were standing close and listening. "Let's leave with Shay Tal before Aoz Roon has us killed—I'm game if these two ladies will come too. We'll head for Sibornal, the group of us."

Oyre said, "My father would never kill you and Laintal Ay. That's wild talk, whatever happened in the past."

Another shrug from Dathka. "Are you prepared to vouch for his behaviour when Shay Tal's gone? Can we trust him?"

"That's all over long ago," Oyre said. "Father's settled happily with Dol now, and they don't quarrel as much as they used, now a baby's coming."

Laintal Ay said, "Oyre, the world's wide. Let's leave with Shay Tal, as Dathka suggests, and make a new start. Vry, we'll take you with us —you'll be in danger here without Shay Tal's support."

Vry had not spoken. In her usual unobtrusive way, she merely formed part of the group; but she said now, firmly, "I can't leave here. Dathka, I am complimented by your kind suggestion, but I must stay, whatever Shay Tal does. My work is yielding results at last, as I hope soon to announce."

"You still can't bear my presence, can you?" he said, looking grim.

"Oh, I almost forgot something," she said sweetly.

She turned, evading Dathka's brooding gaze, and pushed through the women to Shay Tal's side.

"You must measure all distances, Shay Tal. Don't forget. Have a slave count the number of hoxney strides every day, with the direction taken. Write down details every night. Find out how far away the country of Sibornal is. Be as precise as you can."

Shay Tal was majestic in the midst of the weeping and chattering that filled her chamber. Her hawk face preserved a closed look whenever addressed, as if already her spirit was remote from them. She said little, and that little was uttered in unemotional tones.

Dathka, after staring blankly at the walls, with their elaborate patterning of lichen, looked at Laintal Ay with his head on one side and gestured to the door. When Laintal Ay shook his head, Dathka made a characteristic moue and slipped out. "Pity you can't train women like hoxneys," he said, as he disappeared.

"At least he is consistently revolting," Oyre said disdainfully. She and Vry took Laintal Ay into a corner and began whispering to him. It was essential that Shay Tal should not leave on the morrow; he must help persuade her to wait for the following day.

"That's absurd. If she wants to go, she must go. We've been over all this. First you will not leave, now you don't want her to leave. There's a world out beyond the barricades you know nothing about."

She coolly picked a sliver of straw from his hoxneys. "Yes, the world of conquest. I know—I hear enough of it from Father. The point is, there will be an eclipse tomorrow."

"That's general knowledge. It's a year since the last one."

"Tomorrow will be rather different, Laintal Ay," Vry said, warningly. "We simply wish Shay Tal to postpone her departure. If she leaves here on the day of the eclipse, people will associate the two events. Whereas we know there is no connection."

Laintal Ay frowned. "What of it?"

The two women looked uneasily at each other.

"We think that if she leaves tomorrow, ill things may follow."

"Ha! So you do believe there is a connection. . . . The workings of the female mind! If the connection exists, then there's no way we can evade it, is there?"

Oyre clutched her face in exaggerated disgust. "The male mind . . . Any excuse not to do anything, eh?"

"You witches will meddle with what is no concern of ours."

In disgust, they left him standing in the corner and pressed back into the crowd round Shay Tal.

The old women still chattered away, speaking of the miracle at Fish Lake, speaking obliquely, looking obliquely, to see if their reminiscences

registered on the preoccupied Shay Tal. But Shay Tal gave no sign
that she heard or saw them.

"You look proper fed up with life," Rol Sakil commented. "Maybe
when you reach this Sibornal, you'll marry and settle down happily—if
men are made there as they're made here."

"Perhaps they're made better there," another old woman responded,
amid laughter. Various suggestions as to improvements were bandied
about.

Shay Tal continued to pack, without smiling.

Her belongings were few. When she had finally assembled them in
two skin bags, she turned to the crowd in her room and requested them
to leave, as she desired to rest before her journey. She thanked them
all for coming, blessed them, and said she would never forget them. She
kissed Vry on the forehead. Then she summoned Oyre and Laintal Ay
to her side.

She clutched one of Laintal Ay's hands in her two thin ones, looking
with unusual tenderness into his eyes. She spoke only when all but
Oyre had left her room.

"Be wary in all you do, for you are not self-seeking enough, you do
not take enough care for yourself. You understand, Laintal Ay? I'm
glad you have not struggled for the power that you may feel is your
birthright, for it would only bring you sorrow."

She turned to Oyre, her face lined with seriousness.

"You are dear to me, for I know how dear you are to Laintal Ay.
My council to you as we part in this: become his woman with all
speed. Don't put conditions on your heart, as I did, as your father
once did—that leads to inevitable wretchedness, as I understand too
late. I was too proud when young."

Oyre said, "You are not wretched. You are still proud."

"One may be both wretched and proud. Heed what I say, I who
understand your difficulties. Laintal Ay is the nearest thing I shall
ever have to a son. He loves you. Love him—not just emotionally, also
physically. Bodies are for roasting, not smoking."

She looked down at her own dried flesh, and nodded them farewell.
Batalix was setting, true night descending.

Traders came to Oldorando in increasing numbers, and from all
points of the compass. The important salt trade was conducted from
the north and south, whence it arrived often by goat train. There was
now a regular track from Oldorando westwards across the veldt, trodden
by traders from Kace, who brought gaudy things such as jewels, stained
glass, toys, silvery musical instruments, as well as sugar cane and rare
fruits; they preferred money to barter, but Oldorando had no currency, so they accepted herbs, skin, suede, and grain instead. Sometimes

the men from Kace used stungebags as beasts of burden, but the animals became rarer as the weather grew warmer.

Traders and priests still called from Borlien, although they had learned long ago to fear their treacherous northern neighbour. They sold pamphlets and broadsheets that told lurid tales in rhyme, and fine metal pots and pans.

From the east, by divergent ways, came many traders, and sometimes caravans. Dark little men with enslaved populations of Madis or phagors plied regular routes, on which Oldorando was merely one port of call. They brought delicately wrought ornaments and decorations which the women of Oldorando loved. Rumour had it that some of those women fared onwards with the dark men; certain it was that the easterners traded in young Madi women, who looked wild and lovely, but pined away when shut in a tower. Bad though their reputation was, the traders were tolerated for their wares—not decorations only, but woven rugs, carpets, tapestries, shawls, such as Oldorando had never seen before.

All these travellers needed housing. Their encampments became a nuisance. Oldorando's slaves toiled to erect a separate township just to the south of the towers, known ironically as the Pauk. Here all trade was conducted; in narrow alleys, peltmongers and all other mongers carried on their business, with stables and eating houses nearby, and for a while the traders were forbidden entry to Oldorando proper. But their numbers grew, and some settled in the town, importing their arts and vices.

Oldorandans were also learning the artifices of trade. New merchants approached Aoz Roon and asked for special concessions, including the right to mint coin. This question vexed their minds far more than any problems with the academy, which they regarded as a waste of time.

A party of these Oldorandan traders numbering six, comfortably mounted on hoxneys, was returning to Oldorando from a successful expedition. At Freyr-dawn, they paused on a hill to the north, close by the brassimip patch, from where they could see the outskirts of the town, chill in the grey light. The air was so still that distant voices carried to them.

"Look," exclaimed one of the younger traders, shading his eyes as he gazed. "There's some kind of a hullabaloo by the gate. We'd best go by another way."

"Not fuggies, is it?"

They all stared hard. In the distance, a cluster of persons, men and women, could be observed surging from the town. In a space, some of them halted indecisively, causing the cluster to split in two. The others went forward.

"It isn't anything important," said the young trader, and spurred his hoxney. He had a woman in Embruddock he very much wanted to see, and a new bauble for her in his pocket. The departure of Shay Tal meant nothing to him.

Soon Batalix was rising, overhauling its companion in the sky.

The chill, the etiolated morning in which rain threatened, the sense of adventure, served to make her feel disembodied. She experienced no emotion as she clasped Vry to her in mute farewell. Her servant, Maysa Latra, a willing slave, helped her downstairs with her few things. Beside the tower stood Amin Lim, clutchnig the bridle of her own hoxney and Shay Tal's, and saying a sorrowful farewell to her man and her small child; there, thought Shay Tal, is a sacrifice greater than mine. I'm glad to go. Why Amin Lim comes with me, I shall never know. But her heart warmed to her friend, although she also felt a little contempt.

Four women were leaving with her: Maysa Latra, Amin Lim, and two younger disciples, devout pupils of the academy. All were mounted and were accompanied by a male gelded slave, Hamadranabail, who walked, leading two pack hoxneys and a pair of savage hunting dogs with spiked collars.

More people, women and some older men, followed the procession, calling farewells and sometimes advice, serious or jocular as the fancy took them.

Laintal Ay and Oyre waited at the gate to catch a last glimpse of Shay Tal; they stayed close but avoided looking at each other.

Beyond the gate was Aoz Roon himself, standing there in his black furs, arms folded, chin sunk on chest. Behind him was Grey, in the care of Eline Tal, who for once looked no more cheerful than his lord. Several men stood in a huddle behind their silent ruler, faces sober, hands under armpits.

When Shay Tal appeared, Aoz Roon swung himself into his saddle and began to ride slowly, not towards her but rather almost parallel with her path, so that, continuing on undeflected courses, they would collide some way ahead, where trees began.

Before he reached that point, Aoz Roon struck off the track, picking a course parallel with it among the trees. The women's party, with Amin Lim leading, weeping silently, continued sedately along the path. Neither Aoz Roon nor Shay Tal made any attempt to communicate, or even look at each other.

Freyr was hidden as yet in early cloud, so that the world remained without colour.

The ground rose, the track narrowed, the trees grew closer. They came to a fold in the ground where the trees stopped and the ground was marshy. Frogs splashed to safety as the party approached. The hoxneys picked their way slowly through the wet, flexing their paws in distaste, raising yellow mud that curdled under the water surface.

Trees on the far side of the marsh forced the riders more closely together. As if noticing Aoz Roon for the first time, Shay Tal called in her clear voice, "You do not need to follow."

"I am leading, ma'am, not following. I will see you safely away from Oldorando. It's an honour properly owed you."

No more was said. They proceeded farther, coming at last to rising ground studded with bushes. At the crest, they could pick up a clear traders' path leading northeast, to Chalce and distant Sibornal—how distant, no one knew. Trees began again on the downward slope. Aoz Roon reached the crest first, and positioned himself there, bleak of visage, pointing Grey along the lie of the ridge as the women went by.

Shay Tal turned Loyalty's head and approached him, the lines of her face clear and composed.

"It's good of you to come this far."

"Enjoy a safe journey," he said formally, holding himself upright, pulling in his belly. "You observe that no attempt is made to stop you leaving us."

Her voice softened. "We shall never see each other again; from this date on, we are extinct to each other. Have we ruined each other's lives, Aoz Roon?"

"I don't understand what you're talking about."

"Yes, you do. Since we were children we have been up against each other. Give me a word, friend, as I go away. Don't be proud, as I've always been proud—not now."

He firmed up his mouth and regarded her without saying anything.

"Please, Aoz Roon, a true word on parting. I am well aware I said No to you once too often."

At that he nodded. "There's your true word."

She looked about anxiously, then kicked Loyalty one pace nearer, so that the two hoxneys touched each other.

"Now that I'm leaving for ever, just tell me—that in your heart you still feel for me as once you did, when we were younger."

He gave a snorting laugh. "You're mad. You never understood reality. You were too wrapped up in yourself. I feel nothing for you now—or you for me, if you but knew it."

She reached out to clutch him, but he backed away, showing his teeth like a dog. "Lies, Aoz Roon, all lies! Give me then a gesture as I go—give me a parting kiss, damn you, I who have suffered so much from you. Gestures are better than words."

"Many think not. What's said always remains."

Tears burst from her eyes and were gone, falling aslant her lean cheeks.

"May the fessups feed on you!"

She wrenched round the head of her mare and galloped away, plunging into the trees to catch up with her small procession.

He sat for a moment where he was, drawn up rigid in the saddle, staring ahead with his knuckles white about the reins. Gently, he turned Grey's head and coaxed her among the trees, going away from Oldorando at a tangent, ignoring Eline Tal, who discreetly waited some distance behind.

Grey picked up speed as she moved downhill, encouraged by her master. Soon they were going at full gallop, the ground flying beneath them, and all human beings lost to view. Aoz Roon raised his clenched right fist high in the air.

"Good riddance to the hag-bitch," he cried. Savage laughter was torn from his throat as he rode.

Earth Observation Station Avernus saw everything as it passed overhead. All change was monitored and all data transmitted back to Earth. In the Avernus, members of the eight learned families were at work, synthesising the new knowledge.

They charted not only the movement of human populations but also those of the phagorian populations, both white and black. Every advance or retreat was transformed into an impulse which would eventually make its way across the light-years to the globe and computers back in the Helliconian Centronics Institute on Earth.

From the window of the station, the team could observe the planet below, and the progress of the eclipse, as it spread a grey necrosis over the oceans and the tropical continent.

On one bank of monitor screens, another progress was under survey— the progress of the kzahhn's crusade towards Oldorando. By its own peculiar travelling time, the crusade was now precisely one year away from its anticipated target, the destruction of the old town.

In codified form, these signals were relayed back to Earth. There, many centuries later, Helliconia-watchers assembled to see the final agonies of the drama.

The bleak regions of Mordriat, its echoing canyons, its shattered walls of rock, its moors with their unexpected air of privacy, its drab high valleys through which cloud forever smouldered, as if fire rather than ice had moulded the unyielding contours of its desolation, lay behind.

The straggling crusade, broken into many separate groups, was wending its way over lower country, empty save for Madis with their flocks, and dense flights of birds. Indifferent to their surroundings, the phagors continued towards the southeast.

The kzahhn of Hrastyprt, Hrr-Brahl Yprt, led them onwards. Vengeance was still strong in their harneys, as they made their way through the floods of the east Oldorandan plain; yet many of them had died. Sickness and attacks from merciless Sons of Freyr had cut down their numbers.

Nor had they been well received by small components of phagors through whose land they travelled. Those components without kaidaws pursued a settled way of living, often with large gangs of human or Madi slaves, and fiercely resisted any invasion of their territory.

Hrr-Brahl Yrpt had come victorious through everything. Only sickness was beyond his power to command. As news of his columns preceded him, so living things in his path moved away, causing the ripples of his progress to spread across half a continent.

Now the leaders stood with Hrr-Brahl Yprt before a wide-flowing river. The waters of the river were icy; they plunged down, though the phagor host knew it not, from the same Nktryhk uplands from which the crusade against the Sons of Freyr had started, a thousand miles away.

"Here by these torrents we will stay while Batalix makes her way twice across the sky," Hrr-Brahl Yprt said to his commanders. "Leader scouts will diverge to either side and find us a dry crossing; the air-octaves will guide them."

He whistled down his cowbird, who began to search his pelage for ticks. It was done abstractedly, for the kzahhn had other matters on his harneys; but the minute creatures were suddenly irritating. Perhaps it was the warmth of the valley surrounding them. Green cliffs rose on all sides, trapping the unwelcome heat as cupped hands hold water. The third blindness would soon be upon them. Later, a retreat to colder quarters must commence.

But first came vengeance.

He gestured the graceful Zzhrrk away, and strode off to obtain an understanding of the overall situation, his bird remaining above him with an occasional downthrust of its wings.

They could wait while the rest of the force, which straggled back over several dozen miles, caught up. Banners were hoisted, the kaidaws were released to forage. Minions erected tents for the leadership. Meals and rituals were set in train.

As Batalix and the treacherous Freyr sailed above the encampment, the kzahhn of Hrastyprt strode into his tent, unbuckling his face crown. His long head was thrust forward between burly shoulders, and the barrel of his body—trimmed by the ordeals of travel—also leaned forward in his eagerness.

The sweeping lashes of his eyes came down, slitting his cerise stare, as he glared along the curve of his nose to his four fillocks. They stood within the tent, scratching or jostling each other as they awaited his arrival.

Zzhrrk swooped through the opening of the tent, but Hrr-Brahl Yprt brushed it away. It fluttered, caught off balance, and landed awkwardly, to waddle out of the tent. Hrr-Brahl Yprt pulled down the rug behind him, closing the entrance. He began to divest himself of his armour, his sleeveless jacket, his belt and sporran, all the while looking at his four brides, the imperious gaze switching from one to the other. He snuffed at them, smelling their scents.

The fillocks fretted, scratching at ticks, or adjusting their long white coats so that their plump dugs smacked about in his sight. The eagle feathers in their head hair nodded towards him. They snorted and shot their pale milts neatly into their nostril slits.

"You!" he said, pointing to the one female fully in heat. While her companions banged away and squatted at the rear of the tent, the chosen one turned her back on the young kzahhn and stooped forward. He approached, prodding his three fingers deep into her proffered flesh, then wiping them on the black fur of his muzzle. Without further ado, he hoisted himself upon her, his weight bowing her until she was on all fours. Slowly she sank further as he thrust, until her wide forehead rested on the rug.

When the incursion was over, and the other fillocks trotted forward to nuzzle their sister, Hrr-Brahl Yprt pulled on his armour and strode from the tent. It would be three weeks before his sexual interest reawoke.

His crusade commander, Yohl-Gharr Wyrrijk, was stolidly awaiting him. The two stood foresquare, looking into each other's eyes. Yohl-Gharr Wyrrijk gestured up at the sky.

"The day comes," he said. "The octaves tighten."

His kzahhn swivelled his head, waving a fist to clear the sky overhead of cowbirds. He stared up at the usurper Freyr, perceiving how it dragged itself every day, like a spider across its web, closer to Batalix. Soon, soon, Freyr would hide itself in the belly of its enemy. The hosts would then be at their destination. They would strike then, and kill all the progeny of Freyr who lived where Hrr-Brahl Yprt's noble grandstallun had died; and then they would burn down the town and erase it from memory. Only then could he and his followers attain honourable tether. Those thoughts crawled through his harneys like the slow drip of icicles, which splash as they melt and lose shape and make the ground heavy with their drenchment.

"The two seminals draw together," he growled.

Later, he had a human slave sound the stungebag horn, and the keratinous figures of his father and great-grandstallun were presented before him. The young kzahhn noted how both figures had been damaged by the long journey, despite the care that had been taken of them.

Humbly, and with hosts of the component assembled by the black river, Hrr-Brahl Yprt went into his trance. Everyone became absolutely immobile, according to his nature, as if they were frozen in a sea of air.

No larger than a snow rabbit, the image of the great-grandstallun appeared, running on all fours as once it had been with the phagors in the time long gone, when Batalix had yet to be caught in the web woven by Freyr.

"Hold horns high," said the snow rabbit. "Remember enmities, resent the coming of the green, sprinkle it with the red liquids of the Sons of Freyr, who brought the green and banished the white as it was."

The keratinous father also appeared, scarcely larger, bowing to his son, conjuring a sequence of pictures in his pale harneys.

The world was there before the closed eyes, its three divisions pumping. From the steam of its being blew the yellow strands of the air-octaves, writhing like long ribbons about the clenched fists, and about the clenched fists of other worlds nearby, embracing too beloved Batalix and the spiderous shape of Freyr. Things like lice ran along the ribbons, keening with a shrill note.

Hrr-Brahl Yprt thanked his father for the pictures flickering in his harneys. He had seen them many times before. All present were familiar with them. They must be repeated. They were the lodestones of the crusade. Without repetition, the lights were extinguished, leaving the harney-packed skull like some remote cave, piled with the bodies of dead serpents.

With repetition, it was clearly understood that the needs of one phagor were the needs of the whole world, which those departed for the next world had called Hrl-Ichor Yhar, and the needs of Hrl-Ichor Yhar were the needs of a single phagor. There were pictures now of the Sons of Freyr: when the colours of the air-octaves brightened, the Sons were falling ill on the ground, falling or dying or being transformed into smaller sizes. That time had come before. That time would come soon. Past and future were present. The falling would come also when Freyr hid completely in Batalix. And then would be the time to strike—to strike against all, and especially against those whose forebears had slain the Great Kzahhn Hrr-Tryhk Hrast.

Remember. Be valiant, be implacable. Do not deviate an inch from the programme, transmitted through many ancestors.

There was a scent of ancient days, something far, fusty, and true. An angellike array of predecessors was glimpsed, devouring the primal ice-fields. The air turns marched in millions, never mute.

Remember. Prepare for the next stage. Hold horns high.

The young kzahhn emerged slowly from his trance. His white cow-bird had settled on his left shoulder. It slid its curved beak reassuringly among the hairs and folds of his shoulders, and began to feed on the ticks that clustered there. The horn was sounded again, its mournful note carrying across the ice-cold river.

That melancholy note could be heard some distance away, where a group of phagors had become separated from their main component. They were eight in number, six being gillots and two stalluns. They had with them one old red kaidaw, past riding, on whose back weapons and supplies were lashed. A few days previously, when Batalix prevailed auspiciously in the sky, they had captured six Madi men and women, who, with their animals, were trailing behind a migratory caravan heading for the isthmus of Chalce. The animals had been immediately cooked and eaten, their throats bitten out in the approved way.

The unfortunate Madis were tied together and made to follow on. But the difficulty of making them follow, as well as the delay for the feast, had led to the group's separation from the body of the crusade. They got themselves on the wrong side of a brook which swelled to a torrent. Rainstorms broke over the higher ground, the brook flooded, they were cut off.

That Batalix-night, the phagors made camp in a sombre clearing beneath tall rajabarals; they secured the Madis to a slender tree, where the protognostics were allowed to sleep as best they could, huddled together. The phagors flung themselves down close by, lying flat on their backs; their cowbirds came down and settled on their breasts, with heads and beaks tucked into the warmth of the phagors' necks. The phagors went immediately into their dreamless and motionless sleep, as if preparing for tether.

Squawks of cowbirds and cries of Madis woke them. The Madis in terror had broken loose from their tree and fallen upon their captors—not in anger but hopes of protection, relying on their enemies to defend them against a greater menace.

One of the rajabarals was splitting. The air was brittle with the noise of its destruction.

Seams showed vertically, and thick brown sap like pus spurted from the cracks. Steam from the tree shrouded the writhing thing that was emerging from it.

"Wutra worm! Wutra worm!" cried the protognostics, as the phagors scrambled to their feet. The leading phagor crossed to the hobbled kaidaw, handing out spears in a businesslike manner.

The great drum of the active rajabaral was thirty feet high. Suddenly, its top blew, pieces falling like shattered pottery, and out from the top reared a Wutra's worm. Through the clearing poured the characteristic worm stench, in which scumble, festering fish, and decaying cheese mingled.

The creature's head rose like a snake's, glistening in the sun, poised on the flexing column of its neck. It swung about, and the rajabaral cracked open, revealing more slimy coils unwinding, and the discarded skin of a moult. Boring underground, the creature had entered the rajabaral through its roots, to use the tree as a refuge. Increasing warmth encouraged it to moult and metamorphose. Now it required nourishment as its next stage of development forced it through the imperatives of its life cycle.

By now, the phagors were armed. Their leader, a thick-set gillot with black hairs showing in her pelt, gave the order. Her two best marksmen flung their spears at the Wutra's worm.

The beast twisted, the spears flew harmlessly by. It sighted the figures below it, and immediately snaked its head down in attack. Those on the ground were suddenly aware of its true size, as it confronted them—four banked eyes glaring at them above thick fleshy feelers spreading from its mouth. The feelers waved like fingers as the worm poised itself to strike. The mouth, filled with backward-pointing teeth, was curiously baggy, pursing itself in the middle as well as at the sides.

The head was held sideways, sweeping towards them like a wagging asokin's tail. One moment it loomed above the treetops—the next, it was bearing down on the line of phagors. They flung their spears. The cowbirds scattered.

That oddly working mouth, jawless, seemed infinitely capacious. It snatched up one of the phagors in its fangs and half-lifted her. The gillot was too heavy for the musculature of the supple neck to carry. She was dragged croaking across the swampy ground, one arm striking at the scent pits of the monster.

"Kill it!" cried the gillot leader, dashing forward with her knife raised.

But in the dim slimes of the worm's harneys, a decision had been reached. It bit savagely through the flesh in its mouth and dropped the rest. The head jerked upward, out of harm's way, yellow blood pouring off its whiskers. What remained of the gillot beat its fist on the ground and then lay unmoving.

Even as the worm gobbled its morsel, it began to change, its coils crashing down into the young trees round about. Though not given to fright, the seven surviving phagors fell down in terror. The worm was splitting in twain.

It dragged its bloodied head over the grass, some way distant from them. Membranes tore with protracted noise. Something like a mask peeled from the head, which became, grotesquely, two heads. While these heads lay one on top of each other, they still resembled the old one; then the new upper head lifted and the resemblance was gone.

The jaws of the new heads sprouted fleshy feelers, rapidly growing outstretched and stiff to form a circle of spikes, behind which came a mouth, the cartilage fixed wide without the ability to close. The rest

of the head followed this unseemly opening, with two eyes set horizontally in it. A layer of slime, revealed by the torn membranes, dried,
causing a slight colour change to take place. One head became verdi-
gris-hued green, the other a mottled blue.

The heads rose, rearing away from each other in antagonism,
emitting a low roar.

This action caused more membranes to split all along the old body,
which was revealed as two bodies, one green, one blue, both very slender
and winged. A convulsive struggle, similar to a death paroxysm, shook
the old body. The two new javelin bodies came streaming forth from
it, spreading papery wings as they rose. The heads ascended above the
shattered rajabaral, papery wings thrashed. Eight cowbirds flew round
about them, screeching with open beaks.

The two opposed creatures became more stable. In another moment, their long-whiskered tails had left the ground. They were air-
borne, and the light of Freyr glittered on scales and sutured wings. One
monster, the green one, was male, with a double series of tentacle appendages dangling from its middle regions, the other, the blue, female,
its scales less bright.

Now their wings had acquired a steady beat, lifting them above the
treetops. The leading aperture, the mouth, gulped in air, expelling it
through rear vents. The creatures circled the clearing in opposite
directions, watched helplessly by the phagor band. Then they were off
on their maiden flight.

The fliers headed away like flying snakes, one towards the distant
north, one towards the far south, obeying mysteriously musical air-
octaves of their own, and suddenly beautiful in their power. Their long
thin bodies undulated through the atmosphere. They gained height,
lifting themselves above the bowl of the valley. Then they were gone,
each to seek mates in the remoteness of the opposed poles.

The imagos had forgotten their previous existences, imprisoned for
centuries in the hibernal earth.

Grunting, the phagors turned to more immediate things. Their
stares swept about the clearing. Their hobbled kaidaw remained,
placidly cropping grass. The Madis had gone. Seizing their opportunity,
the protognostics had beaten it into the forest.

Madis generally mated for life, and it was rare for a widow or wid-
ower to remarry; indeed, a kind of deep melancholia generally carried
off the survivor of the bond-pair. The fugitives comprised three men
and their mates. The senior pair by a few years was called Cathkaarnit,
that being their merged name since marriage; they were distinguished
as Cathkaarnit-he and Cathkaarnit-she.

All six of them were slender and of small stature. All were dark. The transhuman protognostics, of which the Madis formed one tribe, differed little in appearance from true humans. Their pursed lips, caused by the formation of the bones of the skull and the lie of their teeth, gave them a wistful look. They possessed eight fingers on each hand, with four opposed to four, giving them an amazingly strong grip; and their feet also exhibited four toes forward and four aft, behind the heel.

They ran at a steady jog trot from the clearing where the phagors were, a pace they could maintain for hours if necessary. They ran through groves and through bogs, moving in double file, the Cath-kaarnits leading, then the next oldest pair, then the next. Several wild animals, chiefly deer, went crashing away from their path. Once they flushed a boar. They hastened on without pause.

Their flight led them mainly westwards; the memory of their eight weeks of captivity lent them strength. Skirting the floods, they climbed out of the great saucer of land in which they had made their escape. The heat grew less. At the same time, the inclination upwards of the land, slight but continuous, wore down their energies. The jog trot relapsed into a fast-walking pace. Their skins burned. They pressed on, heads down, breathing painfully through nose and mouth, occasionally stumbling over the rough ground.

At last the rear pair gave a gasp and fell, to lie panting, clutching their stomachs. Their four companions, looking up, saw that they had almost gained the lip of the rise, after which the land could be relied on to level out. They continued, leaning forward, to drop as soon as they climbed from the slope to the flat. Their lungs laboured.

From here they could look back through the preternaturally clear air. Below them were their two exhausted friends, sprawling at the top of an enormous bowl of land. The sides of the bowl were pitted by gulleys down which water poured. The brooks ran down into two immense coils of a river newly enough formed for half-drowned trees still to be standing in it. Dams were forming where branches and other debris had collected. This flood was lost from view where it curved behind a fold of hillside.

Water noises filled the air. They could see where the massive concave rajabarals stood. Somewhere among those rajabarals was the party of phagors from which they had escaped. Behind the rajabarals, thick young forests grew, covering slopes that formed the opposite side of the great bowl. The trees of the forest were generally of a sombre green, rank after rank, punctuated by a tree bearing brilliant gold foliage, known to the Madis as caspiarn; its bitter buds could be eaten in times of famine.

But the landscape did not end with the forests. Beyond them could be seen cliffs which had collapsed here and there to permit a hazardous downward path for animals or men. The cliffs were part of a mountain which spread its rounded contours from one side of the view to the other. Its soft underlying rocks had split, causing ravines from which vegetation sprouted. Where the vegetation was at its most dense, and the collapsed configuration of the mountain most spectacular, a tributary river glinted, foaming as it burst among its gorges towards the valley.

Beyond and above the spongey mountain, yet other mountains stood, harsher, comprising durable basalts, their flanks excoriated by recent centuries of winter. No green mantle covered them. They remained uncompromised, although here and there they were spread with the yellow and orange and white of tiny upland flowers, their colours pure even when viewed from miles away.

Above the domes of those basalt mountains, other ranges, blue, bleak, dreadful, showed. And as if to demonstrate to every living thing that the world had no end, those ranges too permitted a glimpse of objects beyond—land at great distance and great altitude, showing its teeth in a procession of peaks. These were bastions of matter, standing where the blistering colds of the tropopause commenced.

The keen eyes of the Madis took in this prospect, picking out small touches of white among the nearer trees, between the caspiarns, along the cliffs, between the higher defiles of the mountains, even as far as the flashing tributary in its gorges. Those touches of white the Madis correctly identified as cowbirds. Where the cowbirds were were phagors. For almost as many miles as they could see, the stealthy advance of Hrr-Brahl Yprt's host could be marked by cowbirds. Not one phagor could be viewed; yet the mighty landscape probably concealed ten thousand of them.

As the Madis rested and watched, first one and then the other started to scratch at himself or herself. The scratching began like a tickle, but grew more savage as they cooled down. Soon they were rolling about, scratching and swearing, their bodies stung by sweat which cut into the rash of bites mottling their skin. They curled themselves into balls, scratching with feet as well as hands. This frantic itch had assailed them at intervals, ever since their capture by the phagors.

While raking in their crotches, or groping frantically at their armpits, or dragging their nails through the mops of their hair, they gave no thought to cause and effect, never ascribing their rashes to a tick caught from the matted coats of their captors.

That tick was generally harmless, or at least passed on to humans and protognostics nothing worse than a fever or rash which rarely lasted more than a few days. But heat balances were changing as Helliconia moved nearer to Freyr. Ixodidae multiplied: the female tick paid her tribute to Great Freyr in millions of eggs.

Soon that insignificant tick, so much a part of life as to pass unnoticed, would become the vector of a virus inducing the so-called bone fever, and the world would change because of her.

This virus moved into an active stage of development in the spring of Helliconia's great year, at the time of the eclipses. Every spring, the human population was afflicted with bone fever; only something like half the population could expect to survive. The disaster was so comprehensive, its effects so thoroughgoing, that it could be said to wipe itself from such meagre records as were kept.

As the Madis rolled scratching in the leaves, they paid no heed to the untravelled ground behind them.

There, out of the heat of the valley, lush grasses grew, interspersed with thickets of a rank, warted grass known as shoatapraxi, which had a hollow stem and grew hard in old age. Lightly robed men in high turn-down boots emerged from the shelter of the shoatapraxi clumps, ropes in hand. They pounced on the Madis.

The pair of Madis down the slope took their chance and ran away, though it meant going back towards the phagor columns. Their four friends were made captive, still twitching. Their brief, exhausting spell of liberty was over. This time they were the possessions of human beings, to form an insignificant part of another cyclic event, the southward invasion from Sibornal.

They had involuntarily joined the colonising army of the warrior priest Festibariyatid. Little the Cathkaarnits and their two companions cared about that, bowed down as they were by supplies piled on their backs. Their new masters drove them forward. They staggered southwards, still scratching despite their more novel miseries.

As they made their way, skirting the lip of the great bowl to their left, Freyr rose into the sky. Everything grew a second shadow, which shortened as the sun attained its zenith.

The landscape shimmered. The noonday temperature increased. The unregarded ticks swarmed in a myriad unregarded crannies.

XII

LORD OF THE ISLAND

Eline Tal was a large cheerful man, faithful, dependable, lacking in imagination. He was brave, he hunted well, he rode his hoxney with style. He even had the rudiments of intelligence, although he was suspicious of the academy and could not read. He discouraged his woman and children from reading. He was completely loyal to Aoz Roon, with no ambition but to serve him as best he could.

What he was unable to do was understand Aoz Roon. He dismounted from his bright-striped mount and stood patiently some distance away from the Lord of Embruddock. All he could see was the back of Aoz Roon, as the latter stared stolidly forward with his beard on his chest. The lord wore his old stinking black furs, as always, but had draped a cloak of coarse yellow stammel over his shoulders, presumably intending in some obscure way to do honour to his departing sorceress thereby. The hound, Curd, stayed shivering by Grey's heels.

So Eline Tal remained at a distance, one finger in his mouth, picking idly at a back tooth, and did nothing more. His mind was blank.

After a few more curses, uttered aloud, Aoz Roon set his mount in motion. He looked back once over his shoulder, black brows drawn together, but acknowledged his faithful lieutenant in no way, any more than he paid attention to his dog.

He goaded his hoxney at full tilt up to the brow of escarpment, reining Grey so savagely that she reared upon her hind legs.

"Bitch-hag!" shouted Aoz Roon. His voice echoed back to him.

Liking the sound of his own bitterness, he bellowed in rejoinder to the echoes, indifferent that the mare took him farther from Oldorando, while dog and henchman followed if they would.

He reined Grey suddenly, letting foam drip from the bit between her lips. It was only midmorning. Yet a shade had fallen over the world, quelling its life. He scowled upwards through spiked branches, and observed that a bite was taken from Freyr by the dull globe that had slowly outpaced it through the sky. The blindness was encroaching. Curd whined in apprehension and slunk nearer the hoxney's heels.

A night owl burst from a nearby fallen larch, speeding close to the ground. It had speckled feathers and a wingspan wider than a man's outstretched arms. Screeching, it shot between Grey's legs and rose into the sallow sky.

Grey stood high on her hind legs, then she was up and away, no stopping her, plunging forward at full gallop. Aoz Roon fought to cling on, the hoxney fought to dislodge him.

Alarmed by the heavenly phenomenon, Eline Tal followed, wrestling with Drifter, his stallion, to bring him under control. They went like a southern wind, hot in pursuit of the other animal.

When Aoz Roon at last calmed the frightened steed, his blacker mood had lifted. He laughed without mirth, patting the creature and speaking to it more gently than he did to his fellow human beings. Slowly, stealthily, Batalix was eating more deeply into Freyr. The bite of the phagor; old legends came back to mind; the sentinels were not companions, but enemies, doomed to devour each other throughout eternity.

He hunched his shoulders, letting the quieted animal proceed as it would. Why not? He could return to Oldorando and rule as before. Yet would the place be the same, now that *she* was gone, the bitch? Dol was a poor insipid creature, who cared nothing for what he was. Only danger and disappointment lay at home.

Wrenching at the hoxney's head, he made her proceed through a tangle of dogthrush and thorn bushes, sullenly accepting the lash of branches in his face. The world was in disarray too deep for him to fathom. Among the branches were matted reeds, grasses, and straw. So burdened was his mind, he ignored this evidence of recent flooding.

The lower rim of Batalix was lined with silver fire as it continued to devour Freyr. Then it too was eclipsed by cloud, blowing up black from the east. The rain came in increasing force, seething over the cinereous thickets. Aoz Roon kept his head down and pushed on. The downpour hissed in the bushes. Wutra was showing his hatreds.

He kicked his hoxney out of the thicket, to halt where thick grass squelched underfoot. Eline Tal came slowly up behind him. The rain increased, running off the animals to the ground. Looking up from under dripping brows, the Lord of Embruddock saw how the ground rose to one side, where trees grew over a boulder-strewn slope. At the bottom of the slope, a kind of shelter had been built from split stones. Beyond was marshy land, with waterways winding through it. The view faded into the pallor of rainfall; even the outlines of the shelter were indistinct—but not so vague that he failed to see the figures standing at its entrance.

The figures were immobile. They watched. They must have been aware of his approach long before he saw them. Curd stood his ground and growled.

Without looking back, Aoz Roon motioned Eline Tal up to stand with him.

"Scumbing fuggies," Eline Tal said, cheerfully enough.

"They hate water—the downpour may keep 'em safe where they are. Move steady."

He set the pace, a slow walk forward, called Curd to heel.

He would not turn back or show he was afraid. The marsh might be impassable. Best to go up the hillside. Once at the crest—if the phagors let them get that far—they could ride away hard. He was unarmed, except for a dagger at his belt.

The two men moved forward shoulder to shoulder, the dog continuously snarling behind them. To gain the slope, they had to make an oblique approach to the crude building. Because of the murk, it was difficult to be sure of anything; it looked as if no more than five or six of the monsters crouched in the miserable shelter. Behind it stood two kaidaws, rattling their heads to shake away the rain, occasionally clashing horns; they were held by a slave, either human or protognostic, who stared at Aoz Roon and Eline Tal apathetically.

Perched on the roof of the building were two cowbirds, huddling together. Two more were on the ground, fighting over a pile of kaidaw droppings. A fifth, some way off, perched on a boulder, shredding and eating a small animal it had caught.

The phagors made no move.

The two parties were less than a stone's throw away, and the hoxneys were already changing pace to accommodate the slope of the hillside, when Curd dashed from Grey's side and ran towards the shelter, barking furiously.

Curd's action precipitated the phagors forward. They rushed from shelter and charged to the attack. As so often, they seemed to need a prod before they could act, as if their nervous system was inert below a certain minimum level of stimulus. Seeing them run forward, Aoz

Roon shouted a command, and he and Eline Tal spurred their mounts up the slope.

It was treacherous riding. The trees were young, no higher than a man, their foliage spreading from their crowns like umbrellas. It was necessary to ride with the head low. Underfoot, broken boulders formed a constant hazard for the hoxney's paws. Grey and Drifter needed vigilant guidance to maintain anything like a pace.

Behind them came the sounds of pursuit. A spear flashed near them and embedded itself in the ground, but no others followed. More ominous was the noise of kaidaws coming up, and the throaty shouts of their riders. On level ground, a kaidaw could outrun a hoxney. Among the low trees, the larger animals were disadvantaged. Yet fast as Aoz Roon went, he could not shake off the pursuers. He and Eline Tal were soon cursing, and sweating as freely as their mounts.

They struck a patch where water streamed down the hillside. Aoz Roon took the chance to glance round. Two of the shaggy white monsters on their steeds were plunging up behind, each with an immense forearm raised in front of its skull, warding off the backward lash of branches. In their free hand, they carried spears against the flanks of the kaidaws, controlling the animals with their knees and horned feet. The unmounted phagors were doubling up the slope on foot, a long way behind, and no threat.

"The fuggers never give up," Aoz Roon said. "Move, Grey, rot you!"

They plunged on, but the phagors gained.

The downpour faltered, then came on more heavily. It made no difference. The trees flung water as they rode by. The going underfoot was better, but the boulders became more frequent.

Now the two mounted phagors were within spear throw.

Grasping the reins tightly, Aoz Roon stood in the stirrups. He could see above the umbrella trees. Over to the left, the solid ranks of saplings were broken. With a shout for Eline Tal, Aoz Roon wheeled to the left, and for a while lost the phagors behind piles of boulders, the outlines of which seemed to flicker in the weight of the downpour.

They struck a trail of some kind and took it gratefully, spurring upward again. The trees became sparser on either side. Ahead, the ground fell away, subsiding in sluices of mud.

Even as the men felt a flush of hope and goaded on their animals to greater efforts, the pursuing phagors broke from the umbrella trees. Aoz Roon shook his fist and burst ahead. The great yellow dog rushed along, keeping pace by Grey's side, never faltering.

Then it was downhill, with fine gravel underfoot. Ahead lay an entire melancholy landscape, studded with rajabarals, shuttered with trees, its strong verticals counterbalanced by a broad horizontal of water. All was depicted in subdued greens.

Through the midst of this vista wound a turbulent river, overflowing its limits to push out spurs among the stands of larch, creating a maze of reflection. More distantly, dark lines of trees stretched until curtains of haze obscured the sight. Clouds rolled across the sky, dimming the land, hiding the two interlocked sentinels.

Aoz Roon dashed a hand across his face, wiping away rain and sweat. He saw where greatest safety lay. In the river was an island, covered with stones and black-foliaged trees. If he and Eline Tal could get across to that—and its nearer shores were not too distant from the riverbanks—they would be secure from the monsters.

He pointed ahead, shouting hoarsely.

At the same time, he became aware that he rode alone. He turned in the saddle, bracing himself for what he saw.

The bright horizontal stripes of Drifter flashed some way to his left. The animal was riderless, galloping aimlessly towards the river.

Back at the top of the slope, where the umbrellas trees ended, Eline Tal sprawled on the ground. The two shaggy warriors circled round him. One jumped down from his kaidaw. Eline Tal immediately kicked out at him, but the phagor picked him up with an enormous heave. A stain of red showed on Eline Tal's shoulder—they had brought him out of his saddle with a spear. He struggled feebly; the phagor brought its horns down and prepared to use them in a death thrust.

The other phagor did not wait for the coup de grace. It wheeled its steed with a nimble movement and set off downhill towards Aoz Roon, spear held high.

The lord spurred Grey immediately. There was nothing he could do for his unlucky lieutenant. With all speed, he made for the island, leaning forward encouraging Grey, for he felt the animal flagging.

Advantage lay with the pursuing phagor. The kaidaw made superior time over open ground, however willingly the hoxney ran.

Aoz Roon's yellow cloak flapped in the wind as he goaded himself and his mount towards the riverbank. So near, so near, and ever nearer! The swirling waters, the dank foliage, the blur of distant natural features, a rodent scutting for safety in the grass—all flashed before his eyes. He knew he was too late. The pores of the skin between his shoulder blades seemed to turn to liquid as they awaited the fatal spear strike.

A quick glance back. The brute was almost on him, the sinews of the kaidaw's stretched head and neck standing clear, like strands of creeper entwining a tree. It would draw level now, making sure to kill, the damned thing. Its eyes glared.

Old though he was, Aoz Roon's responses were quicker than any phagor's.

Suddenly he dragged on the reins, forcing Grey's head up with savage strength, breaking its stride so that it slewed about in the path of the pursuer. At the same instant he humped from the saddle, rolling over on the sodden ground, absorbing impetus, then flinging himself quickly into the path of the kaidaw.

Grasping his sodden cloak from his shoulders, he swirled it about him and smartly upwards as the spear stabbed down. The coarse cloth folded itself about the enemy's extended weapon arm. Aoz Roon pulled.

The phagor slid forward. With its free arm, it grasped the kaidaw's mane. Tugging his cloak free, Aoz Roon grasped both ends and slammed it down across the beast's throat. One pull, the phagor was jerked loose and struck the ground, its rust-coloured mount bolting onwards.

Its sickly stale-milk stench assailed Aoz Roon. He stood there, gazing down at it, uncertain. Not so far behind, the other phagors were running to the rescue. Grey galloped off. His plight remained as desperate as ever.

He called Curd, but the hound crouched trembling in the grass and would not come.

As the phagor rose, Aoz Roon started to run for the river, clutching the spear. He could swim to the island—it represented his one hope.

Before he reached the edge of the flood, he saw the danger of that swim. The flood water was black, carrying heavy muds in its progress, and worse than muds. There were also drowned animals and semi-submerged branches against which a swimmer would have to battle.

He hesitated. While he did so, the phagor was upon him.

To Aoz Roon came the memory of wrestling with one of the brutes long ago, before his shaming fever. That adversary had been wounded. But this one—this was no youngster, he felt that instinctively, as he grasped its arm and kicked out with his boot. He could heave this one in the river before the others were on him.

But it was not so easy. The brute had enormous strength still. One of them gave a little ground, then the other. Aoz Roon could not bring up the spear or get at his knife. They struggled, proceeding in hops or small runs, groaning, while the adversary tried to bring its horns into play.

He cried in pain as the phagor managed to wrench one arm. He dropped the spear. As he cried, he got an elbow free. He brought it up, sharp under the other's chin. They staggered backwards a few paces, splashing in floodwater almost to the knees. Desperately he called to the hound, but Curd was rushing back and forth, barking savagely to keep off the three phagors approaching on foot.

A large tree bowled along in the flood, currents rolling it so that it turned as it came. A branch emerged like an arm, dripping, striking phagor and man as they stood interlocked in the shallows. They fell, caught by irresistible forces, and were drawn below the plunging water. Another branch rose from the flood, then it too sank, creating yellowish eddies as it was drawn into the undertow.

For four hours, Batalix worried at the flank of Freyr, as a hound worries a bone. Only then was the brighter light entirely engulfed. All the early afternoon, steely shadow lay on the land. Not an insect stirred.

For three hours, Freyr was gone from the world, stolen from the day sky.

By sunset, it had only partially reappeared. Nobody could guarantee that it would ever be whole again. Thick cloud filled the sky from horizon to horizon. So the day died, and an alarming day it was. Whether child or adult, every human being in Oldorando took to bed in a state of apprehension.

Then a wind rose, dispelling the rain, increasing anxiety.

There had been three deaths in the old town, one a suicide, and some buildings had been burnt, or were still burning. Only the heavy rain had saved worse violence.

Light from one of the fires, woken by the wind, lit a sheet of rainwater outside the big tower. Its reflection cast patterns on the ceiling of the room in which Oyre lay sleepless on her couch. The wind blew, a shutter banged, sparks flew up into the chimney of the night.

Oyre was waiting. Mosquitoes troubled her; they had recently returned to Oldorando. Every week brought something that nobody had experienced before.

The flickering light from outside coalesced with the stains on the ceiling, to give her a glimpse of an old man with long ragged hair, dressed in a gown. She imagined she could not see his face, for his head was hidden by a raised shoulder. He was doing something. His legs moved with the ripples the wind raised on the puddle outside. He was silently walking among the stars.

Tiring of the game, she looked away, wondering about her father. When she looked again, she saw that she had been mistaken; the old man was peering over his shoulder at her. His face was blotched and seamed with age. He was walking faster now, and the shutter banged in time with his steps. He was marching across the world towards her. His body was covered with a poisonous rash.

Oyre roused herself and sat up. A mosquito buzzed by her ear. Scratching her head, she looked across at Dol, who was breathing heavily.

"How goes it with you, girl?"

"The pains are coming faster."

Oyre climbed naked out of bed, put on a long cloak, and padded across to her friend, whose pale face she could dimly discern. "Shall I send for Ma Scantiom?"

"Not yet. Let's talk." Dol reached up a hand, and Oyre took it. "You've become a good friend to me, Oyre. I think of such funny things, lying here. You and Vry . . . I know what you think of me. You're both kind, yet you're so different—Vry so unsure of herself, you so sure always. . . ."

"You've got that quite the wrong way round."

"Well, I never knew much. People do fail each other most dreadfully, don't they? I hope I don't fail the child. I failed your father, I know. Now the scumb has failed me. . . . Fancy not being with me, this night of all nights."

The shutter banged again on the floor below. They crouched together. Oyre put a hand on her friend's swollen belly.

"I'm sure he has not gone off with Shay Tal, if that's what you fear."

Dol eased herself up on her elbows and said, turning her face from Oyre, "I sometimes can't bear my own feelings—this pain's welcome by comparison. I know I'm not half the woman she is. Still I said *Yes* and she said No, and that counts. I always said Yes, yet he's not here with me. . . . I don't think he ever ever loved me. . . ." She suddenly started to weep so violently that tears sprang from her eyes. Oyre saw them glint in the flickering light as Dol turned and buried her face in Oyre's broad breast.

The shutter slammed again as the wind gave a sullen howl.

"Let me send the slave for Ma Scantiom, love," Oyre said. Ma Scantiom had taken over the duties of midwife since Dol's mother had become too decrepit.

"Not yet, not yet." Gradually, her tears subsided. She sighed deeply. "Time enough. Time enough for everything." Oyre rose, wrapping the cloak round her, and went barefoot to secure the shutter. Damp wind gusted in on her face, blowing tremendously from the south; she breathed it with gratitude. The immemorial Embruddock sound of geese came to her, as the creatures took shelter under a hedge.

"But why do I keep myself alone?" she asked the darkness.

A bitter savour of smoke reached her while she secured the latch. The building was still smouldering nearby, a reminder of the day's public madness.

When she returned to the worn room, Dol was sitting up, wiping her face.

"You'd better get Ma Scantiom, Oyre. The future Lord of Embruddock is waiting to be born."

Oyre kissed her cheek. Both women were pale and wide-eyed. "He'll be back soon. Men are so—unreliable."

She ran from the room to call a slave.

The wind that rapped on Oyre's shutter had travelled a long way, and was destined to blow itself out among the limestone teeth of the Quzints. Its birthplace had been above the fathomless stretches of the sea that future sailors would name Ardent. It moved along the equator westwards, picking up speed and moisture, until encountering the great barrier of the Eastern Shield of Campannlat, the Nktryhk, where it became two winds.

The northern airstream roared up the Gulf of Chalce and exhausted itself melting the spring frosts of Sibornal. The southern airstream curved about the headlands of Vallgos over first the Scimitar Sea and then the northeast region of the Sea of Eagles, to exhale over the lowlands between Keevasien and Ottassol, with fish on its breath. It roared across a wilderness that would one day be the great country of Borlien, sighed over Oldorando, setting Oyre's shutter banging. It continued on its way, not waiting to hear the first cries of Aoz Roon's son.

This warm stream of air carried with it birds, insects, spores, pollen, and microorganisms. It was gone in a few hours, and forgotten almost as soon as gone; nevertheless, it played its part in altering the scheme of things that had been.

As it passed, it brought some comfort to a man sitting uncomfortably in the branches of a tree. The tree grew on an island in the middle of a fast-flowing flood mightily becoming a tributary of the river Takissa. The man had injured one leg and perched in his place of safety in some pain.

Below the tree squatted a large male phagor. Perhaps he waited to make some kind of attack. Whatever he waited for, he remained without movement, beyond occasionally flicking an ear. His cowbird sat on a branch of the tree, as far as it could get from the injured man.

Man and phagor had been washed onto the shores of the island, half-drowned. The former had climbed to the one point of safety he, in his injured state, could find. He clung to the trunk of the tree when the wind blew.

The wind was too warm for the phagor. He moved at last, standing swiftly and turning without a backward look, to pick his way among the boulders that filled most of the narrow island. After watching for a while with its head craned forward, the cowbird extended its wings and flapped after its host.

The man thought to himself, If I could catch and kill that bird, it would be a victory of sorts—and it would be worth eating.

But Aoz Roon had more pressing problems than hunger. First, he had to overcome the phagor. Through the sheltering leaves as dawn came, he could see the riverbanks from which he had been brushed. There, on marshy ground, stood four phagors, each with a cowbird perched on his shoulder or wheeling lazily above him; one held the mane of a kaidaw. They had been standing there for hours, almost without movement, staring towards the island.

Keeping a safe distance from them along the water margin was Curd. The hound sat uneasily, he whined, he paced back and forth, scanning the darkly swirling floods.

Biting his bearded lower lip against the pain, Aoz Roon tried to slide farther along his branch, so as to watch his immediate adversary's retreat. It moved slowly. Since there appeared to be nowhere to go on the island, he imagined that the monster would merely make a circuit and come back; had he been in better fettle, he might have devised some unpleasant surprise for it when it returned.

He squinted out at the sky. Freyr was disentangling itself from a barrier of trees, apparently intact after its experiences of the previous day. Batalix, having risen already, was lost in cloud. Aoz Roon longed to sleep but dared not. The phagor probably felt the same way.

There was neither sight nor sound of the monster. All that could be heard was the perpetual gargle of water in the rush of its progress southwards. It had been icy cold—Aoz Roon remembered that well. His enemy would be suffering from the immersion.

It seemed likely that the phagor would be setting a trap for him. Despite his pain, he felt a compulsion to climb from the tree and investigate. The decision made, he waited a few minutes to gather his strength. He scratched himself.

Movement was difficult. His limbs had stiffened. His great black skins were still heavy with water. The main problem was his left leg; it was painfully swollen and hard; he could not bend his knee. Nevertheless, he managed to slither down the tree, finally falling flat on the ground. He lay there in agony, panting, unable to rise, expecting at any moment to feel the phagor leap out and kill him.

The phagors on the bank had seen his move and were calling, but their voices, which lacked the carrying power of a man's, could scarcely be heard above the rushing water. Curd also set up a howl.

Aoz Roon got to his feet. By the foaming edge of the water, he found a branch stripped to its bark, which served as a crutch. Fear, cold, sickness, swirled in him like floodwater, almost causing him to collapse. He felt his flesh heavy on him—chill yet enflamed. He stared about in desperation, scratching himself, mouth hanging open, watching for attack. The phagor was nowhere to be seen.

"I'll get you, you scumble, if I never manage anything more. . . . I'm Lord of Embruddock yet. . . ."

He moved forward step by step, keeping the piles of boulders that cluttered the spine of the island between him and the nearer bank, so that the phagors standing vigil could not see him. To his right, stones, debris, lank grass, trailed down into the flood, whose smooth treachery whirled away towards a distant bank. Mist allied itself to the water, curling above its marbled surface.

Malnourished saplings and older trees shared his shipwreck, many dismasted by boulders heaved against them by early inundations. This complex area of natural disaster was no more than twelve metres across at its widest; yet its length—like the spine of a great submerged creature—divided the flood for farther than eye could see.

Like a wounded bear, he limped forward, taking care, in his anxious tour of inspection, to lumber on the margins of the water and keep as much space as he could between himself and possible attack.

A stag, head high, eyes aflash, burst from a fern thicket in front of him. He fell in startlement as it plunged into the flood until only its red-brown head bearing three-pointed antlers was above the water. Uttering a plaintive bellow, it yielded its powerful body to the greater power of the waters, which carried it away in a wide arc. The creature appeared unable to gain the farther bank, and was still swimming bravely when Aoz Roon lost sight of it in banks of mist.

Later, clambering over a fallen tree, he sighted the cowbird again.

It was watching him with its lapidary reptile eye, perched on the sod-and-boulder roof of a hut. The hut's walls were of cut stone; piled shingle, ferns, spavined saplings sought to turn the hut into a natural object. Aoz Roon worked his way round to the front of this refuge, concluding that the phagor must be inside.

Where the ground dipped, water swirled within three feet of the door. Here, the island had broken down. It emerged a few metres farther upstream, to continue its circumscribed course, a thin ship bearing a purposeless freight of stones. Its two parts were divided by a stretch of eddying water no more than knee-deep. The bear-man could wade to better safety. The phagor, with that hatred of water which marked its species, would never follow.

The chill of the current bit into his bones like alligator's teeth. He was groaning loudly as he staggered to the continuation of the island. He fell. He remained prone, scrabbling among rock, twisting to look back at the hut. The adversary must be inside—sick, injured, as he himself was.

He dragged himself up and toured the island, casting about stupidly, eventually using his knife to cut two firm stakes. Tucking them under one arm, he thrust himself back into the cruel stream, hobbling across with the aid of his crutch. He kept his gaze fixed on the hut door.

As he reached it, there was movement over his head. The cowbird swooped down and slashed open his temple with the barb of its beak.

Dropping crutch and stakes, he sliced the air with his knife. The next time the bird plunged, he cut its breast. It banked clumsily and landed on a log, shedding feathers speckled with its red blood.

He staggered forward and jammed the two stakes in place, one under the latch, the other under the upper hinge of the door. The door began immediately to shake. Hammering and bellowing followed, as the phagor fought to get out. The stakes held firm.

He picked up his crutch. As he turned to beat his retreat back to the islet, his gaze fell on the cowbird. It was hopping from one foot to the other, blood dripping from its breast. He lifted his crutch above his head and brought it down hard, killing the bird.

Holding it under one arm, he hobbled through the freezing water a third time.

On the other side, he threw himself down to massage some life back into his legs. He cursed the pain in his bones. The hammering on the hut door continued. Sooner or later, one of the stakes would work out of place, but for the present the phagor was out of action and the Lord of Embruddock triumphant.

Dragging the cowbird, Aoz Roon crawled between two trees that leaned together, pulling stones round himself for protection. Weakness flowed over him in waves. He fell asleep with his face buried in the still warm breast feathers of the bird.

Cold and numbness roused him. Freyr was low in the western sky, drowning in golden haze. By wriggling round in his niche, he could observe the nearer bank. The phagors still waited there. Behind them, the ground rose; he could make out the place where Eline Tal had fallen. Behind that, hazy, loomed the greater sentinel. There was no sign of Curd beside the flood.

The leg was less painful. He worked his way backwards out of his hole, dragging the dead bird, and stood up.

The phagor was waiting only a few metres away across the stream. Behind him was the hut, its door still intact. Its roof was broken, its stones rolled aside; that way had the phagor escaped.

Snorting, the phagor turned his head to one side and then the other, his horns catching the sun as he made this enigmatic gesture. He was a doleful specimen, his coat matted from the recent immersion in the river.

He hurled a clumsy spear as Aoz Roon presented him with a full target. Aoz Roon was too stiff, too surprised, to duck, but the missile went wide. He saw it was one of the stakes he had cut to prop against the door. Perhaps the poor throw signified that the phagor had injured his arm.

Aoz Roon shook his fist. It was going to be dark soon, for a short while. Instinct prompted him to light a fire. He busied himself about the task, thanking Wutra that he was feeling stronger, yet puzzled that he felt mysteriously sick. It might be hunger, he told himself; but food was at hand, once he had a fire.

After collecting twigs and rotted wood, and creating a sheltered place among stones, he set to work like a good hunter, rubbing a stick between his palms. The tinder smouldered. The miracle happened, and a small flame burned. The harsh lines of Aoz Roon's face relaxed slightly as he looked down at the glow between his hands. The phagor stood at its distance and watched, unmoving.

"Son of Freyr, you are make warm," he called.

Looking up, Aoz Roon saw his adversary only in outline, silhouetted against the gold of the western sky.

"I make warm, and what's more I'm going to cook and eat your cowbird, fuggie."

"You give me a share cowbird."

"The floods will go down in a day or two. Then we can both go home. You stay where you are for the present."

The phagor's articulation was thick. He said something Aoz Roon did not understand. The latter squatted by his fire, peering across the dark water at the adversary, whose silhouette was now fading into the general silhouette of trees and hills, black against the sunset. Aoz Roon was scratching himself, raking with his nails under his furs, swaying to and fro.

"You, Son of Freyr, are sick and will die in the night." He had difficulty pronouncing the sibilants, rendering them as heavy z's.

"Zick? Yes, I'm zick, but I'm still Lord of Embruddock, scumb you."

Aoz Roon began to call Curd, but no answer came. It was too dark on the ground to see if the phagor group continued to wait by the flood. The whole world was drowning in night, becoming nothing but a shadowy reflection.

Fearful in his weakness, he thought the phagor crouched, as if it was about to attempt to jump the space that intervened between them.

He waved a fist. "You stick to your world, I'll stick to mine."

Merely uttering the words exhausted him. He held his hands over his eyes, panting as Curd had panted after a day's hunting.

The phagor made no reply for a long while, as if trying to digest the man's remark and finally deciding to reject it. This he did without gesture, saying, "We live and die in zame world, zame world. That is why we muzz fight."

The words came to Aoz Roon over the water. He could not understand their meaning. He remembered only that he had shouted to Shay Tal that they would survive by unity. Now he was confused. It was typical of her not to be at hand when he needed her.

Turning to his fire, he fell upon his knees, pushed more branches on the blaze, and began the bloody job of cutting up the bird. He wrenched off one of its legs, from which sinews dangled, and skewered it on a

XII · LORD OF THE ISLAND 287

stick. He was preparing to push it into the flames when he realised that the agony of the rash on his skin was echoed throughout his bones; his skeleton felt as if it were on fire. Sickness washed over him. The thought of eating anything was suddenly revolting.

He staggered back to his feet, trod in the fire, blundered forward into the water, went in circles, crying, holding aloft the bloody limb. The water noise was loud. It seemed to him that the river became motionless; the island was a slim boat, moving at speed across the surface of a lake; he could not control its flight; and the lake went on forever, into a great cavern of darkness.

The mouth of the cavern closed, swallowing him.

"You have the bone fever," said the phagor. He was called Yhamm-Whrrmar. He was no warrior. He and his friends were itinerant woodmen and fungusmongers. Their kaidaws were stolen. When two Sons of Freyr had appeared in their midst, they had merely done their bounden duty, with the result that Yhamm-Whrrmar was now in some difficulty.

The fungusmongers had been driven westwards by a combination of factors. They were striking in the opposite direction, following favourable air-octaves, when they met humble dwellers like themselves, who spoke of a great crusade advancing, destroying all before it. Although alarmed, the fungusmongers had continued their quest for cooler ground, but had deflected up a long valley where the air-octaves were tainted. Floods had come. They had been forced to retreat. Unkindness and confusion assailed their very eddres.

He stood motionless on the edge of the flood, awaiting the death of the evil seminal being, Freyr. Its disappearance into darkness brought him relief. He unfroze and massaged his injured arm. Night was welcome.

Some distance away, his enemy lay sprawled across a heap of stones. There would be no further trouble from that quarter. After all, parasitic curse though they were, the Sons of Freyr were to be pitied: they all eventually fell sick in the presence of the Ancipital Race. It was no more than justice. Yhamm-Whrrmar stood motionless, letting hours pass.

"You are zick and will die," he called. But he also felt bad air inside him. He scratched his neck with the hand of his good arm, and surveyed the great dark area in which he stood. Complete blackness was already fading. Somewhere to the east, Batalix, that good soldier, Batalix, father of the ancipital race, was already putting forth pale tidings of his presence. Yhamm-Whrrmar retired to the roofless hut and lay down; his magenta eyes closed; he slept without dream or movement.

Over the great floodwaters stole a glimmer from the east, promise of Batalix-dawn. Batalix would rise many times before the floods died, for those floods were fed by enormous reservoirs of water held in the remote Nktryhk. Time would come when the flood scoured for itself a regular riverbed. Later still, shifts in the land mass would deflect the river elsewhere. By the period—still many centuries distant—when Freyr reached its maximum glory, this land would become parched and form a sector of the Madura Desert, traversed by nations as yet a part of futurity unglimpsed.

As man and phagor slept, neither realised that water would flow past their flimsy strip of island for an age to come. It was a temporary inundation: but that inundation would last for another two hundred Batalix-years.

XIII

VIEW FROM A HALF ROON

O n the Earth Observation Station, the term "bone fever" was
well understood. It was part of a complex disease-mechanism
caused by the virus known to the learned families on the
Avernus as the helico virus, and its workings were better understood by
them than by those who suffered and died from it on the planet below.

Research into Helliconian microbiology was far enough advanced for
the Earthmen to know that the virus manifested itself twice in every
1825 years of the Helliconian great year. However it might appear to
the contrary to the Helliconians, these manifestations were not random.
They occurred invariably during the period of the twenty eclipses which
marked the beginning of true spring, and again during the period of the
six or seven eclipses occurring later in the great year. Climatic changes
coincident with the eclipses acted as triggers to the phases of viral hyper-
activity, which formed, as it were, mirror images of each other, their
effects being equally devastating though entirely different at the different periods.

To the inhabitants of the world below, the two scourges were separate phenomena. They raged more than five Helliconian small centuries

(*that is, slightly over seven Earth centuries*) *apart. So they went by separate names, the bone fever and the fat death.*

The disease stream of the virus, like an irresistible flood, affected the history of all through whose lands it swept its ways. Yet an individual virus, like a single drop of water, was negligible.

A helico virus would have to be magnified ten thousand times before it became visible to the human eye. Its size was ninety-seven millimicrons. It consisted of a bag partly covered in icosahedrons, made up of lipids and proteins, and containing RNA; in many ways, it resembled the pleomorphic helical virus responsible for an extinct terrestrial disease called mumps.

Both the scholars on the Avernus and the Helliconia-watchers back on Earth had deduced the function of this devastating virus. Like the ancient Hindu god Shiva, it represented the ancipital principles of destruction and preservation. It killed, and existence followed in its deadly wake. Without the presence of the helico virus on the planet, neither human nor phagorian life would have been possible.

Because of its presence, no person from Earth could set foot on Helliconia and survive. On Helliconia, the helico virus ruled, and set a cordon sanitaire about the planet.

As yet, the bone fever had not entered Embruddock. It was approaching, as surely as was the crusade of the young kzahhn, Hrr-Brahl Yprt. The question in the minds of the scholars on the Avernus was, which would strike first.

Other questions occupied the minds of those who lived in Embruddock. The question uppermost in the minds of the men within sight of the top of the shaky hierarchy was, how could power be attained and, when attained, how could it be retained.

Fortunately for the run of mankind, no permanent answer to this question has ever been devised. But Tanth Ein and Faralin Ferd, venal and easygoing men, had no interest in the question in the abstract. As time passed, and another year—the fateful year of 26 in the new calendar—dawned, and Aoz Roon's absence grew to over half a year, the two lieutenants ran affairs on a day-to-day basis.

This suited them. It suited Raynil Layan less. He had gained increasing say with both the two regents and the council. Raynil Layan saw that an entirely new system was overdue in Oldorando; by introducing it, he would secure power by the sort of nonviolent means which suited him best.

He would appear to yield to pressure from traders and bring in money to replace the age-old system of barter.

From now on, nothing would be free in Oldorando.

Bread would be paid for in his coin.

Satisfied that they would get their share, Tanth Ein and Faralin Ferd
nodded agreement to Raynil Layan's scheme. The city was expanding
every day. Trade could no longer be confined to the outskirts; it was
becoming the centre of life and so it appeared in the centre. And it
could be taxed under Raynil Layan's innovatory thinking.

"Buying food is not right. Food should be free, like the air."

"But we're going to be given money to buy it with."

"I don't like it. Raynil Layan's going to get fat," Dathka said.

He and his fellow Lord of the Western Veldt were strolling towards
Oyre's tower, inspecting some of their responsibilities on the way. Those
responsibilities grew as Oldorando spread. Everywhere they saw new
faces. Learned members of the council estimated—with some wringing
of the hands—that little more than a quarter of the present population
was born locally. The rest were foreigners, many of them in transit.
Oldorando was situated at a continental crossroads which was just beginning to bear traffic.

What had been open land until a few months ago was now a site for
huts and tents. Some changes went deeper. The old regime of the hunt,
by turns harsh and sybaritic, vanished overnight. Laintal Ay and Dathka
kept a slave to feed their hoxneys. Game had become scarce, stungebags had disappeared, and migrants were bringing in cattle which betokened a more settled way of life.

The blandishments of the bazaar had ruined the camaraderie of the
hunt. Those who had gloried in riding like the wind over newly discovered grasslands in the days of Aoz Roon were now content to lounge
about the streets, serving as stall holders, or ostlers, or strong-arm men,
or pimps.

The Lords of the Western Veldt were now responsible for order in
the growing quarter of the city that lay to the west of the Voral. They
had marshals to assist them. Slaves from the south skilled in masonry
were building them a tower in which to live. The quarry was in the
brassimips. The new tower imitated the form of the old ones; it would
command the tents of those the lords sought to control, and stand all
of three stories high.

After inspecting the day's work and exchanging a joke with the over-
seer, Laintal Ay and Dathka headed towards the old town, pushing
through a crowd of pilgrims. Canvas stalls were set up, ready to cater to
the needs of such travellers. Each stall was licenced with Laintal Ay's
office, and displayed its number on a disc.

The pilgrims surged forward. Laintal Ay stepped out of their way,
putting his back against a new wall of canvas. His heel met with air,
he slipped and found himself falling into a hole which the canvas had
concealed. He drew his sword. Three pale young men, naked to the
waist, looked at him in horror as he turned to confront them.

The hole was waist deep, the size of a small room.

The foreheads of the men were painted with central eyes.

Dathka appeared around the corner of the canvas and looked down into the excavation, grinning at his friend's mishap.

"What are you doing?" Laintal Ay demanded of the three men.

Recovering from their astonishment, the three stood firm. One said, "This will be a shrine dedicated to great Naba's Akha, and is therefore sacred ground. We have to ask you to leave at once."

"I own this ground," Laintal Ay said. "Show me your licence to rent a patch here."

While the young men were exchanging looks, more pilgrims gathered round the hole, looking down and muttering. All wore black and white robes.

"We haven't got a licence. We aren't selling anything."

"Where are you from?"

A large man with a black cloth wound about his head stood on the edge of the hole, accompanied by two older women who carried a large object between them. He called down in a pompous voice, "We are followers of the great Naba's Akha and we are proceeding southwards, spreading the word. We plan to erect a small chapel here and we demand you remove your unworthy self immediately."

"I own this ground, every spadeful of it. Why are you digging down if you need to build a chapel up? Don't you foreigners know air from earth?"

One of the young diggers said, apologetically, "Akha is the god of earth and underground, and we live in his veins. We shall spread his good news through all lands. Are we not Takers from Pannoval?"

"You are not taking this hole without permission," Laintal Ay roared. "Get out, all of you."

The large pompous man began to shout, but Dathka drew his sword. He stabbed forward. The object the two older women carried was covered with a cloth. Pricking the cloth with his sword point, Dathka whisked the fabric away. An awkwardly crouching figure was revealed, semihuman, its frog eyes blind but staring. It was carved from a black stone.

"What a beauty!" Dathka exclaimed, laughing. "An ugly mug like that needs to be covered up!"

The pilgrims became furious. Akha had been insulted; sunlight was never allowed to touch Akha. Several men flung themselves at Dathka. Laintal Ay jumped out of the hole shouting, and set about the pilgrims with the flat of his sword. The skirmish brought a marshal and two of his men armed with staves to the scene, and in a short while the pilgrims were battered enough to promise their future good conduct.

Laintal Ay and Dathka continued on to Oyre's new rooms in Vry's tower, which was being rebuilt. Oyre had moved because the square about the big tower had become so noisy, with its wooden stalls and

drinking booths. With Oyre had gone Dol and her small son, Rastil
Roon Den, together with Dol's ancient mother, Rol Sakil. As Aoz
Roon's absence lengthened, Dol had become concerned for her safety
in a building that also housed the two increasingly unruly lieutenants,
Faralin Ferd and Tanth Ein.

At the entrance to the tower, still referred to as Shay Tal's Tower,
four burly young freed Borlienian slaves were on guard. That arrangement was Laintal Ay's doing. He received their salutes as he and Dathka
entered.

"How's Oyre?" he asked, already beginning to tramp upstairs.

"Recovering."

He found his beloved lying in a bed, with Vry, Dol, and Rol Sakil
beside her. He went to her and she put her arms round him.

"Oh, Laintal Ay—it was so horrible. I felt such fear." She stared into
his eyes. He looked upon her face, seeing there weariness, caught in the
faint lines under her eyes. All who went father-communing were aged
by the experience. "I thought I'd never get back to you, my love," she
said. "The world below becomes worse every time you visit it."

Age had bent Rol Sakil double. Her long white hair covered her face,
so that all that could be seen was her nose. She squatted by the bed
nursing her grandson, and said, "It's only them who are old who fail to
return, Oyre."

Oyre sat up and clung more tightly to Laintal Ay. He could feel her
shivering.

"It seemed doubly awful this time—a universe without suns. The
world below is the opposite of ours, with the original boulder like a sun
below everything, black, giving out black light. All the fessups hang
there like stars—not in air but rock. All being sucked slowly down into
the black hole of the boulder. . . . They're so malign, they hate the
living."

"It's true," agreed Dol, soothing her old mother. "They hate us and
would eat us up if they could."

"They snap at you as you go by."

"Their eyes are full of evil dusts."

"Their jaws too . . ."

"But your father?" Laintal Ay prompted, bringing her back to the
reason for her entering pauk.

"I met my mother in the world below. . . ." Oyre could say no more
for a moment. Though she clung to Laintal Ay, the world of air to
which he belonged as yet seemed less real to her than the one she had
left. Not one kind word had her mother for her, only blame and recrimination, and an intensity of hatred that the living scarcely dared reveal.

"She said how I'd disgraced her name, brought her in shame to her
grave. I'd killed her, I was responsible for her death, she had detested
me since she first felt me stir in her womb. . . . All the bad things I

did as a child . . . my helplessness . . . my scumble. . . . Oh, oh, I can't tell you. . . ."

She began to wail horribly to release her grief.

Vry came forward and helped Laintal Ay hold her. "It's not true, Oyre, it's all imagination." But she was thrust away by her weeping friend.

All had been in pauk at some time. All looked on in gloomy sympathy, locked in their own thoughts.

"But your father," Laintal Ay said again. "Did you meet him?"

She recovered sufficiently to hold him at arm's length, regarding him with red eyes, her face glistening with snot and tears.

"He was not there, thanks be to Wutra, he was not there. The time has not yet arrived when he must fall to the world below."

They gazed round at each other in puzzlement at this news. To cover a dread that Aoz Roon was, after all, with Shay Tal, Oyre went on talking.

"Surely he won't become that kind of evil gossie, surely he has lived a life full enough not to turn into one of those little bundles of malevolence? At least he's spared that fate a while longer. But where is he, all these long weeks?"

Dol began to weep by infection, snatching Rastil Roon from her mother, rocking him, and saying, "Is he still alive? Where is he? He wasn't so bad, to be honest. . . . Are you sure he wasn't down below?"

"I tell you he wasn't. Laintal Ay, Dathka, he's still somewhere in this world, though Wutra knows where, that we can be sure of."

Rol Sakil began to wail, now that her movements were not hampered by the infant.

"We must all go down to that terrible place, sooner or later. Dol, Dol, it will be your poor old mother's turn next. . . . Promise you'll come and see me, promise, and I promise I'll say no word against you. I will never blame you for the way you've become involved with that terrible man who has afflicted all our lives. . . ."

As Dol comforted her mother, Laintal Ay tried to comfort Oyre, but she suddenly pushed him away and climbed from the bed, wiping her face and breathing deep. "Don't touch me—I stink of the world below. Let me wash myself."

During these lamentations, Dathka had stood at the back of the room, his stocky figure against the rough wall, his face wooden. Now he came forward.

"Be silent, all of you, and try to think. We are in danger and must turn this news to our advantage. If Aoz Roon is alive, then we need a plan of action till he gets back—if he can get back. Maybe fuggies have captured him.

"I warn you, Faralin Ferd and Tanth Ein plot to take over control of Oldorando. First, they mean to set up a mint, with that worm Raynil

Layan in command of it." His eyes slid to Vry and then away again. "Raynil Layan already has the metal makers at work, minting a coinage. When they control that and pay their men, they will be all-powerful. They will surely kill Aoz Roon when he returns."

"How do you know this?" Vry asked. "Faralin Ferd and Tanth Ein are his friends of long-standing."

"As for that . . ." Dathka said, and laughed. "Ice is solid till it melts."

He stood alert, looking at each, finally letting his gaze rest on Laintal Ay.

"Now we must prove our real worth. We tell nobody that Aoz Roon is still alive. Nobody. Better that they should be uncertain. Leave everyone in doubt. Oyre's news would prompt the lieutenants to usurp power at once. They would act to forestall him before he got back."

"I don't think—" Laintal Ay began, but Dathka, suddenly in command of his tongue, cut him short.

"Who has the best claim to rule if Aoz Roon is dead? You, Laintal Ay. And you, Oyre. Loilanun's son and Aoz Roon's daughter. This infant of Dol's is a dangerous counterargument that the council could seize on. Laintal Ay, you and Oyre must become united at once. Enough shilly-shallying. We'll command a dozen priests from Borlien for the ceremony, and you will make the announcement that the old Lord is dead, so the two of you will rule in his stead. You'll be accepted."

"And Faralin Ferd and Tanth Ein?"

"We can look after Faralin Ferd and Tanth Ein," said Dathka, grimly. "And Raynil Layan. They have no general support, as you do."

They all regarded each other soberly. Finally, Laintal Ay spoke.

"I am not going to usurp Aoz Roon's title while he is still alive. I appreciate your cunning, Dathka, but I will not carry out your plan."

Dathka put his hands on his hips and sneered. "I see. So you don't care if the lieutenants do take over? They'll kill you if they do—and me."

"I don't believe that."

"Believe what you wish, they'll certainly kill you. And Oyre, and Dol and this kid. Probably Vry too. Come out of your dreams. They are tough men, and they have to act soon. The blindnesses, rumours of bone fever—they'll act while you sit and mope."

"It would be better to get my father back," Oyre said, deliberately looking not at Laintal Ay but Dathka. "Things are in flux—we need a really strong ruler."

Dathka laughed sourly at her remark and watched its effect on Laintal Ay without replying.

A heavy silence fell in the room. Laintal Ay broke it by saying awkwardly, "Whatever the lieutenants may or may not do, I am not going to bid for power. It would only be divisive."

"Divisive?" Dathka said. "The place is divided, it's sliding into chaos with all the foreigners here. You're a fool if you ever believed Aoz Roon's nonsense about unity."

During this argument Vry had remained unobtrusively by the trap-door, and was leaning with arms folded against the wall. She came forward now and said, "You make a mistake by thinking only of earthly things."

Pointing towards the baby, she said, "When Rastil Roon was born, his father had just disappeared. That is three quarters ago. The time of double sunset is past. So it is three quarters since the last eclipse, I will remind you. Or the last blindness, if you prefer the old term.

"I must warn you that another eclipse is approaching. Oyre and I have done our calculations—"

Dol's aged mother set up a wail. "We never had these afflictions in the old days—what have we done to deserve them now? One more will finish everybody off."

"I can't explain the why; I'm only just learning to explain the how," Vry said, casting a sympathetic glance at the old woman. "And if I'm correct, the next eclipse will be of much greater duration than the last, with Freyr totally concealed for over five and a half hours, and most of the day filled with the event, which will have begun when the suns rise. You can imagine the kind of panic that may ensue."

Rol Sakil and Dol started to howl. Dathka ordered them abruptly to be quiet, and said, "A day-long eclipse? In a few years, we'll have nothing but eclipse and no Freyr at all, if you're right. Why do you make such claims, Vry?"

She faced him, looking seekingly at his dark countenance. Fearing what she saw, she answered deliberately in terms she knew he could not accept. "Because the universe is not random. It is a machine. There-fore one can know its movements."

Such a deeply revolutionary statement had not been heard in Oldo-rando for centuries. It went entirely over Dathka's head.

"If you are sure, we must try to protect ourselves with sacrifices."

Without bothering to argue, Vry turned to the others, saying, "The eclipses will not last for ever. They will go on for twenty years, getting shorter after the first eleven. After number twenty, they will not return."

Her words were meant to reassure. The expression on their faces showed the pain of their inward thought: in twenty years, none of them was likely to be alive.

"How can you know what's going to happen in the future, Vry? Even Shay Tal couldn't do that," Laintal Ay said heavily.

She wanted to touch him, but was too shy. "It's a matter of observa-tion and gathering old facts, putting everything together. It's a matter of understanding what we know, of seeing what we see. Freyr and Bata-

lix are far apart, even when they appear close to us. Each balances on
the edge of a great round plate. The plates are tipped at an angle.
Where they intersect, there eclipses happen, because our world is in line
with Freyr, with Batalix between. Do you understand that?"

Dathka strode up and down. He said impatiently, "Listen, Vry, I
forbid you to speak of such mad notions in public. The people will kill
you. This is what the academy has led you to. I'm not going to listen to
any more."

He gave her a dark look, bitter, yet oddly imploring. She was transfixed. Dathka left the room without further word. Silence was what he
left behind.

He had been gone only a couple of minutes when there was a commotion in the street outside. Laintal Ay ran down immediately to see what
was happening. He suspected Dathka's intervention, but his friend had
disappeared. A man had fallen from his mount and was crying for help—
a foreigner by his garb. A crowd gathered round him, among them faces
Laintal Ay knew, although none went to help the traveller.

"It's the plague," a man told Laintal Ay. "Anyone who aided this
knave would be sick himself by Freyr-fall."

Two slaves were brought up, and the sufferer was dragged towards
the hospice.

This was the first public appearance of the bone fever in Oldorando.

When Laintal Ay returned to Oyre's room, she had removed her
hoxneys and was washing herself over a bowl, calling out from behind
a curtain to Dol and Vry.

Dol's dimpled face was for once registering expression. She uncoupled
Rastil Roon from her breast and passed him to her mother, saying,
"Listen, my friend, you must act. Call the people together and speak to
them. Explain. Never mind Dathka."

"You should do that, Laintal Ay," Oyre called. "Remind everyone
of how Aoz Roon built Oldorando, and how you were his faithful lieutenant. Don't follow Dathka's plan. Assure everyone that Aoz Roon is
not dead, and will return soon."

"That's right," Dol said. "Remind people how they fear him, and
how he built the bridge. They'll listen to you."

"You've sorted out our troubles between you," said Laintal Ay. "But
you are mistaken. Aoz Roon has been gone too long. Half the people
here scarcely know his name. They're strangers, traders passing through.
Go to the Pauk and ask the first man you meet who Aoz Roon is—he
won't be able to tell you. That's why the question of power is open." He
stood solid before them.

Dol shook her fist at him. "You dare say that! It's lies. If—when he
comes back, he'll rule as before. I'll see that he kicks out Faralin Ferd
and Tanth Ein, too. Not to forget that reptile, Raynil Layan."

"Maybe so, maybe not, Dol. The point is, he is not here. What about Shay Tal? She's been gone just as long. Who speaks of her nowadays? You may still miss her, Vry, but others don't."

Vry shook her head. She said quietly, "If you want the truth, I miss neither Shay Tal nor Aoz Roon. I think they blighted our lives. I believe she blighted mine—oh, it was my fault, I know, and I owe her much, I being the daughter of a mere slave woman. But I followed Shay Tal too slavishly."

"That's right," old Rol Sakil piped, bouncing the baby. "She was a bad example to you, Vry—too virginal by half, was our Shay Tal. You've gone the same way. You must be fifteen now, near middle age, and still not laid. Get on with it, afore it's too late."

Dol said, "Ma's right, Vry. You saw how Dathka marched out of here, furious because you argued with him. He's in love with you, that's why. Be more submissive, that's a woman's job, isn't it? Throw your arms round him and he'll give you what you want. I should think he'd be quite lusty."

"Throw your legs round him, not your arms, that's my advice," Rol Sakil said, cackling with laughter. "There's pretty women passing through Oldorando now—not like when we was all young, when flesh was in short supply. The things they get up to in the bazaar nowadays! No wonder they want a coinage. I know the slot they'll stuff it in. . . ."

"That's enough," Vry said, her cheeks red. "I'll manage my own life without your crude advice. I respect Dathka but I am not at all fond of him. Change the subject."

Laintal Ay took Vry's arm with a consoling gesture, as Oyre emerged from behind her curtain, her hair piled on the top of her head. She had discarded her hoxney skins, which were now regarded as somewhat outmoded among a younger set in Oldorando. Instead, she wore a green woollen dress which trailed almost to the ground.

"Vry's being advised to take a man soon—just like you," Laintal Ay told her.

"At least Dathka's mature and knows his own mind."

Laintal Ay scowled at this remark. Turning his back on Oyre, he said to Vry, "Explain to me about the twenty eclipses. I didn't understand what you were saying. How is the universe a machine?"

She frowned and then said, "You've heard the elements before, but would not listen. You must be prepared to believe that the world is stranger than you give it credit for. I'll try to explain clearly.

"Imagine that the land-octaves extend into the air high above us, as well as into the ground. Imagine that this world, which the phagors call Hrl-Ichor, follows its own octave regularly. In fact, its octave winds round and round Batalix. Hrl-Ichor goes round Batalix once every four hundred and eighty days—hence our year, as you know. Batalix does not move. It is we that move."

"What when Batalix sets every evening?"

"Batalix is motionless in the sky. It is we that move."

Laintal Ay laughed. "And the festival of Double Sunset? What moves then?"

"The same. We move. Batalix and Freyr remain stationary. Unless you believe that, I can explain no further."

"We have all seen the sentinels move, my dear Vry, every day of our lives. So what follows, supposing I believe both of them to be turned to ice?"

She hesitated, then said, "Well, in fact Batalix and Freyr do move as Freyr grows brighter."

"Come—first you'd have me believe that they didn't move, then that they did. Stop it, Vry—I'll believe your eclipses when they happen, not before."

With a scream of impatience, she raised her scrawny arms above her head. "Oh, you're such fools. Let Embruddock fall, what difference would it make? You can't understand one simple thing."

She left the room even more furiously than Dathka.

"There are some simple matters she don't understand either," Rol Sakil said, cuddling the small boy.

Vry's old room showed the change that had come to Oldorando. No longer was it so bleak. Oddments gathered from here and there decked the room. She had inherited some of Shay Tal's—and hence Loilanun's—possessions. She had traded in the bazaars. A star chart of her making hung near the window, with the paths of the ecliptics of the two suns marked on it.

On one wall hung an ancient map, given her by a new admirer. It was painted in coloured inks upon vellum. This was her Ottaassaal map depicting the whole world, at which she never ceased to wonder. The world was depicted as round, its land masses encircled by ocean. It rested on the original boulder—bigger than the world—from which the world had sprung or been ejected. The simple outlined land masses were labelled Sibornal, with Campannlat below, and Hespagorat separate at the bottom. Some islands were formally indicated. The only town marked was Ottaassaal, set at the centre of the globe.

She wondered how far away one would have to be to see the actual world in such a way. Batalix and Freyr were two other round worlds, as she well understood. But they had no support from original boulders beneath them; why then did the world need one?

In a niche in the wall beside the map stood a little figurine which Dathka had brought her. She lifted it down now, cradling it in her palm rather abstractedly. It depicted a couple enjoying coition in a squatting position. Man and woman were carved out of one stone. The hands

through which the object had passed had worn them into anonymity,
age had rendered them both featureless. The carving represented the
supreme act of being together, and Vry regarded it longingly as it
rested in her hand. "That's unity," she murmured, in a low voice.

For all her friends' teasing, she wanted desperately what the stone
represented. She also recognised, as Shay Tal had before her, that the
path to knowledge was a solitary one.

Did the figurine portray a pair of real lovers whose names had been
lost far in the past? It was impossible to tell.

In the past lay the answers to much that was in the future. She
looked hopelessly at the astronomical clock she was trying to construct
from wood, which lay on the table by her narrow window. Not only was
she unused to working in wood, but she still had not grasped the principle that maintained the world, the three wandering worlds, and the
two sentinels in their paths.

Suddenly, she perceived that a unity existed among the spheres—they
were all of one material, as the lovers were of one stone. And a force as
strong as sexual need bound them all mysteriously together, dictating
their movements.

She sat down at her table, and commenced wrenching the rods and
rings apart, trying to rearrange them in a new order.

She was thus engaged when there was a tap at her door. Raynil Layan
sidled in, giving hasty looks about him to see that nobody else was in the
room.

He saw her framed in the pale blue rectangle of window, the light
brooding on her profile. She held a wooden ball in one hand. At his
entrance, she half started up, and he saw—for he watched people closely
—that her habitual reserve had left her for once. She smiled nervously,
smoothing her hoxney skin over the definitions of her breast. He pushed
the door closed behind him.

The master of the tanners had assumed grandeur these days. His
forked beard was tied with two ribbons, in a manner he had learned
from foreigners, and he wore trousers of silk. Recently, he had been paying Vry attention, presenting her with such items as the Ottaassaal map,
acquired in Pauk, and listening closely to her theories. All this she found
obscurely exciting. Although she mistrusted his smooth manners, she
was flattered by them, and by his interest in all she did.

"You work too hard, Vry," he said, cocking a finger and raising an
eyebrow at her. "More time spent outdoors would put colour back into
those pretty cheeks."

"You know how busy I am, running the academy now Amin Lim's
gone with Shay Tal, as well as doing my own work."

The academy flourished as never before. It had its own building, and
was largely run by one of Vry's assistants. They engaged learned men to
speak; anyone passing through Oldorando was approached. Many ideas

were put into practical operation in the workshops under the lecture room. Raynil Layan himself kept a watch on all that was happening.

His eye missed nothing. Catching sight of the stone figurine among the litter on her table, he scrutinised it closely. She flushed and fidgetted.

"It's very old."

"And still very popular."

She giggled. "I meant the object itself."

"I meant their objective." He set it down, looking archly at her, and settled his body against the edge of the table so that their legs were touching.

Vry bit her lip and looked down. She had her erotic fantasies about this man she did not greatly like, and they came crowding back to her now.

But Raynil Layan, as was his style, had changed tack. After a moment's silence, he moved his leg, cleared his throat, and spoke seriously.

"Vry, among the pilgrims just arrived from Pannoval is a man not as blinded with religion as the rest of his crowd. He makes clocks, working them precisely from metal. Wood is no good for your purpose. Let me bring this craftsman to you, and you can instruct him as you will to build your model expertly."

"Mine's no mere clock, Raynil Layan," she said, looking up at him as he stood against her chair, wondering if she and he could in any way be regarded as being made of the same stone.

"That I understand. You instruct the man about your machine. I'll pay him in coin. I shall soon take up an important post, with power to command as I will."

She stood up, the better to assess his response.

"I hear you are to run an Oldorandan mint."

He narrowed his eyes and surveyed her, half-smiling, half-angry. "Who told you that?"

"You know how news travels."

"Faralin Ferd has been blabbing out of turn again."

"You don't think greatly of him or Tanth Ein, do you?"

He made a dismissive gesture and seized her hands. "I think of *you* all the while. I will have power and, unlike those other fools—unlike Aoz Roon—I believe that knowledge can be wedded to power to reinforce it. . . . Be my woman and you shall have what you wish. You shall live better. We will discover all things. We will split open the pyramid that my predecessor, Datnil Skar, never managed to do, for all his prattle."

She hid her face, wondering if her thin body, her torpid queme, could entice and hold a man.

Pulling her wrists from his grasp, she backed away. Her hands, now free, flew like birds to her face to try to conceal the agitation she felt.

"Don't tempt me, don't play with me."

"You need tempting, my doe."

Narrowing his eyes, he opened the purse at his belt, and brought forth some coins. These he extended towards her, like a man tempting a wild hoxney with food. She came cautiously to inspect them.

"The new currency, Vry. Coins. Take them. They're going to transform Oldorando."

The three coins were improperly rounded and crudely stamped. There was a small bronze coin stamped "Half Roon," a larger copper coin stamped "One Roon," and a small gold coin stamped "Five Roons." In the middle of each coin was the legend:

O L D

O R A N

D O

Vry laughed with excitement as she examined them. Somehow, the money represented power, modernity, knowledge. "Roons!" she exclaimed. "That's rich."

"The very key to riches."

She set them on her worn table. "I'll test your intelligence with them, Raynil Layan."

"What a way you do court a man!" He laughed, but saw by her narrow face that she was serious.

"Let the Half Roon be our world, Hrl-Ichor. The big One Roon is Batalix. This little gold one is Freyr." With her finger, she made the Half Roon circle about the Roon. "This is how we move through the upper air. One circle is one year—in which time, the Half Roon has revolved like a ball four hundred and eighty times. See? When we think we see the Roon move, it is we who move on the Half Roon. Yet the Roon is not still. There's a general principle involved, much like love. As a child's life revolves about its mother, so does the Half Roon's about the Roon—and so also does the Roon, I have decided, about the Five Roons."

"You have decided? A guess?"

"No. Simple observation. But no observation, however simple, can be made except by those predisposed to make it. Between winter and spring solstices, the Half Roon moves its maximum to either side of the Roon." She demonstrated the diameter of its orbit. "Imagine that behind the Five Roons there are a number of tiny sticks standing to represent fixed stars. Then imagine you are standing on the Half Roon. Can you imagine that?"

"More, I can imagine you standing there with me."

She thought how quick he was, and her voice shook as she said, "There we stand, and the Half Roon goes first this side of the Roon, then the other. . . . What do we observe? Why, that the Five Roons appears to move against the fixed stars behind it."

"Only appears?"

"In that respect, yes. The movement shows both that Freyr is close compared to the stars, and that it is we who really move and not the sentinels."

Raynil Layan contemplated the coins.

"But you say that the two small denominations move about the Five Roons?"

"You know that we share a guilty secret. There's the matter of your predecessor illegally presenting Shay Tal with information from your corps book. . . . From King Denniss's dating we know that this is the year he would call 446. That is the number of years after someone—Nadir. . . ."

"I've had a better chance than you to puzzle that dating out, my doe, and other dates to compare it with. The date Zero is a year of maximum cold and dark, according to the Denniss calendar."

"Exactly what I believe. It is now 446 years since Freyr was at its feeblest. Batalix never changes its light intensity. Freyr does—for some reason. Once, I believed that it grew bright or dim at random. But now I think that the universe is no more random than a stream is random. There are causes for things; the universe is a machine, like this astronomical clock which seeks to imitate it. Freyr is getting brighter because it approaches—no, vice versa—we approach Freyr. It's hard to shake off the old ways of thought when they are embedded in the language. In the new language, the Half Roon and the Roon are approaching the Five Roons. . . ."

He fiddled with the little ribbons on his beard. Vry watched him thinking over her statement.

"Why is the approach theory preferable to the dim-bright theory?"

She clapped her hands. "What a clever question to ask. If Batalix doesn't fluctuate from dim to bright, why should Freyr? The Half Roon always approaches the Roon, though the Roon always moves out of the way. So I think the Roon approaches the Five Roons in the same way—taking the Half-Roon with it. Which brings us to the eclipses." She circulated the two lower denomination coins again.

"You see how the Half Roon reaches a point each year where observers on it—you and I—would not see the Five because the One would get in the way. That is an eclipse."

"So why isn't there an eclipse every year? It spoils all your theory if one part of it is wrong, just as a hoxney won't run with only three legs."

You're smart, she thought—much smarter than Dathka or Laintal Ay—and I like clever men, even when they're unscrupulous.

"Oh, there's a reason for it, which I can't properly demonstrate. That's why I am trying to build this model. I'll show you soon."

He smiled and took her slender hand again. She trembled as if she were down the brassimip tree.

"You shall have that craftsman here tomorrow, working in gold to your specifics, if you will agree to be mine and let me publish the news. I want you close—in my bed."

"Oh, you'll have to wait . . . please . . . please . . ." She fell trembling into his arms as he clutched her. His hands moved over her body seeking her narrow contours. He does want me, she thought, in a whirl, he wants me in a way Dathka doesn't dare. He's more mature, far more intelligent. He's not half so bad as they make out. Shay Tal was wrong about him. She was wrong about a lot of things. Besides, manners are different in Oldorando now and, if he wants me, he shall have me. . . .

"The bed," she gasped, tearing at his clothes. "Quick, before I change my mind. I'm so divided. . . . Quick, I'm ready. Open."

"Oh, my trousers, have a care . . ." But he was pleased by her haste. She felt, she saw, his rising excitement, as he lowered his bulk onto her. She groaned as he laughed. She had a vision of the two of them, one flesh, whirling among the stars in the grip of a great universal power, anonymous, eternal. . . .

The hospice was new and not yet complete. It stood near the fringes of the town, extending from what had been called Prast's Tower in the old days. Here came those travellers who had fallen sick on their journeyings. Across the street was the establishment of a veterinary surgeon which received sick animals.

Both hospice and surgery had a bad name—it was claimed that the tools of their respective trades were interchangeable; but the hospice was efficiently run by the first woman member of the apothecary's corps, a midwife and teacher at the academy known to all as Ma Scantiom, after the flowers with which she insisted on decking the wards under her command.

A slave took Laintal Ay to her. She was a tall sturdy person of middle age, with plenty of bosom, and a kindly expression on her face. One of her aunts had been Nahkri's woman. She and Laintal Ay had been on good terms for many years.

"I've two patients in an isolation ward I want you to see," she said, selecting a key from a number that hung at her belt. She had discarded hoxneys in favour of a long saffron apron-dress which hung almost to the floor.

Ma Scantiom unlocked a sturdy door at the rear of her office.

They went through into the old tower and climbed the ramps until they were at the top.

From somewhere below them came the sound of a clow, played by a convalescent patient. Laintal Ay recognised the tune: "Stop, Stop, Voral River." The rhythm was fast, yet with a melancholy which matched the useless exhortation of the chorus. The river ran and would not stop, no, not for love or life itself. . . .

Each floor of the tower had been divided into small wards or cells, each with a door with a grille set in it. Without a word, Ma Scantiom slid back the cover over the grille and indicated that Laintal Ay was to look through.

There were two beds in the cell, each bearing a man. The men were almost naked. They lay in locked positions, nearly rigid but never entirely still. The man nearest the door, who had a thick mane of black hair, lay with his spine arched and his hands clenched together above his head. He was grinding his knuckles against the stone wall so that they seeped blood, which ran down the blue-veined paths of his arms. His head rolled stiffly at awkward angles. He caught sight of Laintal Ay at the grille, and his eyes tried to fix on him, but the head insisted on its continued slow-motion movement. Arteries in his neck stood out like cord.

The second patient, lying below the window, held his arms folded tight into his chest. He was curling himself into a ball and then unrolling, at the same time waggling his feet back and forth so that the little bones cracked. His gaze, distraught, moved between floor and ceiling. Laintal Ay recognized him as the man who had collapsed in the street.

Both men were deathly pale and glistening with sweat, the pungent smell of which filtered out of the cell. They continued to wrestle with invisible assailants as Laintal Ay drew the cover across the grille.

"The bone fever," he said. He stood close to Ma Scantiom, seeking out her expression in the thick shadow.

She merely nodded. He followed down the ramps behind her.

The clow was still wearily playing.

> Why do you hurry so?
> Pray this longing takes me to her
> Or else lets me go . . .

Ma Scantiom said over her shoulder, "The first of them arrived two days ago—I should have called you yesterday. They starve themselves; they can hardly be persuaded to take water. It's like a prolonged muscular spasm. Their minds are affected."

"They'll die?"

"Only about half survive attacks of bone fever. Sometimes, when they have lost a third of their body weight, they simply pull out of it. They then normalise at their new weight. Others go mad and die, as if the fever got in their harneys and killed them."

Laintal Ay swallowed, feeling his throat dry. Back in her office, he took a deep inhalation of a bunch of scantiom and raige on the window sill to cleanse the stench in his nostrils. The room was painted white.

"Who are they? Traders?"

"They have both come from the east, travelling with different groups of Madis. One's a trader, one's a bard. Both have phagor slaves, which are at present in the vet's surgery. You probably know that bone fever can spread fast and become a major plague. I want those patients out of my hospice. We need somewhere away from town where we can isolate them. These won't be the only cases."

"You've spoken to Faralin Ferd about it?"

She frowned. "Worse than useless. First of all, he and Tanth Ein said the sick must not be moved from here. Then they suggested killing them and dumping the bodies in the Voral."

"I'll see what I can do. I know a ruined tower about five miles away. Perhaps that would be suitable."

"I knew you'd help." She put a hand on his sleeve, smiling. "Something brings the disease. Under favourable conditions, it can spread like a fire. Half the population would die—we know of no cure. My belief is that those filthy phagors carry it. Perhaps it is the scent of their pelts. There are two hours of Freyr-dark tonight; in that time, I am going to have the two phagors in the vet's surgery killed and buried. I wanted to tell someone in authority, so I'm telling you. I knew you'd be on my side."

"You think they will spread bone fever further?"

"I don't know. I just don't wish to take any risks. There may be another cause entirely—the blindness may bring it. Wutra may send it."

She tucked her lower lip in. He read the concern in her homely face.

"Bury them deep where the dogs can't scratch them up again. I'll see about the ruined tower for you. Are you expecting"—he hesitated—"more cases soon?"

Without changing her expression, she said, "Of course."

As he left, the clow was still playing its plaintive tune, remote in the depths of the building.

Laintal Ay did not think of complaining to Ma Scantiom, although he had laid other plans for the two hours of Freyr-dark.

Dathka's speech of the morning, when Oyre had returned from her pauk-induced spell of father-communing, troubled him deeply. He saw the strength of the argument which said that he and Oyre together represented invincible claimants to the leadership of Oldorando. In general, he wanted what was rightfully his, as anyone else did. And he certainly wanted Oyre. But did he want to rule Oldorando?

It seemed that Dathka's speech had subtly changed the situation. Perhaps he could now win Oyre only by taking power.

This line of thought occupied his mind as he went about Ma Scantiom's business, which was everyone's business. Bone fever was no more than a legend, yet the fact that nobody had experienced the reality made the legend all the more dark. People died. Plague was like the manic stepping-up of a natural process.

So he worked without complaint, conscripting help from Goija Hin. Together, Laintal Ay and the slave driver collected the two phagors belonging to the bone fever victims and sent them into the isolation cell. There, the phagors were made to roll their sick masters into rush mats and carry them away from the hospice. The innocuous-looking mat rolls would cause no panic.

The small group moved with its burdens out of town towards the ruined tower Laintal Ay knew of. With them shuffled the ancient slave phagor, Myk, to take an occasional turn carrying the diseased men. This was designed to hasten the proceedings, but Myk had become so ancient that progress was slow.

Goija Hin, also bent with age, his hair growing so long and stiff over his shoulders that he resembled one of his miserable captives, lashed Myk savagely. Neither lash nor curses hastened the old burdened slave. He staggered onward without protest, though his calves above his fetters were raw from whipping.

"My trouble is, I neither want to wield the lash nor feel it," Laintal Ay told himself. Another layer of thought arose in his mind, like mist on a still morning. He reflected that he lacked certain qualities. There was little he wished for. He was content with the days as they fled.

I've been too content, I suppose. It was enough to know that Oyre loved me, and to lie in her arms. It was enough that once Aoz Roon was almost like a father to me. It was enough that the climate changed, enough that Wutra ordered his sentinels to keep their place in the sky.

Now Wutra has left his sentinels to stray. Aoz Roon has gone. And what was that cutting thing Oyre said earlier—that Dathka was mature, implying I was not? Oh, that silent friend of mine, is that maturity, to be a mass of cunning plots inside? Wasn't contentment maturity enough?

There was too much of his grandfather, Little Yuli, in him, too little of Yuli the Priest. And for the first time in a long while, he recalled his mild grandfather's enchantment with Loil Bry, and of how they had stayed together happily in the room with the porcelain window. It was another age. Everything had been simpler then. They had been so content then, with so little.

He was not content to die now. Not content to be killed by the lieutenants if they thought him involved with Dathka's plotting. And not content either to die of the bone fever, contracted from these two wretches they were carrying away from the city. It was still three miles to the old tower he had in mind.

He paused. The phagors and Goija Hin trudged on automatically with their vile burdens. Here he was again, once more meekly doing what was asked of him. There was no reason for it. His stupid habit of obedience had to be broken.

He shouted to the phagors. They halted. They stood where they were, without moving. Only the burdens on their shoulders creaked slightly.

The group was standing on a narrow track with thickets of dog-thrush on either side. A child had been eaten near here a few days earlier; evidence suggested a sabre-tongue had been the killer—the predators came in close to settlements now that wild hoxneys were scarce. So there were few people about.

Laintal Ay struck in among the bushes. He got the phagors to carry their sick masters into the thicket and set them down. The monsters did so carelessly, so that the men rolled on the ground, still in locked positions.

Their lips were blue, peeled back to reveal yellow teeth and gums. Their limbs were distorted, their bones creaked. They were in some way aware of their position, yet unable to cease a constant motor movement, making their eyeballs roll horribly in their stretched facial skin.

"You know what's the matter with these men?" Laintal Ay asked.

Goija Hin nodded his head and smiled evilly to demonstrate his mastery over human knowledge. "They're ill," he said.

Nor did Laintal Ay forget the fever he had once caught off a phagor.

"Kill the men. Make the phagors scrape out graves with their hands. As fast as you can."

"I understand." The slave master came heavily forward.

Laintal Ay stood with a branch pressing in his back, watching the fat old man do as he was bid, as Goija Hin had always done. At each step in the proceedings, Laintal Ay gave an order and it was executed. He felt himself fully implicated in everything and would not let himself look away. Goija Hin drew a short sword and stabbed it twice through the hearts of the sick men. The phagors scraped graves with their horny hands—two white phagors, and Myk, as obese as his master, prickled with the black hairs of age and working very slowly.

All the phagors had shackles on their legs. They rolled the corpses into their graves and kicked dirt over them, then stood without movement, as was their fashion, awaiting the next order. They were commanded to scrape three more graves under the bushes. This they did, working like mute animals. Goija Hin ran his sword between the ribs of the two strange phagors, afterwards smearing the yellow ichor on their coats as they lay face down, in order to clean his blade.

Myk was made to push them in their graves and cover them with dirt.

As he stood up, he faced Laintal Ay, sliding his pale milt up the slot of his right nostril.

"Not kill now Myk, master. Strike off my chains and allow me to go away to die."

"What, let you loose, you old scumble, after all these years?" Goija Hin said angrily, raising the sword.

Laintal Ay stopped him, staring at the ancient phagor. The creature had given him rides on his back when he was a boy. It touched him that Myk did not attempt to remind him of the fact. There was no feeble appeal to sentiment. Instead, he stood without movement, awaiting whatever would befall.

"How old are you, Myk?" Sentiment, he thought, my sentiment. You couldn't face giving the necessary order to kill, could you?

"I prisoner, don't count years." The s's were dragged like bees from his throat. "Once, we ancipitals ruled Embruddock, and you Sons of Freyr were our slaves. Ask Mother Shay Tal—she knew."

"She told me. And you killed us as we kill you."

The crimson eyes blinked once. The creature growled, "We kept you alive through the centuries when Freyr was sick. Much foolish. Now you Sons will all die. You strike away my chains, leave me go to die in tether."

Laintal Ay gestured to the open grave. "Kill him," he ordered Goija Hin.

Myk put up no struggle. Goija Hin kicked the huge body into the depression and piled dirt about it with his boot. Then he stood among the tanglewood, facing Laintal Ay, moistening his lips and looking uneasy.

"I knew you when you was a little boy, sir. I was good to you. Myself, I always said you should be Lord of Embruddock—you ask my mates if I didn't."

He made no attempt to defend himself with his sword. It fell from his hands and he went down on his knees, blubbering, bowing his hoary head.

"Myk's probably right," Laintal Ay said. "We've probably got the plague in us. We're probably too late." Without another glance, he left Goija Hin where he was and strode back to the crowded city, angry with himself for not striking the fatal blow.

It was late when he entered his room. He stared round it without relaxing his black expression. Horizontal rays of Freyrlight lit the far corner, flaring up brightly, casting the rest of the room into unlikely shade.

He rinsed his face and hands in the basin, scooping up the cool water, letting it run over his brow, his eyelids, his cheeks, and drip from his jaw. He did it repeatedly, breathing deeply, feeling the heat leave him and the self-anger remain. As he smoothed his face, he noted with satisfaction that his hands had ceased to tremble.

The light in the corner slid to one wall and faded to a smouldering yellow, making a square no bigger than a box in which the world's gold decayed. He went round the room, collecting a few items to take with him, scarcely giving a thought to the task.

There was a knock on the door. Oyre looked in. As if sensing immediately the tension in the room, she paused on the threshold.

"Laintal Ay—where have you been? I've been waiting for you."

"There was something I had to do."

She paused with her hand still on the latch, watching, breathing a sigh. With the light behind him, she could not decipher his expression through the thick dusk gathering in the room, but she caught the abruptness in his voice.

"Is anything the matter, Laintal Ay?"

He stuffed his old hunter's blanket into a pack, punching it down. "I'm leaving Oldorando."

"Leaving . . . ? Where are you going?"

"Oh . . . let's say I'm going to look for Aoz Roon." He spoke bitterly. "I've lost interest in—in everything here."

"Don't be silly." She moved a step forward as she spoke, to see him better, thinking how large he seemed in the low-ceilinged room. "How will you seek him in the wilderness?"

He turned to face her, slinging the pack over one shoulder. "Do you think it's sillier to seek him in the real world or to go down in pauk among the gossies to find him, as you do? You were always telling me I had to do something great. Nothing satisfied you. . . . Well, now I'm off, to do or die. Isn't that something great?"

She laughed feebly, and said, "I don't want you to go. I want—"

"I know what you want. You think Dathka is mature and I'm not. Well, to hell with that. I've had enough. I'm going, as I always longed to do. Try your luck with Dathka."

"I love you, Laintal Ay. Now you're acting like Aoz Roon."

He took hold of her. "Stop comparing me with other people. Perhaps you're not as clever as I thought, or you'd know when you were hurting me. I love you too, but I'm going. . . ."

She screamed. "Why are you so brutal?"

"I've lived with brutes long enough. Stop asking stupid questions."

He put his arms round her, dragging her close, and kissed her hard on the mouth, so that her lips were forced back and their teeth slid together.

"I hope to be back," he said. He laughed sharply at the stupidity of his own remark. With a final glance, he left, slamming the door behind him, leaving her in the empty room. The gold had died to ashes. It was almost dark, though she saw points of fire in the street outside.

"Oh scumb," she exclaimed. "Curse you—and curse me, too."

Then she recovered herself, ran to the door, and flung it open, shouting to him. Laintal Ay was running down the stairs and did not respond. She ran after him, clutching his sleeve.

"Laintal Ay, you idiot, where are you going?"

"I'm going to saddle up Gold."

He said it so angrily, wiping his mouth on the back of his hand, that she remained where she was. Then the thought occurred to her that she must get Dathka at once. Dathka would know how to deal with his friend's madness.

Just recently, Dathka had become elusive. Sometimes he slept in the unfinished building across the Voral, sometimes in one tower or another, sometimes in one of the doubtful new places springing up. All she could think of at this hour was to run to Shay Tal's tower to see if he was with Vry. Fortunately, he was. He and Vry were in the middle of a quarrel; her cheek burned and she cowered almost as if Dathka had struck her. Dathka looked pale with fury, but Oyre broke in on them and poured out her tale, oblivious to their troubles. Dathka gave a choking noise.

"We can't let him leave now, just when everything's falling apart." With one deadly glance at Vry, he ran from the room.

He ran all the way to the stables, and was in time to catch Laintal Ay walking out, leading Gold. They confronted each other.

"You're plain mad, friend—behave sensibly. No one wants you to go. Come to your senses and look after your own interests."

"I am sick of doing what everyone wants me to do. You want me here because you need me to play a role in your schemes."

"We need you to see that Tanth Ein and his mate, and that slimy toad Raynil Layan, don't take control of everything we've got." His expression was bitter.

"You don't stand a chance. I'm going to find Aoz Roon."

Dathka sneered. "You're mad. Nobody knows where he is."

"I believe he went with Shay Tal to Sibornal."

"You fool! Forget Aoz Roon—his star's set, he's old. Now it's us. You're getting out of Oldorando because you're afraid, aren't you? It so happens I still have a few friends who haven't betrayed me, including one at the hospice."

"What does that mean?"

"I know as much as you know. You're getting out because you're afraid of the plague."

Afterwards, Laintal Ay repeated obsessively the angry words they exchanged, realising that Dathka was not his ordinary rather emotionless self. At the time, he simply acted on reflex. He struck Dathka with all his might, bringing up his open right hand and dealing his friend an upward blow under the nose with the edge of his palm. He heard the bone go.

Dathka fell back immediately, clutching his face. Blood flowed, and dripped from his knuckles. Laintal Ay swung himself up into the saddle, spurred Gold, and edged through the gathering crowd. Chattering with excitement, the crowd swarmed round the injured man, who staggered about, cursing and bent double with pain.

His temper still raging within him, Laintal Ay rode out of town. He had brought few of the things he intended to bring. In his present mood, it felt good to be leaving with little but his sword and a blanket.

As he went, he felt in his pocket and brought out a small carved object. In the twilight, he could scarcely make out its shape—but it was familiar to him since boyhood. It was a dog which moved its jaw when its tail was worked up and down. He had had it since the day his grandfather died.

He pitched it into the nearest bush.

XIV

THROUGH THE EYE
OF A NEEDLE

Humankind feared the bite of the phagor, but the bite of a phagor tick was more to be dreaded.

The bite of a phagor tick causes a phagor no irritation, and scarcely more to a human. Its mouthparts have adapted over the millennia to piercing skin tissue with a minimum of damage, and to sucking up painlessly the fluid food its requires to further its own complex reproductive cycle.

The tick possesses elaborate genital organs and no head. Its mouthparts are divided into two pairs. One pair consists of modified pincers which penetrate and inject a cocktail of local anaesthetic and anticoagulant into the flesh, the other of sensory organs bearing a complex blade covered with teeth which, projecting backwards, anchor the tick comfortably into position on its host.

There the tick clings, resisting dislodgement, to drop off only when gorged—unless the questing beak of a cowbird discovers it and gobbles it down as a delicacy.

Multitudinous Embruddocks for the helico virus are provided in the cells of the tick. And there the virus tarries, inert, awaiting a certain harmonic which will draw it into the orchestra of life, although it is

313

sparked to quasi-activity if female phagor hosts are on oestrus. Only twice in the cycle of the great Helliconian year does that harmonic trigger the active phase of the virus.

A chain of events then operates that will eventually decide the fate of whole nations. Wutra, the philosophical might claim, is a helical virus.

Obedient to the external signal, the virus streams forth from the cells of the tick, down its mouthparts, and into the body of a human host, where it makes its way along the bloodstream. As if tracing its own air-octaves, the invading force moves through the body until it reaches its new host's brain stem and flows into the hypothalamus, causing severe inflammation of the brain, and frequently death.

Once in the hypothalamus, that ancient sector of awareness, the seat of rage and lust, the virus replicates itself with a reproductive fury which may be likened to a storm over the Nktryhk.

The invasion of the human cell represents an incursion of one genetic system into the precincts of another; the invaded cell capitulates and becomes virtually a new biological unit, complete with its own natural history, much as a city may change hands in a prolonged war, belonging first to one side, then to the other.

Invasion, furious replication: then the outward signs of those events. The victim manifests that manic stiffening and tightening in the sinews witnessed by Laintal Ay at the hospice—and many of his kind before him. On the whole, those who witnessed it left no record, for obvious reasons.

These facts had been established by patient observation and careful deduction. The scholarly families of the Avernus were trained in such matters, and supported by superb instrumentation. The disability of being unable to visit the planetary surface was thus to some extent overcome.

But their imprisonment on the Avernus had drawbacks other than the obvious psychological ones. Firsthand verification of hypotheses was not possible.

Their understanding of the incursions of the so-called bone fever had recently become confused by further knowledge. The situation was again open to debate. For the Pin family had pointed out that it was during the time of the twenty eclipses and the incursions of the virus when—in Oldorando at least—a major change of human diet took place. Rathel had gone out of fashion. The brassimip crop, full of vitamins, which had sustained the community throughout centuries of winter, had fallen from general favour. Was it, the Pins suggested, that this dietary change rendered the humans more susceptible to the bite of the tick, or to the tick's parasite, the virus? The matter was under discussion—often heated. Once more, there were hotheads who voted for an illegal expedition down to the Helliconian surface, despite the dangers.

Not all who contracted bone fever died. It was noticeable that those stricken fell in different ways. Some people were aware of the approach of illness, and had time to suffer apprehension or make their peace with Wutra, according to their disposition; others collapsed in the midst of an activity, unwarned—while talking to friends, when walking in the fields, even when lying in love's embrace. Neither gradual nor sudden succumbing was any warrant for survival. However they sickened, only half recovered. For the rest, it was a lucky corpse—like the patients from Ma Scantiom's hospice—which found a shallow grave; many in the general terror that assailed any stricken community, were left as carrion, while whole populations fled from their homes towards a pestilence that would embrace them on the road.

So it had been as long as there had been human beings on Helliconia. The survivors of the pandemic lost a third of their normal body weight —although "normal" was here a relative term. They never regained the lost weight, nor did their children, nor did their children's children. Spring had arrived at last, summer was ahead—when adaptation would lie in ectomorphism. The leaner shape persisted throughout many generations, though gradually with less marked effect as subcutaneous fat again built up, the disease remaining latent, carried in the nerve cells of the survivors.

This status quo continued until late summer of the Great Year. Then the Fat Death struck.

As if in compensation for such extreme seasonal dimorphic contrasts, the two sexes on Helliconia were similar in stature and in body and brain weight. Both sexes when adult weighed on average about twelve staynes, to use the old Oldorandan measure. If they lived through bone fever, they would emerge as a lanky eight staynes or less. The next generation adjusted to its new skeletal appearance. Succeeding generations then slowly increased average body weight—until the ravages of the more obscene Fat Death brought about another dramatic change.

Aoz Roon was one who survived the first onslaught of this cycle of the pandemic. After him, many hundreds of thousands were destined to suffer and die or pull through. Some, hidden in remote corners of the world wilderness, might entirely escape the plague. But their descendants would be disadvantaged in a new world, would be treated as freaks, would stand small chance of continuance. The two great diseases, to which the phagor tick played vector, were in reality one disease: and that one disease, that Shiva of diseases, that destroyer and saviour, carried on its bloodied sword survival for mankind in the extravagant conditions of the planet.

Twice in two and a half thousand Earth years, Helliconian humanity had to go through the eye of the needle plied by the phagor tick. It was the price of their survival, of their continued development. From the carnage, from the apparent disharmony, came an underlying harmony— as if, among the screams of agony, a reassurance rose from the deepest springs of being to murmur that all was ineffably well.

Only those who could believe would believe such reassurance.

When the sound of cracking muscle faded, in floated a strange watery music. A principle of fluidity established itself over the barrens of pain, manifest first of all to Aoz Roon's hearing. All that presented itself to his returning vision was a collection of rounded shapes, speckled, striated, or of dull uniform hue. They had no meaning, nor did he seek for meaning. He simply remained where he was, back arched, mouth open, waiting until his eyeballs ceased jerking and he could focus his sight.

The liquid harmonies helped his return to awareness. Although he was unable to coordinate his body, he became conscious that his arms were in some fashion imprisoned. Random thoughts visited him. He saw deer running, himself running, leaping, striking; a woman laughed, he was astride, sunlight crackled through head-high trees. His muscles gave sympathetic spasms, like those of an old dog dreaming by a camp-fire.

The rounded shapes resolved themselves into boulders. He was wedged among them, as if himself inorganic. A young tree, uprooted far up river and stripped of its bark, was inextricably mingled with boulders and grit; he lay against it, similarly entwined, hands lost somewhere far above his skull.

With painful care, he drew his limbs together. He sat up after a while, arms resting on knees, and looked long at a teeming river. Deep pleasure welled up in him as he listened to its sound. He crawled forward on hands and knees, feeling his skins flap loose about his body, to a strip of beach no wider than his hand. He gazed with vacant gratitude at the ceaseless flood. Night came. He lay with his face on pebbles.

Morning came. The light of two suns struck down upon him. He became warm. He stood up, steadying himself against an upthrust branch.

He turned his shaggy head, delighted by the ease with which the slight movement was accomplished. A few yards away, separated by narrow frothing water, the phagor stood watching him.

"Zo you come alive again," it said.

Back through years and cycles now remote in antiquity, it had been the custom in many parts of Helliconia, and in the continent of Campannlat in particular, to kill the king of any tribe who showed signs of age. Both criteria and mode of despatch had differed with different tribes. Though kings were regarded as set down on earth by Akha or Wutra, their lives were abruptly terminated. Once he showed grey hair, or became unable to sever a man's head from his body with one blow of an axe, or failed to satisfy the sexual desires of his wives, or could no longer jump a certain stream or chasm—or whatever the tribal criterion might be—then the king was strangled, handed a poison cup, or by other methods disposed of.

In the same way, members of tribes who exhibited symptoms of the killer diseases, who began to stretch and groan, were forthwith despatched. In earlier days, no mercy was known. Burning was often their fate, because of a belief in the healing power of flame, and with the sufferer to the pyre went his family and household. This savage propitiatory rite rarely served to ward off the onslaught of an epidemic, so that the screams of the burning often fell on ears that buzzed already with the first intimations of illness.

Through all adversity, the generations of humankind slowly grew more civilised. This was markedly so if we consider that the first token of civilisation—without which men cannot live together and desperate anarchy prevails—is sympathy for one's fellows, imaginative warmth for their failings. Now hospitals had come into existence, and doctors, nurses, and priests—all bent on alleviating suffering rather than terminating it brutally.

Aoz Roon had recovered without such aid. Perhaps his rugged constitution helped him. Ignoring the phagor, he staggered to the margin of the grey flood, bent slowly, and scooped water in his two hands to sip.

Some of the water, escaping between his fingers, ran from his lips to his beard where, caught by a breeze, it blew to one side, splashing back into the greater flood, to be reabsorbed. Those neglected drops were observed in their fall. Millions of eyes caught the tiny splash. Millions of eyes followed every gesture of Aoz Roon as he stood, panting with wet mouth, on his narrow island.

Ranked monitors on the Earth Observation Station kept many things under close surveillance, including the Lord of Embruddock. It was the duty of the Avernus to transmit all signals received from the Helliconian surface back to the Helliconian Institute.

The Helliconian Institute's receiver was situated on Pluto's moon, Charon, on the extreme margins of the solar system. Much of its financial support came from its Eductainment Channel, through which a continuous saga of Helliconian events was beamed to audiences on Earth and the other solar planets. Vast auditoria stood like conch shells upended in sand in every province; each was capable of housing ten thousands of people. Their peaked domes aspired towards the skies from which the Eductainment Channel was beamed.

On occasions, these auditoria remained almost deserted for years at a time. Then, responding to some new development on the distant planet, audiences would again increase. People came like pilgrims. Helliconia was Earth's last great art form. Nobody on Earth, from its rulers to its sweepers, was unfamiliar with aspects of Helliconian life. The names of Aoz Roon, Shay Tal, Vry, and Laintal Ay were on everyone's lips. Since terrestrial gods died, new figures had arrived to take their place.

Audiences received Aoz Roon as a contemporary, removed only to another sphere, like a platonic ideal casting its shadow on the vast cave of the auditorium. Those audiences were again filling the auditoria to capacity. They entered on sandalled feet. Rumours of the forthcoming plague, of the eclipse, spread round Earth almost as they spread round Oldorando, drawing in thousands whose lives were transformed by their wonder and concern for Helliconia.

A few of those pilgrims who watched reflected on the paradox imposed on them by the size of the universe. The eight learned families on the Avernus lived at the same time as the Helliconians. Their lives were contemporaneous in every sense, though the helico virus decreed that they were sundered indefinitely from the Earth-like world they studied.

Yet how much more sundered were the eight families from that distant world they regarded as their native planet! They transmitted signals back to an Earth where not one single auditorium had been constructed, where even the planners of the auditoria were as yet unborn. The signals took a thousand years to cross the compartments of space between the two systems. In that millennium it was not Helliconia alone which changed.

And those who now sat wordless in the auditoria saw the immense figure of Aoz Roon on the holoscreens, saw him sip water which blew from his lips to merge with the flood below, as it was a thousand years ago, a thousand light-years away.

The imprisoned light they watched, even the life they lived, was a technological miracle, a physical construct. And only a metaphysician with omnipresent understanding could say which lived at the moment the drips returned to the river: Aoz Roon or his audiences. Yet it required no great sophistry to deduce that, despite ambiguities imposed by limitations of vision, macrocosm and microcosm were interdependent, laced together by such phenomena as the helico virus, whose effects were ultimately universal, though perceptible only to the phenomenon of consciousness, the eye of the needle through which the macrocosm and microcosm became actual unity. Understanding on a divine scale

might resolve the compartments between the infinite orders of being;
it was human understanding which brought past and present into their
cheek-by-jowl merging.

Imagination functioned; the virus was merely a function.

The two yelk trotted at a brisk rate, necks held horizontally. Their
nostrils dilated, for they had been trotting for some while. Sweat shone
on their flanks.

Their two riders wore high turn-down boots and long cloaks made of
a grey cloth. Their faces were keen and grey, tufted with small beards
on their chins. Nobody would have mistaken them for anything but
Sibornalans.

The pebbly path they rode was shadowed by a shoulder of mountain.
The regular *plud-plud-plud* of the yelk's hoofs carried out over an expanse of wilderness threaded with trees and rivers.

The men were scouts belonging to the forces of the warrior-priest,
Festibariyatid. They enjoyed their ride, breathing the fresh air, rarely
exchanging words, and always keeping a sharp eye for enemies.

Behind them down the trail other Sibornalans followed on foot,
leading a group of captured protognostics.

The trail wound down to a river, beyond which the land rose in a
rocky promontory. Its sloping cliffs were formed of broken rock strata,
displaced almost vertically and studded with stubby trees. Here was the
settlement ruled over by Festibariyatid.

The scouts forded the river at a shallow place. Assaying the cliffs, the
yelk picked their way cautiously between the strata; they were northern
plains animals, and not entirely happy in mountainous ground. They,
and others like them, had been brought south with the annual incursion
of colonists from the northern continent into Chalce and the regions
bordering on Pannoval; hence the presence of yelk so far south.

The rear guard appeared along the trail. Its four members were armed
with spears and escorted in their midst some luckless protognostics captured during their patrol. Among the captives, Cathkaarnit-he and
Cathkaarnit-she plodded along, still scratching themselves despite weeks
as prisoners on the move.

Encouraged by spear point, they waded across the shallow river and
were forced to make their way up the cliff path, to the confines of which
a scent of yelk still clung, past a sentry, and so to a settlement called
New Ashkitosh.

To this ford, and to this perilous point, many weeks later, came
Laintal Ay. He was a Laintal Ay that few even of his close friends would
have recognised without hesitation. He had lost a third of his body
weight, and was lean, skeletal even, with paler skin, with a different
expression to his eyes. In particular—the finest of disguises because trans-

parent—he moved his body in a new way. He had suffered and survived bone fever.

On leaving Oldorando, he had struck out to the northeast, across what was later known as Roon's Moor, in the direction that Shay Tal and her cortege had taken. He wandered and lost the trail. The country he had known in his extreme youth, when it was covered in white and showed an open face to the skies, had disappeared under a tangle of green.

What had been a solitude was now populated with danger. He was aware of restless movement, not only of harried animals, but of human, semihuman, and ancipital beings, all stirred up by the tide of the seasons. Hostile young faces peered through the bush at every turn. Every shrub had ears as well as leaves.

Gold was nervous in forest. Hoxneys were creatures of the wide open spaces. She grew more and more stubborn, until Laintal Ay dismounted, grumbling, and led the animal.

He found himself at last by a stone tower, to which he had climbed through a seemingly endless forest of birch and fern. He tied Gold to a tree before reconnoitering. All was quiet. He entered the hollow tower, where he rested, feeling ill. When he climbed to the top, he recognised his surroundings; the tower was one he had visited in his carefree wanderings, looking out to bare horizons.

Full of vexation and fatigue, he left the tower. He sank down wearily, stretched, and found himself unable to bring his arms down. Cramps racked him, a fever took him like a blow, and he arched over backwards in delirium, as if he planned to break his spine.

Small dark men and women emerged from hiding and regarded him, creeping stealthily nearer. They were protognostics of the Nondad tribe, hairy creatures who stood no higher than Laintal Ay's waist. Their hands were eight-fingered, but concealed largely by the thick sandy hair that grew like cuffs from their wrists. Their faces resembled asokins, protruding muzzles giving them the same rather wistful appearance as the Madis.

Their language was a mingling of snorts, whistles, and clicks, in no way resembling Olonets, although a few transfusions from the old language had taken place. They consulted themselves, and finally decided to bear the Freyrian away, since his personal octave was good.

A line of proud rajabarals grew on the ridge behind the tower, their boles concealed by the stands of birch. At the base of one such tree, the Nondads entered their earth, dragging Laintal Ay with them, snorting and chuckling at their own difficulty. Gold snorted and plunged at the rein to no avail—her master disappeared.

Among the roots of the great tree, the Nondads had their safe home. This was the Eighty Darknesses. They slept on beds of bracken, to ward off the rodents who shared the earth with them.

Their activities were dictated by custom. It was a custom to select kings and warriors at birth, to rule over and protect them. These rulers were trained to fierceness, and savage battles to the death took place among the Eighty Darknesses. But the kings served as surrogates for the rest of the tribe, acting out their innate violence, so the rank and file of the Eighty Darknesses were meek and loving, clinging close to each other without much sense of personal identity. Their impulse was always to husband life; Laintal Ay's life was husbanded, although they would have devoured him down to the last phalange had he died. That was custom.

One of the females became snoktruix to Laintal Ay, lying against him, caressing and stroking him, sucking his fevers. His deliriums became choked with animals, small as mice, large as mountains. When he woke into the dark, it was to find he had an alien companion close as life, who would do anything to save him and make him whole. Feeling himself to be a gossie, he yielded ardently to this new mode of being, in which heaven and hell delivered themselves in the same embrace.

As far as he could ever understand the word, snoktruix meant a kind of healer: also stealer, dealer, and, above all, feeler.

He lay in the dark in convulsion, limbs contorted, sweating away his substance. The virus raged uncontrollably, forcing him through the terrible eye of Shiva's needle. He became a landscape of sinew, over which the armies of pain battled. Yet the mysterious snoktruix was there, giving of her presence; he was not entirely in isolation. Her gift was healing.

In time, the armies of pain retreated. The voices in the Eighty Darknesses gradually made themselves intelligible, and he began dimly to comprehend what had happened to him. The extraordinary language of the Nondads had no words for food, drink, love, hunger, cold, warmth, hate, hope, despair, hurt, though it seemed that the kings and warriors, battling in the far dark, did. Instead, the rest of the tribe devoted their spare hours, which were many, in prolonged discussion concerning the Ultimates. The necessities of life remained wordless, because contemptible. It was the Ultimates that mattered.

Laintal Ay, amid the suffocations of his succubus, never mastered the language enough to comprehend the Ultimates. But it appeared that the main thrust of the debate—which also was a custom, carried through many generations—was to decide whether all should merge their identity into a state of being within the great god of darkness, Withram, or whether they should cultivate a different state.

Long was the discourse about that different state, unbroken even when the Nondads ate. That they were eating Gold never occurred to Laintal Ay. His appetite had gone. Meditations concerning the different state flowed through him like water.

That different state was somehow equated with a great many things, some extremely uncomfortable, including light and battle; it was the state thrust upon the kings and warriors, and might be roughly translated as individuality. Individuality opposed Withram's will. But in some way, or so the argument seemed to go, as entangled as the roots among which it was unravelled, opposing Withram's will was also following it.

Everything was very confusing, especially when in one's arms lay a small hairy snoktruix.

She was not the first to die. They all died quietly, crawling off among the Eighty Darknesses. At first, he was aware only that fewer voices joined in the harmonics of argument. Then the snoktruix also became rigid. He clutched her tight, in an anguish of which he had not known himself capable. But the Nondads had no resistance to the disease Laintal Ay had brought down into their earth; disease and recovery was not a custom.

Within a short while, she too was dead. Laintal Ay sat and wept. He had never seen her face, though its little meagre contours, behind which such richness seemed to dwell, were familiar to his fingertips.

The discussion of Ultimates came to an end. The last click, snort, whistle, faded into the Eighty Darknesses. Nothing had been decided. Even death, after all, had shown some indecision on the subject; it had been both individual and corporate. Withram alone could say if he was pleased and, in the manner of gods, Withram maintained silence on the subject.

Overwhelmed by shock, Laintal Ay fought to bring together his scattered wits. On hands and knees, he crawled over the corpses of his rescuers, looking for escape. The full, terrible majesty of the Eighty Darknesses was upon him.

He said to himself, endeavouring to maintain the argument, "I have individuality, whatever problems my dear friends the Nondads had. I know I am myself, I cannot escape being myself. I must therefore be at peace with myself. I do not have to undergo that perennial debate they underwent. That's all settled in my case. Whatever happens to me, I know that at least. I am my own man; whether I live or die, I can conduct myself accordingly. It's vain to seek Aoz Roon. He is not my master; I am. Nor has Oyre so much power over me that I must become an exile. Obligations are not slaveries. . . ."

And similarly, on and on, until the words bore little meaning even to himself. The maze among the roots yielded no exit. Many times, when a narrow tunnel took an upward curve, he would crawl forward hopefully—only to come against a blind end in which a corpse lay curled, with rodents conducting their own kind of debate over the entrails.

Passing through a widening chamber, he stumbled over a king. In the darkness, size had less meaning than in the light. The king felt enormous as he landed claws first, roaring. Laintal Ay rolled over, kicking, yelling, struggling to get out his dagger, and the terrible shapeless thing bit and slashed its way towards his throat. He heaved himself over, trying to flatten it, without effect. An elbow in its eye made the assailant momentarily less enthusiastic. Out came the dagger, to be kicked away as the scrimmage was renewed. His searching fingers found a root. Dragging himself closer to it, he pinned one of the king's arms round the root and battered at the sharp-fanged head. Then the raging thing was loose again, flinging itself down on Laintal Ay with unabated fury. The two figures, made one figure in hatred, knocked down on themselves earth, filth, and scuttling things.

Limp after the ravages of bone fever and his long fast, Laintal Ay felt his will to fight weakening. Claws raked his side. Suddenly, something slammed into their joined bodies. Savage roars and clicks filled the air. So total was his confusion that he took a moment to realise there was a third assailant in the dark—one of the Nondad warriors. The warrior was concentrating most of its venom on the king. It was like being caught between two porcupines.

Rolling and kicking, Laintal Ay fought himself loose from the fray, grasped his dagger, and managed to drag himself bleeding into an obscure corner. Drawing his legs up so that his shins protected his body and face from frontal attack, he found a narrow entryway above his head. Cautiously he pushed his way up into a tunnel scarcely wider than his body. Before the fever struck he would never have squeezed himself through; now, with pythonlike contortions, he managed it, eventually dropping into a small round chamber in the earth. He felt dead leaves under his hands. He lay there, gasping, listening with fear to the sounds of combat nearby.

"Light, by the sentinels!" he gasped. A faint greyness like mist pervaded the nook. He had struggled to the edge of the Eighty Darknesses.

Fear drove him to follow the light. He wormed his way out of the earth, and stood trembling beside the bare concave flank of a rajabaral. The light was a cascade, pouring from the tall lake of the sky.

For a long while he remained breathing deep, wiping blood and earth from his face. He looked down at his feet. A savage ferret face stared up at him, then disappeared. He had quit the realm of the Nondads, and his visitation had left most of them dead.

His mind dwelt poignantly on his snoktruix. Sorrow filled him, and amazement and gratitude.

One of the sentinels was overhead. Near the horizon was the other, Batalix, its rays striking almost horizontally through the great silent forest, creating a sinister beauty of its ocean of leaf.

His skins were in tatters. His flesh was incised by long weals, seeping blood, where the claws of the king had raked him.

Although he looked about and called once for Gold, it was without hope. He did not expect to see his hoxney again. His hunterly instincts warned him against staying where he was; he would become prey to something unless he moved, and he felt too faint to fight another battle.

He listened to the rajabaral. Something inside it rumbled. The Nondads had set great store by the trees under whose roots they lived; Withram was said to live at the top of the rajabaral drum, and occasionally to burst out in fury upon a world that was so unjust to protognostics. What would Withram do, he wondered, when all the Nondads died? Even Withram would be forced to a new individuality.

"Wake up," he said, realising how his mind wandered. He saw no sign of the ruinous tower by which he might have oriented himself. Instead, putting Batalix at his back, he began to move among the speckled trunks of the forest. Body and limbs felt pleasantly insubstantial.

Days passed. He hid from groups of phagors and other foes. He felt no hunger; the disease had left him without appetite and with an unclouded brain. He found his mind filling with things that Vry had said to him, and Shay Tal and his mother and grandmother; how much was owed to women—and to the snoktruix . . . things relating to the world as a place to be understood as one world of many, a place in which it was his extraordinary good fortune to be, with the unexpected happening every day, and the breath filling his lungs like a tide. He knew in his bones he was blessed. Worlds inexhaustible lay hived one within the other.

So, lightly stepping, he came to the ford before the Sibornalan settlement known as New Ashkitosh.

New Ashkitosh was in a constant state of excitement. The colonists liked it that way.

The settlement covered a large area. It was circular, as far as the terrain allowed. Huts and fences were built along the perimeter, interspersed with watchtowers, with farm land inside, divided by paths which radiated from the centre like the spokes of a wheel. In the centre was a cluster of buildings and stores, together with the pens in which captives were contained. All of these were arranged round the centremost hub of the settlement, which consisted of a circular church, the Church of Formidable Peace.

Men and women came and went in a businesslike way. No loitering was allowed. There were enemies—Sibornal always had enemies—enemies within and without.

The outside enemy was anyone or anything not of Sibornal. Not that the Sibornalans were hostile; but their religion taught them to be cautious. And in particular to be cautious of anyone from Pannoval, or of the phagorian kind.

Beyond the settlement, scouts ranged, mounted on yelk. They brought news hourly of the progress towards the settlement of scattered bodies of phagors, followed by a veritable army of the ancipitals, descending from the mountains.

The news caused controlled alarm. Everyone was alert. There was no panic. Although the Sibornalan colonists were hostile to the two-horned invaders, and vice versa, they had developed an uneasy alliance which kept conflict to a minimum. Unlike the people of Embruddock, no Sibornalan ever willingly fought a phagor.

Instead, they traded. The colonists were conscious of their vulnerable position, conscious that no retreat to Sibornal was possible—not that they would be at all welcome if they returned, being rebellious and heretical. What they traded was lives, human or semihuman.

The colonists existed on the edge of starvation, even in good times. This colony was vegetarian; every man was a skilled farmer. Their crops thrived. Yet the bulk of their crop went to feeding the mounts they rode. An enormous number of yelk, hoxney, horses, and kaidaws (the latter goodwill gifts from phagors) had to be kept fed in order for the community to survive at all.

For scouts were always patrolling neighbouring territory, keeping the settlement informed of what was happening elsewhere, and capturing anything that came within their sweep. The central pens were well stocked with a transient population of prisoners.

The prisoners were handed over to phagors as tribute. In exchange, the phagors left the settlement alone. Why not? The warrior-priest Festibariyatid had cunningly founded the settlement on a false octave; no phagor was motivated to invade it.

But there remained the enemy inside the camp. Two protognostics giving their names as Cathkaarnit-he and Cathkaarnit-she had fallen ill on arrival and soon died. The pen master had called a doctor-priest, who had identified bone fever. The fever was spreading, week by week. This morning, a scout was found in the bunkhouse, limbs locked tight, eyeballs rolling, sweat pouring from his flesh.

Inconveniently, the disaster happened at a time when the colonists were trying to build up stocks of captives to present to the approaching phagor crusade. Already, they had informed themselves of the name of the ancipital warrior-priest, who was none less than Kzahhn Hrr-Brahl Yprt. A large number of deaths would spoil the tribute. By order of the High Festibariyatid, extra prayers were sung at each declension.

Laintal Ay heard the prayers as he walked into the settlement and was pleased by the sound. He looked with interest at all about him, ignoring the two armed sentries who escorted him to a central guard-house, outside which prisoners were raking dung into piles.

The guard captain was puzzled by a human who was not from Sibornal and yet walked voluntarily into the camp. After talking to Laintal Ay for a while and trying some bullying, he sent a subordinate to fetch a priest-militant.

By this time, Laintal Ay was having to accustom himself to the fact that anyone who had not suffered the plague looked, to his new eyes, uncomfortably fat. The priest-militant looked uncomfortably fat. He confronted Laintal Ay challengingly, and asked what he thought were shrewd questions.

"I met with some difficulties," Laintal Ay said. "I came here hoping to find refuge. I need clothes. The woods are too populated for my liking. I want a mount of some kind, preferably a hoxney, and am prepared to work for it. Then I'm off home."

"What kind of human are you? Are you from far Hespagorat? Why are you so thin?"

"I have come through the bone fever."

The priest-militant fingered his lip. "Are you a fighter?"

"I recently killed off a whole tribe of Others, the Nondads. . . ."

"So you're not afraid of protognostics?"

"Not at all."

He was given the task of guarding the pens and feeding their miserable inmates. In exchange, he was presented with grey wool clothing. The thinking of the priest-militant was simple. One who had suffered from the fever could look after the prisoners without inconveniently dying or passing on the pandemic.

Yet more of the colonists and the prisoners went down with the scourge. Laintal Ay noticed that the prayers in the Church of Formidable Peace became more fervent. At the same time, people kept more closely to themselves. He went where he would and nobody stopped him. He felt that he somehow lived a charmed life. Each day was a gift.

The scouts kept their mounts in a railed compound. He was in charge of a bunch of prisoners whose job it was to carry in hay and fodder to the animals. Here was where the big fodder problem of the settlement lay. An acre of green grass could feed ten animals for a day. The settlement had fifty mounts, used for scouring an increasingly large area; they consumed an equivalent of 24,000 acres per year, or rather less, since some feeding was done beyond the perimeter. This grave problem meant that the Church of Formidable Peace was generally full of half-starved farmers—a rare phenomenon, even on Helliconia.

Laintal Ay refused to shout at the prisoners; they worked well enough, considering their miserable circumstances. The guards stayed at a distance. A light rain made them keep their heads down. Only Laintal Ay took notice of the mounts as they crowded round, thrusting forward their soft muzzles, breathing gently in expectation of a treat. The time was coming when he would select a mount and escape; in a day or two more, the guard would be disorganised enough for his purposes, judging by the way things were going.

He looked a second time at one of the hoxney mares. Seizing up a handful of cake, he approached her. The animal's stripes ran orangey-yellow from head to tail, with a dark powdery blue between.

"Loyalty!"

The mare came over to him, taking the cake and then plunging her nose under his arm. He clung to her ears and petted them.

"Where's Shay Tal, then?" he asked.

But the answer was obvious. The Sibornalans had caught her and traded her to the phagors. She would never get to Sibornal now. By this time, Shay Tal was a gossie. She and her little party, one with time.

The name of the guard captain was Skitosherill. A wary friendship developed between him and Laintal Ay. Laintal Ay could see that Skitosherill was frightened; he touched nobody, and wore a posy of raige and scantiom at his lapel, to which his long nose frequently resorted, hoping to protect its owner from the plague.

"Do you Oldorandans worship a god?" he asked.

"No. We can look after ourselves. We speak well of Wutra, that's true, but we kicked all his priests out of Embruddock several generations ago. You should do the same in New Ashkitosh—you'd have an easier life."

"Barbarian behaviour! That's why you caught the plague, vexing God."

"Nine prisoners died yesterday, and six of your people. You pray too much, and it does no good."

Skitosherill looked angry. They stood in the open, a breeze rippling their cloaks. The music of prayer drifted over to them from the church.

"Don't you admire our church? We're only a simple farming community, yet we have a fine church. There's nothing like it in Oldorando, I'll gamble."

"It's a prison."

But as he spoke, he heard a solemn melody coming from the church which addressed him with mystery. The instruments were joined by voices, uplifted.

"Don't say that—I could have you beaten. Life's in the Church. The circular Great Wheel of Kharnabhar, the holy centre of our faith. If it was not for the Great Wheel, we'd still be in the grip of snow and ice." He made a circle on his forehead with his index finger as he spoke.

"How's that?"

"It's the Wheel that moves us closer to Freyr all the time. Didn't you know that? I was taken to visit it on pilgrimage as a child, into the Shivenink Mountains. You are not a true Sibornalan unless you've made the pilgrimage."

The following day brought another seven deaths. Skitosherill was in charge of the burial party, which consisted of Madi prisoners, scarcely competent enough to dig graves.

Laintal Ay said, "I had a dear friend who was captured by your people. She wished to make a pilgrimage to Sibornal, to consult the priests of that Great Wheel of yours. She thought they might be the source of all wisdom. Instead, your people made her prisoner and sold her to the stinking phagor. Is that how you treat people?"

Skitosherill shrugged. "Don't blame me. She was probably mistaken for a Pannoval spy."

"How could she be mistaken? She rode a hoxney, as did members of her party. Have the people of Pannoval hoxneys? I never heard so. She was a splendid woman, and you brigands handed her over to the fuggies."

"We're not brigands. We just wish to settle here in peace, moving on when the ground's used up."

"You mean, when you've used up the local population. Fancy trading women in exchange for your safety."

Grinning uneasily, the Sibornalan said, "You barbarians of Campannlat, you don't value your women."

"We value them highly."

"Do they rule?"

"Women don't rule."

"They do in some countries of Sibornal. In this settlement, see how well we take care of our women. We have women priests."

"I haven't seen one."

"That's because we take care of them." He leant forward. "Listen, Laintal Ay, I understand you are not a bad fellow, all things considered. I'm going to trust you. I know the state of affairs here. I know how many scouts have gone out and not returned. They've died of the plague in some miserable thicket and had no burial, their corpses probably devoured by birds or Others. It's going to become worse, while we sit here. I am a religious man, and I believe in prayer; but the bone fever is so strong that even prayer cannot prevail against it. I have a wife I love dearly. I wish to strike a bargain with you."

As Skitosherill spoke, Laintal Ay stood on a low eminence, looking down a miserable bit of ground which sloped towards a stream; stunted thorn trees grew along the watercourse. Among the stones littering the slope, the prisoners were slinging back earth, while seven cadavers —the Sibornalan corpses wrapped in sheets—lay in the open awaiting burial. He thought to himself, I can understand why this overweight lump wishes to escape, but what is he to me? He's no more than Shay Tal, Amin Lim, and the others were to him.

"What's your bargain?"

"Four yelk, well fed. Me, my wife, her maidservant, you. We leave together—they'll let me through the lines without difficulty. We ride back with you to Oldorando. You know the way, I protect you, see to it that you have a good steed. Otherwise you'll never be allowed to get away from here—you're too valuable—particularly when matters get worse. Do you agree?"

"When do you plan to leave?"

Skitosherill buried his nose in the posy and looked up searchingly at Laintal Ay. "You say a word of this to anyone and I'll kill you. Listen, the crusade of the phagor kzahhn, Hrr-Brahl Yprt, is due to start passing here before Freyr-set, according to our scouts. We four will follow on afterwards—the phagors will not attack us if we are in their rear. The crusade can go where it will; we shall progress to Oldorando."

"Are you planning to live in such a barbarian place?" Laintal Ay asked.

"We shall have to see how barbarian it is before I answer that. Don't try to be sarcastic to your superiors. Do you agree?"

"I'll have a hoxney rather than a yelk, and choose it myself. I've never ridden a yelk. And I want a sword, white metal, not bronze."

"Very well. You agree, then?"

"Do we shake hands on it?"

"I do not touch other hands. Verbal agreement is enough. Good. I'm a godfearing man, I'll not betray you; see you don't betray me. Get these corpses buried while I go to prepare my wife for the journey."

As soon as the tall Sibornalan had gone, Laintal Ay called the captives to halt their activity.

"I'm not your master. I'm a prisoner as much as you. I hate Sibornalans. Throw those corpses in the water and cover them with stones—it'll save you labour. Wash your hands afterwards."

They gave him suspicious looks instead of thanks, he in his grey woollen garments, tall, standing above them on the bank, he who talked with the Sibornalan guard on equal terms. He felt their hatred and was unmoved by it. Life was cheap if Shay Tal's life was cheap. As they scrambled among the corpses, they brushed the sheet from one of them, so that he glimpsed an ashen face underneath, frozen in its anguish. Then they had the body by feet and shoulders and tossed it down to the stream, where dashing water seized ravenously on the covering, moulding it round the body, which it began to roll unceremoniously downstream.

The watercourse marked the perimeter of New Ashkitosh; on its other bank, beyond a flimsy rail, no-man's land began.

When their task was over, the Madis considered the prospect of escape by fording the stream and running away. Some advocated this course of action, standing on the edge of the water and beckoning their fellows. The more timid hung back, gesticulating towards unknown dangers. All kept glancing anxiously at Laintal Ay, who stood where he was, arms folded. They were unable to make up their minds whether to act individually or corporately, with the result that they did nothing but argue, starting up the bank or down into the stream, but ever returning to a common centre of indecision.

There was reason for their hesitation. The no-man's land on the far side of the river was filling with figures that moved westward. Birds made uneasy by constant disturbance flew up before them, wheeling in the sky and then attempting to realight.

The land rose to a low horizon in the middle distance, where it dropped sharply to reveal a line of drums, the crowns of ancient rajabarals which emitted steam. Beyond their vapour, the landscape continued on a grander scale, revealing hills, stacked distant and serene in misty light. Stone megaliths stood here and there, curiously incised, marking land- and air-octave lines.

The fugitives heading westward turned their faces away from New Ashkitosh, as if fearing its reputation. They were sometimes solitary but more often in groups, frequently large groups. Some drove animals before them, or had phagors with them. Sometimes the phagors were in control.

Progress was not always continuous. One large group stopped on a slope some distance from where Laintal Ay stood. His keen eyes made out the signs of lamentation, with figures alternately bowing down or stretching upward in sorrow. Other groups arrived or passed; people ran from group to group. The plague travelled among them.

He found himself searching the more distant landscape for sight of that from which the refugees fled. He fancied he saw a snow-covered peak between the fold of two hills. The quality of light on it constantly changed, as if shadowy beings sported on its upper slopes. Superstitious fears filled his mind, clearing only when he realised that he was seeing not a mountain, but something closer and entirely less permanent: a flight of cowbirds, converging as they streamed through a pass.

Then at last he broke his reverie. Turning away from the protognostics, who still quarrelled in their ditch, he made his way back to the guard buildings.

It was clear to him that these refugees, many already infected by the plague, would descend on Oldorando. He must return as soon as possible, to warn Dathka and the lieutenants; otherwise, Oldorando would sink under a tide of diseased humanity and inhumanity. Anxiety for Oyre tugged at him. He thought of her too little since the days of his snoktruix.

The suns shed warmth on his back. He felt isolated, but there was no remedy for that at present.

He kicked his heels at the guardhouse, listening for music from the church, but only silence came from that direction. Being uncertain whereabouts on the wide perimeter Skitosherill and his wife lived, he could only wait for the couple to appear. Waiting increased his foreboding.

Three scouts entered the settlement on foot, bringing with them a pair of captives, one of whom collapsed immediately, to lie in a heap by the guardhouse. The scouts were sick and exhausted. They staggered into the guardhouse without a glance at Laintal Ay. The latter looked indifferently at the prisoner who remained on his feet; prisoners were no concern of his anymore. Then he looked again.

The prisoner stood with his feet apart in a defiant attitude, although his head hung as if he were tired. He was of a good height. His thin stature indicated that he also had survived bone fever. He wore clumsy black furs which were draped loosely about his body.

Laintal Ay put his head round the guardroom door, where the newly-arrived scouts were leaning on a table drinking root beer.

"I'm taking the prisoner outside to work—he's needed immediately."

He retreated before they could answer.

With a curt order to the man, Laintal Ay directed him to the Church of the Formidable Peace. Priests were inside at a central altar, but Laintal Ay led the captive to a seat against the wall where the light was dim. The man sank down thankfully, subsiding like a bag of bones.

It was Aoz Roon. His face was gaunt and lined, the flesh of his neck hung like a wattle; his beard had turned almost entirely grey; but, from the knit of his brows and the set of his mouth, there was no mistaking the Lord of Embruddock. At first, he would not recognise the thin man in Sibornalan cloth as Laintal Ay. When recognition came, he gave a sob and clutched him close, his body shaking.

After a while, he was able to explain to Laintal Ay what had happened to him, and how he had come to be stranded on a small island in the middle of a flood. As he recovered from his fever, he realised that the phagor stranded with him was starving to death. The phagor was not a warrior but a humble fungusmonger, by name Yhamm-Whrrmar, terrified of water and consequently unable or unwilling to eat fish. In the anorexia that seized those who recovered from the fever, Aoz Roon himself needed almost nothing to eat. The two of them had talked across the intervening water, and eventually Aoz Roon had crossed to the larger of the two islands, to strike up an alliance with his erstwhile enemy.

From time to time, they saw humans and phagors on the banks and shouted to them, but no one would cross the rapid-gliding water to aid them. Together, they tried to build a boat, which took many vexatious weeks.

Their first attempts were useless. By intertwining twigs and lining them with dried mud, they finally constructed a vessel that would float. Yhamm-Whrrmar was persuaded to climb into it, but leaped out again in fear. After much argument, Aoz Roon pushed off on his own. In the middle of the river, the mud all dissolved and the coracle sank. Aoz Roon managed to swim to a bank some way downriver.

It was his intention to find a rope and return to rescue Yhamm-Whrrmar, but such things as he met were either hostile or fled from him. After many wanderings, he had been captured by the Sibornalan scouts, and dragged to New Ashkitosh.

"We'll go back to Embruddock together," Laintal Ay said. "Oyre will be so delighted." Aoz Roon made no response at first.

"I can't return. . . . I can't . . . I can't desert Yhamm-Whrrmar. . . . You can't understand." He rubbed his hands on his knees.

"You're Lord of Embruddock still."

He hung his head, sighing. He had been defeated, had failed. All he wished for was a peaceful refuge. Again the uncertain movement of hands on knees, on shabby bearskin.

"There are no peaceful refuges," Laintal Ay said. "Everything's changing. We'll go back to Embruddock together. As soon as we can."

Since Aoz Roon's will had deserted him, he must make his decisions for him. He could obtain a suit of the Sibornalan cloth from the guard-room; so disguised Aoz Roon could join Skitosherill's party. He left Aoz Roon with disappointment. This was not what he had expected.

Outside the church, another surprise awaited him. Beyond the wooden buildings that circled the church the members of the colony were gathering. They faced outwards silently, looking across the settlement towards open country, anonymous in their drab greys.

The crusade of the young phagor kzahhn was about to pass.

The flight from the advance of the crusade still continued. An occasional stag plunged along amid the humans and protognostics and Others. Sometimes, the fugitives walked beside groups of the phagors who formed part of the van of Hrr-Brahl Yprt's army. There was a certain blindness about the procession, about its seeming blunders. It was impressive for its numbers rather than its discipline.

Seemingly at random, in fact under control of air-octaves, groups of phagors studded uncounted acres of wild territory. Everywhere, they progressed at their slow remorseless pace with their slow unnatural stride. No haste glowed in their pale harneys.

The way through mountain and valley from the almost stratospheric heights of the Nktryhk down to the plains of Oldorando was three and a half thousand miles. Like any human army travelling mainly on foot over rough terrain, the crusaders seldom averaged better than eleven miles a day.

They rarely marched more than one day in twenty. Most of the time was taken with the customary diversions of large armies: foraging off the land and resting up.

In order to acquire supplies, they had laid siege to several gaunt mountain towns near their path, allying themselves to rocks and crags while waiting for the sons of Freyr inside the town to open their gates and throw down their arms. They had pursued nomadic people, on the threshold of humanity, still ignorant of the power of the seed, and therefore condemned to a life of wandering, tracking them up perilous paths to acquire a few head of scraggy arang for the mess pot. They had been detained at the start by snows and, towards the end, more seriously, by immense inundations crashing towards lower ground from the flanks of the shrinking Hhryggt.

The crusaders had also suffered illness, accident, desertion, and raids by tribes through whose territory they ventured.

Now was the Air-turn 446 according to the modern calendar. In the eotemporal minds of the ancipital race, it was also Year 367 After Small Apotheosis of Great Year 5,634,000 Since Catastrophe. Thirteen air-turns had passed since that day when the stungebag horn had first sounded along the icy cliffs of the home glacier. Batalix and louring Freyr were low in the western sky and close together, as the crusade plodded on the last stage of its journey.

This terrain was soft as a woman's lap compared with the higher lands of Mordriat already traversed, and spoke less nakedly of savage forces. Yet it was scoured and scooped. True, the season had patched it with trees, the acid-green leaves of which spread their points horizontally, as if compressed by invisible air-octaves, but no foliage could disguise the great geological anatomy beneath; that anatomy had been corroded too recently by centuries of frost. It was a land fit to support without sustaining the restless soul of life, in whatever form that soul was cast. It constituted the unedited manuscript of Wutra's great story. The chunky bodies of the phagor army were autochthonous manifestations of the place.

By comparison, the grey-clad inhabitants of the settlement were shadowy things, more transient than those who passed their borders.

Laintal Ay walked along the curved street formed between the church and the surrounding offices, guardrooms, and stores, carrying a suit of Sibornalan clothing for Aoz Roon. As he went, he caught glimpses of the scene between buildings.

All the inhabitants of New Ashkitosh had gathered to watch the crusade pass. He wondered if they waited there from fear, to test whether the human tribute they had paid the ancipital force had indeed secured their safety.

The silent white brutes went by on either side of the settlement. They moved with precision, looking incuriously ahead. Many were thin, their coats moulting; their naked heads by contrast looked enormous. Above them flew the cowbirds, setting up a great racket. Many cowbirds broke ranks, to dive on manure piles lying about the settlement, fighting for them with screams and beating wings.

The people of the settlement sent up their own sound, as if in opposition. As Laintal Ay emerged from the church, the massed ranks broke into song. The words were not Olonets. They carried a harsh yet lyrical texture matched by a powerful melody. The song breathed some grand elusive quality between defiance and submission. Women's voices floated clear above the bass, which developed into a slow chant much like a march.

Now among the ragged army of brutes streaming by could be discerned some on kaidaw-back—not so many kaidaws now as there had been at the start, but enough to make a showing. In the centre of a more orderly phalanx stepped Rukk-Ggrl, red head held low, bearing the young kzahhn himself. Behind the kzahhn came his generals, then his private fillocks—of whom only two survived, and they now haughty gillots. Human prisoners plodded along amid the throng, bearing loads.

Hrr-Brahl Yprt held his head high, his face crown glinting in the sickly light. Zzhrrk fluttered above him like a banner. The kzahhn did not deign to cast his regard upon the human settlement that paid him tribute. Yet the throaty song that rolled out across the land to greet him roused a feeling of some kind in his eddre for, when he came to a point that might be regarded as level with the Church of Formidable Peace, he raised his sword above his head in his right hand—whether as greeting or threat could never be determined. Without pause, he continued on his way.

Seeing that Aoz Roon kept by his side, Laintal Ay led him to the guardhouse. There they waited until Skitosherill arrived, bringing along his wife and a maidservant loaded with baggage.

"Who's this?" Skitosherill demanded, pointing to Aoz Roon. "Are you breaking your side of our bargain already, barbarian?"

"He's a friend of mine, let that suffice. Where are your phagor friends going?"

The Sibornalan shrugged one shoulder, as if denial was hardly worth two.

"Why should I know? Stop them and ask, if you're curious."

"They are heading for Oldorando. Don't you know that?—you brigands, so friendly with the brutes, singing a song to their leader."

"If I knew where every little barbarous town in the wilderness stood, I should hardly rely on you to show me the way to one of them."

They were confronting each other angrily when Skitosherill's wife pushed forward and said, "Why are you arguing, Barboe? Let's get on with the plan. If this man says he can lead us to Ondoro, then encourage him to do so."

"Of course, dear," Skitosherill said, sketching a rictus of a smile in her direction. Scowling at Laintal Ay, he made off, returning very soon with a scout who led several head of yelk. His wife contented herself with surveying Laintal Ay and Aoz Roon in silent contempt.

She was a sturdy woman, almost as tall as her husband, shapeless under her grey garments. What made her remarkable in Laintal Ay's eyes was her fair straight hair and her light blue eyes; despite her harsh expression, they had a pleasant effect. He said to her cordially, "I will take you to Oldorando in safety. Our town is beautiful and exciting, and boasts geysers and stone towers. The Hour-Whistler will amaze you. You are bound to admire all you see."

"I'm not *bound* to admire anything," she said severely. As if regretting this response, she asked his name in more cordial terms.

"Let's move, sunset's upon us," said Skitosherill briskly. "You two barbarians will ride yelk—no hoxneys available. And this scout will accompany us. He has orders to be firm with any trouble."

"With any trouble at all, really," said the scout, from under his cowl.

As Freyr sank to the horizon, they moved out, six of them with seven yelk, one used for baggage. They passed the sentries at the western entrance of the settlement without incident. The guards stood there dejectedly, shadowy in the declining light, staring into the gathering gloom.

The party entered the wilderness, following the last of the kzahhn's shaggy army. The ground was trampled and fouled from the passage of many feet.

Laintal Ay led the others. He ignored the discomforts of the yelk saddle. A suffocating weight lay on his heart and eddre as he thought of the savage phagor army somewhere ahead of him; with growing certainty, he believed that they would encompass Oldorando on their route, whatever their ultimate destination. It was up to him to spur on as fast as possible, outflank the crusade, and warn the city. He kicked the yelk in the ribs, heaving it on by mental force.

Oyre and her smiling eyes represented all that was dear in the city. His long absence was nothing he regretted, since it had brought him new understanding of himself, and new respect for her insight; she had seen his lack of maturity, his dependence on others, and had wished better for him, perhaps without being able to articulate that wish. His return would bring her at least something of those necessary qualities. Provided he arrived in time.

They entered into a murky forest, through which a faint trail glimmered, as Batalix set in golden sheen. The trees were young as yet, growing like weeds, thir crowns scarcely higher than the heads of the riders. Phantoms moved close by. A thin trail of protognostics wended its way eastwards; by holding to its own mysterious octave, it had somehow managed to evade the kzahhn and thread its course through his ranks. Haggard faces moved palely among the eclipsing saplings.

He hunched his thin frame in the saddle and looked back. The scout and Aoz Roon brought up the rear, hardly distinguishable in the twilight. Aoz Roon's head was down; he looked lifeless and broken. Then came the maidservant with the baggage yelk. Directly behind Laintal Ay rode Skitosherill and his wife, their faces shaded by grey cowls. His gaze sought her pale face. Her blue eyes glinted, but something frozen in her expression frightened him. Was death already creeping up on them?

Again he kicked the slow-moving yelk, forcing it towards the dangers ahead.

XV

THE STENCH OF BURNING

S ilence reigned over Oldorando. Few people walked in the streets. Of those who did, most carried some nostrum or other to their face, sometimes keeping it in place with a mask over nose and mouth. Herbs were most highly regarded for this purpose. They fended off plague, flies, and the stink of bonfires.

High over the houses, the two sentinels, only a hairsbreadth apart, glared down like eyes. Beneath the tiles and slates, the population waited. Everything that organisation could do had been done. Now only waiting remained.

The virus moved from one quarter of the city to another. One week, most deaths would be confined to the southern quarter, the so-called Pauk, and the rest of the city would breathe more freely. Then the district across the Voral would be chastised—to the relief of the other districts. But in another few days, the plague might make lightning visitation to its previous haunts, and lamentations would burst out from streets, even households, where similar cries had only recently been heard.

Tanth Ein and Faralin Ferd, lieutenants of Embruddock, together with Raynil Layan, master of the mint, and Dathka, Lord of the

337

Western Veldt, had formed a Fever Committee, on which they themselves sat, together with useful citizens such as Ma Scantiom of the
hospice. Aided by an auxiliary body formed by the pilgrimage from
Pannoval, the Takers, who had stayed in Oldorando to preach against
its immorality, laws had been passed to deal with the ravages of the
fever. Those laws were enforced by a special police contingent.

Notices were posted in every street and alley, warning that the pen-
alties for concealing dead bodies and for looting were the same: execution by phagor bite—a primitive punishment that sent refined
shudders through the rich merchants. Notices posted outside the city
warned all those who approached that the plague ruled. Few of those
fugitives who came from the east were rash enough to ignore the warning: they ringed their foreheads and skirted the city. It was doubtful
whether the notices would provide such effective protection against
those with evil intentions towards the place.

The first carts ever to be seen in Oldorando, clumsy things with two
wheels, pulled by hoxneys, rumbled through the streets regularly. On
them went the day's crop of corpses, some left shrouded in the street,
some thrown unceremoniously out of doorways or dropped naked from
upper windows. No mother or husband or child, however beloved in
life, but caused sickening revulsion when dying, and worse when dead.

Though the cause of the fever was not understood, many theories
existed. Everyone believed that the disease was contagious. Some went
so far as to believe that the mere sight of a corpse was sufficient to turn
one into the same state. Others who had listened to the word of Naba's
Akha—suddenly of persuasive power—believed that venery brought the
fever on.

Whatever their beliefs, all agreed that fire was the only answer for
corpses. The corpses were taken in carts to a point beyond the city, and
there thrown into the flames. The pyre was constantly being rekindled.
Its smoke, the smell of its black fats, drifting across the shuttered
streets, reminded the inhabitants of their vulnerability. In consequence,
those still surviving threw themselves into one or other—and sometimes both—of the extremes of mortification and lechery.

No one as yet believed that the fever was at its height, or that there
was not worse to come. This dread was counterbalanced by hope. For
there was an increasing number of people, mainly young, who survived
the worst that the helico virus could do, and who, in slimmed down
shapes, moved confidently through the city. Among them was Oyre.

She had fallen in the street. By the time Dol Sakil had taken her
into her care, Oyre was locked rigid in pain. Dol looked after her without fear for herself, with that listless indifference which was an established part of Dol's manner. Despite the prognostications of friends,
she did not fall ill herself, and lived to see Oyre come through the eye
of the needle, looking slender, even skeletal. The only precaution Dol

had taken was to send her child, Rastil Roon, to stay with Amin Lim's man and his child. Now the boy was back.

The two women and the child spent their time indoors. The sense of waiting, the sense of an ending, was not unpleasant. Boredom had many mansions. They played with the boy, simple games that took them back to their own childhood. Once or twice Vry joined them, but Vry had an abstracted air these days. When she spoke, she told them of her work, and of all that she aspired to do. On one occasion, she broke out into passionate speech, confessing her involvement with Raynil Layan, of whom they had previously nothing good to say. The affair vexed her; she often felt disgust; she hated the man when he was absent; yet she flung herself on him when he appeared.

"We've all done it, Vry," Dol commented. "It's just that you're a bit late, so it hurts you worse."

"We haven't all done it enough," Oyre said quietly. "I have no desires now. They've gone from me. . . . What I desire is desire. It may return if only Laintal Ay returns." She gazed out of the window at the blue sky.

"But I'm so torn," Vry said, unwilling to be distracted from her own troubles. "I'm never calm, as once I was. I don't know myself any longer."

In her outburst, Vry said nothing of Dathka, and the other women evaded that issue. Her love might have brought her more ease if she did not worry about Dathka; not only was he on her conscience, but he had taken to following her obsessively. She feared for what might happen, and had easily persuaded the nervous Raynil Layan that they meet in a secret room, rather than in their own places. In this secret room, she and her fork-bearded lover had daily tryst, while the city waited on the disease and the sound of saddle animals drifted through their open window.

Raynil Layan wished the window closed, but she would not have it.

"The animals may convey the illness," he protested. "Let's leave here, my doe, leave the city—away from the pest and everything else that worries us."

"How would we survive? This is our place. Here in this city, and in each other's arms."

He gave her an uneasy grin. "And suppose we infect each other with the pest?"

She flung herself back on the bed, her breasts bouncing in his sight. "Then we die close, we die in the act, knotted! Maintain your spirit, Raynil Layan, feed on mine. Spill yourself over—over and over!" She rubbed her hand along his hairy loin and hooked a leg about the small of his back.

"You greedy sow," he said admiringly, and he rolled beside her, pressing his body to hers.

Dathka sat on the edge of his bed, resting his head in his hands. As he said nothing, so the girl on the bed did not speak; she turned her face from him and brought her knees up to her chest.

Only when he rose and began to dress, with the abruptness of one who has suddenly made up his mind, did she say in a stifled voice, "I'm not carrying the plague, you know."

He cast her back a bitter look, but said nothing, continuing hastily to dress.

She turned her head round, brushing long hair from her face. "What's the matter with you, then, Dathka?"

"Nothing."

"You're not much of a man."

He pulled on his boots, seemingly more concerned with them than with her.

"Rot you, woman, I don't want you—you're not the one I want. Get that into your skull and shift yourself out of here."

From a cupboard fitted into the wall he took a curved dagger of fine workmanship. Its brightness contrasted with the worm-scored panels of the cupboard door. He stuck it in his belt. She called to ask where he was going. He paid her no further attention, slamming the door behind him and clattering down the stairs.

He had not wasted the last few bitter weeks since Laintal Ay left and since he had discovered what he regarded as Vry's betrayal of him. Much of his time had been spent building up support among the youth of Oldorando, securing his position, making alliances with foreign elements who chafed at the restrictions Oldorando imposed on them, sympathising with those—and there were many—whose way of life had been disrupted by arduous work patterns imposed by the introduction of a native coinage. The master of the mint, Raynil Layan, was a frequent butt of his criticism.

As he strode into the alley, all was quiet and the side street deserted except for a man he paid to guard his door. In the market, people were about of necessity, attending to their day's requirements. The little apothecary's stall, with its pots ranked imposingly, was doing good business. There were still merchants with bright stalls and bright robes on their backs. Equally, there were also people moving by with loads on their backs, leaving the threatened city before things got worse.

Dathka saw nothing of it. He moved like an automaton, eyes fixed ahead. The tension in the city was one with his personal tension. He had reached a point where he could tolerate it no longer. He would kill Raynil Layan, and Vry too if need be, and have done with it. His lips curled back from his teeth as he rehearsed the fatal blow over and over in his mind. Men started away from him, fearing his fixed look presaged the onset of fever.

He knew where Vry had her secret room; his spies kept him informed. He thought to himself, If I ruled here, I would close down the academy for good. Nobody ever had the courage to make that decision final. I would. Now's the time to strike, using the excuse that classes at the academy spread the pest. That would really hurt her.

"Take thought, brother, take thought! Pray with the Takers to be spared, hear the word of great Naba's Akha. . . ."

He brushed by the street preacher. He would have those fools off the street, too, if he ruled.

Near the Yuli Lane hoxney stables, he was approached by a man he knew, a mercenary and animal trader.

"Well?"

"He's up there now, sir." The man signalled with his eyebrows towards the garret window of one of the wooden buildings facing the stables. These were mainly hostels, rooming houses or drink shops, which acted as a quasi-respectable front to the music rooms and bawdy houses ranged behind them.

Dathka nodded curtly.

He pushed through a bead curtain, to which fresh orling and scantiom had been tied, and entered one of the drink shops. The cramped dark room was empty of customers. On the walls, animal skulls gave dry, serrated smiles. The owner stood against his counter, arms folded, gazing into space. Already primed, he merely lowered his head so that his double chins spread on his chest, a signal to Dathka to do whatever he wished to do. Dathka passed him by and climbed the stairs.

Stale smells greeted him, of cabbage and worse things. He walked by the wall, but the boards still creaked. He listened at the end door, heard voices. Being of nervous disposition, Raynil Layan would be sure to have barred his door. Dathka knocked on the cracked panels.

"Message for you, sir," he said in a muffled voice "Urgent, from the mint."

Smiling a ghastly smile, he stood close, listening as the bolts were drawn inside the room. As soon as the door opened a crack, he burst in, flinging the door wide. Raynil Layan fell back, crying in terror. At the sight of the dagger, he ran to the window and called once for help. Dathka grasped him by the neck and flung him against the bed.

"Dathka!" Vry sat in the bed, pulling a sheet over her nudity. "Get out of here, you rat's eddre!"

For answer, he kicked the door shut without looking round. He went over to Raynil Layan, who was picking himself up and groaning.

"I know you're going to kill me, I can see it, I can tell," the master of the mint said, putting out a tremblingly protective hand. "Spare me, please, I'm not your enemy. I can help you."

"I'm going to kill you with as much compassion as you killed old Master Datnil."

Raynil Layan rose slowly, hiding his nudity, keeping a wary eye on his attacker.

"I didn't do that. Not myself. Aoz Roon ordered his death. It was legal, really. The law was broken. Killing me isn't legal. Tell him, Vry. Listen, Dathka—Master Datnil gave corps secrets away, he showed the secret book of the corps to Shay Tal. Not all of it. Not the worst thing. You ought to know about that."

Dathka paused. "That world's dead, all that corps scumb. You know what I think of the corps. To fessups with the past. It's dead, as you will be."

Vry seized on his hesitation. She had recovered her nerve.

"Listen, Dathka, let me explain the situation. We can help you, both of us. There are things in that corps book that Master Datnil did not dare reveal even to Shay Tal. They happened long ago, but the past is still with us, however we might wish it otherwise."

"If that were so, then you would accept me. So long I longed for you."

Raynal Layan drew his robe round himself and said, mustering his wits, "Your quarrel is with me, not Vry. In the various corps books are records of Embruddock in past time. They prove that this was once a phagor city. Possibly the phagors built it—the record is broken. They certainly owned it, and the corps and the people in it. They kept people as slaves."

Dathka stood regarding them darkly. All he said in his head was, We are all slaves—knowing it to be stupid.

"If they owned Embruddock, who killed them? Who won it back? King Denniss?"

"This happened after Denniss's time. The secret book says little; it records history only incidentally. We understand that the phagors simply decided to quit."

"They were not defeated?"

Vry said, "You know how little we understand the brutes. Perhaps their air-octaves changed and they all marched away. But they must have been here in strength. If you ever studied the painting of Wutra in the old temple, you would know that. Wutra is a representation of a phagor king."

Dathka rested the heel of his hand on his brow. "Wutra a phagor? It can't be. You go too far. This damned learning—it can make white black. All such nonsense stems from the academy. I'd kill it. If I had the power I'd kill it."

"If you want power, I'll side with you," said Raynil Layan.

"I don't want you on my side."

"Well, of course . . ." He gestured frustratedly, tugged the twin points of his beard. "You see, we have a riddle to resolve. Because it seems that the phagors are returning. Perhaps they will reclaim their old city. That's my guess."

"What do you mean by that?"

"It's simple. You must have heard the rumours. Oldorando's alive with the rumours. There's a great force of phagors approaching. Go and talk to the people passing outside the city. The trouble is, Tanth Ein and Faralin Ferd will not protect the city, being too involved with their private interests. They're your enemies—not I. If a strong man killed the lieutenants and took over the city, he could save it. That's just my suggestion."

He watched Dathka scrupulously, seeing the play of emotions on his face. He smiled encouragingly, knowing he had talked his way out of being killed.

"I'd help," he said. "I'm on your side."

Vry said, "I'm on your side, too, Dathka."

He shot her one of his darkly glittering looks. "You'd never be on my side. Not if I won all of Embruddock for you."

Faralin Ferd and Tanth Ein were drinking together in the Two-Sided Tankard. Women, friends, and toadies were with them, enjoying the evening.

The Two-Sided Tankard was one of the few places where laughter could be heard nowadays. The tavern was part of a new administrative building which also housed the new mint. The building had been paid for mainly by rich merchants, some of whom were present with their wives. In the room were furnishings that until recently were unknown in Oldorando—oval tables, sofas, sideboards, rich woven rugs hanging on the walls.

Imported drink flowed, and a fair foreign youth played the hand harp.

The windows were being closed to keep out the chill night air and to shut out an odour of smoke from the alleyways. On the central table, an oil lamp burned. Food lay about, uneaten. One of the merchants was relating a long tale of murder, betrayal, and travel.

Faralin Ferd wore a jacket of suede, untied to reveal a woollen shirt underneath. He rested his elbows on the table, half-listening to the story while his gaze roved about the chamber.

Tanth Ein's woman, Farayl Musk, padded quietly about, ostensibly to see that a slave was securing the shutters correctly. Farayl Musk was distant kinswoman of both Tanth Ein and Faralin Ferd, being descended from the family of Lord Wall Ein Den. Although not exactly beautiful, Farayl Musk had wit and character, which commended her to some people and not to others. She bore a candle in a holder, which she shielded against the draft of her progress with one hand.

The light made her face glow, throwing unexpected shadows on its contours, lending her mystery. She felt Faralin Ferd's eyes on her, but forebore to return his gaze, knowing the value of feigned indifference.

He reflected as he often had done before that he deserved Farayl Musk, rather than his own woman, who bored him. Despite the dangers involved, he had several times made love to her. Now time was short. They might all be dead in a few days; drink did not drown that knowledge. He lusted after her again.

Rising, he stalked abruptly out of the room, casting a significant glance in her direction. The long story was reaching one of its periodic excitements, involving the smothering of a prominent man with the carcass of one of his own sheep. Laughter rose from round the table. Nevertheless, watchful eyes saw the lieutenant disappear—and his fellow lieutenant's woman made her exit after a discreet interval.

"I thought you wouldn't dare follow."

"Curiosity is stronger than cowardice. We've only got a moment."

"Do it with me here, under the stairs. In this corner, look."

"Standing, Faralin Ferd?"

"Feel this, woman—is it standing or is it not?"

She sighed and leaned against him, clutching what he offered with both hands. He recalled from previous occasions how sweet this woman's breath was.

"Under the stairs, then."

She put the candle down on the floor. Ripping open her bodice, she revealed her majestic breasts to him. He set an arm about her and dragged her into the corner, kissing her excitedly.

There they were caught when a party of twelve men under Dathka came in from the street with torches burning and swords naked.

Despite their protests, Farayl Musk and Faralin Ferd were brought forth. They barely had time to draw their clothes together before they were thrust back into the meeting room, where the rest of the lieutenants were already confronted by sword blades.

"This is all lawful," Dathka said, eyeing them much as a wolf regards kid arang. "I am taking the rule of Embruddock into my own hands until such time as the rightful Lord of Embruddock, Aoz Roon, returns. I am his deposed but oldest-serving lieutenant. I mean to see that the city is properly guarded against invaders."

Behind him stood Raynil Layan, his sword sheathed. He said loudly, "And I support Dathka Den. Hail, Lord Dathka Den."

Dathka's eye had found Tanth Ein, lost in the shadows. The older of the two lieutenants had not risen with the rest. He sat still at his place at the head of the table, arms resting on the chair arm.

"You dare defy me!" Dathka cried, leaping forward with his sword raised, to confront the seated man. "Get to your feet, scumb!"

Tanth Ein never moved, except that a rictus of pain traversed his face as his head jerked back. His eyeballs started to roll. As Dathka kicked at the chair, he slid stiffly to the floor with no attempt at breaking his fall.

"It's the bone fever!" someone shouted. "It's among us!"

Farayl Musk began to scream.

By morning, two more lives had gone, and the smell of burning once more tainted the air of Oldorando. Tanth Ein lay in the hospice under Ma Scantiom's courageous care.

Despite the dread of contagion, a large crowd gathered in Bank Street to hear Dathka's public proclamation of his rule. Once on a time, such meetings would have been held outside the big tower. Those days had passed away. Bank Street was more spacious and more elegant. On one side of it, a few stalls dotted the bank of the river. Geese still strutted there, aware of their ancient rights. On the other side was a line of new buildings, with the old stone towers rising behind them. Here, a public platform stood.

On the platform stood Raynil Layan, shifting his weight from foot to foot, Faralin Ferd with his arms bound behind him, and six young warriors of Dathka's guard, armed with sheathed swords and spears, grimly regarding the crowd. Bouquet sellers roved through the people, selling protective nosegays. The pilgrim Takers were there too, dressed in their distinctive black-and-white garb, holding banners urging repentance. Children played on the edge of the crowd, sniggering at the behaviour of their elders.

As the Hour-Whistler blew, Dathka climbed onto the platform and began immediately to address the crowd.

"I am taking up the burden of authority for the sake of the city," Dathka said. It seemed his old silence had dropped from him. He spoke with eloquence. Yet he stood almost motionless, not gesturing, not using his body to help carry his words, as if the habit of silence had quit nowhere but his tongue. "I have no wish to supplant the true ruler of Embruddock, Aoz Roon. When he returns—if he returns—then what is rightfully his will be rightfully handed back to him. I am his lawful deputy. Those he left in command have abused his power, have cast it in the gutter. I could not stand by and see it. We will have honesty in these bad times."

"Why's Raynil Layan beside you then, Dathka?" called a voice from the crowd, and there were other remarks, which Dathka tried to override.

"I know you have complaints. I'll hear them after—you hear me now.

Judge Aoz Roon's usurping lieutenants. Eline Tal had the courage to go into the wilderness with his lord. The other two creatures stayed at home. Tanth Ein has the fever as his reward. Here stands the third of them, the worst, Faralin Ferd. Look at the way he trembles. When did he ever address you? He was too busy about his sly lascivious ways indoors.

"I'm a hunter, as you know. Laintal Ay and I tamed the Western Veldt. Faralin Ferd will die of the pest like his crony, Tanth Ein. Will you be ruled by corpses? I won't catch the plague. Intercourse passes on the plague, and I'm free of it.

"My first deed will be to restore guards all round Embruddock, and to train a proper army. As we are at present, we are ripe to fall to any enemy—human or inhuman. Better die in battle than in bed."

This last remark caused a groundswell of unease. Dathka paused, glaring down at them. Oyre and Dol stood among the people, Dol clutching Rastil Roon in her arms. Oyre cried out loudly as Dathka paused, "You are a usurper. How are you any better than Tanth Ein or Raynil Layan?"

Dathka went to the edge of the platform.

"I steal nothing. I picked up what was dropped." He pointed at Oyre. "You of all people, Oyre, as the natural daughter of Aoz Roon himself, should know that I will return to your father what is his when he returns. He would wish me to do this."

"You cannot speak for him while he's away."

"I can and do."

"Then you speak wrongly."

Others to whom this wrangle meant little, and who cared little about Aoz Roon, also started to shout, calling out complaints. Someone threw an overripe fruit. The guard jostled the crowd, without effect.

Dathka's face grew pale. He raised his fist above his head in passion.

"Very well, you scumble, then I will tell you publicly what has always been kept silent. I'm not afraid. You think so greatly of Aoz Roon, you think he was so admirable, I'll tell you the kind of man he was. He was a murderer. Worse, he was a double murderer."

They fell quiet, their faces upturned to him in a cloud of flesh.

He was shaking now, conscious of what he had started. "How do you think Aoz Roon gained power? By murder, bloody murder, murder by night. There are those of you who will remember Nahkri and Klils, sons of ancient Dresyl, in the days bygone. Nahkri and Klils ruled when Embruddock was just a farmyard. One dark night, Aoz Roon—young then—threw the two brothers off the top of the big tower when they were in their cups. A foul double deed. And who was there as witness, who saw it all? I was there—and so was she—his natural daughter." He pointed accusingly down at the thin figure of Oyre, now clinging in horror to Dol.

"He's mad," a boy shouted on the edge of the crowd. "Dathka's mad!" People were leaving at a run, or running up. General confusion was breaking out, and a struggle developing in one corner of the mob.

Raynil Layan tried to rally the crowd, bringing up his powerful pale presence to shout in a large voice, "Support us and we will support you. We will guard Oldorando."

All this while, Faralin Ferd had been standing silent at the rear of the platform, arms bound, in the grip of a guard. He saw his moment. "Throw Dathka out!" he shouted. "He never had Aoz Roon's approval and he shall not have ours!"

Dathka turned about with a hunter's rapid movement, drawing his curved dagger as he did so. He flung himself on the lieutenant. A high scream came from Farayl Musk, somewhere in the crowd, at the same time as several voices took up the cry, "Throw Dathka out!"

They fell silent almost immediately, stilled by Dathka's sudden action. In the hush, smoke drifted across the scene. Nobody moved. Dathka stood rigid, back to his audience. For a moment, Faralin Ferd was also still. Then he threw up his head and gave a choking groan. Blood gushed from his mouth. He sagged, and the guard let him fall at Dathka's feet.

Then there was uproar. Blood gave the whole crowd voice.

"You fool, they'll slaughter us," Raynil Layan shouted. He ran to the back of the platform and jumped down. Before anyone could stop him, he was disappearing down a side street.

The guard ran about, ignoring Dathka's commands, as the mob closed on the platform. Farayl Musk was screaming for Dathka's arrest. Seeing that it was all over, he also jumped from the platform and ran.

At the rear of the crowd, by the stalls, the small boys jumped up and down, clapping their hands in excitement. The crowd began to riot, finding rioting more lively than death.

For Dathka, there was nothing but to make an ignominious escape. He ran panting, gasping, muttering incoherently, through the deserted streets, his three shadows—penumbral, umbral, penumbral—changing their topology at his feet. His scuttling thoughts similarly dilated and shrank, as he tried to evade the knowledge of his failure, to retch up his disaster from inside him.

Strangers passed him, their belongings loaded on an archaic sledge. An old man, helping a child along, called to him, "The fuggies are coming."

He heard the sound of people running behind him—the mob, avenging. There was one place he could go to for refuge, one person, one hope. Cursing her, he ran to Vry.

She was back in her old tower. She sat in a kind of dream, aware—and frightened of her awareness—that Embruddock was moving to a crisis. When he hammered on her door, she let him in almost with relief. She stood there with neither sympathy nor derision as Dathka collapsed weeping on her bed.

"It's a mess," she said. "Where's Raynil Layan?" He went on weeping, striking the bedding with his fist.

"Stop it," she said mildly. She walked about the room, gazing up at the stained ceiling. "We live in such a mess. I wish I were free of emotion. Human beings are such messes. We were better when the snow contained us, frozen, when we had no . . . hope! I wish there were only knowledge, pure knowledge, no emotion."

He sat up. "Vry—"

"Don't speak to me. You have nothing for me, and never had, you must accept that. I don't want to hear what you have to say. I don't want to know what you've done."

Geese set up a great honking outside.

He sat on the bed, yawned. "You're only half a woman. You're cold. I've always known it, yet I couldn't stop feeling as I did about you. . . ."

"*Cold?* . . . You fool, I steam like a rajabaral."

The noise in the street was louder, loud enough for them to catch the note of individual voices. Dathka ran to the window.

Where were his men now? The people who poured out of nearby alleys were all strangers to him. He could not see one familiar face— none of his men, no Raynil Layan—not that that surprised him—not even one citizen he could identify. Once on a time, every face had been known to him. Strangers were calling for his blood. Real fear entered his heart, as if his only ambition had been to die at the hand of a friend. To be hated by strangers . . . it was intolerable. He leaned from the window and shook his fist in defiance, cursing them.

The faces tipped upwards, opening in the middle almost in unison, like a shoal of fish. They roared and jibbered.

Before that noise, he dropped his fist and shrank back, not meaning to be quelled but quelled nevertheless. He leaned against the wall and examined his rough hands, with blood still moist in the nails.

Only when he heard Vry's voice below did he realise she had left the room. She had flung open the door of the tower and was standing on the platform, addressing the people. The mob surged forward as those at the rear pressed in to hear what she said. Some called out mockingly, but were silenced by others. Her voice, clear and sharp, flew above their tousled heads.

"Why don't you stop and think what you're doing? You're not animals. Try to be human. If we are to die, let us die with human dignity, and not with our hands round one another's throats.

"You are aware of suffering. Both the suffering and the awareness are your badges of humanity. Be proud, rot you—die with that knowledge. Remember the waiting world of the gossies below, where there is only gnashing of teeth because the dead feel disgust for their own lives.

Isn't that a terrible thing? Doesn't it seem to you a terrible thing, to feel disgust—disgust and contempt—for your own lives? Transform your own life from within. Never mind external weather, if it snows or rains or shines, never mind that, accept it, but work to transform your inner self. Create calm in your soul. Take thought. Would Dathka or his murder have the power to cure your personal predicament? Only you have that.

"You think things are going badly. I must warn you that more challenges are to come. I tell you this with the full weight of the academy behind me. Tomorrow, tomorrow at noon, the third and worst of the Twenty Blindnesses is due. Nothing can stop it. Mankind has no power over the skies. What will you do then? Will you run madly through the streets, cutting throats, smashing things, firing what your betters built—as if you were worse than phagors? Decide *now* how filthy, how low, you will be tomorrow!"

They looked at one another and murmured. No one shouted. She waited, instinctively seizing on the right moment at which to launch in again on a new tack.

"Years ago, the sorceress Shay Tal addressed the inhabitants of Oldorando. I remember her words clearly, for I revered everything she said. She offered us the treasure of knowledge. That treasure can be yours if only you will be humble and dare to reach out your hands for it.

"Understand what I tell you. Tomorrow's blindness is no supernatural event. What is it? It is merely the two sentinels passing one another, those two suns you have known since birth. This world of ours is round as they are round. Imagine how large a ball our world must be for us not to fall off it—yet it is small compared with the sentinels. They look small merely because they are so far away.

"Shay Tal, when she spoke, said that there was a disaster in the past. I believe that is not the case. We have added to her knowledge. Wutra has disposed of his world so that everything works through continuous action in all the parts. Your hair grows on your head and body as the suns rise and set. These are not separate actions but one in Wutra's eyes. Our world travels in a circle round Batalix, and there are other worlds like ours which behave likewise. At the same time, Batalix travels in a greater circle round about Freyr. You have to accept that our farmyard is not at the centre of the universe."

Their murmurs of protest grew louder. Vry overrode them by pitching her voice higher.

"Do you understand that? Understanding is harder than slitting throats, isn't it? To comprehend fully what I tell you, you must first understand and then grasp the understanding with your imagination, so that the facts live. Our year is four hundred and eighty days long, that we know. That is the time we take on Hrl-Ichor to make a complete circle about Batalix. But there is another circle to be made, the circle of Batalix and our world about Freyr. Are you prepared to hear the word? It takes eighteen hundred and twenty-five small years. . . . Imagine that great year!" They were quiet now, staring at her, the new sorceress.

"Until our day, few could imagine it! For each of us can expect only forty years of life. It would take forty-six of our lifetimes to add up to one whole circle of this world about Freyr. Many of our lives find no echo, yet are part of that greater thing. That is why such knowledge is difficult to grasp and easy to lose in time of trouble."

She was seized up by her new power, seduced by her own eloquence. "What is the trouble, what is this disaster of which Shay Tal told us, large enough to make us mislay such important knowledge? Why, simply that the light of Freyr varies according to the time of the great year. We have come through many generations of poor light, of winter, when the earth lay dead under snow. Tomorrow you should rejoice when the eclipse comes—the blindness, when distant Freyr slips behind Batalix—for it is a sign that Freyr's light grows nearer. . . . We enter spring of the great year tomorrow. Rejoice! Have the sense, the knowledge, to rejoice! Throw away the mess of your lives that ignorance causes, and rejoice! Better times are coming for all of us."

Shoatapraxi deflected them. The woody grass had been growing in clumps as they approached lower ground. The clumps became thickets. Now they tried to find their way through a region choked with it.

The vegetation rose above their heads. It was broken only by drumlins, up which it was possible to climb occasionally in order to get a bearing. With the shoatapraxi was entwined a thin-stemmed bramble, making progress both difficult and painful. The phagor army ahead had travelled another way. They were forced to follow the more meandering tracks of animals, yet the going remained bad for the yelk. They were nervous of the grass, as if disliking its pungent scent; their sweeping horns caught on the hollow stems, and the thorns underfoot penetrated to the softer parts of their hooves. So the men dismounted, leading their necrogenes as they progressed on foot.

"How much farther, barbarian?" Skitosherill asked.

"Not far, " Laintal Ay responded. It was his stock answer to the stock question. They had slept uncomfortably in the forest, rising at dawn with frost in their clothes. He felt refreshed, still rejoicing in his lighter form, but he saw how weary the others were becoming. Aoz Roon was a shadow of what he had once been; in the night, he had called out in a strange language.

They came to marshy ground, where, to everybody's relief, the shoatapraxi thinned. After pausing to see that all was quiet, they moved on, scattering flights of small birds before them. Ahead loomed a valley, with soft mounds rising on either side. They went that way, rather than moving on to higher ground, chiefly because of their fatigue; but as soon as they entered the neck of the valley, they were assailed by a chill wind, which rushed at them like an animal and bit to their bones. It was a time for struggling on grimly, with the head down.

The wind brought fog with it. The fog curled about their bodies, though their heads were above it. Laintal Ay understood the wind, knowing that a layer of cold air poured down like water from the distant mountains on their left flank, down over the mounds into the valley, seeking lower ground. It was a local wind; the sooner they left its numbing grip, the better.

Skitosherill's wife gave a faint cry and halted, leaning against her yelk and burying her face against her arm.

Skitosherill returned to her concernedly and placed a grey-clad arm round her. The icy air wrapped his cloak about his leg.

He looked worriedly up at Laintal Ay. "She can't go on," he said.

"We'll die if we stay here."

Dashing the moisture from his eyes, he looked forward. In a few hours, he realised, the valley would be warm and harmless. At present it was a death trap. They were in shadow. The light of the two suns slanted across the left slope of the valley above their heads; the light lay in thick vertical bars, where the shadows were cast of giant rajabarals which stood on the opposite crest. The rajabarals were steaming already in the morning sunshine, the vapour pouring up into the sky, casting a rolling shadow.

He knew this place. Its configurations had been familiar to him when snow clothed it. It was normally a welcoming place—the last pass before a hunter gained the plains on the edge of which Oldorando stood. He was too cold even to shiver, body heat snatched by the wind. They could not continue. Skitosherill's wife still leaned sickly against the flank of the necrogene; now that she had given way, her maidservant also felt able to release her miseries and stood screaming with her back to the tide of air.

"We'll get up among the rajabarals," he said, shouting the words into Skitosherill's ear. Skitosherill nodded, still involved with his wife, whom he was trying to help up into the saddle.

"Mount, all of you," Laintal Ay called.

As he shouted, a flutter of white caught his eye.

Above the hillside on their left flank, cowbirds appeared, fighting the cold downdraught, their feathers flickering from white to grey as they rode in the shadows of the rajabarals opposite. Below the birds was a line of phagors. They were warriors; they carried spears at the ready. They moved to the edge of the mound, to poise themselves there as steady as boulders. They looked down at the humans embroiled in the tumbling mists below.

"Fast, fast, up, before we're attacked!" As he shouted, he saw Aoz Roon was staring up at the brutes, without expression, making no move.

He ran to him, clouting him across the back.

"Up. We've got to get out of here."

Aoz Roon said something harsh in his throat.

"You're enchanted, man, you've learnt some of their accursed language and it's rendered you powerless."

By force, he heaved his friend into his saddle. The scout did the same with the servant woman, who was sobbing in terror.

"Up the slope to the rajabarals," Laintal Ay shouted. He slapped Aoz Roon's mare across its shaggy rump as he ran back to mount his own. Reluctantly, the animals started to climb. They made little response to heels in their ribs; a hoxney would have been lighter and faster.

"They won't attack us," the Sibornalan said. "We'll give them the maidservant if there's trouble."

"Our mounts. They will kill us for our mounts. To ride or for food. You stay behind and haggle if you wish."

With a sick look, Skitosherill shook his head and swung himself into his saddle.

He went first up the slope, leading his wife's beast. The scout and the maidservant followed close behind. Then there was a gap as Aoz Roon listlessly rode his yelk, allowing it to stray away from the others, despite Laintal Ay's shouts to keep together. He brought up the rear with the pack yelk, frequently casting glances back at the eminence behind them.

The phagors did not move. It would not be the cold wind that worried them; they were creatures of the cold. Their immobility need not imply decision. It was impossible to know what the brutes thought.

So they mounted the rise. They were soon out of the wind, to their great relief, and tugging with urgency on their reins.

As they came over the brow of the hill, the sunlight shone into their eyes. Both suns, near enough to look amid their dazzle as if linked, glittered between the trunks of the great trees. Just for a moment, dancing figures could be seen in the heart of the gold, lightly tripping—Others at a mysterious festivity; then they vanished as if the acid glory of light had inexplicably dissolved them. The party drew into the protection of the smooth columns, still gasping with cold. With the canopy of steam overhead, it was almost as if they had entered a hall of the gods. There were about thirty of the massive trees. Beyond them lay open ground and the way to Oldorando.

The phagor detachment moved. From complete immobility, it sprang into total action. The brutes came plodding concertedly down the slope on which they had remained poised. Only one of their kind was astride a kaidaw. He led. The cowbirds stayed shrieking above the valley.

Desperately, Laintal Ay looked about for a refuge. There was none, except that offered by the rajabarals. The rajabarals themselves were emitting internal rumbling. He drew his sword and spurred over to where the Sibornalan was lowering his wife from her mount.

"We'll have to stand and fight. Are you prepared for that? They'll be on us in a minute or two."

Skitosherill looked up at him with agony etched in every line of his face. His mouth was open in a kind of snarl of anguish.

"She has the bone fever, she will die," he said.

His wife's eyes were glazed, her body stiffly contorted.

With an impatient gesture of dismissal, Laintal Ay called to the scout, "You and I then. Look lively—here they come."

For answer, the scout gave him a villainous grin, at the same time making a gesture with his finger of slitting windpipes. Laintal Ay was grimly encouraged.

He cast about furiously by the base of the trees, looking for earths down which the Others had disappeared, thinking that here somewhere near at hand might be refuge—refuge and a snoktruix; but never *his* snoktruix, never again.

Despite their abrupt retreat, the Others had left no trace. Well, then there was no alternative to fighting. No doubt they must die. He would not expire until his breath could escape from every wound he received from the spears of the ancipitals.

With the scout by his side, he went to the edge of the mound to challenge the enemy as they appeared.

Behind him, the rumble in the rajabarals grew louder. The mighty trees had ceased to pour out steam and were making a noise like thunder. Below him, the first slanting rays of the linked suns had penetrated almost to the bottom of the valley, where they lit the spectacle of the phagors fording the katabatic wind, their sturdy bodies enmeshed in writhing fog, the stiff hairs of their coats stirred in their progress. They looked upwards and gave a churring cry at the sight of the two humans. They began to move up the hill.

This incident was witnessed from the Earth Observation Station and, a thousand years later, by those who came on sandalled feet to the great auditoria on Earth. Those auditoria were fuller now than they had been at any time over the last century. People who went to view that enormous electronic recreation of a reality that had not been real for many centuries were wishing in their hearts that the humans whose lives they had followed would survive—always using the future tense, which comes naturally to homo sapiens, even for such events as this, so long past.

From their privileged viewpoint, they saw beyond the incident among the grove of rajabarals, across the rolling plain where Fish Lake had once enshrined its terrifying statuary, to Oldorando itself.

And all that landscape was dotted with figures. The young kzahhn was preparing at last to descend upon the city that had torn both life and tether from his illustrious grandstallun. He awaited only the sign. Although his force was arrayed in no great military order, but rather disposed itself like so many herds of cattle, not always looking to the front, numbers alone made it formidable. It would roll across ancient Embruddock, and then roll remorselessly on towards the southwest coasts of the continent of Campannlat, to the very cliffs of the eastern Climent Ocean, to cross if possible to Hespagorat, and the rocky ancestral homelands of Pagovin.

Because of this nonhomogeneous disposition of the phagor crusade, it was still possible for travellers—refugees mainly—to move among the various herds and components without molestation, while hurrying in the direction from which the crusade had come. Generally, these fearful parties were led by Madis, sensitive to the air-octaves avoided by the hulking beasts under Hrr-Brahl Yprt's banner. One such party had the fork-bearded Raynil Layan pushing a timid Madi before him. It passed close by the young kzahhn himself, but the latter, immobile, gave no flicker of interest.

The young kzahhn stood against the eroded flanks of Rukk-Ggrl and communed with those in tether, his father and his great-grandstallun, hearing once more their advice and instruction in his pale harneys. Behind him stood his generals and then his two surviving gillots. He had serviced the gillots rarely but, given favourable fortunes, the time would come again. First must the two future octaves of victory or death be unravelled; if he travelled down the octave of victory, there would be music for mating.

He waited without motion, occasionally sliding his milt up the slots of his nostrils under the black fuzz of his muzzle. The sign would come in the heavens, the air-octaves would convulse themselves into a knot, and he and those whom he commanded would surge forward to burn down that ancient damned city, once Hrrm-Bhhrd Ydohk.

Across this ancient battlefield, where man and phagor had encountered each other more frequently than either side knew, Laintal Ay and the Sibornalan scout stood with their swords ready to greet the first phagors to climb the mound. Behind them, the noise of the rajabarals was like thunder. Aoz Roon and the maidservant crouched by one of the boles, supinely awaiting whatever befell. Skitosherill laid down the rigid body of his wife tenderly, tenderly, shielding her face from the blinding double sun now climbing towards zenith. Then he ran to join his two fellows, drawing his sword as he did so.

The uphill climb disrupted the line of phagors, the fitter arriving at the top first. As the leader charged into view, head and shoulders appearing over the slope, Laintal Ay ran forward. In despatching them one by one lay their only hope—he had counted thirty-five or more of the brutes, and refused to reckon the hopeless odds.

Up came the phagor's throwing arm. It bent back to what to a human was a disconcerting angle, but Laintal Ay dived under the point of the spear, rendering it useless, and stabbed with a straight arm. His elbow took the shock as the blade grated against rib. As yellow blood spurted from the wound, to his mind came the old hunters' tale that ancipital intestines were situated above their lungs; he had proved its truth when he skinned the phagor to deceive its kaidaw.

The phagor threw back its long boney head, lips peeling back from yellow teeth in a gesture of agony. It fell, and went rolling down the slope, to lie at the bottom in the dispersing mists.

But the other brutes were at the breast of the rise now, closing in. The Sibornalan scout was fighting valiantly, every now and again gasping a curse in his native tongue. With a yell, Laintal Ay flung himself into the fray again.

The world exploded.

The noise was so sharp, so close, that fighting immediately stopped. A second explosion came. Black stones flew overhead, most of them landing somewhere on the far side of the valley. Pandemonium ensued.

Each side was governed by its own instincts: the phagors became immobile, the two humans threw themselves flat on the ground.

Their timing was perfect. Concurrent explosions sounded. The black stones flew everywhere. Several hit phagors, carrying them immediately over the brink, scattering their dying bodies. The rest of the phagors turned tail and ran back into the valley for safety, rolling, slipping, sliding, in their haste to escape. The cowbirds flew screeching across the sky.

Laintal Ay sprawled where he was, hands over his ears, looking upwards in terror. The rajabarals were splitting from the top, cracking and peeling open like exploding casks, their staves falling. In the autumn of Helliconia's last great year, they had retracted their enormous fruit-bearing branches into the top of their trunks, sealing the crown over with a cap of resin until the vernal equinox. Over the winter centuries, internal heat pumps, drawing up warmth through the root system from rocks far below, had been preparing the way for this mighty explosion.

The tree above Laintal Ay burst with furious noise. He watched the seeds expelled. Some flew upwards, most were shot out on all sides. The force of the ejaculation threw the black projectiles as much as a half mile away. Steam rolled everywhere.

When silence fell, eleven of the trees had exploded. As their blackened casings peeled back from the top, a more slender crown thrust up inside, whitish, topped by green growth.

That green growth was destined to spread until the grove, which had consisted merely of polished columns, became roofed over in brilliant green foliage, shielding the roots from the more savage suns that were to come, in the days when Helliconia moved close to Freyr—too close to be comfortable for man, beast, or vegetation. Whoever lived or died under their shade, the rajabarals had their own form of life to protect.

These rajabarals formed part of the vegetation of the new world, the world that came into existence after Freyr swam into the clouded skies of Helliconia. Together with the new animals, they were set in ceaseless ecological competition with the orders of the old world, when Batalix ruled in isolation. The binary system had created a binary biology.

The seeds, a mottled black in colour, designed to resemble stones, were each as big as a human head. Over the course of the next six hundred thousand days, some would survive to become adult trees.

Laintal Ay kicked one carelessly away, and went over to see to the scout. The latter had been wounded, pierced by a sharp-edged phagor blade. Skitosherill and Laintal Ay helped him back to where Aoz Roon and the maidservant stood. He was in a bad way, bleeding freely. They squatted helplessly by his side as the life drained from his eddre.

Skitosherill began to go into an elaborate religious ritual, whereon Laintal Ay jumped up angrily.

"We must get to Embruddock as soon as possible, don't you understand? Leave the body here. Leave the woman with your wife. Press on with me and Aoz Roon. Time's running out."

Skitosherill gestured to the body. "I owe him this. It will take a while but it must be done according to the faith."

"The fuggies may return. They don't get scared easily, and we can hardly hope for another turn of fortune like the last. I am going to press on with Aoz Roon."

"You've done well, barbarian. Go forward, and perhaps we will meet again."

As Laintal Ay turned to go, he paused and looked back. "I'm sorry about your wife."

Aoz Roon had had the sense to keep hold of two of the yelk when the rajabarals exploded. The other animals had galloped away in fright.

"Are you fit to ride?"

"Yes, I'm fit. Help me, Laintal Ay. I'll recover. To learn the language of the phagor kind is to see the world differently. I'll recover."

"Mount and let's be off. I'm afraid that we may be too late to warn Embruddock."

They rode off rapidly, one behind the other, leaving the shade of the grove where the grey Sibornalan knelt in prayer.

The two yelk proceeded steadily, heads held low, eyes staring vacantly forward. When they dropped their scumble, beetles emerged from the ground and rolled the treasure to underground stores, inadvertently planting the seeds of future forests.

Seeing was bad, because of the way the plain rippled with ridge after ridge. More stone monuments dotted the landscapes, ages old, their circular signs eroded by weather or ripicolous lichens. Laintal Ay pressed ahead, alert for trouble, ever turning back to urge Aoz Roon to keep up.

The plain contained its travelling groups, moving in all directions, but he gave them as wide a berth as possible. They passed fleshless corpses to some of which garments still clung; fat birds sat by these memorials to life, and once they sighted a slinking sabre-tongue.

A cold front rose like a shawl behind their shoulders to the north and east. Where the sky remained clear, Freyr and Batalix clung together, their discs inseparable. The yelk had passed the site of Fish Lake, where a cairn had been erected to mark Shay Tal's miracle in the vanished waters, many winters ago; they were climbing over one of the tiresome ridges, when a wind rose. The world began to grow dark.

Laintal Ay dismounted and stood fondling the muzzle of his yelk. Aoz Roon remained despondently in the saddle.

The eclipse was beginning. Once more, exactly as Vry had predicted, Batalix was taking a phagor bite from the brilliant outline of Freyr. The process was slow and inexorable, and would result in Freyr's being lost entirely for five and a half hours. Not so many miles away, the kzahhn had his needed sign.

The suns were devouring their own light. A terrible fear took hold of Laintal Ay, freezing his eddre. For a moment stars blazed in the day sky. Then he closed his eyes and clung to the yelk, burying his face in its rusty pelage. The Twenty Blindnesses were upon him, and he cried in his heart to Wutra to win the war in his heavens.

But Aoz Roon looked up to the sky with awe blunting his thin features, and exclaimed, "Now Hrrm-Bhhrd Ydohk will die!"

Time seemed to cease. Slowly, the brighter light faded behind the duller. The day took on the greyness of a corpse.

Laintal Ay pulled himself from his dread and took Aoz Roon by his skeletal shoulders, searching that familiar but transformed countenance. "What did you say to me then?"

Aoz Roon said dazedly, "I'll be all right, I'll be myself again."

"I asked you what you said."

"Yes. . . . You know how the stench of them, that milky smell, clings to everything. Their language is the same. It makes everything different. I was with Yhamm-Whrrmar a half air-turn, talking with him. Many things. Things of which my Olonets-speaking intelligence can make no sense."

"Never mind that. What did you say about Embruddock?"

"It is something that Yhamm-Whrrmar knew would happen as certainly as if it were past, not future. That phagors would destroy Embruddock—"

"I must go on. Follow if you wish. I must return and warn everyone. Oyre—Dathka—"

Aoz Roon grasped his arms with sudden force.

"Wait, Laintal Ay. A moment and I'll be myself. I had the bone fever. I knocked myself out. Cold nailed my heart."

"You never made excuses for others. Now you make excuses for yourself."

Something of the older man's qualities returned to his face as he stared at Laintal Ay. "You are one of the good men, you bear my mark, I have been your lord. Listen. All I say is what I never thought of till I was on that island half an air-turn. The generations are born and fly their course, then they drop to the world below. There's no escape from it. Only to have a good word said after all's over."

"I'll speak well of you, but you're not dead yet, man."

"The ancipital race knows that their time is done. Better times come for men and women. Sun, flowers, soft things. After we're forgotten. Till all Hrl-Ichor Yhar's frame is empty."

Laintal Ay pushed him away, cursing, not understanding what was said.

"Never mind tomorrow and all that. The world hangs on now. I'm riding to Embruddock."

He climbed again into the saddle of the yelk and kicked it into action. With the lethargic movements of a man rousing from a dream, Aoz Roon followed suit.

The greyness was settling in thicker, like fermentation. In another hour, Freyr was half-devoured, and the hush became more intense. The two men passed groups petrified by dusk.

Later in their progress, they sighted a man approaching on foot. He was running slowly but steadily, arms and legs pumping. He stopped on top of a ridge and stared at them, tensed to run away. Laintal Ay rested his right hand on his sword handle.

Even through the twilight, there was no mistaking that portly figure, the leonine head with its forked beard dramatically flecked with grey. Laintal Ay called his name and moved his mount forward.

It took Raynil Layan some while to be convinced of Laintal Ay's identity, still more for him to recognise the skeletal Aoz Roon with no sparkle in his eyes. He came cautiously round the antlers of the yelk to grasp Laintal Ay's wrist with a damp hand.

"I shall be one with our forefathers if I take another step. You've both endured the bone fever and survived. I may not be so lucky. Exertion makes it worse, they say—sexual exertion or otherwise." He held his chest and panted. "Oldorando's rotten with pest. I've failed to escape in time, fool that I am. That's what these revolting signs mean in the sky. I've sinned—though I'm by no means as bad as you, Aoz Roon. Those religious pilgrims spoke true. It's the gossies for me."

He sank to the ground, puffing and holding his head in misery. He rested an elbow on a pack he had been carrying.

"Tell me what news of the city," Laintal Ay said impatiently.

"Ask me nothing, let me be. . . . Let me die."

Laintal Ay dismounted and kicked the lord of the mint in the buttocks.

"What of the city—besides the pest?"

Raynil Layan turned his red face upwards. "Enemies within. . . . As if the visitations of the fever were not enough, your worthy friend, the other Lord of the Western Veldt, has been trying to usurp Aoz Roon's position. I despair of human nature."

He dipped his hand into a purse hanging by his belt, and brought out some bright gold coins, roons freshly minted at his mint.

"Let me buy your yelk, Laintal Ay. You're within an hour of home and scarcely need it. But I need it. . . ."

"Give me more news, rot you. What of Dathka, is he dead?"

"Who knows? Probably so by now—I left last night."

"And the phagor components ahead? How did you get through them —buying your way?"

Raynil Layan gestured with one hand while he tucked his money away with the other. "Plenty of them between us and the city. I had a Madi as a guide, who avoided them. Who can tell what they may be up to, filthy things." As if struck by a sudden recollection, he added, "Understand that I left, not of course for my own sake, but for the sake of those I had a duty to protect. Others of my party are behind me. We had our hoxneys stolen almost as soon as we set out yesterday, and so our progress—"

Growling like an animal, Laintal Ay seized the other's coat and dragged him to his feet.

"Others? Others? Who's with you? Who are you running away from, you bladder? Is Vry there?"

A wry face. "Let me go. *She* prefers her astronomy, I'm sad to relate. She's still in the city. Be grateful to me, Laintal Ay, I have rescued friends and indeed relations of yours and Aoz Roon's. So bestow on me your insufferable yelk. . . ."

"I'll settle with you later." He pushed Raynil Layan aside and jumped on the yelk. Spurring it fiercely, he crossed the ridge and rode forward to the next one, calling.

On the syncline of the ridge, he found three people and a small boy sheltering. A Madi guide lay with his face buried in the bank, still overcome by the stigmata in the sky. Beside him were Dol, clinging to Rastil Roon, and Oyre. The boy was crying. The two women gazed at Laintal Ay in terror as he dismounted and went forward to them. Only when he clung to them and called their names did they recognise him.

Oyre too had been through the eye of the fever needle. They stood and surveyed each other, smiling and exclaiming at their skeletal selves. Then she gave a laugh and a cry at the same time, and snuggled into his arms. While they stood together, faces against each other's flesh, Aoz Roon came forward, clutched his small son's chubby wrist, and embraced Dol. Tears poured down his ravaged face.

The women related some of the recent painful history of Oldorando; Oyre explained Dathka's unsuccessful attempt to take over the leadership. Dathka was still in the city, together with many others. When Raynil Layan had come to Oyre and Dol, offering to escort them to safety, they had accepted his offer. Though they suspected the man was really fleeing to save his own skin, such was their fear that Rastil Roon would catch the pest that they accepted Raynil Layan's offer, and had left hurriedly with him. Because of his inexperience, their goods and mounts had been stolen almost immediately by Borlienian brigands.

"And the phagors? They're going to attack the city?"

All the women could say was that the city still stood, despite the chaos within its walls. And there had certainly been massed ranks of the dreadful fuggies outside the city as they slipped away.

"I shall have to go back."

"Then I return with you—I'm not leaving you again, my precious," Oyre said. "Raynil Layan can do as he pleases. Dol and the boy stay with father."

As they stood talking, clutching each other, smoke drifted across the plains from the west. They were too involved, too happy, to notice.

"The sight of my son revives me," Aoz Roon said, hugging the child and drying his eyes on his sleeve. "Dol, if you are able to let the past die, I'll be a better man to you from now on."

"You speak words of regret, Father," Oyre said. "I should be the first to do that. I know now how wilfully I behaved to Laintal Ay, and almost lost him as a consequence."

As he saw the tears come to her eyes, Laintal Ay thought involuntarily of his snoktruix in the earth below the rajabarals, and reflected that it was only through Oyre's nearly having lost him that they were now able to find each other. He soothed her, but she burst out of his grasp, saying, "Forgive me, and I'll be yours—and wilful no more, I swear."

He clasped her, smiling. "Keep your will. It's needed. We have much else to learn, and must change as times change. I'm grateful to you for understanding, for making me act."

They clung lovingly together, clutching each other's skeletal bodies, kissing each others' fragile lips.

The Madi guide began to come to his senses. He got up and called for Raynil Layan, but the master of the mint had fled. The smoke was thicker now, adding its ashes to the ashen sky.

Aoz Roon started to relate his experiences on the island to Dol, but Laintal Ay interrupted.

"We're united again, and that is miraculous. But Oyre and I must return to Embruddock in all haste. We'll surely be needed there."

The two sentinels were lost in cloud. A breeze was rising, troubling the plain. It was the breeze, blowing from the direction of Embruddock, which carried the news of fire. Now the smoke became denser. It became a shroud, dimming the living beings—whether friend or foe—scattered across the expanses of plain. Everything was enveloped. With the smoke came the stench of burning. Flights of geese winged eastwards overhead.

The human figures clustering about two antlered animals represented between them three generations. They began to move across the landscape as it faded from view. They would survive, though everyone else perished, though the kzahhn triumphed, for that was what befell.

Even in the flames consuming Embruddock, new configurations were being born. Behind the ancipital mask of Wutra, Shiva—god of destruction and regeneration—was furiously at work on Helliconia.

The eclipse was total now.

END OF VOLUME ONE

. . . Alternatively, you may believe that all these things existed before, but that the human race was wiped out by a burst of fiery heat or its cities were laid low by some great upheaval of the world or engulfed by greedy rivers which persistent rains had driven to overflow their banks. All the more reason, then, to concede my point and admit that an end is coming to earth and sky. If the world was indeed shaken by such plagues and perils, then it needs only a more violent shock to make it collapse in universal ruin.

Lucretius: *De Rerum Natura*
55 BC

HELLICONIA
SUMMER

Man is all symmetry,
Full of proportions, one limb to another,
And all to all the world besides;
Each part may call the farthest, brother;
For head with foot hath private amity,
And both with moons and tides.

More servants wait on Man
Than he'll take notice of: in every path
He treads down that which doth befriend him
When sickness makes him pale and wan.
Ah, mighty love! Man is one world and hath
Another to attend him.

George Herbert, *Man*

CONTENTS

I · The Seacoast of Borlien   3

II · Some Arrivals at the Palace   19

III · A Premature Divorce   36

IV · An Innovation in the Cosgatt   46

V · The Way of the Madis   61

VI · Diplomats Bearing Gifts   78

VII · The Queen Visits the Living and the Dead   109

VIII · In the Presence of Mythology   122

IX · Some Botheration for the Chancellor   135

X · Billy Changes Custody   154

XI · Journey to the Northern Continent   175

XII · The Downstream Passenger Trade   194

XIII · A Way to Better Weaponry   215

XIV · Where Flambreg Live   232

XV · The Captives of the Quarry   249

XVI · The Man Who Mined a Glacier   266

XVII · Death-Flight   281

XVIII · Visitors from the Deep   302

XIX · Oldorando   331

XX · How Justice Was Done   353

XXI · The Slaying of Akhanaba   370

Envoi   391

I

THE SEACOAST OF BORLIEN

Waves climbed the slope of the beach, fell back, and came again. A short way out to sea, the procession of incoming surges was broken by a rocky mass crowned with vegetation. It marked a division between the deeps and the shallows. Once the rock had formed part of a mountain far inland, until volcanic convulsions hurled it into the bay.

The rock was now domesticated by a name. It was known as the Linien Rock. The bay and the place were named Gravabagalinien after the rock. Beyond it lay the shimmering blues of the Sea of Eagles. The waves splashing against the shore were clouded with sand picked up before they scattered into flurries of white foam. The foam raced up the slope, only to sink voluptuously into the beach.

After surging round the bastion of Linien Rock, the waves met at different angles on the beach, bursting up with redoubled vigour so as to swirl about the feet of a golden throne which was being lowered to the sand by four phagors. Into the flood were dipped the ten roseate toes of the Queen of Borlien.

The dehorned ancipitals stood motionless. With nothing more than the flick of an ear, they allowed the milky flood to boil about their feet, greatly though they feared water. Although they had carried their royal load half a mile from the Gravabagalinien palace, they showed no fatigue. Although the heat was intense, they showed no sign of discomfort. Nor did they display interest as the queen walked naked from her throne to the sea.

Behind the phagors, on dry sand, the majordomo of the palace supervised two human slaves in the erection of a tent, which he filled with bright Madi carpets.

The wavelets fawned about the ankles of Queen MyrdemInggala. "The queen of queens" was what the Borlienese peasantry called her. With her went her daughter by the king, Princess Tatro, and some of the queen's constant companions.

The princess screamed with excitement and jumped up and down. At the age of two years and three tenners, she regarded the sea as an enormous, mindless friend.

"Oh, look at this wave coming, Moth! The biggest wave yet! And the next one . . . here it comes . . . oooh! A monster, high as the sky! Oh, they're getting ever so big! Ever so bigger, Moth, Moth, *look*! Just look at this one now, look, it's going to burst and—ooh, here comes another, even huger! Look, look, Moth!"

The queen nodded gravely at her daughter's delight in the placid little waves, and raised her eyes to the distance. Slatey clouds piled up on the southern horizon, heralds of the approaching monsoon season. The deep waters had a resonance for which "blue" was no adequate description. The queen saw azure, aquamarine, turquoise, and viridian there. On her finger she wore a ring sold her by a merchant in Oldorando with a stone—unique and of unknown provenance—which matched the colours of the morning's sea. She felt her life and the life of her child to be to existence as the stone was to the ocean.

From that reservoir of life came the waves which delighted Tatro. For the child, every wave was a separate event, experienced without relation to what had been and what was to come. Each wave was the only wave. Tatro still lingered in the eternal present of childhood.

For the queen, the waves represented a continuous operation, not merely of the ocean but of the world process. That process included her husband's rejection of her, and the armies on the march over the horizon, and the increasing heat, and the sail she hoped every day to see on the horizon. From none of these things could she escape. Past or future, they were contained in her dangerous present.

Calling good-bye to Tatro, she ran forward and dived into the water. She separated herself from the little figure hesitant in the shallows, to espouse the ocean. The ring flashed on her finger as her hands sliced the surface and she swam out.

The waters were elegant against her limbs, cooling them luxuriously. She felt the energies of the ocean. A line of white breakers ahead marked the division between the waters of the bay and the sea proper, where the great westbound current flowed, dividing the continents of torrid Campannlat and chilly Hespagorat, and sweeping round the world. MyrdemInggala never swam further than that line unless her familiars were with her.

Her familiars were arriving now, lured by the strong taint of her femininity. They swam near. She dived with them as they talked in their orchestral language to which she was still a stranger. They warned her that something—an unpleasantness—was about to happen. It would emerge from the sea, her domain.

The queen's exile had brought her to this forsaken spot in the extreme south of Borlien, Gravabagalinien, Ancient Gravabagalinien, haunted by the ghosts of an army which had perished here long ago. It was all her shrunken domain. Yet she had discovered another domain, in the sea. Its discovery was accidental, and dated from the day when she had entered the sea during the period of her menses. Her scent in the water had brought the familiars to her. They had become her everyday companions, solace for all that was lost and all that threatened her.

Fringed by the creatures, MyrdemInggala floated on her back, her tender parts exposed to the heat of Batalix overhead. The water droned in her ears. Her breasts were small and cinnamon tipped, her hips broad, her waist narrow. The sun sparkled on her skin. Her human companions sported nearby. Some swam close to the Linien Rock, others skipped along the beach; all unconsciously used the queen as reference point. Their cries rang in competition with the clash of waves.

Away up the beach, beyond the seawrack, beyond the cliffs, stood the white and gold palace of Gravabagalinien, the home to which the queen was now exiled, awaiting her divorce—or her murder. To the swimmers, it looked like a painted toy.

The phagors stood immobile on the beach. Out to sea, a sail hung immobile. The southern clouds appeared not to move. Everything waited.

But time moved. The dimday wore on—no person of standing would venture into the open in these latitudes when both suns were in the sky. And, as dimday passed, the clouds became more threatening, the sail slanted eastwards, moving towards the port of Ottassol.

In due time the waves brought a human corpse with them. This was the unpleasantness of which the familiars had warned. They squealed in disgust.

The body came swinging about the shoulder of Linien Rock as if it still possessed life and will, to be washed up in a shallow pool. There it lay, carelessly, face down. A sea bird lit on its shoulder.

MyrdemInggala caught the flash of white and swam over to inspect. One of the ladies of her court was there already, gazing down in horror at the sight of the strange fish. Its thick black hair was spikey with brine. An arm was wrapped brokenly round the neck. The sun was already drying its puckered flesh when the queen's shadow fell over it.

The body was swollen with putrefaction. Tiny shrimps in the pool scudded to feed off one broken knee. The court lady put out her foot and tipped the carcass over. It sprawled on its back, stinking.

A mass of writhing scupperfish hung from the face, busily devouring mouth and eye sockets. Even under the glare of Batalix, they did not cease their guzzling.

The queen turned nimbly about as she heard the patter of small feet approaching. She seized Tatro and swung the child up above her head, kissing her, smiling warmly at her in reassurance, and then scampering up the beach with her. As she went, she called to her majordomo.

"ScufBar! Get this thing off our beach. Have it buried as soon as possible. Outside the old ramparts."

The servant rose from the shade of the tent, brushing sand from his charfrul.

"At once, ma'am," he said.

Later in the day, the queen, driven by her anxieties, thought of a better way of disposing of the corpse.

"Take it to a certain man I know in Ottassol," she instructed her little majordomo, fixing him earnestly with her gaze. "He's a man who buys bodies. I shall also give you a letter, though not for the anatomist. You are not to tell the anatomist where you come from, you understand?"

"Who is this man, ma'am?" ScufBar looked the picture of unwillingness.

"His name is CaraBansity. You are not to mention my name to him. He has a reputation for craftiness."

She strove to hide her troubled mind from the servants, little thinking that the time would unfold when her honour rested in CaraBansity's hands.

Beneath the creaking wooden palace lay a honeycomb of cool cellars. Some of the cellars were filled with pile on pile of ice blocks, which had been hewn from a glacier in distant Hespagorat. When both suns had set, Majordomo ScufBar descended among the ice blocks, carrying a whale-oil lantern above his head. A small slave boy followed him, clutching the hem of his charfrul for safety. By way of self-defence in a lifetime of drudgery, ScufBar had become hollow-chested, round-shouldered, and pot-bellied, so as to proclaim his insignificance and escape further duties. The defence had not worked. The queen had an errand for him.

He put on leather gloves and a leather apron. Pulling aside the matting from one of the piles of ice, he gave the lantern to the boy and picked up an ice-axe. With two blows, he severed one of the blocks from its neighbour.

Carrying the block, and grunting to convince the boy of its weight, he made his way slowly up the stairs and saw to it that the boy locked the door behind him. He was greeted by hounds of monstrous size, which prowled the dark corridors. Knowing ScufBar, they did not bark.

He made his way with the ice through a back door and into the open. He listened to hear the slave boy bolt it securely from the inside. Only then did he make his way across the courtyard.

Stars gleamed overhead, and an occasional violet flicker of aurora, which lit his way under a wooden arch to the stables. He smelt the tang of hoxney manure.

A stablehand waited in the gloom, shivering. Everyone was nervous after dark in Gravabagalinien, for then the soldiers of the dead army were said to march in search of friendly land-octaves. A line of brown hoxneys shuffled in the gloom.

"Is my hoxney ready, lad?"

"Aye."

The stablehand had equipped a pack hoxney ready for ScufBar's journey. Over the animal's back had been secured a long wicker casket used for transporting goods requiring ice to keep them fresh. With a final grunt, ScufBar slid the block of ice into the casket, onto a bedding of sawdust.

"Now help me with the body, lad, and don't be squeamish."

The body which had been washed into the bay lay in a corner of the stable, in a puddle of sea water. The two men dragged it over, heaved it up, and arranged it on top of the ice. With some relief, they strapped the padded casket lid down.

"What a beastly cold thing it is," said the stablehand, wiping his hands on his charfrul.

"Few people think well of a human corpse," said ScufBar, pulling off his gloves and apron. "It's fortunate that the deuteroscopist in Ottassol does."

He led the hoxney from the stable and past the palace guard, whose whiskery faces peered nervously from a hut near the ramparts. The king had given his rejected queen only the old or untrustworthy to defend herself with. ScufBar himself was nervous, and never ceased to peer about him. Even the distant boom of the sea made him nervous. Once outside the palace grounds, he paused, took breath, and looked back.

The mass of the palace stood out against the star shingle in fretted outline. In one place only did a light punctuate its darkness. There a woman's figure could be discerned, standing on her balcony and gazing inland. ScufBar nodded to himself, turned towards the coast road, and pulled the hoxney's head eastwards, in the direction of Ottassol.

Queen MyrdemInggala had summoned her majordomo to her earlier. Although she was a religious woman, superstition lingered with her, and the discovery of the body in the water disturbed her. She was inclined to take it as an omen of her own threatened death.

She kissed the Princess TatromanAdala good night and retired to pray. This evening, Akhanaba had no comfort to offer, although she had conceived a simple plan whereby the corpse might be used to good effect.

She feared what the king might do—to her and to her daughter. She had no protection from his anger, and clearly understood that as long as she lived her popularity made her a threat to him. There was one who would protect her, a young general; to him she had sent a letter, but he was fighting in the Western Wars and had not replied.

Now she sent another letter, in ScufBar's care. In Ottassol, a hundred miles distant, one of the envoys of the Holy Pannovalan Empire was due to arrive shortly—with her husband. His name was Alam Esomberr, and he would be bringing with him a bill of divorcement for her to sign. Thought of the occasion made her tremble.

Her letter was going to Alam Esomberr, asking for protection from her husband. Whereas a messenger on his own would be stopped by one of the king's patrols, a grubby little man with a pack animal would pass unremarked. No one inspecting the corpse would think to look for a letter.

The letter was addressed not to Envoy Esomberr but to the Holy C'Sarr himself. The C'Sarr had reason to dislike her king, and would surely give protection to a pious queen in distress.

She stood barefoot on her balcony, looking into the night. She laughed at herself, placing faith in a letter, when the whole world might be about to burn. Her gaze went to the northern horizon. There, YarapRombry's Comet burned: to some a symbol of destruction, to others of salvation. A nightbird called. The queen listened to the cry even after it had died, as one watches a knife irretrievably falling through clear water.

When she was sure that the majordomo was on his way, she returned to her couch and drew the silk curtains round it. She lay there open-eyed.

Through the gloom, the dust of the coast road showed white. ScufBar plodded beside his load, looking anxiously about. Still he was startled when a figure materialised out of the dark and called to him to halt.

The man was armed and of military bearing. It was one of King JandolAnganol's men, paid to keep an eye on all who came or went on the queen's business. He sniffed at the casket. ScufBar explained that he was going to sell the corpse.

"Is the queen that poor, then?" asked the guard, and sent ScufBar on his way.

ScufBar continued steadily, alert for sounds beyond the creak of the casket. There were smugglers along the coast, and worse than smugglers. Borlien was involved in the Western Wars against Randonan and Kace, and its countryside was often plagued by bands of soldiers, raiders, or deserters.

When he had been walking for two hours, ScufBar led the hoxney under a tree which spread its branches over the track. The track rose steeply ahead, to join the southern highroad which ran from Ottassol all the way westwards to the frontier with Randonan.

It would take the full twenty-five hours of the day to reach Ottassol, but there were easier ways of making the journey than plodding beside a loaded hoxney.

After tying the animal to the tree, ScufBar climbed into a low branch and waited. He dozed.

When the rumble of an oncoming cart roused him, he slipped to the ground and waited crouching by the highway. The aurora flickering overhead helped him to make out the traveller. He whistled, an answering whistle came, and the cart drew to a leisurely stop.

The man who owned the cart was an old friend from the same part of Borlien as ScufBar, by name FloerCrow. Every week in the summer of the small year, he drove produce from local farms to market. FloerCrow was not an outgoing man, but he was prepared to give ScufBar a lift to Ottassol for the convenience of having an extra animal to take a turn between the shafts.

The cart stopped long enough for the pack hoxney to be secured to a rear rail, and for ScufBar to scramble aboard. FloerCrow cracked the whip, and the cart lumbered forward. It was drawn by a patient drab brown hoxney.

Despite the warmth of the night, FloerCrow wore a wide-brimmed hat and thick cloak. A sword stood in an iron socket by his side. His load comprised four black piglets, persimmons, gwing-gwings, and a pile of vegetables. The piglets dangled helplessly in nets on the outside of the cart. ScufBar wedged his body against the slatted backrest, and slept with his cap over his eyes.

He roused when the wheels were making heavy weather over dried ruts. Dawn was bleaching the stars as Freyr prepared to rise. A breeze blew and brought the aromas of human habitation.

Although darkness clung to the land, peasants were already about, making for the fields. They moved shadowy and silent, the implements they carried giving an occasional clank. Their steady pace, the downward inclination of their heads, recalled the weariness that had attended their way home on the previous evening.

Male, female, young, old, the peasants progressed on various levels, some above the level of the road, some below. The landscape, as it slowly revealed itself, was composed of wedges, inclines, and walls, all of a dull brown colour, like the hoxneys. The peasants belonged to the great loess plain, which formed the central southern part of the tropical continent of Campannlat. It ran to the north, almost to the borders with Oldorando, and east to the River Takissa, where Ottassol stood. The loamy soil had been dug over by countless workers for countless years. Banks and cliffs and dams had been constructed, to be continually destroyed or rebuilt by succeeding generations. Even in times of drought like the present, the loess had to be worked by those whose destiny it was to make crops grow from dirt.

"Whoa," said FloerCrow, as the cart rumbled into a village by the roadside.

Thick loess walls guarded the aggregation of dwellings against robbers. The gateway had broken and crumbled during last year's monsoon and had not been repaired. Although the gloom was still intense, no lights showed from any window. Hens and geese scavenged beneath the patched mud walls, on which apotropaic religious symbols were painted.

One item of cheer was provided by a stove burning by the gate. The old vendor who tended the stove had no need to cry his waies: the wares gave out a smell which was their own advertisement. He was a waffle seller. A steady stream of peasants bought waffles from him to eat on their way to work.

FloerCrow dug ScufBar in the ribs and pointed with his whip to the vendor. ScufBar took the hint. Climbing stiffly down, he went to buy their breakfast. The waffles came straight from the glowing jaws of the waffle iron into the hands of the customers. FloerCrow ate his greedily and climbed into the back of the cart to sleep. ScufBar changed hoxneys, took the reins, and got the cart moving again.

The day wore on. Other vehicles jostled on the road. The landscape changed. For a while, the highway ran so far below the level of the ground that nothing could be seen but the brown walls of fields. At other times, the way ran along the top of an embankment, and then a wide prospect of cultivation was visible.

The plain stretched in all directions, as flat as a board, dotted with bent figures. Straight lines prevailed. Fields and terraces were square. Trees grew in avenues. Rivers had been deflected into canals; even the sails of boats on the canals were rectangular.

Whatever the view, whatever the heat—today's temperature was in the hundreds—the peasants worked while there was light in the sky. Vegetables, fruits, and veronika, the chief cash crop, had to be tended. Their backs remained bent, whether one sun or two prevailed.

Freyr was pitilessly bright in contrast to the dull red face of Batalix. No one doubted which of the two was master of the heavens. Travellers faring from Oldorando, nearer the equator, told of forests bursting into flame at Freyr's command. Many believed Freyr would shortly devour the world; yet still rows had to be hoed and water trickled on delicate growths.

The farm cart neared Ottassol. The villages were no longer visible to the eye. Only fields could be seen, stretching to a horizon which dissolved in unstable mirages.

The road sloped down into a groove, bounded on either side by earth walls thirty feet high. The village was called Mordec. The men climbed down and tethered the hoxney, which drooped between the shafts until water was brought for it. Both of their little dun-coloured animals showed signs of tiredness.

Narrow tunnels led into the soil on either side of the road. Sunlight showed through them, chopped neatly into rectangular shape. The men emerged from a tunnel into an open court, well below ground level.

On one side of the court was the Ripe Flagon, an inn carved out of the soil. Its interior, comfortingly cool, was lit only by reflections of the light striking down into the courtyard. Opposite the inn were small dwellings, also carved into the loess. Their ochre facades were brightened by flowers in pots.

Through a maze of subterranean passageways the village stretched, opening intermittently into courts, many of them with staircases which led up to the surface, where most of the inhabitants of Mordec were labouring. The roofs of the houses were fields.

As they ate a snack and drank wine at the inn, FloerCrow said, "He stinks a bit."

"He's been dead a while. Queen found him on the shore, washed up. I'd say he was murdered in Ottassol, most like, and flung in the sea off a quay. The current would carry him down to Gravabagalinien."

As they went back to the cart, FloerCrow said, "It's a bad omen for the queen of queens, no mistake."

The long casket lay in the back of the cart with the vegetables. Water trickled from the melting ice and dripped to the ground, where a pool marbled itself with a slow-moving spiral of dust. Flies buzzed round the cart.

They climbed in and started on the last few miles to Ottassol.

"If King JandolAnganol wants to have someone done away with, he'll do it. . . ."

ScufBar was shocked. "The queen's too well loved. Friends everywhere." He felt the letter in his inner pocket and nodded to himself. Influential friends.

"And him going to marry an eleven-year-old slip of a girl instead."

"Eleven and five tenners."

"Whatever. It's disgusting."

"Oh, it's disgusting, right enough," agreed ScufBar. "Eleven and a half, fancy!" He smacked his lips and whistled.

They looked at each other and grinned.

The cart creaked towards Ottassol, and the bluebottles followed.

Ottassol was the great invisible city. In colder times, the plain had supported its buildings; now they supported the plain. Ottassol was an underground labyrinth, in which men and phagors lived. All that remained on the scorched surface were roads and fields, counterpointed by rectangular holes in the ground. Down in the rectangles were the courts, surrounded by facades of houses which otherwise had no external configuration.

Ottassol was earth and its converse, hollowed earth, the negative and positive of soil, as if it had been bitten out by geometrical worms.

The city housed 695,000 people. Its extent could not be seen and was rarely appreciated even by its inhabitants. Favourable soil, climate, and geographical situation had caused the port to grow larger than Borlien's capital, Matrassyl. So the warrens expanded, often on different levels, until they were halted by the River Takissa.

Paved lanes ran underground, some wide enough for two carts to pass. ScufBar walked along one of these lanes, leading the hoxney with the casket. He had parted with FloerCrow at a market on the outskirts of town. As he went, pedestrians turned to stare, screwing up their noses at the smell which floated behind him. The ice block at the bottom of the casket had all but melted away.

"The anatomist and deuteroscopist?" he asked of a passerby. "Bardol CaraBansity?"

"Ward Court."

Beggars of all descriptions called for alms outside the frequent churches, wounded soldiers back from the wars, cripples, men and women with horrific skin cancers. ScufBar ignored them. Pecubeas sang from their cages at every corner and court. The songs of different strains of pecubea were sufficiently distinct for the blind to distinguish and be guided by them.

ScufBar made his way through the maze, negotiated a few broad steps down into Ward Court, and came to the door which bore a sign with the name Bardol CaraBansity on it. He rang the bell.

A bolt was shot back, the door opened. A phagor appeared, dressed in a rough hempen gown. It supplemented its blank cerise stare with a question.

"What you want?"

"I want the anatomist."

Tying the hoxney to a hitching post, ScufBar entered and found himself in a small domed room. It contained a counter, behind which a second phagor stood.

The first phagor walked down a corridor, both walls of which it brushed with its broad shoulders. It pushed through a curtain into a living room in which a couch stood in one corner. The anatomist was enjoying congress with his wife on the couch. He rested as he listened to what the ahuman servant had to say, and then sighed.

"Scerm you, I'll be there." He climbed to his feet and leaned against the wall to pull his pants up under his charfrul, which he adjusted with slow deliberation.

His wife hurled a cushion at him. "You dolt, why do you never concentrate? Finish what you're doing. Tell these fools to go away."

He shook his head and his heavy cheeks trembled. "It's the unremitting clockwork of the world, my beauty. Keep it warm till I return. I don't order the comings and goings of men. . . ."

He moved down the corridor and paused at the threshhold of his shop so as to inspect the new arrival. Bardol CaraBansity was a solid man, less tall than weighty, with a ponderous way of speech and a heavy skull shaped not unlike a phagor's. He wore a thick leather belt over his chafrul, and a knife in the belt. Although he looked like a common butcher, CaraBansity had a well-earned reputation as a crafty man.

With his hollow chest and protruding stomach, ScufBar was not an impressive sight, and CaraBansity made it plain he was not impressed.

"I've got a body for sale, sir. A human body."

Without speaking, CaraBansity motioned to the phagors. They went and brought the body in between them, dropping it down on the counter. Sawdust and ice fragments adhered to it.

The anatomist and deuteroscopist took a step nearer.

"It's a bit high. Where did you acquire it, man?"

"From a river, sir. When I was fishing."

The body was so distended by internal gasses that it bulged out of its clothes. CaraBansity pulled it onto its back and tugged a dead fish from inside its shirt. He threw it at ScufBar's feet.

"That's a so-called scupperfish. To those of us who have a care for truth, it's not a fish at all but the marine young of a Wutra's worm. Marine. Sea, not freshwater. Why are you lying? Did you murder this poor fellow? You look like a criminal. The phrenology suggests it."

"Very well, sir, if you prefer, I did find him in the sea. Since I am a servant of the unfortunate queen, I did not want the fact widely known."

CaraBansity looked at him more closely. "You serve MyrdemInggala, queen of queens, do you, you rogue? She deserves good lackeys and good fortune, does that lady."

He indicated a cheap print of the queen's face, which hung in a corner of the shop.

"I serve her well enough. Tell me what you will pay me for this body."

"You have come all this way for ten roon, not more. In these wicked times, I can get bodies to cut up every day of the week. Fresher than this one, too."

"I was informed that you would pay me fifty, sir. Fifty roon, sir." ScufBar looked shifty, and rubbed his hands together.

"How does it happen that you turn up here with your malodorous friend when the king himself and an envoy from the Holy C'Sarr are due to arrive in Ottassol? Are you an instrument of the king's?"

ScufBar spread his hands and shrank a little. "I have connections only with the hoxney outside. Pay me just twenty-five, sir, and I'll go back to the queen immediately."

"You scerm are all greedy. No wonder the world's going to pot."

"If that is the case, sir, then I'll accept twenty. Twenty roon."

Turning to one of the phagors standing by, flicking its pale milt up its slotlike nostrils, CaraBansity said, "Pay the man and get him out of here."

"How muzzh I pay?"

"Ten roon."

ScufBar let out a howl of anguish.

"All right. Fifteen. And you, my man, present Bardol CaraBansity's compliments to your queen."

The phagor fumbled in its hempen gown and produced a thin purse. It proffered three gold coins, lying in the gnarled palm of its three-fingered hand. ScufBar grabbed them and made for the door, looking sullen.

Briskly CaraBansity ordered one of his ahuman assistants to shoulder the corpse—an order obeyed without observable reluctance—and followed him along the dim corridor, where strange odours drifted. Cara-Bansity knew as much about the stars as about the intestines, and his house—itself shaped rather like an intestine—extended far into the loess, with entrances to chambers devoted to all his interests on several lanes.

They entered a workshop. Light slanted down through two small square windows set in fortress-thick earth walls. Where the phagor trod, points of light glinted under his splayed feet. They looked like diamonds. They were beads of glass, scattered when the deuteroscopist was making lenses.

The room was crammed with learned litter. The ten houses of the zodiac were painted on the wall. Against another wall hung three carcasses in various stages of dissection—a giant fish, a hoxney, and a phagor. The hoxney had been opened up like a book, its soft parts removed to display ribs and backbone. On a desk nearby lay sheets of paper on which CaraBansity had drawn detailed representations of the dead animal, with various parts depicted in coloured ink.

The phagor swung the Gravabagalinien corpse from his shoulder and hung it upside down from a rail. Two hooks pierced the flesh between the Achilles tendon and the calcaneum. The broken arms dangled, the puffy hands rested like shelled crabs on the floor. At a blow from Cara-Bansity, his assistant departed. CaraBansity hated having the ancipitals about, but they were cheaper than servants or even human slaves.

After a judicial contemplation of the corpse, CaraBansity pulled out his knife and cut the dead man's clothes away. He ignored the stench of decay.

The body was that of a young man, twelve years old, twelve and a half, possibly twelve years and nine tenners, not more. His clothes were of coarse and foreign quality, his hair was cut in a manner generally used by sailors.

"You, my fine fellow, are probably not of Borlien," said CaraBansity to the corpse. "Your clothes are Hespagorat style—probably from Dimariam."

The belly was so distended that it had folded over and concealed a leather body belt. CaraBansity worked it free. As the flesh sank back, a wound was revealed. CaraBansity slipped on a glove and thrust his fist into the wound. His fingers met with an obstruction. After some tugging, he extracted a curved grey ancipital horn, which had punctured the spleen and sunk deep into the body. He regarded the object with interest. Its two sharp edges made it a useful weapon. It had once possessed a handle, which was missing, possibly lost in the sea.

He regarded the body with fresh curiosity. A mystery always pleased him.

Setting the horn down, he examined the belt. It was of superior workmanship, but the sort of standard thing sold anywhere—at Osoilima, for example, where pilgrims provided a ready market for such goods. On the inner side was a button-down pocket, which he flipped open. From the pocket, he withdrew an incomprehensible object.

Frowning, he laid the object in his grubby palm and walked across to the light with it. It was like nothing he had ever seen before. He could not even identify the metal of which it was chiefly made. A shiver of superstitious fear crossed his pragmatic mind.

As he was washing it under the pump, removing traces of sand and blood, his wife, Bindla, entered the workshop.

"Bardol? What are you doing now? I thought you were coming back to bed. You know what I was keeping warm for you?"

"I love it, but I have something else to do." He flashed her one of his solemn smiles. She was of middle age—at twenty-eight and one tenner almost two years younger than he—and her rich russet hair was losing some of its colour; but he admired the way she was still aware of her ripe charms. At present, she was overacting her resentment at the smells in the room.

"You're not even writing your treatise on religion, your usual excuse." He grunted. "I prefer my stinks."

"You perverse man. Religion is eternal, stinks aren't."

"On the contrary, my leggiandrous beauty, religions change all the time. It's stinks which go on unchanged for ever."

"You rejoice in that?"

He was drying the wonderful object on a cloth and did not answer. "Look at this."

She came and rested a hand on his shoulder.

"By the boulder!" he exclaimed in awe. He passed it to Bindla, and she gasped.

A strap of cunningly interwoven metal, much like a bracelet, supported a transparent panel in which three sets of numbers glowed.

They read the numbers aloud as he pointed to them with a blunt finger.

06 : 16 : 55   12 : 37 : 76   19 : 20 : 14

The numbers writhed and changed as they watched. The CaraBansitys looked at each other in mute astonishment. They watched again.

"I never saw such a talisman before," Bindla said in awe.

They had to look again, fascinated. The figures were black on a yellow background. He read them aloud.

06 : 20 : 25   13 : 00 : 00   19 : 23 : 44

As CaraBansity put the mechanism to his ear to see if it made any noise, the pendulum clock on the wall behind began to chime thirteen. This clock was an elaborate one, built by CaraBansity himself in his younger days. It showed in pictorial form the rising and setting times of the two suns, Batalix and Freyr, as well as the divisions of the year, the 100 seconds in a minute, the forty minutes in an hour, the twenty-five hours in a day, the eight days in a week, the six weeks in a tenner, and the ten tenners in a year of four hundred and eighty days. There was also an indicator to show the 1825 small years in a Great Year; that pointer now stood at 381, the present date by the Borlien-Oldorando calendar.

Bindla listened to the mechanism, and heard nothing. "Is it a clock of some kind?"

"Must be. Middle numbers make it thirteen o'clock, Borlien time . . ."

She always knew when he was at a loss. He chewed his knuckle like a child.

There was a row of studs along the top of the bracelet. She pressed one.

A different series of numbers appeared in the three apertures.

$$6877 \qquad 828 \qquad 3269$$
$$(1177)$$

"The middle one's the year, by some ancient calendar or other. How can that work?"

He pressed the stud and the previous series appeared. He set the bracelet down on the bench and stared at it, but Bindla picked it up and slipped it over her hand. The bracelet immediately adjusted itself, fitting snugly to her plump wrist. She shrieked.

CaraBansity went across to a shelf of worn reference books. He passed over an ancient folio copy of *The Testament of RayniLayan*, and pulled out a calf-bound *Seer's and Deuteroscopist's Calendrical Tables*. After fluttering through several pages, he settled on one and ran his finger down a column.

Although the year by the Borlien-Oldorando calendar was 381, this reckoning was not universally accepted. Other nations used other reckonings, which were listed in the Tables; 828 was listed. He found it under the ancient, discarded "Denniss Calendar," now associated with witchcraft and the occult. Denniss was the name of a legendary king supposed to have ruled all Campannlat.

"The central panel of the bracelet refers to local time . . ." He tested out his knuckle again. "And it has survived inundation in the sea. Where are there craftsmen now who could manufacture such a jewel? Somehow it must have survived from the time of Denniss . . ."

He held his wife's wrist and they watched the numbers busy with their changes. They had found a timepiece of unparalleled sophistication, probably of unparalleled value, certainly of unparalleled mystery.

Wherever the craftsmen were who had made the bracelet, they must be secure from the desperate state to which King JandolAnganol had brought Borlien. Things still held together in Ottassol because it was a port, trading with other lands. Conditions elsewhere were worse, with drought, famine, and lawlessness. Wars and skirmishes wasted the country's lifeblood. A better statesman than the king, advised by a less corrupt scritina, or parliament, would make peace with Borlien's enemies and see to the welfare of the population at home.

Yet it was not possible to hate JandolAnganol—though CaraBansity regularly tried to do so—because he was prepared to give up his beautiful wife, the queen of queens, to marry a stupid child, a half-Madi. Why should the Eagle do that, if not to cement the alliance between Borlien and its old enemy, Oldorando, for his country's sake? JandolAnganol was a dangerous man, all agreed—but as much under the cudgel of circumstance as the lowest peasant.

The worsening climate could be much blamed. The madness of the heat, increasing generation by generation, till the very trees caught fire . . .

"Don't stand dreaming," Bindla called. "Come and get your ridiculous contraption off my wrist."

II

SOME ARRIVALS
AT THE PALACE

The event that the queen feared was already in process. King JandolAnganol was on his way to Gravabagalinien to divorce her. From the Borlienese capital of Matrassyl he would sail down the River Takissa to Ottassol, there to take a coastal ship westward to Gravabagalinien's narrow bay. JandolAnganol would present his queen with the Holy C'Sarr's bill of divorcement in front of witnesses. Then they would part, perhaps forever.

This was the king's plan, and very stormy he looked about it.

Accompanied by a brave sound of trumpets, escorted by members of his Household in finest array, King JandolAnganol was driven in his state coach down the hill from the palace, through Matrassyl's crooked streets, to the quayside. In the coach with him was a solitary companion: Yuli, his pet phagor. Yuli was no more than a runt, with the brown hairs of his infancy still showing through his white coat. He had been dehorned and sat against his master, shuffling in nervous anticipation of the river journey.

As JandolAnganol stepped out of the vehicle, the captain of the waiting ship came forward and saluted smartly.

"We'll get under way as soon as you are ready," JandolAnganol said. His queen had sailed into exile from this very quay some five tenners earlier. Groups of citizens stood along the riverbank, eager to observe the king who had such a mixed reputation. The mayor had come to bid his monarch farewell. The cheering was nothing like the roar that had sped Queen MyrdemInggala on her way.

The king went aboard. A wooden clapper sounded, crisp as hoof on cobble. Rowers began to row. The sails were unfurled.

As the boat slid out from its mooring, JandolAnganol turned sharply to stare at the mayor of Matrassyl, who stood with his attendants drawn stiffly up on the dock in farewell. Catching the king's glance, the mayor bowed his head submissively, but JandolAnganol knew how angry the man was. The mayor resented his monarch's leaving the capital when the city was under external threat. Taking advantage of Borlien's war with Randonan in the west, the savage nations of Mordriat to the northeast were on the move.

As that surly face fell behind the stern of the ship, the king turned his head to the south. He admitted to himself that there was some justice in the mayor's attitude. From the high, restless grasslands of Mordriat came news that the warlord Unndreid the Hammer was active again. The Borlienese Northern Army, to improve its morale, should have had appointed as its general the king's son, Robayday-Anganol. But RobaydayAnganol had disappeared on the day he heard of his father's plan to divorce his mother.

"A son to trust in . . ." said JandolAngonal to the wind, with a bitter expression. He blamed his son for this journey on which he was embarked.

So the king set his profile southwards, looking for loyal demonstration. On the timbers of the deck, the shadows of the rigging lay in elaborate patterns. The shadows doubled themselves when Freyr rose in splendour. Then the Eagle retired to sleep.

A canopy of silk provided shelter in the poop of the ship. There the king remained for most of the three-day journey, with companions by his side. A few feet below his coign of vantage, almost naked human slaves, Randonanese for the most part, sat at their oars, ready to assist the canvas when the wind failed. The scent of them drifted up occasionally, to mingle with the smells of tar, timber, and bilges.

"We will make a stop at Osoilima," the king announced. At Osoilima, a place of pilgrimage on the river, he would go to the shrine and be scourged. He was a religious man, and needed the goodwill of Akhanaba, the All-Powerful, in the test that was to come.

JandolAnganol was of distinguished and morose bearing. At twenty-

five years and a tenner or two, he was still a young man, but lines
marked his powerful face, giving him an appearance of wisdom his
enemies claimed he did not possess.

Like one of his hawks, he had a commanding way of holding his head.
It was to this head that most attention turned, as if the head of the
nation were embodied in his skull. There was an eaglelike look to
JandolAnganol, emphasised by the sharp bladed nose, the fierce black
eyebrows, and the trim beard and moustache, which latter partly concealed a sensuous mouth. His eyes were dark and intense; the darting
glance from those eyes, missing nothing, had brought him his nickname in the bazaars, the Eagle of Borlien.

Those who were close to him and had a gift for understanding character claimed that the eagle was always caged, and that the queen of
queens still held the lock of the cage. JandolAnganol had the curse of
khmir, best described as an impersonal lust, well understood in these hot
seasons.

Often the quick head movements, in marked contrast to the concentrated stillness of the body, were the nervous habits of a man who
hoped to see where he could turn next.

The ceremony under the high rock of Osoilima was soon over. The
king, with blood seeping through his tunic, stepped back on board
ship, and the second half of the journey began. Hating the stench of
the boat, the king slept on deck at night, lying on a swansdown mattress. His phagor runt Yuli slept by him, guarding his feet.

Behind the king's ship, keeping a discreet distance, was a second
ship, a converted cattle boat. In it sailed the king's most faithful troops,
the First Phagorian Guard. It drew protectively closer to the king's ship
as they approached Ottassol's inner harbour, on the afternoon of the
third day of the voyage.

Flags dropped from masts in the muggy Ottassol heat. A crowd
gathered at the quayside. Among the banners and other tokens of pa-
triotism were grimmer signs, saying THE FIRE IS COMING: THE OCEANS
WILL BURN, and LIVE WITH AKHA OR DIE FOR EVER WITH FREYR. The
Church was taking advantage of a time of general alarm, and trying to
bring sinners to heel.

A band marched importantly forward between two warehouses and
began to play a regal theme. The plaudits for his majesty as he stepped
down the gangplank were restrained.

Greeting him were members of the city scritina and notable citizens.
Knowing the Eagle's reputation, they kept their speeches brief, and the
king was brief in his reply.

"We are always happy to visit Ottassol, our chief port, and to find it
flourishing. I cannot remain here long. You know how great events
move forward.

"My unbending intention is to divorce myself from Queen Myrdem-Inggala by a bill of divorcement issued by the Great C'Sarr Kilandar IX, Head of the Holy Pannovalan Empire and Father Supreme of the Church of Akhanaba, whose servants we are.

"After I have served that bill upon the present queen, in the presence of witnesses accredited by the Holy C'Sarr, as in law I must, then, when the Holy C'Sarr receives the bill, I shall be free to take, and will take, as my lawful spouse Simoda Tal, Daughter of Oldorando. Thus shall I affirm by bonds of matrimony the alliance between our country and Oldorando, an ancient linkage, and confirm our common partnership in the Holy Empire.

"United, our common enemies will be defeated, and we shall grow to greatness as in the days of our grandfathers."

There was some cheering and clapping. Most of the audience rushed to see the phagorian soldiery disembark.

The king had discarded his usual keedrant. He was dressed in a tunic of yellow and black, sleeveless, so that his sinewy arms were well displayed. His trousers were of yellow silk, clinging close to his limbs. His turn-over boots were of dull leather. He wore a short sword at his belt. His dark hair was woven about the golden circle of Akhanaba, by whose grace he ruled the kingdom. He stood staring at his welcoming committee.

Possibly they expected something more practical from him. The truth was that Queen MyrdemInggala commanded almost as much affection in Ottassol as in Matrassyl.

With a curt gesture to his retinue, JandolAnganol turned and stalked off.

Ahead lay the shabby low cliffs of loess. A length of yellow cloth had been laid across the quayside for the king to walk on. He avoided it, crossed to his waiting coach, and climbed in. The footman closed the door, and the vehicle moved off at once. It entered an archway and was immediately within the labyrinth of Ottassol. The phagorian guard followed.

JandolAngonol, who hated many things, hated his Ottassol palace. His mood was not softened by being welcomed at the gate by his Royal Vicar, the chill, wench-faced AbstrogAthenat.

"Great Akhanaba bless you, sire, we rejoice to see your majesty's face, and to have your presence among us, just when bad tidings arrive from the Second Army in Randonan."

"I'll hear of military matters from military men," said the king, and paced forward into the reception hall. The palace was cool, and remained cool as the seasons grew hotter, but its subterranean nature depressed him. It reminded him of the two priestly years he had spent in Pannoval as a boy.

His father, VarpalAnganol, had greatly extended the palace. Seeking his son's praise, he had asked him how he liked it. "Cold, copious, ill considered," had been Prince JandolAnganol's answer.

It was typical of VarpalAnganol, never an artist at warfare, not to appreciate that the subterranean palace could never be defended effectively.

JandolAnganol remembered the day the palace was invaded. He was three years and a tenner old. He had been playing with a wooden sword in an underground court. One of the smooth loess walls shattered. From it burst a dozen armed rebels. They had tunnelled through the earth unnoticed. It still vexed JandolAnganol to recall that he had yelled in terror before charging at them with his toy sword.

There happened to be a change of guard assembling in the court, with weapons ready. After a furious skirmish, the invaders were killed. The illegal tunnel was later incorporated into the design of the palace. That had been during one of the rebellions which VarpalAnganol had failed to put down with sufficient harshness.

The old man was now imprisoned in the fortress at Matrassyl, and the courts and passages of the Ottassol palace were guarded by human and ancipital sentries. JandolAnganol's eyes darted to the silent men as he passed them in the winding corridors; if one so much as moved, he was ready to kill him.

News of the king's black mood spread among the palace staff. Festivities had been arranged to divert him. But first he had to receive the report from the western battlefields.

A company of the Second Army, advancing across the Chwart Heights intending to attack the Randonanese port of Poorich, had been ambushed by a superior force of the enemy. They had fought till dusk, when survivors had escaped to warn the main force. A wounded man had been despatched to report the news back along the Southern Highway semaphore system to Ottassol.

"What of General TolramKetinet?"

"He fights on, sire," said the messenger.

JandolAnganol received the report almost without comment and then descended to his private chapel to pray and be scourged. It was exquisite punishment to be beaten by the lickerish AbstrogAthenat.

The court cared little what happened to armies almost three thousand miles away: it was more important that the evening's festivities should not be spoilt by the king's bile. The Eagle's chastisement was good for everyone.

A winding stair led down to the private chapel. This oppressive place, designed in the Pannovalan fashion, was carved from the clay which lay beneath the loess, and lined with lead to waist level, with stone above. Moisture stood in beads, or ran in miniature waterfalls. Lights burned behind stained glass shades. The beams from these lanterns projected rectangles of colour into the dank air.

Sombre music played as the Royal Vicar took up his ten-tailed whip from beside the altar. On the altar stood the Wheel of Akhanaba, two sinuous spokes connecting inner rim with outer. Behind the altar hung a tapestry, gold and red, depicting Great Akhanaba in the glory of his contradictions: the Two-in-One, man and god, child and beast, temporal and eternal, spirit and stone.

The King stood and gazed at the animal face of his god. His reverence was wholehearted. Throughout his life, since his adolescent years in a Pannovalan monastery, religion had ruled him. Equally, he ruled through religion. Religion held most of the court and his people in thrall.

It was the common worship of Akhanaba which united Borlien, Oldorando, and Pannoval into an uneasy alliance. Without Akhanaba there would be only chaos, and the enemies of civilisation would prevail.

AbstrogAthenat motioned to his royal penitent to kneel, and read a short prayer over him.

"We come before Thee, Great Akhanaba, to ask forgiveness for failure and to display the blood of guilt. Through the wickedness of all men, Thou, the Great Healer, art wounded, and Thou, the All-Powerful, art made weak. Therefore Thou hast set our steps among Fire and Ice, in order that we may experience in our material beings, here on Helliconia, what Thou dost experience elsewhere in our name, the perpetual torment of Heat and Frost. Accept this suffering, O Great Lord, as we endeavour to accept Thine."

The whip came up over the royal shoulders. AbstrogAthenat was an effeminate young man, but strong in the arm and assiduous in working Akhanaba's will.

After penitence, the ceremonial of the bath; after the bath, the king ascended to the revelry.

Whips here gave way to the flicking of skirts in the dance. The music was brisk, the musicians fat and smiling. The king put on a smile too, and wore it like armour, as he remembered that this chamber had previously been lit by the presence of Queen MyrdemInggala.

The walls were decorated with the flowers of dimday, with idront and scented vispard. There were mounds of fruit and sparkling jugs of black wine. The peasants might starve, but not the palace.

JandolAnganol condescended to refresh himself with black wine, to which he added fruit juice and Lordryardry ice. He sat staring without much attending to the scene before him. His courtiers kept at a discrete distance. Women were sent to charm him and sent away again.

He had dismissed his old chancellor before leaving Matrassyl. A new chancellor, on probation, fussed at his side. Made at once fawning and anxious by his advancement, he came to discuss arrangements for the forthcoming expedition to Gravabagalinien. He also was sent away.

The king intended to remain in Ottassol for as short a time as possible. He would meet with the C'Sarr's envoy and then continue on with him to Gravabagalinien. After the ceremony with the queen, he would make a forced march to Oldorando; there he would marry Princess Simoda Tal and get that whole business over with. He would then defeat his enemies, with assistance from Oldorando and Pannoval, and impose peace within his own borders. Certainly, the child princess, Simoda Tal, would have to live in the palace at Matrassyl, but there was no reason why he should have to see her. This scheme he would accomplish. It ran constantly through his mind.

He looked about for the C'Sarr's envoy, the elegant Alam Esomberr. He had met Esomberr during his two-year stay in the Pannovalan monastery, and they had remained friendly ever since. It was necessary for JandolAnganol to have this powerful dignitary, sent by Kilandar IX himself, to witness his and the queen's signature to the document of divorcement, and to return it to the C'Sarr himself before the marriage was legally void. Esomberr should be at his side by now.

But Envoy Esomberr had been delayed as he was about to leave his suite. A scruffy little man with a pot belly, mangy hair, and travel-stained clothes had talked his way into the envoy's powdered presence.

"I take it you're not from my tailor?"

The scruffy little man denied the charge and produced a letter from an inner pocket. He handed it to the envoy. He stood and wriggled while Esomberr tore open the letter with an elegant gesture.

"It is, sir, intended—intended for onward delivery. For the eyes of the C'Sarr alone, begging your pardon."

"I am the C'Sarr's representative in Borlien, thank you," said Esomberr.

He read the letter, nodded, and produced a silver coin for the bearer.

Muttering, the latter retreated. He left the underground palace, went to where his hoxney was tethered, and began making his way back to Gravabagalinien to report his success to the queen.

The envoy stood smiling to himself and scratching the end of his nose. He was a willowy, personable man of twenty-four and a half years, dressed in a rich trailing keedrant. He dangled the letter. He sent a minion for a likeness of Queen MyrdemInggala, which he studied. From any new situation, personal as well as political advantages were to be gained. He would enjoy his trip to Gravabagalinien, if that were possible. Esomberr promised himself that he would not be too religious for his own enjoyment at Gravabagalinien.

As soon as the royal boat had docked, men and women had crowded into the forecourt of the palace to seek a word with the king. By law, all supplications had to go through the scritina, but the ancient tradition of making a plea direct to the king died hard. The king preferred work to idleness. Tired of waiting and of watching his courtiers gyrate themselves into states of breathlessness, he agreed to hold audience in a nearby room. His runt sat alertly by the small throne, and the king patted him now and again.

After the first two supplicants had come and gone, Bardol Cara-Bansity appeared before the king. He had thrown an embroidered waistcoat over his charfrul. JandolAnganol recognised the man's strutting walk and frowned as a florid bow was sketched in his direction.

"This man is Bardol CaraBansity, sire," said the chancellor-on-trial, standing at the king's right hand. "You have some of his anatomical designs in the royal library."

The king said, "I remember you. You are a friend of my ex-chancellor, SartoriIrvrash."

CaraBansity blinked his blood-shot eyes. "I trust that SartoriIrvrash is well, sire, despite being an ex-chancellor."

"He has fled to Sibornal, if that can be called being well. What do you want of me?"

"Firstly, a chair, sire, since my legs pain me to stand."

They contemplated each other. Then the king motioned a page to move a chair below the dais on which he sat.

Taking his time about getting himself settled, CaraBansity said, "I have an object to set before you—priceless, I believe—knowing your majesty to be a man of learning."

"I am an ignorant man, and stupid enough to dislike flattery. A king of Borlien concerns himself with politics merely, to keep his country intact."

"We do whatever we do the better for being better informed. I can break a man's arm better if I know how his joints work."

The king laughed. It was a harsh sound, not often heard from his mouth. He leaned forward. "What is learning against the increasing rage of Freyr? Even the All-Powerful Akhanaba seems to have no power against Freyr."

CaraBansity let his gaze rest on the floor. "I know nothing of the All-Powerful, Majesty. He does not communicate with me. Some public benefactor scribbled the word 'Atheist' on my door last week, so that is my label now."

"Then take care for your soul." The king spoke less challengingly now, and lowered his voice. "As a deuteroscopist, what do you make of the encroaching heat? Has humankind sinned so gravely that we must all perish in Freyr's fire? Is not the comet in the northern sky a sign of coming destruction, as the common people claim?"

"Majesty, that comet, YarapRombry's Comet, is a sign of hope. I could explain at length, but I fear to vex you with astronomical reckoning. The comet is named after the sage—cartographer and astronomer —YarapRombry of Kevassien. He made the first map of the globe, setting Ottaassaal, as this city was then called, in the centre of the map, and he named the comet. That was 1825 years ago—one great year. The return of the comet is proof that we circle about Freyr like the comet, and will pass it by with no more than a slight singe!"

The king thought. "You give me a scientific answer, just as Sartori-Irvrash did. There must also be a religious answer to my question."

CaraBansity chewed his knuckle. "What does the Holy Pannovalan Empire say on the subject of Freyr? For Akha's sake, it dreads any manifestation in the sky, and therefore uses the comet only to increase the fear of the people. It declares one more holy drumble to eliminate the phagors from our midst. The Church's argument is that if those creatures without souls are eliminated, the climate will immediately cool. Yet we are given to understand that, in the years of ice, the Church then claimed it was the ungodly phagors which brought the cold. So their thinking lacks logic—like all religious thinking."

"Don't vex me. I am the Church in Borlien."

"Majesty, apologies. I merely speak true. If it offends you, send me away, as you sent SartoriIrvrash away."

"That fellow you mention was all for wiping out the ancipitals."

"Sire, so am I, though I depend on them myself. If I may again speak truth, your favouring of them alarms me. But I would not kill them for some silly religious reason. I would kill them because they are the traditional enemy of mankind."

The Eagle of Borlien banged his hand down on the arm of his chair. The chancellor-on-trial jumped.

"I'll hear no more. You argue out of place, you impertinent hrattock!"

CaraBansity bowed. "Very well, sire. Power makes men deaf and they will not hear. It was you, not I, sire, who called yourself ignorant. Because you can threaten with a look, you cannot learn. That is your misfortune."

The king stood. The chancellor-on-trial shrank away. CaraBansity stood immobile, his face a patchy white. He knew he had gone too far.

But JandolAnganol pointed at the cringing chancellor.

"I tire of people who cower before me, like this man. Advise me as my advisor cannot and you shall be chancellor—no doubt to prove as vexing as your friend and predecessor.

"When I remarry, and take for wife the daughter of King Sayren

Stund of Oldorando, this kingdom will be linked more firmly to the
Holy Pannovalan Empire, and from that we shall derive strength. But
I shall come under much pressure from the C'Sarr to obliterate the
ancipital race, as is being done in Pannoval. Borlien is short of soldiers
and needs phagors. Can I refute the C'Sarr's edict through your
science?"

"Hm." CaraBansity pulled at a heavy cheek. "Pannoval and Oldorando have always hated fuggies as Borlien never did. We are not on
ancipital migratory routes, as is Oldorando. The priests have found a
new pretext to wage an old war. . . ."

"There is a scientific line you might take, sire. Science that would
banish the Church's ignorance, if you'll forgive me."

"Speak, then, and my pretty runt and I will listen."

"Sire, you will understand. Your runt will not. You must know by
repute the historical treatise entitled *The Testament of RayniLayan*.
In that volume, we read of a saintly lady, VryDen, wife of the sage
RayniLayan. VryDen unravelled some of the secrets of the heavens
where, she believed, as I do, that truth, not evil, lives. VryDen perished
in the great fire which consumed Oldorando in the year 26. That is
three hundred and fifty-five years ago—fifteen generations, though we
live longer than they did in those times. I am convinced that VryDen
was a real person—not an invention of an Ice Age tale, as the Holy
Church would have us believe."

"What's your point?" asked the king. He began to pace sharply
about, and Yuli skipped after him. He remembered that his queen set
great store by the book of RayniLayan, and read parts of it to Tatro.

"Why, my point is a sharp one. This same VryDen lady was an
atheist, and therefore saw the world as it is, unobscured by imagined
deities. Before her day, it was believed that Freyr and Batalix were two
living sentinels who guarded our world against a war in heaven. With
the aid of geometry, this same excellent lady was able to predict a series
of eclipses which brought her era to a close.

"Knowledge can build only on knowledge, and one never knows
where the next step will lead. But it leads somewhere, whereas Church
dogma leads only in a circle. The Church's very emblem is that circle."

"Which I prefer to your fumbling steps into darkness."

"I found a way to see through the darkness into light. With the aid
of our mutual acquaintance, SartoriIrvrash, I ground some lenses of
glass like the lens in the eye." He described how they had constructed a
telescope. Through this instrument, they studied the phases of Ipocrene
and the other planets in the sky. This intelligence they kept to themselves, since the sky was not a popular subject in those nations under the
religious sway of Pannoval.

"One by one, these wanderers revealed their phases to us. Soon we could predict their changes exactly. There's deuteroscopy! From there, SartoriIrvrash and I backed our observations by calculation. Thus we came on the laws of heavenly geometry, which we think must have been known to YarapRombry—but he suffered martyrdom at the hands of the Church. These laws state that the orbits of the worlds lie about the sun Batalix, and the orbit of Batalix lies about Freyr. And the radius vector of the solar movements covers equal areas of space in equal times.

"We discovered also that the fast planet, called by VryDen Kaidaw, has its orbit not about Batalix but about Helliconia, and is therefore a satellite body or moon."

The king stopped pacing to ask sharply, "Could people like us live on this Kaidaw?"

The question was so at variance with his previous reluctant interest that CaraBansity was surprised. "It is merely a silver eye, sire, not a true world, like Helliconia or Ipocrene."

The king clapped his hands. "Enough. Explain no more. You could end as did YarapRombry. I understand nothing."

"If we could make these explanations clear to Pannoval, then we might change their out-of-date thinking. If the C'Sarr could be coaxed to understand celestial geometry, then he might come to appreciate a human geometry enough to allow humankind and ancipitals to revolve about each other as Batalix and Freyr do, instead of promulgating his holy drumbles, which upset orderly life."

He was about to launch into further explanation, when the king made one of his impatient gestures.

"Another day. I can't listen to much heresy at a time, though I appreciate the cunning of your thought. You incline to go with circumstances, even as I do. Is this what you came here for?"

For a while, CaraBansity faced the sharp gaze of the king. Then he said, "No, Your Majesty, I came, like many of your faithful subjects, hoping to sell you something."

He brought from his belt the bracelet with the three sets of numbers which he had discovered on the corpse, and presented it to his majesty.

"Did you ever see a jewel like this before, Your Majesty?"

His majesty regarded it with surprise, turning it over in his hand.

"Yes," he said. "Yes, I've seen this very bracelet before, in Matrassyl. It is indeed strange, and it came from a strange man, who claimed to have come from another world. From your Kaidaw." He closed his mouth after this mysterious speech, as if sorry to have spoken.

He watched the numbers in the piece of jewellery writhing and changing for a while, and said, "You can tell me at a more leisurely time how this arrived in your possession. Now this audience is closed. I have other matters to attend to."

He closed his hand over the bracelet.

CaraBansity broke into pained protest. The king's demeanour changed. Rage burned from his eyes, from every line of his face. He leaned forward like a predatory bird.

"You atheists will never comprehend that Borlien lives or dies by its religion. Are we not threatened on every side by barbarians, by unbelievers? The empire cannot exist without belief. This bracelet threatens the empire, threatens belief itself. Its wriggling numbers come from a system that would destroy us. . . ." In a less intense voice, he added, "Such is my conviction, and we must live or die by our convictions."

The deuteroscopist bit his knuckle and said nothing.

JandolAnganol contemplated him, then spoke again.

"If you decide to become my chancellor, return here tomorrow. We will then speak more. Meanwhile, I will keep this atheistic bauble. What will your answer be, do you think? Will you become my chief advisor?"

Seeing the king place the bracelet within his clothes, CaraBansity was overcome.

"I thank your majesty. On that question, I must consult my own chief advisor, my wife. . . ."

He bowed low as the king passed him and swept out of the room.

In a nearby corridor of the palace, the C'Sarr's envoy was preparing to attend the king.

The portrait of Queen MyrdemInggala was painted on an oval piece of ivory cut from the tusk of a sea beast. It showed that unmatched face with a brow of flawless beauty, and her hair piled high above it. The queen's deep blue eyes were shielded by full lids, while the neat chin lent a delicate aspect to an otherwise rather commanding mien. These features Alam Esomberr recognised from earlier portraits he had examined in Pannoval—for the queen's beauty was known far and wide.

As he gazed upon this image, the official envoy of the Holy C'Sarr allowed his mind to dwell upon lascivious thoughts. He reflected that in a short space of time he would be face to face with the original masterpiece.

Two agents of Pannoval who spied for the C'Sarr stood before Esomberr. As he stared at the picture, they reported the gossip of Ottassol. They discussed back and forward between themselves the danger the queen of queens would be in once the divorcement between her and JandolAnganol was complete. He would wish to have her removed entirely from the scene. Entirely.

On the other hand, the general multitude preferred the queen to the king. Had not the king imprisoned his own father and bankrupted his country? The multitude might rise up, kill the king, and place Myrdem-Inggala on the throne. Justifiably.

Esomberr looked mildly upon them.

"You worms," he said. "You hrattocks. You tit-tattlers. Do not all kings bankrupt their countries? Would not everyone lock up his father, given the power? Are not queens always in danger? Do not multitudes always dream of rising up and overthrowing someone or other? You chatter merely of traditional role-playing in the great but on the whole somewhat typecast theatre of life. You tell me nothing of substance. Agents of Oldorando would be flogged if they turned in such a report."

The men bowed their heads. "We also have to report that agents of Oldorando are busy here."

"Let's hope they don't spend all their time rumboing the port wrenches, as you two evidently do. The next time I summon you, I shall expect news from you, not gossip."

The agents bowed more deeply and left the room, smiling excessively, as if they had been overpaid.

Alam Esomberr sighed, practised looking severe, and glanced again at the miniature of the queen.

"No doubt she's stupid, or has some other defect to counterbalance such beauty," he said aloud. He tucked the ivory into a safe pocket.

The envoy to C'Sarr Kilandar IX was a noble of deeply religious Taker family with connections in the deep-dwelling Holy City itself. His austere father, a member of the Grand Judiciary, had seen to it that promotion of his son, who despised him, had come early. Esomberr regarded this journey to bear witness to his friend's divorcement as a holiday. On holiday, one was entitled to a little fun. He began to hope that Queen MyrdemInggala might provide it.

He was prepared to meet JandolAnganol. He summoned a footman. The footman took him into the presence of the king, and the two men embraced each other.

Esomberr saw that the king was more nervous in his manner than previously. Covertly, he assessed that lean bearded profile as the king escorted him into the chambers where revels were still in progress. The runt Yuli followed behind. Esomberr threw him a look of aversion, but said nothing.

"So, Jan, we have both managed to arrive in Ottassol safely. No invaders of your realm intercepted either of us on our way."

They were friends as friendship went in those circles. The king remembered well Esomberr's cynical airs and his habit of holding his head slightly to one side, as if questioning the world.

"As yet we are free of the depredations of Unndreid the Hammer. You will have heard of my encounter with Darvlish the Skull."

"I'm sure the rogues you name are frightful rogues indeed. Would they have been somewhat nicer, one wonders, if they had been given less uncouth names?"

"I trust your suite is comfortable?"

"To speak true, Jan, I abominate your underground palace. What happens when your River Takissa floods?"

"The peasants dam it with their bodies. If the timetable suits you, we shall sail for Gravabagalinien tomorrow. There's been delay enough, and the monsoon approaches. The sooner the divorcement is over the better."

"I look forward to a sea voyage, as long as it is short and the coast remains within earshot."

Wine was served them, and crushed ice added.

"Something worries you, cousin."

"Many things worry me, Alam. It's no matter. These days, even my faith worries me." He hesitated, looked back over his shoulder. "When I am insecure, Borlien is insecure. Your master, the C'Sarr, our Holy Emperor, surely would understand that. We must live by our faith. For my faith, I renounce MyrdemInggala."

"Cousin, in private we can admit that faith has a certain lack of substance, eh? Whereas your fair queen . . ."

In his pocket, the king fingered the bracelet he had taken from Cara-Bansity. That had substance. That was the work of an insidious enemy who, intuition told him, could bring disaster to the state. He clenched his fist round the metal.

Esomberr gestured. His gestures, unlike the king's, were languid, lacking spontaneity.

"The world's going to pot, cousin, if not to Freyr. Though I must say religion never caused me to lose a wink of sleep. Indeed, religion's often been the cause of sleep in me. All nations have their troubles. Randonan and the dreaded Hammer are your preoccupations. Oldorando now has a crisis with Kace. In Pannoval, we are once more being attacked by the Sibornalese. South through Chalce they come, unable to tolerate their ghastly homeland for another instant. A strong Pannoval-Oldorando-Borlien axis will improve the stability of all Campannlat. The other nations are mere barbarians."

"Alam, you are requested to cheer me, not depress me, on the eve of my divorcement from MyrdemInggala."

The envoy drained his glass. "One woman's much like another. I'm sure you'll be blissfully happy with little Simoda Tal."

He saw the pain on the king's face. JandolAnganol said, looking away towards the dancers, "My son should be marrying Simoda Tal, but I get no sense from him. MyrdemInggala understands that I take this step in the interests of Borlien."

"By the boulder, does she indeed?" Esomberr felt inside his silk jacket and produced a letter. "You had better read this, which has just come to my hand."

Seeing MyrdemInggala's bold handwriting, JandolAnganol took the sheet tremblingly, and read.

To the Holy Emperor, C'Sarr Kilandar IX, Head of the Holy Pannovalan Empire, in the City of Pannoval, in the country of that name.

Revered Sire—Whose faith is followed devoutly by the undersigned—

Look favourably upon this supplication from one of thy most unlucky daughters.

I, Queen MyrdemInggala, have been punished where no crime was committed. I was unjustly accused of conspiring against Sibornal by my husband the king, and by his father, and stand in grave danger.

Revered sire, my lord King JandolAnganol has treated me with cruel injustice, banishing me from his side to this forlorn seaside place. Here I must stay until the king disposes of me as he will, a victim of his khmir.

I have been a faithful wife to him for thirteen years, and have borne him a son and a daughter. The daughter is yet little, and remains with me. My son has become wild since this division, and I know not where he is.

Since my lord the king usurped his father's throne, ill things have befallen our kingdom. He has made enemies on all sides. To break from a circle of retribution, he plans a dynastic marriage with Simoda Tal, daughter of King Sayren Stund of Oldorando. As I understand, this arrangement has obtained your approval. To your judgment I must bow. But it will not be enough for JandolAngonol to reject me by a manipulation of the law, he will also require me finally removed from the earthly scene.

Therefore I beseech my revered Emperor to despatch as soon as possible a letter forbidding the king to harm me or my children in any fashion, on pain of excommunication. At least the king professes religious faith; such a threat would have effect upon him.

Your distraught daughter-in-religion,
ConegUndunory MyrdemInggala

This letter will reach you via your envoy in Ottassol, and I pray he will mercifully deliver it to thy cherished hand by the fastest means.

"Well, then we shall have to deal with this," said the king, with a look of pain, clutching the letter.

"I will have to deal with this," corrected Esomberr, retrieving the letter.

The following day, the party set sail westwards along the coast of Borlien. With the king went his new chancellor, Bardol CaraBansity.

The king had developed a nervous habit at this time of looking over his shoulder, as if he felt himself watched by Akhanaba, the great god of the Holy Pannoval Empire.

There were those who watched him—or who would watch him—but they were more remote in space and time than JandolAnganol could imagine. They were to be numbered in their millions. At this time, the planet Helliconia held ninety-six million human beings, and possibly a third of that number of phagors. The distant watchers were still more numerous.

The inhabitants of the planet Earth had once watched the affairs of Helliconia with considerable detachment. The transmissions from Helliconia, beamed to Earth by the Earth Observation Station, had begun as little more than a source of entertainment. Over the centuries, as Great Spring on Helliconia turned to Summer, matters were changing. Observation was developing into commitment. The watchers were being changed by what they watched; despite the fact that Present and Past on the two planets could never coincide, an empathetic link was now being forged.

Schemes were in hand to make that link more positive.

The increasing maturity, the increasing understanding of what it was to be an organic entity, was a debt which the peoples of Earth owed to Helliconia. They now saw the embarkation of the king from Ottassol, not as Tatro saw the wave on the beach, as a separate event, but rather as a strand in an inescapable web of cosmology, culture, and history. That the king possessed free will was never in dispute among the observers; but whichever way JandolAnganol turned to exert his will—a ferocious one—the infinite linkages of the continuum closed behind him again, to leave little more trace than the keel of his ship upon the Sea of Eagles.

Although the terrestrials viewed the divorce with compassion, they saw it less as an individual act than as a cruel example of a division in human nature between mistakenly romantic readings of love and duty. This they were able to do because something of Earth's long crucifixion was over. The upheaval of JandolAnganol's divorce from MyrdemInggala took place in the year 381, by the local Borlien-Oldorando calendar. As the mysterious timepiece had indicated, on Earth the year was 6877 years after the birth of Christ; but this suggested a false synchronicity, and the events of the divorce would become real to the peoples of Earth only when a further thousand years elapsed.

Dominating such local dates was a cosmic one with more meaning. Astronomical time in the Helliconian system was at full flood. The planet and its sister planets were approaching periastron, the nearest point in the orbit to the brilliant star known as Freyr.

It took Helliconia 2592 Earth years to complete one Great Year in its orbit about Freyr, during which time the planet endured extremes of heat and cold. Spring was over. Summer, the enervating summer of the Great Year, had arrived.

Summer's duration would extend over two and a third Earth centuries. To those who lived on Helliconia at this time, winter and its desolations were but legends, although powerful ones. So they would remain yet a while, waiting in the human mind to become fact.

Above Helliconia shone its own local sun, Batalix. Dominating Batalix was its giant binary companion, Freyr, shining at present with an apparent brightness thirty percent greater than Batalix, although it was 236 times more distant.

Despite their involvements in their own history, the observers on Earth watched Helliconian events closely. They saw that strands of the web—the religious strand not the least—had been woven long ago which now entangled the King of Borlien.

III

A PREMATURE DIVORCE

The Borlienese were not a nation of seamen, despite their long seacoast. It followed that they were not great shipbuilders like the Sibornalese, or even some nations of Hespagorat. The ship that took the king to Gravabagalinien and divorce was a small brig with round bows. It kept the coast in sight most of the time and navigated by traverse board, on which the mean course made good during each watch was calculated from the positions of pegs inserted on the board.

An even more tublike brig followed the first, bearing the ancipitals of the First Phagorian Guard.

The king broke from his companions as soon as the ship sailed and went to stand by the rails, staring rigidly ahead, as if anxious to be the first to see the queen. Yuli became miserable at the motion of the sea and sprawled by the capstan. For once the king showed his pet no sympathy.

Its cordage creaking, the brig laboured through calm seas.

The king fell suddenly to the deck. His courtiers ran to him and lifted

him. JandolAnganol was carried to his cabin and placed in his bunk. He
was deathly pale and rolled about as if in pain, hiding his face.

A medical man examined him and ordered everyone to leave the
cabin except CaraBansity. "Stay by his majesty. He has a touch of
seasickness but nothing more. As soon as we get ashore he will be well
again."

"I understood that a characteristic of seasickness was vomiting."

"Hrrrm, well, in some cases. Commoners. Royal personages respond
in a different fashion." The doctor bowed himself out.

After a while, the king's muttered complaints became articulate.
"The dreadful thing I must do. Pray Akhanaba it will soon be over . . ."

"Majesty let us discuss a sensible, important topic, to calm your
mind. That rare bracelet of mine which you hold—"

The king raised his head and said, with his inflexible look, "Get out of
here, you cretin. I'll have you flung overboard to the fish. Nothing is
important, nothing—nothing on this earth."

"May your majesty soon recover himself," said CaraBansity, backing
his awkward bulk out of the cabin.

The ship made fair progress westwards, and sailed into the little bay
at Gravabagalinien on the morning of the second day at sea. Jandol-
Anganol, suddenly himself again, walked down the gangplank and into
the surf—there was no jetty at Gravabagalinien—with Alam Esomberr
close behind him, holding up his cloak tails.

With the latter travelled an escort of ten dignitaries of high ecclesiastical office, referred to by Esomberr as his rabble of vicars. The king's
retinue contained captains and armourers.

The queen's palace waited inland, without a sign of life. Its narrow
windows were shuttered. A black flag flew at half-mast from a turret.
The king's face, turned towards it, was itself as blank as a shuttered
window. No mån dared look long at it, lest he catch the Eagle's eye.

The second brig was coming in, making awkward progress. Despite
Esomberr's impatience, JandolAnganol insisted on waiting until it was
drawn in and a walkway extended from ship to shore, so that his ahuman
troops could reach land without having to set foot in the water.

He then made much of forming them up, drilling them, and addressing them in Native. At last he was ready to walk the half-mile to the
palace. Yuli ran ahead, frisking in the sand, kicking it up, delighted to
be on firm ground again.

They were greeted by an ancient woman in a black keedrant and
white apron. White hairs trailed from a mole on her cheek. She walked
with a stick. Two unarmed guards stood some way behind her.

Close at hand, the white and gold building revealed its shabbiness.

Gaps showed where slates on its roofs, planks from its verandahs, up-rights in its railings, had fallen away and not been replaced. Nothing moved, except a herd of deer cropping grass on a distant hillside. The sea boomed endlessly against the shore.

The king's costume took up the general sombre note. He wore an un-decorated tunic and breeches of a deep blue close to black. Esomberr, by contrast, strolled along in his jauntiest powder blues, offset by a pink short cloak. He was perfumed this morning, to camouflage the stinks of the ship.

An infantry captain blew a bugle to announce their arrival.

The palace door remained closed. The old woman wrung her hands and muttered to the breeze.

Wrenching himself into action, JandolAnganol went up to the door and beat on its wooden panels with the hilt of his sword. The noise echoed within, setting hounds barking.

A key was applied to a lock. The door swung open, propelled by another aged hag, who gave a stiff curtsey to the king and stood there blinking.

All was gloom inside. The hounds that had set up such a din when the door was locked now slunk away into shadowy recesses.

"Perhaps Akhanaba in his somewhat temperamental mercy has sent the plague here," suggested Esomberr. "Thus releasing the occupants from earthly sorrow and rendering ours an unnecessary journey."

The king gave a shout of greeting.

A light showed at the top of the stairs, where all was otherwise dark. They looked up, to see a woman carrying a taper. She bore it above her head, so that her features were in shadow. As she descended the stairs, every step creaked. As she neared those waiting below, the light from outside began to illumine her features. Even before that, something in her carriage declared who she was. The glow strengthened, the face of Queen MyrdemInggala was revealed. She stopped a few paces in front of JandolAnganol and Esomberr and curtseyed first to the one, then the other.

Her beauty was ashen, her lips almost colourless, her eyes dark in her pallid face. Her hair floated in dark abundance about her head. She wore a pale grey gown to the floor which buttoned at the throat to conceal her breasts.

The queen spoke a word to the crone, who went to the doors and closed them, leaving Esomberr and JandolAnganol in the dark, with the intrusive phagor runt behind them. That dark revealed itself as seamed with threads of light. The palace was flimsily built of planking. When the sun shone on it, a skeletal aspect was revealed. As the queen led them to a side room, slivers of light disclosed her presence.

She stood awaiting them in the middle of a room defined by thin geometries of illumination, where daylight slit round shuttered windows.

"Nobody is in the palace at present," MyrdemInggala said, "except for me and the Princess TatromanAdala. You may kill us now, and there will be no witnesses except the All-Powerful."

"We do not intend to hurt you, madam," said Esomberr. He walked over to one of the windows and opened the shutters. Turning in the dusty light, he saw the husband and wife standing close in the almost empty room.

MyrdemInggala pursed her lips and blew out her taper.

JandolAnganol said, "Cune, as I've said, this divorce is a question of state policy." His manner was abnormally subdued.

"You may force me to accept it. You can never make me understand it."

Esomberr opened the window and called for his retinue and for AbstrogAthenat.

"The ceremony will not detain you long, madam," he said. He paraded into the center of the room and bowed to her. "My name is Esomberr of the Esomberrs. I am the Envoy and Representative in Borlien of the Great C'Sarr Kilandar IX, the Father Supreme of the Church of Akhanaba and Emperor of Holy Pannoval. My function is to act as witness on behalf of the Father Supreme, in a brief ceremony. That is my public duty. My private duty is to declare that you are more beautiful than any representation of you could ever be."

To JandolAnganol she said faintly, "After all we have been to each other . . ."

Continuing without altering the tone of his voice, Esomberr said, "The ceremony will absolve King JandolAnganol from any further marital ties. Under this special bill of divorcement granted by the Father Supreme himself, you two will cease to be husband and wife, your vows will be rescinded, and you will renounce the title of Queen."

"Upon what grounds am I to be divorced, sir? What is the pretext? How has the revered C'Sarr been told I have offended, to be treated like this?"

The king stood as in a trance, staring rigidly at the air, while Alam Esomberr pulled a document from his pocket, flapped it open, and read.

"Madam, we have witnesses to prove that while you have been taking your holidays here in Gravabagalinien"—he sketched a sensuous gesture —"you have entered the sea in a state of nudity. That you have there consorted carnally with dolphins. That this unnatural act, forbidden by the Church, has been frequently repeated, often within sight of your child."

She said, "You know this is a complete fabrication." She spoke without fire in her voice. Turning to JandolAnganol, she said, "Can the state survive only by dragging down my name, by disgracing me—and by making you lower than a slave?"

"Here comes the Royal Vicar, madam, who will perform our ceremony," said Esomberr. "You need only stand silent. No further embarrassment will be caused you."

AbstrogAthenat entered, radiating the chill of his personality in the space of the chamber. He raised a hand and pronounced a blessing. Two small boys playing the pipes stood behind him.

The queen said coldly, "If this holy farce must take place, I insist that Yuli be removed from the room."

JandolAnganol broke from his reverie to order his runt outside. After a small fuss, it left.

AbstrogAthenat came forward with a paper on which the words of the wedding ceremony were inscribed. He took the hands of the king and queen, making each hold a side of the paper, which they did as if hypnotised. He then read the bill out in a high, clear voice. Esomberr looked from one to other of the royal pair. They looked at the floor. The vicar lifted a ceremonial sword high. With a muttered prayer, he brought it down.

The paper bond they held was sliced in two. The queen let her half float to the wooden tiles.

The vicar produced a document which JandolAnganol signed, Esomberr signing as witness. The vicar signed it himself, then handed it to Esomberr for its onward transmission. The vicar bowed to the king. He left the room, followed by his two piping boys.

"The deed is done," said Esomberr. Nobody moved.

Heavy rain began to fall. Sailors and soldiers from the ships had crowded to the one open window to catch a glimpse of a ceremony of which they could boast for the rest of their lives. Now they ran for shelter, and officers bellowed at them. The downpour increased. Lightning flashed and presently thunder broke overhead. The monsoons were approaching.

"Ah well, we must make ourselves comfortable," said Esomberr, striving for his usual lightness of tone. "Perhaps the queen—the ex-queen, excuse me—will have some ladies bring us refreshment." He called to one of his men. "Look down in the cellars. The serving maids will be hiding down there or, failing them, the wine will be."

Rain poured in the open window and the unsecured shutter banged.

"These storms blow in from nowhere and are soon over," Jangol-Anganol said.

"That's the way to take it, Jan—with a metaphor," said Esomberr genially. He clapped the king on the shoulder.

Without a word, the queen set down her extinguished taper on a shelf, then turned and left the room.

Esomberr collected two chairs with tapestry seats and set them together, opening up a shutter nearby so that they could watch the fury of
the elements. They both sat down, and the king put his head between his
hands.

"After your marriage to Simoda Tal, I promise you things will take a
turn for the better, Jan. In Pannoval, we are somewhat committed on
our northern front against the Sibornalese. The fighting is particularly
bitter because of traditional religious differences, you know.

"Oldorando is different. After your forthcoming marriage, you should
find that Oldorando will commit themselves to your side. They have
difficulties themselves. Or—and this is quite likely—Kace may sue for
peace after the marriage. Kace, after all, has blood ties with Oldorando.
Right through Oldorando and Kace runs the east-west migratory route
of the phagors and of the subhuman races, like the Madis.

"Rrrhm, as you know, dear Simoda Tal's mother, the queen, is herself
a sub— well, a protognostic, let's say. That little term, 'subhuman' is
prejudicial. And the Kaci . . . well, it's a wild place. So if they make
peace with Borlien, we might even, who knows, induce them to attack
Randonan. That would leave you free to deal with the Mordriat trouble,
and the fellows with the amusing names."

"Which would suit Pannoval well," said JandolAnganol.

Esomberr nodded. "It would suit everyone well. I'm all for being
pleased, aren't you?"

His man returned, accompanied by peals of thunder and five anxious
ladies who bore wine jars and were goaded forward by phagors.

The entrance of these ladies put a different aspect on affairs, even to
the king, who got up and began to walk about the room as if just
learning to use his legs. The ladies, finding no harm was immediately
being offered, began to smile, and fell readily into their accustomed roles
of pleasing male guests and getting them as drunk as possible as soon as
possible. The Royal Armourer and various captains put in an appearance and joined in the drinking.

As the storm continued, lamps were lit. Other pretty captives were
brought in and music was played. Soldiers under canvas canopies
brought a banquet from the brig.

The king drank persimmon wine and ate silver carp with saffron
rice.

The roof leaked.

"I'll speak to MyrdemInggala and see my little daughter, Tatro," he
said, a while later.

"No. That would be inadvisable. Women can humiliate men. You're
the king, she's nobody. We'll take the daughter away with us when we
leave. When the sea is calm. I'm for spending the night in this hospitable
sieve of yours."

After a while, to overcome the king's silence, Esomberr said, "I have a gift for you. This is a good time to present it, before we are too drunk to focus our eyes." He wiped his hands on his velvet suit and felt in a pocket from which he produced a delicate thin box with an embroidered cover.

"This is a gift from Bathkaarnet-she, Queen of Oldorando, whose daughter's hand you are to take in marriage. The queen executed the embroidery herself."

JandolAnganol opened the box. Inside lay a miniature portrait of Simoda Tal, painted on her eleventh birthday. She wore a ribbon in her hair, and her face was half-turned away, as if in bashfulness or possibly coquetry. Her hair curled richly, but the artist had not disguised her parrot looks. The prominent nose and eyes of a Madi showed clear.

JandolAnganol held the portrait at arm's length, trying to read what might be read. Simoda Tal carried a model of a castle in one hand, the castle on the Valvoral which was part of her dowry.

"She's a pretty girl and no mistake," said Esomberr enthusiastically. "Eleven and a half is the most lascivious age, whatever people pretend. Frankly, Jan, I envy you. Though her younger sister, Milua Tal, is even prettier."

"Is she learned?"

"Is anyone learned in Oldorando? Not if they follow the example of their king."

They both laughed and drank a toast to future pleasure in persimmon wine.

By Batalix-fall, the storm had blown away. The wooden palace vibrated with noise and creaked like a ship before coming to anchor in calm. The royal soldiery had found its way into the cellars, among the ice blocks and the wine. They, and even the phagors, were subsiding into drunken sleep.

No watch was kept. The palace seemed too far from any possible trouble, while Gravabagalinien's macabre reputation deterred intruders. As evening wore on, the noise died. There was vomiting, laughter, and cursing, then nothing more. JandolAnganol slept with his head on a maidservant's lap. Soon she detached herself and left him lying in a corner like a common soldier.

The queen of queens kept watch upstairs over the passing hours. She feared for her small daughter; but the site of her exile had been well chosen. There was nowhere to escape to. Eventually, she sent her ladies-in-waiting away. Though reassured by the silence below, she remained alert, sitting in an anteroom to the chamber where Princess Tatro slept.

A knock came at her door. She rose and went to it.

"Who's there?"

"The Royal Vicar, ma'am, begging entrance."

She hesitated, sighing. She slid back the bolt. Alam Esomberr entered the room, grinning.

"Well, not quite the vicar, ma'am, but a near neighbour, and offering more comfort than is perhaps within our poor vicar's power."

"Please leave. I do not wish to talk with you. I am unwell. I shall call the guard." She was pale. Her hand trembled as she rested it against the wall. She mistrusted the smile on his face.

"Everyone's drunk. Even I—even I, model of excellence that I am, son of my worthy father as I am, am just slightly squiffed."

He kicked the door shut behind him and grasped her arm, pushing her before him until she was forced to sit down on the couch.

"Now—don't be so inhospitable, ma'am. Make me welcome, because I am on your side. I have come to warn you that your ex-husband means to kill you. Your circumstances are difficult, and you and your daughter need protection. I can give you that protection, if you behave kindly to me."

"I was not being unkind. I am merely frightened, sir—but I am not to be frightened into anything I would regret later."

He took her into his arms, despite her struggles. "Later! There's the difference between our sexes, ma'am—that for women there's always a *later*. The prevalence of pregnancy among you must account for all the laters. Let me into your fragrant nest tonight and I swear you shall not regret any laters. Meanwhile, I will have my nows."

MyrdemInggala hit him across the face. He sucked his lips.

"Listen to me. You wrote a letter to the C'Sarr in my care, did you not, my lovely ex-queen? In it, you said that King Jan intended to kill you. Your delivery boy betrayed you. He sold the letter to your ex-husband, who has read every mischievous word you wrote."

"ScufBar betrayed me? No, he's always been in my service."

Esomberr took her by the arms.

"In your new position, you have no one you can depend on. No one except me. I will be your protector if you behave."

She broke into weeping. "Jan loves me still, I know it. I understand him."

"He hates you, and lusts for the embrace of Simoda Tal."

He unfastened his clothes. At that moment the door opened and Bardol CaraBansity lumbered in and marched to the center of the room. He stood with his hands on his hips, fingers of his right hand over the hilt of his knife.

Esomberr jumped up, clutching his trousers, and ordered the deuteroscopist out. CaraBansity stood his ground. His face was heavy and flushed. He looked like a man accustomed to butchery.

"I must ask you to cease consoling this poor lady immediately, sir. I venture to trouble you because there is no guard on the palace and an army approaches from the north."

"Find someone else."

"This is an emergency. We are about to be slaughtered. Come."

He led along the corridor. Esomberr looked back at MyrdemInggala, who stood rigid, staring at him with defiant gaze. He cursed and hurried after CaraBansity.

At the end of the corridor was a balcony which overlooked the rear of the palace. He followed CaraBansity onto it and stared out into the night.

The air was warm and heavy, and seemed to hug the sea noise to itself. The horizon lay under the weight of the enormous sky.

Near at hand were small moving tongues of flame, winking in and out of existence. Esomberr stared at them uncomprehendingly, still half drunk.

"Men approaching through trees," CaraBansity said, at his elbow. "Perhaps only two of them by my count. In my alarm I must have overestimated their numbers."

"What do they want?"

"A searching question, sire. I will go down and discover its answer, if you will be all right here, sire. Stay and I shall return with intelligence." He gave the escort a crafty sidelong glance.

Esomberr, leaning on the balcony rail, staggered as he looked down, and leant back against the wall for safety. He heard CaraBansity's shout and a reply from the newcomers. He closed his eyes, listening to their voices. There were many other voices, some angry, calling to him in accusing manner, though he could not grasp what they were saying. The world swayed.

He roused to hear CaraBansity calling him from below.

"What's that you say?"

"It's bad news, sire, not to be shouted aloud. Please come down."

"What is it?" But CaraBansity gave no answer, speaking in a low voice to the newcomers. Esomberr got himself moving, went into the corridor, and nearly fell down the stairs.

"You're drunker than I thought, you fool," he said aloud.

Making his way out through an open door, he almost barged into CaraBansity and a haggard man, covered in dust, who carried a flambeau. Behind him, another man, equally dust-covered, looked about into the dark as if in fear of pursuit.

"Who are these men?"

The haggard man, eyeing Esomberr with distrust, said, "We're from Oldorando, Your Highness, from the court of His Majesty King Sayren Stund, and a hard journey we've had of it, with the unrest in the countryside. I have a message for King JandolAnganol and none other."

"The king's asleep. What do you want with him?"

"It's bad news, sir, which I was entrusted to give to him direct."

Esomberr, growing angry, announced who he was. The messenger eyed him stonily. "If you're who you say you are, sir, then you'll have the authority to lead me to the king."

"I could escort him, sire," suggested CaraBansity.

They all went into the palace, dowsing their flambeaux on the ground before entering. CaraBansity led the way into the main chamber, where sleeping figures lay in confusion on the floor. He went over to where the king slept, and shook his arm without ceremony.

JandolAnganol roused and jumped immediately to his feet, hand on sword.

The haggard man bowed. "I am sorry to awaken you, sire, and I regret coming late. Your soldiers killed two of my escort, and I barely escaped with my life." He produced documents to prove his identity. He had begun to shake violently, knowing the fate of messengers who bring bad tidings.

The king barely glanced at the documents.

"Tell me your news, man."

"It's the Madis, Your Majesty."

"What of them?"

The messenger shuffled his feet and put a hand to his face to stop his jaw rattling. "The Princess Simoda Tal is dead, sire. The Madis killed her."

There was a silence. Then Alam Esomberr began to laugh.

IV

AN INNOVATION
IN THE COSGATT

A lam Esomberr's bitter laughter eventually reached the ears of those
who lived on Earth. Despite the enormous gulf between Helliconia and Earth, that response to the labourings of fate met
with immediate comprehension.

Between Earth and Helliconia a kind of relay was interposed, the
Earth Observation Station called Avernus. The Avernus had its orbit
about Helliconia as Helliconia had its orbit about Batalix, and as Batalix
had its orbit about Freyr. Avernus was the lens through which terrestrial
observers experienced events on Helliconia.

The human beings who worked on the Avernus dedicated their lives
to a study of all aspects of Helliconia. That dedication was not of their
choosing. They had no alternative.

Beneath that dominating injustice, a general justice prevailed. There
was no poverty on the Avernus, no one starving physically. But it was a
narrow domain. The spherical station had a diameter of only one
thousand metres, most of its inhabitants living on the inside of the outer

shell, and within that compass a kind of inanition prevailed, sapping life of its joy. Looking down does not exalt the spirt.

Billy Xiao Pin was a typical representative of Avernian society. Outwardly, he subscribed to all the norms; he worked without industry; he was engaged to an attractive girl; he took regular prescribed exercise; he had an Advisor who preached to him the higher virtues of acceptance. Yet inwardly Billy craved only one thing. He longed to be down on the Helliconian surface, 1500 kilometres below, to see Queen MyrdemInggala, to touch her, speak with her, and make love to her. In his dreams, the queen invited him into her arms.

The distant observers on Earth had other concerns. They followed continuities of which Billy and his kind were unaware. As they watched, suffering, the divorce at Gravabagalinien, they were able to trace the genesis of that division back to a battle which had taken place to the east of Matrassyl, in a region known as the Cosgatt. JandolAnganol's experiences in the Cosgatt influenced his later actions and led—so it appeared by hindsight—inexorably to divorce.

What became known as the Battle of the Cosgatt took place five tenners—240 days, or half a small year—before the day that the king and MyrdemInggala severed their marriage bonds by the sea.

In the region of the Cosgatt, the king received a physical wound which was to lead to the spiritual severance.

Both the king's life and his reputation suffered in the battle. And they were threatened, ironically, by nothing more than a rabble, the raggle-taggle tribes of Driats.

Or, as the more historically minded of terrestrial observers said, by an innovation. An innovation which changed not only the life of the king and queen but of all their people. A gun.

What was most humiliating for the king was that he held the Driats in contempt, as did every follower of Akhanaba in Borlien and Oldorando. For the Driats, it was conceded, were human—but only just.

The threshold between non-human and human is shadowy. On one side of it lies a world full of illusory freedoms, on the other a world of illusory captivity. The Others remained animal, and stayed in the jungles. The Madis—tied to a migratory way of life—had reached the threshold of sapience, but remained protognostic. The Driats had just crossed the threshold, and there abided throughout recorded time, like a bird frozen on the wing.

The adverse conditions of the planet, the aridity of their share of it, contributed to the Driats' permanent backwardness. For the Driat tribes occupied the dry grasslands of Thribriat, a country to the southeast of Borlien, across the wide Takissa. The Driats lived among herds of yelk

and biyelk which pastured in those high regions during the summer of
the great year.

Customs regarded as offensive by the outside world furthered the
survival of the Driats. They practised a form of ritual murder, by which
the useless members of a family were killed after failing certain tests. In
times of near famine, the slaughter of the ancients was often the salvation of the innocents. This custom had given the Driats a bad name
among those whose existence was cast in easier pastures. But they were
in reality a peaceful people—or too stupid to be warlike in an effective
way.

The eruption of various nations southwards along the ranges of the
Nktryhk—particularly those warrior nations temporarily banded together behind Unndreid the Hammer—had changed that. Under pressure, the Driats bestirred their bivouacs and went marauding into the
lower valleys of Thribriat, which lie in the rain shadow of the massive
Lower Nktryhk.

A cunning warlord, known as Darvlish the Skull, had brought order
to their ragged ranks. Finding that the simple Driat mind responded to
discipline, he formed them into three regiments and led them into the
region known as the Cosgatt. His intention was to attack Jandol-
Anganol's capital, Matrassyl.

Borlien already had the unpopular Western Wars on its hands. No
ruler of Borlien, not even the Eagle, could hope really to win against
either Randonan or Kace, since those mountainous countries could not
be occupied or governed even if conquered.

Now the Fifth Army was recalled from Kace and sent into the Cosgatt. The campaign against Darvlish was not dignified with the title of
war. Yet it ate up as much manpower as a war, cost as much, was
fought as passionately. Thribriat and the wilderness of the Cosgatt were
nearer to Matrassyl than the Western Wars.

Darvlish had a personal animus against JandolAnganol and his line.
His father had been a baron in Borlien. He had fought by his father's
side when JandolAnganol's father, VarpalAnganol, had appropriated his
land. Darvlish had seen his father cut down by a youthful Jandol-
Anganol.

When a leader died in battle, that was the end of fighting. No man
would continue. Darvlish's father's army turned and ran. Darvlish retreated to the east with a handful of men. VarpalAnganol and his son
pursued them, hunting them like lizards among the stoney mazes of the
Cosgatt—until the Borlienese forces refused to go further because no
more loot was forthcoming.

After almost eleven years in the wilderness, Darvlish had another
chance, and took it: "The vultures shall praise my name!" became his
war cry.

Half a small year before the king divorced his queen—before the idea even invaded his mind—JandolAnganol was forced to muster new troops and march at the head of them. Men were in short supply and required pay or the loot the Cosgatt would not yield. He used phagors. The phagor auxiliaries were promised freedom and land in return for service. They were formed into the First and Second Regiments of the Royal Phagorian Guard of the Fifth Army. Phagors were ideal in one respect: both the male and female fought, and their young went into battle with them.

JandolAnganol's father before him had also rewarded ancipital troops with land. It was as a result of this policy—forced on the kings by manpower shortage—that phagors lived more comfortably in Borlien than in Oldorando, and were less subject to persecution.

The Fifth Army marched eastwards, through jungles of stone. The invaders melted away before it. Most skirmishes were confined to dimday—neither side would fight either during darkness or when both suns were high. But the Fifth Army, under KolobEktofer, was forced to travel during full day.

It travelled through earthquake country, where ravines ran obliquely across its path. Habitation was scanty. The ravines were a tangle of vegetation, but there, if anywhere, water was to be found—as well as snakes, lions, and other creatures. The rest of the land was pocked with umbrella cactus and scrub. Progress across it was slow.

Living off the land was hard. Two kinds of creature dominated the plain, numberless ants and the ground-sloths which lived off the ants. The Fifth caught the sloths and roasted them, but the flesh was bitter in flavour.

Still the cunning Darvlish withdrew his forces, luring the king away from his base. Sometimes he left behind smouldering campfires or dummy forts on elevated sites. Then a day would be wasted as the army investigated them.

Colour-Major KolobEktofer had been a great explorer in his youth and knew the wilds of Thribriat, and the mountains above Thribriat, where the air finished.

"They will stand, they will stand soon," he told the king one evening when a frustrated Eagle was cursing their difficulties. "The Skull must soon fight, or the tribes will turn against him. He understands that well. Once he knows we're far enough from Matrassyl to be without our supply trains, he'll make his stand. And we must be ready for his tricks."

"What kind of tricks?"

KolobEktofer shook his head. "The Skull is cunning, but not clever. He'll try one of his father's old tricks, and much good they did him. We'll be ready."

The next day, Darvlish struck.

As the Fifth Army approached a deep ravine, forward scouts sighted the Driat host drawn up in battle lines on the far bank. The ravine ran from northeast to southwest, and was choked with jungle. It was more than four times a javelin's throw across from one bank to the other.

Using hand signals, the king mustered his army to face the enemy across the ravine. The Phagorian guards were stationed in front because the ranks of motionless beasts would bring anxiety into the dim minds of the tribesmen.

The tribesmen were of spectral aspect. It was just after dawn: twenty minutes past six. Freyr had risen behind cloud. When the sun broke free of the cloud, it became apparent that the enemy and part of the ravine would be in shadow for the next two or more hours; the Fifth Army would be exposed to Freyr's heat.

Crumbling cliff slopes backed the Driat array, with higher country above. On the royal left flank was a spur of high ground, its angles jutting towards the ravine. A rounded mesa stood between the spur and the cliffs, as if it had been set there by geological forces to guard the Skull's flank. On top of the mesa, the walls of a crude fort could be seen; its walls were of mud, and behind the ramparts an occasional pennant was visible.

The Eagle of Borlien and the colour-major studied the situation together. Behind the colour-major stood his faithful sergeant-at-arms, a taciturn man known as Bull.

"We must find out how many men are in that fort," JandolAnganol said.

"It's one of the tricks he learnt from his father. He hopes we'll waste our time attacking that position. I'll wager no Driats are up there. The pennants we see moving are tied to goats or asokins."

They stood in silence. From the enemy's side of the ravine, under the cliffs, smoke rose in the shadowed air, and an aroma of cooking drifted across to remind them of their own hungry state.

Bull took his officer to one side and muttered in his ear.

"Let's hear what you have to say, sergeant," the king said.

"It's nothing, sire.''

The king looked angry. "Let's hear this nothing, then."

The sergeant regarded him with one eyelid drooping. "All I was saying, sire, is that our men will be disappointed. It's the only way a common man—by which I mean myself—can advance himself, sire, to join the army and hope to grab what is going. But these Driats aren't worth looting. What's more they don't appear to have females—by which I mean women, sire—so that the incentive to attack is . . . well, sire, on the low side."

The king stood confronting him face to face, until Bull backed away a step.

"We'll worry about women when we have routed Darvlish, Bull. He may have hidden his women in a neighbouring valley."

KolobEktofer cleared his throat. "Unless you have a plan, sire, I'd say we have a nigh-on impossible task here. They outnumber us two to one, and although our mounts are faster than theirs, in close combat our hoxneys will be flimsy compared with their yelk and biyelk."

"There can be no question of retreat now that we have caught up with them at last."

"We could disengage, sire, and seek for a more advantageous position from which to attack. If we were on the cliffs above them, for instance—"

"Or could capture them in an ambush, sire, by which I mean—"

JandolAnganol flew into a rage. "Are you officers, or she-goats? Here we are, there stands our country's enemy. What more do you want? Why falter now, when by Freyr-set we can all be heroes?"

KolobEktofer drew himself up. "It is my duty to point out to you the weakness of our position, sire. The smell of some women as booty would have encouraged the men's fighting spirits."

In a passion, JandolAnganol said, "They must not fear a subhuman rabble—with our cross-bowmen we shall rout them in an hour."

"Very good, sire. Perhaps if you would address Darvlish as filth it would increase our men's fighting spirit."

"I shall address him."

A dark look was exchanged between KolobEktofer and Bull, but no more was said, and the former gave orders for the disposition of the army.

The main body of men was dispersed along the ragged lip of the ravine. The left flank was strengthened by the Second Phagorian Guard. The hoxneys, numbering fifty in all, were in poor condition after their journey. They had been used mainly as pack animals. Now they were unloaded so as to serve as cavalry animals, to impress Darvlish's men. Their loads were piled inside a shallow cave in the spur, and guards put on them, human and phagor. If the day was not carried, those supplies would provide booty for the Driats.

While these dispositions went forward, the wing of shadow suspended from the shoulders of the opposite cliffs was retracting, like a giant sundial set to remind every man of his mortality.

The Skull's forces were revealed as no less imposing than they had seemed when shrouded in blue shade. The ur-human tribes wore a tatterdemalion collection of hides and blankets thrown on their bodies with the same negligence as they threw themselves on their yelks. Some wore bright-striped blankets rolled about their shoulders, to give themselves extra bulk. Some wore knee-high boots, many were barefoot. Their headgear inclined to massive biyelk-fur headpieces—often horned or antlered to denote rank. A feature common to many was the penis, painted or embroidered on their breeches in furious erection to denote their rapacious intent.

The Skull was readily visible. His leather and fur headpiece was dyed orange. Antlers thrust forward from it about his moustachioed face. A sword wound sustained in his earlier battles with JandolAnganol had slashed away his left cheek and the flesh of his lower jaw, leaving him with a permanent death-grin, in which bone and teeth played a part. He managed to look fully as ferocious as his allies, whose fur-fringed eyes and prognathous jaws gave them a naturally savage aspect. A mighty biyelk was his steed.

He raised his javelin above his head and shouted, "The vultures shall praise my name!" A ragged cheer came from the throats about him, echoing from the cliffs behind.

JandolAnganol mounted his hoxney and stood in the stirrups. The shout he gave carried clear to the enemy host.

He called in pidgin Olonets, "Darvlish, have you dared to stand before your face rots away?"

A murmur of sounds rose from both confronting armies. The Skull kneed his biyelk to the edge of the precipice and bellowed across to his enemy.

"Do you hear me, Jandol, you woolly-eared dung-beetle? You were farted out of your father's left instep, so why come you here, daring to face real men? Everyone knows your knackers are knocking together in fear. Crawl away, you dropping, crawl away and take those mangey arse-combings of warriors with you."

His voice echoed back and back again from the cliffs. When the silence was complete, JandolAnganol replied in similar vein.

"Yes, I hear your womanish bleatings, Darvlish of the Dunghills. I hear your claim that those clap-ridden three-legged Others beside you are real men. We all know that real men would never associate with the likes of you. Who could bear the stench of your decay but those barbaric monkeys with phagor-scumber for grandmothers?"

The orange head gear shook in the sunshine.

"Phagor-scumber, is it, you dimday hrattock! You know whereof you talk, since a plateful of phagor-scumber is your daily diet, so much do you worship those horned Batalix-buggerers. Kick them into the ravine and dare to fight fair, you crap-crowned cockroach!"

A roar of savage laughter came from the Driat host.

"If you have so little respect for those who are the climax of creation by comparison with your yelk-yobs, then shake the spiders and scabs from your stinking codpiece and attack us, you cowardly little half-faced Driat dildo!"

This address continued for some while. JandolAnganol was revealed as increasingly at a disadvantage, not having the resources of Darvlish's foul mind on which to draw. While the verbal battle was in progress, KolobEktofer sent off Bull with a small column of men to create a diversion of their own.

The heat intensified. Plagues of stinging things visited both armies. The phagors wilted under the gaze of Freyr and would soon break ranks. The insults wound up.

"Epitaph for an ancipital earth-closet!"

"Catamite of a Cosgatt ground-sloth!"

The Borlienese army started to move along the lip of the ravine, shouting and brandishing their weapons, while the Driat horde did the same on the other side.

KolobEktofer said to the king, "How shall we tackle the mesa fort, sire?"

"I'm convinced you are right. The fort is a decoy. Forget all about it. You lead the cavalry, with infantry and the First Phagorian following. I will march the Second Phagorian behind the mesa, so that the Driats lose sight of us. When you engage them, we will charge from cover and attack their right flank, cutting in behind them. It should then be possible to drive Darvlish into the ravine with a pincer movement."

"I shall carry out your orders, sire."

"Akhanaba be with you, major."

The king spurred his hoxney and rode over to the phagorian guard.

The ancipitals were full of complaint and had to be lectured before they would move. Not comprehending death, they claimed that the air-octaves in the valley did not favour their cause; in the event of defeat, they could not find tether here.

The king addressed them in Hurdhu. This back-of-throat language was not the brand of pidgin Olonets in use between races, but a genuine bridge between human and non-human concepts, said to have originated —like so many innovations—from far Sibornal. Thick with nouns, clotted with gerunds, Hurdhu was palatable alike to human brains and the pale harneys of ancipitals.

Native Ancipital was a language with only one tense, the continuous present. It was not a language adapted to abstract thought; even counting, limited to base three, was finite. Ancipital mathematics, however, dedicated itself to the enumeration of sets of years, and boasted a special eotemporal mode. Eotemporal was a sacred speech-form dealing with the concerns of eternity and purporting to be the language of tether.

Natural death being unknown to phagors, theirs was an *umwelt* largely inaccessible to the understanding of human beings. Even phagors did not easily switch from Native to Eotemporal. Hurdhu, devised to solve such problems, used an intraspecific mode of communication. Yet every sentence in Hurdhu bore a weight of difficulty appropriate to its speakers. Humans required its rigid sentence order, corresponding to Olonets. Phagors required a fixed language in which neologisms were almost as impossible as abstracts. Thus, the Hurdhu equivalent for "humanity" was "Sons of Freyr." "Civilisation" was "many of roofs"; "military formation" was "spears on move by orders," and so on. It therefore took JandolAnganol time to make his orders clear to the Second Phagorian.

When they comprehended fully that the foe confronting them was befouling their pastures and spitting their runts like sucking pigs, the stalluns and gillots began to march. They were almost fearless, although the heat had made them visibly less alert. With them went their runts, squealing to be carried.

As the Second Phagorian moved, KolobEktofer shouted orders to the rest of the force. It also got under way. Dust rose. These movements awakened reciprocal movements in the Driat company. Those ragged ranks turned from line abreast into file and marched towards confrontation. The two forces would meet on the expanse at the foot of the cliffs, between the throat of the ravine and the mesa.

The pace on both sides began brisk, slowing as an encounter became inevitable. There was no question of a charge; the chosen battlefield was strewn with broken boulders, memorials to the chthonic upheavals which still dominated the land. It was a question of picking a way towards the enemy.

General shouting gave way to personal insult as the opposed forces drew nearer. Boots tramped without advancing. They faced each other, reluctant to close the gap of a few feet between them. Driat lords in the rear were bellowing and prodding, without effect. Darvlish galloped back and forth behind his men, screaming abuse at them for being scab-devouring cowards; but the tribesmen were unused to this kind of warfare, preferring quick forays and quick retreats.

Javelins were thrown. At last, sword struck against sword and blade into body. Insults turned to screams. Birds began to gather in the sky above. Darvlish galloped the harder. JandolAnganol's detachment appeared round the back of the mesa, and charged at moderate pace towards the right flank of the Driats, as planned.

Whereupon, there were triumphant screams from the hillsides above the battle. There, protected by the shade afforded by the cliffs above them, some of the hags of the tribe—camp followers, harlots, savage dames—had crouched in ambush. They waited only for the enemy to make the anticipated move and skirt the mesa. Leaping to their feet, they rolled boulders down the slope before them, starting a landslide which roared down upon the Second Phagorian. The phagors froze in dismay and were skittled like ninepins. Many of their children died with them.

The faithful Sergeant Bull had been the first to suspect that tribal women must be close at hand. Women were his particular interest. He had moved with a small column of men while the insult address was at its height. Under cover of umbrella cactus, his column climbed down into the ravine, through its thorn entanglements, and up its farther bank, where they managed to skirt the Driat horde and gain the cliffs without being seen.

Scaling the cliffs was a feat. Bull never gave up. He led his men high above the host, where they found a path dotted with fresh human faeces. They smiled grimly at the discovery, which seemed to confirm their suspicions. They scrambled higher still. When they reached another path, life became easier. They crawled along this track on hands and knees, to avoid being seen by either of the armies below. Their reward was the sight of forty or more tribal women, swaddled in blankets and stinking skirts, squatting on the hillside a little way below them. The boulders piled in front of the witches told their own tale.

The climbers had had to leave their spears behind. Their only weapons were short swords. The hill was too rugged to charge down. Their best hope was to fight the hags with their own weapons, and bombard them with stones and boulders.

These had to be amassed in silence, allowing no telltale stones to roll down the slope to give their position away. Bull's column was still gathering ammunition when the Second Phagorian charged round the mesa, and the hags went into action.

"Let them have it, my bullies," the sergeant shouted. They sent a fusillade of stones flying. The women scattered, screaming, but not before their homemade avalanche was in action. Below them, the phagors were obliterated.

With this encouragement, the Driat horde fought the main Borlienese force in fiercer spirit, long-swords flashing in the front ranks, javelins being thrown from the rear. The confused body of men broke into struggling groups. Dust rose above the scene. Thuds, shouts, screams sounded.

Bull viewed the scrimmage from his vantage point. He wanted to be down in the thick of it. He could see, intermittently, the gigantic figure of his major, running from group to group, encouraging, wielding his bloody sword without cease. He could also see into the mud fort on top of the mesa. The king had been mistaken. Warriors were hiding there among asokins.

The tide of fighting surrounded the base of the mesa, except where the cliff fall covered the bodies of the phagors of the Second. Bull yelled to warn KolobEktofer of his danger, but nothing could be heard above the din of battle.

Bull ordered his men to climb down the cliffside to the northwest and rejoin the struggle. He lowered himself down the cliff, slithering and falling until he fetched up on hands and knees on the path where the tribal hags had waited. A young woman, hit on the knee by a stone, lay close by. She drew a dagger and flung herself on Bull. He twisted her arm until it cracked and dragged her face down on the ground, kicking her weapon over the edge.

"I'll deal with you later, you strumpet," he said.

The women had left javelins behind in their flight. He picked one up and balanced it, looking towards the mesa. From this lower elevation, he could scarcely glimpse the backs of the men who crouched behind its walls. But one of them, watching through a slit, had sighted him. This man rose. He raised a mysterious weapon to his chest, the other end of which another man steadied over his shoulder.

Tensing himself, Bull flung the javelin with all his might. It flew true at first, but dropped harmlessly outside the walls of the fort.

As he watched in disgust, Bull saw a puff of smoke issue from the weapon the two men were aiming at him. Something like a hornet whistled by his ear.

Groping among the pots and stained rags the women had left behind, Bull found other javelins. He selected one and again stood poised.

The two men on the mesa had also been busy, ramming something in one end of their weapon. They took up their positions as formerly, and again Bull, as he launched his javelin, saw a puff of smoke and heard a bang. Next moment, something struck him a blow in the left shoulder, sending him spinning as if he had been brutally punched. He fell back, sprawling on the path.

The wounded woman hauled herself to her feet, grabbed one of the javelins, and braced herself to thrust it into his undefended stomach. He kicked her legs away, locked his right arm about her neck, and together they rolled down the hillside.

Meanwhile, the musketmen on the mesa rose to full view and commenced to discharge their novel weapons at KolobEktofer's men. Darvlish screamed with delight and flung his biyelk into the fray. He saw that success could be his.

Dismayed by what had happened to the King's force, KolobEktofer fought on, but the matchlock fire was having a devastating effect on his men. Some were hit. None liked the cowardly nature of this innovation which could kill at a distance. KolobEktofer knew immediately that the Driats had purchased these hand-artillery weapons from the Sibornalese, or from other tribes who traded with the Sibornalese. The Fifth were wavering. The only way to win the battle was to silence the fort immediately.

Summoning six hardened old campaigners to his side, he allowed them no time to pause; the struggle was going against the remnants of the king's party. Sword drawn, the colour-major led a scramble up the one accessible path to the top of the mesa, where rubble formed a slope. As KolobEktofer's party reached the fort, an explosion greeted it. One of the Sibornalese matchlocks had blown up, killing a gunner. At the same time, other guns—there were eleven all told—jammed, or their powder ran out. The Driats were not expert at weapon maintenance. Demoralised, the company allowed themselves to be butchered. They expected no mercy and received none from KolobEktofer. This massacre was observed by the Driats, who surrounded the mesa.

The king's force, or what was left of it, finding its best leaders gone, decided to retire while it was reasonably intact. Some of KolobEktofer's younger lieutenants made attempts to slash their way to the king's side but, their support failing them, they were themselves cut down. The rest of the force turned and ran for safety, pursued by Driats uttering blood-chilling threats.

Although KolobEktofer and his companions put up a brave fight, they were overwhelmed. Their bodies were hacked to pieces and the pieces kicked into the ravine. Mad with victory despite a high casualty list, Darvlish and his cohorts split into groups to hunt down survivors. By nightfall, only vultures and skulking things were still moving on the field of battle. This was the first time that firearms were used against Borlien.

In a notorious house on the outskirts of Matrassyl, a certain ice trader was waking. The whore whose bed he had shared overnight was already padding about, yawning. The ice trader raised himself on one elbow, scratched his chest, and coughed. The time was just before Freyr-break.

"Any pellamountain, Metty?" he asked.

"It's on the boil," she said in a whisper. Since he had known her, Metty always drank pellamountain tea in the early morning.

He sat on the edge of her bed, peering through the thick twilight at her. He covered himself. Now that desire had gone, he was not proud of his thickening body.

He followed her into the little kitchen-cum-washroom which adjoined her cabin. A basin of charcoal had been blown into life with bellows; a kettle sang on it. The glowing charcoal gave the only light in the room, apart from the tatters of dawn filtering through a broken shutter. By this bad light, he observed Metty as she went about the business of making tea as if she were his wife. Yes, she was getting old, he thought, observing her thin, lined face—probably twenty-nine, maybe even thirty. Only five years his junior. No longer pretty, but good in bed. Not a whore any longer. A retired whore. He sighed. She only took old friends nowadays, and then as a favour.

Metty was dressed, neat and conservative, intending to go to church.

"What did you say?"

"I didn't want to wake you, Krillio."

"It's all right." Affection rising in him, he said reluctantly, "I wouldn't want to leave without saying my thanks and farewells."

"You'll be making back to your wife and family now."

She nodded without looking at him, concentrating on arranging a few leaves of the herb in two cups. Her mouth pursed. Her movements were businesslike—like all her movements, he thought.

The ice trader's boat had docked late the previous day. He had come from Lordryardry with his usual cargo, all the way across the Sea of Eagles, to Ottassol, and then up the stubborn Takissa to Matrassyl. On this trip, besides ice, he had brought his son, Div, to acquaint him with the traders on the route. And to introduce Div to Metty's house, to which he had been coming for as long as he had been trading with the royal palace. His lad was backward in all things.

Old Metty had a girl waiting for Div, an orphan of the Western Wars, slender and fair, with an attractive mouth and clean hair. Almost as inexperienced as Div, you'd say, at first glance. He had looked her over, trying with a coin in her kooni to see if she was free of disease. The copper coin had not turned green, and he had been satisfied. Or almost. He wanted the best for his son, fool though the boy was.

"Metty, I thought you had a daughter about Div's age?"

She was not a communicative woman. "Doesn't this girl suit?"

She flashed him a look as if to say, You mind your business and I'll mind mine. Then perhaps relenting because he was always generous with his money and would never come again, she said, "My daughter Abathy, she wants to better herself, wants to move down to Ottassol. I tell her, there's nothing in Ottassol you won't find here, I said. But she wants to see the sea. All you'll see is sailors, I told her."

"So where is Abathy now?"

"Oh, she's doing well for herself. Got a room, curtains, clothes. . . . Earns a little money, she'll be off south. She soon found herself a rich patron, her being so young and pretty."

The ice trader saw the suppressed jealousy in Metty's eye and nodded to himself. Ever curious, he couldn't resist asking who the patron was.

She shot one of her sharp glances at gawky young Div and the girl, both standing by the bunk impatient for their elders to go. Pulling a face—mistrusting what she was doing—she whispered a name into the trader's mottled ear.

The trader sighed dramatically. "Well!"

But both he and Metty were too old and wicked to be shocked at anything.

"You going, Da?" Div asked his father.

So then he had left, to let Div get on with it as best he could. What fools men were when young, what clapped-out wrecks when old!

Now, as morning crept in, Div would be sleeping, his head against the girl's, in some lower cabin. But all the pleasure the trader had experienced the night before, performing a fatherly duty, had gone. He felt hungry, but knew better than to ask Metty for food. His legs were stiff—whores' beds were never meant for sleeping.

In a reflective mood, the ice trader realised that he had unwittingly performed a ceremony the previous evening. In handing his son over to the young whore, he was in effect relinquishing his old lusts. And what when lust died? Women had reduced him to beggary once; he had built up a prosperous trade—and never had he stopped lusting after women. But if that central interest withered . . . something had to enter the vacuum.

He thought of his own godless continent of Hespagorat. Yes, Hespagorat needed a god, though certainly not the god of this religion-infested Campannlat. He sighed, wondering why what lay between Metty's narrow thighs should seem so much more powerful than god.

"Off to church, then? Waste of time."

She nodded. Never argue with a client.

Taking the cup she offered, he cradled its warmth in his paw and went to the threshold of the doorless room. There he paused, looking back.

Metty had not lingered over her pellamountain, but diluted it with cold water and gulped it down. Now she pulled on black gloves which came up to her elbow, adjusting the lace round her wrinkling skin.

Catching his glance, she said, "You can go back to bed. No one stirs in this house yet awhile."

"We've always got on well together, you and I, Metty." Determined to win a word of affection from her, he added, "I get on better with you than with my own wife and daughter."

She heard such confessions every day.

"Well, I hope to see Div next trip, then, Krillio. Good-bye." She spoke briskly, moving forward so that he had to get out of her way. He stepped back into her cabin and she swept past, still fiddling with the top of one glove. She made it clear that the notion of there being any affection between them was just his fantasy. Her mind was on something excluding him.

Carrying his cup back to the bed, he sipped the hot tea. He pushed open the shutter for the pleasure or pain or whatever it was of seeing her walk down the silent street. The crowded houses were pale and closed; something in their aspect disquieted him. Darkness still hung in side alleys. Only one person was to be seen—a man who progressed like a sleepwalker, supporting himself with a hand against the walls. Behind him came a small phagor, a runt, whimpering.

Metty emerged from a door beneath the ice trader's window, took a step into the street. She paused when she saw the man approaching. She knew all about drunks, he thought. Booze and loose women went together, on every continent. But this man was no drunk. Blood ran from his leg to the cobbles.

"I'm coming down, Metty," he called. In another minute, still shirtless, he joined her in the ghostly street. She had not moved.

"Leave him, he's injured. I don't want him in my place. He'll cause trouble."

The injured man groaned, stumbling against the wall. He paused, lifted his head and stared at the ice trader.

The latter gasped in astonishment. "Metty, by the beholder! It's the king, no less . . . King JandolAnganol!"

They ran to him and supported him to the shelter of the whorehouse.

Few of the king's force returned to Matrassyl. The Battle of the Cosgatt, as it came to be called, inflicted a terrible defeat. The vultures praised Darvlish's name that day.

On his recovery—when he had been nursed at the palace by his devoted queen, MyrdemInggala—the king claimed in the scritina that a great force of enemy had been routed. But the ballads the peddlers sold declared otherwise. The death of KolobEktofer was particularly mourned. Bull was remembered with admiration in the lower quarters of Matrassyl. Neither returned home.

In those days when JandolAnganol lay in his chamber, faint from his wounds, he came to the conclusion that if Borlien was to survive he must form a closer alliance with the neighbouring members of the Holy Pannovalan Empire, in particular Oldorando and Pannoval. And he must at all costs acquire that hand artillery which the bandits of the borderland had used so devastatingly.

All this he discussed with his advisors. In their concurrence was laid the seeds of that plan for a divorce and a dynastic marriage which was to bring JandolAnganol to Gravabagalinien half a year later. Which was to estrange him from his beautiful queen. Which was to estrange him from his son. And which, by an even odder fatality, was to confront him with another death, this one attributed to the protognostic race known as the Madis.

V

THE WAY OF THE MADIS

The Madis of the continent of Campannlat were a race apart. Their customs were separate from those of either mankind or the ancipital kind. And their tribes were separate from each other.

One tribe was progressing slowly westwards, through a region of Hazziz which had become desert, several days' journey north of Matrassyl.

The tribe had been on its travels for longer than anyone could tell. Neither the protognostics themselves nor any of the nations which saw them pass could say when or where the Madis began their journeyings. They were nomads. They gave birth while on the move, they grew up and married on the move, they were finally lost to life on the move.

Their word for Life was Ahd, meaning the Journey.

Some humans who took an interest in the Madis—and they were few—believed that it was Ahd which kept the Madis apart. Others believed that it was their language. That language was a song, a song where melody seemed to dominate words. There was about the Madi tongue a complexity and yet an incompleteness which seemed to bind the tribe to its way, and which certainly entangled any human who tried to learn it.

A young human was trying to learn it now.

He had made attempts to speak hr'Madi'h when a child. Now in adolescence, his situation was more serious, and his lessons correspondingly more earnest.

He waited beside a stone pillar on which was inscribed a god symbol. It marked one boundary of a land-octave or health-line, although for that ancient superstition he cared little.

The Madis approached in irregular groups or in file. Their low melody preceded them. They passed him by without looking at him, though many of the adults stroked in passing the stone by which he stood. They wore, men and women alike, sacklike garments loosely tied at the waist. The garments had high stiff hoods which could be raised against bad weather, giving their wearers a grotesque appearance. Their wooden shoes were primitively cut, as if the feet which had to bear them through Ahd were of no consideration.

The youth could see the trail winding back like a thread through the semidesert. There was no end to it. Dust hung over it, veiling it slightly. The Madis moved with a murmur of protognostic language. At any time, someone was singing to some others, the notes passing along the line like blood through an artery. The youth had once assumed this discourse to be a commentary on the way. Now he inclined to the idea that it was some kind of narrative; but what the narrative might concern he had no idea, since for the Madis there was neither past nor future.

He awaited his moment.

He searched the faces coming towards him as if looking for someone loved and lost, anticipating a sign. Although the Madis were human in physical appearance, their countenances held a tantalising quality, their protognostic innocence, which reminded those who looked on them of animal faces or the faces of flowers.

There was one common Madi face. Its eyeballs protruded, with soft brown irises nestled in thick eyelashes. Its nose was pronouncedly aquiline, reminiscent of a parrot's beak. The forehead receded, the lower jaw was somewhat undershot. The whole effect was startlingly beautiful in the youth's eyes. He was reminded of a lovely mongrel dog he had worshipped as a child, and also of the white-and-brown flowers of the dogthrush bush.

By one distinguishing mark could the male face be told from the female. The male had two bosses high on their temples and two on their jaws. Sometimes these bosses were dappled with hair. Once, the youth had seen a male with short stubs of horn emerging from the bosses.

The youth looked with fondness on the array of faces as it passed. He responded to the Madi simplicity. Yet hatred burned in his harneys. He wished to kill his father, King JandolAnganol of Borlien.

Motion and murmur flowed past him. Suddenly, there was his sign!

"Oh, I thank you!" he exclaimed, and moved forward.

One of the Madis, a female driving arang, had turned her gaze away from the trail, to look directly at him, giving him the Look of Acceptance. It was an anonymous look, gone as soon as it came, a gleam of intelligence not to be sustained. He fell in beside the female, but she paid him no further attention; the Look had been passed.

He had become a part of the Ahd.

With the migrants went their animals, pack animals such as the yelk, trapped in the animals' great summer grazing grounds, as well as the semi-domesticated animals: several kinds of arang, sheep, and fhlebiht— all hoofed animals—together with dogs and asokins, which seemed as dedicated to the migratory life as their masters.

The youth, who called himself only Roba and detested the title of prince, remembered with scorn how the bored ladies of his father's court would yawn and wish they were "as free as the wandering Madi." The Madi, with no more consciousness than a clever dog, were enslaved by the pattern of their lives.

Every day, camp was struck before dawn. At sunrise, the tribe would be off, moving to an untidy pattern. Throughout the day, rest periods occurred along the column, but the rests were brief and took no account of whether two suns or one ruled in the sky. Roba became convinced that such matters did not enter their minds; they were eternally bound to the trail.

Some days, there were obstacles on the route, a river to be crossed, a mountainside. Whatever it was, the tribe would accomplish it in their undemonstrative way. Often a child was drowned, an old person killed, a sheep lost. But the Ahd went on, and the harmony of their discourse did not cease.

At Batalix-set, the tribe came to a slow halt.

Then were chanted over and over the two words that meant "water" and "wool." If there was a Madi god, he was composed of water and wool.

The men saw to it that all the animals of their herd had water before they prepared the main meal of the day. The women and girls took down crude looms from their pack animals and on them wove rugs and garments of dyed wool.

Water was their necessity, wool their commodity.

"Water is Ahd, wool is Ahd." The song had no precision, but it recognised truth.

The men sheared the wool from their animals and dyed it, the women from the age of four walked along the trail teasing the wool onto their distaffs. All the articles they made were made from wool. The wool of the long-legged fhlebiht was finest and went to make satara gowns fit for queens.

The woven articles were either stowed on pack animals or else worn by male and female alike under their drab outer garments. Later, they were traded at a town along the route, Distack, Yicch, Oldorando, Akace. . . .

After the evening meal, eaten as dusk thickened, all the tribe slept huddled together, male, female, animal.

The females came on heat rarely. When it was the time of the female Roba travelled with, she turned to him for her satisfaction, and he found delight in that fluttering embrace. Her orgasms were marked by peals of song.

The path the Madis took was as pre-ordained as the pattern of their days. They journeyed to the east or to the west by different trails; those trails sometimes crossed, sometimes wandered a hundred miles apart. A journey in one direction took an entire small year, so that such knowledge of passing time as they had was spoken of in terms of distance— that understanding was Roba's entry point into hr'Madi'h.

That the Journey had been in progress for centuries, and perhaps for centuries before that, was evidenced by the flora growing along its way. These flower-faced creatures, who owned nothing but their animals, nevertheless dropped things all along their route. Faeces and seeds were scattered. As they walked, the women were in the habit of plucking herbs and plants such as afram, henna, purple hellebore, and mantle. These yielded dyes for their rugs. The seeds of the plants were shed, along with the seeds of food plants like barley. Burrs and spores adhered to the coats of the animals.

The Journey temporarily laid waste the grazing along its entire length. Yet it also caused the earth to bloom.

Even in semi-desert, the Madis walked through an avenue of trees, bushes, herbs which they themselves had accidentally planted. Even on barren mountainsides, flowers blossomed which were otherwise seen only in the plains. The eastward and westward avenues—called ucts by the Madis—ran like ribbons, sometimes intertwined, right across the equatorial continent of Helliconia, marking an original trail of scumber.

Endlessly walking, Roba forgot his human connections and the hatred of his father. The Journey through the ucts was his life, his Ahd. At times, he could deceive himself and believe that he understood the murmured narrative that passed through the daily bloodstream.

Although he preferred migratory life to the scheming life of the court, it was a struggle to adapt himself to Madi eating habits. They retained a fear of fire, so their cooking was primitive, though they made a flat unleavened bread, called a la'hrap, by spreading a dough over hot stones. This la'hrap they stored to eat either fresh or stale. With it went blood and milk drawn from their animals. Occasionally, during feasts, they ate raw pulverised meat.

Blood was important to them. Roba wrestled with a whole nexus of words and phrases which had something to do with journeys, blood, food, and god-in-blood. He often meant to clarify his thoughts at night, to write down his knowledge when all was quiet; but directly they had eaten their frugal meal, everyone fell asleep. Roba also slept.

No power could stop his eyelids closing. He slept without dreams, as he imagined his travelling companions did. Perhaps if they ever learnt to dream, he thought, they would turn that mysterious corner which separated their existence from a human one.

When the female, having clung to him for her brief ecstasy, fell away, he wondered in the moment before sleep if she was happy. There was no way he could ask or she answer. And he? He had been lovingly brought up by his mother, the queen of queens, and yet he knew that in all human happiness lies an unremitting sorrow. Perhaps the Madis escaped that sorrow by failing to become human.

Mist coiled over the Takissa and over Matrassyl, but above the city the suns burned. Because the air stifled in the palace, Queen Myrdem-Inggala lay in her hammock.

She had spent the morning dealing with supplicants. Many of her citizens were known to her by name. Now she dreamed in the shade of a small marble pavilion. Her reveries were of the king, who had recovered from his wound and then, without a word of explanation, had gone away on a journey—some said upriver to Oldorando. She had not been invited. Instead, he had taken with him the orphaned phagor runt, a survivor, like the king, of the Battle of the Cosgatt.

Beside the pavilion, MyrdemInggala's chief lady-in-waiting, Mai TolramKetinet, played with Princess Tatro. She amused her with a painted wooden bird which flapped its wings. Other toys and storybooks lay scattered on the tesserae of the pavilion.

Scarcely aware of her daughter's prattle, the queen allowed the bird to fly free in her mind. She had it flutter up into the branches of a gwing-gwing tree, where the ripe fruit hung in bunches. In the magic of her thought, Freyr became a harmless gwing-gwing. Its threatening advance towards the world became nothing more than fructiferous ripeness. Under the same magic which drowsed beneath the queen's lids, she both was and was not the soft gwing-gwing flesh.

Their flesh came down and touched the ground. The globes of their summery weight were furred. They rolled under the hedges, sprawled in the velvets of the moss beneath, their cheeks gentle against the verdure. And the wild boar came.

It was a boar but it was her husband, her master, her king.

The boar pranced upon the fruit, crushed it, devoured it, until juices suppurated at its chin. Even as she filled the garden with her syruped thought, she prayed to Akhanaba to deliver her from the rape—or, rather, to let her enjoy and not to punish her for her excess. Comets flew through the sky, mists boiled above the city, the burn of Freyr fell on them because she allowed herself to dream of the great boar.

The king was upon her now in her reverie. His immense bristled back arched over her. There were nights, there were nights in the summer, when he would call her to his bedchamber. She would go barefoot, annointed. Mai trailed beside her with the whale-oil lamp, its flame carried in a bubble of glass like some incandescent wine. She would appear before him knowing that she was the queen of queens. Her eyes would be wide and dark, her nipples already aglow, her thighs alive with an orchard of gwing-gwings ripe for the tusk.

The pair of them would throw themselves into their embraces with a passion which was ever new. He would call her by her pet name, like a child calling in its sleep. Their flesh, their souls, seemed to rise up like steam from two hot streams mingling.

Mai TolramKetinet's duty was to stand beside their couch and throw a light upon their transports. They were not to be denied the sight of each other's naked body.

Sometimes the girl, staid though she was in her daylight nature, would be overcome, and thrust her hand into her own kooni. Then JandolAnganol, ruthless in his khmir, would harvest the girl down beside the queen and take her as if there were nothing to choose between the two women.

Of this, no word was ever spoken by the queen in daylight. But her intuition informed her that Mai told her brother, now the general of the Second Army, what occurred; she knew by the way that young general looked at her. Sometimes in her hammock, daydreaming, she wondered how it would be if Hanra TolramKetinet also joined in those encounters in the king's bedchamber.

The khmir sometimes failed. On occasions, when dusk moths flew and her lamp again waxed incandescent, JandolAnganol came by secret passage to where she lay. No one else had his footfall. It was, she thought, at once rapid and indecisive, the very footprint of his character. He flung himself upon her. The gwing-gwings were there, but not the tusk. Fury would seize him at this betrayal of his own body. In a court where he trusted few, that was the ultimate treason.

Then intellectual khmir would seize him. He would flagellate himself with a hatred as intense as his previous passion. The queen screamed and wept. In the morning, slave women would go down on their knees, bitter-mouthed and sly-eyed, to mop his blood from the tiles beside her bed.

To this characteristic of her master's, the queen of queens never made reference. Not to Mai TolramKetinet, not to the other ladies of the court. Like his footfall, it was part of him. He was as impatient with his own desires as he was with those of his courtiers. He could not be still enough to face himself, and while his wounds healed he had been alone with his thoughts.

Summoning more branches of gwing-gwings to soften what she was saying to herself, she told herself that the vein of weakness was part of his strength. He would be weaker without it. But she could never tell him she understood. She screamed instead. And the next night, the humpbacked animal would be rooting among the hedgerows again.

Sometimes in the day, when it seemed the gwing-gwings blushed for their devouring, she would plunge naked into her pool, sinking down into the embrace of the water—and looking upwards would see the bright scattered blast of Freyr across the surface. One day—oh, she knew it in her eddre—Freyr would come blasting down into the depths of the pool to burn her for the intensity of her desires. Good Akhanaba, spare me. I am the queen of queens, I too have khmir.

And of course she watched him in the day.

Talking with his courtiers, with wise men or fools—or perhaps even with that ambassador from Sibornal who fixed her with a look she feared—the king would stretch forth a hand and pluck an apple from a bowl. He would snatch without looking. It might be one of the cinnabrian apples, brought upriver from Ottassol. He would bite into it. He would eat it—not as his courtiers ate apples, who nibbled round the flesh and left a fat central spindle to be thrown on the floor. The King of Borlien ate whole-heartedly, yet without apparent enjoyment, and devoured the entire fruit, skin, flesh, core, plump brown pips. All would go, ground down, while he talked. He would then wipe his beard, apparently never giving a thought to the fruit. And secretly MyrdemInggala would think of the boar in the hedges.

Akhanaba punished her for her wanton thoughts. He punished her with the understanding that she would never know Jan, however close they were. By the same token—this was more painful—he would never know her as she desired to be known. As Hanra TolramKetinet mysteriously knew her, without a word being exchanged.

The spell of her reverie was broken by approaching footsteps. Opening one eye, MyrdemInggala saw the chancellor approaching. SartoriIrvrash was the only man in the court allowed into her private garden; it was a right she had granted him on the death of his wife. From her perspective of twenty-four and a half years, SartoriIrvrash was old at thirty-seven years and several tenners. He would not interfere with her women.

Yet she shut her eye again. This was the time of day when he returned
from a certain nearby quarry. JandolAnganol had told her, laughing
harshly, about the experiments SartoriIrvrash carried out on wretched
captives in cages. His wife had been killed by those experiments.

His bald pate shone in the sun as he removed his hat to Tatro and
Mai. The child liked him. The queen would not intervene.

SartoriIrvrash bowed to the recumbent form of the queen, and then to
her daughter. He spoke to the child as if she were an adult, which
possibly explained why Tatro liked him. There were few people in
Matrassyl who could claim to be his friend.

This retiring man, of medium height and dishevelled dress, had been
a power in Borlien for a long while. Thus when the king lay incapacitated by the wound received in the Cosgatt, SartoriIrvrash had ruled in
his stead, directing the affairs of state from his untidy desk. If no one
was his friend, all respected him. For SartoriIrvrash was disinterested.
He played no favourites.

He was too solitary for favourites. Even the death of his wife appeared
to have made no difference to his regime. He did not hunt or drink. He
rarely laughed. He was too cautious to be caught in a mistake.

Nor had he even the customary swarm of relations on whom to
bestow patronage. His brothers were dead, his sister lived far away.
SartoriIrvrash passed muster as that impossible creature, a man without
faults, serving a king who was full of them.

In a religious court, he had only one point of vulnerability. He was an
intellectual and an atheist.

Even the insult of his atheism had to be overlooked. He tried to
convert nobody to his way of thinking. When not occupied with affairs
of state, he worked on his book, filtering truth from lies and legends. But
that did not stop him occasionally showing a more human side of his
nature and reading fairy tales to the princess.

SartoriIrvrash's enemies in the scritina often wondered how he—so
cold-blooded—and King JandolAnganol—so hot-blooded—kept from
each other's throat. The fact was, SartoriIrvrash was a self-effacing man;
he knew how to swallow insults. And he was too remote from other
people to be offended by them—until pressed too far. That time would
come, but it was not yet.

"I thought you weren't coming, Rushven," said Tatro.

"Then you must learn to have more faith in me. I always appear when
I am needed."

Soon Tatro and SartoriIrvrash were sitting together in the pavilion
and the princess was thrusting one of her books at him, demanding a
story. He read the one which always made the queen uneasy, the fairy
tale of the silver eye.

"Once upon a time, there was a king who ruled over the kingdom of

Ponptpandum in the West, where all the suns set. The people and phagors of Ponptpandum feared their king for they thought he had magic powers.

"They longed to be rid of him, and to have a king who would not oppress them, but nobody knew what to do.

"Whenever the citizens thought of a scheme, the king found out. He was such a great magician that he conjured up a huge silver eye. This eye floated in the sky all night, spying on everything that happened in the unhappy kingdom. The eye opened and shut. It came fully open ten times every year, as everyone knew. Then it saw most.

"When the eye saw a conspiracy, the king knew about it. He would then execute all the conspirators, whether men or phagors, outside the palace gate.

"The queen was sad to see such cruelty, but she could do nothing. The king swore that, whatever else he did, he would never harm his lovely queen. When she begged him to be merciful, he did not strike her, as he would have done anyone else, even his advisors.

"In the lowest dungeon of the castle was a room guarded by seven blind phagor guards. They had no horns, because all phagors when they grew up sawed off their horns at the annual fair in Ponptpandum, so as to try and look more human. The guards let the king enter the cell.

"In the cell lived a gillot, an old female phagor. She was the only horned phagor in the kingdom. She was the source of all the king's magic. By himself, the king was nothing. Every evening, the king would beseech the gillot to send the silver eye up into the sky. Every evening, she did as requested.

"Then the king saw all that was happening in his kingdom. He also asked the old gillot many searching questions about nature, which she answered without fail.

"One night when it was bitterly cold she said to him, 'O King, why do you seek such knowledge?'

" 'Because there is power in knowledge,' replied the king. 'Knowledge sets people free.'

"To this the gillot said nothing. She was a wizard and yet she was his prisoner. At last she said in a terrible voice, 'Then the time has come to set me free.'

"At her words, the king fell into a swoon. The gillot walked from her dungeon, and commenced to climb the stairs. Now the queen had long wondered why her husband went to an underground room every night. On this night, her curiosity had got the better of her. She was descending the stairs to spy on him when she encountered the gillot in the dark.

"The queen screamed in terror. In order that she should not scream again, the phagor struck her a heavy blow and killed her. Roused by the sound of his queen's much-loved voice, the king woke and ran upstairs. Finding what had occurred, he drew his sword and slew the phagor.

"Even as she fell to the ground, the silver eye in the sky began to spiral away. Farther and farther it went, growing smaller and smaller, until it was lost to view. At last the people knew they were free, and the silver eye was never seen again."

Tatro was silent for a moment.

"Isn't that an awful bit where the gillot gets killed?" she said. "Would you read it again?"

Raising herself on one elbow, the queen said, teasingly, "Why do you read Tatro that silly story, Rushven? It's a pure fairy story."

"I read it because Tatro likes it, ma'am," he said, smoothing his whiskers, as he often did in her presence, and smiling.

"Knowing your opinion of the ancipital race, I cannot imagine you relish the notion that humankind once looked up to phagors for wisdom."

"Madam, what I relish about the story is that kings once looked up to others for wisdom."

MyrdemInggala clapped her hands with pleasure at the answer. "Let us hope that that at least is no fairy story. . . ."

In the course of their Ahd, the Madis came once more to Oldorando, and to the city bearing that name.

A sector of the city called the Port, beyond the South Gate, was set aside for the migrants. There they made one of their rare halts, for a few days. Celebrations of a modest sort took place. Spiced arang were eaten, elaborate zyganke were danced.

Water and wool. In Oldorando, the garments and rugs woven during the Journey were bartered with merchants for a few necessities. One or two human merchants had gained the trust of the Madis. The tribes always needed pans and goat bells; they were not workers of metal.

It also happened that some members of the tribe always arranged to remain in Oldorando, either until the tribe next returned or permanently. Lameness or illness was reason for leaving the Ahd.

Some years earlier, a lame Madi girl had left the Ahd and gained employment as a sweeper in the palace of King Sayren Stund. Her name was Bathkaarnet-she. Bathkaarnet-she had the traditional Madi face, part flower, part bird, and she would sweep where she was put to sweep without tiring, unlike the lazy Oldorandans. While she swept, small birds would cluster round her without fear, and listen to her song.

This the king saw from his balcony. In those days, Sayren Stund had not surrounded himself with protocol and religious advisors. He had

Bathkaarnet-she brought to him. Unlike most Madis, this girl had an active gaze which could focus like a human's. She was very humble, which suited the nervous Sayren Stund.

He decided to have her taught Olonets, and a good master was employed. No progress was made until the king was inspired to sing to the girl. She sang in response. More language came to her, but she could never speak, only sing.

This shortcoming would have maddened many. It pleased the king. He found that her father had been human and had joined the journey when a youth, running away from slavery.

The king, despite contrary advice, married Bathkaarnet-she, converting her to his faith. Soon she bore him a two-headed son, who died. Then she bore two normal daughters who lived. First Simoda Tal, and then the mercurial Milua Tal.

Prince RobaydayAnganol had heard this story when a boy. Now, as Roba, and dressed as a Madi, he made his way from the Port to one of the gates at the rear of the palace. He wrote a note to Bathkaarnet-she, which a servant bore away.

He stood waiting patiently in the heat, where a nocturnal-flowering zaldal climbed and spread. To the prince, Oldorando was a strange city. Not a phagor was to be seen.

His intention was to learn as much about the Madis as he could from the Madi queen before returning to the Journey. He had determined that he would be the first man to sing the Madi tongue fluently. Before leaving his father's court, he had often talked to Chancellor Sartori-Irvrash, who had inspired in him a love of learning—another reason for his falling out with his father, the king.

Roba waited by the gate. He had kissed the rough cheek of his female, talced with the dust of the roadside, knowing that he could never find her again even when he rejoined the Journey. For then the Look of Acceptance might be flashed by someone else—or, if by her again, how was he to recognise her for sure? He felt strongly that the quality of individuality was a precious thing, granted only to humans and, to a lesser degree, to phagors.

After an hour, he saw the servant returning, watched his self-important human strut, so unlike that Madi shamble which carried them safe across a lifetime. The man walked round two sides of the palace square, under shady cloisters, rather than brave the breath of Freyr in the open.

"Very well, the queen will grant you five minutes' audience. Be sure to bow to her, you rogue."

He slipped through the side gate and began to walk across the square, using the Madi shamble, which kept the spine supple. A man was walking towards him with a hesitant kind of arrogance which needed no display. It was his father, King JandolAnganol.

Roba removed his old sack hood and bent down, sweeping the ground with it, using languid but steady strokes, Madi-fashion. JandolAnganol passed him, talking animatedly to another man, and never even gave him a glance. Roba straightened up and continued on his way to the queen.

The lame queen sat in a silver swing. Her toes were brown and ringed. She was rocked by a green-clad lackey. The room in which she greeted Roba was overgrown with vegetation, among which pecubeas flitted and preets sang.

When she discovered who he was, as she soon did, she refused to sing of her earlier life and instead warbled in fulsome terms about Jandol-Anganol.

This was not to Roba's taste. A kind of madness came over him, and he said to the queen, "I want to sing the song of your birth-tongue. But your song is of my birth-curse. To know that man you praise, you must become his son. There's no room for flesh and blood in that man's heart, only for abstracts. Religion and country. Religion and country, not Tatro and Roba, in his harneys."

"Kings believe in such matters. I know it. I know they are set above us to dream of grand things we cannot," the queen sang. "It's empty where kings live."

"Grandeur's a stone," he said emphatically. "Under that stone he imprisons his own father. And I, his own son—he would imprison me for two years in a monastery. Two years to teach me grandeur! A vow of silence in a Matrassyl monastery, to introduce me to that stone Akhanaba . . .

"How could I bear it? Am I a rickyback or slug, to crawl beneath a stone? Oh, my father's heart is stone, so I ran, ran like a footless wind, to join the Ahd of your kind, kind queen."

Then Bathkaarnet-she began to sing. "But my kind are the scum of the earth. We have no intelligence, only ucts, and in consequence no guilt feelings. What do you call that? No conscience. We can only walk, walk, walk our lives away—except for me who luckily am lame.

"My dear husband, Sayren, has taught me the value of religion, which is unknown to poor ignorant Madis. Fancy to live for centuries and not know that we exist only by the grace of the All-Powerful! So I respect your father for all his religious feelings. He scourges himself every day he is here."

As the singing voice ceased, Roba asked bitterly, "And what is he doing here? Looking for me, a wandering part of his kingdom?"

"Oh, no, no." There was fluting laughter. "He has been here conferring with Sayren, and with Church dignitaries from distant Pannoval. Yes, I saw them, they spoke to me."

He stood before her, in such a way that the lackey had to swing her more gently. "Who confers and never speaks? Who has—and still seeks?"

"Who can tell what kings confer about?" she sang.

One of the bright birds fluttered into his face, and he beat it down.

"You must know what they are planning, Your Majesty."

"Your father has a wound. I see it in his face," she sang. "He needs his nation to be powerful, to smite his enemies to the dust. For that, he will sacrifice even his queen, your mother."

"How will he sacrifice her?"

"He will sacrifice her to history. Is not a woman's life less than a man's destiny? We are nothing but lame things in the hands of men...."

His ways became dark. He had presentiments of evil. His reason fled. He tried to return to the Madis and forget human treachery. But the Ahd required peace or at least absence of mind. After some days of walking, he left the uct and wandered away into the wilderness, living in forest trees or in dens lions had forsaken. He talked to himself in a language all his own. He lived on fruits and fungi and things that crawled beneath stones.

Among the things that crawled beneath stones was a small crustacean, a rickyback. This little humpbacked creature had a tiny face peering from under its chitin shell, and twenty delicate white legs. Rickybacks congregated under logs and stones in their dozens, all packed snug together.

He lay watching them, playing with them, lying on his side with one arm crooked to support his head, flipping them gently over with a finger. He marvelled at their lack of fear, at their laziness. What was their purpose? How could they exist, doing so little?

But these little creatures had survived through the ages. Whether Helliconia was unbearably hot or unbearably cold—SartoriIrvrash had told him this—the rickybacks remained close to the ground, hiding away, and had probably done nothing more since time began.

They were wonderful to him, even as they lay kicking their dainty limbs in ridiculous attempts to right themselves.

His wonder was replaced by unease. What could they be doing if the All-Powerful had not put them here?

As he lay there, the thought was as powerfully presented to him as if someone spoke the words that he might be mistaken and his father might be right; perhaps there was an All-Powerful directing human affairs. In which case, much that had seemed to him wicked was good, and he was deeply mistaken.

He stood up, trembling, forgetting the insignificant creatures at his feet.

He looked up at the thick clouds in the sky. Had someone spoken?

If there was an Akhanaba, then he must surrender his will to the god. Whatever the All-Powerful decreed must be done. Even murder was justified, if the end was Akhanaba's.

At least he believed in the original beholder, that mother figure who saw to the earth and all its works. That misty figure, identified with the world itself, took precedence over Akhanaba.

The days went by, and the suns travelled across them, scorching him. He was lost to the wilderness, hardly knowing he was lost, speaking to no one, seeing no one. There were nondads about, evasive as thought, but he had no business with them. He was listening to the voice of Akhanaba, or the beholder.

As he wandered, a forest fire overtook him. He plunged in a brook full-length, watching the roaring machine of conflagration rush up one slope of a hill and down the other, exhaling energy. In the furnace of its flames he saw the face of a god; the smoke trailing out behind was the god's beard and hair, grey with cosmic wisdom. Like his father, the vision in its passage left destruction behind it. He lay with half his face in the water and both eyes staring, one under water, one above, seeing two universes lit by the visitant. When the visitant had gone by, he rose, going up the hill as if drawn in the wake of the monster, to stagger among smouldering bushes.

The fire god had left a trail of black. He would see it ahead, still pursuing its course like a whirlwind of vengeance.

Prince RobaydayAnganol began to run, laughing as he went. He was convinced that his father was too powerful to kill. But there were those near him who could be killed, whose deaths would lessen him.

The thought roared into his mind like fire, and he recognised it for the voice of the All-Powerful. No longer did he feel pain; he had become anonymous, like a true Madi.

Caught up in the uct of his own life, RobaydayAnganol saw the stars wheel over his head every night. He saw as he fell asleep YarapRombry's Comet blazing in the north. He saw the fleet star Kaidaw pass overhead.

Robayday's keen eyes picked out the phases of Kaidaw when it was at zenith. But it moved rapidly, traversing the sky from south to north. As he watched it hurl itself towards the horizon, it was no longer possible to distinguish the Kaidaw's disc; it sank to a pinpoint of bright light and then disappeared.

To its inhabitants, the Kaidaw was known as the Avernus, Earth Observation Station Avernus. During this period, it was home for some six thousand inhabitants, men, women, children, androids. The human beings were divided into six scholarly families or clans. Each clan studied some aspect of the planet below, or of its sister planets. The information they gathered was signalled back to Earth.

The four planets which circled about the G-class star known as Batalix comprised the great discovery of Earth's interstellar age. Interstellar exploration—"conquest," as the peoples of that arrogant age called it—was conducted at enormous expense. The expense became so ruinous that interstellar flight was eventually abandoned.

Yet it yielded a transformation in the human spirit. A more integrated approach to life meant that people no longer sought to exact more than their fair share from a global production system now much better understood and controlled. Indeed, interpersonal relationships took on a kind of sanctity, once it was realised that, of a million planets within reasonable distance from Earth, not one could sustain human life or match the miraculous diversity of Earth itself.

With emptiness the universe was prodigal beyond belief. With organic life, it was niggardly. As much as anything, it was the scale of desolation of the universe which caused mankind to turn with abhorrence from interstellar flight. By then, however, the planets of the Freyr-Batalix system had been discovered.

"God built Earth in seven days. He spent the rest of his life doing nothing. Only in his old age did he stir himself and create Helliconia." So said one terrestrial wag.

So the planets of the Freyr-Batalix system were of prime importance to the spiritual existence of Earth. And of those planets, Helliconia was paramount.

Helliconia was not unlike Earth. Other human beings lived there, breathed air, suffered, enjoyed, and died. The ontological systems of both planets were parallel.

Helliconia was a thousand light-years from Earth. To travel from one world to the other in the most technologically advanced starship took over fifteen hundred years. Human mortality was too frail to sustain such a journey.

Yet a deep need in the human spirit, a wish to identify with something beyond itself, sought to sustain a bond between Earth and Helliconia. Despite all the difficulties imposed by the enormous gulfs of space and time, a permanent watch post was built in orbit about Helliconia, the Earth Observation Station. Its duty was to study Helliconia and send back its findings to Earth.

So began a long one-sided involvement. That involvement exercised one of mankind's most attractive gifts, the power of empathy. Ordinary terrestrials turned every day—or would turn long hence—to learn how their friends and heroes fared on the surface of the remote planet. They feared phagors. They watched developments at the court of Jandol-Anganol. They wrote in the Olonets script; many people spoke one or other of the languages. To some extent, Helliconia had unwittingly colonised Earth.

This bond continued long after the end of Earth's great interstellar age.

Indeed, Helliconia, prize of that age, was another cause of its decline. There it was, this world of splendour and terror, as beautiful as any dream—and to step on it was death for any human. Not immediate, but certain death.

Pervading the atmosphere of Helliconia were viruses which, through long processes of adaptation, were harmless to the natives. At least they were harmless throughout most of the Great Year. But to anyone from Earth, those unfilterable viruses formed a barrier like the sword of the angel who—in an ancient Earth myth—guarded the entrance to the Garden of Eden.

And to many people aboard the Avernus, a garden of Eden was what the planet below them resembled, at least when the slow cruel centuries of the winter of the Great Year had passed.

The Avernus had its parks, with streams and lakes, and a thousand ingenious electronic simulations with which to challenge its young men and women. But it remained an artificial world. Many aboard it felt that their lives remained artificial lives, without the zest of reality.

This sense of artificiality was particularly oppressive in the case of the Pin clan. For the Pin clan was in charge of cross-continuities. Their responsibility was mainly sociological.

The chief task of the Pin clan was to record the unfolding of the lives of one or two families through the generations throughout the 2592 Earth years of the Great Year and beyond. Such data, impossible to collect on Earth, was of great scientific value. It meant also that the Pin family built up an especially close identification with their subjects below.

That proximity was reenforced by the knowledge which shadowed all their days—the knowledge that Earth was irrecoverably far away. To be born on station was to be born into unremitting exile. The first law governing life on the Avernus was that there was no going home.

Computerborgoid ships occasionally arrived from Earth. These link-ships, as they were called, always provided emergency accommodation in which humans could travel. Possibly some faint hope existed on Earth that one of the Avernians would be able, as a result of new methods, to return to Earth; more likely, the ships, old-fashioned in design, had never been modernised. The gulf of space and time made the thought of such passage a mockery; even bodies sunk deep in cryogenic sleep fell into decay over one and a half thousand years.

Helliconia lay incomparably nearer than Earth. Yet the viruses kept Helliconia sacrosanct.

Existence on the Avernus was utopian—that is to say, pleasant, equable, and dull. There were no terrors to face, no injustices, no shortages, and few sudden shocks. There was no revelatory religion; religious faith hardly commended itself to a society whose duty it was to watch the upheavals on the world below. The metaphysical agonies and ecstasies of individual egos were ruled incorrect.

Yet to some Avernians of every generation, their world remained a prison, its orbit an uct going nowhere. Certain members of the Pin clan, looking down on poor crazed Roba wandering in the wilderness, were consumed by envy of his freedom.

The intermittent arrival of link-ships merely emphasised their oppression. In earlier days, a link-ship had caused a riot. It had come full of casettes of news—ancient news of cartels, sports, nations, artefacts, names, all unknown. The leader of the riot had been caught and, in an unprecedented move, sent down to his death on the surface of Helliconia.

Everyone on the Observation Station had watched avidly his extraordinary adventures before he succumbed to the virus. They had lived vicariously on the planet on their doorstep.

From that time on, there had to be a safety valve, a tradition of ritualised sacrifice and escape. So the ironically named Helliconia Holiday Lottery came into being. The lottery was held once every ten years during the centuries of the Helliconian summer. The winner of the lottery was allowed to descend to his certain death, and to choose any place at which to land. Some preferred solitude, some cities, some mountains, some the plains. No winner ever refused to go or turned aside from fame and freedom.

Lottery time came round again 1177 Earth years after apastron—the nadir of the Great Year.

The three previous winners had been women. On this occasion, the prizewinner was Billy Xiao Pin. He made his choice without difficulty. He would go down to Matrassyl, capital city of Borlien. There he would gaze upon the face of the queen of queens before the helico virus overcame him.

Death was to be Billy's prize: a death in which he would mingle richly with the centuries-long orchestration of Helliconia's Great Summer.

VI

DIPLOMATS BEARING GIFTS

K ing JandolAnganol eventually returned from Oldorando to his
queen. Four weeks passed. He ceased to limp. Yet the incident of
the Cosgatt was not lost. It was midwinter's day, and diplomats
from Pannoval were expected in Matrassyl.

A dead heat lay over the Borlienese capital, enshrouding the palace on
the hill which overlooked the city. The outer walls of the palace shimmered, as if they were a mirage that could be walked through. Centuries
ago, in the winter of the Great Year, midwinter's day had been celebrated in earnest; now it was otherwise. People were too hot to care.

The native courtiers idled in their chambers. The Sibornalese ambassador added ice to his wine and dreamed of the cool women of his home
country. Arriving diplomats, loaded with baggage and bribes, sweated
under their ceremonial robes and collapsed on couches once the official
welcome was over.

The Chancellor of Borlien, SartoriIrvrash, went to his musty room
and smoked a veronikane, concealing his anger from the king.

This occasion would lead to ill things. He had not arranged it. The king had not consulted him.

Being a solitary man, SartoriIrvrash conducted a solitary kind of diplomacy. His inward belief was that Borlien should not be drawn further into the orbit of powerful Pannoval by an alliance with it or with Oldorando. The three countries were already united by a common religion which SartoriIrvrash, as a scholar, did not share.

There had been centuries when Borlien was dominated by Oldorando. The chancellor did not want to see them return. He understood better than most how backward Borlien was; but falling under Pannoval's power would not cure that backwardness. The king thought otherwise, and his religious advisors encouraged him so to think.

The chancellor had introduced strict laws into Matrassyl to govern the comings and goings of foreigners. Perhaps his solitariness included a touch of xenophobia; for he banned Madis from the city, while no foreign diplomat was allowed to enjoy sexual intercourse with a Matrassylan woman, on pain of death. He would have introduced laws against phagors had not the king flatly intervened.

SartoriIrvrash sighed. He desired only to pursue his studies. He detested the way power had been thrust upon him; in consequence, he became a tyrant in petty ways, hoping to steel himself to be bold when the stakes were high. Uncomfortable wielding the power he had, he wished for total power.

Then they would not be in this present dangerous situation, where fifty or more foreigners could lord it in the palace as they liked. He knew with cold certainty that the king intended to bring in change and that a drama was in store which would affect the reasonable tenor of his life. His wife had called him unfeeling; SartoriIrvrash knew it was truer to say that his emotions centred round his work.

He hunched his shoulders in a characteristic way; possibly the habit made him look more formidable than he was. His thirty-seven years—thirty-seven years and five tenners, in the precise way the Campannlatians measured age—had told on him, wrinkling his face round his nose and whiskers to make him resemble an intelligent vole.

"You love your king and your fellow men," he instructed himself, and left the refuge of his chambers.

Like many similar strongholds, the palace was an accumulation of old and new. There had been forts in the caves under the Matrassyl rock during the last great winter. It grew or shrank, became stronghold or pleasure dome, according to the fortunes of Borlien.

The distinguished personages from Pannoval were disturbed by Matrassyl, where phagors were allowed to walk in the street without molestation—and without causing molestation. In consequence, they found fault with JandolAnganol's palace. They called it provincial.

JandolAnganol, in the years when fortune was less against him and his marriage to MyrdemInggala still new, had brought in the best provincial architects, builders, and artists to patch the ravages of time. Particular care had been lavished on the queen's quarters.

Although the general atmosphere of the palace tended towards the military, there was none of the stifling etiquette which marked the Oldorandan and Pannovalan courts. And in places, some kind of higher culture flourished. The apartments of Chancellor SartoriIrvrash, in particular, provided a rat's nest of arts and learning.

The chancellor moved grudgingly on his way to consult with the king. To his mind came thoughts which were pleasanter than affairs of state. Only the previous day he had solved a problem which had long puzzled him, an antiquarian problem. Truth and lies were more easily distinguished in the past than the present.

The queen approached him, wearing one of her flame-red gowns, accompanied by her brother and the Princess Tatro, who ran and clutched his leg. The chancellor bowed. Despite his absorption he saw by the queen's expression that she too was anxious about the diplomatic visit.

"You will have business with Pannoval today," she said.

"I have to consort with a set of pompous asses, and all the while my history is not getting written." Then he caught himself and laughed sharply. "My pardon, ma'am, I meant to say merely that I do not reckon Prince Taynth Indredd of Pannoval a great friend of Borlien . . ."

She sometimes had a slow way of smiling as if she was reluctant to be amused, which started at her eyes, included her nose, and then worked about the curves of her lips.

"We'd agree on that. Borlien lacks great friends at the present."

"Admit it, Rushven, your history will never be finished," said YeferalOboral, the queen's brother, using an old nickname. "It simply gives you an excuse to sleep all afternoon."

The chancellor sighed; the queen's brother had not his sister's brains. He said severely, "If you stopped kicking your heels about the court, you could set up an expedition and sail round the world. How that would add to our knowledge!"

"I wish that Robayday had done some such thing," said MyrdemInggala. "Who knows where the lad is now?"

SartoriIrvrash was not going to waste sympathy on the queen's son. "I made one new discovery yesterday," he said. "Do you wish to hear of it or not? Will I bore you? Will the mere sound of such botherations of knowledge cause you to jump from the ramparts?"

The queen laughed her silvery laugh and held his hand. "Come, Yef and I are no dolts. What's the discovery? Is the world getting colder?"

Ignoring this facetiousness, SartoriIrvrash asked, frowning, "What colour is a hoxney?"

"I know that," cried the young princess. "They're brown. Everyone knows hoxneys are brown."

Grunting, SartoriIrvrash lifted her up into his arms. "And what colour were hoxneys yesterday?"

"Brown, of course."

"And the day before that?"

"Brown, you silly Rushven."

"Correct, you wise little princess. But if that is the case, then why are hoxneys depicted as being striped in two brilliant colours in the illuminations in ancient chronicles?"

He had to answer his own question. "That is what I asked my friend Bardol CaraBansity down in Ottassol. He flayed a hoxney and examined its skin. And what has he discovered? Why, that a hoxney is not a brown animal as we all believe. It is a brown-striped animal, with brown stripes on a brown background."

Tatro laughed. "You're teasing us. If it's brown and brown, then it's brown, isn't it?"

"Yes and no. The lie of the coat shows that a hoxney is not a plain brown animal. It consists of brown stripes. What possible point could there be to that?

"Well, I have hit upon the answer, and you will see how clever I am. Hoxneys were once striped in brilliant stripes, just as the chronicles show. When was that? Why, in the spring of the Great Year, when suitable grazing was available again. Then the hoxneys needed to multiply as rapidly as possible. So they put on their most brilliant sexual display. Nowadays, centuries later, hoxneys are well established everywhere. They don't need to breed exponentially, so mating display is out. The stripes are dulled down to neutral brown—until the spring of the next Great Year calls them out again.

The queen made a moue. "If there is another Great Year spring, and we don't all tumble into Freyr."

SartoriIrvrash clapped his hands pettishly together. "But don't you see, this—this adaptive geometry of the hoxneian species is a guarantee that we don't tumble into Freyr—that it comes near every great summer, and then again recedes?"

"We're not hoxneys," said YeferalOboral, gesturing dismissively.

"Your Majesty," said the chancellor, addressing himself earnestly to the queen, "my discovery also shows that old manuscripts can often be trusted more than we think. You know the king your husband and I are at odds. Intercede for me, I pray. Let a ship be commissioned. Let me be allowed two years away from my duties to sail about the world, collecting manuscripts. Let us make Borlien a centre of learning, as it once was in the days of YarapRombry of Keevasien. Now my wife is dead, there's little to keep me here, except your fair presence."

A shadow passed over her face.

"There is a crisis in the king, I feel it. His wound has healed in his flesh but not in his mind. Leave your thought with me, Rushven, and let it wait until this anxious meeting with the Pannovalans is over. I fear what is in store."

The queen smiled at the old man with considerable warmth. She easily endured his irritability, for she understood its source. He was not entirely good—indeed, she considered some of his experiments pure wickedness, especially the experiment in which his wife was killed. But who was entirely good? SartoriIrvrash's relationship with the king was a difficult one, and she often tried, as now, to protect him from Jandol-Anganol's anger.

Endeavouring to deliver him from his own blindness, she added gently, "Since the incident in the Cosgatt, I have to be careful with his majesty."

Tatro tugged SartoriIrvrash's whiskers. "You mustn't go sailing at your age, Rushven."

He set her down on the ground and saluted her. "We may all have to make unexpected journeys before we are finished, my dear little Tatro."

As on most mornings, MyrdemInggala and her brother walked along the western ramparts of the palace and gazed out over the city. This morning, the mists that little winter usually brought were absent. The city lay clear below them.

The ancient stronghold stood on a cliff looming over the town, in a deep curve of the Takissa. Slightly towards the north, the Valvoral gleamed where it joined the greater river. Tatro never tired of looking down at the people in the streets or on the river craft.

The infant princess extended a finger towards the wharfs and cried, "Look, ice coming, Moth!"

A fore- and aft-rigged sloop was moored by the quayside. Its hatches had recently been opened, for steam poured forth into the air. Carts were drawn up alongside the ship, and blocks of finest Lordryardry ice gleamed for a moment in the sun as they were swung from the hold into the waiting vehicles. As ever, the delivery was on time, and the palace with its guests would be awaiting it.

The ice carts would come rumbling up the castle road, winding as the road wound, with four oxen straining at the shafts, to gain the fortress which stood out like a ship of stone from its cliffs.

Tatro wanted to stand and watch the ice carts come all the way up the hill, but the queen was short of patience this morning. She stood slightly apart from her child, looking about her with an abstracted air.

JandolAnganol had come at dawn and embraced her. She sensed that he was uneasy. Pannoval loomed. To make matters worse, bad news was coming from the Second Army in Randonan. It was always bad news from Randonan.

"You can listen to the day's discussion from the private gallery," he said, "if it won't bore you. Pray for me, Cune."

"I always pray for you. The All-Powerful will be with you."

He shook his head patiently. "Why isn't life simple? Why doesn't the faith make it simple?" His hand went to the long scar on his leg.

"We're safe while we're here together, Jan."

He kissed her. "I should be with my army. Then we'd see some victories. TolramKetinet is useless as a general."

There's nothing between the general and me, she thought—yet he knows there is. . . .

He had left her. As soon as he was gone, she felt gloomy. A chill had fallen over him of late. Her own position was threatened. Without thinking, she linked her arm through her brother's as they stood on the ramparts.

Princess Tatro was calling, pointing to servants she recognised wending their way up the hill to the palace.

Less than twenty years earlier, a covered way had been built up the hillside to the walls. Under its protection, an army had advanced on the besieged fortress. Using gunpowder charges, it blew an entrance into the palace grounds. A bloody battle was fought.

The inhabitants were defeated. All were put to the sword, men and women, phagors and peasants. All except the baron who had held the palace.

The baron disguised himself and—binding his wife, children, and immediate servants—led them to safety through the breached wall. Bellowing to the enemy to get out of his way, he had successfully bluffed a path to freedom with his mock prisoners. Thus his daughter escaped death.

This Baron RantanOborol was the queen's father. His deed became renowned. But the fact was that he could never regain his former power.

The man who won the fortress—which was described, like all fortresses before they fall, as impregnable—was the warlike grandfather of JandolAnganol. This redoubtable old warrior was then busy unifying eastern Borlien, and making its frontiers safe. RantanOborol was the last warlord of the area to fall to his armies.

Those armies were largely a thing of the past, and MyrdemInggala, by marrying JandolAnganol and securing some future for her family, had come to live in her father's old citadel.

Parts of it were still ruinous. Some sections had been rebuilt in JandolAnganol's father's reign. Other grand rebuilding schemes, hastily started, slowly crumbled in the heat. Piles of stone formed a prominent part of the fortress landscape. MyrdemInggala loved this extravagant semi-ruin, but the past hung heavy over its battlements.

She made her way, clutching Tatro's hand, to a rear building with a

small colonnade. These were her quarters. A featureless red sandstone
wall was surmounted by whimsical pavilions built in white marble. Behind the wall were her gardens and a private reservoir, where she liked
to swim. In the middle of the reservoir was an artificial islet, on which
stood a slender temple dedicated to Akhanaba. There the king and
queen had often made love in the early days of their marriage.

After saying good-bye to her brother, the queen walked up her stairs
and along a passage. This passage, open to the breeze, overlooked the
garden where JandolAnganol's father, VarpalAnganol, had once raced
dogs and flown multi-coloured birds. Some of the birds remained in
their cotes—Roba had fed them every morning before he ran away.
Now Mai TolramKetinet fed them.

MyrdemInggala was conscious of an oppressive fear. The sight of the
birds merely vexed her. She left a maid to play with Tatro in the passage,
and went to a door at the far end which she unlocked with a key hidden
among the folds of her skirt. A guard saluted her as she passed through.
Her footsteps, light as they were, rang on the tiled floor. She came to an
alcove by a window, across which drapes had been drawn, and seated
herself on a divan. Before her was an ornate trellis. Through this she
could watch without being observed from the other side.

From this vantage point, she could see over a large council chamber.
Sun streamed in through latticed windows. None of the dignitaries had
yet arrived. Only the king was there, with his phagor runt, the runt that
had been a constant companion ever since the Battle of the Cosgatt.

Yuli stood no higher than the king's chest. Its coat was white and still
tipped with the red tassels of its early years. It skipped and pirouetted
and opened its ugly mouth as the king held out a hand for it. The king
was laughing and snapping his fingers.

"Good boy, good boy," he said.

"Yezz, I good boy," said Yuli.

Laughing, the king embraced it, lifting it off the ground.

The queen shrank back. Fear seized her. As she lay back, the wicker
chair beneath her creaked. She hid her eyes. If he knew she was there,
he made no attempt to call.

My wild boar, my dear wild boar, she called silently. What has become of you? Her mother had been gifted with strange powers: the
queen thought, Something awful is going to overwhelm this court and
our lives. . . .

When she dared look again, the visiting dignitaries were entering,
chatting among themselves and making themselves comfortable. Cushions and rugs were scattered everywhere. Slaves, female and scantily
clad, were busily providing coloured drinks.

JandolAnganol walked among them in his princely way and then
flung himself down on a canopied divan. SartoriIrvrash entered, nodding

sober greetings, and stationed himself behind the king's divan, lighting a
veronikane as he did so. The runt Yuli settled on a cushion, panting and
yawning.

"You are strangers in our court," said the queen aloud, peeping
through her trellis. "You are strangers in our lives."

Near JandolAnganol sat a group of local dignitaries, including the
mayor of Matrassyl, who was also head of the scritina, JandolAnganol's
vicar, his Royal Armourer, and one or two army men. One of the
military was, by his insignia, a captain of phagors but, out of deference
to the visitors, no phagor was present, except for the king's pet.

Among the foreign group, most conspicuous were the Sibornalese. The
ambassador to Borlien, Io Pasharatid, was from Uskut. He and his wife
sat tall and grey and distant from each other. Some said that they had
quarrelled, some that Sibornalese were simply like that. The fact remained that the two, who had lived at the court for more than nine
tenners—they were due to complete their first year in another three
weeks—rarely smiled or exchanged a glance.

"You I fear, Pasharatid, you ghost," said the queen.

Pannoval had sent a prince. The choice had been carefully made.
Pannoval was the most powerful nation among the seventeen countries
of Campannlat, its ambitions restrained only by the war it had constantly to wage against Sibornal on its northern front. Its religion
dominated the continent. At present, Pannoval courted Borlien, which
already paid levies in grain and church taxes; but the courtship was
that between an elderly dowager and an upstart lad, and what the lad
was sent was a minor prince.

Minor he might be, but Prince Taynth Indredd was a portly personage, making up in bulk what he lacked in significance. He was
distantly related to the Oldorandan royal family. Nobody greatly liked
Taynth Indredd, but a diplomat in Pannoval had sent with him as chief
advisor an ageing priest, Guaddl Ulbobeg, known to be a friend of
JandolAnganol since the days when the king had served his priestly term
in the monasteries of Pannoval.

"You men with clever tongues," sighed the queen, anxious behind her
lattice.

JandolAnganol was speaking now in a modest tone. He remained
seated. His voice ran fast, like his gaze. He was in effect giving a
report on the state of his kingdom to his visitors.

"All of Borlien is now peaceful within its borders. There are some
brigands, but they are not important. Our armies are committed in the
Western Wars. They drain our lifeblood. On our eastern borders, too,
we are threatened by dangerous invaders, Unndreid the Hammer and the
cruel Darvlish the Skull."

He looked about him challengingly. It was his shame that he had received a wound from such an unimportant adversary as Darvlish.

"As Freyr draws nearer, we suffer from drought. Famine is everywhere. You must not expect Borlien to fight elsewhere. We are a country large in extent, poor in produce."

"Come, cousin, you are too modest," said Taynth Indredd. "Everyone knows from childhood that your southern loess plain forms the richest land on the continent."

"Richness lies not in land but in land properly farmed," replied JandolAnganol. "Such is the pressure on our borders that we must press peasants into the armies, and let women and children work the farms."

"Then you certainly need our help, cousin," said Taynth Indredd, looking about for the applause he felt his point merited.

Io Pasharatid said, "If a farmer has a lame hoxney, will a wild kaidaw assist him?"

This remark was ignored. There were those who said that Sibornal should not have been present at this meeting.

In the manner of one making everything clear, Taynth Indredd said, "Cousin, you press us for assistance at a time when every nation is in trouble. The riches our grandfathers enjoyed are gone, while our fields burn and our fruits shrivel. And I must speak frankly and say that there is an unresolved quarrel between us. That we greatly hope to resolve, and must resolve if there is to be unanimity between us."

A silence fell.

Perhaps Taynth Indredd feared to continue.

JandolAnganol jumped to his feet, a look of anger on his dark features.

The little runt, Yuli, scrambled up alertly, as if to do whatever his master might bid.

"I went to Sayren Stund in Oldorando to ask for help only against common enemies. Here you gather like vultures! You confront me in my own court. What is this quarrel you dream up between us? Tell me."

Taynth Indredd and his advisor, Guaddl Ulbobeg, conferred. It was the latter, the friend of the king's, who answered him. He rose, bowed, and pointed to Yuli.

"It's no dream, Your Majesty. Our concern is real, and so is that creature you bring here amongst us. From the most ancient times, human kind and phagor kind have been enemies. No truce is possible between beings so different. The Holy Pannovalan Empire has declared holy crusades and drumbles against these odious creatures, with a view to ridding the world of them. Yet your majesty gives them shelter within his borders."

He spoke almost apologetically, his gaze downcast, so as to rob his words of force. His master restored the force by shouting, "You expect aid from us, coz, when you harbour these vermin by the million? They overran Campannlat once before, and will again, given the opportunity you provide."

JandolAnganol confronted his visitors, hands on hips.

"I will have no one from outside my borders interfere with my interior policies. I listen to my scritina and my scritina does not complain. Yes, I welcome ancipitals to Borlien. A truce is possible with them. They farm infertile land that our people will not touch. They do humble work that slaves shrink from. They fight for no pay. My treasury is empty—you misers from Pannoval may not understand that, but it means I can afford only an army of phagors.

"They get their reward in marginal land. Moreover, they do not turn and run in the face of danger! You may say that that is because they are too stupid. To which I reply, that I prefer a phagor to a peasant any day. As long as I am King of Borlien, the phagors have my protection."

"You mean, we believe, Your Majesty, that the phagors have your protection as long as MyrdemInggala is Queen of Borlien." These words were spoken by one of Taynth Indredd's vicars, a thin man whose bones were draped in a black woollen charfrul. Again, tension filled the court. Following up his advantage, the vicar continued, "It was the queen, with her well-known tenderness towards any living thing, and her father, the warlord RantanOborol—whom your majesty's grandfather dispossessed of this very palace not twenty years back—who began this degrading alliance with the ancipitals, which you have maintained."

' Guaddl Ulbobeg rose and bowed to Taynth Undredd. "Sire, I object to the trend this meeting is taking. We are not here to vilify the Queen of Borlien but to offer aid to the king."

But JandolAnganol, as if weary, had sat down. The vicar had sought out his vulnerable spot: that his claim to the throne was recent and his consort the daughter of a minor baron.

With a sympathetic glance at his lord, SartoriIrvrash rose to face the Pannovalan visitors.

"As his majesty's chancellor, I find myself amazed—yet it's an amazement blunted somewhat by custom—to discover such prejudice, I might even say animosity, among members of the same great Holy Pannovalan Empire. I, as you may understand, am an atheist, and therefore observe detachedly the antics of your Church. Where is the charity you preach? Do you aid his majesty by trying to undermine the position of the queen?

"I am grown to the withered end of life, but I tell you, Illustrious Prince Taynth Indredd, that I have as great a hatred of phagors as you. But they are a factor of life we must live with, as you in Pannoval live with your constant hostilities against Sibornal. Would you wipe out all Sibornalese as you would wipe out all phagors? Is it not killing itself that is wrong? Doesn't your Akhanaba preach that?

"Since we are speaking frankly, then I will say that there has long been belief in Borlien that if Pannoval were not engaged in fighting Sibornalese colonists along a wide front to the north, then it would be invading us to the south, as you now attempt to dominate us with your ideologies. For that reason, we are grateful to the Sibornalese."

As the chancellor stooped to confer with JandolAnganol, the Sibornalese ambassador rose and said, "Since the progressive nations of Sibornal so rarely receive anything but condemnation from the Empire, I wish to record my astonished gratitude for that speech."

Taynth Indredd, ignoring this sarcastic interjection, said in the direction of SartoriIrvrash, "You are so much at the withered end that you mistake the reality of the situation. Pannoval serves as a bastion between you and southward incursions of the warlike Sibornalese. As a self-proclaimed student of history, you should know that those same Sibornalese never cease—generation after generation—from trying to quit their loathesome northern continent and take over ours."

Whatever the truth of this last assertion, it was true that the Pannovalans were as offended to find Sibornalese as phagors in the council room. But even Taynth Indredd knew that the real bastion between Sibornal and Borlien was geographical: the sharp spines of the Quzint Mountains and the great corridor between the Quzints and Mordriat called Hazziz which at this period was a scorching desert.

JandolAnganol and SartoriIrvrash had been conferring. The chancellor now spoke again.

"Our pleasant guests bring up the subject of the warlike Sibornalese. Before we enter into further botheration and insults, we should proceed to the heart of the matter. My lord King JandolAnganol was lately grievously wounded in defending his realm, so much that his life hung by a thread. He praises Akhanaba for his deliverance, while I praise the herbs my surgeons applied to the wound. I have here the cause of the injury."

He called forth the Royal Armourer, a small and savagely moustached man dressed in leather who stumped into the centre of the room and then produced a leaden ball, which he held up between thumb and forefinger of a gloved hand. In a formal voice, he announced, "This is a shot. It was dug from out his majesty's leg with a surgeon's knife. It caused great injury. It was fired from a piece of hand artillery called a matchlock."

"Thank you," said SartoriIrvrash, dismissing the man. "We recognise that Sibornal is greatly progressive. The matchlock is evidence of that progress. We understand that matchlocks are now being made in Sibornal in great numbers, and that there is a later development, by name a wheel lock, which will spread greater devastation. I would advise the Holy Pannovalan Empire to show genuine unity in the face of this new development. Let me assure you, this innovation is more to be feared than Unndreid the Hammer himself.

"I must furthermore advise you that our agents report that the tribes which invaded the Cosgatt were supplied with these weapons not from Sibornal itself, as might be expected, but from a Sibornalese source in Matrassyl."

At this statement, all eyes in the court turned to the Sibornalese ambassador. It happened that Io Pasharatid was just refreshing himself with an iced drink. He paused with the glass halfway to his mouth, a look of distress on his face.

His wife, Dienu Pasharatid, reclined on cushions nearby. She rose now, a tall and graceful woman, thin, greyish in cast, severe in appearance.

"If you statesmen wonder why in my country you are called the Savage Continent, look no further than this latest lie of magnitude. Who would be to blame for such arms trading? Why should my husband be always mistrusted?"

SartoriIrvrash pulled his whiskers, so that his face was tugged into an involuntary smile. "Why do you mention your husband in connection with this incident, Madame Dienu? No one else did. I didn't."

JandolAnganol rose again. "Two of our agents, posing as Driat tribesmen, went into the lower bazaar and bought one of these new inventions. I propose a demonstration of what this weapon can do, so that you will be in no doubt that we have entered a new era in warfare. Perhaps then you will see my need to retain phagors in my army and my realms."

Addressing himself directly to the Pannovalan prince, he said, "If your refinement will allow you to tolerate the presence of ancipitals in the room . . ."

The diplomats sat up and stared apprehensively at the king.

He clapped his hands. A leather-clad captain from his cortege went to a passage and called an order. Two dehorned phagors marched smartly into the room. They had been standing motionless in the shadows. Their white pelages picked up the light as they passed by the windows. One of them carried a long matchlock before him. A passage was cleared across the middle of the chamber as he set it down and crouched beside it to prepare for firing.

The hand-artillery piece had a six-foot iron barrel and a stock of polished wood. Both barrel and stock were bound at intervals with silver wire. Near the muzzle was a folding tripod of sturdy design with two clawed feet. The phagor packed powder into the mechanism from a horn carried at his belt, and used a ramrod to tamp a round lead ball down the barrel. He settled himself and lit a fuse. The captain of phagors stood over him to see that all was performed properly.

Meanwhile, the second phagor had moved to the other end of the chamber and stood near the wall, looking forward and twitching an ear. Any humans lolling about on cushions had rapidly cleared a wide space for him.

The first phagor squinted along the barrel, using the tripod to support the muzzle. The fuse spluttered. There was a terrific explosion and a puff of smoke.

The other phagor staggered. A yellow stain appeared high up on its chest, where its intestines were situated. It said something, clutching the spot where the shot had entered its body. Then it fell dead, collapsing with a thud on the floor.

As smoke and smell filled the council hall, the diplomats began to cough. Panic took them. They jumped up, tugging their charfruls, and ran into the open. JandolAnganol and his chancellor were left standing alone.

After the morning's demonstration of fire power, of which the queen had been a secret onlooker, she went and hid herself in her quarters.

She hated the calculations that power entailed. She knew that the Pannoval contingent, led by the odious Prince Taynth Indredd, were not aiming their remarks against Sibornal, for it was taken for granted that Sibornal was a permanent enemy; that relationship, sour though it was, was well understood. JandolAnganol was the target of their talk, for they wished to bind him closer to them. And in consequence she—who had power over him—was also their target.

MyrdemInggala lunched with her ladies. JandolAnganol, by the laws of courtesy, lunched with his guests. Guaddl Ulbobeg earned black looks from his master by pausing at the king's place and saying, in a low voice, "Your demonstration was dramatic, but hardly effective. For our northern armies are having increasingly to fight against Sibornalese forces armed with those very matchlocks. However, the art of their manufacture can be learnt, as you will see tomorrow. Beware, my friend, for the prince will force a hard bargain on you."

After her lunch, scarcely tasted, the queen went alone to her quarters and sat at her favourite window, on the cushioned seat built round its bay. She thought of the odious Prince Taynth Indredd, who resembled a frog. She knew that he was related to the equally disgusting King of Oldorando, Sayren Stund, whose wife was a Madi. Surely even phagors were preferable to these scheming royalties!

From her window, she looked across her garden to the tiled reservoir where she swam. On the far side of the reservoir, a tall wall rose, hiding her beauty from prying eyes, and in the bottom of the wall, just above water level, was a small iron grille. The grille formed the window to a dungeon. There, JandolAnganol's father, the deposed King Varpal-

Anganol, was imprisoned, and had been since shortly after the queen's marriage. In the reservoir were golden carp, visible from where she sat. Like her, like VarpalAnganol, they were prisoners here.

A knock came at her door. A servant opened it, to announce that the queen's brother awaited her pleasure.

YeferalOboral was lolling against the rail at her balcony. They both knew that JandolAnganol would long since have killed him, but for the queen.

Her brother was not a handsome man; all the beauty in the line had been bestowed in superabundance on MyrdemInggala. His features were meagre, his expression sour. He was brave, obedient, patient; otherwise his qualities were few. He never carried himself well, as did the king, as if to emphasise that he intended to cut no figure in life. Yet he served JandolAnganol without protest, and was devoted to a sister whose life he held so much more dear than his own. She loved him for his ordinariness.

"You were not at the meeting."

"It wasn't for the likes of me."

"It was horrible."

"I heard so. For some reason, Io Pasharatid is upset. He's generally so cool, like a block of Lordryardry ice. Yet the guards say he has a woman in town—imagine! If so, he runs a great risk."

MyrdemInggala showed her teeth in a smile. "I detest the way he looks at me. If he has a woman, so much the better!"

They laughed. For a short while, they lingered, talking of cheerful things. Their father, the old baron, was in the country now, complaining of the heat and too old to be reckoned a danger to the state. He had recently taken up fishing, as a cool pursuit.

The courtyard bell rang. They looked down to see JandolAnganol enter the court, closely followed by a guard carrying a red silk umbrella over his head. The phagor runt was close to him, as ever. He called to his queen.

"Will you come down, Cune? Our guests must be entertained during a lull in our discussions. You will delight them more than ever I could."

She left her brother and went down to join him under the sunshade. He took her arm with formal courtesy. She thought he looked weary, though the fabric of the umbrella reflected a flush like fever on his cheeks.

"Are you coming to a treaty with Pannoval and Oldorando which will ease the pressures of war?" she asked timidly.

"The beholder knows what we're coming to," he said abruptly. "We must keep on terms with the devils, and placate them, otherwise they'll take advantage of our temporary weakness and invade us. They're as full of cunning as they are of fake holiness." He sighed.

"The time will come when you and I will be hunting and enjoying life again, as of old," she said, squeezing his arm. She would not rebuke him for inviting his guests.

Ignoring her pious hope, he burst out angrily, "SartoriIrvrash spoke unwisely this morning, admitting his atheism. I must get rid of him. Taynth holds it against me that my chancellor is not a member of the Church."

"Prince Taynth also spoke against me. Will you get rid of me because I am not to his liking?" Her eyes flashed angrily as she spoke, though she tried to keep lightness in her tone. But he replied sullenly, "You know, and the scritina knows, that the coffers are empty. We may be driven to much we have no heart for."

She drew her hand sharply from his arm.

The visitors, together with their concubines and servants, were grouped in a green courtyard, under colonnades. Wild beasts were being paraded; a group of jugglers was entertaining with its paltry tricks. JandolAnganol steered his queen among the emissaries. She noted how the countenances of the men lit up as she spoke to them. I must still be of some value to Jan, she thought.

An old Thribriatan tribesman in elaborate braffista headgear was parading two gorilloid Others on chains. The creatures attracted several onlookers. Away from their arboreal habitat, their behaviour was uncouth. They most resembled—so one of the courtiers said—two drunken courtiers.

The froglike Prince Taynth Indredd was standing under a yellow sunshade, being fanned and smoking a veronikane as he watched the Others perform some limited tricks. Beside him, laughing uproariously at the captives, was a stiff girl of some eleven years and six tenners.

"Aren't they funny, Unk?" she said to the prince. "They're quite like people, except for all the fur."

The Thribriatan, hearing this, touched his braffista and said to the prince, "You like see me make Others fight each other?"

The prince humorously produced a silver coin in the palm of his hand.

"This if you'll make them rumbo each other."

Everyone laughed. The girl screamed with humour. "Unkie, how rude you are! Would they really?"

Mournfully polite, the tribesman said, "These beasts have no khmir like humans. Only every tenner make love, do rumbo. Is more easy make fight."

Shaking his head and laughing, the prince retained his coin. It was as he turned away that MyrdemInggala addressed him. His small companion drifted off, suddenly bored. She was dressed as an adult, and her cheeks were rouged.

When the queen decently could, she left JandolAnganol and Taynth

Indredd talking, and crossed to the fountain to speak with the girl. The latter was staring moodily into the water.

"Are you looking for fish?"

"No, thank you. We have much bigger fish than that at home in Oldorando." She indicated their size in a childlike way, using her hands.

"I see. I've just been talking to your father, the prince."

The girl looked up at her interrogator for the first time, with an expression of contempt. Her face astonished MyrdemInggala, so strange was it, with huge eyes fringed by abnormally long lashes, and a nose like the beak of a little parakeet. By the beholder, thought the queen, this is a half-Madi child! What a funny little thing! I must be nice to it.

It was saying, "Zygankes! Taynth my father! He's not my father. Whatever made you think that? He's only a distant cousin by marriage. I wouldn't have him for a father—he's too fat." As if to strike a pleasanter note, the girl said, "In truth, this is the first time I have been allowed to travel away from Oldorando without my father. My women are with me, of course, but it's terribly boring here, isn't it? Do you have to live here?"

She squinted as she peered up at the queen. A characteristic in her face made her look at once pretty and stupid.

"You know what? You look quite attractive, for an old person."

Keeping a serious face, the queen said, "I have a nice cool reservoir, sheltered from view. Would you like a swim? Is that permitted?"

The girl considered. "I can do what I like, of course, but I don't think a swim would be ladylike just now. I am a princess, after all. That always has to be considered."

"Really? Do you mind telling me your name?"

"Zygankes, it is *primitive* in Borlien! I thought everyone knew my name. I am the Princess Simoda Tal, and my father is the King of Oldorando. I suppose you've heard of Oldorando?"

The queen laughed. Feeling sorry for the child, she said, "Well, if you've come all the way from Oldorando I think you deserve a swim."

"I'll swim when I please, thank you," said the young lady.

And when the young lady pleased was next morning at dawn. She found her way to the queen's quarters and woke her. MyrdemInggala was more amused than vexed. She roused Tatro and they went down with Simoda Tal to the reservoir, accompanied only by their maids, who bore towels, and a phagor guard. The child dismissed the phagors, saying that they disgusted her.

A chill light lay across the scene, but the water was more than tepid. Once, in JandolAnganol's father's time, carts of snow and ice had been brought from the mountains to cool the reservoirs, but considerations of manpower and the stirrings of Mordriat tribes had terminated such luxuries.

Although no windows but her own faced over the reservoir, the queen always swam in a filmy garment which covered her pale body. Simoda Tal had no such reservations. She threw off her garments to reveal a stocky little body prinked with dark hairs, which stood out like pine trees on snowy hillsides.

"Oh, I love you, you're beautiful!" she exclaimed to the queen, rushing up as soon as she was naked and embracing the older woman. MyrdemInggala was unable to respond freely. She felt something inappropriate in the embrace. Tatro screamed.

The young girl swam and surface-dived close to the queen, repeatedly opening her legs as she performed in the water, as if eager to assure MyrdemInggala that she was fully adult where it was most important to be.

At the same time, SartoriIrvrash was being wakened from his couch by an officer of the court. The guards had reported that the Sibornalese ambassador, Io Pasharatid, had left on hoxneyback, alone, an hour before Freyr-dawn.

"His wife, Dienu?"

"She is still in her quarters, sir. She is reported to be upset."

"Upset? What does that mean? The woman's intelligent. I can't say I like her, but she's intelligent. Botheration. . . . And there are so many fools. . . . Here, help me out of bed, will you?"

He drew a gown round his shoulders and roused the slave woman who had served as his housekeeper since his wife died. He admired the Sibornalese. He had estimated that at this time of the Great Year there were possibly fifty million humans living in the seventeen countries of Campannlat; those countries could not agree with each other. Wars were endemic. Empires rose and fell. There was never peace.

In Sibornal, cold Sibornal, things fell out differently. In the seven countries of Sibornal lived an estimated twenty-five million humans. Those seven nations formed a strong alliance. Campannlat was incomparably richer than the northern continent, yet perpetual squabbles between its nations meant that little was achieved—except religions which thrived on desperation. This was why SartoriIrvrash hated the job of chancellor. He had a contempt for most of the men he worked for.

The chancellor had paid bribes, and knew as a result that Prince Taynth Indredd had brought to the palace a chest of weapons—the very weapons discussed yesterday. Clearly, they were designed as bargaining power, but what the bargain would be remained to be seen.

It was not improbable that the Sibornalese ambassador had also gained news of the chest of matchlocks. That could account for his hasty departure. He would be heading north, towards Hazziz and the nearest Sibornalese settlements. He should be brought back.

SartoriIrvrash sipped a mug of pellamountain tea which the slave woman brought and turned to the waiting officer.

"I made a fabulous discovery yesterday regarding hoxneys, which influences the history of the world—a remarkable discovery! But who took account of it?" He shook his bald head. "Learning means nothing, intrigue is everything. So I have to bestir myself at dawn to capture some fool riding north. . . . What a botheration it is! Now. Who's a good hoxneyman near at hand? One we can trust, if such exists. I know. The queen's brother, YeferalOborol. Fetch him, will you? In his boots."

When YeferalOborol appeared, SartoriIrvrash explained the situation.

"Fetch this madman Pasharatid back. Ride hard and you'll catch him up. Tell him—something. Let me think. Yes, tell him that the king has decided to make no commitment to Oldorando and Pannoval. Instead, he wishes to sign a treaty with Sibornal. Sibornal has a fleet of ships. Tell him we will offer them anchorage in Ottassol."

"What would Sibornalese ships be doing so far from home?" Yeferal-Oborol asked.

"Leave him to decide that. Just persuade him to return here."

"Why do you want him back?"

SartoriIrvrash squeezed his hands together. "Guilt. That's why the scerm has left so suddenly. I mean to find out exactly what he has done. There's always more than arm up a Sibornalese sleeve. Now please go, and no more questions."

YeferalOborol rode north through the city, through its streets which were even then crowded with early risers, and through the fields beyond. He rode steadily, trotting and walking his hoxney by turns.

He came to a bridge across the Mar, where that river flowed into the Takissa. A small fort stood, guarding the bridge. He stopped and changed to a fresh hoxney.

After another hour's riding, when the heat was becoming intense, he stopped by a stream and drank. There were fresh hoxney-shoe prints by the water, which he hoped were those of Pasharatid's mount.

He continued north. The country became less fertile. Habitation was scarce. The thordotter blew, parching throats, drying skins.

Giant boulders were strewn about the landscape. A century or so ago, this region had been popular with hermits, who built small churches beside or on top of the boulders. One or two old men could still be seen, but the intense heat had driven most of them away. Phagors worked patches of earth under the boulders; brilliant butterflies fluttered about their legs.

Behind one of the boulders, Io Pasharatid stood waiting for his pursuer. His mount was exhausted. Pasharatid expected capture and was surprised when he saw a solitary rider approaching. There was no accounting for the foolishness of the Campannlatians.

He loaded his matchlock, set it in position, and awaited the right moment to apply his fire. His pursuer was approaching at a steady pace, riding among the boulders and taking no particular care.

Pasharatid lit the fuse, tucked the butt into his shoulder, narrowed his eyes, and aimed the gun. He hated using these beastly weapons. They were for barbarians.

Not every firing was a success. This one was. There was a loud explosion, the bullet flew to its mark. YeferalOborol was blown off his mount with a hole in his chest. He crawled into the shadow of a boulder and died.

The Sibornalese ambassador caught the hoxney and continued his journey north.

It must be said: there were no riches in King JandolAnganol's court to rival the riches of the courts friendly to him in Oldorando and in Pannoval City. In those more favoured centres of civilisation, treasures of all kinds had accumulated; scholars were protected, and the church itself—though this was truer of Pannoval—encouraged learning and the arts to a limited extent. But Pannoval had the advantage of a ruling dynasty which, encouraging a proselytising religion, made for stability.

Almost every week, ships unloaded on to Matrassyl's harbour cargoes of spices, drugs, hides, animals' teeth, lapis lazuli, scented woods, and rare birds. But of these treasures, few reached the palace. For Jandol-Anganol was an upstart king, in the eyes of the world and possibly in his own eyes. He boasted of his grandfather's enlightened rule, but in truth his grandfather had been little better than a successful warlord—one of many who disputed Borlienese territory—who had had the wit to band phagors into formidable armies under human captaincy and so subdue his enemies.

Not all those enemies had been killed. One of the most striking "reforms" of JandolAnganol's father's reign was to appoint a parliament, or scritina; the scritina represented the people and advised the king. It was based on an Oldorandan model. VarpalAnganol had formed the membership of the scritina from two categories of men, from the leaders of guilds and corps, such as the Ironmakers Corps, who had traditional power in the land, and from defeated warlords or their families, thus giving them the chance to air their grievances and him a way of deflating their wrath. Much of the cargo unloaded at Matrassyl went to paying this disaffected body of men.

When the young JandolAnganol deposed and imprisoned his father, he had sought to abolish the scritina. The scritina had refused to be abolished. It met irregularly and continued to harass the king and to make its own members rich. Its leader, BudadRembitim, was also mayor of Matrassyl.

The scritina called an extraordinary meeting. It would certainly demand a fresh attempt to subdue Randonan and stronger defences against the warlike tribes of Mordriat, who were no more than two or three days gallop from their homes. The king would have to answer them and commit himself to a definite line of action.

The king presented himself before the scritina that afternoon, when his distinguished visitors were taking a siesta. He left his runt behind and sank into his throne in grim silence.

After the difficulties of the morning, another set of difficulties. His gaze went round the wooden council chamber as if seeking them out.

Several members of the old families rose to speak. Most of them harped on a fresh theme and a stale one. The stale one was the emptiness of the exchequer. The fresh one was the inconvenient report from the Western Wars that the frontier city of Keevasien had been sacked. Randonanese units had crossed the Kacol River and stormed the city.

This led to complaints that General Hanra TolramKetinet was too young, too unskilled, to command the army. Every complaint was a criticism of the king. JandolAnganol listened impatiently, drumming his fingers on the arm of his throne. He recalled again the wretched days of his boyhood, after his mother had died. His father had beaten and neglected him. He had hidden in cellars from his father's servants, and vowed to himself that, when he was grown up, he would let nobody stand in the way of his happiness.

After he was wounded in the Cosgatt, after he had managed to find his way back to the capital, he lay in the state of weakness which recalled to his mind the past he wished to shut away. Again he was powerless. It was then he had observed the handsome young captain, TolramKetinet, smile at MyrdemInggala, and receive an answering smile.

As soon as he had managed to crawl from his bed, he promoted TolramKetinet to general, and sent him off to the Western Wars. There were men in the scritina who believed—with good reason—that their sons were much more deserving of promotion. Every setback in the stubborn jungles to the west reinforced their belief, and their anger with the king. He knew he needed a victory of some kind very soon. For that he found himself forced to turn to Pannoval.

The next morning, before meeting formally again with the diplomats, JandolAnganol went early to see Prince Taynth Indredd in his suite. He left Yuli outside, where the runt settled down comfortably, sprawling like a dog by the door. This was the king's concession to a man he disliked.

Prince Taynth Indredd was breakfasting off a gout cooked in oatmeal, served with tropical fruits. He listened, nodding assent, to what Jandol-Anganol had to say.

He remarked, with seeming irrelevance, "I hear that your son has disappeared?"

"Robay loves the desert. The climate suits him. He often departs, and is away for weeks at a time."

"It's not the proper training for a king. Kings must be educated. RobaydayAnganol should attend a monastery, as you did, and as I did. Instead, he's joined the protognostics, so I hear."

"I can look after my own son. I require no advice."

"Monastery is good for you. Teaches you that there are things you have to do, even if you don't like them. Bad things loom in the future. Pannoval has survived the long winters. The long summers are more difficult. . . . My deuteroscopists and astronomers report bad things of the future. Of course, it's their trade, you might say."

He paused and lit a veronikane, making a performance of it, breathing out the smoke luxuriously, sweeping the cloud away with languorous gestures.

"Yes, the old religions of Pannoval spoke truth when they warned that bad things came from the sky. Akhanaba's origins were as a stone. You know that?"

He rose and waddled over to the window, where he climbed up on the sill and looked out. His large behind stuck out in JandolAnganol's direction.

The latter said nothing, waiting for Taynth Indredd to commit himself.

"The deuteroscopists say that Helliconia and our attendant sun, Batalix, are being drawn nearer to Freyr every small year. For the next few generations—eighty-three years, to be precise—we move ever nearer to it. After that, if celestial geometries prove correct, we draw slowly away again. So the next generations are the testing ones. Advantage will go increasingly to the polar continents of Hespagorat and Sibornal. For us in the tropics, conditions will become steadily worse."

"Borlien can survive. It's cooler along the south coast. Ottassol is a cool city—below ground, much like Pannoval."

Taynth Indredd turned his froglike face over one shoulder in order to inspect JandolAnganol.

"There's a plan, you see, coz. . . . I know you have little affection for me, but I'd prefer you to hear it from me than have it from your friend, my old holy advisor, Guaddl Ulbobeg. Borlien will be all right at nearpoint, as you say. So will Pannoval, safe in its mountains. Oldorando will suffer most. And both your country and mine need to see Oldorando remain intact, or it will fall to barbarians. Do you suppose you could accommodate the Oldorandan court, Sayren Stund and his like—in Ottassol?"

The question was so startling that JandolAnganol was for once at a loss for words.

"That would be for my successor to say . . ."

The Prince of Pannoval changed his tone of voice, and the subject.

"Coz, take some fresh air at the window with me. See, there below is my charge, Simoda Tal, eleven years and six tenners old, daughter of the Oldorandan line, her ancestry traceable back to the Lords Den ruling Old Embruddock in the chill times."

The girl, thinking herself unobserved, skipped in the courtyard below, dried her hair in a desultory fashion, and whirled her towel about her head now and again.

"Why does she make the journey with you, Taynth?"

"Because I wished you to see her. A pleasant girl, is she not?"

"Pleasing enough."

"Young, it's true, but, from certain signs I have had, of a quite lascivious nature."

JandolAnganol felt a trap was about to spring. He withdrew his head and began to pace the room. Taynth Indredd turned about and settled himself comfortably on the ledge, blowing out smoke.

"Cousin, we wish to see the member states of the Holy Pannoval Empire draw ever closer. We must protect ourselves against bad times— not only now but to come. In Pannoval, we have always had Akhanaba's gift of foresight. That is why we wish you to marry this pretty young princess, Simoda Tal."

The blood sank from JandolAnganol's face. Straightening himself, he said, "You know I am already married—and to whom I am married."

"Face some unpleasant facts, coz. The present queen is the daughter of a brigand. She is not a fit match for you. The marriage degrades you and your country, which demands a better status. Married to Simoda Tal, though, yours would be a force to be reckoned with."

"It cannot be done. In any case, the mother of that girl down there is a Madi. Isn't that so?"

Taynth Indredd shrugged. "Are Madis worse than the phagors you dote on? Listen, coz, we want this new match to go through as smoothly as possible. No hostility, only mutual help. In eighty-three more years, Oldorando will be aflame from one end to the other, with temperatures near to one hundred and fifty degrees, according to calculation. Oldorandans will have to move southwards. Form a dyastic marriage now, and they will be in your power then. They will be poor relations begging at your door. All Borlien-Oldorando will be yours—or your grandsons' at least. It is a chance never to be missed. Now let's have some more fruit. The squaanej are excellent."

"It cannot be done."

"It can. The Holy C'Sarr is prepared to annul your present marriage by a special bill."

JandolAnganol raised a hand as if to strike the prince. He retained the hand at the level of his eyes and said, "My present marriage is my past marriage and my future one. If we need this dynastic marriage, then I will marry off Robayday to your Simoda. It would make an equal match."

The prince leaned forward and pointed a finger at JandolAnganol. "Certainly not. Forget the suggestion. That boy is crazy. His grandma was the wild Shannana."

The Eagle's eyes flashed. "He's not crazy. A little wild."

"He should have attended a monastery, as you did and as I did. Your religion must tell you that your son is inadmissible as a suitor. You must make the sacrifice, if you choose to regard it as such. You will be rewarded for any sense of loss by our considerable aid. When we have your consent, we shall present you with a chest full of the new weaponry, together with all necessary priming. More chests will follow. You can train gunners for use against Darvlish the Skull as well as the Randonanese tribes. You will gain every advantage."

"And what will Pannoval gain?" JandolAnganol asked bitterly.

"Stability, coz, stability. Over the next unstable period. The Sibornalese are not going to grow less powerful as Freyr nears."

He nibbled at one of the purple squaanej.

JandolAnganol stood rooted where he was, looking away from the prince.

"I am already married to a woman I love. I will not put Myrdem-Inggala aside."

The prince laughed. "Love! Zygankes, as Simoda Tal would say! Kings cannot afford to think in such terms. You must put your country first. For Borlien's sake, marry Simoda Tal, unify, stabilise . . ."

"And if I don't?"

Taking his time, Taynth Indredd selected another squaanej from the bowl.

"In that case, you will be wiped from the field of play, won't you?"

JandolAnganol knocked the fruit from his hand. It rolled across the floor and stopped against the wall.

"I have my religious convictions. It would go against those convictions to put my queen aside. And there are those in your Church who would support me."

"You don't mean poor old Ulbobeg?"

Although the prince's hand shook, he bent and selected another fruit.

"First of all, find some pretext to send her away somewhere. Get her out of the court. Send her to the coast. Then think about all the advantages which will accrue when you do as we wish you to do. I must return to Pannoval at the end of the week—with the news that you will make a dynastic marriage which the Holy C'Sarr himself will bless."

The day continued difficult for JandolAnganol. During the morning's meeting, while Taynth Indredd sat silent on his frog-throne, Guaddl Ulbobeg expounded the plan for the new marriage. This time, it was set out in diplomatic terms. When this action was taken, then those benefits would accrue. Great C'Sarr Kilandar IX, Father Supreme of the Church of Akhanaba, would approve both a bill of divorcement and the second marriage.

Wisely, nothing was said about what might or might not accrue in eighty-three years. Most diplomacy was concerned with getting through the next five years.

The royal household gave a luncheon for the guests, over which Queen MyrdemInggala presided, the king sitting at her side without eating, his little phagor waiting behind him. High-ranking members of the Borlienese scritina were also present.

A wealth of roasted crane, fish, pig, and swan was consumed.

After the banquet, Prince Taynth Indredd made his reply. Pretending to reciprocate for the feast, he had his bodyguard give a demonstration of the capabilities of the new matchlocks. Three mountain lions were brought in chains into one of the inner courtyards and despatched.

While the smoke was still clearing, the weapons were given to Jandol-Anganol. They were presented almost contemptuously, as if his assent to the Pannovalan demands was taken for granted.

The reason for the demonstration was clear. The scritina would demand that the king get more matchlocks from Pannoval to fight the various wars. And Pannoval would supply them—at a price.

No sooner was this ceremony concluded than two traders entered the palace grounds, bringing with them a body sewn into a sack, lashed to the back of an ancient kaidaw. The sack was opened. YeferalOboral's body rolled out, with part of its chest and shoulder blown away. It was a tormented king who stalked into his chancellor's chambers that evening. Batalix was setting among roll after roll of cloud, on which Freyr's light intermittently shone. The warm western glow lit the dull corners of the room.

SartoriIrvrash rose from the long cluttered table at which he was sitting and bowed to the king. He was wrestling with his "Alphabet of History and Nature." All about lay ancient sources and modern reports, at which the king's quick eye glared dismissively.

"What decision should I give Taynth Indredd?" demanded the king.

"May I speak clearly, Your Majesty?"

"Speak." The king flung himself untidily into a chair, and the runt stood behind it so as to avoid SartoriIrvrash's gaze.

SartoriIrvrash bowed his head so that the king could see only his expressionless bald pate. "Your Majesty, your first duty lies not to yourself but to your country. So says the ancient Law of Kings. The plan of Pannoval to cement our present good relations with Oldorando by a dynastic marriage is workable. It will render your throne more secure, its tenure less open to question. It will guarantee that in future we may turn to Pannoval for aid.

"I think in particular of aid in the form of grain, as well as weapons. They have great fields in their more temperate north, towards the Pannoval Sea. This year, our harvest is poor, and will become yet poorer as the heat increases. Whereas our Royal Armourer can presumably imitate the Sibornalese matchlocks.

"There is, therefore, everything to be said for your making the match with Simoda Tal of Oldorando, despite her scanty years—everything but one thing. Queen MyrdemInggala. Our present queen is a good and holy woman, and the condition of love prospers between the two of you. If you sever that love, you will suffer harm as a result."

"Perhaps I can come to love Simoda Tal."

"Perhaps you can, Your Majesty." SartoriIrvrash turned to look out of his small window at the sunsets. "But with that love will go the bitter thread of hate. You will never find another woman like the queen; or, if you do, that woman will not bear the name of Simoda Tal."

"Love's not important," said JandolAnganol, beginning to pace the floor. "Survival's more important. So says the prince. Perhaps he's right. In any case, what advice are you giving me? Are you saying yes or no?"

The chancellor tugged at his whiskers. "The phagor question is another botheration. Did the prince bring it up this morning?"

"He said nothing on that subject this morning."

"He will. The people for whom he speaks will. Just as soon as a deal is made."

"So, your advice, Chancellor? Should I say yes to Pannoval or no?"

The chancellor kept his eye on the litter of papers on his table, and sank down on the bench. His hand fluttered a parchment, causing it to rustle like old leaves.

"You tax me, sire, on a crucial matter, a matter where the needs of the heart run into confrontation with the demands of the state. It's not for me to say yes or no. . . . Is this not a religious matter, best taken to your vicar?"

JandolAnganol struck his fist on the table. "All matters are religious, but in this particular matter I must turn to my chancellor. That you reverence the present queen is a quality for which I respect you, Rushven. Nevertheless, put that consideration apart and deliver me your judgment. Should I set her aside and make this dynastic marriage, in order to safeguard the future of our country? Answer."

In the chancellor's mind lay the knowledge that he must not be responsible for the king's decision. Otherwise, he would be made a scapegoat later; he knew the king's volatile disposition, dreaded his rages. He saw many arguments for the coalition between Borlien and Oldorando; to have peace between the two traditionally hostile neighbours would benefit all; in that union, if it was wisely handled—as he could handle it—would be a bulwark against Pannoval as well as against the ever thrusting continent of the north, Sibornal.

On the other hand, he felt as much loyalty to the person of the queen as he did to the king. In his egocentric way, he loved MyrdemInggala like a daughter, especially since his wife had been killed in such horrible circumstances. Her beauty was before him every day to warm his scholarly old heart. He had but to lift a finger, to say vigorously, "You must stand by the woman you love—that is the greatest alliance you can make . . . ," but, peeping up at the stormy face of his king, his courage failed him. There was his great lifelong project, his book, to be defended.

The question was too large for any but the king himself to answer.

"Your majesty will have a nose bleed if you become overexcited. I pray, drink some wine . . ."

"By the beholder, you are all that is worst in men, a very grave of help!"

The old man hunched his shoulders further into his patterned charfrul and shook his head.

"As your advisor, my duty in such a difficult personal matter is to formulate the problem clearly for you. You it is who must decide what resolution is best, Majesty, for you of all people must live with that decision. There are two ways of looking at the problem you face."

JandolAnganol made towards the door and then stopped. He confronted the older man down the length of the room.

"Why should I have to suffer? Why should not kings be exempt from the common lot? If I did this thing demanded of me, should I be a saint or a devil?"

"That only you will know, sire."

"You care nothing, do you—nothing about me or the kingdom, only for that miserable dead past you work over all day."

The chancellor gripped his trembling hands between his knees.

"We may care, Your Majesty, and be unable to do anything. I put it to you that this problem which confronts us is a result of the deteriorating climate. As it happens, I'm studying at present an old chronicle of the time of another king, by name AozroOnden, who was lord of a very different Oldorando almost four centuries ago. The chronicle refers to AozroOnden's slaying of two brothers who had between them ruled the known world."

"I know the legend. What of it? Am I threatening to kill anyone at present?"

"This pleasant story, set in an historical record, is typical of the thinking of those primitive times. Perhaps we are not meant to take the story literally. It is an allegory of man's responsibility for the death of the two good seasons, represented as two good men, and his causing the cold winters and burning summers which now afflict us. We all suffer from that primal guilt. You cannot act without feeling guilt. That is all I say."

The king let out a growl. "You old bookworm, it's love that tears me apart, not guilt!"

He went out, banging the door behind him. He was not going to admit to his chancellor that he did feel guilt. He loved the queen; yet by some perverse streak in him he longed to be free, and the realisation tortured him.

She was the queen of queens. All Borlien loved her, as they did not love him. And a further turn of that particular screw: he knew she deserved their love. Perhaps she took it too much for granted that he loved her. . . . Perhaps she had too much power over him. . . .

And that bastion of her body, ripe as corn sheaves, the soft seas of her hair, the ointments of her loins, the dazzlement of her gaze, the wholeness with which she smiled. . . . But what would it be like to rip into the pubescent body of that pretentious semi-Madi princess? A different thing entirely . . .

His tortuous thoughts, winding this way and that, were penned in among the intricacies of the palace. The palace had accumulated almost by accident. Courts had been filled in by buildings and servants' quarters improvised from ruins. The grand and the sordid lay side by side. The privileged who lived here above the city suffered almost as many inconveniences as those in the city.

One token of inconvenience lay in the grotesque arrangements on the skyline, now visible outlined against the darkening cloud overhead. The air in the valley lay stifling upon the city, like a cat indifferently sprawled upon a dying mouse. Canvas sails, wooden vanes, and little copper windmills had been perched high on air stacks, in order to drag a breath of freshness down to those who suffered in chambers below. This orchestra of semaphoric bids for relief creaked above the king's head as he walked through his maze. He looked up once, as if attracted by a chorus of doom.

No one else was about, except sentries. They stood at every turn, and most of them were phagors. Weapon bearing, marching, or rigidly on guard, they might have been the sole possessors of the castle and its secrets.

JandolAnganol saluted them absently as he went through the gathering shadows. There was one person to whom he could go for advice. It might be advice of a villainous order, but it would be given. The person who gave it was himself one of the secrets of the castle. His father.

As he drew nearer to an innermost part of the palace where his father was confined, more sentries stiffened at his approach, as if by some potent regal quality he could freeze them with his presence. Bats fluttered from nooks in the stonework, hens scattered underfoot; but the place was strangely silent, dwelling on the king's dilemma.

He made for a rear staircase protected by a thick door. A phagor stood there, his high military caste denoted by the fact that he had retained his horns.

"I will enter."

Without a word, the phagor produced a key and unlocked the door, pushing it wide with his foot. The king descended, walking slowly with a hand on the iron rail. The gloom was thick, and thickened as the stair curved down. At the bottom was an anteroom where another guard stood before another locked door. This also was opened to the king.

He came into the damp set of chambers reserved for his father.

Even in his self-absorption, he felt the chill and the damp. A ghost of remorse moved in his harneys.

VarpalAnganol sat in the end room of three, wrapped in a blanket, gazing into a log fire smouldering in a grate. A grille high in one wall let in the last of daylight. The old man looked up, blinking, and made a slapping noise with his lips, as if moistening his mouth preparatory to speech, but he said nothing.

"Father. It's I. Have you no lamp?"

"I was just trying to calculate what year it was."

"It's 381, winter." It was some weeks since he had set eyes on his father. The old man had aged considerably, and would soon be one with the gossies.

He got himself to the standing position, supporting himself with an arm of the chair.

"Do you want to sit down, my boy? There's only the one chair. This place is not very well furnished. It will do me good to stand for a while."

"Sit down, Father. I want to talk to you."

"Have they found your son—what's his name? Roba? Have they found Roba?"

"He's crazy, even the foreigners know it."

"You see, he liked the desert as a child. I took him there, and his mother. The wide sky . . ."

"Father, I am thinking of divorcing Cune. There are state reasons."

"Oh, well, you could lock her up with me. I like Cune, nice woman. Of course, we'd need another chair. . . ."

"Father, I want some advice. I want to talk to you." The old man sank down on the chair. JandolAnganol crossed in front of him and squatted facing him, back to the feeble fire. "I want to ask you about— love, whatever love is. Are you attending? Everyone is supposed to love. The highest and the lowest. I love the All-Powerful Akhanaba, and perform my worship every day; I am one of his representatives here on earth. I also love MyrdemInggala, above all women who ever breathed. You know that I have killed men I thought looked lustfully upon her."

A pause followed while his father gathered his thoughts.

"You're a good swordsman, that I never denied." The old man tittered.

"Didn't a poet say that Love is like Death? I love Akhanaba and I love Cune, yes. Yet under that love—I often ask myself—under that love, isn't there a vein of hatred? Should there be? Does every man feel as I do?"

The old man said nothing.

"When I was a child, how you beat me! You punished me by locking me out. Once you locked me down here in this very cellar, remember? And yet I loved you, loved you without question. The fatal innocent love of a boy for his father. How is it I can love nobody else without that poison of hate leaking in?"

The old man wriggled in the chair as his son spoke, as if possessed of an incurable itch.

"There's no end to it," he said. "No end at all. . . . We cannot tell where one emotion ends and the next begins. Your trouble's not hate but guilt. That's what you feel—guilt, Jan. I feel it, all men feel it. It's an inherited misery bred in the bone, for which Akha punishes us with cold and heat. Women don't seem to feel it the way men do. Men control women, but who's to control men? Hate's not bad at all. I like hate, I've always enjoyed hate. It keeps you warm at nights. . . .

"Listen, when I was young, lad, I hated almost everyone. I hated you because you wouldn't do as you were told. But guilt—guilt's a different matter, guilt makes you miserable. Hate cheers you up, makes you forget guilt."

"Love?"

The old man sighed, blowing his bad breath into the dank atmosphere. It was so dark that his son could not see his face, only the gap in it.

"Dogs love their masters, that I do know. I had a dog once, a wonderful dog, white with a brown face, eyes like a Madi. He used to lie beside me on my bed. I loved that dog. What was his name?"

JandolAnganol stood up. "Is that the only love you've ever felt? Love for some scumbering hound?"

"I don't remember loving anyone else. . . . Anyway, you are going to have a divorcement of MyrdemInggala, and you want an excuse so that you don't feel so guilty about it, eh?"

"Is that what I said?"

"When? I don't remember. What time is it, do you reckon? You must announce that she and YeferalOborol, that brother of hers, plotted to murder the Sibornalese ambassador, and that's how her brother was killed. A conspiracy. There's a perfect excuse. And then when you put her away, you will please Sibornal as well as Pannoval and Oldorando."

JandolAnganol clutched his forehead. "Father—how did you learn of YeferalOborol's death? His body was brought back only an hour ago."

"You see, son, if you keep very still, as I have to with my stiff joints, everything comes to you. I have more time. . . . There is another possibility . . ."

"What's that?"

"You can just have her disappear in the darkness one night. Never seen again. Now that the brother's gone, there's no one interested enough to make a real fuss. Is her old father still alive?"

"No. I couldn't do that. I wouldn't even dream of doing it."

"Of course you would . . ." He panted a little by way of laughter. "But my conspiracy idea is a good one, eh?"

The king went to stand under the window. Waves of light floated on the domed brick ceiling of the prison. Outside was the queen's reservoir. His sorrow accumulated like water. How treacherous this old man still was. . . .

"Good? Full of guile and taking advantage of circumstances, yes. I see clearly where I had my character from."

He hammered on the door for release.

After the cellars, the evening world appeared bathed in light. He took a side door and emerged by the reservoir, where a flight of steps led down to the water. Once a boat had been moored there; he remembered playing in it as a boy; now it had disintegrated and sunk.

The sky was the hue of stale cheese, flecked with wisps of grey cloud. On the far side of the pool, like a cliff, rose the queen's quarters, its elegant outlines black against the sky. A light burned dimly in one window. Perhaps his beautiful wife was there, preparing for her bed. He could go and beg her forgiveness. He could lose himself in her beauty.

Instead, unpremeditatedly, he jumped forward into the reservoir.

He held his hands together above his head as if he were falling from a building. Air belched out from his clothes. The water grew dark rapidly as he sank.

"Let me never rise," he said.

The water was deep and cold and black. He welcomed terror, trying to embrace the mud at the bottom. Bubbles streamed from his nose.

The processes of life commanded by the All-Powerful would not allow him to escape into the avenues of death. Despite his struggles, he found himself drifting upward again. As he surfaced, gasping, the queen's light went out.

VII

THE QUEEN VISITS
THE LIVING AND THE DEAD

The next day dawned hot and heavy. The queen of queens allowed herself to be bathed by her women. She played with Tatro for a while, and then summoned SartoriIrvrash to meet her in the family vault.

There she paid her last respects to her brother. Soon he would be buried in his correct land-octave. His body lay swathed in yellow cloth on a block of Lordryardry ice. She noted with grief how even death had not transformed his plain features. She wept for all things prosaic and exotic, for all that had happened and failed to happen to her brother in his lifetime. So the chancellor found her.

He wore an ink-smeared smock. There was ink on his fingers. He bowed low, and there was ink on his pate.

"Rushven, I have a farewell to say here, but I wish also to greet my brother now that his soul has passed to the world below. I wish you by me while I go into pauk, to see that nobody disturbs me."

He looked troubled. "Madam. May I recall two items to your troubled mind. First, that pater-placation—pauk, if you prefer the old-fashioned term—is discouraged by your church. Second, it is not possible to commune with gossies before their mortal bodies are buried in their land-octaves."

"And third, you believe that pauk is a fairy tale anyway." She gave him a wan smile as she resurrected an old argument between them.

He shook his head. "I know well what once I said. However, times change. Now I confess that I myself have learned to go into pater-placation, to console myself by communing with the spirit of my departed wife."

He bit his lips. Reading her expression, he said, "Yes, she has forgiven me."

She touched him. "I'm glad."

Then the academic rose up in him again, and he said, "But you see, Your Majesty, there is a philosophical difficulty in believing that the pater-placation ritual is other than subjective. There *cannot* be gossies and fessups under the ground with whom living people talk."

"We know there are. You and I and millions of peasants talk to our ancestors whenever we wish. Where's the difficulty?"

"Historical records, of which I have plenty, all report that the gossies were once creatures of hatred, bewailing their failed lives, pouring scorn on the living. Over the generations, that has changed; nowadays, all anyone gets is sweetness and consolation. That suggests that the whole experience is wish-fulfilment, a kind of self-hypnosis. Moreover, stellar geometry has outmoded the antique idea that our world rests on an original boulder, towards which fessups descend."

She stamped her foot. "Must I call the vicar? Am I not under grief and strain enough, without having to listen to your preposterous historical lectures at this hour?"

She was immediately sorry for her outburst, and put an arm through his as they ascended to her room.

"It's a comfort, whatever it is," she said. "Praise be, there's a realm of the spirit beyond knowledge."

"My dear queen, though I hate religion, I recognise sanctity when I am in its presence." When she squeezed his arm, he was emboldened to add, "But the Holy Church has never quite accepted pater-placation as part of its ritual, has it? It does not know what to make of gossies and fessups. In consequence, it would like to ban it, but if it did so, then a million peasants would quit the Church. So it ignores the entire question."

She looked down at her smooth hands. Already she was preparing herself for the act. "How very sensible of the Church," she murmured.

SartoriIrvrash, in his turn, was sensible enough to make no reply.

MyrdemInggala led the way through into her inner chamber. She sank down on her bed, composing herself, controlling her breathing, relaxing her muscles. SartoriIrvrash sat quietly by her bed, circling his forehead with the holy sign, to begin his vigil. He saw that already she was moving into the pauk state.

He kept his eyes tight closed, not daring to gaze upon her defenceless beauty, and listened to her infrequent exhalations.

The soul has no eyes, yet it sees in the world below.

The soul of the queen cast its regard downwards as it began its long descent. Beneath lay space more vast than night skies, more rich, more imposing. It was not space at all: it was the opposite of space, of consciousness even—a peculiar rupellary density without feature.

Just as the land regards an ocean-going ship as a token of freedom, while the sailors confined on that ship regard the land in similar terms, so the realm of oblivion was at once space and non-space.

To consciousness, the realm appeared infinite. In its downward direction, it ceased only where the races of manlike-kind began, in a green and unknown, unknowable womb, the womb of the original beholder. The original beholder—that passive motherly principle—received the souls of the dead who sank back into her. Although she might be no more than a fossil scent entombed in rock, she was not to be resisted.

Above the original beholder were the gossies and fessups, floating, thousands upon thousands upon thousands, as if all the stars of night had been stacked in order, and arranged in accordance with the ancient idea of land-octaves.

The queen's exploratory soul sank down, floating like a feather towards the fessups. At close quarters, they resembled not stars so much as mummified chickens, with hollow eyes and stomachs, their legs dangling clumsily. Age had eroded them. They were transparent. Their insides circulated like luminescent fish in a bowl. Their mouths were open like fish, as if trying to blow a bubble towards a surface they would never see again. In their upper strata, where the gossies were less ancient, little dusts still escaped from phantom larynxes, the very last apostrophes remaining to the possessive case of life.

To some souls venturing there, the ranks of the departed were terrifying. For the queen they held consolation. She looked down upon them, those mouths pickled in obsidian, and was reassured to believe that at least some wreckage remained from existence, and would ever remain until the planet was consumed by fire. And who knew if even then . . .

For venturing souls, no compass bearings seemed possible. Yet there was direction. The beholder was a lodestone. All here had been collected according to plan, as stones on seashores are graded according to size. The ranks of fessups stretched below the whole earth, leading

beyond Borlien and Oldorando to far Sibornal and even to the remote
parts of Hespagorat, to semi-legendary Pegovin beyond the Climent Sea,
even to the poles.

The soul barque moved to a breeze that did not blow, finally drifting
to the gossie of what had once been her mother, the wild Shannana,
wife to RatanOborol, ruler of Matrassyl. The maternal gossie resembled
a battered birdcage, its ribs and hipbones forming tentative golden patterns against the darkness, like a leaf crushed long ago in a child's book.
It spoke.

Gossies and fessups were tormenting things. As negatives of being,
they recalled only the incidents in their lives which were pleasant. The
good had been interred with them; the evil, the dross, lost along with
freedom of action.

"Dear Moth, I come dutifully before you again, to see how you fare."
Her ritual salutation.

"My dear daughter, there are no troubles here. All is serene, nothing
can go awry. And when you appear, everything is gained. My joyous and
beautiful one, how did I squeeze such an offspring from my unworthy
loins? Your grandmother is also here, delighted also to be back in your
presence."

"It is a comfort to be in your presence, too, Moth." But the words
were a formula against entropy.

"Oh, no, but you must not say that, because the delight is all ours,
and often I think how in the hurried days of my life I never cherished
you enough, certainly not as much as your virtue warranted. There was
always so much to be done, and another battle fought, and one may
wonder now why energy was spent on those unimportant things, whereas
the real joy of life was being close with you and seeing you grow up
into—"

"Mother, you were a kind parent, and I not a dutiful enough child. I
was always headstrong—"

"Headstrong!" exclaimed the old gossie. "No, no, you did nothing
to offend. One sees these things differently in this stage of existence, one
sees what the true things are, what's important. A few little peccadillos
are nothing, and I'm only sorry if I made a fuss at the time. That was
just my stupidity—I knew all along that you were my greatest treasure.
Not to pass on life, that's the failure—as those down here without
offspring will testify in endless dole."

She continued joyfully in this vein, and the queen let her ramble on,
placated by her words, for the fact was that in life she had found her
mother self-absorbed and without more than perfunctory kindness. It
delighted her to find that this battered cage should remember events of
her childhood which she had forgotten. Flesh had died; memory was
embalmed here.

At last she interrupted her. "Moth, I came down here half-prepared to meet with YeferalOborol, expecting his soul to have joined you and grandmother."

"Ah . . . then my dear son has come to the end of earthly years? Oh, praise be, that's good news indeed, how glad we shall be to be united with him, since he never mastered pater-placation as you have, you clever girl. How glad you make us."

"Dear Mother, he was shot by a Sibornalese gun."

"Splendid! Splendid! The sooner the better, as far as I'm concerned. That is a treat. . . . And when do we expect him?"

"His mortal remains will be buried within a few hours."

"We shall watch for him, and what a welcome we shall give to him. You'll be here with us one day, too, never fear. . . ."

"I look forward to it, Moth. And I have a request, which you must pass to your fellow fessups. It is a difficult question. There is one on the surface still who loves me, though he has never spoken his love; I have felt it radiating from him. I feel I can trust him as I can trust few men. He has been sent from Matrassyl to fight in a distant land."

"We have no wars down here, sweet child."

"This trusted friend of mine is often in pauk. His father is here in the world below. My friend's name is Hanra TolramKetinet. I want you to pass a message on to his father, to ask Hanra's whereabouts, for it is essential that I get a message to him."

A hissing silence before the shade of Shannana spoke again.

"My sweet child, in your world nobody communicates fully with another. So much is unknown. Here we have completion. There can be no secrets when the flesh is divested."

"I know, Moth," said the soul. It feared that kind of completion. It had heard the statement many times. It explained once more what it required from the revered gossie. After many a diversion, understanding was reached, and the soul's enquiry was passed along the ranks, like a breeze rustling the dead leaves of a forest.

For the soul, there was difficulty in sustaining herself. Phantasms of the upper world seeped in, and a noise like frying. A curtain blew, something rattled with a deadly music. The soul began drifting, despite the cajolings of her mother's gossie.

At last a message returned to her through the obsidian. Her friend was still among the living. The gossies of his family declared that he had spoken with them recently, when his corporeal part was near a village called Ut Pho in the jungles of the Chwart Heights on the eastern margins of the land called Randonan.

"My thanks for what I needed to know," cried the soul. As it poured forth its gratitude, the maternal gossie puffed dust from its throat and spoke again.

"Here we pity your poor disrupted lives, when physical sight blinds you. We can communicate with a greater voice beyond your knowledge, where many voices are one. Come soon and hear for yourself. Join us!"

But the frail soul knew these claims of old. The dead and the living were opposing armies; pauk was only a truce.

With many cries of affection, it left the spark which had once been Shannana, to sail upwards towards the spectrums of movement and breath.

When MyrdemInggala was strong enough, she dismissed Sartori-Irvrash from her suite with suitable courtesies and no mention of what she had learned in pauk.

She summoned Mai TolramKetinet, sister to the friend of whom she had been enquiring in the world below. Mai aided her through the ritual of a post-pauk bath. The queen sluiced down her body with extra care, as if it had been sullied by its journey towards death.

"I wish to go into the city, Mai—in disguise. You will accompany me. The princess will remain here. Prepare two sets of peasant clothes."

When she was alone, MyrdemInggala wrote a letter to General TolramKetinet, apprising him of the threatening events at court. She signed the letter, sealed it with her seal, enclosed it in a leather pouch, and sealed that with a stronger seal.

Dismissing feelings of faintness, she dressed in the peasant clothes Mai brought, and concealed the message pouch in them.

"We shall leave by the side gate."

The side gate attracted less attention. There were always beggars and other importuners at the main gate. There were also heads of criminals on poles at present, which stank.

The guard let them through indifferently, and the women walked down the winding road to the city. At this hour, JandolAnganol was probably asleep. It was his habit, learnt from his father, to rise at dawn and show himself, crowned, on his balcony, for all to see. Not only did this gesture induce a feeling of security in the nation; it impressed everyone with the long hours the king worked—"like a one-legged peasant," as the expression was. But the king generally went back to bed after his appearance.

Heavy cloud rolled overhead. The scorching wind, the thordotter, blew from the southeast, picking at their petticoats, blowing its hot breath in their faces till their eyes dried. It was a relief to gain the narrow alleys at the foot of the hill, despite the dust that whipped at their heels.

"We'll seek a blessing in the church," said MyrdemInggala. There was a church at the end of the street, with steps winding down round its curving wall in the traditional way of Old Borlienese church architecture. Little of the church was above ground except the dome. In this way, the fathers of the church imitated the desire to live underground which possessed the Takers, those holy men of Pannoval who had brought the faith to Borlien, centuries ago.

The two women were not alone in their descent. An old peasant shuffled before them, led by a boy. He held out a hand to them. His story was that he had given up his holding because the heat had killed his crops, and had come to beg in town. The queen gave him a silver coin.

Darkness prevailed inside the church. The congregation knelt in a pool of darkness intended to remind them of their mortal state. Light filtered down from above. The painted image of Akhanaba behind the circular altar was lit by candles. The long bovine face, blue-painted, the eyes kind but inhuman—these were lapped by uncertain shadows.

To these traditional elements was added a more modern embellishment. Near the door, lit by one candle, stood a stylised portrait of a mother, with sad downcast eyes, her hands spread. Many of the women shuffling in kissed the original beholder as they passed her.

No formal service was in progress but, since the church was nevertheless half full, a priest was praying aloud in a high nasal singsong.

"Many come to knock at thy door, O Akhanaba, and many turn away without a knock.

"And to those who turn away and those who stand in all piety knocking,

"Thou sayest, 'Cease to cry "When willst thou open to me, O All-Powerful One?"

" 'For I say that all the while the door stands open, and never has been shut.' These things are there to be seen but you see them not."

MyrdemInggala thought of what her mother's gossie had said. They communicated with a greater voice. Yet Shannana did not mention Akhanaba. Looking up at the face of the All-Powerful, she thought, it's true, we are surrounded by mystery. Even Rushven can't understand it.

"All about you lies all that you need, if you will accept and not take by force. If you would but lay down your self, you would find what is greater than yourself.

"All things are equal in this world, but also greater.

" 'Ask not therefore if I am man or animal or stone:

" 'All these I am and more that you must learn to perceive.' "

The chanting went on, the choir joining in. The queen reflected how excellently the alto voices chimed with the stone vaulting overhead; here indeed were spirit and stone united.

She put a hand under her clothes and placed it on her breast, trying to still the beating of her heart.

Despite the beauty of the singing, the apprehension in her would not be soothed. There was no time to contemplate eternity under the pressure of dire events.

When the priest had blessed them, she was ready to go on. The two women, shawls about their heads, went out again into the wind and daylight.

The queen led them to the quayside, where the River Takissa looked dark and choppy, like a narrow sea. A boat just in from Oldorando was mooring with some difficulty. Small boats were being loaded, but there was less activity than usual because of the thordotter. Empty carts, barrels, timbers, winches, and other equipment essential to river life stood about. A tarpaulin whipped back and forth in the wind. The queen walked on determinedly until they reached a warehouse over which was a sign reading: LORDRYARDRY ICE TRADING COMPANY.

This was the Matrassyl headquarters of the famous ice captain, Krillio Muntras of Lordryardry.

The warehouse had an assortment of doors on all floors, large and small. MyrdemInggala chose the smallest on the ground floor and walked in. Mai followed.

Inside was a cobbled court, with fat men rolling barrels of their own shape over to a dray.

"I wish to speak with Krillio Muntras," she said to the nearest man.

"He's busy. He won't speak to anyone," the man said, regarding her suspiciously. She had drawn a veil across her face, so as not to be recognised.

"He'll speak to me." She withdrew from a finger of her left hand a ring with the colours of the sea in it. "Take this to him."

The man departed, muttering. By his stature and accent, she knew he was from Dimariam, one of the countries of the southern continent of Hespagorat. She waited impatiently, tapping her foot on the cobbles, but after a moment the man was back, his attitude much changed. "Pray allow me to show you to Captain Muntras."

MyrdemInggala turned to Mai. "You will wait here."

"But, ma'am—"

"And do not obstruct the men in their work."

She was shown into a workshop smelling of glues and fresh-shaved wood, where old men and apprentices were sawing up timbers and making them into chests and iceboxes. The workbenches were bearded with long curly shavings. The men watched the hooded female figure curiously as it passed.

Her guide opened a door hidden behind overalls. They climbed a dusty stair to a floor where a long low room commanded a view of the river. Clerks worked at one end of the room, shoulders bent over ledgers. At the other end was a desk with a chair as solid as a throne, from which a fat brown man had risen, to come forward with a beaming face. He bowed low, dismissed the guide, and led the queen into a private room beyond his desk.

Although his room overlooked a stable yard, it was well furnished, with prints on the wall, with an elegance at variance with the functional appearance of the rest of the building. One of the prints depicted Queen MyrdemInggala.

"Madam Queen, I am proud to receive you." The Ice Captain beamed again and set his head on one side as far as it would go, the better to regard MyrdemInggala as she removed her veil and headgear. He was himself simply dressed in a charfrul, the full shift with pockets worn by many natives of the equatorial regions.

When he had her comfortably seated and had given her a glass of wine chilled with fresh Lordryardry ice, he thrust out a hand to her. Opening his fist, he revealed her ring, which he now returned ceremoniously, insisting on fitting it on her dainty finger.

"It was the best ring I ever sold."

"You were only a humble pedlar then."

"Worse, I was a beggar, but a beggar with determination." He struck his chest.

"Now you are very rich."

"Now, what are riches, madam? Do they buy happiness? Well, frankly, they at least permit us to be miserable comfortably. My state, I will admit to you, is better than that of most common folk."

His laugh was comfortable. He hitched a plump leg unceremoniously over the edge of the table and lifted his glass to toast her, evaluating her. The queen of queens raised her eyes to his. The Ice Captain lowered his gaze, protecting himself from a tremor of feeling much like awe. He had dealt in girls almost as widely as ice; before the queen's beauty, he felt himself powerless.

MyrdemInggala talked to him about his family. She knew he had a clever daughter and a stupid son, and that the stupid son, Div, was about to take over the ice trade on his father's retirement. That retirement had been postponed. Muntras had made his last trip a tenner and a half ago, at the time of the Battle of the Cosgatt—only it had proved not to be his last trip, since Div needed further instruction.

She knew the Ice Captain was gentle with his silly boy. Yet Muntras's father had been harsh with him, sending him out as a lad to earn money begging and peddling, in order to prove he was capable of taking over a one-ship ice business. She had heard this tale before, but was not bored by it.

"You've had an eventful life," she said.

Perhaps he thought some sort of criticism was implied, for he looked uncomfortable. To cover his unease, he slapped his leg and said, "I'm not ashamed to say that I have prospered at a time when the majority of citizens are doing the reverse."

She regarded his solid countenance as if wondering if he understood she was also of that majority, but merely said, in her composed way, "You told me once you started in business with one boat. How many have you now, Captain?"

"Yes, Madam Queen, my old father started with but one old hooker, which I inherited. Today, I hand over to my son a fleet of twenty-five ships. Fast seagoing sloops, and ketches, hookers, and doggers, to ply the rivers and coasts, each adapted to the trade. There you see the benefits of dealing in ice. The hotter it gets, the more a block of good Lordryardry ice will fetch in the market. The worse things get for others, the more they improve for me."

"But your ice melts, Captain."

"That's so, and many the jokes people make about it. But Lordryardry ice, being pure off the glacier, melts less rapidly than other ices sold by other traders." He was enjoying himself in her presence, though he had not failed to notice a clouded air about her, so different from her normal disposition.

"I'll put another point to you. You are devout in the religion of your country, Madam Queen, so I do not need to remind you of redemption. Well, my ice is like your redemption. The less there is, the scarcer it becomes, and the scarcer it becomes, the more it costs. My boats now sail all the way from Dimariam, across the Sea of Eagles, up the Takissa and Valvoral rivers to Matrassyl and Oldorando City, as well as along the coast to Keevasien and the ports of the deadly assatassi."

She smiled, perhaps not entirely pleased to hear religion and trade intermingled. "Well, I'm glad someone fares well in a bad age." She had not forgotten the time when she as a young girl on her first visit to Oldorando had met the Dimariamian in the bazaar. He was in rags, but he had a smile; and he had produced from an inner pocket the most beautiful ring she had ever seen. Shannana, her mother, had given her the money. She had returned the next day to buy it, and had worn it ever since.

"You overpaid me for that ring," Krillio Muntras said, "and with the profit I went home and bought a glacier. So I have been in your debt ever since." He laughed, and she joined in. "Now, Madam Queen, you come here not to bargain about ice, since that I supply through the palace majordomo. Can I do you a favour?"

"Captain Muntras, I am in a difficult situation, and I need help."

He looked suddenly cautious. "I do not want to lose the royal favour which permits me, a foreigner, to trade here. Otherwise . . ."

"I appreciate that. All I ask of you is reliability, and of that you will surely avail me. I wish you to deliver a letter for me, secretly. You mention Keevasien, on the border with Randonan. Can you reliably deliver a letter to a certain gentleman fighting in Randonan in our Second Army?"

Muntras's expressive face looked so glum that his cheeks tightened themselves round his mouth. "In war, everything is doubtful. The news is that the Borlienese army fares badly, and Keevasien too. But—but— for you, Madam Queen . . . My boats go up the Kacol River above Keevasien, as far as Ordelay. Yes, I could send a messenger from there. Provided it's not too dangerous. He'd need paying, of course."

"How much?"

He thought. "I have a boy who would do it. When you're young, you don't fear death." He told her how much it would cost. She paid out willingly enough and handed over the pouch with the letter to General TolramKetinet.

Muntras made her another bow. "I'm proud to do it for you. First, I must deliver a freight to Oldorando. That's four days upriver, two days there and two days back. A week in all. Then I'll be back here and straight south for Ottassol."

"Such delay! Do you have to go to Oldorando first?"

"Have to, ma'am. Trade's trade."

"Very well, I'll leave it to you, Captain Muntras. But you understand that this is of vital importance and absolutely secret, between you and me? Carry out this mission faithfully, and I'll see you have your reward."

"I'm grateful for the chance to help, Madam Queen."

When they parted, and the queen had taken another glass of refreshing wine, she was more cheerful and battled almost gaily back to the palace with her lady-in-waiting, the sister of the general to whom her letter was now despatched. She could hope, whatever the king had decided.

Throughout the palace, doors banged and curtains fluttered in the wind. Pale of face, JandolAnganol talked to his religious advisors. One of them finally said to him, "Your Majesty, this state is holy, and we believe that you have already in your heart come to a decision. You will cement this new alliance for holy reasons, and we shall bless you for it."

The king replied vehemently, "If I make this alliance, it will be because I am wicked, and welcome wickedness."

"Not so, my lord! Your queen and her brother conspired against Sibornal, and must be punished." They were already halfway to believing the lie he had set in circulation; it was his old father's lie, but now it had become common property and possessed them one by one.

In their own chambers, the visiting statesmen, awaiting the king's

word, complained about the discomfort of this miserable little palace
and of the poverty of the hospitality. The advisors quarrelled amongst
themselves, jealous of each other's privileges; but one thing they agreed
on. They agreed that if and when the king divorced his queen and
married Simoda Tal, the question of the large phagor population of
Borlien should be reopened.

Old histories told how ancipital hordes had once descended on
Oldorando and burned it to the ground. That hostility had never died.
Year by year, the phagor population was being reduced. It was necessary that Borlien should follow the same policy. With Simoda Tal and
her ministers at JandolAnganol's side, the issue could be pressed harder.

And with MyrdemInggala gone, with her softhearted ways, it would
be convenient to introduce drumbles.

But where was the king, and what was his decision?

The time was a few minutes after fourteen o'clock, and the king stood
naked in an upper chamber. A great pendulum of pewter swung solemnly against one wall, clicking out seconds. Against the other wall
hung an enormous mirror of silver. In the shadows stood serving
wenches, waiting with vestments to dress JandolAnganol to appear before the diplomats.

Between the pendulum and the mirror JandolAnganol stood or paced.
In his indecision, he ran his finger down the scar on his thigh, or pulled
the pallid length of his prodo, or regarded the reflection of those bloody
devotional stripes which stretched from his shoulderblades down to his
thin buttocks. He snarled at the lean whipped thing he saw.

The king could easily send the diplomats packing; his rage, his khmir,
were fully equal to such a deed. He could easily snatch up the thing
dearest to him—the queen—and brand her mouth with hot kisses, vow-
ing never to allow her from his sight. Or he could do the opposite—be a
villain in private and become a saint in the eyes of many, a saint ready
to throw everything away for his country.

Some of those who observed him from afar, such as the Pin family on
the Avernus, who studied the cross-continuities of the king's family,
claimed that the decision was made for the king in a distant past. In
their records lay the history of JandolAnganol's family through sixteen
generations, back to the time when most of Campannlat lay under snow,
back to a distant ancestor of the king's, AozroOn, who had ruled over a
village called Oldorando. Along that line, untraced by those who were
part of it, lay a story of division between father and son, submerged in
some generations but never absent.

That pattern of division lay deep in JandolAnganol's psyche, so deep
he did not notice it in himself. Beneath his arrogance was an even older
self-contempt. His self-contempt made him turn against his dearest
friends and consort with phagors; it was an alienation which early years

had fostered. It was buried, but not without voice, and it was about to speak.

He turned abruptly from the mirror, from that shadowy figure who lurked there in silver, and summoned up the maids. He raised his arms and they dressed him.

"And my crown," he said, as they brushed his flowing hair. He would punish the waiting dignitaries by his distance from them.

A few minutes later, the dignitaries found relief from their boredom by rushing to the windows when marching feet were heard outside. They looked down on great rough heads crowned by gleaming horns, on muscular shoulders and coarse bodies, on hoofs that echoed and war harness that creaked. The Royal First Phagorian Guard was parading—a sight that caused unease in most human spectators, since the ancipitals were so hinged at knee and elbow that lower leg and lower arm could turn in all directions. The march was uncanny, with an impossible forward flexure of the leg at every step.

A sergeant called an order. The platoons halted, going from movement to the instant immobility characteristic of phagors.

The scorching wind stirred the trailing hairs of the platoon. The king stepped from between platoons and marched into the palace. The visiting statesmen regarded each other uneasily, thoughts of assassination in their heads.

JandolAnganol entered the room. He halted and surveyed them. One by one, his guests rose. As if he struggled to speak, the king let the silence lengthen. Then he said, "You have demanded of me a harsh choice. Yet why should I hesitate? My first duty is solemnly pledged to my country.

"I am resolved not to let my personal feelings enter the matter. I shall send away my queen, MyrdemInggala. She will leave this day, and retire to a palace on the seacoast. If the Holy Pannovalan Church, whose servant I am, grants me a bill of divorcement, I shall divorce the queen.

"And I shall marry Simoda Tal, of the House of Oldorando."

Clapping and murmurs of congratulation rose. The king's face was expressionless. As they were approaching, before they could reach him, he turned on his heel and left the room.

The thordotter slammed the door behind him.

VIII

IN THE PRESENCE
OF MYTHOLOGY

Billy Xiao Pin's face was round, as were, in general disposition, his eyes and nose. Even his mouth was a mere rosebud. His skin was smooth and sallow. He had left the Avernus only once previously, when close members of the Pin family had taken him on an Ipocrene fly-past.

Billy was a modest but determined young man, well-mannered like all members of his family, and it was believed that he could be relied upon to face his death with equanimity. He was twenty Earth years old, or just over fourteen by Helliconian reckoning.

Although the Helliconia Holiday Lottery was ruled by chance, it was generally agreed—at least among the thousand-strong Pin family—that Billy was an excellent choice as winner.

When his good fortune was announced, he was sent on a tour of the Avernus by his doting family. With him went his current girl friend, Rose Yi Pin. The moving corridors of the satellite were event-oriented, and those who travelled them often found themselves caught in technological typhoons, or surrounded by animated computer graphics, sometimes of a malignant kind. The Avernus had been in its orbit for 3269 years; every facility available was mustered to counteract the killing disease which threatened its occupants: lethargy.

Together with a group of friends, Billy took a holiday in a mountain resort. There they slept in a log hut high above the ski slopes. Such synthetic pleasure spots had once been based on real Earth resorts; now they were rejigged to imitate Helliconian locations. Billy and his friends appeared to ski in the High Nktryhk.

Later, they sailed the Ardent Sea to the east of Campannlat. Setting out from the one harbour on a thousand miles of coast, they had as background the eternal cliffs of Mordriat, rising out of the foam straight to heights of almost six thousand feet, their shoulders wreathed in cloud. The Scimitar waterfall fell and paused and fell again in its plunge of over a mile towards the racing sea.

Pleasing though such excitements were, the mind was always aware that every danger, each remote vista, was imprisoned in a mirrored room no more than eighteen feet long by twelve feet wide.

At the conclusion of the holiday, Billy Xiao Pin went alone to his Advisor, to squat before him in the Humility position.

"Silence recapitulates long conversations," said the Advisor. "In seeking life you will find death. Both are illusory."

Billy knew that the Advisor did not wish him to leave the Avernus, for the profound reason that the Advisor feared any dynamism. He was devoured by the deadly illusionism which had become prevalent philosophy. In his youth, he had written a poetic treastise one hundred syllables long entitled, "On the Prolongation of One Helliconian Season Beyond One Human Life-Span."

This treatise was a product of, and a sustaining factor in, the illusionism which gripped the Avernus. Billy had no intellectual way of fighting the philosophy, but now that he was about to leave the ship, he felt a hatred of it which he dared to voice.

"I must stand in a real world and experience real joy, real hurt. If only for a brief while, I must endure real mountains and walk along stone streets. I must encounter people with real destinies."

"You still overuse that treacherous word 'real.' The evidence of our senses is evidence only to our senses. Wisdom looks elsewhere."

"Yes. Well. I'm going elsewhere."

But morbidity did not know where to stop. The aged man continued to lecture. Billy continued meekly to listen.

The old man knew that sex was at the bottom of it. He saw that Billy had a sensuous nature which needed to be curbed. Billy was giving up Rose to seek out Queen MyrdemInggala—yes, he knew Billy's desires. He wished to see the queen of queens face to face.

That was a sterile idea. Rose was not a sterile idea. The real—to use that word—was to be found not extraneously but within the mystery of personality: in Billy's case, Rose's personality, perchance. And there were other considerations.

"We have a role to fulfil, our role towards Earth the Obligation. Our deepest satisfaction comes from fulfilling that role. On Helliconia, you will lose role and society."

Billy Xiao Pin dared raise his eyes so as to regard his old Advisor. The huddled figure was planted, each of his out-breaths directing his weight down to anchor against the floor, each in-breath lifting his head towards the ceiling. He could not be perturbed, not even by the loss of a favourite pupil.

This scene was being recorded by ever-watching cameras and broadcast to any of the six thousand who might care to flip to this chamber. There was no privacy. Privacy encouraged dissidence.

Watching the wise simian eyes, Billy saw that his Advisor no longer believed in Earth. Earth!—the subject Billy and his contemporaries discussed endlessly, the ever-interesting topic. Earth was not accessible like Helliconia. But Earth for the Advisor and hundreds like him had become a sort of ideal—a projection of the inner lives of those aboard.

As the voice shaped its crisp nothings, Billy thought he saw that the old man did not believe in the objective reality of Helliconia either. For him, ensconced in the sophistry of argument which formed so large a part of the station's intellectual life, Helliconia was merely a projection, an hypothesis.

The great lottery prize was designed to counteract this withering of the senses. The youthful hope of the ship—which in magical ways centred about that great object of study disrobing its seasons below them—died, generation by generation, until the enforced imprisonment became voluntary imprisonment. Billy had to go and die that others might live.

He had to go to where that sloe-eyed queen thrust her body against the breath of the thordotter as she climbed to the castle.

The speech ceased at last. Billy took his chance.

"Thousand thanks for all your care, Master." Bowing. Leaving. Breathing deeper.

His departure from the Avernus was stage-managed as a great event. Everyone felt strongly about his going. This was the actual proof that Helliconia existed. The six thousand were becoming less able to live imaginatively beyond the station, in spite of all the instruments which were devised to enable them to do so. The prize was a gesture of supreme worth, even to the losers.

Rose Yi Pin turned her neat small face up to Billy's and wrapped her arms round him for the last time. "I believe you will live for ever down there, Billy. I shall watch you as I grow old and ugly. Just beware of their silly religions. Life here is sane. Down there they are mad in the head with religous notions—even that so beautiful queen of yours."

He kissed her lips. "Live your orderly life. Don't fret."

Suddenly fury burst from her. "Why do you ruin my life? Where's the order, with you gone?"

He shook his head. "That you must discover for yourself."

The automated craft was waiting to take him from purgatory. Billy climbed through the passage into the little shell, and the door hissed shut behind him. Terror gripped him; he strapped himself into the seat and enjoyed the emotion.

The choice as to whether to make the descent with the windows shuttered or not was his. He pressed a button. Up flew the shutters and he was rewarded with a view of a magical whale from whose flank he was now excommunicated. A belt of irregular stars spread into the distance like the curl of a comet's tail. Gasping, he realised that these stars were unprocessed rubbish ejected from the Avernus, falling into orbit about the station.

At one moment, the Avernus was an immensity, its eighteen million tons obscuring the field of vision; at the next, it was dwindling, and Billy forgot to look. Helliconia was in view, as familiar as his own face in a mirror, but now seen more nakedly, with cloud drifting across its lit crescent and the peninsula of Pegovin striking like a club into the central sea. The great southern ice cap dazzled.

He looked for the two suns of the binary system as the windows darkened to fend off their light.

Batalix, the nearer sun, was lost behind the planet, only 1.26 astronomical units away.

Freyr, visible as a grey ball behind the opaqued glass, was immensely bright at 240 astronomical units. When at 236 astronomical units distance, Helliconia would reach perihelion, its nearest point to Freyr; that time was only 118 Earth years away. Then once more Batalix and its planets would be carried away on their orbits, not to come so close to the dominant member of the system for another 2592 Earth years.

To Billy Xiao Pin, this set of astronomical figures, which he had learned along with his alphabets at the age of three, made a neat diagram. He was about to land where the diagram became an untidy question of history, of crises and challenges.

His round face elongated at the thought. Although Helliconia had been under constant observation for such a long while, it remained in many ways a mystery.

Billy knew that the planet would survive perihelion, that temperatures at the equator would soar to 150 degrees but nothing worse; that Helliconia had an extraordinary system of homeostasis, at least as powerful as

Earth's, which would maintain as steady a state of equilibrium as possible. He did not share the superstitious fears of the peasantry that Freyr was about to devour them—though he understood how such fears might arise.

What he did not know was whether various nations would survive the testing heat. Tropical countries like Borlien and Oldorando were most threatened.

The Avernus had been in existence and observing since before the spring of the previous Great Year. It had once experienced the slow spread of the Great Winter on the planet below, had witnessed multitudes dying and nations going down. How precisely that pattern would be repeated in the Winter still far distant remained to be seen. The Earth Observation Station would have to function and the six families to exist for another fourteen Earth centuries before that mystery was resolved.

To this awe-inspiring world, Billy had committed his soul.

Trembling took Billy in every limb. He was to embrace this world, he was to be born.

The craft made two orbits of the planet, braking as it did so, and landed on a plateau to the east of Matrassyl.

Billy rose from his seat and stood listening. At last he remembered to breathe. An android had been sent down with him, an alter ego to defend him. The Avernians felt their vulnerability. The product of generations of soft-bred men, Billy was reckoned to need protection. The android was programmed to be aggressive. It carried defensive weapons. It looked human, and indeed its face was moulded to resemble Billy's, which it did in all but mobility; its expressions changed sluggishly, giving it a permanent air of gloom. Billy disliked it. He looked at it as it stood expectantly in a recess shaped to its body.

"Stay where you are," Billy said. "Go back to the Avernus with the craft."

"You need my protection," said the android.

"I will manage as best I can. It's my life now." He pressed a delay switch which would ensure automatic liftoff in an hour's time. Then he activated the door and climbed from the craft.

He stood on the wished-for planet, breathing its scents, letting a thousand strange sounds come to his ears. The unfiltered air bruised his lungs. Dizziness assailed him.

He looked up. All above him stretched a sky of most beautiful resonant blue, without feature. Billy was accustomed to looking at space; paradoxically, the arch of sky appeared vaster. The eye was drawn forever into it. It covered the living world and was its most beautiful expression.

To the west, Batalix in aurioles of gold and tan was preparing to set. Freyr, its disc only thirty percent the size of Batalix's, burned with splendid intensity almost at zenith. All around it swam the great blue envelope which was the first of Helliconia to be seen from space, and the unmistakable imprimatur of it as a life-bearing planet. The visiting life-form lowered his head and passed a hand over his eyes.

At a short distance stood a group of five trees, overhung with fleshy creepers. Towards them Billy made his way, walking as if gravity had only just been invented. He fell against the nearest trunk, embracing it, to have his hands torn by thorns. Nevertheless, he clung tight, closing his eyes, flinching from every inexplicable sound. He could not move. When the craft lifted for its return to the mother station, he wept.

Here was the real, with a vengeance. It penetrated all his senses.

By clinging to the tree, lying on the ground, hiding beside a fallen trunk, he accustomed himself to the experience of being on an immense planet. Distant objects, clouds, and a line of hills, in particular, terrified him with their implications of size and—yes—reality. Just as alarming were all the small live things with random inclinations of their own, whole phyla absent from existence aboard the Avernus. He looked down in anguish as a small winged creature alighted on his left hand and used it as a highway to his sleeve. What was most alarming was the knowledge that all these things were beyond his control; no touch of a switch could tame them.

There was in particular the problem of the suns, which he had not taken into account. On the Avernus, light and dark were largely matters of temperament; here, one had no choice. As dimday was followed by night, Billy felt for the first time the ancient precariousness of his kind. Long ago, mankind had built huddling places against the dark. Cities had developed, had grown to metropolises, and had taken off into space; now he felt himself back at the beginning of history.

He survived the night. Despite himself, he had fallen asleep, to wake unharmed. Doing his accustomed morning exercises brought him back to a sense of himself. He was enough in control to walk from the shelter of the cluster of trees and to rejoice in the morning. After drinking and eating from his rations, he set off in the direction of Matrassyl.

Walking along a jungle path, bemused by bird calls, he became aware of a footstep behind him. He turned. A phagor froze to instant immobility, only a few paces away.

Phagors were part of the mythology of the Avernus. Their portraits and models of them were accessible everywhere. This one, however, had the presence and individuality of life. It chewed as it regarded Billy, saliva leaking from its broad lower lip. Over its bulky figure was a one-piece garment, dyed here and there with saffron. Tufts of its long white hair were similarly dyed, giving it an unhealthy appearance. A dead snake was knotted over one shoulder—evidently a recent catch. In its hand it carried a curved knife. This was neither an idealised museum replica nor a child's cuddly toy. As it stepped nearer, it exuded a rancid odor which made Billy giddy.

He faced it squarely and spoke slowly in Hurdhu. "Can you give me directions to Matrassyl?"

The creature went on ruminating. It appeared to be chewing on some kind of scarlet nut; juice of that colour trickled from its mouth. A drop sprayed onto Billy Xiao Pin. He reached up and brushed it from his cheek.

"Matrassyl," it said, pronouncing the word leadenly as "Madrazzyl."

"Yes. Which way is Matrassyl?"

"Yes."

The look in its cerise eyes—impossible to determine whether it was meek or murderous. He wrenched his gaze away, to find that more phagors stood near, bushlike among the befoliaged shadow.

"Can you understand what I say?" His sentences came from the phrasebook. He was bewildered by the unreality of the situation.

"A taking to a place is within ability."

From a creature that had the natural force of a boulder, good sense was hardly to be expected, but Billy was left in little doubt as to its intentions. The creature rolled forward with an easy motion and pushed Billy along the path. Billy moved. The other figures tramped among the undergrowth, keeping pace.

They reached a broken slope. Here the jungle had been cleared— some trees had been hacked down, and scuttling pigs saw to it that further growth would never reach maturity. Among casual attempts at cultivation were huts or, rather, roofs supported by posts.

In the shade provided by these huts, lumpish figures lay like cattle. Some rose and came towards the foragers, one of whom sounded a small horn to announce their arrival. Billy was surrounded by male and female ancipitals, creaghs and gillots and runts, glaring up at him inquisitively. Some runts ran on all fours.

Billy dropped into the Humility position.

"I'm trying to get to Matrassyl," he said. The absurdity of the sentence made him laugh; he had to check himself before he became hysterical, but the noise had the effect of making everyone stand back.

"The lower kzahhn has proximity for inspection," a gillot said, touching his arm and making a motion of her head. He followed her across a stone-strewn dell, and everyone else followed him. Everything he passed —from tender green shoots to rounded boulders—was rougher than he could have visualised.

Under an awning set against the dell's low cliff sprawled an elder phagor, arms bent at impossible angles. It sat up in smooth movements and revealed itself as an ancient gillot, with prominent withered dugs and black hairs sprouting from her coat. A necklace of polished gwing-

gwing stones hung about her neck. She wore a face bracelet buckled across the prow of her nose as mark of rank. This was evidently the "lower kzahhn."

Remaining seated, she looked up at Billy.

She spoke to him questioningly.

Billy had been a junior in the great sociological clan of Pin, and not a conscientious one at that. He worked in the division which studied the family of Anganols, generation by generation. There were those among his superiors who were conversant with the histories of the present king's predecessors back to the previous spring, some sixteen generations past. Billy Xiao Pin spoke Olonets, the main language of Compannlat and Hespagorat, and several of its variants, including Old Olonets. But he had never attempted the ancipital tongue, Native; nor had he properly mastered the language the lower kzahhn was speaking, Hurdhu, the bridge language used in these times between man and phagor.

"I don't understand," he said, in Hurdhu, and felt a strange sensation when she understood, as if he had stepped from the real world into some strange fairy story.

"Understanding is to me of you being from a far place," she said, translating her own language, noun-choked, into Hurdhu. "What situation is that far place?"

Perhaps they had seen the space-craft land.

He gestured vaguely, and recited a prepared speech. "I come from a distant town in Morstrual, where I am the kzahhn." Morstrual was even more remote that Mordriat, and safe to name. "Your people will be rewarded if they escort me to King JandolAnganol in Matrassyl."

"King JandolAnganol."

"Yes."

She became immobile, gazing ahead. A stallun squatting nearby passed her a leather bottle from which she drank in slobbering fashion, letting the liquid spill. It smelt pungent and spiritous. Ah, he thought, raffel: a deleterious drink distilled by ancipitals. He had fallen in with a poor tribe of phagors. Here he was, dealing capably with these enigmatic beasts, and on the Avernus everyone would be watching him through the optical system. Even his old Advisor. Even Rose.

The heat and the short walk over rough ground had taxed him. But a more self-conscious motive made him sit down on a flat stone and spread his legs, resting his elbows on his knees, to stare nonchalantly at the creature confronting him. The most incredible occurrences became everyday when there was no alternative.

"Ancipital race carry much spears for his crusade for King Jandol-Anganol." She paused. Behind her was a cave. In its shade, dim cerise eyes gleamed. Billy guessed that tribal ancestors would be stored there, sinking through tether to pure keratin. At once ancestor and idol, every undead phagor helped direct its successors through the painful centuries when Freyr dominated.

"Sons of Freyr fight other Sons of Freyr each season, and we lend spears."

He recognised the traditional phagorian term for humankind. The ancipitals, unable to invent new terms, merely adapted old ones.

"Order two of your tribe to escort me to King JandolAnganol."

Again her stillness—and all the others, as Billy looked round, conspiring to that same immobility. Only the pigs and curs trundled about, forever searching for titbits in the dirt.

The old gillot then began a long speech which defied Billy's understanding. He had to halt her in the middle of her ramblings, asking her to start again. Hurdhu tasted as pungent as goat's cheese on his tongue. Other phagors came up, closing round him, choking him with their dense smell—but not as unpleasant as anticipated, he thought—all aiding their leader with her explanation. As a result, nothing was explained.

They showed him old wounds, backs bereft of skin and fur, broken legs, shattered arms, all exhibited with calm insistence. He was revolted and fascinated. They produced pennants and a sword from the cave.

Gradually he took their meaning. Most of them had served with King JandolAnganol in his Fifth Army. Some weeks ago, they had marched against Driat tribes. They had suffered a defeat here in the Cosgatt. The tribes had used a new weapon which barked like a giant hound.

These poor folk had survived. But they dared not go back to the king's service in case that giant hound barked again. They lived as they could. They dreamed of returning to the cool regions of the Nktryhk.

It was a long tale. Billy became vexed by it, and by the flies. He took some of their raffel. It was deleterious, just as the textbooks said. Feeling sleepy, he ceased to listen when they tried to describe the Cosgatt battle to him. For them, it might have happened yesterday.

"Will two of you escort me to the king or will you not?"

They fell silent, then grunted to each other in Native Ancipital.

At length, the gillot spoke in Hurdhu to him.

"What gift is from your hand for such escort?"

On his wrist he wore a flat grey watch, its triple set of flicking figures telling the time on Earth, on Central Campannlat, and on the Avernus. It was standard equipment. The phagors would not be interested in timetelling, for their eotemporal harneys remained set in a temporality which registered only sporadic movement; but they would like the watch as decoration.

The old lower kzahhn's mottled face hung over his arm as he extended it to her gaze. Of her horns, one had been broken halfway and its tip replaced with a wooden peg.

She pulled herself up in a squatting position and called to two of the younger stalluns.

"Do what the thing demands," she said.

The escort stopped when a pair of houses was sighted in the distance. They would go no farther. Billy Xiao Pin removed the watch from his wrist and offered it to them. After contemplating it for a while, they refused to accept it.

He could not understand their explanation. They seemed to have lapsed from Hurdhu into Native. He grasped that numbers were involved. Perhaps they feared the ever changing numbers. Perhaps they feared the unknown metal. Their refusal was made without emotion; they simply would not take it; they wanted nothing. "JandolAnganol," they said. Evidently they still respected the king's name.

As he went forward, Billy looked back at them, partly obscured by a spray of flowering creeper hanging from a tree. They did not move. He feared them; he also felt a kind of marvel, that he had been in their company and was still sane.

Soon he found himself moving from that dream to another just as wonderful, as he walked in the narrow streets of Matrassyl. The winding way took him under the great rock on which the palace stood. He began to recognise where he was. This and this he had seen through the optics of the Avernus. He could have embraced the first Helliconians he saw.

Churches had been built into the rock; the stricter religious orders imitated the preferences of their masters in Pannoval and locked themselves away from the light. Monasteries huddled against the rock, three stories high, the more prosperous ones built in stone, the poorer in wood. Despite himself, Billy lingered, to feel the grain of the timber, running his nails in its cracks. He came from a world where everything was renewed—or destroyed and reconstituted—as soon as it aged. This ancient wood with the grain outstanding: how superb the accident of its design!

The world was choked with detail he could never have imagined.

The monasteries were cheerfully painted red and yellow, or red and purple, carrying the circle of Akhanaba in those colours. Their doors bore representations of the god, descending in fire. Black locks of hair escaped from his topknot. His eyebrows curled upwards. The smile on his half-human face revealed sharp white teeth. In each hand he carried torches. A cloth garment wound itself like a serpent about his blue body.

There were representations too, on banners, of saints and familiars and bogeys: Yuli the Priest, Denniss the King, Withram and Wutra, and streams of Others, large and black, small and green with claws for toenails and rings on their toes. Among these supernatural beings—fat and bald or shaggy—went humans, generally in supplicatory postures.

Humans were shown small. Where I come from, Billy said to himself, humans would be shown large. But here they went in supplicatory postures, only to be mown down by the gods in one way or another. By flames, by ice, by the sword.

Memories of school lessons came to Billy, fertilised by reality. He had learnt how important religions were on backward Helliconia. Sometimes nations had been converted to a different religion in a day—it had happened to Oldorando, he recalled. Other nations, losing their religion as suddenly, had collapsed and disappeared without trace. Here was the very bastion of Borlien's creed. As an atheist, Billy was both attracted and repelled by the lurid fates depicted on all sides.

The monks looked not too stricken by the dreadful state of the world; devastation was merely part of a greater cycle, the background of their placid existences.

"The colours!" Billy said aloud. The colours of devastation were like paradise. There is no evil here, he told himself, bedazzled. Evil is negative. Here everything is robust. Evil was where I came from, in negativity.

Robust. Yes, it's robust. He laughed.

Mouth open, arms out, he stood in the middle of the street. Aromas drifting like colours of the air detained him. Every step of his way had been haunted by smells of various kinds—a dimension of life missing on the Avernus. Nearby, under the shadow of the cliff, was a well, with stalls clustering by it. Monks were flocking from their buildings to buy food there.

Billy was teased by the thought that they were performing just for him. Death might come. It would be worth it just to have stood here and caught these savoury smells, and to have seen the monks lift greasy buns to their faces. Above them, from a monastic balcony fluttered a red and yellow banner, on which he could read the legend, ALL THE WORLD'S WISDOM HAS ALWAYS EXISTED. He laughed to himself at this antiscientific legend: wisdom was something that had to be hammered out—otherwise, he would not be here.

Here in the traffic of the street, Billy's understanding grew of how priest-ridden Helliconian society was, and of how the Akhanaban faith influenced action. His antipathy to religion was deep-rooted; now he found himself in a civilisation founded on it.

When he approached the stalls, a stall holder called to him. She was a tall woman, shabbily dressed, with a big red face. She maintained a bright-burning fire in a basin. Waffles were her trade. Billy had on him forged money, as well as other equipment for his visit. Pulling some coins from a pocket, he paid the woman and was rewarded with a savoury-smelling waffle. The waffle irons had imprinted on them the

Akhanaban religious symbol, one circle within another, the two connected by oblique lines. He thought for the first time, as he bit into it, that the symbol possibly represented in a crude way the orbit of the lesser sun, Batalix, about the greater.

"It won't bite you back," said the waffle woman, laughing at him.

He moved away, triumphant at having negotiated the transaction. He ate more delicately than the monks, conscious of the eyes of the Avernus. Still munching, he continued along the street, a swagger in his step. Soon he was treading up the slopes that led to Matrassyl palace. It was wonderful. Real food was wonderful. Helliconia was wonderful.

The route became more familiar. Having studied the family now called royal through three generations, Billy knew the layout of the palace and its surroundings in some detail. More than once he had watched the archival tapes which showed this stronghold being taken by the forces of the grandfather of the present king.

At the main gate, he asked to speak to JandolAnganol, producing forged documents which showed him to be an emissary from the distant land of Morstrual. After an interrogation in the guard house, he was escorted to another building. A long wait ensued until he was taken to a section of the palace he recognised as the chancellor's domain.

Here he kicked his heels, staring at everything—the rugs, the carved furniture, the stove, the curtains at the window, the stains on the ceiling —in a kind of fever. The waffle had given him hiccups. The world was a maze of fascinating detail, and every strand in the carpet on which he stood—he guessed it to be of Madi origin—had a meaning which led back into the history of the planet.

Queen MyrdemInggala, queen of queens, had stood in this very room, had placed her sandalled feet upon this woven carpet, and the beasts and birds figured there had gratefully received her weight as she passed by.

As Billy stood looking down at the carpet, a wave of dizziness overcame him. No, it couldn't be death already. He clutched his stomach. Not death but that waffle? He sank into a chair.

Outside lay the world where everything had two shadows. He felt its heat and power. It was the real world of the queen, not the artificial world of Billy and Rose. But he might not be up to it. . . .

He gave a loud hiccup. He understood now what his Advisor meant when he had said that Billy might find fulfilment with Rose. But that could never have been while the queen of his imagination stood in his way. The real queen was now somewhere close at hand.

The door opened—even that was a wonder, that wooden door. A lean old secretary appeared, who conducted him to the chancellor's suite. There he sat on a chair in an antechamber and waited. To his relief, the hiccups died and he felt less ill.

Chancellor SartoriIrvrash appeared, walking wearily. His shoulders were bent and, despite a show of courtesy, his manner was preoccupied. He listened to Billy without interest and ushered him into a large room where books and documents took up a major part of the space. Billy looked at the chancellor with awe. This was a figure out of history. This was once the hawkish young advisor who had assisted Jandol-Anganol's grandfather and father to establish the Borlienese state.

The two men seated themselves. The chancellor pulled agitatedly at his whiskers and muttered something under his breath. He seemed not to listen as Billy described himself as coming from a town in Morstrual on the Gulf of Chalce. He hugged his lean body as if comforting himself.

When Billy's words ran out, he sat in puzzlement as silence descended. Did the chancellor not understand his Olonets?

SartoriIrvrash spoke at last. "We'll do whatever we can to be of assistance, sir, although this is not the easiest of times, not by any means."

"I want a conversation with you, if I can, as well as with his majesty and the queen. I have knowledge to offer, as well as questions to ask."

He gave a belated hiccup.

"Apologies."

"Yes, yes. Excuse me. I am what someone once termed a connoisseur of knowledge, but this happens to be a day of deepest—deepest botheration."

He stood, clutching at his stained charfrul, shaking his head as he regarded Billy as if for the first time.

"What is so bad about today?" asked Billy in alarm.

"The queen, sir, Queen MyrdemInggala . . ." The chancellor rapped his knuckles on the table for emphasis. "Our queen is being put away, expelled, sir. This is the day she sails for exile. For Ancient Gravabagalinien."

He put his hands up to his face and began to weep.

IX

SOME BOTHERATION
FOR THE CHANCELLOR

There was an old country saying among the peasants of the land still known locally as Embruddock concerning the continent on which they lived: "Not an acre is properly habitable, and not an acre is uninhabited."

The saying represented at least an approach to the truth. Even now, when millions believed that the world was to die in flames, travellers of all kinds crossed and recrossed Campannlat. From whole tribes, like the migrant Madis and the nomadic nations of Mordriat, down to pilgrims, who counted out their pilgrimage not in miles but in shrines; robber bands, who counted territory in throats and purses; and solitary traders, who travelled leagues to sell a song or a stone for a greater price than it would fetch at home—all these found fulfilment in movement.

Even the fires that consumed the interior of the continent, stopping short only at rivers or deserts, did not deter travellers. Rather, they added to their numbers, contributing refugees in quest for new homes.

One such group arrived in Matrassyl down the Valvoral in time to see

Queen MyrdemInggala leave for exile. The royal press gang gave them little time to gape. Its officers descended on the new arrivals in their leaky tub and marched the men away to serve in the Western Wars.

That afternoon, the natives of Matrassyl had temporarily forgotten the wars—or shelved the thought of them in favour of this newer drama. Here was the most dramatic moment of many dull lives: poverty, committing them to mere endurance, forced them to live vicariously through the illustrious. For this reason, they appointed and tolerated the vices of their kings and queens, so that shock or delight might enter their existences.

Smoke drifted over the town, shrouding the crowds mute along the quayside. The queen came in her coach. It moved between lines of people. Flags waved. Also banners, saying REPENT YE! and THE SIGNS ARE IN THE SKY. The queen looked neither to right nor to left.

Her coach stopped by the river. A lackey jumped down and opened the door for her majesty. She put forth a dainty foot and stepped down upon the cobbles. Tatro followed, and the lady-in-waiting.

MyrdemInggala hesitated and looked round. She wore a veil, but the aura of her beauty was about her like a perfume. The lugger that was to take her and her entourage downstream to Ottassol, and thence to Gravabagalinien, awaited her. A minister of the Church in full canonicals stood on deck to greet her. She walked up the gangplank. A sigh escaped the crowd as she left Matrassylan soil.

Her head was low. Once she had gained the deck and accepted the minister's greeting, she pulled back her veil and lifted a hand in farewell, her head high.

At the sight of that peerless face, a murmur rose from the wharves and walks and roofs nearby, a murmur which rumbled into a cheer. This was Matrassyl's inarticulate farewell to its queen of queens.

She gave no further sign, letting the veil drop, turning on her heel and going below, out of sight.

As the ship weighed anchor, a young court gallant ran forward to stand on the edge of the quay and declaim a popular poem, "And Summer's Self She Is." There was no music, no more cheering.

No one standing there in silent farewell knew of the events at the court that afternoon, though news of fearful deeds would leak out soon enough.

The sails were hoisted. The ship of exile moved slowly from the quayside and began its journey downstream. The queen's vicar stood on the deck and prayed. Nobody in the watching crowd, on the street, on the cliffs, or perched on rooftops, stirred. The wooden hull began to shrink with distance, its detail to be lost.

The people went silently away to their homes, taking their banners with them.

* * *

The Matrassyl court swarmed with factions. Some factions were unique to the court; others had nationwide support. The best-supported of the latter groups was undoubtedly the Myrdolators. This ironically named clique opposed the king on most issues and supported the queen of queens on all.

Within the major groupings were minor groupings. Self-interest saw to it that each man was divided in some way against his brother. Many reasons could be invented for supporting or opposing a closer union with Oldorando, in the continual jockeying for position in court.

There were those—haters of women perhaps—who hoped to see Queen MyrdemInggala disgraced. There were those—dreaming of possessing her perhaps—who wished to see her remain. Of those who wished to see her remain, some of the most fervent Myrdolators believed that she should stay and the king should go. After all, they argued, to look at the affair legalistically—and to ignore her physical attractions—the queen's claim to the throne of Borlien was as valid as the Eagle's.

Envy saw to it that the enemies of both king and queen were perpetually active. On the day of departure of the queen many were ready to take up arms.

On the morning of that day, JandolAnganol had moved against the malcontents.

By a ruse, the king and SartoriIrvrash had the Myrdolators meet together in a chamber in the palace. Sixty-one of them foregathered, some of them greybeards who had professed loyalty to MyrdemInggala's parents, RantanOboral and Shannana the Wild. They stormed indignantly in to the meeting. The Household Guard slammed the doors on them and guarded the chamber. While the Myrdolators screamed and fainted in the heat, the Eagle, with malicious glee on his face, went to a final meeting with his lovely queen.

MyrdemInggala was still overwhelmed by the turn in her fortunes. Her cheeks were pale. There was a feverish look in her eyes. She could not eat. She started at small things. When the king came upon her, she was walking with Mai TolramKetinet, discussing prospects for her children. If she was threatened, so were they. Tatro was small, and a girl. It was upon Robayday that the brunt of the king's vengeance might fall. Robayday had disappeared on one of his wild excursions. She perceived that she would not even be able to say good-bye to him. Nor would her brother be here to exert influence over his wilful nephew.

The two women walked in MyrdemInggala's dimday garden. Tatro was playing with Princess Simoda Tal—an irony which could be borne if not contemplated closely.

This garden the queen had created herself, directing her gardeners.

Heavy trees and artificial cliffs screened the walks from Freyr's eyes. There was sufficient shade for genetic sports and melanic forms of vegetation to flourish.

Dimday plants flowered beside fullday ones. The jeodfray, a fullday creeper with light pink-and-orange flowers, became the stunted albic, hugging the ground. The albic occasionally put forth grotesque scarlet-and-orange buds along a fleshy stem, to attract the attention of dimday moths. Nearby were olvyl, yarrpel, idront, and spikey brooth, all relishing shade. The ground-loving vispard produced hooded blossoms. It was the adaptation of a nocturnal species, the zadal bush, and had moved towards lighter conditions rather than darker.

Such plants had been brought by her subjects from different parts of the kingdom. She had no great understanding of the astronomy which SartoriIrvrash tried to instil in her, or of the slow protracted manoeuvres of Freyr along the heavens, except through her appreciation of these plants, which represented an instinctive vegetable response to those confusingly abstract ellipses of which the chancellor loved to talk.

Now she would visit this favoured place no more. The ellipses of her own life were moving against her.

The king and his chancellor appeared at the gate. She sensed their wish for formality even from a distance. She saw the tension in the king's stance. She laid a hand on her lady-in-waiting's wrist in alarm.

SartoriIrvrash approached and bowed formally. Then he took the lady-in-waiting off with him, in order to leave the royal couple alone.

Mai instantly broke into anxious protests.

"The king will murder Cune. He suspects she loves my brother Hanra, but it is not so. I'd swear to it. The queen has done nothing wrong. She is innocent."

"His calculations run otherwise, and he will not murder her," said SartoriIrvrash. He hardly looked the figure to comfort her. He had shrunk inside his charfrul and his face was grey. "He rids himself of the queen for political reasons. It has been done before."

He brushed a butterfly impatiently from his sleeve.

"Why did he have Yeferal murdered, then?"

"That piece of botheration is not to be laid at the king's door but rather at mine. Cease your prattle, woman. Go with Cune into exile and look after her. I hope to be in touch some time, if my own situation continues. Gravabagalinien is no bad place to be."

They entered into an archway and were immediately embraced within the stuffy complexities of the building.

Mai TolramKetinet asked in a more even voice, "What has overcome the king's mind?"

"I know only of his ego, not his mind. It is bright like a diamond. It will cut all other egos. It cannot easily tolerate the queen's gentleness."

When the young woman left him, he stood at the bottom of the stairwell, trying to steady himself. Somewhere above him, he heard the voices of the visiting diplomats. They waited with indifference to hear how the matter worked out and would be departing soon, whatever happened.

"Everything finally goes . . ." he said to himself. In that moment, he longed for his dead wife.

The queen, meanwhile, stood in her garden, listening to the low, hasty voice of JandolAnganol, trying to thrust his emotions upon her. She recoiled, as from a great wave.

"Cune, our parting is forced on me for the survival of the kingdom. You know my feelings, but you also know that I have duties which must be performed. . . ."

"No, I won't have it. You obey a whim. It is not duty but your khmir speaking."

He shook his head, as if trying to shake away the pain visible in his face.

"What I do I have to do, though it destroys me. I have no wish for anyone at my side but you. Give me a word that you understand that much before we part."

The lines of her face were rigid. "You have traduced the reputation of my dead brother and of me. Who gave the order for the spreading of that lie but you?"

"Understand, please, what I have to do for my kingdom. I have no will that we part."

"Who gave the order for our parting but you? Who commands here but you? If you don't command, then anarchy has come, and the kingdom is not worth saving."

He gave her a sideways look. The eagle was sick. "This is policy I must carry through. I am not imprisoning you but sending you to the beautiful palace of Gravabagalinien, where Freyr does not dominate the sky so greatly. Be content there and don't scheme against me, or your father will answer for it. If the war news improves, who knows but we may be together again."

She rounded on him, by her vehemence making him look into her overflowing face.

"Do you then plan to wed that lascivious child of Oldorando this year and divorce her next, as you do me this? Have you an endless series of matrimonies and divorcements in mind by which to save Borlien? You talk of sending me away. Be warned that when I am sent, I remain forever away from you."

JandolAnganol reached out a hand, but dared not touch her.

"I'm saying that in my heart—if you believe I have one—I am not sending you away. Will you understand that? You live only by religion

and principle. Have some understanding of what it means to be king."
She plucked a twig of idront and then flung it from her.

"Oh, you've taught me what it is to be a king. To incarcerate your
father, to drive off your son, to defame your brother-in-law, to dismiss
me to the ends of the kingdom—that's what it is to be a king! I've learnt
the lesson from you well.

"So I will answer you, Jan, after your own fashion. I cannot prevent
your exiling me, no. But when you put me away, you inherit all the
consequences of that act. You must live and die by those consequences.
That is religion speaking, not I. Don't expect me to alter what is
unalterable."

"I do expect it." He swallowed. He seized her arm tightly and would
not let it go, despite her struggles. He walked her along the path, and
butterflies rose up. "I do expect it. I expect you to love me still, and not
to stop simply from convenience. I expect you to be above humanity,
and to see beyond your suffering to the suffering of others.

"So far, in this pitiless world, your beauty has saved you from suffering. I have guarded you. Admit it, Cune, I have guarded you through
these dreadful years. I returned from the Cosgatt only because you were
here. By will I returned. . . . Won't your beauty become a curse when I
am not by to act as shield? Won't you be hunted like a deer in a forest,
by men the likes of whom you have never known? What will your end be
without me?

"I swear I will love you still, despite a thousand Simoda Tals, if you
will tell me now—just tell me, as we kiss good-bye—that you still hold
me dear, despite what I have to do."

She broke from him and steadied herself against a rock, her face in
shadow. Both of them were pale and sweated.

"You mean to frighten me, and so you do. The truth is, you drive
me away because you do not understand yourself. Inwardly, you know
that I understand you and your weaknesses as does no one else—except
possibly your father. And you cannot bear that. You are tortured because I have compassion for you. So yes, damn you, since you wrench it
from me, yes, I do love you and will do so until I am merged with the
original beholder. But you can't accept that, can you? It's not what you
desire."

He blazed up. "There! You hate me, really! Your words lie!"

"Oh, oh, oh!" She uttered wild cries and began to run. "Go away! Go
away! You're crazed. I declare what you ask and it maddens you! You
want my hatred. Hatred is all you know! Go away—I hate you, if that
satisfies your soul."

JandolAnganol did not attempt to pursue her.

"Then the storm will come," he said.

* * *

So smoke began to flow down and fill the bowl of Matrassyl. The king was like a man possessed after parting from MyrdemInggala. He ordered straw from the stables and had it piled about the doors of the chamber in which the Myrdolators were still imprisoned. Jars of purified whale oil were brought. JandolAnganol himself snatched a burning brand from a slave and hurled it into the kindling.

With a roar, flames burst upwards.

That afternoon, as the queen sailed, the fire raged. Nobody was allowed to check it. Its fury went unabated.

Only that night, when the king sat with his runt drinking himself insensible, were servants able to come with pumps and quench the blaze.

When pale Batalix rose next morning, the king, as was his custom, rose and presented himself to his people by the dawn light.

A larger crowd than usual awaited him. At his appearance, a low inarticulate growl arose, like the noise a wounded hound might make. In fear of the many-headed beast, he retired to his room and flung himself down on his bed. There he stayed all day, neither eating nor speaking.

On the succeeding day, he appeared to be himself again. He summoned ministers, he gave orders, he bade farewell to Taynth Indredd and Simoda Tal. He even appeared briefly before the scritina.

There was reason for him to act. His agents brought news that Unndreid the Hammer, Scourge of Mordriat, was again moving southwestwards, and had formed an alliance with Darvlish, his enemy.

In the scritina, the king explained how Queen MyrdemInggala and her brother, YeferalOboral, had been planning to assassinate the ambassador from Sibornal, who had made his escape. It was for this reason that the queen was being sent into exile; her interference in state affairs could not be tolerated. Her brother had been killed.

This conspiracy must be an object lesson to all in this time of peril for the nation. He, the king, was drawing up a plan by which Borlien would become more closely linked to its traditional friends, the Oldorandans and Pannovalans. These plans he would disclose fully in good time. His challenging gaze swept round the scritina.

SartoriIrvrash then rose, to demand that the scritina look upon new developments in the light of history.

"With the battle of the Cosgatt still fresh in our minds, we know that there are new artilleries of attack available. Even the barbarous tribes of Driats have these new—guns, as they are called. With a gun, a man can kill an enemy as soon as he can see him. Such things are mentioned in old histories, although we cannot always trust what we read in old histories.

"However. We are concerned with guns. You saw them demonstrated. They are made in the great northern continent by the nations of Sibornal, who have a pre-eminence in manufacturing arts. They possess deposits of lignite and metal ores which we do not. It is necessary for us to remain on good terms with such powerful nations, and so we have put down firmly this attempt to assassinate the ambassador."

One of the barons at the back of the scritina shouted angrily, "Tell us the truth. Wasn't Pasharatid corrupt? Didn't he have a liaison with a Borlienese girl in the lower town, contravening our laws and his?"

"Our agents are investigating," said SartoriIrvrash, and went on hastily. "We shall send a deputation to Askitosh, capital of the nation Uskutoshk, to open a trade route, hoping that the Sibornalese will be more friendly than hitherto.

"Meanwhile, our meeting with the distinguished diplomats from Oldorando and Pannoval was successful. We have received a few guns from them, as you know. If we can send sufficient quantities of guns to our gallant General Hanra TolramKetinet, then the war with Randonan will be quickly over."

Both the king's speech and SartoriIrvrash's were received coldly. Supporters of Baron RantanOboral, MyrdemInggala's father, were present in the scritina. One of them rose and asked, "Are we to understand that it is these new weapons which are responsible for the deaths of sixty-one Myrdolators? If so, they are powerful weapons indeed."

The chancellor's reply was uncertain.

"An unfortunate fire broke out at the castle, started by the ex-queen's supporters, many of whom lost their lives in the blaze they had themselves caused."

As SartoriIrvrash and the king left the chamber, a storm of noise broke out.

"Give them the wedding," said SartoriIrvrash. "They'll forget their anger as they coo over the prettiness of the child bride. Give them the wedding as soon as possible, Your Majesty. Make the fools forget one swindle with another."

He looked away to hide his revulsion for his own role.

Tension hung over all who lived in the castle of Matrassyl, except for the phagors, whose nervous systems were immune to expectation. But even the phagors were uneasy, for the stench of burning still clung to everything.

Scowling, the king retired to his suite. A section of the First Phagorian stood duty outside his door, and Yuli remained with them while JandolAnganol prayed in his private chapel with his Royal Vicar. After prostrating himself in prayer, he had himself scourged.

While being bathed by his female servants, he summoned his chancellor back to him. SartoriIrvrash appeared after a third summons, clad in an ink-stained flowered charfrul and rush slippers. The old man looked aggrieved, and stood before the king without speaking, smoothing his beard.

"You're vexed?" JandolAnganol addressed him from the pool. The runt sat a short distance away, its mouth open.

"I'm an old man, Your Majesty, and have endured deep botheration this day. I was resting."

"Writing your damned history, more likely."

"Resting and grieving for the murdered sixty-one, if truth be told."

The king struck the water with the flat of his hand. "You're an atheist. You have no conscience to appease. You don't have to be scourged. Leave that to me."

SartoriIrvrash showed a tooth in a display of circumspection.

"How can I serve your majesty now?"

JandolAnganol stood up, and the women swathed him in towels. He stepped from the bath.

"You have done enough in the way of service." He gave SartoriIrvrash one of his darkly brilliant looks. "It's time I put you out to pasture, like the old hoxneys of which you are so fond. I'll find someone more to my way of thought to advise me."

The women huddled by the earthenware pitchers which had brought the royal bathwater, and listened complacently to the drama.

"There are many here who will pretend to think as you wish them to think, Your Majesty. If you care to put trust in such, that is your decision. Perhaps you will say how I have failed to please. Have I not supported all your schemes?"

The king flung away his towels, and paced naked and dangerous about the room. His gaze was as hasty as his walk. Yuli whined in sympathy.

"Look at the trouble about my ears. Bankrupt. No queen. Unpopular. Mistrusted. Challenged in the scritina. Don't tell me I'll be a favourite of the mob when I wed that chit from Oldorando. You advised me to do this, and I have had sufficient of your advice."

SartoriIrvrash had backed against one wall, where he was fairly safe from the king's pacing. He wrung his hands in distress.

"If I may speak . . . I have faithfully served you and your father before you. I have lied for you. I lied today. I have implicated myself in this gruesome Myrdolators' crime for your sake. Unlike other chancellors you might elect, I have no political ambitions— You are good enough to splash me, your majesty!"

"Crime! Your sovereign is a criminal, is he? How else was I to put down a revolt?"

"I have advised you with your good in mind, rather than my advancement, sire. Never less than in this sorry matter of the divorcement. You will recall that I told you you would never find another woman like the queen and—"

The king seized a towel and wrapped it about his narrow waist. A puddle formed round his feet. "You told me that my first duty lay with my country. So I made the sacrifice, made it at your suggestion—"

"No, Your Majesty, no, I distinctly—" He waved his hands distractedly.

" 'I dizztingtly,' " said Yuli, picking up a new word.

"You merely want a scapegoat on which to vent your rage, sire. You shall not dismiss me like this. It's criminal."

The words echoed about the bath chamber. The women had made as if to escape from the scene, then had frozen in cautionary gestures, lest the king turn upon them.

He turned on his chancellor.

As his face flushed with rage, the colour chased itself down his jaw to his throat. "Criminal again! Am I criminal? You old rat, you dare give me your orders and insults! I'll settle with you."

He marched over to where his clothes lay spread.

Fearing that he had gone too far, SartoriIrvrash said in a shaking voice, "Your Majesty, forgive me, I see your plan. By dismissing me, you can then be free to blame me before the scritina for what has occurred, and thus show yourself innocent in their eyes. As if truth can be moulded that way. . . . It is a well-tried tactic, well-tried—transparent, too—but surely we can agree on how precisely—"

He faltered and fell silent. A sickly evening light filled the room. Traces of an auroral storm flickered in the cloud mass outside. The king had drawn his sword from its scabbard where it lay on the table. He flourished it.

SartoriIrvrash backed away, knocking over a pitcher of scented water, which rushed to escape in a flood across the tiled floor.

JandolAnganol began a complex pattern of swordplay with an invisible enemy, feinting and lunging, at times appearing hard pressed, at times pressing hard himself. He moved rapidly about the room. The women huddled against the wall, tittering with nervousness.

"Heigh! Yauh! Ho! Heigh!"

He switched direction, and the naked blade darted at the chancellor.

As it stopped an inch from his collarbone, the king said, "So, where's my son, where's Robayday, then, you old villain? You know he'd have my life?"

"Well I know the history of your family, sire," said SartoriIrvrash, ineffectually covering his chest with his hands.

"I must deal with my son. You have him hidden in the warren of your apartments."

"No, sire, that I do not."

"I am told you do, sire, the phagor guard told me. And he whispered, sire, that you still have some blood in your eddre."

"Sire, you are overtaxed by the ordeals you have undergone. Let me get—"

"Get nothing, sire, but steel in the gullet. So reliable! You have a visitor in your rooms."

"From Morstrual, sire, a boy, no more."

"So, you keep boys now . . ." But the subject seemed to lose its interest. With a shout, the king flung up his sword so that it embedded itself in the beams overhead. When he reached up and grasped its hilt, the towel fell from him.

SartoriIrvrash stooped to retrieve it for his majesty, saying, falteringly, "I understand from whence your madness comes, and allow—"

Instead of seizing the towel, the king seized the old man's charfrul and swung him about by it. The towel went flying. The chancellor uttered a cry of alarm. His feet slipped from under him, and they fell together heavily, in the flood of water.

The king was back on his feet as nimbly as a cat, motioning to the women to help SartoriIrvrash up. The chancellor groaned and clutched his back as two of them assisted him.

"Now go, sire," said the king. "Get packing—before I demonstrate to you just how mad I am. Remember, I know you for an atheist and a Myrdolator!"

In his own chambers, Chancellor SartoriIrvrash had a woman slave annoint his back with ointments, and indulged in some luxurious groans. His personal phagor guard, Lex, looked on impassively.

After a while, he called for some squaanej juice topped with Lordryardry ice, and then laboriously wrote a letter to the king, clutching his spine between sentences.

Honoured Sire,

I have served the House of Anganol faithfully, and deserve well from it. I am prepared still to serve, despite the attack upon my person, for I know how your majesty suffers in his mind at present.

As to my atheism and my learning, to which you so frequently object, may I point out that they are one, and that my eyes are opened to the true nature of our world. I do not seek to woo you from your faith, but to explain to you that it is your faith which puts you in your present difficult situation.

I see our world as a unity. You know of my discovery that a hoxney is a striped animal, appearances to the contrary. This discovery is of vital importance, for it links the seasons of our Great Year, and gives us new

understanding of them. Many plants and animals may have similar de-
vices by which to perpetuate their species through the Year's conflicting
climates.

Could it be that humanity has, in religion, a similar mode of perpetu-
ation? Differing only as humanity differs from the brute beasts? Religion
is a social binding force which can unify in times of extreme cold or, as
now, of extreme heat. That social binding force, that cohesion, is valu-
able, for it leads to our survival in national or tribal entities.

What it must not do is rule our individual lives and thinking. If we
sacrifice too much to religion, then we are prisoners of it, as Madis are
prisoners of the uct. You must, sire, forgive my pointing this out to you,
and I fear that you will not find it palatable, but you yourself have shown
such a slavishness to Akhanaba—

He paused. No, as usual he was going too far. The king in his anger
would destroy him if he read that sentence. Laboriously, he took a fresh
sheet of parchment and wrote a modified version of his first letter. He
charged Lex with delivering it.

Then he sat and wept.

He dozed. Later, he awoke to find Lex standing over him, his milt
flicking up the slots of his nostrils. He had long grown used to the
silence of phagors; though he hated the creatures, they were less bothersome than human slaves about the place.

His table clock told him it was near the twenty-fifth hour of the day.
He yawned, stretched, and put on a warmer garment. Outside, the
aurora flickered over an empty courtyard. The palace was asleep—
except perhaps for the king. . . .

"Lex, we'll go and speak with our prisoner. Have you fed him?"

The phagor, immobile, said, "The prisoner has his food, sir." He
spoke in a low voice, buzzingly, so that the honorific came out as 'zzorr.'
His Olonets was limited, but SartoriIrvrash, in his abhorrence, refused
to learn Hurdhu.

Among the shelves covering most of a long wall stood a cupboard.
Lex swung it away from the wall to reveal an iron door. Clumsily, the
ancipital inserted a key in the lock and turned it. He pulled the door
open; man and phagor entered a secret cell.

This had once been an independent room. In the days of Varpal-
Anganol, the chancellor had had its external door plastered over. Now
the only means of entry lay through his study. Stout bars had been fixed
over the window. From outside, the window was lost in the muddle of
the castle facade.

Flies buzzed in the room, or hung as if sleeping in the thick air. They
crawled over the table, and over the hands of Billy Xiao Pin.

Billy sat on a chair. He was chained to a strong eye anchored in the floor. His clothes were stained with sweat. The stench in the room was overwhelming.

Producing a sachet of scantiom, pellamountain, and other herbs, SartoriIrvrash pressed it to his nose and gestured towards a cessbucket standing in a corner of the room.

"Empty that." Lex moved to obey.

The chancellor took a chair and placed it beyond the reach of any lunge his prisoner might make. He sat down carefully, nursing his back and grunting. He lit a long veronikane before he spoke.

"Now, BillishOwpin, you have been here for two days. We shall have another discussion. I am the Chancellor of Borlien, and, if you lie to me, it is well within my powers to torture you. You introduced yourself to me as the mayor of a town on the Gulf of Chalce. Then, when I locked you up, you claimed that you were a much grander person, who came from a world above this one. Who are you today? The truth now!"

Billy wiped his face on his sleeve and said, "Sir, believe me, I knew of this secret room before I arrived here. Yet I am ignorant of many aspects of your manners. My initial mistake was to pose as someone I am not—which I did because I doubted if you would believe the truth."

"I may say without vanity that I happen to be one of the foremost seekers after truth of my generation."

"Sir, I know it. Therefore set me free. Let me follow the queen. Why lock me up when I mean no harm?"

"I lock you up because I may get some good out of you. Stand up."

The chancellor surveyed his captive. Certainly, there was something odd about the fellow. His physiology was not the attenuated one of a Campannlatian, nor had he the barrel shape of those freak humans, sometimes displayed at fairs, whose ancestors (according to medical thought) had escaped the near-universal bone fever.

His friend CaraBansity in Ottassol would have said that underlying bone structure accounted for the peculiar rounded quality of the captive's features. The man's skin texture was smooth, with a notable pallor, though his button nose was sunburnt. His hair was fine.

And there were more subtle differences, such as the quality of the captive's gaze and its duration. He seemed to look away to listen, and regarded SartoriIrvrash only when he spoke—although fear could account for that. His eyes were often cast upward, instead of down. In particular, he spoke Olonets in a foreign style.

All this the chancellor observed before saying, "Give me an account of this world above from which you claim to come. I am a rational man, and I shall listen without prejudice to what you have to say." He drew upon his kane and coughed.

Lex returned with an empty bucket and stood motionless against one wall, fixing his cerise glare on an undefined point in the middle distance.

When Billy sat down, his chains rattled. He placed his weighted wrists on the table before him and said, "Merciful sir, I come, as I told you, from a much smaller world than yours. A world perhaps of the size of the great hill upon which Matrassyl Castle stands. That world is called Avernus, though your astonomers have long known it as Kaidaw. It lies some fifteen hundred kilometers above Helliconia, with an orbital period of 7770 seconds, and its—"

"Wait. On what does this hill of yours lie? On air?"

"There is no air about Avernus. In effect, the Avernus is a metal moon. No, you don't have that word in Olonets, sir, since Helliconia possesses no natural moon. Avernus orbits Helliconia continually, as Helliconia orbits Batalix. It travels through space, as Helliconia does, and moves continually, as Helliconia does. Otherwise, it would fall under the pull of gravitation. I think you understand this principle, sir? You know of the true relationships between Helliconia on the one hand and Batalix and Freyr on the other."

"I understand what you say very well." He slapped at a fly crawling over his bald pate. "You are addressing the author of 'The Alphabet of History and Nature,' in which I seek to synthesise all knowledge. It is understood by few men—but I happen to be one of them—that Batalix and Freyr revolve about a common focus, while Copaise, Aganip, and Ipocrene revolve with Helliconia about Batalix. The haste of our sister worlds in their orbits is commensurate with their stature and their distance from the parent body, Batalix. Furthermore, cosmology informs us that these sister worlds sprang from Batalix, as men spring from their mothers, and Batalix sprang from Freyr, which is its mother. In the realm of the heavens, you will find me suitably informed, I flatter myself."

He looked up at the ceiling and blew smoke among the flies.

Billy cleared his throat. "Well, it's not quite like that. Batalix and its planets form a relatively aged solar system which was captured by a much larger sun, which you call Freyr, some eight million years ago, as we reckon time."

The chancellor moved restlessly, crossing and uncrossing his legs, with a peevish expression on his face. "Among the impediments to knowledge are the persecutions of those who seek power, the difficulties of investigation, and—this in particular—a failure to recognise what should be investigated. I set all this out in my first chapter.

"You clearly have some knowledge, yet you betray it by mingling it with falsehood for your own reasons. Remember that torture is a friend of truth, BillishOwpin. I'm a patient man, but this wild talk of millions angers me. You won't impress me by mere numbers. Anyone can invent figures out of thin air."

"Sir, I do not invent. How many people inhabit all Campannlat?"

The chancellor looked flustered. "Why, some fifty million, according to best estimates."

"Wrong, sir. Sixty-four million people, and thirty-five million phagors. In the time of VryDen, whom you like to quote, the figures were eight million humans and twenty-three million phagors. The biomass relates directly to the amount of energy arriving at the planetary surface. In Sibornal there are—"

SartoriIrvrash waved his hands. "Enough—you try to vex me. . . . Return to the geometry of the suns. Do you dare claim there is no blood relationship between Freyr and Batalix?"

From gazing down at his hands, Billy looked askance at the old man who sat beyond his reach. "If I tell you what really happened, honoured Chancellor, would you believe me?"

"That depends whether your tale is within credence." He puffed out a cloud of smoke.

Billy Xiao Pin said, "I caught only a glimpse of your beautiful queen. So what is the point of my being here, dying here, if I fail to tell you this one great truth?" He thought of MyrdemInggala passing, glorious in her floating muslins.

And he began. The phagor stood by the stained wall, the old man sat in his creaking chair. The flies buzzed. No sounds came from the outside world.

"On my way here, I saw a banner saying, in Olonets, 'All the world's wisdom has always existed.' That is not so. It may be a truth for the religious, but for the scientific it is a lie. Truth resides in facts which must be painfully discovered and hypotheses which must be continually checked—although where I come from, facts have obliterated truth. As you say, there are many impediments to knowledge, and to the meta-structure of knowledge we call *science*.

"Avernus is an artificial world. It is a creation of science and the application of science we call—you have no such word—*technology*. You may be surprised to hear that the race from which I come, which *evolved* on a distant planet called Earth, is younger than you Helliconians. But we suffered fewer natural disadvantages than you."

He paused, almost shocked to hear that charged word, *Earth*, pronounced in these surroundings.

"So I shall not lie to you—though I warn you you may find that what I say does not fit into your world-picture, Chancellor. You may be shocked, even though you are the most enlightened of your race."

The chancellor stubbed out his veronikane on the top of the table and pressed a hand to his head. It ached. The prison room was stifling. He could not follow the young stranger's speech, and his mind wandered to the king, naked, and the sword embedded dangerously in a beam above them. The prisoner talked on.

Where Billy came from, the cosmos was as familiar as a back garden. He spoke in matter-of-fact tones about a yellow G4-type star which was some five thousand million years old. It was of low luminosity and a temperature of only 5600K. This was the sun now called Batalix. He went on to describe its only inhabited planet, Helliconia, a planet much like distant Earth, but cooler, greyer, older, its life processes slower. On its surface, over many eons, species developed from animal to dominant being.

Eight million years ago by Earth reckoning, Batalix and its system moved into a crowded region of space. Two stars, which he called A and C, were orbiting each other. Batalix was drawn within the massive gravitational field of A. In the series of perturbations which followed, star C was lost, and A acquired a new companion, Batalix.

A was a very different sun from Batalix. Although between only ten and eleven million years old, it had evolved away from the main sequence of stars and was entering stellar old age. Its radius was over seventy times the radius of Batalix, its temperature twice as great. It was an A-type supergiant.

Try as he might, the chancellor could not listen attentively. A sense of disaster enveloped him. His vision blurred, his heart beat with an irregular throb which seemed to fill the room. He pressed his scantiom sachet to his nose to help his breathing.

"That's enough," he said, breaking into Billy's discourse. "Your kind is known in history, talking in strange terms, mocking the understandings of wise men. Perhaps it is a delusion we suffer from. . . . Small wonder if we do. Only two days ago—only fifty hours—the queen of queens left Matrassyl, charged with conspiracy, and sixty-one Myrdolators were cruelly murdered. . . . And you talk to me of suns swooping here and there as fancy takes them. . . ."

Billy drummed the fingers of one hand on the table and fanned away flies with the other. Lex stood nearby, motionless as furniture, eyes closed.

"I'm a Myrdolator myself. I'm much to blame for these crimes. Too used to serving the king . . . as he's too used to serving religion. Life was so placid. . . . Now who knows what fresh botherations will happen tomorrow?"

"You are too sunk in your own little affairs," Billy said. "You're as bad as my Advisor on the Avernus. He doesn't entirely believe in the reality of Helliconia. You don't entirely believe in the reality of the universe. Your umwelt is no larger than this palace."

"What's an umwelt?"

"The region encompassed by your perceptions."

"You pretend to know so much. Is it correct, as I perceive, that the hoxney is a brown-striped animal which wore coloured stripes in the spring of the Great Year?"

"That is correct. Animals and plants adopt different strategies to survive the vast changes of a Year. There are binary biologies and botanies, some following one star, as previously, some the other."

"Now you return to your perambulating suns. In my belief, established over thirty-seven years, our two suns are set in our skies as a constant reminder of our dual nature, spirit and body, life and death, and of the more general dualities which govern human life—hot and cold, light and dark, good and evil."

"You say my kind is known in history, Chancellor. Maybe those were other visitors from the Avernus, also trying to reveal the truth, and being ignored."

"Revelations through some crazed geometries? Then they perished!" SartoriIrvrash rose, resting his fingers on the table, frowning.

Billy also laboriously rose, rattling his chains. "The truth would free you, Chancellor. Whatever you think, those 'crazed geometries' rule the universe. You half-know this. Respect your intellect. Why not go further, break from your *umwelt*? The life that teems on Helliconia is a product of those crazed geometries you scoff at.

"That A-type sun you know as Freyr is a gigantic hydrogen fusion-reactor, pouring out high-energy emissions. When Batalix and its planets took up orbits round it, eight million years ago, they were subjected to bombardments of X rays and ultraviolet radiation. The effect on the then-sluggish Helliconian biosphere was profound. There was rapid genetic change. Dramatic mutations occurred. Some new forms survived. One animal species in particular rose to challenge the supremacy previously enjoyed by a much older species—"

"No more of this," cried SartoriIrvrash, waving a hand in dismissal. "What is this about species changing into other species? Can a dog become an arang, or a hoxney a kaidaw? Everyone knows at least that every animal has its place, and humans their place. So the All-Powerful has ordained."

"You're an atheist! You don't believe in the All-Powerful!"

Confused, the chancellor shook his head. "I'd prefer to be ruled by the All-Powerful than by your crazed geometries. . . . I had hoped to make a present of you to King JandolAnganol, but you would drive him madder than he is already."

Wearily, SartoriIrvrash realised that the king could not be placated at present by rational means. SartoriIrvrash himself felt far from rational. Listening to Billy, he was reminded of another young madman— the king's son, Robayday. Once a charming child, then overtaken by a kind of mad fancy, espousing the desert like a parched mother, expert at killing game, at times hardly making sense . . . the plague of his royal parents.

He wondered at his own long struggle to make sense of the world. How was it that such an omnipresent problem oppressed so few?

Billy might be a figment of his tired imagination, the darker side of rationality, sent to plague him.

He turned to the phagor. "Lex, guard him. I'll think how to dispose of him and his *umwelts* on the morrow."

In his bedchamber, loneliness overwhelmed the chancellor. The king had seized him and flung him to the floor! He felt the bumps of his bruised spine, felt how ugly his body was growing as the years squeezed it dry. The days contained so much shame.

His slave woman came at his call, looking reluctant as he had looked reluctant when summoned before the king.

"Massage my back," he ordered.

She lay against him, running a rough but gentle hand from his skull to his pelvis. He smelt of veronikane, phagors, and piss. She was Randonanese, with tribal marks cut in her cheeks. She smelt of fruit. After a while, he rolled over to face her, his prodo stirring. There was one comfort given to believers and atheists alike, one refuge from abstraction. The chancellor thrust one hand between the dark exiled thighs and reached with the other into her shift, to clasp the slave woman's breasts.

She drew him close.

Petitions were being signed on the Avernus for a party to descend to the Helliconian surface and rescue Billy Xiao Pin. No serious notice was taken of the petitions. Billy's contract clearly stated that, whatever difficulties he found himself in, no help would be forthcoming. Which did not prevent many young ladies of the Pin family from threatening to commit suicide if the government did not act at once.

But the work of the station continued as usual, as it had done for the previous thirty-two centuries. Little the Avernians knew how Earth's technocrats had programmed them for obedience. The great families continued to analyse all incoming data, and the automatic systems continued to broadcast signals to distant Earth.

Gigantic auditoria shaped like conch shells stood all round that faraway planet.

To the people of Earth, Helliconian events were news. The signals were received first of all on Charon, on the extreme fringes of the solar system. There again they were analysed, classified, stored, transmitted. The most popular transmission went to Earth via the Eductainment Channel, which carried various continuous dramas from the binary system. The events at King JandolAnganol's court were at present the highest-rating news. And that news was a thousand years old.

Those who listened to that news formed part of a global society undergoing a change as profound as any on Helliconia. The Decline of the Modern Ages had been hastened by greatly increased glaciation at

IX · SOME BOTHERATION

the terrestrial poles, leading to the Great Ice Age. In the ninth century of the sixth millennium after the birth of Christ, the glaciers were again retreating, and the peoples of Earth moving northwards in their wake. Old racial and national antipathies were in abeyance. A mood appropriate to the congenial climate of Earth prevailed, in which sophisticated sensibilities were directed to exploring the relationship between the biosphere, its living things, and the gubernatory globe itself.

For once, leaders and statesmen arose who were worthy of their people. They shared a true vision and inspired the populace. They saw to it that the drama of the distant planet Helliconia was studied as an object lesson in folly as well as an endless tapestry of circumstance.

To the great conch shells, millions of terrestrials had come to watch the departure of the queen, the burning of the Myrdolators, the quarrel between the king and his chancellor. These were contemporary events, in that they influenced the emotional climate of those who looked up at the gigantic images. But the events were also fossil events, compressed within the strata of light on which they had arrived. They seemed to burst up with renewed heat and life on reaching the consciousness of terrestrial human beings, as long-buried trees of Earth's Carboniferous Age yield the sun's energies when coal burns in a grate.

Those fires did not touch everyone. In some quarters, Helliconia was regarded as the relic of an age long past, a period of troubled history best forgotten, when human affairs had been little better managed on Earth than on Helliconia. The new men turned their faces to a new way of life in which the human and its engines were not to be the ultimate arbiter. Some who worked towards those goals found time still to cheer for crabbed SartoriIrvrash, or to become Myrdolators.

The terrestrial followers of the queen were many, even in the new lands. Day and night, they awaited their fossil news.

X

BILLY CHANGES CUSTODY

Whether Akhanaba or the "crazed geometries" were in charge of events in Matrassyl—whether those events were pre-ordained or the result of blind happenstance—whether free will or determinism determined—the fact was that the next twenty-five hours were miserable ones for Billy Xiao Pin. All the bright colours he had experienced in his early hours on Helliconia had faded. Nightmare took over.

On that winter's day in the Great Summer when Chancellor Sartori-Irvrash interrogated Billy and did not listen properly, there was a period of night of almost five hours' duration when neither Freyr nor Batalix was in the sky.

YarapRombry's Comet could be seen low on the northern horizon. Then it was swallowed by a freak fog. The thordotter did not blow, as expected, but sent fog in its stead.

The fog arrived the way the queen left, by river. It made itself felt first as a cold shiver down the naked spines of wharfmen, ferrymen, and others whose livelihood lay along the confluences of the Valvoral and the Takissa.

Some of those watermen, going home, took the insidious element with them into the houses which lined the poor streets behind the docks—and made them the poorer for it. Wives, peering out as they dragged shutters across windows, saw godowns dissolve into a universal sepia puddle.

The puddle rose higher, brimming over the cliffs, as cunning as ill health, and penetrated the castle walls.

There, soldiers in their thin uniforms, shaggy-coated phagors, stirred the infection after them as they patrolled, coughed into it, became devoured by it. The palace itself did not long resist the invasion, but took on the aspects of a ghost of a palace. Through the empty rooms where Queen MyrdemInggala had lived, the fog went mournfully without a sound.

The marauder also found entry to the world under the hill. It snuffled amid that nest of gongs and exclamations and prayers and prostrations and processions and suppressions where holiness was manufactured; there, its uncanny breath mingled easily with the exhalations of vigils and congregations, and created purple haloes about devotional candles, as if here, and here alone, it found a kindred place where it was welcome. It coiled along floors among bare feet, and found out the secret places of the mountain.

To those secret places, Billy Xiao Pin was being escorted.

He rested his head wearily on his table once SartoriIrvrash had left him, letting tired thoughts run riot through his head. When he tried consciously to check on them, the thoughts were gone like criminals over a wall. Had he once described Helliconia as a "form of argument"? Well, there was no arguing with the reality. He recalled all his glib debates about reality with his Advisor, back on the Avernus. Now he had a dose of reality, and it would kill him.

The criminal thoughts crept into action again, to be checked when the doglike Lex placed a bowl of food before him.

"Do eating," the ancipital commanded, as Billy looked mistily up at him.

The food was a porridge into which highly coloured fruit had been chopped. He took up a silver spoon and began to eat. The taste was insipid. After a few spoonfuls, drowsiness overcame him. He pushed the bowl away, groaning, and lay his head on the table again. Flies settled on the food, and on his undefended cheek.

Lex went to the wall opposite to the one by which he and the chancellor habitually entered, and tapped on one of the wooden panels. A countertap answered, to which he responded with two wide-spaced answering taps. A section of panelling opened into the room, scattering dust.

A female ancipital entered the cell, moving with the gliding movement of her kind. Without hesitation, she and Lex lifted the paralysed
Billy and carried him into the narrow passage now revealed. She closed
and bolted the panel door behind them.

The palace contained neglected passages in plenty; this one, in its
unfinished state, gave every appearance of having been neglected for
centuries. The two great ahumans filled it.

Phagor slaves were as common about Matrassyl Palace as phagor
soldiers. When employed as stone masons, for which work they had a
rough aptitude, they had walled in a retroversion in the great walls,
roofed it over, and utilised it as one of their own convenient ways about
the building.

Billy, in a state of paralysis, but still conscious, found himself being
carried down stairs that went back and forth as if forever denied an exit.
His head dangled over the gillot's shoulder, knocking against her
shoulderblade at every step.

At ground level, they paused. Damp hung in the air. Somewhere out
of his sight, a torch smouldered. Hinges squeaked. He was being lowered down into the earth through a trapdoor. His terror could escape
only in the faintest sigh.

The torch appeared as his head fell back, to be eclipsed by a shaggy
head. He was somewhere underground and three-fingered hands were
clutching him. Mauve and red pupils glowed in the gloom. Sickly smells
and shuffling sounds surrounded him. A trapdoor slammed, its echoes
shuttling away into distance.

His viewpoint showed little more than a monstrous back. Another
door, more waiting, more stairs, more insane whispers. He passed out—
yet remained aware of jolts of descent which continued for uncounted
time.

They were making him walk like a drunken man. His feet were dead.
Of course—they had drugged his food. Head rolling to one side, he
gathered that they were in a large underground chamber, moving along a
wooden walk set near the ceiling. Banners hung from the walk. Below,
humans in long garments congregated, barefoot. He recalled their name
in a moment: monks. They sat at long tables, where phagors in similar
garments served them. Memories returned to Billy Xiao Pin; he recollected the monasteries under the hill where he had bought a waffle. He
was being taken through the maze of holy ways carved in the rock
beneath JandolAnganol's palace.

The walking revived him. Two phagors escorted him, both gillots.
Probably Lex had returned to do duty for the chancellor, who would
now be asleep. He gave a feeble call to the monks below, but nobody
heard him in the babble of voices. They left the lighted space.

More corridors. He tried to protest, but the females hustled him on.

By his side, a band of carving braided the stone wall. He tried to grip it; his hand was snatched away.

Down again.

Total darkness, smelling of rivers and things unborn.

"Please let me go." His first words. A gate opened.

He was marched into a different world, an underground ancipital kingdom. The very air was different, its sounds and stinks alien. Water lapped. Proportions were different: archways were wide and low, cavernous. The way was rough and uphill. It was like climbing into a dead mouth.

Nothing in the Avernus had prepared Billy for this adventure. Crowds of phagors were gathering to inspect him, thrusting their cow faces into his. They jostled him before a council of ancipitals, male and female. In niches round the walls were stacked their totems, aged phagors sinking further and further in tether; the oldest totem was like a little black doll, almost entirely composed of keratin. Leading the council was a young kzahhn, Ghht-Yronz Tharl.

Ghht-Yronz Tharl was no more than a creaght. The dense white coat over his shoulders was still red-tipped. His long curving horns were painted with a spiral design, and he kept his head thrust low, with a pugnacious gesture, so as not to scrape the tips of those horns on the roof of the chamber.

As for that chamber itself, though its roof was indeed rough and unfinished, its form was approximately circular. Indeed, the auditorium —if such a term was applicable among such an inhuman audience—was built in the shape of a wheel. Ghht-Yronz Tharl stood stiffly upright, puffing out his chest, at the hub of the wheel.

Stalls for the audience radiated like spokes from the hub. Most of the floor was divided into low stalls. Here members of the council stood motionless, or merely twitching a shoulder or ear. In each stall was a trough and a length of chain stapled into the stonework. Runnels for water or urine were cut in the floor and ran to ditches by the perimeter of the wheel.

The fog seemed to have penetrated here, or else the sickly breath of the ancipital race lent a blue aura to the torches. Taking in what he could of this scene as he was examined by rough hands, Billy saw ramps leading upwards, and others, their entrances unwelcoming, leading even further underground.

A perception came to him: in these caves, at this time, phagors gathered to escape the heat; the time would come when men huddled here, to escape the cold. The phagors would then take over the outside world.

Some kind of order was called, and interrogation began. It was evident that Lex had informed Ghht-Yronz Tharl of the content of Billy's conversation with SartoriIrvrash.

Sitting by the kzahhn was a middle-aged female human, a shapeless woman in a dress of stammel, who translated a series of questions from the kzahhn into Olonets. The questions concentrated on Billy's arrival from Freyr—the phagors would hear nothing of Avernus. If this son of Freyr had arrived from otherwhere, then it followed that he came from Freyr, whence, in ancipital eyes, all evil came.

He could hardly understand their questions. Nor could they understand his answers. He had had difficulties with the Borlienese chancellor; here the cultural difference was much wider—he would have said insuperable, except that occasionally he made himself understood. For instance, these nightmarish creatures grasped the point that Helliconia's time of intensifying heat would pass in three or four human lifetimes, to be replaced by a long continued slide towards winter.

At this juncture, the questioning broke off, and the kzahhn sank into a trance in order to communicate with the ancestors of his component present. A human slave brought Billy flavoured water to drink. He begged to be allowed back to the palace, but in a short while his questioning was resumed.

It was curious that the phagors grasped what SartoriIrvrash could not, that Billy had travelled through space, though the Native Ancipital phrase for "space" was an almost untranslatable conglomerate, meaning "immeasureable pathway of air-turns and great year procedures." More briefly, they sometimes spoke of it as "Aganip pathway."

They examined his watch without touching it. He was pushed from one to another of the audience, along the spokes of the council wheel, so that all could see it. His explanation that the three dials showed time on Earth, Helliconia, and Avernus meant nothing to them. Like the phagors he had met outside Matrassyl, they made no attempt to take the instrument and soon reverted to other topics.

His eyes streamed, his nose ran—he had an allergy to their dense coats against which he had been forced to brush.

Between sneezes, Billy told them all he knew about the situation on Helliconia. His fear drove him to reveal everything. When they heard something they could absorb or that interested them especially, the kzahhn would pass on the information to his keratinous ancestor, either for storage or information, Billy was not sure which—phagors had not come within his discipline on the Avernus.

Did they tell him at some point, when he laboured unnecessarily to explain how seasons came and went, that the monastic caverns in the hills were occupied at some seasons by phagors, at others by Sons of Freyr? Once, in a different existence, he had boasted that Avernus held too little otherness for him; now, in a mist of otherness, the curious line of language weaved between Hurdhu, Native, and Eotemporal, between scientific and figurative.

Like a child finding that animals can talk, Billy listened as they spoke to him. "Possibility for revenge against Sons of Freyr at inharmonious season-of-Great-Year has no being. Surviving alone must have all our duty. Watchfulness fills our harneys. All time exists till Freyr-death. Kzahhn JandolAnganol has protective arm for ancipitals' survival in lands of his component. Therefore, the order is for our legions to make formation in a reinforcement of Kzahhn JandolAnganol. Such is our present law of inharmonious season. Carefulness is what you Billy must take not to make a further torment for this kzahhn of weakness named JandolAnganol. Hast comprehension?"

With the noun-freighted sentences whirling in his head, he tried to declare his innocence. But questions of guilt, or freedom from it, were outside their *umwelt*. As he spoke, bafflement reinforced the hostility in the air.

Behind their hostility was fear of a kind, an impersonal fear. They saw JandolAnganol as weak, and they feared that when the alliance with Oldorando was sealed by dynastic marriage, their kind might become as subject to persecution in Borlien as in Oldorando. Their hatred of Oldorando was clear and, in particular, their hatred for its capital, which they called by the Eotemporal name of Hrrm-Bhhrd Ydohk.

While ancipital affairs were a mystery—a blank—to mankind, the ancipitals had a good grasp of mankind's affairs. Such was mankind's arrogant contempt of them that phagors were often present, though ignored, at the most delicate discussions of state. Thus the humblest runt could act effectively as a spy.

Confronting their stolid forms, Billy thought they intended to hold him to ransom, to influence the king against his new marriage; feebly he tried to convey that the king did not even know of his existence.

As soon as the words had left him, he saw that he had put himself in another danger. They might keep him here, in a worse prison than his previous one, if they realised that his presence in the palace was a secret. But the shaggy council was pursuing another line of thought, reverting once more to the question of Batalix's capture by Freyr, an event which seemed of obsessive importance to them.

If not from Freyr, then was he from T'Sehn-Hrr? This question he could not understand. By T'Sehn-Hrr, did they mean the Avernus, Kaidaw? Evidently not. They tried to explain, he tried. T'Sehn-Hrr remained a mystery. He was one with the keratinous figures propped against the wall, doomed to say the same thing many times, in an ever decreasing voice. Talking to phagors was like trying to wrestle with eternity.

The council passed him among them, pressing him here, turning him

there. Again they were interested in looking at the three-faced watch
on his wrist. Its writhing figures fascinated them. But they made no
efforts to remove or even touch it, as if they sensed in it a destructive
force.

Billy was still seeking for words when he realised that the kzahhn and
his council were departing. Clouds gathered in his head again. He found
himself staggering into a familiar chair, let his forehead rest on a familiar table. The gillots had returned him to his cell. A pale shrouded
dawn was at hand.

Lex was there, without horns, emasculated and almost faithful.

"Steps are necessity to bed for a sleep-period," he advised.

Billy started to weep. Weeping, he slept.

The fog reached far and wide and took a turn up the River Valvoral
to view the jungles embracing either bank. Caring nothing for national
frontiers, it penetrated far into Oldorando. There it met, among other
river traffic, the *Lordryardry Lady* heading southeastward to Matrassyl
and the distant sea.

With the last of its ice cargo sold profitably in Oldorando, the flat-
bottomed boat now bore cargoes for the Borlienese capital or Ottassol:
salt; silks; carpets of all descriptions; tapestries; blue gout from Lake
Dorzin, boxed with smashed ice; carvings; clocks; with tusks, horns, and
furs in variety. The small deck cabins were occupied by merchants who
travelled with their goods. One merchant had a parrot, another a new
mistress.

The best deck cabin was occupied by the boat's owner, Krillio Muntras, famous Ice Captain of Dimariam, and his son, Div. Div, who was
slack of jaw and, for all his father's encouragement, would never rival
his father's success in life, sat gazing at the hazily sketched scenery. His
bottom was planted on the deck. Occasionally, he spat into the passing
water. His father sat solidly in a canvas chair and played on a double-
clouth—perhaps with a deliberate sentimentality, for this was his last
voyage before retirement. His last last voyage. Muntras matched a pleasant tenor voice to his tune.

> *The river flows and will not cease, no,*
> *No—not for love or life itself, oh . . .*

The passengers roaming the deck included an arang, which was to
provide the sailors with their supper. Except for the arang, the passengers were markedly respectful to the ice captain.

Fog curled like steam off the surface of the Valvoral. The water
became darker still as they neared the cliffs of Cahchazzerh, whose steep
faces overlooked the river. The cliffs, folded like old linen, rose a few

hundred feet to be crowned with dense foliage which, in its exuberance, appeared to be lowering itself down the overhanging rock by means of creepers and lianas. Much of the cliff had been colonised by swallows and mourner birds. The latter launched themselves and came to investigate the *Lordryardry Lady*, wheeling above it with their melancholy shrieks as it prepared to moor.

Cahchazzerh was remarkable for nothing but its situation between cliff and river, and its apparent indifference to the falls of the one or the rise of the other. At the water's edge, the town consisted of little but a wharf and a few godowns, one of which bore a rusty sign saying LORDRYARDRY ICE TRADING CO. A road led back to scattered houses and some cultivation on top of the cliffs. The town marked a last stop before Matrassyl on the downstream journey.

As the vessel moored up, a few dockhands bestirred themselves, while near-naked boys—indispensable adjuncts of such places—came running. Muntras put down his musical instrument and stood grandly in the bows, accepting the salutations of the men ashore, every one of whom he knew by name.

The gangplank went down. Everybody aboard disembarked to walk about and buy fruit. Two merchants whose journeys terminated here saw to it that the sailors unloaded their possessions safely. The boys dived for coins in the river.

An incongruous item in this sleepy scene was a table, laid with a gaudy cloth, which stood outside the Lordryardry warehouse, a white-clad waiter in attendance. Behind the table were four musicians who, on the instant of the boat's side kissing the wharf, gave forth with a lively rendering of "What a Man the Master Is!" This reception was the farewell present of the local staff of the ice company to their boss. There were three staff. They came forward, smiling, although they had been through the performance before, to conduct Captain Krillio and Div to their seats.

One of the three employees was a gangling youth, embarrassed by the whole affair; the other two were white-haired and older than the man they had served so long. The oldsters managed to shed a tear for the occasion, while covertly summing up young Master Div, in order to estimate to what extent their jobs were threatened by the change in command.

Muntras shook each of the trio by the hand and subsided into the waiting chair. He accepted a glass of wine, into which were dropped sparkling fragments of his own ice. He gazed out across the sluggish river. The far bank could scarcely be seen for mist. As a waiter served them little cakes, there was conversation consisting of sentences beginning, "Do you remember when—" and concluding with laughter.

The birds still wheeling overhead masked a sound of shouts and

barking. As these noises became more obtrusive, the Ice Captain asked
what was happening.

The young man laughed, as the two old men looked uneasy. "It's a
drumble up in the village, Captain." He jerked a thumb towards the
cliffs. "Killing off fuggies."

"They're great on drumbles in Oldorando," Muntras said. "And often
enough the priests use the drumbles as an excuse to kill off so-called
heretics as well as phagors. Religion! Fgh!"

The men continued with reminiscences of the time when they had all
been engaged in building up the inland ice trade, and of the Ice Captain's dictatorial father.

"You're lucky not to have a father such as he was, Master Div," one
of the old men said.

Div nodded as if he was not too sure on that point and left his chair.
He ambled to the river's edge and looked up the cliff, whence came
distant shouts.

In a minute, he called to his father, "It's the drumble."

The others made no response and went on talking, until the youth
called again. "The drumble, Pa. They're just going to heave the fuggies
over the cliffside."

He pointed upwards. Some of the other boat travellers were also
pointing, craning their necks to look up the cliff.

A horn gave a tantivy, and the baying of hounds intensified. "They're
great on drumbles in Oldorando," the captain repeated, getting heavily
to his feet and walking out to where his son stood, open-mouthed, on
the bank.

"You see, it's government orders, sir," said one of the old men,
following and peering into the Ice Captain's face. "They kill off the
phagors and take their land."

"And then don't work it properly," added the Ice Captain. "They
should leave the poor damned things alone. They're useful, are phagors."

Hoarse phagor shouting could be heard, but little action could be
seen. However, in a short time, human shouts of triumph rang out and
the riot of vegetation on the cliffs became disturbed. Broken branches
flew, rocks tumbled, as a figure emerged from obscurity and plunged
downwards, alternately flying and bouncing, to the enormous inconvenience of the mourner birds. The figure crashed onto the narrow bank
under the cliff, made to sit up, and toppled into the water. A three-
fingered hand was raised, to sink slowly as its owner was carried away
by the flood.

Div broke into empty laughter. "Did you see that?" he exclaimed.

Another phagor, endeavouring to escape its human tormentors, began
well by leaping down the cliff. Then it slipped and crashed headlong,
bouncing on a spur of rock and cartwheeling into the water. Other

figures followed, some small, some large. For a spell, figures were raining down the cliff. At the crest of the cliff, where the underpinning was steeper, two phagors jumped free, clutching each other by the hand. They broke through the outermost branches of an overhanging tree, fell clear of the rock, and dropped into the river. An overadventurous dog followed them down, to crash on the bank.

"Let's be away from here," said Muntras. "I don't care for this. Right, men, gangplank up. All aboard who's getting aboard. Look lively!"

He shook hands with his old staff in a perfunctory way and strode towards the *Lordryardry Lady* to see his orders carried out.

One of the Oldorandan merchants said to him, "I'm glad to see that even in these benighted parts they're trying to rid us of those shaggy vermin."

"They do no harm," said Muntras brusquely, his solid figure not pausing in its stride.

"On the contrary, sir, they are mankind's oldest enemy, and during the Ice Age reduced our numbers almost to nothing."

"That was the dead past. We live in the present. Get aboard, everyone. We're pushing off from this barbarous spot with all haste."

The crew, like their captain, were men from Hespagorat. Without argument, they got the gangplank up and the boat under way.

As the *Lady* drifted into midstream, her passengers could see ancipital corpses floating in the water, surrounded by clouds of yellow blood. One of the crew called out. Ahead was a live phagor, making wretched attempts to swim.

A pole was quickly brought and thrust over the side. The boat had no sail up, for there was no wind, but the current was carrying it with increasing speed. Nevertheless, the phagor understood what was happening. After thrashing furiously, he grasped the end of the pole with both hands. The river brought him against the bulwarks, where he was hauled up to safety.

"You should have let him drown. Fuggies can't stand the water," said a merchant.

"This is my vessel, and my word is law here," said Muntras, with a dark look. "If you have any objections to what goes on, I can put you off right now."

The stallun lay panting on the deck in a spreading pool of water. Ichor ran from a wound in his head.

"Give him a dram of Exaggerator. He'll survive," said the captain. He turned away when the fierce Dimariamian liquor was brought forward and retired to his cabin.

Over his lifetime, he considered, his fellow human beings had grown nastier, more spiteful, less forgiving. Maybe it was the weather. Maybe the world was going to burn up. Well, at least he was going to retire in his own home town of Lordryardry, to a stout building overlooking the sea. Dimariam was always cooler than damned Campannlat. People were decent there.

He would call in on King JandolAnganol when in Matrassyl, on the principle that it was always wise to call on sovereigns of one's acquaintance. The queen was gone, together with the ring he had once sold her; he must see about delivering her letter when he reached Ottassol. Meanwhile he would hear the latest news of the unfortunate queen of queens. Maybe he would also call on Matty; otherwise he would never see her again. He thought affectionately of her well-run whorehouse, better than all the squalid knocking-shops of Ottassol; although Matty herself had put on airs and went to church daily since the king rewarded her for her assistance after the Battle of the Cosgatt.

But what would he do in Dimariam when he was retired? That did need thought; his family was not a great source of comfort. Perhaps he could find some minor profitable mischief to keep him happy. He fell asleep with one hand resting on his musical instrument.

The stocky Ice Captain arrived at a city muted by the events recently played out on its stage.

The king's problems were mounting. Reports from Randonan talked of soldiers deserting in companies. Despite constant prayer in the churches, crops were still failing. The Royal Armourer was having little success in manufacturing copies of the Sibornalese matchlocks. And Robayday returned.

JandolAnganol was in the hills with his hoxney Lapwing, walking through a copse beside his mount. Yuli trotted behind his master, delighted to be in the wilds. Two escorts rode behind at a distance. Robayday jumped from a tree and stood before his father.

He bowed deeply. "Why, it is the king himself, my master, walking in the woods with his new bride." Leaves fell from his hair.

"Roba, I need you at Matrassyl. Why do you keep escaping?" The king did not know whether to be pleased or angry at this sudden apparition.

"To keep escaping is never to escape. Though what keeps me prisoner I know not. Difference must be between fresh air and grandfather's dungeon. . . . If I had no parents, then I might be free." He spoke with a roving eye, unfocussed. His hair, like his speech, was tumbled. He was naked except for a kind of fur kilt over his genitals. His ribs showed, and his body was a tracery of scars and scratches. He carried a javelin.

This weapon he now stuck point first in the ground and ran to Yuli, clasping the runt's arms, crying out in affection.

"My dearest queen, how wonderful you look, so well dressed in that white fur with the red tassels! To keep off the sun, to hide your delectable body from all but this lecherous Other, who swings on you, no doubt, as if you were a bough. Or a sow. Or a broken vow."

"You make me hurted," cried the little phagor, struggling to get free.

JandolAnganol reached out to take his son's arm, but Robayday darted to one side. He tugged a flowering creeper which hung from a caspiarn and, with a quick movement, twined it round Yuli's throat. Yuli ran about, calling hoarsely, lips curled back in alarm, as JandolAnganol took tight hold to his son.

"I don't intend to hurt you, but cease this foolery and speak to me with the respect you owe me."

"Oh me, oh me! Speak to me in respect of my poor mother. You have planted horns upon her, you gardener in bogs!" He gave a cry and fell back as his father struck him across the mouth.

"Cease this unkind nonsense at once. Be silent. If you had kept your sanity and had been acceptable to Pannoval, then you might have married Simoda Tal in my place. Then we would have been spared much pain. Do you think only for yourself, boy?"

"Yes, as I make my own scumber!" He spat the words out.

"You owe me something, who made you a prince," said the king with bitterness. "Or have you forgotten you're a prince? We'll lock you up at home until you come back to your right mind."

With his free hand up to his bleeding mouth, Robayday muttered, "There's more comfort in my wrong mind. I'd rather forget my rights."

By this time, the two lieutenants had come up, swords out. The king turned, ordering them to put up their weapons, dismount, and take his son captive. As his attention was distracted, Robayday broke free of his father's grasp and made off, with great leaps and whoops, among the trees.

One of the lieutenants put an arrow to his crossbow, but the king stopped him. Nor did he make any attempt to follow his son.

"I not have liking to Robay," squealed Yuli.

Ignoring him, JandolAnganol mounted Lapwing and rode swiftly back to the palace. With his brows knitted, he resembled more than ever the eagle that gave him his nickname.

Back in the seclusion of his quarters, he submitted himself to pauk, as he rarely did. His soul sank down to the original beholder and he spoke with the gossie of his mother. She offered him full consolation. She reminded him that Robayday's other grandmother was the wild Shannana, and told him not to worry. She said he should not hold himself guilty for the deaths of the Myrdolators, since they had intended treason to the state.

The fragile casket of dust offered JandolAnganol every verbal comfort. Yet his soul returned to his body troubled.

His wicked old father, still alive in the ponderous basements, was more practical. VarpalAnganol never ran out of advice.

"Warm up the Pasharatid scandal. Get our agents to spread rumours. You must implicate Pasharatid's wife, who impudently remains here to carry her husband's office. Any tale against the Sibornalese is readily believed."

"And what am I to do regarding Robayday?"

The old man turned slightly in his chair and closed one eye. "Since you can do nothing about him, do nothing. But anything you could do to speed your divorce and get the marriage over with would be useful."

JandolAnganol paced about the dungeon.

"As to that, I'm in the hands of the C'Sarr now."

The old man coughed. His lungs laboured before he spoke again. "Is it hot outside? Why do people keep saying it's hot? Listen, our friends in Pannoval *want* you to be in the C'Sarr's hands. That suits them but it doesn't suit you. Hurry matters if you can. What news of Myrdem-Inggala?"

The king took his father's advice. Agents with an armed escort were dispatched to distant Pannoval City beyond the Quzints, with a long address beseeching the C'Sarr of the Holy Pannovalan Empire to hasten the bill of divorce. With the address went icons and other gifts, including holy relics fabricated for the occasion.

But the Massacre of the Myrdolators, as that affair was now called, continued to exercise the minds of people and scritina. Agents reported rebellious movements in the city, and in other centres such as Ottassol. A scapegoat was needed. It had to be Chancellor SartoriIrvrash.

SartoriIrvrash—the Rushven once beloved of the king's family—would make a popular victim. The world mistrusts intellectuals, and the scritina had particular reason to hate both his high-handed ways and his long speeches.

A search of the chancellor's suite would be certain to reveal something incriminating. There would be the notes of his breeding experiments with the Others, Madis, and humans he kept captive in a distant quarry. And there were the voluminous papers relating to his "Alphabet of History and Nature." These papers would be full of heresies, distortions, lies against the All-Powerful. How both scritina and Church would lick their chops at that prospect! JandolAnganol sent in a guard, led by no less a personage than Archpriest BranzaBaginut of Matrassyl Cathedral.

The search was more successful than anticipated. The secret room was discovered (though not its secret exit). In that secret room was discovered a secret prisoner of curious quality. As he was dragged away, this prisoner screamed in accented Olonets that he came from another world.

Great piles of incriminating documents were taken into the courtyard. The prisoner was taken before the king.

Although it was now twenty past thirteen in the afternoon, the fog had not cleared; rather, it had deepened, taking on a yellowish tinge. The palace drifted in a world of its own, the ventilation devices on its chimneys like the masts of a sinking fleet. Perhaps claustrophobia played a part in the uncertainty of the king's moods as he swung between meekness and anger, between calm and wild excitement. His hair stood dishevelled on his forehead. His nose bled by fits and starts, as if forced into the role of safety valve. About the corridors he went, followed by a train of unhappy courtiers who infuriated him with placatory smiles.

When SartoriIrvrash was brought forth and confronted by the trembling Billy, JandolAnganol struck the old man. After which he seized up his chancellor like an ancient rag doll, wept, begged forgiveness, and suffered another nose bleed.

It was while JandolAnganol was in a penitent mood that Ice Captain Muntras arrived at the palace to pay his respects.

"I will see the captain later," said the king. "As a traveller, he may bring me news of the queen. Tell him to wait on me. Let the world wait."

He wept and snarled. In a minute, he called back the messenger.

"Bring in the Ice Captain. He shall witness this curiosity of human nature." This was said as he prowled about Billy Xiao Pin.

Billy shifted from foot to foot, half-inclined to blubber, unnerved by the bloody state of the royal nostrils. On the Avernus, such demonstrations of feeling, if they ever occurred, would take place in seclusion. "On the Prolongation of One Helliconian Season Beyond One Human Life-Span" had been firm, if brief, on the subject of feeling. "Sensation: superfluous," it said. The excitable Borlienese believed otherwise. Their king did not look like a sympathetic listener.

"Um—hello," managed Billy, with an anguished smile. He gave a violent sneeze.

Muntras entered the room, bowing. They were in a cramped and ancient part of the palace which smelt of mortar, though it was mortar four hundred years old. The Ice Captain stood on his two flat feet and looked about curiously as he delivered his greetings.

The king barely acknowledged Muntras's courtesies. Pointing to a pile of cushions, he said, "Sit there and don't speak. Observe what we have found rotting in the recesses of this pile. The fruit of treachery!"

Turning abruptly back to Billy, he asked, "How many years have you festered in SartoriIrvrash's clutches, creature?"

Disconcerted by the king's regal brand of Olonets, Billy stammered. "A week—even eight days . . . I forget, Your Majesty."

"Eight days is a week, slanje. Are you the poor results of an experiment?"

The king laughed, and all those present—less from humour than from a care for their lives—echoed him. Nobody wished to seem to be a Myrdolator.

"You smell like an experiment." More laughing.

He summoned up two slaves and told them to wash Billy and change his clothes. As this was done, food and wine appeared. Men came running, bent in the attitude of mobile bows, bearing warmed kid-meat served in orange rice.

While Billy ate, the king marched about the chamber, disdaining food. JandolAnganol occasionally pressed a silken cloth to his nose, or stared at his left wrist where his son, in escaping his grasp, had scratched his flesh. Pacing somewhat awkwardly by his side was the Archpriest BranzaBaginut, an enormous man whose bulk, rigged overall in saffron and scarlet canonicals, caused him to resemble a Sibornalese warship in full sail. His heavy face might have belonged to a village wrestler was it not for a lurking humour in his expression. He was widely respected as a shrewd man and one who supported the king as a benefactor of the Church.

BranzaBaginut loomed over the king, who wore by contrast only breeches, was unbooted, and allowed his dirty white jacket to gape, revealing a boney chest.

The room itself was undecided in its role, being somewhere between a reception chamber and a storeroom. There were plenty of rugs and cushions of a mouldy sort, while old timbers were stacked in one corner. The windows looked out on a narrow passage; men passed that way occasionally, carrying piles of SartoriIrvrash's papers into the courtyard.

"Let me question this person, sire, on religious matters," said BranzaBaginut to the king. Receiving nothing in the way of disagreement, the dignitary sailed in the direction of Billy and asked, "Do you come from a world where Akhanaba the All-Powerful rules?"

Billy wiped his mouth, reluctant to cease eating.

"You know I can easily give you an answer to please you. Since I have no wish to displease you, or his majesty, may I offer it you, knowing it to be untrue?"

"Stand when you address me, creature. You give me your answer to my question and I tell you soon enough whether or not I am pleased by it."

Billy stood before the massive ecclesiastic, still nervously wiping his mouth.

"Sir, gods are necessary to men at some stages of development . . . I mean, as children, we need, each of us, a loving, firm, just father, to help our growth to manhood. Manhood seems to require a similar image of a father, magnified, to keep it in good check. That image bears the name of God. Only when a part of the human race grows to a spiritual manhood, when it can regulate its own behaviour, does the need for gods disappear—just as we no longer need a father watching over us when we are adults and capable of looking after ourselves."

The archpriest smoothed a large cheek with a hand, appearing struck by this explanation. "And you are from a world where you look after yourselves, without the need of gods. Are you saying that?"

"That is correct, sir." Billy looked fearfully about him. The Ice Captain reclined nearby, filling his face with the royal food, but listening intently.

"This world you come from—Avernus, did I hear?—is it a happy one?"

The priest's innocent-seeming question set Billy in a good deal of confusion. Had the same question been put to him a few weeks ago on the Avernus, and by his Advisor, he would have had no trouble answering. He would have responded that happiness resided in knowledge, not in superstition, in certainty, not in uncertainty, in control, not in chance. He would have believed that knowledge, certainty, and control were the singular benefits derived from and governing the lives of the population of the observation station. He would certainly have laughed—and even his Advisor would have spared a wintery chuckle—at the notion of Akhanaba as bringer of felicity.

On Helliconia, it was different. He could still laugh at the idolatrous superstition of the Akhanaban religion. And yet. And yet. He saw now the depth of meaning in the word "godless." He had escaped from a godless state to a barbaric one. And he could see, despite his own misfortunes, in which world the hope of life and happiness more strongly lay.

As he was stuttering over his reply, the king spoke. JandolAnganol had been meditating Billy's previous answer. He said challengingly, "What if we have no sound image of a father to guide us to manhood? What then?"

"Then, sir, Akhanaba may indeed be a support to us in our trouble. Or we may reject him completely, as we reject our natural father."

This reply caused the king's nose to bleed again.

Billy seized the moment to bluff his way out of replying to Branza-Baginut's question by saying to him, with more confidence than he felt, "My lord, I am a person of importance, and have received bad treatment from this court. Let me go free. I can work with you. I can tell you details about your world you need to know. I have nothing to gain—"

The Archpriest clapped his large hands together, and said in a gentle voice, "Don't deceive yourself. You are of no importance whatsoever, except when you condemn further Chancellor SartoriIrvrash of conspiring against his royal majesty."

"You have made no attempt to assess my importance. Supposing I tell you that thousands of people are watching us at this moment? They wait to see how you behave towards me, to test you. Their judgement will influence how you are set down in history."

Colour rose to the dignitary's cheeks. "It is the All-Powerful who watches us, no one else. Your dangerous lies of godless worlds would overturn our state. Hold your tongue, or you will find yourself on a bonfire."

In some desperation, Billy approached the king, displaying his watch with its three faces to him. "Your Majesty, I beg you to free me. Look on this artifact I wear. Every person on the Avernus wears a similar one. It tells the time on Helliconia, on Avernus, and on a distant controlling world, Earth. It is a symbol of the tremendous strides we have made in conquering our environment. To a sympathetic audience, I could convey marvels far in advance of anything Borlien could manage."

Interest woke in the king's eyes. He lowered his silk and asked, "Can you make me a functioning matchlock, the equal of Sibornal's?"

"Why, matchlocks are nothing. I—"

"Wheel locks, then. You could produce a wheel lock?"

"Well, no, I—sir, it's a question of the tensile strengths of the metal. I daresay I could devise— Such things are obsolete where I come from."

"What kind of weapon can you make?"

"Sir, first interest yourself in this watch, which I beg you to accept as a present, in token of my faith." He dangled the watch before the king, who showed no inclination to accept it. "Then let me free. Then let me work from first principles with some of your learned men, such as the Archpriests here. Very soon we might devise a good, accurate pistol, and radio, and an internal combustion engine. . . ."

He saw the expressions on both the king's and the archpriest's face, changed his mind about what he was going to say, and instead held out the watch again in supplicatory fashion.

The little figures wriggled and changed under the king's inspection. His majesty seized the timepiece; he and BranzaBaginut inspected it, whispering. Prophets had spoken of a time when magical machineries would appear and the state would be overthrown and the Empire destroyed.

"Will this jewel tell me how long I have left to reign? Can it inform me of the age of my daughter?"

"Sir, it is science, plain science, not magic. Its case is of platinum trawled from space itself. . . ."

The king brushed it away with a sweep of his hand.

"The jewel is evil. I know it. Kings as well as deuteroscopists are cunning about the future. Why did you come here?" He threw the watch back to Billy.

"Your Majesty, I came to see the queen."

JandolAnganol was disconcerted by this reply and stepped back as if he were confronting a ghost. Said BranzaBaginut, "So you are not only an atheist but a Myrdolator? And you expect to be welcome here? Why should his majesty tolerate any more of your riddling? You are neither lunatic nor jester. Where did you come from? SartoriIrvrash's armpit?"

He advanced threateningly on Billy, who backed against a wall. Other members of the court began to close in, anxious to show their sovereign how they regarded unroasted Myrdolators.

Krillio Muntras rose from his cushions and advanced to where the king stood, looking about sharply in some indecision.

"Your majesty, why not ask your prisoner by what ship he arrived from this other world of his?"

The king looked as if undecided as to whether to become angry. Instead, he said, with his nose still covered, "Well, creature, to please our ice trader—by what vehicle came you here?"

Edging round the perimeters of BranzaBaginut, Billy said, "My ship was of metal, a ship entirely enclosed, carrying its own air. I can make all this comprehensible with the aid of diagrams. Our science is advanced, and could aid Borlien. . . . The ship brought me down to Helliconia safely, then left, to return on its own to my world."

"Has it a mind then, this vessel?"

"That's difficult to answer. Yes, it has a mind. It can calculate— navigate through space, perform a thousand actions by itself."

JandolAnganol bent in a careless way and lifted up a wine jar, elevating it slowly until it was above his head. "Which of us is mad, creature, you or I? This vessel has a mind—yes, yes, it too can navigate all by itself. Look!" He flung it. The jar flew through the air, crashed into a wall and broke, splashing its contents all about. This small violence caused everyone to become as immobile as phagors.

"Your Majesty, I endeavoured to answer your—" He sneezed violently.

"It's guilt and anger only that forces me to try and get reason out of you. But why should I bother? I'm deprived, I have nothing, this place is an empty larder, with rats for courtiers. All has been taken away, yet still more is asked of me. You too ask something of me. . . . I am confronted by demons all the way. . . . I must do penance again, Archpriest, and your hand must not be light upon me. This is SartoriIrvrash's demon, I do believe. Tomorrow, I will endeavour to address the scritina and all will be changed. Today I am merely a father who bleeds a lot . . ."

He said in a lower voice, to himself, "Yes, that's it, simply, I must change myself."

He lowered his eyes and looked weary. A drip of blood fell to the floor.

Ice Captain Muntras gave a cough. As a practical man, he was embarrassed by the king's outburst.

"Sire, I come on you at a bad time, as I see. I am just a trader, and so had best be on my way. For the past many years, I have brought you the best Lordryardry ice straight off the best slice of our glaciers, and at the best prices. Now, sire, I will give my grateful thanks for your custom and hospitality at the palace, and take my leave of you for ever. Despite the fog, it's best I was off back home."

The speech seemed in a measure to revive the king, who put a hand on the Ice Captain's shoulder. The eyes of the latter were round in innocence.

"I would I had such men as you about me, talking plain sense all the time, Captain. Your service has been appreciated. Nor do I forget your assistance to me when I was wounded after that fearsome occasion in the Cosgatt—as I am wounded now. You are a true patriot."

"Sire, I am a true patriot of my own country, of Dimariam. To which I am about to retire. This is my last trip. My son will carry on the ice trade with all the devotion I have shown you and the—hm—the ex-queen. As the weather grows hotter, your majesty will perhaps be needing additional loads of ice?"

"Captain, you good trader in better climates, you should be rewarded for your service. Despite my dreadful state of penury, and the meanness of my scritina, I ask—is there anything I might present you with as a token of our esteem?"

Muntras shuffled. "Sire, I am unworthy of reward, and do not seek one, but supposing I said to you that I would make an exchange? On the journey here from Oldorando, I, being a compassionate man, rescued a phagor from a drumble. He is recovered from a watery ordeal, often fatal to his kind, and must find a living away from Cahchazzerh, where he was persecuted. I will present this stallun to you as a slave if you will present me with your prisoner, whether demon or not. Is it a deal?"

"You may have the creature. Take it away, together with its mechanical jewel. You need give me nothing in return, Captain. I am in your debt if you will remove it from my kingdom."

"Then I will take him. And you shall have the phagor, so that my son may call on you in the same civil terms as I have always done. He's a good boy, sir, is Div, though with no more polish than his father."

So Billy Xiao Pin passed into the keeping of the Ice Captain. And on the following day, when the fog was dispersing before a slight breeze, the king's cloudiness also dispersed. He kept his promise to address the scritina.

To that body, who sat coughing in their pews, he presented the appearance of a changed man. Having attested to the wickedness of Chancellor SartoriIrvrash, and to his major role in the reverses recently suffered by the state, JangolAnganol launched into a confession.

"Gentlemen of the scritina, you swore fealty to me when I ascended the throne of Borlien. There have been reverses to our dearly beloved kingdom, that I do not deny. No king, however powerful, however benevolent, can greatly change the condition of his people—that I now realise. I cannot command droughts or the suns which bring such plagues on our land.

"In my desperation, I have committed crimes. Urged on by the chancellor, I was responsible for the deaths of the Myrdolators. I confess and ask your forgiveness. It was done to set the kingdom right, to stop further dissension. I have given up my queen, and with her all lust, all seeking for self. My marriage to the Princess Simoda Tal of Oldorando will be a dynastic one—chaste, chaste, I swear. I will not touch her except to breed. I will take thought for her years. I shall henceforth devote myself wholeheartedly to my country. Give me your obedience, gentlemen, and you will have mine."

He spoke controlledly, with tears in his eyes. His audience sat in silence, gazing up at him sitting on the gilded throne of the scritina. Few felt pity for him; most saw only the opportunity to exploit this fresh instance of his weakness.

Despite the absence of a moon, there were tides on Helliconia. As Freyr drew nearer, the planet's watery envelope experienced an increase in tidal strength of some sixty percent above conditions at apastron, when Freyr was more than seven hundred astronomical units distant.

MyrdemInggala, in her new home, liked to walk alone by the shore of the sea. Her troubled thoughts blew away for a while. This was a marginal place, the strip between the kingdoms of the sea and the kingdoms of the land. It reminded her of her dimday garden left behind, placed between night and day. She was only vaguely aware of the constant struggle that went on at her feet, perhaps never to be entirely won or lost. She gazed towards the horizon, wondering as she did every day if the Ice Captain had delivered her letter to the general in the distant wars.

The queen's gown was pale yellow. It went with the solitude. Her favourite colour was red, but she wore it no more. It did not go with old Gravabagalinien and its haunted past. The hiss of the sea demanded yellow, to her mind.

When she was not swimming, she left Tatro on the beach to play and walked below the high-tide line. He lady-in-waiting reluctantly followed. Tough grasses grew from the sand. Some formed clumps. A step or two farther inland and other plants ventured. A little white daisy with armoured stem was among the first. There was a small plant with succulent leaves, almost like a seaweed. MyrdemInggala did not know its name, but she liked to pick it. Another plant had dark leaves. It straggled among the sand and grasses in insignificant clusters but, on occasions where conditions were right, raised itself into striking bushes with a lustrous sheen.

Behind these first bold invaders of the shore lay the litter of the tide line. Then came a haggard area, punctuated with tough, large-flowered daisies. Then less adventurous plants took over, and the beach was banished, though inlets of sand seamed the land for some way.

"Mai, don't be unhappy. I love this place."

The dawdling lady put on a sullen expression. "You are the most beautiful and fateful lady in Borlien." She had never spoken to her mistress in this tone before. "Why could you not keep your husband?"

The queen made no answer. The two women continued along the shore, some way apart. MyrdemInggala walked among the lustrous bushes, caressing their tips with her hand. Occasionally, something under a bush would hiss and recoil from her step.

She was aware of Mai TolramKetinet, trailing dolefully behind her, hating exile. "Keep up, Mai," she called encouragingly. Mai did not respond.

XI

JOURNEY TO THE
NORTHERN CONTINENT

The old man wore an ankle-length keedrant which had seen better days. On his head was a scoop-shaped hat, which protected his scrawny neck as well as his bald pate from the sun. At intervals, he lifted a shaking hand to his lips to puff at the stem of a veronikane. He stood all alone, waiting to leave the palace for good.

At his back was a coach of light build, loaded with his few personal belongings. Two hoxneys were harnessed between the shafts. It needed only a driver, and then SartoriIrvrash could be gone.

The wait afforded him a chance to look across the parade to a corner where an old bent slave with a stick was encouraging a mountain of papers to burn. That bonfire contained all the papers ransacked from the ex-chancellor's suite, including the manuscripts which formed "The Alphabet of History and Nature."

The smoke rose into a pallid sky from which light ash occasionally fell. Temperatures were as high as ever, but a grey overcast covered everything. The ash was born on an easterly airstream from a newly erupting volcano some distance from Matrassyl. That was of no interest to SartoriIrvrash; it was the black ashes ascending which occupied his attention.

His hand trembled more violently and he made the tip of his veronikane blaze like a small volcano.

A voice behind him said, "Here are some more of your clothes, master."

His slave woman stood there, a neatly wrapped bundle offered to him. She gave him a placatory smile. "It's a shame you have to go, master."

He turned his worn face fully to her, stepped a pace nearer to look into her face.

"Are you sorry to see me go, woman?"

She nodded and lowered her gaze. Well, he thought, she enjoyed it when we had a little rumbo—and to think I never bothered to ask. I never thought of her enjoyment. How isolated I have been in my own feelings. A good enough man, learned, but worth nothing because I had no feelings for others. Except for little Tatro.

He didn't know what to say to the slave woman. He coughed.

"It's a bad day, woman. Go inside. Thank you."

She gave him a last eloquent glance before turning away. SartoriIrvrash thought to himself, Who knows what slave women feel? He hunched his shoulders, irritated with her, and with himself, for showing feeling.

He scarcely noticed when the driver appeared. He took in only a youthful figure, head shrouded against the heat in a kind of Madi hood, so that its face could scarcely be seen.

"Are you ready?" this figure called, as it swung itself up into the driver's seat. The two hoxneys shuffled as the weight adjusted against their straps.

Still SartoriIrvrash lingered. He pointed with his kane towards the distant bonfire. "There goes a whole lifetime's learning." He was mainly addressing himself. "That's what I can't forgive. That's what I shall never forgive. All that work . . ."

With a heavy sigh, he climbed aboard the coach. It began at once to roll forward, towards the palace gates. There were those in the palace who loved him; fearing the king's wrath, they had not dared to emerge and wave him farewell. He set his face firmly to the front, blinking his eyes rapidly.

The prospects before SartoriIrvrash were dim. He was thirty-seven years and eight tenners old—well past middle age. It was possible that he could get a post as advisor at the court of King Sayren Stund, but he detested both the king and Oldorando, which was far too hot. He had always kept himself apart from his own and his dead wife's relations in Matrassyl. His brothers were dead. There was nothing for it but to go and live with his daughter; she and her husband dwelt in a dull southern town near the Thribriat border.

There he would sink from human ken and attempt to rewrite his life's work. But who would print it, now that he had no power? Who would read it if it were not printed? In despair, he had written to his daughter, and now intended to catch a boat that would take him south. The coach proceeded briskly downhill. At the bottom of the hill, instead of turning towards the docks, it swerved to the right and rattled up a narrow alley. Its hubs on its left side screamed as they rubbed against the walls of the houses.

"Take care, you fool, you've gone wrong!" said SartoriIrvrash, but he said it to himself. Who cared what happened?

The equipage rattled down a back road under the brow of a cliff and entered a small neglected courtyard. The driver jumped energetically down and closed the courtyard gates, so that they could not be seen from the street. He looked in at the ex-chancellor.

"Would you care to climb down? There's someone waiting to see you." He swept off his elaborate headgear in a mock bow.

"Who are you? What have you brought me here for?"

The boy opened the carriage door invitingly.

"Don't you recognise me, Rushven?"

"Who are you? Why—Roba, it's you!" he said in some relief—for the thought had occurred to him that JandolAnganol might be planning to kidnap and murder him.

"It's me or a hoxney, for I move at speed these days. That's how it's all secrecy. I'm a secret even from myself. I have vowed to be revenged on my cursed father again, since he banished my mother. And on my mother, who left without a farewell to me."

As he allowed the boy to help him out, SartoriIrvrash surveyed him, anxious to see if he looked as wild as his words. RobaydayAnganol was now just twelve years old, a smaller and thinner edition of his father. He was toasted brown by the sun; red scars showed on his torso. Smiles came and went like twitches over his face, as though he could not decide whether he was joking or not.

"Where have you been, Roba? We've missed you. Your father missed you."

"Do you mean the Eagle? Why, he nearly caught me. I've never cared for court life. I care even less now. My father's crime has set me free. So I am a hoxney-brother. A Madi-assister. I will never become king, and he will never again become happy. New lives, new lives, and one for you, Rushven! You first introduced me to the desert, and I will not desert you. I'm going to take you to someone important, human, not father or hoxney."

"Who? What's all this about? Wait!"

But Roba was striding off. SartoriIrvrash looked doubtfully at the coach loaded with all his worldly goods and then decided he had better follow. Walking fast, he entered a dim hall only a step or two behind the king's son.

The house was built according to a pattern suited to its overshadowed location: it stretched up to the light like a plant growing between boulders. The old man was panting by the time Roba led them off the shaking wooden stairs and into a room on the third floor, the only room on that level. SartoriIrvrash broke into prolonged coughing and collapsed on a stool someone offered him.

There were three people awaiting them in the room, and he observed that they seized on the opportunity also to cough. A certain rickety elegance in their structure, a certain sharpness of bone structure, marked them out as Sibornalese. One of them was a woman, elegantly dressed in a silk chagirack, the northern equivalent of a charfrul, its delicate fabric patterned with large black and white formal flowers. Two men stood behind her in the shadows. SartoriIrvrash recognised her immediately as Madame Dienu Pasharatid, wife of the ambassador who had disappeared the day that Taynth Indredd had introduced matchlocks into the palace.

He bowed to her and apologised for his coughing.

"We are all doing it, Chancellor. It is the volcano making our throats sore."

"I believe my throat is sore through grief. You must not call me by my old title." He would not ask her to what volcano she referred, but she saw uncertainty in his face.

"The volcanic eruption in the Rustyjonnik Mountains. Its ash carries this way."

She regarded him with sympathy, letting him recover from the stairs. Her face was large and plain. Although he knew her for an intelligent woman, there was an unpleasant asperity about her mouth, and he had often been guilty of avoiding her company.

He looked about. The walls were covered with thin paper which had peeled in places. One picture hung there, a pen-and-tint drawing of what he recognised as Kharnabhar, the holy mountain of the Sibornalese. The only window, which was to one side, lighting Dienu Pasharatid's face in profile, provided a view of rocky cliff from which creepers hung; the vegetation had a coating of gray ash. Roba sat cross-legged on the floor, sucking a straw and smiling from one to another of the party.

"Madame, what do you want with me? I must go to catch a boat before further disasters befall me," SartoriIrvrash said.

She stood before him and clutched her hands behind her back, while gently moving her weight from one foot to another.

"We ask you to forgive us for getting you here in such an unusual way, but we wish to enlist your aid—for which aid, we will pay generously."

She outlined her proposal, turning occasionally to the men for confirmation. All Sibornalese were profoundly religious, believing, as he knew, in God the Azoiaxic, who existed before life and round whom all life revolves. The members of the ambassadorial contingent held the religion of Akhanaba in low regard, considering it little better than a superstition. They were therefore shocked but not surprised when JandolAnganol made the decision to break his marriage and contract another.

Sibornalese—and the Azoiaxic through them—regarded the bond between woman and man as an equal decision to be held through life. Love was a matter of will, not whim.

SartoriIrvrash sat nodding automatically through this part of the speech, recognising its sententious tone as characteristic of the northern continentals and longing to be on his way.

Roba, not even listening, winked at the ex-chancellor and said confidentially, "This is the house where Ambassador Pasharatid used to meet a lady of the town. It's an historical whorish house—but for you this lady will only talk."

SartoriIrvrash hushed him.

Ignoring the interruption, Madame Dienu said that her party felt that he alone, Chancellor SartoriIrvrash, had pretension to knowledge in the Borlienese court. They felt that the king had treated him almost as badly as—possibly worse than—the queen. Such injustice distressed them, as it would all members of the Church of the Formidable Peace. She was now returning home. They invited SartoriIrvrash to join them, in the assurance that he would be given good accommodation in Askitosh and a good advisory position in the government, as well as freedom to complete his life's work.

He felt the trembling which so often overcame him return. Temporising, he asked, What sort of advisory post?

Oh, advice on matters Borlienese, upon which he was such an expert. And they were preparing to leave Matrassyl on the hour.

So overwhelmed was he by this offer that SartoriIrvrash did not enquire why this sudden haste. Gratefully, he accepted.

"Excellent!" exclaimed Madame Dienu.

The two men behind her now showed an almost ancipital ability to change from stillness to intense activity without intervening stages. They were immediately gone from the room, to promote shouting on all floors and a galumphing on all stairs, as luggage and people hastened down into the courtyard below. Carriages emerged from shelters, hoxneys from stables, stable boys with harness from tackrooms. A procession was assembled in less time than a Borlienese could have drawn on a pair

of boots. Prayers were briskly said, all standing round in a circle, and
then they were away, leaving an empty house behind them.

They drove north through the warren of the old town, circled the
great semisubterranean Dome of Striving, and were soon on the road
north with the Takissa gleaming on their left-hand side. Roba yippeed
and sang as they went.

Weeks of travel followed.

A feature of the first part of their journey was the pervading greyness
caused by the volcanic ash. Mount Rustyjonnik, always a source of
grumbling and occasional runs of lava, was in full eruption. The country
in the path of its ash became a land of the dead. Trees were killed by the
substance, fields covered with it, streams clogged with it. After rain, it
turned to paste. Birds and animals died or fled the area. Human families
and phagors trudged away from their blighted homes.

Once the Sibornalese party had crossed the River Mar, the blight
grew less. Then it faded. They entered Mordriat—a name of terror in
Matrassyl. The reality was peaceful. Most of the tribes smiled beneath
sheltering layers of braffista turbans, their chief item of apparel.

Guides were engaged to guarantee their safety, thin villainous-looking
men who abased themselves at every sunrise and sunset. Round their
campfire at night, the head Pointer of the Way, as he called himself,
explained to the travellers how the ornamentation on his braffista indicated his rank in life. He boasted of the numerous ranks below his.

None listened more eagerly than SartoriIrvrash. "Strange, this human
propensity to create ranks in society," he observed to the rest of the
party.

"A propensity the more noticeable the nearer the bottom of the pile
one descends," said Madame Dienu. "We avoid such demeaning gradations in my land. How you will enjoy seeing Askitosh. It is a model for
all communities."

SartoriIrvrash had some reservations about that. But he found a rest-
ful quality in the steady severity of Madame Dienu after years of dealing
with a changeable king. As the wilderness grew more arid, his spirits
rose; equally, Roba's madness grew calmer. But when the others slept,
SartoriIrvrash could not. His bones, which had become accustomed to a
goosedown mattress, could not adapt to a blanket and hard ground. He
lay looking up at the stars and the lightning flickering between them, full
of an excitement he had not known since he and his brothers were
children. Even his bitterness against JandolAnganol abated somewhat.

The weather continued dry. The coaches made fair progress over the
low hills. They arrived at a small trading town called Oysha—"Quite
probably a corruption of the Local Olonets word 'osh,' meaning simply
'town,' " SartoriIrvrash explained to the company. Explanations that
could be attached to things made the journey more enjoyable. However

the word was derived, at Oysha the Takissa, rushing down from the east, met up with its formidable tributary, the Madura. Both rivers had their sources high in the limitless Nktryhk. Beyond Oysha to the north stretched the Madura Desert.

In Oysha, the coaches were exchanged for kaidaw geldings. The Pointer volubly made the deal, during which much striking of foreheads took place. The kaidaw was a reliable animal when it came to crossing deserts. The rust-coloured brutes stood in the dusty market square of Oysha, indifferent to the deal being negotiated beside them.

The ex-chancellor sat on a chest while the trading was in progress. He mopped his brow and coughed. The outfall from Mount Rustyjonnik had given him a sore throat and fever he could not shake off. He stared at the long haughty faces of the kaidaws—those legendary steeds of the warrior phagors in the Great Winter. It was hard to see in these slow beasts the whirlwind which, with phagors astride it, had brought destruction upon Oldorando and other Campannlatian cities in the time of cold.

In the Great Summer, the animals stored water in their single hump. This made them suitable for desert conditions. They looked meek enough now, but excited SartoriIrvrash's sense of history.

"I should purchase a sword," he told RobaydayAnganol. "I was quite a swordsman in my younger day."

Roba turned a cartwheel. "You turn the year upside down, now that you are free of the Eagle. You're right to defend yourself, of course. In those hills lives the accursed Unndreid—our herdsmen here sleep with his multitudinous daughters every night. Murder's as frequent hereabouts as scorpions."

"The people seem friendly."

Roba squatted before SartoriIrvrash and put on a cunning leer. "Why are they outwardly so friendly? Why is Unndreid now armed to the teeth with Sibornalese bang-bangs? Have you discovered why the big black Io Pasharatid left the court so suddenly?"

He took SartoriIrvrash's arm and led him behind one of the coaches for privacy, where only the guileless eyes of the kaidaws were upon them.

"Even my father cannot buy friendship or love. These Sibornalese buy friendship. It's their way. They'd trade their mothers for peace. They have been greasing their safe passage to Borlien by presenting the chiefs along the route with matchlocks, as they say. I say there is no match for them. Even Akhanaba's favourite king, JandolAnganol, son of VarpalAnganol, father of a Madi-lover—but not so mad in that direction as he—even that monarch of Matrassyl was no match for matchlocks. They did for him in the Battle of the Cosgatt. Did you ever see the wound in his thigh?"

"It kept your father abed. I saw only its effects, not the wound."

"He goes without a limp. Lucky not to go without a hard-on! That wound was a kiss from Sibornal."

Lowering his voice, SartoriIrvrash said, "You well know that I never trusted the Sibs. When the matchlocks were demonstrated in court, I advised that no Sibs should be present. My word went unheeded. It was shortly after the demonstration that Io Pasharatid disappeared."

Roba lifted a cautionary finger and wagged it slowly. "Disappeared because his swindles were then revealed—revealed to his wife, our fair companion, and his own ambassadorial staff. There was a local young lady involved, who acted as go-between . . . and whom I also go between, on occasions . . . that's how I know all about Io Pasharatid."

He laughed. "The matchlocks which Taynth Indred had in his possession—which he presented so arrogantly to my eagle-father—which my eagle-father took so pusillanimously, because he would take a plague scab from a beggar if it was offered—those matchlocks were sold to Taynth Indred cheap by Pasharatid. Why cheap? Because they were not his to sell, in which case he could not avoid making a profit. The guns were the property of his government, intended to buy friendship with such as the rogues you see here, and with such as Dervlish the Skull, who has proved his friendship a thousand times over."

"Unusual behaviour for a Sib. Especially one in high office."

"High office, low character. It was because of the young lady. Did you never see the way he eyed my fair mother—I mean, she who was my mother before she went away without farewell?"

"Pasharatid would have been put to death if your father had discovered his crime. I assume he is now back in Sibornal."

RobaydayAnganol shrugged eloquently. "We are following him. Madame Dienu is after his blood. To understand his lust for other ladies, simply contemplate union with her. Would you couple with a matchlock? . . . He'll be busy concocting a lying tale, to cover his sins. She will arrive and seek to destroy it. Ah, Rushven, no drama like a family drama! They will have old Io locked up in the Great Wheel of Kharnabhar, mark my words. It was a place of religion, now they lock up criminals there. Well, monks are also prisoners. . . . What a drama to come. You know the old saying, 'More than an arm up a Sibornalese sleeve.' I almost wish I were coming with you, to see what happens."

"But you are coming! My dear boy!"

"Ah, unky, no affection! Not for Anganols! No protests. I'm leaving you here. You go north with Madame. I go back south with this coach. I have my parents to look after . . . my ex-parents. . . ."

SartoriIrvrash's face showed his distress. "Don't leave me, lad, not with these villains. I shall be dead in no time."

Making funny running-away gestures, the prince said, "Well, that's escaping from being human, isn't it? I'm going to be a Madi in no time. Another escape, another escapade. It's the Ahd for me."

He jumped forward and kissed SartoriIrvrash on his bald pate.

"Good luck in your new career, old uncle. Green things will grow from us both!"

He leaped into the coach, cracked his whip over the hoxneys, and was away at a great pace. The tribesmen fell back in alarm, cursing him in the name of the sacred rivers. A cloud of dust swallowed the speeding vehicle.

The Madura Desert: Matrassyl began to seem a long way off. But the stars came nearer overhead and, on clear nights, the sickle of Yarap-Rombry's Comet blazed like a signpost on their way.

SartoriIrvrash stood shivering in the small hours when the fire had died and the other travellers were sleeping. He could not entirely lose his fever. He thought of BillishOwpin. His story of having come from another world seemed more likely here than it had done at the palace.

He walked by the tethered kaidaws and encountered the Pointer of the Way, standing silently smoking. The two men talked in low voices. The kaidaws uttered sniggering grunts.

"The animals are quiet enough," SartoriIrvrash said. "History pictures them as almost unmanageable brutes. To be ridden only by phagors. I've never seen a phagor riding one, any more than I have ever seen a cowbird with a phagor. Perhaps history was wrong on that point, too. I've spent a lifetime trying to disentangle history from legend."

"Perhaps they aren't so different," the Pointer said. "I can't read a single letter, so I have no strong opinion in the matter. But we smoke these kaidaws when they're mere calves—puff a veronikane up their nostrils. It seems to make them calm.

"I'll tell you a tale, since you can sleep no more than I." He sighed heavily in preparation for the burden of narrative. "Many years ago now, I went eastwards with my master, through the provinces controlled by Unndreid, up into the wilderness of the Nktryhk. It's a different world up there, very harsh world, with little air to breathe, yet people remain fit."

"Less infection at high altitudes," commented SartoriIrvrash.

"That's not what the people of the Nktryhk say. They say that Death is a lazy fellow who doesn't readily bother to climb mountains. I'll tell you one thing. Fish is a popular food. Often the fish may be caught in a river a hundred or more miles away. Yet it doesn't decay. You catch a fish here at dawn, it's bad by Freyr-set. Up in the Nktryhk, it remains good to eat for a small year."

He leaned over the back of one of the patient kaidaws and smiled. "It

was fine up there when you got used to it. Cold by night, of course. No
rain, never. And there, in the high valleys, is land ruled only by fuggies.
They're not as submissive as here. I tell you, it's a different world. The
fuggies ride kaidaws, ride them like the wind—aye, and have cowbirds
to sail at their shoulders. My understanding is that they come down and
invade the lowlands when snow falls here, whenever that may be. When
Freyr fails."

Nodding his head with interest and some disbelief, SartoriIrvrash
said, "But there can be few phagors at those altitudes, surely? What can
they eat, apart from your ever-fresh fish? There's no food."

"That isn't so. They grow crops of barley in the valleys—right up to
the snowbanks. All they need is irrigation. Every drop of water and
urine is precious. There's a virtue in that thin air—they have crops of
barley that ripen in three weeks."

"Half a tenner from sowing? Incredible."

"Nevertheless it is so," said the Pointer. "And the phagors share the
grain and never quarrel or use money. And the white cowbirds drive out
all other winged things bar the eagles. I saw it with my own eyes, when I
stood no higher than this quadruped's shoulders. I mean to go back one
day—no king or laws there."

"I'll make a note of all that, if you don't mind," said SartoriIrvrash.
As he wrote, he thought of JandolAnganol among his abandoned
buildings.

After the Madura, the long desolation of Hazziz. Twice they had to
pass through strips of vegetation, stretching from one bleak horizon to
another like god's hedges. Trees, shrubs, a riot of flowers, drew a line
across the face of the grasslands.

"This is/will be the uct," said Dienu Pasharatid, employing a translation of a Sibish continuous present tense. "It stretches across the
continent from east to west, following the lines of Madi migration."

In the uct, they saw Others. Madis were not the only beings to use the
verdant road. The Pointer of the Way shot an Other from a tree. It fell
to the ground almost at their feet, its eyebrows still twitching with shock.
They roasted it later over the campfire.

One day rain fell, closing across the grasslands like a snake's jaw.
Freyr climbed higher into the sky than it managed in Matrassyl. Sartori-
Irvrash still wished to travel only by dimday, according to upper class
Borlienese custom, but the other travellers would have none of that.

The nights spent sleeping in the open were over. The ex-chancellor
surprised himself by regretting their passing. Sibornalese settlements
were becoming more frequent, and in them the party stayed overnight.
Each settlement was built to the same plan. Smallholdings lay inside a

circle, with guard houses posted every so many paces along the perimeter. Between the smallholdings, roads like spokes of a wheel led in to one or more rings of dwellings which formed the hub. Generally, barns, stores, and offices encircled a church dedicated to the Formidable Peace, standing at the geometrical center of the wheel formation.

Grey-clad priests-militant ruled these settlements, supervising the arrival and departure of the travelling party, which was always given free food and accommodation. These men, who sang the praises of God the Azoiaxic, wore the wheel symbol on their garb and carried wheel locks. They did not forget that they were in territory traditionally claimed by Pannoval.

When it was almost too late, SartoriIrvrash noticed that the Pointer of the Way and his men were not allowed inside the Sibornalese settlement. Touching his braffista, their guide was taking his pay from one of the ambassadorial staff and making off, heading southwards.

"I must bid him farewell," said SartoriIrvrash. Dienu Pasharatid thrust a hand before him. "That is not necessary. He has been paid and he will leave. Our way ahead is clear."

"But I liked the man."

"But he is of no further use to us. The way is safe now, moving from settlement to settlement. They believe superstitious things, these barbarians. The Pointer told me he could lead us this far only because his tribe's land-octave came this way."

Pulling at his whiskers uncomfortably, SartoriIrvrash said, "Madame Dienu, sometimes old habits enshrine truth. The preference for one's own land-octave is not entirely dead. Men and women prosper best when they live along whatever land-octave they were born on. Practical sense lies behind such beliefs. Such octaves generally follow geological strata and mineral deposits, which influence health."

She flicked a smile on and off her boney face. "Naturally, we expect primitive peoples to hold primitive beliefs. It is that which anchors them to primitivism. Things are continuously better where we are going." This last sentence was evidently a direct translation into Olonets of one of many Sibish tenses.

Being of such high rank, Dienu Pasharatid addressed SartoriIrvrash in Pure Olonets. In Campannlat, Pure Olonets, as opposed to Local Olonets, was spoken only by high castes and religious leaders, mainly within the Holy Pannovalan Empire; it was becoming increasingly the prerogative of the Church. The main language of the northern continent was Sibish, a dense language with its own script. Olonets had made little headway against Sibish, except along some southern coasts where trade with the Campannlatian shore was common.

Sibish deployed multiple tenses and conditionals. It had no *y* sound. The substituted *i* was pronounced hard, while *ch*'s and *sh*'s were almost whistled. One result of this was to make a native of Askitosh sound sinister when speaking to a foreigner in the latter's own language. Perhaps the entire history of the continuous northern wars rested on the mockery that Sib-speakers made of a word like "Matrassyl." But behind the brief pursing of the lips involved lay the blind driving force of the climate of Helliconia, which discouraged unnecessary opening of the mouth for half the Great Year.

The travellers left their kaidaws at the southernmost settlement, where the Pointer went his way, and posted northwards from settlement to settlement on hoxneys.

After the twelfth settlement, they progressed up a slope which grew gradually steeper. It climbed for some miles. They were forced to dismount and walk beside their steeds. At the top of the rise stood a line of young rajabarals, high and thin, their bark of the translucence of celery. When the trees were gained, SartoriIrvrash laid a hand against the nearest tree. It was soft and warm, like the flank of his hoxney. He gazed up into the plumes high above him, stirring in the breeze.

"Don't look upward—look ahead!" said one of his companions.

On the other side of the crest lay a valley, sombre in its blue shades. Beyond it was a darker blue: the sea.

His fever had gone and was forgotten. He smelt a new smell in the air.

When they reached the port, even the northerners showed excitement. The port had a defiantly Sibish name, Rungobandryaskosh. It conformed to the general layout of the settlements they had passed, except that it consisted only of a semi-circle, with a great church perched centrally on the cliff, a beacon light on its tower. The other half of the circle, symbolically, lay across the Pannoval Sea in Sibornal.

Ships lay in nearby docks. Everything was clean and shipshape. Unlike most of the races of Campannlat, the Sibornalese were natural scafarers.

After a night in a hostel, they rose at Freyr-rise and embarked with other travellers on a waiting ship. SartoriIrvrash, who had never been on anything larger than a dinghy before, went to his small cabin and fell asleep. When he woke, they were preparing to sail.

He squinted out of his square porthole.

Batalix was low over the water, spreading a pathway of silver across it. Nearby ships were visible as blue silhouettes, without detail, their masts a leafless forest. Near at hand, a sturdy lad rowed himself across the harbour in a rowing boat. The light so obscured detail that boy and boat became one, a little black shape where body went forward as oars went back. Slowly, stroke by stroke, the boat was dragged through the dazzle. The oars plunging, the back working, and finally the dazzle yielding (and soon composing itself again), as the rower won his way to the pillars of a jetty.

SartoriIrvrash recalled a time when he as a lad had rowed his two small brothers across a lake. He saw their smiles, their hands trailing in the water. So much had been lost since then. Nothing was without price. He had given so much for his precious "Alphabet."

There were sounds of bare feet on deck, shouted orders, the creak of tackle as sails were raised. Even from the cabin, a tremor was felt as the wind started to catch. Cries from the dock, a rope snaking fast over the side. They were on their way to the northern continent.

It was a seven-day voyage. As they sailed north-northwest, the Freyr-days grew longer. Every night, the brilliant sun sank somewhere ahead of their bows, and spent progressively less time below the horizon before rising somewhere to the north of northeast.

While Dienu Pasharatid and her friends lectured SartoriIrvrash on the bright prospects ahead, visibility became dimmer. Soon they were enveloped in what one sailor, in the ex-chancellor's hearing, called "a regular Uskuti up-and-downer." A thick brown murk descended like a combination of rain and sandstorm. It muffled the ship's noises, covering everything above and below decks in greasy moisture.

SartoriIrvrash was the only person to be alarmed. The captain of the vessel showed him that there was no need to fear.

"I have sufficient instruments to sail through an underground cavern unharmed," he said. "Though of course our modern exploring ships are even better equipped."

He showed SartoriIrvrash into his cabin. On his desk lay a printed table of daily solar altitudes, to determine latitude, together with a floating compass, a cross-staff, and an instrument the captain called a nocturnal, by which could be measured the elevation of certain first magnitude stars, and which indicated the number of hours before and after midnight of both suns. The ship also had the means to sail by dead reckoning, with distance and direction measured systematically on a chart.

While SartoriIrvrash made notes of these matters, there was a great cry from the lookout, and the captain hurried on deck, cursing in a way the Azoiaxic One would hardly have commended.

Through the drizzle loomed brown clouds and, somewhere in the clouds, men were bellowing. The clouds became shrouds and sails. At the last possible minute, a ship as big as their own slid by, with hardly a foot of leeway between hulls. Lanterns were seen, faces—mainly savage and accompanied by shaking fists—and then all were gone, back into the hanging soup. The Sibornal-bound ship was alone again in its sepia isolation.

Passengers explained to the foreigner that they had just passed one of the Uskut "herring-coaches," fishing with curtain nets off the coast. The herring-coach was a little factory, since it carried salters and coopers among its crew, who gutted and packed the catch at sea, storing it in barrels.

Thoroughly upset by the near collision, SartoriIrvrash was in no mood to listen to a eulogy on the Sibornalese herring trade. He retired to his damp bunk, still wrapped in his coat, and shivered. When they landed in Askitosh, he reminded himself, they would be on a latitude of 30° N, and only five degrees south of the Tropic of Carcampan.

On the morning of the seventh day of the voyage, the banks of fog rolled back, though visibility remained poor. The sea was dotted with herring-coaches.

After a while, a sluggish stain on the horizon resolved itself into the coastline of the northern continent. It was no more than a ruled line of sandstone dividing almost waveless sea from undulating land.

Moved by something like enthusiasm for the sight of her homeland, Madame Dienu Pasharatid delivered SartoriIrvrash a brief geography lesson. He saw how the water was dotted with small ships. Uskutoshk had been forced to became a maritime nation because of the advance of ice southwards from the Circumpolar Regions—these regions being mentioned with hushed tones. There was little land for cultivation between sea and ice. The seas had to be harvested and sea lanes opened to the two great rich grain prairies of the continent—which she indicated as being distant with a sweep of her arm.

How distant, he asked.

Pointing westward and yet more westward, she named· the nations of Sibornal, pronouncing their titles with varied inflections, as if she knew them personally, as if they were personages standing on a narrow strip of land glaring southwards, with cold draughts from the Circumpolar Regions freezing their backs—and all with a strong inclination to march down into Campannlat, SartoriIrvrash muttered to himself.

Uskutoshk, Loraj, Shivenink, where the Great Wheel was situated, Bribhar, Carcampan.

The grainlands were in Bribhar and Carcampan.

Her roll call ended with a finger pointing to the east.

"And so we have rounded the globe. Most of Sibornal, you see, is isolated in the extreme, caught between ocean and ice. Hence our independence. We have mountainous Kuj-Juvec coming after Carcampan—it is scarcely populated by humans—and then the troubled region of Upper Hazziz, leading into the Chalce Peninsula; then we are safe back in Uskutoshk, the most civilized nation. You arrive at a time of year when we have both Freyr and Batalix in the sky. But for over half the Great Year, Freyr is eternally below the horizon, and then the climate

becomes severe. That's the Weyr-Winter of legend. . . . The ice moves
south, and so do the Uskuts, as we call ourselves, if we can. But many
die. Many die." She used a future-continuous tense.

Warm though it was, she shivered at the thought. "Some other people's lifetimes," she murmured. "Fortunately, such cruel times are still
far away, but they are hard to forget. It's a race memory, I suppose. . . .
We all know that Weyr-Winter will come again."

From the docks, they were escorted to a solid four-wheeled brake
with a canopy. Into this vehicle they climbed after human slaves had
piled in their baggage. Four yoked yelk then dragged them off at a good
pace, along one of the radial roads leading away from the quayside.

As they passed under the shadow of an immense church, Sartori-
Irvrash tried to sort out the impressions that thronged in on him. He was
struck by the fact that much of the wagonette in which they rode was
not of wood but metal: its axles, its sides, even the seats on which they
sat, all were metal.

Metal objects were to be seen on every side. The people crowding in
the streets—not jostling and shouting like a Matrassyl crowd—carried
metal pails or ladders or assorted instruments to the ships; some men
were encased in gleaming armoured jackets. Some of the grander buildings on the way flaunted iron doors, often curiously decorated, with
names in raised relief upon them, as if the occupants intended to live on
there perpetually, whatever happened in the Circumpolar Regions.

A haze in the sky warded off the heat of Freyr, which, to the visitor's
eye, stood unnaturally high in the sky at noon. The atmosphere of the
city was smokey. Although Sibornal's forests were thin in comparison
with the riotous jungles of the tropics, the continent had extensive lignite
and peat beds, as well as metal ores. The ores were smelted in small
factories in various parts of the city. Each metal was located in a definite area. Its refiners, its workers, and its ancilliary trades were grouped
about it, and its slaves about them. Over the last generation, metals had
become less expensive than wood.

"It's a beautiful city." One of the men leaned over to favour the
visitor with this observation.

He felt small, sniffed a small sniff, and said nothing.

From the wagonette, he could see how Askitosh's half-wheel plan
worked. The great church by the harbour was the axle. After a semicircle of buildings came a semicircle of farms, with fields, then another
semicircle of buildings, and so on, though various living pressures had in
some places broken down what to Borlienese eyes was an unnatural
symmetry.

They were delivered to a large plain building like a box, in which
slitlike windows had been cut. Its double entrance doors were of metal;
on them, in raised relief, were the words 1st. *Convential, Sector Six*. The

convential proved to be a cross between a hotel, a monastery, a nunnery, a school, and a prison, or so it appeared to SartoriIrvrash, as he explored the cell-like room he was given, and read the rules.

The rules declared that two meals were served per day, at twenty minutes past four and at nineteen, that prayers were held every hour (voluntary) in the church on the top floor, that the garden was open during dimday for relaxed walking and meditation, that instructions (whatever they were) might be had at all times, and that permission was needed before visitors left the establishment.

Sighing, he washed himself and settled down on the bed, letting gloom overcome him. But Uskutoshkan hospitality, like most things Uskutoshkan, was brisk, and in no time came a brisk rap at his door and he was conducted along a corridor to a banquet.

The banquetting hall was long and low, lit by slit windows, from which the activities of the street could be glimpsed in small vertical sections. The floor was uncarpeted, yet a touch of luxury, even grandeur, was added to the chamber by an enormous tapestry on the rear wall which depicted, upon a scarlet background, a great wheel being rowed through the heavens by oarsmen in cerulean garments, each smiling blissfully, towards an astonishing maternal figure from whose mouth, nostrils, and breasts sprang the stars in the scarlet sky.

So struck was SartoriIrvrash by the details of this tapestry that he itched to make a note or even a sketch; but he was thrust forward and introduced to twelve personages who stood waiting to receive him. Each was named for him in turn by Madame Dienu Pasharatid. None shook his proffered hand: it was not the habit in that country to touch the hands of anyone outside one's own family or clan.

He tried to grasp the complex names, but the only one to remain in his head was Odi Jeseratabhar, and that because it belonged to a Priest-Militant Admiral who wore a blue-and-grey striped uniform and was female. And moreover was beautiful in an austere way, with two fair tresses plaited and wound about her head to finish as two blond horns sticking forward with an impressive yet comical air.

All concerned smiled in an affable way upon their guest from Campannlat, and assembled themselves at the table with great noise of metal chairs scraping on the bare floor. As soon as they were seated, silence fell, and the greyest member of the dozen rose to say grace. The rest placed their forefingers on foreheads in the attitude of prayer. SartoriIrvrash did the same. The grace began, intoned in dense Sibish, with dextrous use of continuous present, conditional-eternal, past-into-present, transferential, and other tenses, to carry the message of thanks all the way to the Azoiaxic One. The length of the prayer was perhaps intended to be proportional to the distance.

It was over at last, and a meal of many minute courses, mainly vegetarian except for fish, and relying heavily on assorted raw and steamed seaweeds, was served by slave wenches. Fruit juices and an alcoholic drink called yoodhl, with a seaweed base, were served.

The one exceptional course, the only one which SartoriIrvrash could say he really enjoyed, was a spitted creature brought on with ceremony, which he guessed to be a pig. It was presented still on its spit and covered with a creamy sauce. Of this, he was given a small portion of breast. He was told it was "treebries." Only some days later did he discover that treebries was roast Nondad. It was a prized Uskutoshki delicacy, rarely served except to distinguished visitors.

While the banquet was still in progress, Dienu Pasharatid came round behind SartoriIrvrash's chair and spoke to him.

"Soon, the Priest-Militant Admiral will address us. What she says may alarm you. Do not be alarmed. I know you are not given to fear. Equally, I know you are not given to malice, so do not think ill of me because of my part in this."

The ex-chancellor was immediately alarmed and dropped his knife. "What is going to be said?"

"An important announcement which will affect your country's destiny and mine. Odi Jeseratabhar will give you the details. Just remember, I was forced to bring you here in order to clear my name of any stain shed on it by my husband's actions. Remember that you hate JandolAnganol and all will be well."

She left him and returned to her seat. He found himself unable to take another mouthful of food.

Once the complex meal was finished and spirit served, the speeches began.

First came a welcoming speech from a local panjandrum, couched in almost comprehensible terminology. Then Madame Dienu arose.

After a brief preliminary, she came to her point. Making an oblique reference to her husband, she said she felt she had to atone for his departure from diplomatic procedures. Therefore, she had rescued Chancellor SartoriIrvrash from the melancholy position in which he found himself and had brought him here.

Their distinguished visitor was in a position to do them, and Uskutoshk, and indeed the entire northern continent, a service which would go down in history and secure for his name a place in their annals. What that service was, their loved and respected Priest-Militant Admiral, Madame Odi Jeseratabhar, would now announce.

Premonitions of bad things made SartoriIrvrash feel even worse than the yoodhl had done. He longed for a veronikane but, seeing that nobody else at the table smoked, was smoking, was about to smoke, or was even employing the conditional-eternal to smoke, desisted, and gripped the table instead, as the Admiral rose.

Since she was making a speech, she employed a kind of Mandarin Priest-Militant Sibish.

"Priests-Militant, War Commissions members, friends, and our new ally," began the lady imposingly, tossing her blond horns, "time is always short, so I will/am cut my speech accordingly. In only eighty-three years, Freyr will be/is at its strongest, and in consequence the Savage Continent and its barbarous nations are/should in dire array, prophesying doom for themselves. They are/were incapable of facing the future as we in Uskutoshk—rightly, to my mind—pride ourselves in doing/done/continuing.

"Of the chief nations of that unhappy continent, Borlien in particular is/will in trouble. Unfortunately, our old enemy, Pannoval, continues/grows strong. A random factor not calculated has recently/now become apparent, with our arms trading growing beyond control, owing to delinquent ambassadors. We shall not dwell on that incident.

"Soon, the warlike nations of the Savage Continent will be making imitations of our weapons. We must/can act before that is allowed to happen to any great extent, while we have supremacy.

"As those of my friends on the War Commission already know, our plan is nothing less than to take over Borlien."

Her words struck the banqueters to silence. Then a great murmur of acclamation arose. Many eyes turned towards where SartoriIrvrash sat, white-faced.

"We have not/will not enough troops to hold down all of Borlien by force. Our plans is to annex and subdue by means provided unwittingly by the Borlienese king, JandolAnganol. Once we subdue Borlien, we can strike at Pannoval from the south as well as the north."

The banqueters began clapping before the fair Admiral had finished. They smiled first at each other and then at SartoriIrvrash, who kept his gaze firmly on the finely turned lips of the Admiral.

"We have a fleet ready to sail," said those lips. "We anticipate that Chancellor SartoriIrvrash will sail with it, to play his vital role. His reward will be great."

Again applause, rationed to a few hand claps.

"The fleet will sail westward. I shall be in command aboard the *Golden Friendship*. We intend/shall sail round the coast of Campannlat, finally approaching the Bay of Gravabagalinien, where Queen MyrdemInggala is/will exiled, from the west. The chancellor and I will stop to conduct the queen from that place of exile, while the rest of the fleet intend/will sail on to bombard Ottassol, Borlien's largest port, until it capitulates/has capitulated.

"The queen is/was/will well-loved by her people. SartoriIrvrash will proclaim a new government for Ottassol under the queen, with himself as prime minister. No battle need be fought.

"You will/should appreciate the feasibility of this plan. Our distinguished ally and the barbarian queen, descended from the Thribriat Shannana, are both united in a hatred of King JandolAnganol. The queen will be happy to be reinstated. She will of course be under our supervision.

"Once Ottassol is/can secure, our boats and soldiery will move upriver to take over the capital, Matrassyl. My understanding, based on agents' reports, is that we shall/can find allies there, notably the queen's old father and his faction. The king's insecure rule will be easily ended. His life the same. The world can do without such phagor lovers.

"With Borlien fallen into our hands, we execute a sabre slash northwards, right across the Savage Continent, from Ottassol in the south to Rungobandryaskosh.

"We are hastening matters forward now that you are here. Rest, friends, for action lies ahead, action of a most glorious sort. We plan that a good part of the fleet will/can/should sail at Freyr-rise, two days from now, God willing.

"A great future dawns/will dawn."

This time, the applause was unrationed.

XII

THE DOWNSTREAM PASSENGER TRADE

"The brute, unchanging ignorance of the people. . . . They labour and do not improve their lot. Or they don't labour. It makes no difference. They're interested in nothing beyond their own village—no, beyond their own belly buttons. Look at them, idle lot! If I were that stupid, I'd still be a pedlar in Oldorando City Park . . ."

The philosopher making these comments was sprawling among cushions, with cushions behind his head and another under his bare feet. By his right hand, he had a glass of his favourite Exaggerator, to which crushed ice and lemon had been added, while his left arm was wrapped about a young woman with whose left breast he was idly toying.

The audience to whom he was making these comments—excluding the young woman, whose eyes were closed—were two in number. His son leaned against the rail of the boat on which they were travelling, his eyes half closed and his mouth half open. This youth had a bunch of yellow-blue gwing-gwings by his side to eat and occasionally spat a gwing-gwing stone at other river traffic.

Propped up against the fo'c'sle where he was shaded from the sun lay a pallid young man who sweated a good deal and muttered still more. He was covered by a striped sheet, beneath which he moved his legs restlessly; he was running a fever and had been ever since the boat left Matrassyl on its journey south. This being one of his less lucid intervals, he scarcely seemed any more capable than the gwing-gwing eater of receiving the older man's wisdom.

This did not deter the older man.

"At that last stop we made, I asked one old fool who was leaning against a tree if he thought it was getting hotter, year by year. All he said was, 'It's always been hot, skipper, since the day the world was made.' 'And what day might that be?' I asked him. 'In the Ice Age, as I heard tell.' That was his reply. In the Ice Age! They've no sense. Nothing gets through to them. Take religion. I live in a religious country, but I don't believe in Akhanaba. I don't believe in Akhanaba because I have reasoned things out. These natives in these villages, they don't believe in Akhanaba—not because they have reasoned things out as I have, because they don't reason . . ."

He interrupted himself to take a firmer grasp on the left breast and a long drink of the Exaggerator.

". . . They don't believe in Akhanaba because they're too stupid to believe. They worship all kinds of demons, Others, Nondads, dragons. They still believe in dragons. . . . They worship MyrdemInggala. I asked my manager to show me round the village. In almost every hut, there hung a print of MyrdemInggala. No more like her than I am, but *intended* for her. . . . But, as I say, they're interested in nothing beyond their own belly buttons."

"You're hurting my bips," the young lady said.

He yawned and covered his mouth with his right hand, wondering absently why he enjoyed the company of strangers so much more than that of his own family: not just his rather stupid son, but his uninteresting wife and overbearing daughter. It would suit him to sail for ever down the river with this girl and this youth who claimed to come from another world.

"It's soothing, the sound of the river. I like it. I'll miss it when I'm retired. There's proof that Akhanaba doesn't exist. To make a complicated world like ours, with a steady supply of living people coming and going—rather like a supply of precious stones dug from the earth, polished, and sold off to customers—you would need to be really clever, god or no god. Isn't that so? Isn't it?"

He pinched with his left finger and thumb, so that the girl squealed and said, "Yes, if you say so."

"I do say so. Well, if you were so clever, what pleasure would it give you to sit up above the world and look down at the stupidity of these natives? You'd go out of your mind with the monotony of it, generation after generation, getting no better. 'In the Ice Age . . .' By the beholder . . ."

Yawning, he let his eyelids close.

She jabbed him in the ribs. "All right, then. If you're so clever, tell me who did make the world. If it wasn't Akhanaba, who was it?"

"You ask too many questions," he said.

Ice Captain Muntras fell asleep. He woke only when the *Lordryardry Lady* was preparing to moor for the night at Osoilima, where he was to enjoy the hospitality of the local branch of the Lordryardry Ice Trading Co. He had been enjoying the hospitality of each of his trading posts in turn, so that the journey downriver from Matrassyl had taken longer than was usually the case—almost as long as the upriver journey, when the boats of his ice trading fleet were towed against the stream by teams of hoxneys.

One reason had caused the shrewd Ice Captain, in his younger days, to establish an outpost at Osoilima, and that reason loomed over them as the *Lady* tied up. It towered three hundred feet above the crests of the brassims which flourished hereabouts. It dominated the surrounding jungle, it lorded it over the wide river, it pondered on its reflection in the water. And it drew pilgrims from the fourteen corners of Campannlat, eager for reverence—and ice. It was the Osoilima Stone.

The local manager, a grey-haired man with a broad Dimariam accent, by name Grengo Pallos, came aboard and shook his employer's hand warmly. He helped Div Muntras supervise passenger disembarcation. As phagors unloaded some bales of goods marked OSOILIMA, Pallos returned to the Ice Captain.

"Only three passengers?"

"Pilgrims. How's trade?"

"Not good. Have you nothing more for me?"

"Nothing. They've grown lazy in Matrassyl. Upheavals at court. Bad for trade."

"So I hear. Spears and money never rattle together. Bad about the queen. Still, if we unite with Oldorando, it may encourage more pilgrims here. Hard times, Krillio, when even the devout say it's too hot to travel. Where will it all end, I ask myself. You're retiring at the right time."

The Ice Captain drew Pallos aside. "I've got a special case here, and I don't know what to make of him. He's sick, his name's BillishOwpin. He claims to have come from another world. Maybe he's mad, but what he has to say is very interesting, if you can take it in. He thinks he's dying. But I say he's not. Could your old woman give him some special attention?"

"As good as done. We'll discuss the cost of accommodation in the morning."

So Billy Xiao Pin was helped ashore. Also ashore went the young lady, by name AbathVasidol, who was getting a free cruise down to Ottassol. Her mother, an old friend of the captain's, by name of Metty-Vasidol, kept a house on the outskirts of Matrassyl.

After the two traders had had a drink, they went to see Billy, now installed in the modest establishment ruled over by Pallos's wife.

He was feeling better. He had been scrubbed down the backbone with a block of Lordryardry ice, a sovereign remedy for all ills. The fever had gone, he was no longer coughing or sneezing—as they left Matrassyl, his allergy vanished. The captain told him he was not going to die.

"I shall die soon, Captain, but I am grateful for your kindness, all the same," said Billy. After the horrors of Matrassyl, it was bliss to be in the care of the Ice Captain.

"You won't die. It was that filthy volcano, Mount Rustyjonnick, pouring out its poison. Everyone in Matrassyl fell sick. Same symptoms as you—weepy eyes, sore throat, fever. You are fine now, fit to be on your feet. Never give in."

Billy coughed weakly. "You might be right. My life may have been prolonged by sickness. I shall surely die of helico virus, since I have no immunity to it, but the volcano may have postponed that fate for a week or two. So I must make the most of life and freedom. Help me to stand up."

In no time, he was walking about the room, laughing, stretching his arms.

Muntras and the manager's wife stood by, smiling at him. "What a relief, what a relief!" said Billy, "I was beginning to hate your world, Captain. I thought Matrassyl was going to be the death of me."

"It's not a bad place when you get to know it."

"But religious!"

Muntras said, "Where you have mankind and phagors together, you will have religion. The clash of two unknowns generates that kind of thing."

The wisdom of this remark impressed Billy, but Pallos's wife ignored it and took a firm grip on his upper arm.

"Why, you're fine," she said. "I'll wash you, and you'll feel completely fit again. Then we'll get some scoff into you, that's what you need."

Muntras said, "Yes, and I've another remedy for you, Billyish. I'll send in this pleasant young lady, Abath, daughter of an old friend of mine. Very nice willing girl. Half an hour of her company will do you a power of good."

Billy regarded him quizzically, and his cheeks grew red. "I told you I

am of completely different stock from you, not being born on Helliconia.
. . . Would it work? Well, we're identical physically. Would the young
lady *mind* . . . ?"

Muntras laughed heartily. "She'd probably prefer you to me. I know
how you're set on the queen, Billish, but don't let that put you off. Use
a little imagination, and Abath will be equal to the queen in every
way."

Billy's face was a study in red. "Earth, what an experience. . . . What
can I say? Yes, send her in, please, and let's see if it works . . ."

As the traders went out, Pallos laughed, rubbing his hands together,
and said, "He certainly shows an experimental spirit. Will you charge
him for the girl?"

Knowing Pallos's mercenary nature, Muntras ignored this question.
Perhaps catching the snub, Pallos asked hastily, "All his talk of dying—
do you think he comes from another world? Is that possible?"

"Let's have a drink, and I'll show you something he gave me." He
summoned up Abath, gave her a kiss on the cheek, and sent her in to
see Billish.

The evening shadows were taking on a velvet intensity. Batalix was in
the western sky. The two men sat companionably on Pallos's verandah
with a bottle and a lantern between them. Muntras brought up his heavy
fist, placed it on the table, and opened it.

In his palm lay Billy's watch, with its three dials, where small figures
flickered busily:

$$11:49:2 \qquad 19:06:52 \qquad 23:15:43$$

"It's a beauty. How much is it worth? Did he sell it to you?" Pallos
prodded it.

Muntras said, "It's unique. According to Billish, it tells the time here
in Borlien—this centre dial—and the time on the world he comes from,
and the time on another world he does not come from. In other words,
you could say this jewel is proof of his farfetched tale. To make a
complicated watch like this, you'd need to be really clever. Not mad.
More like a god. . . . Not but what I can't rid my mind of the notion he
is mad. Billish says the world which made this timepiece, the world he
comes from, rides above us, looking down on the stupidity of the natives. And it's a world made entirely by men like us. No gods involved."

Pallos took a sip of Exaggerator and shook his head. "I hope they
can't read my trading figures."

A mist was creeping in from the river. A mother was calling her small
boy home, warning him that greebs would crawl out of the water and eat
him in a single gulp.

"King JandolAnganol had this elegant timepiece in his hand. He took
it for an evil omen, that was plain. Pannoval, Oldorando, and Borlien
have to unite, and it's only their hrattocking religion that unites them.

The king is committed on such a course that he can't allow one element of religious doubt . . ."

He tapped the timepiece with a plump finger. "This amazing jewel is an element of doubt, right enough. A message of hope or fear, depending who you are." He tapped his breast pocket. "Like other messages I have entrusted to me. The world's changing, Grengo, I tell you, and not before time."

Pallos sighed and took a sip from his tumbler.

"Do you want to see my books, Krillio? I warn you takings are down on last year."

The Ice Captain looked across the top of the lantern at Pallos, whose face the light made cadaverous.

"I'm going to ask you a personal question, Grengo. Have you any curiosity? I show this timepiece, I tell you it came from another world. There's this odd feller Billish, getting his first ever rumbo on this earth —what could be going through his harneys? Doesn't all this waken your sense of mystery? Don't you want to know more? Isn't there something beyond your ledgers?"

Pallos scratched his cheek and then worked down to his chin, setting his head to one side to do so. "All those stories we listened to as kids. . . . You heard that woman call to her son that a greeb would get him? There's not been a greeb seen at Osoilima since I came here, and that's getting on for eight years. All killed for their skins. I wish I could trap one. The skins are worth a good price. No, Billish is telling you a story, boss. How would men go about making a *world*? Even if it was true, what then? It wouldn't help my figures, would it now?"

Muntras sighed, shuffling his chair round so as to be able to peer down into the mist, perhaps hoping that a greeb would emerge to prove Pallos wrong.

"When young Billish comes off the kooni, I think I'll take him up to the top of the Stone, if he's strong enough. Ask your old woman to get us some supper, will you?"

Muntras sat where he was when the local manager had gone. He lit a veronikane and remained smoking contentedly, absently watching the smoke ascend to the rafters. He did not even wonder where his son was, for he knew: Div would be in the local bazaar. Muntras's thoughts were much further away.

Eventually, Billy and Abath appeared, holding hands. Billy's face was only just wide enough to accommodate his grin. They sat down at the table without speaking. Without speaking, Muntras offered the Exaggerator bottle. Billy shook his head.

It was easy to see that he had undergone an emotional experience. Abath looked as composed as if she had just returned from church with her mother. Her features resembled a younger Metty's, but there was a lustre about her which Metty had lacked for many a day. Her gaze was bold, where Metty's was slightly furtive, but there was, thought Muntras, who considered himself a judge of human nature, the same kind of reserve to her as to her mother. She was escaping some kind of trouble in Matrassyl, which might account for her guarded manner. Muntras was content just to admire her in her light dress, which emphasised her generous young breasts and echoed the chestnut brown of her hair.

Perhaps there was a god. Perhaps he kept the world going, despite its idiocy, because of beauty like Abath's . . .

At length, Muntras exhaled smoke and said, "So, don't they go in for trittoming between man and woman on your world, Billish?"

"We are taught to trittom, as you call it, from the age of eight. It's a discipline. But down here—I mean with Abath—it's . . . the reverse of discipline . . . it's real. . . . Oh, Abathy . . ." Exhaling her name as Muntras exhaled smoke, he seized her and began to kiss her passionately, breaking off only to utter endearments. She responded in a minor key.

Billy shook Muntras's hand. "You were right, my friend, she is the equal of the queen in every way. Better."

The captain said, "Perhaps all women are equal and it is only in the imagination of men that differences lie. Remember the old saying, 'Every rumbo romps home to the same rhythm. . . .' You have a very vivid imagination, so I imagine that you found her a very good trittom in consequence. . . . Are koonis in our world as deep as in yours?"

"Deeper, softer, richer . . ." He fell to kissing the girl again.

The captain sighed. "Enough of that. Passion is as boring as drunkenness in other men. Go away, Abath. I want some sense out of this young man, if possible. . . . Billish, if you have managed to see over the top of your own prodo since we landed, you may have noticed the Osoilima Stone. You and I are going to ascend it. If you are well enough to mount Abath, you are well enough to mount the Stone."

"Very well, if Abath can come too."

Muntras gazed at him with an expression at once a scowl and a grin. "Tell me, Billish boy—you're really from Pegovin in Hespagorat, aren't you? They're great jokers there."

"Look." He sat down facing the captain. "I'm what I say—from another world. Born and brought up there, recently landed in the space-vehicle I described to you between fever fits. I would not lie to you, Krillio, because I owe you too much. I feel I owe you more than life."

A dismissive gesture. "You owe me nothing. People shouldn't owe others anything. Remember, I was a beggar. Don't think too much of me."

"You've worked with devotion and built up a great enterprise. Now you are the friend of a king. . . ."

Filtering a little smoke between pursed lips, Muntras said stonily, "That's what you think, is it?"

"King JandolAnganol? You are a a friend of his, aren't you?"

"I have dealings with his majesty, let's say."

Billy looked at him with a half-grin. "But you don't like him greatly?"

The Ice Captain shook his head, smoked, and said, "Billish, you don't care much for religion, no more than I. But I must warn you that religion is strong in Campannlat. Take the way his majesty threw your timepiece back at you. He is very superstitious and that's the king of the land. If you showed that object to the peasants of Osoilima, they would riot if you caught them at the wrong moment. They might make you a saint or they might kill you with pitchforks."

"But why?"

"It's the irrational. People hate things they don't understand. One madman can change the world. I tell you this only for your own good. Now. Come on." He stood up, sweeping his lecture away and laying a hand on Billy's shoulder. "The girl, the meal, my manager, the Stone. Practicalities."

What he demanded was done, and soon they were ready for the climb. Muntras discovered that Pellos had never been to the top of the Stone, despite living at the bottom of it for eight years. He was laughed into coming along as escort and marched beside them with a Sibornalese matchlock over one shoulder.

"Your figures can't be too bad if you can afford such artillery," Muntras said suspiciously. He trusted his managers no more than he trusted the king.

"Bought to protect your property, Krillio, and every roon of it hard earned. It isn't as though the pay's good, even when trade's good."

Their way lay along a track that ran back from the wharf to the small town of Osoilima. The mist was less thick here, and the few lights round the central square gave a semblance of cheer. Many people were about, attracted by a cooler breeze that had sprung up with sunset. Stalls selling souvenirs, sweets, or savoury waffles were doing fair business. Pallos pointed out one or two houses where pilgrims lodged which ordered Lordryardry ice regularly. He explained that most of the people wandering about, throwing their money away, were pilgrims. Some came here, drawn by a local tradition, to free slaves, human or phagor, because they had grown to believe it wrong to own another life. "Fancy giving away a valuable possession like that!" he exclaimed, disgusted with the foolishness of his fellow men.

The base of the Osoilima Stone was just by the square—or rather, the town and its square had been built close against the Stone. Closest of all was a hostelry, bearing the name The Freed Slave, where the Ice Captain bought four candles for the party. They went through its garden and began the ascent. Talipots grew by the Stone; they had to push away the stiff leaves in order to climb. Summer lightning flickered round them.

Others were already ascending. Their whispers sounded from above. The steps had been carved in the stone a long while ago. They spiralled round and round the rock, with never a hint of railing for security. The guiding lights of their candles flickered before their faces.

"I'm too old for this sort of thing," Muntras grunted.

But their slow progress led eventually to a level platform, and an arch led them into the top of the rock, where a dome had been hollowed. They could rest their elbows on the parapet and gaze in safety at the spread of mist-shrouded forest all round.

The sounds of the town reached them and the continuous noise of the Takissa. Music was playing somewhere—a double-clouth or, more likely hereabouts, binnaduria, and drums. And all about the forest, where rolls of mist allowed, they could make out dim lights.

"That's what they say," Abath chirped up. " 'Not an acre habitable, not an acre uninhabited.' "

"True pilgrims stay up here all night to watch the dawns," Muntras told Billy. "In these latitudes, there's never a day of the year when both suns aren't visible at some time. Different from where I come from."

"On the Avernus, Krillio, people are very scientific," said Billy, hugging Abath. "We have ways of imitating reality with video, 3D tactiles and so on, just as a portrait imitates a real face. As a result, our generation doubts reality, doubts if it exists. We even doubt if Helliconia is real. I don't suppose you understand what I mean . . ."

"Billish, I've travelled most of Campannlat, as a trader and before that as a beggar and pedlar. I've even been right far to the west, to a country called Ponipot beyond Randonan and Radado, where the continent ends. Ponipot is perfectly real, even if no one in Osoilima believes in its existence."

"Where is this Avernus world of yours then, Billish?" Abath asked him, impatient with the way the men talked. "Is it above us somewhere?"

"Mm . . ." The sky above was fairly clear of cloud. "There's Ipocrene, that bright star. It's a gas giant. No, Avernus is not risen yet. It is below us somewhere."

"Below us!" the girl gave a smothered laugh. "You are mad, Billish. You ought to stick to your story. *Below!* Is it a sort of fessup?"

"Where's this other world, Earth? Can you see that one, Billish?"

"It's too far away to see. Besides, Earth doesn't give out light like a sun."

"But Avernus does?"

"We see Avernus by light reflected from Batalix and Freyr."

Muntras thought.

"So why can't we see Earth by light reflected from Batalix and Freyr?"

"Well, it's too far away. It's difficult to explain. If Helliconia had a moon, it would be easier to explain—but in that case, Helliconian astronomy would be much more advanced than it is. Moons draw men's eyes to the sky better than suns. Earth reflects the light of its own sun, Sol."

"I suppose Sol is too far away to see. My eyes are not what they were anyway."

Billy shook his head and searched the northeastern sky. "It's somewhere over there—Sol and Earth, and Sol's other planets. What do you call that long straggly constellation, with all the faint stars at the top?"

Muntras said, "In Dimariam, we call that the Night Worm. Bless me, I don't see it very clear. Round these parts, they call it Wutra's Worm. Isn't that right, Grengo?"

"It's no good asking me the names of the stars," Pallos said, and sniggered as if to say, "But show me a gold ten-roon piece and I'll identify it for you."

"Sol is one of the faint stars in Wutra's Worm, about where its gills are."

Billy spoke jokingly, being slightly uneasy in the role of lecturer after his years as one of the lectured. As he spoke, the lightning was there again, laying them out momentarily for examination. The pretty girl, her mouth slightly open, staring vaguely where he was pointing. The local manager, bored, gazing into blackness, thumb tucked comfortably into the muzzle of his matchlock. The burly old Ice Captain, flattened hand up to his receding hairline, peering toward infinity with determination written over his countenance.

They were real enough—Billy was becoming used now, since he had been with Muntras and Abathy, to the idea of a *real* reality, abhorrent though it might have been to his Advisor on the Avernus, caught in an *unreal* Reality. His nervous system had been jarred into life by new experiences, textures, stinks, colours, sounds. For the first time, he lived fully. Those who looked down on him would consider him in hell; but the freedom moving throughout his frame told him he was in paradise.

The lightning was gone, sunk to nothing, leaving a moment of pitch before the mild night world returned to existence.

Billy wondered, Can I convince them about Avernus, about Earth? But they'll never convince me about their gods. We inhabit two different thought-*umwelts*.

And then came a questioning of darker tone. What if Earth was a figment of Avernian imagination, the god Avernus otherwise lacked? The devastating effects of Akhanaba and his battles against sin were apparent everywhere. What evidence was there for Earth's existence—

anything more than that fuzzy patch where Sol glimmered in the Worm to the northeast?

He postponed the uncomfortable question for some future time to listen to what Muntras was saying.

"If Earth is so far, Billish, how can the people there be watching us?"

"That's one of the miracles of science. Communication over very long distances."

"Could you write down for me how you do it, when we get to Lordryardry?"

"Do you mean to say that people out there—real people like us—" said Abath, "could be watching us even now? Seeing us big-like, not down the gullet of a worm?"

"It's more than possible, my darling Abath. Your face and your name may already be known to millions of people on Earth—or rather, that is to say *will* be known when a thousand years have passed, for that's how long it takes communications to get from Avernus to Earth."

Unimpressed by figures, she could think of only one thing. Putting her hand to her mouth, she moved her mouth closer to Billy's ear. "You don't suppose they will see us having a go on the bed, do you?"

Overhearing the remark, Pallos laughed and pinched her bottom. "You charge extra for anyone watching, don't you, girl?"

"You mind your own scumbing business," Billy told him.

Muntras pursed his lips. "What possible pleasure can they get, watching us in all our native stupidity?"

"What distinguishes Helliconia from thousands of other worlds," said Billy, returning to something like a dry lecturer's tone, "is the presence here of living organisms."

As they were digesting his remark, a noise reached them from the mist and the jungle, a prolonged shrilling, distant but clear.

"Was that an animal?" asked the girl.

"I believe it was a long horn blown by phagors," said Muntras. "Often a danger sign. Are there many free phagors hereabouts, Grengo?"

"There could be. The freed phagor slaves have learned men's ways and live quite comfortably in their own jungle settlements, I hear tell," said Pallos. "They never get very bright in the harneys, though—you can charge them a good high price for broken ice."

"They buy ice off you, phagors?" asked Abath, in surprise. "I thought it was only King JandolAnganol's Phagorian Guard that got treated to ice!"

"Well, they bring in things to Osoilima to trade—gwing-gwing stone necklaces, skins, and suchlike, so then they've the money to pay me for ice. They crunch it straightaway, standing in my store. Disgusting! Like a man drinking liquor."

Silence descended on them. They stood quiet, peering out at the night, under the limitless vault of stars. To their imaginations, the wilderness seemed almost as limitless, and it was from there that the occasional sound came—once a cry, as if even those rejoicing in newfound freedom suffered. From the stars came only the uninsistent signals of light and, from the great Stone below them, darkness.

"Well, the phagors won't worry us," said Muntras, curtly, breaking in on their speculations. "Billish, over where Sol is, over in that direction somewhere lies the Eastern Range, what people call the High Nktryhk. Very few people visit it. It's almost inaccessible, and only phagors live there, legend has it. When you have been riding on your Avernus, have you ever seen the High Nktryhk?"

"Yes, Krillio, often. And we have simulations of it in our recreation centres. The Nktryhk peaks are generally wreathed in cloud, so that we watch through infrared. Its highest plateau—which covers the top of the range like a roof—is over nine miles high, and protrudes into the stratosphere. It is a most impressive sight—awesome, to be true. Nothing lives on the very highest slopes, not even phagors. I wish I had brought a photograph to show you, but such things are heavily discouraged."

"Can you explain to me how to make—photogiraffes?"

"Photographs. I'll try, when we reach Lordryardry."

"Good, let's go down, then, and never mind hanging about for Akhanaba to appear. Let's get some food and sleep, and we will be off promptly in the morning, before noon."

"Avernus will be up in an hour. It will make a transit of the whole sky in about twenty minutes."

"Billish, you've been ill. You must be in bed in an hour. Food, then bed—alone. I must be your father on Earth—I mean to say, on Helliconia. Then if your parents watch us, they will be happy."

"We don't really have parents, only clans," Billy explained, as they went under the arch and prepared to descend. "Extra-uterine birth is practised."

"I will much enjoy your drawing me a picture of how you manage *that*," the Ice Captain said.

They spiralled back to the ground, Billy clutching Abathy's hand.

Downriver, the scenery changed. First one bank, then the other, became the scene of intensive cultivation. The jungles were left behind. They had entered the land of the loess. The *Lordryardry Lady* slipped into Ottassol almost before its passengers realised, unused as they were to cities which had withdrawn their existence underground.

As Div supervised the unloading of goods onto the quay, Ice Captain Muntras took Billy below decks and into a now empty cabin.

"You're feeling well?"

"Excellent. It can't last. Where's Abathy?"

"Listen to me, Billish, I want you to stay quiet here while I transact a little business in Ottassol. I must see an old friend or two. And I have an important letter to deliver. There are clever Johnnies here, not just country bumpkins. I don't wish anyone to know of your existence, you understand?"

"Why's that?"

Muntras looked him in the eye. "Because I'm an old bumpkin myself and I believe your tale."

Billy smiled with pleasure. "Thank you. You have more sense than SartoriIrvrash or the king."

They shook hands.

The bulk of the Ice Captain seemed almost to fill the little cabin. He leaned forward confidentially. "Remember how those two treated you, and do as I say. You stay in this cabin. No one must know of your existence."

"While you go ashore and get drunk again. Where's Abathy?"

A big hand came up in a cautionary gesture. "I'm getting old and I want no fuss. I will not get drunk. I will return as soon as possible. I want to get you safe to Lordryardry, where you will be well looked after, you and that magical timepiece of yours. There, you can tell me about the vessel that brought you here, and other inventions. But first I have some business to transact, and that letter to deliver."

Billy became more anxious. "Krillio, where is Abathy?"

"Don't make yourself ill again. Abathy has gone. You know she was travelling only as far as Ottassol."

"She's left without saying good-bye? Without a kiss?"

"Div was jealous, so I hustled her away. I'm sorry. She sent you her love. She's got a living to make, like everyone else."

"A living to make . . ." Speech failed him.

Muntras took the opportunity to slip nimbly out of the cabin and lock the door from the outside. He pocketed the key, smiling as he did so.

"I'll be back soon," he said reassuringly as Billy started to hammer on the door. He climbed the companionway stairs, crossed the deck, and strolled down the gangplank. Across the wharf was a tunnel leading into the loess. A notice above it read LORDRYARDRY ICE TRADING CO. TRANSIT GOODS ONLY.

This was a modest wharf. The main Lordryardry wharf was half a mile farther downstream, where the seagoing ships tied up, and a grander affair entirely. But here few eyes pried, and security was good. Muntras walked down the tunnel and entered a checking office.

Two clerks, alarmed to see the owner arrive, stood up, hiding playing cards under ledgers. The other occupants of the office were Div and Abath.

"Thank you, Div. Will you take these clerks away and let me have a moment alone with Abathy?"

In his sullen way, Div did as instructed. When the door had closed behind the three men, Muntras locked it and turned to the girl.

"Sit down, my dear, if you like."

"What do you want? The journey's over—at long last—and I ought to be on my way." She looked huffy and at the same time anxious. The sight of the locked door worried her. In a way she had of drawing down her mouth in displeasure, Muntras recognised her mother's gesture.

"Don't be cheeky, young lady. You've behaved properly till now, and I'm pleased with you. In case you don't realise it, Captain Krillio Muntras is a valuable ally for a young slip of a thing like you, old though I am. I'm pleased with you, and I intend to reward you for how amiable you were with me and Billish."

She relaxed slightly.

"I'm sorry. It's just that you were making a—a bit of a mystery of it. I mean, I would have liked to have said good-bye to Billish. What is wrong in his harneys?"

As she was talking, he was removing some silver pieces from his body belt. He held them out to her, smiling. Abath came closer and, as she reached out to take the money, he grasped her wrist tightly with his other hand. She gave a cry of pain.

"Now, girl, you can have this money, but first I'm going to get a confidence out of you. You know that Ottassol is a big port?"

He squeezed her wrist till she hissed, "Yes."

"You know there are therefore many foreigners in this big port?"

Squeeze. Hiss.

"You know among those foreigners are people from other continents?"

Another squeeze. Another hiss.

"Like Hespagorat, for instance?"

Squeeze and hiss.

"And even far Sibornal?"

Squeeze, hiss.

"Including people of the Uskut race?"

Squeeze—pause—hiss.

Although it seemed from the furrowing of Muntras's brow that this catechism was not over, he let go of the wrist, which had grown red during interrogation. Abath took the silver coins and tucked them into a pocket in the roll of luggage she had by her, making no comment beyond a dark look.

"Sensible girl. Take what you can in life. And I am correct in thinking that you had some dealings with a certain man of Uskut race, in Matrassyl, in the way of the usual commodities. Isn't that so?"

She looked defiant again and stood alertly as if thinking of attacking him.

"What usual commodities might those be?"

"The ones you and your mother trade in, my dear—money and kooni. Look, it is no secret to me, because I had the word off your mother and have kept it under my palm ever since. It's been so long that I need you to remind me of the name of that man of Uskut race with whom you exchanged those commodities."

Abath shook her head. Tears gleamed in her eyes. "Look, I thought you were a friend. Forget it! The feller's left Matrassyl anyhow, and gone back to his own country. He got into trouble. . . . That's why I came south, if you want to know. My mother should have held her slanje tongue."

"I see. Your money supply ran out—or ran away. . . . Now, I just want to hear you pronounce his name, and then you're free."

She put her hands up to her face and said into them, "Io Pasharatid." A moment's silence.

"You did aim high, my little fillock. I hardly believed it. The ambassador of Sibornal, no less! And not only kooni but guns involved. Did his wife know?"

"What do you think?" She was defiant again. She outshone her mother.

He became brisk. "Very well. Thank you, Abathy. You now are clear that I have a hold on you. You have a hold on me. You know about Billish. Nobody else must know about Billish. You must keep quiet and never mention his name, not even in your sleep. He was just one more customer. Now he has gone, and you've been paid.

"If you mention Billish to anyone, I shall slip a little note to the Sibornalese representative here, and you will be in trouble. In this religious land, intercourse between Borlienese ladies and foreign ambassadors is strictly illegal. It always leads to blackmail—or murder. If word gets out about you and Pasharatid, you'll never be seen again. Do we understand each other?"

"Oh, yes, you hrattock! Yes."

"Good. That's sensible. My advice is to keep your mouth and your legs closed. I'm going to take you to a friend of mine whom I have to see. He's a scholar. He needs a housemaid. He will pay you regularly and well. I'm not a natural bully, Abathy, although I enjoy getting my way. So I am doing you a favour—for your mother's sake as well as yours. You'd soon go to the bad on your own in Ottassol."

He paused to see what she said, but she merely watched him with untrusting eyes.

"Remain with my scholarly friend in his comfortable home, and you will have no need to turn into a whore. You can probably find a good husband—you're pretty and not a fool. It's a disinterested offer."

"And your friend'll keep an eye on me for you, I suppose?"

He looked at her and pushed his lips forward in a pout. "He's recently married and won't molest you. Come. We'll go and see him. Wipe your nose."

Ice Captain Muntras called a one-wheeled sedan. He and Abath-Vasidol climbed in and off went the sedan, pulled by two veterans of the Western Wars, who had between them two-and-a-half arms, three legs, and about the same number of eyes.

In this style, they creaked through the underground lanes of Ottassol and eventually entered Ward Court, where daylight shone down brightly from the square of sky overhead. At the bottom of a flight of steps was a solid door with a sign above. They climbed out of the cramped conveyance, the veterans accepted a coin, and Muntras rang the doorbell.

It was hardly to be expected of a man in his profession that Bardol CaraBansity, deuteroscopist, should show surprise, whoever called on him; but he did raise an eyebrow at the girl while shaking the hand of his old acquaintance.

Over wine, which his loving wife served, CaraBansity professed himself delighted to instal AbathVasidol in his household.

"I don't suppose you will wish to carry hoxney carcasses about, but there are less alarming jobs to be done. Good. Welcome."

His wife appeared less delighted by the new arrangement, but said nothing.

"Then, sir, I shall be off, with grateful compliments to you both," said Muntras, rising from his chair.

CaraBansity rose too, and this time there was no mistaking his surprise. Of recent years, the Ice Captain had developed leisurely habits. When delivering his fresh ice—of which the CaraBansity household and its corpses consumed a fair share—the trader generally settled in for a long pleasant talk. This haste must have some meaning, thought Cara-Bansity.

"In gratitude for the introduction to this young lady, I will at least ride with you back to your ship," he said. "No, no, I insist."

And he did insist, to such effect that the discomfitted Muntras found himself in no time with his knees pressed against the deuteroscopist's knees and their noses almost touching, and nowhere to cast his regard except into the eyes in front of his, as they jolted in a sedan towards the TRANSIT GOODS ONLY warehouse.

"Your friend SartoriIrvrash," the Ice Captain said.

"Well, I trust?"

"No. The king's dismissed him and he's disappeared."

"Sartori disappeared! Where?"

"If people knew where, it would not count as a disappearance," said Muntras humourously, dislodging one knee.

"What happened, for beholder's sake?"

"You've heard about the queen of queens, of course."

"She came through here on her way to Gravabagalinien. According to the newsletter, five thousand hats were mislaid, having been thrown carelessly into the air as she arrived at the royal dock."

"JandolAnganol and your friend fell out over the Massacre of the Myrdolators."

"And then he disappeared?"

Muntras nodded his head so gently that their noses scarcely touched. "Into the palace dungeons, where others have gone?"

"Very likely. Or was clever enough to flee the city."

"I must discover what has happened to his manuscripts."

Silence between them.

When the sedan chair reached the warehouse, Muntras said, resting his hand on the other's sleeve, "You are too kind, but there is no need for you to get out."

Looking as confused as possible, CaraBansity climbed out nevertheless. "Come, I know your ruse. A good one. My wife can become better acquainted with your pretty AbathVasidol while you and I have a quiet farewell drink aboard your boat, eh? Don't think I didn't grasp your scheme."

"No, but—" While Muntras was anxiously paying off the sedan men, the deuteroscopist was marching in his ponderous way towards the dock where the *Lordryardry Lady* was tied up.

"I expect you have a bottle of the Exaggerator aboard?" inquired CaraBansity cheerfully, as Muntras caught up with him. "And how did you acquire this young lady you have so kindly deposited with me?"

"She's a friend, of an old friend. Ottassol's a dangerous place for innocent young girls like Abathy."

There lay the *Lordryardry Lady*, with two phagor guards nearby, wearing armbands bearing the name of the company.

"I'm sorry, but I cannot let you aboard, my friend," said Muntras, stepping into CaraBansity's path, so that once more their eyes almost touched.

"Why, what's the matter? I thought this was your last trip?"

"Oh, I shall be back . . . I live only just across the sea . . ."

"But you are always terrified of pirates."

Muntras took a deep breath. "I will tell you the truth, and keep it under your palm. I have a case of plague on board. I should have

declared it to the port authorities but I didn't, being anxious to get
home. I cannot let you on board. Definitely. It would endanger your
life."

"Mm." CaraBansity wrapped a meaty fist round his chin, looking at
Muntras from under his brow. "In my trade, I'm familiar with disease
and probably immune to it. For the sake of the Great Exaggerator, I'll
take the risk."

"No, sorry. You're too good a friend to lose. I will see you again soon
when I'm in less of a hurry, and we'll drink ourselves under the table . . ."
Talking in a distracted manner, he shook CaraBansity's hand and
almost ran from him. Pounding up the ship's gangplank, he called out to
his son and anyone else aboard that they were going to sail immediately.

CaraBansity stood on the quay, watching until the Ice Captain disappeared below decks. He then turned slowly on his heel and began
walking away.

At a certain point into the lanes, he stopped short, snapped his fingers, and began to laugh. He thought that he had solved the minor
mystery. To celebrate a further success to deuteroscopy, he turned into
the next court and walked into a tavern where he was not known.

"A half-Exaggerator," he ordered. A treat for himself, a reward.
People gave themselves away with talk without knowing it, for the
underlying reason that they hated the feeling of guilt and therefore
betrayed themselves. With that understanding, he recalled what Muntras
had said in the sedan.

"Into the palace dungeons . . ." "Very likely." "Very likely" means
neither yes nor no. Of course. The Ice Captain had rescued Sartori-
Irvrash from the king and was smuggling him to safety into Dimariam.
The matter was too dangerous for Muntras to tell even SartoriIrvrash's
friend in Ottassol. . . .

Sipping the fuming drink, he let his mind wander over the possibilities
which this secret knowledge opened up.

In his long and colourful career, Ice Captain Muntras had had to
play some tricks on friend and enemy alike. Many mistrusted him; yet
towards Billy he felt strong paternal affection, reinforced perhaps by the
difficulties he experienced with his own son, the weak-minded Div. Muntras liked Billy's helplessness and valued the store of startling knowledge
which seemed so much a part of Billy. Billy was indeed a herald from
another world; Muntras did not doubt it. He was determined to protect
the strange creature from all comers.

But before setting sail for his homeland of Dimariam, he had a small
piece of business to attend to. His leisurely journey down the Takissa
had not made Muntras forget his promise to the queen. At his main

wharf in Ottassol, he summoned to his office one of his captains, the
man who sailed the coastal trader *Lordryardry Lubber*, and laid
MyrdemInggala's letter before him.

"You're bound for Randonan, yes?"

"As far as Ordelay."

"Then you will deliver this document to the Borlienese general,
Hanra TolramKetinet, of the Second Army. You are personally responsible for putting it into the general's hands. Understand?"

At the main wharf, the Ice Captain transferred Billy onto the fine
oceangoing *Lordryardry Queen*, the pride of his fleet. The ship was
capable of transporting 200 tons of finest block ice. Now, on its homeward journey, it carried cargoes of timber and grain. Together with an
excited Billy and a sullen Div.

A favouring breeze filled the sails until the cordage strained and sang.
The prow swung southwards like the needle of a magnet, pointing to
distant Hespagorat.

*The shores of Hespagorat, together with the doleful animals which
inhabited them, were familiar sights to everyone aboard the Earth Observation Station. They were watched with extra attention as the fragile
wooden ship bearing Billy Xiao Pin approached them.*

*Drama was not a feature of life aboard Avernus. It was avoided.
Emotion: superfluous, as "On the Prolongation of One Helliconian
Season Beyond the Human Life-span" had it. Yet dramatic tension was
evident, especially among the youth of the six great families. Everyone
was forced into the situation of disagreeing or agreeing with Billy's
actions.*

*Many said that Billy was ineffectual. It was more difficult to admit
that he showed courage and considerable ability to adapt to different
conditions. Under the arguments that raged was a wistful hope that
Billy might somehow convince people on Helliconia that they, the
Avernians, existed.*

*True, Billy appeared to have persuaded Muntras. But Muntras was not
considered to be important. And there were indications that Billy,
having convinced Muntras, would take no further steps in that direction,
but merely, selfishly, enjoy his remaining days before the helico virus
attacked him.*

*The great disappointment was that Billy had failed where Jandol-
Anganol and SartoriIrvrash were concerned. It had to be admitted that
they had on their minds matters of more immediate concern.*

*The question that few people on the Avernus asked was, What,
effectively, could the king and his councillor have done had they taken
the trouble to understand Billy and come to believe in the existence of
his 'other world'? For that question led to the reflection that Avernus*

was far less important to Helliconia than Helliconia was to Avernus.

Billy's successes and failures were compared with those of previous Helliconia Holiday winners. Few winners had done much better than Billy, if truth were told. Some had been killed as soon as they arrived on the planet. Women had fared worse than men: the noncompetitive atmosphere on the Avernus favoured equality of the sexes; on the ground, matters were conducted differently, and most women winners ended their lives in slavery. One or two strong personalities had had their stories believed, and in one case a religious cult had grown round this Saviour from the Skies (to quote one of his titles). The cult had died when a force of Takers eradicated the villages where the believers lived.

The strongest personalities to descend had concealed their origins entirely and lived by their wits.

One characteristic all winners shared. Despite often severe warnings from their Advisors, all had enjoyed or at least attempted sexual intercourse with the Helliconians. The moths always headed for the brightest flame.

Billy's treatment merely strengthened a general aversion among the families to the religions of Helliconia. The consensus was that those religions got in the way of sensible, rational living. The inhabitants—believers and unbelievers alike—were seen as struggling in the toils of falsehood. Nowhere was there an attempt to be placid and view one's life as an art form.

On distant Earth, conclusions would be different. The chapter in the long cavalcade of history which concerned JandolAnganol, Sartori-Irvrash, and Billy Xiao Pin would be watched with a grief superior to any on the Avernus, a grief in which detachment and empathy were nicely balanced. The peoples of Earth, for the most part, had developed beyond that stage where religious belief is suppressed, or supplanted by ideology, or translated into fashionable cults, or atrophied into a source of references for art and literature. The peoples of Earth could understand how religion allowed even the labouring peasants their glimpse of eternity. They understood that those with least power have most need of gods. They understood that even Akhanaba paved the way for a religious sense of life which needed no God.

But what they most thoroughly understood was that the reason why the ancipital race was untroubled by the perturbations of religion was that their eotemporal minds would not rise to such disquiet. The phagors could never aspire to a moral altitude where they would abase themselves before false gods.

The materialists of the Avernus, a thousand light-years from such thinking, admired the phagors. They saw how Billy had been better received below than in Matrassyl Palace. Some wondered aloud whether

*the next winner of a Helliconia Holiday should not throw in his lot with
the ancipitals and hope to lead them to overthrow mankind's idols.*

*This conclusion was reached after long hours of well-conducted argu-
ment. Underlying it was jealousy of the freedom of Helliconian mankind
even in its fallen state—a jealousy too destructive to be faced within the
confines of the Earth Observation Station.*

XIII

A WAY TO
BETTER WEAPONRY

The little year advanced, though seasonal effects were virtually obliterated under the great flood of Freyr's summer. The Church celebrated its special days. Volcanoes erupted. The suns swung over the bent backs of the peasants.

King JandolAnganol grew thin from waiting for his bill of divorcement to arrive. He planned another campaign in the Cosgatt, to defeat Darvlish and regain a measure of popularity. He camouflaged his inner anguish with constant nervous activity. Wherever he went, the phagor runt Yuli followed—together with other shades which vanished as the king turned his eagle gaze towards them.

JandolAnganol prayed, suffered a flagellation at the hands of his vicar, bathed, dressed, and strode out to the courtyard of the palace where the hoxneys were stabled. He wore a rich keedrant with forms of animals embroidered on it, silk trousers, and high leather boots. Over the keedrant he buckled leather armour trimmed with silver embellishments.

His favourite steed, Lapwing, was saddled. He mounted her. Yuli ran up, yipping and calling him Father; JandolAnganol pulled the creature up behind him. They set off at a trot into the hilly parkland behind the palace. Accompanying the king at a respectful distance went a detachment of the First Phagorian Guard—in whom, during these dangerous times, JandolAnganol reposed more trust than ever before.

The warm wind was on his cheek. He breathed deep. Everything about was dusted with grey in honour of distant Rustyjonnik.

"It's zzhoodin' today," called Yuli.

"Yes, shooting."

In a dell where brassims sent up their leathery branches, a target had been established. Several men in dark clothes were busy making arrangements. They became immobile as the king arrived, testifying to his power to freeze blood by his very majesty. The Phagorian arrived silently and formed a line, blocking the mouth of the dell.

Yuli jumped from Lapwing and scampered about, insensitive to occasion. The king remained in his saddle, brow ominous, as if he had power to freeze himself.

One of the frozen figures moved forward and saluted the king. He was a small thin man of unusual physiognomy, who wore the harsh sacklike garb of his trade.

His name was SlanjivalIptrekira. The name was regarded as rude and funny. Possibly it was this life's handicap which caused SlanjivalIptrekira in middle age to sport a great amount of gingerish side-whisker, reinforced by a phagor-ear moustache. This lent his otherwise mild aspect a ferocity, as well as creating a countenance with more sideways than vertical dimension.

He licked his lips nervously as he endured the hawkish gaze of the sovereign. His unease was occasioned, not by the innuendo of his name, but by the fact that he was Royal Armourer and Chief Ironmaster of the Ironmakers Corps. And by the fact that six matchlocks built under his direction in imitation of a Sibornalese artillery piece were about to be tested.

This was his second testing. An earlier six prototypes, tested half a tenner previously, had all failed to work. Hence the licking of the lips. Hence a tendency of SlanjivalIptrekira's knees to concatenate.

The king remained upright in the saddle. He raised a hand in signal. Figures came to life.

Six phagor sergeants were delegated to test the guns one by one. They marched forward, bovine faces expressionless, heavy shoulders set, their great shaggy bulks contrasting with the scraggy anatomies of the armourers.

SlanjivalIptrekira's new weapon bore the outward appearance of the original. The metal barrel was four feet long. It was bedded into a wooden stock which curved down to a foot a further two feet long. The barrel was bound to the stock with copper bands. The striking mechanism was forged of the best quality iron that the foundries of the Ironmakers Corps could produce. Silver chasing, decorated with religious symbols, had been added to the stock. As in the original, the weapon was loaded from the muzzle end by means of a ramrod.

The first phagor sergeant came up with the first weapon. He held it while an armourer primed it. The sergeant knelt, his lower leg turning forward instead of back, in a posture no human could achieve. At the muzzle end of the piece, a tripod supported part of the weight. The sergeant took aim.

"Ready, sire," said SlanjivalIptrekira, looking anxiously from weapon to majesty. The king gave an almost imperceptible nod.

The striker came down. The powder fizzled. With a mighty explosion, the gun blew to pieces.

The sergeant fell backwards, giving a guttural cry. Yuli ran squealing into the bushes. Lapwing shied. Birds flew screaming from the trees.

JandolAnganol steadied his mare.

"Try Number Two."

The sergeant was helped away, his face and chest leaking ichor. He made a small bleating noise. A second sergeant took his place.

The second gun exploded more violently than the first. Splinters of wood struck the king's chest armour. The sergeant had part of his jaw blown away.

The third gun would not fire. After repeated attempts, the ball rolled from its muzzle to the ground. The Royal Armourer laughed nervously, face ashen. "Better luck next time," he said.

There was better luck with the fourth gun. It went off as intended, and the ball buried itself near the edge of the target. It was a large target designed for archery and stood only two dozen paces away, but the firing was accounted a success.

The fifth gun cracked dismally along its barrel. The sixth gun fired its ball, although the target was missed.

The amourers stood close together, studying the ground at their feet. SlanjivalIptrekira came to the king's horse. He saluted again. His moustache trembled.

"We make some progress, sire. Our charges are perhaps too strong, sire."

"On the contrary, your metals are too weak. Be back here again in a week's time with six perfect weapons, or I'll flay every member of your corps, from you downwards, and drive you skinless into the Cosgatt."

He took one of the ruined guns, whistled up Yuli, and galloped away towards the palace, across the grey sward.

The innermost part of the palace-fortress—its heart, if palace-fortresses have hearts—was stifling. The sky above was overcast, and an echo of it was to be found on the ground, in every corner, on every ledge, cornice, moulding, nook and cranny, where the exhalations of distant Rustyjonnik refused to be swept away. Only when the king had passed through a thick wooden door, and then a second as thick as the first, did he escape the ash.

As the steps wound downwards, dark and cold thickened about him to embrace him like a soaked rug as he entered the subterranean set of chambers reserved for royal guests.

JandolAnganol strode through three interconnecting rooms. The first was the most fearful; it had served as a guard room, a kitchen, a mortuary, and a torture chamber, and still contained equipment relating to those earlier roles. The second was a bedroom, containing merely a bunk, though it too had served as a mortuary, and looked better suited to that purpose. In the end room sat VarpalAnganol.

The old king remained wrapped in a blanket, his feet against a grate in which smouldered a log fire. A high grille in the wall behind him allowed light to filter in and define him as a darkish lump on top of which a wispy skull was perched.

These things JandolAnganol had seen many times. The shape, the blanket, the chair, the grille, the floor, even the log that never burned properly in the dank atmosphere—all these did not alter through the years. It seemed as if only here, throughout his whole kingdom, could he look on enduring things.

Making a noise suggesting that he might need to clear his throat, the old king half-turned in his chair. His expression was half vacant, half crazy.

"It's I—Jan."

"I thought it was that same path again . . . where the fish jumped. . . . You . . ." He struggled to disentangle himself from his thoughts. "That's you, Jan? Where's Father? What time is it?"

"Nearly fourteen, if that's of any interest to you."

"Time's always of interest." VarpalAnganol gave a ghostly chuckle. "Isn't it time that Borlien bumped into Freyr?"

"That's an old wives' tale. I've something to show you."

"What old wife? Your mother's dead, lad. I haven't seen her for . . . or was she here? I forget. It may warm this palace up a bit . . . I thought I smelt burning."

"It's a volcano."

"I see. A volcano. I thought it might be Freyr. Sometimes my thoughts wander. . . . Do you want to sit down, lad?" He began struggling to his feet, but JandolAnganol pushed him back into the chair.

"Have you found Roba yet? He's born now, isn't he?"

"I don't know where he is—he's out of his wits, certainly."

The old king gave a cackle. "Very shrewd. Sanity can drive you mad, you know. . . . You remember how the fish used to jump in that pool? Well, there always was something wild about Roba. Almost a man now, I suppose. If he's not here, he can't shut you up, can he? Nor can you marry him off. What's her name? Cune. She's gone, too."

"She's in Gravabagalinien."

"Good. I hope he doesn't kill her. Her mother was a fine woman. What about my old friend Rushven? Is Rushven dead? I don't know what you do up there half the time. If you can halve time."

"Rushven's gone. I told you. My agents report that he has fled to Sibornal, much good that will do him."

Silence fell between them. JandolAnganol stood with matchlock in hand, reluctant to break into his father's rambling thoughts. He was getting worse than ever.

"Perhaps he'll see the Great Wheel of Kharnabhar. It's their sacred symbol, you know." With a struggle, and only by letting his blanket slip, he managed to screw his stiff old neck round to look at his son. "It's their sacred symbol, I said."

"I know it."

"Then try and answer when I speak to you. . . . What about that other fellow, the Uskuti, yes, Pasharatid? Did they catch him?"

"No. His wife left too, a tenner ago."

The old man sank back into the chair, sighing. His hands twitched nervously at the blanket. "Sounds to me as if Matrassyl's almost empty."

JandolAnganol turned his face away, towards the grey square of light. "Just me and the phagors."

"Did I ever tell you what Io Pasharatid used to do, Jan? When he was allowed to come and see me? Curious behaviour for a man of the northern continent. They are very self-controlled—not passionate, like the Borlienese."

"Did you scheme with him to overthrow me?"

"I just sat here while he dragged a table through, a heavy table. He used to put it under that little window. Did you ever hear such a thing?"

JandolAnganol began to pace about the cell, darting his gaze into the corners as if seeking a way of escape.

"He wanted to admire the view from your luxurious apartment."

The figure in the chair gave a bleat of laughter. "Precisely so. Admiring the view. Well put. A good phrase. And the view was of . . . well, if you get the table yourself, lad, you will see. You will see the windows of

MyrdemInggala's apartments, and her verandah . . ." He broke off for a
dry cough which rattled in his throat. The king paced faster. "You get a
view of the reservoir where Cune used to swim naked with her ladies-in-
waiting. Before you sent her away this was, of course. . . ."

"What happened, Father?"

"Well, that's what happened. I told you but you didn't listen. The
ambassador used to climb on to that table and watch your queen with
nothing on, or wearing only a piece of muslin. . . . Very . . . very
unorthodox behaviour for a Sibornalese. A Uskuti. Or for anyone really."

"Why didn't you tell me this at the time?" He stood confronting the
ancient shape of his father.

"Heh. You would have killed him."

"I should have killed him. Yes. No one would have blamed me."

"The Sibornalese would have blamed you. Borlien would have been
in worse trouble than it is already. You will not learn diplomatic sense.
That's why I didn't tell you."

JandolAnganol began to pace. "What a calculating old slanje you are!
Surely you must have hated what Pasharatid was doing?"

"No . . . what are women for? I have no objection to hate. It keeps
you alive, keeps you warm of nights. Hate is what brings you down here.
You came down here once, I forget what year it was, to talk about love,
but I only know about—"

"Enough!" cried JandolAnganol, stamping his boot on the flags. "I
shall never speak of love again, to you or anyone. Why do you never
help me? Why didn't you tell me what Pasharatid was up to? Did he ever
meet secretly with Cune?"

"Why don't you grow up?" Spite entered his voice. "I expect he crept
in to her warm nest every night . . ."

He cringed away, expecting a blow from his son's raised hand. But
JandolAnganol squatted by the chair instead.

"I want you to look at something. Tell me what you would do."

He lifted the homemade matchlock which had cracked along the barrel and placed it on his father's knee.

"It's heavy. I don't want it. Her garden's all neglected now . . ." The
ex-king pushed it so that it fell on the floor. JandolAnganol let it lie
there.

"That gun was made by SlanjivalIptrekira's corps. The barrel split on
firing. Out of six guns I had him make, only one worked properly. Of
the previous batch, none has worked. What has gone wrong? How is it
that our weapon-makers' corps, which claims to trace its foundation
back for centuries, cannot make a simple gun?"

The old heap in the chair remained silent for a while, pulling ineffectually at its blanket. Then it spoke.

"Things don't get better for being old. Look at me. Look at the figure

behind you. . . . It may be that too many institutions are too old. . . .
What was I going to say? Rushven told me that the various trades corps
were founded to exist through the Great Winter, to hand on their knowledge in secret from generation to generation, so that their arts survived
the black centuries until spring."

"I have heard him say as much. . . . What follows?"

VarpalAnganol's wheezy voice strengthened. "Why, what follows
spring is summer. What follows seasons is that the corps perpetuate
themselves, maybe losing a little knowledge from one generation to
another but not gaining new knowledge. They become hidebound. . . .
Try to imagine what those centuries of darkness and frost were like—
much like being stuck down in this hole for eternity, I imagine. Trees
died. No wood. No charcoal. No fires for smelting properly. . . . Probably it's the smelting process at fault, by the look of that barrel. The
furnaces . . . they may need renewing. Better methods, as the Sibornalese have . . ."

"I'll flog them all for their idleness. Then perhaps we'll see some results."

"Not idleness, tradition. Try chopping Slanji's head off and then offering rewards. That will encourage innovation."

"Yes. Yes, possibly." He picked up the gun and made for the door.

The old man called feebly to him. "What do you want the guns
for?"

"The Cosgatt. The Western Wars. What else?"

"Shoot the enemies nearest your doorstep first. Teach Unndreid a
lesson. Darvlish. Then you'll be safer to fight farther away."

"I don't need your advice on how to wage war."

"You're afraid of Darvlish."

"I'm afraid of no one. Of myself, sometimes."

"Jan."

"Yes?"

"Ask them to send me logs which burn, will you?" He began to cough
rackingly.

JandolAnganol knew he was only shamming.

To show himself properly humble, the king went to the great dome in
the main square of Matrassyl. Archpriest BranzaBaginut greeted him at
the North Door.

JandolAnganol prayed publicly among his people. Without thought,
he took with him his pet runt, who stood patiently by his master while
the latter prostrated himself for an hour. Instead of pleasing his people,
JandolAnganol displeased them by taking a phagor into the presence of
Akhanaba.

His prayer, however, was heard by the All-Powerful, who confirmed that he should take VarpalAnganol's advice regarding the Ironmakers Corps.

Yet JandolAnganol vacillated. He had enough enemies without taking on one of the corps, whose power in the land was traditional, and whose chiefs were represented on the scritina. After private prayer and scourging, he went lengthily into pauk, to be counselled by the fessup of his grandfather. The battered grey cage floating in obsidian comforted him. Again, he was encouraged to act.

"To be holy is to be hard," he said to himself. He had promised the scritina that he would devote himself wholeheartedly to his country. So it should be. Matchlocks were necessary. They would compensate for lack of manpower. Matchlocks would bring back the golden age.

Accompanied by a mounted troop of the Royal First Phagorian Guard, JandolAnganol went to the quarters of the Ancient Corps of Ironmakers and Swordsmen and demanded admittance. The great shadowy place opened up to him. He entered their quarters, which led into the rock. Everything here spoke of long-dead generations. Smoke had come like age to blacken everything.

He was greeted by officers with ancient halbards in some kind of uniform, who tried to bar his way. Chief Ironmaster SlanjivalIptrekira came running with ginger whiskers bristling—apologising, yes, bowing, yes, but stating firmly that no nonmember of the corps (barring possibly the odd woman) had ever entered these premises, and that they had centuries-old charters showing their rights.

"Fall back! I am king. I will inspect!" shouted JandolAnganol. Giving a command to the phagorian guard, he moved forward. Still mounted on their armoured hoxneys, they surged into an inner courtyard, where the air stank of sulphur and tombs. The king climbed from his mount, going forward surrounded by a strong guard while other soldiers waited with the hoxneys. Corpsmen came running, paused, scurried this way and that, dismayed at the invasion.

Red in the face, SlanjivalIptrekira still fell back before the king, protesting. JandolAnganol, showing his teeth in a holy snarl, drew his sword.

"Run me through if you will," shouted the armourer. "You are for ever cursed for breaking in here!"

"Rhhh! You lurk underground like miserable fessups! Out of my way, slanje!"

He pressed forward. The invading party went in under grey rock, thrusting into the entrails of the establishment.

They came to the furnaces, six of them, pot-bellied, made of brick and stone, patched and repatched, towering up to a murky roof, where ventholes in the rock showed as blackened cavities. One of the furnaces was working. Boys were shovelling and kicking fuel into a gleaming eye of heat, as fire roared and raged. Men in leather aprons drew a tray of red-hot rods from the furnace door, set them on a mutilated table, and stepped back, tight-lipped to see what the excitement was.

Further into the chamber, men were kneeling by anvils. They had been hammering away at iron rods. Their din stopped as they stood to see what was happening. At the sight of JandolAnganol, blank amazement covered their faces.

For a moment, the king too was stopped. The terrible cavern astonished him. A captive stream gushed along a trough to work the enormous bellows placed by the furnace. Elsewhere were piled timbers and instruments as fearful as any used in torture. From a separate side cavern came wooden tubs bearing iron ore. Everywhere, blacksmiths, iron smelters, craftsmen—half naked—peered at him with pink-rimmed eyes.

SlanjivalIptrekira ran before the king, his arms raised, waving, fists clenched.

"Your Majesty, the ores are being reduced by charcoal. It is a sacred process. Outsiders—even royal personages—are not allowed to view these rites."

"Nothing in my kingdom is secret from me."

"Attack him, kill him!" cried the Royal Armourer.

The men carrying glowing iron bars lifted them with thick leather gloves. They looked at each other, then set them down again. The king's person was sacred. Nobody else moved.

With perfect calm, JandolAnganol said, "Slanji, you have uttered a treasonable command against your sovereign, as all those here bear witness. I will have every member of the corps executed without exception if anybody dares make a move against my royal person."

Brushing past the armourer, he faced two men at a table.

"You men, how old are these furnaces? For how many generations has metalcraft continued in this manner?"

They could not answer for fear. They wiped their blackened faces with their blackened gloves, which effected no improvement in their appearance.

It was SlanjivalIptrekira who answered, in a subdued voice. "The corps was founded to perpetuate these sacred processes, Your Majesty. We but do as we are bid by our ancestors."

"You are answerable to me, not to your ancestors. I bid you make good guns and you failed." He turned to the corpsmen who had gathered silently in the fumous chamber.

"You men, all, and apprentices. You carry out old methods. Those old methods are obsolete. Haven't you the wits to understand? There are new weapons available, better than we can make in Borlien. We need new methods, better metals, better systems."

They looked at him with dark faces and red-rimmed eyes, unable to understand that their world was ending.

"These rotten furnaces will be demolished. More efficient ones will be built. They must have such furnaces in Sibornal, in the land of the Uskuti. We need furnaces like the Sibornalese. Then we shall make weapons like the Sibornalese."

He summoned up a dozen of his brute soldiery and commanded them to destroy the furnaces. The phagors seized crowbars and commenced without question to carry out their orders. From the live furnace, when its wall was broached, molten metal burst forth. It flashed across the floor. A young apprentice fell screaming under its flood. The metal set fire to wood shavings and timber. The corpsmen shrank away aghast.

All the furnaces were broken. The phagors stood by for further orders. "Have them built anew, according to directions I shall send you. I will have no more useless guns!" With these words, he marched from the building. The corpsmen came to themselves and threw buckets of water over their blazing premises. SlanjivalIptrekira was arrested and jostled off into captivity.

The following day, the Royal Armourer and Ironmaster was tried before the scritina and convicted of treason. Even the other corps-masters could not save SlanjivalIptrekira. He had ordered his men to attack the person of his king. He was executed in the public view, and his head exhibited to the crowd.

Enemies of the king in the scritina, and not his enemies only, nor only in the scritina, were nevertheless angered that he had ventured into premises by long tradition sacrosanct. This was another mad act which would never have been committed had Queen MyrdemInggala been near to keep his madness under control.

JandolAnganol, however, sent a messenger to Sayren Stund, King of Oldorando, his future father-in-law. He knew that the destruction of the city of Oldorando, when it had been overcome by phagor invasion, had resulted in the craft corps' being reformed, and their equipment renewed. Their foundries should therefore be more advanced than Borlien's. He remembered at the last moment to send his neighbour a gift for Simoda Tal.

King Sayren Stund sent JandolAnganol a dark hunchbacked man called Fard Fantil. Fard Fantil came with credentials showing him to be an expert in iron furnaces who understood new methods. JandolAnganol sent him to work immediately.

Immediately, a delegation from the Ironmakers Corps, ashen of face, came before the king to complain of Fard Fantil's ruthlessness and sullen ways.

"I like sullen men," roared JandolAnganol.

Fard Fantil had the premises of the guild moved to a hillside outside Matrassyl. Here the timber was available for charcoal and the supply of running water was constant. The water was necessary to power stamping mills.

No one in Borlien had ever heard of stamping mills. Fard Fantil explained in supercilious fashion that this was the only way to crush ore effectively. The corpsmen scratched their heads and grumbled. Fard Fantil cursed them. Furious at being turned out of their town quarters, the men did all they could to sabotage the new establishment and bring the foreigner into disgrace. The king still received no guns.

When Dienu Pasharatid disappeared from the court so unexpectedly, following her husband to Uskutoshk, she had left behind some Sibornalese staff. These JandolAnganol had imprisoned. He ordered an Uskut brought before him and offered him his freedom if he would design an effective iron smelter.

The cool young man had perfect manners, so perfect that he made a flourish whenever he addressed the king.

"As your majesty knows, the best smelters come from Sibornal, where the art is advanced. There we use lignite instead of charcoal for fuel, and forge the best steel."

"Then I wish you to design a smelter for use here, and I shall reward you."

"Your majesty knows that the wheel, that great basic invention, came from Sibornal, and was not known in Campannlat until a few centuries ago. Also many of your new crops are from the north. Those furnaces which you destroyed—even that design came from Sibornal during a previous Great Year."

"Now we wish for something more up-to-date." JandolAnganol restrained his temper.

"Even when the wheel was brought to Borlien, Your Majesty, full use was never made of it, not only for transport, but in milling, pottery, and irrigation. You have no windmills in Borlien as we have in Sibornal. It has seemed to us, Your Majesty, that the nations of Campannlat have been slow to adopt the arts of civilisation."

It was noticeable that about the king's jaw a roseate flush mounted as the sun of his anger was dawning.

"I'm not demanding windmills. I want a furnace capable of producing steel for my guns."

"Your majesty possibly intends to say guns imitated from the Sibornalese model."

"No matter what I intend to say, what I do say is that I require you to build me a good furnace. Is that understood, or do you only speak Sibish?"

"Forgive me, Your Majesty, I had thought you understood the position. Permit me to explain that I am not an artisan but an ambassadorial clerk, nimble with figures but not with bricks and suchlike. I am if anything less able to build a furnace than your majesty."

Still the king received no guns.

The king spent an increasing amount of time with his phagor soldiery. Knowing the necessity for repeating everything to them, he impressed upon them every day that they would accompany him in strength to Oldorando, in order to make a grand display in the foreign capital on the occasion of his marriage.

Places were delegated in the palace grounds where king and phagor guard met on equal terms. No human entered the phagorian barracks. To this rule the king subscribed, as VarpalAnganol had before him. There was no question of his venturing beyond a certain point in the way he had invaded the traditional quarters of the Ironmakers Corps.

His chief phagor major was a gillot by name Ghht-Mlark Chzarn, addressed by JandolAnganol as Chzarn. They conversed in Hurdhu.

Knowing the ancipital aversion to Oldorando, the king explained once more why he required the presence of the First Phagorian at his forthcoming marriage.

Chzarn responded.

"Speech has been made with our ancestors in tether. Much speech has formed in our harneys. It is delivered that we make a goance with your sovereign body to Hrl-Drra Nhdo in the land Hrrm-Bhhrd Ydohk. That goance we make at command."

"Good. It is good we make goance together. I rejoice that those in tether are in agreement. Have you further to say?"

Ghht-Mlark Chzarn stood impassive before him, her deep pink eyes almost level with his. He was aware of her smell and of the barely audible sound of her breathing. His long acquaintance with phagors told him that more speech was to come. The members of the guard behind her were equally impassive, pressing together, coat against coat. An occasional fart broke from their ranks.

Impatient man though JandolAnganol was, something in the deliberation of phagors—in that intense impression that what they said came not from them only but rather from a great distance, relayed from some ancestral store of understanding to which he could never have access—soothed him. He stood before his major almost as still as she before him.

"Further sayance." Ghht-Mlark Chzarn went through a formula with which the king was familiar. Before a new subject could be broached, linkages with those in tether must be sustained. Thus was aneotic thought endured.

They confronted each other, as tradition demanded, in a military room called the Clarigate; humans entered at one end, phagors at the other. The walls were painted by phagors in swirling greens and greys. The ceiling was so low that its beams were scarred by tracks of ancipital horn points—possibly a deliberate device to emphasise the fact that the Phagorian Guard were never dehorned.

One god only protected the king, Akhanaba, the All-Powerful; many demons tormented him. Phagors were not among those demons; he was accustomed to the steady calculation of their speech, never regarding them—as did his fellow men—as either slow-witted or convoluted in thought.

And in these days of his inner torment, he found a new factor to admire about his guard. They were not sexually preoccupied. He considered that the streams of lubricious thought which occupied the minds of men and women at court—and his own mind, despite applications of god and rod—were absent from ancipital harneys.

There was a periodicity to phagor sexuality. Gillots came into oestrus every forty-eight days, while the stalluns performed the sexual act every three weeks. Coitus was joined without ceremony and not always privately. Because of this lack of shame in what to humans was an act more secret than prayer, the ancipital race was a symbol of lust. The goat foot, the erect horns, were emblems of rut to humanity. Tales of stalluns raping women—and on occasion men—were common and could lead to drumbles and purges in which many phagors were killed.

When the phagor major arrived at her thought, it was brief. "In our goance to Hrl-Drra Nhdo in the land Hrrm-Bhhrd Ydohk, it is delivered your ancipital host must make great presence. So your power burn bright before Hrl-Drra Nhdo people. Commendation comes that that host on parade must have carriance of . . ." A long pause while the concept struggled through into speech. ". . . Of new weapons."

With considerable pain, JandolAnganol said, "We need the new hand artillery from Sibornal. As yet, we cannot produce them in Borlien."

Beads of condensation stood on the walls of the Clarigate. The heat was overpowering. Chzarn made a gesture the king knew well, signifying "Stand."

He repeated his statement. She repeated the "Stand" gesture.

After consultation both with those living and with those in tether, the phagor major declared that the needed weapons would be obtained. Although the king understood the struggle phagors underwent to verbalise the aneotic, he was compelled to ask them how the weapons would be obtained.

"Much speech has form in our harneys," said Chzarn, after another pause.

There was an answer. She switched to Eotemporal to be clear in her tenses. An answer would be delivered, was even now about to be delivered, but must nevertheless wait upon another time, another tenner. His power would be made great in Hrl-Drra Nhdo. Hold horns high.

He had to be content with that.

For farewell, JandolAnganol leant forward, hands to side, neck extended. The gillot also leaned forward, her head protruding over dugs and great barrel of body. Unhorned head met horned head, foreheads touched, harneys were together. Then both parties turned smartly away.

The king left by the Humans Only door of the Clarigate.

Excitement moved in his eddre. His Phagorian would provide their own arms. What faithfulness was theirs! What devotion, deeper than that of human beings! He did not reflect on other possible interpretations of Chzarn's speech.

Briefly, he thought of the happy days when his flesh invaded Cune's delectable queme flesh; but those times of ease and venery were dead. His concern must now be with these creatures, who would help him rid Borlien of its enemies.

Chzarn and the phagor soldiery departed from the Clarigate in a spirit different from the king's. They could scarcely be said to have an alteration of mood. Blood flow hastened or slowed in response to breathing; so much was true.

What was spoken in the Clarigate was reported by Ghht-Mlark Chzarn to the Matrassyl Kzahhn, Ghht-Yronz Tharl himself. The kzahhn reigned under his mountain, unknown even to the king. At this time of evil, when Freyr flew nearer down the air-octaves with his scorching breath, the ancipitals generally despaired. The ichor became sluggish in their veins. Lowland components allowed themselves to fall wholly under human subjugation. But a sign had been given them and hope stirred in their eddre.

To Kzahhn Ghht-Yronz Tharl had been brought a remarkable Son of Freyr, a captive of the disgraced chancellor, by name Bhrl-Hzzh Rowpin. Bhrl-Hzzh Rowpin came from another world and knew almost as much about the Catastrophe as the ancipitals did. To them under the mountain, Bhrl-Hzzh Rowpin had delivered ancient truths which other Sons of Freyr rejected. The things he spoke had gone unheeded by the chancellor and by the king; but the component of Ghht-Yronz Tharl heeded them and determination took form in their harneys.

For the speech of the strange Son of Freyr reinforced voices from tether which sometimes seemed to grow faint.

The Sons of Freyr were badly made, with poor componentalism. So it was with the king, as the faithful spy Yuli reported. For the weak king now offered them a chance to strike back against their traditional enemy. By seeming to obey him, they could stamp their hurt and harm against Hrl-Drra Nhdo, ancient Hrrm-Bhrrd Ydohk. It was a hate-place cursed long ago by one of the Great Ones now only a keratinous image, the Crusading Kzahhn, Hrr-Brahl Yprt. Red ichor would flow there again.

Courage was needed. Be valiant. Hold horns high.

For the required hand artillery, they had only to follow favourable air-octaves. The phagors were on occasion allies of the Nondads and aided them against the Sons of Freyr. The Nondads struggled against the Sons of Freyr called Uskuts. Uskuts—shame to speak it—devoured dead bodies of Nondads, denying them the comfort of the Eighty Darknesses. . . . The Nondads would with their light fingers take hand artillery from the Uskut race. And the hand artillery would bring dismay to the Sons of Freyr.

So it came about. Before another tenner passed, King JandolAnganol was armed with Sibornalese matchlocks—weapons supplied not by his allies in Pannoval or Oldorando, not forged by his own armourers, but brought by devious routes as a gift from those who were his enemies.

In such a fashion, a better way of killing spread slowly across Helliconia.

Belatedly, after many disputes, Fard Fantil the hunchback established his weapon factory outside Matrassyl. The newly acquired weapons served as models. After much cursing of his work force, the hunchback produced native matchlocks which did not blow up and fired with some accuracy.

By then, Sibornalese manufacturers had improved their designs and perfected a wheel-lock piece, which fired the powder pan by means of a revolving flint wheel rather than the old untrustworthy fusee.

Made confident by his new armoury, the king buckled on his breast-plate, saddled Lapwing, and rode forth to war. Once more he led an ahuman army against his enemies, the rag and bobtail of Driat tribes who terrorised the Cosgatt under Darvlish the Skull.

The two forces met only a few miles from where JandolAnganol had sustained his wound. This time, the Eagle of Borlien was more experienced. After a day-long conflict, victory was his. The First Phagorian followed him blindly. The Driats were killed, routed, thrown into ravines. The survivors scattered among the tawny hills from which they had emerged.

For the last time, the vultures had reason to praise the name of Darvlish.

The king returned in triumph to his capital, with the head of Darvlish mounted high on a pole.

The head was placed above the gate of Matrassyl palace, there to fester until Darvlish was in reality nothing but a skull.

* * *

Billy Xiao Pin was by no means the only male among the inhabitants of Avernus to dream of Queen MyrdemInggala. Such private things were seldom admitted even to friends. They emerged only indirectly in that evasive society—for instance, in a general execration of King Jandol-Anganol's latest behaviour.

The sight of the Thribriatan warlord's head on JandolAnganol's gatepost was enough to provoke a howl of protest from this faction.

One of its spokesmen said, "This monster tasted blood with the death of the Myrdolators. Now he is accumulating the weapons for which he traded the queen of queens. Where will he stop? Plainly, we should check him now, before he plunges all Campannlat into war."

Just as JandolAnganol was enjoying some of the popularity he hoped for in Borlien, he roused unusual opprobrium on the Avernus.

The complaints brought against him had been heard before of other tyrants. It was more convenient to blame the leader than the led; the illogic of that position was seldom remarked. Shifting conditions, short-ages of foodstuffs and materials, guaranteed that Helliconian history was a constant series of bids for power, of dictators gaining wide support.

The suggestion that Avernus should move in to put an end to one particular oppression or another was also far from new. Nor was inter-vention an entirely idle threat.

When Earth's colonising starship entered the Freyr-Batalix system in 3600 A.D., it established a base on Aganip, the inner planet closest to Helliconia. On Aganip, 512 colonists were landed. They had been hatched aboard the starship during the final years of its voyage. The information encoded in the DNA of fertilized human egg cells had been stored in computers during the voyage. It was transferred into 512 arti-ficial wombs. The resultant babies—the first human beings to walk the ship during its one-and-a-half millennium flight—were reared by surro-gate mothers in several large families.

The young humans ranged in age from fifteen to twenty-one Earth years old when they landed on Aganip. The construction of the Avernus was already in process. Automation and local materials were used.

Owing to more than one near disaster, the ambitious construction programme had taken eight years. During that hazardous period, Aganip was used as a base. When the job was complete, the young colonists were ferried aboard their new home.

The starship then left the system. The inhabitants of the Avernus were alone—more alone than any humans had ever been before.

Now, 3269 Earth years later, the old base was a shrine, occasionally visited by the enlightened. It had become part of Avernian mythology.

There were minerals on Aganip. It would not be impossible to shuttle to the planet and there construct a number of ships with which to in-

vade Helliconia. Not impossible. But unlikely, for there were no technicians trained for such a project.

The hotheads who whispered of such things had to work against the
whole ethos of the Earth Observation Station, which was strictly non-
interventionist.

Also, the hotheads were male. They had to contend with the female
half of the population, who admired the troubled king. The women
watched JandolAnganol defeat Darvlish. It was a great victory. Jandol-
Anganol was a hero who suffered much for his country, shortsighted
though that aim might be. He was a tragic figure.

The sort of intervention this female faction dreamed of was to descend to Borlien and be by JandolAnganol's side, day and night.

And when these events at last reached Earth?

There would be much nodding of approval at JandolAnganol's choice
of which piece of Darvlish's anatomy to exhibit. Not the Skull's feet,
which had carried the man into skirmish after skirmish. Not his genitals,
which had fathered so many bastards to create future trouble. Not his
hands, which had silenced many a foe. But his head, where all the other
mischief had been co-ordinated.

XIV

WHERE FLAMBREG LIVE

White shadows filled the city of Askitosh. They lay entangled among grey buildings. When a man walked along the pale roads, he took on their pallor. This was the famous Uskuti "silt-mist," a thin but blinding curtain of cold dry air which descended from the plateaux standing behind the city.

Overhead, Freyr burned like a gigantic spark in the void. Sibornalese dimday reigned. Batalix would rise again in an hour or two. At present only the greater star remained. Batalix would rise and sink before Freyr-set and—in this early spring season—would never attain zenith.

Wrapped up in a waterproof coat, SartoriIrvrash looked upon this phantasmal city as it slipped from view. It sank away into the silt-mist, became bare bones, and then was gone entirely. But the *Golden Friend-ship* was not entirely alone in the mist. From forwards, a well-muffled observer could make out the jolly boat ahead with the ancipital rowers straining as they pulled the warship out of harbour. At hand, too, were glimpses of other spectral ships, their sails hanging limp or flapping like dead skin, as the Uskuti fleet started on its mission of conquest.

They were out in the sullen channel when a blur on the eastern horizon marked Batalix-rise. A wind got up. The striped sails above them began to stir and tighten. Not a sailor on board but felt a lightening in spirit; the omens were right for a long voyage.

Sibornalese omens meant little to SartoriIrvrash. He shrugged his thin shoulders under his padded keedrant and went below. On the companionway, he was overtaken by Io Pasharatid, the ex-ambassador to Borlien.

"We shall do well," he said, nodding his head wisely. "We set sail at the right time and the omens are fulfilled as decreed."

"Excellent," said SartoriIrvrash, yawning. The seagoing priests-militant of Askitosh had mustered every deuteroscopist, astromancer, uranometrist, hieromancer, meteorologician, metempiricist, and priest they could lay hands on to determine the tenner, week, day, hour, and minute on which the *Golden Friendship* should most auspiciously sail. The birth signs of the crew and the wood of which the keel was made had been taken into account. But the most persuasive sign lay in the heavens, where YarapRombry's Comet, flying high in the northern night sky, was timed to enter the zodiacal constellation of the Golden Ship at six-eleven and ninety seconds that very morning. And that was the precise time when the hawsers were cast off and the rowers began to row.

It was too early for SartoriIrvrash. He did not contemplate the long and hazardous voyage with cheer. His stomach felt queasy. He disliked the role that had been thrust upon him. And, to crown his discomfort, here was Io Pasharatid, marching about the ship and being suspiciously friendly, as if no disgrace had ever befallen him. How did one behave to a man like that?

It seemed that Dienu Pasharatid could arrange anything. Perhaps because of her cunning appropriation of JandolAnganol's ex-chancellor into her plans, and the designs of her war commission, she had saved her husband from prison. He had been allowed to sail with the soldiery of the *Golden Friendship* as a hand-artillery captain—perhaps in an understanding by the powers-that-be that a long sea voyage in a 910-ton carrack was as bad as a prison sentence, even a sentence in the Great Wheel of Kharnabhar.

Despite this narrow escape from justice, Pasharatid was more arrogant than ever. He boasted to SartoriIrvrash that, by the time they reached Ottassol, he would command the soldiery; so he stood every chance of commanding the Ottassol garrison.

SartoriIrvrash lay on his bunk and lit a veronikane. He was immediately hit by seasickness. It had not troubled him on the way to Askitosh. Now it made up for lost time.

For three days, the ex-chancellor declined all rations. He woke on the fourth day feeling superlatively well and made his way on deck.

Visibility was good. Freyr was eyeing them across the waters, low to the north of northeast, somewhere in the direction from which the *Golden Friendship* had come. The shadow of the ship danced across the smalts of the fresh sea. The air was steeped in light and tasted wonderful. SartoriIrvrash stretched up his arms and breathed deep.

No land was to be seen. Batalix was set. Of the ships which had escorted them from harbour as guard of honour, only one remained, sailing two leagues to leeward with its flags streaming in the wind. Almost lost in blue distance was a cluster of herring-coaches.

So delighted was he at being able to stand without feeling wretched, so loud was the song of canvas and shrouds, that he scarcely heard the greeting addressed to him. When it was repeated, he turned and looked up into the faces of Dienu and Io Pasharatid.

"You've been ill," said Dienu. "My sympathies. Unfortunately, Borlienese are not good sailors, isn't that so?"

Io said quickly, "At least you feel better now. There's nothing like a good long voyage for the health. The journey is approximately thirteen thousand miles, so with favouring winds we should be there in two tenners and three weeks—off Ottassol, that is."

He devoted himself over the next few days to taking SartoriIrvrash on a tour of the ship, explaining its working in the last detail. SartoriIrvrash made notes of what little interested him, wishing in his Borlienese heart that his own country had such expertise in nautical matters. The Uskuti and other nations of Sibornal had guilds and corps which were in general principle similar to those of the civilised Campannlatian nations; but their maritime and military guilds excelled all others in numbers and efficiency, and had/would (for the tense was conditional-eternal-subjunctive) triumphantly survived the Weyr-winter. Winter, Pasharatid explained, was especially severe in the north. Over the coldest centuries, Freyr remained always below the horizon. The winter was always in their hearts.

"I believe that," said SartoriIrvrash solemnly.

In Weyr-winter, even more than in the Great Summer, the peoples of the ice-bound north depended on the seas for survival. Sibornal therefore had few private ships. All ships belonged to the Priest-Sailors Guild. Emblems of the guild decorated the sails of the ship, making of its functionalism a thing of some beauty.

On the main sail rode the device of Sibornal, the two concentric rings joined by two undulant spokes.

The *Golden Friendship* had a fore-, main-, and mizzen-mast. An artemon projecting over the bowsprit was raised only in favouring winds, to speed progress. Io Pasharatid explained exactly how many square feet of sail could be hoisted at any time.

SartoriIrvrash was not entirely averse to being bored by a stream of

facts. He had devoted much of his life trying to ascertain what was
speculation, what fact, and to have a constant flow of the latter was not
without attraction. Nevertheless, he speculated as to why Pasharatid
should go to such lengths to show friendship; it was hardly a predominant Sibornalese characteristic. Nor had it been in evidence in Matrassyl.

"You stand in danger of tiring SartoriIrvrash with your facts, dear,"
said Dienu, on the sixth day of their voyage.

She left them where they were standing, tucked back at the highest
point of the poop, behind a pen containing female arang. Not a foot of
deck but was used for something—rope, stores, livestock, cannon. And
the two companies of soldiers they had aboard were forced to spend
most of the day, wet or fine, standing about on deck, impeding the
movements of the sailors' guildsmen.

"You must miss Matrassyl," said Pasharatid, speaking firmly into the
wind.

"I miss the peace of my studies, yes."

"And other things as well, I imagine. Unlike many of my fellow
Uskuts, I enjoyed my time in Matrassyl. It was very exotic. Too hot, of
course, but I did not mind that. There were fine people with whom I
came in contact."

SartoriIrvrash watched the arang fighting to turn round in their pen.
They provided milk for the officers. He knew that Pasharatid was coming to his point at last.

"Queen MyrdemInggala is a fine lady. It is a shame that the king has
exiled her, do you not think?"

So that was it. He waited before replying.

"The king saw that his duty lay in serving his country . . ."

"You must feel bitter at his treatment of you. You must hate him."

When SartoriIrvrash did not reply to that, Pasharatid said, or rather,
shouted quietly in his ear, "How could he bear to give up a lady as
lovely as the queen?"

No response.

"Your countrymen call her 'the queen of queens,' is that not correct?"

"That is correct."

"I never saw anyone so beautiful in my life."

"Her brother, YeferalOboral, was a close friend of mine."

This remark silenced Pasharatid. He appeared almost about to
terminate the conversation when, with a burst of feeling, he said, "Just
to be in Queen MyrdemInggala's presence—just to see her—made a
man—affected a man like . . ."

He did not finish his sentence.

* * *

Weather conditions were changeable. A complex system of high and low pressure areas brought fogs, hot brownish rains, such as they had encountered on the voyage across to Sibornal—"regular Uskuti up-and-downers"—and periods of clarity where the featureless coastlines of Loraj could sometimes be glimpsed to starboard. Still they made good time, with pursuing winds either warm from the southwest or chilly from west of northwest.

Boredom drove SartoriIrvrash to become familiar with every part of the ship. He saw how the men were so cramped that they slept on deck on coils of rope, or on bins below deck, their heels propped high on the bulkheads. There was not an inch of spare space.

Day by day, the smell of the ship grew stronger. To perform their solid excretions, the men pulled off their trousers and worked their way along a spar set over the side of the ship, on which they had to balance, with a rope coming down from the yardarm to hold onto. Urination was performed to leeward, over the rail—and in dozens of other places, judging by olfactory evidence. The officers fared almost as badly. The women enjoyed better privacy.

After almost three weeks at sea the course was changed from due west to west by northwest, and the *Golden Friendship* and its companion sailed into Persecution Bay.

Persecution Bay was a great and melancholy indentation over one thousand miles long and five hundred miles deep on the coast of Loraj. Even at its mouth, the sea slackened, while day by day the wind dropped and the temperature fell. Soon they moved through a pearly haze, broken only by the shouts of the duty man calling the depth. They travelled now by dead reckoning.

Impatience seized SartoriIrvrash. He retired to his kennel of a cabin to smoke and read. Even those occupations were unsatisfactory, for his stomach howled like a lost dog. Already, ship's rations were causing him, a thin man at the best of times, to tighten his belt. Men's rations were salted fish, onions, olive or fish oil with bread every morning, soup at midday, and a repetition of breakfast for the evening meal, with hard cheese substituted for fish. A mug of fig wine or yoodhl was served to each man twice a week.

The men supplemented this diet with fresh-caught fish, hooked over the side. Officers fared little better, apart from an issue of pungent arang milk occasionally, to which was added brandy for those on watch. The Sibornalese complained at this diet in no more than a routine way, as if inured to it.

Moving forward at five knots, they crossed the line of 35°N, thus leaving the tropics for the narrow northern temperate zone. On that same day, they heard fearsome crashings through the mist, and a series of huge waves set the ship rocking. Then silence again. SartoriIrvrash

poked his head out of his cabin and enquired of the first seaman who
passed what it was.

"Coast," said the man. And in a fit of communicativeness added a
further word, "Glaciers."

SartoriIrvrash nodded in satisfaction. He turned back to his notebook, which was, for want of better occupation, becoming a diary.

"Even if the Uskuti are not civilised, they are enlarging my knowledge
of the world. As is well known among scholars, our globe is set between
great bands of ice. To the extreme north and the extreme south are lands
consisting only of ice and snow. The miserable continent of Sibornal is
especially loaded with this bothersome stuff, which may account for the
dead hearts of its people. Now it seems they steer towards it, as if drawn
by a magnet, instead of sailing on towards the warmer seas.

"What the purpose of this deviation might be, I shall not enquire—
not wishing to risk further lectures from my personal demon, Pasharatid.
But it may at least permit me to glimpse that horrid expanse which
makes up the alpha and omega of the world."

In the night came a ferocious storm which was on them without
warning. The *Golden Friendship* could only heave to and weather it out.
Immense waves burst against the hull, sending spray high into the spars.
There were also ominious knockings which resounded through the ship,
as if some giant of the deep was asking to be admitted aboard—so
thought the ex-chancellor of Borlien, as he clung terrified to his bunk.

He doused the single whale-oil light in the cabin, as orders demanded.
In the noisy dark he lay, by turns cursing JandolAnganol and praying to
the All-Powerful. The giant of the deep by now had firm hold of the ship
in both hands and was rocking it as some maniac might rock a cradle, in
an attempt to pitch the baby out upon its nose. To his later astonishment, SartoriIrvrash fell asleep while this decanting process was at its
height.

When he roused, the ship was silent again, its movement barely discernible. Beyond the porthole lay more mist, lit by meagre sunshine.

Moving to the companionway, past sleeping soldiers, he stared up at
the sky. Tangled among the rigging was a pallid silver coin. He looked
upon the face of Freyr. Back to memory came the fairy story he had
enjoyed reading in the queen of queens' company to TatromanAdala,
about the silver eye in the sky that had sailed away at last.

The duty man called soundings. On the sea floated floes of ice, many
carved into absurd forms. Some resembled stunted trees or monstrous
fungi, as if the god of ice had taken it into his head to devise grotesque
counterparts to living nature. These were the things that had come
knocking at the heights of the storm, and it was a cause for gratitude
that few bergs were half as big as the ship. These mysterious forms
emerged from the mist, only to recede again into abstraction.

After a while, something made SartoriIrvrash shift his attention and look up. Across a narrow stretch of water were two phagor heads. The eyes in those heads stared not at the passing ship but at each other. . . . There were the long face with its misanthropic jaw, the eyes protected by boney ridges, the two horns curving upwards.

And yet. No sooner had he recognised the beasts than SartoriIrvrash knew he was mistaken. These were no phagors. He was seeing two wild animals which confronted each other.

The movement of the ship caused the mist to swirl apart, revealing a small island, no more than a tussock in the sea, yet with a steep little cliff on the near side. Perched on the island's barren crown stood two four-legged animals. Their coats were brown. Apart from their colour and their stance, they markedly resembled ancipitals.

Nearer view diminished the resemblance. These two animals, for all that they were challenging each other, had none of the stubbornness, the independent look which characterised phagors. It was, in the main, the two horns which had caused SartoriIrvrash to jump to the wrong conclusion.

One of the animals turned its head to look at the ship. Seizing the instant, the other animal lowered its forehead and rammed forward with a powerful shoulder movement. The sound of the blow reached the ship. Though the animal had moved no more than three feet, the whole weight of its body from its rear legs on was behind the butt.

The other animal staggered. It tried to recover. Before its head could go down, a second butt came. Its rear feet slipped. It fell backwards, struggling. It struck the water with a great splash. The *Golden Friendship* drifted onward. The scene was hidden in the mist.

"I expect you recognise them," said a voice at SartoriIrvrash's elbow. "They're flambreg, of the bovidae family."

Priest-Militant Admiral Odi Jeseratabhar had scarcely spoken to SartoriIrvrash during the voyage. He had, however, lost no chance in observing her about her duties. She had a good head and carried herself well. Despite the severe lines of her face, her manner was animated, and the men responded willingly to her orders. The inflections of her voice and her uniform proclaimed her to be a grand person; yet her approach was informal, conveying even a hint of eagerness. He liked her.

"This is a desolate shore, ma'am."

"There are worse. In primitive times, Uskotoshk used to land its convicts here and leave them to fend for themselves." She smiled and shrugged, as if dismissing past follies. Her blond plaits escaped from under the flat nautical cap she wore.

"Did the convicts survive?"

"Indeed. Some intermarried with the local population, the Loraji. In an hour, some of us will be going ashore. To compensate for my discourtesy in ignoring you so far, I invite you to come along as my guest. You can see what Persecution looks like."

"I would be glad to do so." He realised as he spoke how excellent it would be to escape the ship for a while.

The *Golden Friendship*, with the *Union* close behind, was inching through the silent waters. As the mist cleared, a solemn shoreline of cliff was revealed, without colour. At a place where the cliffs were eroded, the land fell to meet the ocean. Towards this point the ships slowly headed, tracing a course through a number of small islands, little more than congregations of stones. Gravel spits also barred the way. From one spit, the ribs of an ancient wreck protruded. But eventually the *Friendship*'s anchor was lowered, and the jolly boat after it. The shouts of the sailors sounded hollow against the desolation.

Odi Jeseratabhar chivalrously helped SartoriIrvrash down the side of the ship. The Pasharatids followed, then six men armed with heavy wheel locks. The phagor rowers bent over their oars, and the boat moved between confining spits towards a ruined jetty.

The phagorlike flambreg were the possessors of the scene. Two large males were fighting with locked horns on a stoney beach, their hoofs clashing on broken shells. Males had small manes; otherwise the sexes could scarcely be distinguished. As with other Helliconian species, there was little sexual dimorphism, owing to the more marked seasonal dimorphism. Both male and female flambreg varied in colour from black to shades of russet, with white underparts. They stood four feet or more high at the shoulder. All wore smooth horns sweeping upwards. Face markings varied.

"This is their mating season," said the Priest-Militant Admiral. "Only the fury of rut drives the beasts to venture into the icy water."

The boat slid against the jetty and the party climbed out. There were sharp stones underfoot. In the distance, detonations could be heard, as ice fell from a glacier into the sea. The cloud overhead was iron grey. The phagor rowers stayed huddled in the boat, clutching their oars, unmoving.

An army of crabs rushed out to surround the landing party, raising their asymmetrical arms in menace. They did not attack. The musketeers killed some with gun butts, whereupon their fellows set on them and wrenched them apart. No sooner was this feast begun, and the crabs off guard, than toothed fish jumped from the shallow water, seized one of the crustacea apiece, and sank away from view.

Lining up smartly in this idyllic spot, the marksmen worked in pairs with their weapons, one aiming, one supporting the muzzle. Their targets were some female flambreg who milled about on the shore a few yards away, oblivious to the party from the *Golden Friendship*. The guns went off. Two females fell, kicking.

The marksmen changed positions and guns. A further three shots. This time, three cows fell kicking. The rest of the herd fled.

Men and phagors now splashed through shallow water and over spits, shouting, cheered on by cries from the ships, where the rails were lined with men watching the sport.

Two of the flambreg were not dead. One marksman carried a short-bladed knife. With this, he slit their spinal cords as they tried to stagger to their feet and run.

Great white birds came winging in upon the scene, to hover above the men on an updraught, their heads flicking this way and that as they scented death. They swooped, fanning the men with their wings and raking one with long talons.

The sailors fought off both crabs and birds as the knifeman went about his work. With one long stroke, he opened up the bellies of the dead animals. Reaching inside, he pulled forth their bowels and livers, casting them aside to steam on the shore. With quick chopping movements, he severed the hind legs from the trunks. Golden blood oozed up his arm. The birds screamed overhead.

Phagors carried the legs and carcasses back to the jolly boat.

Another round of killing took place. Meanwhile, the Pasharatids had brought a sledge from the boat. Four sturdy phagors seized up the traces and pulled it to the shore. SartoriIrvrash was invited to follow.

"We will give you a short trip to view the country," Jeseratabhar said, with a tight smile. He thought that this was their excuse to seize a respite from the ship. He fell in beside her, matching her pace.

A strong smell of farmyard met them. The flambreg were cantering about as if nothing had happened, while the white birds fought for offal. Following the sledge, the humans laboured up the slope. They saw other animals resembling flambreg, but with shaggier, greyer coats and ringed horns. These were yelk. Dienu Pasharatid said disdainfully that yelk should have been shot instead of flambreg. Red meat was better than yellow.

No one responded to this comment. SartoriIrvrash glanced at Io. The man's face was closed. He seemed entirely remote. Was he possibly thinking about the queen?

They made their way up between immense boulders deposited by a vanished glacier. On some boulders were scratched ancient names and dates, where convicts had sought to memorialise themselves.

The party reached more level ground. Breathing deeply, they surveyed the panorama. The two ships lay on the fringes of a black sheet of water to which the shelves of a black sky came down. Small icebergs stood here and there; some, caught in a current, moved rapidly towards the sombre distance and could be mistaken for sails. But there was no other human life.

On their other hand lay the land of Loraj, which stretched into the Circumpolar Regions. The mists were still dispersing, to reveal a plain almost without feature. In its very blankness was a grandeur of a kind. Beneath their feet, the ground was grassless, stamped with the imprints of thousands upon thousands of hoofprints.

"These plains belong to the flambreg, the yelk, and the giant yelk," Dienu Pasharatid said. "And not just the plains, but the whole land."

"It's not a place for men and women," said Io Pasharatid.

"Flambreg and yelk look similar, yet differ anatomically," said Odi Jeseratabhar. "The yelk are necrogenes. Their young are born from their corpses and feed on their carrion instead of milk. Flambreg are viviparous."

SartoriIrvrash said nothing. He was still shaken from the slaughter on the shore. The guns were still firing. The object of the ships' putting in to Persecution was precisely to obtain fresh meat.

The four phagors now pulled the four humans along in the sledge. The plain proved to be sodden, pitted with ponds and muskegs. Progress was slow. To the north stretched low mustard-coloured hills, their flanks patched with dwarf spruce and other hardy trees. The trees had less success on the plain, where their branches were weighed down with the clumsy nests of birds, built from sticks and driftwood. The leaves of the trees were fouled with white droppings.

The ships and the sea sank from view. The air was chill, less loaded with sea taint. A stink of rutting animals lay over the ground. The sound of firing died in the distance. They travelled for almost an hour without speaking, relishing the great space about them.

The Priest-Militant Admiral called a halt beside a striated ochre boulder. They climbed from the sledge, marching about separately, swinging their arms. The boulder loomed over them. The only sounds were bird cries and the sough of the wind, until they detected a distant rumbling.

To SartoriIrvrash, the rumble suggested only a distant glacier breaking. He dismissed it in his pleasure at having ground beneath his feet again. The women, however, looked gravely at each other and climbed without speaking to stand on top of the boulder. They scanned the landscape and gave cries of alarm.

"You, brutes, draw the sledge close under the rock," Odi Jeseratabhar called in Hurdhu to the phagors.

The rumble became a thunder. The thunder rose from the earth, from everywhere. Something was happening to the low slopes to the west. They were in motion. With the terror of someone faced with a natural event beyond the scope of his imagination, SartoriIrvrash ran to the rock and began to climb. Io Pasharatid helped him scramble to a shoulder where there was room for all four of them. The phagors stood against the boulder, milts flicking up their nose slots.

"We'll be safe here till they pass," said Odi Jeseratabhar. Her voice shook.

"What is it?" SartoriIrvrash asked.

Through a thin haze, the distance was rolling itself up like a rug and tumbling towards them. They could only watch in silence. The rug resolved itself into an avalanche of flambreg, advancing on a wide front.

SartoriIrvrash tried to count them. Ten, twenty, fifty, a hundred—it was impossible. The front of the advance was a mile wide—two, five miles wide, and comprised herd after herd of animals. Endless ranks of yelk and flambreg were converging on the plain where the boulder stood.

The ground, the rock, the very air, vibrated.

Necks extended, eyes glaring, saliva flowing free from open mouths, the herds came on. They wove their living streams about the boulder, joined them at its far side, and passed on. White cowbirds sailed above them, keeping pace with no more than an occasional dip of a wing.

In their excitement, the four humans stretched out their arms, screamed, waved, cheered with exhilaration.

Beneath them was a sea of hoofed life stretching back to and beyond the horizon. Not a single beast looked up at the gesticulating humans; each knew that to miss its footing meant death.

The human exhilaration soon faded. The four sat down, huddling close. They looked about with increasing listlessness. Still the herd passed. Batalix rose, Batalix set in concentric aurioles of light. Still there was no sign of the end of the herd. The animals continued to flow by in their thousands.

Some flambreg detached themselves from the stampede to mill about by the bay. Others plunged straight into the sea. Still others galloped in a trance over the cliffs to their death. The main body of animals thundered down into the dip and up the other side, heading towards the northeast. Hours passed. The animals continued with their monotonous drumbeats of noise.

Overhead, magnificent curtains of light unfolded and flashed, rising to the zenith. But the humans became despondent: the life which had exhilarated them earlier now depressed them. They huddled together on their ledge. The four phagors stood pressed against the wall of rock, the sledge before them for protection.

Freyr sloped shallowly towards the horizon. Rain began to fall, at first uncertainly. The lights overhead were extinguished as the fall became heavier, soaking the ground and changing the sound of the hoofbeats.

Icy rain fell for hours. Once it had established itself, it prevailed like the herd, with no variation to its monotony.

The darkness and noise isolated SartoriIrvrash and Odi Jeseratabhar slightly from the others. They clung together for protection.

The hammer of animals and elements penetrated him. He crouched with his brow against the rib cage of the admiral, expecting death, reviewing his life.

It was the loneliness that did it, he thought. A deliberate loneliness, lifelong. I allowed myself to drift away from my brothers. I neglected my wife. Because I was so lonely. My learning sprang from that awful sense of loneliness: by my learning I set myself further apart from my fellows. Why? What possessed me?

And why did I tolerate JandolAnganol for so long? Did I recognise a torment in him similar to mine? I admire JandolAnganol—he lets the pain come to the surface. But when he took hold of me, it was like a rape. I can't forgive that, or the deliberate wanton accursed burning of my books. He burnt my defences. He'd burn the world down if he could. . . .

I'm different now. Severed from my loneliness. I will be different, if we escape. I like this woman Odi. I'll show it.

And somewhere in this ghastly wilderness of life I will find the means to bring JandolAnganol low. For years, I swallowed insults, ate bitterness. Now—I'm not too old—I'll see to it for everyone's sake that he is brought low. He brought me low. I'll bring him low. It's not noble, but my nobility has gone. Nobility's for scum.

He laughed and the cold froze his front teeth.

He discovered that Odi Jeseratabhar was weeping, and possibly had been for some while. Boldly, he clutched her to him, inching his way across their perch until his rough cheek was against hers. Every inch was accompanied by the limitless drumming of hoofs across a dark void.

He whispered almost random words of consolation.

She turned so that their mouths were almost touching. "To me falls blame for this. I should have foreseen it might happen . . ."

Something else she said, snatched away by the storm. He kissed her. It was almost the last voluntary gesture left him. Warmth lit inside him.

The journey away from JandolAnganol had changed him. He kissed her again. She responded. They tasted a mutual rain on their lips.

Despite their discomfort, the humans slipped into a sort of coma. When they woke, the rain had faded to no more than a drizzle. The herd was still passing the rock. Still it stretched to the far horizon on either side. They were forced to relieve their bladders by crouching at one edge of the boulder. The phagors and the sledge had been swept away while they were asleep. Nothing remained.

What caused them to rouse was an invasion of flies which arrived with the herd. As there was more than one kind of animal in the great stampede, so there was more than one kind of animal among the flying invasion; all kinds were capable of drawing blood. They settled in their thousands on the humans, who were forced to fold themselves into a small huddle and cover themselves with cloaks and keedrants. Any skin exposed was instantly settled on and sucked till it bled.

They lay in stifling misery, while beneath them the great boulder shook as if still traveling on the glacier which had deposited it on the plain. Another day went by. Another dimday, another night.

Batalix rose again to a scene of rain and mist. At last the force of the herd slackened. The main body had gone by. Stragglers still passed, often mother flambreg with yearlings. The torment of flies lessened. Towards the northeast, the thunder of the disappearing herd still sounded. Many flambreg still milled about along the coastline.

Trembling and stiff, the humans climbed and slid to the ground. There was nothing for it but to make their way back to the shore on foot. With the stench of animal in their nostrils, they staggered forward, assailed by flies every inch of the way. Not a word passed between them.

The ship sailed on. They left Persecution Bay. The four who had been stranded in the midst of the stampede lay below decks in a fever induced by exposure and the bites of the flies.

Through SartoriIrvrash's delirious brain travelled the herd, ever on, covering the world. The reality of that mass presence would not go away, struggle against it as he would. It remained even when he recovered.

As soon as he was strong enough, he went without ceremony to talk to Odi Jeseratabhar. The Priest-Militant Admiral was pleased to see him. She greeted him in a friendly fashion and even extended a hand, which he took.

She sat in her bunk covered only by a red sheet, her fair hair wild about her shoulders. Out of uniform, she looked gaunter than ever, but more approachable.

"All ships sailing long distances call in at Persecution Bay," she said. "They pick up new victuals, meat chiefly. The Priest-Sailors Guild contains few vegetarians. Fish. Seal. Crabs. I have seen the flambreg stampedes before. I should have been more alert. They draw me. What do you think of them?"

He had noticed this habit in her before. While weaving a spell of Sibish tenses about herself, she would suddenly break out with a question to disconcert the listener.

"I never knew there were so many animals in the world . . ."

"There are more than you can imagine. More than anyone can/should imagine. They live all around the skirts of the great ice cap, in the bleak Circumpolar lands. Millions of them. Millions and millions."

She smiled in her excitement. He liked that. He realised how lonely he was when she smiled.

"I assume they were migrating."

"Not that, to the best of my knowledge. They come down to the water, but do not stay. They travel at all times of the year, not just in spring. They may simply be driven by desperation. They have only one enemy."

"Wolves?"

"Not wolves." She gave a wolflike grin, glad to have caught him out. "Flies. One fly in particular. That fly is as big as the top joint of my thumb. It has yellow stripes—you can't mistake it. It lays its eggs in the skin of the wretched bovidae. When the larvae hatch, they burrow through the hide, enter the bloodstream, and eventually lie in pockets under the skin on the back. There the grubs grow big, in a sore the size of a large fruit, until eventually they burst out of their crater and fall to the ground to begin the life cycle again. Almost every flambreg we kill has such a parasite—often several.

"I have seen individual animals run in torment till they dropped, or cast themselves off tall cliffs, to escape that yellow-striped fly."

She regarded him benevolently, as if this account gave her some inward satisfaction.

"Madame, I was shocked when your men shot a few cows on the shore. Yet it was nothing, I see now. Nothing."

She nodded.

"The flambreg are a force of nature. Endless. Endless. They make humanity appear as nothing. The estimated population of Sibornal is twenty-five million at present. There are many times—perhaps a thousand times—that number of flambreg on the continent. As many flambreg as there are trees. It is my belief that once all Helliconia consisted only of those cattle and those flies, ceaselessly coming and going throughout the continents, the bovidae perpetually suffering a torment they perpetually tried to escape."

Before this vision, both parties fell silent. SartoriIrvrash returned to his cabin. But a few hours later, Odi Jeseratabhar sought him out. He was embarrassed to receive her in his stinking cubbyhole.

"Did my talk of unlimited flambreg make you gloomy?" There was coquetry in her question, surely.

"On the contrary. I am delighted to meet with someone like you, so interested in the processes of this world. I wish they were more clearly understood."

"They are better understood in Sibornal than elsewhere." Then she decided to soften the boast by adding, "Perhaps because we experience more seasonal change than you do in Campannlat. You Borlienese can forget the Great Winter in Summer. One sometimes fears/fearing when alone that, if next Weyr-Winter becomes just a few degrees colder, then there will be no humans left. Only phagors, and the myriad mindless flambreg. Perhaps mankind is—a temporary accident."

SartoriIrvrash contemplated her. She had brushed her hair free to her shoulders. "I have thought the same myself. I hate phagors, but they are more stable than we. Well, at least the fate of mankind is better than that of the ceaselessly driven flambreg. Though we certainly have our equivalents of the yellow-striped fly . . ." He hesitated, wanted to hear more from her, to test her intelligence and sensibilities. "When I first saw the flambreg, I thought how closely they resembled ancipitals."

"Closely, in many respects. Well, my friend, you pass for learned. What do you make of that resemblance?" She was testing him, as her pleasantly teasing manner indicated. By common consent, they sat down side by side on his bunk.

"The Madis resemble us. So do Nondads and Others, though more remotely. There seems to be no family connection between humans and Madis, though Madi-human matings are sometimes fertile of offspring. Princess Simoda Tal is one such sport. I never heard that phagors mate with flambreg." He gave a dry laugh at his uncertainty.

"Supposing that the genethlic divinities who shape us have made a family connection, as you call it, between humankind and Madikind? Would you then accept that there was a connection between flambreg and phagors?"

"That would have to be determined by experiment." He was on the brink of explaining his breeding experiments in Matrassyl, then decided to reserve that topic for another time. "A genetic relationship implies outward similarities. Phagors and flambreg have golden blood as a protection against cold . . ."

"There is proof without experiment. I do not believe as most people do that every species is created separately by God the Azoiaxic." She lowered her voice as she said this. "I believe the boundaries blur with time, as the boundary between human and Madi will blur again when your JandolAnganol weds Simoda Tal. You see where I lead?"

Was she secretly an atheist, as he was? To SartoriIrvrash's amazement, the thought gave him an erection. "Tell me."

"I have not heard of phagors and flambreg mating, that's true. However, I have good reason to believe that once this world held nothing but flambreg and flies—both in countless and mindless millions. Through genetic change, ancipitals developed from flambreg. They're a refined version. What do you think? Is it possible?"

He tried to match her manner of argument.

"The similarities may be several, but they are mainly surface ones, apart from blood colour. You might as well say men and phagors are alike because both species talk. Phagors stand erect like us. They have their own cast of intelligence. Flambreg have nothing of the kind—unless galloping madly back and forth across a continent is intelligent."

"The phagorian ability to walk upright and use language came after the two bloodlines divided. Imagine that phagors developed from a group of flambreg which . . . which found an alternative to ceaseless flight as a way of dealing with the fly problem."

They were gazing at each other with excitement. He longed to tell Odi of his discovery regarding hoxneys.

"What alternative?"

"Hiding in caves, for instance. Going underground. Free of the fly torment, they developed intelligence. Stood upright to see further and then had forefeet free to use tools. In the dark, language developed as a substitute for sight. I'll show you my essay on the subject one day. Nobody else has seen it."

He laughed to think of flambreg performing such tricks.

"Not over one generation, dear friend. Over many. Endless generations. The cleverer ones would win. Don't laugh." She tapped his hand. "If this did not happen in past time, then let me ask you this. How is it that the gestation period for gillots is one Batalix-year—while the gestation period for a flambreg cow is exactly the same length of time? Doesn't that prove a genetic relationship?"

Sailing on, the two ships passed the lowly ports of the southernmost coast of Loraj, which lay inside the tropics. From the port of Ijivibir, a caravel of 600 tons named the *Good Hope* sailed out to join the *Golden Friendship* and the *Union*. It made a brave sight, with its sails painted in vertical stripes. Cannon were fired from the flagship in greeting, and the sailors gave a cheer. On an empty ocean, three vessels were many more than two.

Another occasion was marked when they had reached the most westerly point of their course at a longitude of 29° East. The time was ten to twenty-five. Freyr was below the horizon, trawling an apricot glow above. The glow dissolving the horizon seemed to radiate from the hazy water. It marked the grave from which the great sun would presently rise. Somewhere concealed in that glow lay the sacred country of Shivenink; somewhere in Shivenink, high in the mountains that ran all the way from sea to North Pole, was the Great Wheel of Kharnabhar.

A bugle sounded All Hands. The three ships clustered. Prayers were said, music played, all stood to pray with finger to forehead.

Out of the apricot haze came a sail. By a trick of the light, it appeared and disappeared like a vision. Birds screamed about its masts, newly away from land.

It was an all-white ship, sails white, hull fresh with whitewash. As it drew nearer, firing a gun in salute, those aboard the other ships saw that it was a caravel, no bigger than the *Good Hope*; but on its mainsail stood the great hierogram representing the Wheel itself, inner and outer circles connected by wavy lines. This was the *Vajabhar Prayer*, named after Shivenink's chief port.

The four ships tacked close, like four pigeons nestling together on a branch. A bark of orders from the Priest-Militant Admiral herself. Bowsprits turned, cordage creaked, artemons filled. The little fleet began to sail southwards.

Colours in the water changed to a deeper blue. The ships were leaving the Pannoval Sea astern and entering the northern margins of the vast Climent Ocean. Immediately, they struck rough weather. They had a hard time of it, combatting mountainous seas and hazardous storms, in which they were bombarded by gigantic hailstones. For days, they saw neither sun.

When at last they reached calmer waters, Freyr's zenith was lower than before, and Batalix's somewhat higher. To port lay the cliffs of Campannlat's westernmost redoubt, Cape Findowel. Once they had rounded Findowel they sailed into the nearest anchorage along the coast of the tropical continent, there to rest for two days. The carpenters repaired the storm damage, the members of the Priest-Sailors Guild stitched sails or else swam in a warm lagoon. So welcome was the sight of men and women disporting themselves naked in the water—the puritanical Sibornalese were curiously unprudish on this occasion—that even SartoriIrvrash ventured into the water in a pair of silken underpants.

When he rested afterwards on the beach, sheltering from the power of both suns, he watched the swimmers climb out one by one. Many of the *Good Hope*'s crew were women, and sturdily built. He sighed for his youth. Io Pasharatid climbed out beside him and said to him quietly, "If only that beautiful queen of queens were here, eh?"

"What then?" He kept watching the water, hoping that Odi would emerge naked.

Pasharatid dug him in the ribs in an un-Sibornalese way.

"What then, you say? Why, then this seeming paradise would be paradise indeed."

"Do you suppose that this expedition can possibly conquer Borlien?"

"Given the fortune of war, I'm sure of it. We are organised and armed, in a way JandolAnganol's forces will never be."

"Why, then the queen will come under your supervision."

"That reflection had not escaped me. Why else do you think I have this sudden enthusiasm for war? I don't want Ottassol, you old goat. I want Queen MyrdemInggala. And I intend to have her."

XV

THE CAPTIVES
OF THE QUARRY

A man was walking with a pack slung over one shoulder. He wore
the tattered remains of a uniform. Both suns beat down on him.
Streams of sweat ran down into his tunic. He walked blindly,
rarely looking up.

He was traversing a destroyed area of jungle in the Chwart Heights in
eastern Randonan. All round were blackened and broken stumps of
trees, many still smouldering. On the few occasions when the man
looked about him, he could see nothing but the trail and blackened
landscape all round. Palls of grey smoke rose in the distance. It was
possible that tropical heat had started the blaze. Or perhaps a spark
from a matchlock had been the cause of the death of a million trees. For
many tenners battles had been fought over the area. Now soldiers and
cannon were gone, and the vegetation likewise.

Everything about the man's posture expressed weariness and defeat.
But he kept on. Once he faltered, when one of his shadows faded and
disappeared. Black cloud, rolling up, had blotted out Freyr. A few min-

249

utes later, Batalix too was swallowed. Then the rain came down. The man bowed his head and continued to walk. There was nowhere he could shelter, nothing he could do but submit to nature.

The downpour continued, increasing in ferocity by sudden fits. The ashes hissed. More and more of the resources of the heavens were called in, like reserves being brought into a battle.

Bombardment by hail was the next tactic. The hailstones stung the weary man into a run. He took what refuge he could in a hollow tree stump. Falling back against the crumbling wood, he exposed a stronghold of rickybacks. Deprived of their little fortress, the crustaceans climbed through veritable Takissas of liquid ash, seeking refuge with their puny antennae waving.

Unaware of this catastrophe, the man stared forth from under the brim of his hat, panting. Several bent figures staggered through the murk. They were the remnants of his army, the once celebrated Borlienese Second Army. One man passed obliviously within inches of the tree stump, dragging a terrible wound which bled afresh under the hailstones. The shelterer wept. He had no wound, except for a bruise on his temple. He had no right to be alive.

Like an uncomforted child, his weeping turned to exhaustion; he slept despite the hail.

The dreams that terminated sleep were full of hail. He felt their smart on his cheek, woke, saw that the sky was again clear. He started up, yet still the stones struck his face, his neck. As he gasped with vexation, a stone flew into his mouth. He spat it out, turning in bewilderment.

The gnarled, broomlike plants nearby had been burnt by fire. Fire had hardened their seedcases, ripening their seeds with its flame. In a new day's warmth, the cases untwisted. They made a small noise, like the parting of moist lips. Their seeds were shot out in all directions. The ashy ground would provide fertile conditions for growth.

He laughed, suddenly pleased. Whatever folly mankind got up to, nature went on its uncheckable way. And he would go on his way. He patted his sword, adjusted his hat, hitched his pack, and started walking southeastwards.

He emerged from the devastated area towards noon. The way wound down between thickets of shoatapraxi. Over centuries, the road the soldier travelled had been by turns river, dried bed, ice track, cattle trail, and highway. No man could trace its usages. Humble flowers grew beside its banks, some sprung from parent plants which had seeded far away. The banks became higher on either side. He staggered between them, hampered by shifting gravels underfoot. When they crumbled away at last, under the brow of a hill, he saw cottages standing in fields.

The prospect did little to reassure him.

The fields had long been untended. The cottages were derelict. Many roofs had fallen in, leaving end-walls pointing like old fists to the sky. Hedges topping the banks on either side of the track had collapsed from the weight of dust that had been thrown up. Dust had spread over adjoining fields, over cottages and outbuildings, over abandoned pieces of luggage which dotted the view. Everything was rendered in the same greyish tone, as if created all from one material.

Only a great army passing could have raised so much dust, the man with the pack thought. The army had been his. The Second Army had then been marching forward into battle. He was now returning silently in defeat.

His footsteps deadened, General Hanra TolramKetinet walked down the meandering street. One or two furtive phagors peered at him from the ruins, the long masks of their faces without expression. He did not remember this village; it was just one more village they had marched through on just one more hot day. As he reached the end of the street and the sacred pillar which defined the local land-octave, he saw a wedge-shaped copse which he thought he recalled, a copse which his scouts had reconnoitred for enemy. If he was right, there was a sizeable farmhouse beyond it, in which he had slept for a few hours.

The farmhouse remained intact. It was surrounded by outhouses which had been damaged by fire.

TolramKetinet stood by the gateway, peering in. Both yard and house were silent except for the buzz of flies. Sword in hand, he moved forward. Two slaughtered hoxneys lay in an open stall, bodies black with flies. Their stench met his nostrils.

Freyr was high, Batalix already westering. Conflicting shadows lent the house a drab air as he moved towards it. The windows were dimmed with dust. There had been a woman here, the farmer's woman, with four small children, he recalled. No man. Now there was only the buzz of silence.

He set his pack down by the front doorstep and kicked the door open with his foot.

"Anyone there?" He hoped some of his men might be resting in the rooms.

No response. Yet his alerted senses warned him that there was a living thing in the building. He paused in the stone hall. A tall pendulum clock, with its twenty-five illuminated hours, stood silent against one wall. Otherwise, the impression was one of the poverty common to an area which has long been in a war zone. Beyond the hall everything lay in shadow.

Then he marched determinedly forward, down the passage, and into a low-ceilinged kitchen.

Six phagors stood in the kitchen. They stood motionless, as if awaiting his return. Their eyes glowed deep pink in the shade. Beyond them, through a window, grew a patch of bright yellow flowers; catching the sun, they made the beast shapes indeterminate. Yellow reflections rested on shoulders, on long cheekbones. One of the brutes retained its horns.

They came towards him, but TolramKetinet was ready. He had picked up their scent in the hall. They held spears, but he was a practised swordsman. They were swift, but they got in each other's way. He drove the blade up under their rib cages, where he knew their eddre were. Only one of the ancipitals lunged with its spear. He half-severed its forearm with a single blow. Gold blood flew. The room filled with their heavy sick breathing. All died without making any other sound.

As they fell, he saw by their blazes that they had been trusted members of his guard. Catching the Sons of Freyr in disorder, they had taken a chance and reverted to type. A less wary soldier would have fallen into their ambush. Indeed, one had done so recently. At the back of the kitchen, spread out on a table, was a Borlienese corporal, his throat neatly bitten out.

TolramKetinet went back into the courtyard and leaned against a warm outer wall. After a short while, his nausea passed. He stood breathing in the warm air, until the stench of nearby decay drove him from the courtyard.

He could not rest here. When his strength returned, he picked up his pack and resumed his silent march along the road leading towards the coast. Towards the sea and its voices.

The forest closed about him. The road south led through twisted columns of spirax trees, with their double entwined trunks. Through their avenues walked TolramKetinet. This was not dense tangled jungle. Little grew on its floor, for little sunlight penetrated down to the ground. He walked as in a lofty building, surrounded by pillars of amazing design.

Above spread other layers of the forests which separated Borlien from Randonan. The shrub layer, through which large creatures sometimes crashed. The understory, where Others swung and called, occasionally dropping to the floor, to snatch at a fungus before swarming up to the safety of the branches. The canopy, the true roof of the jungle, decked with flowers TolramKetinet could not see, and birds he could only hear. The emergent layer, formed by the tallest trees, which reared above the canopy, home of predatory birds which watched and did not sing.

The solemnity of the rain forest was such that it appeared to those who ventured into it to be much more permanent than savannah land or even desert. It was not so. Of the 1825 small Helliconian years which made one Great Year, the elaborate jungle organism was able to sustain itself for less than half that period. Closely examined, every single tree revealed, in root, trunk, branch, and seed, the strategies it employed to survive when climate was less clement, when it would endure solitary in a howling waste, or wait in a case, petrified, beneath snow.

The fauna regarded the various layers of their home as unchanging. The truth was that the whole intricate edifice, more marvellous than any work of man, had come into being only a few generations ago in response to the elements, springing up like a jack-in-the-box from a scattering of nuts.

In this hierarchy of plants was a perfect order which appeared random only to an untutored eye. Everything, animal or insect or vegetable, had its place, generally a horizontal zone, to call its own. The Others were rare exceptions to this rule. Phagors had taken refuge in the forest, often living in huts contrived in the angles between high-kneed roots, and Others had gravitated into their company, to play a role somewhere between pet and slave.

Often, settlements of a dozen or more phagors, with their runts, were established about the base of a large tree. TolramKetinet gave such places a wide berth. He deeply mistrusted the phagors, and feared the sorties made by their Others, who came rushing out like watchdogs when strangers were near, brandishing sticks.

Men sometimes lurked in these settlements. A small human hut was to be seen next to—and little to be distinguished from—an ancipital hut. These men, near-naked, were evidently accepted by the phagors as large versions of Others. It was as though the brown-pelted Others, in their alliance with the phagors, gave a licence to the men to live in lowly harmony with them.

Most of the men were deserters from units of the Second Army. TolramKetinet spoke to them, trying to persuade them to join him. Some did so. Others threw sticks. Many admitted that they hated the war and rejoined their old commander only because they were sick of the jungle with its secretive noises and slender diet.

After a day of marching along the aisles of the rain forest, they fell back into their old military roles again and accepted as if with relief the ancient disciplines of command. TolramKetinet also changed. His stance had been that of a defeated man. Now he pulled his shoulders back and took on something of his old swagger. The lines of his face tightened; he could again be recognised as a young man. The more men there were to take orders, the more easily he gave orders, and the more right they seemed. With the mutability of the human race, he became what those about him regarded him as being.

So the small force arrived at the Kacol River.

Powered by their new spirit, they launched a surprise raid and took the shantytown of Ordelay. With this victory, fighting spirit was entirely restored.

Among the craft on the Kacol was an ice ship, flying the flag of the

Lordryardry Ice Trading Company. When the town was invaded, this vessel, the *Lordryardry Lubber*, tried to make its escape downstream, but TolramKetinet intercepted it with a group of men.

The terrified captain protested that he was a neutral and claimed diplomatic immunity. His business in Ordelay was not merely to trade in ice but to hand a letter to General Hanra TolramKetinet.

"Do you know where this general is?" demanded TolramKetinet.

"Somewhere in the jungle, losing the king's war for him."

With a sword at his throat, the captain said that he had sent a paid messenger to deliver the message; there his obligations ended. He had carried out Captain Krillio Muntras's instructions.

"What said the contents of the letter?" TolramKetinet demanded.

The man swore he did not know. The leather wallet which contained it was sealed with the seal of the queen of queens, MyrdemInggala. How would he dare tamper with a royal message?

"You would never rest until you found out what was in it. Speak, you scoundrel!"

He needed encouragement. When crushed under an upturned table, the captain admitted that the seal of the wallet had come unstuck on its own. He had happened to notice, without meaning to, that the queen of queens was being sent into exile by King JandolAnganol, to a place on the north coast of the Sea of Eagles called Gravabagalinien; that she feared for her life; and that she hoped that she might one day see her good friend the general delivered from the dangers of war into her presence. She prayed that Akhanaba would guard him from all ills.

When he heard this, TolramKetinet became pale. He went away and looked over the side of the boat at the dark-flowing river, so that his soldiers should not see his face. Expectations, fears, desires, woke in him. He uttered a prayer that he might be more successful in love than in war.

TolramKetinet's party put the battered captain of the *Lubber* ashore and commandeered his boat. They caroused for a day in town, stacked the ice ship with provisions, and sailed for the distant ocean.

High above the jungle, the Avernus sailed in its orbit. There were those on the observation satellite, unfamiliar with the varieties of warfare practised on the planet below, who asked what kind of force could have defeated the Borlienese Second Army. They looked in vain for a set of swaggering Randonanese patriots who had repelled the invasion of their homeland.

There was no such force. The Randonanese were semi-savage tribes who lived in harmony with their environment. Some tribes cultivated patches of cereal. All lived surrounded by dogs and pigs which, when young, were allowed to suckle indiscriminately at the breasts of nursing mothers if they so desired. They killed for the pot and not for sport. Many tribes worshipped Others as gods, although that did not stop them killing such gods as they encountered swinging among the branches of the great forest home. Such was the mould of their mind that numbers of them worshipped fish, or trees, menses, spirits, or patches of double daylight.

In their humility, the tribes of Randonan tolerated the tribes of phagors, which were torpid, and consisted mainly of itinerant woodmen or fungusmongers. The phagors, in their turn, rarely attacked the human tribes, though the customary tales were told of stalluns carrying off human women.

The phagors brewed their own drink, raffel. On certain occasions, they brewed a different potion, which the Randonanese tribes called vulumunwun, believing it to be distilled from the sap of the vulu tree and from certain fungi. Unable to concoct vulumunwun themselves, they obtained it by barter from phagors. Then a feast would be held far into the night.

On these occasions, a great spirit often spoke to the tribes. It told them to go out and make sport in the Desert.

The tribes would bind their gods, the Others, to bamboo chairs and carry them away through the jungle on their shoulders. The whole tribe would go, babies, pigs, parrots, preets, cats, and all. They would cross the Kacol and enter what was officially Borlien. They would invade the richly cultivated lands of the central Borlienese plain.

This was the land the Randonanese called the Desert. It was open to the skies; the suns blazed down. It had no great trees, no dense shrub, no secret places, no wild boar, no Others. In this godless place—with a final libation of vulumunwun—they dared make sport, setting fire to or despoiling the crops.

The plainsmen of Borlien were sturdy dark men. They hated the pale lizards who materialised like ghosts out of nowhere. They rushed from their little villages and drove off the invaders with any weapon that came to hand. Often they lost their own lives in the process, for the tribesmen had blow tubes from which they blew feathered thorns tipped with poison. Maddened, the farmers would leave their homes and burn down the forests. So it had finally come to war between Borlien and Randonan.

Aggression, defense, attack, and counterattack. These moves became confused in the enantiodromia which, in human minds, constantly turns all things into their opposites. By the time the Second Army deployed its platoons in the jungle-clad mountains of Randonan, the little tribesmen had themselves become, in the eyes of their enemies, a formidable military force.

Yet what had defeated TolramKetinet's expedition was no armed opposition. The defence of the tribes was to slide away into the jungle, shrieking through the night barbaric insults at the invaders, just as they heard the Others do. Like the Others, they took to the trees, to rain darts or urine down on the general's men. They could not properly wage war. The jungle did that for them.

The jungle was full of diseases to which the Borlienese army was not immune. Its fruits brought torrential dysenteries, its pools malarias, its days fevers, and its insects a sordid crop of parasites which fed on the men from the outside in or from the inside out. Nothing could be properly fought; everything had to be survived. One by one, or in batches, Borlienese soldiers succumbed to the jungle. With them went King JandolAnganol's ambitions for victory in the Western Wars.

As for that king, so distant from his army disintegrating in Randonan, he was suffering from difficulties almost as elaborate as the mechanisms of the jungle. The bureaucracies of Pannoval were more enduring than the jungle and so had longer to develop their entanglements. The queen of queens had been gone from JandolAnganol's capital for many weeks, and still his bill of divorcement had not arrived from the capital of the Holy Empire.

As the heat intensified, Pannoval stepped up the drumble against the ancipital species living on its lands. Fleeing phagor tribes sought refuge in Borlien, against the general wishes of the mass of people, who both hated and feared the shaggies.

The king felt differently. In a speech given in the scritina, he welcomed the refugees, promising them land in the Cosgatt on which they would be allowed to settle if they would join the army and fight for Borlien. By this means, the Cosgatt, now safe from the shadow of Darvlish, could be cultivated at low cost, and the newcomers effectively removed from the presence of the Borlienese.

This human hand extended to the phagors pleased no one in Pannoval or Oldorando, and the bill of divorcement was again delayed.

But JandolAnganol was pleased with himself. He was suffering enough to appease his conscience.

He put on a bright jacket and went to see his father. Again he walked through the winding ways of his palace and down through the guarded doors to the cellarage where he kept the old man. The chambers of the prison seemed more dank than ever. JandolAnganol paused in the first chamber which had once served as mortuary and torture chamber. Darkness enclosed him. The sounds of the outer world were stilled.

"Father!" he said. His own voice sounded unnatural to his ears.

He went through the second chamber and into the third, where pallid light filtered in. The log fire smouldered as usual. The old man, wrapped as usual in his blanket, sat before the fire as usual, chin resting on chest. Nothing down here had altered for many years. The only thing that had altered now was that VarpalAnganol was dead.

The king stood for a while with one hand on his father's shoulder. Thin though it was, the flesh was unyielding.

JandolAnganol went and stood under the high barred window. He called to his father. The skull with its wispy hair never moved. He called again, louder. No movement.

"You're dead, aren't you?" said JandolAnganol, in tones of contempt. "Just one more betrayal. . . . By the beholder, wasn't I miserable enough with her gone?"

No answer came. "You've died, haven't you? Gone away to spite me, you old hrattock . . ."

He strode over to the fireplace and kicked the logs all over the cell, filling it with smoke. In his fury, he knocked the chair over, and the frail body of his father fell to the stones, remaining in its huddled position.

The king stooped over this tiny effigy, as if contemplating a snake, and then, with a sudden movement, fell to his knees—not to engage in prayer, but to seize the body by its dry throat and pour a flood of words upon it, in which the accusation that this dead thing had long ago turned his mother against him, quenching her love, was repeated in many forms, hissed forth with spiteful examples, until the words died and the king remained there bent over the body, wrapped in heavy coils of smoke. He beat the flagstones with his fist, then crouched motionless.

The logs strewn across the floor were extinguished by damp, each one by itself. At last, red-eyed, the king took himself away from the darkened place, going upwards with a hurried pace as if pursued, up to warmer regions.

Among the many denizens of the palace was an ancient nurse who lived in the servants' quarters and was bedridden most of the day. JandolAnganol had not entered the servants' quarters since he was a child. He found his way without hesitation through the mean corridors and confronted the old woman, who jumped out of bed and clung to one of its posts in terror. She glared at him aghast, pulling hair before her eyes.

"He's dead, your master and lover," JandolAnganol said, without expression. "See that he is prepared for burial."

Next day, a week of mourning was declared, and the Royal First Phagorian Guard paraded through the city in black.

The common people, starved of excitement by their poverty, were quick to spy upon the king's mood, at second or third hand if need be. Their connections with the palace were close, if subterranean. All knew someone who knew someone who was in the royal employ; and they smelt out JandolAnganol's alternating moods of excitement and despair.

Bareheaded under the suns, they flocked to the holy ground where
VarpalAnganol, with the pomp due to a king, was to be buried on his
correct land-octave.

The service was presided over by the Archpriest of the Dome of
Striving, BranzaBaginut. The members of the scritina were there, housed
in a stand erected for the occasion, and draped with the banners of the
house of Anganol. These worthies showed on their faces more the
heaviness of disapproval of the living king than grief for the dead one;
but they attended nevertheless, fearing the consequences if they did not,
and their wives attended them, for the same reason.

JandolAnganol made an isolated figure as he stood by the open grave.
He gave an occasional darting glance round, as if hoping for sight of
Robayday. This nervous glance became more frequent as the body of his
father, wrapped in a gold cloth, was placed on its side in the place dug
for it. Nothing went down with him. All present knew what waited
below, in the world of the gossies, where material things were needed no
more. The only concession to the rank of the departed was when twelve
women of the court came forward to cast flowers down upon the still
form.

Archpriest BranzaBaginut closed his eyes and chanted.

"The seasons in their processes bear us away to our final octaves. As
there are two suns, the lesser and the greater, so we have two phases of
being, life and death, the lesser and the greater. Now a great king has
gone from us into the greater phase. He who knew the light has gone
down into the dark . . ."

And as his high voice silenced the whispering of the crowd, who
strained forward eagerly as the dogs which also attended the ceremony
were straining their noses toward the grave, the first handfuls of earth
were thrown.

At that moment, the king's voice rang out. "This villain ruined my
mother and myself. Why do you pray for such a villain?"

He took a great leap across the lips of the pit, pushed the Archpriest
aside, and ran, still shouting, towards the palace, the shoulders of which
loomed above the hill. Beyond sight of the crowd, he ran still, and
would not stop until he was at his stables and on his hoxney and riding
madly out into the woods, leaving Yuli to mewl far behind.

This disgraceful episode, this insult to the established religion by a
religious man, delighted the common population of Matrassyl. It was
talked about, laughed over, praised, condemned, in the rudest hut.

"He's a joker, is Jandol," was often the carefully considered verdict,
arrived at in taverns after a long evening's drinking, where death was not
regarded with much affection. And the reputation of the joker rose
accordingly, to the vexation of his enemies on the scritina.

To the wrath not only of the joker's enemies but to that of a slender

young man, bronzed of skin and dressed in rags, who attended the burial
and witnessed the king's departure. Robayday had been not far away,
living on a fisherman's island among the reedy waters of a lake, when
news of his grandfather's death reached him. He had returned to the
capital with the alertness of a deer which attempts a closer inspection of
a lion.

Seeing the joker's retreat, he was emboldened to follow and leaped on
a hoxney, taking a track that had been familiar to him since his youth.
He had no intention of confronting his father and did not even know
what was in his own mind.

The joker, who had anything but humour on his mind, took a path he
had not taken since SartoriIrvrash had been expelled. It led to a quarry,
hidden by the soft waxy stems of young rajabaral trees; these saplings,
with hundreds of years of growth in them, were scarcely recognisable as
the redoubtable wooden fortresses they would become when the summer
of the Great Year yielded once more to winter. His fever over, the king
tied Lapwing to a young tree. He rested a hand on the smooth wood,
and his head on his hand. To his mind came a memory of the queen's
body and of the cadency which had once lit their love. Such good things
had died, and he had not known.

After a while in silence, he led Lapwing past the stump of the parent
rajabaral, as black as an extinct volcano. Ahead stood the wooden
palisade which barred entry to the quarry. No one challenged him. He
pushed his way in.

All was untended in the forecourt. Weeds thrived. The lodge was in
disrepair; a short neglect was leading it to a long decay. An old man
with a straggling white beard came forward and bowed low to his
majesty.

"Where's the guard? Why isn't the gate locked?" But there was carelessness in his challenge, which he uttered over one shoulder, in the act
of approaching the cages ahead.

The old man, accustomed to the king's moods, was too wise to adopt
a matching carelessness, and followed with a lengthy explanation of how
all but he were withdrawn from the quarry once the chancellor was
disgraced. He was alone and still tended the captives, hoping thereby to
incur the king's pleasure.

Far from showing pleasure, the king clasped his hands behind his
back and assumed a melancholy face. Four large cages had been built
against the cliffs of the quarry, each divided into various compartments
for the greater comfort of its prisoners. Into these cages JandolAnganol
sent his dark regard.

The first cage contained Others. They had been swinging there by
hands, feet, or tails as a way of passing time; when the king moved
towards their prison, they dropped down and came running to the bars,

thrusting out their handlike paws, oblivious to the exalted status of their
visitor.

The occupants of the second cage shrank away at the stranger's approach. Most of them flitted into their compartments, out of sight. Their
prison was built on rock, so that they could not tunnel into the earth.
Two of their number came forward and stood against the bars, looking
up into JandolAnganol's face. These protognostics were Nondads, small
elusive creatures often confused with Others, to whom they bore a
resemblance. They stood waist-high to a human and their faces, with
protruding muzzles, resembled Others. Scanty loincloths covered their
genitals; their bodies were covered with light sandy hair.

The two Nondads who came forward addressed the king, flitting
nervously about as they did so. A strange amalgam of whistles, clicks,
and snorts served them for language. The king regarded them with an
expression between contempt and sympathy before passing on to the
third cage.

Here were imprisoned the more advanced form of protognostic, the
Madis. Unlike the occupants of the first two cages, the Madis did not
move when the king approached. Robbed of their migratory existence,
they had nowhere to go; neither the settings of the suns nor the comings
and goings of kings held meaning for them. They tried to hide their faces
in their armpits as JandolAnganol regarded them.

The fourth cage was built of stone, rough-hewn from the quarry, as a
tribute to the greater firmness of will of its occupants, which were
human—mainly men and women of Mordriat or Thribriatan tribes. The
women slunk back into the shadows. Most of the men pressed forward
and began eloquently to implore the king to release them, or at worst to
allow no more experiments on them.

"There's nothing for it now," said the king to himself, moving about
as restlessly as those imprisoned.

"Sir, the indignities we have suffered . . ."

Ash from Rustyjonnik still lay in odd corners, where weeds thrust
from it, but the eruptions had ceased as suddenly as they began. The
king kicked at the ash, raising a small dust storm with his boots.

Although he was most interested in the Madis and studied them from
all angles, sometimes squatting to do so, he was too restless to remain in
one place. Madi males struggled forward with one of their females,
naked, and offered her to him as a condition of their release.

JandolAnganol broke away in disgust, his face working.

Bursting from behind the stone cage into the sunlight, he came face to
face with RobaydayAnganol. Both became rigid like two cats, until
Roba began to gesticulate, arms and fingers spread. Behind him came
the white-haired old guard, shuffling his feet and complaining.

"Imprisoning them for the good of their sanity, mighty king," said
Roba.

But JandolAnganol moved swiftly forward, flung an arm about his son's neck, and kissed him on the lips, as though he had decided on this approach a while ago.

"Where have you been, my son? Why so wild?"

"Can a boy not grieve among leaves, but must come to court to do so?" His words were indistinct as he backed away from his father, wiping his mouth with the back of his hand. As he bumped into the third cage, his other hand went behind him to support himself.

Immediately, one Madi reached out and grasped his forearm. The naked female who had been offered to the king bit him savagely in the ball of his thumb. Roba screamed with pain. The king was at once at the cage with his sword drawn. The Madis fell back and Roba was released.

"They're as hungry for royal blood as Simoda Tal," said Roba, hopping about with his hands clutched between his legs. "You saw how she bit me in the balls! What a stepmotherly act was there!"

The king laughed as he sheathed his sword.

"You see what happens when you put your hand in other people's affairs."

"They're very vicious, sir, and certain they've been wronged," said the old guard from a safe distance.

"Your nature inclines towards captivity as frogs incline towards pools," Roba told his father, still skipping. "But free these wretched beings! They were Rushven's folly, not yours—you had greater follies afoot."

"My son, I have a phagor runt I care for, and perhaps he cares for me. He follows me for affection. Why do you follow me for abuse? Cease it, and live a sane life with me. I will not harm you. If I have wounded you, then I regret it, as you have long given me cause to regret it. Accept what I say."

"Boys are particularly difficult to bring up, sir," commented the guard.

Father and son stood apart, regarding each other. JandolAnganol had hooded his eagle gaze, and appeared calm. On Roba's smooth face was a smouldering rage.

"You need another runt following you? Haven't you captives enough in this infamous quarry? Why did you come up here to gloat over them?"

"Not to gloat. To learn. I should have learned from Rushven. I need to know—what Madis do. . . . I understand, boy, that you fear my love. You fear responsibility. You always have. Being a king is all responsibility . . ."

"Being a butterfly is a butterfly's responsibility."

Irritated by this remark, the king again took to pacing before the cages. "Here was all SartoriIrvrash's responsibility. Maybe he was cruel. He made the occupants of these four cages mate with each other in

prescribed combinations in order to see what resulted. He wrote all
down, as was his fashion. I burnt it all—as is my fashion, you will add.
So, then.

"By his experiments, Rushven found a rule which he called a cline.
He proved that the Others in Cage One could sometimes produce
progeny when mated with Nondads. Those progeny were infertile. No,
the progeny of the Nondads breeding with Madis were infertile. I forget
details. Madis could produce progeny when mated with the humans in
Cage Four. Some of those progeny are fertile.

"He carried on his experiments for many years. If Others and Madis
were forced to copulate, no issue resulted. Humans mating with Nondads produce no issue. There is a grading, a cline. These facts he
discovered. Rushven was a gentle person. He did what he did for the
sake of knowledge.

"You probably blame him, as you blame everyone but yourself. But
Rushven paid for his knowledge. One day, two years ago—you were
absent then, in the wilds as usual—his wife came to this quarry to feed
the captives, and the Others broke out of their cage. They tore her to
pieces. This old guard will tell you . . ."

"It was her arm I found first, sir," said the guard, pleased to be
mentioned. "The left arm, to be partic'lar, sir."

"Rushven certainly paid for his knowledge. Roba, I have paid for
mine. The time will come when you too have to pay a price. It won't
always be summer."

Roba tore leaves from a bush as if he would destroy the bush, and
wrapped the leaves about his wounded hand. The guard went to help
him, but Roba kicked him away with a bare foot.

"This stinking place . . . these stinking cages . . . the stinking palace.
. . . Taking notes of dirty little ruttings. . . . Once, look, before kings were
born, the world was a big white ball in a black cup. Along came the
great kzahhn of all ancipitals and mated with the queen of all the
humans, split her open with his enormous prodo and filled her right up
with golden spume. That rumbo so shook the world that it jarred it out
of its winter frigidity and caused the seasons—"

He could not finish the sentence, so overcome was he by laughter.
The old guard looked disgusted and turned to the king.

"I can assure you, sir, the chancellor never carried out no such experiment here, to my certain knowledge."

The king remained rigid, eyes bright with contempt, not moving until
his son's outburst was over. He turned his back to him then, before
speaking.

"We have no need of that, and no need of quarrelling, not in a time of
grief. Let us return together to the palace. You can ride behind me on
Lapwing, if you wish."

Roba fell to his knees and covered his face with his hands. He made noises that were not weeping.

"Perhaps he's hungry," suggested the guard.

"Get out, man, or I'll slice your head off."

The guard fell back. "I still feed them faithfully every day, Your Majesty. Bring all the food up from the palace, and I'm not as young as I was."

JandolAnganol turned back towards his kneeling son. "You know your grandfather is now one with the gossies?"

"He was tired. I saw his grave yawn."

"I do my best, sir, but really I need a slave to assist me . . ."

"He died in his sleep—an easy death, for all his sins."

"I said he was tired. Self-demented, mother-tormented, granddad-fermented . . . that's three blows you've struck. Where next?"

The king folded his arms and tucked his hands into his armpits. "Three blows! You child—they're my one wound. Why do you plague me with nonsense? Stay and comfort me. Since you're unfit to marry even a Madi, stay."

Roba put his hands on the dirt before him and began slowly to get to his feet. The guard seized his chance to say, "They don't copulate any more, sir. Only among themselves, each cageful, as a way of passing time."

"Stay with you, Father? Stay with you as Grandfather stayed, in the bowels of the palace? No, I'm going back to the—"

As he was speaking, the guard shuffled forward in supplicatory fashion and interposed himself between JandolAnganol and his son. The king struck him a blow which sent him staggering into a bush. The captives began a great to-do, hammering on their bars.

The king smiled, or at least showed his teeth, as he attempted to approach his son. Roba back away. "You'll never understand what your grandfather did to me. You'll never understand his power over me—then—now—perhaps for ever—because I have no power over you. I could succeed only by putting him away."

"Prisons flow like glaciers in your blood. I'm going to be a Madi, or a frog. I refuse to be human as long as you claim that title."

"Rob, don't be so cruel. See sense. I—am about to—have to—marry a Madi girl soon. That's why I came to inspect the Madi here. Please stay with me."

"Trittom your Madi-slave woman! Count progeny! Measure, make notes! Write it down, suffer, lock up the fertile ones, and never forget that there is one running loose about Helliconia fit to send you to an eternal prison. . . ."

As he spoke, the youth was backing away, fingers trailing on the ground. Then he turned and darted away into the bushes. A moment later, the king spied his figure climbing over the quarry cliff. Then he was gone.

The king went and leaned against the trunk of a tree, closing his eyes.

It was the whimpering of the guard which roused him. He went over to where the old man sprawled, and assisted him to his feet.

"Sorry for that, sir, but perhaps a small slave, now I'm getting past it . . ."

Rubbing his forehead with a weary gesture, JandolAnganol said, "You can answer some questions, slanje. Tell me, please, which way is it that Madi women prefer copulation? From the rear, like animals, or face to face, like humans? Rushven would have told me."

The guard rubbed his hands on his tunic and laughed. "Oh, both ways, sir, to my observation, and I've seen it many times, working here with no help. But mainly from the rear, as do the Others. Some say as they mate for life, others as they are promiscuous, but cage life is different."

"Do the Madi sexes kiss each other on the lips like humans?"

"I've not seen that, sir, no. Only humans."

"Do they lick genitals before congress?"

"That is prevalent in all cages, sir. A lot of licking. Licking and sucking mostly, I'd say, very dirty."

"Thank you. Now you may release the prisoners. They have served their purpose. Set them free."

He left the quarry with a slow step, one hand on his sword, one on his brow.

Soft bars of shadow cast by the rajabarals moved across him as he headed back for the palace. Freyr was near to setting. The sky was yellow. Concentric haze aurioles of brown and orange, created by volcanic dust particles, encompassed the sun. It lay near the horizon like a pearl in a corrupt oyster. And the king said to Lapwing, "I can't trust him. He's wild, just as I was. I love him but I'd be better advised to kill him. If he had the sense to work with his mother forming an alliance in the scritina against me, I'd be finished. . . . I love her, but I'd be better advised to kill her, too. . . ."

The hoxney made no response. It moved towards the sunset with no ambition but to get home.

The king became aware of the vileness of his own thoughts.

Looking up at the flaring sky, he saw there the evil his religion taught him to see. "I must chasten myself," he said. "Aid me, O All-Powerful One!"

He stuck a spur in Lapwing's flank. He would go and see the First Phagorian Guard. They raised no difficult moral issues. With them he felt at peace.

The brown aureoles triumphed over the yellow. As Freyr disappeared, the oyster became ashen from its extremities inwards, changing minute by minute as the Batalix sunlight caught it. Its beauty lost, it became just a cloud formation among jumbled cloud as Batalix itself sloped westward. Akhanaba could be saying—and in no enigmatic fashion—that the whole complex scheme of things was about to end.

JandolAnganol returned to his silent palace, to find there an envoy from the Holy Pannovalan Empire. Alam Esomberr, all smiles, awaited his pleasure.

His bill of divorcement had arrived at last. He had but to present it to the queen of queens and he would be free to marry his Madi princess.

XVI

THE MAN WHO MINED
A GLACIER

S ummer of the small year had yielded to autumn in the southern
hemisphere. The monsoons were gathering along the coasts of
Hespagorat.

While on the pleasant northern coast of the Sea of Eagles Queen
MyrdemInggala swam in the blue waters with her dolphins, on the dull
southern coast of that same sea, where it merged with the waters of the
Scimitar Sea, the Avernian prize-winner, Billy Xiao Pin, lay dying.

The port of Lordryardry was sheltered from open sea by the Lordry
islands, two dozen in number, some of which were used as whaling
stations. On these islands, and along the low-lying coasts of Hespagorat,
marine iguanas lived in dense colonies. Wattled, warted, armoured,
these inoffensive beasts grew to twenty feet in length and were sometimes to be seen swimming out to sea. Billy had observed them as the
Ice Captain's *Lordryardry Lady* brought him to Dimariam.

Ashore, the beasts swarmed over rocks and marshes and each other.
Something in their slothful movements and sudden scurries marked
them out as conspirators with the soggy weather which closed in on the

Dimariamian shores at this time of small year; where cold air flowed northwards from the polar ice cap to meet the warm air above the oceans, banks of fog formed, enveloping everything in humid overcast.

Lordryardry was a small port of eleven thousand people. It owed its existence almost entirely to the enterprise of the Muntras family. One of its noteworthy features was that it lay at a latitude of 36.5° South, a degree and a half outside the wide tropical zone. Only eighteen and a half degrees farther south lay the polar circle. Beyond that circle, in the realms of eternal ice, Freyr was never to be seen during the long centuries of summer. In the Great Winter, Freyr would reappear, to remain for many lifetimes dominating the vacant world of the pole.

This Billy was told as he was driven by a traditional sledge from the ship to the ice captain's house. Krillio Muntras recounted such facts with pride, though he fell silent as his home drew near.

The room of the house to which Billy was carried was white. Its windows were framed with white curtains. As he lay locked in illness, Billy could look through trees, over town roofs, to a prospect of white mist. In that mist, an occasional mast loomed.

Billy knew he was shortly to embark on another mysterious journey. Before his ship sailed, he was tended by Muntras's self-effacing wife, Eivi, and by his formidable married daughter, Immya. Immya, he was told, had a high standing in the community as a healer.

After a day's rest, Eivi's and Immya's ministrations took effect, or else Billy enjoyed a remission. The encroaching stiffness partially left him. Immya wrapped him in blankets and helped him into the sledge. Four giant horned dogs, asokins, were harnessed up, and the family drove Billy inland to see the famous Lordryardry Glacier.

The Lordryardry Glacier had carved itself a bed between two hills. The leading face of the glacier fell into a lake which drained into the sea.

Billy observed that Krillio Muntras's manner changed subtly in the presence of his daughter. They were affectionate together, but the respect he showed Immya was not entirely matched by the respect in which she held him—so Billy judged, going less by the way they spoke than by the way Muntras held his backbone and drew in his broad stomach in Immya's presence, as if he felt he must contain himself when her sharp eyes were on him.

Muntras began to describe the workings at the glacier face. When Immya modestly prompted him on the number of men working there, he asked her without rancour to give the account herself. Which she did. Div stood behind his father and his sister, scowling; though he, as the son, was to inherit the ice company, he had nothing to contribute to the narrative, and soon slunk off.

* * *

Immya was not only the chief medical practitioner of Lordryardry; she was married to the chief lawyer of the town the Muntras clan had founded. Her husband, referred to always as Lawyer in Billy's presence, as if that had been his baptismal name, stood as the spokesman and justice of the town against the capital, Oiishat. Oiishat lay to the west, on the frontier between Dimariam and Iskahandi. Oiishat cast envious eyes on the prosperous new Lordryardry, and devised ways of securing some of its wealth by taxation—schemes which Lawyer constantly foiled.

Lawyer also foiled Muntras's local laws, which had been improvised to benefit the Muntras family rather than their workers. So Krillio was of two minds about his son-in-law.

Krillio's wife evidently felt differently. She would hear no complaint about her daughter or the Lawyer. Though submissive, she was impatient with Div, whose behaviour—adversely affected by his mother's dislike—became loutish in the home. "You should reconsider," she told Muntras one day, when they were both standing by Billy's bedside, after another example of Div's awfulness. "Hand over the company to Immya and Lawyer, and then everything will prosper. Under Div, it will be in ruin within three years. That girl has a proper grasp of things."

Certainly, Immya had a grasp of things Hespagoratean. She had never ventured beyond the confines of the continent on which she was born, despite frequent opportunities to do so, as if she preferred to have her front doorstep guarded by the myriad scaley watchdogs which patrolled the shores of Dimariam. But locked in her broad bosom were metaphorical maps, histories, and compass bearings of the southern continent.

Immya Muntras had a good plain square face built like her father's, a face capable of confronting glaciers. She stood foursquare to the ice face as she delivered her account of the family trade, in which she took great pride.

At this spot, they were far enough inland to be free of the coastal fog. The great wall of ice to which Muntras owed his wealth glittered in the sun. Where the glacier lay more distant, Batalix created in its hollows caverns of sapphire. Even its reflection in the lake at its foot gave off diamond glints.

The air was hard, fresh, and alive. Birds skimmed over the lake surface. Where the pure waters yielded to banks of blue flowers, insects were busy in their thousands.

A butterfly with a head shaped like a man's thumb settled on the three-faced watch on Billy's wrist. He stared at it with uncertain gaze, trying to interpret the meaning of the creature.

Things roared overhead, he knew not what. He could hardly look up. The virus was in his hypothalamus, in his brain stem. It would multiply irresistibly; no poultice could check it. Soon he would be locked immobile, like a phagor ancestor in tether.

He felt no regret. Regret only for the butterfly, leaving his hand and making off. In order to live a real life, of a kind his Advisor would not understand, sacrifices were called for. He had glimpsed the queen of queens. He had lain with beautiful Abathy. Even now, incapacitated, he could see distant bays of glacier where the light, conjuring powder- and thunder-blues, made of the ice more a colour than a substance. The excellence of nature had been tasted. Of course it had a price.

And Immya was explaining about the great blocks of ice which rattled overhead. At the ice face, men worked on scaffolding, cleaving the ice with saws and axes. They were Lordryardry's glacier miners. As the blocks fell off, they fell into an open funnel, and from there slipped into the shoot. The shoot, timber-built, was constructed with sufficient slope to keep the blocks of ice moving.

Great tombstones of ice travelled slowly down the shoot, which rumbled in every section as they passed over its stressed wooden legs. The tombstones made their way along two miles of shoot to the docks of Lordryardry.

At the docks, the tombstones were sawn into smaller blocks and loaded into the reed-insulated hulls of the ships of the company's fleet.

So the snows which had once fallen in the polar regions south of 55°, to be compressed and squeezed sluggishly down into the narrow temperate zone, were made to serve the useful purpose of cooling those who lived in far tropics. Here was where nature stopped and Captain Krillio Muntras took over.

"Please take me home," Billy said.

Immya's ready flow of figures ceased. Her tale of tonnages, the length of various voyages, the demand-related costings upon which their little empire was founded: these stopped. She sighed and said something to her father, but a fresh ice-load rumbling overhead erased her words. Then the lines of her face relaxed and she smiled.

"We'd better take Billy home," she said.

"I saw it," he said indistinctly. "I saw it."

And when almost half a Great Year had passed, when Helliconia and its sister planets had journeyed far from Freyr and were once again facing the slow furies of another winter, Billy's huddled form in the old wooden sledge was seen by millions of people on distant Earth.

Billy's presence on Helliconia represented an infringement of terrestrial orders. Those orders had stated that no human being was to land on Helliconia and disrupt the web of its cultures.

Those orders had been formulated over three thousand years earlier. In terms of cultural history, three thousand years was a long period of time. Since then, understanding had deepened—thanks largely to an intensive study of Helliconia undertaken by most of the population.

*There was a much better grasp of the unity—and therefore the strength
—of planetary biospheres.*

*Billy had entered the planetary biosphere and had become part of it.
The terrestrials saw no conflict. Billy's elements comprised the atoms of
dead star matter no different from the elements comprising Muntras or
MyrdemInggala. His death would represent a final union with the
planet, a merging without dissolution. Billy was mortal. The atoms of
which he was constituted were indestructible.*

*There would be a measured sorrow for the winking out of another
human consciousness, for the loss of another identity, unique, irreplaceable; but that was hardly a cause for tears on Earth.*

*The tears were shed long before that on the Avernus. Billy was their
drama, their proof that existence existed, that they themselves had the
ancient power of biological organisms to be moved in response to the
environment. Tears and cheers were the order of the day.*

*The Pin family, in particular, abandoned their usual passivity and
threw a small family storm. Rose Yi Pin, by turns laughing and howling,
was the centre of passionate attention. She had a marvellous time.*

The Advisor was mortified.

The fresh air visited Billy's body and bathed his lungs. It allowed him
to see every detail of the flashing world. But its vividness, its sounds,
were too much. He shut his eyes. When he managed to open them again,
the asokins were moving briskly, the sledge bumped, and coastal pallors
had begun to veil the view.

To compensate for earlier humiliations, Div Muntras insisted on driving the sledge. He threw the reins over his right shoulder, gripping them
under his left arm while clutching the sledge handle with his left hand.
In his right hand he flourished a whip, which he cracked above the
asokins.

"Go steady, Div, lad," Muntras growled.

As he spoke, the sledge struck a hummock of coarse grass and overturned. They were travelling under the shoot, where the ground was
marshy. Muntras landed on his hands and knees. He snatched up the
reins, looking blackly at his son but saying nothing. Immya, forming her
mouth into the shape of a stretcher, straightened the sledge and lifted
Billy back into it. Her silence was more expressive than words.

"It wasn't my fault," said Div, pretending to have hurt his wrist. His
father took up the reins and silently motioned his son round to the back
runners. They then proceeded at a sedate pace home.

The rambling Muntras house was built on one floor only. That floor
was on many levels connected by steps or short flights of stairs, owing to
the rocky terrain. Beyond the room in which Muntras and Immya

placed Billy was the coutryard in which Muntras paid his workers every tenner.

The courtyard was ornamented with smooth boulders, carved from polar mountains which no human had ever seen and delivered to the coast via the glaciers. Compressed into the striations of each stone was a past chthonic history everyone in Lordryardry was too busy to decipher —though electronic eyes aboard the Avernus had done so. Beside each boulder grew tall trees whose trunks forked close to the ground. Billy could see these trees from his couch.

Muntras's wife, Eivi, greeted them on their return and fussed round her husband, as now she fussed about Billy. He was glad when she left him alone in the bare wooden room, to stare out at the bare outlines of the trees. His eyesight became fixed. The slow madness crept on him, moving his limbs, twisting his arms outward until they stretched above his head as rigidly as the wooden branches outside.

Div entered the room. The lad came in cautiously, pushing the door shut behind him and moving quickly to Billy's side. He stared down wide-eyed at Billy in his locked posture. The hand of Billy's left arm was bent back on itself, so that the knuckles almost touched the forearm and his watch cut into his skin.

"I'll take your watch off for you," Div said. He unstrapped it clumsily and laid it on a table out of Billy's line of sight.

"The trees," Billy said, through gritted teeth.

"I want a word with you," said Div threateningly, clenching his fists. "You remember on the Lordryardry Lady, that girl AbathVasidol? The Matrassyl girl?" he asked of Billy, sitting near him, speaking low, looking at the door as he did so. "That really beautiful girl with beautiful chestnut hair and big breasts?"

"The trees."

"Yes, the trees—they're apricot trees. Father distils his Exaggerator from the fruit of those trees. Billish, that girl Abathy, you remember her, Abathy?"

"They're dying."

"Billish, you're dying. That's why I want to talk to you. You remember how Father humiliated me with that girl? He gave her to you, Billish, rot you. That was his way of humiliating me, as he always tries to humiliate me. You understand? Where did my father take Abathy, Billish? If you know, tell me. Tell me, Billish. I never did you any harm."

His elbow joints creaked. "Abathy. Summer ripeness."

"I won't hold it against you because you're foreign rubbish. Now listen. I want to know where Abathy is. I love her. I shouldn't have come back here, should I? Being humiliated by my father and that sister of mine. She'll never let me take over the company. Billish, listen,

I'm leaving. I can make it on my own—I'm no fool. Find Abathy, start my own trade. I'm asking you, Billish—where did Father take her? Quick, man, before they come."

"Yes." The stark gesturing trees at the window were trying to spell out a name. "Deuteroscopist."

Div leant forward, grasping Billy's knotted shoulders. "CaraBansity? He took Abathy to CaraBansity?"

From the dying man came a whispered affirmative. Div let him fall back as if he were a plank of wood. He stood flicking his fingers, muttering to himself. Hearing a sound in the passage, he ran to the window. He balanced his bulk momentarily on the sill. Then he jumped out and was gone.

Eivi Muntras returned. She fed Billy with fragments of a delicate white meat from a bowl. She forced and coaxed; he ate ravenously. In the world of the sick, Eivi was perfectly in command. She bathed his face and brow with a sponge. She drew a gauze curtain over the window to cut down the light. Through the gauze, the trees became ghost trees.

"I'm hungry," he said, when all the food was gone.

"I'll bring you some more iguana soon, dear. You liked it, didn't you? I cooked it in milk especially."

"I'm hungry," he screamed.

She left, looking distressed. He heard her talking to other people. His neck contorted, cords standing out on it as his hearing paid out like a harpoon to fix on what was said. The words made no sense to him. He was lying upside down, so that the sentences entered his ear the wrong way up. When he flipped himself over, everything was perfectly audible.

Immya's voice said, in impartial tones, "Mother, you are being silly. These homemade nostrums cannot cure Billish. He has a rare disease which we scarcely know of except in history books. It is either bone fever or the fat death. His symptoms are unclear, possibly because he comes from that other world as he claims, and therefore his cellular composition may differ in some way from ours."

"I don't know about that, Immya dear. I just think that a little more meat would be good for him. Perhaps he'd like a gwing-gwing . . ."

"He may go into a state of bulimia, coupled with an overactive disposition. Those would be symptomatic of fat death. In that case, we would have to tie him down to the bed."

"Surely that won't be necessary, dear? He's so gentle."

"It is not a case of his disposition, Mother, but of the disposition of his disease." That was a male voice, charged with half-concealed contempt, as if a practical point were being explained to a child. It belonged to Immya's husband, Lawyer.

"Well, I don't know about that, I'm sure. I just hope it isn't catching."

"We don't believe that either fat death or bone fever is infectious at this time of the Great Year," said Immya's voice. "We think Billish must have been with phagors, with whom these illnesses are generally associated."

There was more of the kind, and then Immya and Lawyer were in the room, gazing down at Billy.

"You may recover," she said, bending slightly at the waist to deliver her words and releasing them one by one. "We shall take care of you. We may have to tie you down if you get violent."

"Dying. Inevitable." With a great effort, he pretended not to be a tree and said, "Bone fever and fat death—I can explain. Just one virus. Germ. Different effects. According to time. Of Great Year. True."

Further effort was beyond him. The rigors set in. Yet for a moment he had it all in mind. Although it had not been his subject, the helico virus was a legend on the Avernus, though a dying one, confined to video-texts, since its last outbreak in pandemic form had occurred several lifetimes before those now alive on the station. Those who now looked down helplessly on him from above were witnessing an old story brought back into currency only as the conclusion to every Helliconian Holiday.

The visitations of the virus caused immense suffering but were fortu-nately confined to two periods in the Great Year: six local centuries after the coldest time of that year, when planetary conditions were improving, and in the late autumn, after the long period of heat into which Helliconia had now entered. In the first period, the virus mani-fested itself as bone fever; in the second, as fat death. Almost no one escaped these scourges. The mortality rate of each approached fifty percent. Those who survived became, respectively, fifty percent lighter or fifty percent heavier in body weight, and thus were better equipped to face the hotter and colder seasons.

The virus was the mechanism by which human metabolisms adjusted to enormous climatic changes. Billy was being changed.

Immya was silent, standing by Billy's bedside. She folded her arms over her grand bosom.

"I don't understand you. How do you know such things? You're no god, or you would not be ill . . ."

Even the sound of voices drove him deeper into the entrails of a tree. He managed again. "One disease. Two . . . opposed systems. You as doctor understand."

She understood. She sat down again. "If it were so . . . and yet—why not? There are two botanies. Trees that flower and seed only once in 1825 small years, other trees that flower and seed every small year. Things that are divided yet united . . ."

She closed her mouth tightly as if afraid of releasing a secret, aware that she stood on the brink of something beyond her understanding. The case of the helico virus was not exactly similar to that of Helliconia's binary botanies. Yet Immya was correct in her observations on the divergent habits of plant life. At the time of Batalix's capture by Freyr, some eight million years previously, Batalix's planets had been bathed in radiation, leading to genetic divergences in multitudinous phyla. While some trees had remained flowering and fruiting as before—so that they attempted to produce seed 1825 times during the Great Year, whatever the climatic conditions—others had adapted a metabolism better geared towards the new regime, and propagated themselves only once in 1825 small years. Such were the rajabarals. The apricot trees outside Billy's window had not adapted and were, as it happened, dying off in the unusual heat.

Something in the lines which formed about Immya's mouth suggested she was attempting to chew over these weighty matters; but she switched instead to a contemplaion of Billy's remarks. Her intelligence told her that if the statement proved true, it would be of great importance—if not immediately, then a few centuries ahead, when, the scanty records suggested, fat death pandemics were due.

Thinking so far into the future was not a local habit. She gave him a nod and said, "I will think about it, Billish, and bring your perception before our medical society when next we meet. If we understand the true nature of this malady, perhaps we can find a cure."

"No. Disease essential for survival . . ." He could see that she would never accept and he could never explain his point. He compromised by forcing out, "I told your father."

The remark deflected her interest from medical questions. She stared away from him, swathing herself in silence, seeming to shrink into herself. When she spoke again, her voice was deeper and harsher, as if she too had to communicate from within an imprisonment.

"What else did you do with my father? In Borlien. Was he drunk? I want to know—did he have a young woman on the boat from Matrassyl? Did he have carnal knowledge of her? You must tell me." She leaned over him, to grasp him as her brother had done. "He's drinking now. There was a woman, wasn't there? I ask you for my mother's sake."

The intensity with which these words were spoken frightened Billy; he strove to sink deeper into the tree, to feel the rough bark gripping his eddre. Bubbles came from his mouth.

She shook him. "Did he have carnal knowledge? Tell me. Die if you will, but tell me."

He tried to nod.

Something in his distorted expression confirmed her guess. A look of vindictive satisfaction came on her face.

"Men! That's how they take advantage of women. My poor mother has suffered from his debauchery for years, poor innocent thing. I found out years ago. It was an awful shock. We Dimariamians are respectable people, not like the inhabitants of the Savage Continent, which I hope never to have to visit . . ."

As her voice died, Billy attempted an inarticulate protest. It served to rekindle the fire of Immya's animosity. "And what about the poor innocent girl involved? And her innocent mother? I long ago made that brother of mine, the bane of my life, confess to me everything my father does. . . . Men are pigs, ruled by lust, unable to keep faith . . ."

"The girl." But Abathy's name became entangled with the knots in his larynx.

Gloaming enveloped Lordryardry. Freyr sank to the west. Bird songs became fewer. Batalix took up a position low on the horizon, where it could glare across the water at the scaley things piled on the shore. Mists thickened, obscuring the stars and the Night Worm.

Eivi Muntras brought Billy some soup before she retired to bed. As he drank, terrible hungers rose from his very eddre. His immobility was overcome, he sprang at Eivi, bit her shoulder and tore flesh from it. He ran about the room screaming. This was the bulimia associated with the late stages of fat death. Other members of the family came running, slaves brought lights. Billy was cursed and cuffed and strapped down to his bed.

For an hour he was left, while the sound of ministrations came from the other end of the house. He endured visions of eating Eivi whole, of sucking her brains. He wept. He imagined that he was back on the Avernus. He imagined he was eating Rose Yi Pin. He wept again. His tears fell like leaves.

Boards creaked in the corridor. A dim lamp appeared, behind it a man's face floating as if on a stream of darkness. The Ice Captain, breathing heavily. Fumes of Exaggerator entered the room with him.

"Are you all right? I'd have to throw you out if you weren't dying, Billish." He steadied himself, breathing heavily. "I'm sorry it's come to this . . . I know you're some kind of angel from a better world, Billish, even when you bite like a devil. A man's got to believe there's a better world somewhere. Better than this one, where no one cares about you. Avernus . . . I would take you back there, if I could. I'd like to see it."

Billy was back in his tree, his limbs part and parcel of its agonised branches.

"Better."

"That's right, better. I'm going to sit in the courtyard, Billish, just outside your window. Have a drink. Think about things. It'll soon enough be time to pay the men. If you want me, just give a call."

He was sorry that Billish was dying, and the Exaggerator made him sorry for himself. It was puzzling the way he always felt more comfortable with strangers, even with the queen of queens, than he did with his own family. With them he was constantly at a disadvantage.

He settled himself down outside the window, placing a jug and glass on the bench beside him. In the milky light, the stones resembled sleeping animals. The albic climbing the walls of the house opened its blooms, the blooms opened their beaks like parrots; a tranquil scent floated on the air.

After his plan to bring Billish here in secrecy had succeeded, he found himself unable to proceed further. He wanted to tell everyone that there was more to life than they knew, that Billish was a living example of that truth. It was not just that Billish was dying; Muntras suspected, somewhere in a cold corner of his being, that there might be less to life than he knew. He wished he had remained a wanderer. Now he was back home for good. . . .

After a while, sighing, the Ice Captain pulled himself to his feet and peered through the open window. "Billish, are you awake? Have you seen Div?"

A gurgle in response.

"Poor lad, he's not really fit for the job, that's the truth . . ." He sat down again on the bench, groaning. He took up his glass and drank. Too bad Billish didn't like Exaggerator.

The milky light thickened. Dusk-moths purred among the albic. In the sleeping house at his back boards creaked.

"There must be a better world somewhere . . ." Muntras said, and fell asleep with an unlit veronikane between his lips.

The sound of voices. Muntras roused. He saw his men gathering in the court to be paid. It was daylight. Dead calm prevailed.

Muntras stood and stretched. He looked in through the window at Billish's contorted form, motionless on the couch.

"This is assatassi day, Billish—I'd forgotten, with you here. The monsoon high tide. You ought to see this. It's quite a local event. There'll be celebrations tonight, and no half measures."

From the couch came a single word, forced from a locked jaw. "Celebrations."

The workmen were rough, dressed in rough overalls. They cast their gaze down on the worn paving stones in case their master took offence at being discovered asleep. But that was not Muntras's way.

"Come on, men. I'll not be paying you out much longer. It'll be Master Div's turn. Let's get it over with promptly, and then we'll prepare for the festivities. Where's my pay clerk?"

A small man with a high collar and hair brushed in the opposite direction to anyone else's came darting forward. He had a ledger under his arm and was followed by a stallun carrying a safe. The clerk made a great business of pushing through the workers. This he did with his eyes constantly on his employer and his lips working as if he was already calculating what each man should be paid. His arrival caused the men to shuffle into a line to await their modest remuneration. In the unusual light, their features were without animation.

"You lot are going to collect your wages, and then you're going to hand it over to your wives or get drunk as usual," Muntras said. He addressed the men near him, among whom he saw only common-hire labourers and none of his master craftsmen. But at once a mixture of indignation and pity seized him and he spoke louder, so that all could hear. "Your lives are going by. Here you're stuck. You've been nowhere. You know of the legends of Pegovin, but have you ever been there? Who's been there? Who's been to Pegovin?"

They leaned back against the rounded stones, muttering.

"I've been all over the world. I've seen it all. I've been to Uskutoshk, I've visited the Great Wheel of Kharnabhar, I've seen old ruined cities and sold junk in the bazaars of Pannoval and Oldorando. I've spoken with kings and queens as fair as flowers. It's all out there, waiting for the man who dares. Friends everywhere. Men and women. It's wonderful. I've loved every minute of it.

"It's bigger than you can ever imagine, stuck here at Lordryardry. This last voyage, I met a man who came from another world. There's more than just this world, Helliconia. There's another circling around us, Avernus. And others beyond that, worlds to be visited. Earth, for instance."

All the while he was speaking, the little clerk was laying out his effects on a table under one of the barren apricot trees and removing the key to the safe from an inner pocket. And the phagor was setting the safe down just where needed and flicking an ear as it did so. And the men were shuffling forward to the edge of the table and making their line more definite by moving closer to each other. And other men were coming up, directing suspicious looks at their boss, and joining the rear of the line. And the comfortable seriality of the world was being maintained under the purple clouds.

"I tell you there are other worlds. Use your imagination." Muntras struck the table. "Don't you feel the wanderlust occasionally? I did when I was a young 'un, I tell you. Inside my house even now I have a young man from one of these other worlds. He's ill or he'd come out and speak to you. He can tell you miraculous things that happen lifetimes away."

"Does he drink Exaggerator?"

The voice came from within the ranks of the waiting men. It stopped Muntras in full burst. He paced up and down the line, red of face. Not an eye met his.

"I'll prove what I'm saying," Muntras shouted. "You'll have to believe me then."

He turned and stamped into the house. Only the clerk showed some impatience, drumming his little fingers on the plank table, staring about, pulling his sharp nose, and looking up at the heavy sky.

Muntras ran in to where Billy was, terribly distorted, without motion. He seized Billy's petrified wrist, only to find that the watch had gone.

"Billish," he said. He went over to the invalid, looked down at him, called his name more gently. He felt the cold skin, tested the twisted flesh.

"Billish," he said again, but now it was merely a statement. He knew that Billish was dead—and he knew who had stolen the watch, that three-faced timepiece which King JandolAnganol had once held. There was only one person who would do such a thing.

"You'll never miss your timepiece now, Billy," Muntras said aloud.

He covered his face with a slab of hand and uttered something between a prayer and a curse.

For a moment more, the Ice Captain stood in the room, looking up at the ceiling with his mouth open. Then, recalling his duties, he walked over to the window and gave his clerk a sign to start paying out the men's wages.

His wife entered the room with Immya, her shoulder bandaged.

"Our Billish is dead," he said flatly.

"Oh dear, and on assatassi day, too . . ." Eivi said. "You can hardly expect me to be sorry."

"I'll see his body is conveyed to the ice cellar, and we will bury him tomorrow, after the feast," Immya said, moving over to observe the contorted body. "He told me something before he died which could be a contribution to medical science."

"You're a capable girl, you look after him," Muntras said. "As you say, we can bury him tomorrow. A proper funeral. Meanwhile, I'll go and look to the nets. As a matter of fact, I feel miserable, as if anyone cares."

Taking no heed of the jabbering women who were stringing up lines of net on poles, the Ice Captain walked along the water's edge. He wore high thick boots and kept his hands in his pockets. Occasionally, one of the black iguanas would jump up against him like an importuning dog. Muntras would knee it down again without interest. The iguanas wallowed among thick brown ropes of kelp which swirled in the shallow water, sometimes kicking to get free of the coils. In places, they were banked on top of each other, indifferent to how they lay.

To add to the melancholy abandonment of their postures, the iguanas were commensal with a hairy twelve-legged crab, which scurried in its millions among the forms which kept watch on the breakers. The crabs devoured any fragment of food—seal or seaweed—dropped by the reptiles; nor were they averse to devouring infant iguanas. The characteristic noise of the Dimariamian seashore was a crunch and scrabble of armoured legs against scales; the ritual of their lives was playing out against this clamour, which was as endless as the sound of the waves.

The ice captain took no notice of these saturnine occupants of the shore, but stared out to sea, beyond Lordry, the whaling island. He had checked at the harbour and been told that a light sailing dinghy had been stolen overnight.

So his son was gone, taking the magic watch, either as talisman or for trade. Had sailed away, without so much as a good-bye.

"Why did you do it?" Muntras asked half aloud, staring over the purple sea on which a dead calm prevailed. "For the usual reasons a man leaves home, I suppose. Either you couldn't bear your family any longer, or you just wanted adventure—strange places, amazements, strange women. Well, good luck to you, lad. You'd never have made the world's foremost ice trader, that's certain. Let's hope you aren't reduced to selling stolen rings for a living. . . ."

Some of the women, humble worker's wives, were calling to him to come behind the nets before high tide. He gave them a salute and trudged away from the milling iguana bodies.

Immya and Lawyer would have to take over the company. Not his favourite people, but they'd probably run the whole concern better than he ever did. You had to face facts. It was no use growing bitter. Although he had never been comfortable with his daughter, he recognised that she was a good woman.

At least he'd stand by a friend and see that BillishOwpin got a proper burial. Not that either Billish or he believed in any of the gods. But just for their own two sakes.

He trudged towards the safety of the nets, where the workmen stood. "You were all right, Billish," he muttered aloud. "You were nobody's fool."

The Avernus had company in its orbit about Helliconia. It moved among squadrons of auxiliary satellites. The main task of these auxiliaries was to observe sectors of the globe the Avernus itself was not observing. But it so happened that the Avernus, on its circumpolar orbit, was itself above Lordryardry and travelling north at the time of Billy's funeral.

The funeral was a popular event. The fact is, human egos being frail, other people's deaths are not entirely unpleasureable. Melancholy itself is among the more enjoyable of emotions. Almost everyone aboard the Avernus looked in: even Rose Yi Pin, although she watched the event from the bed of her new boyfriend.

Billy's Advisor, dry-eyed, gave a homily in one hundred measured words on the virtues of submission to one's lot. The epitaph served also as an epitaph to the protest movements. With some relief, they forgot difficult thoughts of reform and returned to their administrative duties. One of them wrote a sad song about Billy, buried away from his family.

There were now a good many Avernians buried on Helliconia, all winners of Helliconia Holidays. A question often asked aboard the Earth Observation Station was, How did this affect the mass of the planet?

On Earth, where the funeral of Billy provoked less interest, the event was seen more detachedly. Every living being is created from dead star-matter. Every living being must make its solitary journey upward from the molecular level towards the autonomy of birth, a journey which in the case of humans takes three-quarters of a year. The complex degree of organisation involved in being a higher life-form cannot be forever sustained. Eventually, there is a return to the inorganic. Chemical bonds dissolve.

That had happened in Billy's case. All that was immortal about him was the atoms from which he was assembled. They endured. And there was nothing strange about a man of terrestrial stock being buried on a planet a thousand light-years away. Earth and Helliconia were near neighbours, composed of the same debris from the same long defunct stars.

In one detail that correct man, Billy's Advisor, was incorrect. He spoke of Billy going to his long rest. But the entire organic drama of which mankind formed a part was pitched within the great continuing explosion of the universe. From a cosmic viewpoint, there was no rest anywhere, no stability, only the ceaseless activity of particles and energies.

XVII

DEATH-FLIGHT

General Hanra TolramKetinet wore a wide-brimmed hat and an old pair of trousers, the bottoms of which were stuffed into the tops of a pair of knee-length army boots. Across his naked chest he had slung a fine new matchlock firearm on a strap. Above his head he waved a Borlienese flag. He waded out to sea towards the approaching ships.

Behind him, his small force cheered encouragement. There were twelve men, led by an able young lieutenant, GortorLanstatet. They stood on a spit of sand; behind them, jungle and the dark mouth of the River Kacol. Their voyage down from Ordelay—from defeat—was over; they had navigated, in the *Lordryardry Lubber*, both rapids and sections of the river where the current was so slight that out from the depths came tuberous growths, fighting like knots of reproducing eels to gain the surface and release a scent of carrion and julip. That scent was the jungle's malediction.

On either bank of the Kacol, the forest twisted itself into knots, snakes, and streamers no less forbidding than the tentacles which rose from the river depths. Here the forest indeed looked impenetrable; there were visible none of the wide aisles down which the general, half a tenner ago, had walked in perfect safety, for the river had tempted to the jungle's edge a host of sun-greedy creepers. The jungle, too, had become more dwarfish in formation, turning from rain forest proper to monsoon forest, with the heavy heads of its canopy pressing low above the heads of the Borlienese troops.

Where river at last delivered its brown waters into sea, foetid morning mists rose from the forest, rolling in ridge beyond ridge up the unruly slopes that culminated in the Randonanese massif.

The mist had been something of a motif of their journey, preluded from the moment when—in undisputed possession of the *Lubber* at Ordelay—they had prized open the hatches, to be greeted by thick vapours pouring from the boat's cargo of melting ice. Once the ice was cast overboard, the new owners, investigating, had discovered secret lockers full of Sibornalese matchlocks, wrapped in rags against the damp: the *Lubber* captain's secret personal trade, to recompense himself for the dangerous voyages he undertook on behalf of the Lordry-ardry Ice Trading Company. Freshly armed, the Borlienese had set sail on the oily waters, to disappear into the curtains of humidity which were such a feature of the Kacol.

Now they stood, watching their general wade towards the ships, on a sandbar that stood out like a spur from a small rocky and afforested island, Keevasien Island, which lay between river and sea. The dark green tunnel, the stench, the insect-tormented silences, the mists, were behind them. The sea beckoned. They looked forward to rescue, shading their eyes to gaze seawards against a brilliance accentuated by the hazy morning overcast.

Rescue could hardly have been more timely. On the previous day, when Freyr had set and the jungle was a maze of uncertain outlines as Batalix descended, they had been seeking a mooring between gigantic roots red like intestines; without warning, a tangle of six snakes, none less than seven feet long, had dropped down from branches overhead. They were pack snakes which, with rudimentary intelligence, always hunted together. Nothing could have terrified the crew more. The man who stood at the wheel, seeing the horrible things land close to him and rapidly disentangle themselves, hissing in fury, jumped overboard without a moment's thought, to be seized by a greeb which a moment before had resembled a decaying log.

The pack snakes were eventually killed. By that time, the boat had swung side on into the current, and was grinding against the Randonanese bank. As they attempted to regain control, their rudder hit an underwater obstruction and broke. Poles were brought forth, but the river was becoming both wider and deeper, so the poles did not serve. When Keevasien Island loomed through the dusk they had no power to choose either the port, the Borlienese, stream, or the starboard, the Randonanese, stream. The *Lubber* was carried helplessly against the rocks on the northern point of the island; with its side stove in, it was beached in the shallows. The current tugged at it, threatening to wash it away. They grabbed some equipment and jumped ashore.

Darkness was coming in. They stood listening to the repetitive boom of the surf like distant cannon fire. Because of the great fear of the men, TolramKetinet decided to camp where they were for the brief night, rather than attempt to reach Keevasien, which he knew was close.

A watch was set. The night around them was given to subterfuge and sudden death. Small insects went shopping with large headlights, moths' wings gleamed with terrifying sightless eyes, the pupils of predators glowed like hot stones; and all the while the two streams of the river surged close by, eddying phosphorescence, the heavy drag of water moaning its way into their dreams.

Freyr rose behind cloud. The men woke and stood about scratching mosquito bites which covered their bodies. TolramKetinet and Gortor-Lanstatet drove them into action. Climbing the rocky spine of the island, they could look across the eastern arm of the river to the open sea and the Borlienese coast ahead. There, protected from the sea by afforested cliff, lay the harbour of Keevasien, the westernmost town of their native land of Borlien, once home of the legendary savant YarapRombry.

A purplish cast to the light obscured the truth from them for a while; they looked on broken roofs and blackened walls for some moments before saying—almost in one voice—"It's been destroyed!"

Phagor herds, denizens of the monsoon forest, had bartered their volumunwun with the Randonanese tribes. The great spirit had spoken to the tribes. The tribes caught Others in the trees, bound them to bamboo chairs, and progressed through the jungle to burn down the port. Nothing had escaped the flames. There was no sign of life, except for a few melancholy birds. The war was still being waged; the men could not avoid being at once its agents and its victims.

In silence, they made their way to the south side of the island, climbing down on a sandy spit to get free of the spikey undergrowth that choked the interior.

Open sea was before them, ribbed with brown where the Kacol joined it, ultimately blue. Long breakers uncurled against the steep slope of the beach, flashing white. To the west they could see Poorich Island, a large island which served as a marker between the Sea of Eagles and the Narmosset Sea. Round the angle of Poorich were sailing four ships, two carracks and two caravels.

Seizing up the Borlienese flag which had been stored among a selec-

tion of flags in the *Lubber*'s lockers, TolramKetinet walked forward into
the foam to meet them.

Dienu Pasharatid was on watch on the *Golden Friendship* as it made
for a safe anchorage with its fleet in the mouth of the Kacol. Her hands
tightened on the rail; otherwise she gave no sign of the elation she felt
on beholding, as Poorich Island slid behind, the coast of Borlien emerge
from the morning mists.

Six thousand sea miles had fallen astern since they repaired the ships
and sailed on from the pleasant anchorage near Cape Findowel. In that
time, Dienu had communed much with God the Azoiaxic; the limitless
expanses of ocean had brought her closer than ever before to his presence. She told herself that her involvement with her husband Io was
over. She had had him transferred to the *Union*, so that she no longer
had to look at him. All this she had done in a cool Sibornalese way,
without showing resentment. She was free to rejoice again in life and in
God.

There was the beautiful breeze, the sky, the sea—why, as she strove
to rejoice, did misery invade her? It could not be because she was
jealous of the relationship which had grown—like a weed, she said to
herself, like a weed—between her Priest-Militant Admiral and the
Borlienese ex-chancellor. Nor could it be because she felt the slightest
spark of affection for Io. "Think of winter," she told herself—using an
Uskuti expression meaning, "Freeze your hopes."

Even the communion with the Azoiaxic, which she was unable to
break off, had proved disconcerting. It seemed that the Azoiaxic had no
place for Dienu Pasharatid in his bosom. Despite her virtue, he was
indifferent. He was indifferent despite her seemly behaviour, her circumspection.

In this respect at least, the Dweller, the Lord of the Church of the
Formidable Peace, had proved dismayingly to resemble Io Pasharatid
himself. And it was this reflection, rather than consolation, which pursued her over the empty leagues of sea. Anything was welcome by way
of distraction. So, when the coast of Borlien appeared, she turned
briskly from the wheel and summoned the bugler to sound "Good
Tidings."

Soon the rails of the four ships were crowded with soldiers, eager
for a first glimpse of the land they were planning to invade and sub-
jugate.

One of the last passengers to arrive on deck was SartoriIrvrash. He
stood for a while in the open air, clapping his clothes and breathing deep
to disperse a smell of phagor. The phagor was gone; only her bitter scent
remained—that, and a fragment of knowledge.

After the *Golden Friendship* had left Findowel, it sailed southeastwards across the Gulf of Ponipot, past ancient lands, and through the
Cadmer Straits, the narrowest stretch of water between Campannlat and
Hespagorat. These were lands that legends told of; some said that
humans had come into being here, some that language was first spoken
here. Here was Ponipot, the Ponpt that little Tatro read about in her
fairy tales, Ponipot almost uninhabited, gazing towards the setting of the
suns, with its old mouldering cities whose names were still capable of
stirring men's hearts—Powachet, Prowash, Gal-Dundar on the frigid
Aza River.

Past Ponipot, to be becalmed off the rocky spines of Radado, the land
of high desert, the southern tail of the Barriers, where it was said that
under one million humans lived—in contrast to the three and a quarter
million in neighbouring Randonan—and certainly fewer humans than
phagors: for Radado formed the western end of a great ancipital migratory route which stretched across the whole of Campannlat, the ultima
Thule to which the creatures came in the summer of every Great Year,
to go about their unfathomable rituals, or simply to squat motionless,
staring across the Cadmer Straits towards Hespagorat, towards a destination unknown to other life forms.

Becalmed or otherwise, in those long hot days on the stationary ship,
SartoriIrvrash had been content. He had escaped from his study into the
wide world. During dimdays, there were long intellectual conversations
to be enjoyed with the lady Priest-Militant Admiral, Odi Jeseratabhar.
The two of them had become closer. Odi Jeseratabhar's first intricacy of
language had dissolved into something less formal. The involuntary
proximities enforced by their narrow quarters had become wished for,
treasured. They turned into circumspect lovers. And the circumnavigation of the Savage Continent had become a circumnavigation also of
souls.

Sitting together on deck during that enchanted becalmment, the aging
lovers, Borlienese and Uskuti, surveyed the almost unmoving sea. The
Radado mainland hung mistily in the background. Nearer at hand,
Gleeat Island lay to port. Away to starboard, three other islands,
submerged mountain peaks, seemed to float on the bosom of the
water.

Odi Jeseratabhar pointed to starboard. "I can almost imagine I can
make out the coast of Hespagorat—the land called Throssa, to be precise. All round us is the evidence that Hespagorat and Campannlat were
once joined by a land bridge, which was destroyed in some upheaval.
What do you think, Sartori?"

He studied the hump of Gleeat Island. "If we can believe the legends,
phagors originated in a distant part of Hespagorat, Pegovin, where the
black phagors live. Perhaps the phagors of Campannlat migrate to

Radado because they still hope to discover the ancient bridge back to their homeland."

"Have you ever seen a black phagor in Borlien?"

"Once in captivity." He drew on his veronikane. "The continents keep their separate kinds of animals. If there was once a land bridge, then we might expect to find the iguanas of Hespagorat on the coast of Radado. Are they there, Odi?"

With a sudden inspiration, she said, "I think they are not, because the humans might have killed them off—Radado is a barren place; anything serves as food. But what about Gleeat? While we are becalmed, we have time to spare, time in which we might add to the fund of human knowledge. You and I will go on an expedition in the longboat and see what we find."

"Can we do that?"

"If I say so."

"Remember our near disaster on the Persecution Bay expedition?"

"You thought I was crazy then."

"I think you're crazy now."

They both laughed, and he clutched her hand.

The Admiral summoned the bo'sun. Slaves were set to work. The longboat was launched. Odi Jeseratabhar and SartoriIrvrash climbed aboard. They were rowed two miles across to the island, over a sea of glass. With them went a dozen armed soldiers, delighted at this chance to leave the hated confines of the ship.

Gleeat Island measured five miles across. The ship's boat beached on a steep sandy shelf at the southeast corner. A guard was set on it, while the rest of the expedition moved forward.

Iguanas basked on the rocks. They showed no fear of the humans, and several were speared to be taken back to the ship as welcome addition to the diet. They were puny beside the giant black iguanas of Hespagorat. These rarely attained more than five feet in length. Their colour was a mottled brown. Even the crabs that lived commensally with them were small and had only eight legs.

As SartoriIrvrash and Odi Jeseratabhar were searching the rocks for iguana eggs, the party came under attack. Four phagors rushed from cover, spears in hand, and fell on them. They were ragged beasts, their coats in tatters, their ribs showing.

With surprise on their side, the phagors managed to kill two of the soldiers, bearing the men down into the water with the force of their charge. But the other soldiers fought back. Iguanas scattered, gulls rose screaming, there was a brief pursuit over the rocks, and the scrimmage was finished. The phagors were dead—except for a gillot whose life Odi Jeseratabhar spared.

The gillot was larger than her companions and covered in a dense black coat. With her arms bound firmly behind her, she was made captive and taken back in the boat to the *Golden Friendship*.

Odi and Sartori embraced each other in private, congratulating themselves on confirming the truth of the old legend of the land bridge. And on surviving.

A day later, the monsoon winds blew, and the fleet was on its way eastwards again. The coast of Randonan was now passing in all its wild splendour on the port side; but SartoriIrvrash spent most of his time below decks, studying their captive, whom he called Gleeat.

Gleeat spoke only Native Ancipital, and that in a dialect. Knowing no Native, or even Hurdhu, SartoriIrvrash had to work through an interpreter. Odi came down into the cramped dark hold to see what he was doing, and laughed.

"How can you bother with this smelly creature? We have proved our point, that Radado and Throssa were once connected. God the Azoiaxic was on our side. The small colony of iguanas isolated on Gleeat Island are an inferior strain, isolated from the main body of iguanas on the southern continent. This creature, living among white phagors, probably represents some kind of survival of the Hespagorat-Pegovin black strain. Doubtless they're dying out on such a small island."

He shook his head. While admiring her quick brain, he perceived that she reached conclusions too hastily.

"She claims that her party were on a ship which was wrecked on Gleeat in an earlier monsoon."

"That's clearly a lie. Phagors do not sail. They hate water."

"They were slaves on a Throssan galley, she says."

Odi patted his shoulder. "Listen, Sartori, it's my belief that we could have proved that the two continents were once linked just by looking at the old charts in the chartroom. There's Purporian on the Radado shore and a port called Popevin on the Throssa shore. 'Poop' means 'bridge' in Pure Olonets, and 'Pup' or 'Pu' the same in Local Olonets. The past is locked up in language, if one knows how to look."

Although she laughed, he was vexed by her superior Sibornalese style. "If the smell is overcoming you, dear, you had better go back on deck."

"We shall soon be approaching Keevasien. A coastal town. As you know, 'ass' or 'as' is Pure Olonets for 'sea'—the equivalent of 'ash' in Pontpian." With that burst of knowledge, smiling, she retired, climbing the ladder to the quarterdeck in practical fashion.

He was surprised next day to find that Gleeat was wounded. There was a golden pool of blood on the deck where she lay. He questioned her through the interpreter. Although he watched her closely, he could detect nothing resembling emotion when she answered.

"No, she is not wounded. She says she is coming on oestrus. She has just undergone her menstrual period." The interpreter looked his distaste but made no personal comment, being of inferior rank.

Such was his hatred for phagors—but it was gone now, like much else from his past life, he realised—that SartoriIrvrash had always neglected their history, just as he had refused to learn their language. Such matters he had left to JandolAnganol—JandolAnganol with his perverse trust in the creatures. However, the sexual habits of phagors had been a target for prurient jest to the very urchins in the Matrassyl streets; he recalled that the female ancipital, neither human nor beast, delivered something like a one-day menstrual flow from the uterus as prelude to the oestral cycle when she came on heat. It might be memories of those old whispers which caused him to imagine that his captive emitted a more pungent odour on this occasion.

SartoriIrvrash scratched his cheek. "What was that word she used for catamenia? Her word in Native?"

"She calls oestrus 'tennhrr' in her language. Shall I have her hosed down?"

"Ask her how frequently she comes into oestrus."

The gillot, who remained tied, had to be prodded before she gave answer. Her long pink milt flicked up one of her nostrils. She finally admitted to having ten periods in a small year. SartoriIrvrash nodded and went on deck for some fresh air. Poor creature, he thought; a pity we can't all live in peace. The human-ancipital dilemma would have to be resolved one day, one way or another. When he was dead and gone.

They drove before the monsoon all that night, the next day, and the night following. The rains were frequently so thick that those aboard the *Golden Friendship* could not make out their sister ships. The Straits of Cadmer were left behind. All about them was the grey Narmosset, its waves streaked with long spittles of white. The world was a liquid one.

During the fifth night, they encountered a storm, and the carrack almost stood on its beam ends. The hollies and orange trees growing along the waist were all lost overboard, and many feared that the ship would founder. The seamen, always superstitious, approached their captain and begged that the captive phagor be cast overboard, since it was well known that ancipitals aboard ship brought bad luck. The captain agreed. He had tried almost everything else.

SartoriIrvrash was awake, despite the late hour. It was impossible to sleep in the storm. He protested against the captain's decision. No one was in any mood to listen to his arguments; he was a foreigner, and in danger of being thrown overboard himself. He went and hid while Gleeat was dragged from her foul hold and thrown into the raging waters.

Within an hour, the worst of the wind died. By the time of false light, when Poorich was just visible ahead, nothing more than a fresh breeze prevailed. By dawn, the other three vessels were disclosed, miraculously unharmed and not too far distant—God the Azoiaxic was good. Soon, the mouth of the Kacol, where Keevasien lay, could be discerned through purplish coastal mists.

An unnatural gloom hovered about the hinges of the horizon. The sea all round the Sibornalese fleet was alive with dolphins, darting just below the surface. Flocks of sea and land birds numbering many hundreds circled overhead. They uttered no cry, but the beat of their myriad wings sounded like a downpour in which no rain fell. The flocks did not swerve as the call "Good Tidings" rolled out from ship to coast.

As the wind died, the cordage slackened and slapped against the masts. The four ships closed as they approached the shore.

Dienu set a spyglass to her eye and stared at where a strip of island lay among the breaking waves. She saw men standing on the strip, and counted a dozen. One was coming forward. During the days of the monsoon, they had skirted the coasts of Randonan; here Borlien commenced—enemy territory. It was important that news of the fleet's coming was not flashed ahead to Ottassol; surprise counted for much, in this as in most warlike enterprises.

The light improved, minute by minute. The *Golden Friendship* exchanged signals with the *Union*, the *Good Hope*, and the white caravel, the *Vajabhar Prayer*, alerting them to danger.

A man in a wide-brimmed hat was wading out into the foam. Behind him, at the mouth of the river, a boat could be seen, hull half-hidden. There was always the possibility that they were moving into an ambush and, getting too far in, would lose the wind and be trapped. Dienu stood tense at the rail of the quarterdeck; for a moment, she wished that her faithless Io were with her; he was always so quick to make up his mind.

The man in the surf unfurled a flag. The stripes of Borlien were revealed.

Dienu summoned artillerymen to line the landward rail.

The distance between ship and shore diminished. The man in the surf had halted, up to his thighs in water. He was waving the flag in an assured manner. The mad Borlienese . . .

Dienu instructed the artillery captain. He saluted, went down the companion ladder to give orders to his men. The men worked in pairs, one operating the wheel lock, the other supporting the muzzle.

"Fire!" shouted the artillery captain. A pause, and then a volley of shots.

So began the battle of Keevasien sandbar.

*   *   *

The *Golden Friendship* was close enough for Hanra TolramKetinet to make out the faces of the soldiery along its rail. He saw the artillerymen taking aim at him.

By now, the insignia on the sails had revealed that these were Sibornalese vessels, surprisingly far from home. He wondered if his opportunist king had concluded a treaty to bring Sibornal into the Western Wars on Borlien's side. He had no reason to believe them hostile—until the weapons were raised.

The *Friendship* swung almost side on to him, to present the artillery men with the best line of fire. He estimated that its draught would allow it to come no farther in. The *Union* was ahead of its flagship, curving round to TolramKetinet's left, getting uncomfortably close to the east end of Keevasien Island. He heard shouted orders coming across the water, as the *Union's* main and mizzen sails were taken in.

The two smaller ships, which had sailed closer to the Randonanese shore, were cutting in to his right. The *Good Hope* was still battling against the broad brown flood from the western arm of the Kacol, the white *Vajabhar Prayer* was past—could indeed be said to be almost behind him, though still some distance away. On all these ships except the *Good Hope*, he could see the glint of gun barrels, pointing towards him.

He heard the artillery captain's order to fire. TolramKetinet dropped his flag, turned about, plunged into the water, and commenced swimming strongly back to the sand spit.

GortorLanstatet was already providing him with covering fire. He got his men down behind a shale ridge and directed half of his fire power at the flagship, half at the white caravel, the *Vajabhar Prayer*. The latter was still coming in fast, heading towards their position. The lieutenant had with him a good crossbowman; he directed him and another man to prepare a pitch fire-thrower.

Lead balls smacked in the water round the general. He swam underwater, coming up for air as infrequently as he could. He was aware of dolphins milling about close by, but they made no attempt to interfere with him.

Suddenly the firing stopped. He surfaced and looked back. The white caravel which bore the hierogram of the Great Wheel upon its sails had unwisely cut between him and the *Golden Friendship*. The Shiveninki soldiery, crowding on the topmost deck, were preparing to fire on the defenders of the spit.

Waves burst over him. The shore was unexpectedly steep. Tolram-Ketinet grasped hold of a root and hauled himself among bushes, working forward a few feet into cover and then collapsing. He lay breathing heavily, his face against the brown sand. He was unhurt.

Before his inward view rose a memory of the lovely face of Queen

MyrdemInggala. She was speaking seriously. He remembered how her lips moved. He was a survivor. He would win for her sake.

Yes, he was not clever. He should not have been made general. He did not possess the natural ability to command men which Lanstatet had. But.

Since he had received the queen of queen's message in Ordelay—the first time she had ever addressed him on a personal level, even at secondhand—he had thought of the king's intention to divorce her. TolramKetinet feared the king. His allegiance to the crown was divided. Although he understood the dynastic necessity for JandolAnganol's action, that royal decision had altered TolramKetinet's feelings. He told himself that the attraction he felt for the queen was treasonable. But the queen in exile was a different matter; treason no longer entered the question. Nor did loyalty to a king who had sent him off out of jealousy to die in a Randonanese jungle. He got to his feet again, and ran for GortorLanstatet's besieged strip.

His Borlienese troops gave him a cheer as TolramKetinet threw himself down among them. He embraced them as he peered out to seaward over the shingle ridge.

In a minute, the scene had changed in certain dramatic respects. The *Golden Friendship* had taken in its sails and lowered fore and aft anchors. It lay about two hundred yards offshore. A lucky fire bolt from the crossbow had set part of its bow and the artemon mast alight. As sailors fought the blaze, two longboats full of soldiers were pulling away from the ship; one of the boats—though the information would have been lost on TolramKetinet—was led by Admiral Odi Jeseratabhar, who stood rigid in the stern; SartoriIrvrash had insisted on accompanying her and sat rather ignominiously at her feet.

The *Union* had almost beached itself away to the left of the small island, and was embarking troops into the shallows; they waded doggedly ashore. Rather nearer was the *Vajabhar Prayer*, stuck in the shallows with sails hanging limp, and a boat full of soldiery making inexpertly for the shore. This boat was the nearest target, and matchlock fire was causing some damage to it.

Only the *Good Hope* had not changed position. Caught in the flow of the outpouring Kacol, it remained with all sail hoist, bowsprit pointing towards Keevasien Island, contributing nothing to the struggle.

"They must believe they are facing the entire Keevasien garrison," GortorLanstatet said.

"We certainly need that garrison, poor devils. If we stay here we'll be slaughtered."

There was no way in which thirteen men, poorly armed, could defend themselves against four boatloads of troops armed with wheel locks.

It was then that the sea rose, opened, and rained assatassi.

* * *

From one end of the Sea of Eagles to the other, assatassi flew like darts from sea to shore.

Fisherfolk who understood the sea kept this day and the following one for celebration and feasting. It was a day which occurred only once early every summer during the Great Summer, at the time of high tide. In Lordryardry, nets were ready. In Ottassol, tarpaulins were spread. In Gravabagalinien, the queen's familiars had warned her to stay away from the deadly shore. What was a feast of plenty for the knowledgeable became a rain of death for the ignorant.

Swimming in from far mid-ocean, shoals of assatassi headed for land. Their migrations during the Great Summer spanned the globe. Their feeding grounds were in the distant reaches of the Ardent Sea, where no man had visited. On reaching maturity, the shoals started their long swim eastwards, against the flow of ocean currents. Through the Climent Sea they went, and on through the narrow gates of the Straits of Cadmer.

This narrowing brought the shoals into greater proximity. The enforced closeness, together with the onset of monsoon weather in the Narmosset Sea, brought a changed behaviour pattern. What had been a long leisurely swim, without apparent aim, became a race—a race which was destined to end in the death-flight.

But for that actual flight, that desired death along thousands of miles of coast, another factor was necessary. The tide had to be right.

Throughout the centuries of winter, Helliconia's seas were all but tideless. After apastron and the darkest years, Freyr again began to make its influence felt. As its gigantic mass beckoned the chill planet back towards the light, so too it stirred the seas. Its pull on the ocean mass was now, only 118 Earth years from periastron, considerable. The time in the small year had arrived when the combined mass of Batalix and Freyr worked together. The result was a sixty percent increase in tidal strength over the winter situation.

The narrow seas between Hespagorat and Campannlat, the strong flow of the current to the west, conspired to make the spring tides mount and break suddenly with dramatic force. On that phenomenal flow of water shoreward, the shoals of assatassi launched themselves.

The ships of the Sibornalese fleet found themselves first with no water under their draught, and then battered by a tidal wave rising precipitously and without warning from the sea. Before the crews could realise what had hit them, the assatassi were there. The death-flight was on.

The assatassi is a necrogenetic fish, or more properly fish-lizard. It reaches a length of eighteen inches at maturity; it has two large mul-

tifacetted eyes; but what chiefly distinguishes it is its straight bill of
bone, supported by a boney cranium. On its death-flight the assatassi
reaches speeds high enough for this bill to penetrate a man to the
heart.

Off Keevasien, the assatassi broke from the surface a hundred yards
further out than the *Golden Friendship*. So full did the air become with
them that those which flew low enough to skim the water and those who
gained heights of fifty feet alike formed part of a solid body of fast-
moving fish-lizard. They gleamed like a myriad of sword blades. The air
became a sword blade.

The flagship was raked by assatassi from stem to stern. Anyone standing on deck was struck. The seaward side of the ship was covered with
creatures, hanging skewered by their bills. So with the three other ships.
But it was the boats, already waterlogged by the tide, which suffered
most. All their company was wounded, and many were killed outright.
The boards were stove in. All four boats began to sink.

Cries of pain and terror sounded—lost beneath the shriek of birds
who plunged down to snatch a meal from the air.

The first wave of assatassi lasted for two minutes.

Only TolramKetinet's men survived without injury. The tidal wave
had washed right over them, so that they were still prostrate and half-
conscious when the assatassi came over.

When the bombardment ceased, they looked up to see chaos all
round. Sibornalese troops were struggling in the water, where large
predatory fish were closing in. The *Good Hope* appeared to be drifting
helplessly out to sea, its main mast shattered. The fire in the masts of the
Golden Friendship was raging unchecked. All round, rocks and trees
were covered with smashed bodies of fish. Many assatassi had impaled
themselves by their bills high up in branches or trunks of trees, or were
lodged in inaccessible crannies in the rocks. The death-flight had taken
many fish a long way inland. The sombre jungles overhanging the mouth
of the Kacol were now interpenetrated by fish-lizards which would be
rotten before Batalix-set.

Far from being some morbid fancy, assatassi behaviour was proof of
the versatility by which species were perpetuated. Like the otherwise
dissimilar biyelk, yelk, and gunnadu, which covered the icy plains of
Campannlat in winter, the assatassi were necrogenes and gave birth only
through death.

Assatassi were hermaphrodite. Formed in too rudimentary a way to
carry within them the normal apparatus of reproduction, assatassi
propagation involved destruction. Germination budded within their gut,
taking the form of threadlike maggots. Embedded safely within the
parental intestine, the maggots survived the impact of the death-flight
and lived to feed on the carrion thus provided.

They ate their way to the outside world. There the maggots metamorphosed into a legged larval stage, closely resembling miniature iguana. In the autumn of the small year, the miniature iguanas, hitherto land-bound, made their way back to the great parent sea, fading down into it, sinking into it as tracelessly as grains of sand, to replenish the cycle of assatassi life.

So startling was the sudden turn in events that TolramKetinet and Lanstatet stood up on their spit to look about them. The huge wave which had drenched all the foreshore was the prelude to an onrushing flood which set the Sibornalese struggling ashore into difficulties.

The first wave had rushed up the Kacol. Its spent waters were now returning, bringing black muds which stained the sea with their eddies. More ominously, to TolramKetinet's left, a stream of bodies was making sodden progress out from the river mouth, accompanied by screaming seabirds. The general's guess was that these were the slaughtered dead of Keevasien, about to find burial.

The incoming wave had overturned the *Golden Friendship*'s longboat. Those who did not stay submerged long enough rose to meet the clouds of fish-lizard.

SartoriIrvrash found himself struggling in the water with the wounded, among whom he soon saw Odi Jeseratabhar. One of her cheeks was torn, and a fish-lizard was embedded in the flesh of the back of her neck. Many of the wounded were being attacked by predatory gulls. SartoriIrvrash himself was uninjured. Fighting his way over to Odi, he lifted her in his arms and began to wade ashore. The water kept getting deeper.

His face came close to the assatassi embedded in her neck, his eye close to its great boney eye, from which all life had not yet faded.

"How can mankind ever build up bulwarks against nature, when it keeps flooding in like a deluge, indifferent to what it carries away?" he said to himself. "So much for you, Akhanaba, you hrattock!"

It was all he could do to keep the unconscious Odi's head above water. There was a spit of land only a few yards distant, yet still the water rose about him. He cried in fear—and then on the spit he saw a man who resembled JandolAnganol's hated general, TolramKetinet.

TolramKetinet and GortorLanstatet were studying the Sibornalese ship, the *Vajabhar Prayer*, which lay only a short distance to their right. The tidal wave had flung it ashore, but a swirling rebate of waters from the Kacol floated it again. Apart from the assatassi peppering its starboard side, it was in good order. The crew, thoroughly demoralised, were throwing themselves ashore and making off into the bushes to safety.

"The ship's ours for the taking, Gortor. What do you say?"

"I'm no sailor, but there's a breeze rising from on shore."

The general turned to the twelve men with him.

"You are my brave comrades. None of you lacks courage. If one of you had lacked courage for a moment, we all would have perished. Now we have one last exploit before we are safe. There is no help for us at Keevasien, so we must sail along the coast. We are going to borrow this white caravel. It's a gift—though a gift we may have to fight for. Swords ready. Follow me!"

As he ran down the strand, his force following, he almost bumped into a bedraggled man struggling for the shore with a woman in his arms. The man called his name.

"Hanra! Help!"

He saw in astonishment that it was the Borlienese chancellor, and the the thought came, Here must be another that JandolAnganol has cheated....

He halted his party. Lanstatet dragged SartoriIrvrash from the flood, two of the men took hold of the woman between them. She was moaning and returning to consciousness. They dashed on to the *Vajabhar Prayer*.

The crew and soldiery of the Shiveninki vessel had suffered casualties. Some were killed; any wounded by the assatassi were mostly ashore. Birds darted over the ship, eating fish-lizards caught on the rigging. There remained a handful of soldiers with their officers to put up a fight. But TolramKetinet's party swarmed up the seaward side of the vessel and took them on. The opposition was already demoralised. After a halfhearted engagement, they surrendered and were made to jump ashore. GortorLanstatet took a party of three below, to round up any hiding and get them off the ship. Within seven minutes of boarding, they were ready to sail.

Eight of the men pushed the caravel. Slowly, the ship swung about and the sails filled, torn though they were by the fish-lizards.

"Move! Move!" shouted TolramKetinet from the bridge.

"I hate ships," GortorLanstatet said. He fell on his knees and prayed, hands above his head. There was an explosion, and water sprayed all over them.

Their piracy had been seen from the *Golden Friendship*. A gunner was firing one of the cannon at them from a range of two hundred yards.

As the *Prayer*, at no more than walking pace, glided out of the shelter of the overhanging jungle, a stronger breeze caught it. Without needing to be told, two gunners among the Borlienese manned one of the cannon on the gundeck. They fired it once at the *Golden Friendship*; then the angle between the ships became so acute that the muzzle of the cannon could not be turned sufficiently in the square gunport to aim at the flagship.

The gun crew in the flagship were faced with the same problem. One more ball flew over, landing in the undergrowth of the island, then silence. The eight men in the water swarmed up boarding nets and climbed on deck cheering as the *Prayer* gathered way.

The island foliage slid away to port. Trees were being attacked by the scavenging birds, devouring impaled assatassi, while the hornets and bees they disturbed buzzed savagely round them. The *Prayer* was about to pass the Uskuti ship, *Union*, still beached with its bows into the land.

"Can you blow it up as we pass?" GortonLanstatet shouted down to the gundeck.

The gunners ran to port, opened the gunport, primed the clumsy cannon. But now they were moving too fast, and the gun could not be made ready in time.

The disgraced Io Pasharatid was among the crew and soldiery on the *Union* who had deserted ship to flee from the death-flight into the island jungle. He went first. His desertion owed more to calculation than panic.

Alone among the Sibornalese in the fleet, he had once visited Keevasien. That had been during his tour of duty as ambassador to the Borlienese court. While he had no love of the place, it was in his mind that he might purchase supplies there to eke out the boredom of ship's rations. His calculation was that he might take off two hours during the general panic without being missed.

Seeing the burnt-out ruins of the town had changed his mind. He returned to the scene of action in time to witness the *Vajabhar Prayer* gliding by his own ship, with Hanra TolramKetinet, favourite of the queen of queens, standing on its quarterdeck.

Io Pasharatid was not entirely sunk in self-interest, though in this instant jealousy played some part in his actions. He ran forward, rallying the men who crouched among the bushes, driving them back aboard the *Union*. The tidal wave had set it on a strip of beach, unharmed.

After some manoeuvring with oars, assisted by the flood tide, they floated the carrack free of the beach. The sails were trimmed and, slowly, her bows drifted round towards the open sea.

Signal flags were run up, reporting that the *Union* was in pursuit of the pirate. The signal was intended for the eyes of Dienu Pasharatid on the *Golden Friendship*; but she would never read another signal. Hers was one of the first human deaths occasioned by the death-flight of the assatassi.

Only when they were out of the bay and a fresh west wind was carrying them slowly against the prevailing ocean stream, did TolramKetinet and SartoriIrvrash take the chance to embrace each other.

When they had given each other some report of their adventures,

TolramKetinet said, "I have little to be proud of. Since I am a soldier, I cannot complain where I am sent. My generalship has been such that my forces dissolved without my being able to fight a single battle. It is a disgrace I shall always live with. Randonan swallows men whole."

The ex-chancellor said, after a moment, "I am grateful for my travels, which were no more planned than yours. The Sibornalese used me, but from the experience has come something valuable. More than valuable."

He made a gesture indicating Odi Jeseratabhar, whose wound was now dressed, and who sat on the deck listening to the men talking, her eyes closed.

"I'm getting old and the loves of the old are always funny to mere youths like you, Hanra. No, don't deny it." He laughed. "And something more. I realise for the first time how fortunate our generations are to live at this period of the Great Year, when heat prevails. How did our ancestors survive the winter? And the wheel will turn, and again it will be winter. What a malign fate, to grow up as Freyr is dying and know nothing else. In parts of Sibornal, people don't see Freyr at all during the centuries of winter."

TolramKetinet shrugged. "It's chance."

"But the enormous scale of growth and destruction. . . . Perhaps our mistake is to think ourselves apart from nature. Well, I know of old that you are less than enthralled by such speculations. One thing I must say. I believe I have resolved one question of such revolutionary nature . . ."

He hesitated, stroking his damp whiskers. Smiling, TolramKetinet urged him to go on.

"I believe I have thought what no man has ever thought. This lady has inspired me. I need to get to Oldorando or Pannoval to lay my thought before the powers of the Holy Pannovalan Empire. My deduction, I should call it. There I shall certainly be rewarded, and Odi and I can then live comfortably."

Scrutinising his whiskery face, TolramKetinet said, "Deductions that are paid for! They must be valuable."

The man's a fool and I always knew it, thought the ex-chancellor, but he could not resist the chance to explain.

"You see," SartoriIrvrash said, lowering his voice so that it could hardly be heard for the slap of the canvas above them, "I could never abide the ancipital race, unlike my master. There lay much of our difference. My thought, my deduction, weighs very much against the ancipitals. Hence it will be rewarded, according to the terms of the Pannovalan Pronouncement."

Rising from her chair, Odi Jeseratabhar took SartoriIrvrash's arm and said to TolramKetinet and Lanstatet, who had joined them, "You may not know that King JandolAnganol destroyed all the chancellor's life's work, his 'Alphabet of History and Nature.' It's a crime not to be forgotten. The chancellor's deduction, as he modestly names it, will revenge him on JandolAnganol, and perhaps allow us both to work together on reassembling the 'Alphabet.' "

Lanstatet said sharply, "Lady, you're our enemy, sworn to destroy our native land. You should be below decks in irons."

"That's past," said SartoriIrvrash, with dignity. "We're simply wandering scholars now—and homeless ones at that."

"Wandering scholars . . ." It was too much for the general, so he asked a practical question. "How are you to get to Pannoval?"

"Oldorando would suit me—it is nearer, and I hope to arrive before the king, if he is not already there, to cause him maximum botheration before he weds the Madi princess. You have no love of him either, Hanra. You'll be the ideal person to take me there."

"I'm going to Gravabagalinien," said TolramKetinet grimly, "if only this tub will sail us there, and we are not overtaken by our enemies."

All looked back. The *Vajabhar Prayer* was now in open sea, making laboured progress eastwards along the coast. The *Union* had emerged from Keevasien Bay, but lay far astern. There was no immediate danger of its catching them.

"You will see your sister Mai in Gravabagalinien," SartoriIrvrash told the general. The general smiled without replying.

Later in the day, distantly, they saw the *Good Hope* also in pursuit, with a jury-rigged main mast. The two pursuing vessels were lost in haze as thunderheads towered from the western sea, their edges cast in copper. Lightning darted silently in the belly of the cloud.

A second wave of assatassi rose from the sea, like a wing unfurling, to cast itself upon the land. The *Prayer* was too far from the coast to suffer ill effect. Only a few of the flying fish-lizard darted past the vessel. The men looked on complacently at what that morning had struck them dumb. As they crawled towards Gravabagalinien, thunderous darkness fell and tiny splinters of light showed ashore, where natives were feasting on the dead invaders.

And something without identity made its way towards the place where the queen of queens resided in her wooden palace: a human body.

RobaydayAnganol had stolen a ride downriver from Matrassyl to Ottassol, keeping ahead of his father. Wherever he went now, he went with a special haste in his gait, half-looking back; did he but know it, this aspect of a man pursued made him resemble his father. He thought of himself as pursuing. Vengeance against his father filled his mind.

In Ottassol, instead of going to the underground palace which his father was due to visit, he went to an old friend of SartoriIrvrash's, the deuteroscopist and anatomist, Bardol CaraBansity. CaraBansity was feeling no great goodwill for the king or his strange son.

He and his wife had staying with them a society of deuteroscopists from Vallgos. He offered Robayday a bed in a house he maintained near the harbour, where, he said, a girl would look after his needs.

Robayday's interest in women was sporadic. However, he immediately found the woman in CaraBansity's harbour house attractive, with her long brown hair and a mysterious air of authority, as if she knew a secret shared by nobody else.

She gave her name as Metty, and he remembered her. She was a girl he had once enjoyed in Matrassyl. Her mother had assisted his father when the latter was wounded after the Battle of the Cosgatt. Her real name was Abathy.

She did not recognise him. No doubt she was a lady with many lovers. At first, Robayday did not enlighten her. He remained inert and let her come to him. To impress, she spoke of a scandalous connection with Sibornalese officials in Matrassyl; he watched her expression as she spoke, and thought of how different her view of the world was, with its clandestine comings and goings.

"You do not recognise me, for I am hard to recognise, yet there was a day when you wore less kohl on your eyes when we were close as tongue to teeth . . ."

Then she spoke his name and embraced him, exhibiting delight.

Later, she said she had cause to be grateful to her mother, to whom she sent back money regularly, for teaching her how to behave with men. She was cultivating a taste for the highborn and powerful; she had been shamefully seduced, she said, by CaraBansity, but now she hoped for better things. She kissed him.

She allowed her charfrul to slip and reveal her pale legs. Seeing cruelty everywhere, Robayday saw only the spider's trap. Eagerly, he entered it. Later, they lay together and kissed, and she laughed prettily. He loved her and hated her.

All his impulses screamed to him to hurry on to Oldorando, yet he remained with her for another day. He hated her and he loved her.

The second evening in her house. He thought that history would cease if he remained for ever. She again let down her beautiful hair and hitched up her skirt, climbing onto the couch with him again.

They embraced. They made love. She was a well of delight. Abathy was starting to undress him for more prolonged enjoyment when there was a thumping at her door. They both sat up, startled.

A more violent thump. The door burst open, and in blundered a burly young fellow dressed in the uncouth Dimariamian fashion. It was Div Muntras, in bull-like quest of love.

"Abathy!" he cried. She yelled by way of reply.

After sailing alone to Ottassol, Div had traced his way to her by
diligent enquiry. He had sold everything he possessed, except for the
talismanic watch stolen from Billish, which reposed safe in his body
belt. And here, at the end of the trail, he found the girl who had
dominated his thoughts ever since she idled voluptuously with his father
on the deck of the *Lordryardry Lady* trittoming with another man.

His face altered into the image of rage. He raised his fists. He bellowed and charged forward.

Robayday jumped up and stood on the couch, his back to the wall.
His face was dark with anger at the intrusion. That the king's son should
be shouted at—and at such a moment! He had no thought but to kill the
intruder. In his belt was a dagger shaped from a phagor horn, a sharp
two-sided instrument. He drew it.

Div was further enraged by the sight of the weapon. He could soon
dispose of this slight lad, this meddler.

Abathy screamed at him, but he paid no heed. She stood with both
hands to her pretty mouth, eyes wide in terror. That pleased Div. She
would be next.

He rushed to the attack, landing on the couch with a leap. He received the point of the horn just below his lowest rib. The tip grated
against the rib as it slid in. His charge ensured that it went into his
flesh to the hilt, penetrating the spleen and the stomach, at which point
the handle broke off in his opponent's hand.

A long baffled groan escaped Div. Liquids gushed over the wall as he
fell against it and slipped to the floor.

Raging, Robayday left the girl to weep. He fetched two men who
disposed of the corpse by tossing it into the Takissa.

Robayday ran from the city, as if pursued by mad dogs. He never
returned to the girl or to the room. He had an appointment which he had
been in danger of forgetting, an appointment in Oldorando. Over and
again, he wept and cursed along the road.

Carried by the current, turning as it went, the body of Div Muntras
drifted among the shipping to the mouth of the Takissa. No one saw it
go, for most folk, even slaves, were indulging in a grand assatassi fry.
Fish moved in to give the corpse their attention as the sodden mass was
taken into the maw of the sea, to become part of the progression of
waters westwards, towards Gravabagalinien.

That evening, when the suns sank, simple people came down to the
beaches and headlands. In all the countries whose boundaries were
lapped by the Sea of Eagles, in Randonan, Borlien, Thribriat, Iskahandi,
and Dimariam, crowds gathered by the water's edge.

The great assatassi feast was ending. Here was a time to pause and
give thanks for such blessings to the spirit who dwelt in the waters.

While women sang and danced on the sand, their menfolk waded into the sea bearing little boats. The boats were leaves, on which short candles burned, giving off a sweet scent.

On every beach, as dusk drew in, whole navies of leaves were launched. Some still floated, burning dim, long after darkness had fallen, forming panoramas reminiscent to the superstitious of gossies and fessups suspended in their more permanent darkness. Some were carried far out to sea before their feeble flames were quenched.

XVIII

VISITORS FROM THE DEEP

Anyone advancing on Gravabagalinien could see from a distance the wooden palace which was the queen's refuge. It stood without compromise, like a toy left on a beach.

Legend said that Gravabagalinien was haunted. That at some distant time in the past a fortress had stood in place of the flimsy palace. That it had been entirely destroyed in a great battle.

But nobody knew who fought there, or for what reason. Only that many had died, and had been buried in shallow graves where they fell. Their shades, far from their proper land-octaves, were still reputed to haunt the spot.

Certainly, another tragedy was now being acted out on the old un-hallowed ground. For the time had come round when King Jandol-Anganol arrived in two ships with his men and phagors, and with Esomberr and CaraBansity, to divorce his queen.

And Queen MyrdemInggala had descended the stairs and had sub-mitted to the divorce. And wine had been brought, and much mischief had been permitted. And Alam Esomberr, the envoy of the C'Sarr, had made his way into the ex-queen's chamber only a few hours after he had conducted the ceremony of divorcement. And then had come the announcement that Simoda Tal had been slain in far Oldorando. And this sore news had been delivered to the king as the first rays of eastern Batalix painted yellow the peeling outer walls of the palace.

And now an inevitability could be discerned in the affairs of men and phagors, as events drew towards a climax in which even the chief participants would be swept helplessly along like comets plunging into darkness.

JandolAnganol's voice was low with sorrow as he tore the hairs from his beard and head, crying to Akhanaba.

"Thy servant falls before thee, O Great One. Thou has visited sorrow upon me. Thou hast caused my armies to go down in defeat. Thou hast caused my son to forsake me. Thou hast caused me to divorce my beloved queen, MyrdemInggala. Thou hast caused my intended bride to be assassinated.... What more must I suffer for Thy sake?

"Let not my people suffer. Accept my suffering, O Great Lord, as a sufficient sacrifice for my people."

As he rose and put on his tunic, the pallid-chopped AbstrogAthenat said casually, "It's true that the army has lost Randonan. But all civilised countries are surrounded by barbaric ones, and are defeated when their armies invade them. We should go, not with the sword, but with the word of God."

"Crusades are in the province of Pannoval, not a poor country like ours, Vicar." Adjusting his tunic over his wounds, he felt in his pocket the three-faced timepiece he had taken from CaraBansity in Ottassol. Now as then, he felt it to be an object of ill omen.

AbstrogAthenat bowed, holding the whip behind him. "At least we might please the All-Powerful by being more human, and shunning the inhuman."

In sudden anger, JandolAnganol struck out with his left hand and caught the vicar across the cheek with his knuckles.

"You keep to God's affairs and leave worldly matters to me."

He knew what the man meant. His reference had been to purging phagors from Borlien.

Leaving his tunic open, feeling its fabric absorb the blood of his latest scourging, JandolAnganol climbed from the subterranean chapel to the ground floor of the wooden palace. Yuli jumped up to welcome him.

His head throbbed as if he were going blind. He patted the little phagor and sank his fingers into its thick pelage.

Shadows still lay long outside the palace. He scarcely knew how to face the morning: only yesterday he had arrived at Gravabagalinien and—in the presence of the envoy of the Holy C'Sarr, Alam Esomberr —he had divorced his fair queen.

The palace was shuttered as it had been the day previously. Now men lay everywhere in the rooms, still in drink-sodden sleep. Sunlight cut its way into the darkness in a crisscross of lines, making it seem like a woven basket that he walked through, heading for the doorway.

When he flung the door open, the Royal First Phagorian Guard stood on duty outside, its ranks of long jaws and horns unmoving. That was something worth seeing anyway, he told himself, trying to dispel his black mood.

He walked in the air before the heat rose. He saw the sea and felt the breeze, and heeded them not. Before dawn, while he still slept heavily from drink, Esomberr had come to him. Beside Esomberr stood his new chancellor, Bardol CaraBansity. They had informed him that the Madi princess he intended to marry was dead, killed by an assassin.

Nothing was left.

Why had he gone to such trouble to divorce his true wife? What had possessed his mind? There were severances the hardiest could not survive.

It was his wish to speak to her.

A delicacy in him restrained him from sending a messenger up to her room. He knew that she was there with the little princess Tatro waiting for him to leave and take his soldiers with him. Probably she had heard the news the men had brought in the night. Probably she feared assassination. Probably she hated him.

He turned in his sharp way, as if to catch himself out. His new chancellor was approaching with his heavy, determined tread, jowls jolting.

JandolAnganol eyed CaraBansity and then turned his back on him. CaraBansity was forced to skirt him and Yuli before making a clumsy bow.

The king stared at him. Neither man spoke. CaraBansity turned his cloudy gaze from the king's.

"You find me in an ill mood."

"I have not slept either, sire. I deeply regret this fresh misfortune which has visited you."

"My ill mood covers not only the All-Powerful but you, who are not so powerful."

"What have I done to displease you, sire?"

The Eagle drew his brows together, making his gaze more hawklike.

"I know you are secretly against me. You have a reputation for craftiness. I saw that gloating look you could not conceal when you came to announce the death of—you know who."

"The Madi princess? If you so distrust me, sire, you must not take me on as your chancellor."

JandolAnganol presented his back again, with the yellow gauze of his tunic patterned red with blood like an ancient banner.

CaraBansity began to shuffle. He stared up abstractedly at the palace and saw how its white paint was peeling. He felt what it was to be a commoner and what it was to be a king.

He enjoyed his life. He knew many people and was useful to the community. He loved his wife. He prospered. Yet the king had come along and snatched him up against his will, as if he were a slave.

He had accepted the role and, being a man of character, made the best of it. Now this sovereign had the gall to tell CaraBansity that he was secretly against his king. There was no limit to royal impertinence —and as yet he could see no way to escape following JandolAnganol all the way to Oldorando.

His sympathy with the king's predicament left him.

"I meant to say, Your Majesty," he began in a determined voice, and then became alarmed by his own temerity, looking at that bloody back. "This is just a trifling matter, of course, but, before we set sail from Ottassol, you took from me that interesting timepiece with three faces. Do you happen to have it still?"

The king did not turn or move.

He said, "I have it here in my tunic."

CaraBansity took a deep breath and then said, much more feebly than he intended, "Would you return it to me, please, Your Majesty?"

"This is no time to approach me for favors, when Borlien's standing within the Holy Empire is threatened." He was the Eagle as he spoke.

They both stood, watching Yuli root in the bushes by the palace. The creature pissed after the retromingent fashion of his species.

The king began to walk with measured pace in the direction of the sea.

I'm no better than a damned slave, said CaraBansity to himself. He followed.

With the runt skipping beside him, the king speeded his step, speaking rapidly as he went, so that the portly deuteroscopist was forced to catch up. He never mentioned the subject of his timepiece again.

"Akhanaba had favoured me and set many fruits in my life's way. And always to those fruits an additional flavour was given when I saw that more were promised—tomorrow, and the day after tomorrow, and the day after that. Whatever I wished, I might have more of.

"It's true I suffered setbacks and defeats, but that within a general atmosphere of promise. I did not allow them to disturb me for long. My personal defeat in the Cosgatt—well, I learnt from it and put it behind me, and eventually won a great victory there."

They passed a line of gwing-gwing trees. The king snatched down a gwing-gwing, biting into it to the stone as he spoke, letting the juice run down his chin. He gestured, clutching the despoiled fruit.

"Today, I see my life in a new light. Perhaps all that was promised me I have already received . . . I am, after all, more than twenty-five years." He spoke with difficulty. "Perhaps this is my summer, and in future when I shake the bush no fruit will fall. . . . Can I any longer rely on plenty? Doesn't our religion warn us that we must expect times of famine? Fah!—Akhanaba is like a Sibornalese, always obsessed with the winter to come."

They walked along the low cliffs separating land from beach, where the queen was accustomed to swim.

"Tell me," said JandolAnganol carelessly, "if you as an atheist do not have a religious construction to put to the case—how do you see my difficulties?"

CaraBansity was silent, setting his beefy red face towards the ground as if guarding it against the king's abrasive look. Work up your courage, he told himself.

"Well? Come, say what you will. I have no spirit! I have been flogged by my whey-visaged vicar . . ."

When CaraBansity stopped walking, the king followed suit.

"Sire, I recently to oblige a friend took into my establishment a certain young lady. My wife and I entertain many people, some alive, some dead; also animals for dissection, and phagors, either for dissection or for bodyguards. None caused as much trouble as that certain young lady.

"I love my wife, and ever continue to do so. But I lusted after that certain young lady. I had a contempt for her, yet I lusted after her. I despised myself, and yet I lusted after her."

"But did you have her?"

CaraBansity laughed, and for the first time in the king's presence, his face lightened. "Sire, I had her much as you have that gwing-gwing, the fruit par excellence of dimday. The juice, sire, ran down. . . . But it was khmir and not love, and once the khmir was quenched—though that was certainly a process . . . that was summer process, sire—once it was quenched, I loathed myself and wanted nothing more of her. I established her apart and told her never to see me again. Since when, I learn that she has taken to her mother's profession, and caused the death of at least one man."

"What's all this to me?" asked the king with a haughty look.

"Sire, I believe the activating principle of your life to be lust rather than love.

"You tell me in religious terms that Akhanaba has favoured you and put many fruits in your path. In my terms, you have taken what you would, done what you would, and so you wish to continue. You favour ancipitals as instruments of your lust, not caring that phagors are in reality never submissive. Nothing really can stand in your way—except the queen of queens. She can stand in your way because she alone in the

XVIII · VISITORS FROM THE DEEP   307

world commands your love, and perhaps some respect. That is why you hate her, because you love her.

"She stands between you and your khmir. She alone can contain your—duality. In you as in me, and perhaps as in all men, the two principles are divided—but the division in you is as great as your state is great.

"If you prefer to believe in Akhanaba, believe now that he has by these supposed setbacks given you warning that your life is about to go wrong. Make it right while the chance is offered."

They stopped on the cliff, ignoring the dull thunders of the sea, and stood face to face, both of them tense. The king heard his chancellor out with never a movment, while Yuli rolled in coarse grass nearby.

"How would you suggest that I make my life right?" A less self-assured man than CaraBansity would have taken fright from his tone.

"This is my advice, Your Majesty. Do not go to Oldorando. Simoda Tal is dead. You no longer have reason to visit an unfriendly capital. As a deuteroscopist, I warn you against it." Under his grizzled eyebrows, CaraBansity kept careful note of the effect of his words on Jandol-Anganol.

"Your place is in your own kingdom, never more so than now, while your enemies have not forgotten the Massacre of the Myrdolators. Return to Matrassyl.

"Your rightful queen is here. Fall before her and ask forgiveness. Tear up Esomberr's bill before her eyes. Take back what you love most. Your sanity lies in her. Reject the cozzening of Pannoval."

The Eagle glared out to sea, eyes rapidly blinking.

"Live a saner life, Majesty. Win back your son. Kick out Pannoval, kick out the phagor guard, live a sane life with your queen. Reject the false Akhanaba, who has led you—"

But he had gone too far.

Matchless fury seized the king. A rage filled him until he was rage personified. He hurled himself bodily upon CaraBansity. Before this anger beyond reason, CaraBansity quailed and fell an instant before the king was on him. Kneeling on his prostrate body, the king drew his sword. CaraBansity screamed.

"Spare me, Your Majesty! Last night I saved your queen from vile rape."

JandolAnganol paused, then stood, sword point directed at the quaking body huddled by his feet. "Who would dare touch the queen when I was near? Answer?"

"Your Majesty . . ." The voice trembled slightly, the lips uttering it were pressed almost to the ground; yet what it said was clear. "You were drunk. And Envoy Esomberr went into her room to ravish her."

The king breathed deep. He sheathed his sword. He stood without movement.

"You base commoner! How could you understand the life of a king? I do not go back along the path I have once trod. You may possess life, which is mine to take, but I have a destiny and shall follow on where the All-Powerful leads.

"Crawl back to where you belong. You cannot advise me. Keep out of my way!"

Yet he still stood over the grovelling anatomist. When Yuli came snuffling up, the king turned suddenly away and strode back to the wooden palace.

The guard roused at his shout. They were to be away from Gravabagalinien within the hour. They would march for Oldorando as planned. His voice, his cold fury, stirred up the palace as if it were a nest of rickybacks disturbed by the lifting of a log. Esomberr's vicars could be heard within, calling to each other in high voices.

This commotion reached the queen in her chambers. She stood in the middle of her ivory room, listening. Her bodyguard was at the door. Mai TolramKetinet sat with two maids in the anteroom, clutching Tatro. Thick curtains were drawn across the windows.

MyrdemInggala wore a long flimsy dress. Her face was as pale as the shadow of a cowbird's wing on snow. She stood breathing the warm air into her lungs and out again, listening to the sound of men and hoxneys, of curses and commands below. Once she went to the curtains; then, as if disdaining her own weakness, withdrew the hand she had raised and returned to where she waited before. The heat brought out beads of perspiration which clung to her forehead like pearls. She heard the king's voice once distinctly, then not again.

As for CaraBansity, he climbed to his feet when the king had gone. He walked down to the bay where he could not be seen, to recover his colour. After a while, he began to sing. He had his liberty back, if not his timepiece.

In his pain, the king went to a small room in one of the rickety towers and bolted the door behind him. Dust drifting down gave phantom substance to slices of gold shining in through a lattice. The place smelt of feathers, fungus, and old straw. On the bare boards of the floor were pigeon droppings, but the king, ignoring them, lay down and cast himself by an effort of will into pauk.

His soul, detached from his body, became tranquil. Like a moth wing falling, it sank into the velvety darkness. The darkness remained when all else had gone.

This was the paradox of the limbo in which the soul now drifted rudderless: that it extended everywhere and was an endless domain, while at the same time being as familiar to him as the dark space under the bedclothes to a child.

The soul had no mortal eyes. It saw with a different vision. It saw beneath it, through the obsidian, a host of dim lights, stationary but seeming to move in relation to each other because of the soul's descent. Each light had once been a living spirit. Each was now drawn to the great mother-principle which would exist even when the world was dead, the original beholder, the principle even greater than—or at least apart from—such gods as Akhanaba.

And the soul moved in particular to one light that attracted it, the gossie of its father.

The spark that had once been no less a personage than Varpal-Anganol, King of Borlien, resembled only a tentative sketch of sunshine on an old wall, with its ribs, its pelvis, scarcely drawn. All that remained of the head which had worn the crown was the suggestion of a stone, with ambers faintly connotating eye sockets. Beneath this little cockle-shell—visible through it—were fessups like trails of dust.

"Father, I come before you, your unworthy son, to beg your forgiveness for my crimes to you." So spoke the soul of JandolAnganol, hanging where no air was.

"My dear son, you are welcome here, welcome whenever you can find time to visit your father, now among the ranks of the dead. I have no reproach for you. You were always my dear son."

"Father, I shall not mind your reproaches. Rather, I welcome your most bitter rebukes, for I know how great is my sin against you."

The silences between their speeches were immeasurable because no breath was exhaled.

"Hush, my son, nobody needs to talk of sin among this company. You were my loving son, and that suffices. No more need be said. Grieve not."

When it seemed time to speak, a dusty fire, the mere death of a candle flame, issued from where a mouth had been. Its smoke could be seen ascending between the cage of the ribs and up the stack of the throat.

The soul spoke again. "Father, I beg you to pour your wrath upon me for all that I did against you in your life, and for causing your death. Lessen my guilt. It is too much to bear."

"You are innocent, my son, as innocent as the wave that splashes on the shore. Feel no guilt for the happiness you brought into my life. Now in the residue of that life, I have no wrath to bring against you."

"Father, I kept you imprisoned ten years in a dungeon of the castle. In what way can I earn forgiveness for that act?"

The flame moved upwards, issuing as sparks.

"That time is forgotten, son. I scarcely remember a time of imprisonment, for you were always there to speak with me. Those occasions were cherished, for you asked advice of me—which I freely gave, as far as it was in my capacity."

"It was a melancholy place."

"It gave me time to think over the failings of my own life, to prepare myself for what was to come."

"Father, how your forgiveness wounds me!"

"Come closer, my boy, and let me comfort you."

But for the living to touch the dead was forbidden in the realm of the original beholder. If that ultimate duality was breached, then both were consumed. The soul floated lightly away from the thing that hung before it in the abyss.

"Comfort me with more advice, Father."

"Speak."

"First of all, let me know whether that tormented son of mine has fallen among you. I fear the instability of his life."

"I shall welcome the boy when he arrives, never worry—but as yet he still journeys in the world of light."

After a moment, the soul communicated again.

"Father, you perceive my position among the living. Advise me where I am to go. Am I to return to Matrassyl? Should I remain in Gravabagalinien? Or shall I continue to Oldorando? Where does my most fruitful future lie?"

"In each place there are those who await you. But there is one who awaits you in Oldorando whom you know not. That one holds your destiny. Go to Oldorando."

"Your advice will guide my actions."

From among the sparkling battalions of the dead, the soul rose, slowly at first, and then with a great urgency. Somewhere, a drum was sounding. The sparks dissolved below, sinking back into the original beholder.

The inanimate anatomy on the floor in the belfry began slowly to move. Its limbs twitched. It sat up. Its eyes opened in a blank face.

The only living thing to meet its gaze was Yuli, who crawled nearer and said, "My poor king in tether."

Without answering, JandolAnganol ruffled the runt's fur and let it snuggle against him.

"Oh, Yuli, what a thing is life."

After a minute, he patted the ancipital across the shoulders. "You're a good boy. No harm in you."

As the creature snuggled against him, the king felt an object against his side, and drew from his pocket the watch with three faces which he had taken from CaraBansity. Whenever he looked at it, his thoughts became troubled, yet he could not find it in himself to throw it away.

Once, the timepiece had belonged to Billy, the creature who claimed to come from a world not ruled by Akhanaba. It was necessary to banish Billy from consciousness (as one banished the thought of those damned Myrdolators), for Billy was a challenge to the whole elaborate structure of belief by which the Holy Pannovalan Empire stood. Sometimes, the fear came to the king that he might become bereft of his religious faith, as he had become bereft of so much else. Only his faith and this humble inhuman pet were left to him.

He groaned. With a great effort, he got to his feet again.

Within the hour, King JandolAnganol was at the head of his force, riding Lapwing with Envoy Alam Esomberr beside him. Behind came the king's captains, then Esomberr's party, and after them the body of the First Royal Phagorian Guard, ears atwitch, scarlet eyes fixed ahead, marching as their kind had done many centuries before towards the city of Oldorando.

The king's departure from the wooden palace, with all its underlying sense of anxiety, made a due impression on the watchers on the Avernus. They were glad to divert their attention from the sight of the king in pauk. Even the devoted female admirers of his majesty felt uncomfortable at the sight of him lying prone with his spirit away from his body.

Throughout the human population of Helliconia, pauk, or paterplacation, came as naturally as spitting. It had no particular religious significance, although it often existed alongside religion. Just as women became pregnant with future lives, so people were pregnant with the lives of those who had gone before them.

On the Avernus, the mysterious Helliconian practice of pauk was regarded as a religious function roughly equivalent to prayer. As such, it embarrassed the six families. The families suffered no inhibitions concerning sex: constant monitoring had ensured that long since; for them love and the higher emotions were no more than side effects of daily functions, to be ignored where possible; but religion was particularly difficult to deal with.

The families regarded religion as a primitive obsession, an illness, an opiate for those who could not think straight. They hoped perpetually that SartoriIrvrash and his kind would become more militant in their atheism and bring about the death of Akhanaba, thus contributing to a happier state of affairs. They neither liked nor understood pauk. They wished it did not happen.

On Earth, other opinions prevailed. Life and death could be perceived as an inseparable whole; death was never feared where life was properly lived. The terrestrials regarded with the liveliest interest the Helliconian activity of pauk. During the first years of contact with Helliconia, they had regarded the trance state as a kind of astral projection of the Helliconian soul, rather similar to a state of meditation. Later, a more sophisticated viewpoint had developed; understanding grew that the people of Helliconia possessed an ability peculiar to them, to shift beyond and return from the boundary set between life and death. This continuity had been given them in compensation for the remarkable discontinuities of their Great Year. Pauk had evolutionary value, and was a point of union between the humans and their changeable planet.

For this reason, the terrestrials were particularly interested in pauk. They had at this period discovered their own unity with their own planet, and related that unity to increasing empathy with Helliconia.

In the days that followed, lassitude took the queen of queens and laid her low.

She had lost the things of value which gave existence its previous fragrance. After the storm, the flowers would never lift their heads so high again. With her deep sense of guilt that she had somehow failed her king went bitter anger against him. If she had failed, it was not for want of trying, and the years of loving bestowed on him as freely as breath were more than wasted. Yet love remained beneath her anger. That was the cruellest thing. She understood JandolAnganol's self-doubt as no one else did. She was unable to break from the bond they had once forged.

Every day, after prayer, she went into pauk, to communicate with her mother's gossie. After her prostrations, recalling how SartoriIrvrash in particular had condemned all pater-placation as superstition, Myrdem-Inggala, in a fury of doubt, questioned whether she had visited her mother at all, whether the phantom was not in her head, whether there could be survival for anyone after death, except in the memories of those who had still to pass beyond that forbidding shore.

She questioned. Yet pauk was her consolation as much as the sea. For her dead brother YeferalOborol was now among the gossies, pouring out love for her as he sank towards the original beholder. The queen's unspoken fear, that he had been murdered by JandolAnganol, was proved baseless. She knew now where the real blame lay. For all that she was grateful.

Yet she regretted not having that additional reason to hate the king. She swam in the sea among her familiars. Peace of mind forsook her each time she returned to shore. The phagors carried her back to the palace in her throne; her resentment grew as she approached its doors.

The days dragged by and she grew no younger. She was scarcely on speaking terms with Mai. She ran up to her creaking chambers and hid her face.

"If you feel so badly, follow the king to Oldorando and plead with the C'Sarr's representatives there to annul your divorce," Mai said in impatient tones.

"Would you like to follow the king?" asked MyrdemInggala. "I would not."

Burnt into her memory was a recollection of how, in spendthrift times, this woman, her lady-in-waiting, had been harvested into the king's bed and the two of them, like low whores, had been pleasured by him at one and the same time. Neither woman spoke of those occasions —but they lay between them as tangibly as a sword.

Chiefly from a need to talk to someone, the queen persuaded Cara-Bansity to stay at the palace for a few days, and then for a day more. He pleaded that his wife awaited him back home in Matrassyl. She pleaded with him to wait a little longer. He begged to be excused, but, cunning man though he was, he found it impossible to say no to the queen. They walked every day along the shore, sometimes coming on herds of deer, and Mai trailed disconsolately behind them.

When JandolAnganol, Esomberr, and their party had been gone from Gravabagalinien for a week and two days, the queen was sitting moodily in her room, gazing to the landward side of her narrow domain. The door was thrown open and in ran TatromanAdala, shrieking a greeting.

The child came halfway across the gulf between the door and the place where her mother crouched. That mother had raised her head and looked from under her disordered hair with such venom that Tatro halted.

"Moth! Can you play?"

The mother saw how the daughter's infant face bore the features of her father's line. The genethlic divinities might have further tragedies yet in store. The queen screamed at Tatro.

"Get out of my sight, you little witch!"

Amazement, scandal, anger, dismay passed across the child's face. It glowed red, it seemed to dissolve, it flowed with tears and sobs.

The queen of queens leaped to her sandalless feet, and rushed at the small being. Twirling it about, she thrust it forward and out of the room, slamming the door on it. Then she herself, flinging her body against a wall, hands above her head, also wept.

Later in the day, her mood lightened. She sought out the child and made a fuss of her. Lassitude gave way to a mood of elation. She put on a satara gown and went downstairs. Her portable golden throne was summoned, though the heat of midday was heavy on Gravabagalinien. Submissive hornless phagors brought it forth. Majordomo ScufBar came, and Princess Tatro with her nursemaid, and the nursemaid's maid, carrying storybooks and toys.

The small procession being assembled, MyrdemInggala mounted her throne, and they started on the way to the beach. At this hour, no courtiers accompanied them. Freyr regarded them, low over a shoulder of cliff, Batalix shone almost at zenith.

Leisurely waves, aglitter as if the world had just begun that day, came in, curling to reveal for a moment their cucumber hearts. About the stand of the Linien Rock, water gargled invitingly. Of the assatassi of the recent past there was no sign, nor would there be until next year.

MyrdemInggala stood for a while on the beach. The phagors stood silently by her throne. The princess rushed excitedly about, issuing her commands to the maids for the building of the strongest sand castle ever, a pianissimo generalissimo rehearsing her role in life. The lure of the sea was not to be resisted. With a bold swing of her arm, the queen released herself from her dress and slid the zona from under her breasts. Her perfumed body was available to the sunlight.

"Don't leave me, Moth!" Tatro shrilled.

"I shall not be long," replied her mother, and ran down the beach to plunge into the beckoning sea.

Once below the surface, the forked creature became a fish herself, as lithe as a fish and almost as speedy. Swimming strongly she passed the dark form of the Linien Rock, to surface only when she was well out into the bay. Here the headland to the east curved round, creating a comparatively narrow passage between it and the solitary stand of rock. She called. The queen of queens was immediately surrounded by dolphins—her familiars, as she spoke of them.

They came, as she knew, in ranking order. She had only to release a spur of urine into the water, and the shapes silvered in, circling about her, closer and closer, till she could rest her arms upon two of them as securely as on the arms of her throne.

Only the privileged could touch her. They were twenty-one in number. Beyond them was an outer court, not less than sixty-four in number. Sometimes, a member of this outer court was permitted to join the inner. Beyond the outer court was a retinue whose numbers MyrdemInggala could only estimate. Possibly one thousand three hundred and forty-four. The retinue contained most of the mothers, children, and oldsters belonging to this school—or nation, as the queen thought of it.

Beyond the retinue, constantly on guard for danger, was the regiment. She rarely saw individual members of the regiment and was discouraged from approaching them, but understood that it numbered certainly as many individuals as the retinue. She also understood that in the deeps were monsters which the dolphins feared. It was the duty of the regiment to guard the retinue and the courts, and to warn them of danger.

MyrdemInggala trusted her familiars more than she trusted her human companions; yet, as in every living relationship, something was withheld. Just as she could not share with them her life on land, they had something in the deeps, some dark knowledge, they could not share with her. Because this thing was unknown, lying beyond her mind, it had its sinister music.

The inner court spoke to her with their great orchestral range of voices. Their pipings near at hand were humble and sweet—truly she was accepted as a queen below water as on land. Further out to sea, long sustained baritone chirps sounded, with basso profundo groans intermingling in a perplexing pattern.

"What is it, my sweetings, my familiars?"

They raised their smiling faces and kissed her shoulders. She knew each member of the inner court by sight and had names for them.

Something worried them. She relaxed, letting her understanding spread out like her urine through the water. She swam deep with them, out to colder water. They spiralled about her, occasionally touching her skin with their skin.

Secretly she hoped to catch a glimpse of the monsters of the true sea. She had not been exiled long enough in Gravabagalinien ever to catch a glimpse of them. However, they appeared to be telling her that this time trouble came from the west.

They had warned her of the death-flight of the assatassi. Although they lacked her time sense, she began to appreciate that whatever was coming was coming slowly but remorselessly, and would arrive soon. Strange thrills worked in her. The creatures responded to her thrills. Every shudder of her body was part of their music.

Understanding her curiosity, the dolphins guided her forward again.

She stared through the zafferine panes of the sea. They had brought her to the brink of a shallow shelf, on which seaweeds grew, bent before the overmastering current. They pushed through. Beyond was a sandy basin. Here were the multitudes of the retinue, line on line, facing westwards.

Beyond them, moving with the wary action of a patrol, was the whole force of the regiment, close together, body almost touching body, making the sea black and extending farther out than vision could penetrate. Never before had the queen been allowed such a close sight of the whole school, or realised how vast it was, how many individuals comprised it. Matching the complex ranks assembled came a tremendous harmony of noise, extending far beyond her human hearing.

She surfaced, and the court followed. MyrdemInggala could remain submerged for three or four minutes, and the dolphins needed to take breath as she did.

She glanced towards the shore. It was distant. One day, she thought, these beautiful creatures that I can love and trust will carry me away from sight of mankind. I shall be changed. She could not tell whether it was for death or life she longed.

Figures danced on the remote shore. One figure waved a cloth. The queen's first response was, indignantly, that they were using her dress for the purpose. Then she realised that they signalled to her. It could only mean a crisis of some kind. Guiltily, her thoughts went to the little princess.

She clutched her breasts in sudden apprehension. To the inner court she gave a word of explanation, before striking back towards the shore. Her familiars followed or plunged before her in arrowhead formation, creating a favourable wake to hasten her strokes.

Her dress lay untouched on her throne, the phagors guarding it, shoulders hunched and acknowledging no excitement. One of the maids, in desperation, had ripped off her own garment to wave. She assumed it again as MyrdemInggala emerged from the water, reluctant to have anyone compare her body with the queen's.

"There's a ship," cried Tatro, eager to be first with the news. "A ship is coming!"

From the headland, using the spyglass which ScufBar brought, the queen saw the ship. CaraBansity was sent for. By the time he arrived on the scene, two further sails were sighted, mere blurs in the murk of the western horizon.

CaraBansity rubbed his eyes with a heavy hand as he returned the spyglass to ScufBar.

"Madam, to my mind the nearest ship is not from Borlien."

"Where, then?"

"In half an hour, its marking will be clearer."

She said, "You are a stubborn man. Where is the ship from? Can't you identify that insignia on its sail?"

"If I could, madam, then I would think it was the Great Wheel of Kharnabhar, and that is nonsense, because it would mean there was a Sibornalese ship very far from home."

She snatched the glass. "It is a Sibornalese ship—of good size. What could it be doing in these waters?"

The deuteroscopist folded his arms and looked grim. "You have been provided with no defences here. Let us hope it is making for Ottassol and its intentions are good."

"My familiars warned me of this," said the queen gravely.

The day wore on. The ship made slow progress. There was great excitement at the palace. Barrels of tar were rolled out to an eminence above the little bay where it was anticipated the ship's boat would have to land if Gravabagalinien was its destination. At least the crew could be confronted by flaming tar if they proved hostile.

The air thickened towards evening. There was no doubt now about the hierogram on the sail. Batalix sank in concentric aureoles of light. People came and went in the palace. Freyr disappeared into the same hazes as its fellow and was gone. Twilight lingered, the sail glinted on the sea; it tacked now, to keep the wind.

With darkness, stars began to appear overhead. The Night Worm burned bright, with the Queen's Scar dim beside it. Nobody slept. The small community feared and hoped, knowing its vulnerability.

The queen sat in her shuttered hall. Tall candles of whale oil fluttered on the table by her side. The wine a slave had poured into a crystal glass and topped with Lordryardry ice was untouched and threw blurred gules on the table. She waited and stared across the room at the bare wall opposite, as if to read there her future fate.

Her aide de camp entered, bowing. "Madam, we hear the rattle of their chains. The anchor is going down."

The queen called CaraBansity and they went to the seashore. Several men and phagors were mustered, to ignite the tar barrels if necessary. Only one torch burned. She took it and strode with it into the dark water. To the wetting of her garments she paid no heed. Lifting the torch above her head, she advanced towards the other advancing lights. She felt immediately the smooth kiss of her familiars about her legs.

Mingled with the roar of surf came a creak of oars.

The wooden wall of the ship, its sails furled, was faintly visible as a backdrop. A boat had been let down. The queen saw men straining, bare-backed, at the oars. Two men were standing amidships, one with a lantern, their faces caught in the nimbus of light.

"Who dares come ashore here?" she called.

And a voice came back, male, with a thrill in it, "Queen Myrdem-Inggala, queen of queens, is that you?"

"Who calls?" she asked. But she recognised the voice even as his response came across the diminishing distance between them.

"It is your general, ma'am, Hanra TolramKetinet."

He jumped from the boat and waded ashore. The queen raised her hand to those on the eminence not to fire their barrels. The general fell before her on one knee, clasping her hand on which the ring with the blue stone gleamed. Her other hand went to his head, to steady herself. In a half-circle round them stood the queen's phagor guard, their morose faces vaguely sketched in the night.

CaraBansity stepped forward with some amazement to greet the general's companion in the longboat. Taking SartoriIrvrash in a great hug, he said, "I had reason to suppose you were in hiding in Dimariam. For once I guessed wrong."

"You're rarely wrong, but this time you were out by a whole continent," said SartoriIrvrash. "I've become a world traveller—what are you doing here?"

"I've remained here since the king left. For a while, JandolAnganol conscripted me to your old post, and almost killed me for it. I've stayed for the ex-queen's sake. She's in a doleful state of mind, poor lady."

Both men looked towards MyrdemInggala and TolramKetinet, but could see no dolefulness about either of them.

"What of her son, Roba?" asked SartoriIrvrash. "Have you news of him?"

"News and no news." CaraBansity's forehead creased in a frown. "It would be some weeks ago that he arrived at my house in Ottassol, just after the assatassi death-flight. The lad's crazed and will cause damage. I let him have a room for the night." He was about to say more, but stopped himself. "Don't mention Robay to the queen."

As the two couples stood conversing on the sand, the boat returned to the *Prayer* to transport Odi Jeseratabhar and Lanstatet ashore. When the oarsmen had dragged the boat safely above the high-tide mark, the whole party made its way up the beach to the palace, following the queen and TolramKetinet. In some of the windows of the palace, lights had been lit.

SartoriIrvrash introduced Odi Jeseratabhar to CaraBansity in glowing terms. CaraBansity became noticeably cool; he made it clear that a Sibornalese admiral was not welcome on Borlienese soil.

"I understand your feelings," Odi said faintly to CaraBansity. She was pale and drawn, her lips white and her hair straggling.

A meal was prepared for the unexpected guests, during which time the general was reunited with his sister Mai and embraced her. Mai wept.

"Oh, Hanra, what's to happen to us all?" she asked. "Take me back to Matrassyl."

"Everything will be fine now," her brother said with assurance.

Mai merely looked her disbelief. She wished to be free of the queen—not to have her as sister-in-law.

They ate fish, followed by venison served with gwing-gwing sauces. They drank such wine as the king's invading force had left, chilled with the best Lordryardry ice. As the meal progressed, TolramKetinet told the company something of the suffering of the Second Army in the jungle; he turned occasionally to Lanstatet, who sat next to his sister, for confirmation of one point or another. The queen appeared scarcely to be listening, though the account was addressed to her. She ate little and her gaze, shielded under long lashes, was rarely lifted from the table.

After the meal, she seized up a candle in its pewter holder and said to her guests, "The night grows short. I will show you to your quarters. You are more welcome than my previous visitors."

The military force with Lanstatet were shown to rear accommodation. SartoriIrvrash and Odi Jeseratabhar were given a chamber near the queen's, and a slave woman to attend them and dress Odi's wounds.

When these dispositions were completed, MyrdemInggala and TolramKetinet stood alone in the echoing hall.

"I fear you are tired," he said in a low voice as they mounted the stairs. She made no answer. Her figure, ascending the steps before him, suggested not fatigue but suppressed energy.

In the corridor upstairs, slatted blinds rattled against the open windows with the stirrings of false dawn. An early bird called from a tower. Looking obliquely back at him, she said, "I have no husband, as you have no wife. Nor am I queen, though by that name I am still addressed. Nor have I been scarcely a woman since I arrived at this place. What I am, you shall see before this night is over."

She flung open the doors of her own bedchamber and gestured to him to enter.

He paused, questioning. "By the beholder—"

"The beholder shall behold what she will behold. My faith has fallen from me as shall this gown."

As he entered, she clasped the neck of her dress and pulled it open, so that her neat breasts, their nipples surrounded by large dark aureoles, sprang before his gaze. He shut the door behind him, calling her name.

She gave herself to him with an effort of will.

During what was left of the night, they did not sleep. The arms of TolramKetinet were round her body, and his flesh inside hers.

Thus was her letter, despatched by the Ice Captain, answered at last.

The next morning brought challenges forgotten in the reunions of the previous night. The *Union* and the *Good Hope* were closing in on the undefended harbour. Pasharatid was drawing near.

Despite the crisis, Mai insisted on getting her brother to herself for half an hour; while she lectured him on the miseries of life in Gravabagalinien, TolramKetinet fell asleep. She threw a glass of water over him to wake him. Staggering angrily out of the palace, he went to join the queen down by the shore. She stood with CaraBansity and one of her old women, looking out to sea.

Both suns were in different sectors of the sky, both shining the more brightly because they were about to be eclipsed by black rain clouds drawing up the slopes of the sky. Two sails glittered in the actinic light.

The *Union* was close, the *Good Hope* no more than an hour's sailing behind; the hierograms on its spread canvas were clear to behold. The *Union* had lowered its artemon, in order to allow its companion to catch up.

Lanstatet was already working with his force, unloading equipment from the *Prayer*.

"They're coming in, Akhanaba help us!" he shouted to Tolram-Ketinet.

"What's that woman doing?" TolramKetinet asked.

An old woman, a servitor of the queen's, a long-term housekeeper of the wooden palace, was helping Lanstatet's men unload the *Prayer*. It was her way of showing her dedication to the queen. A man above her was rolling kegs of gunpowder from the deck onto a gangplank. The old woman was directing the kegs down the slope, releasing a soldier for other duties.

"I'm helping you—what do you think?" she screamed back at the general.

Her attention was distracted. The next keg rolled off the gangplank and struck her shoulder, bowling the old woman over, pitching her face down on the shingle.

She was dragged up, faint but protesting, to lie against a chest on the beach. Blood streamed down her face. MyrdemInggala hurried down from the headland to comfort her.

As the queen knelt by her old servant, TolramKetinet stood over her and laid a hand on the queen's shoulder.

"My arrival has brought trouble on you, lady. That was not my intention. I am trying to regret I did not sail straight on to Ottassol."

The queen made no answer, but took the old woman's head on her lap. The latter's eyes had closed, but her breathing was regular.

"I said, lady, that I hope you don't regret that I did not sail on to Ottassol."

Distress showed in her face as she turned to him. "Hanra, I have no regrets about last night when we were together. It was my wish. I thought to be free of Jan. But it did not achieve what I hoped. For that, I am to blame, not you."

"You are free of him. He divorced you, did he not? What are you talking about?" He looked angry. "I know I'm not a very good general, but—"

"Oh, stop that!" she said impatiently. "It's got nothing to do with you. What do I care if you lost your scerming army? I'm talking about a bond, a solemn state that existed between two people for a long time. . . . Some things don't end when we hope they will. Jan and I—it's like being unable to waken—oh, I'm unable to express—"

With some annoyance, TolramKetinet said, "You're tired. I know how women get upset. Let's talk about such things later. Let's deal with the emergency first." He pointed out to sea, and adopted a no-nonsense voice. "Judging by the nonappearance of the *Golden Friendship*, it was too badly damaged to sail. The Admiral Jeseratabhar says that Dienu

Pasharatid was on it. Perhaps she has been killed, in which case Io Pasharatid on the *Union* will be full of vengeance."

"I fear that man," said MyrdemInggala. "And with excellent reason." She bent her head over the old woman.

Her general gave her a side glance. "I'm here to protect you from him, aren't I?"

"I suppose you are," she said spiritlessly. "At least your lieutenant is doing something about the matter."

JandolAnganol had seen to it that the wooden palace had no weapons with which to defend itself. But the rocks extending out to sea from the Linien Rock meant that any considerable vessel like the *Union* had to sail between the Rock and the headland, and there lay the defender's chance. GortorLanstatet had reinforced his working party on the beach with phagors. Two large cannon from the *Vajabhar Prayer*'s quarter-deck had been winched ashore and were now being manhandled onto the headland, where they would command the bay.

ScufBar and another serving man came up with a stretcher to carry the injured woman back to the safety of the palace and apply iced bandages to her wounds.

Leaving the queen's side, TolramKetinet ran to help position the cannon. He saw the danger of their situation. Apart from the phagors and a few unarmed helpers, the defending forces at Gravabagalinien numbered only his complement of thirteen who had come with him from Ordelay. The two Sibornalese ships now closing on the bay each contained possibly fifty well-armed fighting men.

Pasharatid's *Union* was turning, to present itself broadside on to the coast.

Heaving at the ropes, the men tried to get the second cannon into place.

Confronting the queen with folded arms, CaraBansity said, "Madam, I gave the king good advice which was ill taken. Let me now offer you a similar dose and hope for a kindlier reception. You and your ladies should saddle up hoxneys and ride inland, making no delay."

Her face lit with a sad smile. "I'm glad of your concern, Bardol. You go. Return to your wife. This place has become my home. You know Gravabagalinien is said to be the residence of the ancient ghosts of those who were killed in a battle long ago. I would rather join those shades than leave."

He nodded. "So it may be. I shall stay too, ma'am, in that case."

Something in her expression showed him she was pleased by what he said. On impulse, she asked, "What do you make of this misalliance between our friend Rushven and the Uskuti lady—an admiral, no less?"

"She keeps quiet, but that does not reassure me. It might be safer to pack those two off. There's always more than an arm up a Sibornalese sleeve. We must use our cunning, ma'am—there's little enough else on our side."

"She appears genuinely devoted to my ex-chancellor."

"If so, she has deserted the Sibornalese cause, ma'am. And that may give this man Pasharatid another reason for coming ashore. Pack her off, for everybody's safety."

At sea, smoke billowed, concealing all but the sails of the *Union*. A moment later, explosions were heard.

The shots landed in the water at the foot of a low cliff. With a second salvo, the marksmen would be more accurate. Evidently the lookout had sighted the manoeuvring of the cannon on shore.

But the shots proved to be no more than warnings. The *Union* swung to port and began sailing straight towards the little bay.

The queen stood alone, her long hair, still unbound from the night, streaming in the wind. There was a sense in which she was prepared to die. It might be the best way of resolving her troubles. She was—to her dismay—not prepared to accept TolramKetinet, an honest but insensitive man. She was vexed with herself for putting herself under emotional obligation to him. The truth was, his body, his caresses of the night, had merely roused in her an intense longing for Jan. She felt lonelier than before.

Moreover, she divined with melancholy detachment Jan's loneliness. That she might have assuaged, had she herself been more mature.

Out to sea, monsoon rain created gulfs of darkness and slanting light. Showers burned across the waters. The clouds loomed lower. *Good Hope* was almost lost in murk. And the sea itself—MyrdemInggala looked, and saw that her familiars were choking the waves. What she had mistaken for choppiness was the ferment of their bodies. The rain drove in at speed and dashed itself against her face.

Next second, everyone was struggling through a heavy downpour.

The cannon stuck, its wheels spun in mud. A man fell on his knees, cursing. Everyone cursed and bellowed. The fusee in its perforated tin would be doused if the downpour continued.

Hope of placing the cannon effectively was now dead. The wind veered with the storm. The *Union* was blown towards the bay.

As the ship drew level with the Linien Rock, the dolphins acted. They moved in formation, retinue and regiment. The entrance to the bay was barred by their bodies.

Sailors in the *Union*, half-blinded by rain, shouted and pointed at the teeming backs beneath their hulls. It was as if the ship ran across black shining cobbles. The dolphins wedged their bodies solid against the timbers. The *Union* slowed, groaning.

Screaming with excitement, MyrdemInggala forgot her sorrows and ran down to the water. She clapped her hands, shrieked encouragement at her agents. Sand and salt splashed over her calves, rushing beneath her dress. She plunged forward in the undertow. Even TolramKetinet hesitated to follow. The ship loomed over her and the rain lashed down.

One of her familiars reared out of the water as if he had expected her coming, seizing the fabric of her dress in his mouth. She recognised him as a senior member of the inner court, and spoke his name. In his medley of calls was an urgent message she could recognise: stay away, or gigantic things—she could not determine what—would seize her. Something far off in the deeps had her scent.

Even the queen of queens was frightened by the news. She retreated, guided by the familiar all the way. As she reached the sand, clutching her soaked dress, he sank away below the foam.

The *Union* lay only a few ship's lengths from where the queen and her followers stood. Between beach and carrack were dolphins, both courts and regiment, packed tight. Through the driving torrents, the queen recognised the commanding figure of Io Pasharatid—and he had recognised her.

He stood tall and sinister on the streaming deck, swart-bearded, canvas jacket open to the rain, cap pitched over his eyes. He looked at her and then he acted.

In his fist was a spear. Climbing onto the rail of the ship, clutching the shrouds with one hand, he leaned forward and stabbed down repeatedly into the water. With every stab, crimson spurted up the blade of the weapon. The waters became lashed with foam. Pasharatid stabbed again and again.

To superstitious mariners, the dolphin is a sacred creature. Ally of the spirits of the deep, it can do no wrong in sailors' eyes. Harm it and one places one's own life in jeopardy.

Pasharatid was surrounded by furious mariners. The spear was wrestled from his hand and thrown away. The watchers ashore saw him borne fighting to the deck until his soldiers rushed in and pulled him free. The scrimmage continued for a while. The queen's familiars had successfully barred the way to Gravabagalinien.

The rainstorm was at its height. The waves rose higher, crashing up the beach with splendid fury. The queen screamed her victory, looking in her dishevelment much like her dead mother, the wild Shannana, until TolramKetinet dragged her back, in fear that she would hurl herself into the water again.

Lightning flashed in the storm's belly and then struck with following thunder. Cloud shifted like blown sheet, outlining the *Good Hope* suddenly in silver water. It stood off a third of a mile or less from its companion ship, as its crew fought to keep it offshore.

A line of dolphins streamed from the bay and could be seen heading beyond the *Good Hope* as if summoned by something there.

The sea convulsed. It boiled about the Lorajan vessel. Men ashore swore afterwards that the water boiled. The convulsion grew, with glimpses of things churning. Then a mass rose from the water, shook waves from its head, rose, still rose, till it towered above the masts of the *Good Hope*. It had eyes. It had a great lantern jaw and whiskers that writhed like eels. More of it came out of the sea in thick scaled coils, thicker than a man's torso. The storm was its element.

And there were more coils. A second monster appeared, this one in a rage, to judge by the darting movements of its head. Like a gigantic snake, it rose, then struck at the waves, diving, to leave sections of its roped body still agleam in the viscous air.

Its head emerged again, setting the *Good Hope* rocking. The two creatures joined forces. Careless in their obscene sport, they writhed through the water. One lashing tail smashed against the side of the caravel, breaking planking and treenails.

Then both beasts were gone. The waters lay flattened where they had been. They had obeyed the summons of the dolphins and now were making back towards the depths of the ocean. Although their appearances before the eyes of men were rare, the great creatures still formed part of the cycle of living beings which had adapted to the Great Year of Helliconia.

At this stage of their existence, the great serpents were asexual. Long past was their period of intense mating activity. Then, they had been flighted creatures, and had squandered centuries in amorous anorexy, feeding on procreation. Like giant dragonflies, they and their kind had flirted above the world's two lonely poles, free of enemies or even witnesses.

With the coming of the Great Summer, the aerial creatures migrated to the seas of the south, and in particular to the Sea of Eagles, where their appearance had led some long-dead and ornithologically unversed seamen to name an ocean after them. On remote islands like Poorich and Lordry, the creatures shed their wings. They crawled upon their bellies into the brine, and there gave birth.

In the seas the summer would be spent. Eventually the great bodies would dissolve, to feed assatassi and other marine inhabitants. The voracious young were known as scupperfish. They were not fish at all. When the chills of the long winter came to prompt them, the scupperfish would emerge onto land and assume yet another form, called by such ill names as Wutra's Worm.

In their present asexual state, the two serpents had been stirred into activity by a recollection of their distant past. The memory had been brought them by the dolphins, in the form of a scent trace, infused into the waters by the queen of queens during her menstrual period. In confused restlessness, they coiled about each other's bodies; but no power could bring back what had gone.

Their ghastly apparition had knocked any desire for fighting from the bellies of those aboard the *Union* and the *Good Hope*. Gravabagalinien was a haunted place. Now the invaders knew it. Both ships crammed on all possible sail and fled eastwards before the storm. The clouds covered them and they were gone.

The dolphins had disappeared.

Only the waters raged, breaking high up the Linien Rock with dull booms which carried along the beach.

The human defenders of Gravabagalinien made their way back through the rain to the wooden palace.

The chambers of the palace echoed like drums under the weight of monsoon rain. The tune kept changing as the rain died, then fell with renewed vigour.

A council of war was held in the great chamber, the queen presiding.

"First, we should be clear what kind of a man we are dealing with," TolramKetinet said. "Chancellor SartoriIrvrash, tell us what you know of Io Pasharatid, and please speak to the point."

Whereupon SartoriIrvrash rose, smoothing his bald head and bowing to her majesty. What he had to say would indeed be brief but hardly pleasant. He apologised for bringing up old unhappy things, but the future was always linked with the past in ways that even the wisest among them could scarcely anticipate. He might give as an instance . . .

Catching Odi Jeseratabhar's eye, he applied himself to the point, hunching up his shoulders to do so. In the years in Matrassyl, his duty as chancellor had been to discover the secrets of the court. When the queen's brother, YeferalOboral of beloved memory, was still alive, he had discovered that Pasharatid—then ambassador from his country—was enjoying the favours of a young girl, a commoner, whose mother kept a house of ill-repute. He, the chancellor, also discovered from VarpalAnganol that Pasharatid contrived to look upon the queen's body when naked. The fellow was a scoundrel, lustful and reckless, kept in check only by his wife—whom they had reason to believe was now dead.

Moreover, he wished to retail a rumour—perhaps more than a rumour—gathered from a guide called the Pointer of the Way, whom he befriended on his journey through the desert to Sibornal, that Io Pasharatid had murdered the queen's brother.

"I know that to be so," said MyrdemInggala, dismissively. "We have every reason to regard Io Pasharatid as a dangerous man."

TolramKetinet rose.

He adopted military postures and spoke with rhetorical flourishes, glancing across at the queen to see how his performance was being received. He said that they were now clear how Pasharatid was to be feared. It was reasonable to assume that the scoundrel was in command of the *Union* and, by dint of his connections, could enforce his orders on the commander of the *Good Hope*. He, TolramKetinet, had evaluated the military situation from the enemy's viewpoint, and estimated that Pasharatid would move as follows. One—

"Please make this brief, or the man will burst in upon us at this table," said CaraBansity. "We take it that you're as great an orator as you are a general."

Frowning, TolramKetinet said that Pasharatid would decide that two ships could never take Ottassol. His best plan would be to capture the queen and thus force Ottassol to submit to his demands. They should anticipate that Pasharatid would land somewhere to the east of Gravabagalinien, wherever a favourable beach presented itself. He would then march on Gravabagalinien with his men. He, TolramKetinet (who struck his chest as he spoke), declared that they must immediately muster their defences against this anticipated land attack. The queen's person was safe in his keeping.

After a general discussion, the queen issued orders. As she spoke, rain started to drip down on the table. "Since water is my element, I cannot complain if the roof leaks," she said.

MyrdemInggala advised that defences should be built along the perimeters of the palace grounds and that the general should draw up an inventory of all weapons and warlike impedimenta available, not forgetting the armoury of the *Vajabhar Prayer*.

Turning to SartoriIrvrash, she ordered him and Odi Jeseratabhar to depart from the palace at once. They might have three hoxneys from the stables.

"You are kind, ma'am," said SartoriIrvrash, although the expression on his volelike face suggested he thought otherwise. "But can you spare us?"

"I can if your companion is fit to ride."

"I don't think she is fit."

"Rushven, I can spare you as Jan could spare you. You advised him on the plan of divorcement, didn't you? As for your new consort, I understand that she is or was a close friend of the villainous Io Pasharatid."

He was taken aback. "My lady, there was much botheration. . . . Many questions of policy were involved. I was paid to support the king."

"You used to claim that you supported the truth."

He searched his charfrul absentmindedly, as if looking for a veronikane, then settled for rubbing his whiskers instead.

"Sometimes the two roles coincided. I know that your kind heart and the king's spoke for the phagors in our kingdom. Yet they are the chief cause of all human troubles. In summer, we have the opportunity to rid ourselves of them when their numbers are low. Yet summer is the time we squabble among ourselves and are least capable of seeing them as our ultimate enemy. Believe me, ma'am, I have studied such histories as *Brakst's Thribriatiad*, and have learned—"

She looked at him not unfavourably, but now held up her hand.

"Rushven, no more! We were friends, but our lives have changed. Go in peace."

Unexpectedly, he ran round the table and clasped her hand.

"We'll go, we'll go! After all, I'm used to cruel treatment. But grant one request before we leave. . . . With Odi's assistance, I have discovered something of vital importance to us all. We shall go on to Oldorando, and present this discovery to the Holy C'Sarr, in the hopes that it may merit reward. It will also discountenance your ex-husband, you may be pleased to hear—"

"What is your request?" she broke in angrily. "Be finished, will you? We have more important business."

"The request has to do with the discovery, ma'am. When we were all safe at the palace at Matrassyl, I used to read to your infant daughter. Little you care for that now. I remember the charming storybook that Tatro possessed. Will you permit me to take that storybook with me to Oldorando?"

MyrdemInggala stifled something between a laugh and a scream. "Here we try to prepare for a land attack and you wish to have a child's book of fairy tales! By all means take the book as far as I'm concerned —then be off the premises, and take that ceaseless tongue of yours with you!"

He kissed her hand. As he backed to the door, Odi beside him, he gave a sly smile and said, "The rain is stopping. Fear not, we shall soon be away from this inhospitable refuge."

The queen hurled a candlestick after his retreating back.

To one side of the palace was an extensive garden, where herbs and fruit bushes grew. In the garden was an enclosure within which pigs, goats, chickens, and geese were kept. Beyond this enclosure stood a line of gnarled trees. Beyond the trees lay a low earthworks, grass-covered, which encircled marshy ground to the east—the direction from which Pasharatid's force would come if it did come.

After a businesslike survey of the ground, TolramKetinet and Lanstatet decided they must use this old line of defence.

They had considered evacuating Gravabagalinien by ship. But the *Prayer* had been inexpertly moored. During the storm, it suffered damage and could hardly be considered seaworthy.

Everything of value was unloaded from the ship. Some of its higher timbers were utilised to make a watchtower in the stoutest tree.

As the ground dried off after the storm, some of the phagors were employed to build a defensive breastwork along the top of the earthworks. Others were deployed to dig trenches nearby.

This was the scene of activity which met SartoriIrvrash and Odi Jeseratabhar as they left the settlement. They travelled one behind the other on hoxneys, with a third animal trailing, carrying their baggage. They saw CaraBansity supervising the digging of fortifications, and SartoriIrvrash halted.

"I must bid farewell to my old friend," he said as he dismounted.

"Don't be long," Odi warned. "You have no friends here because of me."

He nodded and walked over to the deuteroscopist, squaring his shoulders.

CaraBansity was working in a patch of marshy ground with some labouring ancipitals. When he looked up and saw SartoriIrvrash, his heavy face went dark, then, as if forced to it by the pressure of excitement, burst into a smile. He beckoned SartoriIrvrash over.

"Here's the past . . . these earthworks form part of an ancient fortification system. The phagors are uncovering the geometries of legend made flesh. . . ."

He walked over to a newly dug pit. SartoriIrvrash followed. CaraBansity knelt at the edge of the pit, heedless of squelching mud. An arm's length below the turf, emerging from the peaty soil, lay what SartoriIrvrash took at first to be an old black bag, pressed flat. It was or it had been a man. His body lay sprawled on its left side. Short leather tunic and boots suggested that the man had been a soldier. Half-concealed beneath his flattened form lay the hilt of a sword. The man's profile, mouth distorted by broken teeth, had been moulded by earth's pressure into a macabre smile. The flesh was a rich shining brown.

Other bodies were being uncovered. The phagors worked without interest, scratching the mud away with their fingers. From the dirt, another mummified soldier appeared, a fearful wound in his chest. The creases of his face were clear, as if in a pencil sketch. His eyeballs had collapsed, giving his expression a melancholy vacancy.

The cellar smell of soil bit into their nostrils.

"The peaty earth has preserved them," said SartoriIrvrash. "They could be soldiers who died in battle, or similar botheration. They may be a hundred years old."

"Far more than that," said CaraBansity, jumping down into the trench. He scratched up one of a number of what SartoriIrvrash had taken to be stones, and lifted it for examination. "This is probably what killed the fellow with the broken teeth. It's a rajabaral tree seed, as hard as iron. It may have been baked, which is why it never germinated. It's over six centuries since spring, when the rajabarals seeded. The attackers used the seeds as cannonballs. This is where the legendary battle of Gravabagalinien was fought. We find the site because we are about to use it again for battle."

"Poor devils!"

"Them? Or us?" He went to the rear corner of the excavation. Lying below the body of the man with the chest wound was a phagor, partly visible. Its face was black, its coat matted and reddened by the bog water, until it resembled a compressed vegetable growth. "You see how even then men and phagors fought and died together."

SartoriIrvrash gave a snort of disgust. "They may equally well have been enemies. You've no evidence either way."

"Certainly it's a bad omen. I wouldn't want the queen to see these. Or TolramKetinet. He's scumber himself. We'd better cover the bodies up."

The ex-chancellor made to turn away. "Not all of us cover up the secrets we find, friend. I have knowledge in my possession which, when I lay it before the authorites of Pannoval, will start a Holy War against the ancipital kind throughout all Campannlat."

CaraBansity looked calculatingly at him through his heavy bloodshot eyes. "And you'll get paid for starting that war, eh? Live and let live, I say."

"Yes, you say it, Bardol, but these horned creatures don't. Their creed is different. They will outbreed us and kill us unless we act. If you had seen for yourself the flambreg herds—"

"Don't fly into a passion. Passion always causes trouble. . . . Now, we'll get on with our job. There are probably hundreds of bodies lying under the earth about here."

Folding his arms tightly about his chest, SartoriIrvrash said, "You give me a cold reception, just like the queen."

CaraBansity climbed slowly out of the trench. "Her majesty gave you what you asked for, a book and three hoxneys." He stuck a knuckle between his teeth and stared at the ex-chancellor.

"Why are you so against me, Bardol? Have you forgotten the time when, as young men, we looked through your telescope and observed the phases of Kaidaw as it sped above us? And from that deduced the cosmic geometries under which we exist?"

"I don't forget. You come here, though, with a Sibornalese officer, a dedicated enemy of Borlien. The queen is under threat of death and the kingdom of dissolution. I have no love of JandolAnganol or of phagors, yet I wish to see them continue, in order that people may still look through telescopes.

"Overturn the kingdom, as both you and she would do, and you overturn the telescopes."

He gazed through the trees towards the sea with a bitter expression, shrugging his shoulders.

"You have witnessed how Keevasien, once a place of some culture, home of the great YarapRombry, has been carelessly erased. Culture may flourish better under old injustice than under new. That's all I say."

"It's a plea for your own way of life."

"I shall always fight for my own way of life. I believe in it. Even when it means fighting myself. Go, take that woman with you—and remember there's always more than an arm up a Sibornalese sleeve."

"Why speak to me like this? I'm a victim. A wanderer—an exile. My life's work's ruined. I could have been the YarapRombry of my epoch. . . . I'm innocent."

CaraBansity shook his large head. "You're of an age when innocence is a crime. Leave with your lady. Go and spread your poison."

They regarded each other challengingly. SartoriIrvrash sighed, CaraBansity climbed back into his trench.

SartoriIrvrash walked back to where Odi Jeseratabhar waited with the animals. He mounted his hoxney without a word, tears in his eyes.

They took the trail leading northwards to Oldorando. JandolAnganol and his party had travelled that way only a few days earlier, on their way to the home of the king's murdered bride-to-be.

XIX

OLDORANDO

The suns blazed down out of a cloudless sky, flattening the veldt with their combined light.

King JandolAnganol, Eagle of Borlien, enjoyed being in the wilderness again. His way of enjoyment was not every man's. It consisted mainly of hard marches interspersed with short rests. This was not to the taste of the C'Sarr's pleasure-loving envoy, Alan Esomberr.

The king and his force, with attendant ecclesiastics, approached Oldorando from the south along one of the old Pilgrim's Ways, which led on through Oldorando to Holy Pannoval.

Oldorando stood at the crossroads of Campannlat. The migratory route of the phagors and the various ucts of the Madis ran east and west close by the city. The old salt road meandered north into the Quzints and Lake Dorzin. To the west lay Kace—slatternly Kace, home of cutthroats, craftsmen, vagabonds, and villains; to the south lay Borlien —friendly Borlien, home of more villains.

JandolAnganol was approaching a country at war, like his own, with barbarians. That war between Oldorando and Kace had broken out because of the ineffectiveness of King Sayren Stund as much as the nastiness of the Kaci.

Faced with the collapse of the Second Army, JandolAnganol had made what was widely regarded as a cowardly peace with the hill clans of Kace, sending them valuable tributes of grain and veronikane in order to seal the armistice.

To the Kaci, peace was relative; they were long accustomed to internecine struggles. They simply hung their crossbows on the back of the hut door and resumed their traditional occupations. These included hunting, blood feuds, potting—they made excellent pottery which they traded with the Madi for rugs—stealing, mining precious stones, and goading their scrawny womenfolk into working harder. But the war with Borlien, sporadic though it had been, instilled in the clans a new sense of unity.

Failing by some chance to quarrel during their extensive victory celebrations—when JandolAnganol's grain tribute was converted into something more potable—the leading clans of Kace accepted as their universal suzerain a powerful brute called Skrumppabowr. As a kind of goodwill gesture on his election, Skrumppabowr had all the Oldorandans living on Kaci land slaughtered, or "staked" as the local term was.

Skrumppabowr's next move was to repair the damage done by war to irrigation terraces and to villages in the southeast. To this end, he encouraged ancipitals to come in to Kace from Randonan, Quain, and Oldorando. In exchange for their labour, he guaranteed the phagors freedom from the drumbles racking Oldorando. Being heathen, the Kaci clans saw no reason to persecute the phagors as long as they behaved themselves and never looked at Kaci women.

JandolAnganol heard of these events with pleasure. They confirmed his sense of himself as a diplomat. The Takers were less pleased. The Takers were the militants of the Holy Pannovalan Empire, with highly placed connections within the See of Pannoval itself. Kilandar IX, so it was rumoured, had been a Taker himself in his young days.

A mounted arm of Takers, striking out from Oldorando City, made a daring raid on Akace, the squalid mountain settlement which served as a capital, and slaughtered over a thousand newly arrived phagors overnight, together with a few Kaci.

This success proved less than a victory. On their way home, the Takers, rendered careless by the outcome of their raid, were ambushed by Lord Skrumppabowr's clans and slaughtered in their turn, many in sadistic ways. Only one Taker returned to Oldorando, more dead than alive, to tell the tale. A thin bamboo rod had been driven through his body from his anus; the sharp end protruded from behind the clavicle of his right shoulder. He had been staked.

Reports of this outrage reached King Sayren Stund. He declared a
holy war on the barbarians and set a price on Skrumppabowr's head.
Blood had since been spilt on both sides, but mainly on the Oldorandan
side. At the present time, half the Oldorandan army—in which no
phagors were allowed to serve—was away making forced marches
among the wilderness of shoatapraxi which abounded on Kace hillsides.

The king soon lost interest in the struggle. After the murder of his
elder daughter, Simoda Tal, he retreated into the confines of his palace
and was rarely seen. He bestirred himself when he heard of Jandol-
Anganol's approach, but then only at the concerted prompting of his
advisors, his Madi queen, and his surviving daughter, Milua Tal.

"How are we to amuse this great king, Sayren, sweetest?" asked
Queen Bathkaarnet-she, in her singing voice. "I am such a poor thing, a
flower, and I am lame. A limp flower. Will you wish me to sing my
songs of the Journey to him?"

"I don't care for the man, personally. He's without culture," said her
husband. "Jandol will bring his phagor guard, since he can't afford to
pay real soldiers. If we must endure the pestilential things in our capital,
perhaps they'll amuse us with their animal antics."

Oldorando's climate was hot and enervating. The eruption of Mount
Rustyjonnik had opened up a chain of volcanic activity. A sulphurous
pall often hung over the land. The flags which the king ordered to be put
out to greet his Borlienese cousin hung limp in the airless atmosphere.

As for the King of Borlien, impatient energy possessed him. The
march from Gravabagalinien had taken the best part of a tenner, first
over the loess farmlands, then across wilder country. No pace was rapid
enough for JandolAnganol. Only the First Phagorian made no complaint.

Bad news continued to reach the column. Crop failure and famine
were everywhere in his kingdom; evidence of that lay all round. The
Second Army was not merely defeated: it was never going to reemerge
from the jungles of Randonan. Such few men as came back slunk to
their own homes, swearing they would never soldier again. The phagor
battalions which had survived disappeared into the wilds.

From the capital, the news was no more encouraging. Jandol-
Anganol's ally, Archpriest BranzaBaginut, wrote that Matrassyl was in a
state of ferment, with the barons threatening to take over and rule in the
name of the scritina. It behoved the king to act positively, and as soon
as possible.

He enjoyed being on the move, delighted in living off what game there
was, rejoiced in the evening bivouac, and even tolerated days of brilliant
sunshine, away from the coastal monsoons. It was as if he took pleasure

from the ferment of emotions that filled him. His face became leaner, tenser, his waywardness more marked.

Alam Esomberr felt less enthusiastic. Brought up in his father's house in the subterranean recesses of Pannoval, he was unhappy in the open and mutinous about the forced pace. The dandified envoy of the Holy C'Sarr called a halt at last, knowing he had the support of his weary retinue.

It was dimday, when fat, brilliant flowers opened among the lustreless grasses, inviting the attention of dusk-moths. A bird called, hammering at its two notes.

They had left the loess farmlands behind and were traversing a farm-less moor which supported few villages. For shade, the envoy's party retreated under an enormous denniss tree, whose leaves sighed in the breeze. The denniss sprouted many trunks, some young, some ancient, which propped themselves up languidly—like Esomberr himself—with gnarled elbows as they sprawled on the ground in all directions.

"What can drive you like this, Jandol?" Esomberr asked. "What are we hurrying for, except for hurrying's abominable sake? To put it another way, what fate awaits you in Oldorando better than the one you revoked in Gravabagalinien?"

He eased his legs and looked up with his amused glance into the king's countenance.

JandolAnganol squatted nearby, balancing on his toes. A faint smell of smoke came to his nostrils, and he searched the distance for its origin. He threw small pebbles at the earth.

A group of the king's captains, the Royal Armourer, and others leant on their staffs, a short distance away. Some smoked veronikanes, one teased Yuli, prodding the creature with his staff.

"We must reach Oldorando as soon as possible." He spoke as one who wants no argument, but Esomberr persisted.

"I'm eager to see that somewhat squalid city myself, if only to soak for a few millennia in one of their famous hot springs. That doesn't mean I'm anxious to *run* all the way there. You're a changed man since your Pannoval days, Jandol—not quite such fun, if I may say so. . . ."

The king threw his pebbles more violently. "Borlien needs an alliance with Sayren Stund. That deuteroscopist who presented me with my three-faced timepiece, Bardol CaraBansity, said I had no business in Oldorando. A conviction seized me at that moment that I had to go there. My father supported me. His dying words to me were—as he lay dying in my arms—'Go to Oldorando.' Since that fool Tolram-Ketinet allowed his army to be wiped out, I can only seek union with Oldorando. The fates of Borlien and Oldorando have always been linked." He flung down a final stone with violence, as if to destroy all argument.

Esomberr said nothing. He plucked a grass blade to suck, suddenly self-conscious under the king's stare.

After a moment, JandolAnganol jumped up, to stand with his feet planted apart.

"Here stand I. While I press upon the earth, the energies of the earth surge up through my body. I am of the Borlienese soil. I am a natural force."

He raised his arms, fingers tensed.

The phagors, armed with their matchlocks, lay about at a short distance, like shapeless cattle, looking over the plain. Some rooted under stone and found grubs or rickybacks, which they ate. Others stood without movement, beyond the occasional swing of the head or a flick of the ears to ward off flies. Winged things buzzed in the shade. Made uneasy, Esomberr sat up.

"I don't understand what you mean, but do enjoy yourself." His voice was dry.

The king scrutinised the horizon as he spoke. "An example for you, so that you understand well the kind of man I am. Although I may have rejected my Queen MyrdemInggala for whatever reason, nevertheless she remains mine. If I discovered that you, for instance, had dared to enter her bedchamber to consort with her while we were in Gravabagalinien, then, notwithstanding our friendship, I would kill you without compunction, and hang your eddre from this tree."

Neither of them moved. Then Esomberr rose and stood with his back to one of the trunks of the denniss. His narrow handsome face had grown as pale as a dead leaf.

"I say, did it ever occur to you that those damned phagors of yours, well armed with Sibornalese weapons, strike fear into ordinary chaps like me? That they will most likely meet with an ill reception in Sayren Stund's capital, where a holy drumble is in progress? Are you ever afraid that you might . . . well, grow to be a bit like a phagor yourself?"

The king turned slowly, with an expression denoting total lack of interest in the question.

"Watch."

He screwed his face into a mixture of grimace and smile, and snorted breath through his nose. He broke into a run, gathered himself, and leaped clear over one of the trunks of the tree, a full four feet above the ground. It was a perfect jump. He recovered himself, turned, and jumped the trunk in the opposite direction, with a force which carried him almost against Esomberr.

The king was half a head taller than the envoy. The latter, alarmed, reached for his sword, then stood without movement, tense against the king.

"I am twenty-five years of age, in fine condition, and fear neither man

nor phagor. My secret is that I am capable of going with circumstances.
Oldorando shall be my circumstance. I gain energy from the geometry of
circumstance. . . . Do not vex me, Alam Esomberr, or forget my words
about the sanctity of what was once mine. I am one of your circumstances, and not vice versa."

The envoy moved to one side, coughed as a reason for moving his
hand from his sword hilt to his mouth, and managed a pale smile.

"You're terribly fit, I see that. That's tremendous. By the beholder,
but I envy you. It's a wretched nuisance that I and my little rabble of
vicars aren't in such fine trim. I've often thought that praying vitiates the
muscles. Therefore, I must request that you proceed ahead with your
party and your favoured species—at your breakneck pace—while we
follow on behind at our own feeble pace, eh?"

JandolAnganol regarded him without change of expression. Then he
gave a fierce grimace. "Very well. The country hereabouts is peaceful,
but guard yourselves. Robbers have scant respect for vicars. Remember
you carry my bill of divorcement."

"Strive ever onwards, if you will. I shall deliver your bill to the C'Sarr
in good time." He gave a wave of his hand and left it dangling in front
of him. The king did not take it.

Instead, JandolAnganol turned away without further word and whistled Yuli to his side. He called the gillot leader of the guard, Ghht-Mlark
Chzarn. The ahuman columns formed up and marched away; the humans followed more informally. In a short while, Alam Esomberr, together with his followers, was left standing silent under the denniss tree.
Then the figures were lost to JandolAnganol amid the shade. Soon the
great tree itself was lost in the shimmering heat of the plain.

Two days later, the king halted his force only a few miles short of
Oldorando. Wisps of smoke trailed across the rolling landscape.

He stood by one of the aged stone pillars which dotted the landscape.
Impatient for the rear of the phagor column to catch up, JandolAnganol
traced with one finger the worn design on the stone, a familiar pattern of
two concentric circles with curving lines running from inner to outer
circle. Just for a moment, he wondered what the pillar and its pattern
could signify; but such enigmas—presumably never capable of resolution, any more than he expected to be told what long-dead king had
erected the stones—occupied his mind only for a moment. His thoughts
were all on what lay immediately ahead.

They had reached a region which was in fact a hinterland of the
fabled city they were approaching.

Of that city, there was as yet no sign. The view comprised low rolling
hills, the foothills of the foothills of the Quzint Mountains, running like

an armoured spine over the continent. Ahead, sprawling across the ground, was one of the ucts, threading its way into the distance on either side.

The uct here formed a tawny rather than a green line, comprising few large trees but many bushes and cyclads, entwined by gaudy mantle flowers, the seeds of which migrant tribes chewed as they progressed.

No road was as wide as this uct. Unlike a road, however, it was not to be travelled by humans. Despite the depredations of arang and fhlebiht, it had become impenetrable. The Madi tribes with their animals travelled along its edge. There, scattering seeds and droppings, the protognostics unthinkingly widened the uct. Year by year it spread, becoming a strip of forest.

Not that the strip was regular. Alien growths like shoatapraxi, introduced as burrs on the coats of animals, had prospered in places where they could take advantage of favourable soil conditions, and spread in thickets. The Madi skirted the new thickets, or else plunged through them leaving a trail later obliterated by further waves of aliens.

What was incidental became established. The uct served as a barrier. Butterflies and small animals found on one side of the barrier were not to be seen on the other. There were birds and rodents and a deadly golden snake which kept to the shelter of the uct and never ventured beyond its confines as they spread across the continent. Several kinds of Others lived their pranksome lives out in the uct.

Humans, too, recognised the existence of the uct by using it as a frontier. This uct marked the frontier between Northern Borlien and the land of Oldorando.

And that frontier was on fire.

A lava flow from a newly erupting volcano had set the uct ablaze. It had begun to burn along its length like a fusee.

Instruments on the Avernus were recording details of increasing volcanic activity on the world approaching periastron below. Data relayed to Earth concerning Mount Rustyjonnik showed that the material from the eruption rose to a height of 50 kilometres. The lower layers of this cloud were carried rapidly eastwards, circling the globe in 15 days. The material rising above 21 kilometres moved westwards with the prevailing flow of the lower stratosphere, to circle the globe in 60 days.

Similar readings were obtained for other eruptions. Dust clouds gathering in the stratosphere were about to double Helliconia's albedo, reflecting the increasing heat of Freyr away from the surface. Thus the elements of the biosphere worked like an interrelated body or machine to preserve its vital processes.

During the decades when Freyr was closest to Helliconia, the planet would be shielded by acidic dust layers from its worst effects.

Nowhere was this dramatic homeostasis observed with more wonder and awe than on Earth.

On Helliconia, the forest fire was the end of the world for many frightened creatures. To a more detached view, it was a sign of the world's determination to save itself and its freight of organic life.

JandolAnganol's forces waited, tucked in a shallow valley. A pall of smoke to the east announced the approach of the fire. Numbers of hairy pigs and deer ran along the line of the uct westwards to safety. Herds of slower fhlebiht followed, setting up a massive bleating as they passed.

Families of Others went by, encouraging their young in a human fashion. They had dark fur and white faces. Some species were tailless. They swung deftly from branch to branch and were gone.

JandolAnganol rose and stood in a crouch to watch the game go by. The little runt Yuli leapt up sportively to join him. The phagors continued to rest impassively like cattle, chewing their day's ration of porridge and pemmican.

To the east, Madis and their flocks were fleeing before the blaze. While some of their animals bolted for freedom or ran in terror into the thicket, the protognostics themselves remained obedient to custom and followed the line of the uct.

"Blind fools!" exclaimed JandolAnganol.

His quick mind devised a plan. Ordering up a section of phagorian guard, he set a trap into action. When the leading Madis came up, a rope draped with thorn-lianas from the thickets suddenly sprang into the air before them. They came to a confused halt, sheep, asokins, and dogs milling about their legs.

Their Madi faces were as innocuous as the faces of parrots or flowers. Foreheads and jaws receded,· eyes and noses were prominent, giving them a permanent look of incredulity before the world. The males had bosses on foreheads and jaws. Their hair was glossy brown. They called to each other in despairing pigeon voices.

Out leaped the phagor section from its concealment. Each phagor closed in on the frightened Madis. Each caught three or four by their arms, arms burned red by the suns and powdered by the dust of the track. They came without fight. A gillot caught the bellwether, an asokin with a can thumping against its chest. The ewes stood meekly by.

Some Madis tried to run. JandolAnganol clubbed two with his fist, sending them sprawling. They lay crying in the dirt. But others were coming up from the rear all the while, and he let them go.

His party forced their way through the uct with their bag. The dense coats of the phagors rendered them immune to thorns. Driving their captives before them, they crossed over from Borlien to Oldorando. They were safely on their way when the fire passed through the strip, travelling at a brisk walking pace, leaving ashes behind it.

It was in this manner that the royal party arrived at the city of Oldorando, more resembling shepherds than royalty. Their protognostic prisoners were torn and bleeding from the uct thicket, as were many of the humans. The king himself was covered in dust.

There was about Oldorando something almost theatrical, perhaps because at its heart lay the gaudy stage on which worship of Akhanaba the ox-faced All-Powerful was at its most resplendent. True worship is solitary; when the religious gather together, they put on pageants for their gods.

Lying in the steamy centre of Campannlat, threaded by the River Valvoral which connected it with Matrassyl and—ultimately—the sea, Oldorando was a city of travellers. Mostly they came to worship or, if not to worship, to trade.

In the physical form of the city was commemorated the long existence of these opposed intentions. The Holyval sector of the city ran in a diagonal line from southwest to northeast, rising above the sprawl of commerce like a fretted cliff. Holyval included the Old City, with its quaint seven-storey towers, in which lived permanent religious communities. Here were the Academicians, a female order. Here, too, were pilgrims and beggars, as well as god's scum, those who beat empty breasts. Here were courts of shadow and places of prayer sunk deep into the earth. Here too stood the Dom with its attendant monastries, and King Sayren Stund's palace.

It was generally agreed—at least by those whose lives were enclosed by Holyval—that this sector of saintliness, this diagonal of decency, ran between sewers of worldly vices.

But set in Holyval's pompous and fretted walls and forbidding ramparts were a variety of doors. Some were opened only on ceremonial occasions. Others allowed access to the Old City only for the privileged. Others admitted only women or only men (no phagors were permitted to sully Holyval). But others, and those among the most used, let even the most secular of persons to come and go as they would. Between the holy and the unholy, as between the living and the dead, was set a barrier which detained nobody from crossing it.

The unholy lived in less grand premises, although even here the rich had built their palaces along the broader boulevards. The wicked prospered, the good made their way through life as best they could. Of the city's present population of eight hundred and ninety thousand humans, almost one hundred thousand were in religious orders, and served Akhanaba. At least as many were slaves, and served believer and unbeliever alike.

It was in keeping with the shows which Oldorando loved that two messengers clad in blue and gold should wait on JandolAnganol's arrival at the south gate, with a coach in which to draw him to King Sayren Stund.

JandolAnganol refused the coach and, instead of taking the triumphal route along Wozen Avenue, paraded his dusty company into the Pauk. The Pauk was a comfortable, down-at-heels area of taverns and markets where there were traders who would buy both animals and protognostics.

"Madis don't fetch much in Embruddock," said one sturdy dealer, using the old country name for Oldorando. "We got enough of them and, like the Nondads, they don't work well. Now your phagors would be a different question, but in this city I'm not allowed to trade in phagors."

"I'm selling only the Madis and animals, man. Your price, or I'll go elsewhere."

When a sum had been agreed on, the Madis were sold into captivity and the animals to slaughter. The king retired in satisfaction. He was now better prepared to meet Sayren Stund. Before the transaction, he had not so much as a roon piece on him. Phagors dispatched to Matrassyl for gold had not returned.

Moving in military order, the First Phagorian proceeded up Wozen Avenue, where crowds had assembled to watch them. The crowds cheered JandolAnganol as he strode along with Yuli. He was popular with the rabble of Oldorando, despite his championship of the officially deplored ancipitals. The common people contrasted a lively, eager man favourably with their fat, idle, domestic breed of monarch. The common people did not know the queen of queens. The common people had sympathy for a king whose bride-to-be had been brutally murdered—even if that bride was only a Madi, or half-Madi.

Among the common people went the religious. The clerics were out with banners. RENOUNCE YOUR SINS. THE END OF THE WORLD IS NIGH. REPENT YE WHILE TIME IS. Here as in Borlien, the Pannovalan Church played on public fears in order to bring the independent-minded to heel.

The dusty progress continued. Past the ancient King Denniss Pyramid. Through the Wozen sector. Into the wide Loylbryden Square. On the far side of the square, across a stream, Whistler Park. Facing on to square and park, the great Dom of Striving and the picturesque town palace of the king. In the centre of the square, a golden pavilion, in which was seated King Sayren Stund himself, waiting to greet his visitor.

Beside the king sat Queen Bathkaarnet-she, wearing a grey keedrant decorated with black roses, and an uncomfortable crown. Between their majesties on a smaller throne sat their one remaining daughter, Milua Tal. The three of them reposed in absurd dignity under an awning, while the rest of the court sweated in the sun. The heat buzzed with flies. A band played. The absence of soldiers was noticeable, but several elderly officers in resplendent uniforms marched slowly about. The civil guard kept the crowd in order along the perimeters of the square.

The Oldorandan court was known for its stifling formality. Sayren Stund had done his best to soften court etiquette on this occasion, but there remained a line of advisors and church dignitaries, many of them in flowing canonicals, drawn up severely as they waited to shake Jandol-Anganol's hand and kiss his cheek.

The Eagle stood with his party of captains and his hunchbacked armourer, surveying them challengingly, the dust of his journey still about him.

"Your parade would do credit to a museum, Cousin Sayren," he said.

Sayren Stund was dressed, as were his officers, in a severe black charfrul to express mourning. He levered himself out of his throne and came to JandolAnganol with arms extended. JandolAnganol made a bow, holding himself stiffly. Yuli stood a pace behind him, sticking his milt up alternate nostrils, otherwise motionless.

"Greetings in the name of the All-Powerful. The Court of Oldorando welcomes you in your peaceful and fraternal visit to our capital. May Akhanaba make the meeting fruitful."

"Greetings in the name of the All-Powerful. I thank you for your fraternal reception. I come to offer my condolences and my grief at the death of your daughter, Simoda Tal, my bride-elect."

As JandolAnganol spoke, his glance, under the line of his eyebrows, was ever active. He did not trust Sayren Stund. Stund paraded him along the ranks of dignitaries, and JandolAnganol allowed his hand to be shaken and his grimy cheek to be kissed.

He saw from Sayren Stund's demeanour that the King of Oldorando bore him ill will. The knowledge was a torment. Everywhere was hatred in men's hearts. The murder of Simoda Tal had left its stain, with which he now had to reckon.

After the parade, the queen approached, limping, her hand resting on Milua Tal's arm. Bathkaarnet-she's looks had faded, yet there was something in her expression, in the way she held her head—submissively yet perkily—which affected JandolAnganol. He recalled a remark of Sayren Stund's which had once been reported to him—why had that lodged in his memory?—"Once you have lived with a Madi woman, you want no other."

Both Bathkaarnet-she and her daughter had the captivating bird faces of their kind. Though Milua Tal's blood had been diluted with a human stream, she presented an exotically dark, brilliant impression, with enormous eyes glowing on either side of her aquiline nose. When she was presented, she gazed direct at JandolAnganol, and gave him the

Look of Acceptance. He thought briefly of SartoriIrvrash's mating experiments; here if ever was a fertile cross-breeding.

He was pleased to gaze on this one bright face among so many dull ones, and said to her, "You much resemble the portrait I was sent of your sister. Indeed, you are even more beautiful."

"Simoda and I were much alike, and much different, like all sisters," Milua Tal replied. The music of her voice suggested to him many things, fires in the night, baby Tatro cooing in a cool room, pigeons in a wooden tower.

"Our poor Milua is overcome by the assassination of her sister, as we all are," said the king, with a noise which incorporated the best features of a sigh and a belch. "We have agents out far and wide, pursing the killer, the villain who posed as a Madi to gain entrance to the palace."

"It was a cruel blow against us both."

Another compendious sigh. "Well, Holy Council will be held next week, with a special memorial service for our departed daughter, which the Holy C'Sarr himself will bless with his presence. That will cheer us. You must stay with us for that event, Cousin, and be welcome. The C'Sarr will be delighted to greet such a valued member of his Community—and it would be to your advantage to pass time with him, as you will realise. Have you met His Holiness?"

"I know his envoy, Alam Esomberr. He will arrive shortly."

"Ah. Yes. Hmm. Esomberr. A witty fellow."

"And adventurous," said JandolAnganol.

The band struck up. They proceeded across the square to the palace, and JandolAnganol found Milua Tal by his side. She looked up brightly at him, smiling. He asked her conspiratorially, "Are you prepared to tell me your age, ma'am, if I keep it a secret?"

"Oh, that's one of the questions I hear most often," she said, dismissively. "Together with 'Do you like being a princess?' Persons think me in advance of my age, and they must be right. The increased heat of the present period brings younger persons on, develops them in every way. I have dreamed the dreams of an adult for over a year. Did you ever dream you were in the powerful irresistible embrace of a fire god?"

He bent to her ear and said in a ferocious whisper, playfully, "Before I reveal to you if I am that very fire god, I shall have to answer my own question. I'd put you at no more than nine years old."

"Nine years and five tenners," she replied, "but it is emotions, not years, which count."

The facade of the palace was long, and three storeys high, with massive polished columns of rajabaral rising through the marked horizontals of the upper storeys. The roof swept flamboyantly upwards, tiled with blue tiles made by Kaci potters. The palace had been first built over three hundred and fifty small years ago, after Oldorando was partially destroyed by phagor invasion; although its timbers had been renewed since, the original design was adhered to. Elaborately carved wooden screens protected the unglazed windows. The doors were of the same type of carving, but veneered in silver and backed by thick wooden panels. A tubular gong was struck within, the doors opened, and Sayren Stund led his guests inside.

There followed two days of banquetting and empty speeches. The hot water springs for which Oldorando was famous also played their part. A service of thanksgiving was held in the Dom, attended by many high-ranking dignitaries of the Church. The singing was magnificent, the costumes impressive, the darkness in the great underground vault all that Akhanaba could desire. JandolAnganol prayed, sang, spoke, submitted to ceremony, and confided in no one.

All were uncertain of this strange man, all kept their eyes on him. And his eyes were on all. It was clear why some called him the Eagle.

He took care to see that the First Phagorian Guard was suitably housed. For a city that hated phagors, they were well provided for. Across the Loylbryden Square from the Dom was Whistler Park, an area of green entirely surrounded by the Valvoral or its tributaries. Here were preserved brassim trees. Here also was the Hour Whistler of continent-wide fame. This geyser blew with a shrill note at every hour, with the greatest accuracy. Days, weeks, tenners, years, centuries, went by; still the Hour Whistler blew. Some said the hour's length, and the forty minutes which divided the hour, had been decided by this noise issuing from the earth.

An ancient seven-storey tower and some new pavilions stood on the margins of the park. The phagors were billeted in the pavilions. The four bridges into the park were guarded, by phagors on the inner and humans on the outer side, so that no one could get into the park to molest the ancipitals.

Crowds soon gathered to watch the ancipital soldiery across the water. These well-drilled, placid-seeming creatures were far different from the phagors of popular imagination, where they rode godlike on great rust-red steeds, travelling at godlike speeds to bring destruction among men. Those riders of the icy storm had little in common with the beasts marching dourly about the park.

As JandalAnganol left his cohorts to return to Sayren Stund, he noticed how restless they were. He spoke to Phagor-Major Chzarn, but could get from her only that the guard needed a while to settle into new quarters.

He assumed that the noise of the Hour Whistler caused them some irritation. Giving them words of reassurance, he left, the runt capering along at his side. A sulphurous volcano smell filled the air.

Milua Tal met him as he entered the silver gates of the palace. In the last two days he had grown increasingly fond of her volatile company, her cooing pigeon voice.

"Some of your friends have arrived. They say they're holy, but everyone seems to be holy here. The chief of them doesn't look holy. He's too handsome to be holy. He looks naughty to me. Do you like naughty people, King Jandol?—because I think I'm rather naughty."

He laughed.

"I think you are naughty. So are most people. Including some of the holy ones."

"So it is necessary to be exceptionally naughty to stand out from the crowd?"

"That's a reasonable deduction."

"Is that why you stand out from the crowd?"

She slipped her hand into his, and he clasped it.

"There are other reasons. Being a fire god is one."

"I find most people are terribly disappointing. Do you know, when my sister was murdered, we found her sitting upright in a chair, fully dressed. No blood visible. That was disappointing. I imagined pools of blood. I imagined people threw themselves all over the place when they were getting killed, as if they hated what was happening."

JandolAnganol asked in a hard voice, "How was she killed?"

"Zygankes, stabbed right through the heart with a fuggie horn! Father says it was a fuggie horn. Right slap through her clothes and her heart." She glanced suspiciously at Yuli, following his master, but Yuli had been dehorned.

"Were you frightened?"

She gave him a scornful look. "I never think about it. At all. Well, I think about her sitting upright, I suppose. Her eyes were still frozen open."

They entered the tapestried reception hall. Milua Tal's warning had served to alert JandolAnganol to the arrival of Alam Esomberr and his "little rabble of vicars," as Esomberr had called them. They were surrounded by a crowd of Oldorandan grandees, from whom a bumble of polite regard arose.

The eagle eye of the king, penetrating to the rear of the chamber, observed another familiar figure who, as the king arrived, was being bustled out of a rear door. The figure turned to look back as he left the room and his gaze, despite all the heads in between, met JandolAnganol's. Then he was gone, and the door closed behind them.

On the entry of the king, Esomberr broke courteously from his companions and came forward to make a bow to JandolAnganol, giving one of his mocking smiles.

"Here we are, as you see, Jandol, my somewhat ecclesiastical party and I. One twisted ankle, one case of food poisoning, one envoy longing for the fleshpots, otherwise all in good order. Travel-stained, of course, from a preposterously long walk across your domains . . ." They embraced formally.

"I'm glad you are preserved, Alam. You will find the fleshpots rather gloomy here, that's my impression."

Esomberr was eyeing the runt standing by the king's side. He made playfully to pat Yuli, and then withdrew his hand. "You don't bite, do you, thing?"

"I'm zivilised," said Yuli.

Esomberr raised an eyebrow. "I don't want to speak out of turn, Jandol, but will this rather stuffy crowd here, Sayren Stund and company, tolerate even a zivilised you-know-what in their midst? There's a drumble on at present—to celebrate the death of your betrothed, I gather. . . ."

"I've met no trouble yet—but the C'Sarr arrives soon. You had better get your fleshpotting in before then. By the way, I have just seen my ex-chancellor, SartoriIrvrash. Do you know anything about him?"

"Hmm. Yes, yes, I do, sire." Esomberr rubbed his elegant nose with a finger. "He and a Sibornalese lady came upon me and my rabble of vicars shortly after you and your phagorian infantry had trotted on ahead in your brisk, forceful manner. Both he and the Sibornalese lady were on hoxney-back. They journeyed the rest of the way with us."

"What business has he in Oldorando?"

"Fleshpots?"

"Try again. What did he tell you?"

Alam Esomberr cast his eyes down to the floor as if seeking to recall an elusive memory. "Zygankes, travel does soften the mind . . . hm. Why, I really cannot say, sire. Perhaps you had best ask him yourself?"

"He had come from Gravabagalinien? Why was he there?"

"Sire, perhaps he wished to view the sea, as I've heard some men do before they die."

"In that case, his wish could have been premonitory," said Jandol-Anganol, with spirit. "You are not helpful this evening, Alam."

"Forgive me. My legs are in such shape that my head is also affected. I may be more effectual after I have bathed and dined. Meanwhile, I assure you that I am no friend of your somewhat gaseous ex-chancellor."

"Except that you both would rid the world of phagors."

"So would most men if they had the courage to act. Phagors and fathers."

They regarded each other. "We had better not get to the subject of courage," said JandolAnganol, and walked away.

He plunged into a group where men in grand ornamental charfruls and exotic hairpieces were conversing with King Sayren Stund, interrupting them without apology. Sayren Stund looked flustered, but reluctantly asked his audience to leave him. A space was cleared about the two kings. Immediately, a lackey came forward with a silver tray, to present glasses of iced wine. JandolAnganol turned. Only half deliberately, he knocked the tray from the man's hand.

"Tut-tut-tut," said Sayren Stund. "No matter, it was an accident, I saw that. Plenty more wine. And more ice, as a matter of fact, delivered now by a *lady* captain, Immya Muntras. We must accustom ourselves to such innovations."

"Brother king, never mind the niceties of conversation. You are sheltering here in your palace a man who was my chancellor, of whom I rid myself, a man I think my enemy, since he went over to the Sibornalese cause, by name SartoriIrvrash. What does he want here? Has he brought you some secret message from my ex-queen, as I fear?"

The King of Oldorando looked about apprehensively.

"The man you mention arrived here only twenty minutes ago, along with gentry of good character, such as Alam Esomberr. I agreed to give him shelter. He has a lady with him. I assure you they are not to be guests under this roof."

"She is Sibornalese. I dismissed that man. I conclude that he cannot be here to do me any favours. Where will they lodge?"

"Dear brother, I hardly think that is business of mine or yours. The dusk-moth must keep to the dusk, as we say."

"Where will he stay? Are you protecting him? Be frank with me."

Sayren Stund had been sitting on a high chair. He rose with dignity and said, "It grows heated in here. Let us take a walk in the garden before we become overheated." He gestured to his wife to remain behind.

They progressed through the room amid a corridor of bows. Only the runt Yuli followed. The gardens were lit by flambeaux set in niches. Since almost as little air circulated as in the palace, the torches burned with a steady flame. A sulphurous smell hung about the neatly trimmed avenues.

"I do not wish to vex you, Brother Sayren," JandolAnganol said. "But you understand that I have unknown enemies here. I perceived just by the look of SartoriIrvrash, by his expression, that he is now my enemy, come to make trouble for me. Do you deny that?"

Sayren Stund had taken better control of himself. He was corpulent and he wheezed as he walked. He said coolly, "You appreciate that the common people of Oldorando, or Embruddock, as some like to say, affecting the old mode, regard men of your country—this is not a prejudice I share, you understand—as barbarians. I cannot educate them out of the illusion, not even by stressing the religion we have in common."

"How does this answer my question?"

"Dear, I'm out of breath. I think I have an allergy. May I ask you if you keep that fuggie following at heel simply to offend me and my queen?" He indicated Yuli with a contemptuous gesture.

It was the turn of JandolAnganol to be at a loss.

"He's no more than—a pet hound. He follows me everywhere."

"It's an insult to bring that creature into this court. It should be housed on Whistler Island with the rest of your animals."

"I tell you, it's just a favourite hound. It sleeps outside my bed-chamber door at night and will bark if there's danger."

Sayren Stund stopped walking, clasped his hands behind his back, and gazed intently into a bush.

"We should not quarrel, we both have our difficulties, I in Kace, you at home in Matrassyl, if the reports that reach me are to be trusted. But you cannot bring that creature into my court—the force of the opinion of the court is against it, whatever I personally may say."

"Why did you not say this when I arrived, two days ago?"

A heavy sigh from the Oldorandan king. "You have had two days' grace. Think of it like that. The Holy C'Sarr arrives shortly, as you know. The honour of receiving him means much, but is a grave re-sponsibility. He will not tolerate the sight of a phagor. You are too difficult for us, Jandol. Since you have exhausted your purpose here, why do you not return to your capital tomorrow, with your troupe of animals?"

"Am I that unwelcome? You invited me to stay for the C'Sarr's visit. What poison has SartoriIrvrash poured in your ear?"

"The occasion when the Holy C'Sarr is present must pass off peace-fully. Perhaps the alliance with powerful Pannoval is more important to me than to you, since my kingdom is nearer. Frankly, fuggies and fuggy-lovers are not popular in this part of the world. If you have no purpose here, then I suggest we give you godspeed tomorrow."

"If I have a purpose?"

Sayren Stund cleared his throat. "What purpose? We are both reli-gious men, Jandol. Let us go and pray and be scourged together now, and part as friends and allies in the morning. Isn't that best? Then your visit can be sweetly remembered. I will give you a boat with which you can sail rapidly down the Valvoral and be home in no time. Can you smell the flowering zaldal? Beautiful, isn't it?"

"I see." JandolAnganol folded his arms. "Very well, then, if that is as deep as your friendship and your religion go—we shall quit your pres-ence on the morrow."

"We shall sorrow to see you leave us. So will our queen and daughter."

"I comply with your request, and poorly I think of it. In return, answer my question. Where is SartoriIrvrash?"

The King of Oldorando showed sudden spirit. "You have no right to think poorly of my request. Do you imagine my daughter would be dead today if you had not been espoused to her? It was a political killing— she had no personal enemies, poor girl. Then you come to my court with your filthy fuggies and expect to be made welcome."

"Sayren, I say truly, I grieve for the death of Simoda Tal. If I found the murderer, I would know how to deal with him. Do not increase my sorrow by laying that evil at my door."

Sayren Stund ventured to rest his hand upon the arm of his brother king.

"Do not worry yourself about—the man you mention, your ex-chancellor. We have given him a room in one of the monastic hostels which lie behind this palace and the Dom. You will not have to meet with him. And we will not part foes. That would not do." He blew his nose. "Just be sure you leave Oldorando tomorrow."

They made each other a bow. JandolAnganol went slowly up to his quarters in a wing of the palace, Yuli following behind.

Indifferent tapestries hung on the walls here, the board floor was filthy. He knocked on his infantry major's door. No answer came. On inspiration, he went along to Fard Fantil's door and knocked. The Royal Armourer called to him to enter. The hunchback sat on his bed, polishing his boots; he jumped to his feet when he saw who entered. A phagor guard stood silent by the window, spear in hand.

JandolAnganol lost no time in coming to the point.

"You're the very man I want. This is your native city and you know local customs as I don't. We leave here tomorrow—yes, it's unexpected, but there's no choice. We sail to Matrassyl."

"Trouble, sire?"

"Trouble."

"He's tricky, is the king."

"I want to take SartoriIrvrash with me, prisoner. He's here, in the city. I want you to find him, overpower him, smuggle him into these quarters. We can't cut his throat—it would cause too much of a scandal. Get him here, unseen."

Fard Fantil began to pace up and down the room, clutching his brow. "We can't do such a thing. It's impossible. The law won't allow. What has he done?"

JandolAnganol smacked a fist into his palm. "I know that dangerous old crank's way of thought. He has developed some mad piece of knowledge to discredit me. It will concern the phagors somehow. Before it gets out, I must have him safe, a prisoner. We leave with him tomorrow, shut in a chest. Nobody will know. He resides in one of the hostels behind this palace. Now, I rely on you, Fard Fantil, for I know you as a good man. Do this, and I will reward you, on my word."

Still the armourer hesitated. "The law won't allow."

In a steely voice, the king said, "You have a phagor here in your chambers. I expressly forbad it. Except for my runt, all ancipitals were to be housed in Whistler Park. You merit a flogging for disobeying my orders—and a demotion."

"He is my personal servant, sire."

"Will you get SartoriIrvrash for me, as I request?"

With a sullen look, Fard Fantil agreed.

The king threw a bag of gold onto the bed. It was the money he had acquired in the market, two days previously.

"Good. Disguise yourself as a monk. Go at once. Take that pet of yours with you."

When man and phagor had gone, JandolAnganol stood for a while in the dark room, thinking. Through the window, he could see Yarap-Rombry's Comet low in the northern sky. The sight of that bright smudge in the night brought a memory of his last encounter with his father's gossie, and its prediction that he would meet one in Oldorando who would control his destiny. Was that a reference to SartoriIrvrash? His brain, like a darting glance, looked over other possibilities.

Satisfied that he had done all that might be done in a hostile place, he returned to his quarters, where Yuli had settled himself for sleep before the door as usual. The king gave him a pat as he climbed past.

By the bed, a tray of wine and ice had been placed. Perhaps it was Sayren Stund's way of showing gratitude to a departing guest. Scowling, JandolAnganol drank off a full glass of the sweet wine, then hurled tray and pitcher into a corner.

Flinging off his clothes, he climbed in among the rugs and immediately slept. He always slept soundly. This night, his sleep was heavier than usual.

His dreams were many and confused. He was numerous things, and at last he was a fire god, paddling through golden fire. But the fire was less flame than liquid. He was a fire god of the sea, and MyrdemInggala was riding a dolphin just ahead of him. He struggled mightily. The sea clutched him.

At last he caught her. He held her tight. The gold was all about them. But the horror that had tagged along on the margins of the dream was moving in rapidly upon him. MyrdemInggala was other than he thought. An immense weight and sickliness emanated from her body. He was crying as he wrestled with her. The gold ran about his throat and eyes. She felt like—

He broke from the dream into waking. For a moment, he scarcely dared open his eyes. He was in the bed in the Oldorandan palace. He was clutching something. He was trembling violently.

Almost against his wish, his eyes opened. Only the gold from the dream remained. It stained the rugs and silken pillows. It stained him.

Crying out, he sat up, flinging back the skins that covered him. Yuli lay close against him. The runt's head had been severed. There was only the body. It was cold. Its copious golden blood had ceased to flow and lay congealing in a pool beneath the corpse, and beneath the king.

The king flung himself down on the bare floor, face to the tiles. He wept. The sobs rose from some inner recess and shook his whole stained body.

It was the custom in the Oldorandan court for a service to be held every morning at the tenth hour, in the Royal Chapel, which was under the palace. King Sayren Stund, to honour his guest, invited Jandol-Anganol each day to read—as was his custom—from the revered "Testament of RayNilayan." Much whispering and speculation filled the chapel on this morning, as the royal members of the faith gathered. Many doubted that the Borlienese king would appear.

The king came down the stairs from his chambers. He had washed himself over and over and dressed, not in a charfrul, but in knee-length tunic, boots, and light cloak. His face was of an extreme pallor. His hands shook. He walked deliberately, taking step by step, and was in control of himself.

As he descended the staircase, his armourer came at the run after him, and spoke.

"Sire, I had no response to my knock at your door earlier. Forgive me. I have the prisoner you named in my room, tied in the garderobe. I will watch him till the ship is ready. Tell me only what time I can smuggle him aboard."

"Plans may be changed, Fard Fantil."

The king's manner as much as his words alarmed the armourer.

"Are you ill, sire?" Said with an ill-favoured glance upwards from under his brows.

"Go back to your room." Without a backward look, the king continued to descend, down to the ground floor and down again to the Royal Chapel. He was the last to enter. The introit was playing on vrach and drums. All eyes turned upon him as he walked stiffly, like a boy on stilts, to mount into the box beside Sayren Stund. Only Stund remained gazing towards the altar, eyes blinking rapidly, as if unaware of anything amiss.

The royal box was set apart, in front of the congregation. It was an ornate affair, its carved sides decorated with silver. Six curving steps led up to it. Ranking just below it was a plainer box, reached by only one step, where Queen Bathkaarnet-she sat with her daughter.

JandolAnganol took his place beside the other king, staring ahead, and the service proceeded. Only after the long hymn of praise to Akhanaba did Sayren Stund turn and gesture to JandolAnganol, just as he had done on previous days, to read a part of the Testament.

With slow pace, JandolAnganol descended the six steps, walked across the black and red tiles to the lectern, turned, and faced the congregation. Absolute silence fell. His face was as white as parchment.

He confronted their massed stoney regard. He read curiosity, covert smiles, hatred. Nowhere did he detect sympathy, except on the face of the nine-year-old girl, who shrank down beside her mother. She, he observed, as he directed his full regard at her, mustered the old Madi Look of Acceptance, as she had when first they met.

He spoke. His voice sounded surprisingly feeble but, after a faltering start, gathered strength.

"I wish to say—that is, Your Royal Highnesses, Nobles, All, I would say—you must excuse me if I do not read, but instead take this opportunity to address you direct in this holy place, where the All-Powerful hears every word, and looks into every heart.

"I know he must look into your hearts and see how much you wish me well. Just as much as I wish you well. My kingdom is a great and rich one. Yet I have left it to come here almost alone—almost alone. We all are in quest of peace for our peoples. That quest has long been mine, and my father's before me. My life's quest is for the prosperity of Borlien. So I have sworn.

"And there is a more personal quest. I am without that thing which a man most desires, even above his service to his country. I lack a queen.

"The stone I set rolling half a year ago still rolls. My resolve was then to marry the House of Stund's daughter; that intention I shall now carry out."

He paused as if himself alarmed by what he was about to say. Every eye in the chapel lit on his face to search out the story of his life inscribed there.

"It is therefore not only in response to what His Royal Highness, King Sayren Stund, has done that I announce here, before the throne of one who is above all earthly power, that I—King JandolAnganol of the House of Anganol—intend to unite the nations of Borlien and Oldorando in a blood bond. I mean to take in marriage as soon as is possible the prized and beloved daughter of His Majesty, Princess Milua Tal Stund. The solemnisation of our nuptials will take place, Akhanaba willing, in my capital city of Matrassyl, since I am desired to leave for there today."

Many in the congregation jumped up, in order to see how Sayren

Stund responded to this astonishing news. When JandolAnganol ceased speaking, they became like statues under his chill gaze, and again there was absolute silence in the chapel.

Sayren Stund had slipped gradually from his seat and could no longer be seen. The tableau was broken by a cry from Milua Tal, who recovered fast from her initial surprise and rushed across the floor to clasp JandolAnganol.

"I will stand by you," she said, "and perform as your nuptial wife in all things."

XX

HOW JUSTICE WAS DONE

F irecrackers exploded. Crowds gathered. Rathel was drunk. Prayers were said in the holier parts of the city.

The population of Oldorando City rejoiced at the news of JandolAnganol's engagement to Princess Milua Tal. They had no logical reason for rejoicing. The royal house of Stund and the church with which it was involved lived well at the populace's expense. But chances for rejoicing are few, and wisely taken.

The royal family had won general sympathy when Princess Simoda Tal was assassinated. Such horrendous events contributed to the emotional life of the people.

That the younger sister was now affianced to the man previously engaged to her dead sister was an enjoyable coup de théâtre. There was prurient speculation as to when Milua Tal experienced her first menses and—as usual—debate about the sexual habits of the Madis. Were they totally promiscuous or entirely monogamous? It was a question never settled, though most male opinion was in favour of the former alternative.

JandolAnganol met with general approval.

In the public view, he was a dashing figure, neither offensively young nor distastefully old. He had married and divorced one of the most beautiful women in all Campannlat. As to why he should now marry a girl younger than his son . . . such dynastic couplings were not rare; while the numbers of child prostitutes in East Gate and Uidok provided one easy answer to the question.

On the subject of phagors, the population was more neutral than the palace supposed. Certainly, everyone knew their folk history, and the famous time when phagor hordes destroyed the city. But that was long ago. There were no marauding fuggie bands now. Phagors had become a rare sight in Oldorando. People liked to go and view them in Whistler Park, gazing across the Valvoral at the First Phagorian Guard. They were, after a fashion, popular.

None of which appeased the bitter resentment of King Sayren Stund.

Never a determined man, he had let the moment slip by when he might have banned the match. He inwardly cursed himself. He cursed his queen. Bathkaarnet-she approved the match.

Bathkaarnet-she was a simple woman. She liked JandolAnganol. As she put it, singing, she "liked his looks." Although she had no fondness for the ancipital kind, she saw in the constant drumbles a sort of intolerance which might easily spill over against her own kind; indeed, the Madis were not popular in Oldorando, and incidents of violence against them were frequent. Therefore she considered that this man who protected phagors would be kind to her sole remaining daughter, a half-Madi.

More tellingly, Bathkaarnet-she knew that Sayren Stund had long had it in mind to marry off Milua Tal to Taynth Indredd, a prince of Pannoval far older and more revolting than JandolAnganol. She disliked Taynth Indredd. She disliked the thought of her daughter living in gloomy Pannoval, buried under the mountains of the Quzint. That was not a fit fate for a Madi, or the daughter of a Madi. JandolAnganol and Matrassyl appeated the better bargain.

So, in her self-effacing way, she opposed her king. He was forced to find another way to show his anger. And a way was at hand.

Outwardly, Sayren Stund preserved a pleasant demeanour. He could not admit any responsibility for the killing of Yuli. He even invited JandolAnganol to a meeting to discuss wedding arrangements. They convened in a room where fans swung from the ceiling, where potted vulus grew, and where bright Madi rugs hung on the walls in place of windows, Pannoval-style.

With Sayren Stund were his wife and an advisor in holy orders, a tall saturnine man with a face like an unshaven hatchet, who sat in the background, looked at no one, and said nothing.

JandolAnganol arrived in full uniform, escorted by one of his captains, a hearty outdoor man who looked bewildered by his new diplomatic role.

Sayren Stund poured wine and offered a glass to JandolAnganol.

The latter refused. "The fame of your vineyards is universal, but I have found the vintage makes me sleepy."

Ignoring the thrust, Sayren Stund came to the point.

"We are content that you should marry the Princess Milua Tal. You will recall that your intention was to wed my murdered daughter in Oldorando. Therefore we request you to hold the ceremony here, under the dispensation of the Holy C'Sarr himself, when he arrives."

"Sire, I understood you to say you were eager for me to leave today."

"That was a misunderstanding. We are given to understand that the tame creature of yours which caused us offence has been disposed of." As he said this, his eyes slid towards the saturnine advisor, as if for support. "We will hold festivities appropriate for you, rest assured."

"Are you certain the C'Sarr will be here in three days?"

"His messengers are already here. Our agents are in touch. His entourage has passed Lake Dorzin. Other visitors, such as Prince Taynth Indredd of Pannoval, are expected tomorrow. Your nuptials will make the occasion a solemn historic event."

Realising that Sayren Stund intended to gain advantage over him by this delay, JandolAnganol retired to a corner of the room to talk to his captain. He wished to leave immediately before more treachery could be worked. But for that he needed a ship, and ships were at the dispensation of Sayren Stund. There was also the pressing question—as the captain reminded him—of SartoriIrvrash, bound and gagged and near suffocation in Fard Fantil's garderobe.

He addressed Sayren Stund. "Have we reason to be certain that the Holy C'Sarr will perform this office for us? He is ancient, is he not?"

Sayren Stund pursed his lips.

"Ageing, certainly. Venerable. Not, I'd say to the best of my judgement, ancient. Possibly thirty-nine and a tenner or two. But he might, of course, have an objection to the alliance, on the grounds that Borlien continues to harbour phagors and refuses to obey requests for a drumble. On that point of doctrine, I would not myself care to be dogmatic; we must naturally hear the judgement from his holy lips."

Points of anger burned on JandolAnganol's cheeks.

In a restrained voice, he said, "There is reason to believe that our beloved religion—to which none is more attached than I—began in simple phagor worship. That was when both phagors and men lived more primitively. Although ecclesiastical history seeks to hide the fact, the All-Powerful once closely resembled an ancipital in appearance. Of more recent centuries, popular images have blurred over that resemblance. Nevertheless, it is there.

"Nobody imagines nowadays that phagors are all-powerful. I know from my personal experience how docile they can be, given firm handling. Nevertheless, our religion hinges centrally upon them. Therefore it cannot be just to persecute them under the edicts of the Church."

Sayren Stund looked back for assistance to his priestly advisor. This worthy spoke, saying in a hollow voice, without looking up, "That is not an opinion which will carry weight with His Holiness the C'Sarr, who would say that the Borlienese king blasphemes against the countenance of Akhanaba."

"Quite," said Sayren Stund. "That is not an opinion which will carry weight with any of us, brother. The C'Sarr must marry you and you must keep your views to yourself."

The meeting concluded briskly. Alone with his queen and the dark advisor, Sayren Stund rubbed his chubby hands and said, "Then he will wait for the C'Sarr. We have three days to see the wedding does not take place. We need SartoriIrvrash. The phagor quarters in Whistler Park have been searched and he is not there. He must then be still in the palace. We will have the king's quarters searched—every nook and cranny."

The dark advisor cleared his throat. "There is the question of the woman, Odi Jeseratabhar. She arrived here with SartoriIrvrash. This morning, she sought refuge in the Sibornalese ambassadorial mansion in some distress, reporting her friend's disappearance. My understanding is that she is an admiral. My agents tell me that she has not been well received. The ambassador may treat her as a traitor. Nevertheless, he will not hand her over—as yet at least."

Sayren Stund fanned himself and took some wine. "We can manage without her."

"There is another point in your majesty's favour which my ecclesiastical lawyers have produced," continued the priestly advisor. "King JandolAnganol's divorcement from MyrdemInggala is contained in a bill which as yet remains in the possession of Alam Esomberr. Although the king has signed it and appears to believe his divorce absolute, by an ancient enactment of Pannovalan canon law the divorce of royal personages is not absolute until the bill has physically passed into the keeping of the C'Sarr. The enactment was passed in order to delay ill-considered dynastic alliances. So at present King JandolAnganol is in a de facto state of decree nisi."

"And therefore cannot marry again?"

"Any marriage contracted before the decree is absolute would be illegal."

Sayren Stund clapped his hands and laughed. "Excellent. Excellent. He's not going to get away with this impertinence."

"But we need an alliance with Borlien," said the queen feebly.

Her husband scarcely bothered to look at her.

"My dear, we have but to undermine his position, to disgrace him, and Matrassyl will reject him. Our agents report further riots there. I may then myself step in as the saviour of Borlien, ruling over both kingdoms, as Oldorando has ruled over Borlien in the past. Have you no sense of history?"

JandolAnganol was well aware of the difficulty of his position. Whenever he felt discouraged he whipped up his anger by thinking of Sayren Stund's malice. When he had sufficiently recovered from the shock of discovering Yuli's headless body to leave his room, he had come upon the head lying in the corridor. A few yards farther down the corridor lay the human guard he had posted, stabbed to death, his face hacked at savagely with a sword. JandolAnganol had vomited. A day later, sickness still overwhelmed him. Despite the heat, there was chill in his body.

After the meeting with Sayren Stund, he walked across to Whistler Park, where a small crowd which had gathered gave him a cheer. Association with the phagorian guard calmed him.

He inspected their premises with greater care than before. The phagor commanders trailed behind him. One of the pavilions had been designed as a kind of guest house, and was pleasantly furnished. Upstairs was a complete apartment.

"This apartment will be mine," JandolAnganol said.

"It make your place. No person in Hrl-Drra Nhdo have entry here."

"No phagors either."

"No phagors."

"You will guard it."

"It izz our understanding."

He saw no reason to worry that the commander used what was an ancient phagorian name for Oldorando, though he knew of their long and seemingly ineradicable memories. He was too used to their archaic speech habits.

As he was walking back across the park, four phagors escorting him, the earth shook. Tremors were frequent in Oldorando. This was the second he had felt since his arrival. He looked across Loylbryden Square at the palace. He wished there would be an earthquake severe enough to shake it down, but he could see that the wooden pillars along its face were designed for maximum stability.

The onlookers and loiterers seemed unworried. A waffle seller carried on business as usual. With an inward tremor, JandolAnganol wondered if the end of the world was coming, despite all the wise men said.

"Let it all end," he said to himself.

Then he thought of Milua Tal.

Towards Batalix-set, messengers ran to the palace to say that Prince Taynth Indredd of Pannoval was arriving at the East Gate earlier than anticipated. A formal invitation was sent to JandolAnganol's party to be present at the welcome ceremony in Loylbryden Square, an invitation he could scarcely refuse.

Indifferent to affairs of state, or to wars in progress elsewhere, Taynth Indredd had been on a hunt in the Quzints, and came loaded with trophies of the hunt—skins, plumes, and ivories. He arrived in a palanquin, followed by several cages of animals he had captured. In one cage, a dozen Others chattered at the crowd or moped dejectedly. A twelve-piece band played lively airs as they marched, and banners flew. It was a more impressive entry than JandolAnganol's. Nor did Taynth Indredd have to stoop to haggling for a little money in the marketplace.

Among the prince's retinue was one of JandolAnganol's few friends in the Pannovalan court, Guaddl Ulbobeg. Ulbobeg looked exhausted from his journey. When the official welcoming ceremony showed signs of turning into a prolonged drinking bout, JandolAnganol managed to talk to the old man.

"I'm getting too frail to undertake such expeditions," Guaddl Ulbobeg said. He lowered his voice to add, "And between ourselves, Taynth Indredd gets more tiresome, tenner by tenner. I greatly desire to retire from his service. I'm thirty-six and a quarter, after all."

"Why don't you retire?"

Guaddl Ulbobeg laid a hand on JandolAnganol's arm. The king was moved by the unthinking friendliness of the gesture. "With the post goes the bishopric of Prayn. Do you not recall I am a bishop of the Holy Pannovalan Empire, bless it? Were I to resign before being retired, I'd lose the post and all that goes with it. . . . Taynth Indredd, by the by, is not best pleased with you, so let me warn you."

JandolAnganol laughed. "I'm universally hated, I do believe. How have I offended Taynth Indredd?"

"Oh, it's common knowledge that he and our pompous friend Sayren Stund intended him to marry Milua Tal until you put your oar in."

"You know about that?"

"I know everything. I also know I'm going to bathe and then to bed. Drink's no good to me at my age."

"We'll talk in the morning. Rest well."

* * *

The earthquakes came again in the early part of the night. This time, they were serious enough to cause alarm. In the poorer parts of the city, tiles and balconies were dislodged. Women ran out screaming into the streets. Slaves spread alarm throughout the palace.

It suited JandolAnganol well. He needed a distraction for his purposes. His captains had investigated the grounds to the rear of the palace and discovered—as was to be expected of a building which had not had to serve as a fortress for a great while—that there were many exits for those who knew. Some had been made by the palace staff for their own convenience. Although there were guards at the front, anyone could leave by the back. As JandolAnganol did.

Only to find that the palace had its own diversions. In the alley that ran outside the northeast side of the palace, a wagon, drawn by six hoxneys, arrived. Four burly men climbed down. One held the lead hoxney, while the other three set about sliding wooden bars away from a side door. They flung the door open and shouted to someone inside the wagon. When there was no answer, two of the men climbed in and, with blows and curses, dragged a bound figure out into the street. A rug had been tied over the captive's head. When he groaned too distinctly, he was fetched a blow across his shoulders.

Without hurry, the three toughs unlocked an iron door and passed into an outbuilding of the palace. The door slammed shut behind them.

JandolAnganol watched this event from the concealment of a portico. Beside him was the fragile figure of Milua Tal. From where they stood, beside the wall, they could smell the heavy fragrance of the zaldal, to which Sayren Stund had drawn JandolAnganol's attention earlier.

In the pavilion in Whistler Park, which they called the White Pavilion, they established their refuge. They would be safe under the protection of the Phagorian Guard. The king was still preoccupied with the sight they had just witnessed in the street.

"I think your father means to kill me before I can escape from Oldorando."

"Killing's not so bad, but he's determined somehow to disgrace you. I'll find out how if I can, but he gives me only black looks now. Oh, how can kings be so difficult? I hope you won't be like that when we escape to Matrassyl. I'm so curious to see it, and to sail down the Valvoral. Boats going downstream can go at a fantastic speed, faster than birds.

"Do they have pecubeas in Borlien? I'd like some in my room, just like Moth has. Four pecubeas at least, maybe five—if you can afford it. Father says that you intend to murder me in revenge and cut my head off, but I just laughed and stuck my tongue out—have you seen how far my tongue comes out?—and said, 'Revenge for what, you silly old king-person?' and that got him so mad. I thought he'd have apolloplexy."

She chattered away happily as she examined the apartment.

Carrying their single light, JandolAnganol said, "I intend you no harm, Milua. You can believe that. Everyone thinks me a villain. I am in the hands of Akhanaba, as we all are. I do not even intend your father harm."

She sat on the bed and stared out of the window, the beakiness of her face emphasized in the shadows. "That's what I told him, or words to that effect. He was so mad, he let one thing slip. You know Sartori-Irvrash?"

"I know him well."

"He's in father's hands again. Father's men found him in that hunch-back's room."

He shook his head. "No. He's still bound and gagged in a garderobe. My captains are going to bring him over here for safekeeping."

Milua Tal gave her bubbling laugh. "He fooled you, Jan. That's an-other man, a slave they put in there in the dark. They found the real SartoriIrvrash when everyone was greeting fat old Prince Taynth."

"By the beholder! That man has trouble for me, that man has trouble. He was my chancellor. What does he know? . . . Milua, whatever happens, I am going to face it out. I must face it out, my honour is involved."

"Oh, zygankes, 'My honour is involved'! You sound like Father when you say that. Aren't you supposed to say you are mad about my infantile beauty or something?"

He caught at her hands. "So I may be, my pretty Milua! But what I'm trying to say is that that sort of madness is no good without something to back it. I have to survive dishonour, to outlive it, to remain uncon-taminated by it. Then honour will return to me. All will respect me for surviving. Then it will be possible to form an alliance between my country and yours, as I have long desired, and I will form it with your father or with whoever succeeds him."

She clapped her hands. "I succeed him! Then we'll have a whole country each."

Despite his tension, his premonition that further ills were about to befall him, he burst into laughter, seized her, and pressed her delicate body against him.

The earth shook again.

"Can we sleep here, together?" she whispered.

"No, it would be wrong. In the morning, we go to see my friend Esomberr."

"I thought he wasn't your friend."

"I can make him be my friend. He's vain, but not a villain."

The earth tremors died. The night died. Freyr rose in strength, again hidden from sight by the yellow haze, and the temperature climbed.

That day, few persons of importance were seen about the palace. King Sayren Stund announced that he would hold no audiences; those who had lost a home or a child in the tremors wailed in vain in the stagnant anterooms, or were turned away. Nor was King JandolAnganol to be seen. Or the young princess.

On the following day, a body of Oldorandan guards, eight strong, arrested JandolAnganol.

They caught him as he descended the staircase leading from his room. He fought, but they lifted him off his feet and carried him to a place of imprisonment. He was kicked down a spiralling stone stair and thrown into a dungeon.

He lay for many minutes panting on the floor, beside himself with anger.

"Yuli, Yuli," he said, over and over. "I was so sick at what they did to you that I never could think through to see what danger I was in. . . . I never could think. . . ."

After some minutes of silence, he said aloud, "I was overconfident. That's always been my fault. I trusted too much that I could ride with the circumstances. . . ."

A long while later, he picked himself off the floor and looked helplessly about. A shelf against one wall served as bed and bench. Light filtered in from a high window. In one corner was a trough for sanitary purposes. He sank down on the bench, and thought of his father's long imprisonment.

When his spirits had sunk still lower, he thought of Milua Tal.

"Sayren Stund, if you harm one lash of her eyes, you slanje . . ."

He sat rigid. Eventually, he forced himself to relax and leaned with his back against the moist wall of the cell. With a roar, he jumped up and began to pace about, up and down, between wall and door.

He ceased only when he heard the scrape of boots coming down the stair. Keys rattled at the lock, and a black-clad member of the local clerisy entered between two armed guards. As he gave a scanty bow, JandolAnganol recognised him as Sayren Stund's axe-faced advisor, by name Crispan Mornu.

"Under what devious law am I, a visiting prince of a friendly country, imprisoned?"

"I am come to inform you that you are charged with murder, and will be tried for that crime tomorrow at Batalix-break, before a royal ecclesiastical court." The sepulchral voice paused, then added, "Prepare yourself."

JandolAnganol advanced in a fury. "Murder? Murder, you pack of criminals? What new scoundrelism is this? Whose murder is laid at my door?"

Crossed spears halted his advance.

The priest said, "You are charged with the murder of Princess Simoda Tal, elder daughter of King Sayren Stund of Oldorando."

He bowed again and withdrew.

The king remained where he was, staring at the door. His eagle eyes fixed upon its boards, never blinking, as if he had vowed they should never blink again until he was free.

He stayed almost motionless throughout the night. The intense active principle within him, being confined, stayed coiled within him like a spring. He maintained a defiant alertness throughout the hours of dark, waiting to leap to attack anyone who ventured to enter the dungeon.

Nobody came. No food was brought, no water. During the night there was a remote tremor—so remote it might have been in an artery rather than the earth—and a powder shower of mortar floated down to the stones. Nothing else. Not so much as a rat visited JandolAnganol.

When light seeped in to the place of confinement, he went over to the stone trough. By climbing onto it and hooking his fingers into a hollow between two stones, carved by previous prisoners, he could look out of the unglazed window. A precious breath of fresh air expired upon his cheek.

His dungeon was at the front of the palace, near to the corner by the Dom, or so he estimated. He could look across Loylbryden Square. His viewpoint was too low to see anything beyond it except the tops of trees in the park.

The square was deserted. He thought that if he waited long enough he would possibly see Milua Tal—unless she was also captive of her father.

His view was towards the west. The tiny patch of sky he could see was free of haze. Batalix cast long shadows across the cobbles. Those shadows paled and then divided into two as Freyr also rose. Then they died as the haze returned and the temperature started to mount.

Workmen came. They brought platforms and poles with them. Their manner was the resigned one of workmen everywhere: they were prepared to do the job, but not prepared to hurry over it. After a while, they set up a scaffold.

JandolAnganol went and sat down on the bench, clutching his temples between his nails.

Guards came for him. He fought them, uselessly. They put him in chains. He snarled at them. They pushed him up the stone stairs indifferently.

Everything had fallen out as King Sayren Stund might have wished it. In the incessant enantiodromia which afflicts all things, turning them into their opposites, he could now crow over the man who had so recently crowed over him. He bounded up and down with glee, he uttered cries of joy, he embraced Bathkaarnet-she, he threw merrily evil glances at his dejected daughter.

"You see, child, this villain you threw your arms about is to be branded a murderer before everyone." He advanced upon her with ogreish glee. "We'll give you his corpse to embrace in a day's time. Yes, just another twenty-five hours and your virginity will be safe forever from JandolAnganol!"

"Why not hang me too, Father, and rid yourself of all your daughters to worry about?"

A special chamber in the palace had been set aside to serve as the courtroom. The Church sanctified it for judiciary purposes. Sprigs of veronika, scantiom, and pellamountain—all regarded as cooling herbs—were hung to lower the stifling temperature and shed their balm into the room. Many luminaries of court and city were gathered to watch the proceedings, not all of them by any means as in accord with their ruler as he supposed.

The three main actors in the drama were the king, his saturnine advisor, Crispan Mornu, and a judge by name Kimon Euras, whose station in the Church was minister of the rolls.

Kimon Euras was so thin that he stooped as if the tautness of his skin had bent the backbone it contained; he was bald or, to be precise, without visible vestige of hair, and the skin of his face displayed a greyish pallor reminiscent of the vellums over which he had parsimonious custody. His spiderish air, as he ascended to his bench, clad in a black keedrant hanging to his spatulate feet, seemed to guarantee that he would handle mercy with a similar parsimony.

When these impressive dignitaries were settled in their places, a gong was struck, and two guards chosen for strength dragged King Jandol-Anganol into the chamber. He was made to stand in the middle of the room for all to see.

The division between prisoner and free is sharp in any court. Here it was more marked than usual. The king's short imprisonment had been enough to make filthy his tunic and his person. Yet he stood with his head high, darting his eagle gaze about the court, more like a bird of prey hunting weaknesses than a man looking for mercy. The clarity which attended his movements and contours remained part of him.

Kimon Euras began a long address in a powdery voice. The ancient dusts from the documents in his charge had lodged in his larynx. He spoke marginally louder when he came to the words, ". . . cruel murder of our beloved Princess Simoda Tal, in this very palace, by the thrust of an ancipital horn. King JandolAnganol of Borlien, you are charged with being the instigator of this crime."

JandolAnganol immediately shouted in defiance. A bailiff struck him from behind, saying, "Prisoners are not allowed to speak in this court. Any interruptions and you will be thrown back in your cell."

Crispan Mornu had managed for the occasion to find a garment of deeper black than usual. The colour reflected up into his jowls, his cheeks, his eyes, and, when he spoke, into his throat.

"We intend to demonstrate that the guilt of this Borlienese king is inescapable, and that he came here with no other purpose than the destruction of Princess Milua Tal, thus ending the lineage of the House of Stund. We shall produce a copy of the instrument with which Princess Simoda Tal was cruelly dispatched. We shall produce also the actual perpetrator of the deed. We shall show that all factors point inescapably to the prisoner as the originator of the cruel plot. Bring forth the dagger."

A slave scurried forward, making a great business of his haste, and presented the article demanded.

Unable to keep out of the proceedings, Sayren Stund reached forward and grasped it before Crispan Mornu could take it.

"This is the horn of a phagor beast. It has two sharp edges, and hence cannot be confused with the horn of any other animal. It corresponds with the configurations of the wound in the late princess's breast. Poor dear girl.

"We do not attempt to pretend that this is the weapon with which the murder was committed. That weapon is lost. This is merely a similar one, newly pulled from the head of a phagor.

"I wish to remind the court, and they shall judge whether or not the fact is relevant, that the prisoner had a phagor runt for a pet. That runt the prisoner blasphemously named after the great warrior-saint of this nation, Yuli. Whether the insult was deliberate or made through ignorance, we need not inquire."

"Sayren Stund, your callousness will be well repaid," JandolAnganol said, and received a hearty blow for it.

When the horn dagger had been passed round, the curved figure of Kimon Euras uncurled enough to ask, "What else has the prosecution to bring against the accused by way of evidence?"

"You have seen the weapon with which the deed was done," the black voice of Crispan Mornu announced. "Now we shall show you the person who used the weapon to kill the princess Simoda Tal."

Into the court a struggling body was half-brought, half-carried. It had a rug tied about its head, and JandolAnganol thought immediately of the prisoner he had seen in the night, evicted from the wooden wagon.

This captive was tugged into the well of the court. At a word of command, the rug was wrenched from it.

The youth thus revealed seemed to consist of a fury of a tousled mane of hair, an empurpled visage, and a torn shift. When he was struck hard and began to whimper instead of struggle, he was recognisable as RobaydayAnganol.

"Roba!" cried the king, and received a chop in the kidneys which doubled him up in pain. He sank down on a bench, overwhelmed by the sight of his son in captivity—Roba, who had always feared captivity.

"This young person was apprehended by his majesty's agents in the seaport of Ottassol, in Borlien," said Crispan Mornu. "He proved difficult to track down, since he posed sometimes as a Madi, adopting their habits and style of dress. He is, however, human. His name is Robayday-Anganol. He is the son of the accused, and his wildness is widely talked of."

"Did you murder the late Princess Simoda Tal?" demanded the judge, in a voice like tearing parchment.

Robayday burst into a fit of weeping, during which he was heard to say that he had murdered nobody, that he had never been to Oldorando before, and that he wanted only to be left in peace to lead his own miserable life.

"Did you not carry out the murder at the instigation of your father?" demanded Crispan Mornu, making each word sound like a small axe descending.

"I hate my father! I fear my father! I would never do his bidding."

"Why then did you murder the Princess Simoda Tal?"

"I didn't. I didn't. I am innocent, I swear."

"Whom did you murder?"

"I have murdered no one."

As though these were the very words he had waited all his life to hear, Crispan Mornu raised a mottled hand high in the air and brought up his nose until it shone in the light as if honed.

"You hear this youth claim he has murdered no one. We call a witness who will prove him a liar. Bring in the witness."

A young lady entered the court, moving freely if nervously between two guards. She was directed to take a stance beneath the judge's platform, while those in the court regarded her avidly. Her beauty and youth were appealing. Her cheeks were brightly painted. Her dark hair was strikingly dressed. She wore a tight-fitting chagirack, the floral pattern of which emphasised her figure. She stood with one hand on her hip, slightly defiant, and managed to look at once innocent and seductive.

Judge Kimon Euras curved his albaster skull forward and was perhaps rewarded by a glimpse down into her zona, for he said in a more human tone than had so far been the case, "What is your name, young woman?"

She said in a faint voice, "Please, AbathVasidol, usually called Abathy by my friends."

"I am sure you have plenty of friends," said the judge.

Untouched by this exchange, Crispan Mornu said, "This lady has also been brought here by his majesty's agents. She came not as a prisoner but of her own free will, and will be rewarded for her efforts on behalf of the truth. Abathy, will you tell us when you last saw this youth, and what the circumstances were?"

Abathy moistened her lips, which were already shining, and said, "Oh, sir, I was in my room, my little room in Ottassol. My friend was with me, my friend Div. We were sitting on the bed, you know, talking. And suddenly this man here . . ."

She paused.

"Go on, girl."

"It's too awful, sir . . ." There was a thick silence in the court, as if even the cooling herbs were drowning in the heat. "Well, sir, this man here came in with a dagger. He wanted me to go with him, and I wouldn't. I don't do such things. Div went to protect me, and this man here struck with his dagger—or horn, it was, you know—and he killed Div. He stabbed Div right in the stomach."

She demonstrated daintily on her own hypogastric region, and the court craned its collective neck.

"And what happened then?"

"Well, sir, you know, this man here took the body away and threw it into the sea."

"This is all a lie, a lying plot!" said JandolAnganol.

It was the girl who answered him, with a spurt of her own anger. She was more at home in the court now, and beginning to enjoy her role.

"It's not a lie. It's the truth. The prisoner took Div's body away and threw it into the sea. And the extraordinary thing was that a few days later it returned, the body I mean, packed in ice, to Ottassol, because I saw it in the house of my friend and protector, Bardol CaraBansity— later to become the king's chancellor for a while."

JandolAnganol emitted a strangled laugh and appealed direct to the judge. "How can anyone believe such an impossible story?"

"It's not impossible, and I can prove it," Abathy said boldly. "Div had a special jewel with three moving faces with figures, a timepiece. The figures were alive. Div kept it in a belt round his waist." She indicated the area she meant on her own anatomy, and again the collective neck was craned. "That same jewel turned up at CaraBansity's and he gave it to his majesty, who probably has it now." She pointed her finger dramatically at JandolAnganol.

The king was visibly taken aback and remained silent. The timepiece lay forgotten in his tunic pocket.

He recalled now, all too late, how he had always feared the timepiece as an alien thing, a thing of science to be mistrusted. When BillishOwpin, the man who claimed to have come from another world, had offered him the timepiece, JandolAnganol had thrown it back to him. Mysteriously, it had returned later through the agency of the deuteroscopist. Despite his intentions, he had never rid himself of it.

Now it had betrayed him.

He could not speak. An evil spell had descended on him: that he saw, but could not say when it had begun. Not all his dedication to Akhanaba had saved him from the spell.

"Well, Your Majesty, well, brother," said Sayren Stund, with relish, "have you this jewel with living figures?"

JandolAnganol said faintly, "It is intended as a wedding gift for the Princess Milua Tal . . ."

A hubbub broke out in court. People dashed here and there, clerics called for order, Sayren Stund covered his face in order to hide his triumph.

When order was restored Crispan Mornu put another question to Abathy. "You are sure this young man, RobaydayAnganol, son of the king, is the man who murdered your friend Div? Did you ever see him again?"

"Sir, he was a great nuisance to me. He would not go away. I don't know what would have happened to me if your men hadn't arrested him."

A short silence prevailed in court while everyone contemplated what might have happened to such an attractive young lady.

"Let me put one last and rather personal question to you," Crispan Mornu said, fixing Abathy with his corpselike stare. "You are evidently a low-born woman, and yet you seem to have well-connected friends. Rumour mentions your name with that of a certain Sibornalese ambassador. What do you say to that?"

"Shame," said a voice from the court benches, but Abathy answered in an untroubled way, "I did have the pleasure of knowing a Sibornalese gentleman, sir. I like the Sibornalese for their good manners, sir."

"Thank you, Abathy, your testament has been invaluable." Crispan Mornu managed a moue which resembled a stiletto's smile. He then turned to the court, speaking only when the girl had left.

"I submit that you need no further proof. This innocent young girl has told us all we need to know. His lies to the contrary, the King of Borlien's son is revealed as a murderer. We have heard how he murdered in Ottassol, presumably at his father's instruction, merely to obtain some bauble to bring here. His preferred weapon was a phagor horn; he had already murdered Simoda Tal, using the same weapon. His father was left to proceed here to enjoy our hospitality, to carry out his evil designs upon his majesty's sole remaining daughter. We have uncovered here as black a plot as ever history related. I have no hesitation in demanding—on behalf of the court, and on behalf of our whole nation—the death penalty for both father and son."

RobaydayAnganol's defiance had collapsed as soon as Abathy had entered the court. He looked no more than an urchin, and his voice sank to a whisper as he said, "Please let me go free. I'm made for life, not death, for some wild plot where the breeze blows. I have no wild plot with my father—that I deny, and all other charges."

Crispan Mornu swung dramatically about and confronted the youth. "You still deny the murder of Simoda Tal?"

Robayday moistened his lips. "Can a leaf kill? I'm merely a leaf, sir, caught in the world's storm."

"Her Majesty Queen Bathkaarnet-she is prepared to identify you as a visitor to this palace a while ago, when you came disguised as a Madi for the express purpose of committing the foul deed. Do you wish her majesty to come to this court to identify you?"

A violent trembling took Robayday. "No."

"Then the case is proven. This youth, a prince, no less, entered the palace and—at his father's command—murdered our much-loved princess, Simoda Tal."

All eyes turned to the judge. The judge turned his gaze down to the floor before delivering judgement.

"The verdict is as follows. The hand that committed this vile murder belongs to the son. The mind that controlled the hand is the father's. So where lies the source of guilt? The answer is clear—"

A cry of torment broke from Robayday. He thrust out a hand as if physically to intercept Kimon Euras's words.

"Lies! Lies! This is a room of lies. I will speak the truth, though it destroy me! I confess I did that thing to Simoda Tal. I did it not because I was in league with my father the king. Oh, no, that's impossible. We are day and night. I did what I did to spite him.

"There he stands—just a man now, not a king! Yes, just a man, while my mother remains the queen of queens. I, in league with him? I would no more kill for his sake than I would marry for his sake. . . . I declare the villain innocent. If I must die your dingy death, then never let it be said even in here that I was in league with him. I wish there was a league between us. Why help one who never helped me?"

He clutched his head as if to wrench it from his shoulders.

In the silence following, Crispan Mornu said coldly, "You might have done your father more harm by keeping silent."

Robay gave him a cold sane look. "It's the principle of evil in men I fear—and I see that principle more rampant in you than in that poor man burdened with the crown of Borlien."

JandolAnganol raised his eyes to the ceiling, as if trying to detach himself from earthly events. But he wept.

With the sound of rippling parchment, the judge cleared his throat.

"In view of the son's confession, the father is of course shown to be blameless. History is full of ungrateful sons. . . . I therefore pronounce, under the guidance of Akhanaba, the All-Powerful, that the father go free and the son be taken from here and hanged as soon as it suits the convenience of his majesty, King Sayren Stund."

"I will die in his stead and he can reign in my stead." The words came from JandolAnganol, spoken in a firm voice.

"The verdict is irreversible. Court dismissed."

Above the shuffle of feet came Sayren Stund's voice.

"Remember, we refresh ourselves now, but this afternoon comes a further spectacle, when we hear what King JandolAnganol's ex-chancellor, SartoriIrvrash, has to say to us."

XXI

THE SLAYING OF AKHANABA

The drama of the court and the humiliation of JandolAnganol had
been watched by a greater audience than the king could have
imagined.

The personnel of the Avernus, however, were not entirely occupied by
the story in which the king played a conspicuous part. Some scholars
studied developments taking place elsewhere on the planet, or continuities in which the king played merely an incidental role. A group of
learned ladies of the Tan family, for instance, had as their subject the
origins of long-standing quarrels. They followed several quarrels through
generations, studying how the differences began, were maintained, and
were eventually resolved. One of their cases concerned a village in
Northern Borlien through which the king had passed on his way to
Oldorando. There the quarrel originally concerned whether pigs belonging to two neighbours should drink at the same brook. The brook had
gone and so had the pigs, yet two villages existed at the spot locked in
hatred and still referring to the killing of neighbours as "hog-sticking."

King JandolAnganol, by passing with his phagors through one village
and not the other, had exacerbated the feud, and a youth had had a
finger broken in a brawl that night.

Of that, the learned Tan ladies were as yet unaware. All their records
were automatically stored for study, while they at present worked over
a chapter in their quarrel which had taken place two centuries ago; they
studied videos of an incident of indecent exposure, when an old man
from one of the villages had been mobbed by men from the other village. After this squalid incident, someone had composed a beautiful
dirge on the subject, which was still sung on festive occasions. To the
learned Tan ladies, such incidents were as vital as the king's trial—and
of more significance than all the austerities of the inorganic.

Other groups studied matters even more esoteric. Phagor lines of
descent were particularly closely watched. The question of phagor mobility, baffling to the Helliconians, was by now fairly well understood on
the Avernus. The ancipitals had ancient patterns of behaviour from
which they were not easily deflected, but those patterns were more
elaborate than had been supposed. There was a kind of "domestic"
phagor which accepted the rule of man as readily as the rule of a kzahhn;
but hidden from the eyes of men was a much more independent ancipital which survived the seasons much as its ancestors had done, taking
what it would and moving on: a free creature, unaffected by mankind.

The history of Oldorando as a unit also had its scholars, those who
were most interested in process. They followed interweaving lives of
individuals in only a general way.

When the eyes of Avernus first turned towards Oldorando, or Embruddock as it was then, it was little more than a place of hot springs
where two rivers met. Round the springs, a few low towers stood in the
middle of an immense ice desert. Even then, in the early years of Avernian research, it was apparent that this was a place, strategically situated,
with a potential for growth when the climate improved.

Oldorando was now larger and more populous than anyone in the six
families had seen it before. Like any living organism, it expanded in
favourable weather, contracted in adverse.

But the story was no more than begun as far as those on the Avernus
were concerned. They kept their records, they transmitted a constant
stream of information back to Earth; present transmissions could be
reckoned to arrive there in the year 7877. The intricacies of the Helliconian biosphere and its response to change throughout the Great Year
could be understood only when at least two complete cycles had been
studied.

The scholars could extrapolate. They could make intelligent guesses.
But they could no more see the future than King JandolAnganol could
see what was to befall that very afternoon.

* * *

Sayren Stund had not been in better humour since before his elder daughter died. Before the afternoon's event, which was to humiliate JandolAnganol further, Stund ate a light meal of Dorzin gout and called a meeting of the inner circle of his council to impress on them how clever he had been.

"Of course it was never my intention to hang King JandolAnganol," he informed the councillors genially. "The threat of execution was simply to reduce him, as that Other of a son of his put it, to a mere man, naked and defenceless. He thinks he can do as he pleases. That is not so."

When he had finished talking, his prime minister rose to make a speech of thanks to his majesty.

"We particularly appreciate your majesty's humiliation of a monarch who cultivates phagors and treats them—well, almost as if they were human. We in Oldorando can have no doubt, must have no doubt, that the ancipitals are animals, nothing more. They have all the stamp of animals. They talk. So do preets and parrots.

"Unlike parrots, phagors are forever hostile to mankind. We know not where they come from. They seem to have been born in the late Cold Period. But we do know—and this is what King JandolAnganol does not know—that these formidable newcomers must be eradicated, first from among human society, then from the face of the earth.

"We still have the indignity of suffering JandolAnganol's phagor brutes in our park. We all anticipate that, after this afternoon's event, we shall be able to show gratitude once more to King Sayren Stund for ridding us for ever both of this pack of brutes, and of their pack master."

There was general clapping. Sayren Stund himself clapped. Every word in the minister's speech echoed his own words.

Sayren Stund enjoyed such sycophancy. But he was not a fool. Stund still needed the alliance with Borlien; he wished to make sure he would be the senior partner to it. He hoped, too, that the afternoon's entertainment would impress the nation with whom he was already in uncomfortable alliance, Pannoval. He intended to challenge the C'Sarr's monopoly of militarism and religion; that he could do by supplying an underlying philosophy for the Pannovalan drive against the ancipital kind. Having talked to SartoriIrvrash, he foresaw that that scholar could provide precisely such a philosophy.

He had struck a bargain with SartoriIrvrash. In exchange for the afternoon's oratory and the destruction of JandolAnganol's authority, Sayren Stund had Odi Jeseratabhar released from the Sibornalese embassy, despite the grumbles of the Sibornalese. He promised SartoriIrvrash and Odi the safety of his court, where they could live and work in peace. The bargain had been agreed upon with glee on all sides.

* * *

The heat of the morning had overwhelmed many of those who attended the court; reports entering the palace spoke of hundreds dying of heart attacks in the city. The afternoon's diversion was therefore staged in the royal gardens, where jets of water played on the foliage and gauzes were hung from trees to create pleasant shade.

When the distinguished members of court and Church had gathered, Sayren Stund came forward, his queen on his arm, his daughter following behind. Screwing up his eyes, he gazed about for sight of Jandol-Anganol. Milua Tal saw him first and hastened across the lawn to his side. He stood under a tree, together with his Royal Armourer and two of his captains.

"The fellow has boldness, grant him that," Sayren Stund murmured. He had had delivered to JandolAnganol an ornate letter apologising for his mistaken imprisonment, while making excuses because the evidence was so much against him. What he did not know was that Bathkaarnet-she had written a simpler note, expressing her pain over the whole incident and referring to her husband as a "love throttler."

When his majesty was comfortably settled on his throne, a gong was struck, and Crispan Mornu appeared, shrouded as ever in black. Evidently the minister of the rolls, Kimon Euras, was too overcome by his morning's activities to manage anything further. Crispan Mornu was in sole charge.

Ascending the platform set in the middle of the lawn, he bowed to the king and queen and spoke in his voice which had about it, as a court wit once remarked, the same redolence as the sex life of a public hangman.

"We have a rare treat this afternoon. We are to be present at an advancement of history and natural philosophy. Of recent generations, we among the enlightened nations have come to understand how the history of our cultures is at best intermittent. It is caused by our Great Year of 1825 small years, and not by wars as the idle have claimed. The Great Year contains a period of intense heat and several centuries of intense cold. These are punishments from the All-Powerful for the sinfulness of mankind. While the cold prevails for so long, civilisation is difficult to maintain.

"We are to hear from one who has pierced through these disruptions to bring us news of distant matters which concern us urgently today. In particular, they refer to our relationship with those beasts which the All-Powerful sent to chasten us, the phagors.

"I beg you, gentles all, to listen well to the scholar Master Sartori-Irvrash."

Languidly polite clapping went about the lawn. On the whole, music and tales of bawdy were preferred to intellectual effort.

As the clapping died, SartoriIrvrash came forth. Although he smoothed his whiskers with a familiar gesture and looked rather furtively to left and right, he did not appear nervous. By his side walked Odi Jeseratabhar in a flowered chagirack. She had recovered from her assatassi wounds and carried herself alertly. Much of her Uskuti arrogance remained in the gaze with which she surveyed the assembly. Her expression was gentler when she looked at SartoriIrvrash.

The latter had adopted a linen hat to cover his baldness. He carried some books which he deposited carefully on the table before he spoke. The magisterial calm with which he began betrayed nothing of the consternation he was about to spread.

"I am grateful to his majesty, King Sayren Stund, for giving me sanctuary in the Oldorandan court. In my long life, vicissitudes have been many, and even here, even here, I have not been free of botheration from those who are the enemies of knowledge. All too often, those who hate learning are the very people on whom we should most rely to promote it.

"For many years, I served as chancellor to King VarpalAnganol, and later to his son, who dares to be present here despite his encounter with justice this morning. By him I was unfairly dismissed from office. During my years in Matrassyl, I was compiling a survey of our world, entitled 'The Alphabet of History and Nature,' in which I sought to integrate and distinguish between myth and reality. And it is on that subject I speak now.

"When I was dismissed, all my papers were most cruelly burnt, and my life's work destroyed. The knowledge I carry in my head was not destroyed. With it, with my experiences since, and in particular with the assistance of this lady by my side, Odi Jeseratabhar, Priest-Militant Admiral of the Sibornalese fleet, I have come to understand much that was previously a mystery.

"One mystery in particular. A cosmological mystery, one which touches on our everyday lives. Bear with me, hot though it is, for I shall be as brief as possible, although I am told that is not always my habit."

He laughed and looked about him. Everywhere was attention, real or feigned. Encouraged, he plunged into his argument.

"I hope to offend no one by what I say. I speak in the belief that men love truth above all things.

"We are so bound to our human concerns that we rarely catch sight of the great business of the planet about us. It is more marvellous than we can credit. It abounds with life. Whatever the season, winged and footed life is everywhere, from pole to pole. Endless herds of flambreg, each herd numbered in millions of beasts, rove ceaselessly across the vast continent of Sibornal. Such a sight is unforgettable. Where have the beasts come from? How long have they been there? We have no answers to such questions. We can only remain mute with awe.

"The secrets of antiquity could be unlocked if only we ceased our warring. If all kings had the wisdom of Sayren Stund."

He bowed in the direction of the Oldorandan king, who smiled back, unaware of what was to come. There were scattered handclaps.

"While life was peaceful at the Matrassyl court, I was privileged in enjoying the company of MyrdemInggala, called by her subjects the queen of queens—merely because they knew not of Queen Bathkaarnet-she, of course—and her daughter, TatromanAdala. Tatro had a collection of fairy tales which I used to read to her. Although all my papers were destroyed, as I have said, Tatro's fairy tales were not destroyed, not even when her cruel father banished her to the coast. We have a copy of Tatro's book here."

At this point, Odi solemnly raised the little book aloft and held it for all to see.

"In Tatro's storybook is a tale called 'The Silver Eye.' I read it many times without perceiving its inner meaning. Only when I travelled could I grasp its elusive truth. Perhaps because the herds of flambreg reminded me strongly of primitive ancipitals."

Until this point, SartoriIrvrash's delivery, free of his old pedantry, had kept his audience listlessly attentive. Many of the audience lounging on the lawn were drumble organisers, with a natural hatred of phagors; at the word "ancipitals," they showed interest.

"There is an ancipital in the story of the Silver Eye.

"The ancipital is a gillot. Her role is advisor to a king in a mythical country, Ponpt. Well, not so mythical: Ponpt, now called Ponipot, still exists to the west of the Barrier Mountains. This gillot is superior to the king, and provides him with the wisdom whereby he rules. He depends on her as a son on a mother. At the end of the story, the king kills the gillot.

"The Silver Eye itself is a body like a sun, but silver and shining only by night. Like a close star, without heat. When the gillot is slain, the Silver Eye sails away and is lost for ever.

"What did all that signify? I asked myself. Where was the meaning of the tale?"

He leaned over the podium, hunching his shoulders and pointing at the audience in his eagerness to tell the tale.

"The key to the puzzle came when I was on an Uskuti sailing vessel. The vessel was becalmed in the Cadmer Straits. Odi, this lady here, and I landed on Gleeat Island, where we managed to capture a wild gillot with a black pelage. The females of the ancipital species have a one-day flow of menses from the uterus as a prelude to the oestral cycle, when they go into rut. Because of my prejudice against the species, I have no knowledge of Native Ancipital or even Hurdhu, but I discovered then that the gillot's word for her period was 'tennhrr.' That was the key!"

Forgive me if such a subject seems too disgusting to contemplate.

"In my studies—all destroyed by the great King JandolAnganol—I had noted that even phagors preserved one or two legends. They could hardly be expected to make sense. In particular, there is a legend which says Helliconia once had a sister body circling about it, just as Batalix circles about Freyr. This sister body flew away as Freyr arrived and as mankind was born. So the legend goes. And the name of the escaping body in Native is T'Sehn-Hrr.

"Why should 'tennhrr' and 'T'Sehn-Hrr' be virtually the same word? That was the question I asked myself.

"A gillot's tennhrr occurs ten times in a small year—every six weeks. We may therefore assume that this heavenly eye or moon served as a timing mechanism for the periods. But did the moon 'T'Sehn-Hrr,' supposing it existed, circle Helliconia once every six weeks? How to check on something which happened so long ago that human history has no record of it?

"The answer lay in Tatro's story.

"Her story says that the silver eye in the sky opened and shut. Possibly that means it grew bigger or smaller, according to distance, as does Freyr. It became wide open or full ten times in a year. That was it. Ten times again. The pieces of the puzzle fitted.

"You understand the unmistakable conclusion to which I was drawn?"

Gazing at his audience, SartoriIrvrash saw that indeed many of them did not understand. They waited politely for him to be done. He heard his voice rise to a shout.

"This world of ours once had a moon, a silver moon, which was lost at a time of some kind of disturbance in the heavens. It sailed away, we don't as yet know how. The moon was called T'Sehn-Hrr—and T'Sehn-Hrr is a phagor name."

He looked at his notes, he conferred briefly with Odi, as the listeners stirred. He resumed his discourse with a note of asperity in his voice.

"Why should the moon have only an ancipital name? Why is there no human record of this missing body? The answer leads us into the mazes and botherations of antiquity.

"For when I looked about, I found that missing moon. Not in the sky, but shining forth from our everyday speech. For how is our calendar divided? Eight days in a week, six weeks in a tenner, ten tenners in a year of four hundred and eighty days. . . . We never question it. We never question why a tenner is called a tenner, because there are ten of them in a year.

"But that is not the whole truth. Our word 'tenner' commemorates the time when the silver eye was open and the moon was full. It does so because humanity adopted the phagor word 'tennhrr.' 'Tenner' is 'tennhrr' is 'T'Sehn-Hrr.' "

The murmurings from the crowd were louder. Sayren Stund was plainly uncomfortable. But SartoriIrvrash held up Tatro's storybook and called for silence. So engrossed was he that he failed to see the trap opening before him.

"Hear the whole conclusion, my friends. There stands King Jandol-Anganol among you, and he must hear the truth as well—he who has so long encouraged the noxious ahumans to breed on his territories."

But no one was interested in JandolAnganol at present. Their angry faces turned to SartoriIrvrash himself.

"The conclusion is clear, inescapable. The ancipital race, to which we can ascribe many of our human difficulties over the ages, is not a race of new invaders, like the Driats. No. It is an ancient race. It once covered Helliconia as flambreg cover the Circumpolar Regions.

"The phagors did not emerge out of the last Weyr-Winter, as the Sibornalese call it. No. That story is based on ignorance. The real story, the fairy story, tells the truth. *Phagors long preceded mankind.*

"They were here on Helliconia before Freyr appeared—possibly long before. Mankind came later. Mankind depended on the phagors: Mankind learned language from the phagors and still uses phagor words. 'Khmir' is the Native word for 'rut.' 'Helliconia' itself is an old ancipital term."

JandolAnganol found his voice at last. The speech was such an onslaught on his religious sensibilities that he had stood as if in a trance, his mouth open, more resembling fish than eagle.

"Lies, heresy, blasphemy!" he shouted. The cry of blasphemy was taken up by other voices. But Sayren Stund had ordered his guard to see that JandolAnganol did not interrupt. Burly men closed in on him—to be met by JandolAnganol's captains with drawn swords. A struggle broke out.

SartoriIrvrash raised his voice. "No, you see your glory diminished by the truth. Phagors preceded mankind. Phagors were the dominant race on our world, and probably treated our ancestors as animals until we rebelled against them."

"Let's hear him. Who dares say the man is wrong?" shrilled Queen Bathkaarnet-she. Her husband struck her in the mouth.

The hubbub from the audience rose. People were standing and shouting or kneeling to pray. Fresh guards ran to the scene, while some court ladies tried to escape. A fight had broken out round JandolAnganol. The first stone was thrown at SartoriIrvrash. Brandishing his fist, he continued to speak.

In that courtly crowd, now moved to fury, there was at least one cool observer, the envoy Alam Esomberr. He was detached from the human drama. Unable to be deeply moved by events, he could derive only amusement from their effects.

Those on Earth, distant in time and space, viewed the scene on King Sayren Stund's lawn with less detachment. They knew that Sartori-Irvrash spoke truth in general, even if his details were sometimes incorrect. They also knew that men did not love truth above all things, as he claimed. Truth had constantly to be fought for, for it was constantly being lost. Truth could sail away like a silver eye, never to be seen again.

When T'Sehn-Hrr sailed away, no human being had witnessed the event. Cosmologists on the Avernus and on Earth had reconstructed the event, and believed they understood it. In the great disruptions which had overtaken the system eight million Earth years previously, the gravitational forces of the star now called Freyr, with a mass 14.8 times that of the Sun, had wrenched T'Sehn-Hrr away from Helliconia's pull.

Calculations indicated that T'Sehn-Hrr had a radius of 1252 km, against Helliconia's 7723 km. Whether the satellite had been capable of supporting life was doubtful.

What was certain was that the events of that epoch had been so near catastrophic that they had remained etched in the eotemporal minds of the phagors. The sky had fallen in and no one had forgotten it.

More impressive to human minds was the way in which life on Helliconia had survived even the loss of its moon and the cosmological events which had caused that loss.

"Yes, I know. This sounds like sacrilege and I am sorry," shouted SartoriIrvrash, as Odi moved close to him and the noise grew. "What is true should be said—and heard. Phagors were once the dominant race and will become so again if allowed to live. The experiments I conducted show, I believe, that we were animals. Genethlic divinities bred mankind from Others—Others who were ancipital pets before the upheaval. Mankind· developed from Others as phagors developed from flambreg. As phagors developed from flambreg, they may again cover the earth one day. They are still waiting, wild, with kaidaws, in the High Nktryht, to descend in vengeance. They will wipe you out. Be warned then. Increase the drumbles. Intensify them. Ancipitals must be wiped out in the summer, when mankind is strong. When winter comes, the wild kaidaws return!

"My final word to you: We must not waste energy fighting each other. We should fight the older enemy—and those humans who protect them!"

But the humans were already fighting each other. The most religious members of the audience were often those, like Crispan Mornu, who were most in favour of drumbles. Here was an outsider offending their deepest religious principles, yet encouraging their violent instincts. The first one to throw a stone was attacked by his neighbour. Missiles were flying all over the garden. Soon the first dagger bit into flesh. A man ran among the flower beds, bleeding, and fell on his face. Women screamed. Fighting became more general as tempers and fears mounted. The awning collapsed.

As Alam Esomberr quietly left the scene, a miniature history of warfare was enacted on the palace lawn.

The chief cause of the commotion looked on aghast. It was beyond belief how people responded to scholarship. Holy idiots! A flying stone caught him in the mouth, and he collapsed.

Odi Jeseratabhar threw herself on SartoriIrvrash, crying and trying to ward off more stones.

She was dragged aside by a group of young monks, who punched her and then began to beat and kick the prostrate ex-chancellor. They at least refused to hear the name of Akhanaba defiled.

Crispan Mornu, in fear that matters were getting so out of hand, stepped forward and raised his arms, opening the black wings of his keedrant. It was slashed by a sword blade. Odi turned and ran; her garments were seized by a woman as she passed, and next moment she was struggling for her life amid a dozen angry women.

The clamour grew, a clamour that before the hour was out would spread into the city. Indeed the monks themselves spread the clamour. Before very long, they emerged bloodstained from the precincts of the palace, bearing above their heads the broken corpses of SartoriIrvrash and his Sibornalese companion, screaming as they went, "Blasphemy is dead! Long live Akhanaba!"

After the fighting in the gardens, there was a rush to the streets, and more scuffles there, while the dead bodies were paraded down Wozen Avenue before finally being thrown to the dogs. Then a terrible quiet fell. Even the First Phagorian in the park seemed to be waiting.

Sayren Stund's plan had terribly misfired.

SartoriIrvrash had intended merely to be revenged on his ex-master and to have the First Phagorian slain. That was his conscious aim. His love of knowledge for its own sake, his hatred of his fellow men, had betrayed him. He had failed to understand his audience. As a result, religious belief was set at an intolerable crisis—and that on the day before the Emperor of Holy Pannoval, the great C'Sarr Kilandar IX, was to arrive in Oldorando to bestow the unction of Akhanaba upon the faithful.

The most living words spring from dead martyrs. The monks unwittingly propagated the heresies of SartoriIrvrash, which found ready soil on which to grow. Within a few days, it would be the monks themselves who were under attack.

What had goaded the crowd into such fury was the aspect of his disclosures to which SartoriIrvrash himself was blind. His listeners would make a connection through their faith of which, with his limited sympathies, SartoriIrvrash was incapable.

They perceived that the rumour long suppressed by the Church now confronted them nakedly. All the world's wisdom had always existed. Akhanaba was—and they themselves, and their fathers before them, had spent their lives in the worship of—a phagor. They prayed to the very beast they persecuted. "Ask not therefore if I am man or animal or stone," said the scriptures. Now the comfortable enigma fell before the banal fact. The nature of their vaunted god, the god that held the political system together, was ancipital.

Which should the people now deny in order to make their lives tolerable? The intolerable truth? Or their intolerable religion?

Even the servants of the palace neglected their duties, asking each other, "Are we slaves of slaves?" Over their masters, a spiritual crisis prevailed. Those masters had taken it for granted that they were masters of their world. Suddenly the planet had become another place—a place where they were comparative newcomers, and lowly newcomers at that.

Heated debates took place. Many of the faithful threw out SartoriIrvrash's hypothesis entirely, affecting to dismiss it as a tissue of lies. But, as ever in such situations, there were others who subscribed to it and added to it, and even claimed they had known the truth all along. The torment mounted.

Sayren Stund took only a practical interest in his faith. It was not to him the living thing it was to JandolAnganol. He cared for it only as oil which smoothed his rule. Suddenly, everything was in question.

The hapless Oldorandan king spent the rest of the afternoon shut in his wife's compartments, with preets twittering round his head. Every so often, he sent Bathkaarnet-she out to attempt to discover where Milua Tal might be, or received messengers who spoke of shops being broken into and a pitched fight being held in one of the oldest monasteries.

"We've no soldiers," wept Sayren Stund.

"And no faith," said his wife, with some complacency. "You need both to keep order in this terrible city."

"And I suppose JandolAnganol has fled to escape being killed. He should have stayed for the execution of his son."

That thought cheered him until the arrival of Crispan Mornu in the evening. The advisor's aspect showed that he had unsuspected reserves of gauntness in him. He bowed to his sovereign and said, "If I diagnose the confused situation correctly, Your Majesty, the central issue has shifted away from JandolAnganol. It now focusses on our faith itself. We must hope that this afternoon's intemperate speech will soon be forgotten. Men cannot long endure to think of themselves as lower than phagor brutes.

"This might be a convenient time to see that JandolAnganol is removed altogether from our attention. In canon law, he remains undivorced, and this morning we exposed his pretentions for what they are. He is a spent force.

"Therefore, we should remove him from the city before he can speak to the Holy C'Sarr—perhaps through Envoy Esomberr or Ulbobeg. The C'Sarr is going to have to face a larger issue, the problem of a spiritual crisis. The question of your daughter's marriage is also one we can settle, with suitable parties."

"Oh, I know what you're hinting at, Crispan," chirped Bathkaarnetshe. Mornu, in his oblique way, had been reminding his majesty that Milua Tal should be speedily married to Prince Taynth Indredd of Pannoval; in that way, a tighter religious grip over Oldorando could be established.

Crispan Mornu gave no sign that he had heard the queen's remark.

"What will you do, Your Majesty?"

"Oh, really, I think I'll take a bath. . . ."

Crispan Mornu brought an envelope from the recesses of his dark gown.

"This week's report from Matrassyl suggests that various problems there may come shortly to a head. Unndreid the Hammer, the Scourge of Mordriat, has died in a fall from his hoxney during a skirmish. While he threatened Borlien, some unity was preserved within the capital. Now with Unndreid dead and JandolAnganol away . . ." He let the sentence dangle and smiled with a cutting edge. "Offer JandolAnganol a fast ship, Your Majesty—two if necessary—to get himself and his Phagorian Guard back down the Valvoral as speedily as possible. He may accept. Urge on him that we have here a situation we cannot control, and that his precious beasts must be removed or massacred. He prides himself on going with circumstances. We will see that he does go."

Sayren Stund mopped his forehead and pondered the matter.

"JandolAnganol will never take such good advice from me. Let his friends put it to him."

"His friends?"

"Yes, yes, his Pannovalan friends, Alam Esomberr and that contemptible Guaddl Ulbobeg. Have them summoned while I have myself voluptuously bathed." Addressing his wife, he asked, "Do you wish to come and enjoy the voluptuous sight, my dear?"

The mob was in action. Its gathering could be traced from the Avernus. Oldorando was full of idle hands. Mischief was always welcome. They came out of taverns, where they had been harmlessly occupied.

They locked up shops and picked up sticks. They rose from outside churches, where they had been begging. They wandered along from hostels and billets and holy places. Just to have a share in whatever was going on.

Some hrattock had said they were inferior to fuggies. Those were fighting words. Where was this hrattock? Maybe it was that slanje standing talking over there . . .

Many Avernian watchers regarded the brawling, and the pretext for brawling, with contempt. Others who reflected more deeply saw another aspect of it. However preposterous, however primitive the issue that SartoriIrvrash had raised, it had its parallels aboard the Earth Observation Station—and there no rioting would solve it.

"Belief: an impermanence." So it said in the treatise "On the Prolongation of One Helliconian Season Beyond One Human Lifetime." The belief in technological progress which had inspired the building of the Avernus had, over the generations, become a trap for those aboard it, just as the accretion of beliefs called Akhanabaism had become a trap.

Settled into an introspective quietism, those who ran the Avernus saw no escape from their trap. They feared the change they most needed. Patronising though their attitude was to the unwashed who ran through Goose Street and Wozen Avenue, the unwashed had a hope denied those far above them. Hot with fight and drink, a man in Goose Street could use his fists or shout before the cathedral. He might be confused, but he did not endure the emptiness the advisors among the six families endured. Belief: an impermanence. It was true. Belief had largely died on the Avernus, leaving despair in its place.

Individuals despair, but not peoples. Even as the elders looked down on, and transmitted wearily back to Earth, scenes of confusion which seemed to reflect their own futility, another faction was taking bold shape on the station.

That faction had already named itself the Aganippers. Its members were young and reckless. They knew there was no chance for them to return to Earth or—as the recent example of Billy Xiao Pin had effectively demonstrated—to live on Helliconia. But on Aganip there was a chance for them. Avoiding the ever watching lenses, they accumulated their stores and marked out a shuttle they could appropriate which would transport them to the empty planet. In their hearts was a hope as bright as any to be found in Goose Street.

The evening grew slightly cooler. There was another earth tremor, but it passed almost unnoticed among the general excitements.

Calmed and refreshed by his bath, well fed, King Sayren Stund was in fit mood to receive Alam Esomberr and the elderly Guaddl Ulbobeg. He

seated himself comfortably on a couch and assembled his wife behind
him to make an attractive composition before summoning the two men
to his presence.

All due courtesies were made, and a slave woman poured wine into
glasses already freighted with Lordryardry ice.

Guaddl Ulbobeg wore an ecclesiastical sash over a light charfrul. He
entered reluctantly and appeared no more comfortable to see Crispan
Mornu present. He felt his position to be dangerous, and showed it in
his nervous manner.

Alam Esomberr, by contrast, was excessively cheerful. Immaculately
dressed as usual, he approached the king's couch and kissed the hands
of both majesties with the air of one immune to bacteria.

"Well, indeed, sire, you did present us with a spectacle this afternoon,
just as you promised. My congratulations. How ably your old rogue of
an atheist spoke! Of course, our faith is merely deepened by doubt.
Nevertheless, what an amusing turn of fate it is that the abhorred King
JandolAnganol, lover of phagors, who only this morning stood trial for
his life, should this evening stand revealed as heroic protector of the
children of God."

He laughed pleasantly and turned to Advisor Mornu to judge his
amusement.

"That is blasphemy," said Crispan Mornu, in his blackest voice.

Esomberr nodded, smiling. "Now that God has a new definition,
surely blasphemy has one too? The heresy of yesterday, sir, is now
perceived as today's true path, which we must tread as nimbly as we
can. . . ."

"I don't know why you are so merry," Sayren Stund complained.
"But I hope to take a small advantage of your good humour. I wish to
ask you both a favour. Woman, serve the wine again."

"We will do whatever your majesty commands," said Guaddl Ulbobeg, looking anxious and clutching his glass.

The king rose up from a reclining position, smoothed his stomach,
and said, with a touch of royal pomp, "We shall give you the wherewithal with which to persuade King JandolAnganol to leave our kingdom immediately, before he can delude my poor infant daughter Milua
Tal into matrimony."

Esomberr looked at Guaddl Ulbobeg. Guaddl Ulbobeg looked at
Esomberr.

"Well?" said the king.

"Sire," said Esomberr, and fell to tugging a lock of hair at the back of
his neck, which necessitated his looking down at the floor.

Guaddl Ulbobeg cleared his throat and then, more or less as an
afterthought, cleared it again. "May I venture to ask your majesty if you
have seen your daughter just of late?"

"As for me, sire, I am almost totally within the power of the King of Borlien, sir," added Esomberr, still attending to his neck. "Owing to a past indiscretion on my part, sir. An indiscretion concerning—most unforgiveably—the queen of queens. So when the King of Borlien came to us this afternoon, seeking our assistance, we felt bound . . ."

Since he allowed the sentence to dangle while he scrutinised the countenance of Sayren Stund, Ulbobeg continued the discourse.

"I being a bishop of the Household of the Holy C'Sarr of Pannoval, sire, and therefore," said Guaddl Ulbobeg, "empowered to act in His Holiness's stead in certain offices of the Church . . ."

"And I," said Esomberr, "still remissly holding in my charge a bill of divorcement signed by the ex-queen MyrdemInggala which should have been rendered to the C'Sarr, or to one of his representatives of the Household, tenners ago—with apologies for using that now opprobrious word—"

"And we both having care," said Guaddl Ulbobeg, now with rather more relish in his voice, "not to overburden His Holiness with too many functions on this visit of pleasure between sister nations—"

"When there will be more contentious matters—"

"Or, indeed, to incommode your majesty with—"

"Enough!" shouted Sayren Stund. "Come to the point, the pair of you! Enough procrastination!"

"Precisely what we both said to ourselves a few hours ago," agreed Esomberr, bestowing his choicest smile on the gathering. "Enough procrastination—perfectly put, Your Majesty. . . . Therefore, with the powers entrusted in us by those above us all, we solemnised a state of matrimony between JandolAnganol and your beautiful daughter, Milua Tal. It was a simple but touching service, and we wished that your majesties could have been present."

His majesty fell off the couch, scrambled up, and roared.

"They were married?"

"No, Your Majesty, they are married," said Guaddl Ulbobeg. "I took the ceremony and heard their vows for His Holiness in absentia."

"And I was witness and held the ring," said Esomberr. "Some of the King of Borlien's captains were also present. But no phagors. That I promise."

"They are married?" repeated Sayren Stund, looking about wildly. He fell back into his wife's arms.

"We'd both like to congratulate your majesties," said Esomberr suavely. "We are sure the lucky couple will be very happy."

It was the evening of the following day. The haze had cleared toward sunset and stars shone in the east. Stains of a magnificent Freyr-set still lingered in the western sky. There was no wind. Earth tremors were frequent.

His Holiness the C'Sarr Kilandar IX had arrived in Oldorando at midday. Kilandar was an ancient man with long white hair, and he retired straight to a bed in the palace to recover from his journey. While he lay prostrate, sundry officials, and lastly King Sayren Stund, in a fever of apology, came to tell the old man of the religious disarray in which he would find the kingdom of Oldorando.

To all this, His Holiness listened. In his wisdom, he declared that he would hold a special service at Freyr-set—not in the Dom but in the chapel of the palace—during which he would address the congregation and resolve all their doubts. The degrading rumour that ancipitals were an ancient, superior race would be exposed as complete falsehood. The voice of atheists should never prevail while strength was left in his ageing body.

This service had now begun. The old C'Sarr spoke out in a noble voice. There was scarcely an absentee.

But two absentees were together in the white pavilion in Whistler Park.

King JandolAnganol, in penitence and gratitude, had just prayed and scourged himself, and was washing the blood from his back with jugs of hot spring water poured by a slave.

"How could you do such cruelty, my husband?" exclaimed Milua Tal, entering briskly. She was shoeless, and wore a filmy white gown of satara. "What are we made of but flesh? What else would you desire to be made of?"

"There is a division between flesh and spirit, of which both must be reminded. I shall not ask you to undergo the same rituals, though you must bear with my religious inclinations."

"But your flesh is dear to me. Now it is my flesh, and if you hurt it more, I will kill you. When you sleep, I will sit on your face with my bottom and sufflicate you!" She embraced him, clinging to him until her dress was soaked. He sent the slave away, and kissed and petted her.

"Your young flesh is dear to me, but I am determined that I will not know you carnally until your tenth birthday."

"Oh, no, Jan! That's five whole tenners away! I'm not such a feeble little thing—I can easily receive you, you'll see." She pressed her flower face to his.

"Five tenners is not long, and it will do us no harm to wait."

She flung herself on him and bore him down onto the bed, fighting and wriggling in his arms, laughing wildly as she did so.

"I'm not going to wait, I'm not going to wait! I know all about what wives should be and what wives should do, and I am going to be your wife in every single particle."

They began to kiss furiously. Then he pushed her away, laughing.

"You little spitfire, you jewel, you posy. We'll wait till circumstances are more propitious and I have made some sort of peace with your parents."

"But now is always a popiters time," she wailed.

To distract her, he said, "Listen, I have a little wedding present for you. It's almost all I possess here. I shall heap gifts upon you when we are back home in Matrassyl."

He took from his tunic the timepiece with the three faces and held it out to her.

The dials read:

$$07:31:15 \qquad 18:21:90 \qquad 19:24:40$$

Milua Tal took it and looked rather disappointed. She tried it on her brow, but the ends would not meet at the back of her head.

"Where am I supposed to wear it?"

"As a bracelet?"

"Maybe so. Well, thanks, Jan. I'll wear it later." She threw the watch down and then, with a sudden movement, pulled off her damp dress.

"Now you can inspect me and see if you are going to get good value."

He began to pray but his eyes would not close as she danced about the room. She smiled lasciviously, seeing in his eyes the awakening of his khmir. He ran to her, seized her, and carried her to the bed.

"Very well, my delicious Milua Tal. Here beginneth our married life."

Over an hour later, they were roused from their raptures by a violent quake. The timbers about them groaned, their little lamp was pitched to the floor. The bed rattled. They jumped up, naked, and felt how the floor rocked.

"Shall we go out?" she asked. "The park jumps about a little, doesn't it?"

"Wait a minute."

The tremors were long sustained. Dogs howled in town. Then it was over, and a dead silence prevailed.

In that silence, thoughts worked like maggots in the king's head. He thought of the vows he had made—all broken. Of the people he loved—all betrayed. Of the hopes he had entertained—all dead. He could not find, in the prevailing stillness, consolation anywhere, not even in the perspiring human body lying against his.

His eyes with their leaden stare fixed on an object which had dropped onto the rush mat on the floor. It was the timepiece once owned by BillishOwpin, the article of an unknown science which had woven its way through the tenners of his decline.

With a sudden shout of rage, he jumped up and hurled the timepiece away, out through the north-facing window. He stood there naked, glaring, as if daring the thing to return to his hand.

After a moment of fright, Milua Tal joined him, resting her hand on his shoulder. Without words, they leaned out of the window to breathe cooler air.

An eerie white light shone to the north, outlining horizon and trees. Lightning danced noiselessly in the middle of it.

"By the beholder, what's happening?" JandolAnganol asked, clutching the slender shoulders of his bride.

"Don't be alarmed, Jan. It's the earthquake lights—they soon die. We often see them after a particularly bad quake. It's a kind of night-rainbow."

"Isn't it quiet?" He realised that there was no sound of the First Phagorian moving about nearby, and was suddenly alarmed.

"I can hear something." Suddenly she ran to the opposite window, and screamed. "Jandol! Look! The palace!"

He ran to her and looked out. On the far side of Loylbryden Square, the palace was alight. The entire wooden facade was ablaze, with clouds of smoke rolling up towards the stars.

"The quake must have caused a fire. Let's go and see if we can help—fast, fast, my poor moth!" Her pigeon voice shrilled.

Aghast, the two dressed and ran out. There were no phagors in the park but, as they crossed the square, they saw them.

The First Phagorian stood armed, staring at the blazing palace, guarding it. They watched without movement as the flames took ever firmer hold. Townspeople stood at a distance, gazing helplessly, kept at bay by the phagors.

JandolAnganol went to break through the phagorian ranks, but a spear was thrust out and his way barred. Phagor-Major Ghht Mlark Chzarn saluted her leader and spoke.

"You may not make a coming to more nearness, sir, because danger. We have made a bringing of flames to all Sons of Freyr in that church-place below the ground. Knowledge reaches our harneys that the evil king and the church-king would bring killing to your all servants of this Guard."

"You had no orders." He could scarcely speak. "You've slain Akhanaba—the god made in your image."

The creature before him with its deep scarlet eyes brought a three-fingered hand to its skull. "Orders have formed in our harneys. Make arrival from long time. Once, this place izz ancient Hrrm-Bhhrd Ydohk. ... Further sayance ..."

"You've slain the C'Sarr, Akhanaba ... everything ... everything. ..." He could scarcely hear what the ancipital was saying, for Milua Tal was holding his hand and screaming at the top of her voice, "My moth, my moth, my poor mother!"

"Hrrm-Bhhrd Ydohk once ancient place of ancipital kind. Not give to Sons of Freyr."

He failed to understand. He pushed against her spear, then drew his own sword. "Let me through, Major Chzarn, or I shall kill you."

He knew how useless threats were. Chzarn merely said, without emotion, "Not go through, sir."

"You're the fire god, Jan—command it die!" As she parrot-screamed, she raked his flesh, but he did not move. Chzarn was intent on explaining something and wrestled with words before managing to say, "Ancient Hrrm-Bhhrd Ydohk good place, sir. Air-octaves make a song. Before Sons of Freyr any on Hrl-Ichor Yhar. In ancient time of T'Sehn-Hrr."

"It's the present, the present! We live and die in present time, gillot!" He tried to wind himself up to strike but was unable to do so, despite the screaming girl at his side. His will failed. The flames burned in the pupils of his narrowed eyes.

The phagor obstinately continued her explanation, as if she were an automaton.

"Ancipitals here, sir, before Sons of Freyr. Before Freyr make bad light. Before T'Sehn-Hrr goance, sir. Old sins, sir."

Or perhaps she just said "old things." In the fury of the blaze, it was impossible to hear. With a roar, part of the palace roof collapsed and a column of fire rolled up into the night sky. Pillars crashed forward into the square.

The crowd cried in unison and stumbled back. Among the watchers was AbathVasidol; she clung to the arm of a gentleman from the Sibornalese embassy as everyone shrank from the heat.

"The Holy C'Sarr . . . all destroyed," cried JandolAnganol in pain. Milua Tal hid her face in JandolAnganol's side and wept. "All destroyed . . . all destroyed."

He made no attempt to comfort the girl or to push her away. She was nothing to him. The flames devoured his spirit. In that holocaust were consumed his ambitions—the very ambitions the fire would fulfil. He could be master of Oldorando as well as Borlien, but in that ceaseless changing of things into their opposites, that chastising enantiodromia which made a god into a phagor, he no longer wished for that mastery.

His phagors had brought him a triumph, in which he saw clearly his defeat. His thoughts flew to MyrdemInggala: but his and her summer was over, and this great bonfire of his enemies was his autumn beacon.

"All destroyed," he said aloud.

But a figure approached them, moving elegantly through the ranks of the First Phagorian, arriving almost at a saunter in time to remark, "Not quite all, I'm glad to say."

Despite his attempt at customary nonchalance, Esomberr's face was pale and he trembled visibly.

"Since I've never worshipped the All-Powerful with any great degree of fervour, whether he's man or phagor, I thought I would excuse myself from the C'Sarr's lecture on the subject. Terribly fortunate as it proved. Let this be a lesson to you, Your Majesty, to go to church less frequently in future."

Milua Tal looked up angrily to say, "Why don't you run away? Both my parents are in there."

Esomberr wagged a finger at her. "You must learn to ride with circumstances as your new husband claims to do. If your parents are perished—and there I suspect you have hit upon a profound truth—then may I be the first to congratulate you on becoming Queen of both Borlien and Oldorando.

"I hope for some advancement from you, as the chief instrument in your clandestine marriage. I may never make C'Sarr, but you both know my council is good. I'm cheerful, even in times of adversity like the present."

JandolAnganol shook his head. He took Milua Tal by the shoulders and began to coax her away from the conflagration.

"We can do nothing. Slaying a phagor or two will solve nothing. We will wait for morning. In Esomberr's cynicism there is some truth."

"Cynicism?" asked Esomberr quietly. "Are not your brutes merely imitating what you did to the Myrdolators? Is there no cynicism in your taking advantage of that? Your brutes have crowned you King of Oldorando."

Written in the king's face was something Esomberr could not bear to see. "If the entire court is wiped out, then what is there for me but to stay, to do my duty, to see that the succession is legally continued in Milua Tal's name? Will I find joy in that task, Esomberr?"

"You will go with the circumstances, I expect. As I would. What's joy?"

They walked on, the princess shambling and needing support.

At length the king said, "Otherwise there will be anarchy—or Pannoval will step in. Whether it calls for rejoicing or weeping, it seems that we do indeed have a chance to make our two kingdoms one, strong against enemies."

"Always enemies!" wailed Milua Tal to her failed god.

JandolAnganol turned to Esomberr, his expression one of blank disbelief. "The C'Sarr himself will have perished. The C'Sarr . . ."

"Failing divine intervention, yes. But one piece of better news for you. King Sayren Stund may not go down in history as its wisest monarch, but he experienced a generous impulse before he perished. He was probably prompted by your new queen's mother. His majesty could not quite stomach hanging his new son-in-law's son, and had him released an hour or so ago. Perhaps as a sort of wedding gift . . ."

"He released Robayday?" His frown left him momentarily.

Another section of the palace collapsed. The tall wooden columns burned like candles. More and more of the inhabitants of Oldorando crept forth silently to stare at the blaze, knowing they would never look on such a night again. Many, in their superstitious hearts, saw this as the long-prophesied end of the world.

"I saw the lad go free. Wild as ever. Wilder. An arrow from a bow would be a fair comparison."

A groan escaped JandolAnganol's lips. "Poor boy, why did he not come to me? I hoped that at last he had lost his hatred of me . . ."

"By now he's probably in the queue to kiss the wounds of the dead SartoriIrvrash—an unhygienic form of amusement if ever I saw one."

"Why did Rob not come to me . . . ?"

There was no answer, but JandolAnganol could guess it: he had been hidden in the pavilion with Milua Tal. It would take many a tenner before the consequences of this day's work were fully borne out, and he would have to live them through.

As if echoing his thoughts, Alam Esomberr said, "And may I enquire what you intend to do with your famous Phagorian Guard, who have committed this atrocity?"

The king threw him a hard glance and continued to walk away from the blaze.

"Perhaps you will tell me how mankind is ever to solve its phagor problem," he said.

ENVOI

The soldiery from the *Good Hope* and the *Union* landed on the Borlienese coast and marched westwards on Gravabagalinien under the leadership of Io Pasharatid.

As the force progressed, Pasharatid gleaned news of the turmoil about to overwhelm Matrassyl. The conscience of the people had been slowly roused as they digested the news of the massacre of the Myrdolators; the king would be unwelcome when he returned.

In Pasharatid's harneys a scheme burned with such conviction that it already seemed actual. He would take the queen of queens; Gravabagalinien would fall to him, and she also. Matrassyl would willingly accept her as queen. He would rule as consort; politically he was not ambitious, not greatly. His past, its evasions, disappointments, disgraces, would be over. One minor military engagement, and all he desired would be his.

His advance scouts reported breastworks about the wooden palace. He attacked at Batalix-dawn, when haze stretched across the land. His gunners advanced two-by-two, wheel locks at the ready, protected by pikemen.

A white flag waved from behind the defences. A stocky figure cautiously emerged into the open. Pasharatid signalled to his soldiery to halt, and walked forward alone. He was conscious of how brave he was, how upright. He felt every inch the conqueror.

The stocky man approached. They halted when no more than a pike's length apart.

Bardol CaraBansity spoke. He asked why soldiers were advancing on an almost undefended palace.

To which Io Pasharatid responded haughtily that he was an honourable man. He required only the surrender of Queen MyrdemInggala, after which he would leave the palace in peace.

CaraBansity made the sacred circle on his forehead and sniffed a resounding sniff. Alas, he said, the queen of queens was dead, slain by an arrow fired by an agent of her ex-husband, King JandolAnganol.

Pasharatid responded with angry disbelief.

"Look for yourself," said CaraBansity.

He gestured towards the sea, lacklustre in the dawn light. Men were launching a funeral barque upon the waters.

In truth, Pasharatid could see it for himself. He left his force and ran to the beach. Four men with heads bowed were carrying a bier on which a body lay beneath layers of white muslin. The hem of the muslin fluttered in a growing breeze. A wreath of flowers lay on top of the body. An old woman with hair growing from a mole in her cheek stood weeping at the water's edge.

The four men carried the bier reverently aboard the white caravel, the *Vajabhar Prayer*; the ship's battered sides had been repaired well enough for a voyage which did not involve the living. They laid the bier under the mast and retired.

ScufBar, the queen's old majordomo dressed in black, stepped aboard the ship carrying a lighted torch. He bowed deeply to the shrouded body. Then he set light to the brushwood piled high on the deck.

As fire took the ship, it began with the favouring wind to sail slowly out from the bay. The smoke billowed out across the water like lank hair.

Pasharatid cast down his helmet into the sand, crying wildly to his men.

"On your knees, you hrattocks! Down and pray to the Azoiaxic for this beautiful lady's soul. The queen is dead, oh, the queen of queens is dead!"

CaraBansity smiled occasionally as he rode a brown hoxney back to his wife in Ottassol. He was a clever fellow and his ruse had succeeded;

Pasharatid's pursuit had been deflected. On the little finger of his right hand, he wore the queen's gift to him, a ring with a sea-blue stone.

The queen had left Gravabagalinien only a few hours before Pasharatid's arrival. With her went her general, his sister, the princess Tatro, and a handful of followers. They made their way northeastwards, across the fertile loess lands of Borlien, towards Matrassyl.

Wherever they went, peasants came from their huts, men, women, and children, and called blessing upon MyrdemInggala. The poorest of people ran to feed her party and help her in any way possible.

The queen's heart was full. But it was not the heart it had been; the heat had gone from her affections. Perhaps she would accept Tolram-Ketinet in time. That remained to be seen. She needed to find her son first and solace him. Then the future could be determined.

Pasharatid remained on the shore for a long while. A herd of deer came down onto the beach and foraged at the high-tide line, ignoring his presence.

The funeral ship drifted out to sea, bearing the corpse of the servant who had died following injuries from a falling gunpowder keg. Flames rose straight up, smoke sank across the waves. A crackle of timber came to Pasharatid's ears.

He wept and tore his tunic and thought of all that would never happen. He fell to his knees on the sand, weeping for a death that had yet to occur.

The animals of the sea circled about the blazing hulk before leaving. They abandoned coastal waters and headed far out towards the deeps. Moving in well-organised legions, they swam where no man yet had sailed, to merge with the liquid wildernesses of Helliconia.

The years passed. That tumultuous generation faded one by one. . . . Long after the queen was lost to mortal sight, much that was immortal of her travelled across the immeasurable gulfs of space and was received on Earth. There, those lineaments and that face lived again. Her sufferings, joys, failings, virtues—all were called up once more for the peoples of Earth.

On Helliconia itself, all memories of the queen were soon lost, as waves are lost on the beach.

T'Sehn-Hrr shone overhead. The moonlight was blue. Even by day, when Batalix shone through the cool mists, the daylight was blue.

Everything perfectly suited the ancipital kind. Temperatures were low. They held horns high and saw no need to hurry. They lived among the tropical mountains and forests of the Pegovin Peninsula of Hespagorat. They were at peace with one another.

As the runts grew slowly to creighthood and then full adulthood, their coats became dense and black. Under that shapeless pelage, they were immensely strong. They threw roughly shaped spears which could kill at a hundred yards. With those weapons they slayed members of other components who infringed their territory.

They had other arts. Fire was their chained and domesticated pet. They travelled with their hearths on their shoulders, and groups of them were to be seen, climbing down to the coast on occasions, where they would trap fish, with flames borne on stone slabs upon their broad shoulders.

Bronze accoutrements were not beyond their understanding. With that metal they decorated themselves; the warm gleam of bronze might be caught about the smoking firesides of their mountain caves. They mastered pottery sufficiently to make coil pots, often of intricate design, shaped to resemble the pods of the fruits they ate. Coarse body coverings were woven from reeds and creepers. They had the gift of language. Stalluns and gillots went out to hunt together, or cultivated their scanty vegetables together in cleared patches. There was no quarrel between male and female.

The ancipital components kept animals as pets. Asokins lived commensally with them, and served as hunting dogs when they went out to hunt. Their Others were of less practical use; the naughty thieving tricks of Others were tolerated for the amusement their antics gave.

When Batalix set and light drained from the cool world, the ancipitals sank indifferently to sleep. They slept humbly as cattle, lying where they had stood. They switched off. No dreams haunted their long skulls during the silent hours of night.

Only when the moon T'Sehn-Hrr was full, they mated and hunted instead of sleeping. That was their great time. They killed any animal they came across, any bird, any other ancipital. There was no reason in the killing; they killed because it was their way.

By daylight, some of the components, those who lived to the south, hunted flambreg. That vast continent, the southern polar continent of Hespagorat, was populated by millions of head of flambreg. With the flambreg went clouds of flies. With the clouds of flies went the yellow fly. So the phagors killed the flambreg, massacred them separately or by the scores, killed the heads of herds, killed does, gravid or otherwise, killed the young, tried to fill the world with their carcasses.

The flambreg were never deterred from charging northwards across the lowlands of the Pegovin Peninsula. The ancipitals never wearied of killing them. The years came and went, and the centuries, and still the great herds plunged towards the untiring spears. There was no history among the components, except the history of this constant killing.

Mating took place at full moon: a year later, parturition occurred at full moon. The runts slowly became adult. Everything was slow, as if heartbeats themselves took their time, and the leisurely pace at which a tree grew was a standard for all things. When the great white disc of moon sank into the mists of the horizon, all was much as it had been when it rose from those same mists. Being one with this sluggish peace, the phagors were governed by its tempo; time did not enter into their pale harneys.

Their pets died. When an Other died, its body was casually cast aside, or thrown outside the area of the camp for vultures to eat. The great black phagors did not know death: death was no more to them than time. As they grew older, their movements slowed. Though they remained within the shelter of their vaguely demarcated families, they became apart. Year by year, their abilities grew more circumscribed. Language was early lost. Eventually movement itself was lost.

Then the tribe showed a sense of caring. They cared not for individuals. They ministered to their infants, but otherwise only to those who succumbed to age. These superannuated phagors were stored safely away, revered, brought out on any ceremonial occasion, as for instance when an attack was intended on a nearby component.

Like embodiments of sluggish time, the elderly phagors passed without perceptible change beyond the shadowy division which distinguished life from other conditions. Time congealed in their eddre. They shrank, to become over many years nothing more than small keratinous images of their former selves. Even then, the flickerings of existence were not entirely spent. They were consulted. They still played a part in the life of the component. Only when they disintegrated could it be said that they were visited with finality: and many were so gently handled that they survived for centuries.

This crepuscular life-style continued long. Summer and winter spelt little change in the club-shaped peninsula, extending almost to the equator. Elsewhere, in the winters, the seas might freeze; in the peninsula, up in the mountains, down in the afforested valleys, a lethargic paradise was maintained unaltered over many, many moons, many moons and many eons.

The ancipital kind was not readily responsive to change. The unknown star—the unheralded and unprecedented star—was a brilliant point long before it entered the calculations of the components.

The first white-coated phagors which appeared were treated with indifference. More of them grew to maturity. They produced white offspring. Only then were they driven out. The outcasts lived along the doleful shores of the Kowass Sea, feeding on iguana. Their tame Others rode on their backs, occasionally throwing twigs of dried seaweed into the portable hearths.

In the gloaming, phagors and Others could be seen, strung out along the shore, flame and smoke at their shoulder, moving disconsolately towards the east. As year succeeded year, white phagors became more numerous, the exodus to the east more steady. They marked their way with stone pillars, perhaps in the hope that some day they could return home. That return was never to be.

Instead, the cancerous star in the skies grew brighter, eclipsing all other stars until, like T'Sehn-Hrr, it cast a shadow by night. Then the ancipital kind, after much consultation with the elders in tether, bestowed on the new star a name: *Frehyr*, meaning fear.

From one generation to another, there appeared no difference in the magnitude of the fear-star. But it grew. And from generation to generation the mutated white phagors spread along the coastlines of Hespagorat. To the west of the Pegovin Peninsula, they were halted by the dreary marshes of a land later to be known as Dimariam. To the east, they slowly covered the alpine lands of Throssa, to come, after two thousand miles, to the Cadmer land-bridge. All this was achieved with the spiritless determination characteristic of the ancipital kind.

Across the land-bridge, spreading over Radado, they entered lands where the climate more nearly resembled that of Pegovin. Some settled there; others, arriving later, foraged further. Always as they went they erected their stone pillars, to mark healthful air-octaves which led back to their ancestral home.

The time of catastrophe arrived. The ageing star, Batalix, with its freight of planets, was captured by the fear-star, young, furious, filling the space around it with radiation. The fear-star possessed a fainter companion. In the cosmic upheaval which followed, as new orbits were established, the fainter companion was lost. It sped away on a new course, taking with it one of Batalix's planets and the moon of Helliconia, T'Sehn-Hrr. Batalix itself moved into a captive position about the fear-star. This was the Catastrophe, never to be forgotten in the harneys of the ancipital kind.

In the subsequent upheavals which afflicted the planet, the ancient land-bridge across the Cadmer Straits was demolished by savage winds and tides. The link between Hespagorat and Campannlat was severed.

During this time of change, the Others changed. The Others were more puny than their mentors, but more nimble and more flexible of mind. Their exodus from Pegovin had transformed their role vis-à-vis the phagors: they were no longer regarded merely as pets of an idle day, but were required to forage for food in order to keep the component fed.

The revolution happened by accident.

A party of Others was foraging in a bay along the Radado coast when the incoming tide cut them off. They were marooned temporarily on an island where a lagoon provided a glut of oil fish. The oil fish were one of the manifestations of a changing ecology; they spawned in the seas in their millions. The Others stayed and feasted.

Later, having lost their mentors, they struck out on their own, moving northwestwards into an almost deserted land they called Ponpt. Here were founded the Ten Tribes, or Olle Onets. Eventually, their greatly modified version of Ancipital, which became known as Olonets, spread throughout Campannlat. But that was not until many a century had passed its hand over the developing wildernesses.

The Others themselves developed. The Ten Tribes broke up and became many. They were quick to adapt to the new circumstances in which they found themselves. Some tribes never settled, and took to wandering the face of the new continent. Their great enemies were the phagors, whom they nevertheless regarded as godlike. Such delusions—such aspirations—were part and parcel of their lively response to the world in which they discovered themselves. They rejoiced, hunted, multiplied, and the new sun shone on them.

When the first Great Winter set in, when that first turbulent summer faded into cold, and the snows fell for months at a time, it must have seemed to the eotemporal minds of the phagors that normality was returning. This was the period during which the Ten Tribes were put to the test: genetically malleable, they were to have their future existences shaped by the degree of success with which they weathered the centuries of apastron, when Batalix crawled through the slowest sectors of its new orbit. Those tribes who adapted best emerged the next spring with new confidence. They had become humanity.

Male and female, they rejoiced in their new skills. They felt the world and the future to be theirs. Yet there were times—sitting about campfires at night with the star-shingle blazing overhead—when mysterious gaps opened in their lives and they seemed to look into a gulf there was no bridging. Back came folk memories of a period when larger creatures had looked after them and had administered a rough justice. They crept to sleep in silence, and words without sound formed on their lips.

The need to worship and be ruled—and to rebel against rule—never left them, even when Freyr again proclaimed its strength.

The new climate, with its higher energy levels, did not suit the white-coated phagors. Freyr, above them, was the symbol of all ills which befell. They took to carving an apotropaic symbol on their air-octave stones: one circle inside another, with rays like spokes connecting the inner with the outer. To the phagorian eye, this was first of all a picture of T'Sehn-Hrr moving away from Hrl-Ichor Yhar. It later came to be regarded as something different, as a picture of Freyr with its rays flattening Hrl-Ichor Yhar beneath it as it drew nearer.

While some of the Olonets-speakers were transformed, generation by generation, into the hated Sons of Freyr, the phagors slowly lost their culture. They remained stalwart and held horns high. For the new climate was not entirely on the side of the Sons.

Though Freyr never departed, there were long periods when it moved to such a distance that it hid its spiderous shape among the star-shingle. Then once again the ancipital kind were able to master the Sons of Freyr. At the next Time of Cold they would obliterate their ancient enemy entirely.

That time was not yet. But it would come.

END OF VOLUME TWO

HELLICONIA
WINTER

In the first place, since the elements of which we see the world composed—solid earth and moisture, the light breaths of air and torrid fire—all consist of bodies that are neither birthless nor deathless, we must believe the same of the Earth as a whole, and of its populations. . . . And whatever earth contributes to feed the growth of others is restored to it. It is an observed fact that the Universal Mother is also the common grave. Earth, therefore, is whittled away and renewed with fresh increment.

Lucretius: *De Rerum Natura*
55 BC

CONTENTS

Prelude   3

I · The Last Battle   12

II · A Silent Presence   29

III · The Restrictions of Persons in Abodes Act   45

IV · An Army Career   59

V · A Few More Regulations   78

VI · G4PBX/4582-4-3   96

VII · The Yellow-Striped Fly   110

VIII · The Rape of the Mother   127

IX · A Quiet Day Ashore   141

X · "The Dead Never Talk Politics"   152

XI · Stern Discipline for Travellers   164

XII · Kakool on the Trail   175

XIII · "An Old Antagonism"   196

XIV · The Greatest Crime   218

XV · Inside the Wheel   232

XVI · A Fatal Innocence   246

XVII · Sunset   266

Acknowledgements   285

PRELUDE

Luterin had recovered. He was free of the mysterious illness. He was allowed out again. The couch by the window, the immobility, the grey schoolmaster who came every day—they were done with. He was alive to fill his lungs with the brisk airs of outdoors.

The cold blew down from Mount Shivenink, sharp enough to peel the bark from the north side of trees.

The fresh wind brought out his defiance. It drew the blood to his cheeks, it made his limbs move with the beast which carried him across his father's land. Letting out a yell, he spurred the hoxney into a gallop. He headed it away from the incarcerating mansion with its tolling bell, away along the avenue traversing the fields they still called the Vineyard. The movement, the air, the uproar of his own blood in his arteries, intoxicated him.

Around him lay his father's territory, a dominion triumphing over latitude, a small world of moor, mountain, valley, plunging stream, cloud, snow, forest, waterfall—but he kept his thought from the waterfall. Endless game roved here, springing up plenteously even as his father hunted it down. Roving phagors. Birds whose migrations darkened the sky.

3

Soon he would be hunting again, following the example of his father. Life had been somehow stayed, was somehow renewed. He must rejoice and force away the blackness hovering on the edges of his mind.

He galloped past bare-chested slaves who exercised yelk about the Vineyard, clinging to their snaffles. The hoofs of the animals scattered mounds of earth sent up by moles.

Luterin Shokerandit spared a sympathetic thought for the moles. They could ignore the extravagances of the two suns. Moles could hunt and rut in any season. When they died, their bodies were devoured by other moles. For moles, life was an endless tunnel through which the males quested for food and mates. He had forgotten them, lying abed.

"Moledom!" he shouted, bouncing in the saddle, rising up in the stirrups. The spare flesh on his body made its own movements under his arang jacket.

He goaded the hoxney on. Exercise was what was needed to bring him back into fighting shape. The spare fat was falling away from him even on this, his first ride out for more than a small year. His twelfth birthday had been wasted flat on his back. For over four hundred days he had lain like that—for a considerable period unable to move or speak. He had been entombed in his bed, in his room, in his parents' mansion, in the great grave House of the Keeper. Now that episode was finished.

Strength flowed back to his muscles, arriving from the animal beneath him, from the air, from the trunks of trees as they flashed by, from his own inner being. Some destructive force whose nature he did not comprehend had wiped him out of the world; now he was back and determined to make a mark upon that flashing stage.

One of the double entrance gates was opened for him by a slave before he reached it. He galloped through without pause or sideways glance.

The wind yelped in his unaccustomed ear like a hound. He lost the familiar note of the bell of the house behind him. The small bells on his harness jingled as the ground responded to his advance.

Both Batalix and Freyr were low in the southern sky. They flitted among the tree trunks like gongs, the big sun and the small. Luterin turned his back on them as he reached the village road. Year by year, Freyr was sinking lower in the skies of Sibornal. Its sinking called forth fury in the human spirit. The world was about to change.

The sweat that formed on his chest cooled instantly. He was whole again, determined to make up for lost time by rutting and hunting like the moles. The hoxney could carry him to the verge of the trackless caspiarn forests, those forests which fell away and away into the deepest recesses of the mountain ranges. One day soon, he planned to fade into the embrace of those forests, to fade and be lost, relishing his own dangerousness like an animal among animals. But first he would be lost in the embrace of Insil Esikananzi.

Luterin gave a laugh. "Yes, you have a wild side, boy," his father had once said, staring down at Luterin after some misdemeanour or other—staring down with that friendless look of his, while placing a hand on the boy's shoulder as if estimating the amount of wildness per bone.

And Luterin had gazed downwards, unable to meet that stare. How could his father love him as he loved his father when he was so mute in the great man's presence?

The distant grey roofs of the monasteries showed through the naked trees. Close lay the gates of the Esikananzi estate. He let the brown hoxney slow to a trot, sensing its lack of stamina. The species was preparing for hibernation. Soon all hoxneys would be useless for riding. This was the season for training up the recalcitrant but more powerful yelk. When a slave opened the Esikananzi gate, the hoxney turned in at walking pace. The distinctive Esikananzi bell sounded ahead, chiming randomly as the wind took its vane.

He prayed to God the Azoiaxic that his father knew nothing of his activities with Ondod females, that wickedness he had fallen into shortly before paralysis had overcome him. The Ondods gave what Insil so far refused him.

He must resist those inhuman females now. He was a man. There were sleazy shacks by the edge of the forest where he and his school friends—including Umat Esikananzi—went to meet those shameless eight-fingered bitches. Bitches, witches, who came out of the woods, out of the very roots of the woods . . . And it was said that they consorted with male phagors too. Well, that would not happen again. It was in the past, like his brother's death. And like his brother's death, best forgotten.

It was not beautiful, the mansion of the Esikananzis. Brutality was the predominant feature of its architecture; it was constructed to withstand the brutal onslaughts of a northern climate. A row of blind arches formed the base of it. Narrow windows, heavily shuttered, began only on the second floor. The whole structure resembled a decapitated pyramid. The bell in its belfry made a slatey sound, as if ringing from the adamantine heart of the building.

Luterin dismounted, climbed the steps, and pulled the doorbell.

He was a broad-shouldered youth, already lofty in the Sibornalese manner, with a round face seemingly built naturally for merriment: although, at this moment, awaiting sight of Insil, his brows were knit, his lips compressed. The tension of his expression caused him to resemble his father, but his eyes were of a clear grey, very different from his father's dark, in-dwelling pupils.

His hair, curling riotously about his head and the nape of his neck, was light brown, and formed a contrast to the neat dark head of the girl into whose presence he was ushered.

Insil Esikananzi had the airs of one born into a powerful family. She could be sharp and dismissive. She teased. She lied. She cultivated a helpless manner; or, if it suited her better, a look of command. Her smiles were wintery, more a concession to politeness than an expression of her spirit. Her violet eyes looked out of a face she kept as blank as possible.

She was carrying a jug of water through the hall, clasped in both hands. As she came towards Luterin she lifted her chin slightly into the air, in a kind of mute exasperated enquiry. To Luterin, Insil was intensely desirable, and no less desirable for her capriciousness.

This was the girl he was to marry, according to the arrangement drawn up between his father and hers at Insil's birth, to cement the accord between the two most powerful men of the district.

Directly he was in her presence, Luterin was caught up once more into their old conspiracy, into that intricate teasing web of complaint which she wove about herself.

"I see, Luterin, you are on your two feet again. How excellent. And like a dutiful husband-to-be, you have perfumed yourself with sweat and hoxney before presuming to call and present your compliments. You have certainly grown while in bed—at least in the region of your waistline."

She fended off an embrace with the jug of water. He put an arm about her slender waist as she led him up the immense staircase, made more gloomy by dark portraits from which dead Esikananzis stared as if in tether, shrunken by art and time.

"Don't be provoking, Sil. I'll soon be slim again. It's wonderful to have my health back."

Her personal bell uttered its light clap on every stair.

"My mother's so sickly. Always sickly. My slimness is illness, not health. You are lucky to call when my tedious parents and my equally tedious brothers, including your friend Umat, are all attending a boring ceremony elsewhere. So you can expect to take advantage of me, can't you? Of course, you suspect that I have been had by stable boys while you were in your year's hibernation. Giving myself in the hay to sons of slaves."

She guided him along a corridor where the boards creaked under their worn Madi carpets. She was close, phantasmal in the little light that filtered here through shuttered windows.

"Why do you punish my heart, Insil, when it is yours?"

"It's not your heart I want, but your soul." She laughed. "Have more spirit. Hit me, as my father does. Why not? Isn't punishment the essence of things?"

He said heatedly, "Punishment? Listen, we'll be married and I'll make you happy. You can hunt with me. We'll never be apart. We'll explore the forests—"

"You know I'm more interested in rooms than forests." She paused with a hand on a door latch, smiling provocatively, projecting her shallow breasts toward him under their linens and laces.

"People are better outside, Sil. Don't grin. Why pretend I'm a fool? I know as much about suffering as you. That whole small year spent prostrate—wasn't that about the worst punishment anyone could imagine?"

Insil put a finger on his chin and slid it up to his lip. "That clever paralysis allowed you to escape from a greater punishment—having to live here under our repressive parents, in this repressive community— where you for instance were driven to cohabit with non-humans for relief . . ."

She smiled as he blushed, but continued in her sweetest voice. "Have you no insight into your own suffering? You often accused me of not loving you, and that may be so, but don't I pay you better attention than you pay yourself?"

"What do you mean, Insil?" How her conversation tormented him.

"Is your father at home or away on the hunt?"

"He's at home."

"As I recall, he had returned from the hunt not more than two days before your brother committed suicide. Why did Favin commit suicide? I suspect that he knew something you refuse to know."

Without taking her dark gaze from his eyes, she opened the door behind her, pushing it so that it opened to allow sunshine to bathe them as they stood, conspiratorial yet opposed, on the threshold. He clutched her, tremulous to discover that she was as necessary to him as ever, and as ever full of riddles.

"What did Favin know? What am I supposed to know?" The mark of her power over him was that he was always questioning her.

"Whatever your brother knew, it was that which sent you escaping into your paralysis—not his actual death, as everyone pretends." She was twelve years and a tenner, not much more than a child: yet a tension in her gestures made her seem much older. She raised an eyebrow at his puzzlement.

He followed her into the room, wishing to ask her more, yet tongue-tied. "How do you know these things, Insil? You invent them to make yourself mysterious. Always locked in these rooms . . ."

She set the jug of water down on a table beside a bunch of white flowers which she had picked earlier. The flowers lay scattered on the polished surface, their faces reflected as in a misted mirror.

As though to herself, she said, "I try to train you not to grow up like the rest of the men here . . ."

She walked over to the window, framed in heavy brown curtains which hung from ceiling to floor. Although she stood with her back to him, he sensed that she was not looking out. The dual sunlight, shining in from two different directions, dissolved her as if it were liquid, so that her shadow on the tiled floor appeared more substantial than she. Insil was demonstrating once more her elusive nature.

It was a room he had not entered before, a typical Esikananzi room, loaded with heavy furniture. It held a tantalising scent, in part repugnant. Perhaps its only purpose was to hoard furniture, most of it wooden, against the day when the Weyr-Winter came and no more furniture would be made. There was a green couch with carved scrollwork, and a massive wardrobe which dominated the chamber. All the furniture had been imported; he saw that by its style.

He shut the door, remaining there contemplating her. As if he did not exist, she began arranging her flowers in a vase, pouring water from the jug into the vase, shuffling the stems peremptorily with her long fingers.

He sighed. "My mother is always sickly, too, poor thing. Every day of her life she goes into pauk and communes with her dead parents."

Insil looked up sharply at him. "And you—while you were lying flat on your back—I suppose you've fallen into the habit of pauk too?"

"No. You're mistaken. My father forbad me . . . besides, it's not just that . . ."

Insil put fingers to her temples. "Pauk is what the common people do. It's so superstitious. To go into a trance and descend into that awful underworld, where bodies rot and those ghastly corpses are still spitting the dregs of life . . . oh, it's disgusting. You're *sure* you don't do it?"

"Never. I imagine my mother's sickness comes from pauk."

"Well, sherb you, *I* do it every day. I kiss my grandmother's corpse-lips and taste the maggots . . ." Then she burst into laughter. "Don't look so silly. I'm joking. I hate the thought of those things underground and I'm glad you don't go near them."

She lowered her gaze to the flowers.

"These snowflowers are tokens of the world's death, don't you think? There are only white flowers now, to go with the snow. Once, so the histories say, brightly coloured flowers bloomed in Kharnabhar."

She pushed the vase resignedly from her. Down in the throats of the pale blossoms, a touch of gold remained, turning to a speck of intense red at the ovary, like an emblem of the vanishing sun.

He sauntered across to her, over the patterned tiles. "Come and sit on the couch with me and talk of happier things."

"You must be referring to the climate—declining so rapidly that our grandchildren, if we live to have any, will spend their lives in near darkness, wrapped in animal skins. Probably making animal noises . . . That sounds a promising topic."

"What nonsense you talk!" Laughing, he jumped forward and grasped her. She let him drag her down on the couch as he uttered fevered endearments.

"Of course you can't make love to me, Luterin. You may feel me as you have before, but no lovemaking. I don't think I shall ever take kindly to lovemaking—but in any case, were I to permit it, you would lose your interest in me, your lust being satisfied."

"It's a lie, a lie."

"It had best stand as the truth, if we are to have any marital happiness at all. I am not marrying a sated man."

"I could never have enough of you." As he spoke, his hand was foraging up her clothes.

"The invading armies . . ." Insil sighed, but she kissed him and put the point of her tongue in his mouth.

At which moment, the door of the wardrobe burst open. Out jumped a young man of Insil's dark colouration, but as frenzied as his sister was passive. It was Umat, brandishing a sword, shouting.

"Sister, sister! Help is at hand! Here's your brave rescuer, to save you and the family from dishonour! Who's this beast? Isn't a year in bed enough for him, that he must rise immediately to seek the nearest couch? Varlet! Rapist!"

"You rat in the skirting!" Luterin shouted. He rushed at Umat in a rage, the wooden sword fell to the floor, and they wrestled furiously. After his long confinement, Luterin had lost some of his strength. His friend threw him to the floor. As he picked himself up, he saw that Insil had flitted away.

He ran to the door. She had vanished into the dark recesses of the house. In the scuffle, her flowers had been spilt and the jug broken on the tiled floor.

Only as he made his way disconsolately back to the village road, letting the hoxney carry him at walking pace, did it occur to Luterin that possibly Insil had staged Umat's interruption. Instead of going home, he turned right at the Esikananzi gate, and rode into the village to drink at the Icen Inn.

Batalix was close to setting when he followed the mournful Shokerandit bell home. Snow was falling. No one was about in the grey world. At the inn, the talk consisted mainly of jokes and complaints concerning the new regulations being introduced by the Oligarch, such as curfew. The regulations were intended to strengthen communities throughout Sibornal for ordeals to come.

Most of the talk was cheap, and Luterin despised it. His father would never speak of such things—or not in his one remaining son's hearing.

The gaslights were burning in the long hall of his home. As Luterin was unbuckling his personal bell, a slave came up, bowed, and announced that his father's secretary wished to see him.

"Where is my father?" Luterin demanded.

"Keeper Shokerandit has left, sir."

Angrily Luterin ran up the stairs and threw open the door into the secretary's room. The secretary was a permanent member of the Shokerandit household. With his beaklike nose, his straight line of eyebrow, his shallow forehead, and the quiff of hair which protruded over that forehead, the secretary resembled a crow. This narrow wooden room, its pigeonholes stuffed with secret documents, was the crow's nest. From here, it surveyed many secret prospects beyond Luterin's ken.

"Your father is off on a hunt, Master Luterin," announced this wily bird now, in a tone mingling deference with reproach. "Since you were nowhere to be found, he had to leave without bidding you farewell."

"Why didn't he let me accompany him? He knows I love the hunt. Perhaps I can catch him up. Which way did his entourage go?"

"He entrusted me with this epistle for you. You would perhaps be advised to read it before dashing off."

The secretary handed over a large envelope. Luterin snatched it from his talons. He ripped open the cover and read what was set down on the enclosed sheet in his father's large and careful hand:

Son Luterin,

There is a prospect in the days to come that you will be appointed Keeper of the Wheel in my place. That role, as you are aware, combines both secular and religious duties.

When you were born, you were taken to Rivenjk to be blessed by the Priest-Supreme of the Church of the Formidable Peace. I believe this to have fortified the godly side of your nature. You have proved a submissive son in whom I am satisfied.

Now it is time to fortify the secular side of your nature. Your late brother was commissioned to the army, as is the tradition with elder sons. It is fitting that you should take up a similar office, especially as in the wider world (of which you so far know nothing), Sibornal's affairs are moving towards a point of decision.

Accordingly, I have left a sum of money with my secretary. He will hand it over to you. You will proceed to Askitosh, chief city of our proud continent, and there enroll yourself as a soldier, with a commissioned rank of lieutenant ensign. Report to Archpriest-Militant Asperamanka, who will be familiar with your situation.

I have instructed that a masque shall be held in your honour, to celebrate your departure.

You are to leave without delay and gather esteem to the family name.

Your father

A blush spread over Luterin's face as he read his father's rare word of praise. That his father should be satisfied with him despite all his failings!—satisfied enough to declare a masque in his honour!

His glow of happiness faded when he realised that his father would himself not be present at the masque. No matter. He would become a soldier and do anything asked of him. He would make his father proud of him.

Perhaps even Insil would warm to the name of glory. . . .

The masque was performed in the banqueting hall of the Shokerandit mansion on the eve of Luterin's departure south.

Stately personages in grand costume enacted preordained roles. A solemn music played. A familiar story was performed telling of innocence and villainy, of the lust to possess, and of the convoluted role of faith in the lives of men. To some characters harm was allotted, to some good. All came under a law greater than their own jurisdiction. The musicians, bent over their strings, emphasised the mathematics which prevailed over relationships.

The harmonies evoked by the musicians suggested a cadence of stern compassion, inviting a view of human affairs far beyond the normal acceptances of optimism or pessimism. In the leitmotifs for the woman forced to give herself to a ruler she hated and for the man unable to control his baser passions, musical members of the audience could detect a fatality, a sense that even the most individual characters were indissolubly functions of their environment, just as individual notes formed part of the greater harmony. The stylised acting of the performers reinforced this interpretation.

Some entrances were politely applauded by the audience, others observed without especial pleasure. The actors were well rehearsed in their roles, but not all by any means commanded the same presence as the principals.

Figures of state, figures of noble families, figures of the church, allegorical figures representing phagors and monsters, together with the various humours of Love, Hatred, Evil, Passion, Fear, and Purity, played their parts on the boards and were gone.

The stage emptied. Darkness fell. The music died.

But Luterin Shokerandit's drama was just beginning.

I

THE LAST BATTLE

S uch was the nature of grass that it continued to grow despite the
wind. It bowed to the wind. Its roots spread under the soil,
anchoring it, leaving no room for other plants to find lodgement.
The grass had always been there. It was the wind which was more
recent—and the bite in it.

The great exhalations from the north carried with them a fast-moving
sky, comprising a patchwork of black and grey cloud. Over distant high
ground the clouds spilled rain and snow. Here, across the steppelands
of Chalce, they purveyed nothing worse than a neutral obscurity. That
neutrality found an echo in the monotony of the terrain.

A series of shallow valleys opened one into the next, without definite
feature. The only movement to be seen was among the grasses. Some
tufts bore insignificant yellow flowers which rippled in the wind like
the fur of a supine animal. The sole landmarks were occasional stone
pillars marking land-octaves. The south-facing sides of these stones
sometimes bore lichens, yellow and grey.

Only keen eyes could have discerned minute trails in the grass, used
by creatures which appeared at night or during dimday, when only one
of the two suns was above the horizon. Solitary hawks, patrolling the

sky on motionless wings, explained the lack of daytime activity. The widest trail through the grasslands was carved by a river which flowed southwards towards the distant sea. Deep and sluggish in movement, its waters appeared partly congealed. The river took its colour from the tatterdemalion sky.

From the north of this inhospitable country came a flock of arang. These long-legged members of the goat family loosely followed the tedious bends of the river. Curly-horned dogs kept the arang closely grouped. These hardworking asokins were in turn controlled by six men on hoxney-back. The six sat or stood in their saddles to vary their journey. All were dressed in skins lashed about their bodies with thongs.

The men frequently looked back over their shoulders, as if afraid of pursuit. Keeping up a steady pace, they communicated with their asokins by whoops and whistles. These encouraging signals rang through the hollow spaces round about, clear above the bleat of the arang. However often the men glanced back, the drab northern horizon remained empty.

The ruins of a place of habitation appeared ahead, nestling in an elbow of the river. Scattered stone huts stood roofless. A larger building was no more than a shell. Ragged plants, taking advantage of the windbreak, grew about the stones, peering from the blank window sockets.

The arangherds gave the place a wide berth, fearing plague. A few miles farther on, the river, taking a leisurely curve, served as a boundary which had been in dispute for centuries, perhaps for as long as there had been men in the land. Here began the region once known as Hazziz, northernmost land of the North Campannlatian Plain. The dogs channelled the arang along beside the river, where a path had been worn. The arang spread into a fast-moving line, face to tail.

They came in time to a broad and durable bridge. It threw its two arches across the wind-troubled face of the water. The men whistled shrilly, the asokins marshalled the arang into a bunch, preventing them crossing the bridge. A mile or two away, lying against the northern bank of the river, was a settlement built in the shape of a wheel. The name of the settlement was Isturiacha.

A bugle sounded from the settlement, telling the arangherds that they had been sighted. Armed men and black Sibornalese cannon guarded the perimeter.

"Welcome!" shouted the guards. "What did you see to the north? Did you see the army?"

The arangherds drove their animals into pens already awaiting them.

The stone farmhouses and barns of the settlement had been built as a fortification along its perimeter. The farms, where cereals and live-stock were raised, lay in the middle. At the hub of the circle, a ring of barracklike offices surrounded a tall church. There was continual coming and going in Isturiacha, which increased as the herdsmen were taken into one of the central buildings to refresh themselves after their journey across the steppes.

On the south side of the bridge, the plain was more varied in contour. Isolated trees betokened increased rainfall. The ground was stippled with fragments of a white substance, which from a distance resembled crumbling stone. On closer inspection the fragments proved to be bone. Few pieces measured more than six inches in length. Occasionally a tooth or wedge of jawbone revealed the remains to be those of men and phagors. These testimonies to past battles stretched across miles of plain.

Over the immobility of this doleful place rode a man on yelk-back, approaching the bridge from the south. Some way behind him followed two more men. All three wore uniform and were equipped for war.

The leading rider, a small and sharp-featured man, halted well before he reached the bridge, and dismounted. He led his animal down into a dip and secured it to the trunk of a flat-topped briar tree before climbing to the level, where he stood peering through a spyglass at the enemy settlement ahead.

The other two men presently joined him. They also dismounted and tied their yelk to the roots of a dead rajabaral. Being of senior rank, they stood apart from the scout.

"Isturiacha," said the scout, pointing. But the officers spoke only to each other. They too scrutinised Isturiacha through a spyglass, conferring together in low tones. A cursory reconnaissance was made.

One officer—an artillery expert—remained on watch where he was. His brother officer galloped back with the scout to pass information to an army which advanced from the south.

As the day passed, the plain became broken by lines of men—some mounted, many more on foot—interspersed by wagons, cannon, and the impedimenta of war. The wagons were drawn by yelk or the less sturdy hoxney. There were columns of soldiers marching in good order, contrasting with baggage trains and women and camp followers in no order at all. Above a number of the marching columns waved the banners of Pannoval, the city under the mountains, and other flags of religious import.

Further back came ambulances and more carts, some carrying field kitchens and provisions, many more loaded with fodder for the animals involved in this punitive expedition.

Although these hundreds and thousands of people functioned like cogs in the war machine, nevertheless each underwent incidents peculiar to his or her self, and each experienced the adventure through his or her limited perceptions.

One such incident occurred to the artillery officer who waited with

his mount by the shattered rajabaral tree. He lay silent, watching his
front, when the whinnying of his yelk made him turn his head. Four
small men, none coming higher than his chest, were advancing on the
tethered mount. They evidently had not observed the officer as they
emerged from a hole in the ground at the base of the ruined tree.

The creatures were humanoid in general outline, with thin legs and
long arms. Their bodies were covered in a tawny pelt, which grew
long about their wrists, half concealing eight-fingered hands. The muzzles of their faces made them resemble dogs or Others.

"Nondads!" the officer exclaimed. He recognised them immediately,
although he had seen them only in captivity. The yelk plunged about
in terror. As the two leading Nondads threw themselves at its throat,
he drew his double-barrelled pistol, then paused.

Another head thrust itself up between the ancient roots, struggled
to get its shoulders free, and then rose, shaking soil from its thick coat
and snorting.

The phagor dominated the Nondads. Its immense box-head was
crowned by two slender horns sweeping backwards. As the bulk of it
emerged from the Nondad hole, it swung its morose bull face between
its shoulders, and its eyes lit on the crouching officer. Just for a moment,
it paused without movement. An ear flicked. Then it charged at the
man, head down.

The artillery officer rolled onto his back, steadied the pistol with
both hands, and fired both barrels into the belly of the brute. An
irregular golden star of blood spread across its pelt, but the creature
still came on. The ugly mouth opened, showing spadelike yellow teeth
set in yellow gums. As the officer jumped to his feet, the phagor struck
him full force. Coarse three-fingered hands closed round his body.

He struck out again and again, hammering the butt of his gun
against the thick skull.

The grip relaxed. The barrel body fell to one side. The face struck
the ground. With an enormous effort, the creature managed to regain
its feet. It bellowed. Then it fell dead, and the earth shook.

Gasping, choking on the thick milky stench of the ancipital, the
officer pulled himself to his knees. He had to steady himself with a
hand on the phagor's shoulder. In amid the thick coat of the body,
ticks flicked hither and thither, undergoing a crisis of their own. Some
climbed onto the officer's sleeve.

He managed to stagger to his feet. He trembled. His mount trembled
nearby, bleeding from lacerations at its throat. Of the Nondads there
was no sign; they had retreated into their underground warrens, into
the domain they knew as the Eighty Darknesses. After a while, the
artillery officer was sufficiently master of himself to climb into the
saddle. He had heard of the liaison between phagors and Nondads, but

had never expected to confront an example of it. There could be more of the brutes beneath his feet . . .

Still choking, he rode back to find his unit.

The expedition mounted from Pannoval, to which the officer belonged, had been operating in the field for some while. It was engaged in wiping out Sibornalese settlements established on what Pannoval claimed as its own territory. Starting at Roonsmoor, it had carried out a series of successful forays. As each enemy settlement was crushed, the expedition moved farther north. Only Isturiacha remained to be destroyed. It was now a matter of timing before the small summer was over.

The settlements, with their siege mentality, rarely assisted each other. Some were supported by one Sibornalese nation, some by another. So they fell victims to their destroyers one by one.

The dispersed Pannovalan units had little more to fear than occasional phagors, appearing in even greater numbers as the temperatures on the plains declined. The experience of the artillery officer was not untypical.

As the officer rejoined his fellows, a watery sun emerged from scudding cloud to set in the west amid a dramatic display of colour. When it was quenched by the horizon, the world was not plunged into darkness. A second sun, Freyr, burned low in the south. When the cloud formations parted about it, it threw shadows of men like pointed fingers to the north.

Slowly, two traditional enemies were preparing to do battle. Far behind the figures toiling on the plain, to the southwest, was the great city of Pannoval, from which the will to fight issued. Pannoval lay hidden within the limestone range of mountains called the Quzints. The Quzints formed the backbone of the tropical continent of Campannlat.

Of the many nations of Campannlat, several owed allegiance through dynastic or religious ties with Pannoval. Coherence, however, was always temporary, peace always fragile; the nations warred with each other. Hence the name by which Campannlat was known to its external enemy: the Savage Continent.

Campannlat's external enemy was the northern continent of Sibornal. Under the pressure of its extreme climate, the nations of Sibornal preserved a close unity. The rivalries under the surface were generally suppressed. Throughout history, the Sibornalese nations pressed southwards, across the land-bridge of Chalce, to the more productive meadows of the Savage Continent.

There was a third continent, the southern one of Hespagorat. The continents were divided, or almost divided, by seas occupying the temperate zones. These seas and continents comprised the planet of

Helliconia, or Hrl-Ichor Yhar, to use the name bestowed on it by its elder race, the ancipitals.

At this period, when the forces of Campannlat and Sibornal were preparing for a last battle at Isturiacha, Helliconia was moving towards the nadir of its year.

As a planet of a binary system, Helliconia revolved about its parent sun, Batalix, once every 480 days. But Batalix itself revolved about a common axis with a much larger sun, Freyr, the major component of the system. Batalix was now carrying Helliconia on its extended orbit away from the greater star. Over the last two centuries, the autumn—that long decline from summer—had intensified. Now Helliconia was poised on the brink of the winter of another Great Year. Darkness, cold, silence, waited in the centuries ahead.

Even the lowest peasant was aware that the climate grew steadily worse. If the weather did not tell him as much, there were other signs. Once more the plague known as the Fat Death was spreading. The ancipitals, commonly referred to as phagors, scented the approach of those seasons when they were most comfortable, when conditions returned most closely to what they once had been. Throughout the spring and summer, those ill-fated creatures had suffered under the supremacy of man: now, at the chill end of the Great Year, as the numbers of mankind began to dwindle, the phagors would seize their chance to rule again—unless humankind united to stop them.

There were powerful wills on the planet, wills which might move the mass of people into action. One such will sat in Pannoval, another, even harsher, in the Sibornalese capital of Askitosh. But at present those wills were most preoccupied with confounding each other.

So the Sibornalese settlers in Isturiacha prepared for siege, while looking anxiously to see if reinforcement would come from the north. So the guns from Pannoval and her allies were wheeled into position to aim at Isturiacha.

Some confusion reigned both at the front and the rear of the mixed Pannovalan force. The elderly Chief Marshal in charge of the advance was powerless to stop units who had looted other Sibornalese settlements from heading back to Pannoval with their spoils. Other units were summoned forward to replace them. Meanwhile, the artillery situated inside the walls of the settlement began to bombard the Pannovalan lines.

Bruum. Bruum. The short-lived explosions burst among the contingent from Randonan, which had come from the south of the Savage Continent.

Many nations were represented in the ranks of the Pannovalan expeditionary army. There were ferocious skirmishers from Kace, who marched, slept, and fought with their dehorned phagors; tall stone-faced men of Brasterl, who came kilted from the Western Barriers;

tribes from Mordriat, with their lively timoroon mascots; together with a strong battalion from Borldoran, the Oldorando-Borlien Joint Monarchy—Pannoval's strongest ally. A few amid their number presented the squat shape of those who had suffered the Fat Death and lived.

The Borldoranians had crossed the Quzint Mountains by high and windy passes to fight beside their fellows. Some had fallen ill and turned for home. The remaining force, fatigued, now discovered their access to the river blocked by units which had arrived earlier, so that they were unable to water their mounts.

The argument grew hot while shells from Isturiacha exploded nearby. The commandant of the Borldoranian battalion strode off to make complaint to the Chief Marshal. This commandant was a jaunty man, young to command, with a military moustache and a concave back, by name Bandal Eith Lahl.

With Bandal Eith Lahl went his pretty young wife, Toress Lahl. She was a doctor, and also had a complaint for the old Chief Marshal—a complaint about the poor standards of hygiene. She walked discreetly behind her husband, behind that rigid back, letting her skirts trail on the ground.

They presented themselves at the Marshal's tent. An aide-de-camp emerged, looking apologetic.

"The Marshal is indisposed, sir. He regrets that he is unable to see you, and hopes to listen to your complaint another day."

"'Another day'!" exclaimed Toress Lahl. "Is that an expression a soldier should use in the field?"

"Tell the Marshal that if he thinks like that," Bandal Eith Lahl said, "our forces may not live to see another day."

He made a bold attempt to tug off his moustache before turning on his heel. His wife followed him back to their lines—to find the Borldoranians also under fire from Isturiacha. Toress Lahl was not alone in noticing the ominous birds already beginning to gather above the plain.

The peoples of Campannlat never planned as efficiently as those of Sibornal. Nor were they ever as disciplined. Nevertheless, their expedition had been well organized. Officers and men had set out cheerfully, conscious of their just cause. The northern army had to be driven from the southern continent.

Now they were less buoyant in mood. Some men, having women with them, were making love in case this was their last opportunity for that pleasure. Others were drinking heavily. The officers, too, were losing their appetites for just causes. Isturiacha was not like a city, worth the taking: it would hold little except slaves, heavy-bodied women, and agricultural implements.

The higher command also was depressed. The Chief Marshal had received word that wild phagors were now coming down from the High Nyktryhk—that great aggregate of mountain ranges—to invade the plains; the Chief Marshal suffered a fit of coughing as a result.

The general feeling was that Isturiacha should be destroyed as soon as possible, and with as little risk as possible. Then all could return quickly to the safety of home.

So much for the general feeling. The fainter of the suns, Batalix, rose again, to reveal a sinister addition to the scene.

A Sibornalese army was approaching from the north.

Bandal Eith Lahl jumped onto a cart to peer through a spyglass at the distant lines of the enemy, indistinct in the light of a new day.

He called to a messenger.

"Go immediately to the Chief Marshal. Rouse him at all costs. Instruct him that our entire army must wipe out Isturiacha immediately, before their relieving army arrives."

The settlement of Isturiacha marked the southern end of the great Isthmus of Chalce, which connected the equatorial continent of Campannlat with the northern continent of Sibornal. Chalce's mountainous backbone lay along its eastern edge. Progress back or forth from one continent to the other entailed a journey through dry steppeland, which extended in the rain shadow of the eastern mountains from Koriantura in the north, safe in Sibornal, all the way down to perilous Isturiacha.

The kind of mixed agriculture practised by the Campannlatians had no place in the grasslands, and consequently their gods no foothold. Whatever emerged from that chill region was bad for the Savage Continent.

As fresh morning wind dispersed the mist, columns of men could be counted. They were moving over the undulant hills north of the settlement by the river tracks along which the arangherds had come the previous day. The soaring birds above the Pannovalan force could, with the merest adjustment of their wingtips, be hovering above the new arrivals in a few minutes.

The sick Pannovalan Marshal was helped from his tent and his gaze directed northwards. The cold wind brought tears to his eyes; he mopped absently at them while regarding the advancing foe. His orders were given in a husky whisper to his grim-faced aide-de-camp.

The hallmark of the advancing foe was an orderliness not to be found among the armies of the Savage Continent. Sibornalese cavalry moved at an even pace, protecting the infantry. Straining animal teams dragged artillery pieces forward. Ammunition trains struggled to keep up with the artillery. In the rear rattled baggage carts and field kitchens. More and more columns filled the dull landscape, winding southwards as if

in imitation of the sluggish river. No one among the alarmed forces of
Campannlat could doubt where the columns came from or what they
intended.

The old Marshal's aide-de-camp issued the first order. Troops and
auxiliaries, irrespective of creed, were to pray for the victory of Campannlat in the forthcoming engagement. Four minutes were to be dedicated to the task.

Pannoval had once, been not merely a great nation but a great
religious power, whose C'Sarr's word held sway over much of the continent and whose neighbouring states had sometimes been reduced to
satrapy under the sway of Pannovalan ideology. Four hundred and
seventy-eight years before the confrontation at Isturiacha, however, the
Great God Akhanaba had been destroyed in a now legendary duel. The
God had departed from the world in a pillar of flame, taking with him
both the then King of Oldorando and the last C'Sarr, Kilandar IX.

Religious belief subsequently splintered into a maze of small creeds.
Pannoval, in this present year of 1308, according to the Sibornalese
calendar, was known as the Country of a Thousand Cults. As a result,
life for its inhabitants had become more uncomfortable, more uncertain. All the minor deities were called upon in this hour of crisis, and
every man prayed for his own survival.

Tots of fiery liquor were issued. Officers began to goad their men
into action.

"Battle Stations" sounded raggedly from bugles all over the southern
plain. Orders went out to attack the settlement of Isturiacha immediately and to overwhelm it before the relieving force arrived. Whereupon
a rifle brigade began almost at once to cross the bridge in a businesslike
way, ignoring shellfire from the settlement.

Among the conscripts of Campannlat, whole families clustered together. Men with rifles were accompanied by women with kettles, and
the women by children with teething troubles. Along with the military
chink of bayonet and chain went the clank of dishpans—as later the
shrieks of the newly weaned would merge with the cries of the injured.
Grass and bone were trampled underfoot.

Those who prayed went into action along with those who scorned
prayer. The moment was come. They were tense. They would fight.
They feared to die this day—yet life had been given them by chance,
and luck might yet save that life. Luck and cunning.

Meanwhile the army from the north was hastening its progress
southwards. A strictly disciplined army, with well-paid officers and
trained subordinates. Bugle calls sounded, the snare drum set the pace
of advance. The banners of the various countries of Sibornal were displayed.

Here came troops from Loraj and Bribahr; tribes from Carcampan and primitive Upper Hazziz, who kept the orifices of their bodies plugged on the march, so that evil spirits from the steppes should not enter them; a holy brigade from Shivenink; shaggy highlanders from Kuj-Juvec; and of course many units from Uskutoshk. All were banded together under the dark-browed, dark-visaged Archpriest-Militant, famed Devit Asperamanka, who in his office united Church and State.

Among these nations trudged phagor troops, sturdy, sullen, grouped into platoons, corniculate, bearing arms.

In all, the Sibornalese force numbered some eleven thousand. The force had moved down from Sibornal, travelling across the steppelands which lay as a rumpled doormat before Campannlat. Its orders from Askitosh were to support what remained of the chain of settlements and strike a heavy blow against the old southern enemy; to this end, scarce resources had been assembled, and the latest artillery.

A small year had passed while the punitive force gathered. Although Sibornal presented a united face to the world, there were dissentions within the system, rivalries between nations, and suppressions on the highest level. Even in the choosing of a commander, indecision had made itself felt. Several officers had come and gone before Asperamanka was appointed—some said by no less than the Oligarch himself. During this period, settlements which the expedition had been designed to relieve had fallen to Pannovalan onslaught.

The vanguard of the Sibornalese army was still a mile or so from the circular walls of Isturiacha when the first wave of Pannovalan infantry went in. The settlement was too poor to employ a garrison of soldiers; its farmers had to defend themselves as best they could. A quick victory for Campannlat seemed certain. Unfortunately for the attacking force, there was the matter of the bridge first.

Turmoil broke out on the southern bank. Two rival units and a Randonanese cavalry squadron all tried to cross the bridge at the same time. Questions of precedence arose. There was a scuffle. A yelk slipped with its rider from the bank and fell into the river. Kaci claymores clashed with Randonanese broadswords. Shots were fired.

Other troops attempted to cross the waters by ropeline, but were defeated by the depth of the water and its surly force.

A conflict of mind descended on everyone involved in the confusion at the bridge—except possibly for the Kaci, who regarded battles as an opportunity to consume huge libations of pabowr, their treacherous national drink. This general uncertainty caused isolated misadventures. A cannon exploded, killing two gunners. A yelk was wounded and ran amok, injuring a lieutenant from Matrassyl. An artillery officer plunged from his steed into the river, and was found, when dragged out, to exhibit symptoms of illness which none could mistake.

"The plague!" The news went round. "The Fat Death."

To everyone involved in the operations, these terrors were real, these situations fresh. Yet all had been enacted before, on this very sector of the North Campannlat plain.

As on earlier occasions, nothing went exactly as planned. Isturiacha did not fall to its attackers as punctually as was expected. The allied members of the southern army quarrelled among themselves. Those who attacked the settlement found themselves attacked; an ill-organised running battle took place, with bullets flying and bayonets flashing.

Nor were the advancing Sibornalese able to retain the military organisation for which they were renowned. The young bloods decided to dash forward to relieve Isturiacha at all costs. The artillery, dragged over two hundred miles in order to bombard Pannovalan towns, was now abandoned, shelling being as likely to kill friendly as enemy troops.

Savage engagements took place. The wind blew, the hours passed, men died, yelk and biyelk slipped in their own blood. Slaughter mounted. Then a unit of Sibornalese cavalry managed to break through the melee and capture the bridge, cutting off those of the enemy attacking Isturiacha.

Among the Sibornalese moving forward at that time were three national units: the powerful Uskuti, a contingent from Shivenink, and a well-known infantry unit from Bribahr. All three units were reinforced by phagors.

Riding with the forward Uskuti force went Archpriest-Militant Asperamanka. The supreme commander cut a distinguished figure. He was clad in a suit of blue leather with heavy collar and belt, and his feet were shod in black leather turnover boots, calf-high. Asperamanka was a tall, rather ungainly man, known to be soft-spoken and even sly when not issuing commands. He was greatly feared.

Some said of Asperamanka that he was an ugly man. True, he had a large square head, in which was set a remarkably rectangular face, as if his parents had had their geometries at cross purposes. But what gave him distinction was a permanent cloud of anger which appeared to hover between the brows, the bridge of the nose, and the lids, which shielded a pair of dark eyes ever on the watch. This anger, like a spice, flavoured Asperamanka's least remark. There were those who mistook it for the anger of God.

On Asperamanka's head was an ample black hat and, above the hat, the flag of the Church and of God the Azoiaxic.

The Shiveninki and the Bribahr infantry poured forward to do battle with the enemy. Judging that the day was already turning in Sibornal's favour, the Archpriest-Militant beckoned his Uskuti field commander to one side.

"Just allow ten minutes until you go in," he said.

The field commander protested impatiently, but was overruled.

"Hold back your force," said Asperamanka. He indicated with a black glove the Bribahr infantry, firing steadily as they advanced. "Let them bleed a little."

Bribahr was currently challenging Uskutoshk for supremacy among the northern nations. Its infantry now became involved in a desperate hand-to-hand engagement. Many men lost their lives. The Uskuti force still held back.

The Shiveninki detachment went in. Underpopulated Shivenink was reputed the most peaceable of the northern nations. It was the home of the Great Wheel of Kharnabhar, a holy place; its honours in battle were few.

A mixed squadron of Shiveninki cavalry and phagor troops was now commanded by Luterin Shokerandit. He bore himself nobly, a conspicuous figure, even among many flamboyant characters.

Shokerandit was by now thirteen years and three tenners old. More than a year had passed since he had said good-bye to his bride-to-be, Insil, on leaving Kharnabhar for military duties in Askitosh.

Army training had helped remove from his body the last traces of the weight he had gained during his period of prostration. He was as slender as he was upright, generally carrying himself with a mixture of swagger and apology. Those two elements were never far from his manner, betokening an insecurity he sought to hide.

There were some who claimed that the young Shokerandit had attained his rank of lieutenant ensign only because his father was Keeper of the Wheel. Even his friend Umat Esikananzi, another ensign, had wondered aloud how Luterin would conduct himself in battle. There remained something in Luterin's manner—perhaps an aftereffect of that eclipse which had followed his brother's death—which could distance him from his friends. But in the saddle of his yelk he was the picture of assurance.

His hair grew long. His face was now thin, hawklike, his eye clear. He rode his half-shaven yelk more like a countryman than a soldier. As he urged his squadron forward, the excitement tightening his expression made him a leader to follow.

Driving his beast forward to the disputed bridge, Luterin rode close enough to Asperamanka to hear the commander's words—"Let them bleed a little."

The treachery of it pierced him more than the shrilling bugle. Forcing through the press, spurring on, he raised a gloved fist.

"Charge!" he called.

He waved his own squadron forward. Their lily-white banner bore the great hierogram of the Wheel, its inner and outer circles connected by wavy lines. It flew with them, unfurled above their heads as they surged towards the foe.

Later, when the struggle was over, this charge by Shokerandit's squadron was reckoned one of its pivotal moments.

As yet, however, the fight was far from won. A day passed, and still the fighting continued. The Pannovalan artillery got itself marshalled at last and began a steady bombardment on the Sibornalese rear, causing much damage. Their fire prevented the Sibornalese guns from pulling forward. Another artilleryman went down with the plague, and another.

Not all the settlers in Isturiacha had been employed shooting down Pannovalans. The wives and daughters, every bit as hardy as their menfolk, were dismantling a barn and ripping out its planking.

By next Batalix-rise, they had built two stout platforms, which were thrown across the river. A cheer rose from the Sibornalese. With thunderous sound, metal-shod yelk of the northern cavalry crossed the new bridges and burst among the ranks of Pannoval. Camp followers who, an hour before, had considered themselves safe were shot down as they fled.

The northerners spread out across the plain, widening their front as they went. Piles of dead and dying marked their progress.

When Batalix sank once more, the fight was still undecided. Freyr was below the horizon, and three hours of darkness ensued. Despite attempts by officers of both camps to continue the fighting, the soldiery sank to the ground and slept where they were, sometimes no more than a spear's throw from their opponents.

Torches burned here and there over the disputed ground, their sparks carried away into the night. Many of the wounded gave up the ghost, their last breath taken by the chill wind rolling over them. Nondads crept from their burrows to steal garments from the dead. Rodents scavenged over the spilt flesh. Beetles dragged gobbets of intestine into their holes to provide unexpected banquets for their larvae.

The local sun rose again. Women and orderlies were about, taking food and drink to the warriors, offering words of courage as they went. Even the unwounded were pale of face. They spoke in low voices. Everyone understood that this day's fighting would be decisive. Only the phagors stood apart, scratching themselves, their cerise eyes turned towards the rising sun; for them was neither hope nor trepidation.

A foul smell hung over the battlefield. Filth unnamed squelched underfoot as fresh lines of battle were drawn up. Advantage was taken of every dip in the land, every hummock, every spindly tree. Sniping began again. The fighting recommenced, wearily, without the previous day's will. Where human blood was voided it was red, where phagor, gold.

Three main engagements took place that day. The attack on the Isturiachan perimeters continued, with the Pannovalan invaders managing to occupy and defend a quarter of the settlement against both the settlers and a detachment from Loraj. A manoeuvre by Uskuti forces, eager to make amends for their previous delay, was held south of the bridge, and involved sections of either army; long lines of men were crawling and sniping at each other before engaging in hand-to-hand fighting. Third, there were prolonged and desperate skirmishes taking place in the Campannlatian rear, among the supply wagons. Here Luterin Shokerandit's force again set the pace.

In Shokerandit's contingent, phagors stood side by side with humans. Both stalluns and gillots—the latter often with their offspring in attendance—fought, and male and female died together.

Luterin was gathering honour to his family's name. Battle lust made him secure from caution and, seemingly, injury. Those who fought with him, including his friends, recognised this fearful enchantment and took heart from it. They cut into the Pannovalan enemy without fear or mercy, and the enemy gave way—at first with stubborn resistance, then in a rush. The Shiveninki pursued, on foot or in the saddle. They cut down the defeated as they ran, until their arms were weary of thrusting and stained to the shoulder with blood.

This was the beginning of the rout of the Savage Continent.

Before the forces from Pannoval itself began to retreat, Pannoval's doubtful allies cast about for a safe way home. The battalion from Borldoran had the misfortune to straggle across the path of Shokerandit, and came under attack. Bandal Eith Lahl, their commander, valiantly called on his men to fight. This the Borldoranians did, taking refuge behind their wagons. A gun battle ensued.

The attackers set fire to the wagons. Many Borldoranians were slain. There came a lull in the firing, during which the noise of other encounters reached the ears of the protagonists. Smoke floated over the field, to be whipped away by the wind.

Luterin Shokerandit saw his moment. Calling to the squadron, he dashed forward, Umat Esikananzi at his side, throwing himself at the Borldoranian position.

In the wilds of his homeland, Luterin was accustomed to hunting alone, lost to the world. The intense empathy between hunter and hunted was familiar to him from early childhood. He knew the moment when his mind became the mind of the deer, or of the fierce-horned mountain goat, the most difficult of quarries.

He knew the moment of triumph when the arrow flew home—and, when the beast died, that mixture of joy and remorse, harsh as orgasm, which wounded the heart.

How much greater that perverted victory when the quarry was human! Leaping a barricade of corpses, Luterin came face to face with Bandal Eith Lahl. Their gazes met. Again that moment of identity! Luterin fired first. The Borldoranian leader threw up his arms, dropping his gun, doubling forward to clutch his intestines as they burst outwards. He fell dead.

With the death of their commander, the Borldoranian opposition collapsed. Lahl's young wife was taken captive by Luterin, together with valuable booty and equipment. Umat and other companions embraced him and cheered before seizing what loot they could gather.

Much of the booty the Shiveninki gathered was in the form of supplies, including hay for the animals, to ease the return of the contingent to their distant home in the Shivenink Chain.

On all quarters of the field, the forces of the south suffered mounting defeat. Many fought on when wounded, and continued to fight when hope had gone. It was not courage they lacked, but the favour of their countless gods.

Behind the Pannovalan defeat lay a history of unrest extending over long periods. During the slow deterioration of climate, as life became harder, the Country of a Thousand Cults was increasingly at odds with itself, with one cult opposed to another.

Only the fanatical corps of Takers had the power to maintain order in Pannoval City. This sworn brotherhood of men lived inside the remotest recesses of the Quzint Mountains. It still clung to the ancient god Akhanaba.

The Takers and their rigid discipline had become a byword over the centuries; their presence on the field might have turned the tide of defeat. But in these troublous times, the Iron Formations judged it best to remain close to home.

At the end of that dire day, wind still blew, artillery still boomed, men still fought. Groups of deserters wended their way southwards, towards the sanctuary of the Quzints. Some were peasants who had never held a gun before. The forces of Sibornal were too exhausted to pursue defeated foes. They lit camp fires and sank down into the daze of battle slumber.

The night was filled with isolated cries, and with the creak of carts making their way to safety. Yet even for those who retreated to distant Pannoval, there remained other dangers, fresh afflictions.

Enmeshed in their own affairs, the human beings had no perception of the plain as other than an arena on which they made war. They did not see the place as a network of interrelated forces involved in the continual slow mechanisms of change, its present form being merely the representative of a forgotten series of plains stretching into the remote past. Approximately six hundred species of grass clothed the North Pannovalan flatlands; they were either spreading or in retreat under the dictates of climate; and with the success of any one kind of grass was bound up the fate of the animal and insect chains which fed on it.

The high silica content of the grasses demanded teeth clad in strongly resistant enamel. Impoverished as the plain looked to a casual human glance, the seeds of the grass represented highly nutritious packages— nutritious enough to support numerous rodents and other small mammals. Those mammals formed the prey of larger predators. At the top of that food chain was a creature whose omnivorous capabilities had once made it lord of the planet. Phagors ate anything, flesh or grass.

Now that the climate was more propitious to them, free phagors were moving into lower ground. To the east of the equatorial continent stood the mass of the High Nyktryhk. The Nyktryhk was far more than a barrier between the central plains and the horizons of the Ardent Sea: its series of plateaux, building upwards like steps of a giant staircase, its complex hierarchies of gorge and mountain, constituted a world in itself. Timber gave way to tundralike uplands, and those to barren canyons, excoriated by glaciers. The whole was crowned nine miles above sea level by a dominating plateau, a scalp on nodding terms with the stratosphere.

Ancipital components who had lived the long centuries of summer in the high grasslands secure from man's depredations were descending to more abundant slopes as their refuges were assailed by the furies of oncoming winter. Their populations were building up in the labyrinthine Nyktryhk foothills.

Some phagor communities were already venturing into territories traversed by mankind.

Into the area of battle, under cover of darkness, rode a company of phagors, stalluns, gillots, and their offspring, in all sixteen strong. They were mounted on russet kaidaws, their runts clinging tight against their parents, half smothered in their rough pelages. The adults carried spears in their primitive hands. Some of the stalluns had entwined brambles between their horns. Above them, riding the chilly night air, flew attendant cowbirds.

This group of marauders was the first to venture among the weary battle lines. Others were not far behind.

One of the carts creaking towards Pannoval through the darkness had stuck. Its driver had attempted to drive it straight through an uct, a winding strip of vegetation which broke the plain in an east–west direction. Although much reduced from its summer splendour, the uct still represented a palisade of growth, and the cart was wedged with saplings between both axles.

The driver stood cursing, attempting by blows to make his hoxneys budge.

The occupants of the carts comprised eleven ordinary soldiers, six of them wounded, a hoxney-corporal, and two rough young women who served as cooks, or in any other capacity required. A phagor slave, dehorned, chained, marched behind the vehicle. So overcome by fatigue and illnesses was this company that they fell asleep one on top of the other, either beside the cart or in it. The luckless hoxneys were left to stand between the shafts.

The kaidaw-phagor component came out of the night, moving in single file along the straggling line of the uct. On reaching the cart, they bunched closer together. The cowbirds landed in the grass, stepping delicately together, making noises deep in their throats, as if anxiously awaiting events.

The events were sudden. The huddled band of humans knew nothing until the massive shapes were on them. Some phagors dismounted, others struck from their saddles with their spears.

"Help!" screamed one of the doxies, to be immediately silenced with a thrust to the throat. Two men lying half under the cart woke and attempted to run. They were clubbed from behind. The dehorned phagor slave began to plead in Native Ancipital. It too was despatched without ceremony. One of the wounded men managed to discharge a pistol before he was killed.

The raiders picked up a metal pot and a sack of rations from the cart. They secured the hoxneys on trailing leads. One of them bit out the throat of the groom-corporal, who was still living. They spurred their massive beasts on into the expanses of the plain.

Although there were many who heard the shot and the cries, none on that vast battlefield would come to the aid of those on the cart. Rather, they thanked whatever deity was theirs that they themselves were not in danger, before sinking back into the phantasms of battle slumber.

In the morning by dim first light, when cooking fires were started and the murders discovered, it was different. Then there was a hue and cry. The marauders were far away by that time, but the torn throat of the groom-corporal told its own tale. The word went round. Once more that ancient figure of dread—horned ancipital riding horned kaidaw— was loose in the land. No doubt of it: winter was coming, old terror-legends were stirring.

And there was another dread figure, just as ancient, even more feared. It did not depart from the battlefield. Indeed, it thrived on the conditions, as if gunpowder and excreta were its nectar. Victims of the Fat Death were already showing their horrifying symptoms. The plague was back, kissing with its fevered lips the lips of battlewounds.

Yet this was the dawn of a day of victory.

II

A SILENT PRESENCE

In Luterin Shokerandit's mind, the sense of victory was mingled with many other emotions. Pride like a shrill of trumpets moved in him when he reflected that he was now a man, a hero, his courage proved beyond everyone's doubt but his own. And there was the excitement of knowing that he now had within his clutches a beautiful and powerless woman. Yet not entirely silenced was the continual unease of his thoughts, a flow so familiar that it was part of him. The flow brought before him continually the question of his duty to his parents, the obligations and restrictions at home, the loss of his brother—still painfully unexplained—the reminder that he had lost a year in prostrating illness. Doubt, in short, which even the sense of victory would not entirely still. That was Luterin's perceptual universe at thirteen years; he carried about with him an uncertainty which the scent, the voice, of Toress Lahl by turn soothed and aroused. Since he had no one in whom he could confide, his strategy was to suppress, to behave as if all were well.

So at first light, he threw himself gladly back into action. He had discovered that danger was a sedative.

"One last assault," said Archpriest-Militant Asperamanka. "Then

the day will be ours." His face of anger moved among the thousand
other grim faces, dry of lip, again preparing to fight.

Orders were shouted, phagors mustered. Yelk were watered. Men
spat as they swung themselves again into the saddle. The plain lightened
with Batalix-dawn and human suffering again took on movement. The
rise of the greater luminary was a more gradual event: weakening Freyr
could not climb far above the horizon.

"Forward!" In went the cavalry at walking pace, infantry behind.
Bullets flew. Men staggered and fell.

The Sibornalese attack lasted a little under the hour. Pannovalan
morale was sinking fast. One by one, its units fell into retreat. The
Shiveninki force under Luterin Shokerandit moved off in pursuit, but
was recalled; Asperamanka had no wish to see this young lieutenant
acquire yet more glory. The army of the north withdrew to the northern
side of the river. Its wounded were taken to Isturiacha, to a field ambu-
lance established in some barns. Tenderly, the broken men were laid to
bleed on straw.

As the opponents withdrew from the plain, the cost of battle could
clearly be seen. As if in a gigantic shipwreck, pallid bodies lay strewn
upon their last shore. Here and there, an overturned wagon burned, its
smoke carrying thin across the soiled ground.

Figures moved among the dead. A Pannovalan artillery officer was
one of them, scarcely recognisable. Sniffing at a corpse like a dog, he
wrenched at its jacket until the sleeve came off. He commenced to chew
at the arm. He ate in snatches, face distorted, raising his head to look
about as he chewed each mouthful.

He continued to chew and stare even when a rifleman approached.
The latter raised his weapon and fired at short range. The artillery
officer was blown backwards, to lie motionless with arms outspread. The
rifleman, with others similarly detailed, moved slowly about the death-
field, shooting the devourers of corpses. These were the unfortunates
who had contracted the Fat Death and, in the throes of bulimia, were
driven to feast on the dead. Plague victims were reported on both sides.

As the main body of the Pannovalan army made its untidy retreat,
it left behind a detail of monumental masons.

The masons had no victory to celebrate. Nevertheless, their trade
had to be exercised. Back in Pannoval, the defeated commanders would
be bound to claim a victory. Here, at the limits of their territory, the
lie had to be reinforced in stone.

Although the plain offered no quarries, the masons found a ruinous
monument near at hand. They demolished it and carried its separate
stones nearer to the bridge by the sullen river.

These guildsmen took pride in their craft. With practised care, they
reerected the monument almost stone for stone on its new site. The
master-mason carved upon the base of the monument the name of the

place and the date, and, in grander lettering, the name of the old Chief Marshal.

All stood back and regarded the stonework with pride before returning to their wagon. None who executed this act of practical piety realised that he had demolished a monument commemorating a similar battle fought here eons ago.

The gaunt Sibornalese watched with satisfaction as the defeated enemy withdrew southwards. They had sustained heavy losses, and it was clear there was nothing to be gained by pressing on farther as had once been planned; their other settlements had been wiped out, as refugees in Isturiacha reported.

Those who survived the battle felt relief that the challenge was behind them. Yet there was also a sense in some quarters that the engagement had been a dishonourable thing—dishonourable and even paltry, after the months of training and preparation which had preceded it. For what had it been fought? For ground that would now have to be conceded? For honour?

To quell such doubts, Asperamanka announced a feast to be held that evening in celebration of the Sibornalese victory. Some arang, newly arrived in Isturiacha, would be slaughtered; they and supplies captured from the enemy would provide the fare. The army rations, needed for the journey home, would not be touched.

Preparations for this celebration went forward even while the dead were being buried in nearby consecrated ground. The graves lay in a great shallow vale, open to the wide skies, where aromas of cooking wafted over the corpses.

While the settlers were busy, the army was content to rest. Their trained phagors sprawled with them. It was a day for grateful sleep. For binding of wounds. For repairs to uniforms, boots, harness. Soon they would have to be on the move again. They could not remain in Isturiacha. There was not enough food to support an idle army.

Towards the end of the day, the smells of woodsmoke and roasting meats overcame the lingering stench of the battlefield. Hymns of thanksgiving were offered up to God the Azoiaxic. The men's voices, and the ring of sincerity in them, brought tears to the eyes of some women settlers, whose lives had been saved by these same hymn singers. Rape and captivity would have been their lot after a Pannovalan invasion.

Children who had been locked in the church of the Formidable Peace while danger threatened were now released. Their cries of delight brightened the evening. They clambered among the soldiery, chuckling at the attempts of the men to get drunk on weak Isturiachan beer.

The feast began according to the omens, as dimday snared the world. The roast arang were attacked until nothing but the stained cages of their ribs remained. It was another memorable victory.

Afterwards, three solemn elders of the settlement council approached the Archpriest-Militant and bowed to him. No hand touching took place since Sibornalese of high caste disapproved of physical contact with others.

The elders thanked Asperamanka for preserving the safety of Isturiacha, and the senior among them said formally, "Revered sire, you understand our situation here is that of the last and southernmost settlement of Sibornal. Once there were/continued other settlements farther into Campannlat, even as far as Roonsmoor. All have been overwhelmed by the denizens of the Savage Continent. Before your army will/must retire to our home continent, we beseech you on behalf of all in Isturiacha to leave a strong garrison with us, that we may not/avoidance suffer the same fate as our neighbours."

Their hairs were grey and sparse. Their noses shone in the light of the oil lamps. They spoke in a high dialect larded with slippery tenses, past continuous, future compulsive, avoidance-subjunctive, and the Priest-Militant responded in similar terms, while his gaze evaded theirs.

"Honoured gentlemen, I doubt if you can/will/could support the extra mouths you request. Although this is the summer of the small year, and the weather is clement, yet your crops are poor, as I perceive, and your cattle appear starved." The thundercloud was dark about Asperamanka's brow as he spoke.

The elders regarded each other. Then all three spoke simultaneously.

"The might of Pannoval will return against us."

"We pray/praying every day for better climates as before."

"Without a garrison we die/will/unavoidable."

Perhaps it was the use of the archaic fatalistic future which made Asperamanka scowl. His rectangular face seemed to narrow; he stared down at the table with pursed lips, nodding his head as if making some sly pact with himself.

It was by Asperamanka's command that young Lieutenant Shokerandit sat next to him in a place of honour, so that some of the latter's glory might be deflected to his commander. Asperamanka turned his head to Shokerandit and asked, "Luterin, what reply would/dare you give these elders to their request—in high dialect or otherwise?"

Shokerandit was aware of the danger lurking in the question.

"Since the request comes not from three mouthpieces but from all the mouths in Isturiacha, sire, it is too large for me to answer. Only your experience can discover the fit reply."

The Priest-Militant cast his gaze upwards, to the rafters and their long shadows, and scratched his chin.

"Yes, it could be said that the decision is mine, to speak for the Oligarchy. On the other hand, it could be said that God has already decided. The Azoiaxic tells me that it is no longer possible to maintain this settlement, or the ones to the north of it."

"Sire—"

He raised one triangular eyebrow in his rectangular face as he addressed the elders.

"The crops fail year by year despite all prayer can do. That's a matter of common record. Once these southern settlements of ours grew vines. Now you are hard put to it to raise barley and mouldy potatoes. Isturiacha is no longer our pride but our liability. It is best that the settlement be abandoned. Everyone should leave when the army leaves, two days from now. In no other way can you escape eventual starvation or subjection to Pannoval."

Two of the leaders had to prop up the third. Consternation broke out among all who overheard this conversation. A woman rushed to the Priest-Militant and clasped his stained boots. She cried that she had been born in Isturiacha, together with her sisters; they could not contemplate leaving their home.

Asperamanka rose to his feet and rapped on the table for attention. Silence fell.

"Let me make this matter clear to you all. Remember that my rank entitles me—no, forces me—to speak on behalf of both Church and State. We must be under no illusions. We are a practical people, so I know that you will accept what I say. Our Lord who existed before life, and round whom all life revolves, has set this generation's steps on a stoney path. So be it. We must tread it gladly because it is his will.

"This gallant army who celebrates with you tonight, these brave representatives from all our illustrious nations, must start almost immediately northwards again. If the army is not on the move, it will starve from lack of fodder. If it remains here in Isturiacha, it will starve you with it. As farmers you understand the case. These are laws of God and nature. Our first intention was to press on to conquer Pannoval; such was our charge from the Oligarch. Instead, I must start my men homewards in two days, neither more nor less."

One of the elders asked, "Why such a sudden change of plan, Priest-Militant, when yours was the victory?"

The rectangular face managed a horizontal smile. He looked about at the greasy faces, lit by firelight, hanging on his words, while he timed his utterance with the instinct of a preacher.

"Yes, ours was the victory, thanks be to the Azoiaxic, but the future is not ours. History stands against us. The settlements to the south where we hoped we might find support and supplies are wiped out, destroyed by a savage enemy. The climate deteriorates faster than we judged—you see how Freyr scarce rises from his bed these days. My judgement is that Pannoval, that heathen hole, lies too far for victory, and near enough only for defeat. If we continued there, none of us would return here.

"The Fat Death spreads from the south. We have it among us. The

most courageous warrior fears the Fat Death. Nobody goes into battle
with such a companion by his side.

"So we bow to nature and return home to report our victory to the
Oligarchy in Askitosh. We leave, as I have said, in fifty hours. Use that
time, settlers, use it well. At the end of that period, those of you who
have decided to return to Sibornal with your families will be welcome
to come north with us, under the army's protection.

"Those who decide to stay may do so—and die in Isturiacha. Sibornal
will not, cannot return here. Whatever you decide, you have fifty hours
to do it in, and God bless you all."

Of the two thousand men, women, and children in the settlement,
most had been born there. They knew only the harsh life of the open
fields or—in the case of the more privileged men—of the hunt. They
feared leaving their homes, they dreaded the journey to Sibornal across
the steppes, they even misdoubted the sort of reception they might
receive at the frontier.

Nevertheless, when the case was put to them by the elders at a meeting in the church, most settlers decided to leave. For longer than anyone
could recall, the climate had been worsening, year by small year, with
few remissions. Year by year, connections with the northern homeland
had become more tenuous, and the threat from the south greater.

Tears and lamentations filled the camp. It was the end of all things.
All that they had worked for was to be abandoned.

As soon as Batalix rose, slaves were sent off into the fields to gather
in all the crops they could, while the households packed their worldly
goods. Scuffles broke out between those who intended to leave and a
smaller group who intended to stay at all costs; the latter shouted that
the crops should be preserved.

Three kinds of slaves were driven out to labour in the fields. There
were the phagors, dehorned, who served as something between a slave
proper and a beast of burden. Then there were the human slaves. Lastly
there were slaves of non-human stock, Madis, or, more rarely, Driats.
Both humans and non-humans were regarded as dishonoured persons,
male or female. They were the socially dead.

It counted as a sign of rank to keep slaves; the more slaves, the higher
the ranking. The many Sibornalese who did not keep slaves looked with
envy on those who did, and aspired to own at least a phagor. In easier
times, slaves in the cities of Sibornal had often been maintained in
idleness, almost as if they were pets; in the settlements, slaves and
owners worked side by side. As times grew harsher, the attitudes of the
owners changed. Slaves became drudges, except in rare cases. The slaves
of the settlement, when they returned from the fields, were now put to
building carts, and given other tasks beyond their competence.

When the Priest-Militant's stipulated two days were up, bugles were sounded and everyone had to assemble outside the confines of the settlement.

The quartermasters of the Sibornalese army had set up field kitchens and baked bread for the start of the homeward trek. Rations were going to be short. After a conference, the chiefs of staff announced that the settlers heading north must shoot their slaves or set them free, in order to cut down the number of mouths to be fed. From this order, ancipitals were spared, on the grounds that they could double as beasts of burden and were able to forage for their own food.

"Mercy!" cried both slaves and masters. The phagors stood motionless.

"Kill off the phagors," some men said, with bitterness.

Others, remembering old history, replied, "They were once our masters . . ."

The settlers were now under military law. Protests were of no avail. Without their slaves, householders would be unable to transport many of their goods; still the slaves had to go. Their usefulness had expired.

Over a thousand slaves were massacred in an old riverbed near the settlement. The corpses were given casual burial by phagors, while hordes of carrion birds descended, perching on nearby fences in silence, awaiting their chance. And the wind blew as before.

After the wailing a terrible silence fell.

Asperamanka stood watching the ceremony. As one of the women of the settlement passed near him, weeping, he was moved by compassion and placed a hand on her shoulder.

"Bless you, my daughter. Do not grieve."

She looked up at him without anger, her face blotched by crying. "I loved my slave Yuli. Is it not human to grieve?"

Despite the edict, many slaves were spared by their owners, especially those who were sexually used. They were concealed or disguised, and assembled with the families for the journey. Luterin Shokerandit protected his own captive, Toress Lahl, giving her trousers and a fur cap to wear as a disguise. Without a word, she tucked her long chestnut hair into the confines of the cap and went to hold Luterin's yelk by its bridle.

The marching columns began to form up.

While this bustle was afoot and carts were being overloaded and arrangements were being made for the wounded, six arangherds left slyly, climbing the perimeter, and made off over the plain with their dogs. Theirs was the wild free life.

Asperamanka stood alone by his black yelk, thinking his dark thoughts. He called an orderly to fetch Lieutenant Shokerandit to him.

Luterin arrived, looking, in his unease, very immature.

"Have you two reliable men on reliable mounts, Lieutenant Shokerandit? Two men who would travel fast? I wish news of our victory to get to the Oligarch by the fastest means. Before he hears from other sources."

"I could find two such men, yes. We from Kharnabhar are great riders."

Asperamanka frowned, as if this news displeased him. He produced a leather wallet, which he then tucked under one arm.

"This message must be taken by your reliable men to the frontier town of Koriantura. It is there to be delivered to an agent of mine, and he will deliver it in person to the Oligarch. Your reliable men's responsibility ends at Koriantura, you understand? Report to me when all is ready."

"Sire, I will."

The wallet was pulled from under the arm and held out towards Shokerandit in a blue-gloved hand. It was sealed with the Archpriest-Militant's seal and addressed to the Supreme Oligarch of Sibornal, Torkerkanzlag II, in Askitosh, Capital City of Uskutoshk.

Shokerandit chose two reliable youths, well-known to him and like brothers back in Shivenink. They left their comrades and their fighting phagors and mounted two shorn yelk, with nothing more than packs of provisions and water at their backs. Within the hour they were off across the grasslands, riding northwards with the message for the dread Oligarch.

But the Oligarch of Sibornal, ruling over his vast bleak continent, had spies everywhere. Already a trusted man of his, placed close to the Archpriest-Militant Asperamanka, had ridden off with the news of the engagement, for one particular interest of the Oligarch's was the progress of the plague northwards.

It was the time for farewells. The trek northwards began in some disorder. Each unit started off with its carts, supply animals, phagors, and guns. Their noise filled the shallow landscape. They jostled for the course they had traversed only a few days earlier. The settlers leaving Isturiacha, many for the first time in their lives, went in greatest disarray, clutching children and precious possessions which had found no place on their overloaded carts.

Tearful good-byes were called to those individuals who had made the decision to remain behind. Those exiles stood outside the perimeter, stiff and upright, hands upraised. In their bearing was a consciousness of playing the honourable role, of defying fate—a consciousness, too, of the elemental forces slowly mounting against them. From now on, only the Azoiaxic and their own competence would be their defence.

Luterin Shokerandit sat at the head of the Shivenink force, aware of how his status had changed since last he passed this way. He was now a hero. His captive, Toress Lahl, disguised in her cap and breeches, was forced to ride behind him on his yelk, clinging to his belt. The death of her husband still burned inside her, so that she spoke no word.

In her pain, Toress Lahl showed no fear of the yelk, a creature of mild habits but ferocious aspect. Its horns curled about its shaggy head. Its eyes, shielded by furry lids, gave the beast a watchful look. The curl of its heavy underlip suggested that it despised all that it saw of human history.

The settlement fell away behind the procession. A succession of wearyingly similar valleys began to unfold ahead. The wind blew. The grass rustled.

Silence closed over the procession. But one of the elders who had elected to leave Isturiacha was a garrulous old man who enjoyed the sound of his own voice; he urged his mount over until he was riding beside Shokerandit and his lieutenants, and tried to pass the time of day with him. Shokerandit had little to say. His mind was on the immediate future and the long journey back to his father's house.

"I suppose it really was the Supreme Oligarch who ordered Isturiacha to be closed," he said.

No response. He tried again. "They say the Oligarch is a great despot, and that his hand is harsh over all Sibornal."

"Winter will be harsher," said one of the lieutenants, laughing.

After another mile, the elder said confidentially, "I fancy you young men do not see eye-to-eye with Asperamanka . . . I fancy that in his position you would have ordered a garrison to stay and defend us."

"The decision was not mine to make," Shokerandit said.

The elder smiled and nodded, revealing his few remaining teeth. "Ah, but I saw the expression on your face when he announced his ruling, and I thought to myself—in fact, I said it to the others—'Now there's a young man with a measure of mercy in him . . . a saint,' I said . . ."

"Go away, old man. Save your breath for the ride."

"But to break up a fine settlement just like that. In the old days, we used to send our food surplus back to Uskutoshk. Then to break it up . . . You'd think the Oligarch would be grateful. We're all Sibornalese, are we not? You can't argue against that, can you?"

When Shokerandit had been given, and failed to take, his chance to argue against it, the elder wiped his mouth with the back of his hand and said, "Do you think I was wise to leave, young sir? It was my home, after all. Perhaps we should all have stayed. Perhaps another of the Oligarch's armies—one with more generous impulses towards its compatriots—will be coming this way again in a year or two . . . Well, this is a bitter day for us, that's all I will say."

He was turning his steed's head and about to ride off when Shokerandit reached out suddenly and grasped the collar of his coat, almost unseating the old man.

"You must know nothing of the world if you can't see the truth of the situation more clearly than that! What I think of the Priest-Militant is immaterial. He gave the only judgement possible. Work it out for yourself instead of airing your grievances. You see what a multitude we are? By dimday, we shall have spread out until we stretch from one horizon to the other. Feet, steeds, mouths to be fed . . . the weather becoming more bleak . . . Work it out for yourself, old man."

He gestured over the moving multitude, gestured towards all the grey, black, and russet backs of the soldiers, each back burdened with a pack containing a three-day ration of hardtack, plus unspent ammunition, each back turned towards the south and the pallid sun. The multitude spread wider and wider, to allow the creaking carts more room. It moved with a dull entombed sound which the low hills returned.

Among the men riding went others on foot, often clinging to a saddlestrap. Some carts were piled with equipment, others with wounded, who suffered at every jog of the axle. Loaded phagors trudged by their masters, backs bent, eyes to the ground; the ancipital fighting corps marched slightly apart with their strange jointless stride.

The halt that night was a confused affair. Not all the shouted orders and bugle calls could discipline it. Units settled where they would, pitching tents or not as the case was, to the inconvenience of other units seeking a better site. Animals had to be fed and watered. The watering entailed sending water carts off into the gloom to one side or the other, to seek out streams in the hills. The mutter of men's voices, the restless movement of animals, were never absent during the brief night.

The clouds parted. It grew colder.

The Shivenink contingent formed a close group. Being young, most of them clustered about Luterin Shokerandit, preparing to drink the night away. Their canteens contained the spirit they called yadahl, fermented from seaweed, ruby red in colour. In yadahl they celebrated their recent victory, Luterin's heroism, and the excitement of being on the plains rather than in the familiar mountains of home—and the pleasure of simply being alive, and anything else that entered their heads. Soon they were singing, despite outcries from groups of would-be sleepers.

But the yadahl did not inspire Luterin Shokerandit to sing. He moved apart from his companions from Kharnabhar, his thoughts dwelling on his fair captive. Though she had been married, he doubted if she was as old as he, despite her assured manner; the women of the Savage Continent married young.

He longed to possess her. And yet his parents had committed him to marry in Kharnabhar. Why should that make a difference to what he did here, in the wilds of Chalce? His friends would laugh at his scruples.

His memories returned to the night before the Sibornalese army had left the frontier town of Koriantura to head south. His contingent had been given leave. His friend Umat had tried to persuade him to come on the rampage, but no, he had hung back like a fool.

While the rest of them had gone drinking and whoring, Luterin had walked the cobbled streets alone. He had entered a deuteroscopist's shop, set in a square next to an old theatre.

The deuteroscopist had shown him many curious things, including a small object like a bracelet, said to come from another world, and a tapeworm in a jar one hundred inches long, which the deuteroscopist had charmed from the entrails of a lady of quality (by using a small silver flute which he was prepared to sell at a price).

"Have I the courage for battle?" Luterin had asked the diviner.

Whereupon the old man had become busy on Luterin's skull with calipers and other measuring devices before saying finally, "You are either a saint or a sinner, young master."

"That was not my question. My question was, am I hero or coward?"

"It's the same question. It needs courage to be a saint."

"And none to be a sinner?" He thought of how he had not dared to join his friends.

Much nodding of the hairy old head. "That needs courage too. Everything needs courage. Even that tapeworm needed courage. Would you care to pass your life imprisoned in someone's entrails? Even the entrails of a beautiful lady? If I told you that such a fate lay in your future, would you be happy?"

Impatient with his procrastination, Luterin said, "Are you going to give me an answer to my question?"

"You will answer it yourself very soon. All I will say is that you will display great courage . . ."

"But?"

A smile that pleaded forgiveness. "Because of your nature, young man. You will find yourself both sinner and saint. You will be a hero, but I think I see that you will behave like a scoundrel."

He had recalled that conversation—and the tapeworm—all the way down to Isturiacha. Now he had become a hero, could he dare to be a scoundrel?

As he sat there, drinking but not singing, Umat Esikananzi grabbed him by the boot and pulled him forcibly nearer the fire.

"Don't be glum, old lad. We're still alive, we've played the hero—you especially—and soon we'll be back home." Umat had a big puddingy face rather like his father's, but it beamed now. "The world's a horribly empty place; that's why we're singing—to fill it up with noise. But you've got other things on your mind."

"Umat, your voice is the most melodious I ever heard, including a vulture's, but I'm going to sleep."

Umat waved an admonitory finger. "Ah, I thought as much. That fair captive of yours! Give her hell from me. And I promise not to tell Insil."

He kicked Umat on the shin, "How Insil had the rotten luck to get a brother like you I'll never know."

Taking another swig of yadahl, Umat said cheerfully, "She's a girl, is Insil. Come to think of it, she might be grateful to me if I took you by the scruff of your neck and made you get a bit of practice in."

The whole group roared with laughter.

Shokerandit staggered to his feet and bid them good night. With an effort, he made for his own pitch, close by a cart. Despite the stars overhead, it seemed very dark. There was no aurora in these latitudes as there so often was in Kharnabhar.

Clutching his canteen, he half fell against the bulk of his yelk, which was staked to the ground by the tether burnt through its left ear. He went down on his knees and crawled to where the woman was.

Toress Lahl lay curled up small, hands grasping her knees. She stared up at him without speaking. Her face was pale in the obscurity. Her eyes reflected minutely the litter of stars in the sky above them.

He caught hold of her upper arm and thrust the canteen at her.

"Drink some yadahl."

Mutely she shook her head, a small decisive movement.

He clouted her over the side of the head and thrust the leather bottle in her face. "Drink this, you bitch, I said. It'll put heart in you."

Again the shake of head, but he took her arm and twisted it till she cried out. Then she grasped the canteen and took a swallow of the fiery liquor.

"It's good for you. Drink more."

She coughed and spluttered over it, so that her spittle lighted on his cheek. Shokerandit kissed her forcibly on the lips.

"Have mercy, I beg you. You are not a barbarian." She spoke Sibish well enough, but with a heavy accent, not unpleasant to his ear.

"You are my prisoner, woman. No fine airs from you. Whoever you were, you are mine now, part of my victory. Even the Archpriest would do with you as I intend, were he in my boots . . ." He gulped at the liquid himself, heaved a sigh, slumped heavily beside her.

She lay tense; then, sensing his inertia, spoke. When not crying out, Toress Lahl had a voice with a low liquid quality, as if there were a small brook at the back of her throat. She said, "That elder who came to you this afternoon. He saw himself going into slavery, as I see myself. What did you mean when you said to him that your Archpriest gave the only judgement possible?"

Shokerandit lay silent, struggling with his drunken self, struggling with the question, struggling with his impulse to strike the girl for so blatantly trying to turn the channel of his desires. In that silence, up from his consciousness rose an awareness darker than his wish to violate her, the awareness of an immutable fate. He threw down more liquor and the awareness rose closer.

He rolled over, the better to force his words on her.

"Judgement, you say, woman? Judgement is delivered by the Azoiaxic, or else by the Oligarch—not by some biwacking holy man who would see his own troops bleed to serve his ends." He pointed to his friends carousing by the camp fire. "See those buffoons there? Like me, they come from Shivenink, a good part of the round globe away. It's two hundred miles just to the frontiers of Uskutoshk. Lumbered with all our equipment, with the necessity for foraging for food, we cannot cover more than ten miles a day. How do you think we feed our stomachs in this season, madam?"

He shook her till her teeth rattled and she clung to him, saying in terror, "You feed, don't you? I see your wagons carry supplies and your animals can graze, can't they?"

He laughed. "Oh, we just feed, do we? On what, exactly? How many people do you think we have spread across the face of this land? The answer is something like ten thousand humans and ahumans, together with seven thousand yelk and whatever, including cavalry mounts. Each of those men needs two pounds of bread a day, with an extra one pound of other provisions, including a ration of yadahl. That adds up to thirteen and a half tons every day.

"You can starve men. Our stomachs are hollow. But you must feed animals or they sicken. A yelk needs twenty pounds of fodder every day; which for seven thousand head comes to sixty-two odd tons a day. That makes some seventy-five tons to be carried or procured, but we can only transport nine tons . . ."

He lay silent, as if trying to convert the whole prospect in his mind into figures.

"How do we make up the shortfall? We have to make it up on the move. We can requisition it from villages on our route—only there aren't any villages in Chalce. We have to live off the land. The bread problem alone . . . You need twenty-four ounces of flour to bake a two-pound loaf. That means six and a half tons of flour to be found every day.

"But that's nothing to what the animals eat. You need an acre of green fodder to feed fifty yelk and hoxneys—"

Toress Lahl began to weep. Shokerandit propped himself on an elbow and gazed across the encampment as he spoke. Little sparks glowed in the dark here and there over a wide area, constantly obscured as bodies moved unseen between him and them. Some men sang; others abased themselves and communicated with the dead.

"Suppose we take twenty days to reach Koriantura at the frontier, then our mounts will need to consume two thousand eight hundred acres of fodder. Your dead husband must have had to do similar sums, didn't he?

"Every day an army marches, it spends more time in quest of food than it does in moving forward. We have to mill our own grain—and there's precious little of anything but wild grasses and shoatapraxi in these regions. We have to make expeditions to fell trees and gather wood for the bakeries. We have to set up field bakeries. We have to graze and water the yelk. . . . Perhaps you begin to see why Isturiacha had to be left? History is against it."

"Well, I just don't care," she said. "Am I an animal that you tell me how much these animals eat? You can all starve, the lot of you, for all I care. You got drunk on killing and now you're drunk on yadahl."

In a low voice, he said, "They didn't think I would be any good in battle, so at Koriantura I was put in charge of animal fodder. There's an insult for a man whose father is Keeper of the Wheel! I had to learn those figures, woman, but I saw the sense in them. I grasped their meaning. Year by year, the growing season is getting shorter—just a day at either end. This summer is a disappointment to farmers. The Isthmus of Chalce is famine-stricken. You'll see. All this Asperamanka knows. Whatever you think of him, he's no fool. An expedition such as this, which set out with over eleven thousand men, cannot be launched ever again."

"So my unfortunate continent is safe at last from your hateful Sibish interference."

He laughed. "Peace at a price. An army marching through the land is like a plague of locusts—and the locusts die when there's no food in their path. That settlement will soon be entirely cut off. It's doomed.

"The world is becoming more hostile, woman. And we waste what resources we have. . . ."

Luterin lay against her rigid body, burying his face in his arms. But before sleep and drink overpowered him, he heaved himself up again to ask how old she was. She refused to say. He struck her hard across the face. She sobbed and admitted to thirteen plus one tenner. She was his junior by two tenners.

"Young to be a widow," he said with relish. "And—don't think you'll get off lightly tomorrow night. I'm not the animal fodder officer anymore. No talk tomorrow night, woman."

Toress Lahl made no reply. She remained awake, unstirring, gazing miserably up at the stars overhead. Clouds veiled the sky as Batalix-dawn drew near. Groans of the dying reached her ears. There were twelve more deaths from the plague during the night.

But in the morning those who survived rose as usual, stretched their limbs, and were blithe, joking with friends of this and that as they queued for their rations at the bread wagons. A two-pound loaf each, she remembered bitterly.

There was no soldier on that long trail homeward who would admit to enjoying himself. Yet it was probable that everyone took some pleasure in the routine of making and breaking camp, in the camaraderie, in the feeling that progress was being made, and in the chance of being in a different place each day. There was simple pleasure in leaving behind the ashes of an old fire and pleasure in building a new one, in watching the young flames take hold of twigs and grass.

Such activities, with the enjoyments they generated, were as old as mankind itself. Indeed, some activities were older, for human consciousness had flickered upward—like young flames taking hold—amid the challenges of mankind's first long peregrination eastwards from Hespagorat, when forsaking the protection of the ancipital race and the status of domesticated animal.

The wind might blow chill from the north, from the Circumpolar Regions of Sibornal, yet to the soldiers returning home the air tasted good in their lungs, the ground felt good beneath their feet.

The officers were less lighthearted than their men. For the general soldiery, it was enough to have survived the battle and to be returning home to whatever welcome awaited them. For those who thought more deeply, the matter was more complex. There was the question of the increasingly severe regime within the frontiers of Sibornal. There was also the question of their success.

Although the officers, from Asperamanka downwards, talked repeatedly of victory, nevertheless, under that terrible enantiodromia which gripped the world, under that inevitable and incessant turning of all things into their opposites, the victory came to feel more and more like a defeat—a defeat from which they were retreating with little to show but scars, a list of the dead, and extra mouths to feed.

And always, to heighten this oppressive sense of failure, the Fat Death was among them, keeping pace easily with the fastest troops.

In the spring of the Great Year was the bone fever, cutting down human populations, pruning the survivors to mere skeletons. In the autumn of the Year was the Fat Death, again cutting down human populations, this time melding them into new, more compact shape. So much and more was well enough understood, and accepted with fatalism. But fear still sprang up at the very word "plague." And at such times, everyone mistrusted his neighbour.

On the fourth day, the forward units came across one of the two messengers whom Shokerandit had sent ahead. His body lay face down in a gully. The torso had been gnawed as if by a wild animal.

The soldiers preserved a wide circle about the corpse, but seemed unable to stop looking at it. When Asperamanka was summoned, he too looked long at the dreadful sight. Then he said to Shokerandit, "That silent presence travels with us. There is no doubt that the terrible scourge is carried by the phagors, and is the Azoiaxic's punishment upon us for associating with them. The only way to make restitution is to slay all ancipitals who are on the march with us."

"Haven't we had slaughter enough, Archpriest? Could we not just drive the ancipitals away into the wilds?"

"And let them breed and grow strong against us? My young hero, leave me to deal with what is my business." His narrow face wrinkled into severe lines, and he said, "It is more necessary than ever to get word swiftly to the Oligarch. We must be met and given assistance as soon as possible. I charge you now, personally, to go with a trusted companion and bear my message to Koriantura for onward transmission to the Oligarch. You will do this?"

Luterin cast his gaze on the ground, as he had often done in his father's presence. He was accustomed to obeying orders.

"I can be in the saddle within an hour, sir."

The wrath that seemed always to lurk under Asperamanka's brow, lending heat to his eyes, came into play as he regarded his subordinate.

"Reflect that I may be saving your life by charging you with this commission, Lieutenant Ensign Shokerandit. On the other hand, you may ride and ride, only to discover that the silent presence awaits in Koriantura."

With a gloved finger, he made the Sign of the Wheel on his forehead and turned away.

III

THE RESTRICTIONS
OF PERSONS
IN ABODES ACT

Koriantura was a city of wealth and magnificence. The floors of its palaces were paved with gold, the domes of its pleasure houses lined with porcelain.

Its main church of the Formidable Peace, which stood centrally along the quaysides from which much of the city's wealth came, was furnished with an exuberant luxury quite foreign to the spirit of an austere god. "They'd never allow such beauty in Askitosh," the Korianturan congregation was fond of saying.

Even in the shabbier quarters of the city, which stretched back into the foothills, there were architectural details to catch the eye. A love of ornamentation defied poverty and broke out in an unexpected archway, an unpremeditated fountain in a narrow court, a flight of wrought-iron balconies, capable of lifting the spirits even of the humdrum.

Undeniably, Koriantura suffered from the same divisions of wealth and outlook to be found elsewhere. This might be observed, if in no other way, from the welcome given to a rash of posters from the presses of the Oligarchy at present flooding the cities of Uskutoshk. In the richer quarters, the latest proclamation might draw forth an "Oh, how wise, what a good idea!"; while, at the other end of town, the same pronouncement would elicit merely an "Eh, look what the biwackers are up to now!"

Most frontier towns are dispiriting places, where the lees of one culture wait upon the dregs of the next. Koriantura was an exception in that respect. Although known at an earlier date in its history as Utoshki, it was never, as the old name implied, a purely Uskutoshk city. Exotic peoples from the east, in particular from Upper Hazziz and from Kuj-Juvec beyond the Gulf of Chalce, had infiltrated it and given it an exuberance which most cities of Sibornal did not possess, stamping that energy into its very architecture and its arts.

"Bread's so expensive in Koriantura," went a saying, "because the opera tickets are so cheap."

Then, too, Koriantura was on an important crossroads. It pointed the way southwards, south to the Savage Continent and—war or no war—its traders sailed easily to such ports as Dorrdal in Pannoval. It also stood at one end of the frequented sea route which led to distant Shivenink and the grainlands of Carcampan and Bribahr.

Then again, Koriantura was ancient and its connections with earlier ages had not been broken. It was still possible to find, in the antiquarian stalls of its back streets, documents and books written in antique languages, detailing lost ways of life. Every lane seemed to lead backwards into time. Koriantura had been spared many of the disasters which afflict frontier towns. Behind it stood, range on range, the foothills of the greater hills which in turn formed a footstool to the Circumpolar Mountains, where the ice cap ground its many teeth in cold fury. Before it lay the sea on one side and, on the other, a steep escarpment up which those must climb who would leave the barren steppes of Chalce and enter the city. No invading Campannlatian armies, having survived the march across the steppes, had ever stormed that escarpment.

Koriantura was easy to defend against everything but the impending winter.

Although many military personnel were stationed in Koriantura, they had not succeeded in downgrading it into a garrison town. Peaceful trade could prosper, and the arts to which trade paid somewhat grudging homage. Which was why the Odim family lived there.

The Odim business ranged along one of the wharfs on Climent Quay. The family house stood not far away, in an area that was neither the smartest nor the shabbiest in town. The day's business done, Eedap Mun Odim, chief support of his large family, saw his employees off the premises, checked that the kilns were safe and the windows bolted, and emerged from a side door with his first mistress.

The first mistress was a vivacious lady by name Besi Besamitikahl. She held various packages for Odim as he fussed over locking the door to his premises. When the task was done to his satisfaction, he turned and gave her his gentle smile.

"Now we go our separate ways, and I will see you at home soon."

"Yes, master."

"Walk fast. Watch out for soldiers on the way."

She had only a short walk, round the corner and into Hill Road. He turned in the other direction, towards the local church.

Eedap Mun Odim kept a straight back against middle age. He tucked his beard inside his suede coat. He had a rather grand walk: more of a strut, which he emphasised despite the wind. He turned in at the church in time for service, as he did every evening after business was done. There, like the good Uskuti round him, he humbled himself before God the Azoiaxic. It was only a short service.

Besi Besamitikahl, meanwhile, had reached the Odim house and knocked to be let in by the watchman.

The Odim mansion was the last in the street leading down to Climent Quay. From its upper windows, good views were obtained of the harbour, with the Pannoval Sea beyond. The house had been built two centuries earlier by prosperous merchants of Kuj-Juveci descent. To avoid high Korianturan ground rents, each floor of the five-storey house was larger than the one below. There was ample room under the roof, where the best views were, and little room on the ground floor for anything but the entrance hall and a lair for a surly watchman with his hound. A narrow staircase twisted up through the building. In the many stuffy rooms of the second, third, and fourth floors, many stuffy Odim relations were housed. The top floor belonged to Odim and his wife and children alone. Eedap Mun Odim was a Kuj-Juveci, despite the fact that he had been born in this very house. About Besi it was more difficult to say.

Besi was an orphan who remembered neither of her parents, although rumour had it that she was the daughter of a slave woman from far Dimariam. Some claimed that this slave woman had been accompanying her master on a pilgrimage to Holy Kharnabhar; he had kicked her out on the streets on discovering that she was about to give birth. Whether true or not (Besi would say cheerfully), the story had a ring of truth. Such things happened.

Besi had survived her childhood by dancing in those same streets into which her mother had been kicked. By that dancing, she had come to the notice of a dignitary on his way to the Oligarch's court in Askitosh. After undergoing a variety of abuses at the hands of this man, Besi managed to escape from the house in which she was imprisoned with other women by hiding in an empty walrus-oil vat.

She was rescued from the vat by a nephew of Eedap Mun Odim's, who traded on his uncle's behalf in Askitosh. She so charmed this impressionable young man, particularly when she played her trump card and danced for him, that he took her in marriage. Their joy, however, was brief. Four tenners after their wedding day, the nephew fell from the loft of one of his uncle's warehouses and broke his neck.

As orphan, ex-dancing girl, slave, other dubious things, and now widow, Besi Besamitikahl had no standing in any respectable Uskuti community.

Odim, however, was a Kuj-Juveci, and a mere trader. He protected Besi—not least from the scorn of her relations by marriage—and so discovered that the girl could think as well as employ her more obvious talents. Since she still had her beauty, he adopted her as first mistress.

Besi was grateful. She became rather plump, tried to look less flighty, and assisted Odim in the countinghouse; in time, she could supervise the complex business of ordering his cargoes and scrutinising bills of lading. The days of the Oligarch's court and the walrus oil were now far behind her.

After a brief exchange with the watchman, she climbed the winding stair to her own room.

She paused at one of the tiny kitchens on the second floor, where an old grandmother was busy preparing supper with a maidservant. The old woman gave Besi a greeting, then turned back to the business of making pastry savrilas.

Lamplight gleamed on pale and honey-coloured forms, the simple shapes of bowls and jugs, plates, spoons and sieves, and on dumpy bags of flour. The pastry was being rolled wafer-thin, as mottled old hands moved above its irregular shape. The young maidservant leaned against a wall, looking on vacantly, pulling at her lower lip. Water in a skillet hissed over a charcoal fire. A pecubea sang in its cage.

What Odim said could not be true: that everyday life in Koriantura was threatened—not while the grandmother's capable hands continued to turn out those perfect half-moon shapes, each with a dimpled straight edge and a twist of pastry at one end. Those little pillows of pleasure spoke of a domestic contentment which could not be shattered. Odim worried too much. Odim always worried. Nothing would happen.

Besides, tonight Besi had someone other than Odim on her mind. There was a mysterious soldier in the house, and she had glimpsed him that morning.

All the lower and less favoured rooms were occupied by Odim's many relatives. They constituted almost a small township. Besi held little communication with any of them except the old grandmother, resenting the way they sponged off Odim's good nature. She patrolled through their rooms with her nose in the air, tilting that organ at an angle which enabled her to see what was happening in those enervating abodes.

Here basked remote female Odims of great age, grown monstrous on sloth; younger female Odims, their figures flowing like loose garments under the impact of bearing multitudinous small Odims; adolescent female Odims, willowy, reeking of zaldal perfume, frugal in all but the spots and pallors of indoor life; and the multitudinous small Odims themselves, clad in bright frocks or frocklets, so that boy could scarcely be distinguished from girl, should anyone wish to do so, scurrying, sicking, scuttling, squabbling, suckling, screaming, sulking, or sleeping.

Scattered here and there like cushions, overwhelmed by the preponderance of femininity, were a few Odim males. Castrated by their dependence on Eedap Mun Odim, they were vainly growing beards or smoking veronikanes or bellowing orders never to be complied with, in an effort to assert the ascendancy of their sex. And all these relations and interrelations, of whatever generation, bore, in their sallow skin colour, their listless eye, their heaviness of jowl, their tendency—if an avalanche may be so termed—towards corpulence, flatulence, and somnolence, such a family resemblance that only loathing prompted Besi to distinguish one odious Odim from the next.

Yet the Odims themselves made clear distinctions. Despite their superabundance, they kept each to their own portion of whatever room they occupied, squabbling luxuriously in corners or lounging on clearly defined patches of carpet. Narrow trails were traced out across each crowded chamber, so that any child venturing onto the territory of a rival, even that of a mother's sister, might expect a clout straight off, no questions asked. At night, brothers slept in perfect and jealously guarded privacy within two feet of their voluptuous sisters-in-law. Their tiny portions of real estate were marked off by ribbons or rugs, or draperies hung from lines of string. Every square yard was guarded with the ferocity normally lavished on kingdoms.

These arrangements Besi viewed with jaundiced eye. She saw how the murals on the walls were becoming besmirched by her master's vast family; the sheer fattiness of the Odims was steaming the delicate tones from the plaster. The murals depicted lands of plenty, ruled over by two golden suns, where deer sported amid tall green trees, and young men and women lay by bushes full of doves, dallying or blowing suggestively on flutes. Those idylls had been painted two centuries ago, when the house was new; they reflected a bygone world, the vanished valleys of Kuj-Juvec in autumn.

Both the paintings and their pending destruction fed Besi's mood of discontent; but what she was chiefly seeking was a place where she could enjoy a little privacy away from her master's eye. As she completed her tour in increasing disgust, she heard the outside door slam and the watchdog give its sharp bark.

She ran to the stairwell and looked down.

Her master, Eedap Mun Odim, was returning from worship, and
setting his foot on the lowest stair. She saw his fur hat, his suede coat,
the shine of his neat boots, all foreshortened. She caught glimpses
of his long nose and his long beard. Unlike all his relations, Eedap
Mun Odim was a slender man, a morsel; work and money worries had
contained his waistline. The sole pleasures he allowed himself were
those of the bedchamber, where—as Besi knew—he kept a cautious
mercantile tally of them and entered them in a little book.

Uncertain what to do, she stood where she was. Odim drew level and
glanced at her. He nodded and gave a slight smile.

"Don't disturb me," he said, as he passed. "I shall not want you
tonight."

"As you please," she said, employing one of her well-worn phrases.
She knew what was worrying him. Eedap Mun Odim was a leading light
in the porcelain trade, and the porcelain trade was in difficulties.

Odim climbed to the top of the house and closed his door. His wife
had a meal prepared; its aromas filtered through the house and down to
those quarters where food was less easily come by.

Besi remained on the landing, in the dusk among the odours of
crowded lives, half-listening to the noises all round her. She could hear,
too, the sound of military boots outside, as soldiers marched along the
Climent Quay. Her fingers, still slender, played a silent tune on the
bannister rail.

So it was that she stood concealed from anyone on the floors below
her. So it was that she saw the old watchman creep from his lair, look
furtively about, and slink out the door. Perhaps he was going to find
out what the Oligarch's soldiery were doing. Although Besi had taken
care to befriend him long ago, she knew the watchman would never
dare let her out of the house without Odim's permission.

After a moment, the door opened again. In came a man of military
bearing, whose wide bar of moustache neatly divided his face along its
horizontal axis. This was the man who had provided the secret motive
for Besi's inspection of her domain. It was Captain Harbin Fashnalgid,
their new lodger.

The watchdog came rushing out of the watchman's lair and began to
bark. But Besi was already moving swiftly down the stairs, as nimbly
as a plump little doe down a steep cliff.

"Hush, hush!" she called. The dog turned to her, swinging its black
jowls around and making a mock charge to the bottom of the stairs. It
thrust out a length of tongue and spread saliva across Besi's hand
without in any way relaxing its menacing scowl.

"Down," she said. "Good boy."

The captain came across the hall and clutched her arm. They stared
into each other's eyes, hers a deep deep brown, his a startling grey. He

was tall and slim, a true pure Uskuti, and unlike the proliferating Odims in every way. Thanks to the Oligarch's troop movements, the captain had been billeted on Odim the previous day, and Odim had reluctantly made room for him among his family on the top floor. When the captain and Besi clapped eyes on each other, Besi—whose survival through a hazardous life had had something to do with her impressionability—had fallen in love with him straight away.

A plan came immediately into her mind.

"Let's have a walk outside," she said. "The watchman's not here."

He held her even more tightly.

"It's cold outside."

All he needed was her slight imperious shake of the head, and then they moved together to the door, looking up furtively into the shadows of the staircase. But Odim was closeted in his room and one woman or another would be playing a binnaduria and singing him songs of forsaken fortresses in Kuj-Juvec, where maidens were betrayed and white gloves, dropped one fateful dimday, were forever treasured.

Captain Fashnalgid put his heavy boot to the chest of the hound—which had shown every sign of following them away from captivity—and whisked Besi Besamitikahl into the outside world. He was a man of decision in the realm of love. Grasping her arm firmly, he led her across the courtyard and out of the gate where the oil lamp burned.

As one they turned to the right, heading up the cobbled street.

"The church," she said. Neither said another word, for the cold wind blew in their faces, coming from the Circumpolar Mountains with ice on its breath.

In the street, winding upwards with it, went a line of pale dogthrush trees, wan between the two enclosing stone cliffs of houses. Their leaves flapped in the wind. A file of soldiers, muffled, heads down, walked on the other side of the road, their boots setting up echoes. The sky was a sludgy grey which spread to everything beneath it.

In the church, lights burned. A congregation cried its evensong. Since the church had a slightly bohemian reputation, Odim never came here. Outside its walls, tall man-high stones stood in rows, more correct than soldiers, commemorating those whose days beneath the sky were done. The furtive lovers picked their way among the memorials and hid against a shadowy sheltered wall. Besi put her arms round the captain's neck.

After they whispered to each other for some while, he slid a hand inside her furs and her dress. She gasped at the cold of his touch. When she reciprocated, he grunted at the chill of her hand. Their flesh seemed ice and fire alternately, as they worked closer together. Besi noticed with approval that the captain was enjoying himself and in no great hurry. Loving was so easy, she thought, and whispered in his ear, "It's so simple . . ." He only burrowed deeper.

When they were united, he held her firmly against the wall. She let her head roll back against the rough stone and gasped his name, so newly learned.

Afterwards, they leaned together against the wall, and Fashnalgid said matter-of-factly, "It was good. Are you happy with your master?"

"Why ask me that?"

"I hope one day to make something of myself. Maybe I could buy you, once this present trouble's over."

She snuggled against him, saying nothing. Life in the army was uncertain. To be a captain's chattel was a steep step down from her present security.

He brought a flask from his pocket and drank deeply. She smelt the tang of spirits and thought, Thank God Odim doesn't booze. Captains are all drinkers . . .

Fashnalgid gasped. "I'm not much catch, I know that. The fact is, girl, I'm worried about this errand I'm on. They've landed me with a real sherber this time, my scab-devouring regiment here. I reckon I'm going mad."

"You're not from Koriantura, are you?"

"I'm from Askitosh. Are you listening to me?"

"It's freezing. We'd better get back."

Grudgingly, he came along, taking her arm in the street, which made her feel like a free woman.

"Have you heard the name of Archpriest-Militant Asperamanka?"

With the wind about her head, she gave him only a nod. He wasn't as romantic as she had hoped. But she had been to listen to the Priest-Militant just a tenner earlier, when he had held an outdoor service in one of the city squares. He had spoken so eloquently. His gestures had been pleasing and she had enjoyed watching. Asperamanka!—what a gift of the gab! Later, she and Odim had watched him lead his army through the city and out by the East Gate. The guns had shaken the ground as they passed. And all those young men marching off . . .

"The Priest-Militant took my oath of fealty to the Oligarchy when I was made captain. That's a while ago." He smoothed his heavy moustache. "Now I'm really in trouble. Abro Hakmo Astab!"

Besi was deeply disgusted to hear this curse spoken in her presence. Only the lowest and most desperate would use it. She tugged her arm from his and quickened her pace down the street.

"That man has won a great victory for us against Pannoval. We heard about it in the mess at Askitosh. But it's being kept secret. Secrets . . . Sibornal lives on sherbing secrets. Why do you think they should do that?"

"Can you tip our watchman so that he doesn't make a fuss to Odim?" She paused as they got to the outer gate. A new poster had been pasted up there. She could not read it in the dark, and did not wish to.

As Fashnalgid felt in his pocket for money as she requested, he said, in a flat way that seemed characteristic, "I have been posted to Koriantura to help organise a force which will ambush the Priest-Militant's army when it returns from Chalce. Our orders are to kill every last man, including Asperamanka. What do you make of that?"

"It sounds awful," Besi said. "I'd better go in first in case there's trouble."

Next morning, the wind had dropped, and Koriantura was enveloped in a soft brown fog, through which the two suns gleamed intermittently. Besi watched the thin, parched form of Eedap Mun Odim as he ate breakfast. She was allowed to eat only when he had finished. He did not speak, but she knew that he was in his usual resigned good humour. Even while she recollected the pleasures that Captain Fashnalgid could offer, she knew that she was, despite everything, fond of Odim.

As if to test out his humour, he allowed upstairs one of his distant relations, a second cousin who professed to be a poet, to speak to him.

"I have a new poem, cousin, an Ode to History," said the man, bowing, and began to declaim.

> "Whose is my life? Is history
> To be considered property
> Only of those who make it?
> May not my finer fancy take it
> Into my heart's morality
> And shape it just as it shapes me?"

There was more of the same. "Very good," said Odim, rising and wiping his bearded lips on a silken napkin. "Fine sentiments, well displayed. Now I must get down to the office, if you will excuse me—refreshed by your ornamental thoughts."

"Your praise overwhelms me," said the distant cousin, and withdrew.

Odim took another sip of his tea. He never touched alcohol.

He summoned Besi to his side as a servant came forward to help him into his outdoor coat. His progress down the stairs, Besi obediently following, was slow, as he underwent the barrage of his relations, those Odims who squawked like starlings on every stair, cajoling but not quite begging, jostling but not quite pushing, touching but not quite impacting, calling but not quite shrieking, lifting tiny befrocked Odims for inspection but not exactly thrusting them in his face, as he performed his daily spiral downwards.

"Uncle, little Ghufla can do his arithmetic so well . . ."

· "Uncle, I am so shamed that I must tell you of yet another infidelity when we are private together."

"Darling Unky, stop a while while I tell you of my terrifying dream in which some terrible shining creature like a dragon came and devoured us all."

"Do you admire my new dress? I could dance in it for you?"

"Have you news from my creditor yet, please?"

"Despite your orders, Kenigg kicks me and pulls my hair and makes my life a misery, Unky. Please let me be your servant and escape him."

"You forget those who love you, darling Eedap. Save us from our poverty, as we have pleaded so often."

"How noble and handsome you look today, Unk Eedap . . ."

The merchant showed neither impatience at the constant supplications nor pleasure at the forced compliments.

He pushed slowly through the thickets of Odim flesh, the odours of Odim sweat and perfume, saying a word here and there, smiling, permitting himself once to squeeze the mangolike breasts proffered by a young great-niece, sometimes even going so far as to press a silver coin into a particularly protruding hand. It was as if he considered—and indeed he did—that life could be got through only by sufferance, dispensing as few advantages to others as possible but nevertheless retaining a general humanity for the sake of one's self-respect.

Only when he was outside, as Besi closed the gate after him, did Odim display emotion. There, pasted to his wall, were two posters. He made a convulsive clutch at his beard.

The first poster warned that the PLAGUE was threatening the lives of the citizens of Uskutoshk. The PLAGUE was particularly active in ports, and most especially in THE RENOWNED AND ANCIENT CITY OF KORIANTURA. Citizens were warned that public meetings were henceforth banned. More than four people gathering together in public places would be subject to severe punishment.

Further regulations designed to restrict the spread of THE FAT DEATH would be introduced shortly. BY ORDER OF THE OLIGARCH.

Odim read this notice through twice, very seriously. Then he turned to the second poster.

THE RESTRICTIONS OF PERSONS IN ABODES ACT. After several clauses in obscurantist language, a bolder clause stood out:

> THESE LIMITATIONS as regards houses, demesnes, lodgings, rooms, and other Dwellings apply in particular to any household where the Householder is not of Uskuti blood. Such Persons are shown to be particularly liable to conduct the Spread of the Plague. Their numbers will henceforth be limited to One Person per Two Square Metres floorspace. BY ORDER OF THE OLIGARCH.

The announcement was not unexpected. It was aimed at doing away with the more bohemian quarters of the city, where the Oligarchy

found no favour. Odim's friends on the local council had warned him
of its coming.

Once more, the Uskuti were demonstrating their racial prejudices—
prejudices of which the Oligarchy was quick to take advantage. Phagors
had been banned from walking untended in Sibornalese cities long ago.

It made no difference that Odim and his forebears had lived in this
city for centuries. The Restrictions of Persons in Abodes Act rendered
it impossible for him to protect his family any longer.

Looking quickly about him, Odim tore the poster from the wall,
screwed it up, and thrust it under his suede coat.

This action alarmed Besi almost as much as the captain's oath had
done the previous evening. She had never seen Odim step outside the
law before. His unswerving obedience to what was legal was well-
known. She gasped and stared at him with her mouth open.

"The winter is coming," was all he said. His face was drawn into
bitter lines.

"Take my arm, girl," he said huskily. "We shall have to do something . . ."

The fog rendered the quayside a place of beauty where a copse of
swaying masts floated in the sepia glow. The sea lay entranced. Even
the customary slap of rigging against mast was silent.

Odim wasted no time admiring the view, turning in at the substantial
arcade above which a sign bore the words ODIM FINEST EXPORT
PORCELAINS. Besi followed him past bowing clerks into his inner sanctum.

Odim stopped abruptly.

His office had been invaded. An army officer stood there, warming
himself before the lignite fire and picking his teeth with a match. Two
armed private soldiers stood close, their faces impervious in usual
bodyguard fashion.

By way of greeting, the major spat the match on the floor and
tucked his hands behind his back. He was a tall man in a lumpy coat.
He had grey in his hair and a lumpish protruding mouth, as if his
teeth, imbued with true military spirit, were waiting to burst through
his lips and bite a civilian.

"What can I do for you?" asked Odim.

Without answering the question, the major announced himself in
a way that exercised his teeth prominently.

"I am Major Gardeterark of the Oligarch's First Guard. Well-known,
not liked. From you I will have a list of all times of sailing for ships
in which you have an interest. Today and coming week." He spoke in
a deep voice, giving each syllable an equal weight, as if words were
feet to be firmly planted on a long march.

"I can do that, yes. Will you sit and take some tea?"

The major's teeth moved a little further forward.

"I want that list, nothing else."

"Certainly, sir. Please make yourself comfortable while I get my chief clerk—"

"I am comfortable. Don't delay me. I have waited six minutes for your arrival as it is. The list."

Whatever its disadvantages, the northern continent of Sibornal had reserves of minerals and seams of lignite unmatched elsewhere. It also boasted a variety of clays.

Both china and glass drinking vessels had been in regular use in Koriantura while the little lords of the Savage Continent were still quaffing their rathel from wooden bowls. As early as the spring of the Great Year, potteries as far afield as Carcampan and Uskutoshk were producing porcelains fired in lignite-fuelled kilns at temperatures of 1400° C. Through the centuries, these fine wares were increasingly sought after and collected.

Eedap Mun Odim took little part in porcelain manufacture, though there were auxiliary kilns on his premises. He exported fine china. He exported the local, prized Korianturan porcelain to Shivenink and Bribahr, but mainly to ports in Campannlat, where, as a man of Kuj-Juveci descent, he was more welcome than his Sibornalese competitors. He did not own the ships which carried his wares. He made his business from the entrepreneurial trade, and from banking and financing; he even lent money to his rivals and made a profit.

Most of his wealth came from the Savage Continent, from ports along its northern coastline, from Vaynnwosh, Dorrdal, Dowwel, and from even farther afield, Powachet and Popevin, where his competitors would not trade. It was precisely this adventurous element of Odim's business which made his hand tremble slightly as he handed his sailing timetable over to the major. He knew without being told that foreign names would be bad for the soldier's liver.

The gaze of the major, as brown and foggy as the air outside, travelled down the printed page.

"Your trade goes mainly to alien ports," he said at last, in the leathery voice. "Those ports are all thick with the plague. Our great Oligarch, whom the Azoiaxic preserve, fights to save his peoples from the plague, which has its source in the Savage Continent. There will be no more sailings for any Campannlat port from now on."

"No more sailings? But you can't—"

"I can, and I say no more sailings. Until further notice."

"But my trade, my business, good sir . . ."

"Lives of women and children are more important than your trade. You are a foreigner, aren't you?"

"No. I am not a foreigner. I and my family have lived in Uskutoshk for three generations."

"You're no Uskutoshi. Your looks, your name, tell me that."

"Sir! I am Kuj-Juveci only by distant origins."

"From today, this city is under military law. You obey orders, understand? If you don't, if one of your cargoes leaves this port for foreign parts, you are liable to be tried by military court and sentenced . . ."

The major let the words hang in the air before adding two further words in his best leather: ". . . to death."

"It will mean ruin to me and my family," Odim said, trying to wrench a smile out of himself.

The major beckoned to one of the privates, who produced a document from his tunic.

The major flung it on the table.

"It's all down there. Sign it to prove you've understood." He let his teeth air while Odim blindly signed, before adding, "Yes, as a foreigner, you report every morning in future to my under officer in charge of this whole area. He has just established an office in the warehouse next door, so you've not far to go."

"Sir, let me repeat, I am not a foreigner. I was born round the corner. I am chairman of the local trades committee. Ask them."

As he made a supplicatory gesture, the wadded-up poster fell from under his coat. Besi stepped forward and put it carefully on the fire. The major ignored her, as he had all along. He merely stuck his tongue between teeth and upper lip, as if considering Odim's impertinence, and then said, "You report every morning in future to my under officer, as I just said. He's Captain Fashnalgid and he is next door." At the mention of this name, Besi leant over the fire. It must have been the flames from the burning poster which caused a brief ruddiness in her cheeks.

When Major Gardeterark and his escort had left, Odim shut the door into the packinghouse and sat down by the fire. Very slowly he leaned forward, picked a chewed match from the carpet, and tossed it to the back of the grate. Besi knelt beside him and held his hand. Neither spoke for a long while.

At last Odim said, with an attempt at brightness, "Well, my dear little Besi, we are in difficulty. How can we meet it? Where can we all live? Here, possibly. Perhaps we could do away with that kiln we scarcely use and house some relations in there. The room could be made nice . . . But if I am not allowed to trade, then . . . well, ruin faces us all. They know that, the scoundrels. These Uskuti would have us all for slaves . . ."

"Wasn't he horrible, that man? His eyes, his teeth . . . like a crab."

Odim sat up in his chair and clicked his fingers. "One stroke of luck, though. First, we start work with this Fashnalgid in the next warehouse. By good fortune, that very captain is at present billeted with me—you may have caught a glimpse of him. He reads books and perhaps he's civilised. And my wife feeds him well. Perhaps we could persuade him to help us."

He lifted up Besi's chin so that she was forced to look him in the eye.

"Always something can be done, my chick. Go round to this nice Captain Fashnalgid and invite him here. Say I have a present for him. He'll bend the regulations for us, for sure. And, Besi . . . he's as ugly as a mountain devil, but never mind. Very very sweet to him, eh, chick? As sweet as you can be, and that's very sweet. Even a little tempting—you know? Even if you have to go to the limit. Our lives depend on such things . . ."

He tapped his long nose and smiled coaxingly.

"Run along, my dove. And remember—stop at nothing to win him over."

IV
AN ARMY CAREER

The Restrictions of Persons in Abodes Act met with the mixed reception customary for proclamations from the Oligarchy. In the more privileged sectors of the city people nodded their heads and said, "How wise—what a good idea." Nearer the docks, they exclaimed, "So that's what the biwackers are up to now!"

Eedap Mun Odim gave no overt expression to his dismay when he returned to his crowded five-storey home. He knew that the police would call soon enough to inform him that he was contravening the new law.

That night, he patted his children, settled his modest anatomy beside the slumbrous bulk of his wife, and prepared his mind for pauk. He had said nothing to his spouse, knowing that her display of anguish, her tears, her undoubted rushing from one end of the room to the other, kissing her three children with huge hydropic kisses en route, would do nothing to resolve the problem. As her breath became as regular as a balmy breeze over the autumn valleys of Kuj-Juvec, Odim gathered together his inner resources and underwent that small death which forms the entrance gate to pauk.

For the poor, the troubled, the persecuted, there was always that refuge: the trance state of pauk. In pauk lay communication with those

59

of the family whose life on earth was ended. Neither State nor Church had jurisdiction over the region of the dead. That vast dimension of death placed no restriction on persons; nor did God the Azoiaxic prevail there. Only gossies and the more remote fessups existed in orderly oblivion, sinking towards the unrisen sun of the Original Beholder, she who took to her bosom all who lived.

Like a feather, the tremulous soul of Eedap Mun Odim sank down, to hold what intercourse it might with the gossie of its father, recently departed the world above.

The father now resembled a kind of ill-made gilt cage. It was difficult to see it through the obsidian of nonexistence, but Odim's soul made its obeisances, and the gossie twinkled a little in response. Odim poured out his troubles.

The gossie listened, expressing consolation in little dreadful gasps of bright dust. It in its turn communed with the guttering ranks of ancestors below it. Finally it uttered advice to Odim.

"Gentle and beloved son, your forebears honour you for your tender duty towards our family. Family must rely upon family, since governments do not comprehend families. Your good brother Odirin Nan lives distantly from you, but he, like you, shares an abiding fondness for our poor people. Go to him. Go to Odirin Nan."

The voiceless voice sank away in an eddy. To which Odim faintly responded that he loved his brother Odirin Nan, but that brother lived in far Shivenink; might it not be better instead to cross the mountains and return to a remote branch of the family which still lived in the vales of Kuj-Juvec?

"These here with me who still can make voice advise no return to Kuj-Juvec. The way over the mountains becomes more hazardous every month, as new arrivals here report." The tenuous framework guttered even as it spoke. "Also, the valleys are becoming stonier, and the cattle herds grow thin of flank. Sail westwards to your brother, beloved one, most dutiful of young men. Be advised."

"Father, to hear the melody of your voice is to obey its music."

With tender expressions on either side, the soul of Odim drifted upwards through obsidian, like an ember through a starry void. The ranks of past generations were lost to view. Then came the pain of finding a feeble human body lying inert on a mattress, and seeking entry to it.

Odim returned to his mortal body, weakened by the excursion but strengthened by the wisdom of his father. Beside him, his ample wife breathed on, undistressed in her sleep. He put an arm about her and snuggled into her warmth, like a child against its mother.

There were those—lovers of secrecy—who rose almost at the time that Odim was settling to sleep. There were those—lovers of night—who liked to be about before dawn, in order to get ahead of their fellow men. There were those—lovers of chill—whose constitutions were such that they found satisfaction in the small hours when human resistance is at its lowest.

At the chime of three in the morning, Major Gardeterark stood in his leather trousers, keeping a watchful eye on his reflection in the mirror while he shaved.

Major Gardeterark would have no nonsense with pauk. He regarded himself as a rationalist. Rationalism was his creed, and his family's. He had no belief in the Azoiaxic—Church Parade was a different matter— and less than a belief in pauk. It would never occur to the major that his thinking had confined him to an *umwelt* of living obsidian, through which no light shone.

At present, with each stroke of his cut-throat razor, he contemplated how to make miserable the lives of the inhabitants of Koriantura, as well as the existence of his under officer, Captain Harbin Fashnalgid. Gardeterark believed he had rational family reasons for hating Fashnalgid, over and above the motive of the latter's inefficiency. And he was a rational man.

A great king had once ruled in Sibornal, before the last Weyr-Winter. His name had come down as King Denniss. King Denniss's court had been held in Old Askitosh, and his retreat had been in the mighty edifices now known as the Autumn Palaces. So legend had it.

To his court, King Dennis had summoned learned men from all quarters of the globe. The great king had fought for Sibornal's survival through the grim centuries of Weyr-Winter, and had launched an invasion force across the seas to attack Pannoval.

The king's scholars had compiled catalogues and encyclopaedias. Everything that lived had been named, listed, categorised. Only the slow-pulsed world of the dead had been excluded, in deference to the Church of the Formidable Peace.

A long period of confusion followed the death of King Denniss. The winter came. Then the great families of the seven Sibornalese nations had joined together to form an Oligarchy, in an attempt to rule the continent on rational and scientific lines, as proposed by King Denniss. They had sent learned men abroad to enlighten the natives of Campannlat, even as far afield as the old cultural centre of Keevasien, in the southwest of Borlien.

The autumn of the present Great Year had witnessed one of the most enlightened of the Oligarchy's decrees. The Oligarchy had altered the Sibornalese calendar. Previously, Sibornalese nations, with the exception of backwaters like Upper Hazziz, had adhered to a "so many years after the coronation of Denniss" formula. The Oligarchy abolished such prescriptions.

Henceforth, the small years were numbered as the astronomers directed, in precedence following the small year in which Helliconia and its feebler luminary, Batalix, were most distant from Freyr: in other words, the year of apastron.

There were 1825 small years, each of 480 days, in a Great Year. The present year, the year of Asperamanka's incursion into Chalce, was 1308 After Apastron. Under this astronomical system, nobody could forget where they stood with regard to the seasons. It was a rational arrangement.

And Major Gardeterark rationally finished shaving, dried his face, and commenced in a rational way to brush his formidable teeth, allowing so many strokes for each tooth in front, so many for each behind.

The innovation of the calendar alarmed the peasantry. But the Oligarchy knew what it was doing. It became secretive; it amassed secrets. It deployed its agents everywhere. Throughout the autumn it developed a secret police force to watch over its interests. Its leader, the Oligarch, gradually became a secret person, a figment, a dark legend hovering over Askitosh, whereas—or so the stories said—King Denniss had been loved by his people and seen everywhere.

All the acts and edicts promulgated by the Oligarchy were backed by rational argument. Rationality was a cruel philosophy when practised by the likes of Gardeterark. Rationality gave him good reason for bullying people. He drank to rationality every evening in the mess, sinking his huge teeth deep over the rim of his glass as the liquor ran down his throat.

Now, having finished his toilet, he allowed his servant to help him into his boots and greatcoat. Rationally clad, he went out into the frosty predawn streets.

His under officer, Captain Harbin Fashnalgid, was not rational, but he drank.

Fashnalgid's drinking had begun as an amiable social habit, indulged in with other young subalterns. As Fashnalgid's hatred of the Oligarch grew, so did his need for drink. Sometimes, the habit got out of hand.

One night, back in the officers' mess in Askitosh, Fashnalgid had been peaceably drinking and reading, ignoring his fellow men. A hearty captain by the name of Naipundeg halted by Fashnalgid's chair and laid his hoxney-crop across the open page of the book.

"Always reading, Harbin, you unsociable dog! Filth, I suppose?"

Closing the volume, Fashnalgid said in his flat voice, "This is not a work you would have come across, Naipundeg. It's a history of sacred architecture through the ages. I picked it up from a stall the other day. It was printed three hundred years ago, and it explains how there are

secrets that we in these later days have forgotten. Secrets of contentment, for example. If you're interested."

"No, I'm not interested, to be frank. It sounds wretchedly dull."

Fashnalgid stood up, tucking the little book into a pocket of his uniform. He raised his glass and drained it dry. "There are such block-
heads in our regiment. I never meet anyone interesting here. You don't
mind me saying that? You're proud of being a blockhead, aren't you?
You'd find any book not about filth dull, wouldn't you?"

He staggered slightly. Naipundeg, himself far gone in drink, began
to bellow with rage.

It was then that Fashnalgid blurted out his hatred of the Oligarchy,
and of the Oligarch's increasing power.

Naipundeg, throwing another tumbler of fiery liquor down his throat,
challenged him to a duel. Seconds were summoned. Supporting their
primaries, they jostled them into the grounds of the mess.

There a fresh quarrel broke out. The two officers drove off their
seconds and blazed away at each other.

Most of the bullets flew wild.

All except one.

That bullet hit Naipundeg's face, shattering the zygomatic bone,
entering the head by way of the left eye, and leaving through the rear
of the skull.

In that casual military society, Fashnalgid was able to pass off the
duel as an affair of honour regarding a lady. The court-martial convened
under Priest-Militant Asperamanka was easily satisfied; Naipundeg, an
officer from Bribahr, had not been popular. Fashnalgid was exonerated
of blame. Only Fashnalgid's conscience remained unappeased; he had
killed a fellow officer. The less his drinking companions blamed him,
the more he judged himself guilty.

He applied for leave of absence and went to visit his father's estates
in the undulating countryside to the north of Askitosh. There he intended to reform, to become less prodigal with women and drink.
Harbin's parents were growing senile, although both still rode daily—
as they had done for the past forty years or more—about their fields and
stands of timber.

Harbin's two younger brothers ran the estate between them, aided by
their wives. The brothers were shrewd, sowing coarser crops when finer
ones failed, selecting strains with more rapid growth periods, planting
cold-resistant caspiarn saplings where gales blew down established trees,
building stout fences to keep out the herds of flambreg which came
marauding from the northern plains. Sullen phagors worked under the
brothers' direction.

The estate had seemed a paradise to Harbin in his childhood. Now
it became a place of misery. He saw how much labour was required to

maintain a status quo threatened by the ever worsening season, and wanted no part of it. Every morning, he endured his father's repetitive conversation rather than join his brothers outdoors. Later, he retired to the library, to leaf moodily through old books which had once enchanted him and to allow himself the occasional little drink.

Harbin Fashnalgid had often grieved that he was ineffectual. He could not exert his will. He was too modest to realise how many people, women especially, liked him for this trait. In a more lenient age, he would have been a great success.

But he was observant. Within two days, he had noticed that his youngest brother had a quarrel with his wife. Perhaps the difference between them was merely temporary. But Fashnalgid began offering the woman sympathy. The more he talked to her, the weaker became his resolve to reform. He worked on her. He spun her exaggerated tales about the glamour of military life, at the same time touching her, smiling at her, and feigning a great sorrow which was only part feigned. So he won her confidence and became her lover. It was absurdly easy.

It was an irrational way to behave.

Even in that rambling two-storey parental house, it was impossible that the affair should remain secret. Intoxicated by love, or something like it, Fashnalgid became incapable of behaving with discretion. He lavished absurd gifts on his new partner—a wicker hammock; a two-headed goat; a doll dressed as a soldier; an ivory chest crammed with manuscript versions of Ponipotan legends; a pair of pecubeas in a gilt cage; a silver figurine of a hoxney with a woman's face; a pack of playing cards in ivory inlaid with mother-of-pearl; polished stones; a clavichord; ribbons; poems; and a fossilized Madi skull with alabaster eyes.

He hired musicians from the village to serenade her.

The woman in her turn, driven to ecstasies by the first man in her life who knew nothing about the planting of potatoes and pellamountain, danced for him on his verandah in the nude, wearing only the bracelets he gave her, and sang the wild zyganke.

It could not last. A lugubrious quality in the countryside could not tolerate such exuberance. One night, Fashnalgid's two brothers rolled up their sleeves, rushed into the love nest, kicked over the clavichord, and bounced Fashnalgid out of the house.

"Abro Hakmo Astab!" roared Fashnalgid. Not even the labourers on the estate were allowed to employ that vile expression aloud.

He picked himself up and dusted himself down in the darkness. The two-headed goat chewed at his trousers.

Fashnalgid stationed himself under his old father's window, to shout insults and supplications. "You and Mother have had a happy life, damn you. You're of the generation which regarded love as a matter of will. 'Will marks us from the animal, and love from lovelessness,' as sayeth the poet. You married equally for life, do you hear, you old fool? Well, things are different now. Will's given way to weather . . .

"You have to grab love when you can now. . . . Didn't you have a parental duty to make me happy? Eh? Reply, you biwacking old loon. If you've been so sherbing happy, why couldn't you have given me a happy disposition? You've given me nothing else. Why should I always be so miserable?"

No answer came from the dark house. A doll dressed as a soldier sailed from one of the windows and struck him on the side of the head.

There was nothing for it but to return to his regiment in Askitosh. But news travelled fast among the landed families. Scandal followed Fashnalgid. As ill fortune would have it, Major Gardeterark was an uncle of the woman he had disgraced, of that very woman who had so recently danced naked on his verandah and sung the wild zyganke. From then on, Harbin Fashnalgid's position in the regiment became one of increasing difficulty.

His money went on obscure books as well as women and drink. He was accumulating a case against the Oligarchy, discovering just how the authoritarian grip on the Northern Continent had increased over the sleepy centuries of autumn. Searching through the rubbish in an antiquarian's attic, he came across a list of entitlements of Uskuti estates of over a certain annual income; the Fashnalgid estate was listed. These estates had "pledged assignments to the Oligarchy." This phrase was not explained.

Fashnalgid fulfilled his military duties while brooding over that phrase. He became convinced that he was himself part of the property assigned.

Between bouts of drinking and wenching, he recalled some of his father's boasts. Had not the old man once claimed to have seen the Oligarch himself? Nobody had seen the Oligarch. There was no portrait of the Oligarch. No vision of the Oligarch existed in Fashnalgid's mind, except possibly a pair of great claws reaching over the lands of Sibornal.

After garrison duties one evening, Fashnalgid ordered his personal servant to saddle up his hoxney and rode furiously out to his father's estate.

His brothers snarled at him like curs. Nor was he allowed as much as a glimpse of his light of love, except for a bare arm disappearing round a door as she was dragged away. He recognised the bracelets on the lovely wrist. How they had rattled when she danced!

His father lay on a day sofa, covered in blankets. The old man was scarcely able to answer his son's questions. He rambled and procrastinated. Sadly, Fashnalgid recognised his own portrait in his father's lies and pretences. The old man still claimed once to have seen Torkerkanzlag II, the Supreme Oligarch. But that had been over forty years ago, when his father was a youth.

"The titles are arbitrary," the old man said. "They are intended to conceal real names. The Oligarchy is secret, and the names of the Members and the Oligarch are kept secret, so that no one knows them. Why, they don't know each other . . . Just as well . . ."

"So you never met the Oligarch?"

"No one ever claimed to have met him. But it was a special occasion, and he was in the next room. The Oligarch himself. So it was said at the time. I know he was there, I've always said so. For all I know, he could be a gigantic lobster with pincers stretching to the sky, but he was certainly there that day—and had I opened the door, I would have seen him, pincers and all . . ."

"Father, what were you doing there, what was this special occasion?"

"Icen Hill, it's called. Icen Hill, as you know. Everyone knows where it is, but even the Members of the Oligarchy don't know each other. Secrecy is important. Remember that, Harbin. Honesty's for boys, chastity's for women, secrecy's for men. . . . You know the old saying my grandfather used to tell me, 'There's more than an arm up a Sibornalese sleeve.' Some truth in that."

"When were you at Icen Hill? Did you assign a tithe of this estate to the Oligarchy? I must know."

"Duties, boy, there are duties. Not just buying women dolls and poems. The estate is entitled to protection if you assign it. Winter's coming, you need to look ahead. I'm getting old. Security . . . There's no need for you to be upset. It was agreed before you were born. I *was* someone then, more than you'll ever—you should be a major by now, son, but from what I hear from the Gardeterarks. . . . That's why I signed the agreement that my firstborn son should serve in the Oligarch's army, in the defence of that state act, when I—"

"You sold me into the army before I was born?" Fashnalgid said.

"Harbin, Harbin, sons go into the army. That's gallantry. And piety. It's piety, Harbin. As taught in church."

"You sold me into the army? What precisely did you get in return?"

"Peace of mind. A sense of duty. Security, as I said, only you weren't listening. Your mother approved. You ask her. It was her idea."

"Beholder . . ." Fashnalgid went and poured himself a drink. As he was throwing the liquid down his throat, his father sat up and said in a distinct voice, "I received a promise."

"What sort of a promise?"

"The future. The safety of our estate. Harbin, I was for many years myself a Member. That's why I signed you over to the army. It's an honour—a good career, fine career. You should cultivate young Gardeterark more. . . ."

"You *sold* me. Father, you sold your son like a slave. . . ." He began to weep and rushed from the house. Without looking back, he galloped away from the place where he had been born.

A few months later, he was posted with his battalion to Koriantura, under his enemy, Major Gardeterark, and ordered to prepare a warm reception for Asperamanka's returning army.

Throughout recorded time, Sibornal had existed more unitedly than had the rabble of nations which comprised Campannlat. The nations of the northern continent had their differences, but remained capable of uniting in the face of an external threat.

In milder centuries, Sibornal was a favoured continent. From early in spring of the Great Year, Freyr rose and never set, permitting the northern lands to develop early. Now that the Year was declining, the Oligarchy was busy tightening the reins of its power—bringing in its own kind of darkness.

Both Oligarchy and common people understood that winter, setting in steadily, could burst society apart like a frozen water pipe. The disruptions of cold, the failure of food supplies, could spell the collapse of civilisation. After Myrkwyr, only a few years away, darkness and ice would be upon the land for three and a half local centuries: that was the Weyr-Winter, when Sibornal became the domain of polar winds.

Campannlat would collapse under the weight of winter. Its nations could not collaborate. Whole peoples would revert to barbarism. Sibornal, under more severe conditions, would survive through rational planning.

Still seeking consolation, Harbin Fashnalgid consorted with priests and holy men. The Church was a reservoir of knowledge. There he discovered the answer to Sibornal's survival. Obsessed as he was with his virtual exile from his father's estates, from those fields and woods where his brothers laboured, the answer had the force of revelation. It was not to the land that Sibornal would turn in extremity.

The huge continent was so largely covered by polar ice that it might best be regarded as a narrow circle of land facing sea. In the seas lay Sibornal's winter salvation. Cold seas held more oxygen than warm ones. Come winter, the seas would swarm with marine life. The durable food chains of the ocean would yield their plenty—even when ice covered those estates of his family from which he had been banished.

The awful working of history gnawed at Fashnalgid. He was used to thinking in periods of days or tenners, not in decades and centuries. He fought his disposition to drink and took to spending as much time with priests as with whores. A Priest-Servitant attached to the military chapel in the Askitosh barracks became his confidant. To this priest, Fashnalgid one day confessed his hatred of the Oligarchy.

"The Church also hates the Oligarchy," said the priest mildly. "Yet we work together. Church and State must never be divided. You resent the Oligarchy because, through its pressures, you had to enter the army. But the flaws in your character under which you labour are yours—not the army's, not the Oligarchy's.

"Praise the Oligarchy for its positive aspects. Praise it for its continuity and benevolent power. It is said that the Oligarchy never sleeps. Rejoice that it watches over our continent."

Fashnalgid kept silent. He took a while to understand why the priest's answer alarmed him. It came to him that "benevolent power" was a contradiction in terms. He was an Uskuti, yet he had been virtually sold into the slavery of the army. As for the Oligarchy not sleeping: anyone who went without sleep was by definition inhuman, and therefore as opposed to humanity as the phagors.

It was a while later that he realised the priest had spoken of the Oligarchy in the same terms he might have used for God the Azoiaxic. The Azoiaxic also was praised for his continuity and his benevolent power. The Azoiaxic also watched over the continent. And was it not claimed that the Church never slept?

From that moment on, Fashnalgid ceased to attend church, and was more confirmed than ever in his opinion that the Oligarchy was monstrous.

The Oligarch's First Guard had escaped being sent with Asperamanka's punitive expedition to Northern Campannlat. Only a few weeks later, however, it received orders to move to Koriantura to man the frontier.

Fashnalgid had dared to question Major Gardeterark on the reasons for the move.

"The Fat Death is spreading," said the major brusquely. "We don't want any rioting in the frontier towns, do we?" His dislike of his junior officer was such that he would look him not in the eyes but in the moustache.

On his last evening in Askitosh, Fashnalgid was with a woman he currently favoured, by name Rostadal. She lived in an attic only a few streets from the barracks.

Fashnalgid liked Rostadal and pitied her. She was a displaced person. She had come from a village in the north. She had nothing. No possessions. No political or religious beliefs. No relations. She still managed to be kind, and made her little rented room homely.

He sat up suddenly in bed and said, "I'll have to go, Rostadal. Get me a drink, will you?"

"What's the matter?"

"Just get me a drink. It's the weight of misery. I can't stay."

Without complaint, she slipped out of bed and brought him a glass of wine. He threw it down his throat.

She looked down at him and said, "Tell me what's worrying you."

"I can't. It's too terrible. The world's full of evil." He began dressing. She slipped into her soiled heedrant, wordless now, wondering if he would pay her. There was only an oil lamp to light the scene.

After lacing up his boots, he collected the book he had set by the bedside and put down some sibs for her. His look was one of misery. He saw her fright but could do nothing to comfort her.

"Will you come back, Harbin?" she asked, clasping her hands together.

He looked up at the cracked ceiling and shook his head. Then he went out.

A spiteful rain fell over Askitosh, setting its gutters foaming. Fashnalgid took no notice. He walked briskly through the deserted streets, trying to wear out his thoughts.

On the previous night, a messenger on an exhausted yelk had ridden through these same streets. He rode to the army headquarters at the top of the hill. Although the incident had been hushed up, the officers' mess soon heard about it. The messenger was an agent of the Oligarch. He brought a report concerning Asperamanka, announcing the victory of the latter's forces against the combined armies of Campannlat, and the relief of Isturiacha. Asperamanka, said the report, was expecting a triumphal reception on his return to Sibornal.

The messenger bearing this letter dismounted in the square and fell flat on his face. He was suffering all the symptoms of the Fat Death. A senior officer shot the man as he lay.

Only an hour or two later, Fashnalgid's mother came to him distraught in a dream, saying, "Brother shall slay brother." He was himself dangling from a hook.

Two days passed and Fashnalgid was posted to Koriantura.

As he took his orders from Major Gardeterark, he saw clearly the plan the Oligarch had devised. There was one factor which would disrupt the scheme for carrying Sibornal through the Weyr-Winter. That factor was more divisive even than the cold: the Fat Death. In the madness the Fat Death carried with it, brother would devour brother.

The death of his midnight messenger warned the Oligarch that the return of Asperamanka's army would bring the plague from the Savage Continent. So a rational decision had been arrived at: the army must not return. The First Guard, of which Fashnalgid was an officer, was in Koriantura for one reason only: to annihilate Asperamanka's army as it approached the frontier. The antiplague regulations, the Restrictions of Persons in Abodes Act, imposed on the city and on Eedap Mun Odim, were moves to make the massacre when it came more acceptable to the population.

These terrible reflections ran through Harbin Fashnalgid's head as he lay in his billet under Odim's roof. Unlike Major Gardeterark, he was not an early riser. But he could not escape into sleep from the vision in his head. The Oligarchy he now saw as a spider, sitting somewhere in the darkness, sustaining itself through the ages at whatever cost to ordinary people.

That was the implication behind his father's remark that he had bought the promise of the future. He had bought it with his son's life. His father had ensured his own safety as an ex-Member of the Oligarchy, at no matter what expense to others.

"I'll do something about it," Fashnalgid said, as he finally dragged himself out of bed. Light was filtering through his small window. All round him, he could hear Odim's vast family beginning to stir.

"I'll do something about it," he said as he dressed. And when, a few hours later, the girl Besi Besamitikahl entered his office, he read in the unconscious gestures of her body a willingness to do his will. In that moment, he saw how he might make use of her and Odim to disrupt the Oligarch's plan and save Asperamanka's army.

The escarpment to the east of Koriantura, which tumbled down to the Isthmus of Chalce, marked the point where the continents of Sibornal and Campannlat joined. The broken land south of the escarpment— through which any army must make its way if approaching Uskutoshk— was bounded to the west by marshes which led eventually to the sea, and was terminated after a few miles by the Ivory Cliffs, standing like sentries before the steppes of Chalce.

Harbin Fashnalgid and the three common soldiers under him reined their yelk at the foot of the Ivory Cliffs and dismounted. They discovered a cave from which to shelter from the stiff breeze, and Fashnalgid ordered one of the men to light a small fire. He himself took a pull from a pocket flask.

He had already made some use of Besi Besamitikahl. She had shown him a way through the back alleys of Koriantura which curved downhill. The route avoided the rest of the First Guard mustering along the ramparts of the escarpment. Fashnalgid was now technically a deserter.

He gave a little misleading information to his detail. They would wait here until Asperamanka's army came from the south. They were in no danger. He had a special message from the Oligarch for Asperamanka himself.

They tethered their yelk in lying positions so that they could crouch against the animals and derive benefit from their body warmth. There they waited for Asperamanka. Fashnalgid read a book of love poetry.

Several hours elapsed. The men began to complain to each other. The fog cleared, the sky became a hazy blue. In the distance, they heard the sound of hoofs. Riders were approaching from the south.

The Ivory Cliffs were the bastions of the inhospitable spine of the highlands which curled about the Gulf of Chalce. They formed canyons through which all travellers must go.

Fashnalgid stuffed the poetry volume into his pocket and jumped up. He felt—as so often in the past—the feebleness of his own will. The hours of waiting, not to mention the languorous tenor of the verse, had sapped his determination to act. Nevertheless, he gave crisp orders to his men to position themselves out of sight and stepped from concealment. He expected to see the vanguard of an army. Instead, two riders appeared.

The riders came on slowly. Both slumped wearily in the saddles of their yelk. They were in army uniform, the yelks were half-shaved, in the military fashion. Fashnalgid ordered them to halt.

One of the riders dismounted and came forward slowly. Although he was little more than a stripling, his face was grey with dust and fatigue. "Are you from Uskutoshk?" he called, in a hoarse voice.

"Yes, from Koriantura. Are you of Asperamanka's army?"

"We're a good three days ahead of the main body. Maybe more."

Fashnalgid considered. If he let them through, the two riders would be stopped by Major Gardeterark's lookouts, and might reveal his whereabouts. He did not consider himself capable of shooting them in cold blood—why, this young fellow was a lieutenant ensign. The only way to halt them was to tell them of the fate which hung over the army, and enlist their cooperation.

He stepped one pace nearer the lieutenant. The latter immediately produced a revolver and braced it against his crooked left arm to aim. As he squinted down the barrel, he said, "Come no nearer. You have other men with you."

Fashnalgid spread wide his hands. "Look, don't do that. We mean you no harm. I want to talk. You look as if you might like a drink."

"We'll both stay where we are." Without ceasing to squint down his gun barrel, the lieutenant called to his companion, "Come and get this man's gun."

Licking his lips nervously, Fashnalgid hoped that his men would come to his rescue; on the other hand, he hoped they would not, since that might lead to his being shot. He watched the second rider dismount. Boots, trousers, cloak, fur hat. Face pale, fine-featured, beardless. Something in her movements told Fashnalgid, an expert in such matters, that this was a woman. She came hesitantly towards him.

As she got to him, Fashnalgid pounced, grasping her outstretched wrist, twisting her arm and swinging her violently about. Using her as a shield between him and the other man, he pulled his own gun from its holster.

"Throw your weapon down, or I'll shoot you both." When his order was obeyed, Fashnalgid called to his men. The soldiers emerged cautiously, looking unwarlike.

The rider, having dropped his gun, stood confronting Fashnalgid. Fashnalgid, still pointing his revolver, reached inside his captive's coat with his left hand, and had a feel of her breasts.

"Who the sherb are you?" He burst out laughing, even as the woman began to weep. "You're evidently a man who likes to ride with his creature comforts . . . and a well-developed creature it is."

"My name is Luterin Shokerandit, Lieutenant. I am on an urgent mission for the Supreme Oligarch, so you'd better let me through."

"Then you're in trouble." He ordered one of his men to collect Shokerandit's pistol, turned the woman about, and removed her hat so that he could get a better look at her. Toress Lahl stood before him, her eyes heavy with anger. He patted her cheek, saying to Shokerandit, "We have no quarrel. Far from it. I have a warning for you. I'll put my gun away and we will shake hands like proper men."

They shook hands warily, looking each other over. Shokerandit took Toress Lahl's arm and drew her beside him, saying nothing. As for Fashnalgid, the feel of breasts had heartened him; he was beginning to congratulate himself on his handling of a difficult situation when one of his men, keeping lookout, called that riders were approaching from the north, from the direction of Koriantura.

A line of mounted men was nearing the Ivory Cliffs, a banner flying in its midst. Fashnalgid whipped a spyglass from his coat pocket and surveyed the advance.

He uttered a curse. Leading the advance was none other than his superior, Major Gardeterark. Fashnalgid's first thought was that Besi had betrayed him. But it was more likely that one of the citizens of Koriantura had seen him leaving the city and reported the fact.

The figures were still some distance away.

He had no doubt what his fate would be if he was caught, but there was still time to act. His manner as much as his words persuaded Shokerandit and the woman that they would be safer joining him than trying to escape—particularly when Fashnalgid offered them two of his fresh yelk to ride. Shouting to his men to stand their ground and tell the major that there was a large body of armed men at the other end of the Cliffs, Fashnalgid flung himself onto his yelk and galloped off at full speed, Shokerandit and Toress Lahl following. He kicked one of the unmounted yelk before him.

Some way along the narrow defile of the Cliffs was a side passage. Fashnalgid drove the unmounted yelk straight forward, but led the other down the defile. He calculated that the sound of the escaping yelk would lead the enemy force to ride straight on.

The defile dwindled to a mere fissure. By setting their mounts determinedly forward, they could scramble up the crumbling slope onto higher ground. They emerged in a confusion of broken rock where small trees and bushes, arched over by the prevailing wind, pointed southwards. From somewhere below them came the thunder of the major's troop galloping past.

Fashnalgid wiped the cold sweat from his brow and picked a course westward among the rocks. Both the suns lay close in the sky, Freyr low as ever in the southwest, Batalix sinking to the west.

The three riders urged their mounts through a series of eroded buttes and round a shattered boulder the size of a house, where there were signs of past human habitation. In the distance, beyond where the land fell away, was the glint of the sea. Fashnalgid halted and took a drink from his flask. He offered it to Shokerandit, but the latter shook his head.

"I've taken you on trust," he said. "But now that we have eluded your friends, you had better tell me what is on your mind. My job is to get word to the Oligarch as soon as possible."

"My job is to evade the Oligarch. Let me tell you that if you present yourself before him, you will probably be shot." He told Shokerandit of the reception being arranged for Asperamanka. Shokerandit shook his head.

"The Oligarchy ordered us into Campannlat. If you believe that they would massacre us on our return, then you are plainly crazed."

"If the Oligarch thinks so little of an individual, he will think no more of an army."

"No sane man would wipe out one of his own armies."

Fashnalgid started to gesticulate.

"You are younger than I. You have less experience. Sane men do the most damage. Do you believe that you live in a world where men behave with reason? What is rationality? Isn't it merely an expectation that others will behave as we do? You can't have been long in the army if you believe the mentalities of all men are alike. Frankly, I think my friends mad. Some were driven mad by the army, some were so mad they were attracted to that area of idiocy, some simply have a natural talent for madness. I once heard Priest-Militant Asperamanka preach. He spoke with such force that I believe him to be a good man. There are good men . . . But most officers are more like me, I can tell you—reprobates that only madmen would follow."

There was silence after this outburst, before Shokerandit said coldly, "I certainly would not trust Asperamanka. He was prepared to let his own men die."

" 'Wisdom to madness quickly turns, If suffering is all one learns,' " quoted Fashnalgid, adding, "An army carrying plague. The Oligarchy would be happy to be rid of it, now there's little danger of an attack from Campannlat. Also, it suits Askitosh to get rid of the Bribahr contingent. . . ."

As if there was nothing more to be said, Fashnalgid turned his back on the other two and took a long swig from his flask. As Batalix descended towards the strip of distant sea, clouds drew across the sky.

"So what do you propose doing, if we are not to be trapped between armies?" Toress Lahl asked boldly.

Fashnalgid pointed into the distance. "A boat is waiting across the marshes, lady, with a friend of mine in it. That's where I'm going. You are free to come if you wish. If you believe my story, you'll come."

He swung himself up slowly into the saddle, strapped his collar under his chin, smoothed his moustache, and gave a nod of farewell. Then he kicked his beast into action. The yelk lowered its head and started to move down the rocky slope in the direction of the distant glimmering sea.

Luterin Shokerandit called after the disappearing figure, "And where's that boat of yours bound for?"

The wind stirring the low bushes almost drowned the answer that came back.

"Ultimately, Shivenink . . ."

The gaunt figure on its yelk moved down into a maze of marshes which fringed the sea; whereupon birds rose up under the shaggy hoofs of the animal as small amphibians disappeared underneath them. Things hopped in rain-pocked puddles. Everything that could move fled from the man's path.

Captain Harbin Fashnalgid's mood was too bleak for him even to question why mankind's position should remain so isolated in the midst of all other life. Yet that very question—or rather a failure to perceive the correct answer to the problem it posed—had brought into existence a world which moved above the planet in a circumpolar orbit.

The world was an artificial one. Its designation was Earth Observation Station Avernus. Circling the planet 1500 kilometres above the surface, it could be seen from the ground as a bright star of swift passage, to which the inhabitants of the planet had given the name Kaidaw.

On the station, two families supervised the automatic recording of data from Helliconia as it passed below them. They also saw to it that that data—in all its richness, confusion, and overwhelming detail—was transmitted to the planet Earth, a thousand light-years distant. To this end, the EOS had been established. To this end, human beings from Earth had been born to populate it. The Avernus was at this time only a few Earth years short of its four thousandth birthday.

The Avernus was an embodiment, cast in the most advanced technology of its culture, of the failure to perceive the answer to that age-old problem of why mankind was divorced from its environment. It was the ultimate token in that long divorce. It represented nothing less than the peak of achievement of an age when man had tried to conquer space and to enslave nature while remaining himself a slave.

For this reason, the Avernus was dying.

Over the long centuries of its existence, the Avernus had gone through many crises. Its technology had not been at fault; far from it— the great hull of the station, which had a diameter of one thousand metres, was designed as a self-servicing entity, and small servomechanisms scuttled like parasites over its skin, replacing tiles and instruments as required. The servomechanisms moved swiftly, signalling to each other with asymmetrical arms, like crabs on an undiscovered germanium shore, communicating with each other in a language only the WORK computer which controlled them understood. In the course of forty centuries, the servomechanisms continued to serve. The crabs had proved untiring.

Squadrons of auxiliary satellites accompanied the Avernus through space, or dived off in all directions, like sparks from a fire. They crossed and recrossed in their orbits, some no bigger than an eyeball, others complex in shape and design, coming and going about their automatic business, the gathering of information. Their metaphorical throats were parched for an ever flowing stream of data. When one of them malfunctioned, or was silenced by a passing speck of cosmic debris, a replacement floated free from the service hatches of the Avernus and took its place. Like the crabs, the sparklike satellites had proved untiring.

And inside the Avernus. Behind its smooth plastic partitioning lay the equivalent of an endomorphic skeleton or, to use a more suitably dynamic comparison, a nervous system. This nervous system was infinitely more complex than that of any human. It possessed the inorganic equivalent of its own brains, its own kidneys, lungs, bowels. It was to a large extent independent of the body it served. It resolved all problems connected with overheating, overcooling, condensation, microweather, wastes, lighting, intercommunication, illusionism, and hundreds of other factors designed to make life tolerable physiologically for the human beings on the ship. Like the crabs and the satellites, the nervous system had proved untiring.

The human race had tired. Every member of the eight families— later reduced to six, and now reduced to two—was dedicated, through whatever speciality he or she pursued, to one sole aim: to beam as much information about the planet Helliconia as possible back to distant Earth.

The goal was too rarified, too abstract, too divorced from the bloodstream.

Gradually, the families had fallen victim to a sort of neurasthenia of the senses and had lost touch with reality. Earth, the living globe, had ceased to be. There was Earth the Obligation only, a weight on the consciousness, an anchor on the spirit.

Even the planet before their view, the glorious and changing balloon of Helliconia, burning in the light of its two suns and trailing its cone *of darkness like a wind sock behind it, even Helliconia became an abstract. Helliconia could not be visited. To visit it meant death. Although the human beings on its surface, scrutinised so devotedly from above, appeared identical to Earthlings, they were protected from external contact by a complex virus mechanism as untiring as the mechanisms of the Avernus. That virus, the helico virus, was lethal to the inhabitants of the Avernus at all seasons. Some men and women had gone down to the planet's surface. They had walked there for a few days, marveling at the experience. And then they had died.*

On the Avernus, a defeated minimalism had long prevailed. The attenuation of the spirit had been embraced.

With the slow crawl of autumn across the planet below, as Freyr receded day by day and decade by decade from Helliconia and its sister planets—as the 236 astronomical units of periastron between Batalix and Freyr lengthened to the formidable 710 of apastron—the young on the Observation Station rose up in despair and overthrew their masters. What though their masters were themselves slaves? The era of asceticism was gone. The old were slain. Minimalism was slain. Eudaemonism ruled in its stead. Earth had turned its back on the Avernus. Very well, then Avernus would turn its back on Helliconia.

At first, blind indulgence in sensuality had been sufficient. Just to have broken the sterile bonds of duty was glory enough. But—and in that "but" lies possibly the fate of the human race—hedonism proved insufficient. Promiscuity proved as much of a dead end as abstention.

Cruel perversions grew from the sullied beds of the Avernus. Woundings, slashings, cannibalism, pederasty, paedophilia, intestinal rape, sadistic penetrations of infants and the ageing became commonplace. Flayings, public mass fornications, buggery, irrumation, mutilation—such was the daily diet. Libido waxed, intellect waned.

Everything depraved flourished. The laboratories were encouraged to bring forth more and more grotesque mutations. Dwarfs with enlarged sex organs were succeeded by hybrid sex organs imbued with life. These "pudendolls" moved with legs of their own; later models progressed by labile or preputial musculature. These reproductive leviathans publicly aroused and engulfed each other, or overwhelmed the humans thrown into their path. The organs became more elaborate, more aposematic. They proliferated, reared and tumbled, sucked, slimed, and reproduced. Both those forms resembling priapic fungi and those resembling labyrinthiform ooecia were ceaselessly active, their colours flaring and fading according to their flaccidity or engorgement. In their later stages of evolution, these autonomous genitalia grew enormous; a few became violent, battering like multicoloured slugs at the walls of the glass tanks wherein they spent their somewhat holobenthic existence.

Several generations of Avernians venerated these strange polymorphs almost as if they were the gods which had been banished from the station long ago. The next generation would not tolerate them.

A civil war, a war between generations, broke out. The station became a battleground. The mutated organs broke free; many were destroyed.

The fighting continued over several years and lifetimes. Many people died. The old structure of families, stable for so long, based on patterns of long endurance on Earth, broke down. The two sides became known as the Tans and the Pins, but the labels had little reference to what had once existed.

The Avernus, haven of technology, temple of all that was positive and enquiring in mankind's intellect, was reduced to a tumbled arena, in which savages ran from ambush at intervals to break each other's skulls.

V

A FEW MORE
REGULATIONS

A system of raised dykes covered the marshlands between Koriantura and Chalce like a network of veins. Here and there, the
dykes intersected. The intersections were sometimes marked by
crude gates, which prevented domestic cattle from wandering. The tops
of the dykes were flattened where animals and men had worn paths;
the sides of the dykes were covered in rough lush grass that merged
into reeds bearding the lips of ditches which ran with black water. The
land divided by these features squelched when walked upon. Heavy
domestic cattle crossed it with slow deliberation. They paused occasionally to drink from dark open pools.

Luterin Shokerandit and his captive woman were the only human
figures to be seen for miles. Their progress occasionally disturbed flocks
of birds, which rose up with a clatter, flew low, and suddenly folded
up the fan of their winged cloud to sink in unison back to earth.

As the man drew nearer to the sea and the distance between him
and the following woman increased, so the little streams which flowed
became more subject to the sea and their waters more brackish. The
slight babble they made was a pleasant accompaniment to the plod-
plod of the yelk's hoofs.

Shokerandit halted and waited for Toress Lahl to catch up. He intended to shout to her, but something stopped him.

He was certain that the strange Captain Fashnalgid was lying about the reception which awaited Asperamanka on the Koriantura ridge. To believe Fashnalgid was to cast doubt on the integrity of the system by which Shokerandit lived. All the same, a certain sincerity about the man made Shokerandit cautious. Shokerandit's duty was to bear Asperamanka's message to Koriantura, to the army headquarters there. It was therefore his duty also to avoid possible ambush. The wisest course seemed to be to pretend to believe Fashnalgid's story, and to escape from Chalce by boat.

The light over the marshes was deceptive. Fashnalgid's figure had disappeared. Shokerandit was not making the progress he wished. Though his mount followed the trail along the top of the dykes, every step seemed sluggish and mired in marsh.

"Keep close to me," he called to Toress Lahl. His voice sounded thickly in his head. He jerked the yelk forward again.

The brownish rain had threatened earlier to turn into a regular Uskuti up-and-downer, as the old phrase had it. Its shawls had now trailed away to the south, leaving confused light patterns over the marshes. To some, the scene might appear dismal; yet even in this marginal land, processes were at work which were vital to the health of those species which contended for the mastery of Helliconia, the ancipitals and the humans.

In the tidal waters which fed the pools to either side of the dykes, marine algae flourished. They were similar to laminaria, and concentrated the iodine in the water in their narrow brown fingers. The algae dissipated this chemical into the air in the form of iodine compounds, notably methyl iodine. As the methyl iodine decomposed back into iodine in the atmosphere, the circulation of the winds carried it to every last corner of the globe.

The ancipitals and humans could not live without iodine. Their thyroid glands harvested it in order to regulate their metabolisms with iodine-bearing hormones.

At this time of the Great Year, after the trigger time of the Seven Eclipses, some of those hormones were ensuring that the human species was more susceptible than usual to the depredations of the helico virus.

As if caught in a maze, his thoughts travelled round and round in familiar patterns. Time and again, he recalled his celebrated exploits at Isturiacha—but no longer with pride. His companions had admired him for his courage; each bullet he had fired, each thrust of his sword which had broken an enemy body now had a legendary glamour attached to it. Yet he shrank in horror from what he had done, and from the exultation he had felt while doing it.

And with the woman. On their lonely journey north, he had possessed Toress Lahl. She had lain unresisting while he had his way. He still rejoiced in the feel of her flesh, and in his power over it. Yet he thought with remorse of his intended wife, Insil Esikananzi, waiting back in Kharnabhar. What would she think if she saw him lying with this foreign woman from the heart of the Savage Continent?

These thoughts returned in distorted and fugitive shape until his skull ached. He had a sudden memory of intruding on his mother when a child. He had run thoughtlessly into her chamber. There stood that dim figure, closeted so frequently in her own room (and more so since Favin's death). She was being dressed by her handmaid, watching the process in her misty silver mirror in which the cluster of her bottles of perfume and unguents was reflected like the spires and domes of a distant city.

His mother had turned to confront him, without reproach, without animation, without—as far as he could remember—a word. She was being helped into her gown in preparation for some special grand reception. The gown was one that learned associations of the Wheel had given her, embroidered all over with a map of Helliconia. The countries and islands were depicted in silver, the sea in a bright blue. His mother's hair, as yet undressed, hung down darkly, a waterfall that flowed from the Northern Pole to the High Nyktryhk and beyond. The gown buttoned down the back. He noticed as she stood there and the maid stooped to do up the buttons that the city of Oldorando in the Savage Continent marked the site of his mother's private parts. He had always been ashamed of this observation.

He saw the thick clumps of marsh grass underfoot like coarse body hair. The grass was getting closer in a puzzling way. He saw small amphibians hop away into hair-fringed clefts, heard the tinkle of water travelling, watched tiny pied daisies fall beneath the hoofs of the yelk as if they were stars going into eclipse. The universe came to him. He was slipping from his saddle.

At the last moment, he managed to pull himself upright and land on two feet. His legs felt unfamiliar.

"What's the matter with you?" Toress Lahl asked, riding up.

Shokerandit found difficulty in moving his neck to look up at her. Her eyes were shielded by her hat. Mistrusting her, he reached for his gun, then remembered it was stashed in his saddle. He fell forward, burying his face in the wet fur on his yelk's rump. He sank to the ground and felt himself sliding down the side of the dyke.

A rigidity had seized him. A disconnection between will and ability had taken place. Yet he heard Toress Lahl dismount and come squelching down to where he lay sprawled.

He was conscious of her arm about him, of her voice, anxious, seeking out his sense. She was helping him up. His bones ached. He tried to cry out in pain, but no noise emerged. The bone ache, the limb pain, crept into his skull. His body twisted and contorted. He saw the sky swing on a hinge.

"You're ill," Toress Lahl said. She could not bring herself to mention the dread name of the disease.

She dropped him and let him lie in the wet grasses. She stood looking round at the vacancy of the marshes and at the distant bald hills from which they had come. There were still moving banners of rain in the southern sky. Tiny crabs ran in the streamlets at her feet.

She could escape. Her captor lay powerless at her feet. She could shoot him with his own gun as he lay. A return to Campannlat overland would be too perilous, with an army approaching somewhere over the steppe. Koriantura was only a few miles away to the northwest; the escarpment which marked the frontier could be discerned as a smudge on the horizon. But that was enemy territory. The light was fading.

Toress Lahl walked a few paces back and forth in her indecision. Then she returned to the prone figure of Luterin Shokerandit.

"Come on, let's see what can be done," she said.

She managed to get him back in the saddle with a struggle, climbing up behind him and kicking the yelk into action. Her yelk followed in fits and starts, as if preferring company to a night alone on the marshes.

Prompted by anxiety, she urged increased speed out of her animal. As dusk closed in, she caught a glimpse of Fashnalgid ahead, his figure silhouetted against the distant sea. Raising Shokerandit's revolver, she fired it in the air. Birds rose in flocks from the surrounding land, screaming as they escaped.

In another half hour, night or its half-brother lay over the land, although shimmering pools here and there picked up a reflection from the southwestern horizon, just below which Freyr lurked. Fashnalgid could no longer be seen.

She spurred on the yelk, supporting Shokerandit's body against hers. Water flooded in on either side of the raised path. Its noise was greater now, which Toress Lahl believed indicated that the tide was rising. She had never seen the sea before, and feared it. In the deceptive light, she came on a small jetty before she knew it. A boat was moored there.

The sallow sea lapped with a greedy sound on the mud. Glumaceous grasses and sedges set up a ghostly rustle. Small waves slapped against the side of the dinghy. There was no sign of any human being.

Toress Lahl climbed from the yelk and eased Shokerandit down on a bank. Cautiously she ventured onto the creaking jetty to which the dinghy was moored.

"Got you, then! Hold still!"

She gave a small scream as the shout came from beneath her feet. A man jumped out from under the jetty and pointed his gun at her head.

She smelled the spirits on his breath, saw his luxuriant moustache, and recognised Captain Fashnalgid with relief. He gave a grunt of recognition, expressing not so much pleasure or displeasure as an admission that life was full of tiresome incidents, each demanding to be dealt with.

"Why did you follow? Are you leading Gardeterark after you?"

"Shokerandit is ill. Will you help me?"

He turned and called towards the boat.

"Besi! Come out. It's safe."

Besi Besamitikahl, wrapped in her furs, emerged from under a tarpaulin where she had been sheltering and came forward. She had listened almost without astonishment as the captain, in one of his ranting moods, had outlined his scheme to snatch Asperamanka from the wrath of the Oligarch—as he dramatically put it. He would go such and such a way to meet the Priest-Militant, and would ride with him to the coast, where Besi would have a boat waiting. This boat would be lent by courtesy of Eedap Mun Odim. She must not fail him. Life and honour were at stake.

Odim had listened to this plan, as the girl related it, with delight. Once Fashnalgid became involved in an illegal enterprise, he would be in Odim's power. By all means he should have a little boat, with a boatman to crew her, and Besi should sail round the bay and meet him and his holy companion.

Even while these arrangements had been made, the laws of the Oligarch were pressing down harder on the population. Day by day, street by street, Koriantura was falling under military control. Odim saw all, said nothing, worried for his herd of relations, and made his own plans.

Besi now helped Toress Lahl to carry the stiff body of Luterin Shokerandit into the boat. "Do we have to take these two?" she asked Fashnalgid, staring down with disfavour at the sick man. "They are probably infectious."

"We can't leave them here," Fashnalgid said.

"I suppose you want us to take the yelks too."

The captain ignored this remark and motioned to the boatman to cast off. The yelks stood on the shore, watching them depart. One ventured forward into the mud, slipped, and withdrew. They remained staring at the small boat as it faded away over the water in the direction of Koriantura.

It was cold on the water. While the boatman sat by the tiller, the others crouched below the tarpaulin, out of the wind. Toress Lahl was disinclined to talk, but Besi plied her with questions.

"Where are you from? I can tell by your accent that you're not from here. Is this man your husband?"

Reluctantly, Toress Lahl admitted that she was Shokerandit's slave.

"Well, there are ways out of slavery," said Besi feelingly. "Not many. I'm sorry for you. You could be worse off if your master dies."

"Perhaps I could find a boat in Koriantura which would take me back to Campannlat—once Lieutenant Shokerandit is safe, I mean. Would you help me?"

Fashnalgid said, "Lady, there will be trouble enough for us when we get back to Koriantura, without helping a slave to escape. You're a good-looking woman—you should find a good billet."

Ignoring this last remark, Toress Lahl said, "What kind of trouble?"

"Ah . . . That is up to God, the Oligarch, and a certain Major Gardeterark to devise," said Fashnalgid. He brought out his flask and took a long swig at its contents.

With some reluctance, he offered it round to the women.

From under the tarpaulin, Shokerandit said, slowly but distinctly, "I don't want to go through this again . . ."

Toress Lahl rested a hand on his burning head.

Fashnalgid said, "You'll find that life is essentially a series of repeat performances, my fine lieutenant."

The population of Sibornal was less than forty percent that of its neighbour Campannlat. Yet communications between distant national capitals was generally better than in Campannlat. Roads were good, except in backward areas like Kuj-Juvec; since few centres of population were at a great distance from the coast, seas acted as thoroughfares. It was not a difficult continent to govern, given a strong will in the strongest city, Askitosh.

A street plan of Askitosh revealed a semicircular design, the centre point of which was the gigantic church perched on the waterfront. The light on the spire of this church could be seen for some miles down the coast. But at the rear of the semicircle, a mile or more from the sea, was Icen Hill, upon which granite mound stood a castle housing the strongest will in Askitosh and all Sibornal.

This Will saw to it that the land and sea roads of the continent were busy—busy with military preparation and with that forerunner of military preparation, the poster. Posters appeared in towns and in the smallest hamlets, announcing one new restriction after another. Often the announcements these posters bore came in the guise of concern for the population: they were for the Prevention of the Spread of Fat Death, or they were for the Limitation of Famine, or for the Arrest of Dangerous Elements. But what they all boiled down to was the Curtailment of Individual Liberty.

It was generally supposed by those who worked for the Oligarchy that the Will behind these edicts regulating the lives of the inhabitants of the northern continent was that of the Supreme Oligarch, Torkerkanzlag II. No one had ever seen Torkerkanzlag. If he existed, Torkerkanzlag confined himself to a set of chambers within Icen Hill Castle. But such edicts as were currently being issued were felt to be consistent with the nature of someone who had so little love for his own liberty that he locked himself up in a suite of windowless rooms.

Those higher up the scale had their doubts about the Supreme Oligarch, and often maintained that the title was an empty one, and that government was in the hands of the Inner Chamber of the Oligarchy itself.

It was a paradoxical situation. At the core of the State was an entity almost as nebulous as the Azoiaxic One, the entity at the heart of the Church. Torkerkanzlag was understood to be a name adopted on election, and possibly used by more than one person.

Then there were the obiter dicta supposed to filter down from the very lips—the beak, some claimed—of the Oligarch himself.

"We may debate here in council. But remember that the world is not a debating chamber. It more closely resembles a torture chamber."

"Do not mind being called wicked. It is the fate of rulers. That the people want nothing but wickedness you can ascertain by listening at any street corner."

"Use treachery where possible. It costs less than armies."

"Church and State are brother and sister. One day we will decide which shall inherit the family fortune."

Such morsels of wisdom passed through the oesophagus of the Inner Chamber and into the body politic.

As for that Inner Chamber, it might be expected that those who belonged to it would know the nature of the Will. Such was not the case. The Members of the Inner Chamber—they were now in session and came masked—were collectively even less sure of the nature of the Will than the ignorant citizens living in the damp streets below the hill. So close to that formidable Will were they that they had to fence it about with pretence. The masks they wore were but an outer cover for a barrier of deviousness; these men of power trusted each other so little that each had developed a posture with regard to the nature of the Oligarch by which truth could not be distinguished—much like insects which, if predatory, disguise themselves as something innocuous whereby to deceive their prey, or, if innocuous, as a poisonous species to deceive their predators.

Thus it might be that the Member from Braijth, the capital city of Bribahr, was a man who knew the truth about the Will that dominated them. He might admit to his cronies the truth of the matter; or he might tell a guarded half-truth; or he might lie about the matter in one way or another, according to what best suited him.

And in the case of that Member from Braijth, in actual fact, the degree of his deceitfulness could scarcely be judged, since, beneath the imposed continental unity, guaranteed by many a solemn pact, Uskutoshk was at war with Bribahr, and a force from Askitosh was besieging Rattagon (as far as it was possible to besiege that island fortress).

Moreover, other Members feigned to trust the Member from Braijth according to their secret sympathies with his country's policy in daring to challenge the leadership of Uskutoshk. Feigning was all. Their very sincerity was feigned.

No one was secure in his understanding. With this they were collectively content, finding security in believing that their fellow Members were even more deluded than they were themselves.

Thus the soul of the most powerful city on the planet had at its core a profound obfuscation and confusion. It was with this confusion that they chose to meet the challenge of the changing seasons.

The Members were currently discussing the latest edict to descend from the unseen hand of the Oligarch for their ratification. This was the most challenging edict yet. The edict would prohibit the practice of pauk, as being against the principles of the Church.

If the required legislation was passed, it would entail in practice the stationing of soldiery in every hamlet throughout the continent in order to enforce the prohibition. Since the Members considered themselves learned, they approached the subject by leisurely discourse. Their lips moved thinly under their masks.

"The edict brings under consideration our very nature," said the Member for the city of Juthir, the capital of Kuj-Juvec. "We are speaking here of an age-old custom. But what is age-old is not necessarily sacrosanct. On the one hand, we have our irreplaceable Church, the very basis of Sibornalese unity, with its cornerstone God the Azoiaxic. On the other hand, unrecognised by the Church, we have the custom of pauk, by which living persons can sink their selves down into a trance state to commune with their ancestral spirits. Those spirits, as we know, are supposed to be descending to as well as being descended from the Original Beholder, that inscrutable mother figure. On the one hand is our religion, pure, intellectual, scientific; on the other hand is this hazy notion of a female principle.

"It is necessary for us to prepare for the harsher, colder times to come. For that, we must arm ourselves against the female principle in ourselves, and eradicate it from the population. We must strike at this pernicious cult of the Original Beholder. We must banish pauk. I trust that what I say merely elucidates the wisdom behind this fresh and inspired edict of the Will.

"Furthermore, I would go so far as to claim—"

Most of the Members were old, were accustomed to being old, had persisted in being old for a long while. They met in an ancient room in which all items, whether iron or wood, had been polished over the centuries by a host of slaves until they shone. The iron table at which they propped themselves, the bare floor beneath their slippered feet, the elaborately wrought chairs on which they sat, all gleamed at them. The austere iron panelling on the walls threw back distorted reflections of themselves. A fire glowed in the prison of its grate, sending more smoke than flame through the bars; because it did little to remove the chill of the chamber, the Members were well shrouded in felts, like mummers in an ancient play. The one furnishing to relieve this gloomy brightness was a large tapestry which decked one wall. Against a scarlet background, a great wheel was depicted being rowed through the heavens by oarsmen in pale blue garments; each oarsman smiled towards an astonishing maternal figure from whose nostrils, mouth, and breasts spurted the stars in the sky. This ancient fabric lent a touch of grandeur to the room.

While one or other of their number held forth, the Members sipped at pellamountain cordial and stared down at their fingernails or out through the slit windows, which provided glimpses of an Askitosh sliced into small vertical sections.

"Some claim that the myth of the Original Beholder is a poetical image of the self," said the Member from the distant province of Carcampan. "But it has yet to be established whether such an entity as the self exists. If it does, it may not even be, if I may coin a phrase, master in its own house. It may exist outside our selves. That is to say, the self may be a component of Helliconia itself, since our atoms are Helliconia's. In which case, there may be some danger attendant on destroying contact with the Beholder. That I must point out to the Honourable Members."

"Danger or not, the people must bend to the will of the Oligarch, or the Weyr-Winter will destroy them. We must be cured of our self. Only obedience will see us through three and a half centuries of ice. . . ." This platitude came from the other end of the iron table, where reflections and shadows merged.

The view of Askitosh was executed in sepia monochrome. The city was enfolded in one of the famous "silt mists," a thin curtain of cold dry air which descended on the city from the plateaux ranged behind it. To this was added the smoke rising from thousands of chimneys, as the Uskuti endeavoured to keep themselves warm. The city faded under a shadow partly of its own making.

"On the other hand, communication with our ancestors in the pauk state does much to fortify our selves," said one greybeard. "Particularly when in adversity. I mean, I imagine that few of us here have not derived comfort from communication with the gossies."

In a querulous voice, a Member from the Lorajan port of Ijivibir said, "By the by, why have our scientists not discovered how it is that gossies and fessups are now friendly to our souls, whereas—as well-authenticated testaments tell—they were once always hostile? Could it be a seasonal change, do you think—friendly in winter and summer, hostile in spring?"

"The question will be rendered immaterial if we abandon the gossies and fessups to their own devices by promulgating the edict before us," replied the Member from Juthir.

Through the narrow windows could be seen the roofs of the government printing press where, after only a day or two of further discussion, the edict of the Supreme Oligarch Torkerkanzlag II was turned into print. The posters that fell in their thousands from the flatbed presses announced in bold type that hereafter it would be an Offence to Go into Pauk, whether Secretly or in Company with Others. This was explained as another precaution against the Encroaching Plague. Penalty for contravening the law, One Hundred Sibs and, for a Second Offence, Life Imprisonment.

Within Askitosh itself was a rail transport system worked by steam cars which pulled carriages at the rate of ten or twelve miles an hour. The cars were dirty but dependable, and the system was being extended outside the city. These cars took bundles of the posters to distribution points on the fringes of the city, and to the harbour, whence they were distributed by ship to all points of the compass.

Thus bundles soon arrived at Koriantura. Bill stickers ran about the town, pasting up the terms of the new law. One of those posters was stuck to the wall of the house where Eedap Mun Odim's family had lived for two hundred years.

But that house was now empty, abandoned to the mice and rats. The front door had slammed for the last time.

Eedap Mun Odim left the family house behind him with his usual stiff little walk. He had his pride: his face betrayed nothing of the griefs he felt.

On this special morning, he took a circuitous route to Climent Quay, going by way of Rungobandryaskosh Street and South Court. His slave Gagrim followed, carrying his bag.

He was conscious with every step that this was the last time in his life that he would walk the streets of Koriantura. Throughout all the long past years, his Kuj-Juveci background had led him to think of it as a place of exile; only now did he realise how much it had been home.

His preparations for departure had been made to the best of his ability; fortunately, he still had one or two Uskuti friends, fellow merchants, who had helped him.

Rungobandryaskosh Street branched off to the left, the street steep. Odim paused at the turning just before the churchyard and looked back down the road. His old house stood there, narrow at the base, wide at the top, its boxed-in wooden balcony clinging to it like the nest of some exotic bird, the eaves of its steep roof curving outwards until they nearly touched the eaves of the house opposite. Inside, no plentiful Odim family: only light, shadow, emptiness, and the old-fashioned murals on the walls, depicting life as it had once been in a now almost imaginary Kuj-Juvec. He tucked his beard more firmly inside his coat and marched briskly on.

This was an area of small craftsmen—silversmiths, watchmakers, bookbinders, and artists of various kinds. To one side of the street stood a small theatre where extraordinary plays were produced, plays which could not fill the theatres in the centre of town: plays trafficking in magic and science, fantasies dealing with both possible and impossible things (for both sorts were much alike), tragedies dealing with broken teacups, comedies dealing with wholesale slaughter. Also satires. Irony and satire were things the authorities could neither understand nor abide. So the theatre was often closed. It was closed at present, and the street looked the drabber for it.

In South Court lived an old painter who had painted scenery for the theatre and porcelain for the factory whose wares Odim exported. Jheserabhay was old now, but he still had a sure hand with plates and tureens; equally important, he had often given work to the ample Odim family. Odim valued him, despite his sharp tongue, and had brought him a farewell present.

A phagor let Odim into the house. There were many phagors in South Court. Uskuti in general had a marked aversion to the ancipital kind, whereas artistic people seemed to delight in them, perversely enjoying the immobility and sudden movements of the creatures. Odim himself disliked their sickly milky stench, and passed as quickly as possible into the presence of Jheserabhay.

Jheserabhay sat wrapped in an old-fashioned heedrant, feet up on a sofa, close to a portable iron stove. Beside him rested a picture album. He rose slowly to welcome Odim. Odim sat on a velvet chair facing him, and Gagrim stood behind the chair, clutching the bag.

The old painter shook his head gloomily when he heard Odim's news.

"Well, it's a bad time for Koriantura and no mistake. I've never known worse. It's a poor thing, Odim, that you should be forced to leave because things are so difficult. But then, you never really belonged here, did you—you and your family."

Odim made no gesture. He said slowly, without thinking, "Yes, I do belong here, and your words amaze me. I was born here, within this very mile, and my father before me. This is my home as much as yours, Jhessie."

"I thought you were from Kuj-Juvec?"

"Originally my family was from Kuj-Juvec, yes, and proud of it. But I am both a Sibornalese and a Korianturan, first and foremost."

"Why are you leaving then? Where are you going? Don't look so offended. Have a cup of tea. A veronikane?"

Odim soothed his beard. "The new edicts make it impossible to stay. I have a large family, and I must do the best I possibly can for them."

"Oh, yes, yes, so you must. You have a very large family, don't you? I'm against that sort of thing myself. Never married. No relations. Always stuck to my art. I've been my own master."

Narrowing his eyes, Odim said, "It's not only Kuj-Juveci families which get large. We're not primitive, you know."

"My dear old friend, you are sensitive today. I was levelling no accusations. Live and let live. Where are you going?"

"That I would rather not say. News gets about, whispers become shouts."

The artist grunted. "I suppose you're going back to Kuj-Juvec."

"Since I have never in my life been there, I cannot go *back* there."

"Someone was telling me that your house is full of murals of that part of the world. I hear they are rather fine."

"Yes, yes, old but fine. By a great artist who never made a name for himself. But it is my house no more. I had to sell it, lock, stock, and barrel."

"Well then . . . I hope you got a good price?"

Odim had been forced to accept a miserable price, but he rationed himself to one word: "Tolerable."

"I suppose I shall miss you, though I've got out of the habit of seeing people. I hardly ever go over to the theatre now. This north wind gets into my old bones."

"Jhessie, I have enjoyed your friendship over twenty-five years, give or take a tenner. I have also much appreciated your work; maybe I never paid you enough. Although I am only a merchant, nevertheless I appreciate artistry in others, and no one in all Sibornal has depicted birds on porcelain so finely as you. I wish to give you a parting present, something too delicate to travel, which I think you will appreciate. I could have sold it in the auctions but I thought you made a worthy recipient."

Jheserabhay struggled into a sitting position and looked expectant. Odim motioned to his slave to open the bag. Gagrim lifted out an article which he handed to Odim. Odim raised the article and held it temptingly before the artist's eyes.

The clock was of the shape and size of a goose's egg. Its dial showed the twenty-five hours of the day round the outer circle, with the forty minutes of the hour inside, in the traditional way. But on the hour, when striking—and the mechanism could be made to strike at any time by pressing a button—the clock revolved, so that a second, rear, face was briefly revealed. The rear face also had two hands, the outer indicating the week, tenner, and season of the small year, and the inner the season of the Great Year.

The faces were enamel. The egg was of gold. It was clutched, top and bottom, by a figure in jade, the ample figure of the Original Beholder, seated on a bank which formed the base of the clock. To one side of her, wheat grew; to the other, glaciers. The finish of the whole was exquisite, the detail perfect: the toes which peeped from the Beholder's sandals had discernible nails.

Reaching out his old seamed hands, Jheserabhay took the clock and examined it for a long time without speaking. Tears came to his eyes.

"It's a thing of beauty, no less. The workmanship is wonderful. And I can't recognise its provenance. Is it from Kuj-Juvec?"

Odim bridled up immediately. "We barbarians are excellent craftsmen. Didn't you know we live in sherb but spend our life killing people and turning out exquisite artwork? Isn't that the idea you proud Uskuti have of us?"

"I didn't mean to offend you, Odim."

"Well, it is from Juthir, if you must know, our capital city. Take it. It will cause you to remember me for five minutes." As he said this, he turned away and looked out the window. A file of soldiers under a noncommissioned officer were searching a house opposite. As Odim watched, two of them brought a man out into the square. The man hung his head, as if ashamed to be seen in such company.

"I'm really sorry you are going, Odim," said the artist, placatingly.

"Evil is loose in the world. I have to go."

"I don't believe in evil. Mistakes, yes. Not evil."

"Then perhaps you are afraid to believe it exists. It exists wherever men are. It's in this very room. Good-bye, Jhessie."

He left the old man clutching the clock and trying to rise from his dusty chair.

Odim looked round warily before leaving the shelter of the house where Jheserabhar had his apartment. The file of soldiers had disappeared with their prisoner. He stepped briskly in the Court, dismissing the encounter with the artist from his mind. These Uskuti were always hard to deal with, after all. It would be a relief to get away from them.

He was all prepared to go. Everything had been done legally, if hastily. Since Besi Besamitikahl had collected the deserter Captain Fashnalgid in the dinghy, two days earlier, Odim had concentrated on getting his affairs in order. He had sold his house to an unfriendly relation and his export business to a friendly rival. He had purchased a ship with Fashnalgid's aid. He would join his brother in distant Shivenink. It would be a pleasure to see Odirin again; they could help each other now that they were not as young as they had been. . . .

Struggle is the true guise of hope, Odim said to himself, straightening his back and walking a little faster. Don't give up. Life will be easier, winter or no winter. You must cease to think only of money. Your mind is dominated by the mighty sib. This adversity will be good for you. In Shivenink, with Odirin's help, I'll work less hard. I will paint pictures like Jheserabhay. Perhaps I will become famous.

Nourishing similar warming thoughts, he turned onto the quay. His soliloquy was shattered by a steam gun trundling slowly by. It was heading eastwards. Word had spread that a great battle was soon to commence; it was another reason for leaving the city as fast as possible. The gun was so heavy that it shook the ground as it rattled over the cobbles. Its fiendish engine, pistons pumping, belched out smoke. Small boys ran beside it, shouting in delight.

The steam gun followed Odim along Climent Quay, its heavy barrel pointing in his general direction. With a sense of relief, he turned in at ODIM FINEST EXPORT PORCELAINS, Gagrim pressing hard at his heels.

The showroom and warehouse were in confusion, mainly because nobody was doing any work. Hired workers and slaves alike had seized on the opportunity to do nothing. Many of them hung about the door, watching the gun go by. In their reluctance to step aside, they revealed a lack of respect for their ex-boss.

Never mind, he said to himself. We will sail on the afternoon's tide, and then these people can do what they like.

A messenger came up and told him that the new owner of the premises was upstairs and would like to see him. A hint of danger ran through Odim's mind. It seemed unlikely that the new owner should be here, since the hand-over was not officially operative until midnight, according to the terms of the contract. But he told himself not to be anxious, and mounted the stairs with determination. Gagrim followed behind.

The reception room was an elegantly furnished gallery with windows overlooking the harbour. On the walls hung tapestries and a series of miniatures which had belonged to Odim's grandfather. Examples of Odim porcelain services lay about on polished tables. This was where special customers were brought and the firm's most important business transacted.

This morning, only one special customer stood in the low room, and his uniform indicated that his business was unlikely to be pleasurable.

Major Gardeterark stood with his back to the window, head thrust forward, heavy protruding mouth and lips swivelling in the direction of Eedap Mun Odim. Behind him stood a pale Besi Besamitikahl.

"Come in," he said. "Close the door."

Odim stopped so abruptly on the threshold that Gagrim bumped into him. Major Gardeterark was contained within his huge greatcoat, a garment of coarse texture with buttons like flambreg eyes positioned on it at intervals as if on metallic sentry go, and pockets which stuck out like boxes. It was in every way a coat that might go about its master's business if its master were ever posted out of it. Gardeterark, however, was very much on duty, and watched from among his buttons as Odim closed the door as instructed.

What most frightened Odim was not so much the major as the sight of Besi beside him. One look at the girl's pale face told Odim that she had been forced to give away his secrets. His mind flew immediately to the secrets he had been prevailed upon to hide on these premises: Harbin Fashnalgid, officially posted as a deserter; a lieutenant from the army of the enemy, now suffering from the Fat Death; and a Borldoranian girl, a slave, who was nursing the lieutenant. He knew that what to him was simple humanity in Gardeterark's bulging eyes was a fatal list of crimes.

Anger burned in Odim's slender frame. He was frightened but the anger overcame the fear. He had loathed this odious, cold officer ever since the moment when he had found him downstairs, bloated with his own power. The creature could not be allowed to interfere with Odim's plans to take everyone away to safety.

Nodding his head towards Besi, Gardeterark said, "This slave woman tells me that you are harbouring an army deserter, by name Fashnalgid."

"He was here waiting. He forced me—" Besi began. Gardeterark brought up his gloved hand, which featured several buttons, and struck her across the face.

"You are hiding this deserter on the premises," he said. He took a step towards Odim, at no time glancing at the girl, who had subsided against the wall, clutching her mouth.

Gardeterark produced from one of his boxes a pistol, and pointed it at Odim's stomach. "You are under arrest, Odim, you foreign sherb. Take me to where you are concealing Fashnalgid."

Odim clutched his beard. Although the sight of Besi being struck had frightened him with its violence, it had also stiffened his resolve. He gave the major a blank stare.

"I don't know who you mean."

Prominent yellow teeth came into view, framed between lips which immediately squeezed shut again. It was the major's patent way of smiling.

"You know who I mean. He lodged with you. He went on an expedi-

tion into Chalce with this woman of yours, no doubt with your con-
nivance. He is to be arrested for desertion. A wharf hand witnessed him
come in here. Lead me to him or I'll have you taken to headquarters
for questioning."

Odim stepped back.

"I'll take you to him."

At the far end of the gallery was a door into the rear areas of the
building. As Gardeterark followed Odim, he pushed aside one of the
tables obstructing his easy passage. The chinaware fell to the floor and
shattered.

Odim made no sign. He signalled Gagrim forward. "Unlock this
door."

"Your slave can stay behind," Gardeterark said.

"He carries the keys during the day."

The keys were in Gagrim's pocket, secured by a chain to his belt. He
unlocked the door with trembling hand, letting the two men through.

They were in a passage leading to the rear offices. Odim led the way.
They went down the passage and turned left, where four steps led up
to a metal door. Odim gestured to the slave to unlock it. An especially
large key was needed.

Once through it, they emerged on a balcony overlooking a yard.
Most of the yard was occupied by cartloads of wood and two old-
fashioned kilns. The kilns were generally unused; one was at present
being fired to meet an emergency order from the local garrison, for
whom no great finesse was needed. Otherwise, most of the Odim porcelain came from companies situated elsewhere in Koriantura. Four
company phagors stood about, tending the active kiln. It was old and
inefficiently insulated, and the heat and smoke from it filled the yard.

"Well?" Gardeterark prompted as Odim hesitated.

"He's in a loft over there," Odim said, pointing across the yard.
Their balcony was connected to the loft he indicated by a catwalk
which spanned the yard. It was almost as ancient as the kilns below;
its single wooden railing was rickety and sooted up by smoke from
below.

Odim started cautiously across the catwalk. Halfway across, as the
smoke billowed up, he paused, steadying himself with one hand on the
rail. "I'm feeling ill . . . I'd better go back," he said, turning towards
the major. "Look at the kiln."

Eedap Mun Odim was not a violent man. All his life, he had hated
force. Even signs of anger disgusted him—his own anger not least. He
had schooled himself to politeness and obedience, following the example of his parents. Now he threw away his training. He brought his
arms round with a wide swinging movement, hands clasped together,
and as Gardeterark glanced down, caught him on the back of his neck.

"Gagrim!" Odim called. His slave never moved.

Gardeterark staggered with his side against the rail and tried to bring up the gun. Odim kicked him on the knee and butted him in the chest. The officer seemed twice his size, the greatcoat impenetrable.

He heard the rail crack, heard the revolver explode, felt Gardeterark begin to fall, dropped to the catwalk on hands and knees to save himself from going too.

Gardeterark gave a terrible cry as he fell.

Odim watched him go, arms flailing, his animal mouth open. It was not far to fall. He hit the middle of the dual-chamber kiln which was being fired. The roof of the kiln was strewn with loose brick and rubble. Cracks ran across it, widening, flaring red. As the heat came up, Odim pulled himself flat on the catwalk to avoid burning.

Screaming, the major made an attempt to get to his feet. The greatcoat smouldered like an old shed. His leg plunged into one of the cracks in the roof. The arch collapsed. Fire spewed upwards like splashing liquid. The temperature inside the kiln was over eleven hundred degrees. Gardeterark, already burning, plunged down into it.

Afterwards, Odim had no idea how long he lay on the catwalk. It was Besi, with her split mouth, who ventured along the walk and helped him return to the gallery. Gagrim had fled.

She was hugging him and wiping his burnt face with a cloth. He realised that he was saying to her over and over, "I killed a man."

"You saved us all," she said. "You were very brave, my darling. Now we must get into the ship and sail as soon as possible, before anyone discovers what has happened."

"I killed a man, Besi."

"Say rather that he fell, Eedap." She kissed him with her burst lips and began to cry. He clutched her as he never had before in daylight, and she felt his thin, hard body tremble.

So ended the well-organised part of Eedap Mun Odim's life. From now on, existence would be a series of improvisations. Like his father before him, he had attempted to control his small world by keeping accurate accounts, by balancing ledgers, by cheating no one, by being friendly, by conforming in every way he could. At one stroke, all that was gone. The system had collapsed.

Besi Besamitikahl had to assist him across the quayside to the waiting ship. With them went two others, whose lives had been equally disrupted.

Captain Harbin Fashnalgid had seen his own face crudely portrayed on a red poster as he stepped ashore with Besi, after they had sailed the twenty miles from the jetty in the marshlands. The poster was newly arrived from the local printing works commandeered by the army, and still glistened with the bill sticker's glue. For Fashnalgid,

Odim's ship served the purpose, not only of escaping from Uskutoshk, but of staying close to Besi. Fashnalgid had decided that if he were to reform his life, then he needed a courageous, constant woman to look after him. He stepped up the gangplank briskly, longing to be free of the army and its shadow.

Behind him followed Toress Lahl, widow of the great Bandal Eith Lahl, recently killed in battle. Since her husband's death and her capture by Luterin Shokerandit, her life had become quite as disoriented as Odim's or Fashnalgid's. She now found herself in a foreign port, about to sail for another foreign port. And her captor lay already in the ship, tied down while he underwent the agony of the Fat Death. She might elude him; but Toress Lahl knew of no way in which a woman of Oldorando could return home safely from Sibornal. So she remained to tend Shokerandit, hoping to earn his gratitude thereby if he survived the plague.

Of the plague, she had less fear than the others. Back home in Oldorando, she had worked as a doctor. The word that inspired fear and curiosity in her was the name of Shokerandit's homeland, Kharnabhar, a word which embodied legend and romance when spoken from the distance of Borldoran.

To acquire his ship, Odim had worked through intermediaries, local friends who knew useful people in the Priest-Sailors Guild. The money from the sale of his house and company had all gone to purchase the *New Season*. It now lay moored alongside Climent Quay, a two-masted brig of 639 tons, square-rigged on fore- and mainmasts. The vessel had been built twenty years earlier, in Askitosh shipyards.

Loading was complete. The *New Season* contained, besides such provisions as Odim could lay his hands on at short notice, a herd of arang, fine Odim porcelain services, and a sick man bearing the plague, with a slave woman to tend him.

Odim had managed to get clearance from the quaymaster, an old acquaintance of his who had been paid liberally across Odim cargoes for many years. The captain of the vessel was persuaded to compress into the shortest possible time all the ceremonies recommended by deuteroscopists and hieromancers for an auspicious voyage. A cannon was fired to mark the departure of a ship from Sibornal.

A brief hymn was sung on deck to God the Azoiaxic. With tide and wind set fair, a gap widened between ship and Climent Quay. The *New Season* began its voyage for distant Shivenink.

VI

G4PBX/4582-4-3

O n the Avernus, fleet Kaidaw of Helliconian skies, the monotony
of barbarism descended. Eedap Mun Odim was rightly proud
of the craftsmanship embodied in the Kuj-Juvecian clock he
presented to Jheserabhay; the very narrowness of societies such as Kuj-
Juvec gives their art a concentrated vitality. But the barbarism prevailing on the Avernus produced nothing but smashed skulls, ambushes,
tribal drumming, simian mirth.

The many generations which had served under Avernian civilisation
had often expressed a longing to escape from the sense of futility, from
a doctrine of minimalism, imposed by the concept of Obligation Earth.
Some had preferred death on Helliconia to a continuation of Avernian
order. They would have said, if asked, that they preferred barbarism to
civilisation.

The boredom of barbarism was infinitely greater than the restraints
of civilisation. The Pins and the Tans had no respite from fear and
deprivation. Surrounded by a technology which was in many respects
self-governing, they were little better off than many of the tribes of
Campannlat, caught between marsh and forest and sea. Barbarism let
loose their fears and curtailed their imaginations.

The sections of the station which had suffered greatest damage were those most intimately connected with human activity, such as the canteens and restaurants, and the protein-processing plants which supplied them. The crop fields dominating the inside of the spherical hull were now battlefields. Man hunted man for food. The great perambulant pudendolls, those genital montrosities created from a perverted genetic inheritance, were also tracked down and eaten.

The automated station continued to flash images on internal screens from the living world below—continued, indeed, to vary the interior weather, so that humanity was not bereft of that eternal stimulus.

The surviving tribes were no longer capable of making the old connections. The images they received of hunters, kings, scholars, traders, slaves, had become divorced from their contexts. They were received as visitants from another world, gods or devils. They brought only wonder into the hearts of those whose forebears had studied them with disdain.

The rebels of the Avernus—a mere dissident handful at the onset— had launched out for greater freedoms than they imagined they enjoyed. They had beached themselves on the shores of a melancholy existence. The rule of the head was taken over by the belly.

But the Avernus had a duty which took precedence over tending its inhabitants. Its first duty was to transmit a continuous signal back to the planet Earth, a thousand light-years away. Over the eventful centuries of the Observation Station's existence, that signal, with its freight of information, had never faltered.

The signal had formed an artery of data, fed back to Earth according to the original plan of a technocratic élite responsible for the grandiose schemes of interstellar exploration. The artery never ran dry, not even when the inhabitants of the Avernus reduced themselves to a state close to savagery.

The artery never ran dry, but somewhere a vein had been cut. Earth did not always respond.

Charon, a distant outpost of the solar system, housed a receiving complex built across the frigid methane surface of the satellite. At this station, on which the nearest approaches to intelligent life were the androids which maintained it, the Helliconia signals were analysed, classified, stored, transmitted to the inner solar system. The outward process was far less complex, consisting merely of a string of acknowledgements, or an order to the Avernus to increase coverage of such and such an area. The news bulletins which had once been sent outwards had long ago ceased, ever since someone pointed out the absurdity of feeding the Avernus with items of news one thousand years old. Avernus knew—and now cared—nothing regarding events on Earth.

As to those events: The crowded nations of Earth spent most of the twenty-first century locked in a series of uncomfortable confrontations: East threatened West, North threatened South, First World helped and cheated Third World. Growing populations, dwindling resources, continuous localised conflicts, slowly transferred the face of the globe into something approaching a pile of rubble. The concept of "terrorist nation" dominated the mid-century; it was at this time that the ancient city of Rome was taken out. Yet, contrary to gloomy expectations, that ultimate Valhalla, nuclear war, was never resorted to. This was in part because the superpowers masked their operations behind manipulated smaller nations, and in part because the exploration of neighbouring space acted as something of a safety valve for aggressive emotions.

Those who lived in the twenty-first century regarded their age as a melancholy one despite exponential developments in technological and electronics systems. They saw that every field and factory producing food was electronically protected or physically patrolled. They felt the increasing regimentation of their life. Yet the structure, the underlying system of civilisation, was maintained. Restrictive though it was, it could be transcended.

Many gifted individuals made the century a brilliant one, at least in retrospect. Men and women arose from nowhere, from the masses, and won enormous fame by their gifts. In their brilliance, their defiance of their underprivileged environment, they lightened the hearts of their audience. When Derek Eric Absalom died, it was said that half the globe wept. But his wonderful improvised songs remained as consolation.

At first, only two of Earth's nations were in competition beyond the confines of the solar system. The number crept up to four and stopped at five. The cost of interstellar travel was too great. No more could play, even in an age when technology had become a religion. Unlike religion, the hope of the poor, technology was a rich man's strategy.

The excitements of interstellar exploration were relayed back to the multitudes of Earth. Many admired intellectually. Many cheered for their own teams. The projects were always presented with great solemnity. Great expenditures, great distances, great prestige: these united to impress the taxpayers back home in their ugly cities.

Occasional automated starships were launched during the heyday of interstellar travel, from approximately 2090 to 3200. These ships carried computer-stored colonists, able to range vacuum continually until habitable worlds were discovered.

The extrasolar planet on which mankind first set foot was solemnly named New Earth. It was one of two moonless bodies orbiting Alpha Centauri C. "Arabia Deserta writ large," said one commentator, but most settled for comfortable awe as the monotonous landscapes of New Earth unrolled.

The planet consisted mainly of sand and tumbled mountain ranges.

Its one ocean covered no more than a fiftieth of the total land area. No life was found on it, apart from some abnormally large worms and a kind of seaweed which grew in the fringes of the salt sea. The air, though breathable, had an extremely low water-vapour content; human throats became parched within a few minutes when breathing it. No rain ever fell on New Earth's dazzling surface. It was a desert world, and had always been so. No viable biosphere could establish itself.

Centuries passed.

A base and rest centre were established on New Earth. The exploration ships moved farther out. Eventually, they covered a sphere of space with a diameter of almost two thousand light-years. This area, though immense in the experience of a species which had only fairly recently tamed the horse, was negligible as a proportion of the galaxy.

Many planets were discovered and explored. None yielded life. Additional mineral resources for Earth, but not life. Down in the gloomy miasmas of a gas giant, writhing things were discovered which came and went in a manner suggesting volition. They even surrounded the submersible which was lowered to investigate them. For sixty years, human explorers tried to communicate with the writhing things—with no success. At this period, the last whale in Earth's polluted oceans became extinct.

On some newly discovered worlds, bases were established and mining carried out. There were accidents—unreported back home. The gigantic planet Wilkins was dismantled; fusion motors, roaring through its atmosphere, converted its hydrogen to iron and heavier metals, and the planet was then broken up. Energy was released as planned—but rather more rapidly than planned. Lethal shortwave radiation killed off all involved in the project. On Orogolak, war broke out between two rival bases, and a short nuclear war was fought which turned the planet into an ice desert.

There were successes, too. Even New Earth was a success. Successful enough, at least, for a resort to be set up on the edge of its chemical-laden sea. Small colonies were established on twenty-nine planets, some of which flourished for several generations.

Although some of these colonies developed interesting legends— which contributed to Earth's rich store—none was large or complex enough to nourish cultural values which diverged from their parent system.

Space-going mankind fell victim to many strange new maladies and mental discomforts. It was a fact rarely acknowledged that every terrestrial population was a reservoir for disease; a considerable proportion of the people of all ethnic groups were unwell for a percentage of their days—for unidentifiable reasons. SUDS (Silent Untreated Disease Syndrome) now clamoured for identification. In gravity-free conditions, SUDS proliferated.

What had been untreated was long to prove incurable. Nervous systems failed, memories developed imaginary life histories, vision became hallucinatory, musculature seized up, stomachs overheated. Space dementia became an everyday event. Shadowy frights passed across the vacuum-going psyche.

Despite its discomforts and disillusions, infiltration of the galaxy continued. Where there is no vision, the people perish—and there was a vision. There was a vision that knowledge, for all its dangers, was to be desired; and the ultimate knowledge lay in an understanding of life and its relationship to the inorganic universe. Without understanding, knowledge was worthless.

A Chinese/American fleet was investigating the dust clouds of the Ophiuchus constellation, seven hundred light-years from Earth. This region contained giant molecular clusters, nonisotropic gravities, accreted planets, and other anomalies. New stars were being created among the palls of inchoate matter.

An astrophysics satellite attached to one of the computerborgoids of the fleet obtained spectrographic readings on an atypical binary system some three hundred light-years distant from the Ophiuchus clouds which revealed at least one attendant planet supporting Earth-like conditions.

The oddity of an ageing G4 yellow star moving about a common axis with a white supergiant no more than eleven million years old had already engaged the interest of the cosmologists attached to the Chinese/American fleet. The spectroanalysis spurred them into active investigation.

The supposedly Earth-like planet of the distant binary system was filed under the appellation G4PBX/4582–4–3. Signals were despatched on their lengthy journey through the dust clouds to Earth.

Berthed inside the flagship of the fleet, then cruising the outer fringes of the Ophiuchus dust clouds, was an automated colonising ship. The ship was programmed and despatched to G4PBX/4582–4–3. The year was 3145.

The colonising ship entered the Freyr-Batalix system in 3600 A.D., to begin immediately the task for which it was programmed, the establishment of an Observation Station.

There was G4PBX/4582–4–3, like something dreamed! Real, but beyond belief, beyond even rejoicing.

As signals from the new station flashed back to Earth, it became more and more clear that the new planet's resemblance to Earth was close. Not only was it stocked with innumerable varieties of life in the prodigal terrestrial manner—and in heartening contrast to previously discovered planets—more, it supported an intriguing cline of semi-

intelligent and intelligent species. Among the intelligent species were a humanlike being and a horned being something resembling a rough-coated minotaur.

The signals eventually reached Charon, on the margins of the solar system, where androids fed the data to Earth, only five light-hours distant.

By the middle of the fifth millennium, Earth's Modern Ages were in slow decline. The Age of Apperception was a memory. For all but a few meritocrats in positions of power, galactic exploration had become an abstraction, another burden inflicted by bureaucracy. G4PBX/4582-4-3 changed all that. Ceasing to feature merely as a mysterious body among three sister planets, it took on colour and personality. It became Helliconia, the marvellous planet, the world beyond the veils of darkness where life was.

Helliconia's suns took on symbolic significance. Mystics remarked on the way in which Freyr-Batalix seemed to represent those divisions of the human psyche celebrated in Asian legend long ago:

> *Two birds always together in the peach tree:*
> *One eats the fruit, the other watches it.*
> *One bird's our individual Self, tasting all the world's gifts:*
> *The other the universal Self, witnessing all and wondering.*

How avidly the first prints of human and phagors, struggling out of a snowbound world, were studied! Inexplicable thankfulness filled human hearts. A link with other intelligent life had been forged at last.

By the time the Avernus was built and established in orbit about Helliconia, by the time it was stocked with the humans reared by surrogate mothers on the colonising ship, the sphere of terrestrial-directed space activity was contracting. The inhabited planets of the solar system were moving towards a centralised form of government, later to evolve into COSA, the Co-System Assemblage; their own byzantine affairs occupied them. Distant colonies were left to fend for themselves, marooned here and there on semihabitable worlds like so many Crusoes on desert islands.

Earth and its neighbouring planets were by this time storehouses of undigested information. While the materials brought back to Earth had been processed, the knowledge had not been absorbed. The enmities which had existed since tribal days, rivalries founded on fear and a lust for possession, remained dormant. The dwindling of space squeezed them into new prominence.

By the year 4901 A.D., all Earth was managed by the one company, COSA. Judicial systems had yielded to profit and loss accounts. Through one chain of command or another, COSA owned every building, every industry, every service, every plant, and the hide of every human on the

*planet—even those humans who opposed it. Capitalism had reached
its glorious apogee. It made a small percentage on every lungful of
oxygen breathed. And it paid out its stockholders in carbon dioxide.*

*On Mars, Venus, Mercury, and the moons of Jupiter, human beings
were more free—free to found their own petty nations and ruin their
own lives their own way. But they formed a sort of second-class citizenry
of the solar system. Everything they acquired—and acquisition still
played a major part in their lives—they paid for to COSA.*

*It was in 4901 that this burden became too great, and in 4901 that a
statesman on Earth made the mistake of using the old derogatory term
"immigrants" about the inhabitants of Mars. And so it was in 4901
that nuclear war broke out among the planets—the War over a Word,
as it was called.*

*Although records of those pre-apocalypse times are scarce, we do know
that populations then regarded themselves as too civilized to begin
such a war. They had a dread that some lunatic might press a button.
In fact the buttons were pressed by sane men, responding to a well-
rehearsed chain of command. The fear of total destruction had always
been there. Nuclear weapons, once invented, cannot be disinvented.
And such are the laws of enantiodromia that the fear became the wish,
and missiles sped to targets, and people burned like candles, and silos
and cities erupted in an unexpungeable fire.*

*It was a war between the worlds, as had been predicted. Mars was
silenced for ever. The other planets struck back with only a fraction of
their total firepower (and so were destroyed). Earth was hit by no more
than twelve 10,000-megaton bombs. It was enough.*

*A great cloud rose above the capital of La Cosa. Dust which com-
prised fragments of soot, grains of buildings, flakes of bodies, vegetable
and mineral, rose to the stratosphere. A hurricane of heat rolled across
the continents. Forests, mountains, were consumed by its breath. When
the initial fires died, when much of the radioactivity sank to the
despoiled ground, the cloud remained.*

*The cloud was death. It covered all of the northern hemisphere. The
sunlight was blotted from the ground. Photosynthesis, the basis of all
life, could no longer take place. Everything froze. Plants died, trees died.
Even the grass died. The survivors of the strike found themselves
straggling through a landscape which came more and more to resemble
Greenland. Land temperatures fell rapidly to minus thirty degrees.
Nuclear winter had come.*

*The oceans did not freeze. But the cold, the dirt in the upper atmos-
phere, spread like discharge over a sheet, poisoning the southern hemisphere as well as the northern. Cold gripped even the favoured lands of
the equator. Dark and chill reigned on Earth. It seemed that the cloud
was to be mankind's last creative act.*

Helliconia was celebrated for its long winters. But those winters were

*of natural occurrence: not nature's death, but its sleep, from which the
planet would reliably arouse itself. The nuclear winter held no promise
of spring.*

*The filthy aftermath of the war merged indistinguishably with an-
other kind of winter. Snow fell on hills which the so-called summer did
not disperse; next winter, more snow fell on what remained. The drifts
deepened. They became permanent. One permanent bed linked with
another. One frozen lake generated another. The ice reservoirs of the
far north began to flow southward. The land took the colour of the sky.
The Age of Ice returned.*

*Space travel was forgotten. For Earthmen, it had again become an
adventure to travel a mile.*

A spirit of adventure grew in the minds of those who sailed in the
New Season. The brig left the harbour without incident, and soon was
sailing westwards along the Sibornalese coast with a fresh northeasterly
in her canvas. Captain Fashnalgid found that he was whistling a horn-
pipe.

Eedap Mun Odim coaxed his portly wife and three children on deck.
They stood in a mute line, staring back at Koriantura. The weather had
cleared. Freyr wreathed itself in fire low on the southern horizon,
Batalix shone almost at zenith. The rigging made complex patterns of
shadow on the deck and sails.

Odim excused himself politely, and went over to where Besi Besamitikahl stood alone in the stern. At first he thought she was seasick, until
the movements of her head told him she was weeping. He put an arm
around her.

"It hurts me to see my precious one waste her tears."

She clung to him. "I feel so guilty, dear master. I brought this
trouble on you. . . . Never shall I forget the sight of that man . . .
burning. . . . It was all my fault."

He tried to calm her, but she burst out with her story. Now she put
the blame on Harbin Fashnalgid. He had sent her out early in the day,
when no ordinary people were about, to buy some books, and she had
been seized in the street by Major Gardeterark.

"His biwacking books! And he said that that was the last of his
money. Fancy wasting the last of your money on books!"

"And the major—what did he do?"

She wept again. "I told him nothing. But he recognised me as one
of your possessions. He took me into a room where there were other
soldiers. Officers. And he made me . . . made me dance for them. Then
he dragged me round to our offices . . . It's me that's to blame. I should
never have been fool enough to go out for those books. . . ."

Odim wiped her eyes and made soothing noises. When Besi was

calmer, he asked seriously, "Have you a real affection for this Captain Harbin?"

Again she clutched him. "Not any more."

They stood in silence. Koriantura was sinking in the distance. The *New Season* was sailing past a cluster of broad-beamed herring-coaches. The herring-coaches had their curtain nets out, trawling for fish. Behind the fishermen were salters and coopers, who would gut and preserve the catch as soon as it was hauled aboard.

Amid sniffs, Besi said, "You'll never forget what happened when you —when that man died on the kiln, will you, dear master?"

He stroked her hair. "Life in Koriantura is over. I have put everything that belonged to Koriantura behind me, and would advise you to do the same. Life will begin again when we reach my brother's home in Shivenink."

He kissed her and returned to his wife.

The next morning, Fashnalgid sought Odim out. His tall clumsy figure dominated Odim's slender and tightly parcelled form.

"I'm grateful to you for your kindness in taking me aboard," he said. "You'll be paid in full when we get to Shivenink, I assure you."

"Don't worry," Odim said, and said no more. He did not know how to deal with this officer, now a deserter, except by his usual method of dealing with people—through politeness. The ship was crowded with people who had begged to be allowed aboard to escape the oligarchic legislation; all had paid Odim. His cabin was stacked with treasures of one sort of another.

"I mean what I say—you will be paid in full," Fashnalgid repeated, looking heavily down at Odim.

"Good, good, yes, thank you," said Odim, and backed away. Out of the corner of his eye, he saw Toress Lahl coming on deck, and went over to her to escape from Fashnalgid's attentions. Besi followed him. She had avoided Fashnalgid's gaze.

"How is your patient?" Odim asked the Borldoranian woman.

Toress Lahl leaned against the rail, closed her eyes, and took a few deep breaths. Her pale, clear features had taken on a translucent quality under strain. The skin below her eyes looked puckered and dirty. She said, without opening her eyes, "He's young and determined. I believe he will live. Such cases generally do."

"You shouldn't have brought a plague case aboard. It endangers all our lives," Besi said. She spoke with a new boldness; she would never have dared speak out previously in front of Odim: but on the voyage all relationships changed.

" 'Plague' is not the scientifically exact term. The plague and the Fat Death are different things, although we use the terms interchangeably. Obscene though the symptoms of the Fat Death are, the majority of young, healthy people who contract it recover."

"It spreads like the plague, doesn't it?"

Without turning her head to reply, Toress Lahl said, "I could not leave Shokerandit to die. I am a doctor."

"If you're a doctor, you should know the dangers involved."

"I do, I do," said Toress Lahl. Shaking her head, she rushed from them and hurried down the companionway below decks.

She paused outside the door of the closet in which she kept Shokerandit. As she rested her head on her arm, she was vouchsafed a glimpse of the turn her life had taken, the misery in which she now lived, and the uncertainty which surrounded all on the ship. What was the reason for this gift of consciousness, which even phagors did not have, this awareness that one was aware, when it was incapable of changing what one did?

She was nursing the man who had taken her husband's lifeblood. And—oh, yes, she felt it—she was already infected with his disease. She knew it could easily leap to everyone else in the confines of this ship; the insanitary conditions on the *New Season* made it a haven for contagion. Why did life happen—and was it possible that, even now, some detached part of her was enjoying life?

She unlocked the door, set her shoulder against its resistance, and entered the closet. There she lived for the next two days, seeing no one, crawling only rarely onto the deck for fresh air.

Besi meanwhile had been given the task of supervising the many relations of Odim who had been stowed in the main hold. Her chief support came from the old grannie who made the delectable pastry savrilas. This aged woman still managed to cook on a small charcoal stove, filling the hold with benevolent aromas, while at the same time soothing the anxieties of the family.

The family lay about on boxes and ottomans and chests, indulging themselves in their customary way even while complaining about the rigours of life at sea. Theatrically, they declaimed to Besi and to anyone who would listen, and was not simultaneously declaiming, of the dangers of sea voyages. But Besi thought, And what of the dangers of plague! If it spreads to this hold, how many of you poor vulnerable bodies will survive? She determined to stay with them whatever happened, and secretly armed herself with a small dagger.

Toress Lahl remained isolated, speaking to no one, even when she crept up on deck.

On the third morning, she saw small icebergs dotting the water. On the third morning, with fever on her, she returned to her vigil as usual. The door was more reluctant than ever to budge.

Luterin Shokerandit was confined in a small irregular area in the bows of the *New Season*. A supporting pillar stood in the middle of the space, leaving enough room only for a bunk to one side of it and a bucket, a bale of hay, a stove, and four frightened fhlebihts, tethered beneath the small porthole. The porthole admitted light enough for Toress Lahl to see stains running across the floor and the gross figure tethered on the lower bunk. She locked the door behind her, rested against it, and then took a step closer to the prostrate figure.

"Luterin!"

He stirred. Under his left arm, which she had strapped by the wrist against the supports of the bunk, his head thrust a short way, tortoise-like, and one eye opened, to regard her through a spike of hair. His mouth opened, making a croaking noise.

She fetched a ladle of water from a casket standing behind the stove. He drank.

"More food," he said.

She knew he would recover. These were the first words he had spoken since they had carried him to this place on the *New Season*. He was again capable of organized thought. Yet she dare not touch him, although his wrists and ankles were tied securely.

On the top of the stove lay the charred remains of the last fhlebiht she had killed. She had dismembered it into joints with a cleaver, cooking it as best she could over the charcoal. The corkscrew horns, the long white fleece of the animal, lay with other rubbish in the corner.

As she threw a joint over to him, Toress Lahl thought for the first time how good the grilled meat looked. Shokerandit wedged it under an elbow and commenced to gnaw at the meat. Ever and again he cast a glance up at her. There was no longer the anger of madness in his eye. The bulimia had passed.

The thought of his previous savage eating tormented her. She looked at his naked limbs, gleaming with the sweat of his earlier struggles, and imagined how it would be to sink her teeth into his flesh. She snatched the charred meat from the stove.

Chains and manacles lay ready. Toress Lahl fell to her knees and crawled to them, securing herself to the central post with them. She locked her wrists together and flung the key clumsily into one corner, out of reach. The halitus of the place came to her, the stench of the man's body mingled with the smell of the confined animals and the odour of their droppings, all flavoured with the fumes from the charcoal. As she choked, a stiffness came on her. She began to stretch as far as the chains would allow, knees out before her in an ungainly position, head slowly rolling at the end of its neck. The animal carcass was cradled under one arm as if it were a child.

The man lay where he was, staring without movement. At last the woman's name came to his lips and he called to her. Her gaze momentarily met his, but it was the stare of an idiot and her eyeballs continued to roll.

Jaw hanging open, Shokerandit wriggled to sit up. He was tightly bound to the bunk. The wildest struggles of his delirium, when the helico virus had raged in his hypothalamus, had not sufficed for him to break the leather thongs securing his wrists and ankles.

As he struggled, he found a pair of brass tongs with claws, such as were used for handling lumps of red-hot charcoal, against his side. The implement was useless for cutting his bonds. For a while he slept. Waking, he tried again to set himself free.

He called. Nobody would come. The fear of the Fat Death was too great. The woman lay almost immobile against her pillar. He could prod her with his foot. The animals bleated, turning restlessly on their straw. Their eyes glowed yellow in the half dark.

Shokerandit had been secured so that he lay face down. The stiffness was leaving his joints. He was able to twist his head and look about. He inspected the webbing of the bunk overhead. Halfway down the bed a wooden crossbar was inserted to strengthen the structure. Into the crossbar a long-bladed dagger had been driven.

Minutes passed as he gazed awkwardly up at the dagger. Its handle was not far above him, but he had no hope of grasping it, tied as he was. He was clear in his mind that Toress Lahl had set it there before she succumbed to the disease. But why?

He felt the brass tongs against his flesh. The connection came at once, and with it a revelation of her cleverness. Wriggling, he managed to work the tongs down the bunk until he could grasp them between his knees. Then came an agony of contortion as he rotated his clenched knees and brought them up under the dagger. He worked for an hour, two hours, sweating and groaning in his pain, until at last he had the handle of the dagger secure between the brass claws. Then it was only a matter of time until he worked the dagger free.

It fell against his thighs. Shokerandit rested until he had recovered strength enough to shuffle the blade up the bunk. At last he could take it in his teeth.

There was the painful labour of sawing through one of the leather thongs, but it was done eventually. Once he had one hand free, he was able to cut himself loose. He lay back, panting. At last he climbed from the foetid bunk.

He took a step or two and then collapsed weakly against the wooden pillar. Hands on knees, he contemplated the figure of Toress Lahl, with its slow distorted movements. Although his mind did not feel like his own, he understood her devotion and her thought for him when she felt herself falling to the plague. While under the madness of the fever, he would never have had the coordination to get the dagger and release himself. Without the dagger, he would have been unable to cut himself free when he recovered.

After a rest, he stood up and felt his filthy body. He was changed.

He had survived the Fat Death and was changed. The painful contortions to which he had been subject had served to compress his spine; he was now, he estimated, three or four inches shorter than he had been. His perverted appetite had caused him to put on flesh. In that phase, he would have devoured anything, the blanket on the bunk, his own faeces, rats, had Toress Lahl not fed him cooked meat. He had no knowledge of how many animals he had devoured. His limbs were thicker. He gazed down at his barrel chest in disbelief. He was now a smaller, rounder, more thickset person. His weight had undergone a radical redistribution.

But he lived!

He had come through the eye of the needle and lived!

No matter what was involved, anything was better than death and dissolution. There was a sort of marvellous sense to life, to the unconscious movements of breathing, to the need for nourishment and defecation, to the ease of gesture, to the casual thought—so often not tied to the present moment. It was a sense, a wisdom, that even degradation and discomfort could not deny. Even as he rejoiced in it, feelings of health pervaded him in the stinking closet.

As if a curtain were drawn back, he saw again scenes from his youth in the mountains of Kharnabhar, at the Great Wheel. He recalled his father and mother. He reviewed again his heroism on the field of battle near Isturiacha. It came back clear, washed, as if it had all happened to someone else.

He recalled again striking down Bandal Eith Lahl.

Gratitude filled him that the widow he had taken captive should not have left him to die. Was it because he had not raped and beaten her? Or was the goodness of her action quite independent of anything he had done?

He bent down to look at her, sad to see her so grey, so overcome. He put an arm about her, smelling her sharp, sick stink. Her lolling head came round as if to rest against him. Her dry lips peeled back from her teeth, and she bit his shoulder.

Shokerandit pulled himself away from her. He handed her the meat at her feet. She took a mouthful but could not chew. That would come later, as the full madness developed.

"I'll look after you," he told her. "I'm going up on deck to wash myself and breathe some fresh air." His shoulder was bleeding.

How long had it been? He dragged the door open. The ship was full of creaks, the companion way of shifting shadows.

Rejoicing in the newfound ease of his limbs, he climbed the companionway and looked about. The decks were empty. There was no one at the wheel.

"Hello!" he called. No one answered, yet furtive movement could be heard.

Alarmed, he ran forward, still calling. A body lay half-naked by the mast. He stared down at it. All the flesh of the chest and upper arm had been crudely hacked away and—oh, yes, he could guess it—eaten. . . .

VII

THE YELLOW-STRIPED FLY

It was not that Icen Hill was impressive as such features go; indeed, compared with many of the hills in Sibornal, it was no more than a pimple. But it dominated its flat surroundings, the outer rings of Askitosh. Icen Hill Castle dominated and almost enveloped the hill.

When the wind from the north brought rain on its breath, the water collected on the roofs, fortifications, and spiteful spires of the castle and flung itself down in gouts upon the population of Askitosh, as if conveying personal greetings from the Oligarch.

One advantage of this exposed position—for the Oligarch and his Inner Chamber if for no one else—was that news could be got rapidly to the castle: not merely by the streams of messengers who laboured up the slippery cobbles of the hill road, but by the tidings flashed by heliograph from other distant eminences. A whole chain of signalling stations was established which girded Sibornal, the main artery of information adhering with fair precision to the line of latitude on which Askitosh lay. Thus was brought to the Oligarch—always assuming he existed—news of the welcome accorded the victorious army returning through Chalce to Koriantura.

That army had halted below the escarpment where Chalce petered out before the brow of Sibornal. It waited there until its stragglers caught up. For two days it waited. Those who died of the plague were buried on the spot. Both men and mounts were more gaunt than when they had set out from Isturiacha, almost half a tenner earlier. But Asperamanka was still in command. Morale was high. The troops cleaned themselves and their equipment, ready for a triumphal entry into Uskutoshk. The military band polished its instruments and practised its marches. Regimental flags were unfurled.

All this was done under the concealed guns of the Oligarch's First Guard.

As soon as Asperamanka's men moved forward, as soon as they were within range, the Oligarch's artillery fired upon them. The steam guns began to pound. Bullets rained down. Grenades exploded.

Down went the brave men. Down went their yelks. Blood in their mouths, faces in the dirt. Those who could scream, screamed. The scene was enveloped in smoke and flying earth. People ran hither and thither, at a loss to understand, rendered senseless by shock. The glittering instruments ceased to play. Asperamanka shouted to his bugler to sound retreat. Not a shot was fired back at their fellow countrymen.

Those who survived this evil surprise lurked like wild beasts in the wilderness. Many became speechless with shock.

"Abro Hakmo Astab!"—that at least they cried, the forbidden Sibish curse which even soldiery hesitated to utter. It was a shout of defiance to fate.

Some survivors climbed into the windswept recesses of the mountains. Some lost their way in the maze of marshland. Some banded together again, determined to recross the grass desert and join forces with those who remained in Isturiacha.

Asperamanka. Using his smooth tongue, he tried to persuade the broken groups to form up in units again. He was foul-mouthed in return. Officers and men alike had lost faith in authority. "Abro Hakmo Astab . . ." They uttered it to his stormy face.

Dire circumstances called forth the ancient curse. Its true meaning was lost in time, like its origins. A polite interpretation was that it recommended befouling both suns. In the northern continent, crouched beneath the chill breath of the Circumpolar Regions, men delivered the curse against the Azoiaxic—and against all other gods remembered or forgotten—as if to call down eternal darkness on the world.

"Abro Hakmo Astab!"—the defilement of the light. Those who hurled the words at Asperamanka then slunk away. Asperamanka made no further command. The thunder gathered below his brow, he tugged his cloak about him, he prepared to look to his own salvation. Yet, as a man of the Church, he felt the ancient curse lie heavy in his mind. He perceived his own defilement.

This much information was carried back by an informer to the Oligarch sitting in his stone hill in Askitosh. Thus the governor of men learned something of the effect of his villainous welcome to Koriantura on Asperamanka's troops.

The Oligarch's next step required little consideration. After the Inner Chamber had deliberated, a poster went out to the farthest corners of the land. It announced that a Plague-ridden Army, intent on spreading Disease and Death throughout the Continent, had been bravely repelled at the Frontier. Let all work harder by way of Celebration.

And the old fisherwomen of Koriantura stood with arms akimbo, reading what was written, and saying, "There you are, always 'work harder'. . . . How are we supposed to work harder than we do?" And they bunched closer and looked askance as units of the First Guard marched by, clattering westward in their noisy boots.

And the remains of that broken army in no-man's-land; it had yet another battle to fight.

Ever since the death of the last C'Sarr of Campannlat, four hundred and seventy-nine years earlier, the phagors had been gathering strength. Even before death-dealing Freyr had expanded to its fullest power and waned again, the components had been growing in numbers. The human will to check them had died in part with the C'Sarr. The more timid ancipitals, who submitted to existence on the plains among the Sons of Freyr, had passed word to the warlike contingents of the High Nyktryhk. The first marauders were out and about earlier in this Helliconian winter.

A group of ancipitals, mounted on kaidaws, could sweep like wind over the grasslands which were so formidable to men. In part this was for a simple reason: stallun, gillot, and kaidaw alike could eat the grass and survive on that diet, where the fragile Sons of Freyr would perish.

Nevertheless, the components of the High Nyktryhk kept away from the grasslands leading to Sibornal unless some special objective lured them there. Sibornal was feared by the ancipitals. In their pale harneys remained a memory of a terrible fly.

That memory—more of a programme than a memory—told them that the chill regions of Sibornal were the resort of flies, and of one fly in particular. That fly made almost intolerable the existence of the countless head of flambreg which inhabited the plains below the Circumpolar Regions. The yellow-striped fly lived on the flambreg herds, the female sinking her ovipositor into the hide of the animals. There the larvae, when they hatched, entered into the bloodstream, eventually to form pockets of putrefaction under the skin until they were ready to burst forth into the world.

The grubs grew as big as the end of a man's thumb. They finally chewed their way through their host's hide, dropping to the ground to pupate.

It might seem that this yellow-striped terror fulfilled no role in life except to make miserable the lives of the flambreg. That was not so. No other animal would venture into the territory ruled by the yellow-striped fly; and so the domain of the flambreg did not become overgrazed in the normal course of events.

Yet the fly remained as a curse, a scourge to the flambreg—who frequently galloped along the most windswept ridges, careless of danger, in a vain attempt to escape their fate. The ancipitals, descended from the flambreg, retained in their eotemporal minds a record of that yellow-striped torment, and steered well clear of its empire.

But a broken human army wandering in the wilds of Chalce represented a special objective to the ancipitals. Travelling into the wind, like the wind, with a supply of spears and rifles in the quivers at their backs, they bore down on the Sons of Freyr.

All they encountered they killed. Even those phagors who served in Asperamanka's army were mowed down with no compunction, and their eddre strewn across the lands.

Some groups of men maintained a semblance of military order. They formed up behind their supply wagons and fired at the enemy in a disciplined way. Many phagors fell.

Then the marauders stood off awhile, watching the men deteriorate from thirst and cold, before attacking again. They spared no one.

It was useless for the soldiers to surrender. They fought to the last, or blew their own brains out. Perhaps in them too was some kind of a racial memory: that summer was the time of human supremacy, when Freyr was bright; that when the long winter came, the ancipitals in their turn prevailed upon the globe, as once they had before mankind arrived upon the scene. So they defended themselves without hope, to die without help. The women who were with the men died too.

But sometimes the ammunition ran out and then the phagors, instead of killing everyone, took the humans into slavery.

Although the Oligarch did not know it, ancipitals proved his best ally. They eliminated what was left of Asperamanka's once great army.

Such phagor components as there were in Sibornal manifested a less warlike spirit. They were largely composed of ancipital slaves who had escaped their masters, or lowland phagors accustomed to generations of hard work and servility. These creatures roamed the countryside in small bands, doing their best to avoid human settlements.

Of course anything vulnerable belonging to the Sons of Freyr became their target; their deep-seated antagonism never died. When one such group sighted the brig *New Season* close to the coast, it became the object of scrutiny. The group followed it as the ship drifted along the bleak Loraj coast to the west of Persecution Bay, where Uskuti territory ended.

Eight gillots, a fillock, three ageing stalluns, and a runt comprised the band. All but the runt were dehorned. They had with them as baggage animal a yelk which was loaded with their chief items of diet, pemmican and a thick porridge. They were armed.

Although a stiff offshore wind blew the brig from the land, the coastal current, running westwards, was slowly bringing it closer. The phagors paced it, mile by unweary mile, as the distance between them lessened. They knew in their eddre that the time would come when they could seize and destroy the vessel.

Visible activity on board was intermittent. Several shots were fired one night. At another time, a man was seen to run to the starboard rail, pursued by two screaming women. Knives flashed in the hands of the women. The man threw himself overboard, made some attempt to swim ashore, and drowned without a cry in the cold sea.

Small icebergs, sailing like swans, moved in a westward direction after spilling out of Persecution Bay. They occasionally banged against the sides of the *New Season*. Luterin Shokerandit heard them as he sat in the wretched closet where Toress Lahl lay.

He had locked the door, but sat clutching a small chopper. The bulimia engendered by the Fat Death made everyone on ship a potential enemy. He used the chopper occasionally to hack into the beams of the ship. The wood was needed to fuel the small fire on which he roasted joints cut from the last flehbiht. Shokerandit and Toress Lahl between them had all but devoured the four long-legged goats in what he estimated was eight or nine days at sea.

The Fat Death generally ran its course in about a week. By that time, the sufferer was dead or on his way to recovery, faculties unimpaired but physiologically altered. He watched as the woman struggled and thickened. In her fight to get free, Toress Lahl had torn the clothes from herself, often using her teeth. She had gnawed the upright to which she was secured. Her mouth was bruised and bleeding. He looked at her with love.

The time came when she was able to return his gaze. She smiled.

She slept for some hours and then was better, with that feeling of well-being which accompanies those who survive the Fat Death.

Shokerandit untied her limbs and bathed her with a cloth and salt water in a bowl. She kissed him as he tried to help her to her feet. She surveyed her naked form and wept.

"I'm like a barrel. I was so slim."

"It's natural. Look at me."

She stared at him through her tears and then laughed.

They laughed together. He took in the marvellous architecture of her new body, still gleaming from its wash, the beauty of her shoulders, breasts, stomach, thighs.

"These are the proportions of a new world, Luterin," Toress Lahl said; he heard her using his first name for the first time.

He threw up his arms, scraping his knuckles on the bulkhead. "I'm relieved that you survived."

"Because you looked after your captive."

It was natural to wrap his arms about her, natural to kiss her bruised mouth, and natural to sink with her to the deck on which they had recently wrestled with agony. There they wrestled with sexual rejoicing.

Later, he said to her, "You are no longer my captive, Toress Lahl. We are now captives of each other. You are the first woman I have loved. I will take you to Shivenink, and we will go into the mountains where my father lives. You shall see the wonders of the Great Wheel of Kharnabhar."

She was already beginning to forget what had happened, and answered indifferently.

"Even in Oldorando we have heard of the Great Wheel. I will come with you if you say so. The ship is very silent. Shall we see how the others fare? They may all be sick with the plague—Odim and his vast brood, and the crew."

"Wait here with me a little longer." Lying with his arms about her, looking down into her dark eyes, he was reluctant to break the spell. At that time he was incapable of distinguishing between love and restored health.

She said briskly, "Back in Oldorando I was a doctor. It's my duty to tend the sick." She turned her face from Luterin.

"Where does the plague come from? From phagors?"

"From phagors, we believe."

"So our brave captain spoke the truth. Our army was going to be prevented by force from returning to Sibornal, just in case we spread the plague; it was among us. So what the Oligarch decreed was wise rather than evil."

Toress Lahl shook her head. She began to comb her hair with slow strokes, luxuriously, looking into a small mirror rather than at him as she spoke. "That's too easy. What the Oligarch decreed is entirely wicked. To destroy life is always wicked. What he did may not only be evil; it may prove ineffective too. I do know something about the contagious nature of the Fat Death—although since the Fat Death is latent for most of the Great Year it is difficult to study. Knowledge hard-learnt one year is forgotten by the next."

He expected her to continue but she fell silent, continuing to regard her face even when she had set down her comb, licking a finger to smooth her eyebrows.

"Be careful what you say about the Oligarch. He knows more than we."

Then she turned to look at him. Their regards met as she said with some emphasis, "I don't have to respect your Oligarch. Unlike the Oligarchy, the Fat Death has elements of mercy in its functioning. It's mainly the old and very young who die of it: a majority of fit adults survive—over half. They successfully metamorphose, as we do." She prodded him with a still moist finger, not without humour. "We in our compact shapes represent the future, Luterin."

"Yet half the population will die . . . whole communities destroyed . . . The Oligarch wouldn't allow that to happen in Sibornal. He'd take strong measures—"

She gestured dismissively. "Such die-back has its merciful side at a time when crops are failing and famine threatens. The healthy survivors benefit. Life goes on."

He laughed. "In fits and starts . . ."

She shook her head as if suddenly impatient. "We must see who has survived on the ship. I don't like the silence."

"I hope to thank Eedap Mun Odim for his kindness."

"I trust you will be able to."

They stood close in the small stale room, gazing at each other through the stramineous light. Shokerandit kissed her, although at the last moment she moved her lips away. Then they ventured into the corridor.

The scene was to come back to him much later. He would see then, as not at the time, how much of herself Toress Lahl withheld from him. Physically, she was very desirable to him; but her attitude of independence was more attractive to him than he could then realise. Only when that independence was eroded by time could they come to any true understanding.

But Shokerandit's proper appreciation of that fact could scarcely be arrived at while his whole outlook was based upon certain misunderstandings which left him, whichever way he turned, insecure, unable to develop emotionally. His innocence stood between him and maturity.

Shokerandit went first. Beyond the companionway, the corridor led to the main hold, where the relations of Odim had been settled. He went to listen at the door and heard stealthy movement within. From the cabins on either side of the corridor came silence. He tried the door of one, and knocked; it was locked, and no answer came.

As he emerged on deck, with Toress Lahl behind him, three naked men ran swiftly into hiding. They left a female corpse spread-eagled beneath the mizzenmast. It had been partially dismembered. Toress Lahl went over and looked at it.

"We'll throw it overboard," Shokerandit said.

"No. This woman is already dead. Leave her. Let the living be fed."

They turned their attention to the situation of the *New Season* itself. The ship, as their senses had told them, was no longer in motion. The ocean currents had brought it slowly to fetch up against the shore. The *New Season* was trapped against a tongue of sand which curled out from the land.

Towards the stern, a small cluster of icebergs had accumulated. At the bows, it would be an easy matter to jump over the side and walk ashore without getting a foot wet. The guardians of this spit of sand were two large rocks, one taller than the masts of the ship, which stood on the shore, deflecting ocean tides. They had probably been thrown to their present position by some long-gone volcanic explosion, though nothing so dramatic as a volcano could be seen inland. The coast offered a vista only of low cliffs, so tumbled that they might have been an old wall part-demolished by cannon fire, and, beyond the cliffs, mustard-coloured moorland, off which a chill wind blew, bringing tears to the viewer's eyes.

Blinking the water away, Shokerandit looked again at the larger rock. He was sure he had seen movement there. In a moment, two phagors appeared, walking with their curious glide away from the shore. It became apparent that they were going to meet a group of four of their kind who materialised over a rise, dragging with them the carcass of an animal of some kind. More phagors appeared from behind the rock to greet the hunters.

The original party of thirteen ancipitals had that morning met up with a second and larger party, a party also comprising escaped slaves, as well as four phagors who had served as transport animals in the Oligarch's soldiery. There were now thirty-six phagors in all. They had a fire burning in a cavity in the landward side of the rock, on which they intended to roast whole flambreg their hunting party had speared.

Toress Lahl looked at Shokerandit in dismay.

"Will they attack us?"

"They have a marked aversion to water, but they could easily get along that spit of sand and board us. We'd better see if we can find any fit members of the crew—and quickly."

"We were the first to go down with the Fat Death, so we may be the first to recover."

"We must see if there are any weapons to defend the ship with."

Their search of the ship horrified them. It had become a slaughterhouse. There had been no escape from the plague. Those who had locked themselves into cabins alone had succumbed and, in some cases, died alone. Where two or three had shut themselves away, the first to show symptoms had perhaps been killed. Any animals aboard had been killed and devoured, their remains fought over. Cannibalism had prevailed in the large hold, where the Odim family was. Of twenty-three members of the family, eighteen were already dead, killed mainly by their relations. Of the five remaining alive, three were still suffering from the madness of the disease and fled when shouted at. Two young women were able to speak; they had undergone the full metamorphosis. Toress Lahl took them to the safety of the closet where she and Shokerandit had sheltered.

The hatches to the crew's quarters were locked in place. From below came animal noises and a peculiar singsong, intoning endlessly

> *"He saw his fair maid's incision*
> *O, that terminal vision . . .*
> *O, that terminal vision . . ."*

In a forward storage cupboard, they discovered the bodies of Besi Besamitikahl and the old grannie. Besi lay staring upwards, a puzzled expression frozen on her face. Both were dead.

In the forward hold, they came on some sturdy square boxes which had remained untouched throughout the disaster which had overwhelmed the ship.

"Praise be, cases of rifles," Shokerandit exclaimed. He opened the nearest box and pulled away some sacking. There, each item wrapped in tissue paper, lay a complete dinner set in purest porcelain, decorated with pleasant domestic scenes. Other boxes contained more porcelain, the finest that Odim exported. These were Odim's presents for his brother in Shivenink.

"This will not keep the phagors off," Toress Lahl said, half laughing. "Something has to."

Time seemed to be suspended as they wandered the bloodied ship. Because it was small summer, the hours of Batalix's daylight were long. Freyr was rarely far above the horizon, rarely far below. The cold wind blew continually. Once a sound like thunder came with its breath.

After the thunder, silence. Only the dull pound of the sea, the occasional knock of a small ice floe against the wooden hull. Then the thunder again, this time clear and continuous. Shokerandit and Toress Lahl looked at each other in puzzlement, unable to imagine what the noise was. The phagors understood it without thought. For them, the noise of a flambreg herd on the move was unmistakable.

The flambreg lived in their millions below the skirts of the polar ice cap. Their progeny filled the Circumpolar Regions. Loraj, of all the countries of Sibornal, offered a variety of territories most suited to flambreg, with extensive forests of the hardy eldawon tree, and a landscape of low rolling hills and lakes. The flambreg, unlike yelk, were mildly carnivorous, with a fondness for any rodents and birds they could catch. Their main diet was of lichen, fungi, and grass, supplemented with bark. The flambreg also ate the indigestible moss called flambreg moss by the primitive tribes of Loraj which hunted them. The moss contained a fatty acid which protected the animals' cell membranes from the effects of cold, enabling the cells to continue efficient functioning at low temperatures.

A herd of over two million individuals was nearing the coast. Many of the Loraj packs were several times larger. This herd had emerged from an eldawon forest and was running almost parallel with the sea. The ground shook under its multitudinous hoofs.

On the shore, the phagors showed signs of unease. Their crude cooking operations were suspended. They marched back and forth, scanning the horizon, manifesting a humanlike uncertainty.

Two escape routes lay open to them. They could climb to the top of the house-sized boulder, or they could attack and take possession of the ship. Either alternative would save them from the approaching stampede.

There was a living forerunner of the herd. Above the heaving shoulders of the animals flew a cloud of midges, intent on drawing blood from the furry noses of the flambreg. The midges were the enemies also of a fly the size of a queen wasp. This fly now darted ahead into freer air. It appeared from nowhere and landed smartly between the eyes of one of the phagors. It was a yellow-striped fly.

The ancipital group broke into an uncharacteristic panic, rushing back and forth. The individual whose face the fly had alighted on turned and ran straight into the rock. He squashed the fly and laid himself out senseless.

The rest of the group gathered together to confer on a plan of action. Some of the newly arrived group carried with them a small and wizened emblem, an ancestor in tether. This shrunken symbol of themselves, this illustrious and moth-eaten great-grandstallun, though almost entirely transformed into keratin, was still a degree or two from nonbeing. In it, some faint spark still served to focus their attempts at ratiocination. Comprehension left their harneys. They communed. The currents of their pale harneys entered into tether.

From an area of total whiteness, a spirit emerged. It was no bigger than a rabbit. The phagor whose ancestor it was said inwardly, "O sacred forebear, now integrating with earth, here you see us in grave danger by the edge of the drowning world. The Beasts-we-were run upon us and will trample us down. Strengthen our arms, direct us from danger."

Through their harneys the keratinous figure transmitted pictures the ancipitals knew well, pictures flowing fast, one to another. Pictures of the Circumpolar Regions with their ice, their bogs, their sombre enduring forests, and of the teeming life that ran there, even there, on the edge of the ice cap. The ice cap then much greater in extent, for Batalix ruled alone in the heavens. Pictures of hunted creatures hiding in caves, making an alliance with that mindless spirit called fire. Pictures of the humble Others taken as pets. Terrifying pictures of Freyr roaming, coming mottled black down the air-octaves, a giant spider-form, eddre-chilling. The retreat of beautiful T'Sehn-Hrr, once silver in the tranquil skies. The Others proving themselves Sons of Freyr, running off carrying the mindless spirit fire on their shoulders. Many, many ancipitals dying, in flood, in heat, in battle with the monkey-browed Sons of Freyr.

"Go fast, remember enmities. Retreat to safety of the wooden thing afloat on the drowning world, kill all Sons of Freyr. Stay safe there against the running of the Beasts-we-were. Be valiant. Be large. Hold horns high!"

The tiny voice fled to lands beyond knowing. They thanked the great-grandstallun with a deep churring in their throats.

They would obey its word. For the voice was his and the voice was theirs and there was no difference. Time and opinion had no place in their pale harneys.

They advanced slowly on the beached ship.

It was an alien thing to them. The sea was their dread. Water swallowed and extinguished them. The ship was outlined against the smouldering orange of Freyr, snoring just below the horizon, ready to leap from its hiding place in that same hungry sea.

They clutched their spears and moved with reluctant step towards the *New Season.*

The sand crunched beneath their tread. All the while, their twitching ears picked up the thunder of the approaching flambreg.

To one side lay the icebergs, no taller than the runt which walked close to its gillot. Some icebergs clung to the sides of the vessel; some, as if possessed by a mysterious will, described slow intricate figures over the still sea, ghostly in the dim light, their reflections caught as if in tether in the water.

As the sand spit narrowed, so the ancipital group had to narrow its front. Finally, two stalluns led the rest. The ship loomed above them without movement.

Things clattered and broke beneath the feet of the stalluns. They tried to halt, but those behind pushed them forward. More breaking, more clattering. Looking down, they saw the thin white shards beneath their feet, and the whiteness stretching cracked all the way to the ship's hull.

"There is ice and it breaks," they said to each other, using the continuous present tense of Native Ancipital. "Go back or we fall into the drowning world."

"We must kill all Sons of Freyr, as it is said. Go forward."

"That we cannot do with the drowning world protecting them."

"Go back. Hold horns high."

Crouching by the rail of the *New Season,* Luterin Shokerandit and

Toress Lahl watched their enemies shuffle back to the shore and seek for shelter by the rock.

"They may return. We have to get the ship afloat as soon as possible," Shokerandit said. "Let's see how many of the crew have survived."

Toress Lahl said, "Before we leave the coast, we should kill some flambreg if they get within range. Otherwise everyone is going to starve."

They looked uneasily at each other. The thought crossed their minds that they sailed with a cargo of the dead and the mad.

Standing with their backs to the mainmast, they set up a great shout, which rolled away across the wastes of water and land. After a pause, an answering cry came. They called again.

A man appeared from the forecastle, staggering. He had undergone the metamorphosis, and presented the typical barrel-figure of a survivor. His clothes were ill-fitting, his once boney face now broad and presenting a curiously stretched appearance. They hardly recognised him as Harbin Fashnalgid.

"I'm glad you're alive," Shokerandit said, going towards him.

The transformed Fashnalgid put out a warning hand and sat down heavily on the deck.

"Don't come near me," he said. He covered his face with his hands.

"If you are fit enough, we need help in getting the ship on course again," Shokerandit said.

The other gave a laugh without looking up. Shokerandit saw that there was blood caked on his hands and clothes.

"Leave him to recover," Toress Lahl said. At this Fashnalgid uttered a harsh cackle and started to shout at them, " 'Leave him to recover!' How can a man recover? Why should he recover . . . I've been through the last few days eating raw arang—yes, and killing a man for the privilege of doing so . . . Entrails—everything . . . And now I find Besi's dead. Besi, the dearest, truest girl there ever was . . . Why do I want to recover? I want to be dead."

"You'll feel better soon," said Toress Lahl. "You scarcely knew her."

"I'm sorry about Besi," Shokerandit said. "But we have to get the ship on course."

Fashnalgid glared up at him. "That's typical of you, you skerming conformist! No matter what happens, do what you're supposed to do. Let the ship rot, for all I care."

"You're drunk, Harbin!" He felt morally superior to this abject figure.

"Besi's dead. What else matters?" He sprawled on the deck.

Toress Lahl motioned to Shokerandit. They crept away.

They took fire hatchets to break into cabins and went below.

As Shokerandit reached the bottom of the companionway, a naked

man threw himself on him. Shokerandit went down on one knee and
was seized by the throat. His attacker—an Odim relation—snarled,
more like a maddened animal than a human being. He clawed at
Shokerandit without any coherent attempt to overcome him. Shokerandit stuck two knuckles in the man's eyes, straightened his arm, and
pushed hard. As the man fell away, he kicked him in the stomach,
jumped on him, and pinned him to the deck.

"Now what do we do? Throw him to the phagors?"

"We'll tie him up and leave him in a cabin."

"I'm not taking any chances." He picked up the hatchet he had
dropped and clouted the prone man across the temple with the handle.
The man went limp.

They tackled the captain's cabin in the stern. The lock broke under
their assault, and they burst in. They found themselves in a comfortably
appointed quarter galley with windows opening above the water.

They drew up short. A man with an old-fashioned bell-mouthed
musket was sitting with his back to the windows, aiming the gun at
them.

"Don't shoot," Shokerandit said. "We intend no harm."

The man rose to his feet. He lowered the weapon.

"I would have blasted you if you were loonies."

He was proportioned in the unaccustomed thickset way. He had
passed through the Fat Death. They recognised him then as the captain. His officers lay about the cabin, their hands tied. Some were
gagged.

"We've had a high old time here," said the captain. "Fortunately,
I was the first to recover, and we have lost only the first mate—for
eating purposes, that was, excuse the expression. A few more hours
and these officers will be back in action."

"Then you can leave them and see to the rest of your ship," said
Shokerandit sharply. "We're beached, and there's a threat from phagors
ashore."

"How's Master Eedap Mun Odim?" asked the captain, as he accompanied them from the cabin, his gun under his arm.

"We haven't found Odim yet."

They found him later. Odim had locked himself in his cabin with a
supply of water, dried fish, and ship's biscuits as he felt the first fever
upon him. He had undergone the metamorphosis. He was now a few
inches shorter, and of much more rounded bulk than before. His characteristic straight-backed stance had disappeared. He wore a floppy
sailor's garb, his own clothes having become too tight for him. Blinking,
he emerged on deck like a hibernatory bear from its cave.

He looked round quickly frowning, as they hailed him. Shokerandit
approached slowly, well aware that it was he who had passed the Fat
Death to all aboard. He humbly reminded Odim of his name.

Ignoring him, Odim went to the rail and gestured over the side of the ship. When he spoke, his voice choked with rage.

"Look at this barbarism! Some wretch has thrown my best plate overboard. It's an atrocity. Just because there's illness on the ship, it doesn't excuse . . . Who did it? I demand to know. The culprit is not going to sail with me."

"Well . . ." said Toress Lahl.

"Er . . ." said Shokerandit. He took a grip on himself and said, "Sir, I have to confess that I did it. We were being attacked by phagors at the time."

He pointed to where phagors could be seen by the rock.

"You shoot phagors, you do not throw precious plates at them, you imbecile," Odim said. He reined in his temper. "You were mad—is that your excuse?"

"The ship has no weapons with which to defend itself. We saw that the phagors were going to attack—they will try again if they get desperate. I threw the plate over the side deliberately, to cover the sand spit. As I expected, the fuggies believed they were treading on thin ice, and retreated. I'm sorry about your porcelain, but it saved the ship."

Odim said nothing. He stared down at the deck, up at the mast. Then he brought a little black notebook out of his pocket and perused it. "That service would have fetched a thousand sibs in Shivenink," he said in low tones, darting swift glances at them.

"It has saved all the rest of the porcelain on the ship," Toress Lahl said. "Your other crates are intact. How is the rest of your family?"

Muttering to himself, Odim made a pencilled note. "Perhaps more than a thousand . . . Thank you, thank you . . . I wonder when such fine ware will again be manufactured? Probably not until the spring of next Great Year, many centuries in the future. Why should any of us care about that?"

He turned bemusedly, to shake hands with Shokerandit while looking elsewhere. "My gratitude for saving the ship."

"Now we'll get it afloat again," said the captain.

The noise of the flambreg herd was louder now. They turned to see the animals pour by, not more than a mile inland. Odim disappeared unnoticed.

Only later did they discover the reason for his slightly eccentric behaviour. It was not his dear Besi's death alone which had unsettled Odim. Of his three children, only the eldest boy, Kenigg, had survived the ravages of the Fat Death. His wife was also dead. Little was found of her bar skull, torso, and a pile of bones.

The flotation was not to come about for several hours. With the captain and a few crew on their feet again, some attempt was made to bring the ship back into order. Those still sick were settled as comfortably as possible in the surgeon's cabin. The injured were tended. The convalescent were brought to fresh air. The dead were wrapped in blankets and lined up in a row on the upper deck. The dead numbered twenty-eight. The survivors were twenty-one in number, including the captain and eleven of his crew.

When everyone had been accounted for and order prevailed, the fit assembled for a service of thanksgiving for their survival to God the Azoiaxic, who ordered all things.

In their innocent hymns, they did not see that the complexity of their survival was beyond the capacity of any local deity.

Helliconia was at this period receding towards something like the original conditions which had existed before its parent sun Batalix became locked into the gravitational field of the A-type supergiant. The planet had then carried a remarkable number of phyla, ranging in size from viruses to whales, while being denied the energy levels or the complexity to support beings with that intensity of cellular organisation required as building blocks for higher mental functions—the thinking, deducing, perceiving functions associated with full consciousness. The ancipitals were Helliconia's supreme effort in this respect.

The ancipitals were a part of the integrated living system of Helliconia's biosphere. One of the functions of that systemic gestalt—of which, needless to say, its component parts were entirely unaware—was to maintain optimum conditions for the survival of all. As the yellow-striped fly could not live without the flambreg, so ultimately, the flambreg could not live without the yellow-striped fly. All life was interdependent.

The capture of Batalix by the supergiant was only an event of the first magnitude and not a catastrophe for Helliconian life, although it was catastrophic for many phyla and many individuals. The impact of the capture was gradual enough for the biosphere to sustain it. The planet looked after its own. Its moon was lost; its vital processes continued, although through a disruption which brought storms and blizzards raging for hundreds of years.

The fierce output of high-energy radiation from the new sun caused more damage. More phyla were eradicated, while others survived only through genetic mutation. Among the new species were some which were, in evolutionary terms, hastily developed; they survived in the new environment only at some cost to themselves. The assatassi in the sea, which were born as maggots from the decaying bodies of their parents; the yelk and biyelk, necrogenes which resembled mammals but were without wombs; and human stock; these were among the new creatures which rose to abundance under the energy-rich conditions which came about eight million years before the present.

The new creatures were products of the biospheric striving for unity, and cobbled into it at the time of maximum change. Before its capture by Freyr, Helliconia's atmosphere had contained a large amount of carbon dioxide, protecting its life with a greenhouse effect, and producing a mean temperature of $-7°$ C. After capture, the atmospheric carbon dioxide was much reduced, combining at periastron with water to form carbonate rocks. Oxygen levels increased to amounts suitable for the new creatures: humans could not live in the oxygen-scarce Nyktryhk, as phagors did. In the seas, greater concentrations of macromolecules led to stepped-up activity all along the food chain. All these new parameters for existence came within the regulatory functions of Helliconia's biosphere.

The humans, as the most complex life form, were the most vulnerable. However they might rebel against the idea, their corporate lives were never more than part of the equipoise of the planet to which they belonged. In that, they were no different from the fish, the fungi, or the phagors.

In order that they might function at optimum efficiency in Helliconia's extremes, evolutionary pressure had introduced a system for regulating the masses of the humans. The pleomorphic helico virus had as its vector a species of arthropoda, a tick, which transferred itself readily from phagor to human. The virus was endemic during two periods of the Helliconian year, in the Spring and in the late Autumn of the Great Year, with minor epicycles between these cycles. These two pandemics were known as bone fever and the Fat Death.

Sexual dimorphism between the sexes was negligible; but both sexes showed seasonal dimorphism. Male and female could be said to average approximately one hundred and twelve pounds over an entire Great Year. But spring and autumn brought dramatic variations in body weight.

Survivors of the spring scourge of bone fever weighed a lanky ninety-six pounds, and presented a skeletal appearance to those who were brought up to the old way of things. This decreased body weight was an inheritable factor. It persisted throughout the generations as a crucial survival trait during the increasing heat. But the effect slowly became less apparent, until populations achieved the median of one hundred and twelve pounds.

Towards winter, the virus returned, partly in obedience to glandular signals. Survivors of these attacks increased in bulk, rather than losing it, generally gaining an average of about fifty percent body weight. For a few generations, the population averaged one hundred and sixty-eight pounds. They had transformed from ectomorph at one extreme to endomorph at the other.

This pathological process performed a vital function in preserving the human stock, with a side effect which benefitted the entire biosphere. As the expanding energy quota of the spring planet demanded a much

more variegated biomass for efficient systemic working, so the contracting energy quota of winter required a decrease in total biomass. The
virus culled the human population to conform with the total food-chain
organisation of the biosphere.

Human existence was not possible without the virus, just as the
flambreg herds would have ceased ultimately to exist without the curse
of the yellow-striped fly.

The virus destroyed. But it was a life-giving destruction.

VIII

THE RAPE
OF THE MOTHER

The stiff breeze blew off the coast. The clouds parted, revealing Batalix overhead. The sea sparkled, tossing up foam made of finest pearl. The *New Season* raced west by southwest, with music in her shrouds.

Along the Loraj coast on the north stood the Autumn Palaces, terrace after terrace of them. The dreams of forgotten tyrants were imprisoned in their stone, extending along the shore in distance and time. According to legend, King Denniss had once lived within their hallowed walls. Since the days of their fashioning, the Palaces, like some inconclusive human relationship, had never been entirely occupied or entirely deserted. They had proved too grandiose for those who created them and for those who followed after. Yet they were used still, long after whatever autumn had first seen the rise of their towers above the granite strand. Human beings—whole tribes of beings—lived in them like birds under neglected eaves.

The learned, who are always attracted to the past, lodged also in the Autumn Palaces. For them, the Palaces were the greatest archaeological site in the world, their ruinous cellars taproots to an earlier age of man. And what cellarage! Mazes of almost infinite depth stretched down into the rock, as if to syphon up warmth from the heart of Helliconia. Here were reckonings inscribed on stone and clay, pot shards, skeletons of leaves from vanished forests, skulls to be measured, teeth to be fitted to jawbones, middens, weapons dissolving in rust . . . the history of a planet patiently awaiting interpretation, yet as tantalisingly beyond complete comprehension as a vanished human life.

The Palaces lay pallid with distance, and the *New Season* passed them far to starboard.

The depleted crew occasionally saw other ships. As they sailed by the port of Ijivibir, they passed fleets of herring-coaches about their business. Farther out to sea, an occasional warship was sighted, reminding them that the quarrel between Uskutoshk and Bribahr was still active. Nobody molested them or even signalled to them. Ice dolphins sported alongside the vessel.

After Clusit, the captain decided to make a landing on the coast. He was familiar with these waters and determined to stock the ship with food before they made the last part of the run for the Shivenink port of Rivenjk. His passengers were doubtful about the wisdom of going ashore after their recent close encounter with the phagor band, but he reassured them.

This part of Loraj was within the northern tropics and still fertile. Behind the coast lay a glittering country of woods, lakes, rivers, and marshes, scarcely inhabited by mankind. Behind that country stood ancient eldawon and caspiarn forests, stretching all the way to the ice cap.

On the shore, helmeted seals basked, roaring as the passengers and crew of the *New Season* walked among them. They offered no resistance as they were clubbed to death. This clubbing was done with an oar. The oar had to hit the creature under the jaw in the vulnerable part of its throat. With its air passages blocked, the seal died of suffocation. This took some while. The passengers averted their gaze while the seals rolled in agony. Their mates often tried to help them, whimpering pitifully.

The heads of the seals were covered by something resembling a helmet. The helmet was an adaptation of horns, the seals having been land animals in the distant past, driven back into the oceans by the cold of Weyr-Winter. The adaptation protected the ears and eyes of the creatures, as well as the skull.

As the human party turned away from the seals they were killing, legged fish heaved themselves out of the waves and rushed up the steeply shelving shingle. They began attacking the dying seals, tearing chunks of their blubbery flesh.

"Hey!" shouted Shokerandit, and struck out at the fish.

Some scattered and ran under stones. One lay wounded by Shokerandit's blow. He picked it up and showed it to Odim and Fashnalgid.

The fish was the best part of a metre long. Its six "legs" were finlike. It had a lantern jaw, behind which trailed a number of fleshy whiskers. As its head flicked from side to side, jaw snapping, its filmy grey eyes stared at its captor.

"See this creature? It's a scupperfish," said Shokerandit. "Soon these creatures will be coming ashore in the thousands. Most of them get eaten by birds. The others survive and tunnel into the earth for safety. Later, they'll become longer than snakes, once the Weyr-Winter's here."

"They're Wutra's worms, that's what they're called," said the captain. "Best throw it away, sir. They're not fit even for the sailors to eat."

"The Lorajans eat them."

The captain said, deferentially but firmly, "Sir, the Lorajans do eat the worms as a delicacy, that's true. They are poison nonetheless. The Lorajans cook them with a poisonous lichen, and 'tis said that the two poisons cancel each other out. I've eaten the dish myself, sir, when wrecked on this coast some years past. But I still hate the sight and taste of the things, and certainly don't want my men filling their bellies with them."

"Very well." Shokerandit flung the still wriggling scupperfish out to sea.

Cowbirds and other sorts of birds were wheeling above them, screaming. The sailors cut up six of the helmeted seals as quickly as possible and carried the chunks of meat over to the jolly boat. The offal was left to the other predators.

Toress Lahl was weeping in silence.

"Get back in the boat," Fashnalgid said. "What are you weeping for?"

"What a horrible place this is," the woman said, turning her face away. "Where things with legs crawl from the sea and everything eats some other living thing."

"That's how the world is, lady. Jump in."

They rowed back towards the ship, and the birds followed, crying, crying.

The *New Season* hoisted sail and began to move over the still water, its bows swinging towards Shivenink. Toress Lahl tried to speak to Shokerandit, but he brushed her to one side; he and Fashnalgid had matters to attend to. She stood by the rail, hand to brow, watching the coastline dwindle.

Odim came up and stood beside her.

"You need not be sorrowful. We'll soon reach the safety of the harbour of Rivenjk. There my brother will take us in, and we can rest and recover from our various shocks."

Her tears burst forth again. "Do you believe in a god?" she asked, turning a tear-stained face towards him. "You've undergone such sorrow this voyage."

He was silent before answering. "Lady, all my life until now I have lived in Uskutoshk. I behaved like an Uskuti. I believed like an Uskuti. I conformed—which means that I regularly worshipped God the Azoiaxic, the God of Sibornal. Now that I have come away from that place, or have been driven away, as one might say, I can see that I am no Uskuti. What is more, I find I have absolutely no belief in God. At his passing, I felt a weight lifting." He patted his chest in illustration. "I can say this to you, since you are not an Uskuti."

She gestured towards the shore they were leaving. "This hateful place . . . those dreadful creatures . . . all I've been through . . . my husband killed in battle . . . the gruesomeness of this ship . . . Everything just gets steadily worse, year by year . . . Why wasn't I born in the spring? I'm sorry, Odim—this isn't like me. . . ."

After a pause, he said gently, "I understand. I've also undergone bereavement. My wife, my younger children, dear Besi . . . But I speak to my wife's gossie in pauk, and she comforts me. Do you not seek out your husband in pauk, lady?"

She said to him in a low voice, "Yes, yes, I sink down to his gossie. He is not as I desire to see him. He comforts me and tells me I should find happiness with Luterin Shokerandit. Such forgiveness . . ."

"Well? Luterin is a pleasant young man, by all I see and hear."

"I can never accept him. I hate him. He killed Bandal Eith. How can I accept him?" She startled herself by her own antagonism.

Odim shrugged his broad shoulders. "If your husband's gossie so advises you . . ."

"I am a woman of principle. Maybe it is easier to forgive when you are dead. All gossies speak with the same voice, sweet like decay. I may cease the habit of pauk . . . I cannot accept the man who has enslaved me—however tempting the terms he uses to bribe me. Never. It would be hateful."

He rested a hand on her arm. "All is hateful to you, eh? Yet perhaps you should try to think as I do that a new life is being presented to us—us exiles. I am twenty-five and five tenners—no chicken! You are much younger. The Oligarch is supposed to have observed that the world is a torture chamber. That is the case only for those who believe so.

"When we walked on the shore, killing off those seals—only six out of thousands, after all!—a feeling overcame me that I was being shaped for the winter season in some wonderful way. I had put on flesh but I had shed the Azoiaxic. . . ." He sighed. "I find difficulty talking profoundly. I'm better at figures. I'm only a merchant, as you know, lady. But this metamorphosis through which we have come—it is so wonderful that we must, *must*, try to live in accord with nature and her generous accountancy."

"And so I'm supposed to yield to Luterin, is that it?" she said, giving him a straight look.

A smile turned the corner of his mouth. "Harbin Fashnalgid has a soft spot for you also, lady."

As they laughed, Kenigg, Odim's one surviving son, ran up to him and hugged him. He stooped and kissed the boy on his cheek.

"You're a marvellous man, Odim, I really think it," Toress Lahl said, patting his hand.

"You are marvellous too—but try not to be too marvellous for happiness. That's an old Kuj-Juvec saying."

As she nodded her head in agreement, a tear shone in her eye.

Worse weather came in as the ship approached the coasts of Shivenink. Shivenink was a narrow country consisting almost entirely of an enormous mountain range—the Shivenink Chain, which had lent its name to the nation. The range divided the territories of Loraj and Bribahr.

The Shiveninki were peaceful, god-fearing people. Their rages had been drained by the original chthonic angers which had built their mountains. In the recesses of their natural fortress, they had built an artifact which embodied their particular brand of holiness and determination, the Great Wheel of Kharnabhar. This wheel had become a symbol, not merely to the rest of Sibornal but to the rest of the globe as well.

Great whales thrust their beaked heads up to observe the *New Season* as it entered Shiveninki waters. Sudden snow blizzards, battering the ship, almost immediately hid them from sight.

The ship was in difficulties. The wind howled through its rigging, spray dashed across the deck; the brig pitched from side to side as if in fury. In something like darkness—though the hour was Freyr-dawn—the sailors were sent up the ratlines. In their new metamorphosed shape, they were clumsy. To the yardarm they climbed, soaked, drenched, battered. The unwilling sails were furled. Then back down to a deck ceaselessly awash.

With the crew depleted, Shokerandit and Fashnalgid, together with some of Odim's more able relations, helped to man the pumps. The pumps were amidships, just abaft the mainmast. Eight men could work on each pump, four on either handle. There was scarcely room for the sixteen together in the pump well. Since this part of the main deck caught the worst of the seas breaking inboard, the pumpers were constantly inundated. The men cursed and fought, the pumps wheezed like old grandfathers, the waters smashed against them.

After twenty-five hours the wind abated, the barometer steadied, the sea became less mountainous. The snow fell silently, blowing off the land. Nothing could be seen of the shore, yet its presence could be felt, as if some great thing lay there, about to wake from its ancient sleep of rock. They all sensed it, and fell silent. They looked for it, peering into the muffling snow, and saw nothing.

Next day brought improvement, a calm passage in the orchestration of the elements.

The snow showers fell away across the green water. Batalix shone through overhead. The sleeping thing was slowly revealed. At first only its haunches were visible.

The ship was reduced to toy dimensions by a series of great blue-green bastions whose tops were lost in cloud. The bastions unfolded as the ship, again under full sail, sped westwards. They were immense headlands, each greater than the last. At sea level, pillars of gigantic proportions irresistibly suggested that they had been sculpted by a hand with intent behind it; they supported brows of rock which went almost vertically up. Here and there, trees could be observed, clinging to folds in the rock. White horizontal veins of snow defined the curves of each headland.

Cleft between the headlands were deep bays—pockets in which the mountains kept reserves of murk and storm. Lightning played in these recesses. White birds hovered where the current raced at their mouths. Strange sounds and resonances issued across the waters from the veiled cavities, touching the minds of the humans like the salt that lighted on their lips.

Fitful bursts of sun, penetrating such bays, revealed at their far end cataracts of blue ice, great waterfalls frozen as for eternity, which had tumbled down from the high homes of rock, ice, hail, and wind concealed almost perpetually by cloud.

Then a bay greater than the previous ones. A gulf, flanked by black walls. At its entrance, perched on a rock where the highest seas could not overwhelm it, a beacon. This token of human habitation reinforced the loneliness of the scene. The captain nodded and said, "There's the Gulf of Vajabhar. You can put in there at Vajabhar itself—it sticks out like a tooth in the lower jaw of the Gulf."

But they sailed on, and the great bulk of the planet to their starboard seemed to move with them.

Later, the coast became more massive still, as they reached the waters off the Shiven Peninsula. Round this they had to sail to reach the port of Rivenjk. The peninsula had no bays. It was almost featureless. Its chief characteristic was its size. Even the crew, when off duty, gathered silently on deck to stare.

The tall slopes of Shiven were shrouded in vegetation. Climbers hung down, falling free as if in imitation of the many small waterfalls which began their descent and never finished, whipped away by winds scouring the sheer faces. Occasionally the clouds would part to reveal the great head of snow-clad rock which climbed to the sky. This was the southern end of a mountain range which curved northwards to join the enormous lava plateau sequences under the polar ice cap.

Within a comparatively few miles of where the ship sailed, the ridge of the peninsula rose to heights of over six and a quarter miles above sea level. Far higher than any mountain peaks on Earth, the Shivenink Chain rivalled the High Nyktryhk of Campannlat in scale. It formed one of the grandest spectacles on the planet. Shrouded in its own storms, its own climatic conditions, the great chain revealed itself to few human eyes, except from the deck of a passing ship.

Lit by the almost horizontal rays of Freyr, the formation clad itself in breathtaking lights and shadows. To the perceptions of the passengers, all appeared brilliant, all new. They became uplifted just to regard such titanic scenery. Yet what they beheld was ancient—ancient even in terms of planetary formation.

The heights that dominated them had come into being four thousand and more million years earlier, when the unevolved Helliconian crust had been struck by large meteors. The Shivenink Chain, the Western Barriers in Campannlat, as well as distant mountains in Hespagorat, were remaining testaments to that event, forming between them segments of a great circle comprising the ejecta material of a single impact. The Climent Ocean, regarded by sailors as of almost infinite extent, lay within the original crater.

For day after day they sailed. As in a dream, the peninsula remained to starboard, unchanging, as if it would never go away.

Once they rounded a small island, a pimple in the ocean, which might have dropped from the overhanging landmass. Although it looked a terrifying place on which to live, the island was inhabited. A smell of wood smoke drifted out to the ship; that and the sight of huts nestling among trees made the passengers long for a spell ashore, but the captain would hear nothing of it.

"Those islanders are all pirates, many of them desperate characters lost off ships in storms. Were we to set foot there, they'd murder us and steal our ship. I'd sooner befriend vultures."

Three long skin canoes put out from the island. Shokerandit passed his spyglass round, and they looked at the men, bent of back, who rowed towards them as if their life depended on it. In the stern of one of the boats stood a naked woman with long black hair. She carried a baby which suckled at her breast.

A snowstorm blew off the mountains at that time, falling like a shawl to the sea. The flakes settled on the woman's bare breasts and melted.

The *New Season* was carrying too much sail for the canoes to catch up. They fell astern. Still the men rowed with undiminished zeal. Still they rowed when lost to sight, like madmen.

Once or twice, cloud and mist parted enough for the passengers to catch a glimpse of the Shiven heights. Then whoever saw the gap would give a cry, and other passengers would come running, and gasp to see how far above their heads stretched those dripping rocks, those vertical jungles, those snows.

Once a landslide started. A part of the cliff fell away. It dropped and dropped, carrying away more rock with it. Where it struck the sea, a great wave was raised. A wedge of ice fell, disappeared under the surface, bobbed up again. Larger wedges tumbled after it—having fallen from the edge of some glacier invisibly housed in the clouds. The falls caused terrifying reverberations of sound.

A colony of brown birds sped out from shore in their thousands, whistling their fright. So great was their wingspan that, when they passed over the ship, the noise of their movements was like low thunder. The colony took half an hour to pass overhead, and the captain shot several for the pot.

When at last the brig rounded the peninsula and began to sail north, within two days of Rivenjk, another storm struck. It was less severe than the previous one. They were whirled up in fog and snow, which arrived in great flurries. For a whole day the light of the suns glittered through thick mists and hail, the hailstones being as large as a man's fist.

As the storm abated and the men at the pumps were able to stagger away and sleep, the coastline slowly revealed itself again.

Here the cliffs were less vertical, though as awesome as ever, husbanding their own clouds and rainstorms. From out of one obscuring storm emerged the gigantic figure of a man, swathed in mist.

The man appeared to be intending to spring from the shore and land on the deck of the New Season.

Toress Lahl cried in alarm.

"That's the Hero, ma'am," said the second mate reassuringly. "He's a sign we're nearly at journey's end—and a good thing too."

Once the scale of the coast was grasped, it was plain that the statue was gigantic. The captain demonstrated with his sextant that it stood over a thousand metres high.

The Hero's arms were upraised and carried slightly forward over the head. The knees were slightly bent. The man's stance suggested that he was either about to jump into the ocean or take flight. The latter alternative was suggested by what might have been a pair of wings, or else a cloak, flowing back from the broad shoulders. For stability, the figure's lower legs had not been separated from the rock face from which it was sculpted.

The statue was stylised, cut with curious whorls as if to confer an aerodynamic shape. The face was sharp and eaglelike, yet not entirely inhuman.

Increasing the solemnity of the sight, a distant bell tolled. Its brazen voice rolled across the grey waters to the brig.

"He's a splendid figure, isn't he?" Luterin Shokerandit said with pride. The passengers in their metamorphosed state all gathered at the rail to stare uneasily across at the gigantic statue.

"What does he represent?" Fashnalgid asked, plunging his hands into his coat pockets.

"He represents nothing. He is himself. He's the Hero."

"He must represent something."

Annoyed, Shokerandit said, "He stands there, that's all. A man. To be seen and admired."

They fell uneasily silent, listening to the melancholy note of the bell.

"Shivenink is a land of bells," Shokerandit said.

"Has the Hero got a bell in his belly?" young Kenigg asked.

"Who would build such a thing in such a place?" Odim enquired, to cover his son's impertinent question.

"Let me tell you, my friends, that this mighty figure was created ages ago—some say many Great Years past," Shokerandit said. "It was built, legend has it, by a superior race of men, whom we call the Architects of Kharnabhar. The Architects constructed the Great Wheel. They are the finest builders the world has ever known. When they finished their labours on the Wheel, they sculpted this giant figure of the Hero. And the Hero has guarded Rivenjk and the way to Kharnabhar ever since."

"Beholder, what are we coming to?" Fashnalgid asked himself aloud. He went below to smoke a veronikane and read a book.

When the desolation of a post-apocalyptic Earth yielded to the ice age, signals had been received from Helliconia for the past three centuries. As the glaciers moved south, there were few who possessed the ability to watch that newly discovered planet's history, apart from the androids on Charon.

At least this could be said for the ice age. It wiped the Earth clear of the festering shells of defunct cities. It obliterated the cemeteries which all previous habitation had become. Voles, rats, wolves, ran where highways had once been. In the southern hemisphere, too, the ice was on the move. Solitary condors patrolled the empty Andes. Penguins moved, generation by generation, towards the desired ice shelves of Copacabana.

A drop of only a few degrees had been enough to throw the intricate mechanisms of climatic control out of gear. The nuclear blast had induced in the living biosphere—in Gaia, the Earth mother—a state of shock. For the first time in epochs, Gaia met a brute force she could not accommodate. She had been raped and all but murdered by her sons.

44448488484848844484448488848444

For hundreds of millions of years, Earth's surface had been steadily maintained within the narrow extremes of temperature most congenial to life—maintained by an unwitting conspiracy between all living things in conjunction with their parent world. This despite increases in the sun's energy, causing dramatic changes in the constitution of the atmosphere. The regulation of the amount of salt in the sea had been maintained at a constant percentage of 3.4. If that had ever risen to a mere 6 percent, all marine life would have ceased. At that percentage of salinity, cell walls disintegrate.

The amount of oxygen in the atmosphere had similarly been maintained at a steady 21 percent. The percentage of ammonia in the atmosphere had also been maintained. The ozone layer in the atmosphere had been maintained.

All these homeostatic equilibria had been maintained by Gaia, the Earth mother in whom all living things, from sequoias to algae, whales to viruses, had their being. Only mankind had grown up and forgotten Gaia. Mankind had invented its own gods, had possessed those gods, had been possessed by them, had used them as weapons against enemies, and against their own inner selves. Mankind had enslaved itself, in hate as much as love. In that madness of isolation, mankind invented formidable weapons of destruction. In committing genocide, it almost slew Gaia.

She was slow to recover. One striking symptom of her illness was the death of trees. Those abundant organisms, which had spread from the tropical rain forests to the northern tundras, were killed by the radioactivity and an inability to photosynthesise. With the disappearance of trees, a vital link in the homeostatic chain was broken; the homes they provided for a myriad of life forms were lost.

Conditions of cold prevailed for almost a thousand years. Earth lay in a chill catalepsy. But the seas lived.

The seas had absorbed much of the large clouds of carbon dioxide released by the nuclear holocaust. The carbon dioxide remained trapped in the water, retained in deep ocean circulation and not to be released for centuries. The ultimate release initiated a period of greenhouse warming.

As had happened before, life came forth from the seas. Many components of the biosphere—insects, microorganisms, plants, man himself—had survived, thanks to isolation, freak winds, or other providential conditions. They again became active, as white gave place to green. The ozone layer, shielding living cells from lethal ultraviolet, reestablished itself. Once more, as the firn melted, the pipe of separate instruments reached towards orchestral pitch.

By 5900, better conditions were evident. Antelope sprang among low thorn trees. Men and women muffled themselves in skins and trudged north after the glaciers.

At night, those humbled revenants huddled together for comfort and gazed upwards at the stars. The stars had scarcely changed since the time of paleolithic man. It was the human race which had changed.

Whole nations had gone forever. Those enterprising people who had developed mighty technologies and had struck out first for the planets and then for the stars, who had forged clever weapons and legends— those peoples had wiped themselves out. Their sole heirs were the sterile androids working on the outer planets.

Races came forth who, under an earlier dispensation, could be regarded as losers. They lived on islands or in wildernesses, at the tops of mountains or on untamed rivers, in jungles and swamps. They had once been the poor. Now they came forth to inherit the Earth.

They were peoples who took delight in life. In those first generations, as the ice retreated, they had no need to quarrel. The world awoke again. Gaia forgave them. They rediscovered ways of living with the natural world of which they were a part. And they rediscovered Helliconia.

From 6000 and for the next six centuries, Gaia could be said to convalesce. The tall glaciers were withdrawing fast to their polar fortresses.

Some of the old ways of life had survived. As the land returned, old bastions of the technophile culture were uncovered—generally hidden underground in elaborate military complexes. In the deepest bastions, there were descendants still living whose ancestors had been part of the ruling elite of the technophile culture; they had ensured their own survival while those who had been subject to them had perished. But these living fossils, on reaching the sunshine, died within a few hours— like fish brought up from the enormous pressures of the ocean deeps.

In their foul warrens, a hope was found—the link with another living planet. Summonses were sent through space to Charon, and a company of androids fetched back to Earth. These androids, with untiring skill, set about building auditoria in which the new population could observe all that happened on the far-distant planet.

The mentalities of the new populations were shaped to a large extent by the unfolding story they saw. Survivors on the other planets, cut off from Earth, also had their links with Helliconia.

In fresh green lands, auditoria stood like conch shells upended in sand. Each auditorium was capable of housing ten thousand people. In their sandalled feet, roughly clothed in skin, and later cloth, they came to look on with wonder. What they saw was a planet not greatly different from their own, emerging slowly from the grip of a long winter. It was their story.

Sometimes an auditorium might remain deserted for years. The new

*populations also had their crises, and the natural catastrophes which
attended Gaia's recovery. They had inherited not only the Earth but
its uncertainties.*

*When they could, the new generations returned to watch the story
of lives running parallel to their own. They were generations without
terrestrial gods; but the figures on the giant screens appeared like gods.
Those gods endured mysterious dramas of possession and religion which
gripped yet puzzled their terrestrial audiences.*

*By the year 6344, living forms were again in moderate abundance.
The human population took a solemn vow that they would hold all
possessions in common, declaring that not only life but its freedom was
sacred. They were much influenced by the deeds of a Helliconian living
in an obscure hamlet in the central continent, a leader called Aoz
Roon. They saw how a good man was ruined by a determination to get
his own way. To the new generations, there was no "own way"; there
was only a common way, the journey of life, the uct of the communal
spirit.*

*As they viewed the immense figure of Aoz Roon, saw water blow from
his lips and beard as he drank from his hands, they watched drops which
had fallen a thousand years earlier. The human understanding of past
generations had made past and present merge. For many years, the picture of Aoz Roon drinking from his hands became a popular ikon.*

*To the new generations, with their empathic feel for all life, it was
natural to wonder whether they could assist Aoz Roon and those who
lived with him. They had no idea of setting out in starships, as preglacial
peoples might have done. Instead, they decided to focus their empathic
sense and broadcast it outwards through conch shells.*

*So it was that signals went from Earth to Helliconia, responding for
the first time to the signals which had long flowed in the opposite direction.*

*The characteristics of the human race were now drawn from a slightly
different genetic pool than formerly. Those who had inherited the Earth
were strong on empathy. Empathy had not been dominant in the preglacial world. That gift of entering into the personality of another, of
experiencing sympathetically his or her state of mind, had never been
rare. But the elite had despised it—or exploited it. Empathy ran against
their interest as exploiters. Power and empathy were not happy team-
mates.*

*Now empathy was widely dispersed among the race. It became a
dominant feature, with survival characteristics. There was nothing inhuman about it.*

*There was an inhuman aspect to the Helliconians. The terrestrials
puzzled greatly about it. The Helliconians knew the spirits of their dead
and communed regularly with them.*

The new race on Earth took no particular account of death. They understood that when they died they were taken back and absorbed into the great Earth mother, their elementary particles to be re-formed into future living things. They were buried shallowly with flowers in their mouths, symbolising the force that would spring up from their decay. But it was different on Helliconia. They were fascinated by the Helliconians' descent into pauk to commune with their gossies, those sparks of vital energy.

And it was observed that the ancipital race had a similar relationship with its dead. Dead phagors sank into a "tether" state and appeared to linger, dwindling, for several generations. The phagors had no burial customs.

These macabre extensions to existence were regarded on Earth as a compensation for the extremities of climate which living things endured in the course of a Helliconian Great Year. There was, though, a marked difference between the defunct of the ancipital kind and the defunct of the human kind.

Phagors in tether supported their living descendants, formed a reservoir of wisdom and encouragement, comforted them in adversity. The spirits of humans visited in pauk, on the other hand, were unmitigatedly spiteful. No gossie ever spoke except to utter reproaches and to complain about a spoilt life.

Why this difference? asked the new intellects.

They answered from their own experience. They said: Dreadful though the phagors are, they are not estranged from the Original Beholder, the Helliconian Gaia figure. So they are not tormented by the spirits about them. The humans are estranged; they worship many useless gods who make them ill. So their spirits can never be at peace.

How happy for the Helliconian peoples—said the empathic ones among themselves—if they could have comfort from their gossies in the midst of all their other troubles.

So a determination developed. Those fortunate enough to experience life, to rise up from the molecular and surface into the great light of consciousness, like a salmon leaping from a stream to take a winged life, should radiate their happiness towards Helliconia.

The living of Earth, in other words, should beam empathy like a signal to Helliconia. Not to the living of Helliconia. The living, estranged from their Original Beholder, busy with their affairs, their lusts and hatreds, could not be expected to receive such a signal. But the gossies—for ever hungry for contact—might respond! The gossies in their event-free existence, suspended in obsidian as they sank towards the Original Beholder, the gossies might be capable of receiving a beam of empathy.

A whole generation discussed the daringly visionary proposal.

Was the attempt worth making? went the question.

It would be a great unifying experience even if it failed, came the answer.

Could we possibly hope to affect alien beings—the very dead—so far away?

Through us, Gaia could address the Original Beholder. They are kin, not alien. Perhaps this amazing idea is not ours but hers. We must try.

But when we are so far distant in space and time . . . ?

Empathy is a matter of intensity. It defies space and time. Do we not still feel for the exile of Iphigenia in that ancient story? Let's try. Shall we?

On all counts, it is worth it. The spirit of Gaia commands.

And so they tried.

The attempt was long-sustained. Wherever they sat and watched, wherever they came or went in their rough sandals, the living generations put away worldly things and radiated empathy towards the dead of Helliconia. And even when they could not resist including the living, such as Shay Tal or Laintal Ay, or whomever they might personally favour, they were still empathising with those long dead.

And over the years the warmth of their empathy took effect. The fessups ceased to grieve, the gossies ceased to chide. Those of the living who communed through pauk were not reproved but comforted. An unpossessive love had triumphed.

IX

A QUIET DAY ASHORE

A biogas fire burned in the grate. Before it sat two brothers talking. Every now and again, the thin brother would reach out to pat the sturdy one, as the latter told his tale. Odirin Nan Odim, referred to by all his kin as Odo, was a year and six tenners older than Eedap Mun Odim. He much resembled his brother, except in the crucial matter of girth, for the Fat Death had yet to make its dread appearance in Rivenjk.

The two brothers had much to tell each other, and much planning to do. A ship bearing the Oligarch's soldiery had recently arrived in the port, and the set of regulations against which Odim had fought was beginning to trouble Odo too. However, the Shiveninki were less ready than the Uskuti to take orders. Rivenjk was still a comfortable place in which to live.

The remaining precious porcelain which Odim had brought to his elder brother had been well received.

"Soon such porcelain will become even more precious," said Odo. "Such fine quality may never be achieved again."

"Because the weather deteriorates towards winter."

"What follows from that, brother, is that fuel for firing the kilns will become short, and so increase in price. Also, as people's lives grow harsher, they will be content with tin plates."

"What do you plan to do then, brother?" asked Odim.

"My trade links with Bribahr, the neighbouring country, are excellent. I even despatch my goods to Kharnabhar, far north of here. Porcelain and china are not the only goods that need to travel such routes. We must adapt, deal in other goods. I have ideas for—"

But Odirin Nan Odim was never allowed peace for long. He, like his brother, housed a number of relations. Some of them, voluble and voluminous, rushed to the fireside now, heads full of a quarrel that only Odo could settle. Some of Eedap Mun's relations, surviving plague and voyage, had been billeted with their Rivenjk relations, and the old question had arisen of floor space being encroached upon.

"Perhaps you would not mind coming with me to see what is happening," said Odo.

"I would be pleased. From now on, I shall be your shadow, brother."

Homesteads in Rivenjk were arranged round a courtyard and protected from the elements by a high wall. The more prosperous the family, the higher the wall. Round this courtyard lived the various branches of the Odim family—very little more enterprising here than the relatives in Koriantura had been.

With the families lived their domestic animals, housed in stalls adjoining the human habitations. Some of the animals had been crowded together to permit the newly arrived relatives shelter. This arrangement was the cause of the present quarrel: the resident relations prized their animals above the newly arrived relations—and with some justice.

The sanitary arrangements of most Shiveninki courtyard homesteads depended on a commensalism between animals and humans. All excretions from both house and stall were washed down into a bottle-shaped pit carved in the rock under the courtyard. The pit could be maintained from an inspection flap in the courtyard, through which all vegetable refuse was also thrown. As the refuse rotted underground, it gave off biogas, chiefly methane.

The biogas rising from the pit was trapped and piped into the houses, to be used for cooking and lighting.

This civilised system had been developed throughout Shivenink to cope with the extremes of the Weyr-Winter.

As the Odim brothers inspected the complaints of their relatives, they discovered that two cousins had been housed in a stall where there was a small gas leak. The smell offended the cousins, who had insisted on bundling into the adjoining house, which was already packed with people.

The gas leak was plugged. The cousins, protesting for form's sake, went back to their appointed stall. Slaves were despatched to see that the biogas tank was not malfunctioning.

Odo took his brother's arm. "The church is nearby, as you will observe when we take you on a tour of the city. I have arranged this evening for a small service of thanksgiving to be held there. Praise will be offered to God the Azoiaxic for your preservation."

"You are most kind. But I warn you, brother, I am free of religious belief."

"This little service is necessary," said Odo, raising a dismissive finger. "There you will be able to meet all our relatives formally. There is something downcast in your spirit, brother, owing to your multiple bereavements. You must take a good woman, or at least a slave, to make you happy. What is the status of that foreign woman in your party, Toress Lahl?"

"She's a slave, belonging to Luterin Shokerandit. A doctor, very spirited. He is a fine young man, and from Kharnabhar. About Captain Fashnalgid, I am less certain. He's a deserter, not that I blame him for that. I started out the voyage, before the Fat Death overcame us, with a woman who meant much to my comfort. Alas, she died in the epidemic."

"Was she from Kuj-Juvec, brother?"

"No, but she became like a dove to the tree of my self. She was faithful and good. Her name, for I must speak it, was Besi Besamitikahl. She was more to me even than my—"

Odim broke off sharply, for up ran Kenigg, with a newfound friend. As Odim smiled and took his son's hand, his brother said, "Let me help you find another dove for that good tree of your self. You have only one brother, but the air is full of doves waiting for a suitable branch on which to alight."

Luterin Shokerandit and Harbin Fashnalgid had been given a small room under the roof, thanks to Odo's generosity. It was lit by one little garret window overlooking the courtyard, from which they could watch the comings and goings of the family and their slaves. In an alcove stood a stove on which their slave could cook their meals.

Both the men had beds of wood, raised above the floor and covered in rugs. Toress Lahl was supposed to lie on the floor beside Shokerandit's bed.

Shokerandit took her in with him while Fashnalgid still slept. He lay all night with his arms round her. Only as he was rising did Fashnalgid stir.

"Luterin, why so energetic?" he asked, yawning cavernously. "Didn't you drink enough of the Odim family's wine last night? Rest, man, and for the Azoiaxic's sake, let's recover from that terrible voyage."

Shokerandit came and looked down at him, smiling. "I had enough wine. Now I want to be off to Kharnabhar as soon as possible. My status is uncertain. I must see how my father is."

"Damn fathers. May their gossies eat shoe leather."

"I have another anxiety too—one you had better heed. Although the Oligarch is well occupied with the war against Bribahr, he has a ship here in port. More may arrive. They may be watching for us both. The sooner I start for Kharnabhar, the better. Why not come with me? There'd be safety and work with my father."

"It's always cold in Kharnabhar. Isn't that what they say? How far north is it from here?"

"The Kharnabhar road covers over twenty-two degrees of latitude."

Fashnalgid laughed. "You go. I'll stay here. I'll find a ship sailing for Campannlat or Hespagorat. Anything rather than your frozen refuge, thanks for all that."

"Please yourself. We don't exactly please each other, do we? Men have to get along well, to survive the drive to Kharnabhar."

Fashnalgid brought an arm up from his furs and held out a hand to Shokerandit. "Well, well, you're a man for the system, and I'm against it, but never mind that."

"You like to think I'm a man for the system, but since my metamorphosis I've broken from it."

"Yes? Yet you long to get back to Father in Kharnabhar." Fashnalgid laughed. "True conformists don't know they conform. I like you well enough, Luterin, though I know you think I wrecked your life by capturing you. On the contrary, I saved you from the claws of the Oligarch, so be grateful. Be grateful enough to heave your Toress over to my bed for the morning, will you?"

A flush spread over Shokerandit's face. "She'll get you water or food while I'm out. Otherwise, she is mine. Ask Odim's brother for what you want—he has plenty of slaves for whom he cares nothing."

They looked each other in the eye. Then Shokerandit turned to leave the room.

"Can I come with you?" Toress Lahl called.

"I shall be busy. You can stay here."

As soon as he was gone, Fashnalgid sat up in bed. The woman was hurriedly dressing. She cast the odd glance across at the captain, who smoothed his moustache and gave a smile.

"Don't be so hasty, woman. Come over to me. Sweet Besi's dead and I want comforting."

When she made no answer, he climbed naked out of bed.

Toress Lahl made a run for the door, but he caught her by the wrist and pulled her back.

"Don't be in such a hurry, I said, didn't I? Didn't you hear me?"
He gave her long brown hair a gentle tug. "Women are generally pleased
to be attended by Captain Fashnalgid."

"I belong to Luterin Shokerandit. You heard what he said."

He twisted her arm and grinned down at her. "You're a slave, so
you're anyone's. Beside, you hate his guts—I've seen the looks you
give him. I never forced a woman, Toress, that's the truth, and you'll
find me a good deal more expert than he, from what I overheard."

"Please let me go. Or I shall tell him and he'll kill you."

"Come on, you're too pretty to threaten me. Open up. I saved you
from death, didn't I? You and he were riding into a trap. He's a fatal
innocent, your Luterin."

He put a hand between her legs. She got her right hand free and
slapped him across the face.

With a burst of anger, Fashnalgid wrenched her off her feet and
threw her down on his bed. He fell on top of her.

"Now you listen to me before you provoke me beyond words, Toress
Lahl. You and I are on the same side. Shokerandit is all very well, but
he is going home to security and position—all the things you and I have
lost. What is more, he plans to drive you countless skerming miles
northwards. What's up there but snow and holiness and that gigantic
Wheel?"

"It's where he lives."

"Kharnabhar's fit only for rulers. The rest die in the cold. Haven't
you heard of the Wheel's reputation? It used to be a prison, the worst
on the planet. Do you want to finish up in the Wheel?

"Throw your lot in with me. I have seen the sort of woman you are.
You've seen the sort of man I am. I am an outcast, but I can fend for
myself. Before you get taken miles to some fortress in the northern ice
from which you will never escape, achieve wisdom, achieve wisdom,
woman, and throw in your lot with me. We'll sail from here to
Campannlat and better climes. Maybe we'll even get back to your
precious Borldoran."

She had gone very pale. His face, close above hers, was a blur, nothing
more than eyebrows, those piercing eyes, and that great dead moustache.
She was afraid that he would strike her or even kill her—and that
Shokerandit would not care. Her will was already ebbing under the
burden of captivity.

"He owns me, Captain. Why discuss it? But you may have your
way with me if you must. Why not? He has."

"That's better," he said. "I'll not hurt you. Throw your clothes off."

Luterin Shokerandit knew the port of Rivenjk well. It had always
been the great city, spoken of in Kharnabhar with longing, visited—

when visited—with excitement. Now that he had seen more of the world, he recognised that it was rather small.

At least there was pleasure in being ashore again. He could swear he still felt a slight rolling movement underfoot. Walking down to the harbour, he went into one of the inns and drank a measure of yadahl while listening to the talk of the sailors.

"They're nothing but a nuisance here, these soldiers," a man nearby was saying to a companion. "You heard, I suppose, that one was knifed last night down Perspicacity Alley, and I don't wonder at it."

"They'll set sail tomorrow," his friend said. "They'll be confined aboard ship tonight, you'll see, and good riddance." He lowered his voice. "They're off under Oligarch's orders to fight against the good people of Bribahr. What harm Bribahr have done the rest of us, I don't know."

"They may have captured Braijth, but Rattagon is impregnable. The Oligarch is wasting his time."

"Set in the middle of a lake, I hear."

"That's Rattagon."

"Well, I'm glad I'm not a soldier."

"You're too much of a fool to be anything but a sailor."

As the two men laughed together, Shokerandit fixed his gaze on a poster on a wall by the door. It announced that henceforth Anyone Entering the State of Pauk committed an Offence. To Enter into Pauk, whether alone or in company, was to Encourage the Spreading of the Plague known as the Fat Death. The Penalty for defying this law was One Hundred Sibs and, for a Second Offence, Life Imprisonment. By Order of the Oligarch.

Although Shokerandit never practised pauk, he disliked the stream of new orders the State was issuing.

Shokerandit thought to himself as he drained his glass that he probably hated the Oligarch. When the Archpriest-Militant Asperamanka had sent him to report to the Oligarchy, he had felt honoured. Then Fashnalgid had stopped him almost at the Sibornalese frontier; and it had taken him some while to believe what the man claimed, that he would have been cold-bloodedly killed with the rest of the returning army. It was even more difficult to realise that all of Asperamanka's force had been wiped out on the Oligarch's orders.

It made sense to take rational measures to keep the plague from spreading. But to suppress pauk was a sign that authoritarianism was spreading. He wiped his mouth with his hand.

As a result of circumstance, Shokerandit was no hero but a fugitive. He could not imagine what his fate would be if he was arrested for desertion.

"What did Harbin mean, I'm a man of the system?" he muttered. "I'm a rebel, an outcast—like him."

It behoved him to get home to Kharnabhar and remain under his father's powerful protection. At least in distant Kharnabhar the forces of the Oligarch would not reach him. Thought of Insil could be left for later.

With this reflection came another. He owed Fashnalgid something. He must take him on the arduous journey north if Fashnalgid could be persuaded to come. Fashnalgid would be useful in Kharnabhar: there he could help bear witness to the massacre of thousands of young Shiveninki by their own side.

He said to himself, I had courage in battle. I must have courage to fight against the Oligarchy if necessary. There will be others at home who feel as I do when they hear the truth.

He paid his coin and left the inn.

Along the waterfront stood a grand avenue of rajabarals. As temperatures dropped, the trees prepared for the long winter. Instead of shedding their leaves, they drew in their branches, pulling them into the tops of their vast trunks. Shokerandit had seen pictures in natural history books of how branches and leaves would dissolve to form a solid resin plug, protecting the featureless and undecaying tree until it released its seed in the following Great Spring.

Under the rajabarals, soldiers from a ship which flew the flags of Sibornal and the Oligarchy were parading. Shokerandit had a momentary fear that someone might recognize him; but his metamorphosed shape was protection. He turned inland, towards the marketplace, where there were agents who handled the affairs of travellers intending to visit Kharnabhar.

The cold winds from the mountains made him turn up his collar and lower his head. But at the agent's door, pilgrims eager to visit the shrines of the Great Wheel were gathered, many poor and scantily clad.

It took him a while to arrange matters to his liking. He could travel to Kharnabhar with the pilgrims. Or he could travel independently, hiring a sledge, a team, a driver, and a jack-of-all-trades. The former way was safer, slower, and less expensive. Shokerandit decided on the latter as more befitting the son of the Keeper of the Wheel.

All he needed was cash or a letter of credit.

There were friends of his father's at hand, some men of influence in the town's affairs. He hesitated, and eventually chose a simple man called Hernisarath, who ran a farm and a hostel for pilgrims on the edge of town. Hernisarath welcomed Shokerandit in, immediately supplied a letter of credit for the agent, and insisted that Shokerandit join him and his wife for a midday meal.

He embraced Shokerandit on the doorstep when it was time to take leave.

"You're a good and innocent young man, Luterin, and I'm happy to help. Every day as Weyr-Winter approaches, farming becomes more difficult. But let's hope we shall meet again."

His wife said, "It's so nice to meet a young man with good manners. Our respects to your father."

Shokerandit glowed as he left them, pleased to have made a good impression; whereas Harbin was probably drunk by now. But why did Hernisarath call him "innocent"?

Snow began to fall from the heights, whirling as it came, like fine white sugar dissolving in a stirred glass of water. It thickened, muffling the sound of his boots on the cobbles. The streets cleared of people. Long grey shadows sprouted penumbras, dark for Freyr, lighter for Batalix, until the cloud extended over the bay and enveloped all Rivenjk in murk.

Shokerandit halted suddenly behind a rajabaral.

Another man came on from behind, clutching his collar to his throat. He walked past the tree, glanced back, shuffled his feet, and hurried into a side street. Shokerandit saw with some amusement that it was called Perspicacity Alley.

With uncharacteristic forethought, he had not told his fellow travellers that on the head of the Hero guarding entry to Rivenjk harbour was a heliograph signalling station. Warning of the deserters aboard the *New Season* could have reached the port long before the brig docked. . . .

He returned to Odo's house by as devious a route as he could contrive. By then, the worst of the snow shower was over.

"How fortunate that you arrive in time," Odo said, as Shokerandit entered the door. "My brother and I and the rest of the family are about to go to church to give thanks for the *New Season*'s survival. You will come along, please?"

"Oh . . . yes, of course. A private ceremony?"

"Absolutely private. Only the priest and the family."

Shokerandit looked at Odim, who nodded encouragingly. "You are about to embark on another journey, Luterin. We who have known each other such a short while must part. The ceremony seems appropriate, even if you don't believe in prayer."

"I will see if Fashnalgid will come too."

He hastened up the winding wooden stair to the room Odo had lent them. Toress Lahl was there, lying under her skins on his bed.

"You're meant to be working, not lying about," he said. "You're not still mourning your husband? Where's the captain?"

"I don't know."

"Find him, will you? He'll be drinking somewhere."

He ran back downstairs. As soon as he was gone, Fashnalgid climbed out from under his bed and laughed. Toress Lahl refused to smile.

"I want food, not prayer," he said, peering cautiously out of the window. "And that drink your friend mentioned would be welcome. . . ."

The Odim clan was gathering in the courtyard, where slaves were still meddling inefficiently with long rods, climbing in and out of the biogas inspection pit, despite the sleet in the air. The place was filled with excited talk.

Shokerandit appeared. Some of the ladies who had been on the *New Season* ran up and embraced him, in a manner more reminiscent of Kuj-Juvec than of the rest of Sibornal. Shokerandit no longer contrasted such free behaviour with his own formal upbringing.

"Oh, this is such a good place, this Rivenjk," said one well-wrapped grand-aunt, taking his arm. "There are many fine buildings, and much statuary. I shall be happy here, and mean to set up a press to print poetry. Do you think your countrymen like poetry?"

But before Shokerandit could reply, the lady had turned in the other direction to grasp Eedap Mun Odim by the sleeve. "You are our little hero, cousin, bringing us safe from oppression. Let me be in the church next to you. Walk there with me and make me proud."

"I shall be proud to walk with *you*, auntie," said Odim, smiling kindly at her. And the whole jostling crowd began to move out of the courtyard gate and along the street to the church.

"And we are proud to have you with us, too, Luterin," said Odim, anxious that Shokerandit should not feel left out of the party. He looked round with pleasure at so many Odims gathered together. Although their ranks had been culled by the Fat Death, the bulk of the survivors was a compensation of sorts.

When they filed into the high-roofed church, Odim ranged himself against his brother, elbows touching. He wondered if Odo, like him, had no belief in God the Azoiaxic. He was far too polite to put such a personal question; secrecy was for men, as the saying went. If his brother wished to confess one evening, over a little wine, that was another matter. For now, it was enough that they were together and that the service allowed them to mourn for those who had died, including his wife and children and the beloved Besi Besamitikahl, and to rejoice in the fact that their own lives were spared.

A treble voice, disembodied, sexless, free of lust, traced a thread of theatrical penitence which rose from the well of the church to its interlaced roof beams.

Odim smiled as he sang and felt his soul lifted towards the rafters. Belief would have been good. But even the wish to believe was consolatory.

As the voices of the congregation were raised in song inside, ten beefy soldiers marched down the street outside accompanied by an officer, and halted outside Odirin Nan Odim's gate. The watchman opened up to them, bowing. The soldiers brushed him aside and marched into the centre of the courtyard, trampling the already trodden carpet of snow.

The officer barked orders to his men. Four men to search the houses set at each point of the compass, remainder to stand where they were and be alert for escapees.

"Abro Hakmo Astab!" Fashnalgid shouted, jumping up from his bed. He had been sitting half-dressed, watching both the window and Toress Lahl, to whom he occasionally read lines of poetry from a small book. She was obeying his orders to prepare a meal, and was carrying a flaming brand obtained from a slave downstairs to light their stove.

She flinched at the obscenity of his oath, although she was used to the swearing of soldiers.

"How I love the sound of a military voice! 'No song like yours under spring skies . . .'" Fashnalgid said. "And the clump of army boots. Yes, there they are. Look at that young fool of a lieutenant, uniform gleaming. All I once was . . ."

He glared down at the scene in the courtyard, where, in front of the soldiers, slaves still worked, rodding out the biogas drains, glancing mistrustfully at the invaders.

A pair of boots started to clump up the stairs to the attic room.

Fashnalgid snarled, showing white teeth under the wave of his moustache. He rushed for his sword and glared round the room like a cornered beast. Toress Lahl stood petrified, one hand to her mouth, the other holding the flaming brand at arm's length.

"Haaa . . ." He dashed forward and snatched the brand from her, trailing the smoke across the room as he ran for the window. Pushing it open, he forced his head and shoulders out and hurled the brand with all his strength.

He had not lost his military skills. No grenade could have flown truer. The flame drew a parabola down the darkened air and disappeared into the open trap of the biogas chamber. For a second, silence. Then the whole place exploded. Slabs of the courtyard went flying. A great flame rose in the midst of everything, burning blue at its core.

With a roar of satisfaction, Fashnalgid crossed to the door and flung it wide. A young soldier stood there, hesitating, looking back the way he had come. Without thought, Fashnalgid ran him through. As the man doubled, Fashnalgid kicked out, sending him head first down the stairs.

"Now we've got to run for our lives, woman," he said, taking hold of Toress Lahl's hand.

"Luterin—" she said, but she was too frightened to do anything but follow him. They ran downstairs. The courtyard was a scene of panic. The gas still burned. Odims too old, too young, or too voluminous to attend the church service, together with their animals, were running about among the soldiers. The smart lieutenant aimed a bullet or two at the clouds. Slaves were screaming. One of the houses had caught fire.

It was an easy matter to skirt the melee and leave by the gate.

Once they were in the street, Fashnalgid dropped to an easier pace and sheathed his sword, so as to be less conspicuous.

They hurried into the churchyard. He pulled the woman against a buttress, panting. Inside, hymns rose to God the Azoiaxic. In his excitement, he gripped her painfully by the upper arm.

"Those sherbs, they're after us. Even in this piddling dump . . ."

"Oh, do let me go. You're hurting me."

"I'll let you go. You're going to go inside this church and get Shokerandit. Tell him that the military have caught up with us. There'll be no escaping by boat now. If he has arranged a sledge, then we all start for Kharnabhar as soon as we can. Go in and tell him." He gave her a push to encourage her. "Tell him they want to hang him."

By the time Toress Lahl reappeared with Shokerandit, many people were about in the street—and not only innocent bystanders. As the Odims ran shouting with distress, Fashnalgid said, "Luterin, have you got a sledge? Can we get out of here right away?"

"Need you have wrecked the Odim home after all they have done for us?" Shokerandit said, regarding the other's disarray.

"Don't trust Odim. He's a tradesman. We have to leave. The army's woken up. Don't forget your lovely Toress Lahl is officially a runaway slave. You know the penalty for that. Where's the sledge?"

"We can get it when the stables open at Batalix-dawn. You have changed your mind suddenly, haven't you?"

"Where do we hide till dawn?"

Shokerandit thought. "There's a family friend, by name Hernisarath. He and his wife will give us shelter until the morning. . . . But I must go and say good-bye to Odim."

Fashnalgid pointed a thick finger at him. "You'll do no such thing. He'll hand you over. Soldiers are swarming everywhere. You *are* an innocent, aren't you?"

"All right, and you're an eccentric. Insults apart, why the change of plan? Only this morning you were going to sail for Campannlat."

Fashnalgid smiled. "Suppose it occurred to me that I ought to be nearer to God? I've decided to come with you and your lady slave to Holy Kharnabhar."

X

"THE DEAD NEVER
TALK POLITICS"

On the sixth day of the sixth tenner of every sixth small year, the Synod of the Church of the Formidable Peace met in Askitosh. The lesser fry met in conventials behind the Palace of the Supreme Priest. The fifteen dignitaries who formed the standing synod lived and met in the Palace itself. They represented both the ecclesiastical and the secular or military arms of the organisation of the Church. The burdens of office were heavy upon them. They were not men given to drollery.

Being human, the fifteen had their faults. One was regularly overcome by alcohol by sixteen twenty every day. Others kept young female or male slaves in their chambers. Some enjoyed peculiar defilements. Nevertheless, at least a part of each of them was dedicated to the good continuance of the Church. Since good men were hard to find, the fifteen could be accounted good men.

And the most dedicated man of all was Chubsalid, a man of Bribahr birth, brought up by holy fathers within the cloisters of their church, now Priest-Supreme of the Church of the Formidable Peace, the ap-

pointed representative on Helliconia of God the Azoiaxic, who existed
before life and round whom all life revolves.

Even the most watchful ecclesiastical eye had never seen Chubsalid
raise a bottle to his lips. If he had any sexual proclivities whatsoever,
they were a secret kept between him and his maker. If he ever experienced anger, fear, or sorrow, no shadows of those emotions ever reached
his rosy face. And he was no fool.

Unlike the Oligarchy, whose meeting place on Icen Hill was not a
mile away, the Synod had wide popular support. The Church genuinely
ministered to the needs of its people; uplifted their hearts and supported
them in adversity. And preserved tactful silence about pauk.

Unlike the Oligarch, who was never seen and whose image in the
fearful popular imagination most resembled a huge crustacean with
hyperactive nippers, Priest-Supreme Chubsalid travelled among the poor
and was a popular visitor with his congregations. He looked every inch a
Priest-Supreme, with his large stature, craggy but kindly countenance,
and mane of white hair. When he spoke, people wished to listen. His
addresses were spun from piety and often fringed by wit: he could
make his congregations laugh as well as pray.

The discussion at the synodical meetings was conducted in the
highest Sibish, with multiple clauses, elaborate parentheses, and spectacular verb formations. But the matter on this occasion was strictly
practical. It concerned the strained relationship between the two great
estates of Sibornal, the State and the Church.

The Church watched with alarm as the edicts of the Oligarchy increased in severity. One of the synodic priesthood was speaking to the
assembly on this subject.

"The new Restrictions of Persons in Abodes Act and similar regulations are/continue represented by the State as a move to curtail the
plague. Already they are causing as much disruption as the plague does/
will/can. The poor are evicted and arrested for vagrancy, or else perish
from the increasing cold."

He was a silvery man and spoke in a silvery voice, but its conviction
carried to the end of the room. "We can see the political thinking behind this iniquitous Act. As more northerly farms fail/failing, the
peasants and small farmers who worked those farms drift into town,
where they must find shelter where they can, generally in overcrowded
conditions. The Act seeks to confine them to their failed farms. There
they will starve. I hope I am not unduly uncharitable when I say that
their deaths would suit the State well. The dead never talk politics."

"You foresee a revolt starting in the towns if the Act were repealed?"
asked a voice from the other end of the table.

"In my youth, it was said that a Sibornalese worked for life, married
for life, and longed for life," replied the silvery voice. "But we never

rebel. We leave that to the people of the Savage Continent. The Church has so far said nothing about these restrictive Acts. Now I suggest that we have reached a sticking point with the Act against pauk."

"We have no policy on pauk."

"Neither had the State till now. Again, the dead have no politics, and that the State has/continuous recognises. Nevertheless, the Oligarchy have now legislated against pauk. This causes/has/will further misery to our congregations for whom—if you will forgive my saying so—pauk is as much a part of life as parturition.

"The poor are being unfairly punished to fit them for the coming winter. I move that the Church speaks out publicly against the recent actions of the State."

An aged and bald man, completely lacking hair or colour, rose with the aid of two sticks and spoke.

"It may be as you say, brother. The Oligarchy may be tightening its grip. I suggest to you that it has to do so. Think of the future. All too soon, our descendants will be faced/facing three and a half centuries of the bitter Weyr-Winter. The Oligarchy reasons that the harshness of nature must be matched by the harshness of mankind.

"Let me remind you of that terrible Sibish oath which must not be spoken. It is regarded as a supreme blasphemy, and rightly. Yet it is admirable. Yes, admirable. I would not/admonitorily have it spoken in my diocese, yet I admire the defiance of it."

He steadied himself. There were those who thought the venerable man was about to defile his lips with the oath. Instead, he took a different tack.

"In the Savage Continent of Campannlat, chaos descends with the cold. They have no overriding order as we have. They crawl back to their caves. Sibornal survives intact. We will/shall/have perpetual survive by organisation. That organisation has to tighten like an iron fist. Many have to die that the state will survive.

"Some of you have complained because all phagors are to be shot regardless. I say they are not human. Get rid of them. They have no souls. Shoot them. And shoot all that defend them. Shoot the farmers whose farms fail. This is no time for individual gestures. Individuality itself must soon/will be punished by death."

In the silence, his sticks rattled like bones as he seated himself again.

A murmur of shock went round the room, but Priest-Supreme Chubsalid from his ermine-lined seat said mildly, "No doubt they make such speeches all the while on Icen Hill, but we must keep to our chosen profession, which involves/continuous tempering our dealings even with failed farmers with mercy. Our Church stands for the individual, for individual conscience, individual salvation, and our duty is to remind our friends in the Oligarchy of this from time to time, so that the people are also clear in their minds on that point.

"The seasons may grow harsh. We do not have to imitate them, so that even in harshest times the essential teaching of the Church may/will/must live. Otherwise there is no life in God. The State sees this time of crisis as one in which it must show its strength. The Church must do at least as much. Who here of the fifteen agrees that the Church should stand against the State?"

All of the fourteen he had addressed turned to mutter with their neighbours down the long table. They could guess the retribution which would follow the move advocated by their leader.

One of the number raised a gold-ringed hand and said, in a quavering voice, "Sire, the time may/potential come when we do indeed have to take the kind of stance you suggest. But for pauk? When we have carefully avoided for eons—when perhaps some doubt as to the legitimacy of challenging—when the myth of the Original Beholder opposes our . . ."

He left that theatrical thought unstated.

The youngest member of the Synod was a Priest-Chaplain named Parlingelteg, a delicate man, though it was whispered that some of his activities were indelicate. He was never afraid to speak up, and he addressed his words directly to Chubsalid.

"That last miserable speech convinces me at least—and I imagine all of you—that we must stand against the State. Perhaps specifically on the issue of pauk. Let's not pretend pauk isn't real, or that the gossies don't exist, just because they don't fit with the Teaching.

"Why do you think the State has tried to forbid pauk? For one reason only. The State is guilty of genocide. It killed off thousands of men in Asperamanka's army. The mothers of those sons thus slain have communed with them after death. The gossies have spoken. Who here said the dead have no politics? That's nonsense. Thousands of dead mouths cry out against the State and the murderous Oligarch. I support the Priest-Supreme. We must speak against Torkerkanzlag and have him thrown out of office."

He blushed red to the roots of his fair hair, as several of his seniors applauded. The meeting broke up. Still they drew back from taking a decision. Had not Church and State always been inseparable? And to speak aloud of that massacre . . . They loved peace—some of them at all costs.

An hour's break followed. It was too chilly to go outdoors. They loitered in the heated withdrawing rooms while scouts served water or wine in porcelain cups. They talked among themselves. Perhaps there was a way of avoiding actual consultation; apart from what the gossies said, there was no real evidence, was there?

A bell rang. They reconvened. Chubsalid spoke privily to Parlingelteg and both looked solemn.

The debate was continuing when a liveried slave knocked and

entered. He bowed low before the Priest-Supreme and handed him a note on a tray.

Chubsalid read the note, then sat for a moment with his elbow on the table before him and his hand touching his tall forehead. The talk died. All waited for him to speak.

"Brothers," he said, looking round at them. "We have a visitor, an important witness. I propose to summon him before us. His words, I fancy, will carry more weight than would further discussion." He gestured to the slave, who bowed and hurried from the room.

Another man entered the chamber. With deliberation, he turned and closed the doors behind him, only then advancing towards the table where the fifteen leaders of the Church sat. He was dressed in deep blue from head to foot; boots, breeches, shirt, jacket, cloak, all were blue; so was the hat he carried in his hand. Only his hair was white, although black remained over each temple. When the Synod had last seen him, his hair had been entirely black.

The white hair emphasised the size of his head. His straight brows, eyes, mouth, emphasised the anger that lurked like thunder there.

He bowed deeply to the Priest-Supreme and kissed his hand. He turned to salute the Synod.

"I thank you for giving me audience," he said.

"Archpriest-Militant Asperamanka, we had been informed of your death in battle," said Chubsalid. "We rejoice in the inaccuracy of our information."

Asperamanka formed his lips into a chilling smile. "I all but died— but not in battle. The story of how I managed to reach Askitosh, almost alone of all my army, is an extraordinary one. I was shot in Chalce, on the very frontiers of our continent, I was captured by phagors, I escaped, I was lost in marshland—well, in brief, it is God's miracle that I stand before you now. God protected me, and sharpened me as an instrument of justice. For I come as proof of a crime of perfidy unequalled in the illustrious history of Sibornal."

"Pray take a seat," said the Priest-Supreme, motioning to a lackey. "We wait to hear what you have to tell us. You will prove a better informant than any gossie."

As Asperamanka told his story of the ambush, of the withering fire directed by the Oligarch's guard against his returning forces, as the full extent of what had happened was borne home to everyone, it became clear that Parlingelteg had spoken truly. The Church would have to confront the State. Otherwise, the Church became party to the massacre.

It took Asperamanka over an hour to unfold the whole story of the campaign and its betrayal. Finally he was silent. Silent only for a minute. Then he unexpectedly hid his face in his hands and burst into tears.

"The crime is mine too," he cried. "I worked for the Oligarch. I fear the Oligarch. To me, Church and State were one and synonymous."

"But no more," said Chubsalid. He rose and rested his hand on Asperamanka's shoulder. "Thank you for being God's instrument and making our duty plain to us.

"The Oligarchy has had jurisdiction over humanity's bodies, the Church over its souls. Now we must gird ourselves to assert the supremacy of the soul above the body. We must oppose the Oligarchy. Is it here so resolved?"

The fourteen members gave cries of assent. Sticks rattled under the table.

"Then it is unanimous."

After more discussion, agreement was reached that the first move should be to send out a firmly worded Bill to all churches the length and breadth of the land. The Bill would declare that the Church defended the ancient practice of pauk, which it regarded as an essential freedom of every man and woman in the realm. There was no evidence that the so-called gossies spoke other than Truth. The Church in no way accepted that the practice of pauk spread the Fat Death. Chubsalid set his name to the Bill.

"This is probably the most revolutionary Bill the Church has ever put out," said the silvery voice. "I just want to state that fact. And by acknowledging pauk, are we not acknowledging also the Original Beholder? And are we not thus allowing heathen superstition into the Church?"

"The Bill makes no mention of the Original Beholder, brother," said Parlingelteg softly.

The Bill was approved and sent to the ecclesiastical printer. From the printer it went out to all the churches in the land.

Four days passed. In the Palace of the Priest-Supreme, churchmen waited for the storm to break.

A messenger, clad in oilskins against the weather, came down from Icen Hill and delivered a sealed document at the Palace.

The Priest-Supreme broke the seal and read the message.

The message said that subversive pamphlets put out by the Synod preached treason, in that they set out deliberately to flout recent Acts promulgated by the State. Treason was punishable by death.

If there was an explanation for these vile offences, then the Priest-Supreme of the Church of the Formidable Peace should present himself before the Oligarch forthwith, and deliver it in person.

The letter was signed with the signature of Torkerkanzleg II.

"I do not believe that man exists," Chubsalid said. "He has reigned for over thirty years. Nobody has ever seen him. No portrait exists of his face. He could be a phagor for all we know to the contrary . . ."

He continued for a while in this vein, tut-tutting absently, and visiting the Synod library to compare signatures, toying with magnifying glasses and shaking his head.

This activity made the Priest-Supreme's advisors nervous; they felt he should be concentrating on the gravity of a summons which, on the face of it at least, appeared to be his death warrant. Senior advisors, speaking among themselves, suggested that the entire centre of the Church should move immediately from Askitosh to a safer place—possibly to Rattagon, although it was under siege, since its position in the middle of a lake rendered it secure; or even to Kharnabhar, despite its extreme climate, since it was a religious refuge.

But Chubsalid had his own ideas. Retreat never entered his mind. After an hour of pottering about comparing signatures, he announced that he would meet the Oligarch. An acceptance note was written by his scribe to that effect. It suggested that the meeting should be in the great entrance hall of Icen Castle, and that anyone who wished might come there and hear the debate between the two men.

As Chubsalid appended his name to the document, Priest-Chaplain Parlingelteg, who was standing nearby, came forward and knelt by the Priest-Supreme's chair.

"Sire, when you go to that place, permit me to accompany you. Whatever there befalls you, let it also befall me."

Chubsalid set his hand on the young man's shoulder.

"It shall be as you suggest. I shall be grateful for your presence."

He turned then to Asperamanka, who was also in the company.

"And you, our Priest-Militant, will you also come to Icen Castle, to bear witness to the Oligarch's crime?"

Asperamanka looked here and there, as if seeking out an invisible door. "You speak better than I, Priest-Supreme. I think it unwise to bring up the subject of the plague. We have no cure for the Fat Death, any more than the State. The Oligarch may have reasons we know nothing of for wishing to suppress pauk."

"Then we will hear them. You will come with Parlingelteg and me?"

"Perhaps we should take doctors with us."

Chubsalid smiled. "We shall be able to stand against him, I trust, without the aid of doctors."

"Surely we ought to try and compromise," said Asperamanka, looking wretched.

"We shall see if that is possible," said Chubsalid. "And thank you for saying you will accompany us."

The day dawned. Priest-Supreme Chubsalid put on his ecclesiastical robes and bade good-bye to his colleagues. One or two he embraced.

The silvery man shed a tear.

Chubsalid smiled at him. "Whatever happens this day, I will require your courage as well as mine." His voice was firm and serene.

He climbed into his carriage, where Asperamanka and Parlingelteg waited. The carriage moved off.

It made its way through silent streets. The police, at the Oligarch's command, had cleared onlookers away, so that there was none of the cheering which usually greeted the appearance of the Priest-Supreme. Only silence.

As the carriage ground its way up the treacherous paving stones of Icen Hill, the presence of soldiery was all too noticeable. At the gates of the castle, armed men stepped forward and fended off those priests who had followed behind their leader's carriage. The carriage passed under the ponderous stone arch. The great iron gates closed behind it.

Many windows looked down on the front courtyard, enforcing silence with their oppressive dead shine. They were mean windows, less like eyes than blunt teeth.

The party of three was led unceremoniously from the carriage into the chill of the building. Their footsteps echoed as they traversed the great entrance hall. Soldiers in elaborate national uniform stood on guard. None moved.

The party was shown to the rear, to a dingy passage where the skirting was scuffed by innumerable boots, as if a tormented animal had tried to fight its way to freedom. After a wait, a signal was given their guide and they ascended by a narrow wooden stair which wound up two flights without a window by way of punctuation. They emerged into another passage, no more congenial to tormented animals than the first, and halted at a door. The guide knocked.

A voice bade them enter.

They came into a room which displayed all the festive cheer for which the Oligarchy was noted. It was a reception room of a kind, lined with chairs on which only the most emaciated anatomies could have found rest. The one window in the room was draped in heavy leather curtains, evidently designed to be capable of repelling the onslaughts of daylight.

The niggardly proportions of the room, in which the height of the ceiling was matched only by the depth of gloom it engendered, was reinforced by its lighting. One fat viridian candle burned in a tall stand in the middle of the otherwise empty floor. A chilling draught caused its shadows to stir wakefully on the creaking parquet.

"How long do we wait here?" Chubsalid enquired of the guide.

"A short while, sire."

Short whiles were of long duration in such a room, but eventually inner doors opened. Two uniformed men with swords dragged the doors apart, allowing the party to view a further room.

This further room was lit by gas flares, which imparted a sickly light over everything but the face of a man sitting berobed in a large chair at the far end of the room. Since the gas lights were behind his throne, his face was cast into shadow. The man made no movement.

Chubsalid said in a clear voice, "I am Priest-Supreme Chubsalid of the Church of the Formidable Peace. Who are you?"

And an equally clear voice came back. "You address me as the Oligarch."

The visiting party, although they had prepared themselves for the encounter, were silenced by a momentary awe. They shuffled forward to the door of the inner chamber, where soldiers barred their way with naked swords.

"Are you Torkerkanzlag II?" asked Chubsalid.

Again the clear voice. "Address me as the Oligarch."

Chubsalid and Asperamanka looked at each other. Then the former spoke out.

"We have come here, Dread Oligarch, to discuss the curtailment of traditional liberties in our state, and to speak with you regarding a recent crime committed—"

The clear voice cut in. "You have come here to discuss nothing, priest. You have come here to speak of nothing. You have come here because you preached treason, in deliberate defiance of recent edicts issued by the State. You have come here because the punishment for treason is death."

"On the contrary," said Parlingelteg. "We came here anticipating reason, justice, and an open debate. Not some sort of tawdry melodramatics."

Asperamanka set his chest against one of the drawn swords and said, "Dread Oligarch, I have served you faithfully. I am Priest-Militant Asperamanka, who, as no doubt you know, led your armies to victory in the field against the thousand heathen cults of Pannoval. Did you not— were not those armies destroyed on their return to your domains?"

The unmoved voice of the Oligarch said, "In the presence of your ruler, you do not ask questions."

"Tell us who you are," said Parlingelteg. "If you are human you give no evidence of it."

Ignoring the interruption, Torkerkanzlag II gave the guard an order: "Draw back the window curtain."

The guide who had led the three into the stifling chamber creaked his way across the floor and grasped the leather curtain with both hands. Slowly, he pulled the curtain back from the long window.

Grey light filtered into the room. While the other two turned to see out, Chubsalid looked back towards the Oligarch. Some of the light filtered even to where he sat motionless on his shadowed throne; something of his features was revealed.

"I recognise you! Why, you're—" But the Priest-Supreme got no further, for one of the soldiers grasped him unceremoniously by the shoulder and swung him to the long window, where the guide stood pointing downwards.

A courtyard lay beneath the window, surrounded entirely by tall grey walls. Anyone walking down there would have been crushed by the weight of disapproving windows ranged above him.

In the middle of the courtyard, a wooden cage had been built. Inside the cage was a tall, sturdy pole. What made this arrangement remarkable was the fact that cage and pole stood on a slatted wooden platform, which was built over piles of logs. Tucked in among the logs were bundles of brushwood. Bunches of twigs and kindling skirted the brushwood.

The Oligarch said, "The punishment for treason is death. That you knew before you entered here. Death by burning. You have preached against the State. You will be burnt."

Parlingelteg spoke up boldly as the curtain was pulled back over the window. "If you dare burn us, you will turn the religion of Sibornal against the State. Every man's hand will be against you. You will not survive. Sibornal itself may not survive."

Asperamanka made a run for the door, shouting, "I'll see to it that the world hears of this villainy."

But there were soldiers outside the door who turned him back.

Chubsalid stood in the middle of the room and said soothingly to him, "Be firm, my good priest. If this crime is committed here in the centre of Askitosh, there will be those who will never rest until the Azoiaxic triumphs. This is the monster who believes that treachery costs less than armies. He will find that this treachery costs him everything."

The unmoving man in the chair said, "The greatest good is the survival of civilisation over the next centuries. To that end all else must be sacrificed. Fine principles have to go. When plague's rampant, law and order break down. So it has always been at the onset of previous Great Winters—in Campannlat, in Hespagorat, even in Sibornal. Armies run mad, records burn, the finest emblems of the state are destroyed. Barbarism reigns.

"This time, this winter, we shall/will survive that crisis. Sibornal is to become a fortress. Already none may enter. Soon, none shall leave. For four centuries, we shall remain a haven of law and order, whilst the cold tears out the gizzards of wolves. We will live from the sea.

"Values will be maintained, but those values must be the values of survival. I will not have Church and State at loggerheads. That is what the Oligarchy has decided. Ours is the only plan which can/determined save the maximum number of people.

"Next spring, we shall rise up strong while Campannlat is still given over to primitivism and its women lug carts like beasts of burden—if they haven't forgotten how to make wheels by then. At that time, we shall resolve the endless hostility with those savage lands for good and all.

"Do you call that wicked? Do you call that wicked, Priest-Supreme? To see our beloved continent triumph?"

Garbed in his canonicals, Chubsalid made a fine figure. He drew himself up. He let silence cover the Oligarch's rhetoric before he replied.

"Whatever you may arrogantly believe to the contrary, yours is the argument of a weak man. We have in Sibornal a harsh religion, forged, like the Great Wheel itself, out of an adverse climate. But what we preach is stoicism, not cruelty. Yours is the ancient argument of ends justifying means. You will find that if you pursue your proposed course the cruel means will subvert the end, and your plan will fail utterly."

The man in the chair moved his hand scarcely an inch as a substitute for a gesture. "We may make mistakes, Priest-Supreme, that I grant. Then we shall simply bury our dead and remain on course."

Parlingelteg's clear young voice rang out: "And all the dead will bear witness against you. Word will go from gossie to gossie. All will hear of your crimes."

The Oligarch's darker tone replied. "The dead may bear witness. Happily, they cannot bear arms."

"When this deed is known, many will bear arms against you!"

"If you have nothing to say beyond the airing of threats, then the time has come for you to meet those unarmed millions below ground yourselves. Or do any of you care to reconsider your loyalty to the State in view of what I have said?"

He motioned to the guards. Parlingelteg shouted the forbidden curse. "Abro Hakmo Astab, damned Oligarch!"

Armed guards marched across the room with heavy tread, to take up positions behind the ecclesiastics.

Asperamanka could say nothing for the trembling of his jaw. He rolled his eyes at Chubsalid, who patted him on the shoulder. The youngest priest took Chubsalid by the arm and called out again, "Burn us and you set all Askitosh afire!"

Chubsalid said, "I warn you, Oligarch, if you cause a schism between Church and State, your plans will never succeed. You will divide the people. If you burn us, your plan will already have failed."

In a composed voice, the Oligarch said, "I shall find others who will cooperate, Priest-Supreme. Dozens of the obedient will rush to fill your place—and think it honourable. I know men well."

As the guards took hold of the captives, Asperamanka broke free. He ran towards the Oligarch's throne and went down on one knee, bowing his head.

"Dread Oligarch, spare me. You know that I, Asperamanka, was your faithful servant in war. You surely never intended that such a valuable instrument should be killed. Do with these other two as you will, but let me be saved, let me serve again! I believe that Sibornal must survive as you say. Harsh times call for harsh measures. Spiritual power must make way for temporal power to secure the way. Just let me live, and I will serve . . . for the glory of God."

"You may do it for your own base sake, but never for God's," said Chubsalid. "Get up! Die with us, Asperamanka—'twill be less pain."

"Living or dying, we accept the role of pain in our existence," said the Oligarch. "Asperamanka, this comes unexpectedly from you, the victor of Isturiacha. You entered here with your brothers; why not burn with your brothers?"

Asperamanka was silent. Then, without rising from his knees, he burst out in a flood of eloquence.

"What has been said here belongs not so much to politics or morals as to history. You wish to change history, Oligarch—perhaps the obsession of all great men. Indeed our cyclic history stands in need of reform—reform which must be brutal to be effective.

"Yet I speak for our beloved Church, which I have also served— served with devotion. Let *these* burn for it. I'd rather live for it. History shows us that religions can perish just like nations. I have not forgotten my history lessons as a child in the monastery of Old Askitosh, where I was taught of the defeat of the religion of Pannoval at the hand of a wicked King of Borlien and his ministers. If Church and State here fall apart, then our Supreme God is similarly threatened. Let me, as a Man of God, serve your ends."

As the other priests were marched out, Parlingelteg took a flying kick at Asperamanka, sending him sprawling on the floor. "Hypocrite!" he called as he was dragged out of range.

"Take those two down to the courtyard," said the Oligarch. "If a little fear is struck into the heart of the Church, the Church may not be so vocal in future."

He sat motionless as Priest-Supreme Chubsalid and Priest-Chaplain Parlingelteg were marched away.

The chamber emptied. Only one guard remained, silent in the shadows, and Asperamanka, still crouching on the floor, face pale.

The Oligarch's cold stare turned in Asperamanka's direction.

"I can always find work for your kind," he said. "Get up on your feet."

XI

STERN DISCIPLINE
FOR TRAVELLERS

Most of Sibornal's rivers ran south. Most of them, for most of the year, were fast and ill-natured, as befitted waters born of glaciers.

The Venj was no exception. It was wide, full of dangerous currents, and could be said to hurtle rather than flow on its way to its outlet at Rivenjk.

In the course of centuries, however, the Venj had scoured itself a valley through which it might flow or flood as the mood took it, and it was along this valley that the road led which would eventually bear a north-bound traveller to Kharnabhar.

The road wound upward through pleasant country, protected from prevailing winds by the mass of the Shivenink Chain. Large bushes, indifferent to frost, grew here, putting out immense blossoms. Small flowers grew by the wayside, picked by pilgrims because they were never seen elsewhere.

The pilgrims were carefree on this, the first stage of their land journey to Kharnabhar. They travelled alone or in groups, dressed in all manner of garb. Some went barefoot, claiming that they controlled their bodies so as not to experience cold. There was singing and music among the groups. This was a serious exercise in piety—one that would stand them in good stead at home for the rest of their lives—but nevertheless it was a holiday, and they rejoiced accordingly. For some miles out of Rivenjk, stalls stood by the side of the way, where fruit or emblems of the Wheel could be bought. Or peasants from Bribahr— for the frontier was close here—climbed up from the valley to sell produce to the travellers. This stage of the way was easy.

The way became steeper. The air grew a little thinner. The blossoms on the leathery-leaved bushes were brighter but smaller. Fewer peasants climbed up from the valley. Not so many of the pilgrims had the lung power to blow their musical instruments. There was nervous talk of robbers.

But still—well, this special trip must be an adventure, perhaps the great adventure. They would all return home as heroes. A little difficulty was welcome.

The hostels where the pilgrims slept for the night, if they could afford it, became rougher, the dreams of the pilgrims more troubled. The nights were filled with the sound of water forever falling—a reminder of the heights lost in the clouds above them. Next morning, the travellers would get silently on their way. Mountains are enemies of talk. Conversation was born a lowland art.

Still the road wound upward, still it followed the ill-tempered Venj. Still the travellers followed the road. And at last they were rewarded by fine views.

They were approaching Sharagatt, five thousand metres above sea level. When the clouds dispersed, views were to be had northwestward, down the tangled mountainsides, into terrifying gorges where vultures soared. Even farther, if the pilgrim was lucky and eagle-eyed, he might see the plains of Bribahr, blue with distance or possibly frost.

Before Sharagatt, a few pokey wayside shops began again. Some had nuts and mountain fruits to sell, some offered paintings of the landscape, as badly drawn as they were highly idealised. Signs appeared. A bend in the road—and yet another bend—and how tired the calf muscles suddenly seemed—and a stall selling waffles—and a glimpse of a wooden spire—and then another bend—and people—crowds—and Sharagatt, yes, that haven!—Sharagatt and the prospect of a bath and a clean bed.

Sharagatt was full of churches, some modelled on the ones in Kharnabhar. Paintings and engravings of Kharnabhar were on sale. Some claimed that, if you knew where to go, you could purchase genuine certificates to say that you had visited the Great Wheel.

For Sharagatt—considerable though the achievement was to reach it—was nothing. It was but a halt, a beginning. Sharagatt was where the real journey to Kharnabhar began. Sharagatt was as far as many travellers ever got. Promising everything, it was a milestone of lost hopes. Many people found themselves too old, too tired, too ill, or simply too poor to get further. They stayed for a day or two. Then they turned round and made their way back down to Rivenjk, at the mouth of the unforgiving river.

For Sharagatt was little past the tropical zone. To the north, further up the mountain, the climate rapidly grew more severe. Many hundreds of miles lay between Sharagatt and Kharnabhar. More than determination was needed to make that journey.

Luterin Shokerandit, Toress Lahl, and Harbin Fashnalgid slept in the Sharagatt Star Hotel. More precisely, they slept on a verandah under the broad eaves of the Sharagatt Star Hotel. For even Shokerandit's careful booking of all details in Rivenjk had not prevented a muddle at the hotel, which was fully occupied. A creaky three-decker bunk bed had been carried onto the verandah for their comfort.

Fashnalgid lay in the top bunk, with Shokerandit next and the woman at the bottom. Fashnalgid had not been pleased with the arrangement, but Shokerandit had bought them each a pipe full of occhara, the weed grown from a mountain plant, and they were full of peace. A light wagon had brought them and other privileged passengers this far. Tomorrow they would take to a sledge. Tonight was for rest. When the mists cleared over the mountain, the night sky blazed with familiar constellations, the Queen's Scar, the Fountain, the Old Pursuer.

"Toress Lahl, you see the stars? Can you name them?" Shokerandit asked in a dreamy voice.

"I name them all—stars. . . ." She gave a faint laugh.

"Then I shall climb down into your bunk and teach you."

"There are so many."

"It will take me a long time. . . ."

But he fell asleep before he could move, and even animal cries from further down the mountainside did not awaken him.

Shokerandit was up early next morning, feeling stale and tired. He pulled his chilly top clothes on before rousing Toress Lahl.

"We sleep in all our clothes from now until the end of the journey," he said. Without waiting for her to follow he was off to the stores to see to the equipment that would be needed for the month ahead. NORTH TRAVEL STORES it announced over the door, with a painting of the Great Wheel.

He was anxious. Fashnalgid, a true Uskuti, thought of Shivenink as a mountainous backwater. Luterin Shokerandit knew better. Remote though it was from the capital, Shivenink was well provided with police and informers. After Fashnalgid's killing of a soldier, both police and military would be on their track. He grieved to think of the trouble he had left with Eedap Mun Odim and Hernisarath.

Using an assumed name, he bought various necessary items at the store, and then went to inspect the team, already booked, which would transport them to Kharnabhar and the safety of his father's estates.

Fashnalgid took the processes of the morning more slowly. Directly Shokerandit was gone from the verandah, he ceased to feign sleep and climbed down into the lower bunk with Toress Lahl. Now that he had broken her spirit, she offered no resistance. The occhara had left her listless.

"Luterin will kill you when he discovers what you are doing," she said.

"Shut up and enjoy it, you hussy. I'll take care of him when the time comes." He seized her in a bear's embrace, and with his ankles wrapped about hers, parted her thighs, and thrust into her. His thrusting set the rickety bunk banging against the rail of the verandah.

Sharagatt was divided into two parts. There was Sharagatt and North Sharagatt. The two parts were close. Little more than a hundred yards and a clifflike corner of rock separated them. Sharagatt was protected by wedges of mountainside above it. On North Sharagatt cold katabatic winds poured, lowering the temperature by several degrees. The teams that made the northward journey were stabled only in North Sharagatt. Sharagatt itself would have made them soft.

It took Shokerandit two hours to see that all was arranged for the journey. He knew the folk he had to deal with. They were mountain people who called themselves Ondod, which meant—according to who was translating from their complex language—either "Spirit People" or "Spirited People."

One Ondod would be driver. With him would be his phagor slave. He had a good sledge and an eight-dog asokin team.

While he was inspecting the harness inch by inch, Toress Lahl appeared, her face pale and sullen.

"It's freezing here," she said listlessly.

He went over to the supplies he had acquired and brought back a woollen one-piece undergarment. Smiling, he handed it to her. "This is for you. Put it on now."

"Where?"

"Here." He caught her meaning, glanced at the Ondod and phagors standing there. "Oh, these people have no shame. Put your new garment on."

"I'm the one with shame," she said. But she did as she was told, while the others watched smiling.

He went back to checking everything and interrogating their Ondod driver, by name Uuundaamp, a small person with brilliant black eyes, pockmarked cheeks, and a narrow moustache that faded out into lashes across his cheekbones. He was fourteen, and had made the difficult journey many times.

As Uuundaamp took Shokerandit out to see the team, Toress Lahl joined them in her new gear, glancing at the Ondod questioningly.

"All drivers are young," Shokerandit told her. "They live on meat, and generally die young."

At the back of the store, a door opened into a yard. Here were the pens, separated by high wire. Dirty snow lay on the ground. The noise of the dogs was deafening.

Uuundaamp walked the narrow path between the pens. On either side, asokins hurled themselves at the wire, teeth snapping, saliva running from their jaws. The horned dogs stood as high as a man's hip, and were covered in thick fur, brown, white, grey, black, or mixed.

"This our team—gumtaa team—very good asokin," Uuundaamp said, pointing out the contents of one pen and glancing slyly up at Shokerandit. "Before we go here, you two give one meat chunk for lead dog, make friend together him. Then you alway friend together him. Ishto?"

"Which is the lead dog, the black one?" Shokerandit asked.

Uuundaamp nodded. "Same black one, he lead dog. He name Uuundaamp, all same me. People say, he same size me, only not so fierce."

The black asokin had finely marked and curled horns, pointing outwards at the ends. Uuundaamp's body was covered with bristling black fur. Only his chest was white, and the underside of his tail. The Ondod Uuundaamp pointed out this latter feature; it was distinctive, making Uuundaamp easy for the rest of the pack to follow.

Uuundaamp turned to Toress Lahl. "Lady, to you warning. You give one meat this Uuundaamp, like I say. Then never no more. You never give no meat other asokin, understand? These asokin, they keep rules. We obey. Ishto?"

"Ishto," she said. That mountain word of acceptance she had picked up on the way from Rivenjk.

He stared up at her, black eyes merry. "You big woman. I no feed you one piece meat. Beside, my woman, she come Kharnabhar together us. One thing more. Most important. Never you try pat these asokin, see? He take him hand like one piece meat."

Toress Lahl shivered and laughed. "I wouldn't dare try to pat them."

"We'll collect Fashnalgid and then we'll be away," Shokerandit said when he had checked everything thoroughly. The stores and provisions were adequate; the sledge would not be overloaded. He linked his arm in hers. "You are well, aren't you? It's completely useless to be ill on the trail."

"Can't we leave Fashnalgid behind?"

"No. He's okay. He'd be a good man if anything happened. Let me tell you that I am anxious in case the Oligarch's agents are on our track. Perhaps they think that if we reach my father and tell him our history, he will turn the army against the Oligarchy. Many of my father's associates are military. I checked here, and one of the sledges is booked to leave at fifteen—just an hour after us. They said that four men hired it. If we can leave earlier, all the better for us. I have a gun."

"I'm frightened. Can you trust these Ondod?"

"They're not human. They're related to the Nondads of Campannlat. He's got eight fingers on each hand—you'll see when he takes his gloves off. They tolerate the phagors but they never really ally themselves with humans. They're tricky. You must pay them and please them, or they can be difficult."

While they were talking, they were walking back from North Sharagatt to Sharagatt. The change in temperature was marked.

She clung to his arm and said resentfully, "Why did you make me strip off in front of them? You don't have to humiliate me just because I'm a slave."

He laughed. "Oh, that was part of pleasing them. They wanted to see. They'll think the better of me for it."

"I don't think the better of you for it."

"Ah, but I am lead dog."

She said viciously, "Why didn't you come into my sleeping bag? Are you weird or something? Aren't I supposed to be yours to biwack whenever you feel the urge?"

"Oh, you want me now? That's a change of tune." He gave a short angry laugh. "Then you'll be pleased about tonight's arrangements."

They collected Fashnalgid, who was drinking spirits at a wayside stall. Shokerandit then spent a while in a small shop, haggling over the price of a bright yellow-and-red striped blanket. The inevitable pattern of the Great Wheel was woven among its stripes.

"Beholder, how you waste your money!" Fashnalgid said. "I thought you'd been so careful to get all the necessary supplies already."

"I like the look of this blanket. Pretty, isn't it?"

He paid up and draped the colourful blanket over his shoulder before starting back for North Sharagatt. Other travellers took no apparent notice of him; all were dressed unpredictably against the cold mountain air. Fashnalgid looked on in amazement as, at another stall, Shokerandit paid dear for a skinned smoked kid.

A man at the North Travel Stores said that Uuundaamp was asleep. Shokerandit went alone to the makeshift dwelling carved from the rock at the back of the store, behind the asokin pens. Some Ondod were sitting on the floor eating strips of raw meat. Others slept with their women on shelves built against the cliff.

Uuundaamp was wakened, and came forward scratching his armpits and yawning, showing teeth almost as sharp as those of his animals.

"You make hard chief, start three hour too much. I no your man till fifteen."

"Sorry. Look, I want to start soonest. I bring you present, ishto?"

He threw the smoked baby goat on the floor. Uuundaamp immediately sat down on the floor and called to his friends. He pulled out a knife and beckoned to Shokerandit with it. "All come eat, friend. Gumtaa. Then make quick start."

As everyone gathered round, Uuundaamp called to his wife as an afterthought. She rolled off the shelf she had shared and came forward, bundled in bedding. All that was visible of her was a round face with black eyes much like Uuundaamp's. She made no attempt to join the greedy circle of men. Instead, she stood meekly behind Uuundaamp, deftly catching a scraggy slice of meat when he tossed it to her over his shoulder.

While Shokerandit chewed his meat, he observed the hands of the men. They were narrow and sinewy, and bore eight fingers. The blunt clawlike nails were uniformly black, gleaming with filth and fat lodged under them.

"Gumtaa," said Uuundaamp, with his cheeks bulging.

"Gumtaa," agreed Shokerandit.

"Gumtaa," agreed the other Ondod. The woman, being a woman, was not called upon to say whether she thought the food was good or not.

Soon, nothing but bones and horns were left of the kid. Uuundaamp rose immediately, wiping his hands on his suit of fur. "By way, chief," he said, still chewing, "this horrid bag behind me with belly full of gas and babies is my woman. Name Moub. You can forget. She come together us. You no mind."

"She is as welcome as she is beautiful, Uuundaamp. I am carrying this blanket for myself, which I did not intend to give away, but in view of Moub's loveliness, I wish you to give it to her as a present."

"Loobiss. You give, chief. Then she not lose it. She kiss you."

So Shokerandit presented the yellow-and-red striped blanket to Moub.

"Loobiss," she said. "Far too good for any bag belong this vile Uuundaamp." She hopped nimbly forward and kissed Shokerandit with her full and greasy lips.

"Gumtaa. Any time you want biwack, chief, you use Moub. She look horrid but she got all that stuff there, ishto?"

"Loobiss!" Their friendship had been properly cemented. Happiness swept through Shokerandit, as he recalled sleigh rides with his mother when he was a child, and playing with Ondod children on their estates. His mother had always found the Ondod coarse and beastly, perhaps because of the peculiar conventions between the sexes, which relied on insult. Later, he and his friends had visited a shack on the edge of the caspiarn forests. His first sexual experiences had been with Ondod females. He remembered a rotund girl called Ipaak. To Ipaak he had always been "the pink stinker."

Stern discipline for asokins, stern discipline for travellers. That was the rule for journeys between Kharnabhar and the outside world.

Uuundaamp sat at the front of the sledge with the whip, Moub lumpish just behind him. The phagor, Bhryeer, rode at the back, standing upright to steer the long vehicle, often jumping off to left or right, sometimes pushing when the incline was steep enough for the asokins to require help. The three humans sat astride the tarpaulin-covered supplies, on one side or the other according to the direction of the wind.

It was easy to fall off the sledge. An eye had to be kept on the driver, for a hint of which way they might be turning. Sometimes Uuundaamp could hardly be seen for the snow that fell in flurries from the heights of the chain above them. They had crossed the treacherous Venj by wooden bridge, and were now proceeding on a roughly north-north-easterly course under the high spine of Shivenink, where ice prevailed above the ten-thousand-metre line for all of the Great Year.

Even when the air was clear of snow, the breath of the dogs rose like steam and concealed them from the passengers. The team included one bitch, to keep the other seven doing their utmost. The dogs frequently broke wind at the start of a new lap of the journey. Their panting could be heard above the shrill of the metal runners. Otherwise, sounds were muffled. There was no visibility, except for white walls on either side. The smell of the dogs and of stale clothes became part of the scene. Monotony dulled the sense of danger. Weariness, the reflections of the snow, reveries that ran half-formed through the mind, these filled the days.

The asokins were attached to the sledge by twenty feet of leather harness. They were allowed to rest for ten minutes every three hours. Then all eight would lie down except for Uuundaamp the leader. The man Uuundaamp was at least as close to his asokins as he was to Moub. They were his life.

During the break, Uuundaamp did not rest. He and Moub would walk restlessly about, studying natural phenomena—the shape of clouds, the flight of birds, any nuance of change in weather, tracks of animals, sounds and signs of landslides.

Sometimes they met pilgrims coming or going, making the great journey on foot. There were other sledges on the route, bells ringing. Once they were caught behind a slow herring-train and forced to tag along slowly before the vehicle moved into a passing place. The herring-train was a land version of the herring-coach. It bore barrels of pickled fish up to the distant rendezvous.

The asokins barked furiously whenever they met with another vehicle, but the rival drivers never moved a muscle in greeting.

The night's break also had its set pattern. Uuundaamp pulled the team off the track in selected places he knew about. He then immediately went about settling the dogs, which had to be staked separately and away from the sledge, so that they did not eat its skins. Each asokin was fed two pounds of raw meat every third day; they worked best when starved. But each night they got a herring apiece,

which Uuundaamp threw to each asokin in turn, starting with Uuundaamp. They caught the fish in midair, swallowing it at a gulp. The
bitch was last to be fed. The lead dog slept some way from the rest
of the team. If snow fell during the night, the dogs remained under
it, in small caverns carved by their own heat. Bhryeer the phagor slept
with them.

At a night's stop, everything had to be made ready for the evening
meal inside fifteen minutes.

"It's not possible. What's the point?" Fashnalgid complained.

"The point is that it's possible and must be done," Shokerandit said.
"Stretch the tent, hold tight."

They were stiff with cold. Their noses were peeling, their cheeks
blackened by frost.

The sledge had to be unloaded. The tent was pitched over it and
secured, which often entailed a battle against wind. Skins were stretched
across the sledge. On this, the five of them slept, to be off the ground.
Belongings required overnight were arranged nearby: food, stove, knives,
oil lamp. Although the temperature in the tent generally remained
below zero, they found themselves sweating in the confined space,
after the cold of the journey.

When Uuundaamp entered on the first night, he found the three
humans quarrelling.

"No more speak. Be good. Anger bring smrtaa."

"I can't stand four weeks of this," Fashnalgid said.

"If you disobey him, he will simply leave," Shokerandit said. "All he
asks is that you put your personality away to sleep for the journey. The
cold will not allow quarrels, or death will strike."

"Let the sherb leave."

"We'd die here without him—can't you understand that?"

"Occhara soon, soon," said Uuundaamp, nudging Fashnalgid. He
handed Moub a pair of silver foxes to cook. They came from traps he
had set on his previous journey.

A pleasant fug arose in the tent. The meat smelt good. They ate
with filthy hands, afterwards drinking melted snow water from a
communal mug.

"Food ishto?" asked Moub.

"Gumtaa," they said.

"She bad cook," Uuundaamp said, as he lit up pipes of occhara and
handed them round. The lamp was providently extinguished and they
smoked in peace. The howl of the wind seemed to die away. Good
feelings overcame them. The smoke filtering through their nostrils was
the breath of a mysterious better life. They were the children of the
mountain and it had them in its care. No harm comes to those who
have eaten silver fox. For all the differences between men and women,
and between men and men, all have this good thing in common—that

the divine smoke pours from their noses, and perhaps from eyes and ears and other orifices. Sleep itself is but another orifice in the mountain god. Sometimes in sleep men become the dream of the silver fox.

In the morning, when they struggled in the dull, bitter air to fold the tent, Toress Lahl said secretly to Shokerandit, "How degraded you are and how I hate you! Last night, you biwacked with that bag of lard, Moub. I heard you. I felt the sledge tremble."

"I was being courteous to Uuundaamp. Pure courtesy. Not pleasure."

He had discovered that the Ondod female was far gone with child.

"No doubt your courtesy will be rewarded with a disease."

Uuundaamp came up smiling with the two silver fox tails. "Carry these at teeth. Gumtaa. Keep off cold from face."

"Loobiss. Have you one for Fashnalgid?"

"That man, he got tail grow along face," said Uuundaamp, indicating the captain's moustache, and laughing merrily.

"At least he means to be kind," Toress Lahl said, hesitatingly placing the tail between her teeth to protect her chapped nose and cheeks.

"Uuundaamp is kind. And when we stop tonight you must be kind to him. Return his favour."

"Oh, no . . . Luterin . . . not that, please. I thought you had some feeling for me."

He turned savagely on her. "I have some feeling for getting us safe to Kharnabhar. I know the conventions of these people and these journeys and you don't. It's a code, a matter of survival. Stop thinking you are so special."

Bitterly hurt, she said, "So you don't care, I suppose, that Fashnalgid rapes me whenever your back is turned."

He dropped the tent and grasped her jacket.

"Are you lying to me? When did he do it? Tell me when. Then and when else. How many times?"

He listened bleakly as she told him.

"Very well, Toress Lahl." He spoke in no more than a whisper, his face hard. "He has broken the honour that existed between us as officers. We need him on this journey. But when we get to my father's home, I shall kill him. You understand? For now, you say nothing."

Without further words, they loaded up the sledge. Smrtaa—retribution. A prominent feature of life in these parts. Uuundaamp was harnessing up the dogs, and in a few minutes they were once more on their way through the mist, Shokerandit and Toress Lahl biting on their fox tails.

The unsleeping machines of the Avernus still recorded events below, and transmitted them automatically back to Earth. But the few humans surviving on the Observation Station took little interest in that primary function; their own primary function was to survive. Their numbers were so far down—lowered by disease as well as fighting—that defence became a less pressing need.

Much time was spent establishing tribes and tribal territory, to obviate pitched battles. In neutral territory between tribes, the obscene pudendolls survived, to become something sacroscanct, something between gods and demons.

Though a measure of "peace" descended, the earlier destruction of food synthesising plants meant that cannibalism was still prevalent. There was almost no meat but human meat. The heavy tabus against this practice fell with great force upon the delicately trained sensibilities of the Avernians. To descend to barbarism and worse within a generation was more than their psyches could easily endure.

The tribes became matriarchies, while many of the younger men, mainly adolescent, developed multiple personalities. As many as ten different personalities could house themselves in one body, differing in inclination, age, and sex, as well as habits. Ascetic vegetarians were common, living an eye's blink away from stone age savages, tempestuous dancers from lawgivers.

The complex separation from nature undergone by the Avernian colonisers had now reached its limits. Not only did individuals not know each other: they were now strangers to themselves.

This adaptation to stress situations was not for everyone. When severe fighting first broke out, a number of technicians left the Avernus. They stole a craft from one of the Observation Station's maintenance bays and fled. They landed on Aganip.

Tempting though the green, white, and blue planet of Helliconia looked, its danger was known to all. Aganip occupied a special place in the mythology of Avernus, for it was here, many centuries ago, that Earth's colonising starship had established a base while the Avernus was being constructed.

Aganip was a lifeless planet, with an atmosphere consisting almost entirely of carbon dioxide, together with a little nitrogen. But the old base still stood, and offered something of a welcome.

The escapers built a small dome. There they lived in restricted circumstances. At first they sent out signals to Earth and then—being naturally unwilling to wait two thousand years for an answer—to the Avernus. But the Avernus had its own problems and did not reply.

The escapers had failed to understand the nature of mankind: that it, like the elephant and the common daisy, is no more and no less than a part and function of a living entity. Separated from that entity, humans, being more complex than elephants and daisies, have little chance of flourishing. The signals continued automatically for a long while.

No one heard.

XII

KAKOOL ON THE TRAIL

And when that massed human spirit we have called empathy reached out across space and communicated with the gossies of Helliconia, what then? Did nothing important happen—or did something unprecedentedly magnificent, something quantally different, happen?

The answer to that question will perhaps remain forever clouded in conjecture; mankind has its umwelt, however bravely it strives to enlarge that confining universe of its perceptions. To become part of a greater umwelt may prove biologically impossible. Or perhaps not. It must be sufficient to admit that if something unprecedentedly magnificent, something quantally different, happened, it happened in a greater umwelt than mankind's.

If it happened, then it was a cooperation, and perhaps a cooperation of various factors not unlike the cooperation forced on differing individuals on the trail to Kharnabhar.

If it happened, then it left an effect. That effect can be traced by looking at the contrasting fates of Earth, where Gaia resided, and New Earth, which was without a tutelary biospheric spirit. . . .

To start with the case of Earth, after which New Earth was named:

The intermission between the two postnuclear ice ages has been understood as the swing of a pendulum. Gaia was trying to regulate her clock. But it was less simple than that, just as the biosphere was less simple than the mechanism of a clock. The truth may be put more accurately. Gaia had been almost terminally ill. She was now convalescent, and subject to relapses.

Or, abandoning the dangers of personifying a complex process, it may be said that the carbon dioxide released by the deep oceans initiated a period during which the ice retreated. At the end of the period of greenhouse heating, there was an overshoot of the return to normal, as the whole biosphere and its ruined biosystems strove for adjustment. The ice returned.

This time, the cold was less severe, the spread of the ice caps less extensive, and the duration of the cold briefer. The period was marked by a series of oscillations, in the way that a clock's pendulum gradually slows to a stationary median position. It was a time of discomfort for many generations of the thin-spread human race. In the remission in the 6900s, for instance, there was a small war in what had once been India, followed by famine and pestilence.

Could that trivial war be likened to a convalescent's tantrum?

The restlessness of the period awoke a corresponding restlessness in the human spirit. Fences were no longer going to be possible. The old world of fences had died, and was never going to be rebuilt.

"We belong to Gaia." And with the declaration went the understanding that human beings were not exactly Gaia's best allies. To see those best allies, a microscope was needed.

Throughout the ages—and long before the invention and development of nuclear weapons—there had been those who prophesied that the world would end because of man's wickedness. Such prophecies were always believed, no matter how many times they had been proved wrong in the past. There was a wish for, as well as a fear of, punishment.

Once nuclear weapons were invented, the prophecies gained plausibility, although now they were couched in lay terms rather than religious ones.

Evidence, the more convincing because governments tried to suppress it, proved that the world could be ended at the touch of a button.

Eventually, the button was touched. The bombs came.

But human wickedness proved too feeble to end the world. Set against that wickedness were industrious microbes of which wickedness took little cognisance.

Large trees and plants disappeared. The carnivores, including man, disappeared from the scene for a while. They were superfluous to requirements. These large beings were merely the superstars in Earth's drama. The dramatists themselves still lived. Under the soil, on the seabeds of the continental shelves, thick microbial life continued Gaia's story, undisturbed by radioactivity or increased ultraviolet. The eco-systems of unicellular life were rebuilding nature. They were Gaia's pulse.

Gaia regenerated herself. Mankind was a function in that regenera-tion. The human spirit was triggered into a quantum leap in conscious-ness.

As nature had formed a diverse unity, so now did consciousness. It was no longer possible for a man or woman merely to feel or merely to think; there was only empathic thinkfeel. Head and heart were one.

One immediate effect was a mistrust of power.

There were people who understood what the greed for power in all its forms had done to the world. That chill faded from the mind. Hu-manity began truly to be adult and to live and enjoy with adult com-prehension. Men and women looked about at the territory they hap-pened to occupy and no longer asked, "What can we get out of this land?" Instead, they asked, "What best experience can we have on this land?"

With this new consciousness came less exploitive ties and more ties everywhere, an abundance of new relationships. The ancient structure of family faded into new superfamilies. All mankind became a loose-knit superorganism. It did not happen at once, nor did it happen to everyone. There were those who could not undergo the metamorphosis. But their genes were recessive and their strain would die away. They were the insensible in a new world of new empathies. They were the only ones not smiling.

When more generations passed, the new race could feel itself to be the consciousness of Gaia. The ecosystems of unicellular life had been given a voice—had, in a sense, invented a voice for themselves.

Even as this was happening, the convalescence of the biosphere con-tinued. While humanity evolved, an entirely new type of being was born to the Earth.

Many phyla had vanished for ever. The cummerbund of tropical forest with its various myriad lives had withered from the equator under the nuclear onslaught. Its fragile soils had been lost into the oceans and could not be recovered. Now a replacement of a startlingly different kind came forth.

The new thing was not born of the oceans. It came from the snows and frosts of the arctic. It fed on ultraviolet radiation and it began moving southward as the glaciers began a fresh retreat northwards.

The first men to meet the new thing fell back in astonishment.

White polyhedrons were slowly advancing. Some of the shapes were no larger than giant tortoises. Others reached as high as a man's head.

Beyond their various planes, they had no features. No visible means of movement. No arms or tentacles. No mouths of any kind. No orifices. No eyes or ears. No appendages whatsoever. Just white polyhedrons. Some sides were perhaps less white than others.

The polyhedrons left no track. They sailed where they would. They moved slowly, but nothing could stop them, although brave men tried to. They were christened geonauts.

The geonauts multiplied and sailed the Earth.

The geonauts provided a new wonder. The old wonder remained. The great conchlike auditoria were still scattered across Earth, maintained by androids who had found no other function, having been programmed to none.

On the holoscreens, the spring of the Great Year turned to summer just as the snows of Earth were dying. The history of the beautiful MyrdemInggala, known as the Queen of Queens, was familiar to all. The new race found much to learn from that thousand-year-old story.

They attended. They gloried in the benevolent effect their empathy had on the gossies. But their own new world was calling urgently, with a fresh beauty that could not be resisted. A thousand years of spring was theirs.

But what of that unprecedentedly magnificent, quantally different something—that empathic linking of two worlds? Were its traces visible to those capable of looking for signs?

So to the case of New Earth:

On the other planets also, some slight recovery had been made. There were no Mother Natures on the dead worlds of Mars and Venus. Their surface temperatures were generally intolerable, their atmospheres coffins full of carbon dioxide. Yet the unfortunate colonists who had settled there managed to survive, by wits and by technology.

These Outlanders had succumbed to a psychosis regarding Earth. Their generations were smothered by cosmic anomie. To Earth they would never return. They felt themselves dispossessed.

When advanced technology was again within their power—and they were quicker to solve technical problems than social ones—they built a starship and set off for the nearest planet which mankind had colonised earlier, so-called New Earth.

This was an all-male expedition. The men left their women at home, preferring to take with them on their journey svelte robotic partners, styled as abstract ideals of womanhood. They enjoyed coupling with these perfect metal images.

New Earth retained breatheable air. Its one small ocean remained surrounded by desert—desert and inhospitable mountain ranges. There was a spaceport on the equator, with a city nearby. The spaceport had not been in use for ages. Nor had the city grown; the roads from it led nowhere. People lived in the city knowing nothing of that great ocean of space above their roofs.

The New Earthers were like neutered animals. Something vital and rebellious had gone from their spirits. They had no aspirations, no feeling for the immensities of space, no love for the world that was their home, no tremulous intimations at dawn and sunset. The degenerate language they spoke had no conditional tense. Music had been entirely lost as an art.

Hardly surprising. Their world was without spirit.

These New Earthers occasionally visited the shores of their salt sea. The visits were not to refresh themselves but to collect cartloads of the kelp which grew in the sea. The kelp was one of the few living things on the planet. The people of New Earth spread it on their fields, growing cereals brought from Earth ages previously.

They did not dream because they existed on a world which had never nurtured a Gaia figure. But they had a myth. They believed that they lived in a giant egg, of which the desert was the yolk and the cloudless sky was the shell. One day, said the myth, the sky would crack and fall. Then they would be born. They would acquire yellow wings and white tails, and they would fly to a better place, where trees like giant seaweeds grew everywhere in pleasant vales and it always rained.

When the Outlanders arrived, they did not like New Earth much.

They flew to examine the neighbouring planet, like New Earth the size of a terrestrial planet.

Whereas New Earth was a world of sand, its sister was a world of ice.

An observation drone was sent out to take computer-corrected photographs of the surface and of what lay below the ice.

It was a forbidding world. Glaciers engulfed mountain ranges. Trackless snowfields filled the lowlands. Helliconia in the grip of apastron winter was never as dead as this rigid globe.

The reconnaissance photographs showed frozen oceans beneath the ice. More. They showed the ruins of great cities and the routes of astonishly wide roads.

The Outlanders descended to the surface. Below an icefield remains of a vast building could be glimpsed. Fragments of it lay about the surface; some fragments had been carried far from source by the glacier. By blasting, the men got down to a sector of the ruins.

One of the first artefacts they brought up was a head, carved in a durable artificial material. The head was of an inhuman creature. In a slender tapering skull four eyes were set, lidless. Small feathers lay under the eyes. A short beak counterbalanced the backward thrust of the skull.

One side of the head was blackened.

"It's beautiful," a robot partner said.

"Ugly, you mean."

"It was once beautiful to someone."

Dating was not difficult. The city had been destroyed 3.2 thousand years earlier, at a time when New Earth was being strenuously colonised.

The whole planet had been destroyed by nuclear bombardment, and the avian race had perished with it.

The Outlanders called this planet Armageddon. They remained on the frigid surface for some while, discussing what should be done, spellbound by melancholy.

One of the powerful leaders spoke. "I think we might agree that we have found here on Armageddon an answer to one of the questions which has plagued mankind for many generations.

"How was it that when man went into space, he found no other intelligent species? It was always assumed that the galaxy would be full of life. Not so. How was it that there were scarcely any other planets like Earth?

"Well, we do realise that Earth is a pretty unusual place, where a number of fine specifications are met. Take just one example—the amount of oxygen in Earth's atmosphere is close to twenty-one percent. If it was twenty-five percent or over, forest fires would be started by lightning—even damp vegetation would burn. On New Earth, the oxygen percentage is eighteen; there are no plants to lock away the carbon dioxide and release oxygen molecules. No wonder the poor boobies there live in a dream.

"Nevertheless, statistics suggest that there must be other planets like Earth. Maybe Armageddon was one. Suppose a race with a wide-ranging diet reaches supremacy and dominates the planet, as happened on Earth before the nuclear war. That race must use technology to do so—from the club and bow-and-arrow onwards. It masters the laws of nature.

"The time comes when technology is advanced enough for the race to choose alternatives. It can put out into space, or it can destroy its enemies with nuclear weapons."

"Suppose there are no enemies on the planet?" someone called.

"Then the race invents them. The pressure of competition which technologies generate makes enemies necessary, as we know. And there's my point. At that stage, poised for a whole new way of life, no longer to be confined to the planet of its birth, on the brink of major discoveries —right then that race is set the big examination question: Can I develop the international social skills required to bring my aggression under control? Can I excel myself and make a lasting truce with my enemies, so that we throw away these vile weapons for good and all?

"You see what I mean? If the race fails the exam, it destroys its planet and itself, and shows that it was unfit to cross that vital quarantine area space provides.

"Armageddon was unfit. Its people failed the exam. They destroyed themselves."

"But you're saying everyone everywhere was unfit. We never have found another space-going race."

The leader laughed. "We're still only on Earth's doorstep, don't forget. Nobody is going to come looking for us until they know we're trustworthy."

"And are we trustworthy?"

Amid general laughter, the leader said, "Let's tackle Armageddon first. Maybe we can get the old place going again, if we press the right button."

Further surveys showed what the world had once been. One notable feature was a considerable high-latitude sea which—before the nuclear disaster—had been only partially ice-covered. After the disaster, atmospheric contamination had cooled the umbrella of air, leaving the water of the high-latitude sea warmer than its overlying air. The air was in consequence heated from below, and moisture drawn upwards. Violent high-latitude storms had resulted, probably enough in themselves to finish off any survivors of the nuclear strike. Plentiful snow fell on middle-altitude ground, a plateau once covered by urbanisation. The major glaciation which set in became self-sustaining.

The Outlanders decided to drop what the leader had called vile weapons on the frozen high-altitude sea, in order to "get things started" again. But the ice wilderness remained an ice wilderness. Here, the local tutelary spirit, the biospheric gestalt, was dead.

They were now almost out of fuel. They decided to return to New Earth and conquer it. Their discoveries on Armageddon had provided them with a strategy. Their idea was that one—just one—thermonuclear device dropped over New Earth's north pole would cause heavy rainfall, transforming the planet. The sea could be enlarged; the local zombies could make themselves useful by cutting canals. More kelp could be encouraged to grow, and eventually more oxygen released into the air. The calculations looked good. To the Outlanders, the decision to try just one more nuclear bomb was a sane one.

So they climbed into their ship, leaving Armageddon to its eons of frost.

For the people who lived on New Earth, one part at least of their only myth came true. The sky cracked and fell.

What were the vital differences here? Why could New Earth never recover, while Earth flourished and put forth new forms like the geonauts?

When the terrestrials developed their empathic link with the gossies of Helliconia, a new factor entered the universe. The terrestrials, *whether or not they knew it, were acting as a focus of consciousness for the whole biosphere. The empathic link was not a weak thing. It was a psychic equivalent of magnetism or gravity; it bound the two planets.*

A more startling way of putting it would be to say that Gaia communicated directly with her lusty sister, the Original Beholder.

Of course it is speculation. Mankind cannot see into the greater umwelts about him. But he can train his ample senses to look for evidence. All the evidence suggests that Gaia and the Original Beholder made contact through their progeny's projecting the link. One can only guess at the ripples of shock that contact caused—unless the second ice age and its ripples of remission provide evidence of that contact.

It is speculation that Gaia's recovery was prompted by the refreshment of encountering a sister spirit in the void nearby.

There were the geonauts: serene, calm, apparently amiable, a new thing. They can be understood not as an evolutionary freak but as an inspiration born of a fresh and powerful friendship . . .

While on Helliconia, the august processes of the seasons were in undeniable stride.

In the northern hemisphere, small summer was nearly over. Frosty nights foretold colder nights ahead. In the winding passes of the Shivenink Chain, frost already ruled, and the living creatures who ventured there were subject to that rule.

It was morning. A screaming windstorm, the frigid breath from the pole. The supplies were being stacked away. The phagor and Uuundaamp were harnessing up their asokins. Seventeen days had elapsed since leaving Sharagatt. They had seen no sign that they were being pursued.

Of the three passengers Shokerandit had fared best. Toress Lahl had lapsed into speechlessness. She lay in the tent at night as if dead. Fashnalgid seldom spoke, except to curse. Their eyebrows and lashes were frosty white within a minute of leaving shelter, their cheekbones black with frostbite.

The last section of the trail ran above six thousand metres. To their right, in fuming cloud, was a solid mountain of ice. Visibility was down to a few feet.

Uuundaamp came to Shokerandit, eyes merry in his frosted face. "Today soft going," he shouted. "Downhill through tunnel. You 'member tunnel, chief?"

"Noonat Tunnel?" It was an effort to talk in the wind.

"Yaya, Noonat. Tonight we be there. Takit drink, bit meal, occhara, gumtaa."

"Gumtaa. Toress tired."

The Ondod shook his head. "She soon make meat together asokin.

No much biwack gumtaa no more, eh?" He laughed with closed mouth.

Shokerandit sensed the man had something more to say. Simultaneously they turned their backs on the others working at lashing up the sledge. Uuundaamp folded his arms.

"Your friend got tail grow along face." One quick sly look from his profile.

"Fashnalgid?"

"Your friend got tail along face. Team no like him. Team give plenty kakool. Make bad time. We lose that sherb in Noonat Tunnel, ishto?"

"Has he been molesting Moub?"

"Mole sting? No, he stick him prodo up Moub las' night again. Biwack the bag, ishto? She no like. She full baby Uuundaamps." He laughed. "So we lose in Tunnel, you see."

"I'm sorry, Uuundaamp. Loobiss for telling me—but no smrtaa in Tunnel, please. I speak him friend in Noonat. No more biwack your Moub."

"Chief, you better lose that friend. Else big kakool, I see." He laughed and scowled, tapping his forehead, then turned abruptly on his heel.

The Ondod rarely showed anger. But they were treacherous—that Shokerandit knew. Uuundaamp remained friendly; without at least an appearance of friendship, the journey could never be made; but he had lost face by telling a human of his wife's disgrace.

Shokerandit had been invited to copulate with Moub. Such was Ondod courtesy, and Shokerandit would have offended by declining the invitation. But Fashnalgid had done it uninvited, and had broken Ondod law. Ondod laws were simple and stark; transgression meant death, smrtaa. Fashnalgid would be killed without compunction. If Uuundaamp had decided to lose Fashnalgid in Noonat Tunnel, Shokerandit's plea would count for nothing.

Both Toress Lahl and Fashnalgid shot him curious looks from their red-rimmed eyes. He gave them no word, though deeply troubled. Uuundaamp was always watching, and would see if Shokerandit passed Fashnalgid a warning. That would count as kakool.

The shaggy bulk of Bhryeer emerged from the murk, trudging down the length of the sledge. His eyes gleamed cerise as he swung his head momentarily to contemplate them. His morose gaze settled on Shokerandit. There was no interpreting the phagor's expression.

He clicked his milt up one ice-encrusted nostril and then shouted above the wind, "Team ready go. Climb your plaze. Hol' tight."

Harbin Fashnalgid pulled a flask from inside his skins, thrust the neck between his flaking lips, and swallowed. As he stowed the flask away, Shokerandit said, "Be advised, don't drink. Hold tight, as he said."

"Abro Hakmo Astab!" Fashnalgid growled. He belched and turned away.

Toress Lahl looked appealingly at Shokerandit. He shook his head severely, mutely saying, Don't give up, bite tightly on the silver fox tail.

As they took their places on the sledge, they could just see the bundles that were Uuundaamp and Moub, the latter wrapped in her bright blanket. The dogs were invisible. Uuundaamp brought the long whip forward over his head. *Ipsssssisiii*. Then the first squeal of the steel runners as they chastised the snow. The place where they had spent the night, marked by yellow stains of human and asokin urine, was immediately lost.

Within an hour, they were moving downhill towards Noonat Tunnel. Shokerandit felt the sickness of fear in his throat. He would lose face himself by allowing an Ondod to kill a fellow human, whatever the justification. His anger turned against both Uuundaamp and Harbin Fashnalgid. The man was next to him, back hunched in misery. No communication passed between them.

Their speed increased. They were moving at perhaps five miles an hour. Shokerandit kept staring ahead, squeezing his eyes between cheeks and brow. Only the eternal grey to be seen, although somewhere above was a suspicion of light. Spectral white trees flitted by.

Beyond the customary noises, the sledge creaks, the whistle of whip, the dog farts, the crack of ice, the wind song, another noise grew, hollow, threatening. It was the sound of the wind keening in Noonat Tunnel. Moub answered it with blasts on a curled goat horn.

The Ondod were giving warning of their presence to other teams which might be coming in the other direction.

The suspicion of light overhead was abruptly cut off. They were in the tunnel. The phagor gave a hoarse cry and applied the rear cross-beam brake to slow their progress. Uuundaamp's whip made a different note as he flicked it just before the nose of his lead dog who bore his name, to slow their pace.

A freezing wind struck them like a solid object. This tunnel through the mountainside was a shortcut to the Noonat station. The road, by which heavier traffic or marching men went, was some miles longer but less dangerous. In the tunnel, there was always the chance of two sledges meeting head on, the traces of the teams entangling hopelessly as the rival asokins fought to the death, a fatal knife fight taking place. Since the tunnel had been cut to show an almost circular cross-section, it was theoretically possible for teams to pass by driving partway up opposite walls, but this chance was so remote that most drivers spurred onwards in terror, screaming warning as they went.

There were nine miles of tunnel. What with rockfalls and the force of the wind, the sledge swayed from one side to the other like a rudderless ship.

The attempt by Uuundaamp to slow down caused greater vibrations. Fashnalgid cursed. The driver and his woman slid to either side of the sledge's front and stuck heels into the snow to increase the braking effect.

Bhryeer leaned forward and shouted to Fashnalgid, "You bottle juzz now drop out."

"My bottle? Where?"

As Fashnalgid leant forward over the side of the sledge, looking where the phagor indicated, the phagor struck him a blow across the small of his back. Fashnalgid fell with a cry, landing on hands and knees and rolling over in the snow.

Immediately, there was a shrill cry from Uuundaamp and he lashed on the asokins. The phagor pulled off the rear brake. They sizzled forward, aided by the slope.

Fashnalgid was already on his feet. Already he was fading into the dimness. He began to run. Shokerandit yelled to him to come on. The wind roared, the Ondod shrieked, the runners screamed. Fashnalgid was catching up. As he came level with the rear of the sledge, his face contorted with effort, the phagor lifted an arm to strike another blow.

To be alone in the long tunnel was to face certain death. Other sledges, thrusting through the gloom, would simply run a man over. This was Ondod smrtaa.

Shouting at the top of his voice, Shokerandit drew his revolver and ran back on his knees over the loaded sledge. He clamped the muzzle against the phagor's long skull.

"I'll blast your sherbing harneys out." The silver fox tail fell from his mouth and was gone.

The phagor cowered back.

"Throw the brake on."

Bhryeer did so, but the downhill impetus was such that it made little difference, beyond sending a spume of fine snow over the running man.

Still the whip whistled and the driver shrieked at his team. Fashnalgid was falling back, mouth open, blackened face distorted. His never-too-certain will was failing him.

"Don't give up," yelled Shokerandit, stretching out a hand to the captain.

Making a new effort, Fashnalgid increased speed. His boots drummed on the snow as he slowly drew level with the rear of the sledge. Bhryeer cowered out of harm's way. The wind shrilled.

Clutching a cord securing the tent with one gloved hand, Shokerandit leant forward and extended his other hand. He shouted encouragement. Fashnalgid was tiring. The sledge was still gaining speed. The two men stared into each other's wide eyes. Their gloved hands touched.

"Yes," yelled Shokerandit. "Yes, leap aboard, man, fast!"

Their grips locked. Just as Shokerandit tugged, Uuundaamp gave a swerve to the left, flicking the runners of the sledge up the sloping side of the tunnel, and almost overturning his vehicle. Shokerandit was flung free. He clutched at and missed a runner as it sizzled past his face. Fashnalgid stumbled over him and they sprawled flat.

When they picked themselves up, the sledge was disappearing in the dimness.

"Lousy biwacking drivers," Fashnalgid said, bending forward and trying to get his breath back. "Animals."

"That was deliberate. That's Ondod smrtaa—vengeance. Because of your ape tricks with the woman." He had to turn his back to the wind flow to speak.

"That stinking tub of lard? He said himself that she was not good enough even for an asokin to enjoy." He bent double, panting.

"That's how they talk, you fool. Now listen, and take in what I say. This tunnel is death. Another sledge may come through at any moment, from one end or the other. There's no way we could stop it, except with our bodies. We have about seven miles to go, I'd guess, and we'd better do it fast."

"How about going back and taking the road?"

"That way's about thirty miles. We've no provisions and we'd still be walking when dark fell. We would be dead. Now, are you going to run? Because I am."

Fashnalgid straightened up, groaning. He said, "Thanks for trying to save me."

"Astab you, you arrogant fool. Why couldn't you have tried to obey the system?"

Luterin Shokerandit started to run. At least it was downhill. His knee hurt from his fall. He listened for the sound of another sledge but heard only the wind roaring in his ears.

The footsteps of Fashnalgid echoed behind him. He never looked back. All his faculties were concentrated on getting through the tunnel to Noonat.

When he thought he could run no further, he made himself keep on. Once there was a gleam of light to one side. In relief, he halted and went to look. Part of the rock of the outer wall had fallen away, revealing daylight. Nothing could be seen but cloud and, just beyond arm's reach, a stalactite of ice. He threw a piece of rock into the void, listened, but never heard it fall.

Fashnalgid caught up with him, blowing hard.

"Let's get out through this hole."

"It's a sheer mountainside."

"Never mind. Bribahr somewhere down there. Civilisation. Not like this place."

"You'll kill yourself."

As Fashnalgid was trying to lever his body through the hole in the rock, a distant horn announced an oncoming sledge—this one also arriving from the south. Shokerandit saw a light looming. He pressed into the natural alcove, forcing himself back against the jagged rock close to Fashnalgid.

Next moment, a long black sledge shot by, teamed by ten dogs. A bell dangling over the driver jangled madly. Several men sat aboard, twelve possibly, all crouching masked against the cold. It was by in a flash.

"Military," Fashnalgid said. "Could they be after us?"

"After you, you mean. What does it matter? With them travelling ahead, clearing the way, this is our best chance to get out of the tunnel safely. Unless you like thousand-foot jumps, you'll come too."

He started off again. After a while, the running became automatic. He could feel the knock of his lungs against his ribs. Ice formed on his chin. The lids of his slitted eyes froze. He lost count of time.

When the brightness came, it assailed him. He could not prise open his eyes. He jogged on before realising that he had at last left the tunnel. Sobbing, he staggered to one side and clung to a boulder. There he lay, panting as if he would never stop. Two sledges passed nearby, horns blowing, but he did not look up.

A lump of falling snow forced him into action. He scrubbed his face with the snow and peered ahead. The light still seemed brilliant. The wind had dropped. There was a break in the cloud. Only a short distance away, people were strolling, smoking veronikanes, wearing blankets. A woman was buying something at a stall. An ancient bowed man was driving horned sheep down the street. A welcoming sign said PILGRIM LODGE: *No Ondods*. He had reached Noonat.

Noonat was the last stop before Kharnabhar. It was nothing more than a halt in the wilds, a place where teams could be changed. But it had something else to offer. The trail between Kharnabhar, Northern Sharagatt, and Rivenjk followed the contours of the chain, taking every advantage of the protection against the polar winds which the mountains provided. But at Noonat there was a junction, and a road led westward, over the great falls and valleys and plateaux of the western chain, to enter at last into the plains of Bribahr. Kharnabhar was now nearer than those plains. But the plains were nearer than Rivenjk, by a long measure.

The state of hostility which existed between Uskutosh and Bribahr might account for an increased number of military uniforms visible in

Noonat, and for the fact that an imposing new wooden building, which would face westwards, was being built.

Shokerandit was almost too exhausted to take much care for himself. But he had the presence of mind to stagger behind the boulder that had sheltered him and follow a footpath uphill until he came to a stone-built goat shed. He climbed in with the goats and fell asleep.

When he woke, he felt refreshed, and was angry with himself for wasting time. He could not greatly care what had happened to Fashnalgid, so great was his need to find Toress Lahl and to get the sledge on to Kharnabhar. Once there, his problems would be over.

The straggle of Noonat lay below him. Its poor houses clung to the mountainside like burrs to an animal's flank. Most of the houses took advantage of eldawon trees, a species with thin multiple trunks, and cowered against them or were actually built into them. Since most of the houses were constructed from the timber of the eldawon, it was difficult to distinguish habitation from vegetation.

Cottages crouched here and there, linked by trails followed by humans, animals, and fowls. They stood higgledy-piggledy, so that one man's doorstep came level with the next man's chimney. Fields were coterminous with roofs. Every homestead boasted a pile of chopped logs. Some piles leant against the houses, some houses against the piles. Woodmen could be heard, busy with axes, adding to either the number of piles or the number of homesteads.

For a short while, the air was free of cloud and possessed a brilliance unique to high mountain places. Batalix shone over a distant crag. Boys in the stoney fields, supposedly herding sheep and goats, flew kites instead.

A crowd of pilgrims had just arrived on foot from Kharnabhar. Their voices carried in the clear air. Most had shaven heads, some went barefoot, despite the hard snow on the ground. All ages were represented among them; there was even an old yellowed woman being carried in a wicker chair to which shafts had been attached. A few local traders were watching them attentively, but without great interest. This lot had already been fleeced on their way northwards.

Having travelled the trail before, Shokerandit knew that Uuundaamp would have to stop here. He and Moub would rest. All the asokins would be staked separately and fed, with extra meat for Uuundaamp, the leader. Sledge and harness would be thoroughly overhauled for the last lap of the journey if the Ondods intended to go on to Kharnabhar. And what would they do with Toress Lahl?

Not murder her. She was too valuable. As a slave, she could be sold; but few humans would buy a human slave from an Ondod. Ancipitals on the other hand . . . He was frightened for her, and forgot Fashnalgid.

Although the ancipital kind were rare in Sibornal as a whole, those who escaped slavery often made their way to Shivenink, finding in the wilderness of the chain congenial habitation. Having experienced slavery themselves, they were the more inclined to use human slaves. Once she vanished into the hills with them, Toress Lahl would be lost to human knowledge.

Negotiating the paths at the rear of the houses, he covered the whole village. On its outskirts, he came to a palisade. Furious barking sounded on the other side as he approached. He peered over and saw trail asokins, staked out separately, or in cages. They launched themselves as far as chain and mesh would allow as he appeared.

This was unmistakably the staging post. He remembered it now. It had been snowing the last time he was through, when almost nothing could be seen in the blizzard. Something like fifty half-starved asokins were waiting in the pound.

Without provoking them further, he moved cautiously round by the side.

The staging post was the last building to the north of Noonat. A shout indicated that he had been sighted, although he saw no one. The Ondod were too cautious to be caught unawares.

Three of them appeared immediately, carrying whips. He knew how deadly they were with whips, halted, made the sign of peace on his forehead.

"I want my friend Uuundaamp, give him loobiss. Speak him loobiss, ishto?"

They were surly. They made no move.

"No see Uuundaamp. Uuundaamp no want loobiss together you. Uuundaamp fat lady plenty kakool."

He said. "I know. I bring help. Moub give birth, yaya?"

Sullenly they let him through. He told himself it was a trap, and that he should be ready for anything.

At the entrance to a barnlike building, the Ondods clustered, pausing, giving each other sullen eye glances. Then they motioned him to go in. The interior was dark and unwelcoming. He smelt occhara.

They thrust him in from behind and slammed the door.

He ran forward and threw himself flat. The sharp tongue of a whip passed lightly across his shoulder. He rolled over and dived to a side wall.

With one swift glance he observed Moub naked except for the blanket he had given her, which was now wrapped round her breasts. She lay on a plank, legs spread wide. Toress Lahl crouched over her. Toress Lahl was tied by the upper arm, in such a way that she could use her hands. The other end of the rope was held by one of three dehorned phagors who stood motionless against the wall opposite the one against which Shokerandit crouched. Uuundaamp's lead dog,

Uuundaamp, was staked in the middle of the barn, snapping savagely at the end of his leash in a futile attempt to eat the nearest portion of Shokerandit.

And Uuundaamp. He had heard or seen—for the barn had slit windows—Shokerandit's approach. With the ability of his kind, he had jumped above the lintel of the door, and stood poised there, about to lash out with his whip again. He smiled as he did so, without mirth.

Shokerandit had his gun in his hand. He knew better than to point it at the Ondod—the gesture would have provoked both Uuundaamp and phagors. Nor would any threat to Moub halt Uuundaamp in his present state of mind.

Shokerandit pointed the gun at the dog.

"I kill you dog dead, finish, gumtaa, ishto? You fall down here smart, drop whip. You come here, boy, you Uuundaamp. Else your dog plenty kakool one second quick!"

As he spoke, Shokerandit rose up, pointing the gun with both hands down the throat of the raging dog.

The whip fell to the floor. Uuundaamp jumped down. He smiled. He bowed, touched his forehead.

"My friend, you tumble off sledge in tunnel. No gumtaa. I very worry."

"You'll have a dead lead dog if you give me that sherb. Untie Toress Lahl. Are you all right, Toress?"

In a shaky voice, she said, "I have delivered babies before, and here comes another. But I am greatly relieved to see you, Luterin."

"What was the plan here?"

"The phagors were going to do something for Uuundaamp. I was the exchange gift. I've been terrified but I'm unharmed. And you?" Her voice trembled.

The phagors never moved. As he worked at the knots in the cord, Uuundaamp said, "This very nice lady, yaya. Shaggie he much enjoy . . . give him chance, yaya. No harm." He laughed.

Shokerandit bit his lip; the creature had to be allowed to save face. Almost penniless, they were forced to rely on him to get them to Kharnabhar.

When she was free, Toress Lahl said to Uuundaamp, "You very kind. When your baby is born, I buy you and Moub pipes of occhara, ishto?"

Shokerandit marvelled at her coolness.

Uuundaamp smiled and whistled through his teeth. "You buy extra pipe for baby too? I smoke three pipe together."

"Yaya, if you will kick out these shaggy brutes while I perform the delivery." Her face was white as she confronted him, but her voice no longer shook.

Still Uuundaamp felt that honours had not yet been made equal. "You give money now. Moub go buy three pipe occhara now. Better leave Noonat before is darkness."

"Moub's water broken, give birth directly."

"Baby no come maybe twenty minutes. She go buy fast. Smoke, give birth." He clapped his eight-fingered hands and laughed again.

"The baby is almost hanging out of her."

"That woman lazy bag." He grasped Moub by the arm. She sat up without protest. Toress Lahl and Shokerandit exchanged glances. When he nodded, she produced some sibs and gave them to the woman. Moub wrapped her entire body in the red and yellow blanket and waddled out of the barn without protest.

"Stay there," Shokerandit said. Toress Lahl sat on the water-stained bench. The lead dog settled down on its haunches, its red tongue lolling. At a gesture from Uuundaamp, the phagors filed out of the far end of the barn, pushing through a broken door. Outside, by the dog cage, stood Uuundaamp's sledge, unharmed.

"Where your friend grow tail on face?" Uuundaamp asked innocently.

"I lost him. Your plan did not work well."

"Ha ha. *My* plan work fine. You still want go Kharber?"

"Are you going that way? You've been paid, Uuundaamp."

Uuundaamp held his hand wide in a gesture of frankness, exposing his sixteen black-gleaming nails.

"If your friend tell police, no gumtaa. Hard for me. That bad man no understand Ondod like you. He want smrtaa. Better we go fast, ishto, once that bag throw her baby from her bottom-part."

"Agreed." No point in quarrelling now. He tucked his gun into his pocket. The apparent friendship of the trail could be resumed.

They remained watching each other, and the asokin waited at the end of its leash. Moub padded back, still swathed in the blanket. She gave two pipes to Uuundaamp and resumed her place on the plank by Toress Lahl, the third pipe in her mouth.

"Baby now come. Gumtaa," she said. And a small Ondod male was born into the world without further ado. As Toress Lahl lifted it, Uuundaamp nodded and then turned away. He spat into a corner of the barn.

"Boy. Is good. Not like girl. Boy do much work, soon have biwack, maybe one year."

Moub sat up and laughed. "You no make good biwack, you fool sherb. This boy belong Fashnalgid."

They both burst into laughter. He went across and hugged her. They kissed each other over and over.

This scene so much took everyone's attention that they did not heed whistles of warning from outside. Three police carrying rifles at the ready entered the barn from the road end.

The leader said coolly, "We have offence orders against you all. Uuundaamp, you and that woman have a number of murders to your name. Luterin Shokerandit, we have followed you from Rivenjk. You are an accomplice in blowing up an army lieutenant, and killing a soldier in the course of his duties. Also guilty of deserting from the army. In consequence of which, you, Toress Lahl, slave, are also guilty of escaping. We have a dispensation to execute you at once here in Noonat."

"Who these humans people?" asked Uuundaamp, pointing indignantly at Shokerandit and Toress Lahl. "I no see them. They just come here one minute, cause plenty kakool."

Ignoring him, the police leader said to Shokerandit, "I have orders to shoot you if you try to escape. Throw down any arms you have. Where is your recent companion? We want him too."

"Who do you mean?"

"You know who. Harbin Fashnalgid, another deserter."

"I'm here," said an unexpected voice. "Drop your rifles. I can shoot you and you can't hit me, so don't try. I'll count three and then I shall shoot one of you in the stomach. One. Two."

The rifles dropped. By then they had seen the revolver poking through one of the slit windows.

"Grab the guns, then, Luterin, look alive."

Shokerandit unfroze and did as he was told. Fashnalgid entered by the rear door, setting all the asokins barking.

"How did you come so providentially?" Toress Lahl asked.

He scowled. "I imagine the same way these dummies did. By following that unmistakable red-and-yellow striped blanket. Otherwise I had no idea where you were. As you see, I'm going in for disguise."

They had noticed. Fashnalgid had had his immense moustache shaved off and his hair cut short. He kept his revolver levelled at the police in a professional manner as he spoke.

"Rifle get much money," Uuundaamp suggested. "Cut these man throat first, ishto?"

"Never mind that, you little scab-devourer. If your shaggie was here, I'd drop him. Luckily he is not, because this place is swarming with police and soldiers."

"We'd better leave fast," Shokerandit said. "Excellent timing, Harbin. You'll make an officer yet. Uuundaamp, if we keep these three police quiet, can you and Moub get the dogs harnessed up really quickly?"

The Ondod became very active. He got the two women to drag the sledge into the barn and grease the runners, which he insisted was necessary. The police were made to stand with their trousers round their ankles and their hands up the wall. Everyone stood back as lead dog Uuundaamp was unleashed and he and the other seven asokins were secured to the traces, each in its appropriate place. As he worked, Uuundaamp cursed each of them in different tones of affection.

"Please hurry," said Toress Lahl once, betraying her nervousness.

The Ondod went and sat down on the plank where his wife had recently given birth.

"Jus' take small rest, ishto?"

They waited it out, no one moving, until his honour was satisfied. Snow came in through the rear door as he methodically checked over the harness.

From the direction of the street they could hear shouts and whistles. The three police had already been missed.

Uuundaamp picked up his whip.

"Gumtaa. Get on."

The rifles were tucked hastily under the sledge straps as they jumped aboard. Uuundaamp called encouragingly to Uuundaamp, and the sledge started to move. The police at once began to shout at the top of their voices. Answering shouts came. The sledge bumped out of the rear door.

Outside, ravening asokins leaped furiously against the mesh of their cage. Uuundaamp raised himself, twirled his whip, sent its tip flying towards the cage door. The hasp of the cage was secured in position by a thick wooden wedge. The whip end flicked the wedge free as the sledge went by.

Under the weight of the dogs, the cage door crashed open, and the brutes hurled themselves to freedom in a torrent of fur and fangs. Into and through the barn they rushed. Ghastly cries came up from the police.

The sledge gathered speed, bumping across rough ground, swinging round. Uuundaamp shouted commands, plying his whip expertly, licking each dog with it in turn, arms tireless. The passengers hung on. The barking and sounds of pain from behind died as they went over the hillside and jarred down onto the northward road.

Shokerandit looked back. No one was following. Faintly through the snow, sounds of growling still reached his ears. Then the road turned. Toress Lahl clutched him. Under one arm, wrapped in a bundle of dirty rag, she sheltered the newborn babe. It looked up at her and grinned, showing sharp baby teeth.

A mile along the trail, Uuundaamp slowed and turned.

He pointed the handle of the whip at Fashnalgid.

"You, kakool man. You jump off. No want."

Fashnalgid said nothing. He looked at Shokerandit, grimaced. Then he jumped.

Within a few yards, his figure was concealed in a whirl of snow. His last words reached them faintly—the terrible oath: "Abro Hakmo Astab!"

Uuundaamp turned to scan the trail ahead.

"Kharber!" he cried.

Avoiding Noonat, Fashnalgid met up with a group of Bribahrese pilgrims, returning from Kharnabhar and Noonat and making their way home, down the winding trails to the western valleys. He had shaved off his moustache in order to avoid identification and had every intention of disappearing from human ken.

Hardly had he been with the pilgrims for twenty-five hours when the group met another party climbing up from Bribahr. The latter had such a tale of disaster to tell that Fashnalgid became convinced that he was heading in the wrong direction. Perhaps right directions did not exist anymore.

According to the refugees, the Oligarch's Tenth Guard had descended on the Great Rift Valley of Bribahr, with orders to take possession of or destroy the two great cities of Braijth and Rattagon.

Most of the rift valley was filled by the cobalt blue waters of Lake Braijth. In the lake was an island on which stood an immense old fortress. This was the city of Rattagon. There was no way of attacking the fortress except by boat. Whenever an enemy attempted to cross, it was sunk by the batteries of the frowning castle walls.

Bribahr was the great grain-producing land of Sibornal. Its fertile plains reached down into the tropical zones. In the north, before the ice sheets began, there stretched the tundra barrier, skirted by mile upon mile of caspiarn trees, which could withstand even the onslaught of Weyr-Winter.

The inhabitants of Bribahr were mainly peasant farmers. But a warrior elite, based in the two cities of Braijth and Rattagon, had recklessly threatened Kharnabhar, the Holy City. Braijth would have liked a greater share of Sibornal's prosperity. Bribahr farmers sent grain to Uskutoshk for little return; to put pressure on the Oligarchy, they had made a tentative move against Holy Kharnabhar, capable of being approached from their plains.

In return for their threats, Askitosh had sent an army. Braijth had already fallen.

Now the Tenth sat on the shores of Lake Braijth, looked towards Rattagon, and waited. And starved. And shivered.

The frosts of the brief autumn had come. The lake also began to freeze.

There would be a time, and the Rattagonese knew it, when the ice would be firm enough to permit an enemy force to cross, walking. But that time was not yet. So far, nothing heavier than a wolf could get across. It might take a tenner before the ice would bear a platoon of soldiers. By then, the enemy on the banks would have starved and crawled away home. The Rattagonese knew the habits of their lake.

They did not entirely starve behind their battlements. The ancient rift valley had numerous faults. There was a tunnel below the lake to the northwestern shore. It was a wet way to travel, the water in it always knee-deep. But food could pass by that route; the defenders of Rattagon could afford to wait, as they had done before in times of crisis.

One night, when Freyr was lost behind dense gales of snow blowing from the north, the Tenth put a desperate plan into action.

The ice was strong enough to bear wolves. It would also bear men with kites flying above them, supporting much of their weight, making them no heavier than wolves, and as ferocious.

The officers encouraged their men by telling them tales of the voluptuous women of Rattagon who stayed by their men in the fortress, keeping their beds warm.

The wind blew, strong and steady. The kites tugged and lifted the shoulders of the men. Bravely they ran onto the thin ice. Bravely they permitted themselves to be carried across the ice, right up to the grey walls of the fortress.

Inside the fortress walls, even the sentries slept, huddled in any warm nook to shelter from the storm. They died with hardly a cry.

The volunteers of the Tenth cut away their kite cords and ran to the central keep. They slew the commander of the garrison in mid-snore.

Next day, the flag of the Oligarchy flew over fallen Rattagon.

This dreadful story, related with great drama over camp fires, persuaded Harbin Fashnalgid that there was wisdom in returning to Noonat and seeking a way southwards.

It's always painful to become involved in history, he told himself, and accepted a bottle that was making the rounds of the pilgrims.

XIII

"AN OLD ANTAGONISM"

The night was alive. So thickly was the snow falling that, brushing against a human face in its descent, it resembled the fur of a great beast. The fur was less cold than suffocating: it occupied space normally taken up by air and sound. But when the sledge stopped, the staid brazen tongue of a bell could be distantly heard.

Luterin Shokerandit helped Toress Lahl down from the sledge. The churn of snowflakes had confused her. She stood with bowed shoulder, sheltering her eyes.

"Where are we?"

"Home."

She saw nothing, only the animal dark, rolling, rolling towards her. Dimly, she made out Shokerandit, a bear walking, as he staggered towards the front of the sledge. There he embraced both Uuundaamp and the Ondod mother, clutching her infant into the coloured blanket.

Uuundaamp lifed his whip in farewell and flashed his unreliable smile. Came the jar-jar of his warning bell, the slice of his whip over the team, and the outfit was swallowed immediately by the whirling murk.

Bent almost double, Shokerandit and Toress Lahl made their way to a gate beyond which a dim light burned. He pulled a metal bell handle. They leaned exhaustedly against the stone pillar of the gate until a muffled military figure appeared from a shelter somewhere beyond the bars. The gate swung open.

They sheltered, panting, saying nothing to each other, until the guard returned after securing the gate and scrutinised them under his lantern.

The guard's lineaments were those of an old soldier. His mouth was tight, his gaze evaded other eyes, his expression gave nothing away. He stood his ground and asked, "What do you want?"

"You're speaking to a Shokerandit, man. Where are your wits?"

The challenging tone made the guard look more closely. With no change of expression, he said finally, "You wouldn't be Luterin Shokerandit?"

"Have I been away that long, you fool? Will you stand there and have me freeze?"

The man allowed his glance to take in Luterin's metamorphosed bulk in one mute, insulting glare. "A cab to take you up the drive, sir."

As he turned away, Luterin, still nettled at not being recognised, said, "Is my father in residence?"

"At present not, sir."

The guard put his free hand to the side of his mouth and bawled to a slave lurking at the rear of the guardhouse. In a short while, the cabriolet appeared through the blizzard, drawn by two yelk already encrusted in snow.

It was a mile from the gate to the ancient house, through land still known as the Vineyard. Now it was rough pasturage, where a local strain of yelk was bred.

Shokerandit alighted. The snow whirled round the corner of the house as if personally interested in turning them to ice. The woman closed her eyes and clutched Shokerandit's skins. Following ghostly materialisations of the structure, they climbed steps to the iron-banded front door. Above them sounded the dismal tolling bell, long drawn out, like a sound heard underwater. Other bells, drowning farther off, added their tongues.

The door opened. Dim guardian figures showed, helping the two new arrivals inside. The snow ceased, the roaring and clanging ceased, as bolts were shot home behind them.

In an echoing darkened hall, Shokerandit exchanged words with a servant unseen. A lamp glittered high on a marble wall, not yielding its illumination beyond the frosty surface which reflected it. They padded upstairs, each step with its own protesting noise. A heavy curtain was drawn back as if to abet the powers of darkness and stealth. They entered. While the woman stood, the servant lit a light and quit the room, bowing.

The room smelt dead. Shokerandit turned up the wick of his lamp.

An impression of space, a low ceiling, shutters ineffectively barring out the night, a bed ... They struggled out of their filthy garments.

They had been travelling for thirty-one days and, since Sharagatt, had been allowed only six and a half hours of sleep a day, rarely more, sometimes less, according to whether Uuundaamp considered the police were closing on them. Their faces were blackened by frost and lined by exhaustion.

Toress Lahl took a blanket from a couch and prepared to lie beside the bed. He climbed into the bed and beckoned her to join him.

"You sleep with me now," he said.

She stood before him, her expression still dazed from the journey. "Tell me what place we are in now."

He smiled. "You know where we are. This is my father's house in Kharnabhar. Our troubles are over. We are safe here. Get in."

She attempted a smile in return. "I am your slave and so I obey, master."

She got in beside him. Her answer did not satisfy him, but he put his arms about her and made love to her. After which, he fell asleep immediately.

When she awoke, Shokerandit had gone. She lay gazing at the ceiling, wondering what he was trying to demonstrate by leaving her on her own. She felt herself unable to move from the comfortable bed, to face the challenges that would have to be met. Luterin was well disposed to her, and more than that; she had no doubts on that score. For him, she could feel only hatred. His casual handing over of her to the animal who drove the sledge, a humiliation still fresh in her mind, was merely the latest of his coarse treatments. Of course, she reflected, he did not do these things to *her* personally; he was merely conforming to fashion and treating her as slaves were treated.

She had good reason to hope that he might restore her social status. She would be a slave no more. But if that entailed marrying him, her husband's murderer, she did not think she could go through with it, even to ensure her own safety.

To make matters worse, she felt a dread of this place to which she had been brought. A spirit seemed to brood over it, chill, hostile.

She rolled over unhappily in the great bed, to discover that a female slave was waiting silently, kneeling by the door. Toress Lahl sat up, pulling the sheet over her naked breasts.

"What are you doing there?"

"Master Luterin sent me in to attend you and bathe you when you woke, lady." The girl bowed her head as she spoke.

"Don't call me lady. I am a slave just as you are."

But the response merely embarrassed the girl. Resigning herself to the situation and half-amused, Toress Lahl climbed naked from the bed. She raised an imperious hand.

"Attend me!" she said.

Nodding compliantly, the girl came forward and escorted Toress Lahl to a bathroom, where warm water ran from a brass tap. The whole mansion was heated by biogas, the slave explained, and the water too.

As Toress Lahl reclined in the luxurious water, she surveyed her body. It had grown less bulky with the rigours of the journey. Down both sides of her thighs, the scratches inflicted by Uuundaamp's claws were slowly healing. Rather worse, she suspected that she might be pregnant. By whom she could not say, but she thanked the Beholder that matings between Ondods and humans were never fertile.

Borldoran and her home town of Oldorando were thousands of miles away. If she ever saw the pleasant land of her birth again, she would be more than lucky. A female slave's life was generally wretched and short. She thought to ask the girl attending her about that, then considered it wiser to hold her tongue. If Luterin married her, she would be a thousand times better off.

What would he say? Would he ask her? Tell her? She would have to go through with it, whatever he did.

After the maid had dried her, she put on a satara gown provided for her. She sank back on the bed and delivered herself into a state of pauk. It was the first time that she had descended into the world of the gossies since leaving Rivenjk. There below her, in obsidian where all decisions had finally been made, waited the spark of her dead husband, calling her to him.

The estate looked as beautiful as ever. The continuing wind from the north had blown most of the night's snow into drifts. Exposed areas were clear. To the south of every tree lay a line of snow, fine honed as a bird's bone. The Chief Steward, an agreeable man Luterin had known since his childhood accompanied him on his survey. Ordinary life was beginning again.

Great caspiarns and brassimips stood in wind-deflecting parade. On all sides, distant or near, rose snowy peaks, the daughters of the chain, generally sulking in cloud. To the north, the cloud allowed glimpses of the Holy Mountain, in which was the Great Wheel. Luterin broke off the conversation to raise his gloved hand in salute.

He wore a warm greatcoat over his clothes, and had attached his hip-bell to his belt. In the stable yard, slaves naked to the waist had brought a young gunnadu for him to ride. These two-legged, large-eared creatures balanced themselves by means of long tails, and ran on clawed birdlike feet. Like the yelk and biyelk with which they associated in the wild, the gunnadu were necrogenes. Thus they belonged to a category of animal which could give birth only through its own death. Luterin's mother had said bitterly to him once, "Not unlike humanity."

Gunnadu were without wombs; the sperm developed into grubs inside
the stomach, where they fed, working outwards until reaching an
artery. From there they exploded throughout the maternal body, causing rapid death. The grubs pupated through several stages, feeding on
the carion, until of a size to survive in the outside world as small
gunnadu.

Fully grown gunnadu made docile mounts, but tired easily. They were
ideal for short journeys, such as an inspection of the Shokerandit estate.

He felt himself safe here. The police would never enter one of the
great estates. While his father was away enjoying the hunt, Luterin was
in charge. Despite his long absence, despite his metamorphosis, he fell
into the role with ease. From the Chief Steward down to the lowest
slave, everyone knew him. It was absurd to think of any other life. And
he was the perfect only son.

He had duties. Those he would attend to. He must introduce Toress
Lahl to his mother. And he would have to speak to Insil Esikananzi;
that might be a little awkward. . . . Meanwhile, there were more important duties.

He had matured. He caught himself reflecting that it was no bad
thing that his father was absent. Always before this, he had missed
him. Lobanster Shokerandit's word hereabouts was law, as it was with
his one remaining son. But the formidable Keeper of the Wheel was
frequently absent. He liked to live rough, he said, and his hunting trips
took up two or three tenners at a time. Off he would go, taking his
dogs and his yelk with him. Sometimes he went accompanied only by
his mute hunt captain, Liparotin. A farewell wave and he would be
away, into the trackless wilds.

From his childhood, Luterin remembered that casual gesture of the
hand upraised. Less a sign of love for him and his mother as they
watched him depart, more a sign of acknowledgement to the spirit
which presided over the lonely mountains.

Luterin had grown up missing his father. His withdrawn mother was
hardly compensating company. Once he had insisted on accompanying
his father and his brother, Favin. He had been proud then, among
the proud caspiarns; but Lobanster had appeared vexed with his sons,
and they had returned home after no more than a week away.

He sniffed. He told himself that he too was a solitary, like his father.
And then his thoughts swung back to Harbin Fashnalgid, last seen when
Uuundaamp had turned him off the sledge. Only now did he realise he
liked Fashnalgid, and should try to do something for him. His jealous
anger at the man for possessing Toress Lahl was over.

Now he could recall Harbin uttering his unseemly oath, and smile.
What an outcast the man was! Perhaps that was why it rankled when
he called Luterin a victim of the system, or whatever the phrase was.
The captain also had had a good side to his nature.

He and the Chief Steward visited the stungebag enclosure. The slow creatures were much as he remembered them. It was said that the Shokerandits had bred stungebags through four Great Years. The stungebags looked like badly thatched caterpillars or, when stretched to their full length, like fallen trees. They were combined animal and plant, a sport born at the melting time when the planet was showered by high-energy radiation.

Slaves were working in the hoxney paddock. Droves of hoxneys had once roved the uplands. Now they were starting to go into hibernation. In one of the corners of the estate, slaves were collecting the animals and storing them away in dry barns, prising them out of the nooks and crannies in which they had hidden. The animals relapsed swiftly into a shrunken, glassy state, their energies draining. They would come to resemble small translucent figures. Already, some were losing their dull brown colour and exhibiting colourful horizontal stripes, as they had done in the Great Spring.

In the hibernatory state, the hoxneys were known as glossies, perhaps not only for their shine, but because, like gossies, they were not entirely dead.

The estate manager, a freeman, came up and touched his hat.

"Glad to see you back, master. We're packing the glossies with hay between, as you may observe, to protect the creatures. They should be all right when spring arrives, if so happen it ever does."

"It'll come. It's only a matter of centuries."

"So you scholars say," said the man, with a conspiratorial grin at the steward.

"The principle is to organise for spring now. By storing these hoxneys safely, instead of leaving them to the vagaries of nature, we guarantee a good riding herd when the time comes."

" 'Twill be long past our lifetimes."

"Someone will be here, I don't doubt, to be grateful for our providence."

But he spoke absentmindedly, with Fashnalgid still on his mind.

When he got back to the mansion, he summoned his father's secretary, a learned withdrawn man called Evanporil. He gave Evanporil instructions that four armed liegemen were to be sent on two giant biyelk as far down the road as Noonat, to seek out Fashnalgid if he was to be found. Fashnalgid was to be brought back to the safety of the Shokerandit estate. The secretary left about his task.

Luterin ate some lunch, and only then thought that he should visit his mother.

The hall of the great house was gloomy. There were no windows on the lower floor, so as to render the structure more impervious to ice, snow, and flood. A great heavy chair stood empty on the marble tiling; as far as Luterin knew, no one had ever sat in it.

Between the dim wall lamps, fed from the biogas chambers, skulls of phagors projected from the walls. These were specimens that Lobanster and other Shokerandits before him had killed. They remained now with their horns held high, their shadowed eye sockets observing with melancholy the far recesses of the hall.

He paused on the way to his mother's quarters, aware of an uproar outside. Someone was shouting in a thick drunken voice. Shokerandit ran for a side door, hip-bell clattering. A slave hastily flung back the bolts to allow him passage.

In a court overlooked by the upper windows of the mansion, a liege-man and two freemen were brandishing swords. They had cornered six dehorned phagors. One of the phagors, a gillot with thin withered dugs which spoke of years in captivity, was calling out in a hoarse voice, in Sibish, "You not to kill, you vile Sons of Freyr! This Hrl-Ichor Yhar come back belong to us, the ancipitals! Stop! Stop!"

"Stop!" Shokerandit said.

The men had already killed one of the ahumans. A swordsman had disembowelled a stallun with a downward slash of his sword. Ancipital eddre lodged in their carcasses above their lungs. As Shokerandit bent over the corpse, which was still in spasm, the intestines slithered forth on a tide of yellow blood.

The mass loosened itself and began slowly to evacuate the cavern of the ribs like a concoction of soft-boiled eggs in jelly. Beige shadows ran between little glistening mounds which came creeping out of the wound like a living mass, flowing thickly over the flags and into the cracks between the flags, flowing until all poured forth, separate organs no longer distinguishable in the general exodus, leaving a hollow behind them.

Shokerandit tugged back the dead creature's ear to expose its blaze mark.

He glared at the men.

"These are our slave ancipitals. What are you doing?"

The liegeman was scowling. "Best mind out the way, master. Orders are to kill off all phagors, whether ours or otherwise."

The five phagors began shouting hoarsely and scrambling to get past the men, who immediately brought their swords to the ready.

"Stop. Drikstalgil, who gave you these orders?" He remembered the liegeman's name.

Keeping one eye on the ancipitals and his sword ready, the liegeman dipped into his left pocket and brought out a folded paper.

"Secretary Evanporil issued me this this morning. Now, stand back, if you would not mind, master, or you'll get crushed."

He handed Shokerandit a poster, which Shokerandit flapped open with an angry gesture. It was printed in heavy black letters.

The poster announced that a New Act had been passed, in a further attempt to keep down the Plague known as the Fat Death. The Ancipital Race had been identified as the main Carrier of the Plague. All Phagors must therefore be killed. Phagor slaves must be put down. Wild Phagors should be shot on sight. A bounty would be paid of One Sib per ancipital head by the appropriate authority in each District. Henceforth, the possession of Phagors was illegal, under Penalty of Death. By Order of the Oligarch.

"Put up your swords until I give you further orders," Shokerandit said. "No more killing till I say so. And get this corpse away from here."

When the men reluctantly did as he instructed, Shokerandit went back into the house, marching angrily upstairs to see the secretary.

The mansion was full of ancient prints, many of them engraved by a steel process in Rivenjk, when that city had boasted an artistic colony. Most of the prints depicted scenes suitable to wild mountainous areas: hunters coming unexpectedly upon bears in clearings, bears coming unexpectedly upon hunters, stags at bay, men mounted on yelk leaping into chasms, women being stabbed in gloomy forests, lost children dying in pairs upon exposed crags.

Beside the secretary's door was a print of a soldier-priest on guard before the very portals of the Great Wheel. He stood stiffly upright while spearing to death an immense phagor which had leaped from a hole to attack him. The engraving was entitled—the Sibish lettering executed with many a curlicue—"An Old Antagonism."

"Very appropriate," Shokerandit said aloud, thumped on Evanporil's door, and entered.

The secretary was standing by his window, looking out, and enjoying a cup of pellamountain tea. He inclined his head and looked slyly at Shokerandit without speaking.

Shokerandit spread the poster out on his desk.

"You did not tell me about this when I was here earlier. How's that?"

"You did not ask me, Master Luterin."

"How many ancipitals do we employ on the estate?"

The secretary answered without hesitation. "Six hundred and fifteen."

"It would be a tremendous loss to slaughter them. The new Act is not to be complied with. First, I am going into town to see what the other landlords make of it."

Secretary Evanporil coughed behind his fingers. "I wouldn't advise a visit to town just now. We have reports of some disturbance there."

"What kind of disturbance?"

"The clergy, Master Luterin. The live cremation of Priest-Supreme Chubsalid has caused a great deal of disaffection. A tenner has passed since his death, and I'm given to understand that the occasion was marked this morning by the burning of an effigy of the Oligarch. Member Ebstok Esikananzi led some men to quell the display, but there has been trouble since."

Shokerandit sat himself on the edge of the desk.

"Evanporil, tell me, do you consider that we can afford to kill over six hundred phagors out of hand?"

"That's not for me to say, Master Luterin. I am only an administrator."

"But the Act—it's so arbitrary. Don't you think so?"

"I would say, since you ask me, Master Luterin, that, if scrupulously carried out, the Act will rid Sibornal of the ancipital kind for ever. An advantage, wouldn't you say?"

"But the immediate loss of cheap labour to us . . . I don't imagine my father will be best pleased."

"That may be, sir, but for the general good . . ." The secretary let the sentence hang.

"Then we will not implement the Act until my father returns. I shall write to Esikananzi and the other landlords to that effect. See that the managers are clear on that score immediately."

Shokerandit spent the afternoon happily riding about the estate, ensuring that no more phagors were harmed. He rode out some miles to call on his father's cousins, who had another estate in a mountainous region. With his mind full of plans, he forgot entirely about his mother.

That night he made love to Toress Lahl as usual. Something in the words he uttered, or in the way he touched her, woke a response in her. She became a different person, yielding, imaginative, fully alive. An exhilaration beyond mere happiness filled Luterin. He thought he had won a great gift. All the pains of life were worth such delight.

They spent the whole night in the closest embraces, moving slowly, moving wildly, moving scarcely at all. Their spirits and bodies were one.

Towards morning, Luterin fell asleep. He was immediately in the dreamworld.

He was walking through a sparse landscape almost bereft of trees. It was marshy underfoot. Ahead lay a frozen lake whose immensity could not be judged. It was the future: all-powerful night prevailed in a small winter during the Weyr-Winter. Neither sun was in the sky. A lumbering animal with rasping breath followed him.

It was also the past. On the shores of the lake were camped all the men who had died violently in the Battle of Isturiacha. Their wounds still remained, disfiguring them. Luterin saw Bandal Eith Lahl there, standing apart with his hands in his pockets, gazing down at the ground.

Under the ice of the lake, something gigantic was penned. He recognised that this was where the breathing came from.

The being surged forth from the ice. The ice did not break. The being was a huge woman with a lustrous black skin. She rose and rose into the sky. No one saw her but Luterin.

She cast a benevolent gaze on Luterin and said, "You will never have a woman to make you entirely happy. But there will be much happiness in the pursuit."

Much more she said, but this was all Luterin could remember when he woke up.

Toress Lahl lay beside him. Not only were her eyes shut: her whole countenance presented a closed appearance. A lock of hair lay across her face; she bit it, as recently she had bitten the fox tail to preserve her from the cold of the trail. She scarcely breathed. He recognised that she was in pauk.

Finally she returned. She stared and looked at him almost without recognition.

"You never visit those below?" she said in a small voice.

"Never. We Shokerandits regard it as gross superstition."

"Do you not wish to speak with your dead brother?"

"No."

After a silence, he clutched her hand and asked, "You have been communing with your husband again?"

She nodded without speaking, knowing it was bitter to him. After a moment, she said, "Isn't this world we live in like an evil dream?"

"Not if we live by our beliefs."

She clung to him then and said, "But isn't it true that one day we shall grow old, and our bodies decay, and our wits fail? Isn't that true? What could be worse than that?"

They made love again, this time more from fear than affection.

After he had done the rounds of the estate the next day, and found everything quiet, he went to visit his mother.

His mother's rooms were at the rear of the mansion. A young servant girl opened the door to him, and showed him into his mother's anteroom. There stood his mother, in characteristic pose, hands clasped tightly before her, head slightly on one side as she smiled quizzingly at him.

He kissed her. As he did so, the familiar atmosphere that she carried round with her enveloped him. Something in her attitude and her gestures suggested an inward sorrow, even—he had often thought it—an illness of some kind: and yet an illness, a sorrow, so familiar that Lourna Shokerandit drew on them almost as a substitute for other marked characteristics.

As she spoke gently to her son, not reproaching him for failing to come earlier, compassion rose in his heart. He saw how age had increased its tyranny upon her since their last meeting. Her cheeks and temples were more hollow, her skin more papery. He asked her what she had been doing with herself.

She put out a hand and touched him with a small pressure, as if uncertain whether to draw him nearer or push him away.

"We won't talk here. Your aunt would like to see you too."

Lourna Shokerandit turned and led him into the small wood-panelled room within which much of her life was spent. Luterin remembered it from childhood. Lacking windows, its walls were covered with paintings of sunlit glades in sombre caspiarn forests. Here and there, lost among representations of foliage, women's faces gazed into the room from oval frames. Aunt Yaringa, the plump and emotional Yaringa, was sitting in a corner, embroidering, in a chair upholstered somewhat along her own lines.

Yaringa jumped up and uttered loud soblike noises of welcome.

"Home at last, you poor poor thing! What you must have been through . . ."

Lourna Shokerandit lowered herself stiffly into a velvet-covered chair. She took her son's hand as he sat beside her. Yaringa perforce retreated to her padded corner.

"It's happiness to see you back, Luterin. We had such fears for you, particularly when we heard what happened to Asperamanka's army."

"My life was spared through a piece of good fortune. All our fellow countrymen were slain as they returned to Sibornal. It was an act of deep treachery."

She looked down at her thin lap, where silences had a habit of nestling. Finally she said, without glancing up, "It is a shock to see you as you are. You have become so . . . fat." She hesitated on the last word, in view of her sister's presence.

"I survived the Fat Death and am in my winter suit, Mother. I like it and feel perfectly well."

"It makes you look funny," said Yaringa, and was ignored.

He told the ladies something of his adventures, concluding by saying, "And I owe my survival in great part to a woman called Toress Lahl, widow of a Borldoranian I killed in battle. She nursed me devotedly through the Fat Death."

"From slaves, devotion is to be expected," said Lourna Shokerandit. "Have you been to see the Esikananzis yet? Insil will be eager to see you again, as you know."

"I have not yet spoken to her. No."

"I shall arrange a feast for tomorrow night, and Insil and her family shall come. We will all celebrate your return." She clapped her hands once, without sound.

"I shall sing for you, Luterin," said Yaringa. It was her speciality.

Lourna's expression changed. She sat more upright in her chair.

"And Evanporil tells me that you are countermanding the new Act to destroy all phagors."

"We could cull them gradually, Mother. But to lose all six hundred at once would be to disrupt the working of the estate. We are hardly likely to get six hundred human slaves to replace them—apart from the greater expense of human slaves."

"We must obey the State."

"I thought we would wait for Father's return."

"Very well. Otherwise, you will comply with the law? It is important for us Shokerandits to set an example."

"Of course."

"I should tell you that a foreign female slave was arrested in your rooms this morning. We have her in a cell, and she will go before the local Board when they meet next."

Shokerandit stood up. "Why was this done? Who dared intrude into my rooms?"

With composure, his mother answered, "The servant you had ordered to attend the slave woman reported that she went into a state of pauk. Pauk is proscribed by law. No less a personage than Priest-Supreme Chubsalid has gone to the stake for refusing to comply with the law. Exception can hardly be made for a foreign slave woman."

"In this case, an exception will be made," Shokerandit said, pale of face. "Excuse me." He bowed to his mother and aunt and left their rooms.

In a fury, he stamped through the passages to the Estates Office. He relieved his anger by bellowing at the staff.

As he summoned the estate guard captain, Shokerandit said to himself, Very well, I shall marry Toress Lahl. I must protect her from injustice. She'll be safe, married to a future Keeper of the Wheel . . . and perhaps this scare will persuade her not to visit the gossie of her husband so often.

Toress Lahl was released from the cell without trouble and restored to Shokerandit's rooms. They embraced.

"I bitterly regret this indignity imposed on you."

"I have become used to indignity."

"Then you shall become used to something better. When the right opportunity arises, I will take you to meet my mother. She will see the kind of person you are."

Toress Lahl laughed. "I am sure that I shall not greatly impress the Shokerandits of Kharnabhar."

The feast to mark Luterin's return was well attended. His mother had shaken off her lethargy to invite all local dignitaries as well as such Shokerandit relations as were in favour.

The Esikananzi family arrived in force. With Member Ebstok Esikananzi came his sickly-looking wife, two sons, his daughter Insil Esikananzi, and a train of subsidiary relations.

Since Luterin and Insil had last met, she had developed into an attractive woman, though a heaviness in her brow prevented true beauty—as well as suggesting that tendency to meet fate head-on which had long been a quality of the Esikananzis. She was elegantly dressed in a grey velvet gown reaching to the floor, adorned by the sort of wide lace collar she favoured. Luterin noted how the formal politeness with which she covered her disgust at his metamorphosis studiedly emphasised that disgust.

All the Esikananzis tinkled to a great extent; their hip-bells were very similar in tone. Ebstok's was the loudest. In a loud whisper, he spoke of his bottomless sorrow at the death of his son Umat at Isturiacha. Luterin's protest that Umat was killed in the great massacre outside Koriantura was swept aside as lies and Campannlatian propaganda.

Member Ebstok Esikananzi was a thickset man of dark and intricate countenance. The cold endured on his frequent hunts had brought a maze of red veins creeping like a species of plant life over his cheeks. He watched the mouths, not the eyes, of those who addressed him.

Member Ebstok Esikananzi was a man who believed in being unafraid to speak his mind, despite the fact that this organ, when spoken, had only one theme to sound: the importance of his opinion.

As they demolished the maggoty fists of venison on their plates, Esikananzi said, addressing both Luterin and the rest of the table, "You'll have heard the news about our friend Priest-Supreme Chubsalid. Some of his followers are kicking up a bit of trouble here. Wretched man preached treason against the State. Your father and I used to go hunting with Chubsalid in better days. Did you know that, Luterin? Well, we did on one occasion.

"The traitor was born in Bribahr, so you don't wonder. . . . He paid a visit to the monasteries of the Wheel. Now he takes it into his head to speak against the State, the friend and protector of the Church."

"They have burnt him for it, Father, if that's any consolation," said one of the Esikananzi sons, with a laugh.

"Of course. And his estates in Bribahr will be confiscated. I wonder who will get them? The Oligarchy will decide on what is best. The great thing is, as winter descends, to guard against anarchy. For Sibornal, the four main tasks are clear. To unify the continent, to strike rapidly against all subversive activity, whether in economic, religious, or academic life . . ."

As the voice droned on, Luterin Shokerandit stared down at his plate. He was without appetite. His eventful time away from Shivenink had so widened his outlook on life that he was oppressed by the sight

and sound of the Esikananzis, of whom he had once been in awe. The
pattern of the plate before him penetrated his consciousness; with a
wave of nostalgia, he realised that it was an Odim export, despatched
from the warehouse in Koriantura in better times. He thought with
affection of Eedap Mun Odim and his pleasant brother—and then, with
guilt, of Toress Lahl, at present locked in his suite for safety. Looking
up he caught Insil's cool gaze.

"The Oligarchy will have to pay for the death of the Priest-Supreme,"
he said, "no less than for the slaughter of Asperamanka's army. Why
should winter be an excuse for overturning all our human values? Excuse me."

He rose and left the room.

After the meal, his mother employed many reproaches in order to
induce him to return to the company. Sheepishly, he went and sat with
Insil and her family. They made stiff conversation until slaves brought
in a phagor who had been taught to juggle. Under guidance from her
master's whip, the gillot jiggled a little from one foot to another while
balancing a plate on her horns.

An ensemble of slaves appeared next, dancing while Yaringa Shokerandit did her party piece and sang love songs from the Autumn Palaces.

> *If my heart were free, if my heart were free,*
> *And wild as the dashing Venj is . . .*

"Are you being uncivil or merely soldierly?" Insil asked, under cover
of the music. "Do you anticipate our marrying in a kind of dumb
show?"

He gazed at her familiar face, smiled at her familiar teasing tone. He
admired the froth of lace and linen at shoulders and breasts, and observed how those breasts had developed since their last meeting.

"What are your expectations, Insil?"

"I expect we shall do what is expected of us, like creatures in a play.
Isn't that necessary in times like these—when, as you tactfully reminded
Pa, ordinary values are cast off like garments, in order to meet winter
naked."

"It's more a question of what we expect from ourselves. Barbarism
may come, certainly, but we can defy it."

"Word has it that in Campannlat, following the defeat you administered to their various savage nations, civil wars have broken out and
civilisation is already crumbling. Such disturbances must be avoided
here at all costs . . . Notice that I have taken to talking politics since
we parted! Isn't that barbarism?"

"No doubt you have had to listen to your father preaching about the
perils of anarchy many times. It's only your neckline I find barbaric."

When Insil laughed, her hair fell over her brow. "Luterin, I am not sorry to see you again, even in your present odd shape, disguised as a barrel. Let's talk somewhere privately while your relation sings her heart out about that horrible river."

They excused themselves and went together to a chill rear chamber, where biogas flames hissed a continual cautionary note.

"Now we can trade words, and let them be warmer than this room," she said. "Ugh, how I hate Kharnabhar. Why were you fool enough to come back here? Not for my sake, was it?" She gave him a look askance.

He walked up and down in front of her. "You still have your old ways, Sil. You were my first torturer. Now I've found others. I am tormented—tormented by the evil of the Oligarchy. Tormented by the thought that the Weyr-Winter might be survived by a compassionate society, if men thought that way, not by a cruel and oppressive one like ours. Real evil—the Oligarch ordered the destruction of his own army. Yet I can also see that Sibornal must become a fortress, submitting to harsh rules, if it is not to be destroyed as Campannlat will be by the oncoming cold. Believe me, I am not my old childish self."

Insil appeared to receive the speech without enthusiasm. She perched herself on a chair.

"Well, you certainly don't look yourself, Luterin. I was disgusted at the sight of you. Only when you condescend to smile, when you are not sulking over your plate, does your old self reappear. But the size of you . . . I hope my deformities remain inside me. Any measures, however harsh, against the plague, are justified if they spare us that." Her personal bell tinkled in emphasis, its sound calling up a fragment of the past for him.

"The metamorphosis is not a deformity, Insil; it's a biological fact. Natural."

"You know how I hate nature."

"You're so squeamish."

"Why are you so squeamish about the Oligarch's actions? They're all part of the same thing. Your morality is as boring as Pa's politics. Who cares if a few people and phagors are shot. Isn't life one big hunt anyway?"

He stared at her, at her figure, slender and tense, as she clutched her arms against the chill of the room. Some of the affection he had once felt broke through. "Beholder, you still argue and riddle as before. I admire it, but could I bear it over a lifetime?"

She laughed back. "Who knows what we shall be called upon to endure? A woman needs fatalism more than a man. A woman's role in life is to listen, and when I listen I never hear anything but the howl of the wind. I prefer the sound of my own voice."

He touched her for the first time as he asked, "Then what do you want from life, if you can't even bear the sight of me?"

She stood up, looking away from him. "I wish I were beautiful. I know I haven't got a face—just two profiles tacked together. Then I might escape fate, or at least find an interesting one."

"You're interesting enough."

Insil shook her head. "Sometimes I think I am dead." Her tone was unemphatic; she might have been describing a landscape. "I want nothing that I know of and many things I know nothing of. I hate my family, my house, this place. I'm cold, I'm hard, and I have no soul.

"My soul flew out of the window one day, maybe when you were spending your year pretending to be dead . . . I'm boring and I'm bored. I believe in nothing. No one gives me anything because I can give nothing, receive nothing."

Luterin was pained by her pain, but only that. As of old, he found himself at a loss with her. "You have given me much, Sil, ever since childhood."

"I am frigid, too, I suspect. I cannot bear even to be kissed. Your pity I find contemptible." She turned away to say, as if the admission cost her dear, "As for the thought of making love with you as you are now . . . well, it repels me . . . at least, it does not attract me at all."

Although he had no great depth of human understanding, Luterin saw how her coldness to others was part of her habit of maligning herself. The habit was more ingrained than formerly. Perhaps she spoke truth: Insil was always one for truth.

"I'm not requiring you to make love with me, dear Insil. There is someone else whom I love, and whom I intend to marry."

She remained half turned from him, her narrow left cheek against the lace of her collar. She seemed to shrink. The wan gaslight made the skin at the nape of her neck glisten. A low groan came from her. When she could not suppress it by putting hands to mouth, she began to beat her fists against her thighs.

"Insil!" He clutched her, alarmed.

When she turned back to him, the protective mask of laughter was back on her face. "So, a surprise! I find that there was after all something I wanted, which I never expected to want. . . . But I'm too much of a handful for you, isn't that true?"

"No, not that, not a negative."

"Oh, yes . . . I've heard. The slave woman in your quarters . . . You want to marry a slave rather than a free woman, because you've grown like all the men here, you want someone you can possess without contradiction."

"No, Insil, you're wrong. You're no free woman. You are the slave. I feel tenderly for you and always will, but you are imprisoned in yourself."

She laughed almost without scorn. "You now know what I am, do you? Always before you were so puzzled by me, so you said. Well, you are callous. You have to tell me this news without warning? Why did you not tell my father, as convention demands? You're a great respecter of convention."

"I had to speak to you first."

"Yes? And have you broken this exciting news to your mother? What of the liaison between the Shokerandits and the Esikananzis now? Have you forgotten that we shall probably be *forced* to marry when your father returns? You have your duty as I have mine, from which neither of us has so far flinched. But perhaps you have less courage than I. If that day comes when we are forced into the same bed, I will repay you for the injury you do me today."

"What have I done, for the Beholder's sake? Are you mad because I share with you your lack of enthusiasm for our marriage? Speak sense, Insil!"

But she gave him a cold look, her eyes dark under her disordered hair. Collecting up her heavy skirt with one hand, she set the other hand pale against her cheek and hastened from the chamber.

Next morning, after Toress Lahl had bathed and a slave woman had dressed her, Luterin took her before his mother and announced formally that he intended to marry her and not Insil Esikananzi. His mother wept and threatened—and in particular threatened the wrath of Luterin's father—and finally retreated to her inner room.

"We shall go for a ride," Luterin said coolly, strapping on his revolver and clipping a sling onto a short rifle. "I'll show you the Great Wheel."

"Am I to ride behind you?"

He regarded her judiciously. "You heard what I said to my mother."

"I heard what you said to your mother. Nevertheless, at present I am not a free woman, and this is not Chalce."

"When we return, I will have the secretary issue you a declaration of your freedom. There are such things. Just now, I wish to be outside." He moved impatiently to the door, where two stablemen stood holding the reins of two yelk.

"I'll teach you the points of a yelk one day," he said, as they moved into the grounds. "These are a domestic breed—bred by my father, and his father before him."

Once outside the grounds of the estate, they moved into the teeth of the wind. There was no more than a foot of snow underfoot. On either side of the track, striped markers stood, awaiting the time when the snow was deep.

To get to Kharnabhar, the peak, they had to pass the Esikananzi estates. The track then wound through a tall stand of caspiarns, the branches of which were fuzzy with frost. As they advanced, bells of differing voice told of Kharnabhar, as it emerged gradually from the cloud.

Everything here was bells, indoors and out. What had once had a function—to guard against the possibility of being lost in snow or fog— was now a fashion.

Toress Lahl reined her yelk and stared ahead, holding a cloaked arm up to her face to protect her mouth. Ahead lay the village of Kharnabhar, the lodgings for pilgrims and the stalls on one side of the main track, the housing for those who worked with the Great Wheel on the other side. Most of the buildings had bells on their roofs, housed in cupolas, each with its distinctive tongue; they could be heard when the weather was too bad for them to be seen.

The track itself led uphill to the entrance to the Great Wheel. That entrance, almost legendary, had been adorned by the Architects with gigantic bird-faced oarsmen. It led into the depths of Mount Kharnabhar. The mount dominated the village.

Up the face of the mountain the buildings climbed, many of them chapels or mausoleums erected by pilgrims on this holiest of sites. Some of them stood boldly above the snow, perched on rock outcrops. Some were in ruins.

Shokerandit gestured largely ahead. "Of all this my father is in charge."

He turned back to her. "Do you want to look more closely at the Wheel? They don't take you in there by force. These days, you have to volunteer to get a place in the Wheel."

As they moved forward, Toress Lahl said, "I somehow imagined that we should see a part of the Wheel from outside."

"It's all inside the mountain. That's the main idea. Darkness. Darkness bringing wisdom."

"I thought it was light brought wisdom."

Jostling locals stared at their metamorphosed shapes. Some locals bore prominent goitres, a common malady in such mountainous inland regions. They superstitiously made the symbol of the circle as they moved towards the entrance of the Wheel with Shokerandit and Toress Lahl.

Nearer, they could see a little more: the great ramplike walls leading in from either side, as if to pour humanity down the gullet of the mountain. Above the entrance, protected from landslides by an apron, was a starkly carved scene embodying the symbolism of the Wheel. Oarsmen clad in ample garments rowed the Wheel across the sky, where could be recognised some of the zodiacal signs: the Boulder, the Old Pursuer, the Golden Ship. The stars sprang from the breast of an amazing maternal figure who stood to one side of the archway, beckoning the faithful to her.

Pilgrims, dwarfed by the statuary, knelt at the gateway, calling aloud the name of the Azoiaxic One.

She sighed. "It's splendid, certainly."

"To you, it may be no more than splendid. To those of us who have grown up in the religion, it is our life, the mainspring that gives us confidence to face the vicissitudes of this life."

Jumping lightly from his yelk's back, he took hold of her saddle and said, looking up at her, "One day, if my father finds me fit enough, I may in my turn become Keeper of the Wheel. My brother was to have been heir to the role, but he died. I hope my chance will come."

She looked down at him and smiled in a friendly way, without understanding. "The wind's dropped."

"It's generally calm here. Mount Kharnabhar is high, the fourth highest mountain in the world, so they say. But behind it—you can't see it for cloud—is the even grander Mount Shivenink, which shelters Kharnabhar from the winds of the pole. Shivenink is over seven miles high, and the third highest peak. You'll catch a glimpse of it some other time."

He fell silent, sensing that he had been too enthusiastic. He wished to be happy, to be confident, as he had been. But the encounter with Insil the previous evening had upset him. Abruptly he jumped back on his yelk and led away from the entrance to the Wheel.

Without speaking, he wended a way through the village street, where pilgrims were crowding among the clothing shops and bell stalls. Some munched waffles stamped with the sign of the Great Wheel.

Beyond the village was a steep ravine, with a path winding down into a distant valley. The trees grew close, with massive boulders between them. Drifts of snow lay here and there, making the route treacherous. The yelk picked their way with care, the bells on their harness jingling. Birds called in the branches high above them and they heard the sound of water falling onto rock. Shokerandit sang to himself. Batalix weakly lit their way. In the chasmlike valley below them, shadow ruled.

He halted where the track divided. One fork ran upwards along the slopes, one down. When she caught up with him, he said, "They say this valley will fill with snow when the Weyr-Winter really comes—say in my grandchildren's time, if I have any. We should take the upper track. It's the easiest way home."

"Where does the lower track lead?"

"There's an old church down there, founded by a king from your part of the world, so you might be interested. And next to it is a shrine my father built in memory to my brother."

"I'd like to see."

The way became steeper. Fallen trees obstructed their way. Shokerandit pursed his lips to see how the estate was being neglected. They passed under a waterfall, and picked their way through a bed of snow.

Cloud clung to the hillside. Every leaf about them shone. The light was bad.

They circled past the cupola of the chapel. Its bell hung silent. When they reached level ground, they saw that a great drift of snow had sealed the door of the building.

As a native of Borldoran, Toress Lahl recognised immediately that the church was built in what was known as the Embruddockan style. Most of it lay below ground level. The steps which wound down its curving outer dome were intended to give worshippers a chance to clear their minds of worldly things before entering.

She scooped away snow so that she could peer through a narrow rectangular window set in the door. Darkness had been created inside, such light as there was penetrating from above. An old god's portrait gazed down from behind a circular altar. She felt her breath come faster.

The name of the deity eluded her memory, but she knew well the name of the king whose bust and titles stood, sheltered from the elements, under the porch above the outer door. He was JandolAnganol, King of Borlien and Oldorando, the countries which later became Borldoran.

Her voice shook when she spoke. "Is this why I am brought here? This king is a distant ancestor of mine. His name is proverbial where I come from, though he died almost five centuries ago."

Luterin's only response was to say, "I know the building is old. My brother lies nearby. Come and see."

In a moment, she collected herself and followed him, saying, "JandolAnganol . . ."

He stood contemplating a cairn. Stone was piled on stone, and capped with a circular block of granite. His brother's name—FAVIN— was engraved on the granite, together with the sacred symbol of circle within circle.

To show reverence, Toress Lahl dismounted and stood with Luterin. The cairn was a brutal object in comparison with the delicately worked chapel.

Finally, Luterin turned away and pointed to the rocks above them. "You see where the waterfall begins?"

High overhead, a spur of rock protruded. Water spouted over its lip, falling clear for seventy feet before striking stone. They could hear the sound of its descent into the valley.

"He rode out here one day on a hoxney, when the weather was better. Jumped—man and mount. The Azoiaxic knows what made him do it. My father was at home. He it was who found my brother, dead on this spot. He erected this cairn to his memory. Since then, we have not been allowed to speak his name. I believe that Father was as heartbroken as I."

"And your mother?" she asked, after a pause.

"Oh, she was upset too, of course." He looked up again at the waterfall, biting his lip.

"You think greatly of your father, don't you?"

"Everyone does." He cleared his throat and added, "His influence on me is immense. Perhaps if he were away less, he would not be so close to me. Everyone knows him hereabouts for a holy man—much like your ancestor, the king."

Toress Lahl laughed. "JandolAnganol is no holy man. He is known as one of the blackest villains in history, who destroyed the old religion and burnt the leader of it, with all his followers."

"Well, we know him here as a holy man. His name is revered locally."

"Why did he come here?"

He shook his head impatiently. "Because this is Kharnabhar. Everyone wants to be here. Perhaps he was doing penance for his sins . . ."

To that she would say nothing.

He stood staring down into the valley, into the confused hillsides.

"There is no finer love than that between son and father, don't you agree? Now I have grown up, I know other kinds of love—all with their lure. None has the purity—the clarity—of the love I bear for my father. All others are full of questions, of conflicts. The love for a father is unquestioning. I wish I were one of his hounds, that I could show him unquestioning obedience. He's away in the caspiarn forests for months at a time. If I were a hound, I could be forever at his heel, following wherever he led."

"Eating the scraps he threw you."

"Whatever he wished."

"It's not healthy to feel like that."

He turned towards her, looking haughty. "I am not a lad anymore. I can please myself or I can subdue my will. So it must be with everyone. Compassion and firmness are needed. We must fight unjust laws. As long as anarchy does not take over, Weyr-Winter will be endurable. When spring comes, Sibornal will emerge stronger than ever. We are committed to four tasks. To unify our continent. To rectify work, and consolidate it organisationally with regard to depleted resources . . . Well, all that's no concern of yours. . . ."

She stood apart from him. The clouds of their breath formed and dispersed without meeting. "What role do I play in your plans?"

He was uneasy with the question, but liked its bluntness. Being in Toress Lahl's company was like occupying a different world from Insil's. With a sudden impulse, he turned and grasped her, staring into her eyes before kissing her briefly. He stepped back, drawing deep breath, drinking in her expression. Then he moved forward again and this time kissed her with greater concentration.

Even when she made some response, he could not banish the thought of Insil Esikananzi. For her part, Toress Lahl too struggled against her late husband's phantom lips.

They broke apart.

"Be patient," he said, as if to himself. She gave no answer.

Luterin climbed back on his mount, and led the way up the track which wound through the dark trees. The bells on the animals' harness jingled. The little snowbound chapel sank behind them, soon becoming lost in the obscurity.

When he returned, a sealed note from Insil awaited him. He opened it with reluctance, but it contained only an oblique reference to their quarrel of the previous evening. It read:

Luterin:

You will think me hard, but there are those who are harder. They offer you greater danger than ever I could.

Do you recall a conversation we once had about the possible cause of your brother's death? It took place, unless I dreamed it, after you had recovered from that strange horizontal interlude which followed the death. Your innocence is heroic. Let me say more soon.

I beg you use guile now. Hold "our" new secret for a while, for your own sake.

Insil

"Too late," he said impatiently, screwing the note up into a ball.

XIV

THE GREATEST CRIME

But how could anyone be sure that those tutelary biospheric spirits, the Original Beholder and Gaia, had a real existence?

There was no objective proof, just as empathy cannot be measured. Microbacterial life has no knowledge of mankind: their umwelts are too disparate. Only intuition can permit mankind to see and hear the footsteps of those geochemical spirits who have managed the life of a functioning whole world as a single organism.

It is intuition, again, which tells humanity that to live according to the spirit it must not possess, must refrain from dominating. It was precisely those men who met so secretively on Icen Hill, shut away from human contact, secure from contact with the outside world, who most feverishly tried to possess the world.

And if they succeeded?

The biospheric spirits are forgiving and adaptable. Intuition tells us that there are always alternatives. Homeostasis is not fossilisation but the balance of vitality.

The early tribal hunters who burned the forests to secure their prey gave birth to the ecosystems of the great savannahs. Mutability informs Gaia's cybernetic controls.

The Original Beholder's grey cloak was sweeping across Helliconia. Human beings defied it or accepted it, according to their individual natures.

Beyond the pale of human possession, the creatures of the wild made their own dispositions. The brassimip trees greedily stored food resources far below ground, in order that they might continue to grow. The little land crustaceans, the rickybacks, congregated in their thousands on the underside of stones of alabaster, working lodgements for themselves in the stone with secretions of acid; they would derive such light as they needed to sustain them through the stone itself. The horned sheep of the mountains, the wild asokin, the badgered timoroon, the flambreg on their scoured plains, indulged in fierce courtship battles. There was time for one more mating and perhaps one more: the number of living offspring born would be decided by temperature, by the food supply, by courage, by skill.

All those beings which could not be described as part of the human race, but remained suspended by a quirk of evolution just outside the hearths of humanity—wistfully looking towards the camp fires—those beings too made their dispositions.

The Driat tribes, given the gift of language and well able to curse in it, cursed and moved down from the hills to rocky shores of their continent, where they would find food in abundance. The migratory Madis were driven from their dying ucts to seek shelter in the West and to haunt the ruined cities mankind had deserted. The Nondads burrowed down between the roots of great trees, living their elusive lives little differently from in the scorching days of summer.

As for the ancipital race, each generation saw global conditions reverting to what they had been before the invasion of Freyr into their skies. To their eotemporal minds, the stereotype of the future was coming more nearly to resemble the stereotype of the past. On the broad plains of Campannlat, phagors became increasingly dominant, relying for meat on the herds of yelk and biyelk, which appeared in growing numbers, and becoming bolder in their attacks on the Sons of Freyr. Only in Sibornal, where their presence had never been strong, were they subject to organised counterattacks from humanity.

All these creatures could be seen as vying with one another. In a sense it was true. But in a wider sense, all were a unity. The steady disappearance of green things destroyed their numbers, but they remained intact. For all of them depended on the anaerobic muds on the Helliconian seabeds, working to bury carbon and maintain the oxygen of the atmosphere, so that the great processes of respiration and photosynthesis were maintained over land and ocean.

All these creatures, again, could be seen as the vital life of the planet. In a sense it was true. But fully half of the mass of Helliconian life lived in the three-dimensional pasturages of the seas. That mass was com-

posed for the most part of single-celled microflora. They were the true
monitors of life, and for them little changed, whether Freyr was close
or distant.

The Original Beholder held all living forces in balance. How was life
possible on the planet? Because there was life on the planet. What
would happen without life? There could be no life. The Original Beholder was a spirit who dwelt over the waters: not a separate spirit
endowed with mind, but a vast cooperative entity, creating well-being
from the centre of a furious chemical storm. And the Original Beholder
was forced to be even more ingenious than her sister goddess, Gaia, on
nearby Earth.

Somewhat apart from all other living things, from algae and rutting
sheep and rickybacks, were the humans of Helliconia. These creatures,
although fully as dependent on the homeostatic biosphere as other units
of life, had nevertheless elevated themselves to a special category. They
had developed language. Within the wordless universe, they had assembled their own umwelt of words.

They had songs and poems, dramas and histories, debate, lament and
proclamation, with which to give tongue to the planet. With words
came the power to invent. As soon as words came, there was story. Story
was to words as Gaia was to Earth and the Original Beholder to Helliconia. Neither planet had a story until mankind came chattering onto
the scene and invented it—to fit what each generation saw as the facts.

There were visionaries on Helliconia who, at this time of crisis in
human affairs, divined the existence of the Original Beholder. But
visionaries had always been there, often inarticulate because they worked
close to the thresholds of inarticulacy. They perceived something azoiaxic in the universe, something beyond life round which all life revolves,
which was itself at once unliving and the Life.

The vision did not fit easily into words. But because there were words,
their listeners could not tell whether the vision was true or false. Words
have no atomic weight. The universe of words has no ultimate criteria
corresponding to life and death in the tongueless universe. This is why
it can invent imaginary worlds which have neither life nor death.

One such imaginary world was the perfectly functioning Sibornalese
state as visualised by the Oligarchy. Another was the perfectly functioning universe of God the Azoiaxic as visualised by the elders of the
Church of the Formidable Peace. With the defiance of the Oligarch's
edicts and the subsequent burning of Priest-Supreme Chubsalid and his
fellow ecclesiastics, the two imaginary perfections ceased to coincide.
After long periods of near identity, Church and State discovered to their
mutual horror that they were in opposition.

Many of the leading clergy, like Asperamanka, were too much in the pocket of the State to protest. It was the rank and file of the Church, the lowly friars, the unlovely monks, those closest to the people, who raised the alarm.

One Member of the Oligarchy cried out against "those preachers in their cowls running to and fro, spreading false rumours among the common folk"—thus unconsciously echoing Erasmus on Earth many centuries earlier. But the Oligarchy was no defender of humanism. It could respond to the oppressed only with more oppression.

Enantiodromia once more. Just when the ranks were closing, a gulf opened; when unity was within reach, the divisions became widest.

The Oligarchy turned everything to its advantage. It could use the new unrest in its countries as an excuse for yet firmer measures. The army returning from its success in Bribahr was redeployed in the towns and villages of Uskutoshk. A sullen and cowed population stood by while its village priests were shot.

The dissention reached even Kharnabhar.

Ebstok Esikananzi called upon Luterin to discuss the trouble, and watched his mouth rather than his eyes when Luterin counselled caution. Other worthy officials representing one side or other also called. Luterin found himself closeted with Secretary Evanporil and staff for many hours. With his own fate hanging over him, he was unable to decide the fate of his province.

The Great Wheel was involved in the dispute. While it was itself run by the Church, its territory was under the control of a lay governor appointed by the Keeper. The gulf between lay and ecclesiastic widened. Chubsalid was not forgotten.

After two days of argumentation, Luterin did what he had done before when feeling oppressed. He escaped.

Taking with him a good hound and a huntsman, he rode off into the wilds, the almost limitless wilderness of mountain round Kharnabhar. A blizzard was blowing, but he disregarded it. Lost here and there among the valleys, or punctuating breaks in the caspiarn forests, were hunting lodges and shrines where a man could stable his mount, shelter, and sleep. Like his father, he simply disappeared from human ken.

Often he hoped that he might encounter his father. He saw the meeting in his mind's eye. Saw his father the centre of a group of heavily garbed hunters, the snow swirling about them. Masked hawks sat on leather shoulders. A biyelk dragged a sled carrying dead game. The breath of the hounds rose up. His father descended stiffly from his saddle and came towards him, arms outstretched.

Always his father had learnt of his heroism at Isturiacha, and congratulated him on his escape from death at Koriantura. They embraced . . .

He and his companion met no one, heard nothing but the clash of glaciers. They slept in remote lodges, where the aurora flickered high above the forests.

However tired he was, however many animals they had slain, the nights brought bad dreams to Luterin. The obsession overwhelmed him that he was climbing, not amid forests, but through rooms stuffed with meaningless furniture and ancient possessions. In those rooms, a sense of horror gathered. He could neither find nor evade the thing that hunted him.

Often he awoke and imagined that he was again laid flat by paralysis. Knowledge of his real surroundings returned only slowly. Then he would try to calm his mind with thoughts of Toress Lahl; but ever and again Insil stood beside her.

At least his mother had taken to her bed after the feast she had given in his honour, so news that he would not marry Insil had not spread.

He saw in how many ways Insil was fitted to be his wife in the years to come; in her was the true unyielding Kharnabhar spirit.

Toress Lahl, by contrast, was an exile, a foreigner. Had he said he would marry her merely to prove his independence?

He hated the fact that he was still undecided. Yet he could not decide finally until his own uncertain situation was made clear. That entailed a confrontation with his father.

Night after night, lying with beating heart inside his sleeping bag, he came to see that confrontation there must be. He could marry Insil only if his father did not force him to it. His father must accept his viewpoint.

He must be hero or outcast. There were no other alternatives. He had to face rejection. Sex, when all was said, was a question of power.

Sometimes, as the aurora cast its glow inside the dark lodges, he saw his brother Favin's face. Had he also challenged his father in some way—and lost?

Luterin and the huntsman rose early every dawn, when night birds were still in flight. They shared their food together as equals, but never a private thought did they let pass from one to the other.

However badly the nights passed, the days were all happiness. Every hour brought a changing light and changing conditions. The habits of the animals they stalked differed from hour to hour. With the decline of the small year, the days grew shorter, and Freyr remained always close to the horizon. But sometimes they would climb a ridge and see through foliage the old ruler himself, still blazing, throwing his light into another valley brimming in its depths with shadow like a sea, as a king might carelessly fill a glass with wine.

The stoic silence of nature was all about them, increasing their sense of infinity. Infinity came through all their senses. The rocks down which they scrambled to drink at some snow-bearded mountain stream seemed new, untouched by time. Through the silence ran a great music, translated in Luterin's blood as freedom.

On their sixth day in the wilderness, they spied a party of six horned phagors crossing a glacier on kaidaw-back. The cowbirds sailing above their shoulders gave them away. They stalked the phagors for a day and a half, until they could get ahead of them and ambush them in a ravine.

They killed all six ancipitals. The cowbirds fled, screeching. The kaidaw were good specimens. Luterin and the huntsman managed to round up five of them and decided to drive them back to the family estate. It was possible that the Shokerandit stables could breed a domesticated strain of kaidaw.

The expedition had ended in modest triumph.

The tongues of the sullen bells of the mansion could be heard to toll long before the building loomed out of the blue mists.

So Luterin returned home, to find uproar, and his father's yelk being combed down in the stables, dead game lying everywhere, and his father's bodyguard throwing back fresh-brewed yadahl in the gunroom.

Unlike Luterin's imagined meeting with Lobanster Shokerandit, the real reunion between father and son contained no embraces.

Luterin hurried into the reception hall, throwing off only his outer garments, retaining his boots, his revolver, his bell. His hair was long and unkempt. It fluttered about his ears as he ran towards his father.

Skewbald hounds skulked about the chamber and pissed against the wall hangings. A group of armed men stood by the door, backs to the main party, looking round suspiciously as if plotting.

About Lobanster Shokerandit were gathered his wife, Lourna, and her sister, and friends such as the Esikananzis—Ebstok, his wife, Insil, and her two brothers. They were talking together. Lobanster's back was turned to Luterin, and his mother saw him first. She called his name.

The talk ceased. They all turned to look at him.

Something in their faces—an unpleasant complicity—told him they had been discussing him. He faltered in mid-stride. They continued to regard him and yet, curiously, their true attention still remained with the black-clad man in their midst.

Lobanster Shokerandit could command the attention of any group. This was less by his stature, which was no more than average, than by a sort of stillness which emanated from him. It was a quality all noticed, yet no one had word for it. Those who hated him, his slaves and servants, said that he froze you with a glance; his friends and allies said that he had an amazing power of command or that he was a man apart. His hounds said nothing, but slunk about his legs with their tails tucked down.

His hands were neat and precise, his nails pointed. Lobanster Shokerandit's hands were noticeable. They were active while the rest of him remained rigid. They frequently travelled up to visit his throat, which was always swathed in black silk, moving with a startled action not unlike that of crabs or hawks searching for concealed prey. Lobanster had a goitre, which his cravat concealed and his hands betrayed. The goitre lent a pillarlike solidity to the neck, sufficient to support a large head.

The white hair of this remarkable head was brushed straight back as if raked, receding from a broad forehead. There were no eyebrows, but the pallid eyes were surrounded by thick dark lashes—so thick that some people suspected Madi blood somewhere. The eyes were further bolstered by grey pillows or bags below them; these pillows, having a certain goitrous quality, acted as embankments behind which the eyes watched the world. The lips, though ample, were almost as pale as the eyes, and the flesh of the face almost as pale as the lips. A sebacious sheen covered forehead and cheeks—sometimes the busy hands went up to wipe at the film—so that the face gleamed as if it had recently been recovered from the sea.

"Come near, Luterin," said the face now. The voice was deep and somewhat slow, as if the chin was reluctant to disturb the mound of goitre lying below it.

"I am glad you are back, Father," said Luterin, advancing. "Had you good hunting?"

"Well enough. You are so metamorphosed that I scarcely recognised you."

"Those fortunate enough to survive the plague take on compact shape for the Weyr-Winter, Father. I assure you I feel excellently fit."

He took his father's neat hand.

Ebstok Esikananzi said, "We may assume that phagors feel themselves to be fit, yet they are proven carriers of the plague."

"I have recovered from the plague. I cannot carry it."

"We certainly hope you can't, dear," said his mother.

As he turned to her, his father said sternly, "Luterin, I wish you to retire to the hall and await me. I shall be there presently. We have some legal matters to discuss."

"Is there something the matter?"

Luterin took the full force of his father's stare. He bowed his head and retired.

Once in the hall, he paced about, heedless of the tongue of his bell. What had made his father so cold he could not guess. True, that august figure had always been distant even when present, but that had been merely one of his qualities, as much taken for granted as the hidden goitre.

He summoned a slave and sent him to fetch Toress Lahl from her quarters.

She came questioningly. As she approached, he thought how appealing her metamorphosed shape was. And the frost prints on her face had healed.

"Why have you been so long away? Where have you been?"

There was a hint of reproach, although she smiled and took his hand.

As he kissed her, he said, "I'm entitled to vanish on the hunt. It's in the family blood. Now listen, I am anxious for you. My father's back and evidently displeased. This may be something that concerns you, since my mother and Insil have been talking to him."

"What a pity you were not here to welcome him, Luterin."

"That can't be helped," he said dismissively. "Listen, I want to give you something."

He led into an alcove off the hall, where a wooden cupboard stood. With a key taken from his pocket, he unlocked the cupboard. Within hung dozens of heavy iron keys, each labelled. He ran a finger along the rows, frowning.

"Your father has a mania for locking things," she said, half laughing.

"Don't be silly. He is the Keeper. This place has to be fortress as well as home."

He found what he wanted and picked out a rusted key almost a hand's span long.

"Nobody will miss this," he said, locking up the cupboard. "Take it. Hide it. It is the key to that chapel built by your countryman, the king-saint. You remember, in the woods? There may be a little trouble—I can't tell what. Perhaps about pauk. I don't want you harmed. If anything happens to me, you will be in danger of arrest at the least. Go and hide in the chapel. Take a slave with you—they're all longing to escape. Choose a woman who knows Kharnabhar, preferably a peasant."

She slipped the key into the pocket of her new clothes.

"What can happen to you?" She clutched his hand.

"Nothing, probably, but—I just feel an apprehension. . . ."

He heard a door opening. Hounds came scurrying, nails clicking on the tiles. He pushed Toress Lahl into the shadows behind the cupboard, and stepped forth into the hall. His father was emerging. Behind him came half a dozen of the conspiratorial men, bells clanking.

"We'll speak together," said Lobanster, lifting one finger. He led into a small wooden room on the ground floor. Luterin followed, and the conspiratorial men moved in behind them. The last one in locked the door on the inside. The biogas hissed when turned up.

This room had a wooden bench and table and little else in the way of furniture. People had been interrogated here. There was also a wooden door fortified with iron straps, which was kept locked. It was a private way down into the vaults, where the well was whose waters never froze. Legend had it that precious brood animals had been preserved down there in the coldest centuries.

"Whatever we discuss should be said privately, Father," Luterin said.

"I don't even know who these other gentlemen are, though they make free in our house. They are not your huntsmen."

"They are returned from Bribahr," said Lobanster, speaking the words as if they gave him a cold pleasure. "Eminent men need bodyguards in these times. You are too young to understand how plague can cause the dissolution of the state. It breaks up first small communities and then large. The fear of it disintegrates nations."

The conspiratorial men all looked very serious. In the limited space, it was impossible to stand away from them. Only Lobanster was separate, poised without movement behind the table, on the surface of which he played his fingers.

"Father, it is an insult that we should have to converse before strangers. I resent it. But I say to you—and to them, if they are capable of hearing—that although there may be truth in what you say, there is a greater truth you neglect. There are other ways of disintegrating nations than by plague. The harsh measures being brought against pauk—the common people, the Church—the cruelty behind those measures—will eventually bring greater destruction than the Fat Death—"

"Cease, boy!" His father's hands went to the region of his throat. "Cruelty is also part of nature. Where is mercy, except with men? Men invented mercy, but cruelty was here before them, in nature. Nature is a press. Year by year, it squeezes us tighter. We cannot fight it but by bringing to bear cruelty of our own. The plague is nature's latest cruelty, and must be fought with its own weapons."

Luterin could not speak. He could not find, under that chill, pale gaze, words to explain that while there might be a casual cruelty in circumstances, to formulate cruelty into a moral principle was a perversion of nature. To hear such pronouncements from his father turned him sick. He could only say, "You have swallowed utterly the words of the Oligarch."

One of the conspiratorial men spoke in a loud, rough voice. "That is everyone's duty."

The sound of this stranger's voice, the claustrophobia of the room, the tension, his father's coldness, all mounted to Luterin's brain. As if from afar, he heard himself shouting, "I hate the Oligarch! The Oligarch is a monster. He murdered Asperamanka's army. I'm here as a fugitive instead of a hero. Now he will murder the Church. Father, fight this evil before you are yourself devoured by it."

This he said and more, in a kind of seizure. He was scarcely aware of their bringing him from the room and helping him outside. He felt the bite of the chill wind. There was snow in his face. He was pushed through a courtyard where the biogas inspection pit was, and into a harness room.

The stablemen were sent away, the conspiratorial men were sent away. Luterin was alone with his father. Still he could not bear to look

at him, but sat clutching his head, groaning. After a while he listened
to what his father was saying.

". . . only son left to me. You I must groom to take over the role of
Keeper. For you there are particular challenges, and you must meet
them. You must be strong—"

"I am strong! I defy the system."

"If the order is to wipe out pauk, then we must wipe it out. If to
destroy all phagors, then we must destroy all phagors. Not to do so is
weakness. We cannot live without a system—all else is anarchy.

"I hear from your mother that you have a female slave who has influence over you. Luterin, you are a Shokerandit and you must be strong.
That slave must be destroyed, and you will marry Insil Esikananzi, as
we have planned since your childhood. There is no question but that
you must obey. You obey not for my sake, but for the sake of freedom
and Sibornal."

Luterin gave a laugh. "What freedom would there be in such circumstances? Insil hates me, I believe, but for you that's neither here
nor there. There's no freedom under the laws now being imposed."

Lobanster moved as if for the first time. It was a simple gesture, a
mere removal of one hand from the throat, to extend it in appeal towards Luterin.

"The laws are harsh. That's understood. But there is no freedom, nor
any life, without them. Without laws firmly applied, we shall die. Just
as Campannlat dies without law, though the climate favours it above
Sibornal. Campannlat already disintegrates under the coming of the
Great Winter. Sibornal can survive.

"Let me remind you, my son, that there are one thousand eight
hundred and twenty-five small years in a Great Year. This Great Year
has but five hundred and sixteen more years to run before its death,
before the time of greatest cold, the winter solstice, when Freyr is
farthest from us.

"We have to live like iron men until that time. Then the plague will
be gone, and conditions will improve once more. We have known these
facts since birth, for we hold Kharnabhar. The life of the Great Wheel
is dedicated to getting us through that black time, to bringing us again
to the light and warmth—"

Now Luterin confronted his father and spoke composedly.

"Agreed, the Wheel does as you say, Father. Why, then, do you
approve—as I gather you must—these wicked deeds whereby Chubsalid,
Priest-Supreme of our Church, is burnt and the Church in general
attacked?"

"Because the Wheel is an anachronism." Lobanster made a throaty
noise resembling a laugh, so that his goitre trembled under its black
covering. "It is an anachronism, without meaning. It cannot save Helliconia. It cannot save Sibornal. It is a sentimental concept. It functioned

properly only when it imprisoned murders and debtors. It conflicts with
the scientific laws of the Oligarchy. Those laws, and those alone, can
bring us through the Weyr-Winter which will be upon our children.
We cannot have two sets of laws in conflict. Therefore the Church must
be demolished. It was as a first step towards that demolition that the
Act against pauk was passed."

Again Luterin found no words.

"Is that what you brought me here to tell me?" he asked at last.

"I was not going to have others hear our discussion. I'm chiefly concerned with your contempt for the laws concerning pauk and the ex-
termination of phagors, as reported by Evanporil. If you weren't my son,
I would have killed you. Do you understand?"

Luterin shook his head once. He cast his gaze to the floor of the
tack room. As in childhood, he was unable to face his father's eyes.

"Do you understand?"

Still Luterin could not speak. He was utterly dismayed by his father's
imperviousness to his feelings.

Lobanster wiped his shining brow and crossed to the table, on which
lay a saddle bag among other pieces of harness. He flicked open the
buckle on the saddle bag so that a wad of posters came spilling out. He
handed one to his son.

"Since you are so fond of Acts, have a look at the latest one."

Sighing, Luterin took it. He barely glanced at it before letting it drop.
The sheet sailed into a corner of the room. It stated in black letters that,
as a further measure to prevent plague, persons found in a metamorphosed state would be put to death. By Order of the Oligarch. Luterin
said nothing.

His father spoke. "You see that if you do not obey my wishes I cannot protect you. Can I?"

At last Luterin stared at his father in misery. "I have served you,
Father. I have done as you wished all my life. I went into the army
without protest—and acquitted myself well. I have been—and desired
nothing better than to be—your *possession*. No doubt something of the
same was in Favin's mind when he leaped to his death. But now I have
to oppose you. Not for my sake. Not even for religion's sake, or for the
State. After all, what are they but abstractions? I must oppose you for
your own sake. Either the season or the Oligarch himself has driven you
mad."

A terrible fire shone on his father's face, while the eyes remained as
stoney as ever.

He snatched a long black shoeing knife from the table and held it out
to his son. "Take this, you fool, and come outside with me. You must be
made to see who is mad."

The snow was coming down fast, whirling round a grey angle of the mansion as if bent on filling up the courtyard to the very top of its walls as soon as possible. The conspiratorial men stood in a group, hands tucked under their belts, waiting under a porch, heels knocking together for warmth. To one side stood yelk, still saddled, with an anxious stableman still standing among them. Near at hand was a pile of phagor corpses; they had been dead for some while: the snow settled on them without steaming.

To one side, close to an outer gate, a row of rusty iron hooks stuck out from the wall above head level. The naked bodies of four men and a woman dangled by ropes from the hooks.

Lobanster pushed his son in the back, urging him forward. The touch was like fire.

"Cut these dead things down and look at them. Have a good look at their monstrousness and then ask if the Oligarch is not just. Go on."

Luterin drew near. The killing appeared recent. Moisture stood on the distorted faces of the dead. All five corpses were of people who had survived the Fat Death and metamorphosed.

"Laws have to be obeyed, Luterin, obeyed. Laws are what make society, and without society men are only animals. We caught these people on the way to Kharnabhar today, and we hanged them here because of the law. They died so that society can survive. Do you now think the Oligarch mad?"

As Luterin hesitated, his father said harshly, "Go on, cut them down, look at the agony in their faces, and then ask yourself if you prefer that state to life. When you reach an answer, you can get down on your knees to me."

The lad looked in appeal at his father. "I loved you as a dog its master. Why do you make me do this?".

"Cut them down!" One hand flew convulsively to the throat.

Choking, Luterin came level with the first corpse. He raised the knife and looked up into its distorted face.

It was someone he knew.

For a moment, he hesitated. But there was no mistaking that face, even without its moustache. Luterin recalled vividly seeing it in the Noonat Tunnel, livid with exertion. Swinging the knife, he cut down the remains of Captain Harbin Fashnalgid. At the same time, his mind opened. Just for a second, he was the boy about to prefer a year's paralysis to the truth.

He turned to his father.

"Good. That's one. Now the next. To rule you must obey. Your brother was weak. You can be strong. I heard of your victory at Isturiacha when I was in Askitosh. You can be Keeper, Luterin, and your children. You can be more than Keeper."

Flecks of spittle flew from his mouth, to be carried along in a vortex of snow. The expression on his son's face made him pause. In an instant, his demeanour altered. His bell rattled at his hip almost for the first time as he turned to look for his conspiratorial men.

The words burst from Luterin. "Father, you are the Oligarch! You! That's what Favin discovered, wasn't it?"

"No!" Lobanster suddenly changed. All command was gone. As he raised his crablike hands, every line of his body expressed fear. He clutched his son's forearm as Luterin drove the knife up under his rib cage, straight into his heart. Blood burst from the torn clothing and covered both their hands.

The courtyard became a scene of confusion. First to move was the saddler, who cried in terror and rushed out of the gate. He knew what befell menials who witnessed murder. The conspiratorial men were less quick to respond. Their leader was falling to his knees in the snow and then collapsing slowly, one reddened hand tugging weakly at his goitre, over the body of Fashnalgid. They stared at the sight as if paralysed.

Luterin did not wait. Horrified though he was, he ran over to the yelk and flung himself on one of them. As he galloped from the yard, a shot came, and he heard the men behind him rushing to follow.

Slitting his eyes against the snow, he spurred on the yelk. Across the rear square. Men shouted. His father's recently returned cavalcade was still being unloaded. A woman ran, shrieking, slipped, fell. The yelk leaped over her. At the gate there was a move to stop him. It was ill-coordinated. He struck out with his revolver, trying to smash the face of a guard who made to grab his rein. Then he was in the grounds.

As he rode, heading for a belt of trees and the side road, he was saying something over and over again. His mind had lost its rationality. Only a while later could he grasp and understand what he said.

What he constantly repeated to himself was, "Patricide is the greatest crime."

The words formed a rhythm to his escape.

Nor did he make any conscious decision as to where he was going. There was but one place in Kharnabhar where he might be safe from pursuit. The trees flashed by on either side, smeared across his slitting vision. He rode with his head low on the yelk's neck, breathing its misty breath, shouting at the creature to tell it what the greatest crime was.

The gates of the Esikananzi estate loomed out of the flying twilight. There was a flicker of lamplight at the lodge, and a man ran out. Then he was torn from view. Beyond the drum of the yelk's hoofs, above the whistle of the wind, came sounds of pursuit.

He was into the village before he knew it. Bells clashed about his ears as he passed the first monastery. There were people about, muffled to the eyes. Pilgrims screamed and scattered. He glimpsed a waffle stall overturned. Then it too was gone and there were only guardhouses before him until—out of the murk—loomed the ramparts of Mount Kharnabhar. The tunnel with its mighty figures was before him.

Without waiting to do more than check the yelk's pace, Luterin flung himself off the animal and ran forward. Above, a great bell tolled. It spoke in solemn tones of his guilt. But the instinct for self-preservation drove him onwards. He ran down the ramp. Priestly figures came forward.

"The soldiers!" he gasped.

They understood. The soldiers were no longer their allies. They hurried him into the gloom, while the great metal doors clanged fast together behind him.

The Great Wheel had claimed him.

XV

INSIDE THE WHEEL

The geonauts were the first life systems on Earth not to consist of living cells, and therefore not to depend on bacteria. They formed a complete break from all life that had gone before, including those amazing gene cities, humanity.

Perhaps Gaia had turned her metaphorical thumbs down on humanity. They had proved themselves more of a curse than an adjunct to the biosphere. Possibly they were now being phased out, or merged with a greater thing.

At all events, the white polyhedrons were now everywhere, covering every continent. They appeared to do no harm. Their ways were as inscrutable as the ways of kings to cats, or of cats to kings. But they emitted energy.

The energy was not the old energy which mankind had used for centuries and termed electricity. The humans called the new energy egonicity, perhaps in memory of the old.

Egonicity could not be generated. It was a force which flowed only from large white polyhedrons when they were about to replicate, or were meditating on the subject. It could, however, be felt. It was felt as a mild singing noise in the lower stomach or hora region. It did not register on any instrument the post–ice age humans could devise.

The post–ice age humans were itinerant. They no longer wished to possess land but rather to be possessed by it. The old world of fences was dead for ever.

Wherever they went, they walked. And it so turned out that it was the easiest thing to follow a suitable geonaut. Humanity had not lost its old ingenuity, or its skill with its hands. As generations passed, a group of men on one of the new continents discovered a way of harnessing enough egonicity to move a small carriage. Soon, small carriages were to be seen everywhere, moving at a slow rate over the land, trundling in front of a geonaut.

When the geonaut replicated, letting slip a stream of tiny polyhedrons like sheets of paper in the wind, the egonicity ceased, and those who sat in the carriage had to push it to another source.

However, that was just a beginning. Later developments would bring different arrangements.

The human race, greatly reduced from its former numbers, roamed the new Earth, and developed a dependence on the geonauts which increased generation by generation.

Nobody worked as once people had worked, bent double planting rice or sowing potatoes in the dirt. They did plant vegetables occasionally, but that was for pleasure; and others inherited the fruits of their labours, since they had by that time moved on—though rarely by more than a mile a day. Egonicity was not a violent power source.

Nobody worked at desks. Desks were extinct.

It might have been supposed that these people were always on holiday, or perhaps that they inhabited some rather spartan version of the Garden of Eden. Such was not the case. They were intensely involved with work of their own specific kind. They were doing what they termed rethinking.

The storms of radioactivity which had followed the nuclear war had left their brand upon the genetic pool. The survival of mankind increasingly favoured those with new connections among the neural pathways of their brains. The neocortex had been, in geological terms, a hasty development. It had functioned well on ordinary occasions but, in times of stress, it had been bypassed by emotion. In prenuclear times, this deficiency had been regarded as a norm, sometimes as a desirable norm. Violence was regarded as an acceptable solution to many problems which would never have originated had violence not been in the air in the first place.

In these more pacific times, violence was unwelcome. It was seen as a failing, never as a solution. Generation by generation, the neocortex developed better connections with other parts of the brain. Mankind began to know itself for the first time.

These itinerant people did see themselves as on holiday. Such are the ways that Gaia works through evolution. They found pleasure in doing exactly those things which improved their stock, and those couples excelled whose children in the next generation would do best at the new sport of rethinking.

Mainly they searched for deep structures in the human consciousness. While seeking out those guiding determinants which had shaped the history of the human race so far, they were guided by what happened on Helliconia. The records of terrestrial history before the nuclear destruction were almost entirely destroyed; only one or two caches of knowledge had been disinterred from the ruins. But Helliconia was reckoned to present in its people a fair parallel of the deep structures which had once prevailed on Earth.

Those terrestrials who had so feared their own violent nature, who had walled themselves about with fences, armaments, and harsh laws— so it was reckoned—were not greatly different from the troubled young man who killed his father. Aggression and killing had been an escape from pain: in the end, the planet itself had been murdered by its own sons.

Although there was scarcely a person on the whole planet who had not heard of the Great Wheel of Kharnabhar, few had visited it. None had seen it in its entirety.

The Great Wheel lay underground, buried in the heart of Mount Kharnabhar. The Architects had built it, and none had come after them who could even emulate their work.

Nothing was known of the Architects of Kharnabhar, but one thing was certain. They were devout men. They had believed that faith could move worlds. They had set about building a machine of stone which could haul Helliconia across the darkness and cold until it docked again to bask in the warmth of God the Azoiaxic's favour. So far, the machine had always worked.

The machine was powered by faith, and the faith was in the hearts of men.

The way by which men entered the Wheel had been unchanged throughout the ages. After a preliminary ceremony at the gates of the tunnel, the newcomer was led down a wide flight of stairs which curved into the mountain. Biogas jets lit the way. At the bottom of the steps was a funnel-shaped chamber, the far wall of which was a section of the Wheel itself. The newcomer was then helped or propelled, depending on his state of mind, into the cell of the Wheel there visible. After a while, after a jerk, the Wheel began to rotate. Slowly, the view of the outer world was cut off from the cell's new occupant by the rock face. The outer world disappeared from view. Now the newcomer was alone

—except for all the occupants of all the other cells nearby, who would remain unseen throughout his tenure of the Wheel.

Luterin Shokerandit was not untypical of those who entered the Wheel. Others had sought refuge there. Some had been saints, some sinners.

Originally, the plan of the Architects had been followed by the Church. There had been no shortage of volunteers to take their places in the Great Wheel and row it across the firmament to its rightful port beside Freyr. But when the long centuries of light returned at last, when Sibornal was again bathed in daylight, then the faith declined. It became more difficult to attract the faithful, to persuade them into the darkness.

The Wheel would have come to a standstill had not the State stepped in to aid the Church. It had sent its criminals to Kharnabhar, in order that they might serve their sentences in the Wheel and, crouched deep in rock, haul their world and themselves to remission. Thus had come about the close collaboration of Church and State which had sustained the strength of Sibornal for more Great Years than could be remembered.

Throughout the summer and the long lazy autumn, the Wheel was hauled as often by malefactors as by priests. Only when life became more difficult, when snows began to fall and crops to fail, did the old faith grow strong again. Then the religious returned, begging for a guaranteed place among the righteous. The criminals were sent off to become sailors or soldiers, or were dumped unceremoniously in Persecution Bay.

> *Father father what headwaters are these*
> *The rock so red hot like a forehead*
> *And me so fevered in the rude red darkness*
> *Are you there above below me*
> *Waiting not to die   O death*
> *Its energies   You scream in the walls*
> *Of my existence by my side   The lights go by*
> *Go by and are gone and I in the snoring*
> *Rock   I revile myself   That thing*
> *I never did in mind but of a sudden*
> *With your knife cutting our mutual*
> *It was I swear our mutual artery*
> *This place of terror screaming*
> *Where I'll forever bleed like lava*
> *Clogging the rude red rock darkness*

His thoughts ran in curious patterns, seemed to him to flow through him forever. Time was marked in the entombed soul by protracted squeals of rock against rock and by hideous groans. Gradually, the groans caught his attention. His mind became quieter listening to them.

He was uncertain of his whereabouts. He imagined himself lying in the subterranean stall of some great wounded beast. Though close to death, the beast was still searching for him, looking here, looking there. When it found him, it would fall upon him and crush him to death in its own final agonies.

At last he roused himself. It was the wind he heard. The wind blew down the orifices of the Wheel, creating a harmony of groans. The squealing was the movement of the Wheel.

Luterin sat up. The priests of the Wheel had not only let him in, thus saving him from his father's avengers, they had absolved him from all his sins before guiding him into his cell. Such was their standard practice. Men who were imprisoned with their sins upon them were more likely to go mad.

He stood up. The terrible thing he had done filled all his mind. He looked with horror at his right hand, and at the bloodstain on his right sleeve.

Food arrived. It could be heard rumbling down a chute in the rock overhead. It consisted of a round loaf of bread, a cheese, and a chunk of something which was probably roast stungebag, tied up in a cloth. So it was Batalix-dawn overhead. Soon the small winter would prevail, and then Batalix would not be seen again for several tenners. But little difference that made in the entrails of Mount Kharnabhar. As he munched on a piece of bread, he walked about his cell, examining it with the attention a man gives his surroundings when he knows that a narrow box is to become his life.

The Architects of Kharnabhar had arranged every measurement to correspond in some way with the astronomical facts which governed life on Helliconia. The height of the cell was 240 centimetres, corresponding to the six weeks of a tenner times the forty minutes of the hour, or to five times the six weeks times the eight days in a week.

The width of the cell at its outer end was 2.5 metres—250 centimetres, corresponding to the ten tenners of a small year times the number of hours in a day.

The depth of the cell was 480 centimetres, corresponding to the number of days in a small year.

Against one wall was a bunk, the cell's sole furniture. Above the bunk was the chute down which provisions came. On the far side of the cell was the opening which served as a latrine. The wastes fell down a pipe to biogas chambers below the Wheel, which, supplemented by vegetable and animal wastes from the monastery overhead, supplied the Wheel with its methane lighting.

Luterin's cell was separated from those on either side by walls .64159 metres in thickness—a figure which, added to the cell width, gave the value of pi. As he sat on his bunk with his back against this partition, he regarded the wall on his left. It was solid unmoving rock, and formed the fourth wall of the cell with scarcely a crack between it and its neighbours in the Wheel. Carved in this rock were two sets of alcoves: a high series containing the biogas burners, which provided the cells with what light and warmth they enjoyed, and, set twice as frequent, a lower series containing lengths of chain, firmly stapled into place.

Still munching his bread, Luterin crossed to the outer wall and lifted the heavy links of chain. They seemed to sweat in his hands. He dropped them. The chain fell back into its narrow alcove. It consisted of ten links, each link representing a small year.

He stood there without movement, his gaze locked on the length of chain. Beside the horror of his deed, another horror was growing, the horror of imprisonment. By these ten-link chains, the Great Wheel was to be moved through space.

He had not yet taken his turn with the chains. He had no notion how long he had lain in a delirium, while words winged like birds through his head. He recalled only the shrill noise of trumpets from the monks somewhere above the Wheel, and then the lurching horizontal movements of the Wheel itself, which continued for half a day.

Contemplating the outer wall frightened Luterin. The time would come when he would feel differently. That wall was the only changing element of his environment. Its markings formed a map of the journey; by those excoriations, a practised prisoner could chart his way through time and granite.

The inner walls, the permanent walls of the cell, had been elaborately incised by previous occupants. Portraits of saints and drawings of genital organs testified to the mixed occupancy of the cell. Poems were engraved here, calendars, confessions, calculations, diagrams. Not an inch had been spared. The walls preserved fossils of spirits long dead. They were palimpsests of suffering and hope.

Revolutionary slogans could be read. One was cut on top of an earnest prayer to a god called Akha. Many of the earliest markings were obliterated by later ones, as one generation obliterates another. Some of the early inscriptions, though faint, were legible and delicately formed. Some were in ornate scripts which had disappeared from the world.

In one of the faintest, most elaborate scripts, Luterin read the basic details of the Wheel itself. These were figures which had a power over all who were incarcerated here.

The Wheel might more properly be described as a ring, revolving about a great central finger of granite.

The height of the Wheel was a uniform 6.6 metres, or twelve times 55, the northern latitude of the Wheel itself. Counting its base, its thickness was 13.19 metres, 1319 being the year of Freyr-set, or Myrkwyr, at latitude 55°N, dating the years from the nadir year of apastron. The diameter of the Wheel was 1825 metres, the number of small years in one Great Year. And 1825 was the number of cells set in the outer circumference of the Wheel.

Close to this numeration, and allowed to remain intact, was an intricately engraved figure. It represented the Wheel in its correct dimensions, set in the rock. Above it was the cavern, large enough to permit the monks from the monastery to walk on top of the Wheel and drop supplies to the prisoners below. Entry to the cavern could be gained only through Bambekk Monastery, which perched on the hillsides of Mount Kharnabhar, above the buried Wheel.

Whoever had incised the figure on the granite had evidently been well informed. The river that ran below the Wheel, assisting its revolutions, was also depicted. Other schematic lines carried a connection from the heart of the Wheel out to Freyr and Batalix and to the constellations of the ten houses of the zodiac—the Bat, Wutra's Ox, the Boulder, the Night Wound, the Golden Ship, and the others.

"Abro Hakmo Astab!" Luterin exclaimed, uttering the forbidden oath for the first time. He hated these supposed connections. They lied. There were no connections. There was only himself, embedded in rock, no better than a gossie. He flung himself down on the bunk.

He used the oath again. As one of the damned, he was permitted it.

The dimmer the vision, the louder the noises. Luterin presumed that the other occupants of the Wheel slept when it was not moving. He lay awake, gazing vacantly about the dull box he inhabited.

His water supply ran down into a trough near the foot of his bunk. Its drips and splashes were close, and as regular as the tick of clocks.

Deeper in tone were the flows of water beneath the mobile floor. These were lazy noises, like a continuous drunken monologue. Luterin found them soothing.

Other watery noises, drips and plops, coming more distantly, reminded him of the outside world of nature, of freedom, of the hunt. He could imagine himself wandering free in the caspiarn forests. But that illusion could not be sustained. Ever and again he saw his father's face in its final agony. The brooks, waterfalls, torrents, disappeared from his mind's eye, to be replaced by blood.

His lethargy was pierced only when he opened his daily woven bundle of food, and found a message in it.

He carried the scrap of paper over to the blue flame in the outer wall and peered at it. Someone had written in small script, "All is well here. Love."

There was no signature, not even an initial. His mother? Toress Lahl? Insil? One of his friends?

The very anonymity of the message was an encouragement. There was someone outside who thought well of him and who could—at least on one occasion—communicate with him.

That day, when the priests' trumpets sounded, he leaped up and seized hold of the chain hanging in its alcove in the outer wall. Bracing his feet against the partition wall, he heaved on the chain. His cell moved—the Wheel moved.

Another heave, and the movement was less reluctant this time. A few centimetres were gained.

"Pull, you biwackers!" he shouted.

The encouraging bugles sounded at intervals for twelve and a half hours, then fell silent as long. By the end of a day's work, Luterin had advanced himself by some 119 centimetres, almost half the width of his cell. The flame which lit his cell was close to the dividing wall. By the end of another day's work, it would be eclipsed—would be in the following cell—and a new one would be revealed.

A mass of 1284551.137 tons had to be shifted: that was the burden which holiness had placed on the incumbents of the Wheel. It appeared to be merely a physical labour. But, as the days were to pass, Luterin would find himself regarding it more and more as a spiritual task; while more and more it became apparent to him that there were indeed connections out from his heart, and from the Wheel, to Freyr and Batalix and to the far constellations. The perception would come that the Wheel contained not merely hardship but—as legend claimed—the beginnings of wisdom.

"Pull!" he shouted again. "Pull, you saints and sinners."

From then on, he became fanatical, leaping up eagerly from his bunk as soon as the awaited bugle blew. He cursed those who, in his imagination, did not rise as swiftly to the task as he did. He cursed those who would not labour at their chains at all, as he had once done. It was beyond his understanding why the work periods were not longer.

At night—but here only night existed—Luterin lay down to sleep with a head full of the image of that great slow-grinding Wheel, crushing men's lives away like a grindstone. The Wheel moved every day, as it had done since the great Architects had established it.

It revolved about a harsh irony. The captives, nested like maggots each in separate cells on the perimeter of the Wheel, were forced to propel themselves into the heart of the granite mountain. Only by submitting to that cruel journey, by actively collaborating in it, was it possible to emerge. Only by that collaboration was it possible to effect the revolution of the Wheel which meant freedom. Only by plunging deep into the entrails of the mountain was it possible to issue forth a free man.

"Pull, pull!" shouted Luterin, straining every muscle. He thought of the 1824 others, captive each in his separate cell, each bound to pull if ever they were to escape.

He knew not what crises prevailed in the outside world. He knew not what sequence of events he had precipitated. He knew not who lived or died. Increasingly, as the tenners went by, his mind was filled with loathing for those other prisoners—some perhaps sick or even dead— who did not pull with a whole heart. He felt that he alone was bearing the weight of rock on his sinews, he alone heaving the Wheel through its firmament of granite towards the light.

The tenners passed, and the small years. Only the scratchings on the outer rock wall changed. Otherwise, all remained always the same.

The sameness overpowered his youthful mind. He became dull, resigned. He did not always move now when the priests' trumpets blew overhead, their noise made reedy by the thickness of roof.

His thoughts of his father receded. He had come to terms with his guilt by believing that his father had himself been overwhelmed by guilt, and had handed his son the knife before taunting him in order that he might meet death. That face, always shining with sebum, had been a face of misery.

It took him a long while to contemplate the possibility of visiting his father in pauk. But the idea preyed on his mind. In the second year of his incarceration, Luterin climbed onto his bunk and lay flat. He scarcely knew what to do. Gradually, the pauk state overcame him, and he drifted down into a darkness greater than any in the heart of the mountain.

Never before had he entered into that melancholy world of the gossies, where all who had once lived and lived no more sank slowly through the terrible silences into nonbeing. Disorientation overwhelmed him. At first he could not sink; then he could not stop himself sinking. He drifted down towards the sparks dim below him like guttering stars, all arranged in a static uniformity possible only within the regions of death.

The barque of Luterin's soul moved steadily, peering without sight into the fessup ranks which filtered down all the way to the heart of the Original Beholder. Viewed closely, every gossie resembled something like singed poultry, hanging to dry. Through their rib cages, their transparent stomachs, particles could be seen, circulating slowly like flies in a bottle. In their sketchy heads, little lights flickered through hollow eye sockets. Obeying a direction no compass could detect, the soul of Luterin fluttered before the gossie of Lobanster Shokerandit.

"My father, you need say one word only and I shall be gone, I who loved you best and harmed you most."

"Luterin, Luterin, I wait here, sinking towards extinction, only in the hope of seeing you. What sight could be more welcome to my eyes than you? How fare you, child, in the ranks of those who must still undergo the hour of their mortality?" On the last word, puffs of sparks were transpired.

"Father, ask not of me. Speak of yourself. My thoughts are never free of that crime I committed. Those terrible moments in that fatal courtyard always haunt me."

"You must forgive yourself, as I forgave you when I reached this place. We were of different generations, your mind had not yet composed itself, you were unable to take the long view of human affairs that I could. You obeyed a principle, just as I did. There's honour in that."

"I did not intend to kill you, my beloved father—only the Oligarch."

"The Oligarch never dies. There is always another." As the gossie spoke, a cloud of dull particles issued from the cavity where once a mouth had been. They hung and dispersed but slowly, like snow sinking into coal dust.

The cinder of Lobanster described how he had taken on the duties of the Oligarch because he believed that there were values in Sibornal worth preserving. He spoke long about these virtues, and many times his discourse wandered.

He spoke of the way he had hidden the truth of his august position from his family. His long hunting trips were no such thing. Somewhere in the wilderness of the mountains, he had a secret retreat. There his hunting dogs were kept, while he went on with a small guard to Askitosh. He collected the hounds on the way home. Once his older son had discovered the hounds and pieced the truth together. Rather than speak of what he found, Favin had leaped to his death.

"You may easily imagine the grief that overwhelmed me, son. Better to be here, to be safe in obsidian, knowing that no more bitter shocks can assail flesh and spirit."

The soul of the son was overcome but not convinced by this eloquence.

"Why could you not confide in me, Father?"

"I let you guess when I believed the time to be right. The plague must be stopped, the people must learn obedience. Otherwise, civilisation will sink and die under the impact of centuries of cold. Only with that thought in mind could I persevere as I did."

"Respected Father, you could not represent civilisation when the blood of thousands was on your hands."

"They are here with me now, son, those men of Asperamanka's army. Do you imagine they have a single complaint against me? Or your brother, also here?"

The soul uttered the equivalent of a cry. "Matters are different after death. There is no real feeling, only benevolence. What about that unnecessary war you caused to be waged against our neighbors in Bribahr, when the ancient city of Rattagon was destroyed? Was that not sheer cruelty?"

"Only if necessity is cruelty. My speediest way from Kharnabhar to distant Askitosh was to turn westwards from Noonat and speed down the Bribahrese river, the Jerddal—a much more easily navigable river than our ill-tempered Venj. So I came to the coast where ships awaited me, and was not recognised, as in Rivenjk I would have been recognised. Do you comprehend me, my son? I speak only to set your mind at rest.

"It is important that the Oligarch remain anonymous. It lessens danger of assassination and jealousy between nations. But a party of nobles from Rattagon sailing on the Jerddal did recognise me. In view of the hostility between our countries, they planned to dispose of me. I disposed of them instead, in self-defence. You must do likewise, my dear son, when your turn comes. Protect and cherish yourself."

"Never, Father."

"Well, you have plenty of time to mature," said the glimmering shade indulgently.

"Father, you have also struck out against the Church." The soul paused. It was unable to master its feelings, at once of respect and hatred, towards this smokey fragment. "I must ask you—do you think that God ever listens or speaks?"

The hollow which had once been mouth made no movement when it replied. "It is given to us gossies here below to perceive wherefrom our visitors come. I know well, my son, that you come from the heart of our nation's holiness. Therefore I ask you: in this purgatory, do you hear God speak? Do you feel him listen?"

In the questions moved a kind of leaden evil, as if misery could be happy only in propagating itself.

"If it were not for my sins, he might listen, he might speak. That I believe."

"If there were a God, boy, do you not reckon that we here below in all our legions would know of him? Look around you. There's nothing here but obsidian. God is mankind's greatest lie—a buffer against the bleak truths of the world."

For the soul, it was as if a strong current was drawing it towards an unknown place, and it felt close to suffocation.

"Father, I must leave."

"Come nearer to me that I may embrace you."

Accustomed to obey, Luterin drifted nearer to the battered cage. He was about to hold out a hand in a gesture of affection when a strong rain of particles shot up from the gossie, enveloping it as if with fire. He scudded away. The glow died. Just in time, he recalled the stories which claimed that the gossies, for all their resignation to death, would seize a living soul and change places with it if they could.

Once more, he uttered his protestations of affection and rose up slowly through the obsidian, until the whole congregation of gossies and fessups was not more than a dwindling star field. He returned to his own prostrate form in its cell. Sluggishly, he became aware of the warmth of the living body.

There were still eight years to go before his cell was hauled round to the exit, still three before his cell had reached even halfway, in the heart of the dolorous mountain.

The environment never changed. But Luterin's revulsion for himself began to stale, and change came to colour his thought. He began to brood on the division which had been growing between the Church and the State. Supposing that division became still wider and, for whatever reason, recruitment to the Wheel ceased. Supposing that ten-yearers continued to be released and were not replaced. Gradually the Wheel would slow. There would be too few men to budge its mass. Then, despite all the world's bugles, the Wheel would stop. He would be entombed deep within the mountain. There would be no escape.

The thought pursued him like a yellow-striped fly, even in his slumbers. He did not doubt that it pursued many another prisoner. Certainly the Wheel had never failed since the Architects finished their work long ago; but the past was no guarantee for the future. He lived in a suspense that was scarcely life, thinking with resignation of the old saying, "A Sibornalese works for life, marries for life, and longs for life." Apart from the clause regarding marriage, he would have sworn that the proverb originated in the Wheel.

He was tormented by the thought of women, and by the lack of male companionship. He tried to signal through the rock to his nearest fellow sufferers, but no response came. Nor did he receive any more messages from outside. Hope of them died. He had been forgotten.

Through the spells of work and silence, a riddle rose to haunt him. Of the 1825 cells of the Wheel, only two had access to the outer world at one time, the cell by which one entered and the adjacent cell by which one left. How, then, had the Wheel been loaded with its pilgrims in the first instance? How had the giants who had erected this machine started it into motion?

He burdened his mind with visions of ropes and hawsers and pulleys, and of gushing underground rivers which turned the Wheel into a waterwheel. But he could never resolve the riddle to his satisfaction.

Even the processes of his mind remained incarcerated within the holy mountain.

Occasionally a rickyback would make a journey across his cell floor. With joy, he seized it up, holding it gently, watching its fragile legs wave as it struggled to be free. The rickyback understood freedom and was undividedly interested in the subject. Infinitely more complex humans were more divided.

What transcendental pain caused men to imprison themselves for a large portion of their lives within the Great Wheel? Was this indeed the path towards self-understanding?

He wondered if the rickyback understood itself. His efforts to identify with the tiny creatures, so as to enjoy a fraction of their freedom, left him feeling ill. He lay for hours at a time on the floor of the cell, staring at minute moving things, small white ants, microscopic worms. Sometimes he caught pink-eyed rats and mice observing him. If I died, he thought, these would be my only witnesses. The unconsidered.

Many men must have died during their confinement in the intestines of the Wheel. Some had confined themselves from choice, as some were celibate from choice. Perhaps they had been goaded by a wish to escape into changelessness, away from the bustle of the world—that bustle framed, if he understood the astronomers, within the greater commotion of the universe.

But for him, the changelessness of the cell was a kind of death. There had been no yesterday. There would be no tomorrow. His spirit fought against a withering process.

Then the day's trumpets echoed, and he scrambled up, ran to the outer wall of his cell, and grasped the nearest chain. Heaving the Wheel through the rock had become the only meaningful activity left. By 119 centimetres a day, the machine progressed each of its occupants through the darkness.

He never sank into pauk again. But the visit to his father's ember had removed the burden of his guilt. He found after a while that he had ceased to think of his father; or, if he thought at all, he thought only of the spark spluttering in the world beyond mortality.

The father who had been real to him, the brave hunter, forever stalking with his gallant friends through the wilds of the caspiarn forest, was lost, had never existed. Instead there was a man who—in place of that free life—had chosen to incarcerate himself in Icen Hill, in the slatey castle in Askitosh.

There were curious parallels between the dead man's life and Luterin's own. Luterin was also self-imprisoned.

For the third time, his life had come to a standstill. After the year's paralysis, on the threshold of adulthood, the hiatus of the Fat Death, with its subsequent metamorphosis; now this. Was he at last to cease to be what Harbin Fashnalgid had called a creature of the system? Was there a last metamorphosis awaiting him?

It remained to be seen if he could throw off his father's influence. His father, though head of the system, had also been its victim, as had his family through him. Luterin thought of his mother, for ever incarcerated in the family mansion: she might as well be where he was.

As the years passed, he saw Toress Lahl more dimly. The glow of her presence went out. By becoming a slave, she had become no more than a slave; as his mother had pointed out, her devotion was merely the devotion of a slave, self-seeking, self-preserving, not from the heart. Without social status—dead to society, as people said of slaves—the heart did not move. There could be only tactical moves. He thought he understood that a slave must always hate its captor.

Insil Esikananzi glowed more brightly as the tenners and centimetres passed. Incarcerated in her own home, entombed within her own family, she carried the spark of rebellion; her heart beat strongly under her velvets. He spoke to her in the dark. She answered always mockingly, teasing him for his conformity; yet he was comforted by her concern, and by her perception of the world.

And he hauled on his chain whenever the trumpets blew.

High above the Great Wheel rode a structure to some extent resembling it. The Earth Observation Station Avernus also relied on faith for its working.

That faith had failed. Matriarchal societies ruled over small groups of people now entirely devoted to the spiritual playacting of multiple personalities. The giant aberrant sexual organs, the pudendolls, had all been ceremonially put to death—often by aberrant means. But a revulsion from all things mechanical or technological had left the tribes prey to a spiritless eudaemonism in which the sexual motif predominated.

The genders became hopelessly confused. From childhood, individuals adopted female and male personalities, sometimes as many as five of each. These multiple personalities might remain forever strangers to each other, speaking different dialects, pursuing different ways of life. Or they might fall into violent quarrels with each other, or become hopelessly enamoured of another.

Some of these personalities died, while their originator lived on.

Gradually, a general disintegration took place, as if the genetic coding on which inheritance depended had itself become confused.

A diminishing population continued to play its intricate games. But the sense of an ending was in the air. The automatic systems were also breaking down. The drones programmed to service faulty circuits were becoming themselves fit only for regeneration. Regeneration required human supervision, which was not forthcoming.

The signals passing back to Earth became more partial, less coordinated. Soon they would cease entirely. It needed only a few more generations.

XVI

A FATAL INNOCENCE

I t was summer in the northern hemisphere of Earth in a year that
would once have been called 7583.

A group of lovers was travelling in a slowly moving room. Other
rooms were moving nearby, also at a leisurely pace. They perambulated
before a mountainous geonaut. The geonaut perambulated in the
tropics.

Sometimes, one of the lovers would climb down from the room and
cross to another room. Seventy rooms clustered round the geonaut.
Soon it would replicate.

A man called Trockern was talking, as he liked to do in the after-
noons, when the morning's rethinking session was over. Like the others
present, male and female, Trockern wore nothing but a light gauze
veil over his head.

He was a lightly built olive-skinned man, with good features and an
irrepressible smile which broke forth even when he was speaking
seriously.

"If I've got the fruits of this morning's rethink right, then the bizarre
peoples who lived in the ages before the nuclear war failed to realise one
fact which now seems obvious to us. They had not developed suffi-

*ciently to escape from the same sort of territorial possessiveness which
still governs birds and animals."*

He was addressing two sisters, Shoyshal and Ermine, who were currently sharing his room with him. The sisters looked much alike; but
there was a greater clarity about Shoyshal, and she was the leader of
the pair.

"At least part of the old race denounced the evils of landownership,"
Ermine said.

"They were regarded as cranks," Trockern said. "Listen, my theory,
which I hope we can explore, is that possession was everything for the
old race. Love—for them, even love was a political act."

"That's far too sweeping," Shoyshal said. "Admittedly, over most of
the globe in those times one sex dominated the other—"

"Possessed them as slaves."

"Well, dominated them, you argumentative hunk. But there were
also societies where sex became just good clean fun, without any spiritual or possessive connotations, where 'liberation' was the watchword,
and—"

Trockern shook his head. "Darling, you prove my point. That mi-
nority was rebelling against the predominant ethos, so they too treated
—were forced to treat—love as a political act. 'Liberation' or 'free love'
was a statement, therefore political."

"I don't suppose they thought like that."

"They didn't see clearly enough to think like that. Hence their perpetual unease. My belief is that even their wars were welcome as an
escape from their personal predicaments. . . ." Seeing that Shoyshal was
about to argue, he went on hastily, "Yes, I know war was also linked to
territory. That sense of territoriality extended from the land to the
individual. You were supposed to be proud of your native land and to
fight for it, and equally you were supposed to be proud of and fight for
your lover. Or wife, as they then called it. Do you imagine I am proud
of you or would fight for you?"

"Is that a rhetorical question?" Ermine asked, smiling.

"Look, take an example. This obsession the old race had with owner-
ship. Slavery was a common condition on Earth up to and including
the Industrial Revolution. Long after that, in many places. It was just
as bad as we witness it on Helliconia. It gave you power to possess
another person—an idea now almost past belief to us. It would bring us
only misery. But we can see how the slave owner also becomes enslaved."

As Trockern raised both his left hand and his voice for emphasis, the
old man sleeping away the afternoon on a nearby bunk muttered irri-
tably, snorted, and rolled over onto his other side.

"Again, darling, there were plenty of societies without slaves," Shoyshal said. "And plenty of societies which abhorred the idea."

"They said they abhorred it, but they kept servants when they could

—possessed them as far as possible. Later they employed androids. Officially nonslave societies went in for multiple possessions instead. Possessions, possessions . . . It was a form of madness."

"They were not mad," Shoyshal said. "Just different from us. They'd probably find us pretty strange. Besides, it was the adolescence of mankind. I've listened to your preaching often enough, Trockern, and can't deny I've enjoyed it—more or less. Now listen to what I am going to say.

"We're here because of astonishing luck. Forget about the Hand of God, about which the Helliconians are always agonising. There's just luck. I don't mean only luck that a few humans survived the nuclear winter—though that's a part of it. I mean by luck the series of Earth's cosmic accidents. Think of the way plantlike bacteria released oxygen into an otherwise unbreathable atmosphere. Think of the accident of fish developing backbones. Think of the accident of mammals developing placenta—so much cleverer than eggs—though eggs, too, were winners in their day. Think of the accident of the bombardment which altered conditions so sharply that the dinosaurs failed, to give mammals their chance. I could go on."

"You always could," said her sister half-admiringly.

"Our old adolescent ancestors feared accident. They feared luck. Hence gods and fences and marriage and nuclear arms and all the rest. Not your possessiveness, but the fear of accident. Which eventually befell them. Perhaps such prophecies are self-fulfilling."

"Plausible. Yes. I'll agree, if you will allow that possessiveness itself might have been a symptom of that fear of accidents."

"Oh, well, Trockern, if you're going to agree, let's get back to the subject of sex." They all laughed. Outside their windows, the mobile city could be seen trundling on its inelegant way, drinking egonicity from the white polyhedrons.

Ermine put an arm about her sister's shoulder and stroked her hair.

"You talk about one person possessing another; I suppose you would say that the old institution of marriage was like that. Yet marriage still sounds rather romantic to me."

"Most squalid things are romantic if you get far enough away from them," Shoyshal said. "Anything seen through a haze . . . But marriage is the supreme example of love as a political act. The love was just a pretence, or at best an illusion."

"I don't see what you mean. Men and women did not have to marry, did they?"

"It was voluntary in a way, yes, but there was the pressure of society to marry. Sometimes moral pressure, sometimes economic pressure. The man got someone to work for him and have sex with. The woman got someone to earn money for her. They pooled their cupidities."

"How awful!"

"All those romantic postures," continued Shoyshal, enjoying herself. "Those raptures, those love songs, that sticky music, that literature they so prized, the suicide pacts, the tears, the vows—all just social mating displays, the baiting of the trap they couldn't see they were setting or falling into."

"You make it sound awful."

"Oh, it was worse than that, Ermine, I assure you. No wonder so many women chose prostitution. I mean, marriage was another version of the power struggle, with both husband and wife battling for supremacy over the other. The man had the bludgeon of the purse strings, the woman the secret weapon between her legs."

They all burst out in laughter. The old man on the other bunk, SartoriIrvrash by name, began to snore in self-defence.

"It's a long while since yours was secret," Trockern said.

When a city became too crowded for someone's liking, it was not difficult to change to another geonaut and head off in a new direction. There were many other cities, other alternatives. Some people liked to follow the long light days; others travelled to enjoy spectacular scenery; others developed longings to view the sea or the desert. Every environment offered a different kind of experience.

And those kinds of experience were of a different order from the kinds that once had been. No longer did the people cry out. Their agile brains had at last led their emotions to accept a role of modesty, subordinate but never acquiescent to Gaia, spirit of Earth. Gaia did not seek to possess them, as their imagined gods had once done. They were themselves part of that spirit. They had a vision.

In consequence, death ceased to play the leading role of Inquisitor in human affairs, as once it had done. Now it was no more than an item in the homely accounting which included mankind: Gaia was a common grave from which fresh increment continually blossomed.

There was also the dimension of a real involvement with Helliconia. From watchers, men and women had graduated to participators. As the images failed to arrive from the Avernus, as the mere pictures died in the shell-like auditoria, so the empathic link was forged ever more strongly. In a sense, humankind—humanmind—leaped across space to become the eye of the Original Beholder, to lend strength to their distant fellows on the other planet.

What the future might bring to that spiritual extension of being was a matter for expectation.

By accepting a role proper and comfortable to them, the terrestrials had again entered the magic circle of being. They had forsworn their old greeds. Theirs was the world, as they were the world's.

When it was growing dark, Ermine said, "Talking about love as a political act. It takes a little getting used to. But what was that legalistic arrangement the old race suffered when a marriage broke up? Jandol-

Anganol had one? Oh, a divorce. That was a quarrel over possessions, wasn't it?"

"And over who possessed the children," Shoyshal said.

"That's an example of love all entangled in economics and politics. They didn't understand that the random cannot be escaped. It's one of the caprices by which Gaia keeps herself up to date."

Trockern glanced out the window and gestured at the geonaut. "I wouldn't be surprised if Gaia hasn't sent that object to supersede us," he said, with an air of mock gloom. "After all, geonauts are more beautiful and more functional than we are—present company excepted."

As the stars came out, the three climbed down onto the earth and walked by the side of their slow-trundling room. Ermine linked arms with the other two.

"We can judge from the example of Helliconia how many lives of the old race were ruined by territoriality and the lust to possess those who were loved. No matter that it killed love. At least the nuclear winter freed our race from that sort of territoriality. We have risen to a better kind of life."

"I wonder what else is wrong with us that we don't know about?" Trockern said, and laughed.

"In your case we know," said Ermine, teasingly. He bit her ear. Inside the room, SartoriIrvrash stirred on his bunk and grunted, as if in approval, as if he would have relished biting that pink lobe himself. It was about the hour when he generally decided to wake and enjoy the hours of tropical darkness.

"That reminds me," Shoyshal said, looking up at the stars. "If my randomness theory is in any way correct, it might account for why the old race never found any other life forms out there, except on Helliconia. Helliconia and Earth were lucky. We were accident-prone. On the other planets, everything went according to some geophysical plan. As a result, nothing ever happened. There was no story to tell."

They stood looking up into the infinite distances of the sky.

A sigh escaped Trockern. "I always experience intense happiness when I look up at the galaxy. Always. On the one hand, the stars remind me that the whole marvellous complexity of the organic and inorganic universe resolves itself down to a few physical laws awesome in their simplicity—"

"And of course you are happy that the stars provide a text for a speech. . . ." She imitated his posturing.

"And on the other hand, darling, and on the other hand . . . Oh, you know, I'm happy that I'm more complex than a worm or bluebottle, and thus able to read beauty into those few awesome physical laws."

"All those age-old rumours about God," Shoyshal said. "You can't help wondering if there isn't something in them. Perhaps the truth is that God's a real old bore you wouldn't want to be seen dead with. . . ."

"... *Sitting brooding for ever over planets piled with nothing but sand* ..."

"... *And counting every grain,*" finished Ermine.

Laughing, they had to run to catch up with their room.

The years went by. It was simple. All one had to do was haul on the chains, and the years passed. And the Wheel moved through the starry firmament.

Despair gave way to resignation. Long after resignation came hope, flooding in without fanfares, like dawn.

The nature of the graffiti on the encompassing outer wall changed. There were representations of nude women, hopes and boasts about grandchildren, fears about wives. There were calendars counting down the final years, the figures growing larger as the tenners shrank.

Yet still there were religious sayings, sometimes repeated obsessively on every few metres of wall until, after many tenners, the writer grew tired. One such which Luterin read musingly was ALL THE WORLD'S WISDOM HAS ALWAYS EXISTED: DRINK DEEP OF IT THAT IT MAY INCREASE.

Once, as he hauled on his chains with the rest of the unseen host, as trumpets blew and the whole structure shrieked on its pinions, Luterin Shokerandit was aware of a faint luminosity in his cell. He worked. Every hour hauled the mass of the Wheel under 10 centimetres forward, but every hour increased the luminosity. An halosis of yellow twilight crept in.

He thought himself in paradise. Throwing off his furs, he tugged at the ten-link chain with extra vigour, shouting for his unhearing fellows to do the same. Near the end of the twelve-and-a-half-hour work period, the cell's leading wall slipped forward to reveal the merest slit of light. The cell became filled with a holy substance which flickered and flowed into the least corner of the cell. Luterin fell down on his knees and covered his eyes, crying and laughing.

Before the work period ceased, all of the slit was contained within his outer wall space. It was 240 millimetres wide—and there was now half a small year to go before Luterin had hauled his cell once more to the exit under Bambekk Monastery. Concisely engraved lettering in the granite read: YE HAVE BUT HALF A YEAR LEFT AWAY FROM THE WORLD: SEE YE BENEFIT FROM IT.

The window was cut deep into the rock. It was difficult to see how far it extended before it became a window to the outside. Bars were secured over it at the far end. Through the bars a distant tree could be seen, a caspiarn blowing before a storm wind.

Luterin stared out for a long while before going to sit on his bunk to contemplate the beauty about him. The cleft by which the daylight entered was silted with rubble. Through it filtered a precious quality which brimmed the entire volume of the cell with transforming fluids of beauty. All the light in the world seemed to him to be pouring blessing on his head. Before him lay both the brightest of illuminations, as well as exquisite shadows which painted the corners of the modest room with such gradations of tone as he had never observed in the world of freedom. He drank the ecstasy of being a living biological creature again.

"Insil!" he cried into the twilight. "I shall be back!"

He did not work the next day, but watched the life-giving window being moved by others across the outer wall. On the following day, when again he refused to work, the window moved again and all but disappeared. Even the crack remaining was sufficient to spill an exquisite pearly luminosity into his confinement. When, on the fourth workday, even that vanished—presumably to charm the inmate of the following cell—he was disconsolate.

Now began a period of self-doubt. His longing to be free changed to a fear of what he would find. What would Insil have done with herself? Would she have left the place she hated?

And his mother. Perhaps she was dead by now. He resisted the impulse to sink into pauk and find out.

And Toress Lahl. Well, he had set her free. Perhaps she had made her way back to Borldoran.

And what of the political situation? Was the new Oligarch carrying out the old Oligarch's edicts? Were phagors still being slain? What of the quarrel between Church and State?

He wondered how he would himself be treated when he emerged into the world. Perhaps a party of execution would await him. It was the old question, still unanswered over almost ten small years: was he saint or sinner? A hero or a criminal? Certainly he had forfeited any claim to the position of Keeper of the Wheel.

He began talking to an imagined woman, achieving an eloquence that was never his when he was face to face with anyone else.

"What a maze life is to humans! It must be so much simpler to be a phagor. They aren't tormented by doubt or hope. When you are young, you enjoy a sustained illusion that sooner or later something marvellous is going to happen, that you are going to transcend your parents' limitations, meet a wonderful woman, and be capable of being wonderful to her.

"At the same time, you feel sure that in all the wilderness of possibility, in all the forests of conflicting opinion, there is a vital something that can be known—known and grasped. That we will eventually know it, and convert the whole mystery into a coherent narrative. So that then one's true life—the point of everything—will emerge from the mist into a pure light, into total comprehension.

"But it isn't like that at all. But if it isn't, where did the idea come from, to torture and unsettle us? All the years I've spent here—all the thought that's gone by . . ."

He tugged mightily at each heavy chain that presented itself in that endless succession of chains. The days on the stone calendar dwindled. That impossible day would be upon him when he would be free again to move among other human beings. Whatever happened, he prayed to the Azoiaxic that he might make love to a woman again. In his imagination, Insil was no longer remote.

The wind blew from the north, carrying with it the taint of the permanent ice cap. Very few things could live within its breath. Even the tough leaves of the caspiarns furled themselves like sails against the trunks of the trees when the wind blew.

The valleys were filling with snow. The snow was packing down. Year by small year, the light grew less.

There was now a covered way to the small chapel of King Jandol-Anganol. It was roughly built of fallen branches, but it served to keep a path clear to the sunken door.

For the first time in many centuries, someone lived in the chapel. A woman and a small boy crouched over a stove in one corner. The woman kept the door locked, and screened the stove so that its light could not be seen from outside. She had no right to be here.

All round the chapel she had set traps which she found rusting in the vestry of the chapel. Small animals were caught in her traps, providing food enough. Only rarely did she dare show herself in the village of Kharnabhar, although she had a kind friend there who had established a store to sell fish brought up from the coast—for the old route she had once travelled was kept open, whatever the weather.

She taught her son to read. She drew the letters of the alphabet in the dust, or carried him to see the letters painted on the walls in various texts. She told him that the letters and words were pictures of ideal things, some of which existed or could exist, some of which should not exist. She tried to instil morality with his reading, but she also invented silly stories for him which made them both laugh.

When the child was asleep, she read to herself.

It was a perpetual source of wonder to her that the presiding presence in this building was a man from her own city of Oldorando. Their lives were united in a curious way, across miles and centuries. He had retreated to this place to be in seclusion and to do penance for his sins. Late in life, he had been joined by a strange woman from Dimariam, a distant country of Hespagorat. Both had left documents, through which she wandered by the hour. Sometimes she felt the king's restless spirit by her side.

As the years passed, she told the story to her growing son.

"This naughty King JandolAnganol did a great wrong in the country where your mother was born. He was a religious man, yet he killed his religion. It was a terrible paradox under which he found it hard to live. So he came to Kharnabhar and served in the Wheel for the full ten small years, as now does the one who is your father.

"JandolAnganol left two queens behind him to come here. He must have been very wicked, though the Sibornalese think him holy.

"After he emerged from the Wheel, he was joined by the Dimariam woman I told you about. Like me, she was a doctor. Well, she seems to have been other things besides, including a trader of some sort. Her name was Immya Muntras, and she, feeling the call of religion, sought out the king. Perhaps she comforted his old age. She stood by him. That's no ill thing.

"Muntras possessed learning which she thought precious. See, here is where she wrote it all down, long ago, during the Great Summer, when people thought the world was going to end, just as they do now.

"This lady Muntras had some information from a man who arrived in Oldorando from another world. It sounds strange, but I have seen so many amazing things in my life that I believe anything. Lady Muntras's bones now lie in the antechapel, beside those of the king. Here are her papers.

"What she learned from the man from another world concerned the nature of the plague. She was told by the strange man that the Fat Death was necessary, that it brought to those who survived a metamorphosis, a change in bodily metabolism which would enable them best to survive the winter. Without that metamorphosis, humans cannot hope to live through the heart of the Weyr-Winter.

"The plague is carried by ticks which live on phagors and transfer to men and women. The bite of the tick gives you plague. The plague brings metamorphosis. So you see that man cannot survive the Weyr-Winter without phagors.

"This knowledge the lady Muntras tried to teach in Kharnabhar, centuries past. Yet still they are killing phagors, and the State does everything in its power to keep the plague at bay. It would be better to improve medicine, so that more people who caught the plague could survive."

So she used to talk, scanning her boy's face in the semidarkness.

The boy listened. Then he went to play among the treasures left in the chests which had once belonged to the wicked king.

One evening, as he was playing and his mother reading by the firelight, there came a knocking at the door of the chapel.

Like the slow seasons, the Great Wheel of Kharnabhar always completed its revolutions.

For Luterin Shokerandit, the Wheel at last came full circle. The cell that had been his habitation returned to the opening. Only a wall 0.64 metres thick separated it from the cell ahead, into which a volunteer was even then stepping, to commence ten years in the darkness, rowing Helliconia towards the light.

There were guards waiting in the gloom. They helped him from his place of confinement. Instead of releasing him, they took him slowly up a winding side stair. The light grew steadily brighter; he closed his eyes and gasped.

They took him into a small room in the monastery of Bambekk. For a while he was left alone.

Two female slaves came, regarding him out of the corner of their eyes. They were followed by male slaves, bearing a bath and hot water, a silver looking glass, towels and shaving equipment, fresh clothes.

"These are by courtesy of the Keeper of the Wheel," said one of the women. " 'Tisn't every wheeler gets this treatment, be sure of that."

As the scent of hot water and herbs reached him, Luterin realised how he stank, how the methaney odours of the Wheel clung to him. He allowed the women to strip off his ragged furs. They led him to the bath. He lay glorying in the sensation as they washed his limbs. Every smallest event threatened to overwhelm him. He had been as if dead.

He was powdered and dried and dressed in the thick new clothes.

They led him to the window to peer out, although the light at first almost blinded him.

He was looking down on the village of Kharnabhar from a great height. He could see houses buried up to their roofs in snow. The only things that moved were a sledge pulled by three yelk and two birds circling in the sky overhead, creating that eternal spectre of the wheel.

Visibility was good. A snowstorm was dying, and clouds blew away to the south, leaving pockets of undiluted blue sky. It was all too brilliant. He had to turn away, covering his eyes.

"What's the date?" he asked one of the women.

"Why, 'tis 1319, and tomorrow's Myrkwyr. Now, how about having that beard cut off and looking a few thousand years younger?"

His beard had grown like a fungus in the dark. It was streaked with grey and hung to his navel.

"Cut it off," he said. "I'm not yet twenty-four. I'm still young, aren't I?"

"I've certainly heard of people being older," said the woman, advancing with the scissors.

He was then to be taken before the Keeper of the Wheel.

"This will be merely a formal audience," said the usher who escorted him through the labyrinth of the monastery. Luterin had little to say. The new impressions crowding in were almost more than he could receive; he could not help thinking how he had once regarded himself as destined to be Keeper.

He made no response when eventually he was left at one end of what seemed to him an immense chamber. The Keeper sat at the far end on a wooden throne, flanked by two boys in ecclesiastical garb. The dignitary beckoned Luterin to approach.

He stepped gingerly through the lighted space, awed by the number of paces it required to reach the dais.

The Keeper was an enormous man who had draped himself in a purple gown. His face seemed about to burst. Like his gown, it was purple, and mottled with veins climbing the cheeks and nose like vines. His eyes were watery, his mouth moist. Luterin had forgotten there were such faces, and studied it as an object of curiosity while it studied him.

"Bow," hissed one of the attendant children, so he bowed.

The Keeper spoke in a throttled kind of voice. "You are back among us, Luterin Shokerandit. Throughout the last ten years, you have been under the Church's care—otherwise you would probably have been poisoned by your enemies, in revenge for your act of patricide."

"Who are my enemies?"

The watery eyes were squeezed between folds of lid. "Oh, the slayer of the Oligarch has enemies everywhere, official and unofficial. But they were mainly the Church's enemies too. We shall continue to do what we can for you. There is a private feeling that . . . we owe you something." He laughed. "We could help you to leave Kharnabhar."

"I have no wish to leave Kharnabhar. It's my home." The watery eyes watched his mouth rather than his eyes when he spoke.

"You may change your mind. Now, you must report to the Master of Kharnabhar. Once, if you remember, the offices of Master and Keeper of the Wheel were combined. With the schism between Church and State, the two offices are separate."

"Sir, may I ask a question?"

"Ask it."

"There's much to understand . . . Does the Church hold me to be saint or sinner?"

The Keeper endeavoured to clear his throat. "The Church cannot condone patricide, so I suppose that officially you are a sinner. How could it be otherwise? You might have worked that out, I would have thought, during your ten years below. . . . However, personally, speaking ex officio . . . I'd say you rid the world of a villain, and I regard you as a saint." He laughed.

So this must be an unofficial enemy, thought Luterin. He bowed and turned to walk away when the Keeper called him back.

The Keeper heaved himself to his feet. "You don't recognise me? I'm Wheel-Keeper Ebstok Esikananzi. Ebstok—an old friend. You once had hopes of marrying my daughter, Insil. As you see, I have risen to a post of distinction."

"If my father had lived, you would never have become Keeper."

"Who's to blame for that? You be grateful that I'm grateful."

"Thank you, sir," said Luterin, and left the august presence, preoccupied by the remark regarding Insil.

He had no idea where he was supposed to go to report to the Master of Kharnabhar. But Keeper Esikananzi had arranged everything. A liveried slave awaited Luterin with a sledge, with furs to protect him from the cold.

The speed of the sledge overwhelmed him, and the jingle of the animals' harness bells. As soon as the vehicle started to move, he closed his eyes and held tight. There were voices like birds crying, and the song of the runners on the ice, reminding him of something—he knew not what.

The air smelt brittle. From what little he glimpsed of Kharnabhar the pilgrims had all gone. The houses were shuttered. Everything looked drabber and smaller than he remembered it. Lights gleamed here and there in upper windows or in trading stores which remained open. The light was still painful to his eyes. He slumped back, marshalling his memories of Ebstok Esikananzi. He had known this crony of his father's since childhood, and had never taken to the man; it was Ebstok who should be called to account for his daughter Insil's bitterness.

The sledge rattled and jolted, its bells merrily jingling. Above their tinny sound came the tongue of a heavier bell.

He forced himself to look about.

They were sweeping through massive gates. He recognised the gates and the gatehouse beside them. He had been born here. Cliffs of snow three metres high towered on either side of the drive. They were driving through—yes—the Vineyard. Ahead, roofs of a familiar house showed. The bell of unforgettable voice sounded even louder.

Shokerandit was visited by a warming memory of himself as a small boy, pulling a little toboggan, running towards the front steps. His father was standing there, at home for once, smiling, arms extended to him.

There was an armed sentry on the door now. The door was three parts enclosed in a small hut for the sentry's protection. The sentry kicked on the panels of the front door until a slave opened up and took charge of Luterin.

In the windowless hall, gas jets burned against the wall, their nimbuses reflected in the polished marble. He saw immediately that the great vacant chair had gone.

"Is my mother here?" he asked the slave. The man merely gaped at him and led him up the stairs. Without emotional tone, he told himself that he should be the Master of Kharnabhar, as well as Keeper.

At the slave's knock, a voice bade him enter. He stepped into his
father's old study, the room that had so often been locked against him
during earlier years.

An old grey hound lay sprawled by the fire, woofing pettishly at
Luterin's arrival. Green logs hissed and smouldered in the grate. The
room smelt of smoke, dog's piss, and something resembling face powder. Beyond the thick-paned window lay snow and the infinite wordless
universe.

A white-haired secretary, the hinges of whose lumbar region had
rusted to force on him a resemblance to a crooked walking stick, approached. He munched his lips by way of greeting and offered Luterin
a chair without any needless display of cordiality.

Luterin sat down. His gaze travelled round the room, which was
still crammed with his father's belongings. He took in the flintlocks and
matchlocks of earlier days, the pictures and plate, the mullions and
soffits, the orreries and oudenardes. Silverfish and woodworm went
about their tasks in the room. The sliver of crumbling cake on the
secretary's desk was presumably of recent date.

The secretary had seated himself with an elbow by the cake.

"The master is busy at present, with the Myrkwyr ceremony to come.
He should not be long," said the secretary. After a pause, he added,
regarding Luterin slyly, "I suppose you don't recognise me?"

"It's rather bright in here."

"But I'm your father's old secretary, Secretary Evanporil. I serve the
new Master now."

"Do you miss my father?"

"That's hardly for me to say. I simply carry out the administration."
He became busy with the papers on his desk.

"Is my mother still here?"

The secretary looked up quickly. "She's still here, yes."

"And Toress Lahl?"

"I don't know that name, sir."

The silence of the rooms was filled with the dry rustle of paper.
Luterin contained himself, rousing when the door opened. A tall thin
man with a narrow face and peppery whiskers came in, bell clanking
at waist. He stood there, wrapped in a black-and-brown heedrant, looking down at Luterin. Luterin stared back, trying to assess whether this
was an official or an unofficial enemy.

"Well . . . you are back at last in the world in which you have
caused a great deal of havoc. Welcome. The Oligarchy has appointed
me Master here—as distinct from any ecclesiastical duties. I'm the
voice of the State in Kharnabhar. With the worsening weather, communications with Askitosh are more difficult than they were. We see
to it that we get good food supplies from Rivenjk, otherwise military
links are . . . rather weaker. . . ."

This was drawn out sentence by sentence, as Luterin made no response.

"Well, we will try to look after you, though I hardly think you can live in this house."

"This is my house."

"No. You have no house. This is the house of the Master and always has been."

"Then you have greatly profited by my act."

"There is profit in the world, yes. That's true."

Silence fell. The secretary came and proffered two glasses of yadahl. Luterin accepted one, blinded by the beauty of its ruby gleam, but could not drink it.

The Master remained standing rather stiffly, betraying some nervousness as he gulped his yadahl. He said, "Of course, you have been away from the world for a long time. Do I take it that you don't recognise me?"

Luterin said nothing.

With a small burst of irritation, the Master said, "Beholder, you are silent, aren't you? I was once your army commander, Archpriest-Militant Asperamanka. I thought soldiers never forgot their commanders in battle!"

Then Luterin spoke. "Ah, Asperamanka . . . 'Let them bleed a little' . . . Yes, now I remember you."

"It's hard to forget how the Oligarchy, when your father controlled it, destroyed my army in order to keep the plague from Sibornal. You and I were among the few to escape death."

He took a considered sip at his yadahl and paced about the room. Now Luterin recognised him by the anger lines incised into his brow.

Luterin rose. "I'd like to ask you a question. How does the State regard me—as a saint or a sinner?"

The Master's fingernails tapped against his glass. "After your father . . . died, there followed a period of unrest in the various nations of Sibornal. They're used to harsh laws by now—the laws that will see us safe through the Weyr-Winter—but then it was otherwise. There was, frankly, some bad feeling about Oligarch Torkerkanzlag II. His edicts weren't popular. . . .

"So the Oligarchy circulated the rumor—and this was my idea—that they had trained you to assassinate your father, whom they could no longer control. They put out the idea that you had been spared at the massacre at Koriantura only because you were the Oligarchy's man. The rumour increased our popularity and brought us through a difficult time."

"You wrapped up my crime in a lie."

"We just made use of your useless act. One outcome of it was that the State recognised you officially as a—why do you say 'saint'?—as a

hero. You've become part of legend. Though I have to say that personally I regard you as a sinner of the first water. I still keep my religious
convictions in such matters."

"And is it religious conviction that has installed you in Kharnabhar?"

Asperamanka smiled and tugged at his beard. "I greatly miss Askitosh.
But there was an opportunity open to govern this province, so I took
it. . . . As a legend, a figure in the history books, you must accept my
hospitality for the night. A guest, not a captive."

"My mother?"

"We have her here. She's ill. She's no more likely to recognise you
than you were to recognise me. Since you are something of a hero in
Kharnabhar, I want you to accompany me to the public Myrkwyr ceremony tomorrow, with the Keeper. Then people can see we haven't
harmed you. It will be the day of your rehabilitation. There'll be a
feast."

"You'll let me *feed* a little . . ."

"I don't understand you. After the ceremony, we will make what
arrangements you wish. You might consider it best to leave Kharnabhar
and live somewhere less remote."

"That's what the Keeper also hoped I might consider."

He went to see his mother. Lourna Shokerandit lay in bed, frail and
unmoving. As Asperamanka had anticipated, she did not recognise him.
That night, he dreamed he was back in the Wheel.

The following day began with a great bustle and ringing of bells.
Strange smells of food drifted up to where Luterin lay. He recognised
the savoury odours as rising from dishes he would once have desired.
Now he longed for the simple fare he had reviled, the rations that came
rolling down the chutes of the Wheel.

Slaves came to wash and dress him. He did as was required of him,
passively.

Many people he did not know assembled in the great hall. He looked
down over the bannisters and could not bring himself to join them.
The excitement was overpowering. Master Asperamanka came up the
stairs to him and said, taking his arm, "You are unhappy. What can I
do for you? It is important that I am seen to please you today."

The personages in the hall were flocking outside, where sleighbells
rattled. Luterin did not speak. He could hear the wind roar as it had
done in the Wheel.

"Very well, then at least we will ride together and people will see us
and think us friends. We are going to the monastery, where we shall
meet the Keeper, and my wife, and many of Kharnabhar's dignitaries."

He talked animatedly and Luterin did not listen, concentrating on the
exacting performance of descending a flight of stairs. Only as they went

through the front door and a sleigh drew up for them, did the Master say sharply, "You've no weapon on you?"

When Luterin shook his head, they climbed into the sleigh, and slaves bundled furs round them. They set off into the gale among cliffs of snow.

When they turned north, the wind bit into their faces. To the twenty degrees of frost, a considerable chill factor had to be added.

But the sky was clear and, as they drove through the shuttered village, a great irregular mass appeared through its veils to loom over Mount Kharnabhar.

"Shivenink, the third highest peak on the planet," said Asperamanka, pointing it out. "What a place!" He made a moue of distaste.

Just for a minute the mountain's naked ribbed walls were visible; then it was gone again, the ghost that dominated the village.

The passengers were driven up a winding track to the gates of Bambekk Monastery. They entered and dismounted. Slaves assisted them into the vaulted halls, where a number of official-looking people had already gathered.

At a sign, they proceeded up several staircases. Luterin took no interest in their progress. He was listening to a rumble far below, which carried through the monastery. Obsessively, he tried to imagine every corner of his cell, every scratch on its enclosing walls.

The party came at last to a hall high in the monastery. It was circular in shape. Two carpets covered the floor, one white, one black. They were separated by an iron band which ran across the floor, dividing the chamber in half. Biogas shed a dim light. There was one window, facing south, but it was covered by a heavy curtain.

Embroidered on the curtain was a representation of the Great Wheel being rowed across the heavens, each oarsman sitting in a small cell in its perimeter, wearing cerulean garments, each smiling blissfully.

Now at last I understand those blissful smiles, thought Luterin.

A group of musicians was playing solemn and harmonious music at the far side of the room. Lackeys with trays were dispensing drinks to all and sundry.

Keeper of the Wheel Esikananzi appeared, raising his hand graciously in greeting. Smiling, half-bowing to all, he made his portly way towards where the Master of Kharnabhar and Luterin stood.

When they had greeted each other, Esikananzi asked Asperamanka, "Is our friend any more sociable this morning?" On receiving a negative, he said to Luterin, with an attempt at geniality, "Well, the sight you are about to witness may loosen your tongue."

The two men became surrounded by hangers-on, and Luterin gradually edged his way out of the centre of the group. A hand touched his sleeve. He turned to meet the scrutiny of a pair of wide eyes. A thin woman of guarded mien had approached, to observe him with a look of real or feigned astonishment. She was dressed in a sober russet gown, the hem of which touched the floor, the collar of which rioted in lace. Although she was near middle age and her face was gaunter than in bygone times, Luterin recognised her immediately.

He uttered her name.

Insil nodded as if her suspicions were confirmed and said, "They claimed that you were being difficult and refusing to recognise people. What a habit this lying is! And you, Luterin, how unpleasant to be recalled from the dead to mingle with the same mendacious crowd— older, greedier . . . more frightened. How do I appear to you, Luterin?"

In truth, he found her voice harsh and her mouth grim. He was surprised by the amount of jewellery she wore, in her ears, on her arms, on her fingers.

What most impressed him were her eyes. They had changed. The pupils seemed enormous—a sign of her attention, he believed. He could not see the whites in her eyes and thought, admiringly, Those irises show the depth of Insil's soul.

But he said tenderly, "Two profiles in search of a face?"

"I'd forgotten that. Existence in Kharnabhar has grown narrower over the years—dirtier, grimmer, more artificial. As might be expected. Everything narrows. Souls included." She rubbed her hands together in a gesture he did not recall.

"You still survive, Insil. You are more beautiful than I remembered." He forced the insincerity from him, conscious of pressures on him to be a social being again. While it remained difficult to enter into a conversation, he was aware of old reflexes awakening—including his habit of being polite to women.

"Don't lie to me, Luterin. The Wheel is supposed to turn men into saints, isn't it? Notice I refrain from asking you about *that* experience."

"And you never married, Sil?"

Her glare intensified. She lowered her voice to say with venom, "Of course I am married, you fool! The Esikananzis treat their slaves better than their spinsters. What woman could survive in this heap without selling herself off to the highest bidder?"

She stamped her foot. "We had our discussion of that glorious topic when you were one of the candidates."

The dialogue was running too fast for him. "Selling yourself off, Sil! What do you intend to mean?"

"You put yourself completely out of the running when you stuck your knife into that pa you so revered. . . . Not that I blame you, seeing that he killed the man who took away my cherished virginity—your brother Favin."

Her words, delivered with a false brightness as she smiled at those around them, opened up an ancient wound in Luterin. As so often during his incarceration in the Wheel, he thought of the waterfall and his brother's death. Always there remained the question of why Favin, a promising young army officer, should have made the fatal jump; the words of his father's gossie on that subject had never satisfied him. Always he had shied away from a possible answer.

Not caring who was looking on among the pale-lipped crowd, he grasped Insil's arm. "What are you saying about Favin? It's known that he committed suicide."

She pulled away angrily, saying, "For Azoiaxic's sake, do not touch me. My husband is here, and watching. There can be nothing between us now, Luterin. Go away! It hurts to look at you."

He stared about, his gaze darting over the crowd. Halfway across the chamber, a pair of eyes set in a long face regarded him in open hostility.

He dropped his glass. "Oh, Beholder . . . not Asperamanka, that opportunist!" The red liquid soaked into the white carpet.

As she waved to Asperamanka, she said, "We're a good match, the Master and I. He wanted to marry into a proud family. I wanted to survive. We make each other equally happy." When Asperamanka turned with a sign back to his colleagues, she said in venomous tones, "All these leather-clad men going off with their animals into the forests . . . why do they so love each other's stink? Close under the trees, doing secret things, blood brothers. Your father, my father, Asperamanka . . . Favin was not like that."

"I'm glad if you loved him. Can't we escape from these others and talk?"

She deflected his offer of consolation. "What misery that brief happiness inherited . . . Favin was not one to ride into the caspiarns with his heavy males. He rode there with me."

"You say my father killed him. Are you drunk?" There was something like madness in her manner. To be with her, to enter into these ancient agonies—it was as if time stopped. It was as if a fusty old drawer was being unlocked; its banal contents had become hallowed by their secret nature.

Insil scarcely bothered to shake her head. "Favin had everything to live for . . . me, for instance."

"Not so loud!"

"Favin!" she shouted, so that heads turned in her direction. She began to pace through the crowd, and Luterin followed. "Favin discovered that your father's 'hunts' were really journeys to Askitosh and that he was the Oligarch. Favin was all integrity. He challenged your father. Your father shot him down and threw him over the cliff by the waterfall."

They were interrupted by officious women acting hostess, and separated. Luterin accepted another glass of yadahl, but had to set it down, so violently was his hand shaking. In a moment, he found his chance to speak to Insil again, breaking in on an ecclesiastic who was addressing her.

"Insil—this terrible knowledge! How did you discover about my father and Favin? Were you there? Are you lying?"

"Of course not. I found out later—when you were in your fit of prostration—by my customary method, eavesdropping. My father knew everything. He was *glad*—because Favin's death punished me. . . . I could not believe I had heard aright. When he was telling my mother she was *laughing*. I doubted my senses. Unlike you, however, I did not fall into a year-long swoon."

"And I suspected nothing . . . I was fatally innocent."

She gave him one of her supercilious looks. Her irises appeared larger than ever.

"And you still are fatally innocent. Oh, I can tell . . ."

"Insil, resist the temptation to make everyone your enemy!"

But her look hardened and she burst out again. "You were never any help to me. My belief is that children always know intuitively the real natures of their parents, rather than the dissembled ones which they show the world. You knew your father's nature intuitively, and feigned dead to avoid his vengeance. But I am the truly dead."

Asperamanka was approaching. "Meet me in the corridor in five minutes," she said hastily, as she turned, smiling and gaily raising a hand.

Luterin moved away. He leaned against a wall, struggling with his feelings. "Oh, Beholder . . ." he groaned.

"I expect you find the crowds overpowering after your solitude," someone who passed by said pleasantly.

His whole inner life was undergoing revolution. Things had not been, he had not been, as he had pretended to himself. Even his gallantry on the field of battle—had that not been powered by ancient angers released, rather than by courage? Were all battles releases from frustration, rather than deeds of deliberate violence? He saw he knew nothing. Nothing. He had clung to innocence, fearing knowledge.

Now he remembered that he had experienced the actual moment when his brother died. He and Favin had been close. He had felt the psychic shock of Favin's death one evening: yet his father had announced the death as occurring on the following day. That tiny discrepancy had lodged in his young consciousness, poisoning it. Eventually—he could foresee—joy could come that he was delivered from that poison. But delivery was not yet.

His limbs trembled.

In the turmoil of his thoughts, he had almost forgotten Insil. He feared for her in her strange mood. Now he hurried towards the corridor she had indicated—reluctant though he was to hear more from her.

His way was barred by bedizened dignitaries, who spoke to him and to each other roundly of the solemnity of this occasion, and of how much more appalling conditions would be henceforth. As they talked, they devoured little meat-filled pastries in the shape of birds. It occurred to Luterin that he neither knew nor cared about the ceremony in which he had become involved.

Their conversation paused as all eyes focussed on the other side of the chamber.

Ebstok Esikananzi and Asperamanka were leaving by a spiral stair which wound to an upper gallery.

Luterin took the opportunity to slip into the corridor. Insil joined him in a minute, her narrow body leaning forward in the haste of her walk. She held her skirt up from the floor in one pale hand, her jewellery glittering like frost.

"I must be brief," she said, without introduction. "They watch me continually, except when they are in drink, or holding their ridiculous ceremonies—as now. Who cares if the world is plunged into darkness? Listen, when we are free to leave here, you must proceed to the fish seller in the village. It stands at the far end of Sanctity Street. Understand? Tell no one. 'Chastity's for women, secrecy's for men,' as they say. Be secret."

"What then, Insil?" Again he was asking her questions.

"My dear father and my dear husband plan to kick you out. They will not kill you, as I understand—that might look bad for them, and that much they owe you for your timely disposal of the Oligarch. Simply evade them after the ceremony and go down Sanctity Street."

He stared impatiently into her hypnotic eyes.

"And this secret meeting—what is it about?"

"I am playing the role of messenger, Luterin. You still remember the name of Toress Lahl, I suppose?"

XVII

SUNSET

Trockern and Ermine were asleep. Shoyshal had gone somewhere. The geonaut they preceded had come to a halt, and stood gently breathing out its little white hexagonal offspring.

SartoriIrvrash woke and stretched, yawning as he did so. He sat up on his bunk and scratched his white head. It was his habit to sleep for the second half of the day, waking at midnight, thinking through the dark hours, when his spirit could commune with the travelling Earth, and teaching from dawn onwards. He was Trockern's teacher. He had named himself after a dangerous old sage who once lived on Helliconia, whose gossie he had met empathically.

After a while, he heaved himself up and went outside. He stood for a long while looking at the stars, enjoying the feel of the night. Then he padded back into the room and roused Trockern.

"I'm asleep," Trockern said.

"I could hardly waken you if you weren't."

"Zzzz."

"You stole something of mine, Trockern. You stole my explanation of why things went awry on Earth, in order to impress your ladies."

"As you see, I impressed fifty percent of them." Trockern indicated

*the peacefully sleeping Ermine, whose lips were pursed as if she was
awaiting the chance to kiss someone in her midsummer dream.*

"Unfortunately you got my argument wrong. That possessiveness
which was once such a feature of mankind was not a product of fear,
as you claimed—although I believe you called it 'perpetual unease.' It
was a product of innate aggressiveness. The old races did not fear
enough: otherwise they would never have built the weapons they knew
would destroy them. Aggression was at the root of it all."

"Isn't aggression born of fear?"

"Don't get sophisticated before you can walk. If you take Helliconia
as an example, you can see how every generation ritualises its aggression
and its killing. The earlier terrestrial generations you were talking about
did not seek to possess only territory and one another, as you were
claiming."

"In truth, SartoriIrvrash, you cannot have slept well this afternoon."

"In truth I sleep, as I wake in truth." He put an arm about the
younger man's shoulders. "The argument can be taken to greater heights.
Those ancient people sought to possess the Earth also, to enslave it
under concrete. Nor did their ambitions die there. Their politicians
strove to make space their dominion; while the ordinary people created
fantasies wherein they invaded the galaxy and ruled the universe. That
was aggression, not fear."

"You could be right."

"Don't abandon your point of view so easily. If I could be right I
could be wrong. We ought to know the truth about our forebears who,
wicked though they were, have given us our chance on the scene."

Trockern climbed from his bunk. Ermine sighed and turned over,
still sleeping.

"It's warm—let's take a stroll outside," said SartoriIrvrash.

As they went out into the night, with the star field above them,
Trockern said, "Do you think we improve ourselves, master, by rethinking?"

"We shall always be as we are, biologically speaking, but we can
improve our social infrastructures, with any luck. I mean by that the
sort of work our extitutions are working on now—a revolutionary new
integration of the major theorems of physical science with the sciences
of mankind, society, and existence. Of course, our main function as
biological beings is as part of the biosphere, and we are most useful in
that role if we remain unaltered; only if the biosphere in some way
altered again could our role change."

"But the biosphere is altering all the time. Summer is different from
winter, even here so close to the tropics."

SartoriIrvrash was looking towards the horizon, and said, rather absently, "Summer and winter are functions of a stable biosphere, of Gaia
breathing in and out in her stride. Humanity has to operate within the

limits of her function. To the aggressive, that always seemed a pessi-
mistic point of view; yet it is not even visionary, merely common-
sensical. It fails to be common sense only if you have been indoctrinated
all your life to believe, first, that mankind is the centre of things, the
Lords of Creation, and, second, that we can improve our lot at the
expense of something else.

"Such an outlook brings misery, as we see on our poor sister planet
out there. We have only to step down from the arrogance of believing
that the world or the future is somehow 'ours' and immediately life
for everyone is enhanced."

Trockern said, "I suppose each of us has to find that out for our-
self." He found it delightful to be humble after sunset.

With sudden exasperation, SartoriIrvrash said, "Yes, unfortunately
that's so. We have to learn by bitter experience, not blithe example.
And that's ridiculous. Don't imagine that I think the state of affairs is
perfect. Gaia is an absolute ninny to let us loose in the first place. At
least on Helliconia the Original Beholder planted phagors to keep mankind in check!" He laughed and Tockern joined in.

"I know you think me wanton," the latter said, "but isn't Gaia herself a wanton, spawning so riotously in all directions?"

His senior shot him a foxy look. "Everything else must bring forth
in abundance, so that everything else can eat it. It's not the best of
arrangements, perhaps—cooked up and cobbled together on the spur
of the moment from a chemical broth. That doesn't mean to say we
can't imitate Gaia and adopt, like her, our own homeostasis."

The moon in its last quarter shone overhead. SartoriIrvrash pointed
to the red star burning low by the horizon.

"See Antares? Just north of it is the constellation Ophiuchus, the
Serpent Bearer. In Ophiuchus is a large dark dust cloud about seven
hundred light-years away, concealing a cluster of young stars. Among
them lies Freyr. It would be one of the twelve brightest stars in the sky,
were it not for the dust cloud. And that's where the phagors are."

The two men contemplated the distance without speaking. Then
Trockern said, "Have you ever thought, master, how phagors vaguely
resemble the demons and devils which used to haunt the imagination
of Christians?"

"That had not occurred to me. I have always thought of an even
older allusion, the minotaur of ancient Greek myth, a creature stuck
between human and animal, lost in the labyrinths of its own lusts."

"Presumably you think that the Helliconian humans should allow the
phagors to coexist, to maintain the biospheric balance?"

" 'Presumably . . .' We presume so much." A long silence followed.
Then SartoriIrvrash said, reluctantly, "With the deepest respect to
Gaia and her Serpent-Bearing sister out there, they are old biddies at

*times. Mankind learnt aggression in their wombs. I mean, to use an-
other ancient analogy, humans and phagors are rather Cain and Abel,
aren't they? One or other of them has to go . . ."*

Trumpets sounded above the heads of the gathering. Their voices
were muted and sweet, and in no way reminiscent of those work trumpets buried far below their feet—except to Luterin Shokerandit.

The dignitaries in the great chamber swallowed their last bird-shaped
pastries and put on reverential faces. Luterin moved among them feeling cumbersome among so many ectomorphic shapes. He lost sight of
Insil.

The Keeper and the Master, Insil's father and husband, were returning down the spiral stair. They had assumed silken robes of car-
mine and blue over their ordinary clothes, and put on odd-shaped hats.
Their faces were as if cast from an alloy of lead and flesh.

Side by side, they paraded to the curtained windows. There they
turned and bowed to the assembly. The assembly fell silent, the
musicians tiptoed away over creaking boards.

Keeper Esikananzi spoke first.

"You all know of the reasons why Bambekk Monastery was built,
many centuries ago. It was built to service the Wheel—and of course
you know why the Architects built the Wheel. We stand on the site of
the greatest act of faith ever achieved/to be by mankind. But perhaps
you will/permissive allow me to remind you why this particular position
was chosen by our illustrious ancestors, in what some people regard as
a remote part of the Sibornalese continent.

"Let me draw your attention to the iron band running under your
feet which divides this dome in half. That band marks the line of
latitude on which this edifice is built. We are here fifty-five degrees
north of the equator, and standing upon that actual line. As you scarcely
need reminding, fifty-five degrees north is the line of the Polar Circle."

At this point, he gestured to a servant. The curtains concealing the
windows were drawn apart.

A view over the town was revealed, looking south. The visibility was
good enough for everything to be seen clearly, including the far horizon,
bare except for a thin line of denniss trees.

"We are fortunate on this occasion. The cloud has cleared. We are
privileged to witness a solemn event which the rest of Sibornal will be
commemorating."

At this point, Master Asperamanka stood forward and spoke, stiffening his speech with High Dialect. "Let me echo my good friend and
colleague's word, 'fortunate.' Fortunate we are/tend indeed. Church
and State have kept/keeping/will the people of Sibornal united. The

plague has been/aspirational eradicated, and we have slain most of the phagors on our continent.

"You know that our ships have mastery of the seas. In addition, we are now/will building a Great Wall to serve as an act of faith comparable with our formidable Great Wheel.

"This is/proclamatory a New Great Age. The Great Wall will run right across the north of Chalce. There will be watchtowers on it every two kilometres, and the walls will be seven metres high. That Wall, together with our ships, will keep/keeping out all enemies from our territory. The Day of Myrkwyr is the harbinger of Weyr-Winter ahead, but we shall live through it, our grandchildren will live through it, and their grandchildren. And we shall emerge in the spring, the next Great Spring, ready to conquer all of Helliconia."

Cheers and handclaps had sounded throughout this speech. Now the applause was clamorous. Asperamanka stared down to hide the gleam of satisfaction on his face.

Ebstok Esikananzi raised a hand.

"Friends, it is five to noon on this solemn day. Watch the southern horizon. Since it is small winter, Batalix is below that horizon. She will rise again with her puny light in another four tenners, but—"

His words were lost, as everyone pressed to the windows.

Down in the village below, a bonfire had just been lit. The villagers were seen as ants, running about it, arms upraised, swaddled in woollens or furs.

Fresh drink was brought to the watchers in the dome. Mostly, it was drunk as soon as received, and the empty glasses thrust out for more. An unease had settled on the privileged crowd, whose faces made a gloomy contrast to the merry gestures of the ants far below.

A bell began to sound noon. As if in response to its brazen tongue, a change took place on the southern horizon.

On that horizon, the road could be seen as it wound from the village. Elsewhere was unbroken white, trees and buildings standing in frosty outline. Wisps of snow perpetually blew from lodgements, streaming out on the wind like smoke from candles newly extinguished. The horizon itself was clear, and bright with dawn—with sunrise.

Above its crusty line rose a rim of red, a red of heaviness, of congealing blood, the upper part of Freyr's orb.

"Freyr!" came the exclamation from the throats of all who watched, as if by naming the star they could have power over it.

A shaft of light spread upon the world, casting shadows, flooding a range of far hills with pink light till they gleamed against the slatey sky behind them. The faces of the privileged in the dome were made red. Only the village below, where the ants were circling, remained in shadow.

The privileged glared upon that sliver of disc. It remained as it was, growing no greater. The most intense scrutiny could not determine the instant at which, instead of increasing, it began to shrink. Sunrise was enantiodromic sunset.

Light was withdrawn from the world. The range of far hills faded, was absorbed into the increasing murk.

The precious slice of Freyr shrivelled still further. By now, the giant sun had in actuality set: what remained behind was an image of it, a refraction through the thickness of atmosphere of the real thing below the horizon. None could tell the image from the real. Myrkwyr had already begun, without their knowing it.

The red image shrivelled.

It divided itself into bars of light. Shattered.

Then it was gone.

In the centuries ahead, Freyr would hide like a mole beneath the mountain, never to be seen again. In the small summers, Batalix would shine as previously; the small winters would remain unlit, under the shadow of the greater winter. Auroras would unfold their mysterious banners in the skies above the mountain. Meteorites would briefly glitter. Comets would occasionally be sighted. The stars would still shine. Throughout the next ninety revolutions of the Great Wheel, the major luminary, that massive furnace which had given life to the Sons of Freyr, would be little more than a rumour.

For all who experienced it, Myrkwyr was a day of doom. The faceless deity who presided over the biosphere was powerless to intervene, relying perhaps on the shortsightedness of the humans, on their involvement in their own affairs, to damp down its psychic shock. She was carried along with her world. Seen in wider perspective, Freyr continued to shine, and ever would do until its comparatively brief lifespan was finished: its darkness was merely a local condition, of small duration.

For most of nature, there could be only submission to fate. On land, the sap, the seed, the semen, would wait, dormant for the most part. In the sea, the complex mechanisms of the food chain would continue unabated. Only mankind could lift itself above direct necessity. In mankind lay reserves of strength unknowable to those who held them, reserves which could be drawn upon in situations where survival demanded.

Such reflections were far from the minds of those in the assembly who watched Freyr shatter into fragments of light. They were touched by fear. They wondered for their family's survival and their own. The most basic question of existence faced them: How am I to keep fed and warm?

Fear is a powerful emotion. Yet it is easily overcome by anger, hope, desperation, and defiance. Fear would not last. The great processes of the Helliconian year would grind on towards apastron and the winter solstice. That turning point of the year was many generations away. By

then, the twilights of Weyr-Winter would have long since become all
that northern Sibornal knew. The rise of Freyr once more, majestic in
the Great Spring, would be greeted with the same awe as its departure.
But fear would have died long before hope.

How mankind would survive the centuries of Weyr-Winter would
depend upon its mental and emotional resources. The cycle of human
history was not immutable. Given determination, better could succeed
worse; it was possible to row into the light, to navigate in the tide of
Myrkwyr.

Keeper Esikananzi said solemnly, "The long night holds no fear for
those who trust in the Lord God the Azoiaxic, who existed before life,
and round whom all life revolves. With his aid, we shall bring this
precious world of ours through the long night, to bask again in his
glory." And Master Asperamanka shouted spiritedly, "To Sibornal—
united throughout the long Weyr-Winter to come!"

Their audience responded bravely. But in every heart lay the knowledge that they would never see Freyr again; nor would their children,
nor their children's children. On the latitude of Kharnabhar the brighter
sun of Freyr would never shine in the sky until another forty-two
generations had been born and died. Nobody present could ever hope
to see that brilliant luminary again.

A choir sang distantly the anthem, "Oh, May We All Find Light at
Last." Gloom settled in every heart. The loss was as sharp as the loss of
a child.

The lackey solemnly drew the curtains again, hiding the landscape
from view.

Many in the assembly stayed to drink more yadahl. They had little
to say to each other. The musicians played, but a mood of sullen
resignation had settled which would not be dispelled. Singly or in
groups, the guests were leaving. They evaded each other's gaze.

Stone steps wound down through the monastery to the entrance. A
carpet had been laid on the stairs in honour of the occasion. Cold drafts,
blowing upwards, lifted the edges of the carpet. As Luterin was descending, two men emerged from an archway on a landing and seized him.

He fought and shouted, but they locked his arms behind him and
carried him into a stone washroom. Asperamanka was waiting there.
He had divested himself of his ceremonial robes, and was putting on a
coat and leather gauntlets. His two men wore leather and carried guns
at their belts. Luterin thought of what Insil had said: "All those leather-
clad men . . . doing secret things."

Asperamanka put on a genial tone. "It isn't going to work, is it,
Luterin? We can't have you going free in a tight-knit community like
Kharnabhar. You'll be too disruptive an influence."

"What are you trying to preserve here—apart from yourself?"

"I wish to preserve my wife's honour for one thing. You seem to think there is evil here. The fact is, we have to fight to survive. The good—and the bad—will naturally survive in us. Most people understand that. You don't.

"You are inclined to play the part of a holy innocent, and they always make trouble. So we are going to give you a chance to help the whole community. Helliconia needs to be hauled back into the light. You are going to go into the Wheel for another ten-year spell."

He fought free and ran for the door. One of the huntsmen reached it in time to slam it in his face. He struck the man on the jaw, but was made captive again.

"Tie him," Asperamanka ordered. "Don't let him go again."

The men had no cord. One reluctantly yielded up the broad belt of his jacket, and with that they lashed Luterin's hands behind his back.

When Asperamanka opened the door, they marched down the rest of the stairs, the men flanking Luterin closely. Asperamanka seemed greatly pleased with himself.

"We said farewell to Freyr with courage and ceremony. Admire power, Luterin. I admired your father for his ruthlessness as Oligarch. What a fateful generation ours is. Either we'll be wiped out or we'll decide the course of the world. . . ."

"Or you'll choke on a fish bone," Luterin said.

They descended to the entrance hall. Through the broad archway, the outer world could be seen. The chill came in, and also the noise of the crowd and the bonfire. The simple people were dancing round the fires they had lit, faces gleaming in the light of the flames. Traders scurried about, selling waffles and spitted fish.

"For all their religion, they believe that lighting fires may bring Freyr back," Asperamanka said. He lingered at the entrance. "What they are really doing is ensuring that wood becomes short before it need be. . . . Well, let them get on with it. Let them go into pauk or do whatever they please. The elite is going to have to survive on the backs of just such peasants as these for the next few centuries or more."

There was shouting and a stir from the back of the crowd. Soldiers came into view as the crowd parted to make way for them. They carried something struggling between them.

"Ah, they've caught another phagor. Good. We'll see this," Asperamanka said, with a hint of ancient angers under his brows.

The phagor was lashed upside down to a pole. It struggled violently as its captors brought it to one of the fires.

Behind came a figure of a man, lifting his arms and shouting. Luterin could not hear what he said for the general hubbub, but he recognised him by his long beard. The man was his old schoolmaster, who had taught him—long ago in another existence—when he was lying paralysed in bed. The old man had kept a phagor as servant, being too poor to afford a slave. It was clearly his phagor which the soldiers had captured.

The soldiers dragged the creature nearer to the fire. The crowd ceased its dancing and shouted with excitement, the women egging the soldiers on along with the men.

"Burn it!" shouted Asperamanka, but he merely echoed the voice of the mob.

"It's just a domestic," Luterin said. "Harmless as a dog."

"It's still capable of spreading the Fat Death."

Fight though it would, the ancipital was pulled and pushed to the largest of the fires. Its coat began to burn. Another inch—a yell from the crowd—a heave—and then a mournful call sounded from beyond the gathering. Distant human screams. Into the marketplace poured armed ancipitals on kaidaws.

Each ancipital wore body armour. Some wore primitive skull shields. They rode their red kaidaws from a position behind the animals' low humps, at the crouch. In this position they could strike out with spears as they went.

"Freyr die! Sons of Freyr die!" they cried from their harsh throats.

The crowd began to move, less as separate individuals than as a wave. Only the soldiers made a stand. The captive phagor was left with its pale harneys boiling in its skull, but it rose up and made off, coat still smouldering.

Asperamanka ran forward, shouting to the soldiers to fire. Luterin, as an observer, could see that there were no more than eight of the invaders. Some of them sprouted black hairs, a mark of ancipital old age. All but one had been dehorned—a sure sign that these were no kind of threat from the mountains, such as tremulous imaginations in Kharnabhar fed on, but a few refugee phagors who had banded together on this special day, when conditions in Sibornal reverted to virtually what they had been before Freyr entered Helliconia's sky, many epochs ago.

He saw how members of the crowd who were impeded in some way fell first to the stabbing spears: pedlars with trays, women with babies or small children, the lame, the sick. Some were trampled underfoot. A baby was scooped up and flung into the heart of a fire.

As Asperamanka and his two bullies drew guns and started firing, the horned ancipital wheeled its russet-haired mount and charged at the Master. It came straight, its skull low over the massive skull of the kaidaw. In its eye was no light of battle, simply a dull cerise stare: it was doing what it did according to some ancient template set in its eotemporal brain.

Asperamanka fired. The bullets lost themselves in the thick pelage of animal. It faltered in mid-stride. The two bullies turned and ran. Asperamanka stood his ground, firing, shouting. The kaidaw fell suddenly on one knee. Up came the spear. It caught Asperamanka as he turned. The tip entered his skull through the eye socket and he fell back into the monastery entrance.

Luterin ran for his life. He had wrenched his arms free of the belt. He jumped down into the street, into the trampled snow, and ran. There were other running figures nearby, too concerned with saving their own lives to bother with his. He hid behind a house, panting, and surveyed the scene.

Blue shadows and bodies lay on the marketplace. The sky overhead was a deep blue, in which a bright star gleamed—Aganip. Hues of sunset lay to the south. It was bitterly cold.

The mob had surrounded one kaidaw and was pulling its rider to the ground. The others were galloping off to safety—another sign that this was not an arm of a regular ancipital component, which would not have abandoned a fight so easily.

He made his way without trouble towards Sanctity Street and his appointment with Toress Lahl.

Sanctity Street was narrow. Its buildings were tall. Most had been constructed in a better age to house the pilgrims who came to visit the Wheel. Now the shutters were up; many doors were barricaded. Slogans had been painted on the walls: God Keep the Keeper, We Follow the Oligarch—presumably as a form of life insurance. At the rear of the houses and hostels, the snow was piled up to the eaves.

Luterin started cautiously down the street. His mood was one of elation at his escape. He could see beyond the end of the street, where it seemed eternity began. There was an unlimited expanse of snow, its dimensions emphasised by occasional trees. In the distance stretched a band of pink of the most delicate kind, where the sun Freyr still lit on a far cliff, the southern face of the northern ice cap. This vista lifted his spirits further, suggesting as it did the endless possibilities of the planet, beyond the reach of human pettiness. Despite all oppression, the great world remained, inexhaustible in its forms and lights. He might be gazing upon the face of the Beholder herself.

He passed an entranceway where a figure lurked. It called his name. He turned. Through the dusk, he saw a woman wrapped in furs.

"You are almost there. Aren't you excited?" she said.

He went to her, clutched her, felt her narrow body under the furs. "Insil! You waited."

"Only partly for you. The fish seller has something I need. I am sick after that performance in there, with the silly drama and speeches. They think they have conquered nature when they wrap a few words round it. And of course my sherb of a husband mouthing the word Sibornal as if it were a mouthwash . . . I'm sick, I need to drug myself against them. What is that filthy curse which the commoners use, meaning to commit irrumation on both suns? The forbidden oath? Tell me."

"You mean, 'Abro Hakmo Astab'?"

She repeated it with relish. Then she screamed it.

Hearing her say it excited him. He held her tight and forced his mouth against hers. They struggled. He heard his own voice saying, "Let me biwack you here, Insil, as I've always longed to do. You're not really frigid. I know it. You're really a whore, just a whore, and I want you."

"You're drunk, get away, get away. Toress Lahl is awaiting you."

"I care nothing for her. You and I are meant for each other. That's been the case ever since we were children. Let's fulfill ourselves. You once promised me. Now's the time, Insil, now!"

Her great eyes were close to his.

"You frighten me. What's come over you? Let me be."

"No, no, I don't have to let you be now. Insil—Asperamanka is dead. The phagors killed him. We can be married now, anything, only let me have you, please, please!"

She wrenched herself away from him.

"He's dead? Dead? No. It can't be. Oh, the cur!" She started screaming and ran down the street, holding up her trailing skirt above the trodden snow.

Luterin followed in horror at her distress.

He tried to detain her but she said something which he at first could not understand. She was crying for a pipe of occhara.

The fish seller was, as she had said, at the end of the street. A short passage had been constructed beyond the original shop front, allowing passengers to enter without bringing the cold in with them. Above the door was a sign saying ODIM'S FINEST FISH.

They entered a dim parlour where several men stood, warmly wrapped, all of them metamorphosed winter shapes. Seals and large fish hung on hooks. Smaller fish, crabs, and eels were bedded in ice on a counter. Luterin took little notice of his surroundings, so concerned was he for Insil, who was now almost hysterical.

But the men recognized her. "We know what she wants," one said, grinning. He led her into a rear room.

One of the other men came forward and said, "I remember you, sir."

He was youthful and had a vaguely foreign look about him.

"My name is Kenigg Odim," he said. "I sailed with you on that journey from Koriantura to Rivenjk. I was just a lad then, but you may recollect my father, Eedap Odim."

"Of course, of course," said Luterin distractedly. "A dealer in something. Ivory, was it?"

"Porcelain, sir. My father still lives in Rivenjk, and organises supplies of good fish to come up here every week. It's a paying business, and there's no demand for porcelain these days. Life's better down in Rivenjk, sir, I must say. Fine feelings is about as much good as fine porcelain up here."

"Yes, yes, I'm sure that's so."

"We also do a trade in occhara, sir, if you would care for a free pipe. Your lady friend is a regular customer."

"Yes, bring me a pipe, man, thank you, and what of a lady called Toress Lahl? Is she here?"

"She's expected."

"All right." He went through into the rear room. Insil Esikananzi was resting on a couch, smoking a long-stemmed pipe. She looked perfectly calm, and regarded Luterin without speaking.

He sat by her without a word, and presently the young Odim brought him a lighted pipe. He inhaled with pleasure and immediately felt a mood strangely compounded of resignation and determination steal over him. He felt he was equal to anything. He understood now Insil's expanded irises, and held her hand.

"My husband is dead," she announced. "Did you know that? Did I tell you what he did to me on our wedding night?"

"Insil, I've had enough confidences from you for one day. That episode in your life is over. We are still young. We can marry, can make one another happy or miserable, as the case may be."

Wreathing herself in smoke, she said from the centre of it, "You are a fugitive. I need a home. I need care. I no longer need love. What I need is occhara. I want someone who can protect me. I want you to get Asperamanka back."

"That's impossible. He's dead."

"If you find it impossible, Luterin, then please be quiet and leave me to my thoughts. I am a widow. Widows never last long in winter. . . ."

He sat by her, sucking on the occhara, letting his thoughts die.

"If you could also kill my father, the Keeper, this remote community could revert to nature. The Wheel would stop. The plague could come and go. The survivors would see the Weyr-Winter through."

"There will always be survivors. It's a law of nature."

"My husband showed me the laws of nature, thank you. I do not wish for another husband."

They fell silent. Young Odim entered and announced to Luterin that Toress Lahl awaited him in an upper room. He cursed and stumbled after the man up a rickety stair without a backward look at Insil, certain that she would remain where she was for some while.

Luterin was shown into a small cabin, before which a curtain did duty for a door. Inside, a bed served as the only furniture. Beside the bed stood Toress Lahl. He was astonished at her girth until he remembered that he was much the same size.

She had certainly grown older. There was grey in her hair, although she still dressed it as she had done ten years ago. Her cheeks were rough and florid with the abrasion of frost. Her eyes were heavier, although they lit as she smiled with recognition. In every way, she seemed unlike Insil, not least in the kind of calm stoicism with which she presented herself for his inspection.

She wore boots. Her dress was poor and patched. Unexpectedly, she removed her fur hat—whether in welcome or respect he could not tell.

He took a step towards her. She immediately came forward and embraced him, kissing him on both cheeks.

"Are you well?" he asked.

"I saw you yesterday. I was waiting outside the Wheel when they let you free. I called to you but you did not look my way."

"It was so bright." Still confused by the occhara, he could think of nothing to say. He wanted her to make jokes like Insil. When she did not, he asked, "Do you know Insil Esikananzi?"

"She has become a good friend of mine. We've supported each other in many ways. The years have been long, Luterin . . . What plans do you have?"

"Plans? The sun's gone down."

"For the future."

"This innocent is again a fugitive. . . . They may even try to blame me for Asperamanka's death." He sat down heavily on the bed.

"That man is dead? It's a mercy. . . ." She thought and then said, "If you can trust me, Luterin, I could take you to my little hideout."

"I would only be a source of danger."

"That's not what our relationship is based on. I'm still yours, Luterin, if you will have me." When he hesitated, she said pleadingly, "I need you, Luterin. You loved me once, I believe. What choices do you have here, surrounded by enemies?"

"There's always defiance," he said. He laughed.

They went down the narrow stairs together, taking care in the dark. At the bottom, Luterin looked into the rear room. To his surprise, the couch was empty and Insil had gone.

They bid good-bye to young Odim and made their way into the night.

In the gathering darkness, the Avernus passed overhead, making its swift transit of the sky. It was now a dead eye.

At last the splendid machine had run down. Its surveillance system was only partly functional. Many other systems—but not the vital ones—were still operational. Air still circulated. Cleaning machines still crawled through walkways. Here and there, computers still exchanged information. Coffee machines still regularly brought coffee to the boil.

Stabilisers kept the Earth Observation Station automatically on course. In the port departure lounge, a toilet regularly flushed itself, like a creature unable to suppress weeping fits.

But no signals were returning to Earth.

And Earth no longer had need of them, although there were many who regretted the termination of that unfolding story from another world. For Earth was moving beyond its compulsive stage, where civilisation was measured by the quantity of possessions, into a new phase of being where the magic of individual experience was to be shared, not stored; awarded, not hoarded. The human character became involuntarily more like that of Gaia herself: diffuse, ever changing, ever open to the adventures of the day.

As they went through the dusk, leaving the village behind them, Toress Lahl tried to talk of superficial things. Snow fell, blowing in from the north.

Luterin did not reply. After a silence, she told him how she had borne him a son, now almost ten years old, and offered Luterin anecdotes about him.

"I wonder if he will grow up to kill his father," was all Luterin said.

"He is metamorphosed, as we are. A true son, Luterin. So he will survive and breed survivors, we hope."

He trudged behind her, still with nothing to say. They passed a deserted hut and were heading for a belt of trees. He glanced back now and again.

She was following her own train of thought. "Still your hated Oligarchy is killing off all the phagors. If only they understood the real workings of the Fat Death, they would know that they are killing off their own kind too."

"They know well enough what they're doing."

"No, Luterin. You generously gave me the key to JandolAnganol's chapel, and I've lived there ever since. One evening, a knock came at the door and there was Insil Esikananzi."

He looked interested. "How did Insil know you were there?"

"It was an accident. She had run away from Asperamanka. They were then newly married. He had brutally sodomised her, and she was in pain and despair. She remembered the chapel as a refuge—your brother Favin had taken her there once, in happier days. I looked after her and we became close friends."

"Well . . . I'm glad she had a friend."

"I showed her the records left by JandolAnganol and the woman Muntras, with the explanations of how there was a tick which travelled from phagors to mankind carrying the plagues necessary to mankind's survival in the extreme seasons. That knowledge Insil took back with her, to explain to the Keeper and the Master, but they would take no notice."

He gave a curt laugh. "They took no notice because they already knew. They would not want Insil's interference. They run the system, don't they? They *knew*. My father knew. Do you imagine those old church papers were secret? Their knowledge became common knowledge."

The ground sloped. They picked their way more carefully toward where the caspiarn forest began.

Toress Lahl said, "The Oligarch *knew* that killing off all phagors meant ultimately killing the humans—yet still he passed his orders? That's incredible."

"I can't defend what my father did—or Asperamanka. But the knowledge did not suit them. Simply that. They felt they had to act, despite their knowledge."

He caught the scent of the caspiarns, inhaled the slight vinegary tang of their foliage. It came like the memory of another world. He drew it gratefully into his lungs. Toress Lahl had two yelk tethered in the shelter of the trees. She went forward and fondled their muzzles as he spoke.

"My father did not know what would happen if Sibornal was rid of phagors for ever. He just believed that it was something necessary to do, whatever the consequences. We don't know what will happen either, despite what it may say in some fusty old documents. . . ." More to himself, he said, "I think he felt some drastic break with the past was needed, no matter what the cost. An act of defiance, if you like. Perhaps he will one day be proved right. Nature will take care of us. Then they'll make a saint of him, like your wicked saint JandolAnganol.

"An act of defiance . . . that's mankind's nature. It's no good just sitting back and smoking occhara. Otherwise we should never progress. The key to the future must lie with the future, not the past."

The wind was getting up again; the snow came faster.

"Beholder!" she said. She put a hand up to her rough face. "You've grown hard. Are you going to come with me?" she asked.

"I need you," she said, when he did not answer.

He swung himself up into the saddle, relishing the familiarity of the act, and the response of the animal beneath him. He patted the yelk's warm flank.

He was an exile in his own land. That would have to change. Asperamanka was done for. The obscene Ebstok Esikananzi would have to be brought to an accounting. He did not wish for what Esikananzi had; he wanted justice. His face was grim as he gazed down at the yelk's mane.

"Luterin, are you ready? Our son is waiting for us in the chapel."

He stared across at the blur of her face and nodded. Snowflakes settled on his eyelids. As they nudged their mounts down among the trees, a wind cut through the forest, slicing down from the slopes of Mount Shivenink. Snow cascaded across their shoulders from branches overhead. The ground sloped towards the hidden chapel. They wound by what had once been a waterfall and was now a pillar of ice.

At the last moment, Luterin turned in the saddle to catch a last glimpse of the village. The light of its fires was reflected on the low cloud cover blowing in.

Holding the reins more firmly, he urged the yelk faster down the slope and into the thickening murk. The woman called to him with anxiety in her voice, but Luterin felt exhilaration rising in his arteries.

He raised a fist above his head.

"Abro Hakmo Astab!" he shouted, hurling his voice into the distances of the forest.

The wind took the sound and smothered it in the weight of falling snow.

THE END

For the nature of the world as a whole is altered by age. Everything must pass through successive phases. Nothing remains for ever what it was. Everything is on the move. Everything is transformed by nature and forced into new paths. One thing, withered by time, decays and dwindles. Another emerges from ignominy, and waxes strong. So the nature of the world as a whole is altered by age. The Earth passes through successive phases, so that it can no longer bear what it could, and it can now what it could not before.

Lucretius: *De Rerum Natura*
55 BC

My dear Clive,

There you have it. Seven years have passed since I began to consider these matters. This volume will achieve first publication in a year when we both reach a new decade, and when my age will be exactly double yours.

As I walk in Hilary's garden wondering what form of words to use, it occurs to me that the question to ask is, Why do individuals of the human race long for close community with each other, and yet remain so often apart? Could it be that the isolating factor is similar to that which makes us feel, as a species, apart from the rest of nature? Perhaps the Earth mother you meet in these pages has proved less than perfect. Like a real mother, she has had her troubles—on a cosmic scale.

So the fault is not all ours, or hers. We must accept a lack of perfection in the scheme of things, accept the yellow-striped fly. Time, in which the whole drama is staged, is, as J. T. Fraser puts it, "a hierarchy of unresolved conflicts." We must accept that limitation with the equanimity of Lucretius, and be angry only at those things against which one can be effectively angry, like the madness of making and deploying nuclear weapons.

Such matters are not generally the subject of literature. But I felt the necessity, as you see, to have a shot at incorporating them.

Now at last I have done. The rambling edifice of Helliconia is before you, with my hopes that you will enjoy the results.

Your affectionate
Father

Boars Hill
Oxford

APPENDICES

PHAGOR

APPENDIX 1

Cosmological

Star A (later known as Freyr) once had a companion star (Star C).

Eight million years before the narrated events, Star B (later known as Batalix) came within the gravitational field of Star A. In the orbital disturbances which followed, Star C escaped entirely, while Star B was captured. Henceforth, it formed the inferior partner of a binary system. The properties of the binary suns are as follows:

STAR A

Mass	14.8 mass of Sol (Earth's sun)
Luminosity	60,000 × solar luminosity
Temperature	11,000 Kelvin
Radius	65 × radius of Sol or 28,112.500 miles
Spectral class	A type supergiant
Colour	white

Star A is between 10 and 11 million years old. It has evolved away from the main sequence and is already entering old age.

At the time of its capture of Star B, it was less luminous but hotter. So for the first million years or so after capture, the planets of Star B were subjected to far more UV radiation than at present. X-ray and UV radiation resulted in accelerated evolution of present species.

Star A evolved no planetary system. Orbiting stellar debris was drawn into it and consumed.

STAR B

Mass	0.96 × mass of Sol
Luminosity	0.8 × solar luminosity
Temperature	5690 K
Radius	0.94 × solar radius or 406,550 miles
Spectral class	G4
Colour	yellow

Star B has four planets in orbit. They are, working from inner to outer, Copaise, Aganip, HELLICONIA, and Ipocrene.

In the period before Star B's capture, a moon was in orbit about Helliconia which was lost during the disruption of capture.

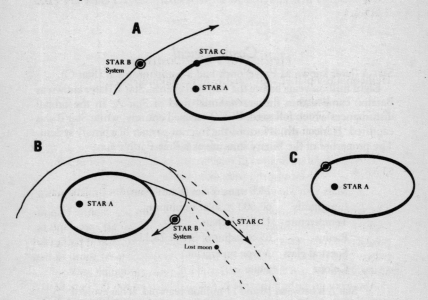

Figure 1. Birth of a new binary system.

A shows the solar system of Star B (Batalix) and its four planets coming close to a binary system consisting of a large A type supergiant star, Star A (Freyr), and its companion, the G type star, Star C. Disturbance begins.

B shows resulting gravitational disruptions, causing Star C to "escape", as the Star B system is drawn into Star A's influence. The moon of one of the planets of Star B (Helliconia) is lost to the system, drifting away in the general direction of Star C.

C shows that now a new binary system has been formed. Star B and its attendant planets are in orbit about the supergiant Star A.

Locations

As located from Earth, the binary system of stars A and B lies in the constellation Ophiuchus (The Serpent-Bearer). The main body of a dark dust cloud lies close to the neighbouring constellation of Scorpius, at a distance of 700 light years from Earth. It conceals a cluster of comparatively young stars, with Star A among them.

Star A is just north of Antares. Location: Right Ascension 16h 25m. Declination: -24° 30'.

Helliconia's first designation on terrestrial charts: Planet G4 PBX/ 4582-4-3.

Helliconia's Composition

Helliconia is a planet with roughly terrestrial properties.

Radius	4800 miles
Circumference	30,159 miles
Mean density	4.09
Mass	equivalent to 1.28 Earth's mass

Axial inclination of rotation axis to the plane of orbit 55°
This compares with about 66° for Earth.
This widens the range of temperatures within climatic zones.

The atmospheric composition varied slightly from pre-capture to post-capture. A greater amount of carbon dioxide in the air, pre-capture, produced a mean temperature of -7°C. After capture, and at periastron (when Star B and planets are at their closest to Star A) some of this atmospheric CO_2 combined with water to form carbonate rocks.

Atmospheric carbon dioxide is thus reduced, so too the benefit of a 'greenhouse' effect is reduced, yielding a mean temperature of +10°C.

In other words, pre-capture conditions were better than might be expected, while post-capture conditions are more severe.

Orbital Motions

Helliconia's "Small Year", that is to say its annual orbit about its parent Star B, is equal to 1.42 Earth years.

The motions of stars A and B are such that B orbits A in the equivalent of 2592 Earth years. Star B, in accordance with Kepler's laws, moves in its orbit at a varying speed, slowing as it reaches the most distant point (apastron) from Star A, speeding up when it nears Star A (at periastron). In consequence, its planets, Helliconia included, spend less time enjoying maximum energy than they do receiving minimum energy.

Fig. 2 shows the "Great Year" of Helliconia about the giant primary, where t = time in Earth years from apastron.

It is the Great Year which has predominant influence over Helliconia's climate, and Star A which provides most of Helliconia's heat and energy.

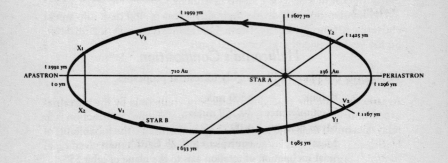

Figure 2. Orbit

The x_1 to x_2 sector marks the 500 E years of deepest winter on either side of apastron.

The y_1 to y_2 sector marks the period at periastron when Star A appears brighter than Star B in Helliconia's skies.

Points V_1, V_2, and V_3 indicate approximately the periods in which the three books of the volume are set.

> The time from 311 to 633 E years marks a period of fairly rapid improvement in climatic conditions. After that, a slow warming process sets in towards periastron. From 1929 E years, a fairly rapid decline takes place. On either side of apastron is a period of over five E centuries when the climate is either severe or unsettled; a minor ice age is either building up or else in slow decline. This contrasts with a more brief 238 E years of high summer, over periastron.

The orbits of the four Star B planets are at the following (E) distances from their primary:

Copaise	0.31AU	Aganip	0.82AU
Helliconia	1.26AU	Ipocrene	1.53AU

An Avernian shrine stands on Aganip (Bk. 2 x), it marks the spot where the 512 future occupants of the Avernus satellite were housed during the construction of the Earth Observation Station.

HELLICONIA'S MOON

The Helliconian satellite lost during the period of capture was known to the phagors as *T'Sehn-Hrr*. It holds the key to one of the discomfitting secrets of human life on Helliconia. (The truth is uncovered by SartoriIrvrash in Vol. 2, xxi, to his detriment.)

Helliconian humans divide their small year of 480 days into weeks and tenners. One week is eight days. One tenner is 6 weeks (i.e. 48 days). So the year is divided into ten equal parts.

AVERNUS AS SATELLITE

Avernus is a satellite placed in orbit about Helliconia by the terrestrial expedition. It is designated Earth Observation Station. Its function is to relay data on all facets of Helliconia back to Earth. To the inhabitants of Helliconia, the OES is known as *Kaidaw*, because of its perceived rapid motion against the stars.

Avernus has an almost circular circumpolar orbit, its mean distance above planetary surface being:

Orbital radius measured from centre of planet   5731 miles
Orbital period   2hrs 9mins 30 secs
Shape: spherical   Diameter   0.62 miles
Mass   18,000,000 tonnes
                                                $(1.8 \times 10^{10}$ Kg)

Depending on the latitude of an observer, Avernus takes about 20–24 minutes to cross the sky, from rising to setting. From the ground, its maximum angular diameter when overhead presents 137.5 seconds of arc. Inhabitants can observe Avernus undergoing rather complex phases when it is passing overhead.

Some Avernus History

When the starship from earth was closing into orbit about Star B, 512 colonists were hatched, almost full-grown (i.e. as late adolescents). The DNA of fertilized human egg cells were computer-stored in nanowombs. The colonists were reared in six "families" or clans, each destined for specific duties.

Once they had been landed at a base on Aganip, automated construction units began the building of the EOS, using local stellar material. Owing to difficulties and set-backs, construction took eight

E-years. The colonists were then ferried to their new home on Avernus to begin an intensive study of Helliconia.

Information transmitted back to Earth takes a thousand years to reach its target. So the early signals sent in Spring are received on Earth in approximately AD 6344.

By the time of "Helliconia Summer", Avernus has been in orbit for thirty-two E-centuries. Its population now numbers close to 6000 people. Copulation is taught from the age of eight, but all procreation is by extra-uterine birth.

Among the six clans, the PIN family is the "Cross-Continuity Family". Its duty is to follow the unfolding of one or two Helliconian family groupings through generations over the cycle of a Great Year (60 generations).

The GO family deals with questions of theology, philosophy, ontogeny, phylogeny, etc.

The TAN family studies the origins of long-standing quarrels, from personal to national and specific.

As a safety valve against confinement sickness, Avernians can enter a "Helliconia Holiday" lottery; winners are allowed to visit the planet below. This is a one-way ticket.

Helliconia and Earth: Relative Dates

The colonising starship left Earth in the year AD 2100, arriving in the vicinity of Star B in AD 3600. The journey of 1000 light years took 1500 years to accomplish. Avernus was operative by AD 3608. On the Helliconian Great Year, this is 500 years After Aphelion.

In Book 1 Avernus has already been operative for more than a Great Year.
    i.e. about 2592 + 134 E years = 2726 E years
In Book 2 Avernus operative for a further 543 years = 3269 E years
        So dates now will be: On Earth, AD 6877
                                On Helliconia, 1177 E years AA
                                On Avernus, 3269
In Book 3 Avernus operative for a further 696 years = 3965 E years
        So dates will now be: On Earth, AD 7573
                                On Helliconia, 1873 E years AA
                                On Avernus, 3965
Myrkwyr is an ominous day in 1873. Freyr sinks below the horizon on the Polar Circle, not to rise again for a further eighteen or so human generations.

CALENDARS

Helliconian Time reckoned as Earth Time

Helliconia units	Equivalent Earth units
1 small year	480 days or 10 tenners
1 day	25.92 hours
1 hour	1.04 hours (62.4 minutes)
1 minute	1.56 minutes
1 second	0.936 seconds

A Helliconian inhabitant living to the ripe
old age of 70 would be 99.4 E years old

The Earth–Avernus method of reckoning Helliconian years is simply to date them After Apastron (AA). On Helliconia itself, various nations have, at various times, their own means of reckoning calendar time. Generally, such calendars begin from the start of the reign of a local despot.

For example, in "Summer" four different calendars are mentioned. Taking these into account, Book 2 opens in

(Terrestrial dateline	AD 6877)
Earth years AA	1177
Helliconia year AA	
"Denniss" calendar	828*
Oldorando-Borlien After Union	381 (some claim 408)
Ancipital year	749ˢ

HUMAN AGES COMPARED

Because the Small Year on Helliconia is longer than a terrestrial year, age differentials exist.

The following table (years) gives comparable ages of humans on the two planets.

*The legendary King Denniss was ruling in Year 249 before apastron, and foresaw disaster.

His calendar has been discarded.

ˢThe full and correct name of this year in the Ancipital calendar, forged in the ancipital cotemporal brain, is:

"Year After Small Apotheosis of Great year 5,634,000 Since catastrophe".

That is, since Freyr's capture of Batalix, some 8,000,280 years previously.

HELLICONIA

Earth	Helliconia
5	3.5
10	7
12	8.45
15	10.56
18	12.67
20	14
22	15.49
25	17.6
30	21
35	24.67
40	28
50	35.21
60	42
70	49
75	52.8
80	56

Life spans are longer in summers of the Great Year

Phagors

The struggle for supremacy on Helliconia is between humans and phagors. Phagors, a two-horned, shaggy-coated species, were the original dominant inhabitants of the planet before Batalix (Star B) was captured by Freyr, the supergiant sun (Star A). They are also known as *ancipitals* (two-edged), a reference to their sharp horns.

This cowlike species probably evolved from *flambreg*, vast herds of which graze the northern wilds of Sibornal. They are kin to older pre-Freyr species, such as the *kaidaws*.

Kaidaws are the large horned animals, somewhat resembling horses, which phagors ride. These older species have physical traits in common, such as ball-joints at knees and elbows. This greater dexterity is counterbalanced by a sporadically firing nervous system; hence frequent bursts of immobility.

Phagors stand upright and possess three fingers on each hand.

BRAIN

A major distinction between phagor and human lies in brain structure. A phagor brain is uni-hemispheric, unlike a human brain with its two hemispheres. There is no equivalent to the neocortex. Inasmuch as the phagor brain resembles a human's, it consists largely of hypothalamus, overlaid with a kind of cerebellum controlling motion.

It may be said in consequence that phagors live in their own perceptual Umwelts. Theirs is an eotemporal consciousness (Eos was the goddess of dawn, sister to Selene), where endings and beginnings cannot be distinguished from one another. For them, time is no indicator of progression as registered in a human mind. Events are monitored as a series of milestones from which direction has been obliterated; thus a trail is indicated, without an arrow of perception to point direction. A rudimentary nervous system permits only action and reaction. But *tether* (See Appendix 4) greatly extends ancipital awareness.

Ancipitals were masters of the cool dawn world before Freyr capture.

With their cowbirds, commensal avians which feed in part on their hosts' parasites, they dominated a world, from the lowlands of Pegovin to Mt Estakhadok in the High Nktryhk. In those remote ages, they kept Others as pets.

BLOOD

Ancipital blood is golden, containing as it does an anti-freeze system which (together with their stiff pelage) renders the phagors impervious to cold. Cowbirds, kaidaws, and other dawn animals, share this characteristic. Red blood, free of anti-freeze, represents a more recent evolutionary development.

Moss forms a large part of phagor diet during cold periods. Mosses contain high percentages of arachidonic acid, which is highly polyunsaturated. A concentration of this fatty acid in the phospholipids of cell membranes makes the membranes more fluid. This serves to lower the temperature at which the lipid in the membranes undergoes a phase shift from liquid-crystalline to a more solid or gel-like state. Hence the acid from the moss protects cell membranes from the effects of cold; the cell is then able to function at low temperatures. Humanity, of course, has no such reinforcement.

SEXES

Linked with their sporadic endocrine system, female phagors come on heat ten times a year (*tenners* is the Eotemporal term, equivalent to the terrestrial term "monthlies"). Phagors copulate infrequently. As with terrestrial gorillas, the penis is small. Phagors never commit rape; that is a piece of human mythology. Females are viviparous and lactate; parturition takes place one small (or Batalix) year after conception. Both sexes carry the Helico virus within the mitochondria of their cells.

stallun	adult male
creaght	young male
gillot	adult mare
fillock	young mare
runt	child, either sex

LANGUAGE

Phagors used two intertwined languages. *Native ancipital* is an everyday language, employing only one tense, the continuous present. *Eotem-*

poral is a sacred speechform, also used for counting on the base three. It is supposedly the language spoken by those ancipitals sunk in *tether*.

Language, phagor-to-phagor, is generally accompanied by gesture. Thus the exhortation on parting is "Hold horns high", accompanied by the ceremony of both sides leaning forward, arms to side, foreheads touching, harneys meeting. Then smartly away.

APPENDIX 3

Other species

Following the capture by Freyr of Batalix and its planetary system, the proximity of the A-type supergiant bathed the planets in high energy radiation.

The effect on the atmospheric composition of Helliconia was to raise the oxygen level, due to the photolysis of CO_2, H_2O, etc. The oceans were also affected. Greater concentrations of macromolecules led to increased activity all the way up the food chain.

For something like a million years, the upheaval of capture bathed Helliconia in high UV radiation and X-ray levels. The result was a fairly rapid evolution of species. The human species evolved from a small Hespagorat ape. Some species perished – the *childrim* for one.

In evolving, the Others escaped from captivity, but remained in proximity with phagors in loose commensal communities, while going through a protognostic stage of development. Hence the survival of ancipital terms into the Olonets language (the main language of Campannlat). Phagors long retained a shadowy dominance (hence the god Akha). Eventually various tribes fled from Hespagorat and the Pegovin region, crossing to Campannlat. The crossing was effected via an ancient landbridge between the two continents.

East–West phagor migratory routes were established at the time of the crossing, or just thereafter.

The tribes crossing the landbridge were known as the Olle Onets. This name was derived from the glut of oil-fish found in the shallows on either side of the isthmus. It became in turn the name of the chief language of Campannlat, Olonets.

Many of the "winter" tribes were driven eastwards before the advancing newcomers. Clans later occupying the lower Nktyrhk, such as the Mordriats, are descendants of such defeated tribes.

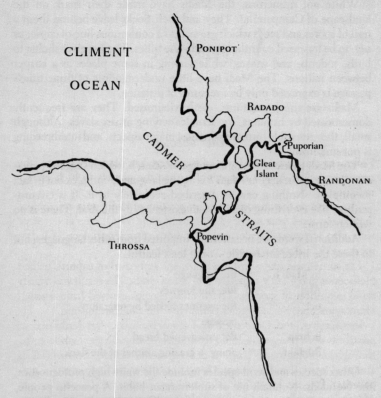

Figure 3. The ancient landbridge
  Landbridge in heavy outline. Present land configuration in light outline.
  The isthmus between the Climent Ocean and the Narmoset Sea. The
land on either side, following the destruction of the isthmus when the polar
caps melted, eventually became the countries of Throssa and Radado, now
separated by the Cadmer Straits.

THE MADIS

These transhumance peoples have never achieved a fully human
consciousness. Madis are categorised as protognostics. Travel is their
whole existence, pursued whether there is one sun in the sky or two.
This fixed pattern of behaviour suggests that they existed before solar
capture, living much as they do at present.

While not numerous, the Madis have made their mark on the landscape of Campannlat. They and their flocks leave behind them a trail of spores and seeds which grows into a continuous line of copse, or *uct*, to be traversed countless times by the tribes. The uct gives shelter to birds, rodents, and snakes, while serving in some places as a barrier between nations. The Madi have little understanding of time; time's passage is expressed only by measures of distance.

Madis are meek creatures, easily victimised. They are frequently domesticated by humans, the females serving as sex slaves. Although small, they resemble humanity in most major aspects, and interbreeding is not unknown.

The Madi tribes call their language *hr'Madi'h*, which suggests pervasive phagor influence. *hr'Madi'h* is a sung language, complex but in fact incomplete. Nothing can be described accurately in it. It is circumscribed, like everything else in Madi existence, by the *Ahd*. There is no written form.

Additional words are occasionally imported from other languages, but to these the tribes are hostile – or at least fearful.

hr'Madi'h	the language
Ahd	life, the journey
uct	the avenues seeded by migratory passage
la'hrap	flat unleavened bread
fhlebiht	arang, a grazing animal of the flock

Other species and semi-species include the waist-high protognostics, the Nondads. Nondads are of subterranean habit. A peaceful people, they leave it to a warrior caste to fight. Thus, they discuss ultimate questions in a language of "clicks, whistles, and snorts", while their warrior kings do battle in the Eighty Darknesses.

Nondads are hunted and eaten by Uskuts; when roast, they are known as *treebries*.

Nondads live in Campannlat, the Africa of Helliconia.

A related people, the Ondods, live in the harsher climates of the northern continent, Sibornal.

NECROGENES

Descending the evolutionary scale, the necrogenes represent a dead end to one line of pre-Freyr development.

These species of fish and animals give birth only through their own

death. Examples are the assatassi (fish or, more properly, fish-lizards)
yelk, biyelk, and gunnadu.

Necrogenes are hermaphrodite, without such mammalian adjuncts
as ovaries and wombs.

For instance, assatassi, a sharp-beaked fish, semi-winged at maturity,
flies ashore in its millions during the great summer along the coasts of
the Sea of Eagles. Their mating grounds lie deep in the Ardent Sea.
After mating they swarm eastwards, against the ocean currents, through
the Cadmer Straits, working up considerable speeds for their death
flight.

They then launch themselves onto the shores of Hespagorat, some
managing to fly a distance inland. Where they fall, there they die. The
young have been carried in their bellies. They live as maggots on the
decaying bodies of their mothers, before metamorphosing to a legged
and tailed form, and crawling back to the sea. [Assatassi first feature in
terrestrial literature in "Star Millenia", in *Galaxies Like Grains of Sand*
(Signet Books, New York, 1960).]

Larger land necrogenes follow similar patterns. After yelk mate, the
sperm seed develops into maggot-like creatures which live off the double
stomachs of their mothers. When they enter an artery, the maggots
explode through the parental body, causing rapid death. They devour
the carcase – and each other – until after metamorphosis, when they
emerge to survive in the outside world as young adult yelk.

WUTRA

In the great hubbub of Helliconian life, one other life form deserves
special mention.

In the centuries of Great Winter, Wutra's Worm is a kind of
devouring dragon. Flighted, it destroys all it comes upon. To the
embattled tribes of humanity – in Pannoval and elsewhere – Wutra is
God of the Skies. In time, the idea becomes a god.

During the Great Summer, a transformation takes place in the life
cycle. The worm retreats to the warming oceans in a marine stage.
Having passed its flighted period in higher latitudes, where it mated, it
now lives out the rest of its life in the sea. The oceans teem with food.
Into this rich environment, the offspring are born.

These fish-like offspring are as vulnerable as they are plentiful, and
are known to coastal peoples as scupper-fish. Scupper-fish make a
nourishing and tasty dish.

After some centuries, when the Great Autumn sets in, the scupperfish crawl to land (much like Earth's mudskippers) and develop wings. A few more years, and Wutra's Worm is again aloft in darkening air.

Even during the period when it is being eaten in its thousands and hundreds of thousands, Wutra's Worm has gained a niche in the night sky.

Most nations of Campannlat and Sibornal recognise ten houses of the Zodiac, the plane of the ecliptic traversed by the two suns and the other planets. One of these houses is Wutra's Worm, sometimes known as the Night Worm. Somewhere within this constellation lies a dim star, Sol.

Houses of the Zodiac

The Bat
Devil Bull (also known as Wutra's Ox)
The Boulder
Wutra's Worm (The Night Worm)
The Queen's Scar (Akha's Wound)
The Old Pursuer
The Fountain
The Golden Ship
The Two Dogs
The Sword

APPENDIX 4

Helliconian Humanity

Terrestrial interest in Helliconia stems from the fact that, after many centuries of interstellar exploration, a planet was discovered on which human life thrives, part of a diverse biomass. However, researches conducted on Avernus soon showed that Helliconian humanity differs in interesting psychological and physical ways from their earthly counterparts.

PSYCHOLOGICAL DIFFERENCE

One divergence from normal terrestrial existence seems so great, even so uncanny, that it must be regarded as pervasively psychological and phylogenic. Indeed, centuries of dispute on Earth failed to resolve the question of whether Helliconians should be categorised as human, or as a separate species.

The aberration (as some call it) lies in a much gentler gradation between life and death than terrestrial humanity experiences. Terrestrial human existence is binary; one is either alive or dead. On Helliconia, two further states follow bodily demise.

The burnt out souls of the dead descend into an obsidian realm of entropy. In this realm, this negative of life, are stored two stages of psychic decay, *gossies*, the residues of the more recently deceased, and, further down the stack, *fessups*. Gossies are subject to febrile mood swings, from bitter recrimination to saccharine sweetness, perhaps related to climatic conditions. Fessups, increasingly less articulate, sink towards ultimate disintegration and the Original Boulder – as early understanding has the term.

[Later this term is understood as the Original Beholder. That is to say, Gaia, the presiding unconscious will of the biomass which maintains the difficult equilibrium of the planet.]

The living are able to commune with *gossies* if they enter a trancelike state resembling death known as *pauk*.

After physical death, phagors undergo a similar gradual diminution towards ultimate disintegration. This is called *tether*.

PHYSICAL DIFFERENCE

Male and female humans exhibit little sexual dimorphism. They undergo instead a dramatic weight/shape transformation before and after the Great Winter. This is in response to the diminished or increased energy reaching the planet. It amounts to an evolutionary survival strategy.

THE HELICO VIRUS

The agent of the weight/shape transformation is a pleomorphic helical virus, somewhat similar to a terrestrial mumps pathogene. Its shell in the shape of an icosahedron consists of lipids and proteins, and contains nucleic acid RNA. It is 97 millimicrons long. The Avernus has not the means to filter out the virus. For this reason, Avernians are unable to visit in person the planet they orbit (except under unusual – and fatal – circumstances).

The helico virus is endemic twice in a Great Year, firstly approximately 600 E years after apastron. It then rages for many small years, coincidental with improving climatic conditions and increased solar energy. Its second appearance is during a decline into wintery conditions, some 1800 E years after apastron.

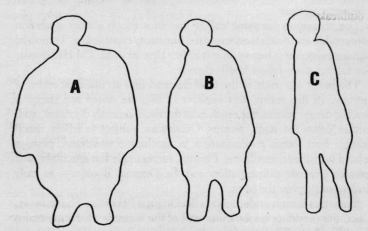

Figure 4. Human form changes throughout Great Year shown in diagram
  A Survivor of Fat Death towards Winter
  B Median figure
  C Survivor of Bone Fever in Spring

At its every visitation, the virus brings widespread death. It strikes at the hypothalamus, causing encephalitis (inflammation of the brain) and delirium. Its manifestations at this stage resemble meningitis. Populations are usually reduced to about half. Survivors take on altered form, gaining (in autumn) fifty per cent of normal body weight, as fatty tissue is built up. This phase is marked by unquenchable bulimia: their own children, faeces, asokins – sufferers will seize on and eat anything living. The survivors of the spring epidemic shed a corresponding amount of weight, marked by anorexia and self-starvation.

In the course of several generations, surviving populations shed the extremes of their thin or heavyweight forms, tending to return to a more average constitution. In so doing, they also lose immunity to the virus.

It will be seen that this terrible scourge has a positive aspect. It forms part of a natural process, ensuring human survival throughout the climatic changes wrought by cosmic upheaval.

In more primitive times, the two phases of the helico pandemic were not recognised as springing from one and the same cause. They were known (in autumn) as the Fat Death, and (in spring) as Bone Fever. By the period covered by Book 3 ("Winter"), the doctor, Toress Lahl, has gained a clear understanding of Fat Death – and of its survival rate. A great chain of eclipses occurs at this period, making Bone Fever outbreaks even more terrifying. A total of twenty eclipses takes place between 630 and 658 E years AA. *

VIRUS CARRIER

The carrier of the helico virus is a species of arthropoda or tick. This vector transfers readily from phagors to humans. Phagors are immune to the virus. The human habit of using phagors as slaves or soldiers during the Great Summer and onwards ensures the survival of both tick and virus (even when the latter is latent) among human populations.

The helico virus is a reminder (for those who can understand) of the

---

*Eclipses occur in the following manner. The orbits of Helliconia and her sister planets lie at a 10° inclination to the orbit of Batalix and Freyr about each other. Helliconia's orbit crosses the greater orbital plane at two points. Joining these two points is the line of the nodes. When the line of the nodes passes through Freyr, so that Helliconia, Batalix, and Freyr are aligned, then eclipses of the greater light will occur.

A lesser eclipse cycle occurs on the other side of periastron, lasting for 9.45 years. In accordance with Kepler's laws, Batalix speeds up when closer to Freyr. It therefore takes less time to move from the Fat Death eclipses to the post-periastron position than from the post-periastron position to the Fat Death position in 630 E yrs AA. So the second eclipse series commences in the year 1424 E yrs AA.

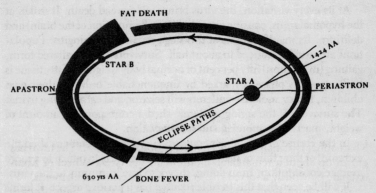

Figure 5. Diagram of human biomass governed by Helico virus.

connection between the present deadly hostility of phagor and humanity and a distant past when the two species were commensal.

Terrible though the disease is, human survival is largely dependent upon the violent weight/shape transformation which it effects. Thus, if the humans succeed in eliminating their enemies, they cause their own undoing.

Or so it seems. If the nations of Summer ceased to war among themselves, if they could then defeat the phagor legions, if they could maintain a selected number in the equivalent of zoological gardens, then humanity could break free from its present limitations. But these are large Ifs . . .

APPENDIX 5

Kharnabhar

Kharnabhar is a small town in a remote region of Sibornal. The town has grown up about a remarkable monument, the Great Wheel of Kharnabhar. Previously a sacred site, it now houses criminal elements.

The fame of the Great Wheel is universal. When SartoriIrvrash arrives in Ashkitosh (Bk. 2, xi), he sees a tapestry bearing an allegorical depiction of the Wheel. "Upon a scarlet background, a great wheel [was] being rowed through the heavens by oarsmen in cerulean garments, each smiling blissfully, towards an astonishing maternal figure from whose mouth, nostrils, and breasts sprang the stars in the scarlet sky."

The main and almost only route to Kharnabhar is from the port of Rivernjk, on the Climent Sea coast, northwards through the mountains of the Shivenink Chain. The distance is about 2400 miles, equivalent to a journey from Gibraltar to the north of Norway.

The Great Wheel

The Wheel is a granite ring, carved inside a granite mountain of the Chain. It revolves within Mount Kharnabhar, only one small segment being accessible from outside the mountain. The Architects long ago created the Wheel encoding with its dimensions the external world, in a bid for astrological symmetry. "As Above, so below." The holy men who first occupied the Wheel intended it as an instrument by which to propel their world across the heavens, out of Winter and into the welcoming light and warmth of Freyr.

Originally, the Great Wheel was dedicated to God the Azoiaxic (meaning "something which revolves beyond life" – later interpreted to mean "one who existed before life and round whom all life revolves").

Penned within the confines of the mountain, the Wheel is inclined at 5° to the horizontal. It rotates above a floor inclined at 4°. This slight difference permits the river flowing round the base of the Wheel to carry mud beneath it, acting as lubricant.

Three-walled cells like alcoves line the outer surface of the ring. The ring is kept in slow movement, day by day. The immoveable fourth wall is not part of the Wheel, although it closes off all the cells; it consists of solid unmoving rock, Mt Kharnabhar itself. Into the rock is inset lengths of chain, stapled firmly into the wall. These chains hang at 125 cm intervals.

With these chains, prisoners in the one thousand and eighty-five cells can haul themselves into and through the dark night of granite. When priests' trumpets sound throughout, all prisoners must pull in unison on their chains. So the Wheel is shifted in its journey through rock or – as some still claim – through the heavens.

Some technical data

Wheel diameter		1825 metres (Number of Small Years in one Great Year)
	thickness	13.19 m (1319 being the year of Freyr-set or Mrykwyr at latitude of Kharnabhar, counting from apastron)
	height	6.60 m (12 times 55, the latitude of the Wheel)
Cell height		240 cm (= the 6 wks of 1 tenner × the 40 mins of 1 hr)
	width	250 cm (+ the 10 tenners of 1 yr × the hrs in a day)
	depth	480 cm (= no. of days in Small Year)
Wall thickness		
	between cells	0.64159 m (+ cell width gives value of *pi*)

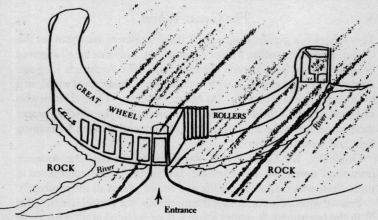

Figure 6. Diagram of the Great Wheel within the granite of Mt. Kharnabhar. (Bambeck projection).

After ten years, the Wheel has been tugged by a captive back to the point at which he started his imprisonment. A revolution has been completed. On that final day, one prisoner finds daylight instead of stone for the fourth wall of his cell, and may make his exit to freedom; in the cell leading his, another man will be entering for his first day of the ten year journey into and through the rock.

This ceaseless revolution has been seen by some to be echoed by the ceaseless orbiting of the Avernus, high above Kharnabhar.

APPENDIX 6

Populations

Helliconia is a sparsely populated world, at least as far as human and phagor densities are concerned. The following table shows how those densities fluctuate between the periods of extreme cold and heat. Phagor populations are more stable than human ones.

	APASTRON		PERIASTRON	
	HUMANS	PHAGORS	HUMANS	PHAGORS
	in millions			
SIBORNAL	3.5?	10	25	14
CAMPANNLAT	8	23	64	35
HESPAGORAT	4	11	9	19
Sub-totals	15.5	44	98	68
Totals	59.5		166	

The weight of planetary biomass is in direct proportion to the solar energy absorbed by the planetary surface. At the time of apastron, the total mass is almost one third that at periastron.